S0-ABQ-398

Colette's Prayer

By

DeVa Gantt

authorHOUSE™
1663 Liberty Drive, Suite 200
Bloomington, Indiana 47403
(800) 839-8640
www.AuthorHouse.com

This book is a work of fiction. People, places, events, and situations are the product of the author's imagination. Any resemblance to actual persons, living or dead, or historical events, is purely coincidental.

© 2005 DeVa Gantt. All Rights Reserved.

No part of this book may be reproduced, stored in a retrieval system, or transmitted by any means without the written permission of the author.

First published by AuthorHouse 10/07/05

ISBN: 1-4208-2151-2 (sc)

Library of Congress Control Number: 2005900358

Printed in the United States of America
Bloomington, Indiana

This book is printed on acid-free paper.

Colette's Prayer could not have taken shape without the help and support of family and friends. We'd like to expressly thank:

Our brother, Chris, for supplying our 1830s calendar and for sharing his vivid recollections

Our medical consultant, Marguerite

Our proofreaders, Mom, Pat, Karen & Marie,
whose critical eyes were amazing!

Those who read the first drafts for the fun of it,
giving us constructive criticism and encouragement:
Dave, Marie, Dawn, Valerie, Betsy, Sherry & Mom

Those who contributed real-life incidents and various facts that made their way into these pages:

Allen
"Never mind who told me. I found out!"
Joan
"Hoc est enim corpus meum."
Tami & Steven
Trees of the Caribbean

Our brother, Bob, president and CEO of Ganttco Enterprises,
as well as our Mom
for their financial backing

Our husbands and children, who put up with our three-year obsession

And most importantly
—Our inspiration—
THE BOYS
"Wherever you are… you are here."

Book One

****

The Charade

Fall 1833
A Prayer

Prologue

An evening mist settled over the moss-scarred walls of the stone church, shrouding it in hopelessness. A solitary man slumped forward in one pew, muttering disparaging phrases to the looming shadows. He needed another drink. Expensive whisky hadn't yielded peaceful oblivion, hadn't even dulled his senses. And yet, if he wasn't drunk, what the hell was he doing in a house of God? *What indeed!* He chortled insanely, the inebriated laugh ending in a dizzying hiccup. He'd come to pray – pray for death. Not his own death. He wasn't quite so noble. Not yet, anyway. Instead, he petitioned the Almighty to bring about the demise of another. Retribution – justice. His lips twisted with the delicious thought of it. *Death – so simple a solution.*

"Put him out of his misery. Put me out of *my* misery," he slurred, confronting the wooden crucifix that hung above the barren altar. *"Do you hear?"*

His sudden movement sent the walls careening, the statues a nauseating blur of spinning specters. He grasped for the bench, attempting to right his toppling world, but his hand missed its mark. Not so his forehead. It met the back of the wooden pew with a resounding crack, shooting shards of pain through his skull. With a groan, he crumbled to the stone floor, his agony blanketed in a palette of smoky-blue, a vision that dissolved into the consuming void of blessed unconsciousness.

Marie Ryan hurried along the dimly lit courtyard, her heel catching sharply on the stone pathway and echoing across the vacant enclosure. In all her years at the St. Jude Refuge, deep in the heart of Richmond, she had never acquired the soft footfalls of the diminutive nuns who routinely tread the very same cobblestone in their contemplative procession toward vespers. This evening was no different.

She was very late, and the interview awaiting her tardy arrival had been arranged for her. Now it would have to be cancelled. She would not leave the refuge again. This was her home, where she belonged, and neither the threat of her husband, nor her ill-fated past, would send her scurrying from its protective walls again. This evening was different; she had received a sign.

The Almighty had intended that she serve Him from the day she had been abandoned as a young child on the steps of St. Jude's thirty years ago. For the past sixteen years, she had ignored His call; tonight she would not. Life beyond the church walls no longer lured her with empty promises. The real world was comprised of two separate, yet contingent, factions of humanity: those who suffered life's travesties and those who ministered to the many who struggled under its burdensome yoke. On this eve, she would circumvent the former and embrace the latter. Her penance had been paid in full. God had sent her a sign.

She entered the rectory and nodded demurely to its three occupants: Sister Elizabeth, Father Michael Andrews, and Joshua Harrington. The latter was an elderly gentleman and prosperous businessman, who was seeking a suitable companion for his wife. With five sons married and moved away, Loretta Harrington was suffering the effects of an empty nest.

"Please don't think me ungrateful, Mr. Harrington," Marie apologized when the introductions were over, "but I'm afraid I've changed my mind."

Father Andrews stood stunned. The gentle woman had shown great interest in the Harrington position and had asked him to set up this meeting. He knew its handsome salary would prove a blessing. "Marie, is something wrong?"

She hesitated. "I've finally realized that this is where I belong, here at the refuge. Yes, I know I have a home, but I want to work at St. Jude's as well, with those who really need me."

The priest's astonishment doubled. Though Marie's daughter attended the rudimentary school that Sister Elizabeth conducted, Marie rarely crossed the church's threshold herself. "But your husband–" he began.

"Will be made to understand," she replied.

"I'm not certain *I* understand. I thought you needed this employment."

Marie sighed. "There was a man in the church tonight. He was ill."

"Another beggar," Michael scoffed, his voice unusually harsh.

"No, not a beggar," Marie refuted, surprised by his reaction. "He was dressed in fine clothing, finer than any I've ever seen. And yet, he was in a sad state: unconscious. I believe he struck his head on the pew. I had Matthew carry him to the common room, and I remained with him until he awoke. I fear he has suffered greatly, and not just physically. I want you to look at him, Michael."

"I fail to comprehend how this man has influenced you."

"It was something he said," Marie remarked distantly. "I believe the Good Lord sent him not only to St. Jude, but to me, to make me see that this is where I'm needed, where I belong. Again, I apologize, Mr. Harrington. I shouldn't have drawn you away from your wife. But I must remain at the refuge. I hope you understand."

With a mixture of relief and dread, exultation and pain, Michael Andrews smiled down at Marie. He'd been denied this woman's presence for sixteen years. Tonight she had returned.

Rising from the rickety chair he had perched before the window, John Ryan strutted across the small kitchen like a proud peacock. He massaged his inflated chest, then raked long yellow fingernails through his graying hair. It fell back over his indelible scowl.

Turning away in disgust, Charmaine Ryan threw herself into preparing dinner. Her father's pompous promenade repulsed her to the core, and when he paraded so, she thanked the Lord for making her a girl.

She sighed. Her mother was unusually late. The appointment with Joshua Harrington had begun over two hours ago, and though her father deemed the lengthening delay a favorable sign, she did not.

"What time did your mother say she was supposed to meet with 'em?"

Charmaine jumped. "I think she said five."

"*Think?* Jesus Christ, girl, don't you know?"

"No, I don't know for certain," she responded peevishly, her eyes already flashing fire until he, with a grumbling shake of the head, meandered into the bedroom.

Charmaine struggled to gain control of her ire. These days, anything her father said brought her to anger, one that was becoming exceedingly difficult to master. Unlike her mother, who cowered under John Ryan's verbal assaults, they incensed Charmaine. Perhaps she was brave because he had never raised a hand to her. Marie was less fortunate. Educated in the folly of questioning her husband's supremacy, she kept silent in order to preserve a fragile peace.

With mind revolting, as it always did when she pondered the union of John Ryan and Marie St. Jude, Charmaine stared absently across the humble kitchen, beyond the dilapidated walls of the three room cottage, and past the barriers of time, hoping to perceive some understanding of nature, the twist of circumstance that had sanctified the marriage of her parents. If she knew little about her mother's past, save the fact that she had been abandoned on the steps of St. Jude Thaddeus Church, she knew even less about her father, a man who appeared and disappeared as the mood struck him, often leaving his wife and daughter for days at a time, which suited Charmaine just fine. The less she saw of him the better. Did he have a family aside from his wife and daughter? It was only one of many unanswered questions. All she really knew of John Ryan was that he was an ill-bred, uneducated drunk. He rarely worked, and then, only when he needed money for spirits, sauntering about the Richmond docks seeking odd jobs.

How had such a scapegrace won the heart of her mother? Another unfathomable question. Marie should have entered the novitiate, taken sacred vows that would have wed her to God and His Holy Church. Instead she had left St. Jude's at the age of eighteen to marry a man whom she claimed had been kind to her. A single child had been born of their union. Charmaine had been christened Haley Charmaine Ryan after her paternal grandmother, a woman she had never met. However, only her father used the name Haley, and now it was all but forgotten, for her mother fancied the name Charmaine, a name that still haunted the older woman's memory from a time and place she couldn't quite recall.

"Maybe we oughta eat without her."

Charmaine flinched. The man had perfected his penchant for sneaking up on people. "Yes, perhaps we should," she agreed, setting the meal on the humble table. She'd purchased a small slab of pork with the money she'd saved from running errands for the elderly spinster next door. Tonight they'd celebrate her mother's good fortune.

"I hope that Harrin'ton fella knows a good thin' when he sees it," he said, straddling the stool at the head of the table. Charmaine held silent as he pulled the wooden platter and knife nearer and proceeded to manicure the fat from the steaming roast. Then, he set aside the choice slices for himself and placed the remaining cuts on his daughter's dish. "Your mother is a hard worker," he continued. "There ain't none what can match her skill when she puts her mind to it, and I wouldn't want this fella thinkin' otherwise."

"No, sir," Charmaine whispered sullenly, appalled by his demand that a stranger respect the virtues of a woman whom he continually debased. His convoluted reasoning would never cease to amaze her, and if the situation weren't so decidedly sad, she would have laughed outright at his pathetic proclamation.

"I just hope he intends to pay her well," he proceeded, his words muffled as he shoved a forkful of meat into his stubbled mouth. "I ain't allowin' no kin of mine to work cheap. No, sir. For his sake, I hope he ain't some high and mighty a-ris-to-crat who thinks he can get away with payin' some miserly amount, 'cause I won't have it."

Again Charmaine bit her tongue. It was pointless to accuse him of sending his wife to labor for wages that he would assert his right to claim. Besides, it would benefit Marie to hold such a position, one that would grant her a life apart from her derelict husband. Charmaine attended the St. Jude School on a daily basis with the other orphaned children. She looked to it as an escape from her father's cruelty. But what did her mother have? Where was her haven? Up until today, Marie had nothing but the bungalow in which they lived and dared not hope for anything better to come along. But something *had* come. The Harrington household offered a refuge of her own.

"Jesus Christ, woman, how could you *be* so goddamn dumb?"

"I'm sorry, John," Marie placated, "but there was nothing to be done."

"*Nothin' to be done?*" he sneered. "You expect me to believe that? I know what you've been up to. You didn't want that job! Workin's too good for you."

"That's not true, John. I told you, Mr. Harrington was seeking someone younger and more impressionable, someone his wife could take under wing."

The remark elicited another oath. "Then send Haley," he said.

"What?"

"You heard me," he responded with a growing grin, the infant idea taking root. "She's young enough for all them things you been sayin' them Harrin'tons want. She oughta suit his fancy wife jus' fine."

"No, John. Charmaine is too young, and she has her schooling to finish."

"Schoolin'!" he spat. "She's had enough of that damned church. What good has it done her, 'cept to teach her how to sass me? It's time she earned her keep!"

"That won't be necessary," Marie unwisely rejoined. "I'll continue to look for a job, and until I find something suitable, we'll get by on the money you earn at the warehouse. I know it isn't much, but we've managed before and–"

"I ain't workin' there no more," he cut in.

"Why not?"

"John Duvoisin is a drunk, and I ain't workin' for no drunk. So we're just gonna have to let Haley work for them Harrin'tons and live on what she brings home. Then when you find somethin', we'll be sittin' pretty."

"But, John, she's young," Marie reiterated softly him. "Surely they won't pay her well. No, there a we'll use the money that I've–" *Too late!*

"And what money might that be, Mother?" h assessing her as if she had somehow managed to

"The money I've earned taking in laundry."

"The money you've earned taking in laund how did you manage to keep all this money a secret

"It wasn't a secret, John. It was my money, and I was saving

"*Your* money? *Your* money?" he bellowed, his face suffused with "That money belongs to me. *All of it!* I'm your husband! I'm the one who clothes and feeds you and your daughter and puts a roof over your heads, ain't I?"

"Yes, John, but–"

"Shut up! And don't be givin' me them saintly looks either!"

"Stop it!" Charmaine shouted. And then, fearing how the ensuing row would ultimately end, she reined in her anger. "Please, just stop it!"

Her unexpected outburst only succeeded in diverting her father's fury. "Now let me tell you somethin', young lady. I'm sick and tired of them looks you been givin' me – looks you think I can't see – believin' you're better than your pappy. It's about time you showed me some respect instead of sassin' me with that spiteful mouth of yours. As long as you're livin' under my roof, you'll be doin' as I say without any lip. You hear me?"

Her pulse quickened. "I hear you, Father, and I'll do just as you say."

He showed great surprise, and his rage ebbed.

Charmaine raised her chin. "I would love to work for the Harringtons. That is, if they'll have me."

"Oh, they'll have you all right," he reasoned, "unless your mother here has been lyin' 'bout what them folks are lookin' for."

Marie ignored her husband's remark. "Charmaine, you can't do this."

"Why not?" she queried.

"Yeah, why not, Mother?"

"Because of your life at St. Jude's, your education."

"What life?" Charmaine countered. "I don't have a life there, and I certainly don't have one here." Ire and pain sparked in her brown eyes, daggers of hatred that she shot at her father. "I want to leave, because once I'm employed by decent people, I'll no longer be living under *your* roof!"

But the declaration did not rile him, for he had gotten exactly what he wanted.

Chapter 1

Friday, September 9, 1836
Richmond, Virginia

John Duvoisin watched the Raven make its labored passage from the harbor. The ship groaned under her weighty cargo, cutting across the uncompromising current of the James River, her huge canvas sails bellied out, harnessing the wind that propelled her toward her destination – three islands nestled in the northeastern waters of the West Indies. Les Charmantes was often considered the foundation of the Duvoisin fortune. To John, Charmantes meant much more. He tracked the vessel and his mind meandered with the James. She was now but a toy on the wide river, and still, he stared after her as if, by mere eye contact, he could transport himself to her decks. Frustration and anger had kept him from boarding the vessel this morning, his reward: bitter reflection alone and a raging spirit that chastised him for doing nothing. His internal war reached its pinnacle as she traversed the river's bend and vanished from view. He drove rigid fingers through his tousled brown locks as if to liberate his turbulent thoughts, then strode from the bustling wharf, oblivious to the business negotiations of Richmond's busy waterfront. He mounted his horse and turned it into the crowds, leaving thoughts of the Raven and Charmantes behind.

"We're moving! We're finally moving!" Charmaine exclaimed as she peered through the porthole of her small cabin. Turning, she smiled triumphantly at Loretta Harrington, who sat complacently on the only anchored chair. "Won't you come and see?"

"No thank you, my dear," Loretta replied, returning the radiant smile. "I'll allow the ship to take care of itself and pray that my stomach does the same." It was the one reservation the middle-aged woman had about this entire trip: seasickness. But Charmaine Ryan was well worth any discomfort she might endure in the next four or five days, so she bent her mind to the task at hand. "Why don't we practice a bit more for the interview, Charmaine? It will take my mind off the rocking of the ship."

"I'm quite prepared," Charmaine replied, but she did as Loretta suggested and came and sat beside the woman who had become a second mother to her...

Charmaine had been welcomed into the Harrington house nearly three years ago. Marie Ryan had contacted the couple when she realized that her daughter would not be talked out of her decision to leave home, and Joshua Harrington had taken an immediate liking to the sensitive yet talkative fifteen-year old. In her large brown eyes, he saw a determination rarely found in one so young, and in her words, noted a firm conviction for what was right and good. After that first meeting, he was certain that Charmaine Ryan would make an excellent companion for his wife, who sorely missed her five grown sons. He hoped that the girl would become the daughter that Loretta never had.

Within a fortnight, all the arrangements had been made, and Charmaine left one life behind to begin another. She moved into a pretty, whitewashed house in a residential section of Richmond, taking her meager belongings with her. She would live with the Harringtons during the week and spend the weekends with her parents.

Charmaine's only regret was leaving her mother to fend for herself. But Marie began spending time at the St. Jude Refuge, drawing solace from the work there, content to shoulder the woes of others rather than dwell on her own, happy in fact. Thus, Charmaine found it strange when she grew unusually distant one weekend, surmising that some misfortunate troubled her. Though Marie avoided the details, she said, "I used to think that only the poor suffer, but I was wrong. Perhaps the greater the wealth, the deeper the pain."

Within the month, John Ryan decided to put a stop to his wife's 'charity' work. Charmaine was determined to thwart him. Due to the fact that her wages exceeded what he'd expected her to earn, she had secretly retained half. Now she insisted that her mother use it. "Tell father the church is paying you," she conspired. "Then he will be happy that you are working there." Sure enough, his grumbling ceased when the cold cash was placed in his hand.

Life with the Harringtons was a breath of fresh air. Under their roof, Charmaine felt secure. In this home, the husband treated his wife with respect and adoration. Joshua Harrington was everything a spouse should be. Likewise, Loretta was devoted to him. A dear and kind woman, she never had a harsh word for anyone. Charmaine benefited the most from the matron's fine character, blossoming in her affection.

"You are more than a companion to me," Loretta had insisted within the first year. "I consider you a part of my family, Charmaine."

Charmaine came to believe this, and it was only when the Harrington sons ventured home that she felt unhappy, envying the relationships between husbands and wives, children and parents, fathers and daughters. Although she was always included in their gatherings, Charmaine was careful to remain aloof, for this loving family didn't belong to her, not as long as her own parents lived. Her mother and father were a constant reminder of who she really was.

For two years, she guarded her background, frightened that the Harringtons would send her packing if they learned the truth. Though her mother was a good woman, she was but an orphan whose only stroke of fortune had been her adoption and education at the St. Jude Refuge. Marie's parentage was probably no better than John Ryan's, and he was nothing more than white trash in the eyes of civilized Richmond gentry such as the Harringtons.

Loretta and Joshua pondered her pensive moods, which usually occurred after her visits home. They sensed that she suffered, yet reasoned that she needed time to overcome her reticence. Time, however, was not on Charmaine's side.

Her father confronted her one weekend. "You been workin' for them Harrin'tons gone two years now. When are they plannin' on payin' you more?"

Charmaine *had* received an increase, but since she continued to share half her wages with her mother, she'd set the additional money aside for herself.

"I'll ask them, Father," she blurted out, the vow apparently appeasing him.

Not so; her hasty response fed his suspicions, and for a week, he mulled it over. Then, late one Friday night, he decided to set things right. It took him a bottle of whisky to muster the courage to lumber up to the Harrington house on wobbly legs and pummel the front door. When the maid opened it, he pushed his way in, demanding to see Joshua Harrington.

"I wanna know how much you been payin' my daughter," he slurred when Joshua appeared, "and I also wanna collect her wages personally from now on. I ain't gonna be cheated outta what's my right to claim!"

"Man, you're drunk!"

"You're damn right I'm drunk! But I'll tell ya one goddamn thing, drunk can make a man see clear. I know Haley's been tryin' to rook her ol' pappy, and I'll be havin' none of it! *Do you hear?"* He slammed his fist into his hand.

"Go home and sleep it off," Joshua cajoled, taking Ryan by the elbow and leading him to the door. "We can discuss this when you're sober."

"Oh no you don't!" John Ryan objected, twisting free. "I know what you're up to. You're in on this little conspiracy. I want them extra wages I ain't been getting', and I want 'em now!" He tried to grab Joshua's lapels, but lost his balance and staggered into the wall.

Joshua flung the door open and spoke in a low, clipped tone. "I've not withheld any wages from your daughter. Clearly, this is a matter to discuss with her, but now is neither the time nor the place. Charmaine has retired for the evening. Now, I ask you politely to leave. Go home and sleep off your sorry state." Joshua pointed toward the walkway.

John Ryan finally shuffled from the house, mumbling under his breath. "If you ain't part a this rotten scheme, then my wife must be behind it. I shoulda known she was lyin' to me."

Charmaine remained unaware of the confrontation; Joshua thought to spare her the humiliation. But he regretted this decision when the following Monday arrived, and she did not return from her visit home. Loretta grew worried. They didn't know where the Ryans actually lived and had no way of contacting her. After a second day passed without word, Joshua went to see Father Michael. The priest had, after all, arranged the initial meeting between the Harringtons and Marie. But Michael had no idea where they lived either. Apprehension set in when Joshua related the story of John Ryan's drunken tirade. Marie had been absent from the refuge for four days. Michael had suspected that her home life was unhappy, and though he had asked her about bruises that appeared overnight, she would brush his concerns aside with excuses. "Just a fall I took… I'm all right," or "I just bumped into the door last night when it was dark… I'm very clumsy." Michael feared the truth, but what could he do? Today, his anger eclipsed the vows he had taken twenty-five years ago. If John Ryan had hurt Marie and Charmaine…

Late Wednesday night, Charmaine gathered the courage to return to the Harringtons. Her mother was dead. Slowly, painfully, she described the squalid life she had endured under her father's roof, culminating with the past weekend when she had found her mother lying unconscious. Even though her father was nowhere to be found, Charmaine knew what had happened. She'd run from the house, crying for help. The neighbors had taken pity on her, summoning a doctor. For three days, her mother lie clinging to life, words occasionally spilling from her lips, begging her husband to stop. Charmaine wept when she learned that a dispute over her wages had instigated the fatal beating.

The following morning, Joshua visited the local sheriff, demanding the immediate arrest of John Ryan. Because Joshua was an upstanding citizen, the sheriff quickly issued the necessary warrant. If John Ryan were in the area, he would be apprehended.

Marie was buried the next day, a quiet funeral attended by the Harringtons and friends from the refuge. Many mourners cried, including Father Michael. As the last prayers were spoken and the small crowd departed, the priest took Charmaine aside. "I'm sorry, Charmaine," he murmured. "Your mother will be deeply missed. If you're ever in need, please don't hesitate to come to me."

"I will be fine, Father," she said. "The Harringtons have offered me a permanent home, but thank you all the same."

One week passed, followed by the next, and it became clear that John Ryan was either far from Richmond or cleverly hiding. The chances of making him pay for his heinous crime grew slimmer by the day. Many nights Charmaine lie awake, fearful that he might be waiting for the opportunity to corner her alone. Although the Harringtons assured her that he would never show his face again, she was ever wary of the shadows, especially when she walked down the city streets. Was he lurking between the buildings, in the doorways, watching and waiting? To calm her fears, she prayed for her mother, resolute in her belief that Marie had found peace in the afterlife and watched over her from paradise.

A year went by and Charmaine began to relax. In that time she had become a daughter to Loretta in nearly every way. The truth about her background *had* changed the Harrington's opinion of her. They loved her all the more.

Loretta took her further under wing, determined to mold her into a graceful lady, certain that she would recognize her value if her station in life were elevated. To this end, an elaborate tutelage commenced. Loretta prided herself on etiquette, and Charmaine found that by following this gentlewoman's perfect example, grace and dignity became second nature. Loretta built upon Charmaine's rudimentary orphanage education, introducing her to literature, fine art, and classical music. She taught Charmaine how to dance, how to sew, and they spent many happy hours in front of a blazing hearth with needlepoint in hand.

Of all the subjects she studied with Loretta, Charmaine cherished her music lessons most. She excelled at the pianoforte, her talent perfected by the melodies themselves and the happiness and sense of well-being she experienced each time she mastered a particular piece. The salubrious effect did not go unnoticed, and one day, Joshua surprised them with a most unexpected and extravagant gift – a 'piano', touting it as the innovation of the century. Unlike its predecessor, the piano's resonance was deep and full-bodied. Loretta took to the new instrument like a duck to water. Inspired, Charmaine strove to fine tune her skill, and with time, had to congratulate herself, for whenever the Harrington sons came to call, their children would gather around the keyboard, requesting that *she* play.

She looked forward to these convivial visits, though they led to new yearnings. Loretta saw it and knew that Charmaine wondered where her life was leading. "She needs a husband," Loretta told Joshua one evening. "Don't you see how longingly she looks at our boys and their children?" When Joshua snorted, she fretted the more. "If only one of our sons weren't married..."

Loretta began inviting eligible young men to the house; but none of them caught Charmaine's fancy. In fact, she was certain the girl had no idea what she was up to until one day Charmaine put a stop to it. "Mrs. Harrington, I'm not interested in the gentlemen you've invited here to meet me." When Loretta feigned confusion, she continued with, "I don't think I'll ever marry. I never want to live the life my mother did."

Loretta anguished over the declaration. "Charmaine, not all men are like your father. Take Joshua, for instance. He is kind and loving. You can have such a husband someday, too. But it won't happen if you see your father in every man."

"Better that I remember the likes of my father than to turn a blind eye to reality. I felt my mother's pain – lived with it. I cannot forget that so easily."

"Charmaine, you're too young to give up on all mankind. There is someone out there for you, but you must open your heart." One look at Charmaine's stormy countenance, and Loretta knew it would take more than words to convince her.

From that day forward, Loretta was determined to change Charmaine's way of thinking, to nudge her from the safe but isolated haven of the Harrington house and into the world of the living. Easier said than done. Just as exasperation was setting in, a new and unprecedented opportunity presented itself. Loretta knew that if she failed to capitalize on it, Charmaine's life was destined to stagnate and with time, turn bitter.

A letter from her sister mentioned that Frederic and Colette Duvoisin were seeking a governess for their three young children. Loretta knew the name well. The Duvoisin family owned large stretches of land in Virginia. In fact, her brother-in-law was an overseer to the Duvoisin holdings on the Caribbean island where the family lived. Les Charmantes was a fabled paradise. Although Loretta had never made the journey there herself, her sister's occasional letters always praised its beauty, and Loretta began to believe that Les Charmantes was just what Charmaine needed: a new home far away, with children, new acquaintances, and God willing, a future!

Her mind made up, Loretta began her artful maneuvers to win Charmaine over to the idea. "I've had a lovely letter from Caroline," she casually mentioned one evening as they sat in the front parlor. Charmaine's eyes lifted from her needlepoint, and Loretta continued. "She's written of the Duvoisin family."

"Duvoisin family?" Charmaine queried, and because her pronunciation wasn't correct, Loretta repeated the French name: Doo-*vwah*-zan.

"Apparently, Frederic and Colette Duvoisin need a governess for their twin girls and young son. According to Caroline's letter, they are considering only young applicants. It would be a wonderful opportunity in such a fine house and serene setting. Something like this only comes along once in a lifetime, if that." Loretta looked up from her sewing to find Charmaine studying her intently.

"You think *I* should apply?" Charmaine asked, certain that Loretta had broached the subject for a very definite reason.

"Yes, I do."

Joshua cleared his throat. "I don't think that is a wise idea, my dear."

"And why not?" *If he says one word to waylay me, he will regret it!*

"The Duvoisin men are a wild lot," he muttered, despite the look his wife was giving him.

"Charmaine would be caring for three young children."

"It is not the children I am worried about," Joshua rejoined.

Loretta shook her head, dismissing his protestations with, "Now, Joshua, we don't live in the Middle Ages. Besides, I intend to accompany Charmaine to the island. If we find the position unsuitable, she need not accept it."

"Island?" Charmaine queried, "but I thought–"

"Les Charmantes," Loretta explained. "I've mentioned it before, Charmaine. It is where Caroline, Harold, and Gwendolyn have lived these past ten years. It is also the Duvoisin homestead."

"Yes, I know where your sister lives, but I thought the position would be here, in Virginia. The island–" she breathed deeply "–it must be very far away."

"Only as far away as a letter, and Duvoisin vessels are constantly en route between Richmond and the islands. The family is as much involved in shipping as it is in tobacco and sugar." Loretta paused before continuing. "Of course, it is your decision, my dear, and it needn't be hastily made. Think on it for a while. Isn't that right, Joshua?"

"Absolutely," he mumbled factitiously, cognizant of his wife's tactics.

Days passed with no mention of the island or the position available there. But Charmaine thought long and hard about traveling to Les Charmantes. Governess of three small children. It was better than maid or housekeeper, and she wouldn't always have Loretta to depend on. Where would she be twenty years from now? This opportunity was before her now, and another might never come her way again. More importantly, if she moved away, she'd no longer be fearful of her father's whereabouts.

Loretta seemed to sense when she was ready to capitulate and broached the subject from another angle. "You are an incredible young woman, Charmaine."

"Incredible indeed," Charmaine scoffed.

"I'll hear none of that," Loretta scolded. "Your worth is in your heart. The Duvoisin children would benefit from the love brimming there. If you speak as if you are unworthy, you make it so."

That fervent declaration left an impression. Perhaps Loretta was right. This was an unusual opportunity, and something might be waiting for her there. It couldn't hurt to visit Les Charmantes and see. Maybe her mother *was* watching over her. She'd leave it in God's hands.

Within the week, Loretta sent a letter to Caroline informing them of their impending visit. By month's end, Joshua had booked passage for the three of them aboard the Raven, one of the Duvoisin cargo vessels that would be delivering supplies to the island.

On the eve of the journey, Charmaine worried over her decision. But today, with the sky so blue, the river so calm, and her anticipation riding high, she was caught up in the exuberance of the moment and happy she had favored action over complacency, chosen the new over the old. If Loretta felt she could claim the coveted position of governess to the Duvoisin children, claim it she would. So, she sat beside her mentor in the small cabin and practiced the answers she would give to the questions that might be asked during her upcoming interview.

"That's fine," Loretta smiled. "And remember, Charmaine, you don't have to tell them *everything*."

"But what if they ask about my family?"

Loretta patted her hand and said, "My mother, God rest her soul, died a year ago. Unfortunately, my father left us long ago."

"But is that acceptable? Will they be satisfied with that?"

"As I told you before, I will see to it that they are."

"All is well!" the robust Joshua Harrington boomed as he fell into the chair that his wife had vacated.

Charmaine and Loretta looked up from the small bunk, the skirt they had been mending momentarily forgotten as they considered the man turned boy again. It was clear that he had enjoyed the last five hours above deck as the vessel forged into the Atlantic.

"Jonah Wilkinson tells me that he foresees no difficulties with our crossing, and, my dear wife, you will be glad to hear that the good Captain believes we will sight the islands in under four days, provided the winds remain with us."

"That *is* good news," she replied cheerfully.

"You know, my dear, we can't really call your affliction seasickness," he pointed out. "After all, you've never actually been–"

"Please, Joshua," she implored, "let us not speak about it."

"How thoughtless of me. Would you prefer to hear about our departure?"

"That would be lovely," she replied enthusiastically, winking at Charmaine.

"I knew it was going to be an exceptional voyage the moment we hoisted sail and started to move," he began. "And not due to the gusting wind. Luck was with us from the start. Captain Wilkinson had expected to be delayed by Mr. Duvoisin, but a message was delivered that he wouldn't be boarding the Raven to inspect the cargo as planned. Needless to say, that saved precious time. But the true good fortune lies in the fact that we were not subjected to Mr. Duvoisin's deplorable comportment and snide comments."

"Joshua!"

"Now Loretta, I've spoken of the man's questionable character before. Everyone in Virginia knows that where John Duvoisin travels, ridicule follows.

I tell you now, if he were residing on Les Charmantes, I would have grave misgivings in allowing our Charmaine to live there."

John... Charmaine thought... *How I despise that name!*

Saturday, September 10, 1836

Jonah Wilkinson charted his ship's passage, pleased that they'd experienced favorable weather thus far. The Raven would make excellent time if she did not encounter the tropical storms that often brewed in these waters in late August and September. But if yesterday's winds were indicative of the future, the voyage to Charmantes would be uneventful and completed in less than four days time. From there, he would steer his ship to New York, then to England, and finally back to Virginia, completing a four-month journey. Although he did not own the decks upon which he tread, Frederic Duvoisin had made him feel as if he alone were master of the Raven. For that reason, he'd work for no other.

He was scrutinizing his charts when Charmaine walked over to him. Although he knew every inch of this part of the Atlantic, he found it comforting and often times commanding to pour over the well-worn maps. The rustle of clothing distracted him, and he turned to look at her. They'd been introduced amid the confusion and flurry of their departure, and he hadn't given her a second thought, until now.

She did not have a stunning face like the rare beauties he'd seen during his travels. It did, however, possess a captivating quality if one cared to look. Well-shaped eyebrows highlighted her most alluring feature – her large brown eyes, framed to perfection by sooty lashes. Her nose was long and slim and turned up on the end. Her lips were neither thick nor thin, coming to life when she spoke. As Jonah stared down at her, he realized her loveliness would never truly be appreciated as long as her dark locks were subdued in a severe bun. But that was for the best, as was her plain apparel, which detracted from her trim figure. Any overt displays of femininity would unleash the uncouth manners of his wild crew.

"Good afternoon, Captain." She smiled up at him, making him feel much taller than his five feet seven inches. "I didn't mean to disturb you, but Mr. Harrington encouraged me to come above deck while he sees to his wife."

"How is the dear woman?" Jonah inquired, remembering that one of his passengers was not faring so well, even during this calmest of voyages.

"She's much improved, thank you. The first day was the worst. When she occupies her mind with a distraction, her constitution is the better for it."

"That's the way of it with many people, until they get their sea legs. But with you, Miss...?"

"Ryan," Charmaine supplied.

"Miss Ryan," he smiled, "you don't seem the least unsettled by this maiden voyage. I'm correct in assuming that this is your first time at sea?"

"Yes, but it's too beautiful to upset me." A radiant smile lit the whole of her face. She drew a deep breath, grasped the railing, and looked out at the endless expanse.

"It is breathtaking, is it not?" he asked, turning to the horizon as well, applauding the young woman's fledgling admiration.

"It makes me realize how small I am in comparison."

"Just as the waves crashed to shore before our birth," he observed in kind, "they will pound the sand after our death. Our passing will make no difference."

The words displeased her. "You think not?"

"There are those who would disagree. Are you one of them?"

"I'd like to believe that everyone makes a difference, if only a minor one."

Jonah marveled over the philosophical statement. She couldn't be more than eighteen. "Once you've reached my age, you may begin to wonder. But that's neither here nor there. Let me show you my pride and joy."

He motioned toward the stern, and Charmaine realized he meant the ship. Inclining her head, she indulged him, spending an hour walking the upper decks, learning each by name: forecastle, waist, and quarter. He told her that the one-hundred-twenty-five-foot vessel had been commissioned in Britain and had, since her maiden voyage over thirty years ago, traversed the high seas with him as her captain. He pointed out everything, from helm to capstan, describing the manpower required to raise the Raven's great length of chain and heavy anchor. Her masts were square-rigged, raked at a slight angle aft for optimum propulsion. Charmaine shielded her eyes and looked up at the three sky-piercing spars, politely humoring him as he went on with a litany of sails, from flying jib, soaring on the bowsprit and spearheading their journey, to the spanker, which acted with the rudder and forged their course. Unfortunately, he mistook her smile for interest and rambled on with his detailed dissertation.

Joshua finally joined them, and Charmaine sighed in relief, ready to escape to her own cabin. But the conversation unexpectedly turned to the Duvoisins, piquing her interest, so she hugged the rail instead.

"...very wealthy," the captain was saying, "ten ships, three islands, thousands of acres, and God knows what other investments. But that fortune comes at a high price. Frederic and his sons have been dealt their share of turmoil, a weighty load that I'd not care to carry..."

The greater the wealth, the deeper the pain... Charmaine thought.

"...There are many who resent their power and covet their money, but those very same men would likely abuse such power and wealth. At least the Duvoisin men come by it honestly, with hard work and keen minds."

Joshua grew circumspect. Over the past two days, Jonah Wilkinson had proven to be a man of integrity, and Joshua had come to respect his opinion. "You speak highly of them," he commented dubiously.

"I'm not placing Frederic on a pedestal, but he is a fair man, as fair as any I've known. It's a trait that he's passed on to his sons."

"Even John?" Joshua snorted. "A few words came to mind when we were introduced last year, but 'fair' was not one of them."

Jonah chuckled. "I'm not surprised. John can be decidedly caustic, his tongue as quick as his mind, but more often than not, he *is* fair. His sarcasm is just a shield."

"A shield?"

"Against the anger, against the guilt," Jonah replied. "It is rumored that he brought on a severe seizure that left his sire crippled. The stroke, or whatever it was, victimized both father and son. Frederic was once a strong and forceful man. Now he never leaves the confines of his estate. John suffers, too. He fled the island three years ago and hasn't returned since. As far as I know, he's had no contact with his father. He continues to manage all the Virginia and shipping assets out of Richmond, while Frederic relies on his other son, Paul, to run Charmantes. Unfortunately, that's created more problems."

"How so?" Joshua queried, enthralled.

"The brothers view matters differently. At times, their conflicting ideas pull those in between in opposite directions. There can only be one captain of a ship, lest it founder."

"So, the two sons struggle for the upper hand."

"It goes back to childhood rivalry. Paul enjoys a bond with his father that John, the legitimate son, never had."

"Legitimate?"

Jonah cleared his throat. He'd said too much, yet felt compelled to explain. "Frederic adopted Paul as an infant and raised him as his own, but his was an illegitimate birth. He's Frederic's son," Jonah finished, anticipating the next query. "Of that I'm certain."

"But why would a man favor a bastard child over–"

The inappropriate epithet was out before Joshua could catch himself. He reddened and looked at Charmaine, but her composure remained intact; apparently, she hadn't understood.

Jonah, however, did not seem pleased with the crude appellation. "Frederic respects both of his sons, but Paul works harder than John, so I suppose it has forged a stronger relationship."

"And John's mother?" Joshua asked, further surprised. "What is her reaction to all this?"

"Elizabeth died in childbirth over twenty-five years ago. Some say that Frederic blamed John for her death, but that's nonsense. Canards of that kind stemmed from the fact that Frederic grieved for many years after her death."

Charmaine was suddenly confused. "But I thought–" she faltered "–then Colette Duvoisin is Mr. Duvoisin's *second* wife?"

"He remarried ten years ago," Jonah answered succinctly.

Frederic grieved for many years after her death...

Charmaine canted her head, sensing evasiveness, unable to pinpoint the heart of her perplexity. Frederic Duvoisin, clearly an older man, had two grown sons, one by his first wife, another by a lover, and he had three other children, the youngest a baby really, these brought forth by a *second* wife.

"Is she an islander?" Charmaine asked.

"Who? Miss Colette? Oh my, no," the captain chuckled. "She is French, pure aristocrat. Arrangements were made by her mother, I believe," he added, uncomfortable with Charmaine's intense frown, attempting to thwart the gossip that he knew she was bound to hear.

"Her mother?"

"Colette was quite young at the time."

"How young?"

Jonah, who had waxed loquacious for the past hour, grew laconic. To Charmaine's further trepidation, Joshua Harrington allied himself to the man. "Arrangements of this sort are made all the time by the upper classes, aren't they, Captain Wilkinson?"

"Just so," Jonah hastily agreed.

Charmaine shivered in the blazing sun. She had thought that the wealthy enjoyed unlimited choices, yet here was a young woman, much like herself, imprisoned more surely than she would ever be.

"An arrangement?" she mused. "A more apt word would be bondage."

"Bondage?" Jonah objected with a false laugh, then added, "Miss Colette may have borne her husband three children, but I assure you, she enjoys a most comfortable life," as if that fact made their coupling palatable.

Charmaine bit her bottom lip, terribly troubled, and her mind ran far afield, to an island she had yet to tread. *A loveless marriage.* Her mother had suffered such a union. Suddenly, Charmaine's life no longer seemed suffocating. She had never appreciated how free she truly was.

The evening meal was served in the Captain's cabin with Charmaine and the Harringtons as his guests. The food, though mediocre, was tempered with good conversation. Even Loretta ate without discomfort, quickly approving of their warm host. Charmaine had shared all the things she had learned that afternoon, so Loretta didn't hesitate to ask her own questions, artfully starting with the Duvoisin's more distant past, one that seemed shrouded in a web of mystery. Jonah, who'd spent many evenings in the company of three generations of Duvoisin men, was happy to oblige...

In the early 1700's Jean Duvoisin left his native France and traveled to the American colonies. The younger son of a wealthy and politically connected family, he set out to find his own fortune, taking with him a sizeable sum of money, a fast ship, and his father's blessings. He settled in Newportes Newes, a thriving community and burgeoning shipping center at the mouth of the James River. When he heard of William Byrd II's plans to establish a new town some ninety miles northwest, he moved his young family to the site in 1737. Richmond was so dubbed in honor of Richmond on the Thames, England, and it was Jean Duvoisin who helped bolster her success. The Byrd trading post and warehouse, or Shocco as the Indians called it, was in need of a full-time shipper. Jean saw financial potential in assuming such a role and had a second ship commissioned in Newportes Newes. Byrd sanctioned the lucrative endeavor, then guaranteed its success by awarding him substantial acreage west of Richmond. In less than ten years, the entire parcel had been cleared and planted. In addition, Jean now owned three merchantmen that not only brought him wealth through the supplies he shuttled from Europe, but enabled him to transport his own tobacco inexpensively and expediently. When he died some twenty years later, both ventures had exceeded his wildest expectations. The plantation had tripled in size, he owned vast stretches of land throughout the Virginia territory, and the shipping operation belonged exclusively to his eldest son.

Jean Duvoisin II followed in his father's footsteps of expanding the Duvoisin empire, but he took to the seas to do so. The shipping industry became his obsession, the prosperity of the future. Upon his sire's demise, the family plantation was left to the care of other men. Jean II had already conquered the deserted islands he named Les Charmantes (pronounced 'lay shar-mont', meaning 'the charming ones'). Searching for a base location amidst the expanding routes of his ever-growing fleet, he tamed the wilderness of the largest island and built himself a villa that would allow him privacy. Rumors spread that the house, the very isle, was nothing more than a prison where he locked away his beautiful wife, gleaning him the title of gentleman pirate. Island lore held that he had kidnapped her from under the nose of a Richmond rival and feared losing her while he was at sea for many months, so he brought her to his isolated paradise so that she'd never escape him.

She was the first to give birth on Charmantes, bringing into the world six children. The three middle sons perished in a fire that claimed her life as well, leaving behind an eldest son, Jean III, a daughter, Eleanor, and a youngest son, Frederic, twelve years his brother's junior. Years later, Jean and Frederic both traveled to Virginia, taking charge once again of the investments there.

When Jean II fell ill in 1796, his elder son returned to Charmantes and became involved in the American and French West Indies dispute. It cost him his life. Within the year, Jean II died as well, and the Duvoisin fortune fell into Frederic's lap. He was only twenty-three. Finding it impossible to guard Charmantes while residing in Virginia, and fearing its possible loss, he journeyed back as well, expanding his father's farming enterprise into a full-fledged sugarcane plantation run on the work of slaves and indentured servants whom he personally hand picked.

He was already in his thirties when he married Elizabeth Blackford, a young Englishwoman fifteen years his junior. She left her family – a mother, father, brother, and sister – and traveled from Liverpool to the islands where she began her life with her new husband. But she died in childbirth less than a year later, leaving behind an embittered husband.

"The island has grown over the years," Jonah went on to say. "The sugarcane operation led to the building of a harbor where ships could unload supplies and take on raw sugar for transport. From there a town emerged, built by the freed bondsmen. Having served their time, Frederic encouraged the better men to continue on in his employ for set wages. These were the first men to truly settle Charmantes, some sending for families. Frederic's close associates insisted that he was mad, his idea sheer folly; in Europe, these men were criminals. But many had been punished for petty crimes. Poverty can make a man do foolhardy things. On Charmantes, they had an opportunity to start over, and most were happy to take it. They are rough around the edges, but there is little crime on the island. In a manner of speaking, they keep the peace. As the population multiplied, Frederic sponsored other businesses. First Thompson's Mercantile was built, supplying the islanders with all the staples. After that, a cooper opened up shop, crafting all the watertight casks necessary for sugar transport. Of course, Dulcie's was next."

"Dulcie's?" Loretta asked.

"The saloon," Jonah explained, stopping to take a sip of his black coffee. "Then a livery went up, and next a meetinghouse which serves as a church on Sundays. That was constructed about ten years ago. Miss Colette is a devout Catholic and insisted on it for the townspeople."

"Do they truly have a reverend to conduct services?" Loretta queried, astonished. "I thought my sister exaggerated when she mentioned Sunday Mass in one letter."

"No exaggeration there. The man is a Roman Catholic priest and has resided on Charmantes for years now."

"Isn't that a bit strange?" Joshua asked. "It seems to me that the Church wouldn't be sending priests to small, distant islands."

"You underestimate the size and scope of Charmantes," Jonah replied. "They even have a bank. It's run by one of Frederic's friends from Virginia. Many influential men have invested in Duvoisin enterprises, primarily the shipping end of his business, while a good many islanders are purchasing land on the outskirts of town, an option open to them as long as they build a house or business on it. The Duvoisin wealth intrigues them, whets their appetite. They feel they can grasp Frederic's good fortune just by owning a parcel of his land."

"And have they?" Joshua asked.

"In a day or two you'll set foot on Charmantes and see her people. Then you can decide if they live the good life or not."

Loretta leaned forward. "I know my sister and her husband are pleased with their move to the Caribbean. And I must admit, after your description, Captain, I'm looking forward to arriving. It sounds wonderful, doesn't it, Charmaine?"

But the girl was pensive, deaf to their conversation.

"Charmaine?"

"I'm sorry – what did you say?"

"Just that Les Charmantes sounds like a lovely place to call home," Loretta prompted. "But you seemed awfully far away."

Charmaine rubbed her brow. "No," she murmured, "I'm listening."

Loretta knew better. The girl had lamented Colette and Frederic Duvoisin's courtship throughout the afternoon, imagining the most wretched scenarios, refusing to consider other possibilities. Loretta was determined to ascertain the truth before Caroline had a chance to bend their ears.

"Captain Wilkinson," she began, "if I'm not being too presumptuous, could you tell us a bit more about Colette Duvoisin?"

Jonah responded with a frown, and Loretta diplomatically digressed. "My sister loves to prattle, but hates to write. Her short letters are few and far between. Charmaine may soon be working for Mr. and Mrs. Duvoisin. Surely you can appreciate her eagerness to become acquainted with them."

"What would you like to know?" he finally relented, realizing there was no point in trying to avoid what they'd eventually find out.

"Charmaine seems to think that Miss Colette is young enough to be Mr. Duvoisin's daughter."

"She is. Younger than his two sons, in fact."

Charmaine gave Loretta an 'I told you so' look.

Jonah read it, too. Folding his arms across his chest, he said, "Miss Colette's family was suffering from financial difficulties. Frederic saw them through all of that. There was also a brother, who was quite ill. Frederic's wealth defrayed the expenses from his prolonged malady. Now, some might call such an arrangement 'bondage', but I'm sure it's not the word Miss Colette would use."

Charmaine ignored Jonah's final assertion, horrified. Her mother's life had been deplorable, but at least that had been Marie's choice. Colette Duvoisin, on the other hand, had been married off for monetary reasons, much like chattel. Charmaine felt terribly sad for the woman.

Jonah leaned back in his chair. "Miss Colette is not as unhappy as you imagine her to be, Miss Ryan."

"That is something I will have to decide for myself, Captain," she replied.

Loretta patted Charmaine's hand, certain that the Captain was right. "At least the mistress of the manor will be someone closer to your own age," she placated. "You may become friends."

Charmaine hadn't thought of this and hoped that might come true.

Monday, September 12, 1836

She awoke early the morning of her fourth day at sea. Captain Wilkinson expected to sight the islands with the break of dawn, and she wanted to be above deck as they came into view. She dressed quickly, choosing her best Sunday dress of pale green, and was brushing out the last tangles in her thick, unruly hair when the awaited shout resounded from above. "Land ho!"

Indecisive for only a moment, she threw the dark brown locks over her shoulder, where a cascade of curls fell to her waist. No bun today, lest she forfeit the coveted sight. Let the wind take the tresses where it would; they'd not spoil this glorious day, which promised the start of a new life. Stealing a final peek in her hand mirror, she smiled in satisfaction, then hastened from the cabin

Captain Wilkinson took no notice of her when she reached the upper deck, his eyes raised to the rigging and the crew that prepared the Raven for docking, some climbing the ratlines to adjust the sails. Surmising that Joshua was still abed, Charmaine moved out of harm's way to a vacant spot at the port railing.

The tarrying men began to ogle her, and she bowed her head to their crude comments. Although she'd turned their heads a number of times during the voyage, their perusal had never come close to a leer. She glanced down at her dress wondering if her attire was somehow indiscreet, but finding nothing there, she focused on the great expanse of ocean, hoping to catch sight of land. They were forging into a stiff headwind, and the gales swirled round her, capturing her unbound hair one moment and molding her skirts against her legs the next.

When one man whistled, Jonah's attention was snared. He chuckled. By all outward signs, the girl was trying to ignore his surly crew. Wiping the sweat from his brow, he walked over to her. "Good morning, Miss Ryan."

Relieved, Charmaine faced him.

Jonah took in her ebullient smile, the sparkling eyes alight with anticipation, and the wild tresses that framed her delicate face, evincing a comeliness thus far obscured. No wonder his men were behaving this way.

"I heard the heralding of land, but I can't see it," she complained. "Are the islands still so far away that I need a spy glass?"

"No, my dear. It's just that you are searching the wrong part of the sea."

Embarrassed, she dropped her gaze, but he took her elbow and led her to the opposite railing, pointing to the southeast. There, on the horizon, was land.

He returned to his work, but she remained starboard side, watching the dark smudge grow larger until the whitest of beaches came into view, a great expanse that seemed tremendous for a mere island. Beyond the shore, she detected shrubs and long grasses that meandered into shaded areas cast by huge, bowing palm trees, willows and silk cottons. She marveled at its untouched beauty, suddenly realizing that she had yet to see any human habitation. There were no docks, no houses, and no people. She looked over her shoulder to question the Captain about this, but he was nowhere to be found, so her curiosity would have to wait. They were now riding parallel to the seemingly deserted island. She felt much like Jean Duvoisin II, discovering his paradise for the first time – untamed, yet free. There couldn't be a more serene place on earth, she thought, concluding that this was probably not the main island, but rather one of the smaller two that had not been settled.

By and by, the beaches turned rocky, and cliffs dominated the coastline, jutting ever higher as they trekked east. Huge waves sent sea spray spiraling upwards as they bombarded the palisades, showering a mist that reached as far as the decks. They closed in on a lighthouse that marked the northernmost point. Once they passed it, her eyes fell back to the bluffs, which curved to the right far into the distance.

The hour lengthened, and Captain Wilkinson returned, Joshua Harrington at his side. "We're circling Charmantes," he said, "and should reach the cove shortly."

"The cove?" she asked.

"That is where the dock is built, on the eastern coast. Most Caribbean islands have a leeward or western port. During hurricane season, they are safe from those storms. But Charmantes boasts an almost landlocked harbor, a bay that is protected by a peninsula. Because he was able to construct his harbor in the east, Jean II chose the safer western side of the island to erect his mansion, where the beaches are sandy and beautiful. When we enter the inlet, this untouched beauty will be replaced by the bustling town I spoke of the other evening."

He pointed to the eastern horizon. "If you look carefully, you'll see the other two islands that comprise Les Charmantes." Shielding their eyes, Charmaine and Joshua were able to discern two tiny landmasses.

Shortly thereafter, the main island curved sharply away, and the Raven tacked south, hugging the peninsula now. Charmaine was once again left alone as Joshua accompanied the Captain. Seabirds appeared from nowhere, darting between the towering masts, swooping low and hovering over the water, squawking loudly as if welcoming their approach.

They reached the cape's tip, and Charmaine's eyes returned to the spider web rigging. Ropes groaned as the triangular sails were trimmed. Instantly, they billowed taut, harnessing the wind. The stern veered out, and the vessel pivoted right, completing a wide one-hundred-eighty-degree loop starboard side. 'Wearing ship', the captain called it, and Charmaine marveled at how the huge merchantman was navigated north and into Charmantes' estuary. She gasped when the deserted land gave way to a busy wharf and thriving community.

As the Captain skillfully maneuvered the Raven closer to port, angling the packet against the largest of three docks, Charmaine ran hungry eyes over every visible portion of the island, buildings everywhere. When she had her fill, her gaze turned toward the people, ordinary people she quickly assessed. Why had she thought they'd be different?

The crowd was increasing; the merchantman's arrival of paramount interest, the pier a sea of faces now – white, black, and every shade in between – all modestly garbed, though far from impoverished. There were women among them, some clutching infants to their breasts as they waved to their sailor husbands. These crewmen were not the wanderers Charmaine had supposed them to be, but had families waiting for them here.

The Raven was secured in a frenzy, as scores of men labored with the massive vessel. Finally, the gangplank was lowered, and those on the quay scurried to her decks. Friends slapped large callused hands across the backs of those they had not seen for many months. Plans were already being made for a night at the town's saloon. Husbands rushed to the wharf to hug their wives and children. For the moment, all thoughts of labor were suspended as handshakes, embraces, and short stories were exchanged.

A hush came over the throng as a tall, dark man boarded the vessel and came to stand in their midst. He radiated a magnetism that commanded everyone's attention, and Charmaine's eyes were riveted, admiring him in a way she had never admired a man before. His face was swarthy, testifying to many hours spent under the tropical sun, his jaw, sharp. Intense eyes hinted of a keen mind. Chestnut-brown locks fell on a sweaty brow, and his straight nose plunged down to a dark moustache and full lips. His stance was easy, yet his bearing was self-assured, proud – aristocratic. "Let's go men!" he bellowed, white teeth flashing against his bronzed skin. "The sooner we get this ship unloaded, the sooner the drinks are on me at Dulcie's!"

Loud cheers went up, and all was in chaos as the men fell into their work. The tall stranger stood his ground, feet planted apart, issuing a spate of orders to all quarters of the deck. The main hatch was thrown open, equipment was rolled forward, and a pulley and boom were quickly assembled. He smiled broadly as he surveyed the enthusiastic laborers before him.

Charmaine could not tear her eyes away, pleased that she'd gone unnoticed.

With a sweep of his forearm, he mopped the sweat from his brow. Then, in imitation of the seamen and longshoremen, he ripped off his own white shirt, revealing a broad, furry chest and wide shoulders. He flung the garment over the railing and threw himself into unloading the vessel.

Charmaine's heart took up an unsteady beat. In Richmond, gentlemen never doffed their shirts, and astounded, she gaped at the play of muscles across his tanned back and arms. Obviously, he was not afraid to work; rather, he enjoyed it. She felt the blood rise to her cheeks as her eyes traveled down his back, which glistened with sweat, to his muscular legs, sculpted against the fabric of his form-fitting trousers. She turned away, unsettled by the overwhelming emotions that assaulted her. She couldn't breath. He was, by far, the most handsome man she'd ever beheld.

"Charmaine!" Joshua called, pushing his way through the commotion to reach her. "I've located Harold and Caroline Browning."

"They're here?"

"Waiting on the wharf," he answered, taking hold of her arm and leading her to the stern of the ship. "Apparently, they expected us to be on the Raven once they realized it was coming from Richmond."

Charmaine nodded, though her regard rested on the captivating stranger. He and three other men were rolling the first casks across the deck, one to the other.

"Who is that man?" she asked.

"Paul Duvoisin," Joshua replied gruffly, noting the blush on Charmaine's cheeks. "We've already been introduced."

"When?"

"Just a few moments ago on the wharf. But come, Charmaine, we must hurry. The ocean breezes are all but gone, and I do not care to spend the remainder of the day in this heat. It's only going to get worse as the sun rises higher."

They neared the gangplank, and Joshua gestured over the side of the ship to a pleasant looking couple waving up at them. "I have to fetch Loretta. Why don't you make your way down to her sister?"

"But I have to get my belongings," she replied. "They're still in my cabin."

"Not to worry. I'll fetch them for you."

"Don't be silly! You go ahead and help Mrs. Harrington, and I'll meet you on the pier with the Brownings in ten minutes time."

Finally in agreement, Joshua departed, taking the stairs of the companionway quickly down. But Charmaine's steps were halted as her gaze fell once again upon Paul Duvoisin. Her heart raced, awed by the realization that a fortune rested in the hands of someone so young and handsome. Best not to dwell on it. With that thought, she descended to the deck below and collected her baggage.

When she once again stepped into the midday sun, Joshua was nowhere in sight. Certain that she had finished her packing before him, she began her search for Captain Wilkinson. It would be impolite to leave without thanking him.

She learned from one of the seamen that he was in his cabin. Crossing to the quarterdeck, she knocked on his door and was told to come in. He was seated at his desk, with Paul Duvoisin leaning over his right shoulder. Neither man looked up from the sheets spread before them, but the captain motioned toward her with a brusque command, "Don't dally boy! Bring them here!"

Charmaine was stunned and didn't answer.

He looked up. "Oh, Miss Ryan, I apologize," he said. "I thought you were Wagner. He was fetching some documents for me."

With the mention of the unfamiliar name, Paul straightened, his attention instantly snared. *This is unusual. What a comely lass: wavy hair, pretty face, and curvaceous figure. Why is she on the Raven?* He inhaled. He had never seen her before. "Is this a beautiful niece you've kept hidden from us, Jonah?"

"You know I have no kin, Paul."

"So you've said," Paul mused, dissatisfied with the response.

His eyes remained fixed on the young woman, but before he could pose another question that might reveal her identity, the cabin boy rushed in. Paul snatched the documents from him, sat down, and began reading them.

Dismissed, Charmaine's heart sank, but she quickly recovered and thanked Jonah Wilkinson for his hospitality. He, in turn, kissed her hand and wished her the best. Glancing toward the desk, she quietly left his cabin.

Above deck, the heat had intensified. She retrieved her trunk and lumbered toward the gangway, certain the Harringtons were waiting for her.

Joshua spotted her and boarded the vessel, taking her luggage in one hand and grabbing hold of her elbow with the other. In no time, she was standing on the solid dock, marveling at how her feet compensated for a motion that did not exist, as if she were still on the rocking ship.

"So, you are Charmaine," Caroline said as introductions were made, her husband smiling pleasantly. "You're as lovely as my sister wrote."

"I'm afraid Mrs. Harrington is too kind."

"Nonsense," the plump woman replied. "You are nearly as pretty as my Gwendolyn."

Her husband coughed loudly, but she silenced him with a cold glare.

Charmaine was glad to climb into the Browning's carriage. "Is it always so hot here?" she complained, dabbing at her brow.

"There's normally a breeze," Harold replied, "but you get used to it."

"Not if she wears her hair that way," Caroline countered.

Charmaine lifted the mane off her neck. "I was trying to wrap it in a bun–"

"Charmaine," Loretta interrupted, squeezing her hand, "it's lovely."

Caroline raised her nose, but quickly turned her attention to the road. "Look – over there!" she exclaimed, pointing across the thoroughfare, motioning for her sister to shift to her side of the coach. "That's Dulcie's. Oh, the goings on at that establishment! But men will be men. Isn't that right, Harold?"

"I wouldn't know," he mumbled, talking to his lap.

"What was that?"

This time he answered clearly. "I said, only you would know."

She eyed him suspiciously, then ignored him altogether as the town continued to roll by. "And over there is the mercantile. It carries a wide variety of goods, nearly as fine a selection as any general store you'll find in the States. But you don't want to shop there on the weekends. That's when the bondsmen make their purchases. What a filthy lot they are!"

"Caroline," the man reprimanded, offended, "many of them are good men."

"How can you say that?" she demanded, every bit as offended as he. "Murderers – that's what they are!"

"They're not murderers. They wouldn't be working here if they were. You know that. Most are poor men paying the price of a minor offense."

"Oh, don't be so addlebrained!" she accused, insulted by his contradictions. "They're common criminals. Why must you always make excuses for them?"

"I know them, or have you forgotten I oversee most of their work?"

"Ssh!" she hissed, her indignation and revulsion surpassed by her shame. "Do you want everyone to know that you associate with those people?"

"I'm not going to hide what I do for a living on this island," he replied in exasperation, "or worse still, lie about it, as you do."

"Harry, please," she protested, her nervous eyes flitting over those in the coach, "not in front of my family!"

When her bottom lip stopped quivering, she peered out the window and complained anew. "Now look what you've done! We're on the outskirts of town and have missed all the sights!"

She remained petulant for all of one minute. "It's a shame you missed meeting Paul Duvoisin, Loretta," she said, warming to a new topic. "Quite a fine specimen of a man he is. But a rogue, if you know what I mean, with quite an eye for the ladies. They say the apple doesn't fall far from the tree. Following in his father's footst–"

"Caroline!" Harold objected again, appalled by her audacity.

"Well, it's true!" she returned in kind, annoyed that her husband would dare squash the bit of gossip that begged telling. "Imagine, remaining a widower for all those years – sampling his fill – only to up and marry a girl young enough to be his daughter! And to think that Colette–"

"Caroline!" Harold exploded. "Hold your tongue!"

"But Harold!" the virago mewled, shaken by his uncharacteristic outrage.

His irate manner cooled as swiftly as it had spiked, and he pulled at his shirt collar in evident distress. "I'm sorry," he apologized lamely. "But my wife shouldn't be spreading rumors."

Caroline clicked her tongue, muttering, "They're not rumors, they're facts."

The remainder of the trip was passed in silence, leaving Charmaine to wonder over the woman's temperament, so unlike that of her sister. Beyond that, Charmaine's thoughts traveled to Colette Duvoisin, the same questions resurfacing, no less troubling. Was the young woman content bound to a man old enough to be her father? What revelations would the next few days bear?

When they finally arrived at the Browning cottage, a girl of perhaps fifteen emerged from within. Like her mother, she was plump, but she had a charming smile and rushed forward to greet them. "Aunt Loretta? Uncle Joshua?"

"Gwendolyn?" Loretta queried. "My, how you've grown!"

As hugs were exchanged, Harold drew his wife aside and whispered to her in heated tones. "If I hear so much as another syllable concerning Frederic and Colette, I swear I will send you packing." When Caroline's mouth dropped open, he rushed on. "Do you want me to lose my position here? Would it please you to see me banished like Clayton Jones? Remember what happened to him?"

Caroline's eyes grew wide as saucers. "Yes – but no – of course not."

"Or perhaps you'd like to be the next Alma Banks? That would really give the townspeople something to talk about, *now wouldn't it*?"

Caroline's expression bordered on the horrific.

"Yes," Harold nodded with a twisted grin, realizing he was finally getting somewhere. "You'd best think about that the next time you feel like wagging your tongue. Frederic might be ill, but I have it on good authority that he's not as incapacitated as everyone seems to believe he is." Harold sighed. "Beyond that, I respect Colette, as much as I do her husband. If not for them, who knows what I'd be doing today? Therefore, you will cease your prattling!"

She nodded meekly, took a moment to compose herself, and finally beckoned everyone inside.

Loretta sighed reflectively. *Some things never change.*

Chapter 2

Wednesday, September 14, 1836
Charmantes

Sunlight poured into the bedroom that Charmaine shared with Gwendolyn Browning. Her eyes opened and she stretched, enjoying the gentle breezes that whispered through the windows. In just a few hours, the coolness of the early morning would yield to the intense rays of the Caribbean sun. This was summer on Charmantes, but according to the Brownings, the other seasons were not much different, just a bit milder.

Crawling from the small double bed, Charmaine looked down at her slumbering friend. Yes, she could call Gwendolyn her friend. The girl was talkative and bubbly, her gaiety infectious.

Yesterday, they had toured the town with Caroline. Today, Gwendolyn wanted to show Charmaine the other, more beautiful spots Charmantes had to offer. Charmaine was looking forward to it. She didn't relish Mrs. Browning's company and was happy to leave the woman with her sister for the day.

As she sat at the dressing table and unbraided her hair, Gwendolyn stirred. "Good morning," she greeted with a yawn. "Why are you up so early?"

"I couldn't sleep. So, what do you have in store for me today?"

"The beaches. They're lovely compared to the ugly town."

Charmaine brushed out the riotous locks. "I didn't think it was ugly." In truth, she had been quite impressed by it. Even with Captain Wilkinson's description aboard the Raven, she had not been prepared for the self-sufficiency she'd witnessed yesterday. Besides the mercantile, saloon, meetinghouse, and bank, the town had a skilled cooper at the cooperage, a farrier and blacksmith at the livery, a tanner, potter, and cobbler sharing space in one of the three large warehouses, and a lumberyard of sorts, which supplied various building materials for all the cottages being erected. According to Mrs. Browning, most of the wood came from the northern pine forests and was milled right there. Additional hardwoods were transported from Virginia. Jonah Wilkinson had been correct; many families intended to make Charmantes their permanent home. Construction was visible everywhere, and only the sea stood as a reminder that this bustling 'city' was on an island and not part of a greater country.

Gwendolyn watched Charmaine coif her thick tresses into a respectable bun. "Your hair is so unusual, Charmaine. How ever did it get so curly?"

"I don't know. My parents had straight hair, and I curse my misfortune."

"But it's beautiful! If I had your hair, I'd set my sights for Paul Duvoisin!"

"Oh, Gwendolyn, you do have high aspirations!"

"Maybe I'd have to lose a bit of flesh around my middle," the girl sulked, looking down at her plump figure. "But after that – well – there'd be no stopping me!" When Charmaine shook her head, she pressed on. "If you saw him, you'd understand what I mean!"

"I have seen him, and I know what you mean."

"You have?" Gwendolyn asked, jumping from the bed. "When? Where?"

"The day we arrived, on the ship."

"Oh… isn't he the most handsome man you've ever seen?" she declared dreamily. "I could just swoon every time he looks my way. Only, when he does look my way, he's never looking at me." She pouted until struck by a new thought. "If I had your curves and hair, I'd have a chance, a *real* chance!"

"A chance at what?"

"A marriage proposal, of course! And I'd accept immediately, before he could change his mind!"

Charmaine smiled at the juvenile declaration. Her friend babbled on.

"I know I'm only romancing. But look at you. You have all those things a man looks at, especially your lovely figure and beautiful hair."

"I'm sorry to say that you are wrong, Gwendolyn. I was wearing my hair like this when Mr. Duvoisin and I first met, and he wasn't interested in introductions."

"He was probably busy," the girl reasoned. "He's always like that when a ship comes into port. All work, all business. But wait until you're living under his roof, seeing him every day, perhaps taking meals with him. Things are bound to change, aren't they? And then you will be the envy of every girl on this island, because you'll have that once in a lifetime chance that we've all been pining for. You mark my words if Paul doesn't notice you then!"

Paul Duvoisin's house... living under his roof... taking meals with him... seeing him every day! The full import of working for the Duvoisins took hold. Why hadn't she thought of him living there? It was his home! Charmaine felt giddy, seized by a host of paradoxical emotions: apprehension and expectation, dread and elation.

They left the bedroom some time later, dressed and ready for a day's excursion. Loretta was sitting at the kitchen table, finishing a letter of introduction that she would send off to the Duvoisin manor. In it, she had requested an audience with Madame Colette Duvoisin, stating that her companion, Charmaine Ryan, had traveled to Les Charmantes from Richmond in order to apply for the position of governess.

"That should do it," she said, patting the folded missive. She set her hand to another, informing her housekeeper that they had arrived and would spend no more than a month abroad. By the time the girls had eaten, she was finished and asked Gwendolyn to post the letter. "Here is some money," she added. "Caroline tells me there will be a fee to have it shipped to the Richmond post office."

Gwendolyn nodded. "What about the other one to Mrs. Duvoisin?"

"Your father said he will deliver it today," Loretta replied.

The waterfront town wilted in the morning sun, but it did not seem to impede any of the islanders. Charmaine and Gwendolyn ambled toward the general store, and still Charmaine felt faint, reaching the shade of the mercantile porch none too soon. The heat had not affected her companion.

"Come, Charmaine," she encouraged, "I see Rebecca Remmen. Her brother doesn't generally allow her to walk about town on her own."

"You go," Charmaine said. "I have to rest a minute. Why don't you give me your aunt's letter and I'll post it while you talk with your friend?"

"All right! I'll meet you inside in a few minutes."

Charmaine entered the general store and was surprised to find it empty, save its proprietress, Madeline Thompson, the comely widow introduced to her yesterday. "May I help you?" the woman asked, her sultry voice laced with a mild, southern accent.

"Yes, please," Charmaine replied. "I have a letter that I'd like to post."

Madeline scrutinized the item she handed over. "Richmond... Hmm... It's a shame you didn't get this to me sooner. The post was carted off yesterday. But I suppose I could deliver it to the Raven myself, after I close up my shop."

Charmaine nodded gratefully and began fishing in her reticule for the coins Gwendolyn had passed to her. She was oblivious to the mercantile bell. "Now if you'll just tell me how much–"

"Excuse me one moment," Madeline said, moving around the corner of the counter. "May I be of some service?" she inquired of her newest patron.

"No thanks, Maddy–"

Charmaine's stomach lurched as she recognized the voice of Paul Duvoisin.

"–I can find the things I need. But if you'd like," and he removed a piece of paper from his shirt pocket, "you could gather the items on *this* list. Miss Colette asked if I could pick them up for her when I left the house this morning."

Madeline smiled and slipped the paper from his fingers, her hand lingering a bit longer than necessary near his. "And may I ask a favor of you?" she queried coquettishly. "That is, if you're headed to the Raven today?"

"I am. What would you have me do?"

The woman looked down at the correspondence she held in her other hand. "I've just received a letter intended for Virginia, but Buford took the post already. Could you possibly give this to the captain for me? I'd be eternally grateful."

"*Eternally*, Maddy? You're not using your feminine wiles on me, are you?"

"If only they would work!"

Charmaine looked on. He seemed to be enjoying the woman's coy overtures.

"All right, Maddy," he said, pocketing the letter. "I'll deliver this if you'll have Miss Colette's items ready by the end of the day."

"Perfect," she purred. "I'll have the pleasure of your company not once, but twice today."

Paul winked at her, then stepped away. Briefly, he looked in Charmaine's direction, and her heart missed a beat. At that moment, she fervently wished she were as adept at conversation as Madeline Thompson, flirtatious as it might be. She shook her head, knowing that such thoughts could only lead to trouble. Suddenly, he was standing next to her, depositing a handful of items on the counter. Charmaine realized how foolish she looked just lingering there. "I think I owe you money for the postage on my letter, Mrs. Thompson." He glanced down at her, but she didn't look up, her bonnet concealing her face.

"That will be two cents," Madeline said as she moved behind the counter.

Charmaine quickly produced the coins, but before the proprietress could take the money, Paul was asking if she could add his items to those he would retrieve later that afternoon. With her nod, he bade them a good day. To Charmaine's relief and disappointment, he walked out the door and into the blazing sun.

She stepped out of the mercantile a few minutes later, but there was no sign of him. Gwendolyn waddled over to her, exuberant. "Charmaine, you've just missed Paul Duvoisin! And he even spoke to me! 'Course, he rushed right off, but Rebecca was ecstatic! If you think I'm bad, you should hear her talk. She's so in love with him..." and so it went. Gwendolyn's happiness was contagious, and despite the heat, Charmaine had to smile and enjoy herself.

"This last week has been unusually warm," Gwendolyn confided. "Our weather is normally beautiful all year long. Wait, you'll see, and I know you'll come to love it here!"

They headed southwest and within an hour were walking along white beaches where it was quiet, the town a distant memory. They collected seashells while Gwendolyn chatted away. Charmaine found it amazing that so many people inhabited Charmantes, yet no one bothered to enjoy its most wondrous spots, for they were alone on the long expanse of sand, save the gulls that scattered with their approach, caterwauling in objection, soaring high on extended wings, then landing moments later in the wake of their steps.

When the searing sun of midday became too intense, they found refuge among the many overhanging boughs of the palm trees. They rested in their shade, their low voices the only indication that they were there. Charmaine smiled as a pair of flamingos walked along the water's edge, but seeing them, turned direction and disappeared into the shaded wood.

"Now," Gwendolyn breathed, "where would you like to go next?"

"I don't know," Charmaine answered, looking up at the girl who had stood to brush away the moss and sand that clung to her skirts.

"It's your choice," Gwendolyn continued. "We're close enough to walk to the Duvoisin mansion. It's probably only a half-hour away from here. Of course, we won't be allowed on the grounds. It's fenced off. But you could get a good look at where you'll be working."

"Where I'll be working?" Charmaine queried with raised brow. "I haven't even gone on an interview yet, Gwendolyn. You sound so sure that I'll get the governess' position."

"You will. Your name alone guarantees it."

Charmaine frowned bemusedly. "What do you mean?"

"Charmaine... Charmantes... It's destiny, don't you think? How many other girls have a name so similar to the home in which they live? It's as if the island were calling to you."

"You are a wonder, Gwendolyn," Charmaine laughed, "and I hope you are right, because I think I will enjoy living here, especially with you as a friend."

She declined the visit to the Duvoisin mansion, fearing that someone important might see her. They were getting hungry, and Gwendolyn suggested that they go back to town and eat at Dulcie's. "I brought some money."

"The saloon?" Charmaine asked, aghast.

"It's not that bad, not during the day anyway, and the food is very good."

Charmaine disagreed. "It's a gaming establishment and worse."

"Only at night, Charmaine, and mostly on weekends. During the day, we'll be fine. None of the indentured servants or freed darkies are allowed in there."

"Freed darkies?" Charmaine queried, finding the statement strange. She had noticed quite a few Negroes walking the streets without restriction, but just now wondered about it, for such sights were uncommon in Richmond.

"All the islands in this area of the West Indies are under British rule," Gwendolyn explained as they meandered back the way they had come, "and a few years ago, slavery was abolished both in England and on the islands."

"But I thought that Frederic Duvoisin owned and governed Charmantes."

"He does," Gwendolyn affirmed. "But according to Father, he also wishes to appease the British. He transports a great deal of sugar to them. He also receives British protection against pirate attacks on the high seas and here on Charmantes. His cargo would not be well received if the English felt it was bought and paid for with slave labor."

"So, he's keeping the peace."

"And not just with the British monarchy. His wife holds slavery as an abomination as well."

"Really?" Charmaine was surprised. She'd grown up with slavery all around her and accepted it as commonplace.

Gwendolyn delved into a sketchy tale about a Negro named Nicholas and a severe beating. Apparently, Colette Duvoisin had come to the man's defense, which fed some nasty gossip. Finally, Frederic Duvoisin put a stop to it, making an example of two islanders at the heart of the problem by expelling them from Charmantes. There were also rumors of a murder, and Gwendolyn insisted that a great taboo still clung to the story, frightening people into silence. Eventually, all the Negroes were liberated.

"If we're not going to Dulcie's," Gwendolyn said, "how about the harbor?"

Charmaine regarded her quizzically. Within the hour, she was being pulled along the boardwalk. As they drew nearer the dock, Charmaine wrenched free, comprehending her friend's scheme. Gwendolyn intended to spy on Paul Duvoisin. But the capricious girl hurried ahead, closer to the Raven, which was still moored there, her quick step unhampered by her girth.

"Gwendolyn – no!" Charmaine called. "We shouldn't be here!"

The girl only giggled, finally stopping to catch her breath. "Don't be silly! He'll never see us, I promise. Leastwise he never has before!"

"Before? You've done this before?"

Gwendolyn nodded persuasively. Though Charmaine shook her head, she realized the busy wharf offered them a measure of anonymity: the passersby ignored them. They were soon concealed in a small alcove formed by one of the huge warehouses and an empty tool shed, a reasonable distance from the ship and the longshoremen who tarried at loading the packet. Barrels and crates obstructed the men's view of them more than their view of the men, for they peered through the slats, hungrily searching the ship for some sign of Paul Duvoisin.

"This was foolish," Charmaine whispered. "What if he *does* see me?"

"He won't," Gwendolyn promised. "Besides, if you watch for a while, you'll get used to seeing him and won't be nervous when you start living at the mansion. After all, it will probably be deliciously difficult those first few days in the house."

A series of load oaths put the discussion to rest. "Jesus Christ Almighty! Not that way! The other way!"

Standing not fifteen feet away at the foot of a beveled gangplank was a disheveled man, his eyes flashing, his yellow teeth grinding down hard on a wad of tobacco. "Goddamn it! I told you to roll it the other way!" He threw down the rope he'd been attempting to loop around a huge oak cask and motioned to a boy of perhaps twelve. "Stand over here, goddamn it! I'll push while you slide the parbuckle underneath. Then we can hoist it up."

The lad, whose shoulder was braced against the horizontal barrel, did not budge, his neck taut and face reddened. "This one's gotta weigh five-hundred pounds. The wharf ain't level, I tell ya. I think it's gonna run away if I let go!"

"I got it!" the dockworker sneered. "Now grab the goddamn rope!"

Reluctantly, the youth obeyed. The barrel instantly broke loose and rolled down the pier. The boy grimaced as it hit three other casks standing on end, his face breaking into a smile when it stopped, undamaged.

"Jesus Christ, boy!" the man cursed lividly. "How could you *be* so goddamn dumb? Why didn't you wait until I got me a proper grip?" Cold hatred gleamed in his eyes, but the lad did not take heed and snickered in relief. "You wouldn't be laughin' if I kicked your damned ass!"

Charmaine had seen enough. "Let's go, Gwendolyn. That man reminds me of someone I'd rather forget."

"What is going on here?"

The older man drew himself up as Paul Duvoisin approached. "This young snip don't know how to be puttin' in a day's work," he grumbled.

"Is that so?" Paul queried. "What do you have to say for yourself, boy?"

"I'm just learning, sir. Today's my first day. I need some trainin' is all."

"What you be needin'," the older man hissed, "is a good swift kick in the pants. Maybe that'd wipe that brazen smile off your goddamn face!"

"All right, that's enough!" Paul commanded. "Since the boy is new, I expect you to be patient with him. If you don't think you can manage that, I'll place him with someone else who can instruct him properly."

"That's fine by me. No way in hell I need help like that!"

"Good," Paul said coolly. "What's your name, lad?"

"Jason, sir. Jason Banner."

"Well now, Jason, we'll see if Buck Mathers can use you today."

"*Buck?*" the older man expostulated. "Why the hell are you givin' him to that big nigger? He don't need no help!"

Paul raised a dubious brow. "If Jason is more of a hindrance than a help, that shouldn't matter to you, should it, Mr. Rowlan?" Receiving no answer, Paul turned back to Jason. "You'll find Buck at the bow of the ship. He's the biggest black man on deck, so you shouldn't have any trouble spotting him."

"Yes, sir. I know who he is."

"Good," Paul replied, clapping a hand on the boy's shoulder. "Do whatever he tells you to do. Tell him that I sent you along, and I'll speak to him later."

"Yes, sir! Thank you, sir!" In a moment, he was gone.

Paul faced Jessie Rowlan. "Back to work."

"You're gonna find someone else to help me, ain't ya?"

"You had help, but you turned it aside. Now, finish this job without further incident or collect your wages from the Duvoisin purser. Either way, I don't want to hear your foul mouth again!"

Rowlan received the ultimatum, but could not contain his outrage. "The Duvoisin purser," he grumbled under his breath as he shuffled over to the awaiting barrels. "Don't that sound fancy? We all know it's 'Do-voy-sin.' Leave it to the rich to take an ugly name–"

"It's 'Doo-*vwah*-zan', Mr. Rowlan, fancy or not," Paul responded smoothly. "Pronounce it correctly or don't bother looking for work here."

Rowlan's eyes narrowed, his hatred poorly concealed.

"Was there something else you wanted to say – to my face this time?"

The man didn't answer, though his manner spoke volumes as once again he readied the cask for hoisting.

Paul rubbed the back of his neck and walked away. *Why didn't I fire him?* But the thought of making the sloth sweat for his wages was highly satisfying.

Charmaine watched Paul return to the Raven's deck, and she imagined a similar confrontation between him and her father. Her lips curled in unbridled delight as she envisioned John Ryan cowering before Paul, and the fear that had stalked her in Richmond was gone.

"Wasn't he wonderful?" Gwendolyn whispered in adulation.

"Yes," Charmaine sighed. Paul Duvoisin was suddenly more than just handsome.

Rowlan coaxed another worker into helping him. A length of rope was doubled around the heavy barrel, the ends of which were pulled through a loop to form a sling. Eventually, it was hoisted up the concave plank with a pulley. Once on deck, it was released and rolled across the waist of the ship to the hatch.

The hour lengthened. Men tarried at the same operation fore and aft, but with ease and camaraderie. Quite abruptly, work shifted from loading the vessel to unloading two crates of tea. Charmaine wondered why, but Gwendolyn only shrugged. A buckboard drew alongside the vessel, ready to receive them, but splintering wood rent the air and the pulley let go, one large container plummeting to the pier below. The men on the quay shouted and scattered, stumbling with the shuddering impact. The crate hit the wharf just shy of the wagon and split open, spilling tea leaves everywhere. The horses reared, and the driver clutched the reins tightly to keep them from bolting.

Paul looked up from the invoices. His scowl was black, his jaw clenched by the time he reached the wharf. "Whose work is this?"

Jake Watson, his harbor foreman, shook his head in disgust. "I don't know."

Paul glared into the circle of men who gathered around the damaged goods. "Who's at fault?" he demanded again, his voice cutting the air like a whip.

A towering Negro stepped forward, Jason Banner at his side. "It was ol' Jessie Rowlan's fault, sir. I saw him liftin' that crate with the wrong pulley."

Paul gritted his teeth. He should have sacked the ornery albatross when he'd had the chance. "Where the hell is he?"

The black man pointed toward the deck, and all eyes followed. Jessie Rowlan was leaning on the railing. Paul strode purposefully up the gangway, his irate regard unwavering.

Jessie Rowlan turned to meet the attack, wearing a vengeful grin. "What can I do for you, Mr. Doo-*vwah*-zan?" he queried snidely.

"Are you responsible for that mess down there?"

"What do you mean 'responsible'? The way I sees it, ain't no one 'responsible'. Just a little accident, is all."

Rowlan's breath reeked of whisky and tobacco, and Paul resisted the urge to shrink back. "The way I see it," he growled, "the wrong equipment was used. We have block and tackle for crates and we have block and tackle for casks, something you might have remembered if you weren't so drunk! But since you were the one working the pulley, I'm holding you *directly* responsible for the 'accident' as you call it. I cannot abide such stupidity, and I certainly can't afford it. Tomorrow you may collect your wages from Jake Watson, out of which I shall deduct the money not only lost on the damaged goods, but on the equipment as well. After that, I never want to see your sorry face again."

Renewed loathing welled up in Jessie Rowlan's eyes. "Well, if it ain't the high and mighty Paul Duvoisin, who thinks he owns the whole goddamn place. Well, sir, I got me some friends, and you'll be regrettin' you ever said that. You think you're better than everybody else. Well, you ain't. You ain't even as good as most of the men here. At least we ain't *bastards* – rich or otherwise!"

Paul seized him by the throat, lifting him clear off the deck. "Utter that word again and I swear you're a dead man! *Hear me?* A dead man!"

"Yes!" Jessie Rowlan choked out.

In an instant, Paul sent him sailing, and he lay sprawled on the deck. He jumped to his feet and dashed off the ship, the dockworkers stepping back as he retreated, all unusually quiet.

"What did he mean?" Charmaine whispered. "Why was Paul so angry?"

"I'll explain later," Gwendolyn hushed, straining to hear.

"All right, Jake," Paul called down to the pier, "let's see what the men can salvage with a few shovels and a couple of barrels. I should have sent the lot back to John when I realized it was still in the hold."

"I don't think it was your brother's fault, sir," Jake shouted up. "I should have checked the labeling more carefully. I thought it said–"

"No matter, Jake! It looks like a storm is rolling in, and we'll have a bigger mess on our hands if it pours before that tea is cleared away. There's a bonus if the job is finished before the first drops hit!"

Hearing this, the men scrambled to do his bidding. Satisfied, Paul turned back to his invoices.

"What did that man mean?" Charmaine pressed as she and Gwendolyn rushed home. "Why did Jessie Rowlan call Paul that nasty name?"

"What name?"

"You know what I'm talking about, Gwendolyn. Mr. Harrington used it during our voyage here and grew uncomfortable when he remembered I was present. I know it's not a nice word. Why won't you tell me?"

"There's nothing to tell," Gwendolyn said, embarrassed by a subject she was not supposed to know about. "The man was cussing, and Paul became angry."

"No, it was more than that. Paul didn't lose his temper until Jessie Rowlan said *that* word." Still, Gwendolyn refused to shed light on the subject. "Is it because Paul is adopted – illegitimate?" she pressed.

"How did you know that?"

"Captain Wilkinson mentioned it."

"Did he also mention what the townspeople whisper?"

"He didn't gossip, if that's what you mean."

Gwendolyn lifted her nose. "And that's exactly why I won't repeat it."

The gleam in Gwendolyn's eyes told Charmaine that the girl was dying to tell all. "It won't go any further than me, if that's what you're afraid of."

"Well," Gwendolyn hesitated, looking around. "People say that Paul is Frederic Duvoisin's *bastard* son," and she whispered the word 'bastard' as if the wind had ears.

"What does that mean? Isn't that the same thing as illegitimate?"

"Yes, but worse! It means that his father had an affair with a woman, probably a prostitute, and that Paul is a product of their liaison. Otherwise, Frederic Duvoisin would have done the gentlemanly thing and married the woman. They say the infant came from abroad, and that Frederic adopted the baby because he was certain *he* was the father."

Charmaine's heart swelled in sadness for Paul. He was wealthy, handsome, and from all outward signs, an honorable man, and yet, he had to endure the gossip and rebuke of those around him.

Pelting rain washed her mind clean.

"Come quickly, Charmaine! We're going to get soaked to the bone!"

They raced through the streets, coming to the residential section of town as swiftly as their legs would carry them. But they weren't fast enough, for their clothes were drenched before they reached the Browning's front porch.

"Goodness me!" Caroline protested as she took in her daughter's appearance. "Just look at yourself, young lady! Your dress is ruined!"

"I'm sorry, mother, but Charmaine and I ran as fast as we could."

"*You what?*"

"We ran from town."

"*You ran from town?* And what will my friends think?"

"Mrs. Browning," Charmaine placated, "everyone was running for shelter."

"Well let me tell you something. Dignified young ladies do not run in public, rainstorm or not! What would Colette Duvoisin say if she saw you?"

Loretta stepped from the sitting room. "She would say, 'There go two intelligent young women. Unlike the *proper* ladies on this island who traipse slowly about town during a rainstorm in wet, clinging clothes, these two run for cover so as not to be struck by lightning.' "

Miffed, Caroline flounced past her sister, but Loretta smiled at the bedraggled girls. "To your room and out of those dresses before you catch cold."

Caroline remained in a huff until dinner, when her true anxieties were revealed. Though she loved the island, she feared her daughter would never learn the social graces necessary to obtain a respectable husband some day. By the end of the meal, Loretta empathized with her sister and, much to the dismay of Gwendolyn and Charmaine, agreed to take Gwendolyn back to Virginia when she and Joshua departed. Noting her niece's downcast eyes, she soothed, "You will come to love Richmond, Gwendolyn. Think of it as an extended holiday, and if you are not happy after a week or two, you can always return home."

Gwendolyn brightened; however, Charmaine felt empty. She had hoped to have a friend on the island whom she could visit and confide in. It seemed she was destined to be alone.

Friday, September 16, 1836
The Duvoisin Mansion

Chapter 3

The open carriage rocked gently from side to side as it turned off the main thoroughfare and proceeded at a leisurely pace through the tree-lined passage that led directly to the Duvoisin mansion. The four occupants soon sampled the tranquility of Les Charmantes. Very few people traveled the isolated road, and the quiescent forest enveloped them. Heading west, their destination was the opposite side of the nine-mile wide island, the paradise of Jean Duvoisin II preserved. Although the eastern coast was heavily populated, the western shore remained the sole dominion of one family: the Duvoisins. Not even the far off sugarcane fields and orchards to the south, nor the lumber mill and pine forests to the north trespassed on the serenity to the west, where the island remained untamed save for the mansion they were swiftly approaching.

"What is the matter, my dear?" Loretta whispered.

Charmaine inhaled. "I'm very nervous. What if they don't like me?"

"We shall leave."

"Oh, Mrs. Harrington, you make everything sound so simple."

"That's because it is," she stated with a fortifying smile.

Yesterday, they had received Colette Duvoisin's reply, written in her own hand, suggesting that the interview be held on the sixteenth of September at four in the afternoon. Charmaine had found it exceedingly difficult to sleep last night, smiling weakly when Harold Browning suggested accompanying them. "Less formal," he had said. She knew he hoped to ease her mind, and she had thanked him, but his presence did not lessen her anxiety.

When it seemed the ride would go on forever, the pine trees began to thin. Charmaine was the first to see it – the magnificent mansion nestled on a lush blanket of rich green, a white pearl set on an emerald carpet. As the carriage closed the distance to the metal fencing that guarded the grounds, it loomed larger than any edifice she had ever seen, grander than any of Virginia's great estates. Palatial and breathtaking, it required no words of compliment or description; in truth, not even the greatest poet would do it justice.

Ten Doric columns rose heavenward from a wide portico, supporting not only a second floor veranda, but a third story as well. The massive colonnade ended beneath a broad, red-tiled roof with dormer windows. Both porch and balcony ran the length of the main structure and wrapped around either side, disappearing along the wings set at right angles. They boasted evenly spaced French doors, all thrown wide to catch the afternoon breezes. The manor's main entrance luxuriated in the shade of two towering oak trees that grew on either side of the central drive. The entire edifice was framed by papaya and palm trees, which extended along the side wings of the house from front to back. But the eye was drawn back to the enormous oaks, unusual, yet majestic. Harold told them that Frederic's father had transplanted saplings from Virginia in memory of his deceased wife. Now, some fifty years later, they flourished on Charmantes, a reminder that the Duvoisin fortune had its origins in America. The pair accentuated the symmetry of the stately mansion, and not even the small stone structure attached to the south wing could mar the perfect balance and beauty.

No one spoke as the carriage passed through the main gates and rolled along the cobblestone driveway. It stopped in the shade of the oaks, where the company of four alighted, each acutely aware of their station in life. With stomach churning, Charmaine allowed Harold Browning to escort her up the short, three-step ascent, across the porch, and to the only set of oak doors.

The butler was awaiting their arrival, for the portal swung inward before they could knock. "If you will kindly step this way," he said, "I shall tell Miss Colette that you are here."

The spacious foyer had a lofty ceiling, crown moldings, an ostentatious chandelier, marble floors, and an enormous grandfather clock. Directly opposite the main entryway was an elaborate staircase. Its ornate railing followed curved steps up to a wide landing, above which hung a stunning, life-sized portrait of a young woman. There, the stairway split in two, each rising to opposite wings of the house. Overlooking these were huge mullioned windows, capturing the afternoon sun and bathing the awed assembly in its golden light.

They were led through the north wing and into the library where they were invited to make themselves comfortable. Volumes of books lined three of the four walls. A huge desk, sofa and armchairs graced the center of the room. It was dark within, but not unpleasantly so, for the dimness embraced the cool ocean breezes that whispered through the open French doors.

Loretta settled in a wing chair. "It's quite humbling, is it not?"

"Yes," Charmaine murmured, doing the same.

"And did you notice the painting in the foyer?" Loretta asked. "I wonder who the beautiful young lady might be?"

"That is Miss Colette," Harold offered.

Loretta smiled. "Well Charmaine, now we know why Mr. Duvoisin married her. I don't think you'll have a problem convincing Mrs. Duvoisin to hire you."

Charmaine was astounded. "Why do you say that?"

"Didn't you study her face?"

"I didn't have time!"

Loretta's smile deepened. "It's something you should have seen immediately. If the painter captured his subject, as I'm certain he did, Mrs. Duvoisin is a warm and loving individual who will recognize the same qualities in you. She should be very pleased when we leave today. I doubt she's had many applicants who are as young, caring, and vibrant as you."

Charmaine began to respond, but the door opened, and the woman of the portrait preceded Paul Duvoisin into the room: quintessential femininity and rugged masculinity, Colette and Paul Duvoisin, stepmother and stepson. Their relationship struck everyone instantaneously. They were close in age and looked more like husband and wife. In truth, they would have made the handsomest couple gracing Richmond society. Yet theirs was a stranger connection. All eyes traveled to the doorway in expectation of Frederic Duvoisin, but he did not cross the threshold.

Colette broke the suspect silence, greeting everyone in turn, the French lilt in her voice enthralling. She suggested that they move to the adjacent drawing room, where it was brighter. This room looked out onto the front and side lawns with two sets of French doors thrown open. It contained a brace of sofas, a number of armchairs and end tables set along the perimeter of an intricately woven Oriental rug, and a massive fireplace, seemingly out of place in a house situated on a Caribbean island. Above the mantel hung a portrait of a man holding a small boy upon one knee, with another boy off to one side. But Charmaine's gaze did not linger there. It was drawn to the grand piano of polished ebony, unlike any she had ever seen, nestled in a corner of the room, between the two doors that opened onto the foyer and library.

As Harold Browning made all the introductions, Colette encouraged everyone to sit as she herself had done. She was clad in an unadorned, yet becoming gown of pale blue. Her golden hair of the palest wheat was pulled to her nape, framing her lovely face. Her slate blue eyes were spellbinding, her nose slim and delicate, her lips full and inviting. But it was her smile that brought all her exquisite features to life and, as Loretta Harrington had averred, put everyone at ease, everyone that is, except Charmaine.

Colette sat with her hands in her lap, lending her complete attention to her guests, while her stepson elected to stand close behind her, feet planted apart, much like that day on the Raven. It was as if he were protecting her from some unknown misery. His darkly handsome features contrasted with her graceful fairness, and once again, Charmaine thought of them as husband and wife.

"Miss Ryan," Colette began, "how do you like our island?"

"It is very beautiful," Charmaine answered.

Colette saw herself in Charmaine. Without warning, she was reliving her own arrival at the Duvoisin mansion nine years ago, those overwhelming feelings that assaulted her as she entered this very room. Of course, her meeting was not an interview for the post of governess. On the contrary, she was to meet Frederic Duvoisin and make a first impression. Even now, she could feel the quickening of her pulse and the racing of her heart when he turned to greet her. He had been exceedingly handsome and extremely intimidating. The intensity of his regard had pierced her soul. He had taken her breath away. Yes, she knew what it was to feel ill at ease in the presence of the Duvoisins. She extended a smile to Charmaine. "You've been here for… three days now?"

"Four," Charmaine corrected. "We arrived Monday morning on the Raven."

That's where I've seen her! Paul mused, her elusive face suddenly recalled and attached to the unidentified woman in the Captain's cabin. But her hair had been down – long, and curling about her face, neck, and arms. That's why he hadn't been able to place her immediately. Now it was clear how she had come to be on Jonah Wilkinson's ship. She'd traveled from Richmond. He wondered if John knew her, perhaps met her on the vessel before its departure. But no, he reasoned, she wouldn't be acting the trapped rabbit if she had met his brother first. Then again, John may have put her ill at ease for the entire family. *It's a shame she wears her hair pinned up... She was so lovely with it down and unruly.*

"...isn't that correct, Paul?" Colette was asking.

"I'm sorry. What were you saying?"

"Just that Miss Ryan has seen the most beautiful parts of Charmantes if she has seen the beaches," she answered, turning in her chair to better look at him.

"Yes," he murmured, but said no more.

Charmaine shuddered under his scrutiny, wondering if she had offended him in some way, for his scowl had darkened. She was grateful when the door opened and another woman joined their company, turning Paul's attention aside.

"Agatha," Colette greeted, "please, come and meet our guests."

The woman was older, yet every bit as striking and statuesque as Colette. Her dark auburn hair was coiled in a thick coiffure. Her face possessed high cheekbones, perfectly shaped eyebrows that arched over piercing green eyes, and a long aristocratic nose, which ended above expressive lips. She swept into the room with an air of authority and smiled pleasantly at the assembly.

"I didn't know you were entertaining visitors today," she said in a thick English accent. "Do you think this wise after Robert's instructions of yesterday?"

"Agatha, I'll adhere to your brother's advice when it is reasonable."

The woman responded by insisting on refreshments. She rang for a servant, who was instructed to prepare a pitcher of lemonade.

Introductions were once again made. Charmaine learned that Agatha Blackford Ward was the sister of Frederic Duvoisin's first wife, Elizabeth. Recently widowed, she'd taken up permanent residence on Charmantes in order to be near her twin brother, Robert Blackford, the island's sole physician, and her closest living relative.

"Miss Ryan is inquiring about the governess position," Colette finished.

Agatha Ward's manner, which had been decorous and welcoming, grew rigid. "Really? She seems very young."

Paul cleared his throat. "I believe Colette is conducting this interview, Agatha. Why don't you allow her to ask the questions?"

The older woman was startled by the polite reprimand, but maintained her aplomb as she went to the door and received the arriving tray of lemonade. She poured a glass for everyone, and took a chair near Colette.

Colette regarded Charmaine once again, her gaze assuasive. "May I ask about your background, Miss Ryan?"

"Please, call me Charmaine."

"Very well, Charmaine. Where have you been employed?"

"I've been working for the Harringtons these past three years, since I was fifteen."

"And your duties there?"

"For the most part, I acted as companion to Mrs. Harrington."

"And before you began working there?"

"I attended school in Richmond. In addition to reading, writing and mathematics, I am quite proficient in a great many scholastic disciplines."

"Which school?"

"St. Jude's."

Colette eyes lit up. "St. Jude Thaddeus… patron saint of the hopeless."

"Yes," Charmaine concurred in surprise. "Many people don't know that."

"The hopeless do," Colette breathed. "Are you Roman Catholic, then?"

"Yes. My mother was devout, and I try to follow her example."

Colette nodded in approval. "And have you had any further education? Attended a lady's academy, perhaps?"

Charmaine hesitated, but Loretta quickly interceded. "Charmaine's education continued throughout her years living with me. She enjoys fine literature and classical music, is quite proficient at needlepoint and is able to sew her own clothing. She knows a great many dance steps and demonstrates a fine hand at the piano. In addition, you'll find that she embraces all the finer points of decorum that you will expect her to impart to your daughters."

"I see," Colette replied. "And do you speak French?"

"Do I have to?" Charmaine gushed in alarm.

"No," Colette chuckled, "it is not a requirement. I was just hoping that we could converse in my native tongue."

Charmaine sighed, but her relief was momentary, for Agatha spoke once again. "You may not be interested in my advice, but I feel it would behoove you to search for someone more mature when considering your children's education. Miss Ryan may very well know all the things Mrs. Harrington insists she does; however, that does not ensure her capability of conveying that knowledge to the children. Surely her education has not included pedagogic training. With Frederic's money, you could procure the most learned professor to instruct the girls and Pierre. Why rush into such a decision? Why not advertise in Europe?"

Charmaine's face fell. She could not fault the woman's observation. In fact, what she said made perfect sense. Why would Frederic Duvoisin hire someone like her when his money could purchase so much more? To her utter dismay, Paul spoke next, and his remarks were no less devastating.

"Perhaps Agatha is right, Colette. Father can well afford the most expensive tutors money can buy, as he did with John, George, and me. When Pierre gets older, it will greatly benefit him to have learned what a true scholar can edify. Why not hire someone like Professor Richards? Thanks to Rose's husband, our education was expansive, and we were well prepared for university. Miss Ryan, on the other hand, has acted as a lady's companion for three years. For all her education, where is her experience with children? It appears to be deficient."

"On the contrary," Loretta argued. The conversation had taken a wrong turn, and it was time to intervene. "There have been many occasions when Charmaine has been left in charge of my grandchildren for days at a time. She is excellent with them, and they beg to come and visit just to spend time with her."

Charmaine was momentarily stupefied, and Paul noted her unguarded surprise. *So, Loretta Harrington is playing games here. No matter, I can play, too.* "Still," he pondered aloud, his eyes sparkling victoriously, "Miss Ryan seems better equipped to fill another role in this house – something less demanding than running after three young and energetic children who are active from morning 'til night. Perhaps a maid?"

"I am quite strong, thank you," Charmaine snapped, "and capable of running after three children. Before I began working for the Harringtons, I used to lend a hand with the orphans at the St. Jude Refuge. I was good at it. I enjoyed playing with them. It wasn't that long ago that I was young myself."

"Exactly," Colette interrupted irenically. "I am seeking more than a governess for my children. As Agatha inferred earlier, my health is not what it should be. And when I am not feeling well, I want to know that I have placed my children in capable hands, hands that will do more than educate them. The governess I hire *must be* energetic, loving and compassionate, and eager to engage in all those impetuous things that young children do. I want my children to run free, I want them to learn to ride a horse and swim in the ocean. I want them to dance – to live! I don't want them closeted in their nursery day in and day out, never enjoying Charmantes' gentle breezes. We live in a paradise. I want my children to embrace that paradise – to grow healthy *in body* as well as in mind, to be happy. Do you appreciate what I'm saying?"

Her rhetorical question was not directed at anyone in particular, but rather everyone in the room. The query held for a moment.

"That being understood," she proceeded. "I have just a few more questions for Miss Ryan. Your family–" she paused as if she knew she were headed for stormy seas "–you have not mentioned them. May I ask why the Harringtons have accompanied you all the way from Virginia and not them?"

Charmaine bowed her head. For all her hours of practice, the memories were incredibly painful. "My mother passed away last year. My father left us long ago. I don't know where he is." She raised glistening eyes to Colette. "If it weren't for the Harringtons, I don't know where I would be today. They have been very kind. They are my family now."

Very good, Loretta thought, *honest and to the point.* One look at Colette and she knew that Charmaine had touched the woman's heart.

"I'm so sorry," Colette murmured, embracing a moment of silence. Then she was speaking again. "I would like my children to meet you. I shall base a portion of my decision upon them. Would you indulge me, Miss Ryan?"

"Please, call me Charmaine. And yes, I was hoping to meet them."

Agatha stood. "Shall I have Rose bring them down?" she asked.

Colette nodded and the older woman departed.

"Rose Richards, or Nana Rose as the children call her, is our nursemaid of sorts," Colette explained. "She's been in the Duvoisin employ for nearly sixty years, raising not only Paul and John, but their father as well. Rose's husband,

Professor Harold Richards, educated two generations of Duvoisin males. She is a dear woman," Colette concluded, "but getting on in years. Certainly not the person to run after three youngsters.

"Now, let me tell you a bit about my children. The girls are the oldest and turn eight the end of this month. Although they are identical twins, they are completely contrary to one another, as different as night and day, so you shouldn't have any trouble telling them apart. Yvette is very precocious, unlike her sister, Jeannette, who appears quiet and shy. My son is two and a half, a troublesome age to be sure. Not so with Pierre; he's very dear and brings only happiness."

The door opened, and a pretty girl with pale blue eyes entered the room. Her flaxen hair was only half plaited, but she seemed oblivious to it as she surveyed each stranger and singled out Charmaine. "Who are you?" she demanded.

"Yvette," her mother reproved. "Our guests will think you've no manners. That is not the proper way to introduce yourself."

"But I don't want to introduce myself, Mama. I would like her–" and the girl pointed a finger toward Charmaine "–to tell me who she is."

"Yvette," Paul corrected curtly, "pointing at someone is not polite either."

Yvette scowled briefly, then plopped into a chair, sulking.

Colette ignored her and invited Jeannette and Pierre to join them. The young boy immediately ran into his mother's outstretched arms. When Jeannette, Rose, and Agatha were settled, Colette proceeded to introduce her children to the visitors. "This is Mr. and Mrs. Harrington of Richmond, Virginia–"

Yvette perked up. "That's where Johnny lives."

"–and this is Miss Ryan, a friend of the Harringtons."

"Do you live in Richmond, too?" Yvette asked.

"I grew up there," Charmaine replied.

"Do you know my older brother?"

"No, I'm sorry to say that I don't."

Yvette was not deterred. "Do you think you could track him down?"

"Yvette," her mother chided, "that's enough."

The girl smiled sweetly. "But Mama, you said the Duvoisin name is well-known. Maybe Miss Ryan could find out where Johnny lives."

Charmaine laughed. "I suppose I could, if I tried."

This seemed to please the girl. "Good, because when you go back to Richmond, I wonder if you might take a letter to him. I've wanted to write to him before, but Mama says she doesn't know where to send his post, and Father... well, he and Johnny had a terrible–"

"Yvette!" Paul barked. "Our guests have no interest in such matters!"

The girl rolled her eyes and turned aside in her chair, pouting the harder when Rose Richards cornered her. "Next time," the elderly matron whispered as she began brushing Yvette's golden hair, "you're not to run out of the room until you look presentable."

Charmaine's eyes traveled to Jeannette, who had remained ever so quiet. The girl smiled timidly and said, "You're very pretty."

Charmaine chuckled. "Thank you, Jeannette. And may I say, so are you?"

"How did you know my name?"

Yvette grunted. "Mama told her before we came into the room, silly!"

"Your sister is correct," Charmaine concurred. "But your mother didn't have the chance to tell me much more than that. And I'd like to know more about both of you, unless of course, you'd like to know something about me."

"I'd like to know your name," Yvette replied.

Colette clicked her tongue. "Yvette, you've been told Miss Ryan's name."

"I mean her first name. What is your first name?"

"Charmaine."

Jeannette canted her head. "That's funny! It sounds like Charmantes."

"It does, doesn't it?" Charmaine agreed. "My friend said the same thing the other day, but I hadn't thought of it before."

"Can we call you Charmaine?" Yvette asked.

"No," Colette interjected, "but you *may* call her Mademoiselle Charmaine."

Yvette attempted to pull away from Rose, but succeeded in yanking her hair. "Ouch!" she squealed, gaining another scolding from her nana.

"If you'd stop your fidgeting, I'd have plaited your hair already."

"Why do I have to have it brushed and braided, anyway? I've told you, I'd rather be a boy and cut it off!"

Charmaine chuckled again. "I sympathize with you, Yvette. I hate brushing my hair and think about trimming it short nearly every morning."

Yvette studied her with something akin to admiration. "Why haven't you?"

"I've been told that it is my most beautiful possession."

Yvette seemed displeased with the answer.

"Besides, what would I do if I looked horrid when I was finished? I'd be in a fine fix. It would take years to grow back."

"True," Yvette ceded, crossing to Charmaine now that her second braid was finished. "When do you begin taking care of us?"

Colette was astonished. "Why ever did you ask that, Yvette?"

The girl faced her mother. "Nana's been saying she can't keep up with us the way she did with Johnny, Paul, and George. And I heard Mrs. Ward suggest a governess."

Colette frowned pensively. "And how did you overhear that, young lady?"

"I don't know," Yvette shrugged. "I just did."

"And would you like Miss Ryan to be your governess?"

"*I* would," Jeannette answered eagerly. She turned to her baby brother, who sat contentedly in his mother's lap, and asked, "What about you, Pierre? Would you like Mademoiselle Ryan to come and take care of us?"

The little boy smiled, rubbed his eyes, and yawned.

"He's tired," Jeannette supplied, "but I think he likes her."

"And what about you, Yvette?" Colette asked. "Would you like Mademoiselle Charmaine to come and live with us?"

"I guess so," she replied flippantly.

Paul spoke sharply. "Yvette, your mother is asking for your opinion. It would be polite to give it."

"It's difficult to say," Yvette returned, finger upon chin, "but I think I'll like her better than I do Felicia."

One look at Paul, and the entire company realized that Yvette had inferred something best left unmentioned. It was equally evident that Colette knew exactly what her daughter meant. Before Paul could reply, Colette said, "Yvette, I am very disappointed in you."

The girl burst into tears, her impertinence swept away with her mother's disapproval. "I'm sorry, Mama," she cried. "I'm sorry, Paul!" Humiliated, she ran from the room.

Colette exhaled. "I think it best to end the interview now. I know you are anxious, Miss Ryan, but I must consider the matter at greater length. I shall send word to you by Monday, if that is agreeable?"

Charmaine smiled weakly. "Yes, of course. That will be fine."

Sensing Charmaine's chagrin, Jeannette walked over to her. "I like you very much. I promise to help convince Mama and Papa to offer you the job."

Papa – Frederic Duvoisin – Charmaine had forgotten about him. Of course Colette would want to discuss this with her husband. Suddenly, all did not seem so bleak, and she smiled at the child. "Thank you, Jeannette, and I hope to see you again very soon."

Caroline Browning was eagerly awaiting their arrival. "Come quickly," she beckoned as they alighted from the carriage. "What happened? Did it go well? Did you get the position?"

Charmaine breathed deeply. "I don't know. I mean, I won't know until Monday. Mrs. Duvoisin wants to speak to her husband first."

"Frederic wasn't there?" Caroline asked as if scandalized. "Then it *is* true."

"What is true?" Loretta asked.

"That Frederic doesn't leave his chambers."

"We don't know that, do we?" Loretta replied. "He could have been attending to business elsewhere."

Such speculation seemed implausible to Charmaine. Paul had found time to be there, and according to Gwendolyn, he was always busy.

Caroline echoed her thoughts. "Everyone knows he never ventures from the mansion. Isn't that so, Harold?"

Her husband did not disagree.

"No, his condition must be grave." Her mind continued to work. "And what of Miss Colette? Is she also as ill as everyone whispers?"

Loretta frowned. "You knew her health was failing and didn't tell us?"

"I can't think of everything," Caroline said, drawing herself up and running a hand down her bodice. "Was it important?"

"It would have explained why Mrs. Duvoisin is seeking someone young and energetic to assist in the care of her children," Loretta stated, her annoyance apparent. "We went to that interview believing that education was the primary qualification for the position, when in fact, the children's supervision is Mrs. Duvoisin's greatest concern. Had we known that, Charmaine could have been better prepared."

"So you think it went badly?" Gwendolyn timidly asked.

"On the contrary," Loretta replied. "It went very well."

Sunday, September 18, 1836

The day was cool, refreshing in its promise of milder weather, but it was drizzling, and Colette sighed as she realized the rainy season was upon them. They'd have overcast weather on and off now until December. She sat at her desk in her private chambers, reveling in the gentle breezes that swirled past the palm and paw-paw branches beyond the balcony and wafted through the French doors. Moments such as these were rare, and she had come to guard this precious time, insisting that she have an hour to herself after Mass every Sunday. So far, everyone had respected her wishes. With Pierre sound asleep in the center of her bed, she was almost content.

Returning to the business at hand, her eyes fell to her partially penned letter:

> *Dear Miss Ryan,*
>
> *Having reflected on our interview of Friday afternoon, I feel it would be beneficial to meet once again in order to discuss more fully the requirements designated to the care of my children. I would, therefore, like to extend a second invitation. If possible, could you meet with me privately this afternoon at four o'clock? I'm certain that if this visit includes just the two of us in my chambers, it will give us the chance to become better acquainted.*

What else to write? She didn't want to alarm the young woman by asking her to come alone, but there had been too many people present on Friday afternoon, hardly the proper way to conduct an interview. She liked Charmaine Ryan and, in all probability, would offer her the governess position before the day was over.

A knock fell on the outer door. *Was it noon already?*

"Come in," she beckoned, grimacing when Agatha Ward opened the portal.

She despised the woman. But Agatha had made herself at home from the moment she crossed the mansion's threshold six months ago. Unlike past visits, this one had never come to an end. According to Rose Richards, the dowager had been making her sporadic treks to the island since Paul and John were young boys. With her parents dead and herself barren, she made a point of staying in touch with her only living relatives: specifically her brother, Robert, and nephew, John. From the day of her first visit some twenty years ago, Frederic had welcomed her, and she would often stay for weeks at a time, usually when her mariner husband, an officer in the British Royal Navy, put to sea. That husband died in January, leaving Agatha alone in the world. By March, she had swept into Colette's world, taking up quarters in the north wing of the Duvoisin manor – permanently. When Colette unwisely suggested a separate residence, Agatha informed her that long ago Frederic had extended a standing invitation to live in the manse, should the need ever arise. The need had arisen, and Agatha Ward was here to stay. To make matters worse, she had masterfully ingratiated herself to the staff, insisting that she was Colette's personal companion of sorts. Colette had neither the will to fight the woman, nor the courage to discuss her misgivings with her husband. Today, she chastised herself for her faintheartedness.

"I thought you were resting," the woman chided lightly.

Fighting an instant headache, Colette attempted to be civil. "I am."

"But you are writing a letter."

"Yes," Colette breathed, "hardly a strenuous activity." She folded the missive as Agatha approached. "Is there a reason why you are here, Agatha? I thought I'd expressly stated an hour – that I'd like one hour to myself."

"The girls were asking for you."

"How can that be? George took them into town today."

Agatha's brow gathered in confusion, yet she shrugged nonchalantly. "I'm sorry. I thought Fatima had complained about them running around the kitchen. Perhaps she was referring to yesterday. But after last week's incident in Paul's chambers, I thought it best to inform you of any inappropriate behavior as soon as it arises. Yvette is the one who takes advantage of your private time."

"Agatha, we've been over this before. She is only a child."

"And as such, should know her place. After all, what kind of young lady will she grow up to be if she is allowed–"

"You are speaking of my daughter."

"And of course you would defend her," Agatha continued with hardened voice. "Colette, I don't mean to upset you, but Yvette does so on a daily basis. According to Robert, it is the worst thing for you. Listen to me!" and she held up a hand when Colette attempted to argue. "Yvette's behavior grows worse by the day. I realize your failing health, your inability to supervise her at all times, has exacerbated the problem, but that is no reason to ignore it. As your friend, your companion, I feel I must warn you of the consequences of such unbridled conduct. She's in need of a firm hand to suppress her already wanton–"

"Mrs. Ward!" Colette blazed. "You are my husband's guest in this house."

"On the contrary, I am your companion."

"That is your title, not mine. You are a guest in this house, nothing more. Therefore, take heed: I love my children. Tread carefully where they are concerned, lest I revoke the gracious invitation my husband has extended to you. Do you understand?"

"My dear," Agatha rejoined condescendingly. "It is you who do not understand. Your husband is distressed over your failing health and has expressed his concerns not only to Robert, but also to myself. It is owing to Frederic that I have agreed to remain on Charmantes. He has requested that I not only tend to your every need, but that I make certain you follow my brother's every instruction. You are, for all intents and purposes, my charge." She smiled triumphantly. "Please, don't look so chagrined, Colette. Frederic is, after all, only worried for you – and his children."

Defeated, Colette bowed her head, unable to comprehend her husband and the further suffering he would now inflict. But then again, she knew all too well the hold Agatha had over him, and she hated the woman for it. When the dowager departed, Colette walked out of the stifling room and onto the balcony, welcoming the rain that kissed her face, washing away the tears that were suddenly there. *Frederic – why? Why would you choose her over me?*

Colette could still remember that night. The twins had just turned one, and Frederic hadn't once, in all that time since their birth, made love to her. It was her own fault, she knew. He thought she hated him. *She* thought she hated him. But she also loved him, loved him fiercely, loved him until it hurt, a love that frightened her in its paralyzing intensity. In addition, there was the doctor's insistence that she never attempt to have more children. Agatha had arrived a few days earlier. She'd come with a number of business associates of her deceased father. Frederic was interested in commissioning a new ship, the Destiny, for his ever-growing fleet. These were the men who would take back the specifications and see the vessel built. There was one gentleman in particular, a younger, handsome man, quite taken with Colette's youth and beauty. It had been easy to flirt with him. She enjoyed watching Frederic across the table: jaw set in tight lines, brow furrowed, his volatile temper perilously close to the surface. Perhaps it was just what he needed to push him over the edge and bring him back to her arms. She gave him a coquettish smile, daring him to speak. Later, she paced a frightened trek back and forth across her carpet, fearful that she'd overstepped her bounds. He'd come to her tonight, of that she was certain, but would she be equipped to deal with his wrath? Her pulse raced with the thought of his lovemaking, heart thudding in her ears. But the hours accumulated, and Frederic did not come. Frustrated, she abruptly decided to go to him. She would swallow her pride and admit that she wanted him, loved him. Heavy breathing came from his bedchamber. There was no need to go further. Agatha's clothes were strewn on the dressing room floor. Frederic had found release in the arms of his sister-in-law. Colette tiptoed back to her own suite, finding release in the many tears she shed on her pillow, her heart dead.

Frederic never knew what she had seen. But every time Agatha came to visit, Colette surmised that he welcomed her to his bed. She wondered if, even now, in his crippled state, he embraced the woman who had come to stay.

Colette returned to her letter. It would be pleasant to meet with Charmaine Ryan, even more pleasant to have someone closer to her own age residing in the manor. She decided to hire the young woman.

"Charmaine, whatever are you doing?" Loretta questioned from the bedroom doorway. "It's nearly half-past three. You'll be late for your appointment."

"I must look my best, but I can't seem to get this clasp."

"Here," Loretta scolded lightly, "allow me."

The brooch was secured, and Charmaine stepped back for inspection. "How do I look? Will I pass the final test?"

"You look lovely," Loretta answered, taking hold of Charmaine's hands in reassurance. "My goodness, you are shaking like a leaf in a windstorm. No wonder you couldn't fasten that clasp."

"I'll be fine," Charmaine said tremulously, her smile faint, her eyes beseeching. "And if I fail to get the position…?"

"It will be their loss," Loretta replied. "But, you must think positively. And remember, a white lie here or there is not beneath you."

"Oh, I couldn't!"

"Nonsense. You saw how effective my fibbing was. And no one in the Duvoisin household was the wiser for it."

"But what if they were to discover the truth?"

"How could they, Charmaine? You must learn to deal with people as you find them, use their tactics, so to speak. Take Paul Duvoisin for example. He exploited your inexperience, and I answered in kind. You *are* capable of caring for my grandchildren, even if you haven't had the opportunity to do so."

"You don't like him, do you?" Charmaine queried.

"Who? Mr. Duvoisin? On the contrary, he's most likely a fine gentleman. However, until you know him better, be on guard." Loretta smiled encouragingly. "Now come, Charmaine, the carriage is waiting to take you to a new life, and in my heart I know you won't be disappointed."

Charmaine settled into the landau that Colette Duvoisin had provided. Sitting alone, she was left to contemplate her fears. Loretta was so sure of her future, but Charmaine could not muster the same confidence. She'd always found comfort in silent prayer, yet those she'd offered at the noon Mass did not help. The island priest, Father Benito St. Giovanni, had delivered a longwinded, inauspicious sermon, and although Colette Duvoisin's letter seemed favorable, Charmaine experienced a sense of impending doom. Perhaps the magnitude of the Duvoisin dynasty blotted out the importance of her humble existence. What did she matter? But more importantly, if Paul disapproved of her, what real happiness could she hope to find within the mansion's walls?

The master and mistress' chambers were located to the rear of the south wing, far from the noise and activity of the thriving house. One story above the dormant ballroom, these lavish chambers provided the quiet solitude that both master and mistress sought, and those who were intent upon living did not trespass there.

This was Frederic Duvoisin's self-imposed prison, a place to brood over the life he had lived. Seated in the massive chair that occupied his outer chamber, he would often contemplate the oak door closed before him. There were three doors leading from the room: one that opened onto his bedchamber and another leading to the hall. But they were of no interest to him. The heavy door sitting directly across from him, not more than ten paces away, the portal that opened onto his wife's sitting room – *that* was the one he cared about.

He was acutely aware of her movements on the other side of that barrier, as he was every night when he lay abed, listening to the ritual of her nightly toilette. And when the chamber was plunged into a despairing silence, he would turn to stare at that door as well, the one connecting bedroom to bedroom, but not husband to wife...

He found himself grinding his teeth, unable to control the fulminating anger that seized him. In all his sixty years, he had never been a man to sit idly by and allow time or circumstance to control him. He had always forged forward: relentless, demanding, and above all else, stubborn. These traits had led to this hell of non-existence: half man mentally as well as physically, a decision fashioned eight years ago, a decision cemented five years later on the day he learned the devastating truth, the day of his seizure. Colette... how he loved her.

But dwelling on his love scorned would do him no good. It was the very emotion he fought to control. He had no rights where his wife was concerned. He had renounced them long ago, a punishment that he hoped would gain her forgiveness. But had she? Even the memory of his first wife, Elizabeth, no longer brought him solace, for he had failed her as well.

"What must you think of me?" he mumbled, his heart aching for her gentle understanding. Why wouldn't she come to him in his greatest need? He knew the answer. Even now, she remained with Colette.

"Enough!" he grumbled, his guilt tangible today. Mustering his minimal strength, he repressed the revolutionary thoughts, lest they destroy his sanity as well. If after three years he hadn't died, he must force himself to live. "I've sat too long and relinquished too much."

With great effort, he stood, his height mocking his crooked frame. The stroke had not completely purloined his strength. In days gone by, he had been a formidable opponent to any man, the envy of his peers, and many would be amazed at his determination now, yet those who knew the man of old would be repulsed.

His left side remained partially paralyzed, the leg giving him more trouble than the arm, and he scowled deeply as he leaned on the black cane he required for support. Trapped inside a useless body, he half limped, half dragged himself to the oak door. As always, his eyes traveled to the full-length mirror that he had demanded be placed in the corner of the room. And as always, he was revolted. Even so, it served its purpose, a constant reminder of what he'd become, why he must remain closeted away. He'd not endure the stares, the whispers, the comments, and most destructive, the pity.

Colette displayed none of these. In fact, she was the only person who did not avert her gaze, choosing instead to meet his regard directly and without repugnance. Yet, in her eyes, he read the most pain of all, was certain she blamed herself. He knew she longed for his forgiveness, but he could not bring himself to utter the words that would sever the only tie that bound them. Funny how he thought about it every time he prepared himself to see her...

Colette surveyed the sitting room, satisfied that everything was in order. She turned to her personal maid, a smile lighting her blue eyes. "That's fine, Gladys, just fine. I'm certain Miss Ryan will find the room inviting. Perhaps you could ask Cookie – I mean, Fatima – ask Fatima to prepare some refreshments."

"Yes, Ma'am," Gladys replied, retreating from the chamber.

Colette stood in the balcony doorway, the breeze buffeting her face. *When am I going to forget?* The sound of the door reopening drew her back to the present. "Did you forget–"

The query died on her lips as Frederic hobbled in. It had been three years since he had entered her boudoir, and this unexpected visit disturbed her. Of late, their only common ground was the neutral territory of the children's nursery.

"I didn't mean to disturb you," he apologized, his speech slightly slurred.

"You didn't," she replied, forcing herself calm, her eyes fixed on him.

He limped closer. "I see you are preparing for a guest. Someone I know?"

"A woman I'd like to hire as governess to the children."

"And the woman's name?"

"Charmaine Ryan."

"Paul says she's very young. Most probably inexperienced."

Astonished and instantly agitated, Colette spoke without thought. "He discussed this with you? How dare he go behind my back?"

"I may ask the same of you, Madame," Frederic snarled derisively. "I am your husband and master of this house. Paul shouldn't be informing me of matters concerning the children – you should. Or is that too much to ask?"

"No," she whispered, lowering her gaze to the floor, fighting the tears that rushed to her eyes, "it is not too much to ask."

Frederic heard the tremor in her voice and gritted his teeth, his outrage engulfed by self-loathing. "Tell me about Miss Ryan," he urged.

Colette composed herself. "She is from Richmond and heard of the governess position through Harold Browning. Harold's wife is related to her previous employers, the Harringtons. She worked for them for three years and has had quite a bit of experience with their grandchildren. She is well educated and–"

" –you highly recommend her for the position," he finished for her.

"Yes," Colette murmured. She was losing this battle of wills. In an attempt to regain her poise, she retreated to a chair a few feet away from him.

But he moved to where she sat, towering above her. "This is all fine and good, Colette, but it doesn't make one whit of sense to me. You, who have never left your children unattended for even a moment, are looking for someone else to tend them? And don't tell me this has anything to do with their education. You could teach them all they'd ever need to know. Why, then, are you situating a stranger in this house, forfeiting the care of our children to someone else?"

"I'm not forfeiting their care, but I'm not as strong as I was a year ago. Robert insists that the children are a burden. Though I don't agree, I don't want my limitations to restrict their activities."

"You should never have had the boy," Frederic stated sharply. "You were told no more children after the twins."

"It wasn't Pierre. I was fine after his birth. It was the fever last spring."

Frederic's scowl deepened, forcing her mute. The minutes ticked uneasily by until he cleared his throat. "And Robert recommended a governess?"

"His sister did."

"She doesn't approve of this one."

"And how would you know that?" Colette asked suspiciously.

"She asked Paul to speak with me. According to Agatha, Charmaine Ryan is too young and vivacious." He limped back to the adjoining door, paused, then faced Colette again, his eyes briefly sparkling. "I'd say Miss Ryan is exactly the type of governess our children need."

Colette smiled, and for the first time in months, Frederic's heart expanded. Tears sprang to his eyes, and he swiftly turned away. "I promised Paul that I would speak to you on Agatha's behalf, and I have." When she didn't respond, he opened the door and returned to his own chambers. Colette had won his approval.

Despite her tardy departure from the Browning house, Charmaine arrived at the Duvoisin doorstep on time. Shaking her skirts free of any wrinkles, she faced the formidable manor and, with the deepest of breaths, began the short ascent up the portico steps. The front door opened, and a man rushed out, head down, oblivious of her. His pace increased, and Charmaine stepped aside to avoid the collision. Too late! He ran headlong into her, nearly knocking her to the ground. Impulsively, he grabbed her arms and steadied them both.

"Excuse me," he chuckled self-consciously, but as he set her from him, his perusal turned fastidious, and his smile deepened. "My, my!"

Charmaine couldn't help but smile in return, completely at ease with this lanky stranger.

"I shouldn't have come galloping out of the house like that, but bumping into you made it all worthwhile." Without further ado, he grasped her elbow and assisted her with the remaining steps. "And might you have a name?"

Her eyes never left his lean face. "Charmaine Ryan."

"Oh, the new governess."

"Am I?" Charmaine queried.

His face sobered, and he groaned inwardly. "Not exactly, but you are being considered. I'm sorry for getting your hopes up, though I'm certain–"

"George, weren't you supposed to help Wade sharpen the saw at the mill?"

Paul Duvoisin stood in the main doorway, arms folded across his chest, a scowl marring his face. Charmaine hadn't noticed him there, and suddenly her cheeks burned crimson. "Well?" he queried.

"It's Sunday," George replied defensively. "The saw can wait until tomorrow. Besides, I've spent the better part of the afternoon with *your* sisters, having just now returned them to my grandmother. The rest of the day is mine."

Paul didn't respond, yet Charmaine read the silent exchange that passed between the two men. "I guess I could look in on Alabaster," George added.

Paul's brow lifted. "Why?"

"Phantom bit him a little while ago."

"How in the hell did that happen?" Paul demanded.

George cleared his throat, adding emphasis to the slight nod he effected in Charmaine's direction. But Paul ignored the gesture, unmoved by her presence. Finally, George answered. "Yvette was–"

Paul held up a hand, highly perturbed. "I don't want to hear it! But I promise you this – and you can tell Rose for me – one of these days Yvette is going to go too far, and when she does, I'm going to put her over my knee and take the greatest pleasure in giving her a damn good spanking!"

George coughed again, louder this time, and glanced at Charmaine, whose face was scarlet. Paul was looking at her, too, a smile replacing his scowl, and she became the recipient of his remarks. "But maybe, where everyone else has failed, Miss Ryan will have some positive effect on my *sweet little sister.* If she does, it will attest to her experience with children."

"I'll check on Alabaster," George broke in. "Good day, Miss Ryan. I hope to enjoy your company in the near future. Good luck!"

"Thank you," she said, grateful that someone was interested in putting her at ease. "It was nice to meet you, even though we were never introduced."

"I'm George," he replied. "George Richards."

"Mr. Richards," she nodded. "And thank you, again."

"The pleasure was all mine," he said. On impulse, he grabbed her hand and kissed it. Then he was striding happily down the steps and across the lawns, unable to suppress the urge to give Paul a backward glance. His friend's jealous scowl did not disappoint him. Yes, Paul *had* been warning him off.

"Miss Ryan," Paul said as he dragged his eyes from George, "I see you have arrived promptly."

"It was very kind of your family to send the carriage for me," she answered, her voice steadier than she believed possible.

"Yes… Shall we go into the house? I know Colette is anxious to see you." He didn't wait for a reply, stepping forward to fill the spot George Richards had vacated. With the slightest pressure to her elbow, he prodded her forward.

Her breathing grew shallow with the trip-hammer of her heart. No words were spoken as he directed her through the doors, across the foyer, and up the south staircase, presumably to the Lady Colette's private chambers. Charmaine welcomed the silence, for it gave her time to compose herself.

"It's not much further," he finally said. "Colette thought you'd be more comfortable in her suite. Unfortunately, it's at the far end of the house."

"I knew the manor was large, but…"

"You didn't realize *how* large," he concluded, a hint of a smile tugging at the corner of his mouth.

"This is the south wing," he explained, stopping at the crest of the massive staircase. "The rooms on this side of the house are relegated to the family. The north wing–" he motioned across the empty cavity below, where the staircase dropped and rose again on the other side "–is vacant for the most part, and used only when my father entertains guests."

"I see," Charmaine said with great interest, noticing that a hallway ran the length of the front of the house, connecting north wing to south wing. Ten other rooms opened onto this gallery.

Paul's eyes followed her avid gaze. "The rooms at the front of the house face east and receive the sun in the morning. My brother's former room," he pointed out, not far from where they stood, "and the children's nursery, complete with bedchamber and playroom," which sat opposite the south wing corridor, "and if you follow this closed hallway, you enter into the south wing of the manor."

He led her down that passageway now. She was becoming accustomed to his voice. Without thinking, she asked, "What of your room?"

If he thought her brazen, he gave no such indication. "We just passed them. They are directly opposite the staircase."

"You have more than one?"

"Yes, a dressing room and a bedroom. Most of the rooms on the second floor were designed that way. It allows the occupants freedom and space."

"Freedom from what?" Charmaine asked, astonished by the grandeur.

"The world, if they choose. But if they decide differently, the sitting room can be changed into a dressing room, as I have done."

"It is good to know that you're not escaping from the world," she answered a bit too enthusiastically.

They had reached the end of the hallway, and Paul turned toward her, smiling roguishly. He was so close she could see the flecks of green in his olive eyes.

"No, I'm not doing that," he reassured softly, sending shivers of delight up her spine. "Shall we?" he asked, inclining his head toward the last door on the left. When she nodded, he knocked, and at Colette's insistence, they entered the mistress' private quarters.

Colette Duvoisin's sitting room was elegantly appointed, yet far from grandiose. There were only a few items of great and expensive beauty, catching the eye quickly and holding it. In the center of the chamber was an Oriental rug, a miniature of the huge carpet that adorned the oak floor of the drawing room. To one side there was a high-backed ottoman, and in front of it, a serving table with marble top. Two mahogany chairs were set to either side, facing the divan. Across the room was an armoire and chest of drawers adorned with fresh cut flowers arranged in a tall vase. Next to this was a dressing table with jewelry chest. On the far wall, nestled between two sets of French doors, was a desk. Colette had moved its chair slightly and sat in front of the open glass doors.

She rose slowly, allowing Charmaine a moment to admire the room, then suggested they sit on the sofa. Paul bade them good afternoon and left, allowing them the private meeting that Colette had suggested in her letter.

They spent an hour together, alone: no children and no introduction to the master of Charmantes. Charmaine surmised that this interview had been arranged to make her feel at ease and to reach an understanding that Colette would remain an active participant in her children's lives as long as her health permitted.

"Mrs. Duvoisin," Charmaine dared to say, "excuse my impertinence, but from what illness do you suffer?"

Colette leaned forward. "Please, I insist that you call me Colette. If I can call you Charmaine, you must use my Christian name as well."

"Very well," Charmaine ceded, "Colette."

Satisfied, Colette said, "It is not an illness, really. I had a difficult delivery with the girls, and the doctor recommended no more children. When I realized I was expecting again, everyone grew concerned. Thankfully, my son's birth proved easy. But when I fell ill earlier this year, Doctor Blackford claimed that the strain of carrying Pierre made it difficult to fight the unknown malady. I fear he is right, for I have yet to recover. Even so, Robert is optimistic and foresees an improvement if I don't exert myself. Hence, the need for a governess. And with that accomplished now, I leave the rest in God's hands."

Charmaine sat stunned, uncertain of Colette's meaning until she stood and extended her arms with the words, "Welcome to the Duvoisin family." Charmaine laughed outright, then cupped a hand over her mouth, rose, and fell into her embrace. *She had the job!*

While sharing tea, they discussed her salary, a figure that was tantamount to a king's ransom in Charmaine's eyes. Her wages would be nearly thrice what she had earned while working for the Harringtons. Once a month, the money would be deposited in the town's bank where she could draw upon it whenever she liked. Her services would be required seven days a week, although only the weekdays would be set aside for studies. The weekends could be spent in any manner she wished, so long as the children were included. Neither her room and board, nor her meals would be deducted, and Charmaine surmised that after a few years in the Duvoisin employ, she would be an independent woman.

As she rode back to the Browning house, she was both happy and relieved and about to embark on a new life.

Monday,
September 19, 1836

Chapter 4

Charmaine arrived at the mansion early the next morning. Colette had insisted that she take a full day to settle into her room on the third floor. Thus, she wouldn't step into her role as governess until Tuesday. Loretta and Gwendolyn had accompanied her, and together, they entered the huge foyer, where Charmaine stifled the first of many giggles. Gwendolyn's "oohs" and "ahs" were plentiful.

"It is beautiful, isn't it, Gwendolyn?" she whispered, awaiting Colette's introductions of the house staff.

Charmaine met Mrs. Jane Faraday, an austere widow and head housekeeper of the manor. Falling directly under her authority were Felicia Flemmings and Anna Smith, two maids, a bit older than Charmaine, whose duties included house cleaning, laundry service, and table waiting at each meal. Next, there were the Thornfields, Gladys and Travis, and their two children, Millie and Joseph. Millie was Gwendolyn's age, and Joseph twelve. They accomplished odd jobs around the mansion and its grounds while their parents attended to the personal needs of the master and mistress. When Travis was not serving as Frederic Duvoisin's valet, he assumed the role of butler. Unlike Mrs. Faraday and her two charges, the Thornfields seemed very pleasant. But of all the servants Charmaine met, Mrs. Fatima Henderson, the rotund black cook, became her favorite. Warm and loud with a devilish twinkle in her eye, Charmaine liked her from the start.

With Travis and Joseph's help, Charmaine's belongings were carried up to the third floor via the servant's staircase at the back of the north wing. She spent the morning unpacking and arranging the bedroom more to her liking, the finest she had ever slept in, Loretta and Gwendolyn offering their advice.

Just before noon, Millie invited them downstairs for lunch, not in the servant's kitchen, but rather, the family's dining room.

Forty feet long and nearly as wide, it was situated between the library and kitchen of the north wing's ground floor. Two of its four walls were comprised of continuous French doors, all open, leading out to the wrap-around veranda on one side and an inner courtyard on the other. Like a crystal palace, the chamber dazzled the eye in the midday sun. In the center was a lustrous red mahogany table, with matching chairs to seat fourteen. The table could accommodate twice as many, yet was dwarfed in the magnificent room. Suspended above it were three chandeliers, sparkling in imitation of the French doors. On the wall abutting the library was a liquor cabinet, opposite that, a baroque cupboard displaying an array of fine chinaware.

A splendid meal awaited them. The children were there, and in a matter of minutes, the discourse turned spontaneous, the girls delighting in the company they were entertaining. When Charmaine marveled over the manor, they insisted on showing her the entire house, but Colette told them that that would have to wait for the next day, as Charmaine's duties didn't begin until then.

When the last dish was cleared away, Charmaine walked Gwendolyn and Loretta to the front portico, taking a deep breath when Loretta turned to hug her goodbye. Charmaine read joy in her eyes.

"You are going to be fine here, Charmaine."

"I know I am," Charmaine concurred, battling a pang of melancholy. "You'll be leaving for Richmond soon, won't you?"

"Not until I'm certain you're happy. I can withstand my sister's company for another week or two." When Gwendolyn laughed, so did Loretta and Charmaine. "Besides," Loretta added, "we don't know when the next ship will put into port."

Charmaine watched as they boarded the carriage and drove away. Turning back into the mansion, she realized the rest of the afternoon belonged to her. With nothing to do, she wished she had taken the girls up on their offer to investigate the house. Nevertheless, Colette had told her the manor was her home now and that she was free to roam wherever she liked.

She ambled into the drawing room and was drawn to the piano. Ever so carefully, she lifted the lid and stroked the beautiful ivory keys. But before she could sit down to play, a voice came from the doorway. "There you are!"

It was Yvette, and she was alone. Paul's words of yesterday surfaced: *One of these days Yvette is going to go too far... But maybe Miss Ryan will have some positive effect on my sweet little sister. If she does, it will attest to her experience with children...* Obviously, Paul's opinion of her remained unfavorable. What Charmaine wouldn't give to prove him wrong and, in the process, demonstrate that children could be handled without spanking them.

"Yvette?" she queried. "You are Yvette, aren't you?"

"Yes, it's me," the girl replied. "Have you finished unpacking?"

With Charmaine's affirmation, she continued. "Perhaps you can spend the rest of the day thinking of some fun things to do with us tomorrow."

"Fun things?" Charmaine asked. "Why do you say that?"

"Everything has been so boring lately. Nana Rose is old, *very* old! And with Mama feeling ill all the time, we never do anything that's fun or exciting anymore. We're always cooped up in that silly nursery!"

"I see. I will think about it. How does that sound?"

Unconvinced, Yvette's shoulders sagged. She flung herself into a chair and mumbled, "It sounds wonderful."

Charmaine took stock; the child's discontent might work in her favor. "I've an idea. You look like the kind of a girl who enjoys a good bargain."

She had Yvette's complete attention. "Yes?"

"I've heard you can be very difficult."

"Who told you that?"

"It's not important. But if we could come to an agreement, I'm certain that we'd both be happy with the outcome."

"What sort of an agreement?" Yvette asked suspiciously.

"Last Friday you mentioned your brother, John, in Richmond."

"What about him?"

"I could possibly get a letter to him."

Yvette's eyes widened. "Really?" Then, as if she knew she was being duped, she said, "How? You're staying here now."

"But my friends, the Harringtons, are returning to Richmond in a few weeks. And Mr. Harrington has met your brother. He could locate him."

"*Really?*"

"I believe so," Charmaine replied, tickled by the girl's renewed exuberance.

Yvette grew cautious again. "What do I have to do?"

"Be well-behaved," Charmaine answered simply.

"Well-behaved? That's it?"

"From what I've heard, that will be a great deal for you. You are to obey and respect me the way you do your mother. No mischief making."

A myriad of expressions ran rampant across the girl's face as she weighed the pros and cons of the pact.

"Of course," Charmaine pursued, "it might be too difficult for–"

"You've got a deal!" the girl cut in. "Do you want to shake on it?"

Charmaine nodded, reaching for Yvette's extended hand, puzzled when it was abruptly withdrawn. "One other thing," Yvette said, arm tucked behind her back. "You had better not tell Mama or Papa, or I won't be allowed to send it."

Charmaine was perplexed. Certainly the child's parents wouldn't forbid her to write a simple letter to her older brother. "Why would they mind?"

"They are angry with Johnny. That's the real reason I haven't been able to send him a letter. I'm not supposed to tell you this, but he caused Papa's seizure. It's the *big family secret!* But you were bound to find out. Everybody in the house knows what happened. Johnny didn't mean it, I know he didn't! At least Papa didn't die!" The girl sighed. "Now I'm not even allowed to mention his name. I know they won't let me write to him."

"I'll speak to your mother about it," Charmaine reasoned gently. "

"Nope!" the girl persisted. "No secret, no deal! Because if you tell her about the letter, it will never leave this island."

Charmaine frowned. She didn't like being manipulated, and she certainly didn't want to go behind Colette's back. "I shall have to think about it."

"Never mind," Yvette groaned, clearly upset. "I knew you'd be too scared to do something daring."

"Yvette," Charmaine cajoled, certain she was courting an enemy now rather than a friend, "if it means that much to you, I promise we'll get a letter to your brother one way or another."

A long silence ensued. Charmaine stood her ground, allowing Yvette her assessment. Finally, the girl smiled hesitantly. "Are you certain? You're not just saying that?"

"I'm certain, and I do promise. Now come, I'll take you back to the nursery before Nana Rose or your mother comes looking for you."

Yvette artfully turned to the piano. "Do you play?"

"Yes, I do."

"Would you teach me?"

"I suppose I could. You'll be my first student, though."

"I don't care. I'd like to learn. Johnny plays very well," she imparted, striking one key. "He'd be very surprised if he came home and could hear me play. I'd really like to surprise him."

Charmaine smiled down on the girl, who so obviously cherished her elder brother. "Very well, Miss Duvoisin. If you are willing to practice an hour a day, by Christmastide you should be able to play a number of simple melodies. Would you like to begin now?"

Receiving an alacritous nod, they sat at the piano. "Now, this is middle C."

It was thus that Colette found them. She smiled contentedly.

When Yvette tired of the piano, Charmaine accompanied her back to the nursery and insisted that the girls give her the grand tour. She was in awe of all the things they pointed out, most especially the water closet situated near the crest of the south wing staircase and its companion washroom on the first floor directly below. Complete with washstand and chamber seat, its interior plumbing was fed by a water system devised by the girls' grandfather at the time of the mansion's construction. Rainwater was collected off the roof and funneled into a holding tank one story above. Charmaine jumped back when Yvette cranked a huge lever and a surge of water 'flushed' the toilet. The girl laughed merrily. "Haven't you ever seen a privy before?" This type, she hadn't. Not even the Harringtons had so modern a lavatory facility.

In the south wing, she was shown the grand ballroom and banquet hall, huge and empty, comprising the entire ground floor of that wing, echoing their hollow footfalls as they crossed to a side doorway that led to the family chapel. The stone edifice was built eight years ago, and was the only structure oddly out of balance with the entire house.

Next, the girls took her to the gardens nestled in the courtyard between the north and south wings. Frederic's father had hired a gardener to plant out the nearly enclosed area with various shrubs and exotic flowers. Travis and Gladys tended it now. It was remarkably cool amongst the many overhanging boughs of scarlet cordia and frangipani trees, their abundant blooms of deep orange, white, pink, and yellow vibrant and sweet smelling. Marble benches were placed along the cobblestone walkway, beckoning any wanderer to sit and enjoy the placid beauty and fragrant flowers. A grand fountain graced the very center, water spurting upward, dropping back to marble basins of graduating diameter, three melodious waterfalls spilling to a shallow pool below.

"You have a little paradise right here," Charmaine said to the girls.

"Still," Yvette commented, "once you've gotten used to it, it's boring."

"Yes," Jeannette agreed, "it's much more fun to go on picnics or riding the way we used to before Mama became ill."

So, Charmaine thought, there is the crux of the matter. They were tired of the same old thing, and she couldn't really blame them. Children were meant to run free. Tonight, she would start planning how she could make their lives more adventurous. Though she knew their studies were important – Colette had already made certain that her daughters could read and write – Charmaine remembered that the manner in which they spent the weekends would be up to her choosing. Perhaps a few picnics would be nice, so long as the rainy weather they were due to experience cooperated.

At seven o'clock, everyone headed for the dining room. Charmaine was to have her first supper with her new family. As at lunch, Rose and Yvette walked to the far side of the table and took two center seats. Colette helped Pierre into the chair adjacent to her own, there at the foot of the table, nearest the kitchen. Charmaine assumed that when Frederic joined them, he would sit opposite his wife at the head of the table. Colette beckoned Charmaine to once again take the chair to Pierre's right, and Jeannette quickly sat next to Charmaine.

"Is this all right, Mama?" she asked politely.

"As long as Nana doesn't mind being cast aside."

Rose shook her head. "Let Jeannette sit near Charmaine. That's fine."

Voices resounded from the hallway, and George Richards and Paul appeared. To Charmaine's utter surprise, Paul sat at the head of the table, while George took the chair to his right. Evidently, Frederic Duvoisin would not be joining them. Unbidden came the thought of Paul and Colette as husband and wife.

Agatha Ward was the last to enter the room. Charmaine had only seen the dowager once the entire day, when she had insisted that Colette take a nap. She graciously greeted everyone, then sat across from Pierre.

The family fell into easy banter, and dinner was served. Charmaine enjoyed the food immensely, not realizing how hungry she was, although the noontime fare had been delectable. She helped with Pierre's plate, while talking with the girls, Rose, and Colette. Halfway through the meal, George spoke to her. "Well, Charmaine Ryan, how was your first day as governess?"

"It was wonderful."

Colette chuckled. "Charmaine wasn't supposed to begin her duties until tomorrow. However–" she sent a mock frown down the table toward her daughter "–Yvette took it upon herself to obtain a piano lesson from Miss Ryan."

All eyes went to the girl, save Paul's, whose gaze rested on Charmaine.

"That's right," Yvette piped up, "Mademoiselle is teaching me how to play."

"She's going to teach me as well!" Jeannette chimed in.

Paul leaned back in his chair. "Miss Ryan is full of surprises, isn't she?"

Charmaine looked directly at him. "There is nothing surprising about playing the piano, Mr. Duvoisin. Mrs. Harrington spoke of my ability to do so during Friday's interview."

"So she did," Paul agreed with the hint of a smile. "Tell us, Mademoiselle, what else do you intend to teach my sisters and Pierre?"

"Whatever they would like to learn."

As his smile broadened, butterflies took wing in her stomach. Flustered, she looked away.

"We've shown Mademoiselle Charmaine the entire house," Jeannette supplied. "And she thinks it's beautiful."

"Yes," Paul mused, "I'm certain she does."

Charmaine was grateful when the conversation turned to other things. Having dinner night after night with Paul in attendance was going to be disconcerting. But at least he had noticed her, and of course, his presence at the table was preferable to his absence.

She wondered why George was there, then his last name registered. *George Richards, Rose Richards... I've just now returned your sisters to my grandmother.* George was Rose's grandson. She remembered Yvette's remarks during her interview. *She can't keep up with us the way she did with Johnny, Paul, and George.* Apparently, Rose had been a surrogate mother to all three boys. Now she understood why George was at the table and why there appeared to be a great camaraderie between him and Paul. Like his grandmother, he was more than an employee; he was considered a part of the family.

When the meal was over, Anna and Felicia cleared the dishes away. Charmaine watched as the latter fawned over Paul a second time. Earlier, Charmaine had been uncertain of the serving girl's intentions, but there was no mistaking the signals Felicia was sending now: the batting eyes and swinging hips. With olive skin, dark hair, and shapely curves, Felicia Flemmings was fetching. More than once, Paul leered at her.

Colette noticed it, too. "Felicia," she sharply remarked, "I'd like to speak with you tomorrow morning, in my chambers."

The maid's face dropped. She curtseyed and scurried away, not to be seen again for the remainder of the evening.

After dessert, Colette rose, and the family retired to the drawing room. Paul and George declined to join them. "We have a number of things to accomplish in the study," Paul told Colette. "Unfortunately, a few of these matters I need to discuss with Father. Nothing taxing, just–"

"That's fine, Paul," Colette interrupted. "It would be good for him to get involved in Duvoisin business, the more taxing the better. He's sat too long."

With a nod, he and George entered the library. Charmaine suddenly realized that the library and the study were one and the same room.

By nine o'clock, the children were asleep, and she returned to her room on the third floor. So much had happened during her first day in the grand house, and both her mind and heart were full. It had been a good day, and she looked forward to tomorrow. With a sigh, she climbed into bed and fell swiftly to sleep.

But her dreams were disturbing. At first, she was on the wharf, watching Paul scowl at Jessie Rowlan. Then, Jessie Rowlan was her father, and Paul was lifting him clear off the dock, his fist knotting the shirt at the base of her father's neck. Next, John Ryan lay sprawled on the floor of the meetinghouse, and Paul was snarling to the island priest, "Tell Mr. Ryan who his daughter is married to."

She awoke in a cold sweat. Though her heart fluttered with Paul's insinuation that *she* was his wife, images of John Ryan remained vivid. *You're safe now... Paul will protect you. That's what your dream was telling you.* He *will* protect you. Even with that thought, it was a long time before she fell back to sleep.

Sunday, September 25, 1836

Charmaine's first week as governess passed without incident. True to her word, Yvette was the perfect child, and Charmaine began to wonder if Paul's anger of the Sunday past had been exaggerated. Nevertheless, Rose and Colette commended the girl on her good behavior. When her praises were sung, Yvette's eyes would travel to her governess, a silent reminder of Charmaine's end of the bargain. A wink sufficed to confirm their pact.

Yvette continued with her piano lessons, her sister in attendance. Their interest had not diminished; both girls practiced over an hour each day, and by Friday, they were able to play a few simple tunes with ease.

When Saturday proved sunny, Charmaine decided to take them on a picnic. Doctor Blackford had arrived early in the day, and Colette was closeted away with him. When Rose insisted on caring for Pierre – "You'll have a better time with the girls if he stays behind" – Charmaine and the girls set out for the nearby southern beaches, a hearty picnic lunch in hand. They collected seashells, waded knee-deep in the warm water, ran and laughed and told stories. The girls wanted to hear all about Charmaine's past, which she recounted, omitting the sordid details of her family life. They were interested in 'being poor' as they put it and decided that it would be a far more exciting life than the one they led 'being rich'. Charmaine snorted. She wished she'd had so terrible a childhood as they.

On Sunday, everyone attended Mass in the small stone chapel, everyone except Frederic. Charmaine began to wonder if she were ever going to meet the Duvoisin patriarch.

Like the week before, Father Benito's verbose sermon was uninspiring and fraught with condemnation. Charmaine's mind wandered to Father Michael Andrews. His homilies had been eloquent, his redeeming message of love and forgiveness, fulfilling. She thought of her mother, recalling her words of praise whenever she spoke of the spiritual priest. Father Benito could derive some inspiration from Father Michael.

Charmaine was glad when the Mass came to a close. The girls had fidgeted, Pierre was cranky, and Paul's eyes were constantly upon her, leaving her ill at ease. Did he think it was her fault that the children could not sit still? Colette withdrew to her chambers, saying she was not feeling well, and it fell to Charmaine and Rose to care for the children for the remainder of the day. After the noonday meal, Charmaine took Pierre upstairs for his nap. The girls wanted to practice their piano lesson, so Rose decided to remain downstairs with them.

The boy fell asleep almost immediately, and Charmaine tiptoed from the room to retrieve a book from her bedroom. Fear gripped her when she returned to the children's chambers: Pierre's bed was empty. *Where could he be?* She ran from the nursery in a panic, reaching the stairs in a heartbeat. Then she heard it: giggling coming from the apartments directly behind her. Relief flooded in. The door was standing slightly ajar, and Charmaine pushed it open. There stood Pierre, thigh-deep in Paul's riding boots.

"Pierre!" she scolded, her eyes darting about the dressing room. "Come here this instant!" He only giggled again, attempting to walk with the boots on. "Pierre, you're not supposed to be in here. Come here, please!"

He tripped and laughed harder, wiggling out of the boots and scurrying into his older brother's bedroom. The chase was on; she had no choice but to dash across the suite, stopping just shy of the bedroom doorway. Thankfully, it was empty as well, save a huge, four-poster bed, under which Pierre was crawling.

"Don't make me come after you, young man!" Charmaine futilely admonished. Groaning, she rushed forward, realizing the faster she got the boy out of Paul's private quarters, the better. Lying flat on the floor, she caught hold of his legs and was just pulling him out from under the bed, when a cough startled her. Afraid to look, but knowing that she must, she let go of Pierre and, standing, turned to face Paul, her cheeks flaming red.

"Have you lost something, Miss Ryan?" he asked devilishly, his shoulder propped against the doorframe, arms and legs casually crossed. "Or perhaps you've come to my chambers for another reason?"

"No, sir – I mean – yes, sir," she stammered, her mortification nearly unbearable. "I've lost something, sir."

"Have you?"

Mercifully, Pierre wriggled out from under the bed and ran directly into his older brother's arms. Paul scooped him up, his brow cocked in Charmaine's direction. "So, it's Pierre you've lost? Amazing... Rose is minding the girls in the drawing room, and you were supposed to be caring for Pierre. Tell me, Miss Ryan, is it too difficult to keep track of one small boy?"

"I thought he was sleeping, sir," she answered, highly offended. "I only left him for a moment to–"

"No need to explain, Miss Ryan. As I mentioned during your interview, running after a child can be quite demanding, perhaps too much for you."

"Sir, you are wrong," she bit out, "and someday, you will eat your words."

He burst into hearty laughter, inciting another round of giggles from Pierre.

Charmaine's temper peaked, and she had to quell the urge to step forward and slap the mirth from his face.

He recorded her anger, and though his eyes remained merry, his demeanor changed. "I think you've proven your worth to my family, Miss Ryan. You've done a fine job with the children, especially where Yvette is concerned."

His unexpected words were sincere. She didn't know what to say.

"Do you accept my compliment, then?" he asked with a lopsided grin.

"Yes sir," she replied, her throat dry and raspy.

"Why don't you call me Paul? That is, if you'll allow me to call you Charmaine? We're not so formal on Charmantes, leastwise not as formal as Richmond society can be. I promise, it is quite easy to pronounce."

The mild barb prompted her to reply. "Paul," she said softly.

"Charmaine," he returned with a slight nod. "Now, *Charmaine*, let's get Pierre back to his playroom. We wouldn't want Mrs. Faraday to find us alone in my bedchamber. I fear she'd be scandalized."

Charmaine's cheeks burned anew, and again Paul chuckled.

In a matter of minutes, Pierre was back in his bed and Paul had left them. But Charmaine trembled for a good hour afterward, her insides pleasantly warm. Paul approved of her, he finally approved of her!

Later that afternoon, Gwendolyn and Loretta paid her a visit. They spent an hour on the portico while the girls and Pierre played hide-and-seek nearby. Gwendolyn nearly swooned when Paul emerged from the manor and greeted them. He headed toward the stable and carriage house, which comprised the southern front lawns of the compound. When he was out of earshot, she said, "You are so lucky, Charmaine!"

Loretta frowned disapprovingly. "Charmaine had best keep a level head."

"Don't worry, Mrs. Harrington. I know I'm only the governess. But it is nice to dream."

"So long as it remains a dream."

Soon it was evening, and Charmaine's first week in the Duvoisin employ came to a close. But as she tucked the girls into bed, Yvette whispered to her, "You haven't forgotten about my letter, have you?"

"No, I haven't forgotten," Charmaine whispered back.

"Good, because I finished it yesterday. I even drew a picture! When are your friends leaving for Richmond?"

"Not for another week or so. They have to wait for a ship to make port. But I haven't forgotten, Yvette, and I promise that I'm sticking to our pact. May I read your letter tomorrow?"

Yvette's eyes widened. "Of course not! It's private."

Charmaine chuckled and gave her a kiss. "You've been a fine girl this week, Yvette. I hope that after your letter leaves the island you'll continue to behave."

"Don't worry, Mademoiselle," she yawned. "I like you, so I'll be good." With a contented smile, she snuggled under her blankets.

Jeannette was already asleep, but Pierre grew obstinate, crying for his mother, whom he hadn't seen for most of the day.

Thankfully, Colette appeared, her face pallid, her legs unsteady. It didn't look as though Doctor Blackford's Saturday visit had done her much good. She stayed only long enough to rock her son to sleep. Charmaine decided that as soon as Colette seemed up to it, she would broach the subject of Yvette's letter.

Monday, September 26, 1836

The second week began much like the first with the exception of her newly won respect from Paul. She was glad that he no longer treated her with indifference. During that first week he'd been courteous to a fault: *Good morning, Miss Ryan. Good evening, Miss Ryan.* By Saturday, Charmaine had been certain that the man didn't know how to be friendly, only polite. All that had changed on Sunday, and she smiled with the memory of it. By the end of Monday, she had become comfortable calling him Paul, and he in turn called her Charmaine, inquiring pleasantly as to how her day had been with the children.

Her new 'friendship' with Paul did not go unnoticed by the two maids of the manor, and late that night when she reached her room on the third floor, Felicia and Anna cornered her there. "So it's Paul, is it?" Felicia sneered. "You wouldn't be falling into his bed now, would you?"

Charmaine was appalled by the maid's vulgarity. "Are you jealous, Felicia? I don't suppose that Paul respects a woman who throws herself at him. I know that Miss Colette doesn't approve."

The housemaid's eyes flashed. "I don't care about *Miss* Colette. And what would you know of Paul's likes or dislikes, anyway? Just stay away from him, you hear me? Stay far away!"

"Please step aside," Charmaine replied condescendingly.

Stunned, the voluptuous woman threw a vexed look to her cohort, the considerably plainer Anna Smith. Charmaine seized the moment and pushed into her room, shutting the door in the servant's face. Leaning back against the portal, she closed her eyes and breathed deeply, wishing her room wasn't on the same floor as Felicia Flemmings'. She didn't think the taunting would end with this one confrontation. Annoyed, she grabbed her book and decided to read until her eyes were tired and she'd be able to sleep.

Tuesday, September 27, 1836

Where Monday had been rainy, Tuesday dawned sunny. On Colette's request, Charmaine spent the morning in town. Tomorrow was the twins' birthday, and Colette needed someone, preferably a woman, to travel to the mercantile. She provided the carriage, and Charmaine had the driver stop at the Browning house to see if Gwendolyn would like to join her. They had great fun fetching the gifts Colette had ordered for her daughters months ago, the most remarkable, two miniature glass horses to add to their animal collection. "The girls love the stable," Colette had said. "Now they'll have horses of their own."

As noon approached, Charmaine said goodbye to Gwendolyn and had the driver take her back to the manor. Once there, she rushed up to her bedroom and deposited the packages on her bed. She reached the table just in time for lunch.

"Where have you been?" Yvette demanded.

"You'll find out tomorrow," was all Charmaine would say.

Later that evening, when everyone was abed, Charmaine wrapped the gifts, spending a great deal of time on the ribbons. Colette had recommended that she hide them in the back of the girls' armoire, behind all their dresses. It was best if she crept down there now, when they were sound asleep. Sure enough, no one stirred. When she was finished, she headed down to the library, crossing paths with Jane Faraday on the stairs.

"Are you in need of something, Miss Ryan?" the head-housekeeper queried brusquely.

Charmaine decided not to take offense. The older woman's comportment was generally curt. "I was just going to the library to get a book."

"At this time of night?"

"I'm not tired, and I find that a novel always does the trick."

The woman eyed her suspiciously. "Then I suggest you choose a book quickly and take it back to your room on the third floor." Without further explanation, she continued her ascent.

Puzzled, Charmaine proceeded on her quest, selecting a novel entitled *Pride and Prejudice.* The study was inviting, the lighting good, and because she had spent a great deal of time in her bedroom already, she ignored the matron's directive and settled into one of the high-backed chairs. For an hour, she was lost to the story, unlike any she had ever read, and the characters of Mr. Darcy and Elizabeth Bennett, imagining Paul and herself as the hero and heroine. Oh, to live such a romance!

Muffled giggles interrupted her revelry. Mrs. Faraday thought everyone was abed. Not so. Charmaine recognized the voices: Felicia and Anna were scurrying about. Paul hadn't dined with them this evening, and Charmaine wondered if he had just come in. Whenever he was in the house, Felicia and Anna were never far away. *What were they up to?*

Charmaine lit a candle and doused the lamp, then crossed the room and cautiously opened the door. The hallway was surprisingly empty and dark, though light cascaded through the French doors in the dining room. She walked toward them, head cocked. No one was there either.

She stepped into the courtyard, breathing in the soft fragrance of the garden flowers. The breeze was a bit chilly, yet refreshing. The cool air carried the scent of ocean spray, sweet against her face as it washed away the remnants of the hot day. On impulse, she wandered along the garden path, her candle unnecessary, for lamps were lit here and there and a full moon bathed the sanctuary in heavenly light. She blew it out and set it atop her book on a nearby bench.

She sat down and closed her eyes, thinking about her new life and all that happened over the past month. So many changes, all for the better, she realized. Was she happy? Yes, she answered; she had made the right decision in coming to Charmantes. Like Yvette and Jeannette, she had yearned for adventure and had miraculously found it. Her life was no longer dull, but exciting.

The hour grew late. It was time to retire. Sighing, she finally rose.

"Going so soon?"

Startled, she spun halfway around to confront the deep voice that spoke from the shadows. "I'm sorry," Paul said as he stepped away from the tree he had been leaning on, "I didn't mean to frighten you."

"How long have you been standing there?"

He walked closer. "Long enough to watch you meander through the gardens and sit down on that bench. Actually, I've been intrigued. So many emotions crossing your brow, some of them quite vexing, I'd say."

Charmaine stepped back, her legs connecting with the bench she had just vacated. "Vexing?" she queried. "They weren't vexing, I assure you."

"What could someone so young be worrying about?" he pondered aloud, ignoring her remark to the contrary, stilling the hand that wanted to caress her cheek. Her blushes were intoxicating, and he had found himself thinking of her often during the past week, more often since Sunday.

"I told you, sir, I wasn't worrying about anything."

"Sir?" he queried. "I thought we'd dispensed with that formality."

"Paul," she acquiesced, heart hammering in her chest.

"Are you content here?"

"I think so," she whispered. "Actually – I *am* content. That is what I was thinking about before you spoke."

"You've been here less than a fortnight. How can you be certain?"

"I can't, but for now, my heart tells me I'm content."

He chuckled softly as if he approved of her conclusion, then stepped in so close that their bodies were nearly touching. Charmaine closed her eyes, certain of his next move. She was desperately frightened, yet scintillatingly excited. But he didn't take her in his arms, and her eyes flew open, both relieved and annoyed to find that he was now sitting on the bench.

"Stay awhile longer," he demanded, grabbing hold of her wrist and pulling her down beside him. "There's no reason why we should feel uncomfortable in one another's presence. I know you think of me as your employer, but I'd much prefer our relationship to grow into that of... *friends.* Would you like that?"

"Yes," she replied. "I'd like that very much."

"Good... And perhaps, in time, our *friendship* will blossom into something more. Would that be agreeable to you?"

He edged closer, his warm thigh coming in contact with hers, branding her through her dress, making it difficult to concentrate on his words. "I think so," she whispered tremulously.

He threw his arm around the back of the bench and leaned forward. "Life can be full for you here, Charmaine. I can see to that. You're a very beautiful young woman, and I can offer you fulfillment." With a rakish smile, he leaned back, allowing her to take his lead. She seemed to puzzle over his words, leaving him to contemplate the depth of her innocence.

"You've been too kind already, Paul. Just this past Sunday, you could have been angry when I allowed Pierre to run into your rooms, but you weren't. You've insisted that I use your given name. I couldn't ask for more than that. Between you and Colette, I've been made to feel very welcome."

So, she believed him to be a gentleman, he mused, in the strictest sense of the word. He had played the game well thus far. But she had been living under his roof for nearly ten days now, and governess or not, she had caught his fancy. He knew she found him disconcerting. How many times had she blushed in his presence? More times than he could count. But those blushes were born of an attraction as well. Just now she was dying to have him kiss her. But he wanted more than a casual kiss. He would have preferred bedding a housemaid than the children's governess. When his efforts to hire her on as a servant had been thwarted, he'd changed his tactics. He had played the gentleman, until tonight. Suddenly, his need to have her was great, the time for the plucking, ripe.

"I'm not speaking of kindness, Charmaine. I'm speaking of comfort."

"I'm quite comfortable, Paul," she replied, completely misreading his cue. "My room is immaculate and finer than any other I've ever had. As for the rest of the manor, it's beautiful, and I feel very fortunate to be allowed to roam about, using the library and the piano whenever I wish. From the very first day, everyone has made me feel at home."

Paul ran his hand through his hair in mild derision. *Must he spell his meaning out for the girl? Had she no knowledge of men?* He found that hard to believe; her comeliness must have captured many a young man's eye. It wasn't as if she were a southern belle, smothered every minute of the day by a hovering chaperone. No, Charmaine Ryan must have had experience in the realm of domination and submission. She was only playing her own game here, perhaps to further her own reward, but that would soon end.

"*Miss Ryan*," he began again, "I'm certain you're not as naïve as you would lead me to believe. I'm pleased that you find my house satisfactory. At present, however, that is the furthest thing from my mind. Let us say I'm more interested in our sleeping arrangements – yours and mine."

Slowly, the light began to dawn, and Charmaine's cheeks flamed scarlet. She tore herself away from the bench and the hand that had come to rest on her thigh. "*How dare you suggest such a thing?*" she spat out, her ire conquering her shame. "I'm a good girl, and I'd never, *never* do what you are suggesting. I was hired to see to the children's care – not yours!" Her eyes flooded with unwanted tears, and she suppressed the urge to run from the courtyard; she'd not grant him the satisfaction of laughing at her as well.

Groaning inwardly, Paul cursed himself for the fool that he was. He had known she was different, but in his eagerness to have her, he'd ignored the signs of her possible virtue. Was he so conceited to believe that every girl on the island would eagerly jump into his bed? He should have waited. But no; he had overstepped the bounds of propriety. She would leave the gardens tonight with her chastity intact, and he, with the brand 'cad' stamped across his chest. From this evening on, she'd be wary of him. Somehow, he must mitigate the damage done, perhaps purge her mind of its dark conclusions.

"Charmaine, whatever is the matter?" he asked with great concern. "Is it something I said? What has brought you to tears?" He stood, produced a handkerchief, and moved toward her.

"Don't come near me!"

Her tone, rather than her command, stilled his advance. With five paces between them, he spoke. "Please, tell me what I've said to upset you."

"You know what you've said. I'll not explain it to you!"

"I fear you misjudge me," he cajoled, a simple plan formulating in his mind. "Surely you don't think that I was suggesting that you…" He allowed his shocked query to trail off as if embarrassed. "Charmaine," he breathed, braving a step closer, "you've misconstrued my remarks. Please believe me when I tell you I was only considering the *'sleeping'* arrangements. There, I've said it again!"

She eyed him skeptically, uncertain of herself. He seemed bent upon exonerating himself. If his intention had been to proposition her, why would he bother? She relaxed somewhat, accepting the handkerchief he held out to her.

"Charmaine," he whispered again, taking another step forward. "I'm sorry, truly I am. I didn't mean to offend you. We're very blunt on Charmantes. But if you'd indulge me a moment longer, I think I can explain. I've been considering your room on the third floor. You're far too removed from the children there, and with Colette's poor health, it seems more practical for you to take up quarters next to the nursery. In that way, you'll be able to comfort them, especially little Pierre, should they awaken in the middle of the night."

He was winning her over. He could see it in her eyes, in her very being, her body no longer rigid. Inspired, he pressed on. "In fact, if you took the room adjacent to the children's bedchamber, I could have a door installed between the two, opening your room onto theirs." He stepped closer still, watching her dab at her eyes. "If that would be agreeable?"

"I don't know, sir," she faltered, relying on a formal address for fortification.

"Charmaine, you're not going to revert to calling me that again, are you?"

"I think 'sir' is more appropriate. Perhaps you think I'm naïve, and I suppose I am. However, being naïve does not make me a fool. I know right from wrong, decency from indecency. If I accept your offer to switch bedrooms, the move will be for the children's comfort, not yours. I hope *my* meaning is understood."

He *had* misjudged her. By the end of her reproof, he was simmering. *Who does she think she is, berating me as if I were a schoolboy? Why did I attempt to placate her? I should have kissed her passionately and been done with it – to hell with her objections.* But the moment was lost, and now he said, "Our meanings are the same, Mademoiselle. What is your answer?"

She hesitated. "Yes, but–"

"But what?" he queried snidely.

"The playroom abuts the children's bedroom on one side, and according to Yvette, your brother's chambers, the other side. Certainly either room is out of the question."

"John's room sits unoccupied. I'll have George break through the wall and mill a door for the frame."

"But what if your brother should return? Surely he won't be happy to find the governess in his room."

"He won't."

"He won't what?"

"Return. John won't return." The declaration was delivered with such conviction that the matter was closed as quickly as it had been opened. "Now," he proceeded, his temper poorly concealed, "if we're in agreement, I'll say goodnight. The hour grows late, and I have to be at the dock at sunrise. I'm expecting a ship from Europe."

"Yes," she replied. "Goodnight and thank you..."

Her words were directed at his back. He'd already dismissed her, quickly retreating through the gardens and leaving her perturbed.

Paul was glad to reach his room, fulminating over the wretched scene he had generated. He was grateful for only one thing: his brother John hadn't been there to witness the complete ass he'd just made of himself; otherwise, he'd never live it down. *Well, Miss Ryan,* he thought as he stretched out on his bed, *tomorrow you can have your fancy room and your fancy airs all to yourself! I want no part of them. There are too many women on the island just clamoring for my attention. I have no need of one lovely governess. But when you grow lonely, when you're ready to become a woman, then you can come crawling back to me, and maybe, just maybe, I'll take you to my bed.* Satisfied with that thought, he finally fell asleep.

Wednesday,
September 28, 1836

Chapter 5

Construction on the new door began the next morning. The sound of splintering wood echoed throughout the house, confounding those at the breakfast table. The twins dropped their spoons and ran from the room, ignoring their mother's admonition to wait for her. Charmaine and Colette found them in the nursery, wide-eyed over the hole in the wall and the debris littering the floor.

"What is this?" Colette demanded as Rose and Pierre drew up alongside her.

George peeked through the opening from the bedroom beyond. "The new doorway," he offered.

"Doorway?" Colette queried, clearly irate. "What doorway?"

"The one that Paul told me to begin working on today."

"Why would Paul ask you to break a hole through that wall, George?"

George's eyes flew to Charmaine, and she cringed. "For the children's benefit," he replied. "Paul thinks Miss Ryan should be nearer the nursery, so he's given her this room – and a door in order to provide easy access should they awaken during the night."

"That's John's room!" Colette fumed. "You've no right to desecrate it."

"*Desecrate it?* I'd hardly say I was desecrating it. And it's not my idea, anyway. I'm just following orders."

"And what if John were to come home?"

"He's not coming home, Colette. You know that."

"Someday he will," she murmured, her anger spent, "and he'll be hurt to find his chambers have been given to someone else."

Jeannette grabbed hold of her mother's hand. "Don't be upset, Mama. There are so many rooms in our house, I'm sure Johnny won't mind using another one. Besides, it will be nice to have Mademoiselle Charmaine nearby. Maybe that was Paul's birthday gift to us."

Colette smiled down at her daughter. "Perhaps you are right. I just wonder what your father is going to say when he sees this mess."

George said, "According to Paul, he approved the project."

Colette rubbed her forehead. "Yes, I suppose he would." She motioned to the children. "Come, let us step out of George's way."

"Oh please, can't we watch?" they begged.

Colette relented, advising them to remain seated on the far bed.

For a full hour, they chatted happily away. George, Travis, and Joseph indulged them whilst sawing, banging, and removing the wood and plaster that seemed to be everywhere.

When Pierre tired of the spectacle, Colette and Charmaine withdrew into the adjoining playroom. Realizing that she was not needed, Rose excused herself.

Charmaine inhaled. "Colette," she said, "I'm sorry that Paul didn't speak to you about the room. I didn't know he was going to start on it immediately. I should have insisted that he get your permission first."

Colette's brow dipped in consternation. "You knew about this?"

"Paul mentioned it to me last night. He suggested–"

"Last night? Paul arrived home very late last night."

Charmaine was too embarrassed to reply, and Colette deduced the obvious.

"Charmaine," she began, folding her hands as if in prayer and bringing them to her lips. "I think I should warn you about Paul. Maybe I should have done so sooner. He's a ladies' man – a womanizer." When Charmaine hung her head, Colette attempted to ease her distress. "I don't want to see you hurt."

"Don't worry, Colette, I won't bring shame to your home."

"I'm not speaking about shame, Charmaine. I'd hate to see you give your heart to someone who has no intention of returning your love."

Charmaine was stung by the words, though she knew they rang true. Her initial assumptions had been correct: Paul *had* propositioned her. When he'd realized she was not about to be compromised, he'd enacted a grand charade of misunderstanding. Her mother had warned her of such men, and Colette was doing the same. There was only one thing that Paul desired from her, and it wasn't 'friendship', not even love.

"I'll take heed," she whispered and added as a dismal afterthought, "If you don't want me in that room–"

"Nonsense," Colette countered. "Moving you into John's room is actually a fine idea, and the damage to the wall is done."

Charmaine reflected on the Duvoisin son she had yet to meet, the strange reaction his name had evoked that morning. Her thoughts circled to Yvette and the letter she'd written. Best to ask now and get it over with. "Yvette would like to send a letter to her brother in Richmond. I promised that if she were good, and you gave your permission, I'd ask Joshua Harrington to deliver it."

"Let Yvette write her letter," Colette answered without hesitation. "I'm certain John could use some happy news from home."

Relief washed over Charmaine. "She already has."

Colette didn't seem surprised.

After a time, she called to the girls, insisting they do a bit of reading. Together, they finished a narrative on Eleanor of Aquitaine, the French noblewoman of the twelfth century, who, at the age of fifteen, married the King of France, and later, the King of England. The girls pestered their mother for details, knowing that Colette's family, the Delacroixs, hailed from Poitiers, the same village where Eleanor grew up. When Colette spoke of the death of Eleanor's twenty-seven-year-old mother, Jeannette lamented. "That is so sad, Mama. You will be twenty-seven soon."

Colette squeezed her, promising to live a long life, then sent them over to Charmaine, who had been preparing a series of spelling lists. The girls were already good readers, but she was showing them the letter patterns in words.

Not five minutes later, Yvette was complaining. "This doesn't make sense!"

Charmaine looked over her shoulder. "What doesn't?"

"This stupid list," she grumbled. "oil, boil, soil, foil…"

"Yes, what about it?"

"Well, if 'o-i' makes the 'oy' sound in those words, Du-*vwah*-zan should be pronounced Du-*voy*-zan… and Mademoiselle… Mad-um-*oy*-zel."

Charmaine chuckled. "Very good, Yvette," she praised. When the girl eyed her skeptically, she added, "it shows you're paying attention and really learning. As for your surname and Mademoiselle, I think the 'o-i' is pronounced differently because both words are French."

Colette looked up from where she was now reading to Pierre. "Mademoiselle Charmaine is correct, Yvette," she interjected. "In the French language, 'o-i' is pronounced 'wah'. But you know that. There are quite a few French words that have made their way into the English language: 'armoire', 'reservoir', and 'repertoire' for instance. Your Papa's other island 'Espoir' is also pronounced with the 'wah' sound."

"It's very confusing," Yvette grumbled.

"That is English," Charmaine concluded. "Linguists say it is one of the most difficult languages to learn because it has so many variations."

"Is that true, Mama?" Jeannette asked.

"Is what true?"

"That English is difficult to learn?"

"Yes, I suppose it is. I learned the rudiments when I was young, but I didn't become proficient until... until I moved here."

"Did Papa teach you?"

Colette grew reticent. "A bit," she whispered. When Jeannette probed further, she said, "It is nearly lunch time. Let us finish up."

After the meal, the girls rushed to the piano for their daily lesson. An hour later, everyone retreated to Colette's chambers where it was considerably quieter and the promise of birthday gifts more enticing than the construction site. Charmaine volunteered to get them. She had just reached the end of the corridor when Agatha Ward appeared.

"Miss Ryan," the matron criticized, "are you being employed to decorate the hallway or were you hired to care for the children?"

The obtrusive statement left Charmaine dumbfounded, for she had had little contact with the woman, passing a friendly 'good day' now and then, but nothing more. Agatha avoided the children, and Charmaine only saw her at mealtimes or when she insisted that Colette rest. Most days, Colette politely ignored her.

"Well, Miss Ryan?" she pressed.

"I've been sent on an errand–" Charmaine stammered "–for Miss Colette."

"An errand?" Agatha scoffed. "And where are the children?"

"With Miss Colette, in her chambers."

"Young lady," she scolded, "Miss Colette is not well. *You* are the one who should be looking after the children, not she! They continue to contribute to her failing health."

Charmaine's ire had been primed. "Miss Colette seems most indisposed after she passes an afternoon with your brother, Mrs. Ward. On the other hand, her health always improves when she spends time with her children."

Agatha Ward's eyes widened briefly, then narrowed into slits of animosity. Charmaine realized too late that she had just made an enemy. "What are you inferring, Miss Ryan – that my brother is incompetent? Let us hope that you are never in need of a physician's care while on this island. I don't think Robert would appreciate ministering to someone who eagerly maligns his good name."

"I didn't mean–"

"Didn't you?" the widow hissed. "You had better scurry back to your–"

"What goes on here?"

Startled, Agatha's hostility faded, her attention focused over Charmaine's left shoulder. "Why Frederic," she recovered, "isn't this a surprise?"

Charmaine pivoted around, stunned to find the splendent Frederic Duvoisin standing before her. He leaned heavily on a polished black cane, his posture crooked. Even so, he radiated a power that negated the rumors she had heard. He was tall, taller than Paul, his attire casual, yet finely tailored, and he was handsome, very handsome. Liberal touches of gray highlighted a full head of hair, not quite as dark as his son's. He was clean-shaven, with squared jaw, long, curved nose, and thin lips. His steely eyes were keen and bored through her, scrutinizing her more surely than she did him.

"Are you pleased with your assessment, Miss Ryan?" he asked, irony lacing his deep voice, his speech slightly slurred. He knew who she was! "I asked you a question, Mademoiselle. Does the invalid meet your expectations?"

"You're not an invalid, sir," she answered truthfully.

The remark surprised him, but he snorted derisively, then confronted Agatha. "Has Miss Ryan done something to annoy you?"

"She has left the children unattended."

"Where?"

The dowager lifted her nose a notch. "In Colette's chambers."

"And where is my wife?"

"With them."

"I'd hardly call that unattended, Agatha. Colette is, after all, their mother."

"Yes, Frederic, but she is not well. That is the only reason Miss Ryan was hired. What is the point of a governess, if she does not tend to her pupils?"

"Miss Ryan?" Frederic queried, giving her the chance to defend herself.

"Your wife asked me to get the twins' birthday gifts, sir."

"I see," he said, focusing on the widow again.

"Had I known," Agatha lamely objected. "Miss Ryan said nothing of gifts."

"You didn't give me a chance," Charmaine rejoined.

Agatha gritted her teeth. She was losing this debate. Best to swallow her pride, apologize, and quickly excuse herself.

Charmaine watched her hasten down the stairs, then faced Frederic again. Suddenly, she understood why Colette might be attracted to a man old enough to be her father. Unlike Paul, who at times possessed a youthful mien, this man was hardened, lordly, and completely disarming. In his younger days, she could only wonder over the women who fell at his feet. Did he know how intriguing he was? Yes, he definitely knew. Even now, in his crippled state, he knew.

Presently, he was awaiting her next move. "Miss Ryan," he said, breaking the prolonged silence. "I believe you were sent to retrieve something for my wife?"

"Yes," she said and headed toward the nursery, intimidated when he followed her, acutely aware of his handicap now that he attempted to walk. She knew he would not appreciate her pity, so she kept her gaze averted, rummaging instead inside the armoire for the girls' presents. When she finally turned around, he was standing before the broken wall, studying it. According to Paul, he'd agreed to the door's installation. She wondered what he was thinking now. Work had come to a halt; the men must have gone off for lunch.

As if reading her thoughts, he said, "I heard all the banging and wanted to see for myself the progress. I also wanted to spend time with my daughters."

He faced her. "My wife is very pleased with you, Miss Ryan."

"I'm very happy to be here, sir. I like your children very much, and Miss Colette is a lovely woman."

"Yes, she is," Frederic agreed, his eyes intense. "And with your new room, she shall sleep soundly knowing that you are not far from the children."

"Yes, sir," she replied, thinking, he *had* given his permission. Although Frederic Duvoisin might not often leave his chambers, he was fully aware of everything that happened in his home. Most of the gossip was untrue.

"I see you have all your packages. Shall we?" He inclined his head toward the hallway, intending to accompany her.

"Yes. The girls will be wondering what has kept me."

Again, Frederic followed, and she slowed her pace in an effort to diminish his incapacity. The gesture annoyed him. "Hurry up, Miss Ryan, we don't have all day!" Flustered, she quickly complied.

When they reached Colette's suite, he asked if she might fetch another three parcels. "There are additional gifts in my dressing room."

The master's apartments were congruent to Colette's boudoir: the same dimensions, doors equally positioned. Yet the similarity ended there. These lavishly appointed quarters were masculine: bold and ornate, dark and somber, with heavy, elaborately carved furniture.

Charmaine didn't dally. She skirted across the spacious room, re-stacked the parcels, and returned to the passageway moments later. The packages were cumbersome, and she shifted them uneasily, relieved when Frederic finally rapped on his wife's door.

Yvette opened it, clearly surprised to find him there. "Papa?"

He raised a dubious brow. "Yvette, am I to stand forever in the hallway? Or will you invite us in? Miss Ryan is overburdened with birthday presents."

"Come in, Papa," she invited, stepping aside. "We didn't expect you to visit us today. Mama promised to take us to your room after dinner tonight."

"The schedule has been changed," he said, limping into the chamber. "I heard the racket coming from the nursery and went to have a look at the door being installed for your benefit. But you weren't there. Instead, I have had the pleasure of meeting your new governess."

Yvette wasn't listening, her attention diverted. "Oh, my!" she exclaimed, scanning the packages Charmaine carried. "How many are there?"

"Allow Miss Ryan to put them down, Yvette."

Frederic reached the settee and fell into it with an exhaustive 'oomph', his face drawn as if in pain. When the moment passed, he looked about the room. "Where is your mother?"

"In the bedroom, with Pierre. He needed to have his nappy changed. There is an odd number of packages here," she observed, lifting the largest.

"One is for Pierre," her father explained.

"Pierre? Why does he get a present? His birthday isn't until March."

"Now Yvette, would you deny him the pleasure of opening a gift? I realize it's not his birthday, but he'll be upset if there's nothing for him to tear into."

Charmaine was taken by the man's thoughtfulness, his tender voice.

"May I open one of them now, Papa?"

"First, tell your brother and sister that I have come for a visit."

She jumped to do his bidding, calling from the doorway, "Papa is here."

Jeannette scampered into the room and embraced him. "Papa!"

"You are looking well, Jeannette."

"So are you, Papa. I'm glad you came to visit us today! Does this mean you are getting better?"

"If I am, it is because of you." He stroked her hair, his eyes glowing.

The endearing moment was broken when Colette stepped into the room, Pierre in her arms. Frederic looked up, missing her smile of greeting, and spoke sharply. "Do you think that wise, Colette?"

Her face dropped. "Wise?"

"Carrying the boy so," he replied. "You've been told not to exert yourself."

She bit her bottom lip, enduring his stern brow, and immediately set Pierre on his feet. He was off and running, crying, "Mainie's back!"

"Mainie?" Jeannette and Yvette asked in tandem.

Colette understood and laughed, shaking off Frederic's cutting disapproval and reveling in Pierre's candid joy. "I think you have a new name, Charmaine."

Charmaine scooped the child up and gave him a hug. "And I like it."

"Mainie," Pierre said again, before giving her a big, wet kiss.

Charmaine returned the affectionate gesture, which elicited a repeat performance from the lad.

The curious scene fascinated Frederic. It was the first time his wife had ever handed the child over to anyone, save Rose, the first time the two-year-old had willingly left his mother's embrace.

After a moment, Charmaine walked over to the sofa. "Your father has come to see you, Pierre," she said, placing the boy on the man's lap.

Pierre immediately began to squirm, and Frederic struggled to hold him in place. Before he could wriggle free, Colette crossed the room and sat next to them. Frederic relaxed his grip, and Pierre crawled into her lap, happy again.

Colette found strength in his contentment and looked up at her husband, instantly unsettled by his hardened regard. He shifted nearer, their thighs touching now. She drew an uneven breath, certain he willed her to look away. She raised her chin in defiance, refusing to be intimidated, or worse, subjugated.

A stray, flaxen lock caressed her cheek. Frederic stilled the hand that yearned to loop it back behind her ear. The contact would be exquisite, but painful as well. Her beauty mesmerized him, made his heart pound and loins quicken.

Charmaine felt extremely uncomfortable. No words had passed between the couple, and yet so much had been said, the room electric, the tension mounting. Even the girls could feel it, for they remained mute, waiting for someone else to break the silence. Only Pierre appeared unscathed, happily playing with the buttons on his mother's dress, oblivious to the tumult.

"Perhaps you'd like some time alone," Charmaine suggested, and not waiting for a reply, she turned to leave.

"A moment longer, Miss Ryan," Frederic commanded. "Would you please distribute my gifts to the children? Each one is marked."

Charmaine attended to his request. Yvette ripped the wrapping from the present. Jeannette held her parcel a moment longer, studying her parents instead.

Frederic looked up at her. "Aren't you going to open your gift, Jeannette?"

"Yes, Jeannette," Yvette urged, "open it quickly. I want to see if you got something better than a stupid old doll so that we can trade." She held up a lovely china doll with eyes that opened and closed.

Charmaine winced, wary of Frederic's reaction. Would he admonish the girl for her rudeness? He only chuckled, as if the declaration were ingenuous, rather than pert. "What is this, Yvette? I thought all little girls played with dolls."

"No, sir. I'd much prefer to have a horse than a silly old doll!"

"A horse?" he pursued in jest. "And how would I manage to get him in a box of that size?"

"He wouldn't have to be in a box, Papa," she replied in earnest. "You could have him hidden in the stables, with a big blue ribbon around his neck!"

"Really? And what would you do with him once you'd found him?"

"Ride him, of course!"

"But horseback riding isn't ladylike."

Yvette mistook his facetious remark and wrinkled her nose disdainfully. "I don't want to be a lady, Papa. I'd much rather be a boy."

"Would you now? And why is that?"

"It's no fun being a lady, that's why! You always have to worry about keeping your dress clean. *You always have to wear a dress!* Boys can wear trousers. They can be rude and spit. They can learn to swim and climb trees! But if you're a girl, you're not allowed to do any of those things. A girl has to have *proper manners*, and I hate it! I want to do the things my brother does."

"Pierre?" Frederic asked, baffled. "Surely you're allowed more than he?"

"Not Pierre, Papa. Johnny. He always does fun things. When he was living here, we had such a wonderful time! Every day we did something new, and he never once told me I couldn't because I was–"

"Yvette," her mother remonstrated, "that's enough."

"No, it's not enough! I'm tired of being told not to mention his name. I love Johnny!" With arms akimbo, she turned accusatory eyes on her father. "And when is he coming home, anyway? When are you going to stop being angry with him? *When?*"

"Not for a very long time," Frederic snarled irascibly, jaw clenched.

"*Why?*" she demanded, stomping her foot.

"He is a menace to certain members of this household. Now, you'll not speak of him again! Is that understood, young lady?"

Undaunted, Yvette's eyes flashed fire for fire, refusing to answer.

"*Is that understood?*"

"No – it's not!" she shouted, throwing down the expensive doll. Its head shattered into a thousand pieces, shards of glass flying everywhere. She tore from the room, ignoring her father's repeated bellows of: "Yvette, come back here!"

Colette weathered the storm, speaking softly, yet firmly when the man leveled his wrathful gaze on her. "There was no need to speak to her that way."

"You think not?"

"She loves her brother and doesn't understand–"

"Damn it, woman!" he roared, astounded by her audacity. "Why do you defend him? It is time you taught the children to respect me! I refuse to tolerate such insolence from an eight-year-old child. My daughter will not decide *if* she obeys. *She will obey!*"

Gulping back her pride, Colette bowed her head to his public chastisement.

Belatedly, Frederic remembered that the governess was there, and his foul temper turned to sour disgust. "Where is Pierre's present?" he asked gruffly.

Charmaine relinquished the package she held for support, and Frederic extended it to his son. "Look, Pierre, I have a gift for you. Come, sit here and open it with me."

The boy would not budge from Colette's protective lap.

"Come," Frederic persisted, quelling his agitation, "sit on my knee so you can open this. Your mother is right here. She would like to see what's inside."

The more he cajoled, the more the child withdrew, balled fists holding tightly to his mother's dress, face buried in her bosom, his muffled whimpers echoing in the turbulent room. He had no interest in the package with its ribbons.

Colette began her own appeal. "Here, Pierre, I will help you. Voici, mon caillou, your father would–" the statement caught in mid-sentence, a minute flinch as her gaze clashed with Frederic's "–come, Pierre, we can open it together."

Frederic had had enough. "Give me my son!" he demanded, grabbing hold of the boy's arm. "Give him here! *Now!*"

Defeated, Colette ignored Pierre's struggles and allowed Frederic to pry him loose. At last, she was free and stood quickly. Embarrassed and deeply hurt, she averted her face, squared her shoulders, and walked with dignity from the room. Once the door closed, however, she ran – ran to escape the demon that chased her, ran down the passageway, the stairs, ran until her side hurt, coming up abruptly as the main door in the foyer swung open and Paul strode in. She turned from him and ran again, to the back of the house and into the gardens.

"Colette?"

Jeannette was silently weeping when her father spoke to her. "Come, Princess, help your brother open his package."

The girl looked from Frederic to Charmaine as if she hadn't heard. "What was the matter with Mama?" she asked.

"I don't know, Jeannette," Charmaine whispered.

Hoping to still her quaking limbs, she scooped up the discarded doll and began picking up the pieces of glass that littered the floor. Perhaps it could be mended. Jeannette crouched down to help.

"Leave that!" Frederic barked.

Charmaine dropped the fragments. "I'd best see to Yvette," she said, determined to escape the wretched room. But unlike Colette, who had maintained her composure, she fled like a petrified rabbit, the broken doll still in her arms.

Jeannette was right on her heels, until Frederic stopped her. "Jeannette, come help your brother." With a sigh, she complied.

Paul walked briskly into the dining room; it was empty. Noise from the kitchen sent him in that direction. He was surprised to find Travis, Joseph, and George sitting at the rough-hewn wooden table. Fatima was serving the three men a late lunch, the very meal that had brought him home. "Have you seen Colette?" he asked.

"No," George replied. "Why?"

"She wasn't upset about the new door, was she?"

"In the beginning. But not anymore. Why?"

"She was crying. Just now – in the foyer."

George shook his head. "She wasn't that upset."

Paul ran a hand through his hair. She *was* upset. He had to find her. *The gardens – she must have gone into the gardens.* Inspired, he headed there.

Charmaine found Yvette on her bed, toying with an envelope that she tapped on her knee. She looked up, her eyes red. "I may as well burn this," she said, and Charmaine realized it contained the letter she had written to John.

"No, Yvette. It's being sent directly to your brother just as I promised. Your mother gave her permission this morning."

Yvette frowned in momentary disbelief, then smiled, wiping away the last of her tears. "Thank you." She turned serious again. "I don't know why Papa is so angry with Johnny. His seizure happened three years ago! Johnny is his son. Why won't he forgive him?"

"It's not just a matter of forgiveness, Yvette. I think your father is very embarrassed about the way he looks right now. His arm, his leg, the way he walks, the cane he has to use for support. He sees himself as a cripple, and that's not an easy thing for any man to live with. If an argument with your brother caused that condition, I can understand his bitterness. The pain and humiliation that's deep inside of him has turned into anger."

"He's more than angry, Mademoiselle Charmaine. He hates Johnny."

Charmaine shook her head. "No, Yvette, I don't believe your father hates him. No man hates his own son." Even as she spoke the words, she wondered if she were wrong. After all, she hated her father. And if that were possible, why couldn't Frederic hate John? She shuddered with the thought of it, for in this relationship, so many others were involved.

"Yvette," she began cautiously, "I'd like you to do something that I know will be very difficult. I'd like you to go back to your mother's apartments and apologize to your father."

Yvette's face turned crimson. "*Apologize?* You want me to apologize after what he said? He should apologize to me and to Johnny! I'll never apologize to him! He'll be lucky if I ever speak to him again! I thought you understood!"

Charmaine allowed the barrage of protests to ebb before she attempted to explain. "Do you want your brother to come home again, Yvette?"

"Of course I do!"

"The only way you're going to get your father to change his mind about John is by setting the example you want him to follow."

Yvette weighed the wisdom of her governess' supposition and grimaced in revulsion. "*But apologize?* I don't see how that can possibly help."

"Your father is very resentful, Yvette. How much greater will those feelings become if he thinks he's lost your love to John as well?"

"He'll only hate him more," she muttered, realizing that she'd only make matters worse if she stayed angry with her parent. "I suppose I have no other choice," she groaned. "And I've ruined that silly doll. I can't fix that!"

"I don't think your father cares about the doll. But he does love you."

"I know he does," she ceded. "Will you come with me?"

"I'll be along in a minute," Charmaine promised as the girl walked to the door. "But Yvette, don't mention the letter to your father."

The girl rolled her eyes. "Don't worry. I'm not that stupid!"

When Yvette had gone, Charmaine went in search of Colette.

Was there nowhere to turn? No quiet haven where the past wouldn't haunt her? How much longer would she bear this heavy burden of guilt? How much more could she endure? Colette was in the courtyard before the kaleidoscopic questions converged into one ostensible answer, too terrible to face. *Peace, there would be no peace until she died.* She sat hard on a bench deep in the garden, buried her face in her hands, and wept.

Where was she? Paul scoured the pathways, hearing, rather than seeing her first. He knew who had reduced her to tears. This had nothing to do with the new door. Or did it? He regarded her for countless minutes, uncertain how to confront her misery. It had been years since she'd cried on his shoulder. His chest ached at the sight of her anguish.

"Colette?" he called, his throat constricted.

The golden head lifted, and her face glistened with moisture, her eyes red and swollen. Embarrassed, she stood and quickly attempted to wipe her cheeks dry. But the tears spilled forth faster than she could brush them away.

"Colette," he breathed again, this time stepping closer, gathering her into his strong arms, a bulwark to shoulder her pain. When she tried to push him away, he pulled her tighter into his embrace, murmuring tender words to soothe her. "Ssh… there now… Cry… cry if you need to cry."

It had been too long since she'd been held – too long. Relinquishing the battle, she collapsed against him, crying until it hurt, until the well was dry and a strange calm settled over her.

"Cela est fini," he murmured against the top of her head.

Charmaine reached the gardens through the ballroom. She didn't want to meet Mrs. Faraday, or worse still, Agatha Ward along the way, so she took a route that avoided the main house. Surely Colette would be here, for the courtyard offered a secluded sanctuary.

Soft words spoken in melodic French caught her ear. Colette used it every day when instructing her children, and Charmaine had learned quite a few phrases, but this was the first time she had been privy to an entire conversation. She peered through the branches and watched Paul lead Colette to the very bench they had shared the night before. And like the night before, he produced a handkerchief, pressed it into her hand, and said, "Tu vas mieux maintenant?"

"Me pardonnera-t-il jamais?" came her desperate response.

He shook his head, studying the delicate hand that he held. "J'éspère que je pourrais te donner la réponse que tu désires entendre."

She lowered her eyes. "Comment est-ce-que je peux demander pardon quand je sais ce que j'ai fait? Je ne devrais pas te demander d'être compréhensif. Tu devrais me reprocher aussi…"

His voice grew hard, and he released her hand. "Tu sais que cela n'est pas vrai! Je ne t'ai jamais reprochée."

She began wringing the handkerchief. "Je ne m'attends pas à ce qu'il me pardonne," she whispered, her eyes raising to his. "Peut-être pourrais-je supporter sa douleur ainsi que la mienne."

"Sa douleur?" he snorted.

"Oui. Je lui ai fait plus de peine qu'à moi-meme." She inhaled and shuddered. "Il m'a aimée. Le savais-tu? Il m'a aimée, mais j'étais trop aveugle pour le voir. Je croyais que ma vie était terminée, alors j'ai choisi de mener une nouvelle vie, plus désastreuse que la première… Mon Dieu… Je me suis mentie à moi-même pendant si longtemps, je ne sais pas où se trouve le vrai bonheur."

"Avec les enfants," Paul answered. "You have the children."

"Yes," she sighed, "I have the children."

The words were spoken reverently, as if she were drawing sustenance from them. But as the conversation continued in English, Charmaine tiptoed away, not wanting to eavesdrop. She knew Colette was in good hands.

She returned to the mistress' chambers, surprised to hear happy voices. Yvette was nestled next to her father, his arm around her shoulders. Someone had cleaned up the mess; there was no sign of the madness that had trespassed there only a short time ago.

Frederic finally bade them good day, his eyes apologetic. "Thank you," he murmured to Charmaine, and she knew he was speaking of Yvette. She nodded and bowed her head, uncomfortable with his taciturn regard.

When they were alone, she breathed deeply. "Come children, let us find your mother." They eagerly agreed, and together, they went downstairs.

Saturday, October 1, 1836

Charmaine woke to the sun in her eyes. She blinked once and, realizing that she'd overslept, jumped from her bed. Swearing under her breath, she flew about the room, splashing water in her face, dressing quickly, and brushing her hair haphazardly. She had no time to pin it up; instead, she tied it back with a ribbon, unmindful of the curly wisps that refused to be tamed.

The Harringtons were leaving at seven, and Paul had promised to take her into town to see them off. She was supposed to be ready at the crack of dawn, but she hadn't slept well last night. Felicia had cornered her in the hallway again, making ribald comments about her new sleeping quarters. "Couldn't be much closer to Paul's." Now Charmaine was terribly late. She ran from her room on the third floor and down the servants' stairwell that led to the kitchen.

Fatima Henderson bustled between table and wood stove, the smell of bacon and eggs filling the air. She was humming to herself, but one look at Charmaine and she clicked her tongue. "Miss Charmaine, why are you runnin' like that?"

"I'm late!" she heaved, completely out of breath. "Have you seen Master Paul? He hasn't left without me, has he?"

"Slow down, child. He's in the dinin' room waitin' for his breakfast. Now, sit yourself down and I'll fix you somethin', too."

"I couldn't eat a thing. Are you certain that Master Paul hasn't left?"

"See for yourself."

Paul was indeed at the table. As she entered the room, he stood, his eyes raking her from head to toe, causing her heart to race.

She hadn't spoken two words to him since the night in the gardens, save a courteous good morning or good evening. That had changed last night when he informed her that the Destiny would be leaving with the tide first thing in the morning. Her beloved Harringtons would be aboard, and it would please him to accompany her to the harbor to bid them farewell. When she had fretted over the imposition, withholding her reservations about riding into town with him alone, he brushed her objection aside, saying he needed to inspect the cargo. It was all arranged; he would escort her.

He was still staring at her, a lopsided grin that amplified the leering quality of his perusal. Charmaine glanced down at her dress, wondering if something in her appearance was amiss. "Is something wrong?" she asked.

"On the contrary," he answered, coming around the table and insisting that she join him. "You look lovely."

She blushed. Suddenly, she felt lovely.

He led her to the chair on his left and pulled it out for her. When she hesitated, he said, "Charmaine, we don't have all day. I promise, I won't bite."

She cringed and sat quickly, cursing her Irish blood, which advertised her every emotion. Obviously, her blushing amused him. She must learn to control her feelings. *But how?*

"I'm sorry I've kept you waiting," she said when he was seated again.

"You haven't. I've just come in to eat," and he took a sip of his coffee.

Fatima was there, filling his plate. When she made her way round the table, Charmaine declined the aromatic food. "I'm not hungry, really I'm not."

Paul's brow raised. "You'll be famished by lunchtime."

"I'll have coffee instead. I don't want to miss the ship's departure."

"The captain won't set sail until I give the order."

When they left the house, she was surprised to find a chaise waiting for them. "I was busy while you were sleeping," he needled as he helped her in. This time she willed her face passive. He circled round the back of the vehicle and climbed in, taking up reins and flicking the horse into motion.

The trip was pleasant, and Charmaine was amazed at how easily Paul drew her into casual conversation. By the time they reached the town, she felt comfortable with him, more comfortable than ever before.

The Destiny was waiting just as he had promised. With heavy heart, she boarded the ship, knowing that this farewell was going to be very difficult.

Loretta and Gwendolyn were just emerging from their cabins, and Charmaine's eyes immediately filled with tears. She fell into Loretta's embrace and hugged her tightly. Finally, she drew away, wiping her face.

"I'm going to miss you," she whispered hoarsely.

"And I you, Charmaine. But you have a new life here. I will write." Loretta faced Paul, who had stepped to one side, permitting them their maudlin farewell. "Charmaine is like a daughter to me, Mr. Duvoisin," she imparted pointedly. "Today I leave her in your care. I pray that I am not remiss in doing so."

Paul responded urbanely. "Your misgivings are unwarranted, Madame. Miss Ryan will be well protected while residing in my home."

"Good," Loretta replied.

Charmaine went in search of Mr. Harrington who was with the ship's captain. She was glad she had stuffed Yvette's letter in her apron pocket the night before. After bidding the man farewell, she pressed the correspondence into his hand, asking if he would see it delivered. He nodded and gave her another hug. She looked up to find Paul closely watching her, a strange expression on his face.

Then it was time to leave. She forced a smile from the boardwalk as the Destiny cast off. Paul remained at her side, watching as she continued to wave to her friends. As the vessel slipped further south toward the mouth of the cove, she finally turned away. Loretta and Gwendolyn were no longer visible; there was no point in staying.

She was frowning when she faced Paul. "I thought you had to check on the ship's cargo before she left."

Paul rubbed his chin. "Everything was in order, just as I had hoped."

"So you weren't needed to see the Destiny off."

"Now, Charmaine, if you had known that, you would have insisted upon journeying to the harbor on your own this morning, and I would have been denied the pleasure of your company."

"Are you saying you lied to me?"

"Something like that." He was smiling, his deviltry irrepressible.

"Come, Charmaine. There is another reason I accompanied you into town today." He read her confusion and took hold of her elbow, leading her away from the wharf. "Colette asked me to take you into the bank and introduce you to Stephen Westphal. He is the town financier and will calculate the deposits made to your register each month. Unconventional by Richmond standards, but expedient on Charmantes. I'd like to check and make certain that the account is in force and that you are able to withdraw your salary whenever you like."

They spent the next hour conversing with Mr. Westphal, a strange man by Charmaine's estimation. He was of medium height, balding, probably a bit younger than Frederic Duvoisin, but not at all handsome. His eyes were too small, his eyebrows too feminine, and his lips too thin. He looked every bit the European aristocrat, which Paul confided he was; his family boasted a Duke as a distant relative, though he himself was born in Virginia. His fingers were long and perfectly manicured. His clothing was very expensive and accentuated his paunch, attesting to his own wealth and good fortune. He knew who Charmaine was. News of the Duvoisin governess had spread rapidly on Charmantes.

"Why don't you join us for dinner this evening, Stephen?" Paul asked. "In fact, come a bit earlier, perhaps six? My father and I have a few matters we'd like to discuss with you."

The man eagerly accepted the invitation, then nodded to Charmaine.

As they left the bank, Paul inquired whether she'd like to get a bite to eat. They strolled across the street, and Charmaine felt many eyes on them. She was thrilled knowing that she was the envy of every young maid today. However, the pleasant feel of Paul's arm beneath her own evaporated when they reached the saloon. "I can't go in there!" she gasped.

"It's not a brothel, Charmaine," he chuckled. "I assure you, Dulcie's food is quite good."

"I – I didn't suggest that it was!" she stammered. "I must get back to the house. The girls are waiting to help me move my belongings into the new bedroom."

"Ah yes, the new bedroom," he chuckled again, but said no more.

The ride home was disconcerting. Unlike their earlier conversation, Paul set her heart to palpitating, touching on indelicate subjects best left alone. Did he enjoy making her uncomfortable now that the Harringtons were gone? Was he reminding her that she had nowhere to turn with them far from Charmantes?

"I hope you find your new bed pleasing," he began. "It might be overly large for just you."

Charmaine's cheeks burned. "If Pierre awakens in the night, there will be plenty of room for him to join me," she courageously returned.

"Hmm... best not to nurture that type of habit. He'll become spoiled."

"I doubt Pierre will ever be spoiled. He's a dear little boy."

To Charmaine's dismay, Paul revisited the subject of her new bedroom. "Now that you are on the second floor with the rest of the family, you will enjoy having the French doors at your disposal." When she didn't respond, he expounded. "During the summer, they are left open to catch the ocean breezes. The rooms on the second floor are always pleasantly cool. And of course, there is the *other* convenience they afford."

Charmaine knew he wanted her to ask him about that *other* convenience. She resolved not to, then did. "What convenience?"

"Every room opens onto the balcony: my bedroom, the children's rooms, even your room now. It's an inconspicuous way to travel from one chamber to the next..." His gaze, which had remained fixed on the road in front of him, now rested on her. "Just another convenience."

The lecherous overture evoked Colette's warning: *He's a ladies' man, Charmaine... I wouldn't want you to get hurt...* Was Paul propositioning her here, in the chaise, in broad daylight? "What are you suggesting, sir?" she bit out.

"Sir?" he queried. "Charmaine, when are you going to drop the formal title? What is it going to take to have you call me Paul permanently? You're not still upset by what you *think* happened in the gardens the other night, are you?"

He was trying to confuse her again. "I shall never call you Paul."

"Perhaps an agreement," he continued, completely ignoring her declaration, his brow raised in thought. "What if I promised to never again say anything to embarrass you?"

"I would say – that is impossible for you."

He threw back his head and laughed. When his glee subsided, he pressed on in the same vein. "What if I vowed to never do anything that you yourself didn't want me to do? Would you drop the title 'sir' then?"

Was he serious? Had he been toying with her to see if he could make her blush? What should she say? She decided it was safer to say nothing.

"Well, Charmaine?" he probed. "We're almost home. Maybe you'd like to think on it. But when you do, remember what I said to your Mrs. Harrington this morning. I meant every word."

They were home, and Charmaine inhaled before facing him. The buggy stopped, and their eyes locked as each tried to read the other's thoughts. The approach of another carriage intruded upon the moment. Doctor Robert Blackford had arrived for his weekly visit. Paul swore under his breath, jumped from the chaise, and rushed around to help her down. The faintest "thank you" fell from her lips as she hastened up the steps and into the house.

Paul stared after her, a wide grin mirroring his mood. She was something to behold, and all the more enchanting in her innocence and ire. Yes, she was innocent. He was certain of that now, and for that reason alone, he couldn't remain angry with her. She was too lovely for that. Today, he had enjoyed teasing her, but he also wanted her to feel at ease in his presence. Perhaps this 'agreement' he'd contrived was the best way to do that. He also had to consider what Colette asked of him in the courtyard the other day. *I don't want you toying with Charmaine's affections. I don't want her to become another conquest. The children will need her should anything happen to me. Please promise me that you won't hurt her.* Because he respected Colette, he had reassured her that he would be on his best behavior. As for Charmaine, he'd make good his 'agreement'. He was certain that if he did, she would come to enjoy his company. It would only be a matter of time before she recognized her own desires, and he'd be there when she was ready to enjoy them. *Yes, Charmaine Ryan, I can wait.*

Robert Blackford interrupted his musings, and they exchanged a few words before going into the house. The doctor was early; it was just after twelve.

"Quickly, Jeannette!" Yvette implored on a strained whisper. She was crouched near the top of the staircase, peering through the rungs of the balustrade into the nursery. "If you don't hurry, we shall miss it!"

"Miss what?" Charmaine asked from the landing.

Yvette swiftly straightened up. "Mademoiselle," she said sweetly.

Perhaps it was the manner in which the girl smiled, or the fact that she didn't give Charmaine a direct answer, but Charmaine knew she was up to something.

"Miss what?" she asked again.

Yvette knew how to handle this: be as truthful as possible without telling the truth. She gave a big, healthy, exasperated huff. "There's a horse in the corral that I wanted Jeannette to see."

The explanation sounded veracious enough, yet Charmaine wasn't convinced. "Why were you sneaking?"

"I wasn't sneaking. I was just telling Jeannette to hurry."

Jeannette appeared, smiling just as sweetly, but her demeanor was natural and honest.

"Where is your mother and Nana Rose?" Charmaine asked suspiciously.

"In the dining room, finishing lunch," Jeannette answered.

"And they've given their permission? This horse isn't dangerous, is it?"

"Oh no," Jeannette answered sincerely, "Chastity is quite tame."

"Chastity?"

"Mama's horse," Yvette supplied with foot tapping.

"And why is this horse of such interest to you?"

"George has something he wants to show us," Yvette replied, inspired.

"What do I want to show to whom?"

Yvette grimaced. *Rotten luck!*

George joined the threesome, a biscuit in hand, another in his mouth. "Was someone talking about me?" he asked, swallowing.

Charmaine turned a critical eye on him. "You know nothing about this?"

"About what?"

"The horse in the corral. The one you wanted to show the girls."

"No."

Yvette was more than exasperated now. "Yes you do, George," she argued. "Remember, last time, when Paul said we were too young? You promised that next time we could watch. Well, now it's next time."

George shrugged. "I don't know what you're talking about."

"Let's have it out, Yvette," Charmaine demanded. "You are obviously concocting mischief."

Jeannette sighed. "Tell her, Yvette."

"Oh, all right," she capitulated with an overly loud expulsion of air, "but George did promise! Joseph said that Gerald and the other stable-hands are supposed to be helping Phantom and Chastity mate, and I want to watch."

Charmaine's hands flew to her face, her fingers fanning her cheeks.

But George's convulsive coughing surpassed her mortification, the biscuit he'd been eating lodged firmly in his throat. "I think – I'd better – go now–" he sputtered, fist thumping his chest "–if you'll – excuse me."

Once he was gone, Charmaine turned her humiliation on the girls. "What a disgusting remark! Why, in heaven's name, would you want to see such a thing?"

"I was just interested," Yvette shrugged lackadaisically.

"I suggest you become uninterested. Whether you like it or not, Yvette, you are a young lady. Even gentlemen don't speak of such things–"

"What things?"

Charmaine winced.

"Charmaine?" Paul queried, drawing up behind her, his eyes shifting to Yvette when she refused to look at him. "A gentleman doesn't speak of what things?" he probed further, the context of the conversation dawning.

"Horses mating," Yvette supplied without shame, arms akimbo.

Charmaine held her breath against his certain anger, surprised when he said, "Mademoiselle Charmaine is correct. Gentlemen don't speak of such things, not freely anyway. I'm surprised that you are causing her grief today. This is hardly the way to show your appreciation. If I'm not mistaken, she delivered a letter to the Destiny for you, didn't she?"

Yvette's stormy eyes turned contrite. The moment held, the silence growing awkward. "I'm hungry," Charmaine finally said.

Colette was wiping Pierre's mouth clean when they entered the dining room. Agatha's face brightened at the sight of her brother. "Why Robert, you've arrived early today." He seemed equally pleased to see her, an unusual smile breaking across his face.

Colette straightened. "Doctor Blackford," she breathed. "I do not require your services today."

The man bristled, throwing back his shoulders. "Madame, that is not a decision for you to make. Your husband has requested that I restore you to good health. I cannot do so unless I minister to you on a regular basis. I thought you understood that when we agreed on weekly treatments."

"I'll tell you what I do understand, Robert," she returned heatedly. "I felt fine before you arrived last Saturday. But after you left, I was dreadfully ill for the remainder of that day and well into Sunday."

The man took offense again, his brow severe. "It must be the new compound. It's quite potent. But it needs to be, especially since you refuse to take it when I'm not here."

Colette's eyes shot to Agatha, and Robert nodded. "Yes, I've heard how difficult you can be. If you'd be reasonable and consume the elixir as prescribed, a lower dosage might be more appropriate. I'll have to consult my medical journals to see what can be done."

"Consult all you like, Doctor, but you will *not* be treating me today."

Agatha clicked her tongue. "It's the governess," she accused, indicating Charmaine. "She has been filling your head with her medical opinions."

Colette frowned. "I don't know what you are talking about, Agatha. But I do know how poorly I've been feeling."

"Exactly," the older woman agreed, "and that is why Robert is here. Think of your children and how it will affect them if your condition worsens."

Colette faltered, and Agatha capitalized on her reaction, nodding toward Charmaine again. "If Miss Ryan thinks my brother is incompetent, I would like to hear why she feels that way."

All eyes rested on Charmaine who was forced to defend herself. "I never said Doctor Blackford was incompetent, Mrs. Ward. I merely said that the best therapy for Miss Colette was the company of her children."

Paul cleared his throat. "Why don't we leave your visit until next Saturday, Robert?" he suggested in an attempt to placate all parties. "In that time you can consult your journals and determine the proper dosage for Colette. Meanwhile, she can see how she fares without her weekly treatment."

Robert gave a cursory nod, clutched his sister's arm before she could protest, and led her out of the house.

When Colette heard the front door close, she sighed. "Thank you, Paul."

He responded with a suave smile, then spoke of a different matter. "I've invited Stephen Westphal to dine with us this evening. My father has agreed to meet with him. I think you are right. It *will* do him good to get involved in island business again."

Colette's eyes lit up. "Did Frederic mention dining with us?"

"Not that involved," Paul replied flatly, "not yet, anyway."

Charmaine and the girls spent the better part of an hour transferring her belongings to her new room. Certain that she'd never use the dressing room, she had insisted that George and Travis move the armoire into the bedchamber where her dresses would be within easy reach. When the girls had finished tucking the last handkerchief away, she stood back to survey the final result, pleased.

Yesterday, the suite had been aired out. The masculine tones were all but gone: feathery curtains replaced the heavy draperies at the French doors, and the dark quilt that had covered the huge, four-poster bed was exchanged for a downy white comforter. Colette had removed all of John Duvoisin's possessions. Charmaine prayed that Paul and George were correct when they declared that the man would never come home. She fretted over Colette's assertion that he'd be upset to find his quarters given to someone else, let alone the governess.

The dinner hour arrived. Colette reminded her daughters that they were to have a guest at their table, and they promised to be on their best behavior. When they reached the dining room, Paul and Stephen Westphal were already there. They had spent an hour in Frederic's apartments, but as Paul had predicted, his father did not join them. Colette was annoyed to find Agatha positioned directly to Paul's left and opposite Stephen, but said nothing. George arrived and said quite tactlessly, "Mr. Westphal, you are in my seat."

"Mr. Richards, really!" Agatha castigated. "Stephen is Paul's guest this evening and has important business to discuss with him. There are plenty of other chairs from which to choose."

George's face reddened, but he didn't respond. Instead, he took a place near Charmaine and avoided glances toward the head of the table. The food was set before them, a sumptuous feast that everyone enjoyed, and though he fell into the meal, he simmered at Agatha's insult.

Agatha Ward – how he despised the woman! For as long as he could remember, he and John fell in her disfavor and stayed far out of her way when she came to visit. But Paul, ever polite and the apple of his father's eye, gained her approval from the start. Agatha was always trying to please Frederic, and if Paul were his father's favorite, Agatha would champion him as well. But today, something else was brewing. *Today? Bah! For months!* Perhaps it was Frederic's malady, perhaps it was Paul's good looks, so much like that of the older man, but Agatha's eyes had been diverted from father to son. George snorted in revulsion. Maybe he should warn his friend before the hag dug her claws in too far. He snorted again. *No, Paul hadn't come to his defense tonight, hadn't put the shrew in her place the way John would have, so no, he wouldn't be speaking to Paul about Agatha Ward.*

The meal progressed and the banter was pleasant. Duvoisin business did not dominate the discussions, though Agatha attempted to drive the conversation in that direction. Paul avoided the topic of sugarcane crops and the shipping industry. After a time, it became obvious that he either didn't want Agatha to know anything about island operations or had covered all the important elements earlier in his father's chambers.

Charmaine considered Colette. Though she played the perfect hostess, she seemed agitated. At first, Charmaine thought Pierre was the source of her irritation, for he played with his food and couldn't be coaxed to eat. But one glance at George, and Charmaine read the same expression there. She felt badly for him, knowing he didn't deserve Agatha Ward's sharp rebuke.

Hoping to mellow his mood, she struck up a conversation, pleased when he responded impishly. In no time, they were chuckling over his whispered comments, "I think Agatha and Stephen make a handsome couple. He looks like a proud rooster. Perhaps he fancies being pecked to death by a clucking hen."

The gaiety coming from the foot of the table chafed Paul. He threw George a nasty scowl, but the man's head was inclined toward Charmaine, and he missed it. Charmaine noticed, however, and quickly straightened up. Reading her expression, George looked round, finally making eye contact with Paul.

Satisfied that the tacit message had been received, Paul turned back to the banker. "So, Stephen, have you any news from your daughter?"

The man swallowed, then patted his mouth with his serviette. "Why, yes. Anne is in fine spirits and no longer wearing widow's weeds."

"Anne London is Stephen's daughter," Paul elaborated for those listening. "She lives in Richmond, but was recently widowed – last year I believe?"

The banker smiled down the table, growing garrulous now that he'd been offered the floor. "A year ago, May. She was quite distraught over the loss of Charles, God rest his soul, but he left her a small fortune, and for that, she is grateful. She has begun socializing again. Of course, I've cautioned her a level head when receiving suitors. She must be wary of blackguards who will be after her money and not her heart."

"I'll bet," George mumbled, eliciting a giggle from Charmaine.

Again Paul scowled, his jaw clenched.

Charmaine blushed at her own impropriety, especially when Yvette demanded, "What's so funny?" She was glad when Agatha piped in.

"Has your daughter been receiving anyone, Stephen?"

"I'm not supposed to say," he chuckled, looking from one face to the other, his gaze coming to rest on Paul, "but, in her last letter, Anne wrote that your brother has been paying her court."

Paul was surprised. "John? She's been receiving John?"

"That's what she writes."

"Johnny?" Yvette inquired. "Does your daughter know Johnny?"

He began to respond, but was cut off by Agatha. "Children should be seen and not heard. This is an adult conversation, young lady."

Colette's restraint wore thin. "Agatha – I am Yvette's mother and will do the reprimanding when necessary." She ripped her turbulent eyes from the widow and spoke to Stephen. "Mr. Westphal, please answer my daughter's question."

"Yes," he said, clearing his throat, uncomfortable with the clash of wills across the table, "my daughter knows your elder brother. She writes fondly of him. Perhaps she will be your sister-in-law someday."

Colette's smile did not reach her eyes. "Tell me, Mr. Westphal, does your daughter have any children by her deceased husband?"

"No, Madame," he answered, confused by the question. "She never really liked children, so I suppose it was for the best. Why do you ask?"

"I was just wondering." She sipped her wine, her gaze traveling to Paul. He considered her momentarily, then returned to his dinner.

The meal ended without further incident, and much later, when Charmaine retired to her second-floor chamber, her thoughts were far from Stephen Westphal, Anne London, or Agatha Ward. She was thinking of the Harringtons and George and Paul. The dreams she would dream tonight would be wondrous in her new bed, for the mattress was luxurious, the pillows soft, and the comforter warm in the cool night air. Bravely, she left the French doors open and fell into a blissful slumber.

Paul and Agatha sent Stephen on his way and climbed opposite staircases to their chambers. Only Colette and George remained behind in the parlor. "George," she said when he rose to retire, "I must speak with you."

"Yes?" he said on a yawn.

"Have you noticed the way Agatha is *mooning* over Paul?"

He laughed with the comment. "You've noticed it as well? I thought it was just me! I was going to warn him about it, Colette, really I was." He shook his head, disgusted. "I could have wrung her neck tonight! Who does she think she is, talking to me like that?"

"I know, George. I was angry, too. Aside from that, I'm uncomfortable with the way she's been looking at Paul. For weeks now, I've tried to convince myself that I've been misreading it. But tonight, when I saw her seated near the head of the table, leaning close to Paul, interested in his every word, I know I'm not."

"Don't worry, Colette, Paul is not going to fall for Agatha Ward. And if he does, what does it matter?"

"*What does it matter?* Do you think I want her living in this house permanently? She's at least ten years older than he."

"More like twenty. Elizabeth was her younger sister, and if I'm not mistaken, *she* was eighteen when she had John. That would make Agatha fifty."

"One would never know. She's a handsome woman."

George only snorted. "Looks are only skin deep, Colette. Paul will be considering more than her beauty if he looks her way."

Colette rubbed her brow. "He never has before."

"Colette, don't fret over it," George soothed, just now realizing how upset she was. "I don't see how you can think *any man* would be interested in Agatha. She's downright cruel. Besides, Paul is far more taken with Charmaine Ryan. Did you see how angry he was with me tonight? He's been giving me that *'she's mine – I saw her first'* look for two weeks now. If you want to place some distance between Paul and Agatha, make certain Charmaine sits next to him at the table. He won't be looking at anyone else in the room. I guarantee it."

Colette forced a smile, and George knew he had not put her at ease.

"I'll talk to him about it. Is that what you want?"

"I don't know, George... But I would like Agatha Ward out of my life."

George nodded in understanding.

Much later, when she was abed, Colette mulled over her predicament. If only she could talk to her husband the way she had during their first year of marriage. They'd been quite happy then, certainly able to communicate once they'd worked their way through those first stormy months. What had happened? She knew: *The twins... the birth of the twins had happened, and she had been forbidden to have any more children.* Frederic was a passionate man, and the strain this placed on their relationship had been destructive. How often had she caught him ogling her in the months following the birth of their daughters, those months when he had never once made love to her? But it was more than that. Much more. Frederic had longed to hear her speak three simple words, words he had often murmured when he climaxed inside of her. Why then had she withheld the love she knew he craved, the love she readily possessed? Why hadn't she told him that she loved him in return? *Because I was frightened,* her mind screamed, *frightened of yielding him a greater power over me!* And so, she had remained silent, allowing him to believe the worst, that she was still very angry with him, hated him. And then something else happened. Agatha Ward had come to visit, and Agatha Ward had found his bed. Frederic's intense perusals stopped, and Colette was left desolate.

Tonight, she worried anew. She'd been mistaken in believing that Agatha still sought Frederic's embrace. Evidently, the disabling effect of his stroke had left the woman wanting. Was Paul her next target? Colette shuddered with the thought. Not that she cared about Paul's sexual proclivities. She did, however, fear the possibility of an enduring relationship. The woman was devious and capable of manipulating a younger man. Colette was strong enough to combat Agatha today, but what of tomorrow? What would happen to her children if she were not well or, worse still, not there to protect them? If Agatha gained a greater foothold in the Duvoisin home, her children would suffer. Colette prayed to God that she was wrong, but she wasn't about to wait for God to answer. Though she didn't want to send Charmaine to the wolves, she did have Paul's promise to respect the young governess. Perhaps with time, he would look beyond Charmaine's lovely face and see the beauty beneath. Yes, Colette sighed, finally able to close her eyes in pursuit of sleep... *Beginning tomorrow, before Agatha becomes accustomed to sitting next to Paul, there will be a new and permanent seating assignment at my table. Let Agatha fume.*

Friday, December 16, 1836

Chapter 6

It was Charmaine's nineteenth birthday, though no one in the house knew.

As soon as she was dressed, she went into the nursery. The children were still asleep, but Pierre sensed her standing over his bed, for he sat up, rubbed his eyes, and stretched out his arms. Charmaine cuddled him, as she did every morning. She had come to cherish him as if he were her son, and he reciprocated that love, an ever-growing bond that made his mother's frequent absences bearable.

Colette's health was deteriorating. Robert Blackford had indeed consulted his journals, changing the compounds he'd been prescribing to a more potent tonic. Throughout the month of October, Colette had improved dramatically. Unlike September, she'd be up and about after his Saturday visits, insisting that she felt fine. Over the last month, however, the fatigue she'd experienced in late summer began setting in again. Charmaine noted that by week's end, Colette's cheeks were pale and her meager energy depleted. She often complained of headaches and dizziness. By Saturday, she desperately needed another dose of the doctor's elixir. She no longer spent Fridays with the children; she was too ill.

Therefore, Charmaine was surprised when she swept into the nursery this morning, proclaiming that she felt fit as a fiddle. "I think it did me good to see the doctor yesterday. As much as I hate to admit it, perhaps I should allow him to visit twice a week."

I just wish his ministrations had a lasting effect, Charmaine thought as she smiled at Colette, her friend. Over the past two months, they had grown so close that Charmaine couldn't imagine life without her. Their similar age had a lot to do with it, but there was something deeper that drew them together: an unspoken, almost reverent, sympathy for one another.

"Good morning, my little Pierre."

Pierre held out his arms to his mother. When she sat on his bed, Charmaine deposited him in her lap. "Mama, I missed you!"

Colette chuckled. "How could you have missed me, mon caillou? You were sleeping."

"I dreamed you was far away, and I was wookin' for you," he said in earnest. "It was scary!"

"Really?" Colette asked, feigning fearful eyes. "What happened?"

"There was so many peoples I couldn't find you. And someone was callin' me, but I was scared so I kept runnin'." His brow, which had furrowed over stormy eyes, suddenly lifted, and his face brightened. "But I found you."

"Where was I?"

"In heaven," he answered simply, happily. "It was very boo-ti-ful there."

A baleful chill rushed up Charmaine's arms, but Colette's countenance remained unscathed. She hugged her son and laughed. "Oh, Pierre! Someday, we'll all be in heaven together, with everyone we love. It's a wonderful place."

Once the girls were up and dressed, they went down for breakfast. Paul was at the table, an unusual sight. He was normally gone long before they had risen and wouldn't return until evening.

Complying with Colette's strange request, Charmaine sat down next to him. Two months ago, she had approached the new seating arrangement with demure reluctance. But she had survived that first day and the day after that. Today, she could honestly say that she enjoyed sitting near him. Ever since their private carriage ride home, he had been the perfect gentleman, and though Charmaine often noticed that assessing look in his eyes, he hadn't once embarrassed her. True to his word, she was safe in his home. Any indecent proposition remained a memory of the past, and she could now spend an entire evening in his presence without blushing. Colette seemed pleased with their blossoming 'friendship', and Charmaine wondered if she were now playing matchmaker.

"What keeps you at home this morning, Paul?" Colette asked while helping Pierre into his chair.

"I've been into town and back already," he answered. "Now I have an important matter to discuss with my father."

His voice was hard, and they realized he was irate. His fingers drummed a short stack of letters on the left side of his plate. Charmaine wondered if they were the cause of his anger.

"Is something wrong?" Colette asked in genuine concern.

"Just my brother."

Yvette perked up. "Johnny? Did he write to you?"

"He wrote to me all right," Paul replied. He leafed through the correspondence and pulled two letters from the rest. "Here, Yvette, Jeannette, at least someone will be happy today."

"From Johnny?" Jeannette queried, her face radiant as she accepted the post.

"Why did you get one?" Yvette sulked. "I'm the one who wrote to him."

"Yvette," her mother remonstrated lightly, "don't be envious. It's not becoming. Besides, you received a letter, too. Why don't you read it to us?"

The girl wrinkled her nose. "It's private, Mama. That is the only reason I learned to read and write in the first place, remember? So that Johnny could send me my own *private* mail."

"Very well," her mother said. "Maybe Jeannette will read *her* letter to us."

The girl was quietly devouring the missive. When she looked up, her eyes twinkled. "Oh no, Mama," she breathed, "mine is a secret, too!"

Getting nowhere with the twins, Colette turned back to Paul. "What has John done this time?" she asked.

He'd begun to eat and didn't answer. If Charmaine didn't know better, she would have thought the topic dismissed, but she had learned to read his moods. He remained agitated, his scowl similar to the one he'd worn the day he'd confronted Jessie Rowlan.

Colette buttered and handed Pierre a piece of toast. He ate it greedily. "Slow down, mon caillou, you have too much in your mouth, and you are going to choke!" Pierre tried to respond, but with his mouth so full, no one could understand what he said. Colette just shook her head, smiling.

She regarded Paul again, seemingly unable to let the matter rest. "Well?"

"John has changed all the shipping routes," he replied curtly, shuffling through the letters again and producing one addressed to Charmaine. "You wanted to know why the mails were delayed," he said, tapping the envelope on the table before passing it to her. "The ships that usually come directly to us from Virginia have now been redirected. Since November they've traveled to Europe first, and *gradually* make their way to us en route back to Virginia. In short, we have to wait on our post and our supplies."

"Why?" Charmaine asked.

"John loves to interfere."

"That is not true," Colette objected.

"*Isn't it?*" Paul demanded, full-voiced, his temper unleashed.

Charmaine sat stunned. He had never spoken a harsh word to Colette.

Colette responded calmly. "If John changed those routes, he had a good reason."

"Why are you always defending him?" he growled, his query strikingly reminiscent of Frederic's remark on the twins' birthday.

"I'm not defending him," she argued diplomatically. "I'm merely stating a fact. John will inherit his father's fortune someday. Why would he jeopardize it by setting up shipping routes that would undermine Duvoisin enterprises?"

Paul was chafed by her logic. "Clearly you are blind to his maneuverings. Therefore, there is no point in discussing it."

"Paul – you and John were close once," she rejoined, unaffected by the fury in his eyes. "Why are you allowing money to come between you now? When I think of the three of you, George included, I can't believe what I see and hear."

"I said I don't want to discuss it!"

Colette sighed, but did not press her point.

Yvette finished eating quickly and ran from the room, saying that she was going straight to the nursery to write another letter.

"You have lessons!" her mother called.

They had developed a routine. After breakfast, the children returned to the playroom. For two hours, they read, did arithmetic problems, and studied geography or world history. If Paul or Frederic were available, they would question them about the travels of the newest ship that had put into port. After lunch, Pierre took his nap while the girls had their piano lessons. Most days, Colette would listen to them, happy with their progress. Other days, she would retire to her own room to rest. The late afternoon was left for the outdoors. The rainy season of autumn was behind them, the weather beautiful, a bit cooler than the summer, and quite unlike the Decembers in Virginia. Now that the children had a governess, Nana Rose had more time to herself. Nevertheless, she was available when the weekends arrived and Charmaine chose to take the girls into town or on a picnic. Sometimes it was best if Pierre stayed home, and if Colette was indisposed, Rose stepped in.

Presently, Charmaine stood from the table. She looked to Paul, who hadn't said another word to anyone; he was reading a periodical that accompanied the perplexing letters. "Thank you," she whispered.

It was a moment before his head lifted and another before he realized she had spoken to him. "Excuse me?" His eyes were grave, but not angry.

"I said, 'thank you'… for the letter from my friends in Virginia."

"You're welcome, Charmaine. I hope they are well."

"I'll soon find out," she said. "How much do I owe you for the postage?"

"Nothing," he replied with a debonair smile. "Any charges are taken out of the island account."

"Are you sure?"

"I'm sure."

She nodded a second 'thank you' and, with heart thumping, called to Jeannette. "Come, Sweetheart, it is time we got on with today's lessons."

Jeannette complied, grasping her own letter. But as she passed behind her mother, she stopped as if remembering something and hugged her, capping the capricious gesture with a kiss.

Stunned, Colette laughed. "What was that for?"

"It's a secret, too," she whispered, turning to Pierre next.

He struggled against the embrace until Colette said, "Your sister is trying to give you a kiss."

Charmaine heard tears in Colette's voice and realized she was trying not to cry. But the moment passed, and she was lifting Pierre to the ground, speaking to Paul at the same time. "Please don't upset your father with talk of John."

He frowned. "This is all about John, Colette. I can't pretend that he doesn't exist – leastwise not while he controls the purse strings from Virginia."

It was futile to argue, so Colette took Pierre by the hand and followed Charmaine and Jeannette from the room.

Later, while the girls were busy working, and Pierre was playing with his blocks, Charmaine turned pensive. *John Duvoisin.* Any time his name was mentioned, emotions ran high. The men of the family spoke of him as if he were an adversary, the women, his proponent. Charmaine began to wonder if she were ever going to meet the man and form her own opinion of him.

"Mademoiselle Charmaine?" Jeannette queried, cutting across her thoughts. "You haven't read your letter. Look, it's under my paper!"

Charmaine was embarrassed. For the better part of a month she'd complained over the delayed mails. Now that she had finally received word from her friends, she'd spent her spare moments thinking about someone she'd never met. Chuckling, she tore into the missive and began to read, happy to find that all was well with the Harrington clan. The letter had been a wonderful birthday present. She'd have to write to them tonight.

Paul entered his father's chambers, nodding to Travis as the man left them alone. Frederic sat in his abominable chair, staring out the French doors, past the gardens and toward the pine forest that ensconced the family's private lake. Beyond that was the ocean and, farther still, the States – Virginia in particular. His eyes did not waver as he said, "You needed to speak with me?"

"Yes, sir," Paul answered, purposefully placing himself between his father and the glass panels. When the man finally looked up, Paul handed over the documents he carried. "John has changed the shipping routes."

"Why?"

Strange question... Paul thought his father would explode with the revelation. "According to his letter, it's an issue of the trade winds. But that has never been a factor before, not when we were in need of supplies."

"How have the routes changed?" Frederic asked, disregarding the papers.

"He's established two circuits: a Richmond, Europe, Charmantes course, and a Richmond, New York, Europe course. Thanks to him, we won't see half the fleet, and the five that do eventually reach us will be hauling staples all the way to Europe first. It's ludicrous. On top of that, if we want to sell sugar in the north, the cargo will have to change ships in Richmond."

"Is this such a bad thing?"

"It's an annoying thing, Father!" Paul railed. "John is looking for an excuse to upset the apple cart. It is his way of exacting retribution."

Frederic rubbed his brow. "Those are harsh words."

"Don't tell me *you* are defending him!" Frederic's eyes narrowed, and Paul cringed. "I'm not trying to stir up trouble, Father. But I am tired of John controlling *everything* – at his whim, I might add."

Silence pervaded the room, and Paul could see the man's mind working, a mind unaffected by the stroke that had damaged him in every other way. Paul, in turn, experienced a wave of righteousness, Colette's assertion surfacing. "To be fair, John may have rerouted the ships for another reason."

Frederic showed surprise. "Really? What is it?"

"For the past two years, the sugar crop has been deplorable. I've had difficulty filling the ships' holds to capacity, sending quite a few back to John with room to spare. In our need to meet the increased demand, we've overworked the soil, using fields that should have lain fallow. This season alone, the yield was two-thirds what it was three years ago, and that was with an increased number of acres harvested. The land is effete and requires a more relaxed rotation if the necessary elements are to be restored. We should either suspend planting for a year or two, or turn the next few tracts over to tobacco."

Frederic grunted. "Tobacco is just as taxing on the land, and then we'd have to consider the other adjustments we'd be forced to make: training the bondsmen, equipment, buildings. And even if it were to flourish, we'd be placing all our coins on one bet. I'll not have the Duvoisin fortune left to the whim of one crop. The Virginia plantation is relegated to tobacco. Charmantes produces sugar."

Paul threw up his hands in exasperation. "Tobacco is just a suggestion, a crop the family has experience with, but if some dramatic changes aren't made, Charmantes will be in deep trouble. She's bringing in minimal revenue now."

"I can see you have something else in mind. What is it?"

Paul inhaled. "Go back to the other island and finish what you started there four years ago."

Frederic's countenance blackened. "The land is cursed."

"That's ridiculous, Father. What happened on Charmantes had nothing to do with Espoir."

"If I had been here–"

Paul's own anger flared. "We're not going to go over this again! What's done is done! The other island is there. It's fertile. It's partially cleared. You've built a bondsmen keep – constructed a dock. It's begging to be developed!"

"You do it," Frederic interrupted.

"What?"

"You heard me. I give it to you. It's yours, Paul. Do with it as you will."

Paul frowned in disbelief. "You're serious? You'll allow me free rein?"

"I'll do better than that. I'll give you enough money to contract the building of three ships – your ships – expressly designed to transport your sugar. You will also need a fourth vessel for the treks between Espoir and Charmantes. Purchase a considerably smaller packet, something ancient. In addition, I'll supply the funds to acquire an indentured crew. How many men will you need: twenty, thirty?"

"Twenty will be more than sufficient," Paul breathed, his jaw slackened in amazement.

"Very well then," Frederic continued, his mind working rigorously now. "Set up a meeting with Stephen Westphal. We'll need to liquidate some funds, but for the balance, our bank seal and the Duvoisin name should hold some weight in the States and Europe. I suggest that you commission the ships in Newportes Newes or Baltimore. Best to check with shipbuilders in New York as well. If the southern costs come in too high, quote the New York estimates to them."

"American-built vessels? But what about the British tariffs?"

"Construction costs should come in at least twenty percent lower than any bark you could commission in Britain. From what I've been reading, European shipbuilders can't compete with the States plentiful lumber. If you contract the building of three vessels, the savings should be considerable. That alone will outweigh any British import tax. The newest clippers have proven advantageous to many shipping magnates, and America seems to be leading the fray in perfecting them. Speed, not imposed tariffs, should be the deciding factor."

"What of steam propulsion as opposed to fully-rigged sail?" Paul asked in waxing excitement. "They are cutting crossing times in half. I'd like your permission to look into that as well."

Frederic nodded, feeding off his son's exuberance. "By all means. You'll have to travel to Britain for the bondsmen. While there, contact the Harrison shipping firm. They can vouch for the progress being made with the paddlewheel. Perhaps they could be persuaded to share information concerning the success of their own steam fleet. Now, if you are as excited about this as you appear to be, it would be prudent not to delay. I suggest you leave as soon as monies are made available through Stephen."

Paul's mind was reeling. *This couldn't be happening!* All these years, he had dreamed of owning a piece of the Duvoisin fortune. To John, the prospect meant nothing. John was the legitimate heir, therefore, the Duvoisin fortune had always been there for the taking. Paul, on the other hand, had labored long and hard for his father, and still, after ten years, remained his loyal son, nothing more. Today, the long journey had come to an end. Somewhere along the way, he had proven himself worthy; he was finally being offered his deepest desire – his rightful share of the Duvoisin holdings. Suddenly, he was smiling broadly, and Frederic was happy to know he had pleased at least one son this day.

"It will be mine?" he whispered. "Not to be shared with John?"

"It will be yours, Paul," his sire avowed, "all yours. No interference from John, no conferring with John, no dependence upon John. I should have done this a long time ago. You've been a good son. You deserve more."

"Thank you, sir," Paul said with the utmost respect. "I'll contact Stephen."

Paul's mood was far different when everyone gathered at the dinner table that evening. The children were equally lighthearted, and Charmaine regarded

George, Rose, and Colette, who seemed part of the same merry conspiracy. As the meal progressed, she grew more befuddled and finally petitioned Jeannette for an answer. "Why is everyone so happy?"

"You'll see," was all the girl would say, and Charmaine caught Colette's wink. But Pierre was unable to keep silent and blurted out, "Mainie's birfday!"

"Pierre!" Yvette scolded. "You've gone and spoiled the surprise!"

"The surprise?" Charmaine asked, her eyes arcing around the table until they rested on Paul, who raised a brow in pretended confusion.

"Da-tay... da-tay... *ta*-day is Mainie's birfday!" Pierre happily repeated.

The kitchen door swung open, and Fatima barreled into the room carrying a cake. In unison, the children shouted, "Happy Birthday!"

Charmaine's hands flew to her mouth. "How did you know?" she asked, missing Agatha's disdainful scowl.

Colette smiled. "You mentioned it to Jeannette months ago during your first picnic, and she told me right away. I just hoped that she wasn't mistaken about the date, but I had no way of asking without making you suspicious."

"I don't know what to say," Charmaine murmured, realizing just how much this family had come to mean to her.

"You don't have to say anything," Jeannette piped in.

"Yes she does," Yvette insisted. "She has to say how old she is!"

"I'm nineteen. And I hope to share many more birthdays with all of you."

Satisfied, the children began begging her to cut the cake.

Colette helped Pierre down from his chair, and he ran to Charmaine with a small package in his hand. "Happy Birfday!" he said, giving her a kiss.

"What is this?"

"A birfday pwesent."

Charmaine lifted the lid to find a lovely, and certainly expensive, set of ivory hair combs within. "Wherever did you get them?" she asked Colette.

"At Maddy's Mercantile. I asked Paul to select them." Colette indicated her accomplice.

"And you had better wear them," he warned drolly. "It took me all morning to decide which ones would suit you."

"Thank you," she said, wondering how she could ever reciprocate their generosity. "Each of you must share your birth date with me. Colette?"

Yvette answered for her mother. "Mama and Pierre's birthdays are the same: March thirty-first."

"Truly?"

With Colette's nod of confirmation, Charmaine looked at Paul.

"Don't worry, Charmaine," he said, cognizant of her motives for asking, "Fatima remembers every birthday in this house."

Satisfied, Charmaine began cutting the cake.

Wednesday, December 21, 1836

Paul was leaving Charmantes. He was traveling on the Black Star, a ship that had berthed on the island yesterday and would set sail the day after Christmas.

He was headed to several southern ports: Newportes Newes, Richmond, and Baltimore, then up to New York and finally on to Britain. In his three months abroad, he would commission the construction of three ships, purchase a fourth, and hire a new crew of indentured servants to clear and cultivate his new island, 'Sacré Espoir', pronounced 'Sock-ray Es-pwahr', meaning 'Sacred Hope'. When finished, he'd travel home and begin developing it. He was very happy.

Charmaine was melancholy. Though Paul promised to be back before Easter, the coming weeks would be long and empty. She was falling in love with him, a disturbing condition exacerbated by the fact that he'd kept her at arm's length for nearly three months now. Still, she would miss him, miss his presence in the house each night, miss his easy banter, miss the times when he'd pull out her chair or hold the door open for her, miss his handsome smile that set her heart racing. If only he had kissed her, just once.

Tonight Stephen Westphal was to visit again. He, Paul, and Frederic would make final arrangements. Frederic would sign vouchers, and Paul would be set for the voyage ahead of him. Mr. Westphal would stay for dinner.

Agatha Ward seemed pleased and traipsed happily about the house the entire day, leaving Colette and Charmaine to wonder over her uncommon behavior.

In the late afternoon, just after the banker had arrived, Colette and Charmaine enjoyed a glass of iced tea on the front portico. The weather was pleasant, and the children were playing on the lawn, running here and there. Jeannette took charge of Pierre, always mindful of his well-being. They chuckled over their antics.

When the moment seemed right, Charmaine withdrew two envelopes from her apron pocket. Both Jeannette and Yvette had written to their brother this time, and she looked to Colette for advice. "Do you think Paul would mind if I asked him to deliver these letters to John? He mentioned stopping in Richmond."

"He will not mind," she answered firmly, aware of Charmaine's misgivings. "For all their rivalry, they're still brothers and very close."

"That is not the way it appears."

"They're brothers," Colette reiterated, "and brothers often fight. I know I used to with Pierre."

"Pierre?"

Colette laughed now. "My brother, Pierre. He and my mother died shortly after the twins were born."

"I'm sorry," Charmaine whispered.

Colette suppressed the painful memory. "He was born a cripple and unable to walk. Now he is at peace… in heaven."

"What of your father?" Charmaine asked cautiously.

"He died when I was very young," she answered, her voice no longer sorrowful. "I hardly remember him. My mother had a difficult time raising us. We were gentry, so my father lost a great deal of his fortune in the years following the French Revolution. By the time I attended a lady's school in Paris, my mother's funds were nearly depleted."

"Why Paris then?"

Colette grew distant. "It was near the university and offered an opportunity to meet a rich gentleman... or at least the son of a rich gentleman. You see, my brother was constantly ill, the physicians' fees mounting. A wealthy husband could resolve my mother's financial difficulties, perhaps foster Pierre's cure. Or so I was told."

"Is that why you married Mr. Duvoisin?"

Colette knew the question was coming, had encouraged it. "That was one of the reasons, but there were others. The situation became complicated."

"He must have been very handsome," Charmaine encouraged.

"He still is," Colette averred, smiling now. "And I was attracted to him from the moment we met. But I was intimidated by him as well."

The minutes gathered, and finally she spoke again. "Frederic is a good man, Charmaine. He's instilled in his sons values they don't even credit to him. And he's been a good husband to me. I know at times he appears gruff, but his stroke has left deep scars."

"I realize that," Charmaine said.

"When we were first married, he restored my mother to a comfortable life. In addition, he took care of my brother and all his doctor's expenses. Pierre wanted for nothing that last year, receiving the best treatment the Duvoisin money could buy. And of course, he gave me two beautiful daughters... and a handsome son."

Charmaine breathed deeply. "Did you ever love him?" she probed, sad that this woman had sacrificed herself for the welfare of her family.

"I love him still," she said, her voice cracking. "But it wasn't easy for Frederic after the girls were born. I was forbidden to have any more children."

"It had to be just as difficult for you," Charmaine reasoned.

"Yes and no," she replied, turning away. "As I said, it became very complicated." The subject was closed, and they fell silent.

Colette considered Charmaine and wondered when the younger woman would speak about her own past. She instinctively knew that Charmaine's recollections contained elements of pain as well. *If not today, soon.* Her musings were interrupted by a most unexpected question.

"What is John like?"

Colette weighed her answer, determined to give an unbiased opinion. "He's an enigma – a one of a kind."

"The good kind or the bad kind?"

Colette smiled. "That depends on who's describing him. There are those who despise him to the core, and there are those who love him until it hurts. With John there is no middle ground. You either hate him or love him, and it's usually in that order."

"The men of this family certainly don't love him."

Colette hesitated again, as if she were looking for the right words to explain a paradoxical dilemma. "Due to my husband's stroke, Paul and Frederic *think* they hate John, and he, in turn *thinks* he hates them. I'm certain you've heard all the rumors, Charmaine. Most of them are true. John and Frederic had a terrible fight and when it was over, Frederic was left as he is today – crippled, in mind as well as body. Paul was there, and he blames John for what happened. Unfortunately, the wound has yet to heal."

"Why don't you blame John?"

Colette sighed forlornly. "He isn't to blame and was hurt as well. Everyone sided with Frederic, including me. I'm afraid that John hates me for it. He carries the same bitterness that eats away at his father. They are alike in so many ways. Yet, each of them would vehemently deny any similarity."

"Alike?" Charmaine pursued. "How so?"

"Their charisma, their self-assuredness, the manner in which they assess a person. Once John sizes you up and passes judgment, he rarely changes his mind, and more often than not, his assessment is correct. Heaven forbid if his judgment is damning. There is all hell to pay, and hell is a sight more lenient than John's sharp tongue. Frederic is the same way – uncompromising to a fault."

"Do *you* like him?"

"Who? John?" Colette laughed. "Look at my daughters, Charmaine. They'd have my head if they heard me say otherwise. But when I first met John, I despised him." She grew thoughtful, her eyes cast beyond her surroundings as if she could see across time. "Someday," she said softly, "you will meet him and understand what I mean… Just remember, Charmaine, you hate him first."

The front doors clapped open, and Paul and Stephen strode onto the portico with Agatha tucked comfortably between them. Colette frowned at the trio, but her attention was diverted as the children came bounding across the lawn. Yvette was shouting enthusiastically, reaching the colonnade first. "Mama!" she heaved, completely out of breath. "Chastity is going to have a foal!"

Jeannette and Pierre drew up alongside her. All three had wandered over to the paddock when Gerald, the head groom, had led the chestnut mare into the yard. "That's right, Mama," Jeannette added, "Gerald says she'll have her baby sometime in August. Isn't that wonderful?"

"That is wonderful," Colette answered with a smile. "And I can just imagine what's going to happen when that filly or colt is born. Mademoiselle Charmaine and I won't be able to get the three of you out of the barn."

Yvette agreed with a happy nod. "Do you think Martin will have to come when it's time for her to foal?"

"Perhaps… but only if there is some difficulty," Colette replied. "Why?"

"He was teaching me how to spit the last time he was here," Yvette answered proudly. "But I don't have it down just right."

"Yvette!" her mother chastised, mumbling something about Martin being a vile man.

Dinner was served at seven. Charmaine brushed out her hair and decided to wear it down. Using the combs she'd received for her birthday, she swept it back from her face and placed a comb high above each ear. The entire mane cascaded down her back. She was a fetching sight when she entered the dining room, and

Paul drew a ragged breath, glad to know that her birthday gift would encourage her to wear the lovely locks in such a fashion.

Stephen Westphal was astonished when Paul beckoned the governess to sit in the chair that Agatha had occupied the last time he had dined at the Duvoisin manor. *So the pretty governess has caught Paul's fancy*, he thought. *Agatha's concerns are warranted.*

A five-course meal was served, beginning with a delicious pea soup. Fatima Henderson, her wide hips swinging, bustled in and out of the kitchen with more ease than Felicia and Anna, who often dawdled. Since Colette's reprimand, Felicia found the evening meal less interesting – she was no longer allowed to flirt with Paul – and she dillydallied over her serving chores. Why the maid was kept on at the manor, Charmaine could only wonder.

George appeared minutes later. He'd obviously been apprised of the banker's visit this time, for he greeted the man cordially and elected to sit near Charmaine. With Jeannette between them, he leaned in and struck up a conversation. Before long, Charmaine and Jeannette were giggling.

Paul preferred having George sit opposite the governess, where he was able to control their repartees, but now their heads were bent overtop his sister, and he experienced an unusually sharp stab of jealousy. *It's time George and I had a little talk*, he decided.

Thus resolved, he turned back to Stephen. "I'll be contacting Thomas and James Harrison when I arrive in Liverpool. Father dealt with their shipping line when he had the Vagabond manufactured. Though I'll be commissioning the vessels in the States, they've become renowned, so I'll take under advisement any recommendation they can make concerning steam propulsion."

"Right," the banker agreed, and so it went for the better part of the dinner.

Agatha chafed at the seating arrangement that placed her far from the financier. She had hoped to participate in Paul's business discussion. She couldn't do so from here; there was too much chatter between them.

As dessert was served, the conversation turned to personal matters. "I'll need an endorsed check for the Bank of Virginia," Paul said. "I'll deposit funds there, liquidate half, and then draw from one resource." He paused for a moment. When he spoke again, his words were hard. "John is not to be involved, Stephen, so I'd prefer that you not share this with your daughter."

"Anne?" he asked in surprise.

"You mentioned some months ago that John was courting her."

"Yes," Stephen confirmed. "In fact, I just received a letter from her. She hints that an engagement is imminent. A marvelous match, wouldn't you say?"

"Marvelous," Paul muttered, thinking of all the money his brother would come into. But John had never cared about such things. How then, had the widow London caught his fancy? She was attractive, most likely in her late twenties, but Paul didn't think she was John's type.

As if reading his thoughts, Yvette added her own two cents. "I don't think Johnny will marry her."

George chuckled. "Why not, Yvette?" he asked.

"He told me that the woman he loved was already married and that he'd never marry anyone else."

"There you have it!" the banker piped up. "All these years he's harbored the hope that one day Anne would be free to wed. I knew he was enamored of her when I visited Richmond some years ago."

Paul snorted.

"You don't believe me?" the man queried, clearly insulted. "Well then, time will tell the tale."

Paul's stormy gaze shifted to Colette, but the woman was whispering to Pierre. "You are right, Stephen," he said. "But in either case, Anne is in contact with my brother, and I do not want him informed of this undertaking."

Westphal grunted derisively. "And how do you expect to keep him from finding out once you've contacted the Virginia Bank and completed your transactions there?"

"I don't," Paul answered smugly, savoring the thought of John in the dark for a change. "But by the time he figures it all out, contracts will be signed, monies will be withdrawn, and any unpleasantness will have been avoided."

"Unpleasantness?"

"Come, Stephen, you know my brother. Is an explanation necessary?"

"What of the legal issues? Richecourt or Larabee is sure to contact him."

"I'll be in touch with their firm as soon as I reach Richmond. John has made an enemy of Edward Richecourt. That being said, Mr. Richecourt will be more than happy to deal with this matter in an expeditious, yet confidential, manner. He is well aware that my father's business dealings keep his practice solvent. Therefore, he can be trusted to keep quiet about Espoir."

Colette cringed over Paul's surreptitious plans. Not that she blamed him. John's needling was relentless. It was that very type of unpleasantness that Paul was trying to avoid. However, this scheme was certain to backfire on him. John always found out, simply because he was far more unscrupulous than Paul. John was the inventor of breaking all the rules.

"That being understood," Paul continued, "can I count on you to keep this to yourself, Stephen?"

"If that is what you want, Anne won't be told."

Satisfied, Paul leaned back in his chair. "So, what else does Anne write? Any Richmond events that I need to know about before traveling there?"

"Actually..." the banker said, clearing his throat, his eyes darting down the room, catching Agatha's raised brow. "She writes about your new governess."

Intensely interested with this unexpected topic, Paul leaned forward and gave Westphal his complete attention. "Really? What does she write?"

"Well," he said, clearing his throat again and shifting uneasily in his chair, aware that every eye was on him. "I don't think I should say – not in front of the children, anyway."

Charmaine's heart accelerated. Disaster was about to strike, and she had no way of stopping it.

Paul scratched his head. The man had obviously uncovered something scandalous if he felt it was only fit for adult ears. "How would your daughter know about our governess?" he mused. "Are you saying that some sordid information accidentally fell into her lap and she just happened to write to you about it?"

"Actually, Mrs. Ward expressed her concerns a few months ago," he replied. "She was anxious about Miss Ryan's background. She came into the bank and asked if Anne might make some inquiries."

"Agatha?" Paul queried, bemused yet annoyed. He peered down the table and questioned her directly. "On whose request?"

"My own," she replied haughtily. "I took it upon myself to petition Stephen. I had legitimate misgivings about Miss Ryan, and when no one else seemed concerned, when no references were required other than those Loretta Harrington provided, I was compelled – for the sake of the children – to investigate." She breathed deeply. "Thank goodness Stephen's daughter agreed to assist. I fear the children are at grave risk. Not even I was prepared for what she uncovered. It is far worse than any of us could have imagined."

Colette checked her anger. "I think Mr. Westphal's allegations, whatever they may be, had best be left for another day. My children have no place in this conversation."

"Colette is right," Paul concurred. "Rose, would you take the children to the nursery?"

Charmaine's reprieve lasted but a moment; Rose quickly jumped to do his bidding, ushering the children from the room, unmindful of Yvette's protests.

Colette cast turbulent eyes down the table at Paul, her stormy countenance rivaled only by George's. Paul remained unperturbed. "All right, Stephen," he breathed. "You now have leave to speak. Tell us, what have you found out?"

Mortified, Charmaine pushed from the table. But Paul foiled her escape, grasping her arm and holding her to the spot. She would be forced to listen to the macabre story, relive it, while those she had come to love sat in judgment over the terrible secrets she had kept. Tonight, they would brand her the offspring of a maniac, a murderer, and she had no defense against the horrific truth. Great shame washed over her, and she bowed her head.

Paul's grip tightened, the pain igniting her wrath, and she glared at him furiously. But he seemed oblivious, his eyes fixed on the banker. "Out with it man!" he snarled, aggravated by Westphal's hesitation.

"If I had known sooner," the man wavered, uncertain if Paul really wanted the truth, "I would have come to you with the information immediately. But as you know, the ships were delayed. Anne's letter is weeks old."

"Yes, yes, get on with it."

"Actually," he faltered again, beads of perspiration dotting his upper lip. "I regret that it has fallen to me to reveal the deplorable facts." He glanced down the table. Colette appeared as irate as Paul. Only Agatha remained smug.

"Tell him, Stephen," the dowager prompted, her satisfied eyes leveled on Charmaine "It is best that he and Colette know the type of person they have hired and are harboring in their home."

"Yes, Stephen," Paul agreed. "You've primed us for this terrible tale. Let's have it out! What has Miss Ryan done that we must know about, lest the children come to harm?"

"It is not what *she's* done. It's her father."

"And?"

"He is – a murderer."

The room fell deadly silent, all of Charmaine's deepest fears realized. Even the sounds from the kitchen ceased, as if ears were pressed against the swinging door. The truth was out, and now Paul, who had allied himself with Agatha during her interview, could gloat. He'd been right about her all along.

Charmaine refused to look his way again. With her disgrace mounting, she renewed her efforts to escape, twisting against his unyielding fist. "Please," she whimpered, to no avail.

"What exactly are you saying, Stephen?"

"Miss Ryan's father is a murderer," he reiterated, "did in fact murder her mother."

"Have you proof?"

"Most assuredly," the financier stated, taking courage from Paul's sudden interest in the facts. "According to Anne, who spoke to one of the Harrington's housemaids, John Ryan barged into the Harrington house late one night. When Joshua Harrington sent him on his way, he went home and attacked his own wife. Of course, Anne wanted to make certain the story wasn't fabricated, so she contacted the sheriff and was shocked to find that not only had John Ryan committed murder, but is still at large, a fugitive. Apparently, the sheriff was relieved to let the case drop once the hullabaloo calmed down, because the Ryans were nothing more than white trash, living in a shanty in the slums of the city."

"How did Mr. Ryan kill his wife?"

"He beat her to death. According to the sheriff, those beatings were a common occurrence. This time it just got out of hand. Miss Ryan–" and the banker nodded across the table toward Charmaine "–came home to find the body near death and cried on the Harringtons' shoulders once it had grown cold in order to get the sheriff involved. Sheriff Briggs conveyed to Anne his disdain for being pulled into the nasty affair."

Charmaine had had enough. She had allowed the man to humiliate her, to expose her deception and label her as riffraff, no better than her father. But she refused to allow him to degrade her mother. With eyes flashing, she shot to her feet. "That 'body' as you call it, was *my mother*, a good and kind woman, whom I loved and lost because of my wretched father!" In spite of her anger, her eyes were flooding with unwanted tears, her anguish painfully apparent in the words she could barely force out. "And yes," she hissed, "he beat her, beat her often, and there was no one to turn to, no one to stop him! Not even when she lay dying. If it wasn't for Joshua and Loretta Harrington, no one would have even cared. Mr. Harrington petitioned the sheriff, but little good that did! It's over a year since my mother's death, and still, my father walks free. I know he will never pay for his heinous crime. So cringe if you will, but let me tell you this, there is no one who despises John Ryan more than I do, and no one who seeks justice as much as I do. *But that will never happen, will it?*" The rhetorical question echoed about the room.

Paul sympathized with the young woman who had yet to look his way. *This is why she is wary of me.* Her father had never given her a reason to love any man, had in fact terrified her. Paul was filled with the desire to comfort her, to hold her in his arms and shield her from all she had suffered.

"No, I thought not," she said in answer to her own question. "There is only one reason my father remains at large, and that is owing to people like you, Mr. Westphal, who are more interested in blaming the innocent rather than looking for the guilty." She turned on Paul. "Punish an easy victim. I'm right here. Now," she snarled, twisting against his hand, "if you'd release my arm, I'd like to retire. I refuse to be further humiliated!"

George stood, enraged. The inquisition had gone on too long. "You are too polite, Charmaine," he growled, his eyes riveted on her manacled wrist. "This room reeks of a different kind of trash, and I, for one, have lost my appetite." He pushed the chair aside and placed a comforting arm around her shoulder, challenging Paul to hold her one moment longer.

The threat was acknowledged, and Paul's hand relaxed. Charmaine pulled free and turned in George's embrace. When they reached the foyer, she broke down and cried. "You had best go back," she heaved, "or they'll be angry with you as well."

George snorted. "I don't care how angry they get."

"I was so happy here. I don't know where I will go now."

"What do you mean?" he asked. "You can't believe that Colette would dismiss you on account of a bit of scandalmongery? If you do, you're not giving her credit for the good and kind woman that she is."

Charmaine considered him, her tears subsiding.

"Colette loves you, Charmaine. The children love you. Even Paul... I'll wager he is in there right now telling them where they can go, if you get my meaning."

"Then why did he treat me like that? Holding me like a trapped animal?"

"He wanted you to face them, with your head held high. Paul has endured years of ridicule because of his illegitimacy and has learned never to allow the accuser the upper hand. Cow-towing, running away – it gives credence to every insinuation, fact or not. I'm just annoyed that he allowed them to badger you for as long as they did."

Charmaine comprehended his wisdom and prayed that he was right. If so, she had sorely misjudged Paul.

"Everyone has something to hide, Charmaine, something they're not proud of. My mother ran off with a sailor when I was only a year old, leaving my father with a broken heart. It was a good thing that my grandmother was here to raise me. We all have secrets we'd prefer to keep."

Charmaine looked tenderly at the man who had just revealed an aspect of his own life that had to be painful. "Thank you, George," she whispered.

"Don't mention it," he smiled, thinking how lovely she looked tonight. If Paul weren't so damned possessive, he'd court Charmaine Ryan himself.

She sighed raggedly. "I think I'll check on the children."

With George's nod, she turned and climbed the stairs to the nursery.

The aspersions continued to mount. The contention: John Ryan's blood ran through his daughter's veins and would someday manifest itself with mortal consequences.

"I've heard enough!" Paul sneered.

"And so have I," Colette agreed, throwing down her napkin and standing, her poise long gone. "I've neglected my children and would like to give them a kiss before they go to sleep." She stepped from the table, but abruptly stopped. "I also need to speak with Miss Ryan. Despite your mean-spirited warnings, she will retain her position here."

Stephen had risen with Colette and attempted to apologize. "Madame, I only had the children's best interest–"

"Mr. Westphal," she accused, disgusted by his pretentious contrition, "if you had *anyone's* best interest at heart, you would have brought this matter to me privately and not to my dinner table. What you forced Miss Ryan to endure tonight was revolting." Without a backward glance, she left the room.

Stephen sent imploring eyes to Paul, who only shrugged. "I'm afraid I have to agree with her, Stephen. Charmaine Ryan is an asset to this family and will remain in my father's employ as long as Colette sees fit. I've never held to the belief that the sins of the father are visited upon his children. If that were the case, most men would be damned. Your sentiments smack of European aristocracy." He paused a moment, allowing his statements to sink in, deploring the classes and labels established by bluebloods and their countless imitators. "I have much to do in the morning," he concluded. "I don't want to appear a poor host, Stephen, but I think it is time to call for your carriage." Not waiting for a reply, he walked to the foyer, pleased when the banker scurried after him.

Charmaine patted her face dry and opened the nursery door.

"Mademoiselle!" Jeannette called, running to her. "Are you all right?"

Yvette did the same, and together, they pulled her into the chamber. "You were crying," she said, her voice quivering.

"I'm fine now," Charmaine answered, sitting on the girl's bed. She glanced at Rose, who also wore a worried expression.

"You're still our governess, aren't you?" Jeannette pleaded.

Charmaine's eyes welled again. "I don't know," she whispered.

"We won't let anyone send you away!" Yvette expostulated, arms wrapped around her. "We love you!"

Charmaine returned the embrace, profoundly touched.

Jeannette noticed her mother standing in the doorway first. "Mama!" she cried, "you're not going to send Mademoiselle Charmaine away, are you?"

"Absolutely not," she replied, her serious face giving way to a smile, then a giggle, and soon they were all laughing.

Later, Charmaine and Colette strolled along the balcony, their soft whispers melding with the evening breezes. They wound up in Colette's boudoir, where Charmaine disclosed the details of her home life. Colette was a compassionate confidante. By the time Charmaine returned to her own room, a heavy yoke had been lifted from her shoulders.

Paul had wanted to speak to Charmaine, but she was not in the nursery, nor in her room. Tomorrow… he would talk with her tomorrow.

Saturday, December 24, 1836

Fatima bustled around the kitchen, humming carols as she put the finishing touches on the dozen food baskets she had prepared at Colette's request. She'd cooked non-stop for two days. Now, she stood back and smiled at the delicious Yuletide delights that would be delivered to the bondsmen's keep that afternoon, an annual tradition, which had commenced nine years ago. Fatima very much approved of Colette's charity, but her exuberance turned to worry when the mistress of the manor entered the kitchen well before noon.

"Miss Colette, what a' you plannin' on doin' dressed like that?"

"You know very well what I'm planning," she answered.

"But Mastah Paul tol' me he was takin' care of the victuals this year."

"His idea, not mine," Colette replied, arranging the loaves of crusty bread into one basket. "I'm quite capable of riding out to the fields in a carriage."

Fatima sucked in her cheeks. "That ain't a good idea."

"Why not? Why should this Christmas be any different?"

"'Cause you been feelin' poorly, that's why," the stern cook replied. When it appeared as if Colette wasn't listening, Fatima pressed on. "Master Frederic ain't gonna like it!"

Colette only laughed. "He didn't like it the first time, either."

"No, he didn't. That's why–"

"And he adjusted his way of thinking, did he not?" Colette interrupted.

"That was then and this is now. He's a mite more concerned 'bout your health than the men-folk gnawing on this here food."

"He won't even know I am gone. Unless, of course, you tell him."

Fatima shook her head, realizing the folly of further argument. When Colette got her dander up, there was no stopping her. A slow smile broke across Fatima's face. It had been a long time since she'd seen even a fleck of that dander, a hint of the Colette of old. A spark had flared the night of the banker's visit, and Fatima was of a mind to see it burn brightly again. Therefore, she set aside her perturbation with one final injunction. "No liftin' them baskets. Joseph can go with you to do the carryin'."

"That is fine, but I am also taking the girls along to help distribute the food."

Fatima stopped dead in her tracks. "Why are you gonna do that?"

"It is time they learn that a life of privilege comes with certain responsibilities. I don't want them growing up pampered beauties with warm smiles and cold hearts."

Even after nine years, Colette's wisdom and concern, the depth of her heart, amazed Fatima. Nodding her approval, she turned back to her work.

The preparations were completed and the carriage readied. When the baskets were secured in the landau's boot, the girls, Colette, and Joseph Thornfield departed the grounds, leaving Charmaine and Pierre to wave their good-byes from the top step of the portico. No one noticed Frederic standing on the second story veranda, a scowl marking his brow.

Later that evening, when Colette had retired and Charmaine coaxed the girls into bed, the twins were still whispering about the huge building they had visited and the strange men they had met. Jeannette had thoroughly enjoyed herself, but Yvette wrinkled her nose in disgust. "I don't know why we had to go out there," she complained. "It was horrible: smelly and filthy!"

"Mama says we wouldn't be half so rich if those men didn't work for Papa," Jeannette offered affably. "She says we should be thankful, and that bringing a Christmas feast is just a small way to show our gratitude."

"I know what she said," Yvette replied peevishly.

Jeannette shrugged and snuggled deep into her covers.

Charmaine gave them a kiss, pulled a blanket over an already slumbering Pierre, and tiptoed from the room. She knew what Colette had hoped to teach her daughters today, but evidently, only Jeannette embraced the charitable lesson.

Colette was brushing out her hair when Frederic stepped into her boudoir. Though he had knocked, he hadn't waited for an answer. She studied him through the looking glass, unnerved as he moved toward her, self-conscious of her state of undress.

"You went out to the keep today," he commented.

"It is Christmas Eve," she answered.

"With the twins."

"Yes." She pushed out of her chair and faced him, struggling to maintain her composure. "Should I not teach them to care for those less fortunate than they? Isn't that what tomorrow is all about – the Christ child born in a lowly manger?"

His eyes swept her from head to toe, an assessing perusal that took her breath away. "They are criminals, Colette," he finally rasped. "I'm concerned for the girls' safety – your safety. Beyond that, you are not well. I don't want you leaving the grounds without telling me."

Colette stiffened. "Am I a prisoner in my own home? You attempted to make it so once before. I tell you now, it will not happen. I will come and go as I please!"

Frederic clenched his teeth. "And I told you that I didn't care if you left. My daughters, on the other hand, *are* my concern."

Colette felt a surge of tears rush to her eyes. She would not allow him to see her anguish, the pain he could so easily inflict. Belting her robe, she pushed past him and marched into her bedroom, slamming the door behind her.

Frederic stared long and hard at it. Coming to an abrupt decision, he rushed forward. But his impaired foot caught the edge of the carpet, and he stumbled. His right hand flew out, grabbing hold of a chair just in time. As his cane clattered to the floor, he swore under his breath. His heart was racing and his limbs shook fiercely. Only when his breathing grew regular did he let go. Beads of perspiration dotted his brow, and he wiped them away with his forearm. Bending over, he retrieved the crutch, realizing that it marked what he had become. Appalled, he slowly returned to his own quarters.

Sunday, December 25, 1836

Charmaine's first Christmas with the Duvoisin family was happy. After Mass and a bountiful breakfast, Colette had taken the children to their father's chambers. Frederic generally visited them once a week in the nursery. Charmaine was grateful that these encounters occurred in that safer territory, a neutral arena of civility, painful civility.

Today, however, the children were in Frederic's apartments, and Charmaine had some time to herself. She walked into the drawing room and found Paul there. They had not spoken since the night of Stephen Westphal's visit. He'd been preoccupied with his upcoming trip, pouring over documents in preparation of his imminent business negotiations. Tomorrow, at dawn, he'd be leaving. As she stepped into the room, he stood.

"I'm sorry," she apologized. "I didn't mean to disturb you."

"You didn't. I wanted to speak with you, anyway. Where are the children?"

"With your father."

"Come and join me then," he invited, indicating the chair opposite him.

When she had complied, he tossed his papers aside, sat, and studied her at length. "I want to apologize," he finally began.

"For what?"

"For allowing you to think that I wasn't on your side the other night. When I realized you were going to flee, I was compelled to stop you. I've learned it's best never to turn your back on the enemy. I feared you were going to do just that."

She was astonished. George had been right.

"If you had looked my way," he was saying, "I would have conveyed that advice to you, but you were far too determined to lambaste Mr. Westphal. I'm sorry if I bruised your wrist."

She had been absentmindedly massaging her arm. "It's fine," she whispered self-consciously. "Thank you for defending me – even in light of the truth. I know you did not approve of me at first."

"I was wrong," he replied. "The children are fortunate to have you here."

"Still, you could have judged me by the deeds of my father."

His eyes were warm on her, and he shifted forward in his chair. "No," he breathed, "I could never have done that."

She was so lovely, and he was going to miss her during his months away. He realized that she'd be missing him, too, perhaps more so. He'd been the perfect gentleman over the past few months, true to his word and true to his agreement. It had worked in his favor. He knew that she was attracted to him. Right now, she longed to be kissed. Unlike two months ago, she felt at ease in his presence. Nevertheless, she was distraught that he had made no further advances. Poor Charmaine Ryan; she was very confused! The woman in her demanded passion, the little girl, safety, and then there was the female her father had molded, the one that screamed, *Every man must be avoided at all costs.* How he longed to wash away her fears and show her the way to womanhood.

Absence… His three-month absence would make her heart grow fonder, and when he returned, he'd read hunger in her eyes. Let her dream of him while he was away. It would make his homecoming that much sweeter. He just needed to give her something to remember him by.

"Come dawn, I'll be sailing with the tide," he murmured. "I shall miss you."

Charmaine was reeling. He was going to kiss her; his hands had gripped the arms of her chair, and she was trapped between them. She closed her eyes, but did not lean away. His cheek brushed against hers as he nuzzled her ear. Her heart was pounding so loudly she couldn't understand what he whispered. To steady her soaring senses, she grabbed hold of his arms.

"There you are!"

The moment was shattered as Agatha entered the room. Paul broke away and immediately stood. Charmaine averted her crimson face. Once composed, she retreated to the foyer without a glance in Paul's direction.

Tuesday,
March 7, 1837

Chapter 7

"Quickly, Robert!" Agatha urged. "She's having trouble breathing!"

Charmaine huddled in the archway of the drawing room, the twins drawn tight against her and Pierre clasped to her breast. As the doctor rushed up the stairs, Jeannette began to cry. "Is Mama going to be all right, Mademoiselle?"

"Of course she is," Charmaine breathed, attempting to disguise her own anxiety. "Now that Doctor Blackford is here, she'll be fine." She carried Pierre back into the room and sat him on the piano bench. "Let us sing together. A few songs might help us feel better."

The children brightened, but Charmaine remained worried. *Why had she encouraged Colette to accompany them on their Sunday outing?* Of course, no one could have predicted the storm that had blown in, not from the beautiful skies that morning. By the time they reached the house, they were drenched to the skin and chilled to the bone. Colette fell prey to a fever almost immediately.

Pneumonia – that's what Doctor Blackford called it, explaining that she suffered from mucus in the lungs, which made breathing difficult. Agatha's alarmed mien added to Charmaine's perturbation; this had to be serious.

The day drew on. Robert finally departed Colette's chambers. He reached the open doorway of the nursery and cleared his throat, startling them.

"How is my mother?" Yvette demanded.

"There has been a minor improvement," he stated sourly.

Robert Blackford could have been a handsome man – tall and lean, with dark, aristocratic features. But he never smiled, his brow permanently severe, his jaw perpetually clenched.

"If you want her well again," he continued, "you are not to disturb her until I give permission. She has pneumonia thanks to your little outing on Sunday."

Charmaine had a great deal of trouble getting the girls to sleep that night. She thought Pierre would present the bigger problem, for he had cried nearly an hour the evening before. Without Nana Rose's able hands – the old woman had been abed for the better part of a week with a bad case of rheumatism – Charmaine feared she was in for another bout of torrential tears. Not so; he fell asleep quite quickly. The girls, on the other hand, were guilt-ridden and anguished over their mother. Charmaine encouraged them to pray, but it was only as she read to them that their eyes grew heavy, and they finally succumbed to exhaustion.

Now she was free to fret on her own. Colette had not been well for the better part of two months, her health deteriorating rapidly since Christmas. Charmaine had thought that the fresh air and sunshine of Sunday would do her some good. But Agatha was right. She wasn't a physician and should have left well enough alone; thanks to her, Colette was worse than ever. Robert Blackford's every-other-day visits would certainly turn into daily visits now.

She went down to the kitchen and chatted with Fatima Henderson. "This house is just too empty," the cook complained. It was true. Because Paul was away, George was overburdened. Over the past weeks, they'd seen very little of him. Charmaine despaired anew. While Paul resided in the house, she felt protected. In his absence, havoc had reigned, the days longer, the nights wretched. Once the children were abed, there was little to do to while away the hours.

She needed a distraction and meandered into the drawing room, walking over to the piano. Maybe if she played something elaborate it would serve such a purpose and cheer her. She rummaged through the side table drawer until she found the dog-eared pages of a complicated piece. She propped them up, rearranged her skirts, and set her fingers on the keys.

She played the first sixteen measures, the last four a sequence that introduced the secondary theme. She sighed. The arrangement was difficult, lovely, yet sad. She played it again and again, reveling in the resonance of the finely crafted piano. This composition would never have sounded so beautiful on Loretta Harrington's upright. It was a masterpiece intended for a master instrument, its haunting strains echoing off the drawing room walls.

One more time over the ivory keys and Charmaine smiled. The notes were becoming familiar. She had faltered only once that last time, and now the rapturous rhapsody blossomed in all its glory, like an anxious flower bud bursting open to the beckoning sun.

Though the dissonant secondary theme defiled the perfect harmonies of the first, they were suitably entwined: lovers racing to the climax, expectancy building with each successive, addictive chord, exploding into a furious arpeggio that thundered up the keyboard, then tumbled back down. After three full measures of silence, a solitary, naked chord finally answered the fury, bringing the piece to a close: desolate, lost, hopeless…

The evening was too warm, the quiescent air too stifling in the confining chamber, and Colette knew the panic of suffocation. She left the bed and pattered barefoot across the soft carpet to the French doors, pulling them open. There she stood, welcoming the brisk March wind that buffeted her face and carried her golden hair off her shoulders, praying that it would clear her senses.

This is only a minor setback, she reasoned. Yes, her head throbbed, her throat was constricted with needling pain, and her chest was congested. *But a severe infirmity of the lungs?* No, she silently denied, she wasn't that ill, though Agatha and Robert would like everyone to believe she was. And yet, after two days of coughing and fever, this afternoon she had lost the will to oppose their ministrations. She succumbed to Robert's wicked serum and Agatha's demanded round-the-clock bed rest.

That had been hours ago. Tonight, with the mansion so quiet and her contaminated room so oppressive, she escaped to the veranda. Breathing deeply, she welcomed the rejuvenating night air, until a hearty gale hit her full force. Shivering, she quickly latched the glass panels and wrapped herself in a plush velvet robe. Just as quickly, the sweats returned.

She should lie down. *No!* She'd not return to the rumpled bed where she had passed the better part of three days. Instead, she slipped her numb feet into soft slippers. She'd check on the children.

She was abreast of the staircase when she first heard it – a torpid melody long abandoned yet well remembered… Then, it was gone, indifferent of the emotion it had evoked. She hadn't heard it. It was all in her clouded mind. She shouldn't have stood in the night air. The exertion was taking its toll. Perhaps she should return to her apartments. No, that was foolish. She'd come this far, and she needed to see her children. If she just steadied herself for a moment, she'd be fine. There, she felt better already.

The children slept soundly. Thanks to Charmaine, they'd been tenderly mothered in her absence. She kissed each child's forehead, tucked in a cover here, moved a head back on the pillow there. Content, she tiptoed from the room.

Everything was shrouded in silence, and yet, as Colette crossed the hallway, the familiar strain was there again, meeting her at the top of the staircase. It was beckoning to her, tugging at her very soul. Yes, it was stronger now and not a bitter disappointment of the imagination. It was real! All she had to do was reach the drawing room. Already her heart beat wildly with incautious desire, the rhapsody embracing her, mocking her turmoil and demanding but one thing: that she come!

Charmaine played on, the power of the piece quintessential. No poet could pen words more plaintive than the haunting sorrow dwelling in this composer's masterpiece. She was merely the medium called upon to give it life, its spellbound prisoner, just now realizing that there was more here than just the music, much more. Her hands floated flawlessly across the keyboard, her fingers exalting the untamed territory. The composition consumed her in its desire to proclaim its plight: to scorn the charades that hide the truth, the injustices that persecute the living, and the endings that remain unresolved… Charmaine had lived them all and wanted to weep.

The door slapped open, and she jumped, her hands crucifying the keys.

Relief flooded over her as she faced the startling wraith. "*Colette?*"

The mistress of the manor appeared dazed, her liquid eyes distant and dilated, her face flushed, and her breathing erratic. When she didn't respond, Charmaine crossed the room and placed an arm around her frail shoulders. Colette swayed and began coughing fitfully. When the spasm passed, Charmaine coaxed her into the nearest chair. "Are you all right? Can I get you something? Perhaps a drink? Or should I have Travis send for the doctor?"

The last query snared Colette's attention, and her detachment receded. "No," she whispered. "I'll be fine… in a minute. Just give me a minute." Her eyes darted about the room as if she were looking for someone. Eventually, they came to rest on Charmaine. "You… it was you playing the piano just now?"

"Yes."

Colette frowned. "I didn't know you could play so – well." Her words trailed off, and again she scanned the darkened room. *Was he standing in the shadows?*

"I didn't think I could play like that either. It was as if the composition possessed me."

Colette's regard sharpened.

Unnerved by that gaze, Charmaine said, "You should be in bed."

"No, I'm fine. I was just checking on the children when I heard the music. You played it so beautifully, almost as if… as if you'd composed it…"

Charmaine laughed softly, incredulously. "I could never have done that."

"…as if you were a part of it," Colette continued, ignoring Charmaine's denial. "As if you belonged to it."

Charmaine could not disagree. "It's exquisite. I just wish I were able to play it properly."

"You will," Colette encouraged, "with time and patience, you will."

"Perhaps, but it will take a great deal of practice." Charmaine lifted the sheets of music from the piano and studied them in the lamplight. "There are a few chords here that flow in the most peculiar direction. I need to better understand their placement before I do it justice. Right now, my fingers are inclined to change the dissonant measures; they're too unhappy."

Colette's eyes sparkled with tears. "An astute observation. The piece needs your touch to see it resolved."

"Resolved?" Charmaine declared, upset that she'd suggested interfering with the imperfectly perfect score. "I wouldn't dream of tampering with it."

"Not tamper," Colette corrected, "enhance. The music as it stands cries out to be understood. The manner in which it is played – a gentle hand, a commitment to each measure – will enrich it. A few notes sent in a new direction will replace the sadness and sorrow with happiness and joy. You have the strength of character to do that, Charmaine, to bend the masterpiece, but not break it, to possess it, as it has possessed you. And when your love *is* the music, the harmony will be perfect."

Peculiar sentiments, Charmaine thought. "Who composed it?" she asked.

"Obviously someone who has borne a great deal of pain."

"Yes," Charmaine agreed, "and that pain must have become his inspiration."

Colette nodded, content for a second time that night. "Would you play it again? It has been so long. I'd like to hear it one last time."

Charmaine placed her fingers on the keys and resurrected the rhapsody.

Wednesday, March 8, 1837

Colette sat at her desk, respiring as deeply as her constricted lungs would allow. Agatha and Robert had finally left her, and she had a moment's peace. She refused to stay abed, certain she had exerted more energy arguing with the doctor and his sister than walking the short distance from bedchamber to sitting room. Still, she admitted that the physician's remedies had had some positive effect. Though her cough persisted, his mustard plaster had eased the piercing pain she'd experienced yesterday when her hacking had been uncontrollable. His constant care had also cured her of a two-day fever and chills.

She had slept very little last night, and yet, this morning she felt strangely untroubled and refreshed. Charmaine Ryan had pointed the way; she knew what she must do.

Picking up her quill, she began to write, allowing her heart to determine the words. More than once, tears splattered the stationery, but she chased them away with the back of her hand. Tears were for the past, smiles were for tomorrow. She would think only of smiles.

So deep were her thoughts that she did not hear her chamber door open.

"Colette, why are you out of bed?"

She jumped, nearly upsetting the inkwell, a hand flying to her mouth.

"Frederic," she gasped, "what are you doing here?" *Had he read over her shoulder?* No, his eyes betrayed only concern.

"I've come to see how you are," he answered gently.

She sighed in relief, but the expulsion of air ended in another coughing fit. When she finally looked up at him, he was scowling.

"Robert told me you've refused his advice. Must I set Gladys up as guard to make certain you stay in bed?"

"Do what you like, Frederic," she retaliated, "but I won't be bullied!"

She remembered a time when such a retort would have incensed him further, but today his countenance softened dolefully. "I am not trying to bully you, Colette. I only wish to see you well again."

"Why?" she asked, suddenly on the verge of tears. "What does it matter?"

"The children need you."

"The children... *Just* the children?" She bit her bottom lip and, for one breathless moment, thought he was going to speak the words she longed to hear.

Instead he asked, "Where were you last night?"

Confused, a multitude of thoughts raced through her mind: the suffocating room, the need to see the children, the music... and then, this peculiar question. "You were here?" she asked, noting the accusatory gleam that flickered in his eyes. *Dear God, he still mistrusts me!*

"Robert has painted a grim picture. I was worried and couldn't sleep."

"Neither could I. I went to check on the children."

"Strange," he snorted, "I did the same thing, and you weren't there."

"I *did* look in on the children," she said. "Afterward, I went downstairs. But if you want to believe the worst about me, if that eases your pain–"

She was coughing again, so fiercely that she doubled over, unaware of his despair. "Colette," he urged, his hale arm pulling her to her feet, "you must get back into bed. I won't disturb you if you'd remain in bed."

Friday, March 31, 1837

Colette's health continued to deteriorate after her bout with pneumonia, and her absences from the nursery became commonplace. Not so today. If Colette couldn't come to the children, the children would go to her. It was her birthday. Charmaine made all the preparations: a day's excursion with the girls and Pierre, and a visit to their mother's chambers after dinner, where they would give her the locket they had picked out at the mercantile earlier that week.

Charmaine had just finished tying Pierre's laces, when Frederic appeared in the nursery doorway. "Are you going somewhere?" he asked.

"Yes, sir," she answered, quickly straightening up.

She remained ill at ease with the man, their first encounter forever etched in her mind. It was a condition she'd been forced to confront on a daily basis now. Over the past month, he'd come to visit nearly every morning, as if he were attempting to make up to his children the time they'd normally have spent with their mother, that precious time that had been stolen from them.

"Mademoiselle Charmaine is going to take us on a picnic," Jeannette offered. "Would you like to come, Papa?"

"I think not. But I do have a present for Pierre. I believe he is three today."

The little boy beamed in delight. "I am! Where's my pwesent?"

Frederic produced a package from behind his back, and the boy quickly dove into the wrapping. He lifted from the paper a wooden ship, a replica of the Duvoisin vessels that sailed the Atlantic. Laughing, he gave his father a fierce hug. "Tank you, Papa!"

Charmaine smiled down at him, satisfied with his manners and delighted with his joy. Already he was on hands and knees pretending to sail the toy.

Yvette frowned in disappointment. "Pierre got a present on our birthday," she remarked sullenly. "Why don't we get one on his?"

"Would a visit to see your mother suffice?" her father asked. "I know she would love a visit from you. She's feeling a bit better today."

The invitation had a magical effect, Charmaine's planned outing quickly forgotten. As they raced out of the room, Frederic called after them. "One thing," he lightly warned. "No jumping on her bed, and don't forget to say 'Happy Birthday' to her."

"Of course we wouldn't forget that!" Yvette exclaimed.

In an instant they were gone, and Charmaine was left alone with the taciturn man. He stepped slightly aside and, with the wave of his hand, encouraged her to precede him down the hallway. She did so, wondering if she had become accustomed to his labored steps, or if those steps had improved in the months she had come to know him; he did not seem to struggle as fiercely as he had before.

They found the children in Colette's bedroom. Though the French doors were thrown open and sunlight spilled into the chamber, the room was dismal. Colette, propped among many pillows, did not look well. Large, dark circles lay claim to sunken eyes, and the smile that reached them was more sad than happy.

The children seemed immune to the severity of her illness. Pierre was nestled beside her, Jeannette sat next to him, and Yvette stood opposite them, near her mother's pillow, grasping one of her hands. They were innocently happy just to be in her presence.

"We are going on a picnic today," Yvette was saying. "We can't wait until you are well enough to come with us again!"

"That's a lovely way to spend Pierre's birthday," Colette answered. "Next year, when I'm better, we'll plan something very special to do together."

"I'm fwee!" Pierre announced proudly.

"Yes I know, mon caillou," she replied. "You are growing so handsome. Soon you will look just like your father." She brushed back the soft brown hair that fell on his brow and drew him close for a tender kiss. "I missed you."

"When are you gonna be better, Mama?"

"Soon, I hope… very soon."

Frederic cleared his throat. "I didn't hear anyone say: 'Happy Birthday'."

"Oh yes, Mama," they all chimed in, "Happy Birthday!"

"I'm so glad we're visiting now," Jeannette said. "Mademoiselle didn't think we'd be allowed until later, but Papa knew we wanted to see you this morning."

Colette's eyes filled with tears as she looked from one child to the next. Then she met her husband's gaze across the room. "Thank you," she whispered, her gratitude rivaled only by her astonishment.

Earlier that morning, she had had a dispute with Robert Blackford, gaining nothing save a warning that she not leave her bed lest he summon her husband.

When Agatha had hurried off to do just that, Colette had been certain that she'd be denied yet another visit with her children. But Frederic had defied them.

The children spent only a short time with her, presenting the wrapped gift that Charmaine remembered to bring. She kissed each of them, savoring those they offered in return. Her eyes remained wistful after they'd left.

Frederic stepped closer and, sitting on the edge of the bed, took her hand in his. In spite of her illness, her pulse quickened and her fingers tingled. *Was he aware of the emotions he evoked?* His eyes told her, *No.*

"Thank you," she whispered again. "They will cure me faster than any of Robert's tonics."

Frederic didn't respond, the weight of his regard unsettling. "If you promise to heed Robert's advice," he finally said, "I will bring the children in to see you whenever you wish. How would that be?"

She weakly squeezed his hand. "That would be wonderful."

He patted her hand before tucking it beneath the coverlet. With some effort, he pushed off the bed and turned to leave. "I need you, too," he murmured.

She watched him limp from the room, blinking back tears. Though her strength was waning, his vigor was waxing. It was too late for them, she realized. In resignation, she accepted that as best for everyone concerned.

Sunday, April 2, 1837

Wade Remmen climbed the front steps and stood before the large oak doors of the Duvoisin mansion. He knocked on the portal and waited, turning to survey the beautiful lawns from the height of the portico. A mere two years ago, his life had been wretched. He'd certainly come up in the world. But he wanted more. Someday, he'd acquire his own fortune and build a palatial estate such as this; then his future could mock his past. *My sister would love to be here right now. Someday...* The front door opened, and the butler invited him in.

George was eating heartily. He motioned for Wade to take the seat across from him and asked Fatima to dish up the same fare.

After a good portion of the meal was consumed, Wade was still pondering the reason for his second invitation to the manor. The first had come months ago – a luncheon offered in gratitude for his intervention at the mill the day before. He'd kept a level head, and a crisis had been averted, one that could have cost a man his life.

In all his nineteen years, Wade had never panicked in an emergency. Likewise, he never feared standing up for himself. These two attributes, in combination with his determination to work hard, had earned him Paul Duvoisin's respect. When the sawmill's foreman severed his arm in early November, exposing the bone and nearly bleeding to death on the spot, Wade had swiftly wrapped a tourniquet on the upper limb and ordered a man to run for the doctor. After he'd sent another man in search of Paul or George, he returned to the labor at hand. The crew began to grumble, but he insisted that a bit of blood wasn't going to shut down production. When their objections grew vehement, his scowl deepened. Then he threw himself into the strenuous effort, ignoring their protests. In less than five minutes, everyone was back to work. In the end, a life had been saved, and just as much lumber milled. Paul had been very pleased.

Today, Wade wondered what feat awaited him, for he knew that Paul was away and George had been carrying the workload of two. His intrigue was piqued when Harold Browning entered the room and the same meal was set before him.

"I have a problem," George finally said. "I must leave Charmantes for a couple of weeks, and I need the two of you to take over while I'm away, or until Paul returns, which I'm hoping will be any day now."

Harold was befuddled. "May I ask where you are traveling?"

"Virginia," he replied tersely, his manner closing the topic to further probes. "Now, can I count on you at the mill, Wade? You've handled it before. This time you'll be in complete control for a fortnight, perhaps more."

"As long as the men know I'm boss, there shouldn't be a problem."

"I'll speak to them first thing in the morning," George answered, shifting his consideration to Harold. "You'll have the greater challenge, managing both the sugarcane and tobacco crews. Jake and Buck can take care of the harbor: warehousing the harvests, coordinating the unloading and loading of any ships that make port. With any luck, Paul will be on the first one from Europe. Once he's home, he can take over."

"Does Frederic know you are leaving?" Harold asked.

George leaned back in his chair. "He will soon enough," he replied vaguely, pleased when Charmaine and the children entered the room.

"George," she greeted with a buoyant smile. She could count on her fingers the number of times she had seen him since Paul's departure three months ago, and she was truly happy to find him at the table now. "What brings you home?"

Before he could answer, her attention was drawn to the other two men, who'd come to their feet as she stepped closer. She nodded to Harold Browning and then the younger man beside him. She couldn't remember his name, though he'd dined with them once before in the fall. The hint of a grin tweaked the corners of his mouth, and she was instantly struck by his good looks, recalling Colette's admiration when he'd departed the house last time. Tall and lanky, he was clean-shaven with a broad nose and full lips. His lazy smile reached his dark eyes. They matched the color of his hair, which was cropped short. Muscular arms and swarthy skin attested to the many hours he'd toiled under the blazing tropical sun. He was young, perhaps her age, yet very sure of himself as if he were much older.

"I remember Miss Ryan," he said as George introduced them.

George didn't dally. "I've a great deal to do today."

With a dejected spirit, Charmaine watched all three men depart. She would have liked to socialize with George, but instead she was left to the company of the children. Only when she looked at Jeannette did she realize that her own downtrodden expression was mirrored there.

"What is the matter, Sweetheart?" she asked.

"I wish Mr. Remmen could have stayed awhile longer, that's all."

Mr. Remmen *and* Mr. Richards, Charmaine thought.

Thursday, April 6, 1837

Dark clouds gathered swiftly, blotting out the sun and rumbling with thunder, but the growling masses did not match the lamentations that shook Charmantes' mansion from within. The entire household was aware of the plight of their frail mistress, who lay near death. The pneumonia had taken a greater hold; any imagined improvement was just that, a delusion, and now Colette was fighting for her life.

Frederic was consumed with despair. He paced his chambers in broken misery, as impotent to fight his wife's infirmity as he was powerless to heal himself. The heavy thump of one boot, the crisp click of the cane, and the sad scrape of his lame leg, could be heard without, again and again and again… He had left Colette's bedside only a short while ago, but Robert's hushed words continued to haunt him: "I fear she is dying, Frederic. All we can do now is pray."

Dear God, it couldn't be so! She was too young, too beautiful, so full of life. *No*, he admitted to himself in sour self-contempt, *the last hadn't been true for a very long time*, not since the day he had shackled her to him with manacles of guilt. The flashing-eyed wench grew into a reserved lady. Sorrow and defeat had snuffed out laughter and fire, her once brilliantly blue eyes now smoky-gray. He was about to lose her more surely than he had all those years ago, and it was his own fault. She didn't want to live, for he'd seen to it that her life was not worth living. Sadly, there was nothing he could do at this late hour but pace and pray.

The house shook beneath the violent storm. The door banged open and was swiftly slammed shut, a mock echo of the tempest. Drenched, Paul mopped the hair from his eyes, doffed his saturated mantel, and handed it to Travis.

"How was your trip, sir?" the manservant asked.

"Fine – fine!" Paul snapped. "What the hell is going on around here? I return after three and a half months abroad to find the island in chaos. George is nowhere to be found. Jake Watson and Harold Browning are tight-lipped as to his whereabouts, and only Wade Remmen is man enough to suggest that he's left Charmantes altogether. But that's insane! To make matters worse, we're in the middle of a raging thunderstorm with little of the island secured."

"Certainly it is nothing to fret over, sir," Travis placated, "after all, it's not yet hurricane season."

Paul snorted. "Why did I expect things to run smoothly in my absence?"

"The house has been in turmoil over the past two days," Travis attempted to explain, his voice taut. "Miss Colette is dreadfully ill. Doctor Blackford has been in constant attendance and allows no one to enter her chambers without his authorization. Even Mrs. Ward is beside herself with worry."

Paul's irritability vanished. The butler's manner left little doubt to the gravity of the situation. "My father–" he demanded urgently "–does he know?"

"Everyone knows, sir, and everyone is praying, most especially the children."

The children, Paul thought. They'd be devastated if anything happened to their mother. Unbidden came thoughts of Charmaine, but he shook off the profane musings. The dampness was seeping in. "I'm in need of a bath and a change of clothing. After I've eaten, I'd like to see my father."

"Yes, sir," Travis nodded eagerly, glad to be put to work. "I'll have Joseph draw the water, and I'll tell Fatima to prepare you a tray of food. Then I'll let your father know you are home."

Paul was halfway up the stairs before he remembered the first news that had accosted him when he'd set foot on Charmantes. "Travis, where *is* George?"

"He left three days ago on the Rogue, sir."

"*What?* Why?"

Travis recalled George's instructions: *Tell Paul or Frederic only if they ask*, and quickly relayed the message, "Miss Colette asked him to deliver a letter to Virginia–"

"*Jesus Christ Almighty! Has he gone mad?* Does my father know?"

"No sir, he never asked me."

"God Almighty," Paul cursed again as the impending scenario played out before him. George's absence would create many managerial problems over the course of the next few weeks, especially progress on Espoir; however, thoughts of George's desertion were far from pertinent in light of the greater disaster awaiting them all. Paul rubbed his throbbing forehead, but the pain only intensified.

He considered Colette. She must be contemplating death if she sent George on such a mission. *But why?* What would it gain her, save pain and havoc for everyone concerned? Ultimately, it threatened the collapse of this faltering fortress – on their heads. Paul shuddered.

Charmaine attempted to amuse the children, but their minds were far from the game of hide-and-seek she had suggested they play. "Come away from the door, Jeannette," she pleaded. "Your father will call us when your mother awakens."

"He said that yesterday, but still we weren't allowed to see her."

"And the day before, we only saw her for ten minutes!" Yvette chimed in.

Charmaine sighed, at a loss for encouraging words. "Yes, I know, but still, we must wait. If your mother needs rest, it's best we don't disturb her. You want to see her completely well again, don't you?"

Jeannette nodded in resignation, but Yvette was not so inclined. "We've been told that over and over and over again! I'll wager Father never comes today. He's so worried, he's forgotten about us."

Jeannette's eyes filled with tears. "Do you think that's true, Mademoiselle Charmaine? Papa promised we would see Mama today."

"I wanna see her, too!" Pierre began to cry, crawling from beneath the bed, where he'd been hiding. "I miss Mama. When are we gowin' to her room?"

Charmaine picked him up and sat on his bed. "Now listen to me," she said. "I know that Doctor Blackford and your father are doing all they can to make your mother better; therefore, we must heed their advice. But, if your mother asks to see you – which I'm certain she will – you'll not be forgotten, will you?" When they shook their heads 'no' and Pierre's tears subsided, she continued. "We must be patient. All right?" They nodded.

Colette's chest pulsated with pain, her breathing shallow as if the weight of the world pressed down on it. Hot one moment and cold the next, she quaked beneath dampened bed clothing, changed not an hour ago, yet already saturated with perspiration. Still, she fought valiantly, her eyes snapping open when a cool cloth was placed to her burning brow.

"Ssh…" Rose Richards whispered, "lie still… don't try to talk."

Colette sighed. The old woman had been so good to her, more of a mother than her own mother had ever been, and she felt comforted. Time wore on, and Rose continued to apply the compresses.

"Try to sleep, Colette," Rose encouraged, "a nice, deep sleep."

The words had the opposite effect; Colette's eyes opened again. "Nan–"

"Ssh…" she admonished. "Save your strength. There's no need to talk."

Colette licked her cracked lips. "Nan," she pressed weakly. "I need to know… did George…"

"Yes, child," Rose soothed. "He left Charmantes days ago. He will deliver your letter. Now, lie back and rest. You must close your eyes and rest."

"It's important… so important…"

"Yes, yes, I know."

"No!" she argued, alarmed by the thread of pacification she heard in the old woman's voice, struggling now to sit up. "I'm not trying to make more trouble."

"Colette, you've never made trouble, and the letter *is* in George's hands. It *will* be delivered. Lie back and sleep."

Drained, yet satisfied, Colette relaxed into the pillows and closed her eyes.

"What the deuce…?"

Robert Blackford was livid as he took in the French doors thrown wide to the raging storm and the cold compress Rose Richards was applying to the brow of his flushed patient. "I thought I told you the woman is in my care!"

Rose met fire with fire. "My remedies may seem old-fashioned to you, Robert, but they will do Colette more good than this contaminated room."

"Woman, you are mad! I tell you now, I've tried *everything*, even cupping."

Rose's mind raced. "Surely you haven't bled her!"

"Of course not! She's too weak to withstand that absurd treatment. But your concoctions are not helping her either. You'd best take out your rosary beads and visit the chapel. That will be the best home remedy you can practice today."

Rose paled with the baleful declaration, and Robert's anger ebbed. "I'm sorry," he muttered bleakly. "I'm at a loss as to what do to do for her."

Rose had only seen him like this once before – the night his sister had died – and the memory filled her with dread. "Surely she'll recover."

"The congestion in her lungs is not the only complication threatening her life. But that is a matter between Colette, Frederic, and the priest."

"Father Benito?" Rose asked, her alarm multiplying two-fold.

Robert nodded solemnly. "She asked for him this morning. He's come and gone only an hour ago. Perhaps he has left her with some measure of peace."

Peace? There was no peace in Colette's contorted face. Her serene smile had been stolen away, her beauty supplanted by hollow eyes and protruding cheekbones that cut harshly into her once angelic visage.

"Come, Rose," the physician cajoled. "She's sleeping now. At present, there is nothing you can do for her. Go, say your prayers. This family needs them."

Rose left the room, a morose nod given to Agatha as they passed on the chamber's threshold.

"Papa, can we see Mama now?" Jeannette implored.

Frederic limped into the nursery. "She is sleeping, Princess, but I will take you to her room once she awakens. I told Doctor Blackford I would be here," he continued, reading Yvette's stormy countenance. "When he calls for me, you may come, too, if that pleases you."

They nodded optimistically.

"What have you been studying today?" he asked, quickly changing the subject. "Perhaps I can help Miss Ryan with your lessons."

For the first time, Charmaine was pleased that Frederic had come to visit.

He must be with Colette, Paul thought when he found his father's chambers empty. He knocked on the adjoining door. Agatha opened it.

"Paul," she exclaimed, stepping forward to hug him, "you're home!"

He suffered the unexpected greeting as she drew him into the room. "Where is my father?"

"I don't know. I thought he was in his apartments."

"How is Colette?"

Her manner turned lugubrious. "Not well, I'm afraid. Not well at all."

"May I see her?"

"I don't think that's wise. Robert is with her now–"

"I'd like to see her," Paul stated.

He crossed the room and opened the bedroom door, ignoring her objections, and reached the foot of the bed just as Robert glanced around. "I must ask you to leave," the man ordered sharply, "she is not well enough to receive visitors."

Paul was not listening, his face a mask of horror as he looked down at Colette. Her eyes were closed, and he was grateful for that, fearing what they might tell him if they opened. Then they were open, and he nearly cried as she attempted to smile. "Good God, Colette," he muttered impulsively.

"Do I look that awful?"

A spasmodic, racking cough erupted from her lame laugh.

"Out!" Robert commanded, "I want you out of here! You're upsetting her!"

"No!" she begged. "Please–" Before she could finish, she was coughing again.

"I said, you're upsetting her!"

Paul was hearing none of Robert's fulminating nonsense. He rounded the far side of the bed and attempted to help Colette sit up to catch her breath. She burned beneath his touch.

"I'm all right now," she finally whispered. "I'd just like a drink."

"Paul, you must leave!"

"Get her a goddamn drink!" Paul barked.

Agatha scurried to the pitcher and poured a glass of water, bringing it to him. Colette swallowed only a sip before collapsing back into the pillows. Beads of perspiration dotted her brow, and Paul wiped them away.

"Thank you," she breathed, clearing her throat.

"Can I get you anything else?"

"The children… Robert refuses… but I want to see my children…"

Paul nodded. "Then you shall."

As he returned to the sitting room, Robert was right on his heels, closing the door between the two chambers. "You cannot mean to bring them here. She doesn't have the strength–"

"What kind of physician are you, anyway?" Paul growled, facing him. "She's been under your care for nearly a year now and look at her!" Receiving no answer, he snorted in disgust. "Stay out of my way!"

"This is not my fault!" Blackford rallied, calling to his back. "She has pneumonia. Your little governess took her on a picnic in the pouring rain. She caught a chill, and her lungs have filled with mucus. She's been fighting this newest malady for a full month now."

Paul rounded on him, but his ire flagged as swiftly as it had spiked. He shook his head and left the room.

"One moment, Yvette!" Charmaine reproved as she opened the door.

"Miss Ryan," Paul greeted, her lovely face erasing the memory of Colette's ghastly visage.

"Paul!" she exclaimed, glad beyond words.

At the mention of his name, everyone in the room perked up, and even Frederic brightened, releasing Pierre who had been sitting in his lap. "Come in, please come in," she invited. "When did you arrive home?"

"An hour ago," he answered, ruffling Pierre's hair and hugging Jeannette who had scampered over to greet him.

Yvette remained next to her father, who sat at her desk. "Mama is very ill," she informed him, as if that were the only thing that mattered now.

"Yes, I know. She's been asking for you. Would you like to see her?"

"Oh yes!" they answered in unison.

"But–" he admonished "–she has a high fever. You mustn't force her to talk, and you may stay only a short time. Do you understand?"

They nodded.

He had just lifted Pierre into his arms when Agatha appeared in the doorway, her face ashen. "It is time. Robert fears it is time."

Death… it hung in the room with a life of its own. The gathered assembly could feel it – smell it – taste it. There was no escaping the sound of it: Colette's labored wheezing, the dogged coughing, and now the whimpers of her loved ones. Charmaine closed her eyes to the telltale finale. *Why in heaven's name did I bring the children here?*

In the throes of her extremity, Colette's unique beauty was only a memory, scarred by the unholy battle she had fought: hooded eyes sunken, lips chafed raw, sallow complexion drawn over skeletal cheeks, lovely hair matted and coarse.

Yvette embraced the truth first, bravely inching closer, silent tears trickling down her cheeks. "Mama, I'm here," she said, taking her hand.

Colette attempted to smile up at her.

Jeannette followed, falling to her knees beside the bed. When Colette closed her eyes, she buried her face in the bed linen and wept.

"Don't cry," Colette beseeched, mustering the strength to stroke her daughter's hair. "I'm happy–" The remark hung unfinished as she suffered through another fitful cough.

Blackford sidestepped Paul, who stood sentry against interference. "The children have had their time," he directed, reaching the bed. "This visit is upsetting everyone, specifically Colette. No good will come of it."

It was true, but Paul couldn't ignore Colette's tormented entreaty of: "No! Please! A moment longer…" He passed Pierre to Charmaine, then pulled Robert aside. "I want you to stay," Colette was saying, her voice low and raspy.

"We will, Mama," Yvette whispered, fighting the fire in her throat. "We'll stay as long as you like."

Colette considered Jeannette again, the child's sobs increasing. "Sweetheart, you mustn't cry…"

"I – I can't help it!" Jeannette gasped. "You can't die! I – I – won't let you die! I love you too much!" She rose from her knees, leaned across the bed, and wrapped her arms around her mother, as if she could squeeze the demon of death from her.

Charmaine's embrace quickened around Pierre. His whimpers had intensified, yet, she took succor from him, grateful to have someone to hold. She pressed his head to her bosom and shielded him from the avalanche of grief.

Rose stepped out of the shadows and bent over Jeannette. "Come, Darling," she comforted, separating the girl from Colette, "say goodbye to your mother."

"No!" Jeannette cried, struggling to be free. "I won't leave her!"

Colette broke into another rattling cough, unable to catch her breath this time, the convulsion worse than the others.

Robert rushed forward again, pulling her upright and striking her back until the spasm subsided. "She cannot withstand this strain!" he remonstrated sharply, his accusatory gaze leveled on Jeannette, who'd retreated, terror-stricken, to the edge of the bed.

"I'm all right," Colette panted, sucking in shallow pockets of air.

"Come, Jeannette," Rose cajoled, gathering her in tender arms, "your mother must rest. Give her a kiss."

Jeannette finally obeyed, her lips lingering on her mother's cheek. "Mama?" Colette's hand found hers. "I love you Mama! I will always love you."

"And I love you!" Colette murmured, her grip tightening momentarily before falling away.

Jeannette abruptly stood and tore from the room, never looking back.

Paul followed.

Yvette stood fast, her eyes fixed on her mother, aware that Rose had come round to her side of the bed. "Mama? You'll be all right without me?"

Colette shook her head slightly. "I won't be without you. I'll always be here… in this house… with you, Yvette." She cleared her throat. "Yvette… you'll take care of your brother and sister for me? You're very strong. Promise me… promise me that you'll always stay together."

"I promise, Mama. Don't worry about them."

Satisfied, Colette beckoned for a final embrace, her arms like dead-weights as they closed over Yvette's shoulders.

"Goodbye, Mama," Yvette choked out. "I love you!" With a swift kiss, she broke free and fled.

Colette turned her head aside and, unmindful of the doctor's reprimands, wept. Her anguish spiraled when she realized Rose and Charmaine were leaving as well. "Please!" she gasped, her voice barely audible. "Please… my son… I want to hold my son."

No one seemed to hear. Robert was wiping her brow, and Agatha was whispering in his ear. The governess was leaving, and she had not kissed her son goodbye. "Please!" she called out desperately.

As Charmaine reached the doorway, Frederic detained her, allowing only Rose to pass. "My wife wants to see Pierre," he said, nodding toward the bed.

Slowly, Charmaine turned back into the room.

"Pierre," Colette sighed, reaching out feebly. "Pierre," she called again, smiling weakly when Charmaine sat him on the bed.

Her joy was swiftly snuffed out. The three-year-old was terrified and wanted nothing to do with her, moaning loudly as she caressed his head. He clambered to the edge of the mattress, reaching for Charmaine.

The woman in this bed was not his mother. His mama was gentle and beautiful, not ravaged and worn. He pulled himself to his knees and buried his face in Charmaine's skirts.

Colette closed her eyes to sorrow. When she opened them again, they held the light of resignation. "Charmaine," she breathed, hand extended.

Charmaine grabbed hold quickly and squeezed Colette's fingers.

"You'll… you'll take care of him?"

"You needn't worry. Colette. I'll take good care of Pierre and the girls."

"And… you'll give him… all the love he needs."

"Yes, Colette. I shall love him as if he were my own. Now, please, don't try to speak anymore. Please rest."

"But him!" Colette struggled anew, as if Charmaine hadn't understood. Frantically, she grasped at Pierre in an attempt to reach his governess. "He needs you the most… because he's the most vulnerable… and I wasn't able to give him… what he–"

"Pierre will be fine," Charmaine promised, lifting him clear off the bed, chasing away her tears with the back of one hand.

Colette nodded and, drained, closed her eyes again.

"Goodbye, Colette," she forced out, returning Pierre's tenacious hug. "Thank you for all you've given me, my dear, *dear* friend."

Colette heard the earnest declaration, took it to her heart. *Love him*, she prayed again.

The door closed softly behind Charmaine, leaving only three to their grim vigil. Frederic's deep voice shattered the solemnity. "Leave us."

Robert faced him. "Frederic, there is little time for that now."

"Leave us, man, and leave us now. I will give my wife everything she needs. Now clear out!"

The physician's mouth clamped shut. In less than a minute, he and his sister were gone, the bedroom suddenly empty. Empty – so cruel in its irony. Would his heart always brim with grief when he felt most empty? He had made it so.

It was a long time before Colette's children slipped into the oblivion of sleep. Paul and Rose attempted to console them, and Rose finally succeeded in getting Pierre to close his eyes. But in the end, Charmaine's gentleness dried the girls' tears. When Paul and Rose departed, they spoke for a long time. Charmaine had, after all, lost her own mother. But she refused to listen to talk of death. "Your mother is sleeping just down the hallway," she insisted. "We're not giving up hope. Let us say our prayers. Let us pray to St. Jude. Miracles can happen."

When they were finally asleep, Charmaine made her way down to the drawing room, something she hadn't done for a very long time. She was happy to find Paul there, even though he was discussing Colette's condition with Agatha, Robert, and Rose. As she entered the parlor, Agatha threw her a nasty look, but Paul welcomed her into their company.

"As I was saying," the doctor continued, "any strength Colette possessed deteriorated long before the pneumonia set in. She was, and still is, ill equipped to fight such a malady. The next twenty-four hours should tell the tale."

"Meaning?" Paul bit out.

"If she can hold on until the fever breaks, she may have a chance."

"Is there nothing you can give her in the interim?"

"Unfortunately, she has eaten little and has vomited the rest, including my strongest compounds." Blackford shook his head. "No, she must fight this on her own. Now, if you'll excuse me, I must see–"

Paul grabbed hold of his arm. "Robert, my father is with her. Give them some time alone."

The doctor looked down at the hand that waylaid him and abruptly pulled away. "An hour – I'll give him one hour." With that, he was gone.

"Paul," Agatha began, "Robert has tried, really, he has. I can attest to the hours he's passed over Colette's bedside. He's forfeited his other patients just to be here, round the clock."

"I'm sure," Paul grumbled, rubbing the back of his neck.

"Agatha is right," Rose interjected. "Robert has done everything in his power to combat this illness."

"It's my fault," Charmaine added, guilt-ridden over the part she had played. "Colette was feeling better a month ago, and I suggested a picnic. If we had arrived home before the rainstorm, she would never have caught a chill."

"Exactly!" Agatha piped in disdainfully. "It is beyond my comprehension that an *educated* person would coerce a frail woman into traipsing far from her home in the first place."

"Coerce?" Paul replied. "Come, Agatha, if Colette didn't feel well enough to go on this picnic, she would have had the good sense to stay home. As for Charmaine, how could she have predicted inclement weather? No one is to blame here. I'm just trying to determine if something else can be done. Colette is a young woman with three children who will be devastated if she–" He feared finishing the thought.

Insulted, Agatha left the room.

Paul turned to Rose. "I've more faith in your remedies than all of Robert's prescriptions combined. If you will consider passing the night at Colette's bedside, I will tell him not to step foot in that room unless he is summoned."

"I'm at a loss," she confided woefully, "but I would be pleased to sit beside Colette for as long as I am permitted."

Paul nodded, then watched her leave.

Charmaine regarded him. She'd so looked forward to his return, felt terrible that he'd come home to heartache. "It has been miserable here without you."

In spite of himself, he smiled. "I guess that means you missed me."

"I *did* miss you. It was as if disaster befell Colette the moment you left."

"She hasn't been ill all that time, has she?"

"She's never been truly well," Charmaine insisted. "After Christmas her health continued to decline. Doctor Blackford's biweekly visits became every other day visits. Some days, she'd seem improved, but when we grew hopeful, she'd have another relapse. Then she contracted this 'pneumonia'. After that, Doctor Blackford was here nearly every day. It has been a terrible ordeal, as much for the children as for Colette."

"At least they have you, Charmaine. Colette is a wise woman. She was right about you."

Embarrassed, Charmaine lowered her eyes, but Paul pressed on. "I don't want you blaming yourself. Colette has been weak for a very long time. She should never have had Pierre…"

His words trailed off and he stared far into the distance – across time.

"I must check on the children," she said. "They've not been sleeping well."

Her voice drew him away from a multitude of disturbing thoughts. "Yes, and I had better find Robert. Tonight he will not disturb Colette with *his* educated ministrations."

Frederic mopped Colette's brow with the cool cloth.

Her eyes fluttered open. "You don't have to stay–"

"Yes, I do," he interrupted, his voice stern, but not harsh. "Close your eyes and rest, Colette."

But her gaze remained fixed on him as he turned back to the basin of water, her parched lips trembling when she spoke. "Promise – promise me you'll not send Charmaine away if I–"

Frederic's head jerked round, his severe regard stifling the ominous words.

"Please, Frederic... promise me," she finished instead.

"If you will close your eyes, I will promise you anything, Colette. Charmaine will always be welcome in this house, you needn't fear otherwise."

Allayed, her eyelids sagged shut.

With difficulty, Frederic dragged the heavy armchair close to the head of the bed. There he remained, continually changing the compresses as soon as they became warm, thankful when no one returned to steal away this private time.

After a while, the heat gave way to severe chills, and though Frederic thought she slept, Colette's eyes flew open, and she began to shiver uncontrollably. At a loss for what to do, he stood and walked round the bed, settling on the mattress. He drew her into his embrace and tucked the coverlet around her. Soon the warm cocoon relieved the violent shudders. Her cheek rested upon his chest, and slowly he felt her arm encircle his waist. He shifted, pulling her more tightly against him. As he stroked her hair, her rapid breathing grew easy and regular. He knew exactly when she had fallen asleep.

The minutes ticked by, and Frederic thought back on all they'd been through together, everything that had propelled them to this moment. He savored the scorching heat that radiated from her cheek, breasts, belly and legs, branding him through the clothing and healing his body with an infusion of pleasure.

The door creaked open, and Rose softly entered. Her eyes immediately fell on the couple. Frederic's finger came to his lips, warning her to remain silent. She nodded and withdrew to the sitting room, where she reclined on the settee. A great calm swept over her, and she wondered if maybe God had sent this egregious tribulation to rectify the pain that the family had suffered these past few years. For the first time in years, Rose entertained the possibility of *hope.*

Frederic, too, experienced an enormous surge of contentment. Kissing his wife's head, he pressed his own back into the pillows, closed his eyes, and slept.

Friday, April 7, 1837

Morning dawned glorious. The storm had washed Charmantes clean, and the mistress' suite reveled in the same redolent splendor. Colette was improved.

She woke to find her cheek pressed to her husband's chest and his arms encircling her. He was snoring, and she cherished the sound of it. Her nightgown clung to her, but she luxuriated in the warmth of his body and, with a soft cough, cuddled closer. The movement awoke him. Before he could speak, she hugged him. His embrace quickened in response. Then, he stroked her brow and caressed her cheek.

Cool to the touch. Frederic closed his eyes in silent prayer, thankful that God had listened to his supplication. He'd never waste another moment with this woman.

Someone knocked, and he attempted to move, but Colette held him fast. He smiled down at her, pleased when she shifted to look up at him.

"Tell whomever it is to go away," she whispered.

His fingers spanned her jaw, his thumb resting under her chin, nudging her head further back into his shoulder. Leaning forward, he tenderly kissed her parched lips. She was unhappy when he drew away.

"I'll not leave you again, ma fuyarde précieuse," he vowed, "not ever again."

She choked back tears, devouring the words 'my precious runaway', that special endearment that she had not heard for so many years.

Rose and Paul were at the door. "How is she?" they asked.

"Better," Frederic answered, "the fever broke during the night."

"Thank God."

Frederic nodded. "Rose, could you have Fatima prepare broth, something light? She hasn't eaten for days. And Paul, would you tell the children they might visit later in the morning? They went through a terrible ordeal last night."

"What about you?" Paul asked. "Don't you want to eat? Get some rest?"

Frederic shook his head. "I'm fine. I'm going to stay right here."

Paul's brow tipped upward, befuddled. His father should be tired, instead he was cheerful, energized, the aura emanating from him more than relief. Rose must have felt it, too, for as they left the mistress' quarters, she was humming.

Paul's thoughts rapidly turned to the other island. He'd be able to transport the bondsmen there today and get them settled, something he thought would have to wait.

Charmaine and the children were breakfasting when he delivered the miraculous news. The twins became animated and bubbly, already planning for the wondrous future. Charmaine's exuberance ebbed, however, when Paul mentioned spending the day and upcoming night on Espoir, insisting that he must take advantage of Colette's recovery and at least establish the new crew on the island. In his three-month absence, doom had reigned supreme. His return had chased it away. But now he was leaving again, and Charmaine feared the consequences of his desertion.

The arrival of Agatha and Robert in the dining room heightened her anxiety, their somber faces overshadowing the children's ebullience.

Paul leaned back in his chair and regarded them. "The fever broke," he informed them.

Blackford's brow rose in surprise. "And shall I commend Rose Richards for her nursing prowess?" he queried sarcastically.

"Actually, my father cared for Colette throughout the night," Paul replied. "Apparently, he was all she needed."

"I would warn against an early celebration," Robert rejoined. "We've seen her improve before, just to have our hopes dashed."

Paul's face hardened, aware of the children's interest in the matter. "She will recover *completely* this time, Robert," he threatened.

The doctor snorted. "What is being done for her this morning?"

"When I left, Gladys and Millie were drawing her a bath, and Fatima is preparing her something to eat."

"*A bath?* They are preparing her a bath? Have they gone mad? Even if the fever has abated, she could easily catch another chill and fall more gravely ill than before."

Paul shrugged. "It is what she requested."

Robert rubbed his brow before throwing his sister a beseeching look, as if no one in the house, save her, would support him. "The food," he continued, "I hope it is something light, like soup or broth?"

"I believe so. But you can check with Fatima."

Fatima scurried around the kitchen, preparing not one, but two trays. If the mistress was up to eating, so was the master, she told Rose.

Rose agreed and helped lay serviettes and utensils on the trays. "She's better, Robert," the elderly woman blithely announced as the physician and his sister entered the kitchen, "and ready to eat something."

"So I've heard."

He watched as the broth was ladled out, the toast buttered, and the coffee poured. "I'll take this one," he offered as he picked up Colette's tray of food. Fatima nodded and turned to ring for Anna or Felicia. "That won't be necessary," he said. "Agatha is coming with me. She can carry Frederic's tray."

Fatima held open the swinging door as sister and brother headed for the mistress' chambers.

Frederic ate most of the food laid before him. But Colette's tray would have to wait. His wife was in the middle of her bath, he informed Robert and Agatha, and when she was finished, *he* would make sure that she consumed something. Colette wanted to rest, *undisturbed.*

Again, Agatha bristled at the intended slight and sauntered toward the door. Robert, on the other hand, warned Frederic of the danger he was courting. "Her condition is fragile, Frederic. You and I both know she has had relapses before. As for this bath, it is sheer folly. Mark my words: her fever will return before day's end. If you are wise, you will insist that she eat and rest, nothing more."

Frederic nodded, but refused to speak.

"I will remain at the house," Blackford continued, "in case I am needed."

Supported on either side by Gladys and Millie, Colette stepped from the tepid tub water and walked the short distance to the armchair, where they helped her dress. Though she shivered, she was glad to be clean.

Millie began brushing out her hair, clicking her tongue in dismay as many golden strands were pulled free. "I fear this illness has damaged your hair, Miss Colette," she lamented, gaining her mother's immediate frown and swift shake of the head. The last thing Gladys needed was her mistress asking for a mirror and fretting over her cadaverous appearance. Colette needed happy words right now.

They had just finished changing the bed linens when Frederic rejoined his wife. Millie cast nervous eyes to the floor and curtseyed, but Gladys smiled. "I'll send Joseph in for the tub, sir," she said as she ushered her daughter from the room. "Will there be anything else, sir?"

"Would you bring the food tray in?"

She complied, then quickly departed.

Frederic turned loving eyes on Colette. "Fatima prepared something for you to eat. Do you think you could manage some broth?"

She nodded with smiling eyes. Her face was so very drawn, and yet today, it possessed a radiance he'd not seen for years. To Frederic, she was beautiful.

She took a small bite of toast and found even chewing an effort. When she reached for the spoon, her fingers refused to work. "My hands are numb," she complained.

Frederic drew a chair closer and took the utensil from her. "I never thought I'd live to see this day, Colette," he quipped, "or perhaps you'd have me believe that I'm the stronger one."

"We do make a pair," she jested with a chuckle. It only served to trigger another convulsive cough, which she struggled to subdue, exhausted by the time it had subsided. "I'm afraid it will be some time before I'm improved."

"You've improved already," he countered lightly. "No more talk of illness. We are going to nurse one another back to health."

He extended the first spoonful of broth to her lips, but the liquid had grown cold. The tray was sent back to the kitchen with Joseph, who had come in for the tub, with orders that the coffee and broth be reheated.

In the interim, Frederic encouraged Colette to enjoy the fresh air out on the veranda, and a chair was moved into the morning sun. It was there that the children found her.

"Mademoiselle Charmaine was right," Jeannette laughed, "miracles can happen! I'm going to say extra prayers to thank Jesus and Mary *and* St. Jude."

Frederic smiled at his daughters, happy for their happiness. He regarded Pierre, who sat on a bench next to his mother, content to let her stroke his hair. Today, he did not cry or pull away; today, he recognized the woman who leaned forward and kissed his head. Frederic would also thank God.

When Colette's tray of food arrived, Charmaine nudged her charges. "Come children, we have lessons, and it is important that your mother eat and rest so she recovers completely."

Their father concurred. "You may see your mother again tomorrow."

Pacified, they gave Colette one last kiss and scampered happily across the balcony and back to the nursery. Once again, Frederic proceeded to feed his wife. This time, the broth was hot and the coffee, heavenly.

"Now," he breathed as she finished the last few drops, surprised by how much she had actually eaten, "it is time you were back in bed, napping. I'll send Rose in to sit with you while I see to myself." When her eyes grew alarmed, he added, "I won't be gone for more than a half hour, and I promise, no pestering from Agatha or Robert today. I told them to stay far away earlier this morning."

"Thank you, Frederic."

He gently drew her out of the wing chair and into his arms. Her frail body was soft and feminine against him, evoking exquisite, scintillating sensations where the two met. For the first time in years, he kissed her as a man kisses a woman, the tender embrace blossoming into passion as his mouth opened hers and his tongue tasted its fill.

She grabbed hold of him to steady her reeling senses, intoxicated by the power, the smell, the feel, the very essence of him. Slowly, his lips traveled on, across her cheek and to her neck, where he buried his head in her hair and whispered endearments near her ear.

"I love you, Colette. I've always loved you."

Recalling the last time she had heard those words, she turned her face into his shirtfront and whimpered joyfully.

When she was back in bed, she remembered the letter she had written and wondered if she had done the right thing. A voice deep within her whispered that she had. She closed her eyes and fell into a peaceful sleep.

Frederic had barely finished dressing when an insistent knock resounded on his dressing room door. Travis opened the portal with an irritated frown, muttering something about patience. His wife stood there, ashen-faced. "It's Miss Colette! She's ill again!"

Robert Blackford was quickly summoned. Frederic was thankful the man had remained in the house, but he cursed himself for ignoring the physician's advice. Her fever raged anew, and now, she was vomiting with acute stomach cramps. *What had happened?* He knew: the bath, the food on an empty stomach, and her excursion from the bed.

Blackford attempted to give her a draught of elixir, but she expelled that right away, doubling over in agony. He stood, shook his head in trepidation, and glared contemptuously at Frederic.

Frederic was grateful that he didn't say, "I warned you."

Rose took up her post at Colette's bed, mopping her fiery brow with a cool cloth. Agatha demanded that Gladys wash the chamber pot, bring fresh linens, and draw cool water.

Frederic threw himself into the nearest armchair and buried his head in his hands. A relapse… how many times had she had them over the past year? Many, though none this severe. Still, she had had them. *Why then, had he tempted fate?*

The day drew on, and Colette remained violently ill, coughing and laboring to breathe. She didn't have the strength to sit up and needed help to lean forward when overcome with a wave of nausea. She became delirious, soiled the bed, and slipped in and out of a fitful slumber in which she uttered strange words and names.

Frederic forbade anyone to tell the children, and so, their afternoon passed by happily. But Charmaine began to worry when they took supper alone. No Rose, no Agatha, and no Robert Blackford, though she knew they were all in the house. If only Paul were home...

As twilight fell, a calm pervaded the infirm room. Colette's vomiting had subsided. Only the fever remained. Still, the two men and two women kept up their bedside vigil. When the clock tolled nine, Frederic broke the solemnity. "Robert, Agatha, Rose, why don't you three have supper and retire? Colette has been resting for some time now. If I need you, I will send Travis."

They nodded, knowing there was little more anyone could do, except wait and pray. Perhaps this night would be as kind as the last.

"If there is any change whatsoever – if she deteriorates or improves," Robert admonished, "I want to be called immediately. I will not abide any more of these old-fashioned remedies. She is my patient. I'm the one who will see her well again, God willing."

His heart heavy with guilt, Frederic nodded. "As you say, Robert."

When they were alone, he limped to the bed. This morning he'd felt whole; tonight, he was weary, crippled again. "Colette?" he queried softly, the mattress sagging under his weight. "Colette?" he called again, grasping her fiery hand.

She was awake, the glassy gaze now regarding him, revealing that she had heard every word. He was shaken by her scrutiny. It was as if she were trying to see into his heart, to know whether the last hours they had spent together had been real. Suddenly, he wanted her to see every fiber of his agony, and his eyes welled.

"I love you, too," she whispered.

He was astounded, and the ache in his breast ruptured. "Oh God, Colette, for so many years I've waited to hear those words. Why now?"

"I thought I hated you," she choked out. "Because of my injured pride, I wanted to hate you... I was a fool, Frederic. Later, when I knew, when I longed to tell you, I thought it was too late... I thought you despised me." She was crying, too, her eyes swimming with tears. "Frederic, I'm sorry. Can you forgive me?"

She struggled to reach his arm, the fist pressed against mouth, but her hand dropped away. He grabbed hold of it and drew her fingers to his lips. "Only if you can forgive me," he pleaded hoarsely.

"I did that a long time ago."

She yearned for him to hold her again, yet she knew she must broach the subject that could send him away forever. "John," she breathed, bravely forging forward, "he needs your love, even more than I do… I'm worried for you both, Frederic. I'm not going to get better. Please promise me–"

"Ssh," he said, placing a finger to her lips. "I love him as much as I love you, Colette. The past is over. Let us look to the future – together."

The hatred of yesterday was gone. Today, love finally prevailed, and for the first time in her life, she didn't fear tomorrow. Closing her eyes, a great calm washed over her. "Hold me tightly like you did last night," she entreated. "I want your arms around me again."

Frederic doffed his clothing and climbed into the bed. Like the night before, she was burning up with fever and shivered as a wave of cool air wafted beneath the blanket. Quickly, she nestled against him, caressing his chest, savoring the warmth of his body stretched full length next to hers, the strong arms that encircled her. He stroked her hair, her shoulders, her back as he kissed the top of her head again and again. She closed her eyes in unsurpassed happiness. *Is there any better way to leave this world?* she wondered with a prayer of thanksgiving. They fell into a peaceful slumber, one from which Colette never awoke.

Sunday,
April 9, 1837

Chapter 8

In a shower of spring brilliance and crystal-blue skies, Colette Duvoisin was laid to rest. As the sun climbed to its zenith, a throng of mourners left the manor's chapel and headed north to the estate's private cemetery, a gnarled, ill-kept plot of land populated with brambles, wild flowers, and stark, jutting headstones that reached heavenward. Here the morbid procession stopped, allowing the pallbearers room to lay their feather-light burden down on the cushioning briars. Then the circle closed around the pine coffin, the mourners drawing solace from one another as they awaited the closing eulogy.

Finality greater than death gripped them, an overwhelming loss that continued to intensify. Yesterday, they had walked in a daze. But today, the firmament illuminated the unfathomable truth, the mortal truth: Colette Duvoisin was dead, and no one – no private prayers, nor dreams of the past – would bring her back. She was gone from them forever, and many weeks would pass before the plethora of pain subsided.

The twins were unusually silent, their blue eyes spent of tears, their stoic stance belying the torture that Charmaine knew ravaged their hearts. Yesterday, those eyes had not been dry for more than a moment at a time, and poor little Pierre, too young to truly comprehend the finite event, was caught up in their acute remorse, sobbing over their distress. Today, Rose had remained behind with him, insisting that the cemetery was no place for a three-year-old and that she would visit it soon enough. But Colette's daughters were determined to join the procession, sitting ramrod straight throughout the entire funeral Mass, standing and following the pallbearers from the chapel without so much as a glance in anyone's direction, their eyes trained on the coffin that held the body of their beloved mother. Charmaine's breast ached for their terrible loss, all the more excruciating in her inability to comfort them.

She remembered Jeannette's innocent query when they received the devastating news. "What happened to our miracle, Mademoiselle Charmaine?"

"I know what happened!" Yvette burst out. "God was only pretending to hear our prayers! I'm never going to pray to Him *or* St. Jude ever again!"

"You don't mean that," Charmaine consoled. "It's your pain talking."

"I do mean it!" she shouted, erupting into tears. "I do!"

Charmaine had searched for words of solace, but they eluded her. She attempted to recall Father Michael Andrew's eulogy at her own mother's funeral, to no avail. Either her grief had been too profound to hear the priest's kind words or his remorse too great to impart them. She embraced Yvette instead and allowed her to cry into her skirts, stroking her hair until she was worn out and heaving. Jeannette wept next, and it was thus that they passed that first awful day.

Today, as Charmaine stood on the knoll, memories of her own mother's death besieged her. She relived the suffering of those first few days, her feelings of abject hopelessness. She had been older than the girls, an adult really. Yvette and Jeannette, on the other hand, were so young. How would they endure? Suddenly, Charmaine's prayers changed. She no longer offered them for Colette. The fair woman rested in heaven. Instead, Charmaine prayed for the twin sisters, that the weeks ahead would heal their hearts. Last night, they had cried out in their sleep for her, and that was a good sign. Charmaine would always be there for them, just as she had promised Colette.

As Father Benito St. Giovanni stepped forward, Charmaine surveyed the assembly that numbered nearly a hundred strong. It seemed the entire town, or at least its workers, had traveled the nine-mile distance to pay their final respects. As for those who lived and worked on the Duvoisin estate, only George and his grandmother were absent.

Again she puzzled over the man's whereabouts this past week and remembered Rose's words. "He's attending to an errand for Colette." *What did that mean?* Charmaine thought it wise not to ask. But just yesterday, she'd been privy to the whispered gossip coming from Felicia and Anna. "He's traveled to Virginia." *But why?* The answers would have to await his return.

Charmaine's gaze continued to travel from face to foreign face, alighting on two she recognized: Harold Browning and Wade Remmen. Slowly, warily, her eyes left the arc and settled for one uncomfortable moment upon the two men standing apart from the crowd.

Frederic shunned the large circle of mourners, leaning heavily on his black cane, dismissing the stalwart son who flanked his left side. Like his daughters, his heart was locked away. He had not emerged from his chambers since leaving his wife's deathbed, and Charmaine surmised that those quarters would once again become his prison. She was mistaken in believing that he'd come to console the children yesterday or this morning, for he refused to even look their way, his eyes trained on his wife's coffin. Charmaine sadly realized that his easy dismissal of the girls and Pierre was as much a punishment for himself as it would become for them. Their mutual sorrow and the comfort they could have drawn from each other might have been the start of healing, but such was not to be the case. Why, then, had he labored from chapel to graveyard, this man who wanted to brood alone, who wanted no one to console him, who rarely left his rooms, this effete man whose love of wife Charmaine had often doubted? Why had he taken up his place beside Colette's casket this morning? *Because he loved her... just as Colette had loved him.*

As the crowd pressed forward to better hear Father Benito's final benediction, Frederic held his ground, his eyes barren, the polar opposite of Friday, when they had visited Colette on the balcony. Instantly, Charmaine's heart was rent by another devastating thought: Colette's dreadful illness had drawn them together, ending their estrangement. How terribly tragic that love had come too late – that their eleventh hour affection had been laid to waste at the toll of twelve. No wonder Frederic wanted to mourn alone. He was damning the world, damning himself. Charmaine shuddered, though the April sun was quite warm. With growing alarm, she wondered where the mortal event would lead this already embittered man. Instinctively, she knew the days and weeks ahead would be bleak, more so than she had feared at the start of this dreadful day.

Late the next evening, Paul knocked on the nursery door. Charmaine, happy to finally have a moment alone with him, stepped out into the hallway.

"How are they?" he whispered.

"They're sleeping now, but I don't know for how long."

He studied her face compassionately. "How are you?"

"Better than the girls," she murmured.

"But you've been crying."

"For them. They're devastated, Paul. I don't know who's more upset, the girls or Pierre." Her voice grew raspier. "He doesn't understand why he can't go to see his mother and–"

Paul was not immune to her tears, and his eyes welled in response, but he hid the unmanly display behind the hand that he brought to his brow.

"They refuse to eat," she finally continued. "I'm at a loss as to what to do."

"There is nothing you can do, Charmaine. Give them time. They need to be sad for a while."

"Do you think your father would let them visit his chambers?" she asked hopefully. "I think he would be a comfort to them, and they to him."

"No," Paul replied, unsettled by the suggestion. "His grief is too great."

Though dissatisfied with his answer, she didn't press him. She needed to draw strength from someone. "At least you're here for them," she said instead.

He inhaled. "Actually – I have to leave for Espoir at dawn. I spent today getting the business on Charmantes in order, but I'm needed there. Until George returns, I'm extremely pressed. You do understand, don't you?"

"Yes, you're abandoning us again," she blurted out.

"That's a harsh statement," he objected, grimacing inwardly. "The lumber has been delivered, the foundation for the new house laid, and now, before the rains are upon us, I need to enclose the building. I've hired carpenters and contracted an architect, who can only remain in the Caribbean for a month. Aside from that, the men are awaiting work. I have to be there."

"You're right," she tried to agree. "It will be better for you to keep busy."

Her conciliatory sentiment cut more deeply than her accusatory one, and he found himself torn. "I promise to return by week's end. We can take the children on an outing together, lift their spirits."

"They should like that," she replied, forcing a smile.

"Good. Then it's a date."

The weekend came, but Paul never returned. Word was sent that a 'catastrophe' prevented him from leaving Espoir. He'd see them sometime during the following week. It was just as well. The girls were still grieving; they'd never have agreed to go anywhere.

Sunday, April 30, 1837

Colette had been dead for three weeks, and conditions in the manor had not improved, leastwise not where the children were concerned. The 'date' Paul had planned weeks ago had finally arrived, but the girls refused to participate, their remarks disdainful.

"If they do not want to go, don't force them," he rejoined curtly, annoyed that he'd suspended his grueling schedule specifically to be with them. A confrontation with his father earlier in the morning had set the mood for an aggravating day, and now he wished he hadn't returned at all.

Exasperated, Charmaine decided to leave them to lament. She and Pierre would accompany Paul into town, and maybe as they departed the grounds, the girls would change their minds. They didn't, and only Rose waved goodbye when the landau pulled away, promising to look in on the twins throughout the afternoon.

Unlike his sisters, Pierre was happy, recovered. Innocent of the grave event that had shaken the rest of the house, he showered Charmaine with the love he had once bestowed upon his mother and blew kisses to Nana Rose as he tried to lean further out the window of the conveyance and shout 'bye - bye'.

The closed carriage bobbed down the quiet road, but the silence within was not peaceful. Paul stared pensively out the window, his countenance dour.

Charmaine spoke first. "How is your father?"

He snorted, then rubbed the back of his neck. "Not well, I'm afraid. More despondent than my sisters, in fact. I think I made matters worse this morning."

"I don't see how," she commented derisively. "The children haven't seen him since the funeral. They've not only lost their mother, but their father as well."

"I'm afraid you're wrong, Charmaine. Matters *can* grow worse, much worse. My father has vowed to follow Colette to the grave," he whispered, fearful that Pierre might understand, "and I'm beside myself as to what to do."

Charmaine shuddered at the thought. "Perhaps he *should* see the children, see what he'd be leaving behind."

"Do you really want to put them through that, Charmaine?"

Again she shuddered, and the remainder of the ride passed in silence.

Charmaine was uncertain if it was Pierre's exuberance or the bustling town that finally brightened their moods, but the afternoon turned somewhat pleasant as they strolled along the boardwalks, greeting people they met, mostly Paul's acquaintances. They finally arrived at the mercantile where Madeline Thompson welcomed them. "My goodness, Pierre, how you've grown in just a month!"

The boy giggled and happily accepted the peppermint stick she offered him.

"Where are the girls?"

"I'm afraid they're still in mourning, Maddy," Paul explained.

The woman's eyes filled with tears. "Why don't you take them two sweets as well?" she offered, allowing Pierre to choose.

They browsed a bit. Charmaine kept returning to a bolt of yard goods and finally decided to purchase a length of the pretty fabric. "This might do the trick. Jeannette's taken quite an interest in sewing, and Yvette may perk up if I let her design her own frock."

Paul smiled down at her, glad that his sisters had Charmaine to fret over them. He refused to allow her to pay, telling Maddy to add the cost of the material to his monthly bill. He insisted that she select something for herself, but she dismissed the idea, telling Pierre to choose a toy instead.

Shortly afterward, they left the store. They'd been away from the house for little more than two hours, but when Paul asked, "Where to next?" he knew Charmaine had had enough of the town.

"I really should be getting back to check on the girls."

"You are a wonder, Miss Ryan," he said, white teeth flashing for the first time that day. She looked innocently up at him, and he had the impulse to kiss her right there in the middle of the thoroughfare for all eyes to see. But that would surely inhibit the friendship that was growing between them, a friendship similar to the one he had shared with Colette. His passionate bend was swept away. He scooped up Pierre instead, and together, they crossed the street.

They had just arrived at the livery when Buck Mathers hailed them down, out of breath. "They need you at the dock, Mastah Paul. There's a big problem."

Paul shook his head in vexation, but Charmaine soothed the situation. "You go ahead. We have a carriage and a driver. We can find our way home."

"I'll be there for dinner," he promised, setting Pierre to the ground.

Charmaine nodded, encouraging the three-year-old to wave as the two men rushed off.

Thursday, May 11, 1837

Charmaine massaged her throbbing temples and collapsed into the armchair. The evening air was silent, but not peacefully so. Not one sniffle wafted on the breeze, though the French doors were open in the adjoining room. The unknowing ear would assume the children slept, but she knew better, certain that at this very moment two sets of eyes stared dismally into space.

She hadn't meant to speak harshly to them, upsetting little Pierre in the process, but Yvette and Jeannette's depression – the drawn looks they wore – could no longer be borne. They consumed very little food, and the effect was haunting. They'd become miniature replicas of their mother in the days before her death and, from what Charmaine had heard whispered, imitators of their father. Time would heal them, everyone kept insisting, time and limitless love, yet these had yielded little solace. Even Rose seemed incapable of mitigating their grief.

The blessing of sisterhood was nothing of the kind, and the desolation they read in one another's faces was beginning to affect Pierre, who already cherished memories of his mother. Just tonight, they cruelly chastised him when he innocently called Charmaine 'Mama' instead of 'Mainie.' With bottom lip quivering, he ran to her, crying hysterically as he buried his face in her skirts.

It was the last straw. "Don't you think this sniveling has gone on long enough?" she struck out, furious. "Look what you've done, making Pierre feel guilty just because he's happy again. *Why?* Do you want to add to your mother's suffering?"

Yvette retaliated with: "Mama isn't suffering anymore – only we are!"

"You think not?" Charmaine countered. "You think she's found peace knowing that her children can't be happy without her? How can she even think about heaven when the two of you hold her bound to earth, imprisoned in this very room with your constant wails of self-pity?"

The plausible words sent Jeannette into tears. "You – you make it sound as if we shouldn't miss her – as if – as if we shouldn't cry for her!"

Charmaine's face softened, yet her voice remained hard. If a dose of severity were efficacious in getting them to talk to her, she'd lace her words with it. "You're not crying for your mother. You're crying for yourselves."

"What's wrong with that?" Yvette demanded.

"Not a thing, had it been a month ago or a few times each day. But you have been crying every hour of every day for too many days now. You're not even trying to accept the Good Lord's decision to take your Mama to paradise with Him. She should be at peace now, not worrying over you. But no, you've not thought of anyone but yourselves – not your brother, not your father, nor anyone else in this house who grieves as you do. Poor Mrs. Henderson, she's so upset that you won't touch the special treats she's prepared just for you, that you're withering away. And Nana Rose, she's known your mama longer than the two of you have, and have you hugged her even once? Or your brother Paul, who took time out of his busy schedule to spend the day with you and lift your spirits, but you cast him aside, making him feel terrible that he even attempted to console you. I'm ashamed of you! I really am. And what about me? Do you realize how difficult it's been for me to watch you like this?"

Charmaine sighed deeply, her voice growing irenic. "I understand your tears, and I know there will be many more over the months to come, *but not like this.* Right now, they've become a terrible burden to all of us. If you really miss your mother, if you truly want to make her happy, you'd best dry those eyes and start living. I'm certain that wherever you run, wherever you play, your mother will be watching from heaven. I'm equally certain that she'd enjoy seeing you smile a great deal more than she would seeing you cry."

The room fell silent. Surprisingly, neither offered a rebuttal.

Charmaine walked over to Pierre, pleased to find her lecture had lulled him to sleep. She crossed to the doorway and stopped. "You can't bring your mother back with tears," she concluded. "I wish you could, but you can't. She's been dead for over a month now, and during that month, you've ravaged her soul in much the same way her illness ravaged her body. It is time to show her how much you really love her. It is time to let go of your pain."

Now, minutes later, sitting alone in her bedroom, Charmaine wondered if they had listened or shut her out. Had she been too hard on them? Hurt them? Suddenly, she was angry with herself. Returning to the nursery, she was astonished to find them asleep. Maybe they had heard. Maybe God would answer her prayers this night.

Wednesday, May 17, 1837

Disgusted, Agatha Ward lifted the untouched tray of food and left the master's quarters. Frederic refused to eat, deciding two weeks ago that this was the easiest way to follow his wife to the grave. He had not wavered from his insane plan. Neither had he budged from the chair that faced Colette's bedchamber, as if she still lay on the other side of the connecting portal.

Starvation would be an ugly thing to witness, but Agatha would not allow him that final triumph. She'd arrest the situation before it was too late. To that end, she swiftly stepped in for Travis Thornfield, horrified to learn that ten days had already lapsed. The manservant, beside himself with worry, was only too happy to allow her to take charge.

That had been three days ago, three days of ineffectual empathizing, coaxing, reasoning, entreating, and finally, ranting. Agatha's thoughts raced to Paul, wishing him home. But even if the younger man were here, what could he do that she hadn't already tried? Nothing.

Frederic, refusing everything but water, was a wretched sight to behold, with a full fortnight's beard, disheveled hair, gaunt cheeks, and crazed eyes. His tailored clothing hung limp from his emaciated body. But his weakness was deceptive: cross the line, challenge his suicidal crusade, and his despondency evaporated like a drop of water in a scorching desert, replaced by a rabid fury that shook even his stalwart sister-in-law.

Tonight, Agatha would not be shaken or deterred. Tonight she would win this unholy war. She looked down at the tray once more, then back at the closed portal. If Frederic wanted to dwell on his dead wife, she would make him think again. The time had come to remind him exactly what type of woman Colette had been – to make him reconsider his misplaced affections. A drastic measure, perhaps, but dire circumstances called for merciless intervention.

Robert Blackford hastened to the Duvoisin estate and waited patiently in the drawing room as Travis went in search of his sister. He didn't need to be told why he'd been urgently summoned at so late an hour, though Agatha's swiftly penned note painted a gruesome picture. He'd heard of Frederic's 'grief' from any number of patients throughout the week; the entire island loved gossip, especially Duvoisin gossip. Apparently, Frederic was not adjusting to his wife's demise.

If the rumors were as bad as they sounded, present conditions threatened to eclipse those of the distant past. He chuckled with the irony of it. Even the players were the same, save the wives. A score and eight years ago, that role had been played by his younger sister, Elizabeth Blackford. Her death had shaken the great Frederic Duvoisin's sanity as surely as Colette's death did now. There had also been a child involved, an infant – John. Robert shuddered with the memory, and even today, wondered how Frederic had survived intact. He remembered fearing for his own life; Frederic had held him responsible for Elizabeth's death. But then, Robert blamed himself as well. True, the baby had been breech, a dangerous delivery at best, but he had needed her to live, his own happiness contingent upon her recovery. Yet, she slipped into unconsciousness and never awoke, and Frederic had never forgiven him.

But Elizabeth was not the problem this night, Colette was: A new time, a new event, and for all the mirrored circumstances, a new pain. There was Frederic's age to consider, as well. He was no longer a man of thirty-three, in the prime of life. He was over sixty and badly beaten by a harsh world. He was also intent upon giving up, bolstering the probability of success. Though the outcome should have pleased Robert, bringing the long and winding road to an end, he feared that Frederic's death would destroy Agatha. This compelled him to intercede. For his twin sister, he would put a stop to the man's self-destruction.

At the sound of the drawing room door opening, he pivoted around, placing under lock and key the painful decision he had just made. "Miss Ryan," he acknowledged in surprise, having expected a servant or his sister.

"Doctor Blackford," she nodded, equally surprised. She had not seen the man since Colette's death and wondered why he was here now.

"I suppose the children are abed?" he asked.

"Well over an hour ago," Charmaine answered. "It's quite late."

"So it is," he said, checking his pocket watch. He snapped it shut, replaced it, then considered her speculatively. Agatha held the girl both inadequate and insubordinate. Still, Robert wondered what information he might garner if he drew her out. "How *are* the children?"

Stunned, Charmaine canted her head. The man had never conversed with her before. "Better," she replied cautiously. "They've finally accepted their mother's passing, but as for their grief, it remains. They have not forgotten her."

"Nor should they. Nevertheless, you are to be congratulated on seeing them through this terrible time," he praised. "Agatha tells me you have worked wonders. If only I could be that effective when meeting with their father tonight."

Charmaine didn't require an explanation. Frederic had not emerged from his impenetrable quarters since Colette's death, and the rumors that he was starving himself had taken root. Thankfully, Jeannette had stopped asking to visit him. Charmaine didn't want the children exposed to that horror.

Agatha arrived and whisked Robert away. Feeling lonely, Charmaine rummaged through the music drawer and found the piece she was seeking. It was perfect for this night: why not a haunting melody to release the ghosts that trampled her soul? She propped the pages on the piano stand, arranged her skirts, and let her fingers sing.

Frederic remained slumped in the high-backed armchair, contemplating death and the ease with which it evaded him. A knock at the door, and his listlessness gave way to ire. *Damn them!* When would they accept his decision to die? Was he not master of this house? Why, then, was everyone hell-bent on stopping him? He *would* follow Colette into the next world, and those of this world be damned if they didn't like it!

He ignored the second rap, the third, and the fourth. But the persistent intruders would not retreat. After the fifth knock, they entered without permission. Now, sister and brother hovered nearby, assessing him as if he were not present. Robert stepped closer still, abruptly gripping the arms of his chair. He leaned over and looked him square in the face, willing his hooded eyes to lift in acknowledgement. "Frederic?" he demanded.

Frederic remained impassive, affording not the slightest indication that he'd heard, that he was aware of the 'visitors' who had come to converse with him.

Blackford straightened up and faced his sister, hands on hips.

"Didn't I tell you?" Agatha whispered as if she knew he was listening, yet not hushed enough to be inaudible. "He has been like this for the better part of two weeks – since Paul left for Espoir."

"And this will come to an end," Blackford snarled. "Frederic – look at me!"

Frederic tilted his head back and shot him a piercing glare.

The raw condemnation shook Robert. "That's better," he muttered, nervously adjusting his waistcoat. He dragged a chair even with Frederic, sat, and forced himself to meet the enraged gaze levelly. With Agatha standing behind him, he could do this. "It is time we talked," he began. "This foolishness stops tonight. Colette is dead, and nothing can change that. You, on the other hand, are very much alive. To convince yourself otherwise is sheer lunacy."

The declaration elicited no reply, and though the eyes remained stormy, Robert began doubting the man's coherency. "Frederic – are you listening to me?" he pressed. "Do you understand what I'm trying to tell you? You cannot go on like this! Surely you don't intend to meet such an end?" Still no response, just the branding eyes. "I tell you now man, I won't permit it!" he threatened. "Even if I have to order you held down and force fed, you will not die of starvation! *Do you hear me?*"

"The *good* doctor come to save my life," Frederic remarked, his deep voice raspy, as if he worked hard at speaking. But for all his difficulty, the chilling statement was not lost on brother and sister, who were taken aback by the sudden and most unexpected reply.

"Yes," Blackford reaffirmed as he squirmed in his chair, "if need be."

Frederic grunted. "I desire death, and you, *dear friend*, come to interfere?"

The query was a slap in the face. "You don't know what you are about!" Robert railed, reflecting on the countless services he had performed for this man for the better part of thirty years. "You are mad if you think that the afterlife is going to reward you with what you desire!"

"*What I desire?*" Frederic thundered. "*What I desire?* I'll tell you what I desire. I desire what you've taken from me! Not once, but twice!"

Blackford bristled. The man *did* blame him! "I've taken nothing from you," he answered softly.

"Haven't you?" Frederic sneered through parched lips. "Elizabeth wasn't enough–"

"There was nothing I could do!" Blackford expostulated, losing his composure. "John's was a breech birth and he – *he alone* stole Elizabeth's life. I thought you comprehended the severity of that delivery!"

Frederic's eyes grew baleful. "Leave me alone. I don't want to hear your excuses. I accepted them once, but never again." He bowed his throbbing head and grumbled, "You cannot explain away Colette's death so easily."

"And I refuse to be blamed again for a situation that was out of my control!"

Frederic's head snapped up. "*Out of your control, man?* She was under your constant care for nearly a year! How, in God's name, did the situation get out of your control? And don't talk to me about this fancy condition you call 'pneumonia'! If it was as deadly as you knew it to be, it should have been arrested in its infancy. You were by her bedside for weeks! So tell me *doctor* – how do you have the gall to stand there and insist that the situation was 'out of your control'?"

"Because it was," Robert bit out malignantly. "Colette did not die of *pneumonia*, though it did contribute to her weakness. I told you years ago: *No more children.* Delivering twins was too much for her. But did you listen? No, you pressed yourself on her and she found herself carrying Pierre."

Frederic's jaw grew rigid, but Robert callously continued. "Again, another strain, yet you were lucky, and she survived. But she did not recover unscathed. Last spring, you almost lost her; the most minor illness can easily take hold. And that is exactly what happened with the pneumonia. But there's more, Frederic. Not one week after she contracted that infirmity, she suffered a miscarriage."

Frederic inhaled sharply, and Robert fed on the man's horrified expression, his courage suddenly limitless. "That's right – a miscarriage. Her weakened constitution made it impossible to carry the baby to term, and for days, I was unable to stem the bleeding. That bath was the worst thing for her. I warned her. She knew the risks."

Then the shock was gone, supplanted by a demonic rage that brought Frederic up and out of his chair like a man possessed.

Robert did not cower or gloat, his gaunt visage merely compassionate now.

Frederic halted in his tracks, revolted by the man's show of pity. "You realize what you are inferring?"

"I realize what I have withheld from you," Blackford answered flatly.

"*By God, why?*" he exploded, his cane sweeping across a nearby table and swiping it clean. The childish tantrum only incensed him further. "Why was this information withheld? *Why*?"

Robert came to his own feet, feeling at a disadvantage while the fulminating man towered above him. "I knew the child could not be yours," he admitted freely, "and in Colette's best interest, I did as she requested. I held silent."

Frederic felt a wave of nausea rising in the back of his throat. He swallowed it, focusing instead on the questions he must ask. "And after her death? Why didn't you tell me then?"

"I feared for *your* well-being. What good would it do, except to put you through the turmoil you now suffer? I had hoped to spare you that."

"When – when did she conceive?"

"Before Christmastide – perhaps November," Blackford answered coolly, "judging by the baby's size."

Frederic glared at him – Agatha next – but found nothing in their faces to refute the brand of infidelity. "Get out," he snarled.

Robert faltered, his sorrowful eyes questioning the edict.

"You heard me, man! The two of you, *out!* I won't be deterred by a lie!"

Agatha stepped forward beseechingly. "Frederic, you are torturing yourself, but this will never do. You have three children to consider. They need you, and I think you need them. Colette..." she paused, carefully choosing her words "*...was not Elizabeth.* Yes, I know what you saw in her, the many similarities. I saw them too!" She breathed deeply, reading Frederic's stunned surprise, pleased to know that she was getting somewhere. "It was only natural that you were attracted to her. You thought of Colette as your second chance. *But she was not Elizabeth!* Elizabeth was a good and decent person, a faithful wife. *Elizabeth* loved you. But Colette, she never loved you as–"

"I've heard enough! I've made my decision – will see it to its end."

Robert just shook his head. "Very well, Frederic. Think what you will. Believe that we are mendacious villains. But while you sit in your chair and contemplate what I've told you, remember that in discrediting me, you've danced to the tune Colette has piped. Not many a man would mourn a woman who has cuckolded him in his own home, under his very nose."

"Get out!" Frederic hissed, spitting venom at the man who had completely overstepped his bounds. "Get out, or I'll have you thrown out!"

Robert relented and, with his sister close behind, left the tortured man. Frederic would have to make up his own mind.

Frederic had been alone for all of five minutes, yet that short space of time seemed an eternity, an eternity to ponder that one word: betrayal. He'd been betrayed, not once, but again and again! This last time, the worst of all! How had she lain in his arms those last two nights of her life, pretending at love, uttering precious words that were nothing more than another lie? How he would love to hold her again, for he'd take great pleasure in squeezing that life from her with his bare hands! Yes, his thoughts were murderous, and he wanted to murder, longed to taste its satisfying, bittersweet flavor.

He had mourned her for weeks, cursed himself for the hell he had created for the both of them. Now he laughed with the ironic insanity of it! He was the only one who had suffered, while she surreptitiously crept from her rooms in the middle of the night to seek solace in the arms of another. He'd been a fool – even in that last month, when he had been beside himself with worry. He remembered that one night when he'd gone to check on her. She wasn't resting as Blackford had ordered, and *she wasn't with the children!* Again the cane slammed down on the table with a violent crack. He knew where she'd been; the question was, *with whom?*

How she must be laughing! She had slyly made him feel guilty. Well, no more! She had been the cause of his misery for nearly ten long years – a whore today, a whore since the day they'd met and all those days in between! Agatha was right: he'd hoped to replace Elizabeth with a snip of a girl who stirred sweet memories. But she was not Elizabeth! She was a highborn slut that had connived and nearly destroyed his family.

Once again the bile rose in his throat, and as he heaved into the chamber pot, spewing the bitter acid that ate away at his soul, he hated more fiercely than ever before.

No one answered the bell-pull. With clenched jaw, he forfeited a third yank and savagely pulled open the hallway door. He limped from his prison, surprised when the foyer clock tolled ten. But the late hour did not deter him, and he nearly bumped into Millie Thornfield as he reached the staircase.

The maid stifled a shriek, a hand flying to her mouth. "May I help you, sir?"

"Where is your father?" he demanded, leaning heavily on his cane, bone weary and irked by the girl's gawking.

Millie hesitated, shaken by the master's maniacal eyes. She didn't know her father's whereabouts, but didn't dare say so. "I'll – I'll find him, sir," she quickly replied.

"When you do, have him summon Benito Giovanni to the house. Immediately!"

"Father Benito?"

"You heard me girl! Now be about it! You are wasting precious time!"

She bobbed before him, then raced down the stairs. But just when she thought she was safe, his voice halted her. Looking up, she awaited a possible countermand. But he stood deathly still, head cocked to one side, eyes staring into space as he registered the strains of the melody that carried from the drawing room. "Sir?" she incautiously interrupted. "Was there something else?"

"Where is that music coming from?"

"From the front parlor, sir. Miss Ryan has been practicing that piece all evening, sir."

"Well, tell her to stop practicing it! Tell her to destroy it!"

"Sir?" Millie queried in renewed consternation.

"Tell her that I *forbid* her to play it. Tell her that if I hear so much as one note of that particular piece again, she will be dismissed. *Go! Tell her!"*

He is mad! Millie chanced one last look at the man. In a flurry of skirts, she scrambled down the remaining stairs and fled the foyer. Moments later, the haunting melody ceased and silence blanketed the great house.

Father Benito St. Giovanni was rudely awoken at the ungodly hour of eleven. The pummeling of a fist on his cabin door brought him up and out of bed. In less than an hour, the priest, who owed his life to both John and Paul Duvoisin, stood before their notorious father. Aware of Frederic's suicidal fast, he had expected to find the man near death. Not so. Why, then, had he been summoned? Frederic's stormy eyes cued him that the reason was not pleasant. Thus, he bowed his head slightly and waited for Frederic to speak.

"Now, Father," the patriarch of Charmantes began, taking one long draw off a tall glass of brandy, relishing the fiery path it blazed down his throat. It hadn't dulled his senses or eased his anguish. So much the better; it fueled his wrath and kept him focused. "I want a name, and I want it now."

Benito frowned slightly, but wisely held his tongue, forcing the tormented man to expound.

Frederic leaned back in his chair, bemused by the padre's charade of ignorance. The initial query had been spoken levelly. Obviously, Giovanni thought he had nothing to fear. Well, he'd soon find out how mistaken he was. If this man of the cloth needed further explanation, Frederic would oblige him. "Come, Father, there's no need to pretend that you don't know why you're here. Surely you knew I'd find out?" Frederic chuckled wryly.

The priest's gaze remained fixed on the floor, and Frederic began to enjoy his discomfiture. "Now," and he paused for effect, taking another swig. "I know my wife received the Last Rites at your hands. Therefore, I'm certain you hold the information I seek." His voice turned sharp and deadly. "I want the name of the man who fathered the bastard child she was carrying!"

Benito closed his eyes and digested the unexpected, searing declaration. *Where had Frederic obtained this information? What am I to say to him?* He held silent, fighting his pounding heart and channeling his racing thoughts.

"*Well?*" Frederic demanded, his patience spent. The game was up. Time to have it out! "Don't deny that you have the name. I knew my wife too well. For all her adultery, I'm certain that she'd confess every mortal sin if she knew she was dying. And she knew. Now, I was here when you were called to her bedside. I know you absolved her of her sins – all of them. Again, I want the name of my wife's lover, and if you know what is good for you, you will tell me quickly. I promise he will wish he had never been born, and not you, nor anyone else on this goddamned island, will deny me the satisfaction of confronting him!"

The priest paled, certain that no matter how he answered, his position on Charmantes was in jeopardy. Somehow, he must appease the man. He raised his head and responded with compassion. "Sadly, you believe the worst about your deceased wife. However, what she did or did not reveal to me under the Sacrament of Extreme Unction will never leave my lips. You know I am sworn to silence. You cannot ask me to break my sacred vow."

"Damn it, man! I will have his name, and he will pay!"

"No, Frederic," the priest countered placidly. "Even if she confessed this sin, she needn't have spoken a name to receive absolution."

Frederic sat stunned. Either Giovanni was smarter than he thought, or he spoke the truth. "You lie. She named her lover. I can see it in your eyes."

"Whoever he is, God forgive him," Benito rejoined, noting the man's waning vehemence. "Forget this libertine and bury the past, Frederic. Murder is a far greater offense than adultery. Your wife is dead and her sins forgiven. Why contaminate your own soul with thoughts of retribution?"

"Get out, old man!" Frederic ordered. "You are no better than Robert and Agatha – laying all blame on Colette. Yes, I would love to confront her face-to-face and reward her for her unfaithfulness, but she is gone. However, there is another here on Charmantes, alive and well. I tell you now: he will suffer for his venery. Before I leave this world – he *will* suffer!"

Sunday, May 21, 1837

Frederic sat on Pierre's bed awaiting the return of his children and their governess from Mass. He was more presentable than last week this time. Even so, he was extremely thin, having not yet regained his appetite.

Charmaine was humming as she swept into the room behind Pierre. She was hoping to see Paul today, but her eyes widened when Pierre shouted, "Papa!" and Jeannette rushed past her. "Papa, you're here! We missed you!" She hugged him fiercely. "I'm so glad you've finally come to visit us! We were so worried!"

"Me too!" Pierre giggled. "Where were you?"

The man swallowed hard, suddenly realizing how very foolish he had been. How could he have thought to abandon this world – that his son was better equipped to take his place? He regarded Yvette, who stood ramrod straight, so much like Colette. "I've been mourning the death of your mother," he said softly, "but that is over now. It is time to move on."

"That's what Mademoiselle Charmaine told us," Yvette said, pleased with his explanation. She embraced him, too. "You loved Mama, didn't you?"

"Yes," he whispered.

Charmaine was not so forgiving. No matter how great his suffering, Frederic had selfishly added to his children's terrible ordeal. Unable to set aside her condemnation, she started toward her bedchamber. "I shall leave you alone."

He must have read her thoughts. "Miss Ryan, stay," he petitioned. "I want to apologize to you, as well as to my children. I'm sorry I wasn't here for them over the past few weeks. I'm also sorry that it fell to you to comfort them."

What could she say? It served no purpose to remain angry. "I am glad you've recovered, sir," she offered. "The children were worried about you. Even I was worried about you."

"Worried?"

Agatha stood in the nursery doorway, her haughty inquiry hanging in the air.

Charmaine grimaced. The dowager had taken great pleasure in berating her over the past six weeks. With Colette gone and Paul away most of the time, no one was there to put the widow in her place.

"I was merely commenting on the children's happiness to see their father again," Charmaine attempted to explain.

"Really? It sounded to me as if you were speaking of your own happiness."

"Agatha," Frederic interceded, "I am spending some time with my children. You wouldn't infringe on that, would you?"

"Certainly not, Frederic," she replied with a striking smile, departing as quietly as she had come.

Later that evening, she visited Frederic in his apartments. It was time to make her ardent dream a reality – now – before another young woman, and the governess no less, stepped in. He was in desperate need of comforting, famished for a woman's love. Tonight, he'd forget those other two, who pretended at love just to enjoy his fortune.

Wednesday, June 14, 1837

"*Are you mad?*" Paul expostulated in disbelief. "You *are* mad, that is the only explanation for this lunacy!"

The day had been all but pleasant. First, he'd been forced to return to the main island mid-week due to a shipping mix-up that threatened to delay the next stage of development on Espoir. No sooner had he set foot on Charmantes and a score of other crises demanded his immediate attention, each one more pressing than the one before. Without George there, his troubles continued to multiply. He snorted when he numbered the weeks his *friend* had been gone – over ten to date, and it greatly irritated him. How long did it take to travel to Richmond and back again? Was George on holiday now? Unfortunately, there was nothing he could do about it. However, the last thing he needed, the last thing he expected to be embroiled in at the end of this deplorable day was this absurd conversation with his father, whose sudden silence could have been mistaken for deep reflection had his visage been pensive. But the man's eyes were stormy, his jaw set behind grinding teeth. Frustrated, Paul took to pacing, no closer to understanding the workings of his parent's mind, his polar loyalties.

In the months before Christmas, Paul would have sworn that the only sentiments existing between Colette and his sire were those of mistrust and anger. Then, after his return from Europe, he'd witnessed a myriad of astonishing emotions: ostensible despair when Colette had hovered near death, relief and happiness when it seemed she'd overcome her malady, and finally, incomprehensible grief when her shaky recovery had ended in death. After the third week of mourning, Colette's words, spoken in the gardens, haunted him: "He loved me once... did you know that? He loved me once." *Had that love never died?* Possibly. Nevertheless, Paul could not dismiss the distant past, and remained uncertain. Yet today, as he walked the streets of Charmantes, he heard the gossip: *Yes, he's on the mend... He's given up thoughts of starvation... of course he still loves her, but he's thinking of the children now...*

Paul recalled the suicidal scheme that his father had initiated in early May. When he arrived home, Rose confirmed the aborted effort. Though he was relieved to hear that it was over, he was ashamed that he'd been absent for it all, annoyed that no one had sent word to Espoir. Today he was ready to admit that his sire had loved Colette, even into the grave, and for the first time, Paul comprehended why the man had been so embittered for all those years. It wasn't just hate, it was heartbreak. He thought he had it all figured out.

But no, just moments ago, his father had changed course again, annihilating those logical deductions. Colette was suddenly to be 'forgotten'. That was the word he'd used. Aside from the children, no one nearest him was to speak of her: no utterance of her name, no reminders of her in his room, no artifact that might spoil the pristine world from which he would purge her memory.

Fine! He could tolerate that, humor his parent, pretend that Colette no longer existed. *But this other thing? Never!* He would never condone this day's nonsense! And he'd be damned if he'd allow the revolting idea to be kindled. He would snuff it out before it flared out of control.

"I tell you again, you are mad! And I won't allow it!"

"*Allow it?*" Frederic returned. "I'm the father, or have you forgotten that?"

Paul flung himself into a chair. "No, I haven't forgotten," he mumbled.

"Good. Then I can count on you to make all the arrangements?"

"No," Paul answered tightly, his eyes every bit as turbulent as his father's. "I'll play no part in it."

Frederic cocked his head to one side, attempting to read his son's mind, unprepared for *this* reaction, erupting before he had a chance to explain. "Why are you so opposed to this?" he finally asked. "What does it matter to you?"

"It matters because it is a grave mistake that you will live to regret. Have you no regard for Colette? Yes–" he bit out "–I dare to speak her name! She has been dead for two months. *Two months!* Not even the lowest wife would be set aside so quickly. But Colette was not lowly. She was good and kind, fair inside and out. *And no,* don't you *dare* argue that point!" He held up a hand to wave off any objection. "For all your condemnation, for all your accusations, you know my words are true."

"I know no such thing!"

"The hell you don't!" Paul exploded. "She made a mistake, one terrible mistake that you mean to crucify her for over and over again! Can't you see the forest for the trees? How can you judge Colette so severely and not see Agatha for what *she* is! To mention them in the same breath is abhorrent!"

"Do not speak of her so. She is to become my wife."

"Haven't you heard a single word I've said?" Paul shouted. "You cannot mean to wed this woman! You cannot!"

"She will make me forget," Frederic answered tightly, straying far from the issue now. "I need to forget."

"She'll make you *wish* to forget! Nothing more. If you think you knew what hell was married to Colette – if you think you know what it is now – just wait!"

"That's enough!" Frederic snarled, further perplexed by his son's outburst. Yet it was Paul's fierce opposition that cemented his resolve to make Agatha Blackford Ward his third wife. "I do not expect you to see it my way. Not now, anyway. But all of this is done for a very good reason. All I ask is that you respect that reason."

"Reason?" Paul choked out, far from appeased. "I see no reason. You haven't spoken of anything remotely linked to reason."

"Isn't it enough that I say it exists? Would you strip me of all pride by suggesting that I'm incapable of making my own decisions?"

Paul faltered; he'd overstepped his bounds. "As you say, it is your decision to make," he capitulated. "But, be warned, Father, my sentiments will not change. And I will never, *never* acknowledge Agatha as my stepmother."

"I don't expect you to," Frederic grumbled, suddenly ambivalent of his noble intentions.

Saturday, July 1, 1837

Not three months after Colette's death, Frederic took Agatha Blackford Ward for his third wife. The couple ventured to the mansion's stone chapel early one Saturday morning for the very private ceremony. Without the knowledge of family and friends, Benito St. Giovanni blessed the peculiar marriage in the presence of only two witnesses: Paul and the island's doctor. Robert Blackford became Frederic's brother-in-law for a second time.

If Frederic had hoped to receive a more favorable response from his younger children, he was disappointed. As he left Agatha and entered the nursery to tell them of his marriage, he was greeted by Yvette's stormy face. "Is it true?" she demanded, pushing past Charmaine. "Tell me it's not true?"

"Is what true?" Frederic asked in surprise.

"Joseph said that his father told him that you were marrying Mrs. Ward today. It's not true, is it? He was lying. Please tell me he was lying, Father!"

Frederic experienced an overwhelming pang of regret. "It *is* true," he answered curtly. "Agatha and I were married a short while ago."

Charmaine's stomach plummeted. In a panic, she grabbed hold of a bedpost, distantly aware of Pierre hugging her legs.

Yvette's belligerent cry, "See, Mademoiselle Charmaine!" ricocheted off the walls. "I told you it was true! Joseph never lies to me."

Jeannette burst into tears. "But Father, why? Why would you marry *her*?"

When he did not explain, Yvette berated him fiercely. "If you had to remarry, why didn't you pick Mademoiselle Charmaine?"

Charmaine was aghast, and she found Frederic assessing her as if he were weighing his daughter's words. *Where did Yvette come up with her ideas?*

The man took the comment in stride, a lopsided smile tugging at the corner of his mouth. "Is that why you are upset? You'd rather Mademoiselle Charmaine replace your mother?"

"I didn't say that!" Yvette scolded, annoyed that her father had misunderstood. "No one can replace Mama. You should know that! You told me you loved her. Were you lying? Mama was good and kind and beautiful. How could you marry someone who is bad and mean and ugly? Now we have a stepmother worse than any we've ever read about in fairytale books!"

Frederic's eyes narrowed. "That will be enough, young lady! Agatha *is* your stepmother now, and as such, you will respect her." He indicated Charmaine menacingly. "And your governess will see to it that you do."

Charmaine's moment of sympathy vanished, but she bit her tongue, willing herself not to side with the twin. "Sir," she said instead, "Yvette is only speaking from her grief. She misses her mother. Surely you can understand that."

"That does not give her the right to grow ill-mannered," he returned stiffly. "I'll not abide insults directed at my new wife. Is that understood?"

"Yes, sir," Charmaine answered meekly, her position precarious.

Perhaps the children sensed her dilemma, for they, too, fell mute.

Yvette's eyes welled with tears, and she blinked them away. The unusual sight shook Frederic more surely than her ire had, but there was no turning back. Certain that it was best to guard a harsh resolve, he bade them good day.

"You must not anger your father," Charmaine cautioned once they were alone. "There is nothing you can do to change the situation, but if you insist on insulting your new stepmother, you will definitely make matters worse."

Thankfully, the girl and her sister nodded.

"Remember," she continued, forcing smile, "I'll always love you." She hugged them, determined to overcome this newest impediment to their recovery.

Later, Charmaine wondered over the strange circumstances that led Frederic to remarry so soon after his second wife's demise. How could he dismiss Colette so quickly, set her from his heart with so little respect? Why had he attempted to end his own life, if his love had not been intense and consuming? *What did it all mean?* Perhaps Agatha charmed him when nobody else was around and offered him solace. If nothing else, she *had* helped save his life. In the end, Charmaine concluded that Frederic had never seen Agatha's cruel side. If he had, surely he wouldn't subject his children to this utterly repulsive arrangement.

Agatha inhaled deeply, enjoying the salty scent of the ocean air, sighing as she retreated to her sitting room. "That will be all, Gladys. You won't be needed until I ring for you tomorrow morning."

Gladys, who had just finished removing Colette's clothing, bobbed and left.

Agatha moved to the jewelry chest atop the dressing table. She lifted the lid and smiled down at the many gems sparkling within the velvet-lined box. She had stopped Gladys before they, too, were taken to some unknown destination, stored until the twins were old enough to wear them. She smiled when she found Elizabeth's valuables amongst Colette's. If the second wife could enjoy the jewels belonging to her predecessor, then so would she. Of course, she knew why Frederic had allowed Colette to touch his *precious* Elizabeth's possessions. He thought of the two women as one and the same. Agatha dismissed the disturbing thought. Today was too wonderful to dwell on the past. For the first time, the future belonged to her. She closed the chest and moved about the chamber, arranging things more to her liking.

When Frederic entered, she gave him a dazzling smile. He limped over to her, as handsome as he'd been this morning, as handsome as ever.

He caressed her cheek. "Happy?" he queried softly.

Her eyes filled with tears. "Very happy," she whispered. "I've loved you Frederic… for so very long."

He nodded soberly. "I know. Perhaps we *are* destined to be together."

"Perhaps? No, Frederic," she insisted, "there is no 'perhaps' on this glorious day. I *shall* make you happy, and the sadness of the past will remain there."

"For my children's sake, I hope you are right. I am tired of being thought of as the sinister patriarch."

Agatha laughed. "Sinister, Frederic? Never! But then, no one understands you the way I do." She stroked his chest, her eyes clouded with passion. "Come," she whispered, pulling him into his chambers and the bed that awaited them.

Sunday, July 2, 1837

On Sunday, Paul joined Charmaine and the children for Mass. As she smiled up at him, she was rewarded with a wink that set her heart to racing. She wondered how long he'd remain on Charmantes, but hesitated to ask, putting aside such depressing thoughts to enjoy the splendid moment while it lasted.

It didn't. At the close of the service, Agatha intercepted the house staff at the chapel door, and Paul rushed off. She instructed them to reconvene in the great hall in one hour's time.

"I will be assigning additional duties to each of you," she stated obtrusively. The underlying message was inauspicious, and Charmaine fretted over the lecture that awaited them. "That will be all," she concluded, turning her attention to Father Benito, who had requested a minute of her time.

Charmaine gathered the children together, stifling a smile when it became apparent that Agatha was annoyed at the priest.

"I don't see why I should have to donate anything," she hissed.

"Mrs. Duvoisin," Benito petitioned pointedly, "you are not only mistress of this grand manor, but the whole of Charmantes as well. As the wife of its benefactor, altruistic obligations fall to you. Surely you were aware of that." Agatha glowered at him, but the priest smiled benevolently. "Miss Colette was extremely charitable, until she fell so *violently* ill."

Charmaine followed the children through the ballroom, Agatha's voice receding behind her. *So, the new Mrs. Duvoisin was about to find out that her life of luxury came with a price.* Hopefully, the priest's philanthropic work proved long and arduous.

An hour later, she returned to the banquet hall and withstood Agatha Duvoisin's dictatorial oration. In less than five minutes, the new mistress revoked any shred of freedom the staff had previously enjoyed. Charmaine watched as Mrs. Faraday left in a huff, followed by a fiery Fatima Henderson and a downtrodden Gladys Thornfield. Felicia and Anna skulked away, permitting Charmaine a moment of vicarious pleasure; finally, the two maids would have to work for their wages. With that happy thought, she headed for the foyer, certain that Rose would be glad when she returned.

"Miss Ryan, you seemed amused."

Charmaine's head snapped up from her daydreams. "I'm sorry?"

"I was wondering if you found my instructions amusing?" Agatha inquired stiffly. "You seem quite pleased with yourself."

"No ma'am," Charmaine replied, her smile wiped clean.

"Good. I would like to speak with you privately in the study. The comfortable position you've held in this house is in need of a review."

"Review?" Charmaine asked with growing dread.

"We shall discuss it later, at four o'clock. And Miss Ryan – do be prompt."

Charmaine was left quaking; this private meeting portended trouble, and even Rose could not convince her otherwise. She remembered Frederic's threatening words of just the morning before. If she didn't tread carefully, she would be sent packing. Sadly, she realized that she would sustain as great a heartache as the children if she were dismissed; she loved them so.

At three-thirty, Charmaine once again left them with Rose. She'd be more than punctual, limiting the ammunition that Agatha might use against her.

Of late, nothing was going Paul's way. He crossed the expanse of emerald lawn with an agitated gait, took the stone steps of the portico in two strides, and stormed the manor's double doors. He slapped a brown folder against his left thigh, the rhythm working his revolving thoughts into a frothing frenzy, until he found himself contemplating the circle's inception once again: his father's mismatched marriage, his ponderous schedule between Charmantes and Espoir, George's prolonged absence, the new manor's halted construction, and finally, the circle's end – the sorest point of all – his brother, John, and the missing shipping invoices that were not with the other, unimportant, papers he held in his hand.

"Why does he do this to me?" he seethed aloud, the habit of talking to himself most prevalent when John provoked him. "I know why," he ground out, barging into the study and slamming the portal shut with such force that the glass rattled in the French doors across the room. "He knows it will foster havoc on Charmantes and that I will have to deal with it! I bet he's been snickering for months just thinking about it."

He reached the desk in another five strides, flinging the folder atop the other papers lying there, its contents spilling out. The childish act yielded momentary gratification; he swung around to find Charmaine staring at him wide-eyed from the high-backed chair. "How long have you been sitting there?" he demanded, his temper spiking as he realized what she had witnessed. "Well? *Answer me!"*

"A long time, sir," she replied docilely, fueling his feeling of foolishness.

Instantly, his anger was gone, and he closed his eyes and rubbed his brow. *Sir... she's calling me sir again.* "I'm sorry, Charmaine. I didn't mean to snap at you like that. It's just that I've had so much on my mind lately that I'm at my wit's end."

"I guess we're in the same predicament," she replied.

He heard the apprehension in her voice. "Is something wrong?"

Is something wrong? she thought. *Surely he's joking!* But how would he know of the troubles facing the entire Duvoisin staff, and her in particular? "There will be many changes in the house within the next few days," she said, dropping her eyes to the hands in her lap. "Some of them frighten me."

"What changes could possibly frighten you?"

"I'm to have a private meeting with Mrs. Duvoisin in a few minutes."

Agatha... his stepmother... the new Mrs. Duvoisin... Suddenly, he was rankled by more than the title she bore. He didn't need an explanation to deduce the woman's motives, nor the distasteful outcome she would attempt to script.

He immediately summoned Travis Thornfield and dispatched a message. The manservant was to inform the new mistress that her meeting with the governess had been cancelled. "If she complains," Paul concluded, "refer her to me. Miss Ryan is firmly established in this house. There is no pertinent reason to interrupt her strict schedule. That will be all, Travis."

The butler departed, an uncommon smile tweaking the corners of his mouth.

Charmaine was astonished. Once again, Paul stood beside her. When was she going to realize that she had nothing to fear from him? *Perhaps today,* her heart whispered, the thought leaving her giddy. *Was it possible that he'd grown more handsome in the past moments?* She had her answer as he casually walked across the room and towered over her, her heart beating wildly in her chest.

"There," he said with a wicked smile, his teeth flashing white below his dark moustache. "She'll not be pleased, but she'll think twice before threatening your position again."

Charmaine was not so certain, though she was very grateful for his efforts. "I don't know..."

"Charmaine," he chided lightly, sitting in the chair adjacent to hers. He leaned forward and lifted her hand from her lap, cradling it in his. "You needn't fear the power Agatha is attempting to wield. She's out to prove that she's now mistress of the manor. I assure you I have my father's support in this matter. He'll not dismiss you, no matter how vehemently she might protest."

"Thank you, Paul," she said in a small voice. His warm hand made breathing difficult, and she found it equally difficult to concentrate. "You have lifted a heavy burden. I don't know what I'd tell the children if I were forced to leave. I've become quite attached to them."

His smile turned warm. "I know you have, Charmaine, and they feel the same way about you. Don't you think my father knows that?"

"I hope he does. After yesterday, I'm not so certain."

Paul frowned. "What happened?"

She told him about the girls' reaction to Frederic's unexpected marriage, and his smile returned. "Yvette has gained my respect," he said. "I told my father much the same thing. I'm glad he's heard it from someone other than me. I can imagine how upset he was."

"Yes, but it doesn't make any difference, does it? What's done is done."

"Unfortunately, you are right about that, Charmaine. It is just one of many things that has added to a deplorable week."

"I'm sure. I wish I could resolve your dilemmas as swiftly as you have mine. Unfortunately, all I can offer is sympathy."

Paul's demeanor abruptly changed. His eyes sparkled beneath raised brows, and a roguish smile spread across his face. "Don't depreciate that offer. I'd love to indulge in a bit of sympathy and forget my troubles for a time."

She knew where his words were leading, where the invitation would take her if she allowed it. That was the key, allowed it. She'd enjoyed his company for almost a year now. Once his flirtatious advances had frightened her; today she found them exciting. Suddenly, she wanted more, wanted to know that he wasn't just toying with her, that he was truly attracted to her, wanted to know what it felt like to have his mouth upon hers. Intuitively, she knew that the lust that had sparked his first proposition in the gardens those many months ago had blossomed into something more. And yet, he had never kissed her. Why? On Christmas Day, he had almost done so, but they had been interrupted. And once he'd returned home, they'd been thrown into the turmoil of Colette's death. Beyond that, there was Espoir and his merciless work schedule, his treks home few and far between. Today was the first time they'd been alone in ages. She returned his dazzling smile. Let him think what he would. She wanted him to kiss her right here and now. As if reading her thoughts, his gaze traveled to her lips.

Paul had watched numerous emotions play across her comely face, and yet he was no closer to figuring her out. The risqué invitation didn't seem to upset her, yet she didn't speak. She was so lovely, and he longed to make love to her, slowly and sweetly. He had no use for this little cat and mouse game and was annoyed with himself. "Charmaine? Did you hear what I said?"

Her coyness vanished. "I heard," she replied, more evenly than she thought possible.

"And?"

He released her hand to cradle her cheek and chin, his thumb brushing across her lips. She closed her eyes to the sensual caress. She couldn't breathe and broke away, standing and turning her back to him.

"And?" he pressed again, moving behind her.

"And–" she faltered "–I don't see how I could possibly help you."

So, he thought, *she's playing to a new set of rules: Don't act offended, but don't give in.* He had dallied too long, and the dreamy moment was dissolving. He felt cheated and chuckled ruefully, his breath catching in her hair.

Embarrassed now, she stepped further away and composed herself. Finally, she faced him. "Perhaps if you explained some of your problems…"

"*Some?*" he derided suavely. "Where would you like me to begin? Agatha? George? Or perhaps John, the biggest problem of all. There's nothing you can do to rectify that headache."

"Let me be the judge of that," she said.

He laughed outright. But when her stance remained set, arms folded one over the other, her eyes serious, he strode to the desk and lifted the sheaf of papers he'd thrown there earlier. "All right. These are invoices. They–"

"I know what invoices are," she cut in.

He nodded, then explained why those he held were so perplexing.

Apparently, a ship had docked on Charmantes mid-week and had sat in the harbor for five days, her cargo untouched. The Captain and Jake Watson had disputed over which goods were intended for Charmantes and which were to be shipped on to Virginia.

"The captain insisted that the supplies packed for Charmantes were at the rear of the hold," Paul was saying. "Jake was confused and demanded to see both the European and Virginia invoices. He didn't believe that even a new captain could be so dimwitted as to bury our goods behind those that would be discharged at a later time. The captain bristled, probably because Jake's estimation of him was accurate. Again, Jake insisted on seeing John's invoices, informing the captain that not one cask would be hoisted without proof of merchandise. The captain hemmed and hawed, finally admitting that – although he *thought* John had given him the proper paperwork – the invoices he carried were, in fact, invalid. When Jake saw these, he had had enough."

"Enough of what?" Charmaine asked.

"*Enough of John's antics!* I didn't rant and rave when he changed the shipping routes last year, so he has come up with another scheme to impede the work on Charmantes. Once our staples were loaded in Richmond, John removed the legitimate paperwork and gave the captain these instead."

Paul waved a pile of papers under her nose. When they stopped flapping, Charmaine caught sight of several crude drawings with accompanying notes, which he abruptly withdrew and shoved back into the folder.

"He used invoice sheets for his artwork just to make certain that I knew the entire mix-up was intentional." Paul slapped the folder against his thigh again, his agitation escalating. "When Jake saw the sketches, he was furious. Apparently, he called the captain a few choice names and informed the man that if his crew unladed the packet, he was storing every last cask, including the merchandise for Virginia, in our warehouses until I returned from Espoir and decided otherwise. The captain lost his temper and stood sentry against Jake's threat. And so, the ship has sat in our harbor for five days! *Five days!*" he bellowed in exasperation. "Her European cargo losing hundreds of dollars in market value."

"But you arrived home on Friday," Charmaine observed in confusion. "Why didn't Mr. Watson talk to you then?"

"Friday *night*, Charmaine," he corrected. "*Late* Friday night. Everyone was at Dulcie's, and I just assumed the ship had been unloaded, reloaded with sugar, and ready to depart for Richmond. *I should have known better!* We spent the better part of two hours climbing over barrels to find out whether those in the stern contained island supplies. Without the invoices, I couldn't be certain, and John would love to learn that I had spent the entire day shifting hogsheads just to find that nothing at the back was for us in the first place!"

Charmaine knew he was chasing circles and felt sorry for him. "Why would your brother create such confusion? He has just as much to lose as your father and you do, doesn't he? That's what Colette used to say."

"He will pay any price, Charmaine, *any price*, if he knows he's upset me or, better yet, made my hard day's work harder."

She was appalled. "If that's true, you have to turn the tables on him."

"How could I possibly do that?"

"Send the ship back to him, just the way it is. Or better still, keep all the merchandise."

Paul disagreed. "Sending it back will deprive us of valuable supplies, especially grain. Keeping it would cost my father a fortune. His buyers in Virginia would be none too pleased either. And John knows all this."

Charmaine nodded to his final declaration, but turned back to her original suggestion. "Are you certain Charmantes couldn't survive without the grain?"

"Of course we could survive, but it accomplishes nothing."

"Nothing, except sending the problem back to your brother. Maybe you should include your own set of drawings, telling him a thing or two!"

Paul chuckled. He certainly would love to see John's face when he began unloading the vessel and found that his mean-spirited tomfoolery had backfired – that *he* was the one facing a laborious day on the docks. Let the captain talk his way out of that one, and let John deal with the buffoon he had hired. Yes, it was a most pleasing fantasy... Then Paul was struck by a new thought. Perhaps John knew about Espoir and had hoped to sabotage his efforts by creating more work on Charmantes. But no, Stephen Westphal and Edward Richecourt were sworn to secrecy, so John couldn't know – unless George had spilled the beans. But that was impossible. The Heir would have left Richmond before George got there.

"Paul?"

He came around when Charmaine called his name a second time. "I'm sorry, Charmaine. Not to worry. I'll sort it out."

"Very well, but I wouldn't stand for such nonsense!"

Her eyes flashed with fervor, and thoughts of his brother vanished. Damn, she was desirable, and he ached to hold her, to release the dark locks pinned at her nape and stroke the abundant mane as it cascaded down her back, to possess her petulant mouth. He stepped closer, but her eyes remained hard, oblivious to the fire she had stoked. He stopped. *Now is not the time*, he thought, steeling himself against his carnal appetite. *You'll only be interrupted again. But soon, very soon, another opportunity will present itself. Perhaps late one night when everyone else is abed...* Yes, he fancied that idea. Then he would conquer her.

"Excuse me, sir."

Paul chuckled with the anticipated interruption. "Yes, Travis?"

"I'm afraid that Mrs. Duvoisin wants to speak to you now, sir. I tried to tell her you were preoccupied–"

Before he could finish, Agatha pushed her way into the room. "So," she accused, "the governess is over-burdened with her duties and cannot make time for an interview with me. And here I thought those duties involved the children."

"At present, Miss Ryan happens to be helping me," Paul replied stiffly.

Agatha's eyes raced up and down Charmaine's slender form, eagerly searching for some incriminating evidence to feed her evil assumptions. "Helping you? I can just imagine how."

"Charmaine *is* helping me, Agatha," Paul bit out, his jaw twitching with contained anger. "If you'd care to notice, we are sorting through a stack of invoices that accompanied the Heir." He produced the folder to support his statement. "John has created another headache by misplacing the most important papers. Charmaine was merely–"

Agatha's face turned livid. "John – always John. How do you put up with it? Why does your father *force* you to put up with it?"

"I don't know," Paul answered, baffled by her reaction, "but I'm not about to discuss it with you. I believe you wanted to speak to me about Miss Ryan?"

"Yes," she agreed reluctantly, scrutinizing Charmaine again. "I think that I have the right, as the children's stepmother, to determine who cares for and educates them."

"No, Agatha, you don't have that right," Paul countered. "Your marriage to my father changes nothing. However, since we disagree, I suggest that we take the matter to him right now, and have *him* settle it once and for all."

"Very well," she hesitated.

"Good. Let's have done with it."

Charmaine was trembling as she preceded Paul out of the study, bewildered when he led her to the nursery. "There's no need to accompany us, Charmaine. I'll let you know how everything turns out." With that, he nudged a miffed Agatha toward his father's quarters.

Charmaine entered the nursery. Rose, who had been reading to the children, lifted her brow in silent inquiry, but Charmaine only shrugged, aware that Yvette was all ears. "Well?" the precocious twin asked. "Don't you think we should know what happened?"

"Yes, Mademoiselle," Jeannette agreed. "We're worried. We don't ever want to lose you."

"I don't think you will," Charmaine offered gently. "Paul is determined to override any harsh decisions your stepmother attempts to make."

"What does that mean?" Jeannette asked.

"It means that he is doing what Johnny would do if he were here," Yvette explained, "and I'm proud of him."

Charmaine chuckled, remembering Paul's earlier words about Yvette. "Paul is speaking with your father right now. He wasn't in the mood to hear Agatha's complaints."

"Why not?" Yvette asked.

Charmaine eyed her for a moment, uncertain if she should tell the eight-year-old what she had learned from Paul. "He was upset with your brother over some missing invoices."

"Johnny? Do you think Paul is talking to father about him, too?"

"I don't know... Maybe... Why?"

"No reason," Yvette answered nonchalantly. "I don't want to see Johnny get into any more trouble, that's all."

Not long after, she left the nursery saying she needed to use the water closet.

Agatha cast a series of aspersions against the governess, saving the worst for last: Charmaine Ryan's background.

Renitent, Frederic sat back in his chair, folded his arms across his chest, and looked her straight in the eye. Thanks to Paul, he'd heard it all many months ago. "Charmaine Ryan was chosen by Colette to care for the children," he said. "They remain her children, not yours, Agatha. If for no other reason than to respect her wishes, Miss Ryan will retain her position in this house."

"But Frederic–" she demurred.

"No buts, no more discussion. I am very pleased with Miss Ryan. Regardless of her past, she's demonstrated great love and affection while mothering my children. That's what they need right now, Agatha, a mother. I do not see you lending a hand with them."

Chastised, Agatha turned aside, saying, "I shan't bring the matter up again."

"Good."

She recovered quickly, spurred on by a new thought. "I fear the entire incident was blown out of proportion. I had only intended to speak with Miss Ryan today. I would never have dismissed her as Paul has led you to believe. He was upset over other matters and jumped to all the wrong conclusions."

"What other matters?" Frederic asked, his regard diverted to his son.

Paul still clutched the folder from the Heir. "John, just John," he answered, tossing the invoices into his father's lap.

"What has he done this time?"

His ire rekindled, Paul delved into the aggravating story, forgetting that Agatha was there. His father listened patiently, shaking his head on occasion. His eyes hardened as he viewed the lecherous sketches, complete with obscene remarks. "He's up to no good again," Frederic snarled, "as if he has nothing better to do with his time."

"May I see those?" Agatha asked, arm outstretched.

"No." Frederic shoved the papers back into the folder and threw them into the dustbin.

Agatha bristled. "Why do you force Paul to deal with such nonsense?"

"Yes, Father," Paul interjected, capitalizing on Agatha's propitious allegiance. "Why do I have to put up with his malicious antics? We're not children any longer. John refuses to behave like an adult, and yet, he's in charge."

Frederic smiled sardonically. "You are in charge here, and John is in charge in Virginia."

"That's not how I see it. John is in charge above and beyond the Virginia operations. John changed the shipping routes, which led to this fiasco. If the packets came directly to us from Richmond, they would be carrying island supplies, nothing else, and we wouldn't be going through this 'which cask is for us?' business."

Frederic nodded, but said nothing.

Paul pressed on, venting his anger. "Beyond that, you and I both know John controls the purse strings that affect the growth of your entire estate."

"That is owing to the fact that he is on the mainland," Frederic said, bringing folded hands to his lips. "What would you have me do?"

"Take him off the will!" Agatha cut in. "Then he shall see where his vicious games have gotten him."

"Really? You think we have problems now?" Frederic paused for a moment, allowing the question to sink in. "We need John in Virginia. For all his faults, Paul knows that no one else could command John's end of the family business as well as John does. As for removing him from the will, well now, if John enjoys a prank when he holds a vested interest in Duvoisin enterprises, what kind of games do you think he'll play if he knows his actions hurt or benefit only one person – Paul? You can't even begin to guess. He'd have a heyday."

Paul had never considered this; his father was a wise man. He glanced at Agatha, who seemed to be searching for a rational rebuttal. There was no love lost between aunt and nephew. John was downright cruel to her, and she preferred that John remain abroad. With her marriage to Frederic, Paul surmised that she worried over her future should his father die and John inherit. He snickered to think of his brother ousting Agatha from the house, if not the island. Clearly, she needed an ally, and he had been chosen. But the Duvoisin empire needed John. As long as John resided in Virginia, he would remain the heir apparent.

Yvette had been gone a long time. Suspicious, Charmaine left the nursery. "Yvette?" she called, knocking on the privy door. "Are you all right?"

"I had a stomachache. But I'm feeling better now. I'll be out in a minute."

She returned, followed by Paul. He had wonderful news: Charmaine had his father's approval. Agatha would not question her position again.

"Mademoiselle said that a ship docked from Virginia," Yvette interjected when the adult discourse ebbed. "Were there any letters from Johnny?"

"No, there weren't any *letters* from Johnny," he answered curtly. "But there was a letter for Miss Ryan, which completely slipped my mind."

Paul pulled an envelope from his shirt pocket, addressed in Loretta Harrington's hand. Charmaine eagerly accepted it. It had been months since she'd heard from the woman, and her eyes flew over the contents.

"What does it say, Mademoiselle Charmaine?" Jeannette asked.

"Mrs. Harrington writes of the new railway into Richmond."

"Railway?"

"Last year there was much ado about it, but I left Richmond before I had the chance to see the station. She, Gwendolyn, and Mr. Harrington booked passage to Fredericksburg, where two of her sons live, and rode directly behind the huge steam engine."

Charmaine looked from eager face to eager face. Even Pierre showed interest the moment he'd heard the words 'steam engine'. The children had been reading about the great locomotives in a periodical that Paul brought back from Europe.

"In just over an hour they traveled fifty miles and arrived in Fredericksburg without delay!"

"Was that city named after Papa?" Jeannette asked innocently.

"No, Sweetheart," Charmaine replied as Pierre climbed into her lap.

"That is why I want to visit Johnny in Virginia," Yvette announced. "I want to have a ride on that great big steam engine."

"Me too!" Pierre piped in.

Charmaine hugged him. "Maybe someday we will visit there," she said, befuddled to find Paul frowning when she smiled up at him.

Saturday,
July 16, 1837

Chapter 9

Agatha sorted through the papers strewn atop her husband's desk. He was visiting with the children, which afforded her an hour to tidy up. She was astonished when she came across his will. Had he removed it from the safe because he intended to change something? Had he given some thought to her comments concerning John?

She had just finished reading it when Frederic entered the room. He instantly realized what she held and turned livid. "How dare you rummage through my personal things?"

Agatha attempted to hide nothing, replacing the document with a great show of dignity. "I wasn't rummaging, Frederic. I was merely straightening out this mess. Your will was amid the papers." She crossed the room, then stopped. "I am your wife now. I didn't think it was a secret. Obviously, I was wrong, and now I know why."

Frederic's rage diminished. "If there is something you want to know, ask."

"Paul is going to be devastated," she choked out, tears glistening in her eyes. "You realize that, don't you? If he finds out, he's going to be devastated."

"Finds out what?"

Frederic grimaced. Paul stood in the doorway. "Agatha has read my will," he replied hesitantly. "It names Pierre as second in line to inherit – after John."

The room plummeted into a paralyzing silence. Only a sense of betrayal hung in the air. Finally, Paul forced himself to speak, to break free of his father's perfidy. "I see… I mean, it makes sense… After all, he is legitimate."

"Paul," his father beseeched, his sorrowful eyes growing steely when it looked as if Agatha would interrupt. "*You know* this has nothing to do with legitimacy. I have tried to provide for all three of you. That is why I've given you Espoir. My will is merely a formality should anything happen to me. In fact, I was preparing a new document that–"

"Father, you don't have to explain your motives to me," Paul cut in, his throat constricted with emotion. He was angry with himself, revolted by the wave of jealousy that engulfed him, the harsh judgment he'd been ready to pass. "As you say, you've given me Espoir. You've financed the entire operation, including the shipping. I've no right to ask for more, to be envious of Pierre or John."

"But I should have told you about Pierre," Frederic murmured. "I'm sorry you found out this way."

"No, Father," Paul countered. "There's no need to apologize, not when you've given me so much."

Sunday, July 30, 1837

Frederic poured over the documents he held, studying each element and computing each figure with swift precision. When the papers offered no further information, he placed them aside and turned a satisfied smile on his son, who waited patiently for his opinion. "They appear to be in order."

Paul concurred. "I'm very pleased. In fact, I'm surprised that we've not confronted any delays since taking over the defaulted contracts in January. The shipbuilders have been prompt in meeting our schedule. They were relieved to have someone step in and purchase the titles. The financial panic made it difficult for them to come up with the capital to finish the vessels. We enabled them to put their men back to work and remain solvent at the same time."

Paul gestured toward the papers on his father's desk. "Once you've signed the remaining documents, I'll see them transported to Mr. Larabee when the next ship sets sail. On his end, he'll liquidate the securities and instruct Edward Richecourt to proceed with the final installment of funds. It was wise to go with the New York firm, and a stroke of luck to boot. Newportes Newes and Baltimore held promise, but I'm glad that I continued north. Because the vessels were well under construction, they'll be ready in a third of the time, and we've obtained three ships for one hundred and fifty thousand dollars when we expected to pay one-eighty."

"You are not disappointed with fully-rigged merchantmen?"

"From what Thomas Harrison indicated, it will be years before the merits of steam outweigh wind propulsion. Paddlewheels may be faster, but fueling their engines becomes a concern. No, we're better off waiting until they are perfected.

I'm quite pleased with the three-masted clippers. Their hulls sit high out of the water, a brilliant bit of engineering that will greatly reduce the time at sea."

Frederic nodded. "And on this end?" he queried. "Will Espoir be ready?"

"We've expanded the dock. Two ships can berth simultaneously. The house is nearly completed and beautiful. The architect proved reputable. He returned to Europe two months ago with a list of furnishings, which he will purchase on my behalf and transport to Espoir when the vessels make their maiden run. As for island operations, the men have cleared half the land, and three fields have been sown. By next year, they will be on a one-tract-per-month rotation."

"We may need to increase the size of the fleet," Frederic said with a smile.

"Let's see how the routes work out first," Paul advised.

Frederic's smile broadened. His son had a good head on his shoulders. "I'm proud of you, Paul, very proud. You've met your own grueling schedule despite the chaos and tragedy of the past four months. I realize the burden hasn't been light, and yet, you've continued to manage operations on Charmantes amid the press of Espoir's development. You haven't shirked your responsibilities, even though you've lost George's able hands."

Paul frowned. He hadn't mentioned George and wondered how his father knew of his prolonged absence. He doubted Travis had shared the information.

"I know about George," Frederic said. "When do you expect him back?"

"I have no idea," Paul grunted. "You realize he went to Virginia?"

"So I've heard."

"What do you think is going to happen?"

"I don't know, Paul," his father replied, rubbing his chin, "I don't know."

"If it hasn't happened by now, George will probably come home alone."

Frederic remained silent, deep in thought as he stared into the distance. When he did speak, he was directing his attention back to the documents, lifting them from his desk and rereading them.

"I know you were upset about Pierre and my will," he commented, to Paul's discomfort. "But I want you to know that I realize which son has remained beside me, who deserves the credit for nurturing enormous profits here on Charmantes, even in the face of our depleted cane fields. It was for this reason that I placed Espoir in your hands and invested in its future. I would like to know that when I die, you will own a share of what you've helped to build."

"Yes, sir," Paul said, embarrassed under the weight of his father's praise. "Thank you, sir."

They were interrupted by a knock on the door. "Agatha, come in," Frederic invited. "I would like to place you in charge of something."

Though he knew she was pleased with his enthusiastic welcome, she eyed him suspiciously as if she feared what he might tell her. He chuckled. "I've been thinking about this for some time now, but I shall need help with the details. I'm certain it will meet with your approval." He breathed deeply, then shifted in his chair. "Paul has projected that the ships will make their maiden crossing before Christmastide. Correct?"

"Yes," Paul confirmed, though he, too, appeared apprehensive.

"This is what I propose: we plan a grand celebration on Charmantes over the Christmas holiday."

"Celebration?" The word dropped in unison from Paul and Agatha's lips.

"Yes." Frederic regarded his son. "According to you, it will take a year before Espoir is in full production. In that time, it would be foolish to forge the Atlantic with ships half-empty. I say we bring Paul Duvoisin to the public eye, set him before the world marketplace. Why not advertise to farmers – both in Virginia and the Caribbean – the availability of your new fleet, and allow these tobacco, cane, and cocoa farmers, as well as their brokers, to bid on your transport services?"

He paused, enjoying their reactions. His wife's eyes twinkled in burgeoning excitement, while his son appeared thunderstruck.

He pressed on. "Why place all your coins on one bet? Yes, I'm certain that Espoir will produce profitable harvests for years to come, but the ships may prove more lucrative in the long run. Additional vessels can always be commissioned if need be, and so much the better if that becomes necessary."

Agatha was elated. "This is marvelous, Frederic, just marvelous! If Paul is jumping into the shipping world, men of influence must be told. And what better way than to invite them here to Charmantes for an unforgettable event?"

"Exactly," Frederic agreed. "We shall plan a week of activities, which will include the unveiling of Espoir, the christening of Paul's fleet, and the signing of contracts. We'll extend invitations to well-known businessmen, brokers, and prosperous farmers both in Virginia and the West Indies. Let these landowners see what we Duvoisins have built; witness our undisputed success. Let them bid on cargo space or better still, invest in additional ships."

"Let them long for a piece of it!" Agatha interjected dramatically.

Frederic nodded. "And then, after all the proper connections have been made, we will culminate the week-long festivities with a grand dinner and ball."

"Father," Paul breathed, "what can I say?"

"I gather you approve of the idea?" Frederic asked.

"Yes, but..." His words dropped off as concern for his father's health came to the fore.

"But what?" Frederic queried.

"But – are you up to this?"

"I'll be up to it," he vowed. "For you, Paul, I'll make every effort to be up to it. I will write to Larabee and Richecourt in Virginia. They can supply the names of the men we should contact in the States. After the invitations go out and the positive responses begin to reach us, I'll rely on you, Agatha, to coordinate the other arrangements. You can do that, can't you?"

"Absolutely!" she purred.

"Then it's settled. My only reservation is burdening you with additional work, Paul."

"On the contrary," his son responded. "Espoir has fallen into its own routine, the overseers conscientious. By the end of next month, I should be able to handle its production from Charmantes, traveling there every week or so. As for this venture–" and he shook his head, still in awe of what his father had planned "–it sounds as if you and Agatha will be taking on far more than I. I'm dumbfounded, actually. This is just wonderful!"

When Frederic was alone, he sighed, happy for the first time in months.

Charmaine entered the drawing room. Pierre was sound asleep, and now she turned her attention on the girls. They begged to stay up a bit longer, playing a duet on the piano. When Paul smiled her way, Charmaine capitulated. He'd dined with them for the first time in two weeks and hadn't rushed off as he normally did directly after dinner. He'd been exceptionally charming throughout the meal, his countenance every bit as amiable now. If she insisted that the twins retire, she'd no longer have a reason to return to the drawing room once they were in bed. She'd be wise to make the most of the next few minutes.

Unfortunately, they were not alone. Agatha sat with her needlepoint, Rose with her knitting. Bravely, Charmaine crossed the room and settled next to Paul on the settee, gaining a lazy smile that widened into an intense perusal.

He relaxed into the cushions, his arm outstretched across the back of the sofa. "Now, isn't this nice?" he whispered.

She blushed.

"I wish I were home more often," he continued softly.

"You're returning to Espoir in the morning?" she asked.

"Unfortunately, yes. However, the work is progressing nicely there, the house nearly finished. It won't be long before I can rely on my overseers full-time. Then, you'll be seeing a great deal more of me." He shifted a discernible degree closer. "Would you like that?"

Her blush deepened. It was answer enough. Her innocence and visible discomfiture fed a quickening in his loins. It was what he loved most about her.

Shortly afterward, Rose stood to say goodnight, and Charmaine and the girls did the same. Paul watched them go, then flipped open a periodical.

Agatha looked up. They were finally alone, an unprecedented occasion. She set her needlepoint aside and studied him. He was so very handsome, so much like his father. "Paul," she began cautiously, waiting for him to give her his full attention, accepting the frown of annoyance he shot her way as he dragged his eyes from the newspaper. "I know you don't like me."

He began to object, but she waved him off. "Please, allow me to say what I have to say, and then you can respond."

He leaned forward.

"I realize you were upset when your father and I married, but I want you to know that I intend to make him happy, truly happy. I've loved him for a very long time."

"Since I was a boy," he supplied.

"Yes," she agreed. "But I wasn't at liberty to marry him then." She bit her bottom lip, distraught. "Don't judge me harshly, Paul. Thomas, God rest his soul, was a good man, and I loved him as well, but never as I have loved your father."

"And?"

"And I thought perhaps we could come to an understanding."

"What type of understanding?"

"I like you, Paul. When you were young and I would come to visit, you were always polite, always respectful – unlike your brother." She grimaced in repugnance, pausing for emphasis. "This afternoon, I was proud to be included in these plans your father is making. I would like this enterprise to succeed beyond your wildest expectations. But mostly, I'd like your approval as I lend a hand in the coming months."

"Agatha, any effort that contributes to the success of this event will gain my approbation. I am glad my father is attempting to meet the world again, and if this new venture gives him purpose, so much the better. Likewise, if you've had a hand in raising him out of his misery, I commend you on that as well."

"Thank you, Paul." Her smile was genuine – beautiful. "I've no doubt that you will do well for yourself. You are more than just a handsome young man…" She let her words fall where they would, then stood and bade him goodnight.

For the second time that day, he was astonished.

Friday, August 18, 1837

By nine o'clock the children were sound asleep, and Charmaine had time to herself. She dismissed the idea of spending the remainder of the evening in the drawing room. Only Agatha and Rose would be there, and although Agatha no longer harassed her, Charmaine still avoided her. She did not need companionship that badly, so she rang for Millie, deciding to take a bath instead.

An hour later, she was finished and sat at her dressing table, working out the tangles in her damp hair. "It's too darn curly!" she grumbled. Like so many other nights, she tossed the comb aside and grabbed her wooden hairbrush, but it failed just as miserably. She was not in the mood and abruptly sent the brush sailing, where it hit the door before dropping to the floor. Dissatisfied still, she fingered the sewing shears on the table. In the building humidity, it would take hours for the thick mane to dry. How easy it would be to clip it short. But she couldn't bring herself to do it. Pushing back from the dressing table, she moved to the French doors. There she stood, allowing the evening breeze to lift the heavy locks off her neck, her fingers absentmindedly raking through the snarls.

Footsteps resounded on the portico below. Paul was on his way to the stable. Charmaine hadn't realized he was home and frowned at her decision to remain in her chambers. Nothing was going right. If she had known he was in the house, she'd have gladly withstood Agatha's disapproving airs to be in his presence.

She shook her head of the thought. He'd upset her greatly over the past two months: setting her heart to racing, yet remaining aloof, always flirting, suggesting that he found her attractive, yet never whispering words of endearment. He had turned her world upside down, and she found she didn't like it. She had always been sure of herself, not flustered and confused.

A sound from across the lawns drew her away from her musings. She looked toward the paddock. Paul emerged from the stables and walked back to the house. Evidently, he wasn't leaving, just checking on Chastity, the mare due to foal.

She hung her head, knowing it was best to stop thinking about him. She'd come to the conclusion that she was merely a distraction – someone to toy with when she was present, but easily forgotten when she wasn't. Hadn't he dismissed her from his thoughts each time he left for Espoir? Certainly, she didn't plague his waking hours as he did hers. After all, she was only the governess. He had made it quite clear that she would please him in bed. As for a decent proposal, it would never happen. Thus, she'd be wise to avoid him. What had Colette said? *He's a ladies' man... I'd hate to see you give your heart to someone who has no intention of returning your love.* If she didn't heed Colette's warning, she'd be nursing a broken heart. *Put him from your mind,* she reasoned, *forget what his kiss would have been like. Be happy that you were in your room tonight. The less you see of Paul, the better.*

A knock resounded on her door, and she invited Millie and Joseph Thornfield into the chamber. They'd come to empty the tub and take it away. Charmaine waited until the boy had waddled off with two brimming buckets, then spoke nonchalantly to his sister. "I noticed Master Paul going into the stables, but he didn't leave. It's awfully late. Is something amiss?"

"He is worried about the mare," Millie replied as she straightened from the tub, a third bucket in hand. "She's been whinnying all evening, but it's too early for her to foal. He's sent for Martin."

"Martin?"

"The town farrier," Millie explained, then shuddered in exaggerated revulsion. "A disgusting man, who's full of himself, if you know what I mean. Once he's been asked to help with the horses, he makes himself right at home. I just hope he doesn't barge in here like he did the last time – midnight it was – rousing the entire house so someone would make him something to eat."

Charmaine had never met this Martin, but she seemed to remember Yvette mentioning him once. "I don't think you have to worry," she soothed. "Surely he won't behave badly with Master Paul at home."

"You think not?" Millie countered. "He's downright rude to Master Paul, and Master Paul indulges him – all because Doctor Blackford refuses to minister to horses anymore."

Joseph returned and refilled his buckets. This time, Millie left with him. One more trip, and the tub was removed, and Charmaine was once again alone.

Thunder rumbled far off, and the drapes flapped in a hearty breeze. She closed the French doors and tiptoed into the children's room. Yvette was sleeping ramrod straight, her thin blanket tucked under each arm. Jeannette's linens had been kicked aside, and Charmaine drew them over her again. Pierre was nearly snoring, one fat thumb stuck in his pudgy mouth, the other hand clutching his stuffed lamb. Stroking back his hair, she kissed him on the forehead, her love abounding as she considered him a moment longer. Then, hearing the first droplets of rain, she latched the glass doors and returned to her room.

The storm was rapidly approaching, the thunder growing louder, bringing with it a sense of dread. She turned down the oil lamp on the night table, knelt to say her prayers, and finally climbed into bed. Already the night resurrected memories of Colette, simulating that terrible day before her demise. Charmaine hugged her pillow and squeezed her eyes shut, awaiting the worst…

But the worst did not come. The foyer clock tolled eleven, and the storm continued to toy with them. Though it rumbled, it did not roar, as if it were purposefully holding back, circling them, waiting for the kill.

Footsteps on the staircase eased the tension. Paul was retiring. Perhaps now she'd be able to sleep, knowing that he was close by and would protect her.

That comforting thought soon took wing. The heavens ripped apart, and the tempest unleashed its full fury on the house. Violent, sporadic wind drove sheets of rain into the French doors. They rattled loudly in objection. Blinding lightning lit up the room, and earsplitting thunder replied, the former rivaling the latter in its power, as if the two were fighting for the upper hand. Then, they were lashing out simultaneously, and Charmaine shrunk under the blanket, curled up and trembling, bracing herself for each explosion, frightened of the interim silence as well, a void that amplified other eerie sounds…

She attempted to ignore the rustling of clothing near her bed, but the cold, clammy hand that touched her arm was real, and she screamed, throwing back the linens to escape. Thankfully, the sound was swallowed by another roar of thunder, for there, standing next to her bed, was a quaking Jeannette and in the doorway to the children's room, Yvette, patting back a wide yawn.

"Sweet Jesus!" Charmaine cried, clamping a hand over her bosom. "I'm sorry, Jeannette, but you frightened me." She laughed in gargantuan relief, holding out her arms to the petrified girl, who eagerly fell into them.

Yvette moved to the foot of the bed. "You're afraid of this storm?" she queried in disgust.

Charmaine nodded, feeling quite foolish now. "Even more than Jeannette."

"She isn't frightened of thunderstorms," Yvette countered.

"No? Then why are you here?" Charmaine asked, looking down at the twin who had yet to speak.

"Someone was standing over my bed," Jeannette whimpered, trembling.

"That's what woke her," Yvette added. "She didn't believe me when I said it was you, coming to check on us."

Charmaine smoothed back Jeannette's hair. "Yvette is right. I did look in on you, Sweetheart. I even covered you up. I'm sorry if I disturbed you."

But the girl shook her head adamantly, fear sparkling in her wide eyes. "It wasn't you. It was a ghost that ran away when I turned over!"

Charmaine gave her another hug. "You must have been dreaming, a nightmare brought on by the storm, no doubt. Come," she encouraged, taking the lamp from her night table, "back to bed with you."

"I wasn't dreaming!" Jeannette cried. "I wasn't! I saw it, and it wasn't you. It ran out the French doors. It's on the veranda right now, waiting for me!"

"I wouldn't let anything harm you, Jeannette," Charmaine averred, "but I can't be brave alone. Won't you help me? We'll go back into your room together, and with the light of the lamp, you will see that there is nothing there to frighten you. All right?"

Jeannette nodded tremulously, taking Charmaine's hand. As they entered the nursery, they were buffeted by a chilling draft. The French doors were swinging on their hinges, the room at the mercy of the storm.

"Why didn't you close them?" Charmaine demanded, placing the lamp on the dresser. But as she rushed over to the wind-beaten panels, face turned away from the pelting rain, a spine-tingling aura took hold, and she came up short. Petrified, she slammed the doors shut, slipped the latch into place, and jumped back, grateful that no ghost had appeared from beyond.

Expelling a shuddering breath, she surveyed the damage. The drapes and rug were drenched. Laundering them would have to wait until morning, but she pulled a towel from the bureau and mopped up the floor.

Next she checked on Pierre. He hadn't budged, which seemed almost unnatural. The storm hadn't subsided. In fact, with the French doors open, it had been magnified, yet he'd slept through it all.

"As you can see, there was no one on the balcony," she finally said. "I think your ghost was nothing more than those billowing drapes, Jeannette. After all, your bed is the closest to the veranda."

The girl remained unconvinced, complaining that without a lock, the doors could open again.

"I know what will help you go back to sleep," Charmaine announced, hoping to defuse Jeannette's fears, "warm milk and cookies. Now, climb into bed, and I'll go get them. How would that be?"

Jeannette nodded, but jumped into bed with Yvette. "I'll wait here," she whispered. In the next moment, they were snuggling under the covers together, giggling softly.

Charmaine donned her robe, then lifted the lamp. But Jeannette immediately objected, begging her to leave it, so Charmaine lit a small candle instead. "I'll be back in a short while," she said.

As she walked down the hallway, the flickering flame cast grotesque shadows on the far walls, feeding her apprehension. Though she was getting good at timing the lightning and thunder, she was unprepared for the first toll of midnight and nearly jumped out of her skin when the foyer clock struck the hour. "Goodness," she scolded herself, grabbing hold of the stairway balustrade, "what's the matter with me? I'm acting like a frightened rabbit. There is no such thing as ghosts!" Then she began her descent.

With his dressing room door slightly ajar, Paul heard the sound of footfalls beyond, a shaky voice accompanying them. He opened the portal and leaned casually against the frame, admiring the lovely vision before him. Charmaine Ryan was indeed a fetching sight, even more so in her state of dishabille: hair unbound and thin robe drawn taut, accentuating her slender waist and shapely hips. She had turned into a temptress, and his mind wandered back to the night in the drawing room, some two weeks ago, when she had brazenly chosen to sit next to him. She was ready for the plucking, of that he was certain, but it was exceedingly difficult to corner her alone... until tonight. He smiled wickedly. Hadn't he hoped for an occasion such as this? What better time than when everyone else was in bed, his desires were stoked, and no one would interrupt? Yes, what better time indeed!

Although the storm had lulled, Charmaine was by no means relieved. The house was shrouded in darkness, her passage illuminated only by the candle and the erratic flashes of lightning. Beyond that, she could not shake the feeling that she was being watched, though it appeared as if everyone had retired. Fear tied a knot in the pit of her belly, and she hastened past the study, through the dining room, and into the kitchen. "I was a fool to suggest coming down here."

She began humming to blot out the creaks and ticks emanating from the dark recesses of the kitchen. The haunting melody that she had been forbidden to play on the piano spontaneously came to her lips, and oddly, she felt at ease, secure. Haunting indeed! She warmed the milk without spilling it and found the cookies that Mrs. Henderson had baked that morning, placing everything, including her nearly extinguished candle, on a serving tray. Then she retraced her steps.

As she emerged from the dining room, a burst of lightening silhouetted the figure of a man standing near the study doorway. Darkness instantly enveloped the corridor, and he was gone. Charmaine gasped, but the ensuing roar of thunder muffled the sound.

"*Who's there?*" she called, praying that her eyes had deceived her.

The apparition was real. Paul stepped into the circle of candlelight, bringing with him a draining relief that left her weak in the knees. "I didn't mean to startle you," he said, moving closer, his hair mussed, his robe askew.

"I didn't know anyone was awake," she sputtered, slowly recovering.

"I heard you on the stairs and thought that perhaps you were in need of company. But I can see that I was mistaken." He indicated the tray she balanced in her arms. "It was hunger, and not loneliness, that has you roaming the house at this late hour."

Charmaine glanced down and laughed self-consciously. "This isn't for me. It's for the twins. They were awakened by the storm, and I thought a snack might help them fall back to sleep."

"I suppose I shouldn't detain you," he said with a dynamic smile, "but I shall. Come..." He walked into the dark study.

Though his manner seemed benign, an inner voice counseled her not to follow. She went no further than the door. "I really must see to the children. They were frightened," she added lamely, "and if I don't return shortly, they'll begin to worry."

"I'm certain they'll survive a few moments longer," he replied. "In fact, when you do return, you are likely to find them asleep." He hoped his words proved true; the hour would be late when she left him. "Besides, Charmaine, aren't you the least interested as to why I really followed you down here?"

She was intrigued, but before she could reply, he turned his back on her again and felt his way to the table with the tinderbox. There he struck the flint and lit the lamp, adjusting the wick. Its flame flared high, chasing the darkness to the far reaches of the library.

The rumbling storm lost its ferocity, and Charmaine relished a sense of security that made it easy to ignore her rational mind and enter the room. She obeyed him when he spoke over his shoulder and casually told her to set the tray of food down. But her momentary calm was shattered when he faced her and she read the raw passion in his eyes. Cauterized, a sudden spasm shook her.

"Are you cold?" he inquired softly.

"No," she whispered, his magnetism pulling at the core of her being. It was as if she weren't in her own body, but floated above the two figures, an observer of the scene unfolding below.

"Are you afraid of me?" he queried.

Yes, her mind screamed, *and of myself! Dear Lord, we're alone, and I am bewitched.* But she said none of this. Heaven forbid! "Should I be afraid of you?" she asked instead, cleverly setting aside his question.

"That depends on what you're afraid of," he answered just as cleverly, cocking his head to one side.

Dear Lord, he's handsome, Charmaine thought, one stray lock of hair curling on his brow, bidding her to stroke it back into place. She dismissed the temptation, certain that such familiarity would send her straight into his arms.

Lightning flashed again, and the thunder answered. A fierce draft skirted across the floor, grabbing at her robe and wrapping it around her legs; then it was gone. In that eternity of passionate thoughts, neither of them spoke.

Paul's eyes blazed brighter as he admired her lithe form, her innocent beauty highlighted by the copious tresses that fell over her shoulders to her waist. His smoldering gaze returned to her lovely face and the dark eyes that lacked the carefree abandon the moment demanded. There, he noted the last shred of wariness. He moved toward her, much like a panther stalking its prey.

Though unknowingly she flinched, Charmaine did not flee. Rather, she stood her ground until they were but a breath apart. She tilted her head back to look up into his face, her heart leaping in exquisite expectation when his callused hand caressed her cheek.

"You are most desirable, my sweet," he murmured huskily, confident of the romantic web he was spinning about her, savoring the spell she had cast on him as well, his own pulse thundering in his ears. "That is why I sought you out, and now, I would ask for a kiss."

His eyes lingered on her lips, and her eyelids fluttered closed in exhilarating anticipation. There was no turning back – she didn't want to turn back – and she leaned forward as he grasped her shoulders and slowly drew her into his embrace. His head descended, he delivered a tender kiss meant to put her at ease. Then his mouth turned persuasive, testing and tasting, his moustache coarse and prickly, masculine. Further gentleness eluded him. He pulled her hard against him, his mouth cutting across her lips and devouring them. One hand traveled to her nape, the other caressed her back, her hair.

Charmaine's head was spinning with the onslaught of his seduction, and she kissed him in return, rising on the tips of her toes, her hands creeping up his sinewy arms and grasping his shoulders, molding her body to his. Her brazen response belied her innocence, and her unleashed ardor sent his desires soaring.

The quintessential moment was shattered when sharp laughter rang from the doorway. Paul quickly disengaged himself, an oath dying on his lips.

"That's the ticket, Paul. Bring her home, put a roof over her head, strip the bit of clothing off her back, bed her, and then, when you've tired of her, out she goes on her fondled ass with little money spent!"

Mortified, Charmaine turned toward the doorway and the resonant voice that dared utter such vulgarity. A bedraggled stranger stood there, badly beaten by the storm, drenched from face to foot, with the stubble of a beard on his cheeks, and a leather cap cocked to the back of his head. With the slightest movement, she espied Paul out of the corner of her eye. He was straightening his robe, a mock display at dignity, yet he held silent, making not the slightest inquiry as to why the man was in the house.

The intruder strode unceremoniously into the room, and though his wet attire should have placed him at a disadvantage, he did not seem ill at ease. He proceeded to audaciously circle them, and Charmaine was unable to move out of sheer embarrassment, appalled when his assessing regard raked her from head to toe, measuring her worth as if she were on display at an auction. His arrogant eyes met hers, and she dropped her gaze to his boots. He'd tracked a considerable amount of mud on the carpet, as if he had come from the stables. And then she knew: He was the livery hand who'd been called to help with the foal. Still, she couldn't understand why Paul would suffer such insolence.

But there was no time to think, for the derelict held them captive. His wandering gaze fell on the tray of cookies and milk, and a smile broke across his face, revealing gleaming white teeth that were not perfectly straight, but perfectly aligned with his sardonic demeanor.

"How cozy," he mused wickedly, "a passionate kiss followed by refreshments." He settled into one of the chairs, crossed his arms over his chest, and said, "Do carry on! I was very *moved* by the romantic performance. Your lines were fabulous! Could you repeat that one again, Paul, about wanting a kiss? I never thought to ask before." He chuckled deeply.

Charmaine's ire boiled over. "You rude, despicable cur!" she spat out, emboldened by her temper. "What filthy hole did you crawl out of? No!" she quickly added, holding up a hand and wrinkling her nose in over-emphasized revulsion. "I don't want to know!"

His smile broadened, the whole of his face one enormous jeer now. It could not be borne, and she lashed out again. "Thank God I live here and need never place name to your arrogant face!"

The grin ruptured into rich laughter, trampling her bravado. She lifted her chin and grabbed hold of the snack tray. But as she marched from the room, his voice followed her. "Give us a kiss, you saucy, brazen wench!"

Once outside the study, Charmaine gave in to her trembling, unable to steady her frayed nerves, let alone soothe her wounded pride. *A wench. A brazen wench. A saucy, brazen wench! She had never been called a wench in her life!* She looked down at the tray and saw that the candle was snuffed out. If she didn't know better, she'd place the blame on the reprobate who was still closeted in the study with Paul. At least he lived in town, and she wouldn't have to see him again. Pacified by that thought, she pushed the debasing episode out of her mind and groped her way up the stairs, no longer afraid of the dark.

"What are you doing here, John?" Paul asked pointedly, moving to the brandy decanter and pouring himself a stiff drink.

"It was high time I checked on business."

"Really?" Paul snorted.

"Really. Lucky for me that the ship was delayed by the storm–" With Paul's raised brow, he added "–or I would have missed you pressing the house help into working overtime on the night shift. You horny bastard!" He smiled. "She really *loves* her job, doesn't she?"

"Drop it, John."

The room fell silent while Paul took a draught of brandy.

"She cares not who I am," John mused. "Perhaps she'll change her mind in the morning."

"I doubt it," Paul answered listlessly, his plans for the evening neatly laid to waste. Leave it to John to screw things up for him. "She's different."

"Really? Not from what I just saw."

"Just leave her be!" Paul growled, unable to check his anger any longer.

"Leave her for you, you mean. Isn't that right, Paulie? So… you haven't had your way with her yet."

"I'm not going to discuss this with you."

"No?" John clicked his tongue and canted his head, giving the matter some thought. "My assumption must be correct. Tonight was your first tryst with the vixen."

"It wasn't a tryst!" Paul sneered.

"Then you're in love with her?" John pressed, receiving only a scowl. "I didn't think so. In that case, she is fair game. We shall see who is the better player." Chuckling again, he stood and strode from the room, leaving a puddle of murky water at the foot of the chair he had vacated.

When she needed the lightning to illuminate the way, it refused to burst forth, and Charmaine realized that the storm was over. The staircase was very dark, and she clutched the balustrade tightly. When she reached the top, she fumbled down the wide hallway, straining to see. Finally her hand found the doorknob to the children's room. She was never more relieved as when she pushed the portal inward and was bathed in the light of the lamp she'd left there.

The girls were asleep, much as Paul had predicted. What a fool to have wandered the house at midnight! Not even the memory of Paul's kiss annulled the humiliation she had suffered. *No! She'd not think about that!*

She turned her mind to the twins, coaxing a sleep-drugged Jeannette back into her own bed, frowning when she glanced at the French doors and found them slightly ajar. A shiver chased up her spine, and she walked cautiously toward the glass panels, securing them again. She could not shake the uneasiness that engulfed her, for it was ludicrous to think that either the girls or Pierre had opened them. It must be a faulty latch. Yes, that seemed plausible. She would mention it to Travis Thornfield in the morning.

She lit another candle and turned the lamp down low. Taking the tray of treats, lest the children eat them before breakfast, she stepped into her own bedchamber and closed the door, safe at last.

In his aggravation over the unpleasant turn the evening had taken, Paul hadn't considered John's destination after leaving the study. Even now, he did not remember that the governess occupied his brother's former bedchamber, for his mind was still relishing the taste of her sweet lips, the feel of her soft body in his arms, her impassioned response to his advance. Had he set aside his glass of brandy and allowed his mind to clear, the implications of the bedroom arrangements would have been manifest, and he'd have been none too pleased.

John fumbled in the darkness as he entered his dressing room. "Blast it all!" he snarled. "Where's the confounded tinderbox?" Despite his rummaging, his efforts came up futile. Frustrated, he groped his way to the bedroom door, hoping to have more success there. He was wet and miserable, and in desperate need of a hot bath. He knew the bath would have to wait until morning, but a good night's sleep in a dry bed after a week aboard the Destiny, which had traveled from New York, would be a pleasant accommodation.

He was stunned when he flung the door open and found his brother's concubine climbing into his bed. In fact, he was so surprised, he gave little thought to her reaction: the speed with which she jumped up. He drew a deep breath and released it slowly, his shock giving way to a crooked grin. She was bewitching. Perhaps he didn't need that full night's sleep after all.

"Well, well, well, and well again, aren't you the little minx?" he chuckled knowingly. "Do you always entertain total strangers?"

Charmaine was too petrified to speak. She only knew that she had been set upon by a beast, one that was tracking her now, and in her mounting fear, all she could do was plaster herself against the wall.

"Now how did you know where I'd be bedding down for the night?" he pondered amusedly, closing the distance between them.

Charmaine realized that she must act, or all would be lost. Pushing off from the wall, she flew like a wild thing, reaching the children's door in a heartbeat.

But in the instant it took to grab the doorknob, her arm was caught from behind, and she was pulled back with one forceful tug. Her scream was stifled as the man's other hand clamped down on her mouth and she was propelled around, coming face to face with the tormenting demon. Her eyes grew wide at his leering grin, her face turning crimson as she fought to hold her breath against the foul odor she was sure he radiated.

Reading the repugnance and terror in her eyes, John relaxed his grip. She didn't seem to know who he was, but that didn't coincide with the fact that she knew where his chambers were located.

Perceiving his moment of weakness, she began to struggle again. Given an inch, she had taken a yard, and John released her mouth to subdue her thrashing feet that were doing little in the way of assaulting his shins, but much in the way of inflaming his ardor.

"Calm yourself, Madame," he hissed, pinning her against the door when she didn't comply. "I just want some answers to my questions. However, if you'd like me to continue where Paul left off, I'd be more than happy to oblige."

She submitted, quaking now. His words buffeted her cheek, and she cringed, anticipating acrid, whisky breath. She smelled wet clothing, little more.

"Why are you in here?" he demanded.

"This is my bedroom!" she pleaded. "I work here! This is where I sleep!"

The conviction in her voice held the ring of truth. "So you *don't* know who I am?"

She grew courageous when his hands dropped away. "You're probably a convict escaped from some filthy prison!" she rallied, bent upon insulting him as he had her. "You should have rotted there!" But even as she blurted out the retort, the light began to dawn: *He wasn't Martin, the livery hand.*

She gasped when he pulled her to his chest and buried his face in her hair, his lips close to her ear. "Ah, a prison indeed," he whispered passionately, "but can you guess what I was convicted of?"

"I'll scream if you don't release me!" she cried, the tremor in her voice nullifying her threat. In truth, she was far too frightened to scream, certain that any such an outburst would prompt him to ravish her.

His head lifted from the sweet fragrance of her wild hair. When he chuckled softly, Charmaine knew he was only toying with her. Then his laughing eyes became serious, and quite abruptly, he released her, stepping back apace.

She was an all too feminine distraction, and he was finding it exceedingly difficult to leave her company. But, he would not cajole her to his bed like his brother, and he certainly wouldn't force her. She'd come of her own accord, or not at all, and he knew she wasn't going to do that. He backed away, grateful that he was as tired as he was.

Still, he was having fun with this little encounter, so he wasn't of a mind to leave just yet. *She must be the governess*, he surmised. *Colette must have moved her into his room to be close to the children.*

He moved around the chamber, noticing the feminine changes she had made. Her possessions were meager, but they warmed the room in a way that his belongings never had. He exhaled, causing her to jump. She hadn't moved from the doorway, and he realized that something besides the change of inhabitant was different, but he couldn't pinpoint what it was.

"Are you going to leave?" she inquired, hugging herself rigidly against his penetrating gaze.

"Patience, patience," he chided, eyeing the tray of cookies. He took one and popped it into his mouth, chasing it down with a glass of milk. "Wouldn't you like to join me? It would be a shame to waste these, and since Paul won't be *coming,* not here anyway, we might as well–"

"Won't you *please* leave?" she cut in, ignoring his chuckle. "It is very late, and I have a great deal to do in the morning!"

"Oh, don't worry about that," he reassured with the wave of his hand, "I'll see to it that you're allowed to sleep in the morning, especially since you've entertained not one, but two gentlemen this evening. A hard night's work!"

When her mouth flew open to protest, he only winked at her, popped another cookie into his mouth and turned to leave. As he strode to the hallway door, something splintered underfoot. He picked up the hairbrush she had thrown across the room earlier that evening. It was broken in two. He studied the pieces for a moment, then tossed them onto the bed. With that, he tipped his cap, opened the door, and left the room.

Charmaine flew to the portal and locked it. She ran to the dressing room door to do the same, only to find that it did not have a lock. She fretted for a time, but when the adjoining room remained mercifully silent, she began to relax. She got into bed and picked up the remnants of her hairbrush, letting out a sigh of relief.

Paul sat heavily on his bed, realizing just how desolate his bedchamber was... "*Shit!*" he swore, shooting to his feet. "*Shit!*"

He sped to the door, but thinking better of it, exited through the French doors. In seconds, he was around the corner of the south wing balcony, past the children's rooms, and standing at the glass portals of John's old bedroom. The doors were closed, but he peered in. Mercifully, Charmaine was sitting in the middle of her bed, alone. He pushed into the room, his eyes raking the chamber, making certain that his brother wasn't lurking in the shadows.

Startled, she gasped, but when she realized it was Paul, her hand dropped from her breast.

"Are you all right?" he queried with genuine concern.

"I am now!" she bit out.

"Was he here?"

"Of course he was here! This is his room!"

"Did he–"

"No!"

Paul's apparent relief fueled her ire. "Why didn't you tell me who he was downstairs? I made a complete fool of myself, ranting and raving the way I did! And if that wasn't bad enough, you let me come up here and..."

Her words dropped off as he rounded the foot of the bed. Again, she jumped off the mattress. *You've entertained not one, but two gentlemen this evening...* Already John Duvoisin's words were haunting her, and she was furious with Paul for placing her in such a humiliating situation. "You told me he'd never return! You promised me that when you suggested I move into this room!"

"He shouldn't have come back," Paul admitted softly, "and I was just as surprised as you were. That's why I was at loss for words."

Charmaine read the displeasure in his eyes, and her anger waned.

"I also thought to save you further embarrassment by avoiding an introduction. John would have just loved that. And I *completely* forgot about the sleeping arrangements until I got to my own room. I'm sorry, Charmaine."

He continued to advance, so close now that her heart thudded in her ears, the beat no longer heated but heady.

"Forgive me?" he petitioned.

With her slight nod and timid smile, he leaned forward.

The moment was at hand. But above the sound of her racing pulse came a resonant, mocking voice: *Well, well, well, and well again... Aren't you the little minx? You saucy, brazen wench!*

Charmaine stepped back; she'd play no part in those vulgar declarations. "You had better go."

Paul accepted her refusal with a soft snort of disappointment. His gaze swept the length of her, then he departed the room the way he had come, leaving her confused and shaken. She had been vulnerable, and again he had acted the gentleman.

She climbed into bed, sitting on the broken brush. She pulled the two pieces from beneath her and thought of John and Paul. *Two gentlemen tonight...* She'd hardly call John Duvoisin a gentleman. She set the hairbrush aside. At least it was the only thing she had lost this night.

Book Two

****

The Charm

Saturday
August 19, 1837

Chapter 1

Paul knocked on Frederic's chamber door at dawn. His father might still be sleeping. He knocked again, and the door opened to a quizzical Travis Thornfield. "Your father is in his bedroom having his breakfast."

"I must speak with him right away."

Travis stepped aside, and Paul crossed the antechamber for the inner room.

Frederic looked up in surprise and closed the journal next to his plate.

"John is back," Paul stated.

Frederic sat back in his chair and allowed the news to sink in, his heart besieged with elation, apprehension, and finally, despair.

Uncomfortable with his parent's pensiveness, Paul felt compelled to say more. "He arrived on the Falcon. She was delayed by the storm and didn't lay anchor until evening."

"Did you see him?"

"I was in the study when he got home."

"Did you speak with him?"

"Briefly. It was late. I was tired. He was soaked." Paul tried hard to read his father's expression, one that he'd never seen before. "He's come home to check on business, or so he says."

Frederic stood, leaned heavily on his cane, and limped to the French doors. "Thank you for letting me know," he finally murmured.

When he realized his father would say no more, Paul left.

Frederic stared down into the courtyard. John was home. He'd been afraid to hope for this day. Now that it had come, he wasn't truly prepared for it.

Charmaine hadn't fallen asleep until the first rays of dawn streaked the sky an inky orange, only succumbing to fatigue after she'd relived her ordeal at least a thousand times. Now, light poured into her room, and she awoke with a start. It had to be late morning. She rose and hurriedly crossed to the children's bedchamber. A sheet of paper had been slipped under the adjoining door.

> *Mlle. Charmaine,*
> *It is morning and you are still sleeping. We are with Nana Rose.*
> *Jeannette, Yvette, and Pierre*

Charmaine smiled in relief; Jeannette and Yvette must have told Rose that they had kept her up very late last night. *Last night...* the storm... the children... the specter... the midnight snack... Paul – *John!*

She sat down on her bed, rubbing her throbbing temple, and looked at the clock on her dresser: eight-thirty. She didn't want to face the day, inevitably confronting John Duvoisin along the way, but she knew she must. Otherwise, she could never save face.

John Duvoisin. She'd finally met the heir to the Duvoisin fortune, the man she'd heard so much about, mostly bad. Now she knew why. In their two brief encounters, hadn't he proven himself worthy of every epithet? She cringed, recalling the words she had spat in his face. *You rude, despicable cur... What filthy hole did you crawl out of?... Thank God I live here and need never place name to your arrogant face... You're probably a convict broken out of some filthy prison...* She groaned and buried her face in her hands.

A convict indeed! How could she have been so verbal—dimwitted? Even if she hadn't figured out who he was in the study, his identity had been glaringly obvious once he'd invaded her bedchamber. He hadn't been stalking her, and he wasn't some stable-hand either! He was merely seeking his bed. Her cheeks flushed as she remembered the assumption *he* had made when he'd found her climbing into his bed. *Do you always entertain total strangers?* Dear God! It was too much to think about! Her head pounded, and her eyes stung from lack of sleep.

She had nothing to be embarrassed about, she resolved, then moaned. Who was she fooling? She *did* have something to be embarrassed about. He'd caught her in his brother's arms. She might not be guilty of 'entertaining' a total stranger, but she was guilty of a late-night rendezvous with Paul. To make matters worse, he had found them in their nightclothes and had drawn all the worst conclusions. She couldn't even enjoy the memory of her first thrilling kiss, for the prurient man defiled it.

John Duvoisin. What would she say to him? If nothing else, she must face him with her head held high.

The nursery door burst open, and the children came bounding in, unmindful of the impropriety of storming her room. Fully dressed, they bounced on the bed in glee, their laughter ricocheting off the walls.

"Have you just awoken?" Yvette exclaimed incredulously. "It is so late! You must hurry and get dressed, Mademoiselle Charmaine."

"Why? What is the rush?"

"Nana Rose told us that we are not to go downstairs for breakfast without you, and we are ready for breakfast now!"

There was a knock on the outer door, and Charmaine opened it to Mrs. Faraday, who bustled into the chamber with a stack of fresh linens.

"You must hurry, Mademoiselle Charmaine, or we'll be too late!" Jeannette piped in, taking up where her sister had left off.

"Huwwy, Mainie!" Pierre echoed.

Confused, Charmaine took in their effervescent faces. "Too late for what?"

Mrs. Faraday explained. "Master John returned late last night, and the children are anxious to see him. He is in the dining room, eating as we speak."

"Master John?" Charmaine queried in feigned ignorance.

"Their elder brother. The girls expect him to shower them with gifts as he did the last time he arrived unexpectedly from Virginia. Apparently, Master Paul was still awake when he came in and has just now told Rose."

Charmaine felt the blood rush to her cheeks. The telltale blush was not lost on the housekeeper, whose assessing eye rested momentarily on her face. Then she babbled on. "She is the only one in the house truly pleased to have him back, though I cannot, for the life of me, figure out why. She is as bad as the children, rushing off to her room to make herself presentable before seeing him."

"We're glad he's come home!" Yvette countered. "I'll wager he has a great stack of presents for us! Maybe something bigger than a piano this time!" She stood on her tiptoes and reached as high as she could in indication of the magnitude of wonders that awaited them with the return of her beloved brother.

"And Pierre wants to meet him!" Jeannette added. "Don't you, Pierre?"

"Uh huh!" he agreed with an alacritous nod. "I neber saw him before."

Tying back the drapes, Mrs. Faraday shook her head. "He can be a rascal," she proceeded, eager to impart what she knew of the man, "a bad influence on the children, teaching them disrespect the likes of which I've never seen." She leveled her gaze on Yvette as if to fortify her point, then motioned toward the tray of half-eaten cookies. "What would you have me do with this, Miss?"

"I'm finished with it, thank you."

Yvette eyed the discarded snack. "You *did* bring them for us! We waited and waited for you, but you never came back last night."

Charmaine caught the housekeeper's raised brow. "It took a while to warm the milk. By the time I returned, the two of you were fast asleep."

"So you ate the cookies yourself?"

"No – I mean – I didn't eat them all."

Mrs. Faraday frowned in bewilderment, taking the tray with her as she left.

"Oh Mademoiselle Charmaine, please hurry and get dressed! We want to see Johnny before he's gone for the day!"

"Very well," she ceded. Best to get the introduction over with.

The children returned to the nursery, and she began washing up, splashing water in her face, brushing out her hair and securing it in a tight bun. As she pulled a dress from her armoire, she realized that her heart was racing. She inhaled deeply. What would Mrs. Harrington do if she were in this predicament? Perhaps the situation wasn't so dire. If she presented herself with dignity and grace, a warm smile and friendly greeting, they could start afresh. She recalled Joshua Harrington's opinion of John Duvoisin and grimaced. Somehow, she knew this was wishful thinking. But see the man she must. *You owe him nothing,* she thought, and then groaned. *Nothing but respect.*

She was fastening the last button on her plain dress when a pummeling resounded on the door. "All right, all right!" she laughed artificially as she opened it. Three eager bodies spilled into the room, dashing to the hallway door.

"What are you waiting for?" Yvette cried over her shoulder, disappearing into the corridor. "Come quickly!"

Charmaine followed, but by the time she reached the crest of the staircase, the twins were far below, slowed only by Pierre, who was trying to keep pace. Even in her excitement, Jeannette lovingly took his hand and helped him along. Next, they were jumping off the landing and racing out of sight, the patter of feet marking their passage. Charmaine lifted her skirts and hurried her descent, knowing it would be better to enter the dining room with the children. She was too late; their voices echoed in unison, attesting to their boundless joy.

"Johnny!"

The name shook her to the core. He was still present at the table, most probably alone. But even if he wasn't, she felt certain that he'd take pleasure in taunting her. She passed the study and braced herself, sighing in relief when she reached the archway and found that his back was turned to her. She could observe him first, inconspicuously.

He lounged in Paul's seat, his boots propped on George's chair. The children were clustered around him. Jeannette was sitting in his lap, Pierre leaned tentatively against his left leg, wearing the widest of grins he'd ever bestowed upon a stranger, and Yvette, his staunchest ally, stood to his right, fiercely hugging his arm. Charmaine was astounded by the raw emotion betrayed with this reunion. One look at the girls' adoring faces, and she knew that she had seriously underestimated how much they loved him. Even more striking was her impression that the man reciprocated the feelings, his attention fixed on the twins, a hand rubbing Pierre's back.

"Where are our presents?" Yvette asked presumptuously.

"Presents?" John queried. "What presents? I didn't bring any presents." His voice was deep and crisp, and quite pleasing to the ear.

"Oh really? Then why did you wink at Jeannette just now?"

"I wasn't winking," he insisted, "I had something in my eye."

Yvette wasn't fooled. "Well then, what's in that large sack under the table?"

"My, haven't we sharp eyes," he laughed in that chuckle that was already disturbingly familiar to Charmaine. "See for yourself."

Yvette clambered under the table to fetch her loot. She was soon forgotten as Pierre tugged on John's leg. "We hab a gubberness," he said, smiling up at the man, who leaned forward to lend his full attention.

"Oh really?" John asked, and Charmaine could tell he was smiling. "And is she old and ugly like Nana Rose?"

"Oh no," Pierre pronounced seriously, the cruel remark lost on the innocent child. "She's boo-tee-full and I love her!" He hugged John's leg all the harder to emphasize his point, exacting another chuckle from the man.

"There she is!" Yvette pointed as she crawled out from beneath the table.

John turned, and Charmaine's breath caught in her throat. Lifting Jeannette off his lap and setting her on her feet, he stood, and their eyes met, his lazy gaze holding her prisoner as he assessed her in the light of this new day.

So this is John Duvoisin, Charmaine thought. He was tall, though perhaps not as tall as his brother, with broad shoulders and a slender waist. Unlike last night, he appeared distinguished, his attire that of a gentleman. The cut of his face possessed a rugged handsomeness she had missed as well. Now there was no mistaking his identity. The resemblance to Frederic was distinct: brown eyes, long curved nose, square jaw, and thin lips. Even had his visage been blank, she would have known he was a Duvoisin, such was his bearing and stance – one that radiated the power wielded by the men of this family.

As if reading her mind, his thick brow tipped upward, touching the light brown locks that covered the whole of his forehead. She wanted to look away, except that he seemed to challenge her to do so, his scrutiny condescending, mocking her fear. She shivered at the thought of her future resting in his hands: she'd never be free of the tormenting fires he had stoked just a few short hours ago when he came barging into her sheltered life. An inkling of the pain that he would bring her caused her to recoil.

"I believe we've already met," he said with a crooked smile, "though we don't know each other's name."

"I know who you are!" she responded heatedly, her anxiety gone.

His brow raised further. "Well now, for someone who thanked God never to 'place name to my arrogant face', it certainly didn't take you long to get all the vital information."

She gaped at him, nettled by his precise recollection. His respectable appearance was not going to foster polite conversation.

He, in turn, was amused by her blatant outrage. She was playing the lady wronged, though he knew she was no lady. Her self-righteousness would prove interesting indeed. "Come, Mademoiselle – it is Mademoiselle, isn't it?" With her rigid nod, he continued, "You act as if I'm still the water rat come in from the rain. Or perhaps in dry attire, I'm just a rat?"

"I never called you a rat!" she replied defensively.

"No?" he queried snidely. "What else but a rat 'crawls out of a filthy hole'? But then, considering we've only just met, perhaps I'm wrong. Surely you couldn't have formed a fair opinion of me, unless someone has influenced you. My brother hasn't been filling your head with nasty stories about me, has he?"

Her silence was answer enough, and he chuckled softly.

His merriment pierced her deeply, yet she could only glare at him, realizing that he had manipulated her into betraying Paul.

"Don't look so chagrined, Mademoiselle," he commented. "You haven't told me anything that I didn't already know."

"I haven't told you anything!"

"That's right, you haven't, Miss…?" He didn't know her name, and suddenly feeling at a disadvantage – he never tolerated that; putting people at a disadvantage was his forte – he pressed on. "You do have a name, don't you?"

Charmaine was intimidated by his directness. She thought of Anne London and grew wary of his motives. According to Stephen Westphal, John was engaged to the widow. He had to know her name – and more! She'd not open herself to further ridicule by answering. Instead, she spoke to the children, who were seated at the table, watching them avidly. "I'm going to ask Mrs. Henderson to prepare a breakfast tray. We can eat–"

"I asked for your name, Mademoiselle," John cut in curtly.

There was no avoiding it. "Charmaine Ryan," she threw over her shoulder, praying that she was wrong, yet hastening toward the kitchen in case she wasn't.

"Well then, Charmaine Ryan," he replied slowly, testing the sound of it. "You and the children shall breakfast with me. Come now, no need to be afraid."

Though his gibe halted her step, curiosity turned her about face; his voice betrayed not the slightest indication that he knew who she was.

He, in turn, canted his head to study her. Somehow, she seemed familiar, though he was certain he had never met her before. "Charmaine Ryan," he murmured again as he pulled out the chair he had propped his feet on and gestured for her to sit. "Since you are guardian of the children, I would just like to talk – become better acquainted with you *and* your *moral* conduct in my home."

She stood stunned. How would she ever reclaim her dignity? She considered leaving the room, but that would lend credence to his lewd conclusions. More importantly, she couldn't abandon the children; he'd hold that against her as well.

"I'm sorry, John," Paul called as he entered the room, "but Miss Ryan and the children are breakfasting with me."

Charmaine sighed in relief.

"How charming!" John chortled, leaning back against the table and crossing his arms and legs. "If it isn't the knight in shining armor come to rescue the damsel in distress." The twins giggled. "And I'm not invited?"

"You can join us, Johnny!" Yvette interjected.

Paul grunted. "Come Charmaine," he said, taking her arm, "we can eat in the kitchen."

"Don't bother," John replied, pushing off from the table. "I know when I'm not wanted."

"Don't go, Johnny!" Jeannette implored. "We haven't visited with you yet."

"I will come to see you later," he promised. And then, on an afterthought, he asked, "Why hasn't your mother joined you this morning? Is she taking breakfast in her chambers?"

The girl froze, her tortured expression mirrored by Yvette. He turned befuddled eyes upon Paul, who struggled with a response.

"John – I–"

Then Jeannette was crying, and John's mounting perturbation was diverted. "What is it? What is the matter, Jeannette?"

"Mama is dead, Johnny," Yvette whispered unsteadily. "She died in April."

Charmaine watched a tumult of emotions run rampant across John's face, and suddenly, she felt sorry for him. He obviously had no idea about Colette's death.

"When were you planning on telling me this, Paul?" he snarled.

"I didn't know you hadn't been told–"

"The hell you didn't!"

The moment held until John headed toward the foyer in large, angry strides. Paul rushed after him. "Where are you going?"

"To see *Father* and find out what other secrets he's been keeping!"

Paul grabbed his arm. "No, John! You hurt him enough last time."

John ripped free, his face contorted, a feral gleam in his eyes. "*I hurt him?*" he thundered. "*I* hurt him?" Then he fell on Paul in volcanic fury, grabbing great fistfuls of his shirtfront and slamming him into the wall.

Charmaine wasn't sure if the impact or her scream brought Fatima Henderson racing from the kitchen.

"What's goin' on in here?" the cook demanded, her voice bringing John to his senses. "Mastah John, what's gotten into you?"

John's grip relaxed, and Paul pushed him away. They glared at one another, refusing to meet the woman's reprimanding eyes, Paul adjusting his jacket as if he were the conqueror instead of the vanquished.

"Miss Charmaine," Fatima pressed when neither man would answer her, "what are these two up to, already at each other's throats and Mastah John not even home a day yet? Are they fighting over you?"

"No, Fatima," Paul refuted coldly, his eyes fixed on his brother. "We're not fighting over Charmaine. John just doesn't like hearing the truth."

Reality began to sink in, and John's wrath caved in to desolation. His face had gone white, and Charmaine read his anguish. He bowed his head and left.

She regarded Paul, silently beseeching an explanation.

"Fatima," he directed, "please feed the children while I speak to Charmaine."

Fatima took charge of Pierre's plate, giving Jeannette a comforting pat on the shoulder. The girl continued to sniffle, her cheeks wet.

Paul looked to Yvette. "When you're finished, you are to take your brother and sister back to the nursery. Mademoiselle Ryan will meet you there."

Yvette nodded. It was clear from his tone that he'd brook no resistance.

John reached the landing, head down, when his eyes fell upon the bottom of her gown. His gaze lifted, taking in the folded hands, her bust, and finally, her breathtaking face, smiling down at him from the portrait, young and innocent and suddenly dead. *Too late, he'd arrived home too late.*

His name echoed from above. He tore his eyes from Colette's lovely face and looked at his aunt.

"So it *is* true," Agatha said as she descended, "you've returned."

"So I have," John muttered, "but unfortunately, you're here."

Unperturbed, she raised a well-shaped brow and smiled triumphantly. "Yes, I'm here. Apparently, you haven't heard *all* the news."

He instinctively knew that she wasn't speaking about Colette.

"Unlike Colette's unfortunate passing," she pressed on, "there has been a joyous wedding in the manor. I am pleased to tell you that your father and I were married in July."

John thought he would vomit. His aunt's smug mien fired him anew, and he took a threatening step toward her.

She smiled amusedly, unalarmed. "It was inevitable. Frederic and I have been in love for many years now. Had I been widowed sooner, I would have become the second Mrs. Duvoisin, rather than the third. Colette was much too young for your father, really. After all, she could have been his daughter. He needs a *woman* to love him, not a little girl."

John would have taken great pleasure in slapping her face if Rose had not called to him from the crest of the north wing staircase.

"John, you *are* home! I was just coming down to see you."

He spun around, masking his emotions. "I'm afraid I can't talk right now, Nan. My father is waiting to see me."

"John," Rose admonished gently, warily, "please... be kind."

"Sure, Nan, sure," he bit out, before pushing past Agatha.

His mind was a maelstrom of words and images. What had George said? *Colette fears Agatha... fears the hold she may exert over Paul... fears for the children...* Clearly, his aunt had been after bigger game and had bagged it.

Agatha's twisted smile followed him. When he was gone, she threw a knowing look to Rose, then turned and climbed the stairs.

Rose offered a silent prayer. She had hoped to have a moment alone with John, but she was too late and headed to the dining room instead.

Paul closed the study door and leaned back against it.

"What happened out there?" Charmaine finally asked.

"You needn't be concerned about it," he replied with an exasperated sigh.

"Needn't be concerned? I was terrified! He attacked you!"

"My brother is easily incensed. He imagines slights against him when none exist, and then he carries on like he did just now."

"But not having been told about Colette *is* a slight. And although I'm not fond of your brother, surely he was justified in being angry about that!"

"He was informed about her failing health months ago," Paul stated flatly. "Her death shouldn't have come as a shock."

"Then why was he so angry?"

"As I said, he doesn't like to hear the truth. He's hurt members of this family with this sort of behavior. Even Colette, as good and kind as she tried to be to him, suffered at his hands."

Charmaine gaped at him in disbelief. She shuddered to think that episodes similar to the one she'd just witnessed had taken place in the past. God forbid, had the man been violent to Colette? She didn't dare ask. "But why?"

"Ever since I can remember, John has been determined to do things his way, and his way invariably runs afoul of our father's wishes. My father has good reason to be angry with him on many accounts. Likewise, John hates the fact that our father is still in charge. It is the very thing that fuels his fury."

She could not speak. The picture Paul painted was all too reminiscent of her parents' home. Fear was nipping at her heels again, that same gnawing apprehension she had constantly lived with when her father was around.

"Charmaine, you've heard me speak of my brother before. You saw for yourself how he is, both last night and this morning. Even so, you needn't worry. You can trust me to watch out for you."

"I hope I can."

"You must. Rough times are ahead. John will see to it. He always does."

"Master John?"

Grave concern creased Travis Thornfield's brow, and he stood his ground, blocking John's entrance to his father's chambers.

"Let him in, Travis."

Travis stepped back, and John stalked into the bright dressing room.

Frederic was standing, and though he appeared at ease, his pulse was racing.

"Leave us alone, Travis," John growled, his anger fed by his father's calm demeanor and restored health.

"Sir?" the manservant questioned, his eyes traveling to Frederic.

Frederic only nodded, and Travis deserted the electrified room.

The day was still in its infancy when Charmaine carried her breakfast tray upstairs. Her steps were slow and burdened, lack of sleep making the prospect of a full day with three healthy children wearisome before it had truly begun.

She gritted her teeth when she found the nursery vacant, angry that the girls had disobeyed Paul's instructions. Her morning was already spoiled, and she could thank John Duvoisin for that, too. Her meal would once again have to wait; she had to find the children before Agatha did. Her head was pounding and her eyes still burned, conditions she was certain she would never shake off as long as John Duvoisin was around. But damning him would not locate her charges. She headed toward the north wing, knocking on the chamber door adjacent to her own.

There was a rustling sound, then nothing. She rapped on the door again and called out to them. No answer, just the sound of scurrying footfalls. "Yvette, Jeannette," she called again, "are you in there?" Still, no reply. She pondered momentarily what to do. Perhaps it wasn't the children. Jeannette would not have held silent. And yet, anyone else would have responded. Without a second thought, she opened the door.

A gust of wind rushed past her, swirling around her legs and taking up her skirts, sweeping a ream of stationery off the nearby desk and raining its many sheets on the immaculate floor. As she stepped into the chamber, a second gale burst through the French doors, taking more paper to wing. The chamber was empty, but before Charmaine could resume her search, she had a mess to clean up.

She closed the door to stem the stiff breezes crossing the room, then set to work. There were scores of blank sheets, and slowly, she straightened and replaced them. She abruptly stopped. There was a letter here – a very wrinkled and worn letter. Charmaine recognized the hand immediately, and her heartbeat quickened. It belonged to Colette. She quickly placed the three pages in order and gasped when she found the first sheet.

> *My dearest John,*
> *I cannot know your present state of mind. It is not my intention to cause you greater pain...*

John stood before his father, seething.

"Why don't you sit down, John?" Frederic offered.

"I won't be staying long," came the rigid reply.

Frederic exhaled. "Welcome home."

John snorted, further revolted by the false greeting. "I see Colette's painting still hangs in the center hallway, Father. When will you be commissioning the artist to paint your third wife's portrait?"

Frederic received the heavy sarcasm evenly. "You've seen Agatha?"

"Right after I found out about Colette's death," John answered virulently. "Not one slap in the face, but two! Tell me, Father, couldn't you wait for Colette's body to turn cold before you took another wife?"

"My marriage to Agatha has nothing to do with Colette."

"You amaze me, Father. I think I've left a cripple behind, but look at you: you're up and about, a veritable newlywed! Poor Paul, he thinks you can't withstand another confrontation with me, but you *have* withstood two young wives, the last of which gave you a real *run for your money*... And here you are, only four months after Colette's death, remarried and working on number three!" He shook his head in theatrical astonishment. "You must be slipping, though. Agatha's rather old. I would have put money on the new governess catching your eye. She's more in line with your taste for virgin flesh, isn't she?"

If Frederic had hoped that John's journey home was for any reason other than continuing where they had left off four years ago, he was mistaken. With his prayers for the morning swiftly desecrated, his heart took up a new beat, and his blood began to boil. And still John was talking, his words ruthless and baiting.

"Or could it be that you're ready to admit you're too old for someone as young and beautiful as Miss Ryan?" He paused for a moment, pretending at thought. "No, that can't be it. You still have all that money to spend! And any young, impressionable maiden would salivate at your feet if you wagged that fortune in front of her, wouldn't she?" He paused again, placing a fist under his chin as if the problem were too perplexing to figure out. Then, he lifted a finger in mock comprehension. "I know what it must be! Paul has laid claim to her and you wouldn't dream of interfering. After all, he's your shining star."

Frederic had heard his fill. "You've come home to insult me, is that it?"

"Not quite," John denied. "I came home because Colette wrote to me. You were aware of that, weren't you?"

He relished the fire in his father's eyes and eagerly pressed on. "She feared for the children. Now, let me see, what were her exact words? Ah yes: 'If your father cannot put his bitterness behind him, the only love the children will have when I am gone is that of their governess and Nana Rose.' But here's the problem: Rose is terribly old, their governess is a little trollop falling all over Paul, and then there's you, the *father* they never see – the bitter one. Such a happy family, isn't it? Oh, but I forgot, now they have a stepmother. Won't she make their lives just *wonderful*?"

"That's enough!" Frederic ground out, his jaw clenched and twitching.

John smiled wickedly; he'd gained the desired result. "How does it feel, Father, to know that your wife wrote to her *stepson* to request his aid in supplying the children with the love and affection they'd never get from you?"

"I am not surprised that she wrote such a letter, John," his father fired back. "She's played you for the fool more than she has me."

"And what is that supposed to mean?"

"Let us just say that I was married to her for *nine long years* and came to know her in ways that you can't even hope to imagine."

John resisted the urge to deliver a hammering blow to his sire's face. Instead, he damned him silently, a hatred unmatched, then turned away and escaped the room, slamming the door behind him. Agatha stood in the hallway, a tight smile of victory on her lips. John contemplated striking her, but curbed that weakness as well. With blood pounding in his ears, he headed for his chambers.

"Some things never change," Frederic mumbled as he slouched into the armchair. "When will I accept that?" Burying his face in his hands, he massaged his brow. He had an excruciating headache.

Charmaine's hands were trembling as her eyes flew over the letter. *My God! Why would Colette write to John, especially after the way he treated her?*

She quickly folded the sheets and placed them back on the desk. But they unfolded slowly, inviting her to read on, and she glimpsed the date at the top of the first page: Wednesday, the eighth of March, eighteen hundred thirty seven – exactly one month before Colette's death!

The penned endearment shouted up at her. *My dearest John...* Why had Colette addressed her stepson with words usually reserved for a loved one? *Dear God,* Charmaine gasped, unable to attach reason to it. According to Paul, Colette had suffered at John's hands, and Colette said that John was very angry with her. Then again, Colette was so kind and good, she would put aside any rancor to make peace, to convert the demon with temperance. Charmaine picked up the letter again, her eyes falling to the first paragraph, drinking in phrases that she knew were not intended for her eyes.

> *... I pray that you receive this letter. I have every faith in George to deliver it into you hands.*

George? The gossip was true! He *had* traveled to Virginia! The letter must have been extremely important to warrant the abandoning of his duties these many months. Charmaine continued to read, this time somewhere in the middle.

> *... I do not want to die knowing that he will shortly follow me in such a state of mind. The ferocity of his anger belies the depth of his love, but he needs somebody to show him the way. I was unable to do so, but I know that you are. If you have ever truly...*

Suddenly, the hallway door banged open, and John stormed the chamber, grabbing hold of the rebounding portal and slamming it shut with such force that the walls vibrated. He was halfway into the room before he realized she was there, her loud gasp breaking through his violent thoughts.

What is she doing here?

And then he knew: clutched to her breast was a letter – his letter. This unsavory act was the last straw, and he exploded. "How dare you sneak into my room and rummage through my drawers for what you could find?"

Charmaine was too terrified to speak, her slackened jaw quivering. She was guilty of violating his privacy, and nothing could exonerate her.

"I'm waiting for an answer, *demoiselle!"*

"I – I'm sorry!" she sputtered, bursting into tears.

The letter slipped to the floor, and her legs propelled her forward. She didn't get far. He caught hold of her as she skirted past, jerking her around to face him.

"Not so fast!" he snarled. "Why are you in my room?" He gave her a hard shake, his hands like vises biting into her flesh.

"I'm sorry!" she sobbed, writhing against his brutal fingers. "I didn't know it was your room!"

Although her contrition was convincing, a torrid torment roiled in his heart, making it easy, satisfying in fact, to vent his wrath on this guilty wench, who was digging herself into a deeper hole of dubious conduct every time he ran into her. Perhaps she wasn't the vicious, manipulative Agatha Blackford Ward, the new Mrs. Frederic Duvoisin, but she was a conniving Jezebel all the same.

"You expect me to believe that?" he chortled insanely.

"I was looking for the children!" she cried.

"*In my desk drawer?*"

She wrenched one arm free, but his fist yanked the other painfully higher. "You're hurting me!"

"Just as I suspected!" he sneered demonically. "You have no answer!"

He pushed her away, and she fell backward into the bed, sitting with a thump, massaging her throbbing arm. Although tears smudged her cheeks, her eyes were suddenly dry. They flashed with hatred, hatred for this man, another '*John*', who was so much like her father. He had just sealed his fate. From this moment forward, their discourse could never be civil. He was a dog and would forever remain so. No matter that Colette had written kind words to him, trying to reach his blackest of souls. But Charmaine was not Colette, did not have the fortitude to selflessly forgive. Experience had taught her that such attempts at peacemaking were futile. With jaw set, she pushed off the bed.

John didn't falter under her display of courage. The moment she moved, so did he, checking her escape. "Now," he growled icily, "I want the truth from you, or you'll have more than a sore arm to rub when you leave this room!"

Charmaine shivered momentarily, but the embers of hatred had been stoked, and its fire eclipsed her fear. "I've told you the truth. I was searching for the children. I heard noises coming from inside this room, but when I called to them and they didn't answer, I assumed they were up to some mischief. That's when I opened the door. A draft blew the papers to the floor. I was merely picking –"

"Behind closed doors?" he demanded incredulously. "Do you take me for a fool, Mademoiselle? I placed that letter in the desk drawer. So tell me, Charmaine Ryan, how did the wind manage to blow it from *that* spot?"

Charmaine fleetingly puzzled over his declaration and dismissed it as swiftly as she thought: *The desk drawer? Colette's letter was not in a drawer. He's hell bent upon venting his anger, and I've become an easy victim.*

John perceived her confusion, her partial innocence, and his temper cooled.

"I've told you the truth," she hissed, squaring her shoulders. "Let me pass."

"You've lied."

"I haven't lied, but I can see that the truth makes little difference to the likes of you. Go ahead and strike me if you must. I'm sure it will be the victory you've been seeking all morning."

Stung by the accurate remark, John hesitated, then stepped aside.

Charmaine was shocked and could not move.

"Well, *my Charm...*" he drawled obsequiously, the mock endearment of her name as cruel as a slap in the face. "What keeps you from departing? Perhaps you are awaiting my leave?"

She stiffened, then raised her chin and dashed around him. As she reached the door, she threw a defiant glare over her shoulder, but the gesture offered little satisfaction, for he responded by bowing low like a courtesan showing great respect for a noble lady.

Once free, she was overcome by blinding tears and collided with George just as she reached the nursery. "Charmaine?" he queried. "What is the matter?"

She struggled to pull away until she realized who he was. "George! You're home!" Then she sobbed harder, luxuriating in the safety of his arms.

"There, now," he soothed, taking courage to stroke her back. "It's all right." He had only seen her in this state once before, and he wondered what could have upset her so. Then, as if struck by a bolt of lightning, he knew.

Charmaine shyly lifted her head, wiping dry her cheeks. "I'm sorry, George," she laughed self-consciously, "I didn't mean to cry on your shoulder like that."

"That's all right," he countered. "What are shoulders for, anyway?" Then the levity was gone. "Would you mind me asking why you were crying?"

"It was nothing," she lied, averting her gaze.

"Nothing but John," he mumbled.

Astonished, her eyes shot back to his face. "How did you know that?"

"I just know. What did he say to upset you?"

"I don't want to talk about it."

She seemed about to cry again, so he refrained from pressing her for details. "You would be wise to avoid John for a while. He's come home to sad news. I'm certain he's not taking it well."

"Why are you telling me this?" she asked charily. "Are you defending him?"

"John is like a brother to me. He's not a bad man, just a troubled one."

"I'm sorry, George, but I'm afraid I've seen the real John Duvoisin, a side that he'd never show another man – that of the devil!"

George willed himself not to smile, having heard similar sentiments many times before. "Very well," he sighed. "Just stay away from him. *Far* away."

"Don't worry," Charmaine avowed. "I intend to."

"Good. Now, before I talk with the *devil,* I'm supposed to tell you that the children are with my grandmother in her chambers."

"How did you know where they were?"

"After four months away, my first order of business was to visit my grandmother. The children were with her when I knocked on her door."

"I had better see to them," Charmaine replied.

George watched her go. Shaking his head, he strode to the guestroom that John now occupied. According to his grandmother, the man had been apprised of all the events leading up to his return home, namely Colette's death and Agatha's reign. John had to be furious if he'd confronted Frederic already. George cringed with the thought of facing his friend just yet. Perhaps this is not a good time, he concluded, the fist that he'd held suspended finally dropping to his side.

Monday, August 21, 1837

Sunday was mercifully uneventful, and when the day ended, Charmaine thanked the Lord that she had been spared John Duvoisin on the Sabbath. She'd anxiously anticipated another rancorous altercation with him, but her worries had been needless. He hadn't attended Holy Mass and was absent for all three meals, locking himself away in his chambers, his presence signaled only by the footfalls of Anna or Felicia as they scurried to his door to deliver another bottle of spirits. Nevertheless, Charmaine had been afraid to venture from her own quarters. Their dispute over Colette's letter was too fresh in her mind, and she hoped to postpone their next confrontation for as long as possible.

For that reason, she rose early today and hastily ushered the children down to breakfast. With any luck, the detestable man would abstain from eating again, or would rise late, and she could successfully evade him for a second day.

As Fatima set four steaming bowls of porridge on the table, Charmaine reeled with the realization that she loathed a man she had only known for forty-eight hours. Her conscience chastised her, but she reasoned that others were suffering his return as well, the house balanced on an undercurrent of tension. Family and servants alike seemed to be awaiting his next move, the thundering crash, the ultimate explosion. Charmaine vowed to be absent for it.

To that end, she was determined to finish breakfast with the children as quickly as possible and retreat to the safety of their rooms. However, Yvette was just as determined to sabotage her purpose. She dallied through the meal, distracting Jeannette and Pierre. Every time Charmaine pointed a finger at her cereal, the girl protested. "Too many lumps!" So, the oatmeal grew cold, and Charmaine had run out of threats.

"I'm going to get some milk!" Yvette announced. "I'm incredibly thirsty!"

"You stay right there," Charmaine enjoined. "I will get it for you."

Upon returning to the dining room, Yvette was nowhere in sight. "Where is your sister?" Charmaine demanded.

"Gone," Pierre replied, taking hold of his glass and sloshing milk down his shirt before greedily drinking it.

"Back to our room," Jeannette elaborated. "She changed her mind."

Charmaine did not believe it for a second, and wiped Pierre's dampened chest in rigid restraint. Sure enough, the nursery proved empty. Now she feared the worst: the eight-year old had begged all weekend long to *visit* her older brother's apartments. *That* was her destination.

When Jeannette promised to read to Pierre, Charmaine took a deep breath and set out in pursuit of the errant twin. She walked quietly along the veranda, stopping just shy of John's quarters, head cocked, listening. No voices, though the French doors were open. Tip-toeing closer, she peered in at an angle, a small section of the chamber visible. Nothing – nobody. She leaned forward and spied the foot of the bed. A little further, and boots came into view. She jumped back, stumbling over her own feet and nearly falling, plastering herself against the face of the manor. Someone was reclining there – *John!* When her heart stopped hammering, she chuckled softly, foolishly, and finally relaxed. He was alone; she'd been wrong.

Where to look now? She crossed through her room and began with the second floor of the north wing, next the servant's staircase to the kitchen, then the kitchen itself. No Yvette. With great care, she cracked the door that opened onto the dining room, relieved to find only Anna and Felicia moving around the table, setting down teacups and saucers. She walked casually across the room, ignoring their sidelong glances, and entered the study. It was empty as well. She was growing more frustrated by the minute and feared that her original assumption was correct: Yvette had stealthily made her way up to John's chambers.

Gritting her teeth, she stepped into the drawing room and circled the piano, the two sofas, the high back chairs, and finally, the low coffee table. She looked behind the curtains. Still, no Yvette. She moved to a table near the French doors.

It was covered with a lace cloth that fell to the floor. She had just bent over to peer under it when a crisp, masculine voice resounded behind her.

"Searching for something, Mademoiselle?"

Charmaine's heart leapt into her throat, and she straightened so quickly that she nearly toppled the table.

John leaned placidly against the hallway doorframe, arms and legs crossed, a bemused smile on his lips. The easy portrait ended there: his eyes were bloodshot, his complexion ruddy, and his cheeks covered in stubble. He seemed oblivious of his unsteady state as he persisted in demeaning her.

"You didn't have to straighten up so fast. Your derrière is the finest bit of fluff I've had the pleasure to see in quite some time, save for the other night."

Charmaine reddened, irate more than embarrassed.

His smile broadened. "What are you searching for so diligently? Perhaps I could help locate it? If not, I'd be happy to assist with anything else that comes to mind." His eyes, which had scanned the room, now raked her from head to toe, indifferent that she was deeply offended.

She steeled her emotions and walked briskly toward the archway where he stood. He did not step aside; rather he placed his palm flat against the opposite doorframe, blocking her path.

"Once again, Mademoiselle," he stated in irritation, "you haven't answered my question. Perhaps you thought the wind had blown a letter under the table, and you felt it your duty to pick it up and *read it*."

He expected an angry response and was unprepared when she ducked under his extended arm and raced into the main foyer. She had reached the steps by the time he'd whirled around, but his chuckle followed her up the stairs.

Safe in her bedchamber, she cursed herself for running from him like some frightened child, or worse yet, a guilty one. She should have stood up to him, and she stamped her foot. "Oh, that miserable, miserable man! How I *despise* him!"

She entered the nursery, praying that by some miracle Yvette had returned.

"Did you find her?" Jeannette asked, looking up from the book.

"No," Charmaine replied in exasperation, only half-aware of Pierre, who had left his sister's lap to give her a big hug. "Jeannette, do you have any idea where she could be?"

Jeannette's negative response set her to pacing. Soon the household would be stirring, and she fretted over the mistress' severe reprimand should Yvette turn up in some forbidden area. Her heart missed a beat when there was an unexpected rap on the hallway door. *Agatha already?*

Charmaine reached the portal, cringing when it was pushed open and Yvette bounded in, leaving her to face not Agatha, but John.

"I'm returning one missing twin to where she belongs at this hour in the morning," he said. "She was what you were looking for, yes?"

"Yes," Charmaine replied curtly. "Thank you."

She pushed the door closed, not caring that it would shut in his face. But he braced his hand against it, stopping it midway. "Before you lock me out," he smirked, "I'd like to have a word with you."

"You've already had a word with me," she rejoined audaciously.

"I'll have another word with you, then," he countered sharply, gesturing for her to step into the hallway.

For all her bravado, his temper was unsettling, and so she complied, counseling herself calm as he closed the door, hands folded primly before her, eyes lowered.

"Aren't you the least bit interested in where I found her?"

"No," she replied stubbornly.

"I see," he mused. "Incompetent *and* stupid."

Charmaine's eyes widened, both hurt and angry, but she didn't have the opportunity to defend herself.

"You would be wise to remember, Mademoiselle, that the children are your responsibility – at least for the present time. Yvette has no business eavesdropping on adult conversations, which she undoubtedly will hear when she escapes your eye and takes cover in the drawing room. Yes, that is where I found her."

"*Really?*" Charmaine seethed, burning over his smug stance, his twisted smile, his limitless arrogance. "May I ask you if you are annoyed with me – or yourself?"

His brow raised in surprise. "Mademoiselle, Yvette is your responsibility."

"And I fail to see how she would have come to any harm in the drawing room, unless, of course, you are embarrassed by what she did, in fact, overhear: *your adult conversation* spoken by you alone – derrière and all! Furthermore, if you hadn't interrupted my search, she wouldn't have remained hidden for long."

John found her outburst entertaining, her large eyes just as diverting. But it wouldn't lead to victory, not even a small one. He'd sparred with intimidating opponents in his day and always won. What else could he say to fire her up and provide more ammunition to hold over her head?

"I don't care what she heard, Miss Ryan, and even less by whom. But *I* am the exception in this household. I know that Mrs. Duvoisin, or even my dear brother wouldn't take too kindly to Yvette eavesdropping on them. If *they* find her in some hidden niche, I guarantee there will be all hell to pay, and the bill that hell charges will come directly to you. That will be all, *my Charm*."

It was the last straw. As he walked away, Charmaine stalked after him. "No, that won't be all!" she spat at his back, drawing him round as he reached the crest of the staircase and took one step down. She stepped in front of him, closer to eye level now, her temper out of control. "There is one more thing, *Master* John. You needn't remind me of my duties, and I take offense that you've judged me incompetent. Obviously, you are unaware that I have managed quite well with the children for close to a year now, and not once has their welfare been jeopardized. But you are right about Mrs. Duvoisin: her reaction would have been just like yours. As for Paul, he has *always* supported me."

For the first time, John appeared stymied, and Charmaine smiled triumphantly. But he didn't remain mute for very long. "Miss Ryan, I know you've made it well worth my brother's while to 'support' you, but you really do underestimate me."

"*Really?*" she returned, shocked by the scope of his crude conclusions. "You should know that your father has also commended me."

John's eyes hardened. "*Miss* Ryan, you have no idea how miserable I can make your life if it strikes my fancy. It hasn't come to that – yet. But, use *my father* to threaten *me,* and it will."

Charmaine felt the blood drain from her face.

Mercifully, Agatha emerged from the south wing hallway, an unlikely buffer for her sudden intimidation. "What goes on here?" she demanded.

"Miss Ryan was just comparing the two of us," her nephew replied.

"Comparing us?" she choked out. "Surely there is no comparison!"

"Indeed!" John agreed wryly, raising his hand in salute.

Then he was gone, leaving Charmaine to contend with the confused woman. With a mumbled 'good morning', she quickly retreated to the nursery.

There she spent the next four hours lamenting her loose tongue. Why had she spoken so brashly, boastfully? *Pride goeth before a fall…* She'd grown over-confident and *had* underestimated John's authority. Should she take the matter up with Paul and tell him everything that had happened? She instantly discounted that idea; it could lead to more trouble. Yes, Paul might support her, but he was second in line. And if he went to his father, Frederic would never condone such unscrupulous behavior, no matter how desperately she pleaded her case. Somehow, her future had been placed in John's hands. He held all the cards, had held them since Saturday morning. And if that wasn't bad enough, she'd just added more fuel to the fire. He was right – *she was stupid!*

The morning wore on, and the children grew bored. Charmaine had repeatedly quelled their requests to leave their sanctuary, but as lunchtime neared, she couldn't quarantine them any longer. Panic seized hold as they approached the dining room. What if John were there? Thankfully, he wasn't. Even so, his wraith was present; every little noise made Charmaine jump.

"Where is Johnny?" Yvette finally asked.

"I don't know," she replied, then added under her breath, "As long as he's not here, he can be anywhere he likes."

"You don't like him, do you?" Yvette demanded, canting her head.

"I never said that!"

"It doesn't matter. You'll change your mind sooner or later."

Charmaine nearly choked on her food. The child had never been more wrong in her life. She'd sooner declare her father a 'man of God'.

Lunch was over, but the children refused to return to the playroom. "I'm tired of playing with those silly toys or reading those fairytale books," Yvette protested. "We haven't left that stupid room for days!"

She was right. They couldn't spend the rest of their lives sequestered in the nursery. "Then let us have our piano lesson," Charmaine offered.

Yvette objected again. "Johnny might hear us, and I want to surprise him."

Charmaine sighed, but Jeannette's suggestion met with everyone's approval. "We wouldn't be spoiling the surprise if you played for us, Mademoiselle."

Minutes later, they clustered around the piano, and Charmaine placed her hands to the keys, performing her usual repertoire of children's tunes while they sang along. Even Pierre joined in, the serious tremor in his voice spawning contagious giggles. All their woes were forgotten, and gaiety ruled the afternoon.

John was contemplating the ceiling and the dust motes suspended above him when the strains of a childhood melody floated into his bedchamber. "Damn good whisky," he mumbled, swinging his legs over the side of the bed. Still, he wasn't as drunk as he wanted to be. Grabbing the bottle he'd retrieved from the dining room earlier that morning, he uncorked it and poured a brimming glass. As he took a swig, the sound caught his ear again. His eyes went to the French doors where the curtains billowed in the breeze. The tune wasn't in the bottle, and it wasn't his besotted imagination either. Finding the music a welcome reprieve from his dismal abyss, he rose and headed to the balcony.

He wasn't prepared for the piercing light and squinted sharply, reaching for the balustrade, holding fast until his world stopped spinning and the throbbing in his head ebbed. The strains were clearer now, and he pictured the twins as they sang along. A feminine soprano rose above their voices, embellishing the melody. *How sweet,* he mused acrimoniously, *the governess plays the piano, too.* He looked at the glass he held, then hurled it over the banister, relishing the sound of shattering glass when it struck the cobblestone drive.

"My, aren't we happy today!"

John leaned further over the railing. An impish George Richards smiled up at him, his smile broadening when they made eye contact.

"You almost got me in a place I shouldn't mention."

"It would have done you some good, Georgie," John chortled. "What have you been up to today?"

"A better question is what *haven't* I been up to? Paul keeps me going."

"Poor George," John cut in with pretended sympathy, "paying the piper for an extended excursion to America. Did he save all the work for you?"

"Not quite, but we've spent the morning going from one operation to the next. He's made a few changes and wanted to acquaint me with them."

"Changes?"

"He's put Wade Remmen in charge of the sawmill," George offered.

"Wade Remmen?"

"You don't know him. He arrived on the island about two years ago: ambition, brawn, and a sharp mind for business. He'll keep the lumber supply stocked while Paul turns his attention to tobacco. I'm glad Espoir is nearly running itself now. Even with Paul here, it will be a chore preparing the tracts for a new crop."

John listened, then snorted. "If Paul is going to be around, I guess we'll have more time to antagonize one another."

"Only if you want to, John," George stated bluntly, hating his role as middleman and peacemaker.

"That's right, George," John agreed coldly, "and he must want it pretty badly if he's shelved the building of his royal palace to plant tobacco and duel with me. But I'm up to the challenge, don't you worry about that!"

"John," George chided, "remember when the three of us ran around Charmantes from dawn to dusk? He's your brother, for God's sake!"

Running a hand through his tangled hair, John shook his head, unable to explain his festering misery. "I'm in a foul mood," he finally mumbled, suddenly feeling childish. "It's that blasted piano and the off-key singing."

"It's the liquor," George corrected.

"Yes, I suppose it is."

"You ought to give it up, John. It isn't doing you any good. Besides, the twins have been asking for you. They're anxious to see you."

"Yes, yes," John replied dismissively.

"Why don't you join us for dinner tonight?" George suggested. "I'll be there. So will my grandmother. She wants to see you. She's worried, you know."

John considered the invitation, then nodded. "Perhaps I will."

"Good," George said, hoping that his friend was ready to face life again. "I have to keep moving. There's plenty to finish between now and then."

"Don't let me stop you," John quipped. "I wouldn't want to be blamed if Paul docks your pay for slacking off."

George chuckled and climbed the steps to the portico. He'd just ridden back from the harbor with Paul. Best to warn him that John might show up for dinner. Not that he regretted coaxing John out of his isolation. Still, the man was drunk and bitter, a dangerous combination that could add up to fireworks.

He found Paul in the kitchen wolfing down a chicken leg and a thick slice of bread. "I invited John to join us for supper tonight," he said, nodding a thank-you to Fatima as she set a glass of cold water in front of him.

Paul coughed, swallowed, and then glared at him.

"I just thought you should know," George added.

"I assume then, he accepted your *kind* offer?" Paul queried caustically.

"I think he did."

"Thank you, George, for all of us. I'm sure the meal will be as enjoyable as this one." He waved the bread in George's face before turning to leave.

George delayed him. "Paul, have a care, will you? John's your brother. He's licking his wounds, and they're deep. He could do with a bit of compassion."

"Those *wounds*, as you call them, are of his own making."

"Perhaps, but they are still there."

Paul's eyes traveled to Fatima, who was dabbing her eyes with her apron. Uncomfortable with the converging fronts, he brusquely strode from the room.

Deep were his thoughts when he heard the piano. His perturbation evaporated as he moved to the drawing room doorway. He had ignored the music only minutes earlier in his rush to eat and get back to work. Now he needed it.

Charmaine struck the last chord of the long sonata she'd been playing in the hope that the children would grow bored and ask to return to the playroom.

"Well done, Mademoiselle."

She cringed for only a second, then regarded her admirer, who stood tall and handsome in the archway. Paul returned her smile, and her heart soared. She rose from the piano bench as he stepped into the room, his gaze unwavering.

"Children," he directed, "run along and play outside. I want to speak with Miss Ryan. She will join you in a moment."

"Why should we?" Yvette objected, rolling her eyes at her sister. "We aren't babies anymore!"

Charmaine was appalled, but Paul was angry. "Yvette, I have told you what to do. Now, you will respect my wishes."

One look at his hardened face and Yvette capitulated, marching from the room in a huff, Jeannette and Pierre right behind her.

"Just like John," Paul mumbled under his breath.

"What is it that you wanted?" Charmaine asked.

He stepped closer. *Would the children, the servants, and now, John, forever interrupt them? When would he find release from this gnawing desire?*

"Paul?" she queried, summoning him away from his dilemma.

"I'd like to escort you to dinner tonight," he said, "if you would permit me. I have reason to believe that, unlike last night or the night before, my brother will be present at the table this evening. He's been drinking, and knowing him as I do, he will do his level best to ruin an excellent meal. If I am at your side, he will think twice before he tries to taunt you, as I suspect he might."

"Oh thank you, Paul! I do appreciate your concern."

He smiled down at her, impassioned by her ebullient gratitude. "Do you think I'd ever allow you to come to harm?" he murmured huskily.

Suddenly, she was discomposed. It was as if this were the first time she'd faced him after his fiery kiss on Friday night. She stepped back and dropped her gaze to the floor. "What time will you come for me?"

"I will be at your door just before seven o'clock."

"I'll be ready," she replied. Then, uncomfortable with the blood thundering in her ears, she quickly skirted past him and rushed outdoors.

Paul watched her go and smiled in satisfaction. "Here's to you, John!" he toasted, raising an imaginary glass to his brother. *You make it so easy to play the chivalrous hero. And doesn't every impressionable young maiden love the hero?*

Rose took charge of the children while Charmaine dressed for dinner. Washing away the perspiration of the hot day, she donned her best dress, then stood before the full-length mirror, pirouetting to check herself at every angle. Though modest, it hugged her trim figure and shapely curves. Satisfied, she began brushing her hair. After a good hundred strokes, she wound it into a loose bun. The combs she'd received for her birthday were the finishing touch.

Before the clock tolled seven, she left her chamber and, with a tremulous smile on her ruby lips, made her way through the children's bedroom and into the playroom. To her surprise, only Paul was there, turning around at the sound of the door opening behind him.

"Good evening," she greeted shyly.

"Good evening," he returned suavely, an appreciative gleam lighting his eyes.

She looked away as he stepped forward. Her heart was already pounding, and she attempted to break the spell. "Where are the children?"

"I sent them downstairs with Rose. They were anxious for dinner, and I was anxious to see you again." He stepped closer. "Lovely," he murmured huskily, his hand caressing her cheek, "you are so lovely. I fear I haven't been of much use to anyone these past few days, for you have haunted my every waking hour."

The declaration was intoxicating, opening a floodgate of possibilities and leaving Charmaine vulnerable to the hand that traveled to her hair. Before she could protest, he released the thick tresses, catching hold of the locks as they tumbled down her back. Gently, persuasively, he pulled her head back. His mouth loomed above hers, his lips barely touching as he whispered an endearment. "You are the wraith that invades my dreams... the vision that follows me when I awake... my beautiful Charmaine..." He claimed his prize, his lips moving over hers with a ferocity that forced them apart, his probing tongue tasting its fill.

She fell into him, thunderstruck, eagerly returning kiss for flaming kiss, arms wrapped around his broad shoulders, pulling him closer as she reveled in the strong, sturdy body that held her. This time, no one interrupted, no one desecrated the rapturous embrace.

Abruptly, he pulled away, held her at arm's length, then turned his back on her, leaving her shaky and confused. She suffered the first pangs of lust, a foreign sensation of yearning and disappointment.

"I'm sorry, Charmaine," he murmured over his shoulder. *What was wrong with him?* He would have taken her here, in the nursery, without a care about who might walk in on them. *Damn! She was too damn tempting!*

"Is something wrong?" she queried, her voice small and laced with shame.

He inhaled before facing her again, commanding control of his raging desires. "Nothing," he reassured, a neat smile painted on his lips, "nothing at all."

"Then why did you apologize?"

"Because now is not the time nor the place to kiss you like that. But you make me do wild things, Charmaine."

"Wild things?"

"Yes, like dreaming of you every night."

She delighted in his poetry, the musical sound of his voice, and her heart was fluttering again. "I'm sorry I plague you so," she whispered coyly.

"You may plague me, Charmaine, but it would be far worse if you fled me."

"Would it?" she asked seriously.

"It would," he answered earnestly. "Now come, we've a dinner to attend."

Dinner... Amazingly, her earlier dread was no longer there. Paul's growing love eclipsed his brother's vicious hatred. With this man at her side, she could combat anything that John hurled her way. Tonight, she would reign victorious.

Paul noted her poise. "You don't seem upset about the impending ordeal."

"With you there, how could I think of it as an ordeal?"

"You're a funny one, Charmaine Ryan," he laughed, recalling how she used to avoid him. "But you are correct. I will be at your side, and John will regret his efforts to come between us. Remember, I won't allow him to hurt you."

"I'll remember," she murmured, her throat tightening against her burgeoning emotions. Once, not so long ago, she had dreamed of laying all her burdens upon Paul's shoulders. Now, under his gentle insistence, she was finally moving in that direction. Could her dreams be coming true? It was best to remain anchored in reality, so she pushed the thrilling thoughts to the back of her mind.

He took her hand and began to lead her to the door, but she stopped. "Can you wait just a moment? I have to fix my hair."

"No," he objected, catching her arm before she dashed away. "No," he said again more gently. "Please leave it this way. It looks lovely."

She accepted his compliment and complied. The combs were still in place, holding the riotous curls away from her face. Unfortunately, she would be very warm with her hair down, but for Paul, she could endure the discomfort. With a final, wistful glance, they left the room.

For all her intrepid words, her hands turned clammy as they stepped into the dining room. The power of Paul's presence fortified her, but Charmaine prayed that it would vanquish any defamatory information his brother might divulge concerning her actions of Saturday morning.

They were the last to arrive. Rose was seated between the twins and Pierre, helping them with their napkins. Although she had sworn not to, Charmaine's eyes went involuntarily to the end of the table, where John had lounged last Saturday morning – Paul's usual spot. She knew he was there; why did she bother to look? She was relieved to find that her entrance was not having the same momentous effect upon him; he was engrossed in conversation with George.

George noticed her first, and his face lit up. "Good evening, Charmaine."

Grimacing, her eyes returned to John. She'd gained his attention. Though his face was clean-shaven and his apparel neat, alcohol had left its mark, his demeanor unsteady, his eyes bleary.

Paul stepped to the table and pulled out a chair for her. She would be seated close to John, but not directly to his left. She took her place with as much grace as she could muster.

When Paul turned to the chair she usually occupied, John appeared amused that his brother intended to sit between them. But Paul did not take his seat. The chair seemed glued to the floor and would not budge.

"Are you going to sit down, Paul?" he queried merrily as he straightened up, "Or must we start without you? I daresay, we've been waiting for you and *Miss* Ryan for quite some time now. Whatever could have detained you?"

Irked, Paul yanked the stubborn chair, but instead of holding stiffly to the floor, it came up easily, and he stumbled backward, regaining his balance just short of a fall. The twins laughed, but he ignored them as he took his seat.

Charmaine cast cold eyes across the table, stifling the girls' mirth to an occasional snicker. She wondered what trick had caused the misfortune, her suspicions lying with the newcomer, whose eyes sparkled deviously.

The table fell quiet as the meal was laid before them – though not for long.

"I heard someone playing the piano today," John mused aloud.

Everyone looked up, save Charmaine, who fixed her gaze on her plate.

"The music was quite good… whoever was playing it."

Mutinously, her eyes connected with his. "Yes, quite good," he reiterated casually, his regard steadfast and challenging. "An assortment of lullabies and even an attempted sonata... Very – how shall I say –? *Sweet*."

Silverware clanked on china and Charmaine cursed the blood that rushed to her cheeks, advertising her disquiet. His jeering gaze refused to release her, and so, she broke away first.

Thus dismissed, John turned his attention to his brother, who seemed oblivious to his calculated comments. Evidently, Paul had not yet recovered from his skirmish with the chair. Well, Paul's fatal flaw was his temper. John's was never leaving well enough alone. Even now, he was wondering: *How far need I push the governess before she lashes out and Paul rushes to the rescue?*

"Might I ask who was playing that beautiful piece this afternoon?" he continued most politely, a masterful performance of cordiality.

Charmaine knew he was goading her and refused to answer, picking up her fork instead.

"Nobody knows?" he pressed, eyeing Yvette. "Perhaps it was a ghost."

"I know who it was!" the girl offered eagerly.

Charmaine groaned inwardly. *Why didn't I just answer the ridiculous question, instead of allowing him to intimidate me?*

"Well?" John probed.

"Information costs money," Yvette informed him curtly. "How much are you willing to pay?"

Charmaine was revolted, but George chortled softly.

"Don't laugh, George," John quipped, "I fear your avaricious streak is rubbing off on my sister."

George's face dropped, and John turned back to Yvette, who was waiting for a monetary bid. "Now Yvette, you wouldn't be attempting to bribe me, would you? For if you are, Auntie over there might be interested in that little matter we discussed in the drawing room this morning."

Agatha leaned forward, suddenly interested in the story that was emerging from the opposite end of the table.

Yvette answered quickly. "Mademoiselle Charmaine was playing."

Charmaine was livid. Now that the answer was out, she simmered over the methods used to extract it. To think that the man would actually coerce an eight-year-old child for his own gain! Unfortunately, his tactics had worked, and his laughing eyes were upon her again. Charmaine gulped back the bile rising in her throat, surprised when a reprieve came from the foot of the table.

"What is this matter concerning Yvette?" Agatha demanded of John.

He raised a hand to wave her off. "You can live without it, Auntie."

Sputtering momentarily, she quickly regained her aplomb. "You may call me Madame Duvoisin if you wish to address me!"

"Address you?" John shot back. "Rest assured, I will *never* wish to address you – *Auntie*. But if necessity warrants it, I certainly won't use *my* name when speaking to you. No, you will always be 'Auntie' to me."

"Well, I never! Your father will hear of this!"

"Fine," John responded wryly, "why don't you rush up there right now and tell him? Then perhaps the rest of us can eat in peace."

Seething, Agatha glared at him, but dismissed his suggestion. Then, unable to sling an equally debasive remark, she made a great show of ripping her gaze from him and turning her unspent fury upon her plate, forcefully plying her knife and fork into a slice of meat.

"Now," John sighed, turning back to Charmaine. "Is it true that you play the piano, Mademoiselle Ryan?" His eyes rested momentarily on Paul, who shifted irately in his chair. "*Do* you play the piano?" he asked again.

"Yes," Charmaine answered flatly, looking directly at her tormentor now.

"You play quite well. Few maestros are acquainted with the instrument and pound on it as if it were a pianoforte or harpsichord. Did you receive lessons?"

His belittling sarcasm stymied her.

Rose sensed Charmaine's distress, aware that John was no more interested in finding out where she had learned to play the piano than he was in giving up the alcohol he'd been nursing. It was time to intervene. "John," she scolded, "eat your dinner before it grows cold."

To Charmaine's stunned relief, John leaned back in his chair, glanced at Yvette, who found the reprimand quite delightful, then lifted a fork to eat. Charmaine turned back to her own plate, grateful for Rose's deliverance.

George studied John, his intimidation of Charmaine unfathomable. He remembered her tears on Saturday and sympathized with her plight. Over the years, he had seen many an unfortunate go down in defeat once they were in John's crosshairs, but those victims had always deserved it. He couldn't imagine what Charmaine, as sweet as she was, could have done to provoke John's wrath. "I saw Bummy Hoffstreicher in town yesterday, John," he began with a crooked smile and a dose of levity. "He actually asked me how you were doing!"

"And did you tell him that I've been rather miserable lately?" John replied gruffly. "He should be pleased to hear that."

"After what you did to him," George chuckled, "I'd say he would!"

"What did Johnny do?" Yvette asked.

George's chuckle deepened. "When we were boys," he reminisced, "perhaps a bit older than you, John, Paul and I used to go fishing off the main wharf in town. Fatima always packed a large lunch, and we'd be off for the day. Anyway, that's where Bummy always used to be."

"Bummy?" Jeannette queried. "Why was he called that?"

"John gave him that name. His real name is Buford, but we called him Bummy because he was always lurking about the harbor, scavenging for hooks and food, like a bum."

The twins lit up, giggling at what Charmaine thought to be cruel. Looking askance at John, she noticed that he was listening, but eating as well, his mind far from her. The conversation turned spontaneous, and she finally relaxed.

"He wasn't poor, mind you," George was explaining, "just too lazy to bring his own lunch. So, if we didn't give him something to eat, he would steal the sandwiches out of our lunch sack when we weren't looking. Every day, we were one sandwich short, until John got angry enough to do something about it."

Felicia entered the room with a pitcher of water. Charmaine watched from the corner of her eye as the maid arrived at the head of the table. She leaned over to refill John's glass, her ample bosom straining against the tight uniform, top buttons undone, her obtrusive pose affording him a generous view. *What a lovely couple they make*, Charmaine mused. *They deserve one another!*

"The next day," George snickered, reliving the delicious revenge, "John cut open some fish and scraped out the guts. Then he poked out theirs eyes. Finally, he took the sandwiches and spread some eyes and guts on each one."

Charmaine's stomach heaved. George, however, was not so squeamish, guffawing with glee, tears brimming in his eyes and running down his gaunt cheeks. "I'll never forget Bummy's face when he bit into that sandwich. He spit it out so fast, well, I thought he was going to lose his breakfast, too!" His merriment washed over the table as Paul and John, then the children and Rose, began to laugh.

"And what about the eyes staring up at us from the dock?" Paul added, drawing an even louder howl from George.

"That was the last thing Bummy ever stole, at least from John, anyway!"

Charmaine found the entire tale very distasteful, and she turned disbelieving eyes upon Paul, who was chortling even harder than George. Everyone found the tale hilarious, save Agatha and herself.

"I can find no humor in such barbarism!" the mistress declared.

Without thinking, Charmaine looked to John, certain that his retort would be swift and sure. However, he caught her eyes upon him and said instead, "You see, Miss Ryan, my aunt and I are really not alike at all."

"That is precisely what I indicated this morning!" Agatha added.

In response, John raised his glass of brandy. "Here's to you, Auntie, I believe that is the first and only time we will ever agree!" He took a long draw.

Charmaine gasped when Yvette imitated him. Rose quickly confiscated her glass of water and reprimanded her softly. "That is not befitting a young lady."

But Yvette's eyes remained fixed on John, wide and wistful with her brother's wink of approval.

Everyone went back to eating, and the table began to hum with clustered conversations. Paul and George exchanged ideas, but John remained reticent. With him unoccupied, Charmaine's nerves grew taut. Why had she surrendered Pierre to Rose's capable hands? Though the child ate his meal passively, seeing to his dish was the type of distraction she needed. Nevertheless, when she smiled at the boy who smiled back at her, she found that John's gaze rested on him as well, and she thought better of having the child sitting next to her.

Thus, she concentrated on eating, forever mindful of her antagonist. *Surely he isn't constantly watching me!* She looked his way and cursed her stupidity. He instantly sensed her regard. The brow arched, and the amber-brown eyes mocked her. She rose to the challenge. She would not allow him the satisfaction of relentless intimidation. She would not!

As if comprehending her resolution, he addressed her directly. "Miss Ryan, I don't recall seeing you on Charmantes before I left a few years ago. I realize you would have been younger; however, you don't speak like an islander. In fact, I detect a southern accent. I'd like to know how you obtained your position here."

To Charmaine's relief, Paul intervened, sparing the details. "Miss Ryan was accompanied by close friends specifically to apply for the position of governess. She possessed all the necessary qualifications and was offered the job."

John propped his elbows on the table and tapped laced fingers against his lips. "Who decided that Miss Ryan 'possessed all the necessary qualifications'? You? If so, perhaps those qualifications are not in the *children's* best interests."

His meaning was not lost on Charmaine or Paul. The latter's jaw twitched menacingly, but his reply was temperate. "Colette conducted the interview. Miss Ryan was her choice."

Their eyes held in a silent, meaningful exchange.

"A most foolish choice if you ask me," Agatha interjected, drawing John's regard. "Miss Ryan has a most questionable past. She is nothing more than a sly opportunist who managed to slither her way into this household by clever pretense, preying on certain members of this family."

Paul's mouth flew open to protest, but John beat him to the punch. "Are you describing Miss Ryan or yourself, Auntie?"

She gasped loudly, and he savored her outrage before continuing. "I don't think Miss Ryan is quite the calculating schemer you say she is. The refined conniver is never caught."

Fuming, Agatha fell into a stony silence.

Charmaine, on the other hand, shuddered at the man's tacit reference to Colette's letter, amazed at how effortlessly he discredited two people at the same time. Had she not been included in his double-edged remark, she would have appreciated the fact that the mistress of the manor had met her match.

"Now, Miss Ryan," he proceeded, "what prompted you to leave your home and family, even your friends, to apply for a position so very far away?"

For a second time, Paul attempted to answer, but John held up a hand. "Miss Ryan has a tongue, has she not? Allow *her* to answer the question, Paul. I fear that when you tell a story, I have to keep digging and digging until I get down to the truth of the matter."

The ensuing silence sent Charmaine's mind into a spiraling frenzy. Spontaneously, Paul winked at her, a gesture that drew a callous grunt from John. But it imbued her with valor; she could answer as concisely as he had. "My home was in Richmond," she said. "When my mother died, I needed to make a new life for myself. Friends in Richmond – the people I worked for – informed me of the opening for a governess here. They have family on the island."

"Really?"

"Yes, really! When I heard of the position and showed an interest in seeking an interview, they generously paid my passage and accompanied me."

The inevitable question followed. "And what of your father?"

Here it comes, Charmaine thought, *Anne London's nasty allegations.* She'd been right: John knew all about her past and had bided his time, carefully choosing the moment to defame her, and in front of the children, no less! She thought to flee. *I've learned never to turn my back on the enemy.*

"My father disappeared one day," she replied boldly, catching sight of Agatha's smug smile, "never to return."

"He just disappeared?" John scoffed. "Never to return? People don't just disappear, Miss Ryan. There must have been a reason why he deserted you. What type of man does such a thing?"

Rose's sympathetic eyes rested on the dedicated governess. Charmaine was undeserving of this insensitive inquisition. "John," she chided, "will you please stop talking and start eating? Your potatoes are getting cold."

"They're already cold," he stated flatly, not backing down as he had before, his eyes unwavering, "and my question has yet to be answered. I find your story hard to believe, Miss Ryan. Did your father really do that?"

"Yes," she whispered.

"Why?"

Charmaine clenched her jaw. Anger and humiliation collided, their union tantamount only to her loathing of this man. He played the game so well, pretending not to know the answers he probably had memorized, while insinuating that she was the liar. "My father was responsible for my mother's death," she hissed. "He disappeared in order to escape punishment for his crime."

John regarded her skeptically. Her acting was superb – a hint of tears welling in her doe-like eyes – and for that she deserved credit. *But murder? Was she suggesting that her father was guilty of murder?* One look at Paul's stark face and the macabre revelation was verified. "A great man," he commented mordantly.

"Are you satisfied?" she demanded. "Do you derive pleasure by demeaning me in front of the children, or are you out to prove me unfit to care for them?"

"I don't hold you responsible for your father's actions, if that is what you're implying, Miss Ryan, only your own. The man should have been horsewhipped and then hung at dawn for his evil deed. In future, when I ask a question, you should speak the truth immediately, rather than try to hide it. I'm an honest man, and I respect those who are honest with me. Perhaps we will get along if you heed my words."

Charmaine was both stunned and revolted by his condescending tirade. *An honest man? Bah!* "I fear you contradict yourself, sir, for when I dared to speak the truth to you on Saturday morning, you refused to believe a word I said!"

She immediately regretted bringing up the topic; Paul's puzzled regard was upon her. Even so, she could sense his applause.

John was not so easily captivated and laughed outright. He stood and walked over to the liquor cabinet, where he selected a bottle of wine. He uncorked it and poured himself another glass. "Don't play me for the fool, Miss Ryan," he sneered, turning back to her. "Poor innocent Charmaine Ryan just happened to venture into my chambers in search of her charges, when a gale force wind came along, opening a drawer and scattering papers on the floor. And just as she was doing her first good deed of the day by picking them up and *reading them,* that nasty ogre of a man, John Duvoisin, came storming into the room to persecute and defile her wholesome kindness with his blackhearted evilness–"

Paul shot to his feet, slamming his fists down on either side of his plate and sending the china clattering across the table. "You insist on making everyone here miserable, don't you?" he exploded. "*Don't you?*"

George jumped to his feet as well, shaking his head at a seething Paul before moving to John, whose eyes were dark with hatred. "John, just sit down and shut up," he ordered, prodding him back to the table.

Surprisingly, John did not resist, and Paul, who awaited his brother's retreat, slowly sat as well. An implacable silence enveloped the room, leaving Charmaine to ponder this latest outburst. Surreptitiously, she glanced from Paul to John. The former blindly contemplated some object on the table, while the latter studied the crystal wineglass he rotated in his hand.

Minutes lapsed and the main course was finally finished. Only dessert remained. Felicia returned with a generous tray of assorted cakes and turnovers. Charmaine declined, having lost her appetite long ago. Paul did the same, contenting himself with a cup of black coffee. John chose to nurse the wine in front of him. George, however, took three.

"You glutton," John commented, eyeing the stack.

Charmaine's anger flared. There wasn't a civil bone in the man's body.

"Why waste?" George shrugged, taking a large bite of the tart on top. "Besides," he continued with his mouth full, "tomorrow, they'll be stale."

"Yuk!"

All eyes turned to Jeannette, who had pushed her pastry away. "I hate nuts!"

Standing, she reached across the table for another, but Agatha swiftly confiscated the tray, slapping her hand away. "You've already chosen your dessert, young lady. You must be satisfied with it."

"But–"

"No buts!" Agatha reprimanded. "Nuts or no, you must eat the one you selected. A girl of your age and class should know it is uncultured to call attention to your plate and then attempt to snatch a second helping." The woman turned her accusatory eyes upon Charmaine, and the remonstration took on a twofold purpose. "It seems the children haven't received any lessons in table manners. First you–" and she flicked her hand at Yvette "–raising your glass like a common seaman at a pub, and you–" she wrinkled her nose at Jeannette "–grabbing at the desserts like a starving beast. A proper young lady would be appalled!"

Charmaine bowed her head and said nothing, knowing full well that Agatha would love to receive an acid retort from her. So, she sympathized silently with a dejected Jeannette.

"Furthermore, it is sinful to waste food," Agatha concluded.

To Charmaine's amazement, John rose and walked to the foot of the table. His aunt cringed as he lifted the pastry tray. "Jeannette, if Auntie here is a *proper* lady, then God help us. Personally, I think you are a fine young lady."

Enraged, Agatha's mouth flew open. "I can't believe that you would–"

"I don't care what you believe, Auntie," he cut in. "You've made it abundantly clear that you are now the 'Duchess-Countess-Empress-Queen Agatha', and I, for one, care not to have it shoved down my throat for dinner!"

Holding her breath, Charmaine glanced at Paul. He was smiling. One sweep around the room told her that he was not the only one enjoying the duel. Anna and Felicia had stepped out of the kitchen, and Charmaine could vividly imagine Fatima Henderson listening from within, an ear pressed to the door.

"I will not tolerate your insolence!" Agatha fulminated. "I am now mistress of this house and insist on your respect!"

"I believe you are forgetting who *I* am," John expostulated. "Take heed, Auntie. One day I will be in charge here. It would be wise to stay in my good graces, for once my father passes from this world to the next, I won't hesitate to expel anyone who irritates me, relative or no."

"Your father will hear of this insult, I assure you!" Agatha screeched back, her face ruby red. "He shall hold you directly responsible for what you have said. Your drunken daze will not excuse you come the morrow!"

"I *intend* to be responsible for my remarks," he replied, his voice menacingly low, "for drunk or no, I always mean what I say. So you take your little complaint to Papa as fast as your spindly legs will carry you. However, you will *never* receive an ounce of respect from me."

Though Agatha trembled with rage, John appeared impassive, dismissing her as quickly as he presented the tray of pastries to Jeannette. "Which one would you like, Jeannie?" he asked kindly.

"I wanted crème," she said softly, "but stepmother took the last one."

"Crème it shall be," John agreed before turning toward the kitchen and calling an unfamiliar name. "Cookie!"

Fatima hobbled into the room. "You want somethin', Mastah John?"

How clever, Charmaine thought wryly, *he nicknamed the cook 'Cookie'.*

He requested a crème pastry for Jeannette, and Yvette immediately jumped in, asking for another one, too. "And what about you, Pierre?" he inquired, looking across at the boy who immediately turned around, a good portion of his half-eaten dessert smeared across his face. "I guess not. Make that two crème pastries, Cookie, and next time, leave out the nuts. Jeannette doesn't like them."

"I like them!" George protested, plate miraculously clean, eyeing the one that Jeannette had rejected.

"George, you would eat anything," John commented dryly. "If you were Bummy, we wouldn't have had a story to laugh over tonight."

He picked up the discarded tart, but instead of giving it to George, he placed it in front of Agatha. "Here you go, Auntie, you finish it. It's sinful to waste."

George laughed loudly, gladly forfeiting the pastry for Agatha's dressing down. Everyone else gaped. John's impudence was boundless, leaving Charmaine to wonder if he ever left well enough alone. Agatha continued to seethe, but said not a word. Finally, John returned to his seat.

Charmaine stole sidelong glances at the head of the table, studying him curiously. He had certainly fallen into his role of master of the house. How much power would Agatha wield with him countering her every move? A storm was brewing to be sure, and most exciting would be the final showdown, when the battle, as Agatha threatened, would be brought before Frederic. Who would the man stand by: his prodigal son or his witch of a wife?

Dessert was finished, and Paul stood. "Ladies, George," he suggested invidiously, "why don't we retire to the drawing room for the remainder of the evening?" He motioned toward the hall, then assisted Charmaine with her chair.

"I quite agree," Agatha added as if nothing untoward had happened, standing regally and running a hand over her costly gown. "Perhaps we could enjoy a glass of port. Yes, port would do me a world of good."

"I doubt anything would do her a world of good," John mumbled to George, rising as well, "excluding, of course, a stampede of wild boars."

George chortled again. "Why don't you join us?" he invited, leaving the table and patting John jovially across the back. "I need your advice on a land deal I've heard about near Richmond."

When John agreed, Charmaine's plans for the evening immediately changed. She moved around the foot of the table and lifted Pierre into her arms, placing a tender kiss on his chubby cheek.

"Mainie," he said, laying his head on her shoulder.

John's attention was drawn to the spectacle, and he frowned.

"This little one is ready for a bath and bedtime story," Rose commented as she stood and squeezed Pierre's pudgy leg. "Let me settle him in for the night."

"You've minded him for the entire dinner," Charmaine said, anxious to return to the nursery. "I'll take him."

Yvette stomped her foot. "I don't want to go to bed! It's too early. I want to go to the drawing room with everybody else."

"I didn't say that you had to–"

"She is right, my Charm," John interrupted pleasantly. "It is much too early for the girls to retire."

Charmaine tensed; Paul was rankled by John's endearment of her name. "If you would have allowed me to finish," she replied stiffly, "I was about to say that Yvette and Jeannette didn't have to come with us."

"How very noble of you," John taunted. "You relieve Nana Rose of caring for a small three-year-old, then ask her to mind two eight-year-olds."

"John," Rose admonished gently, "I love the children."

His face softened, and he considered Pierre, who snuggled contentedly in Charmaine's embrace. "I never doubted that. I know he's safe in *your* hands."

Insulted, Charmaine's arms quickened around the boy, but Rose was already coaxing him away.

"Allow Rose to see to Pierre tonight," Paul interjected. "We rarely have the pleasure of your company."

Defeated, she smiled across the table at him. Then her eyes traveled to John who was moving toward her, his raised brow and crooked grin unsettling.

"Let me," he said, reaching for Pierre. "I'll carry him upstairs for Rose."

The boy buried his head deeper into Charmaine's shoulder and refused to be cajoled into his brother's outstretched arms.

"I'll take him," Paul said, coming around the table.

This time Pierre lifted his head and smiled. Charmaine passed him over, perturbed by the anger that smoldered in John's eyes.

"He knows me, John," Paul placated before leaving the room with Rose.

"Shall we?" George interrupted, defusing the vexing moment.

When they reached the front parlor, Jeannette crossed to John and clutched his hand. "Johnny? Is it true what Auntie Agatha said?"

"About what?" he asked.

"Are you really drunk?"

John seemed taken aback by her frank question. "Not quite yet," he finally said, bowing his head. "But a glass or two should see me to that end."

"Why haven't you visited us?" Yvette demanded, drawing up alongside her sister. "We waited in that stupid playroom all weekend!"

"I was preoccupied with other matters, Yvette. I'm afraid that I would not have been entertaining company."

He settled into a sofa, and the twins situated themselves on either side of him, a safe distance from Agatha, who took up the needlepoint that she never seemed to finish. Paul returned, and he and George started discussing work priorities for the next day. As Charmaine suspected, the next unpleasant episode began.

"Wielding the whip again, Paul?" John observed dryly, joining them.

"That's right. After all, that is how we keep the business running, is it not?"

"Or how you keep George running," John retaliated, straddling the chair he'd pulled out and placed directly across from his brother. He folded his arms over the back and leaned forward. "You don't waste much of his time, do you?"

"No," Paul replied, "unlike you, I don't waste much of George's time."

"I thought you could run Charmantes with your hands tied behind your back."

"Once again, you are mistaken," Paul replied, his patience wearing thin. "I'm the first to admit my limitations, which happen to be far greater when George is not around to pull his weight."

George's chest inflated.

"But you did manage without him," John countered.

"Yes, I did. I'm not completely without resources."

George's chest deflated.

Pretending great interest, John continued his assiduous pestering. "You never cease to amaze me, Paulie, turning to virgin resources so that the construction of your palace would not be delayed."

Paul was dumbfounded. "How did you know–?" He threw George a scowl and shook his head. "Never mind. It's a *house*, John, not a mausoleum."

"Well then," John proceeded with a chuckle, "if it's *only* a house, no wonder you were able to manage without George. And no, George didn't tell me. I already knew. So, how *did* you manage without him?"

"By relying on more dependable help," Paul answered, casting another emphasized glare at George. "In fact, the only real complication I had to confront and then rectify was of *your* making, dear brother."

Charmaine shuddered with the appellation, knowing that it portended trouble. She watched John's lips curl amusedly, the devil dancing in his eyes.

"Complication?" he inquired innocently. "What complication?"

Paul resisted the urge to launch into the subject of missing invoices.

"Is there something wrong?" John asked, his tone all courtesy and concern. "No? Then may I ask a question?"

"Ask away," Paul ceded impatiently.

"You mentioned resources. Would it be too impertinent to ask who managed my inheritance when you went gallivanting across the seas to New York and Europe or onto your soon not-to-be-deserted island?"

"Father – he handled everything."

"Then he's only an invalid when he wants to be? I can't imagine him mounting his mighty steed and riding out to the fields each day. So, who *was* in charge when you were away? Or is that why the sugar crop has been so bad?"

Paul's temper flared. "You cannot be serious! I work my hands raw for the likes of you, while you sit back and wait for Father's fortune to fall squarely into your lap. Don't talk to me about gallivanting when it's *you* who've gallivanted on the mainland for these past ten years, choosing to do as little as possible!" When he received nothing more than John's crooked smile, he was needled into reproving his brother further. "In the words of Socrates: 'Let him that would move the world, first move himself'."

"Really?" John yawned. "Well, Paulie, I'm more inclined to believe that it's: 'better to do a little well, than a great deal badly.'"

Paul dropped the asinine volley.

John sighed loudly. "Now that we've gotten that all figured out, may we get back to the subject at hand?"

"And what would that be?" Paul ground out.

"The men you've put in charge – here on Charmantes." When Paul began to object again, John cut him off. "Just the names, please. That's all I want."

"Damn it, John, you know them all!"

"George mentioned a Wade Remmen. Who the hell is he?"

"Wade Remmen?" Jeannette inquired.

John nodded, looking to his sister. "Do you know him, Jeannie?"

"Oh yes! He's a handsome man!"

Charmaine smiled, aware of Jeannette's infatuation.

"He's quite handsome, is he?" John asked, his mien merry.

"Oh yes," Jeannette nodded eagerly.

"And who told you that?" he probed. "Miss Ryan perhaps? Tell me, does Mr. Remmen have a moustache?"

"No, Johnny," she denied, "Mama said he was handsome. Then I noticed."

Paul's furrowed brow gave way to a gratified grin.

John matched smile for smile. "Did you hear that, Paul? You have nothing to fear: Miss Ryan has eyes *only* for you."

"I don't need you to tell me that!" Paul bit out, belatedly realizing how ridiculous he sounded.

Charmaine groaned inwardly, displeased that her private affections were being broadcast to the entire room, breathing easier when Paul revisited the topic of Wade Remmen. "When George disappeared four months ago, I asked Wade to run the lumber operation. He's managed it very well, his decisions sound. For that reason, I've placed him in charge permanently. George will now be free to oversee other important matters."

"Free to be at your beck and call, you mean," John rejoined. "Tell me, George, how do you like having your strings constantly pulled like a marionette?"

"I don't mind at all – just as long as I'm being paid well."

"I guess some things never change," John mused.

"That's an understatement," Paul mumbled.

Clapping his hands together, John pressed on. "This Mr. Remmen sounds quite industrious. How long has it taken him to reach such an elevated stature?"

Paul knew that John could care less about Wade Remmen or any other island employee, for that matter. The sole purpose of this inquisition was to perpetuate the game John enjoyed playing – that of heir to the family fortune – a game John knew chafed him greatly. So Paul steeled himself and put on a face of disinterest, determined not to allow his brother to succeed.

"Wade is from Virginia. When his parents died, he and a younger sister were left destitute. Unable to find work, they stowed away on one of our ships, hoping to build a better life here. The captain found them aboard the packet two days out of port and turned them over to me when the vessel docked. That was two years ago. Wade was seventeen, well built, and used to hard labor. He pleaded his case and promised to pay for the ship's passage if I gave him the chance. I had nothing to lose and haven't been disappointed. So it was only natural that I relied on him when George deserted us."

"What a story!" John exclaimed with a dramatic shake of his head.

"Anything else you'd like to know?" Paul asked, ignoring the theatrics.

"Did Mr. Remmen ever pay for his passage?"

Charmaine was astounded at the man's stinginess, but Paul seemed accustomed to the financial interrogation and laughed spuriously. "Tell me John, must I account for every penny that might slip past your wallet?"

"If you don't, our resident money-monger George will. Right, George?"

"Right, John. And no, I don't believe Wade paid for either fare."

"And why not?" John asked, his eyes leveled on Paul again.

"Because he has needed his wages to get settled," Paul replied, ripping his furious regard from George. "His salary has gone into purchasing the rundown Field's cottage. He's done a fine job fixing it up."

"I should think so, having had two passages waived. A bit unfair, I'd say."

"I didn't waive them–"

"Miss Ryan wasn't given a grace period, was she? Two years can earn a fortune in interest."

"Impossible," Paul snorted, "it's impossible to speak intelligently with you."

"Since you are meting out charity from my pocket, shouldn't everyone get a share of the bounty?"

"Miss Ryan was not indigent," Paul responded snidely, certain that John was pressing the issue simply to pit Charmaine against him. It wasn't working: not a hint of anger flashed in her lovely eyes. "Nor was she penniless. She held a comfortable position in Virginia, and could afford the crossing costs."

"Then why did she leave?" John demanded.

"We have been over this, John. She wanted to make a new life for herself."

"And *that* she has," John smiled wickedly, entertained by his brother's deepening scowl. "I'd like to meet this Wade Remmen. Indeed, I would."

"He's at the mill," Paul stated. "Whenever you come out of your inebriated *daze* you can look for him there."

He stepped over to the serving tray and poured three glasses of port, passing one to Agatha and another to Charmaine.

Charmaine accepted the libation grudgingly, taking a sip before setting it on the table. This evening had served as a vivid reminder of the detrimental effects of alcohol. It made angry men angrier. She'd be happy to never see a bottle of spirits again.

Yvette took advantage of the lull in the conversation and scurried over to the grand piano. "Johnny," she said in great excitement, "I have a surprise for you!"

Charmaine cringed. *Here it comes*, she thought. John had inferred that her abilities at the instrument were sadly lacking. Now he was about to discover that she had taken it upon herself to teach his sisters the little she knew.

"What's that, Yvette?" he queried, the timbre of his voice unusually gentle.

"Just listen!" she exclaimed, commencing to play her favorite tune.

Charmaine resolved not to look John's way, yet her eyes mutinied. He did not seem to notice; he remained transfixed upon the simple recital.

"What do you think?" Yvette asked, swiveling when she had finished.

"I'm impressed. That was beautiful."

The girl was beaming, and Jeannette quickly joined her. "May I play now?"

With John's assent, she began. This time, his eyes traveled to Charmaine and remained there. She was uncertain what she read in his expression, but it was more than astonishment. Triumphant for the first time that night, she smiled defiantly at him.

"That was lovely, too, Jeannie," he said, turning his regard on both sisters. "I suppose Miss Ryan has been teaching you to play?"

Jeannette nodded. "But we swore her to secrecy so we could surprise you."

"Now I understand," he said, his half-smile sardonic. "Your governess wasn't at the keyboard after all this afternoon. You were just pretending it was she."

"Oh no, Johnny," his sister refuted earnestly. "It *was* Mademoiselle Charmaine. We don't play that well!"

"Do you think we play that well?" Yvette piped in.

"Nearly," he replied, satisfied that he'd squashed Charmaine's gloating.

Jeannette moved from the piano to the chessboard across the room. "Will you teach me how to play chess, Mademoiselle? You promised you would."

"It's been so long since I've played. I wouldn't be a good teacher."

Paul capitalized on the request and left John and George, pulling a chair up to the table. "I challenge you to a game, Miss Ryan. Jeannette, I will instruct you as we play."

Charmaine stammered with an excuse. "I'm afraid I won't be much of an opponent. Perhaps George would like to play in my stead."

Her objection had fallen on deaf ears, for Paul was rotating the board so that the white pieces were on her side. "Come, Charmaine," he coaxed debonairly, "I haven't played in a very long time either. We shall be equally matched."

She gave in reluctantly. Joshua Harrington had taught her the game's basic strategies, but she had never committed them to memory. Paul would handily gain control of the board, and although she didn't care in the least if she lost, she preferred that her inadequacy not be exposed to his brother. And yet, John was conversing with George; perhaps he wouldn't notice.

"...but George, if you purchase land that is nothing more than a swamp, you'll soon find yourself sinking into a quagmire of debt with that little devil of a lawyer Edward 'P.' Richecourt knocking on your cabin door. Now I know you fantasize about accumulating unlimited wealth overnight," he continued facetiously, as Rose stepped into the room and moved closer to them, "but it won't happen if you go looking for bargains. Part with the money you've been hoarding, however, and I've a few prospects that might interest you – sound investments that could prove a real windfall over time."

Paul's eyes left the chessboard and shifted to John, but Rose interrupted. "How many times must I tell you not to sit in a chair that way, John Duvoisin? You are going to topple over."

John, who'd been balancing the chair on its back legs, stood and rearranged it. "I've been sitting that way for as long as I can remember," he complained good-naturedly, "and I have yet to fall."

"Don't argue with me," his one-time nanny warned, shaking a crooked finger at him. "I'm older than you, and if need be, I can still take a switch to you!"

The statement elicited giggles from the twins, who had lost interest in the chess game. "Did you really take a switch to his backside?" Yvette asked, her laughter renewed as John feigned a grimace of fear.

"On more than one occasion," he interjected, placing an affectionate arm around the older woman's bent shoulders and walking her nearer his sisters. Noticing that he had everyone's attention where he liked it, he said, "In fact, I remember one occasion in particular when I was nine – not always a lucky number–"

"Do you mind?" Paul cut in. "I'm trying to concentrate."

Amazingly, John forfeited his story and gave Rose another squeeze before releasing her. "Is Pierre settled for the evening?"

"Sleeping like a newborn," she whispered, taking a seat near Charmaine.

"He's quite a boy," John commented, talking across the chessboard now. "I'm impressed by how well he speaks for a boy of–"

"John," Paul bit out, and then, "Please – take your conversation elsewhere."

"Am I not allowed to speak in my own parlor?" John asked innocently.

Turning slowly in his chair, Paul regarded his brother. "You may speak wherever you wish. I just ask that you spare me your domestic whims until I've finish playing this game with Miss Ryan."

"Now Paul, I'd hardly be a gentleman if I allowed you to *play games* with Miss Ryan. Therefore, I will act as a chaperone and watch – *quietly*."

Vexed, Paul turned back to the chessboard, conscious of John surveying the game behind him. Sliding his bishop five squares diagonally, he proclaimed Charmaine's king in check.

She was in a fine mess, and everyone was watching. Distracted, she pretended intense deliberation before edging her king one square forward. Belatedly, she realized she had laid her valuable queen open to attack.

Paul closed his eyes to the critical blunder, for capturing her queen would place her king in checkmate. Ignoring the decisive move, he took hold of his bishop. But John swiftly brushed his hand aside. "What sort of game is this, Paulie?" he needled, grabbing his brother's black queen and sweeping the white queen off the board. "That's checkmate."

Charmaine's eyes flew from John's taunting visage back to the chessboard. She was indeed in checkmate.

"You couldn't have missed that move!" John remarked with relish. "You were always better at this game than I. Or were you just allowing Miss Ryan a small victory before closing in for the kill?"

"That's it!" Paul snarled, his ire doubly stoked by the twins' chorus of laughter. "You've been at me all night, pressing my patience!"

"Have I now?"

"You know damn well you have!" Paul barked, coming out of his chair and standing toe to toe with his brother.

"Watch your language!" John admonished jovially, unperturbed. "There are ladies present, and we must at least *act* decently."

"What would you know about decency?"

"I don't know Paul, why don't you – Mr. Epitome of Decency – tell me? Why don't you begin with an accounting of the money you've spent on Espoir and an explanation as to why you've concealed its development from me? Or could it be that you don't want me to know how much of Charmantes' profits are financing your building project there?"

"So – the real issue comes to light! Why don't you take the matter up with Father?"

"I have all the figures," John smiled crookedly. When Paul turned on George, he added, "No, I didn't get them from George."

"Then who?"

"Your lawyer and mine, the distinguished Edward Richecourt."

"The hell you did!" Paul roared. "He was given explicit instructions–" As if caught, his words died in mid-sentence.

John paid no mind to what he already knew. "Ah, but given a choice, Mr. Richecourt wisely spoke up. You see, even though he despises me, he knows better than to bite the hand that will one day feed him."

"Very good," Paul applauded ruefully. "But what are you going to do about it, John? Tell Father how to spend *his* money? It's not yours yet!"

"I could care less how *Papa* manages his affairs, and even less about his great estate. I've done fine on my own, and unlike you, will continue to do so without taking a single penny from his pocket."

"*How dare you suggest that I've taken money from this estate?*"

"I wasn't *suggesting* at all, Paulie. I was merely stating the facts."

"Well let me state a few facts for you, dear brother!" Paul thundered. "Unlike you, I don't draw a salary every month – which I'm certain has secured you a great many investments, not to mention the purchase of that additional plantation of yours in Virginia. Yes, John! I, too, know what's going on! So, let's just say I'm cashing in on ten years of wages that I've never laid claim to."

"Any salary I draw is coming out of *my* future inheritance," John retaliated. "I believe I'm still first on father's will, am I not? Amazing that, loyal as you are to him, *you* are not even mentioned in that document." John shook his head once, and clicked his tongue for emphasis. "That being the case, *your* island operation is costing *me* dearly!"

Paul stepped in close, his red face only inches from John's, his fists balled white. "You've gone too far this time!"

Before he could act, George grabbed John's arm. "You've had too much to drink," he chided sternly. Next, he scolded Paul. "And you've taken the bait. Now, John and I are going to say 'goodnight'." He gave a slight nod, then shoved John toward the door.

When they were gone, Paul slumped into his chair, and Charmaine heaved a shuddering sigh of relief.

"Are you out of your mind?" George asked, his voice rising as they reached John's suite. "Why the hell did you say that to him? Why do you perpetuate this rivalry? It isn't Paul's fault that your father favors him, is it?"

"I can't stand how he exploits it – he's a real *daddy's* boy."

"He may be a daddy's boy, John, but Paul was the one who held this family together four years ago. He was the shoulder that all the tears were cried upon. He was the one who calmed everybody down and got life back to normal here."

John grunted in renewed disgust, but George wasn't silenced. "You were dead wrong accusing him of embezzling money from this estate!"

"Shut up, George," he growled, pushing into the room.

"No, I won't shut up!" George expostulated, stepping in front of the man to get his attention. "You were at it all evening long, and not just with Paul. Why in heaven's name were you picking on Charmaine, of all people?"

"She's a sneaky little actress," John sneered.

"Charmaine?" George exclaimed incredulously. "You can't be serious!"

"She's you fooled, too, George?"

George frowned. "What are you talking about?"

"I caught her in here the other day rifling through my papers."

"Charmaine? I find that hard to believe. Are you sure?"

"No," John fired back sarcastically, "she was a mirage!"

"This doesn't sound like Charmaine. Did you give her a chance to explain?"

"She made up a lame excuse when she realized she was caught red-handed."

"She's not a liar," George insisted. "She's a decent, honest young lady."

John remained unconvinced. "And what's this business about her father?"

George's eyes narrowed. "He was a wife-beater. One day it went too far. It has nothing to do with who she is, but it does upset her to talk about it.

"Ah..." John muttered snidely, "that explains it."

"Leave her alone, John, or you'll have me to contend with."

John was perturbed by George's adamant defense of the governess. Fleetingly, he wondered how she'd managed to charm both his brother and his friend. "You know what, George? You talk too much."

"Aye, I talk too much," George agreed, grabbing John's arm as he attempted to brush past him, pulling him round and looking him square in the eye. "But somebody needs to tell you a thing or two!"

"You can't tell me what I want to hear," John replied bitterly, "so why don't you get out and leave me alone?"

He wrenched free, but George beat him to the brandy decanter on the other side of the room, confiscating it. "No, I can't tell you what you want to hear, but liquor isn't going to wash it away, and even if it could, I doubt that the past was any better than the present."

"I just want the oblivion of unconsciousness for a while."

"You've been unconscious for three days now! If you can't pull yourself out of this stupor, you should leave. Go back to Virginia, so that Yvette and Jeannette will remember you as you were four years ago, and Pierre, well..."

"Finish it, George," John prodded, his eyes sparking back to life. "So that Pierre won't remember me at all. Right?"

"Damn it, John! Do you want him to grow up thinking of you as a drunk – an obnoxious oaf who spreads misery to everyone around him? Is that what you want?"

There was no point in preparing for bed; she would never fall asleep. Instead, Charmaine reread the letter she'd recently received from Loretta Harrington. A response was in order, the diversion she needed. She sat at the desk and set quill to paper. But when she had finished, she was no closer to tranquility. Yes, she had written about a variety of things, but the dominant subject was John Duvoisin. She scanned the missive.

> *I was pleased to receive your letter... I am quite well... The children are a constant comfort to me... I still do not understand Mr. Duvoisin's marriage to so cruel a woman as Agatha Ward... I avoid her whenever possible... Paul is the consummate gentleman, and aside from Rose and George Richards, I sometimes feel he is the only friend I have in the house... George finally returned this past week, but you should not harbor hope of him as a possible suitor... my thoughts have been far from such concerns... John Duvoisin has ventured home, even though it is whispered that his father forbade him to do so. His presence has rekindled my former reservations concerning matrimony. I can understand Frederic Duvoisin's disdain for his own flesh and blood, for John is a rude, ill-bred, detestable cur who spends his days closeted in his apartments drinking from dawn to dusk. I've tried to avoid him at all costs, but he appears at the worst possible times, and I find myself poorly equipped to respond to his cruel sarcasm. He has taken a dislike to me for a number of reasons. He's learned of my father, no doubt through his intended bride, the widow Anne Westphal London... Do you know her? But I am not the only person he ridicules. He wages war with practically everyone, including his aunt or stepmother, as the case may be... Tell Mr. Harrington that he was never more correct in his opinion of a person than he was of this man. Please give everyone my love...*

Charmaine stared down at the pages. Committing her turbulent thoughts to paper had not exorcised the demon. It had only succeeded in anchoring his face more firmly before her. *Wide awake... she was still wide awake!* How was she to enjoy the serenity of this lavish bedroom when her mind returned over and over again to the night that he had invaded her privacy here? With everything that had occurred since then, why did she still picture it so vividly – feel his hands on her, his hard body drawn up against hers, his breath buffeting her cheek? *No! I won't think about him! I won't! I'll think about Paul, his kiss before dinner, or his passionate embrace that stormy night when* – It was useless! She needed to escape. Suddenly, the night air beckoned, and she thought of the courtyard gardens. Yes, the gardens, where the ocean breezes mingled with the sweet scent of exotic flowers, a haven that might vanquish the odious image of John Duvoisin.

Paul propped his elbows on his knees and rested his chin on laced fingers. The cool breeze that wafted off the ocean did not ease his turmoil, for phantom figures continued to spurn and mock him. George was right. He had played the buffoon, played it to the tune his brother piped, leaving Charmaine sorely abused, and his dignity battered. John would never allow him to forget his illegitimacy, would always ridicule his efforts to prove himself worthy of the Duvoisin name. Why did it matter? *Because, down deep, you still respect him,* Paul admitted. Bastard… the label had dogged him for as long as he could remember, but up until four years ago, it had never mattered to John. Now, John used it as a weapon, skewering him every chance he got. Paul exhaled and closed his eyes. Suddenly, his father stood before him, hard and condescending. For all of Frederic's praise of his adopted son and vocal disapproval of his legitimate son, John remained sole heir to the Duvoisin empire, with Pierre second in line. Perhaps Paul had no right to pretend at something that he wasn't, to claim a rank among the Duvoisin men who had gone before him. The circumstances of his birth denied him that right. Hadn't his uncontrolled temper this evening proven his worth as a gentleman? A true gentleman would never have behaved so badly, justified or not.

"Good evening…" The soft greeting was angelic.

"Good evening," Paul returned, standing and stepping closer to the feminine vision before him. "I thought you had retired long ago."

"No," Charmaine said shyly. "And what of you? Couldn't you sleep?"

"I had the good sense not to try. Would you walk with me?"

Charmaine agreed without hesitation, though she was disappointed when he turned pensive, clasping his hands behind his back, rather than taking her elbow.

"I'd like to apologize for my brother's behavior tonight," he finally said. "Actually, I'd like to apologize for *my* behavior. I allowed John to test my patience and, in so doing, hurt you. I'm sorry that I broke my promise."

Charmaine studied him in confusion.

"Am I forgiven?" he inquired in earnest.

"Forgiven? Whatever for? You said you would be at my side, and you were. How could I ask for more? As for your brother, you need not plead forgiveness for him. He will have to do that himself, though I'll not hold my breath waiting. I find it amazing that such a man can be called a gentleman. Why, a gentleman sets aside arguments diplomatically, as you attempted to do a number of times this evening. But when one is not dealing with a gentleman then –"

"Charmaine," Paul chuckled, suddenly grasping her hand and squeezing it jubilantly, "you must have been sent by the very gods this night – you with your determination and conviction."

"I'm sorry?"

Though befuddled, she was caught up in his surge of joy.

"You've just restored my self-confidence, and I'm very grateful. You see, John can have a sobering effect on people, forcing them to look at themselves no matter how hard they resist. And this evening, I fell victim."

"Sobering? That's one word I would never use in describing your brother."

"So it would appear," he agreed. "But just wait until he *is* sober. His mordant wit was a bit dull tonight. Normally he's much worse."

The moment's gaiety vanished.

"*Worse?*" she declared apprehensively. "Then, how am I to avoid him?"

Paul's elation did not diminish. "Take the children outdoors. The weather is beautiful. I'm certain they would enjoy a day abroad. Plan a picnic or two."

"That is a fine idea for tomorrow," Charmaine replied dejectedly, "but what of the next day, and the day after that?"

"John will tire of his little games. He has no reason to remain here."

"Then why *is* he here?"

Noting her deep interest, Paul deliberated his reply. "He's curious about Espoir. Once he's looked everything over and is satisfied with his assessment, he'll return to Virginia."

"Do you really think so?"

"I know so. Future chess games will be far different from tonight's."

"And next time you'll allow me to win?" she asked coyly, bravely.

Paul chuckled softly. "Mademoiselle, surely you didn't take my brother's assertions to heart?"

"Did he speak true? *Were* you allowing me to win?"

"And if I answer honestly, will you offer a reward?"

"That depends on what you request," she answered tremulously.

His eyes settled on her lips. "A kiss," he murmured.

"Very well," she responded breathlessly, their playful banter taking her into uncharted territory.

"Charmaine, I would let you win any game if it would afford me a kiss."

His words were muted by the thud of her heart and the sweeping motion that pulled her into his arms. She tilted her head back and closed her eyes, allowing him full access to her lips, savoring the coarseness of his moustache on her soft skin. When it seemed that he couldn't hold her any tighter, his embrace quickened, his ravenous mouth bruising, cutting across her lips and forcing them apart, his tongue thrusting into her mouth. This time he did not withdraw, and the splendid moment lengthened. Charmaine clung to him for support, returning his searing kiss with an ardor of her own. When his mouth finally traveled to her throat, she sighed, his breath warm on her neck, sending a chill of sensate pleasure down her spine. She was keenly aware of the love words he whispered close to her ear: "Sweet Jesus, Charmaine, my need is great… I long for you… long to make love to you… Come with me to my room…"

Reality took hold, overpowering that odd mixture of expectancy and yearning. "I can't!" she cried, bracing her palms against his chest. "I just can't."

Tormented, Paul's iron embrace fell open, and the woman whom he wanted more than any other disappeared beyond the hedge. Although he was left in agony, he reassured himself that time was on his side. It wouldn't be long before she succumbed.

Safe in her room, Charmaine went through the motions of preparing for bed, tears of frustration giving way to the pleasing memory of Paul's embrace. Yes, he had propositioned her again, but she was warmed by the knowledge that he wanted her as a man wants a woman, yet respected her enough to set aside his passion in deference to her wishes. Perhaps in time the two would become one.

Chapter 2

Tuesday, August 22, 1837

Peace of mind! Oh, the oblivion of peaceful peace of mind! They were Charmaine's last thoughts as she drifted off to sleep. Like a prayer answered, she succumbed to a deep and restful slumber, the first she'd had in three long nights.

Songbirds in the great oak just outside her window awoke her, and she lay abed enjoying nature's symphony, a harbinger of the brilliant day ahead, one that was perfect for a picnic. She rose and peeked into the children's room. They were still asleep. She began to dress, determined to get an early start.

As she sat at her dressing table and brushed out her hair, the serenity of the morning was shattered by a series of vociferous oaths that brought her straight to her feet and into the corridor. Joseph Thornfield was racing down the stairs, a wooden bucket tumbling after him, ricocheting off the walls and splattering water everywhere.

"Damn it, boy! I love hot baths almost as much as I love music, but I refuse to be scalded into singing soprano in a boy's choir!"

Charmaine turned toward the bellowing voice, and her jaw dropped. There stood John Duvoisin, dripping wet from head to toe, leaning far over the banister, and shouting after the servant boy. He was naked save a bath towel clasped around his waist, unperturbed by his indecent state of undress. Charmaine compared him to Paul – the gold standard by which she assessed all men – annoyed to find that his toned body rivaled his brother's: wide shoulders, corded arms, and taut stomach, which sported a reddish hue. Belatedly, she realized she was no longer staring at his back. She grimaced as she lifted her gaze and her eyes connected with his. A jeering smile broke across his face, his pain apparently forgotten now that he had an audience.

"You're as red as a ripe apple, my Charm. I thought my brother had shown you a man's body, or did I interrupt that lesson in anatomy the other night?"

Her degradation complete, Charmaine marched back into her bedchamber, slamming the door as hard as she could in his face. Her gratification was meager; it was a full minute before his laughter receded from the hallway.

It was still early when she left her room again. Her plans for a quiet breakfast had been dashed. John had effectively roused the entire household, except for Agatha, who ate in her boudoir. Paul, George and Rose converged on the staircase. Charmaine prayed that John would be delayed, but lately, none of her prayers were being answered. He appeared just as they reached the dining room.

"Good morning, everyone!" he greeted brightly, winking at her.

She glowered in response, but he dismissed her, settling at the table with the children, who were thrilled to see him. She hesitated, debating where to sit. With Paul still talking to George in the archway, she remained indecisive.

John noticed at once. "Do you plan on eating, Mademoiselle, or will you just stand there and watch us? You paint the picture of a wounded dog awaiting table scraps."

The demeaning declaration stung like salt in an open wound, the promise of a brilliant day rapidly fading. Taking courage, she stepped closer, but did not sit.

"Ah yes," he mused, pretending ignorance of her quandary and coming to his feet, "the lady expects a gentleman to help her with her chair, but since Paul is preoccupied right now, I suppose a *convict* like me will just have to do!"

He rounded the table and pulled the chair out for her. With a great flourish, he whisked a napkin through the air and dusted off the seat cushion, finishing his theatrics with a servile bow and a gesture that she be seated. She did so with as much aplomb as she could rally, but as she spread her serviette in her lap, her eyes went to Paul, whose jaw was clenched in monumental self-control.

John returned to his own chair, and chatted with George, Rose, and the children, the meal uneventful until Jeannette produced the letter Charmaine had written to Loretta Harrington.

"Shall I give this to Joseph to post, Mademoiselle?"

Charmaine cringed. "Yes, please," she hastily replied.

Too late! The man's interest was piqued, his brow raised. She knew that expression: it meant trouble. Sure enough, he stopped Jeannette as she passed behind him and removed the envelope from her hand. "What have we here?"

"A letter," Paul snapped, annoyed at this violation of Charmaine's privacy.

"A letter?" John mimicked. "Thank you for explaining, Paul. I'd almost forgotten what a letter looked like. But Miss Ryan hasn't forgotten, has she?"

Charmaine paled, but John pressed on, tapping the envelope against his lips. "Mrs. Joshua Harrington of Richmond, Virginia. Harrington… where have I heard that name before? Ah yes, the merchants' convention last year. Joshua Harrington was leading the protest against import tariffs. I remember him quite well now. A short-tempered man, if my memory doesn't fail me, short and short-tempered."

"I found him quite the contrary," Paul argued.

"Now, Paul," John countered jovially, "he isn't a *tall* man by any measure."

George snickered, but Paul's brow knitted in vexation. "I was speaking of his temperament!"

"Well, I don't know which side of him you saw, but he quickly lost his *temper* when I spoke with him."

"Were you taunting him, John?"

"Why would I do that? He just doesn't have a sense of humor, that's all. I simply commented that with a name like Joshua, he had to be a prophet and should consult with God before delivering his next ludicrous speech. After that, he wanted nothing to do with me, which suited me just fine."

Paul closed his eyes and shook his head in exasperation.

"But that is neither here nor there, is it, Mademoiselle?" John continued, serious again. "You have correspondence to post, and Joseph normally sees to such errands. However, he is busy cleaning up the mess in my room. Therefore, I volunteer to deliver it to the mercantile for you."

"That is very noble of you, John," Paul responded before Charmaine could object. "However, Miss Ryan would like to know that it *was,* in fact, delivered."

"Now Paulie, are you suggesting that I would drop this by the wayside?"

"Let us just say that I, too, am gallant, John. Since you have no reason to travel into town, while that is my very destination today, let me take it."

"No, I think not, Paul. You see, I *do* have a reason to ride into town. I have my own letters to post, and since Miss Ryan doesn't trust me, this is the perfect opportunity to prove to her that I'm not the scoundrel she imagines me to be – that her letter will be delivered to the mercantile, intact."

"John–"

"Admit it, Paul. You have an ulterior motive for visiting the mercantile. A tête-à-tête with Maddy Thompson perhaps?"

"I'm finished playing games with you, John," Paul snarled. "If you insist on posting the letter, then by all means, go ahead."

"Oh goodie!" John exclaimed, inciting a chorus of giggles from the girls.

For Charmaine, however, the fate of her correspondence was far from settled. "If I had known that my letter would cause such a quibble," she laughed artificially, "I would never have allowed Jeannette to carry it to the table. Perhaps it would be better if I just posted it myself." She leaned forward to remove it from John's hand, but he held it out of reach and disagreed glibly.

"The children have lessons, do they not? Surely you don't intend to allow a personal matter to interfere with that? No? I didn't think so. But fear not! I give you my solemn oath as a gentleman that your letter will remain safe in my hands. If there is something else that troubles you, George will vouch for me when I tell you that – unlike a certain individual who shall remain unnamed – I have never bent so low as to read someone else's private mail."

Charmaine reddened.

"Besides, I don't need to read your letter to know what you think of me. You've made that abundantly clear on a number of occasions."

Charmaine remained closeted in the playroom with the children, hoping upon hope that John would leave for town and she'd be free to arrange a picnic lunch with Fatima. It was nearly eleven and, unlike Paul, who had spent the morning in the study with George, John had dawdled the last three hours away. Where was his ambition to carry out the task he had so eagerly begged for at breakfast?

Presently, she turned her mind to an arithmetic lesson, trying not to dwell on her two latest predicaments: the postponed picnic and John's delivery of her letter to the mercantile. Would he read it? He could, and she'd never know! Fool that she was, she had committed her hatred to paper, and now the devil himself possessed it!

John Duvoisin. Yes, she hated him! Hated how he scorned and mocked her. Hated how he singled her out and ridiculed her just for the fun of it. Hated how he presumed to know so much about her character. Hated how he loved to make everyone miserable. Hated him like she hated her father. Hated him, hated him, hated him! Colette's words of long ago haunted her: *Just remember... you hate him first.* Hate him first? What came after that? She seemed to remember something about loving him. Ridiculous! She'd hate him first, second, third, and forever. She prayed fervently for the day when he would pack his bags and return to Richmond. It couldn't come soon enough.

Beyond the confining room, doors banged shut and footfalls resounded in the corridor, setting her on edge. She left Jeannette and Yvette to their problems, and stepped onto the veranda. The breeze was invitingly cool for August, rustling their leaves of the tall oak overhead. Looking toward the paddock, she was rewarded with the fine sight of Paul, who stood with arms akimbo, conversing with George and two stable-hands. Charmaine admired the authority he projected, lingering on his broad shoulders and lean torso, slim waist and well-defined legs, the muscles in his thighs sculpted against the dark fabric of his trousers. Highly polished ebony riding boots finished the lusty figure he cut. She closed her eyes to the heart-thundering image and remembered that first day on the Raven, his shirt doffed, the play of muscle across his broad back and arms, deeply tanned from the island sun. He was the embodiment of the perfect man, like the great Roman statues in the museums of Europe.

She thought of their kiss in the gardens last night, and her heart raced. His embrace had been passionate and longing, and despite her inhibition, she relished the pleasurable memory. His racy invitation simmered in her ears, and she breathed deeply, counseling herself to tread cautiously. She was playing with fire. It would be best to avoid another such encounter. Even now, she realized how difficult that would be, for as he clasped an easy arm around the shoulders of a young stable lad, she fancied herself in those strong arms once again.

The main door banged shut, and the vision was lost. Charmaine gingerly stepped forward and peered down, jumping back when the devil incarnate descended the portico steps. He wore a brown leather cap, white shirt, light brown trousers and matching boots. His gait was lazy, yet deliberate, a self-assuredness that she would love to see crushed. In her brief three-day experience, she knew this would never happen. She had never met anyone who exuded such confidence, not even Paul. Colette's remarks once again echoed in her ears: *He's an enigma...a one of a kind.* Thank God, one was quite enough!

He was halfway to the stables when Paul stepped out of the circle of men. Charmaine held her breath when they reached one another and Paul initiated an exchange, a concise remark that she couldn't hear. John waved a letter in his brother's face: *one single solitary letter.* He spoke next, another short phrase that drew Paul around and sent his eyes traveling up the face of the mansion. Within a moment, he found her, a smile breaking across his lips. Charmaine shook her head. John must have known she was standing there, watching them. *How did he know?* Or did he? He was probably playing Paul for the fool and got lucky.

John disappeared into the stable, emerging minutes later with a great black stallion in tow: Phantom, according to the twins. The proud beast fought the bridle, his sable coat shimmering in the late morning sun.

A groom led another horse out. When George took the reins, Paul threw his hands up. "I won't be long!" George called from the saddle.

Everyone seemed to be waiting for John to mount up as well. No one, not even Paul, rode the 'demon of the stable', so dubbed because he was constantly breaking out of his stall, jumping the corral fencing, evading stable-hands or nipping the other horses. Hence, great care was taken to segregate him. Clearly, John intended to do what his brother had the good sense to avoid, and Charmaine planned to laugh loudly when the stallion threw him onto his conceited rear end.

The steed was growing zealous for the freedom of the road, pulling fiercely at the bit, but John appeared oblivious as he conversed with George. He casually produced something from his shirt pocket and raised it to the animal's large muzzle. The horse gobbled it up. John stroked his satin flank and then, with one fluid motion, swung into the saddle. The horse bolted, but John reined him in, his momentum ending in a lunging halt. With a loud whinny and a violent shake of his huge head, the horse began to circle in place. Charmaine snickered; the man was no horseman. Finally, a weakness that she could exploit when the moment was ripe! If Paul were on the stallion, this wouldn't be happening.

"He's rarin' to go!" George averred. "He hasn't been ridden in ages."

John concurred. "I see my brother wasn't brave enough to work him out!"

"No, John, I value my neck too much!" Paul called back. "If he throws you, it will be your own folly. You won't control him until he's had a good long run!"

"We'll see, Paulie," John countered. "It won't take him long to remember all the tricks."

As if to fortify his contention, he leaned forward and patted the animal's sleek neck. A nudge to the flank, and the beast trotted toward Paul. John reached out and ruffled his brother's hair, laughing heartily as the horse completed a wide sweep of the area, hooves finally tapping out a perfect rhythm on the cobblestone drive. John snapped the reins hard, and the steed shot forward, speeding past George and exiting the compound, his legs a blur, tail and mane sailing in the wind. George spurred his own mount into motion and followed in hot pursuit, disappearing in a cloud of dust kicked up by the vagabond stallion.

Charmaine stepped out of the house and felt liberated. The children were gay, chasing butterflies and picking exotic flowers that grew with abandon in the grassy fields. Though it was hot, the sky was a deep azure and the breeze carried the sweet scent of ocean spray. The tropical paradise was a balm for her turbulent mind, a welcome respite from days of sequestration in the nursery.

They traipsed northwest through three fields, their destination a special picnicking spot the twins had chosen. Ahead was a wooded area, breached only by a dark, narrow path of craggy rocks that appeared to lead nowhere. They entered the copse, trudging up an incline that wasn't quite as treacherous as Charmaine had at first imagined. Soon the path leveled off and quite unexpectedly, opened onto a lush, grassy bluff that was enclosed on three sides by thick foliage. The western edge offered a lofty view of the ocean, unmatched in breathtaking majesty. The water below shimmered in the midday sun.

"Oh girls, this is just beautiful," Charmaine breathed, returning their ebullient smiles. "Look at the flowers! And the ocean – look how very blue it is!"

They giggled in reply, setting down the picnic basket. With her help, they spread a blanket in the shade of a tall cotton tree and laid out the bounty Fatima had packed for them: fried chicken, crusty bread, fresh oranges and bananas, cookies, and lemonade. Charmaine remembered many an evening in her impoverished home where soup and bread were the main course, portioned over a few days to make it last. If she were lucky, a feast such as this would adorn their Christmas table. She silently thanked God for her good fortune and prosperity this day. If only her mother could know how happy her life had become.

They delved into lunch, famished after their long hike. Even Pierre ate heartily, and Charmaine chuckled as he stuffed a third cookie into his greasy mouth. She wiped his face and hands clean as he squirmed away. Then he settled on the other side of the blanket and fell asleep from sheer exhaustion, content to take his afternoon nap in the open air.

John meandered into the kitchen in an attempt to shrug off the boredom that pervaded the study. The afternoon was drawing on, and there was no sign that lunch would be served any time soon. He had declined George's invitation to eat at Dulcie's. He wasn't in the mood to mingle with the men who caroused there.

So, he returned alone. He'd grown accustomed to being alone, and most of the time, he preferred it that way. But now he was hungry.

"'Afternoon, Mastah John," Fatima greeted as she bustled around the sweltering room, setting a tray of warm muffins on the kitchen table.

"Good day, Cookie," he returned as he sat down. "God, it's hot in here! I still say that stove should be out in the cookhouse where it belongs."

"Mind your mouth and don' be givin' your pa any ideas," she warned. "I like it right here. Saves me a lot of runnin'. And don't go touchin' those muffins!" she threatened, catching sight of his avid eyes on them. "They're for dinner."

"I'm not after your muffins, but it's nearly two. Where's lunch?"

His question drew a grumble from Fatima, who was now stoking the oven. As she bent over, John snatched a muffin and concealed it under the table.

"There ain't no table lunch today, Mastah John."

"And why is that? Are you holding out for a raise in wages?"

"You know me better than that," she chided, well aware that he teased her. "I already sent a tray of food up to your pa and Missus Agatha. I didn't expect you back for lunch."

"What about the children and their governess?" John asked, stealing a bite of his muffin when Fatima visited the pantry and dropped potatoes into her apron.

"Miss Charmaine took the children on a picnic," she explained, turning back to the table to dump them there. "I fixed 'em a basket of food before they left."

"A picnic?"

Fatima eyed him suspiciously. "I know what you're thinkin', Mastah John."

"What am I thinking?"

"If you're hungry, I'll fix you somethin', jus' leave Miss Charmaine alone."

"Leave her alone?"

"I heard you pickin' on her last night. She's a nice girl, and she don't know you. So you leave her be, before you frighten her right out of this house."

Fatima fetched a loaf of bread to make him a sandwich.

"A nice girl, eh?" he asked skeptically, grabbing another muffin and raising it to his mouth. "I keep hearing that. George is sweet on her, and my brother–"

His words were cut short when Fatima caught him red-handed. "My muffins!" she bellowed. "Now you put that back before I take a stick to you!"

John scrambled from the chair and was out the back door before she could maneuver her wide girth around the table. He sidestepped several frantic chickens that squawked as they scattered out of his way, then he nearly got tangled in the laundry on the clothesline. But he laughed loudly, knowing he'd escaped her.

"Go on now," she scolded from the doorway, shaking a knife at him, "and don't you come back here 'til dinner!"

He tipped his cap, bowed cordially, and walked down the back lawn, chewing on the warm muffin that he'd nearly swallowed whole. It only whetted his appetite; now he was really hungry. He knew where he could eat – and a fine lunch at that! He laughed again, realizing that the afternoon would not be boring after all. Poor Miss Ryan! She'd be alone with him; no Paul to come to her rescue. Well, at least the children would be pleased to see him. His destination was simple, since he knew exactly where they'd be enjoying their picnic.

Charmaine removed her bonnet, relaxed on the blanket, and took in her surroundings again. "How very romantic," she murmured, imagining herself in this paradise with Paul. "However did you girls find this place?"

"We didn't," Yvette replied matter-of-factly, "Johnny did. A long time ago."

At the mention of the man's name, Charmaine's eyes darted around, searching the shaded areas. *He's not going to jump out at you*, she reasoned. *He rode off to town, and you were gone before he returned. He has no idea where you are now.*

"What's the matter, Mademoiselle Charmaine?" Jeannette asked.

"Nothing. Tell me more about this spot. When did John show it to you?"

"When Mama was well. When we were little."

"And if we close our eyes," Yvette suggested, "we can pretend that Mama is with us again..."

Jeannette approved the idea, and Charmaine indulged their poignant fantasy. "But you mentioned your brother," she finally said. "He discovered this place?"

Yvette nodded. "When he was a boy, he used to go on expeditions with George. That's when they found these cliffs. Johnny swore George to secrecy. He told us that, from then on, whenever he got angry with Paul or Papa, he would come to this hideaway because it was the one place on the island that Paul didn't know about, the one place where he could be alone. When he knew that we could be trusted, he brought us here, too. But we had to promise *never* to tell Paul."

Charmaine gritted her teeth. The gall of the man – setting the children against Paul.

"I decided you could be trusted too," Yvette added thoughtfully. "And if..."

"And if what?" Charmaine asked suspiciously.

"And if Johnny wants company today, he's sure to look for us here."

Wants company? First he has to return from town, then discover that we've left the house. Certain that both could not possibly happen, Charmaine dismissed the thought, pleased when Yvette suggested a game of hide and seek.

She and her sister scurried off, declaring that their governess was the seeker and the blanket, 'home'. Charmaine covered her eyes and counted to fifty. Then she scanned the far edges of the encroaching forest, searching for any movement that would betray the girls' hiding places.

The crunch of leaves caught her ear, and she headed down the path by which they'd arrived. A snapping twig pointed to the brambles straight ahead. Determined to surprise them, she broke into a run and rounded the brush at top speed, lunging to a sudden halt when she nearly landed in John's arms, her bun falling loose and spilling its bounty onto her shoulders.

"Well now," he exclaimed, "I didn't expect you to be *that* happy to see me!"

Fuming, she snubbed him, making a great show of turning away.

"Aren't you going to tag me?" he pressed.

"*No!*" she threw over her shoulder as she stomped back to the clearing, pulling pins free of her hair. Unfortunately, the man fell in step alongside her.

"Johnny!" Yvette and Jeannette called in tandem, running from opposite sides of the bluff to greet him. "You did find us!"

"I was looking for lunch, and Cookie told me she packed a picnic for you."

"You can have some!" Jeannette offered, pointing to the leftover food.

John walked over to the blanket and stared down at the slumbering Pierre. After a moment, he lifted a discarded plate and piled it high with food. Then he settled against the trunk of a tree and delved into his meal. Yvette sat next to him, while Jeannette prepared him a plate of cookies.

They ignored Charmaine, who continued to simmer as she coifed her hair. He obviously intended to stay. After an interminable silence, she found the nerve to speak. "Do you always intrude upon people uninvited?"

"Only when it's worth it. And always when they're unsuspecting."

"And what exactly is that supposed to mean?"

"Let's take you for example: My, my, the secrets I've uncovered by intruding on you!" His eyes twinkled, but he waved away her displeasure with the chicken bone he held, tossing it over his shoulder. "Today I'm only intruding for lunch. This is delicious. The blisters I got on the journey here were a small price to pay."

Charmaine bit her tongue and focused on cleaning up, grateful when the twins engaged his attention, asking him for stories about America.

Their voices woke Pierre, who sat up, rubbed his sleepy eyes, and smiled when he recognized John. Yawning, he left the blanket and walked deliberately toward the man, made a fist, and plunged a targeted punch into his shoulder.

"Pierre!" Charmaine cried in disbelief. The boy had never raised a hand to anyone before. She feared John's reaction, certain that he'd use the child's bad behavior to discredit her. Instead, he doubled over as if seriously injured and, with a loud groan, flopped to the grass, where he lay perfectly still.

With great trepidation, Pierre stepped closer, oblivious of his sisters, who were winking at one another. No sooner had he crouched down, and John's eyes popped open with the cry: "Boo!" Pierre jumped, then chortled in glee, not satisfied until he'd played 'boo' three more times.

When John tired of the game, he drew the boy into his lap, pulled his cap from his back pocket, and placed it on his head. It was too large and slid over his eyes and nose. Only his grinning lips were visible.

Charmaine leaned back against the tree and watched them guardedly. Pierre was warming up to his elder brother. Just what she needed, a third child begging to see John all day long.

"How'd ya get here?" the boy asked, peering up at John from under the cap.

"On Fang, silly!" Yvette interjected, casting all-knowing eyes to John.

"Fang?" Charmaine asked.

"Johnny's horse," Yvette replied presumptuously.

"Horse?" Charmaine expostulated, turning accusatory eyes upon the man. "I'm sure you'll never recover from your large *blisters*."

"I said I had blisters," he rejoined, "I didn't say where."

The girls bubbled with laughter.

Charmaine was not amused. "Your horse's name is Fang? If it's the horse you were riding this morning, I thought his name was Phantom."

"The grooms call him that because of his bad manners. A phantom stallion. Surely you've heard that expression before, my Charm?"

"Of course I have!" she snapped, thinking: *like master, like horse.*

John's smile broadened. "Anyway, his real name is Fang."

"Fang," she repeated sarcastically, "why, that's a dog's name."

"Dog or horse, it's still an animal's name." John winked at Yvette when Charmaine turned away. "And he was given the name for a very good reason."

On cue, Yvette skipped to Charmaine and grabbed her hand, insisting that she examine the horse so that she would understand his bizarre name. "Come, Mademoiselle Charmaine, we'll show him to you."

Unwittingly, she was drawn into the girl's enthusiasm, and before she could object, was trekking the pathway with Yvette. She glanced over her shoulder to find John close behind, Jeannette at his side and Pierre on his shoulders.

The boy attempted to wave from his lofty perch, but quickly changed his mind, clasping both hands over John's eyes. John peeled them away with the complaint: "I can't see, Pierre! If I trip, we'll be like Humpty Dumpty and all fall down." Charmaine giggled when the three-year-old let go of John's face only to grab great fistfuls of his hair.

"That's not Humpty Dumpty," he declared, "that's Ring a Ring a Rosy."

Moments later, they found 'Fang' grazing in the middle of a wild field, his great head bent to the long grass, his tail swishing in the breeze.

"Come quickly!" Yvette urged, breaking into a run.

"Yvette!" John shouted. "Wait for me."

She stopped immediately, arms akimbo. "Then hurry up!"

When he reached her, he set Pierre down and squatted, looking her straight in the eye. "I've told you never to go near Fang without me. I thought you understood."

Yvette bowed her head. "But–"

"There *are* no buts, Yvette. The horse can be dangerous if he's startled. You are not to go near him unless you are with me. Agreed?"

"Agreed," she replied meekly.

John's genuine concern surprised Charmaine. After patting Yvette's back, he placed his cap on her head, a privilege that regained her friendship. Now she tugged at his hand and called for Charmaine to follow.

"So, this is Fang," Charmaine remarked apprehensively, jumping when the horse shook its head.

"Yes," John acknowledged, stroking the black mane, "this is my horse." He threw an arm over the animal's neck and proceeded to introduce them. "Fang, this is Miss Ryan, formerly of Richmond, Virginia. Miss Ryan, this is Fang, my loyal steed."

The twins were giggling and Pierre joined in.

Suddenly, the horse stepped forward and, to John's delight, neighed a greeting that petrified Charmaine. "That means 'pleased to make your acquaintance' in horse talk," he explained, drawing more laughter from the children.

Charmaine smiled in spite of herself.

"Do you like him, Mademoiselle Charmaine?" Jeannette asked.

"He is quite remarkable," she replied nervously, "however, I have yet to see why he's named Fang. I still say that's a dog's name."

John stepped closer. "You use the perfect word to describe Fang, Miss Ryan," he replied, taking hold of her wrist to lead her nearer the steed. "You see, Fang has a *remarkable* characteristic that distinguishes him from other horses."

She cringed with the contact of his warm hand and pulled away quickly.

"He was born with one overly large, *very sharp*, front tooth. Right, girls?"

They nodded vigorously.

"One overly large front tooth?" she asked. "Surely you jest."

"No, I do not. Fang has a reputation for nipping fingers and other horses. That's why they all steer clear of Fang. He uses his tooth as a weapon."

The twins hadn't stopped laughing. How had she been drawn into this ridiculous conversation? If the children weren't enjoying themselves so immensely, she'd be walking back to the blanket.

"You don't believe Johnny, do you?" Yvette demanded. "It's really true!" She looked up at her brother. "You better show her."

John pulled the stallion's head up from the grass and grabbed his muzzle. When Fang whinnied in objection, Charmaine stepped back.

"Why are you moving away?" he asked. "Don't you want to see the oddity of the century? You'd pay a fee to glimpse something like this at the circus."

"Actually," Charmaine faltered, "I'd hate to put you through all that trouble. I'm sure I can do without seeing the 'oddity of the century'."

"Go ahead, Mademoiselle," Yvette implored. "He won't bite you."

Charmaine wondered whether the girl was referring to the horse or John. She decided to placate them and be done with it, or she'd never hear the end of it.

John produced a lump of sugar from his pocket. The stallion's lips curled back, and the treat was devoured, but Charmaine witnessed nothing unusual.

"Did you see it?"

"Well, actually, no."

"How could you miss it? It was right there, plain as the nose on your face!"

"Now Yvette," John chided, "give Miss Ryan a chance. She doesn't know where to look like you do. Perhaps if she stepped a bit closer, she'd see better."

This time when John held out the sugar, he drew back the horse's lips and Yvette pointed to the area of interest. "Look! See it there? See that big fang?"

Charmaine didn't see a thing, but the girl's huff of frustration prompted her to scrutinize the animal's mouth further.

John let go of the huge head and pressed his brow into the steed's neck. Charmaine frowned. *Was he ill?* He looked heavenward, his entire face one tremendous smile. Great tears were welling in his eyes, and in a flash, she realized that he was laughing. The twins rivaled his mirth, doubling over in painful glee, unable to speak. Even Pierre was giggling.

"You are the first grownup that prank has worked on!" Yvette gasped.

Charmaine's heart plummeted. They were enjoying themselves at her expense! Suddenly, insidiously, her throat constricted with tears. Why was this man so determined to make a fool of her? Now he had the children ridiculing her! In great despair, she grabbed Pierre's hand and set a brisk pace back to the bluff.

"Mademoiselle!" Jeannette called after her, running to catch up. "You're not angry, are you? We didn't mean to make you angry. It was only a joke, but we wouldn't have done it if we thought you wouldn't find it funny, too!"

Charmaine struggled not to cry and was comforted when she received an affectionate hug from the gentle twin. Yvette and John were fast approaching, and she quickly composed herself, not wanting the man to know that he had once again reduced her to tears.

He saw her dab at her eyes. *Such a deft little actress. Now I'm supposed to feel guilty because I made the little lady cry.* He shook his head derisively and chuckled to himself. *She is quite fetching with her curvaceous figure and long wild hair – her best assets by far. And she uses that sidelong glance to disarm a man. No wonder Paul and George have fallen for her. Well, George is Mr. Earnest, and Paul likes to be the hero so he can seduce her. And Johnny? Well, Johnny isn't taken in so easily. Still, if she wants to play, then why not? Johnny has nothing to lose. With Paul in her pocket, she thinks she can take on the best of them. But she hasn't played with the likes of Johnny. Well, Miss Ryan, you shall see what it's like to play with Johnny.*

"Race you back to the blanket!" Yvette challenged. "The last one there has to carry the picnic basket home!" The girl broke into a run and bounded into the path, Jeannette and Pierre in hot pursuit.

John drew alongside Charmaine. "Don't you have a sense of humor?"

She was determined to ignore him and stared off into the distance. But he wasn't about to be dismissed, so he stepped in front of her. When she turned her face aside, he grabbed her chin and forced her to look at him. She slapped his hand away. "Don't touch me!"

He only chuckled. When she sidestepped him, he hastened to catch up. "I'm sorry if my jest offended you," he apologized, garnering her utter astonishment. "It's a prank that the twins enjoy playing. I thought you'd go along with it."

Doubting his sincerity, Charmaine withheld comment, relieved when they reached the bluff.

"You didn't even try to catch us!" Yvette complained.

John scooped up Pierre, who had run to greet them, then set him down again. "Now Yvette, you would have been pouting all day if I had outraced you."

"You couldn't have done that if you tried!"

Pulling his cap off her head, she brandished it before him. "I still have this! Let's play 'keep away' from Johnny!"

When John lunged at her, she darted out of reach. As he closed in, she sent the cap sailing through the air to her sister.

He grinned. "All right, Jeannie, now give it back."

She hesitated, then squealed as he dove at her, scurrying away with his cap in hand. Then she, too, sent it flying.

John played along, indulging their tossing escapade for minutes on end. With hands on hips, he strategically placed himself between them. But Yvette recognized the ploy and threw the cap to Charmaine this time. She caught it and was drawn into the game as well. Now John was tracking her.

"Are you going to give me the cap, my Charm?" he asked, arm extended.

"Don't give it to him, Mademoiselle!" Yvette cried. "Throw it to me!"

Charmaine launched the cap in Yvette's direction, breathing easier when John swung away. When it eventually came sailing back, it fell short of its mark, hitting the ground near Pierre. He picked it up, giggled, and clumsily shuttled it to her, enabling John to close in. Charmaine tucked it behind her back and blindly retreated. John steadily advanced, blocking her view altogether. Her foot struck the trunk of the tree. She was trapped!

He was only inches away, and as her eyes traveled up from the buttons on his shirt, past his neck to his clean-shaven face, memories of their first encounter rushed in. Somehow, he seemed taller than that night, even more imposing than the morning he'd barged into his room and found her reading Colette's letter. But he wasn't angry now. He leaned in close and, with a victorious grin, placed his hands flat against the tree trunk, imprisoning her there. His eyes were magnetic. At that moment, he struck her as being very handsome, his wavy hair falling low on his brow, his usually stern features turned boyish. He seemed to read her thoughts, and the rakish smile widened, boring deep dimples into his smooth cheeks. All at once, the blood was thundering in her ears, and she felt her face grow crimson.

"May I have my cap back, my Charm?" he asked huskily, "or must I remove it from your backside forcibly?"

Her limbs were quaking as she handed it over. He stood there a moment longer, restoring it to its original shape, complaining of the damage done. "I'm afraid it hasn't fared well in the battle. It will never be the same."

Yvette was outraged. "You're lucky you even got it back!" She turned on Charmaine. "You're no fun! You didn't even try to keep it away from him!"

"Well, Yvette," John said, "all good things must come to an end. *Even games*." Though he spoke to his sister, his eyes remained fixed on Charmaine, who was still leaning against the tree. He placed the cap on his head and walked over to Pierre, affectionately ruffling his hair.

The twins sneaked up behind him, bent upon dislodging the cap and engaging him in the game again. But he stepped out of their reach. They danced around him still, trying to jump high enough to snatch it off his head. Charmaine had never seen them so gay.

"Up to no good again, eh?" he accused mischievously.

"Just like you, Johnny!" Yvette rejoined.

"Just like me? Since when am I up to no good?"

"You're always up to no good," Yvette exclaimed, as if it were common knowledge. "That's what Father says."

A black scowl darkened John's face. Impulsively, Charmaine took a step closer to Yvette, fearful that he might strike the girl. Instead, he demanded more information. "He told you that?"

"No, not me. Just Paul."

"But you were there."

"Not exactly. Paul had something important to discuss with Father, and I wanted to know what it was. So, I went to the kitchen and took a glass from the cupboard and listened through the wall of the water closet next to Papa's dressing chamber. It worked fine, because I could hear every word they said. Paul was angry about something you did, something about sending a ship here without papers. Anyway, that's when Papa said you were up to no good."

Suddenly, John was laughing heartily. "A glass against the wall," he murmured, shaking his head in amazement.

Yvette nodded, finally pleased with his reaction. "You remember when you showed me how to do that, don't you?"

"Ah, yes," he sighed. "You are an astute pupil, Yvette."

Charmaine was both astonished and irate. "So, her eavesdropping on Saturday was my fault, but this incident is just splendid because the instruction came from you, is that it?"

John laughed harder and spoke to Yvette. "My advice to you, my little spy, is: keep up the good work, but take care *not* to get caught. If Paul finds you with that glass, he'll lock you up in the meetinghouse cellar with all the drunkards."

"Where you belong, no doubt!" Charmaine snapped.

"What is that supposed to mean?" John asked.

"You had better think twice before you teach the children your antics. They may come back to haunt you."

"I'll make a note of that," John replied in overemphasized seriousness. With a theatrical flourish, he produced an imaginary paper and quill and pretended to write. "Miss Ryan, an authority on high morals and untainted virtue, warns me that I had better watch my step, or else!"

"Or else what?" Yvette asked.

"Paulie will come and beat me up. Isn't that right, Mademoiselle?"

Charmaine's eyes narrowed, but she refused to answer, as once again her caustic retort failed to meet its mark.

When John saw she had nothing more to say, he chuckled softly and bid the children a farewell. He turned back to her, pulled the cap off his head, and held it over his heart. "Thank you, Miss Ryan, for graciously allowing me to join your picnic luncheon. I'm sure you'll agree that it was most enjoyable, but please don't beg me to stay any longer, since I really must be leaving now."

Enjoyable indeed! She almost laughed outright at the absurd statement. Still, she sighed with relief when she realized that he really meant to depart. Not even the children were able to change his mind, and he soon disappeared down the pathway. Not long afterward, they, too, headed for home.

Saturday, August 26, 1837

It was an hour past daybreak and Charmaine and the children were already out of the house. Late last night, George had informed the twins that Chastity would finally foal. And so, they were up and dressed at the crack of dawn, pestering Charmaine to visit the stables. Once there, they reveled in the miracle of new life. But Pierre had quickly tired of the spectacle.

Presently, he giggled uncontrollably as Charmaine spun him round and round in wide circles. Dizzy and exhausted, they collapsed onto the dewy lawn, where Charmaine affectionately kissed the top of his head. He scrambled away and stood before her, his cheeks rosy. "I wanna do it again!" he demanded, presenting his back to her and throwing his arms up into the air.

"Pierre," she complained breathlessly, "you are going to be ill!"

"One more time!" he pleaded, turning his baby-brown eyes upon her.

"That is what you said the last time," she replied, placing a finger to his protruding belly and marking her words with a tickle. He squirmed and giggled. "Very well," she sighed, rising again. "But this will be the last time, yes?"

He shrugged with head cocked, an adorable pose that made it impossible to say 'no'. She chuckled and gave him a fierce hug, then twirled him again. His glee echoed off the façade of the manor. When she set him down, he scrutinized her with another tilt of the head. Spontaneously, he threw his arms around her waist and hugged her as tightly as she had him moments ago.

Tears sprang to her eyes. "I love you, Pierre – so very much!"

As she released him, he espied a butterfly flitting over the flowers in the lawns and was off, chasing it down. He stopped to examine it each time it alighted. Charmaine sat in the grass and watched his carefree pursuit.

John strode back into his bedchamber, perplexed. Laughter had awoken him, drawing him out onto the veranda. He stood in awe of Charmaine Ryan's gentle play and genuine affection for Pierre. Quite unexpectedly, he felt reassured that the orphaned boy had found the surrogate mother he needed. Perhaps the young governess was not just another of Paul's hussies. He rubbed the back of his neck. Perhaps he had misjudged her.

The butterfly forgotten, Charmaine watched Pierre toss pebbles across the cobblestone drive. Though she appeared a tranquil figure in the cool morning breeze, her thoughts were turbulent.

The week had ended less eventfully than it had begun. After Tuesday's picnic, she came to accept the futility of hiding from John. Though the past three days had been a tedious exercise in self-control, she was getting better at holding her tongue, learning the hard way that it was impossible to win a war of words with him. He was far too quick on the comeback, another trait that rankled her.

As for Paul, he'd grown aloof, resuming his hectic work schedule on Charmantes. They hadn't shared another moment alone. It was for the best, she reasoned. The last thing she needed was for John to catch her in his brother's arms again. Nevertheless, Paul had been at dinner every evening, and for that, she was grateful. Tonight would be different. He had headed for Espoir before daybreak and wasn't expected back until very late. This evening, she would have to face John alone.

The twins scampered through the stable doorway, shattering the serenity as they raced up the lawns shouting and waving. "Mademoiselle Charmaine, don't you want to pet the new foal?"

"I think he and his mother need to be alone, and we must go inside to eat."

"Only for a little while," Jeannette pleaded as they reached her.

"And we can tell Johnny that Phantom sired a colt!" Yvette exclaimed.

"Johnny?" Charmaine queried quizzically. "Phantom sired?"

"Well of course! Why else would his coat be so very black?"

"Why else indeed?" she murmured.

It wasn't until they had eaten, and Pierre, who'd grown cranky by the end of the meal, was settled for an early nap, that Charmaine accompanied the girls back to the stable. The foal was a sight to behold: jet black, long of leg, and fuzzy all over. He began nursing just as George returned. Confident that the twins were in safe hands, Charmaine left them in order to check on Pierre.

The boy was not in his bed. She entered the playroom, but it, too, was empty. She checked her own room next. Nothing. Where could he be? She headed toward the stairs, counseling herself calm. Pierre was fine. He'd awoken and left the nursery looking for her. Maybe he was in Paul's chambers again.

The sound of shattering glass told her she was wrong. It had come from further down the corridor, from Colette's sitting room, a place where Pierre had often played, a place now forbidden to him. Instantly, Charmaine was at the door, cursing her ill fortune when the opposite portal was yanked open and the mistress of the manor swept out of her husband's quarters.

Agatha's eyes narrowed, but when a child's giggle drew their attention, those eyes turned evil. In a rush, she pushed past Charmaine and threw the door open. Pierre was crouched amid shards of glass and fresh flowers.

"You spoiled little brat!" she hissed, descending upon him in a fury. She grabbed him by the arm and lifted him clear off the floor. "I'll teach you not to touch what doesn't belong to you!"

Charmaine flew at the woman. Stunned, Agatha let go, and Pierre scrambled behind Charmaine, where he pinned his quaking body against her legs and buried his face in her skirts.

"How dare you?" Agatha demanded.

"I – I'm sorry–"

"*Sorry?* Is that all you have to say? You allow him to escape your supervision, enter my private chambers and break a priceless vase, presume to interfere, and then assume that an apology will suffice?"

"It was an accident. You can take the cost of the vase out of my wages."

"Take the cost out of your wages?" Agatha echoed snidely. "You underestimate the value of that piece. But even if I were able to replace it, I refuse to tolerate your insubordination. Somehow you have gotten the idea that you can speak to me as if you are part of this family – initiate an assault of my person! Well, let me remind you who you are – an employee, an inferior!"

"I did not mean to be insolent–"

"Step aside, Miss Ryan, and hand the boy over. Since you are unable to discipline the children, it is time somebody taught you how."

"No, please!" Charmaine begged, shielding Pierre with her arms.

"I said, step aside," Agatha ordered, incited by the boy's whimpers as she tried to pry him from Charmaine, "or I shall dismiss you!"

Charmaine had no choice. Agatha had the authority to carry out her threat, especially today, with Paul gone. In great shame, her arms dropped away.

"Mama! Mama!" Pierre desperately cried, clutching her legs.

Agatha yanked him free and carried him across the room to her dressing table chair, where she sat, laid him across her lap, and bared his bottom. She grabbed her hairbrush and struck him with it.

"Don't!" Charmaine shrieked. "Please, don't!" But her horror was muffled beneath Pierre's screams, which grew louder with each brutal whack, an ocean of tears spilling on the carpet. She finally dove at the woman. "*Let him go!*"

"*What in hell do you think you're doing?*"

Startled, Charmaine broke away. But Agatha cowered, for a livid John stood over them, beholding her defenseless victim. The boy's bottom and lower back were covered in purple welts. Repulsed, he turned acid eyes on his aunt.

"My God, woman, *what is the matter with you?*"

Ashen-faced, Agatha abruptly released Pierre, who ran to Charmaine. Then, she rose regally from her chair and smoothed her rumpled skirts, a pathetic pretense at dignity.

"The boy needed a firm hand," she replied imperiously, attempting to conceal the hairbrush in the folds of her skirt.

"*A hand?*" John snarled, seizing her arm and ripping the brush away. "*You nasty bitch!* I should take this to you!"

Agatha flinched when he hurled it across the room, then gasped at his profanity. "*How dare you?* I am mistress of this manor! I demand your respect! You will not to speak to me like that! You will apologize!"

"Hell will freeze over before I apologize to the likes of you!"

"*How dare you?*"

"How dare *you* abuse the boy over a vase that can easily be replaced?" he shot back. "I warn you now, Agatha, if you ever raise a hand to any child in this house again, I will tear it off and cast it to the dogs!"

"*How dare you? How dare you?*" she shrieked.

John ignored her, turning to Charmaine, who cradled Pierre to her breast, the boy's grip tenacious, face buried in her hair, his muffled sobs little more than shuddering whimpers. John placed a comforting hand to his back, then grasped Charmaine's elbow. "Come with me, before I strangle her."

He nudged her forward, faltering momentarily. Frederic stood in the corridor doorway, his face grim. John pressed on, and the elder immediately stepped aside. Charmaine felt a frigid gale of resentment pass between them, the icy tentacles made manifest by Agatha's cries of indignation. "He has abused me, Frederic! You didn't hear what he called me in front of the house staff! I am…"

They continued down the south wing corridor. When they reached the nursery, Charmaine looked at John askance, bracing herself for a battery of irate questions. "Where are the girls?" he asked instead.

"In the stables with George, watching the new foal."

She was surprised when the inquiry ended there. John was already at the bell-pull, summoning a maid.

Charmaine placed Pierre on his bed and sat down next to him. He cuddled his pillow for comfort, compounding her misery. She had failed him, and her heart was heavy with guilt. "Pierre, I'm sorry – so sorry," she whispered.

He shoved a thumb into his mouth and closed his eyes to the world.

A hand came down on her shoulder, and Charmaine looked up at John. He had rescued them both. "Thank you," she choked out, uttering words she never thought she'd say to him.

"For what?" he asked softly, his eyes earnest.

"For stopping Mrs. Duvoisin, for–"

"I was a bit late."

Charmaine gazed down at the boy, silently shouldering her culpability; she should never have handed him over to the wicked woman. "How could she do that to an innocent child?" she lamented.

"It is beyond reason," John snorted. "Horsewhipping is too good for her."

A knock fell on the outer door, and John opened it to Anna. "We need a basin of cold water and fresh washcloths," he directed.

With a bob, the maid disappeared, returning minutes later with the requested items. Rolling up his sleeves, John dipped the cloth in the water and wrung it out, gently laying the cool compress across Pierre's buttocks.

"This should keep the swelling down."

Pierre awoke with a start, not at all pleased with the comfort placed upon his bruised posterior. He moaned, and Charmaine knelt beside him, massaging his back while John continued to apply the cloth.

"I'm sorry, Mainie."

"I know you are, Pierre, but you mustn't go near those rooms again."

"I won't go there no more."

"Good," she murmured and placed a kiss on his forehead.

Pierre turned his head deep into the pillows. Charmaine took the cloth from John. The welts had already gone down, but she feared that he wouldn't be able to sit for the next day or two.

"Don't worry, Miss Ryan," John reassured, reading her mind. "Children heal quickly. I'm sure we can find a soft pillow for Pierre's bottom."

"This should never have happened. I should never have left him alone, and I should never have allowed that woman to raise a hand to him, threats or no."

"You're being too hard on yourself, Mademoiselle. It would have been far worse if you weren't there. You saved Pierre from Agatha, and he knows that. There is no sense in punishing yourself over it."

She was astonished; his words were compassionate and comforting. Just as amazing, he hadn't taken her to task for allowing Pierre to escape her supervision.

"Better?" he queried.

She nodded, nonplussed.

"Good. Then I'll be on my way. Take care of him for me now, will you?"

When she nodded a second time, he smiled at her – a genuine smile, one that was devoid of mockery. Then he was gone, leaving her in stunned disbelief over all that he had done for them.

Sunday, August 27, 1837

John and Pierre sat at the dining room table. Almost everyone, family and servants alike, was at Sunday Mass. But the wooden pews of the chapel were too hard for the boy's bruised buttocks, so John had suggested that Pierre remain behind with him. Thus, the boy's injury had allowed them this time to be alone together.

John leaned forward, pretending to study Pierre as raptly as the three-year-old studied him. A fine boy, he decided. "Well, Pierre, what are we going to do for the next hour?"

"Go fishin'."

"Fishin'? How do you know about fishin'?"

"Jawj said you fish-ed wif Bummy off'a the dock, 'member?"

John chuckled, amazed by the boy's recollection. "One day we shall go fishing," he promised, "but we will use a rowboat."

Pierre tilted his head to one side. "What's a woeboat?"

"It's a small boat that only a few people can sit in at one time," John explained patiently. "It's the best way to fish in a lake or on a river. Maybe I'll purchase one for your birthday, and we can go fishing then. Would you like that?"

"Uh-huh," Pierre nodded emphatically.

"Good. In fact, where I live, there's a large river called the James. Do you think you'd like to go fishing there?"

Pierre puzzled over his elder brother's words. "Where you live?"

"Yes – in Virginia. I'll have to travel back there soon."

"Why?"

"Because I have work to do there."

"Why?"

"Because..." John was at a loss and chuckled again. "Because I just do. Do you think you'd like to come with me? We would captain a giant ship across the ocean and sail right up the James River. And when we landed, you could see the buildings in the big city and my house. Do you think you'd like that?"

Pierre studied him speculatively. "Would I live in your house?"

"Would you like to live with me?"

"Only if Mainie could live there, too."

"Only if Mainie could live there, too," John mumbled under his breath. "Well, Pierre, we'll have to see about that." He ruffled the lad's hair affectionately.

Father Benito droned on, and Charmaine caught herself daydreaming. Agatha sat directly in front of her, a constant reminder of John's profanity. *Bitch*... the label had had an effect. Agatha had kept to her boudoir until this morning, and Charmaine could thank the man for that, too. Nevertheless, she anguished over Frederic's reaction. He hadn't confronted her as yet; surely he would.

John. By no means did his blessed intervention excuse his reprehensible behavior, but it had brought about a most unexpected cease-fire. For this reason, she bowed her head and said a prayer for him. It was as if her mother were there, telling her that it was the right thing to do. Even at dinner last night, he had been pleasant. With Paul and Agatha absent, the mood had been relaxed, and to the children's delight, he and George carried on throughout the meal, telling jokes, playing tricks, and acting silly. Not once did he send a cutting remark her way, and so it had been easy to place Pierre in his care this morning. Perhaps the worst was behind them; perhaps they had reached a truce.

When the Mass ended, Stephen Westphal approached Paul.

"What brings you to services here?" Paul asked.

Westphal, who hadn't returned to the manor since that terrible dinner last December, glanced at Charmaine. "It is difficult to track you down during the week, so I had hoped to catch you here."

"What is it?"

Agatha moved to Paul's side, and Stephen nodded a greeting. "Perhaps we should go to the library. This is a business conversation, private in nature."

"You can tell me here," Paul replied, suspicious of the man's reticence.

Westphal plunged in. "Some of the Richmond accounts you attempted to liquidate were closed out earlier this year."

"Closed out? What do you mean, closed out?"

"The funds were withdrawn in March–" Westphal cleared his throat "–by John. By all indications, there are no monies left in the Virginia State Bank."

Paul massaged the back of his neck, perplexed.

"This is outrageous!" Agatha exclaimed.

Westphal rushed on. "Don't worry, I had Edward Richecourt contact the Bank of Richmond. Those accounts are still intact, and he saw to it that the shipping firm was paid out of them; however, it would be prudent to find out whether other accounts have been terminated before future notes are written against them."

"We can find that out right now," Paul replied, "that is, if I can locate John. He's probably still sleeping."

"No he's not!" Yvette piped in. "He's in the dining room with Pierre."

"Pierre?" Paul queried, noticing for the first time that the three-year-old was absent. "Alone?" he added, his anxious eyes now leveled on Charmaine. "You left the boy alone with John?"

"Yes–" Charmaine faltered "–but I'm certain that he is fine."

Paul rushed from the chapel. Stephen threw a quizzical look at Agatha and hastened after him. Trembling, Charmaine and the girls did the same. She worried over the expression on Paul's face, the implication that Pierre was in some sort of peril. Surely John wouldn't endanger his own brother.

They found Pierre seated in John's lap, giggling.

"What's the matter, Paul?" John asked as his brother stepped up to the table, a small entourage behind him. "You look as if you've seen a ghost."

Paul exhaled.

Greatly puzzled, Charmaine studied both men, but their faces bore no answers. *Pierre is fine – so why the alarm?*

Stephen broke the perplexing tableau, stepping forward with hand extended. "John, how good it is to see you again."

John made no move to rise. "It is?" he asked, ignoring the proffered hand, which hung suspended in mid-air long enough to become embarrassing.

"Of course it is," the banker rejoined in confusion, his arm dropping to his side. "Anne has written so much about you of late. I'm pleased to hear that the two of you have been getting along so famously."

John snorted. "Famously? Is that how she puts it?"

"Well, yes."

Westphal began fiddling with his collar. He'd forgotten how brutally blunt John could be. Ten years in America hadn't smoothed the man's rough edges.

"Did your daughter write that she was chasing me all over Virginia and that I traveled to New York to get away from her?"

"No – no, of course not!" Westphal blustered, then laughed pretentiously as if John were only joking. "She led me to believe that – that – well that –"

"Well, Mr. Westphal, it appears that your daughter has *misled* you. So let me clear the matter up for you right now: I have no intention of *ever* proposing marriage to her. Is there anything else you've been led to believe?"

To Charmaine's delight, the banker's face reddened in disgrace. "I don't know what to say," he jabbered further. When John held silent, he beat a hasty retreat toward the foyer.

"I know he's annoying," Paul commented as everyone took their seats, "but you didn't have to break it to him quite like that."

"No? Believe me Paul, it is for the best. Unlike Mrs. London, he *got* the message, so perhaps he will convince her that she is wasting her time. I'm tired of her incessant pestering and would see an end to it."

Paul shook his head, but didn't pursue the matter. "I need to speak with you about the Virginia bank accounts. You closed two of them. Why?"

John leaned back in his chair. "I felt it unwise to have all our money in the South, so I transferred funds to New York. Why do you ask?"

"I wrote notes against those accounts. Why didn't you let me know that they'd been moved?"

"I didn't know about the notes. Why didn't *you* let *me* know?"

Paul didn't answer. He grabbed a journal, sat, and began to read.

The children had just finished changing out of their formal Sunday attire and into clothing suited for the stable when a knock fell on their nursery door.

Jeannette opened the portal. "Papa!"

Charmaine finished tying Pierre's shoelace and stood slowly, bracing herself for the man's upbraiding.

"Good morning, Jeannette," he greeted. "Where are you off to today?"

"The stables, Papa. We're going to check on the new colt!"

"Chastity foaled yesterday," Yvette added. "We've spent so much time at her stall, the colt thinks we're his masters. Maybe he could be mine?"

"I don't know, Yvette," her father answered seriously. "If the foal grows to be anything like his sire, he may be too much stallion for you to handle."

Yvette grumbled, but he chuckled softly. "Why don't you and your sister run along to the paddock now? I'd like to speak with your governess."

They needed no further encouragement. Other than Pierre, who was on hands and knees playing with his blocks, Charmaine and Frederic were suddenly alone.

He must have read her apprehension, for he spoke directly. "Miss Ryan, I apologize for my wife's conduct yesterday morning. It won't happen again." Charmaine was dumbfounded, but he didn't seem to notice, his attention on Pierre. "How is he?"

"Recovering," she said, and then, by way of justification, "I thought he was napping, sir. When I returned to check on him, he was gone. I suppose he went into Mrs. Duvoisin's chambers because they used to belong to his –"

"Charmaine, I'm not asking for an explanation. I am quite pleased with your care of my children. It is the single thing that I don't worry about."

Amazingly, the ugly episode was closed, Frederic calling to the boy and requesting a hug, which the child eagerly bestowed.

That evening, John came to the nursery to say goodnight to the children. He hesitated on the threshold, his eyes resting on Charmaine, who was struggling to dress Pierre for bed. The boy giggled up at him, squirming against the garment.

"He's improved throughout the day," she commented with a tentative smile.

"Johnny," Yvette interjected before he could respond, "is it true that you're not going to marry Mr. Westphal's daughter?"

"I'm not going to marry her," he reassured.

"Good," she said. "I don't want you to marry *anyone*, especially her!"

John smiled at her naked honesty.

"Is she really rich like her father says she is?" she pressed.

"Her husband was a wealthy man, and she'll most likely inherit her father's money some day, too." He eyed her quizzically. "Why do you ask?"

"If she is already rich, why would she want to marry you?"

John laughed heartily. "Because I'm so charming, of course!"

Charmaine rolled her eyes, not caring that he had turned to see her reaction.

"I don't think so!" Yvette refuted. "That's why it doesn't make sense."

"For some people, no matter how much money they have, it's never enough, so they make their fortunes bigger by marrying someone with even more."

"But you won't do that, will you, Johnny?" she asked.

"If I marry, Yvette, it will be to a woman who won't care about the size of my fortune; a woman who is happy just to be married to me. And someday, that's how it should be for you, too."

Charmaine was stunned by his declaration and bowed her head, not wishing him to see that she approved of the values he was imparting to his sisters.

"Like Cinderella?" Jeannette interjected, bright-eyed.

"Like Cinderella," John nodded.

"Only the wicked stepmother will belong to the prince's family," Yvette added. "But she'll never get you to sweep the floors, will she, Johnny?"

Monday, August 28, 1837

With Fatima at market and the children hungry, Charmaine prepared a snack tray in the kitchen. She looked up when Anna and Felicia entered the room, then set knife to bread and tried to ignore them.

"Like I was sayin'," Felicia began pointedly, chafed by Charmaine's aloofness, "I'll satisfy him. Just you wait and see, and it won't be by pretendin' to be some innocent virgin. He don't want some backward chit, anyway. What do you think, 'Ma-de-mwah-zelle'? Do I got a chance?"

Charmaine began buttering the slices. "A chance at what?"

Felicia laughed spuriously. "There you go again, actin' all naïve, with your high and mighty airs. You think you're better than me, don't ya? Ever since you got your room moved to the second floor. Well, you might think you're somethin' special, but you ain't. You're still hired help, just like me and Anna. So you oughta stop pretendin' 'cause everyone knows you're just the riffraff daughter of a murderer! Worse than us, in fact."

Charmaine grimaced, hurt, yet perplexed. The maid's verbal abuse had died down long ago, so why this?

"What I'd like to know is what you're up to," Felicia proceeded. "You've been stringin' Paul along for a year now, and that ain't worked. So maybe you think you can make him jealous by fishin' for a bigger catch. Is that what she's up to, Anna?"

Anna nodded, bolstering Felicia's fantastic theory.

The jaded woman smiled wickedly and continued to speak to Anna as if she weren't there. "Ma-de-mwah-zelle Ryan will have her hands full if she thinks she can mewl after John the way she's mewled after his brother."

"*John?*" Charmaine gasped. "I leave him to you, Felicia!"

"Ain't that generous of you!" the serving maid exclaimed, eyes hard as granite, voice cold as ice. "But I've seen the changes 'round here – enemies one day, friends the next. What did ya do, lift your skirts behind Paul's back?"

Revolted, Charmaine grabbed the tray rushed up the servant's staircase.

"That's right, Ma-de-mwah-zelle," Felicia called after her, "you run back to the children and leave the men in this house to me. But if you're gonna keep playin' your games, stick to Paul and stay away from John!"

Charmaine was still simmering when she reached the nursery. She forced a smile for Rose and Pierre, offered them the snack, then settled next to Jeannette, who was absorbed in a book. "It must be very interesting," she commented, pushing Felicia from her mind.

"Hmm?" the girl queried, her eyes rising slowly to Charmaine. "Oh, yes it is! "Mademoiselle, do you really think a person can become a vampire?"

"A vampire? Is that what your book is about?"

"Yes! They're terrible creatures that awaken from the dead," Jeannette explained, her eyes wide with wonderment and fear. "By day, a vampire's body remains asleep in its tomb, but at nightfall, the vampire rises up and stalks the earth, searching for victims –"

"Jeannette, you'll frighten your brother! Why ever would you want to read such a novel, anyway?" She took the book and leafed through the pages of folklore. "Wherever did you get this?"

"Yvette found it in the library a couple of days ago," Jeannette explained. "She's going to read it after she finishes *Frankenstein*."

"*Frankenstein?*" Charmaine asked, her eyes going to Yvette, who lay on the floor next to the French doors, also reading.

"This is even more frightening than vampires," the girl imparted. "Just listen…" and she began reading excerpts from the ghastly story.

Having heard enough, Charmaine walked over to the girl and wrenched the book from her hands. "Mary Shelley… Where did you get this?"

"From Johnny. And Mary Shelley claims that a corpse stood over her–"

"*Corpse?*" Charmaine gasped. "Why would anyone, let alone a woman, want to write something like this?"

"To win a wager," Yvette replied.

"A wager?"

"Johnny said that Mary Shelley and her friends were trying to see who could write the most frightening story."

"And did she succeed?"

"I think so. After all, wouldn't you be frightened by Dr. Frankenstein's experiments to bring the dead back to life?"

"Bring the dead back to life? Yvette, this story is sacrilegious–"

" –and he collected the bodies from graves– "

"That's enough, Yvette!" Charmaine scolded, snapping the book shut.

Rose concurred.

"No more talk about desecrated graves or reanimated corpses," Charmaine decided. "And just to make certain, I'll hold on to this until you are a bit older."

"But you can't! I have to finish reading it or else–"

"Or else what?" Charmaine pressed, noting the glance Yvette threw Jeannette's way. "Out with it, or you won't be seeing this book *ever* again."

"That's unfair!" she replied in a huff, and then: "Joseph was teasing me. He called me a ninny and said that I'd be crying before I finished it. So now I must!"

"Yvette, why do you allow that boy to taunt you? He is five years older than you are. He knows he can get the better of you."

"Well, he can't! And once I've won the wager, I can call him a ninny!"

"Wager?" Charmaine asked. "I hope this doesn't involve money."

Yvette shook her head emphatically, but Charmaine remained unconvinced. Nevertheless, she relinquished the book with the agreement that once Yvette had proven her point to Joseph, the macabre storytelling would cease.

Tuesday, August 29, 1837

"Rose isn't feeling well," John explained from the nursery door.

"Yes, I know," Charmaine replied timidly.

"She mentioned the girls' lessons. I thought I might lend a hand with Pierre."

Charmaine nodded warily, allowing him to enter, and so it was settled. John hadn't spent thirty minutes with Pierre before the twins coaxed him over to their desks, and soon, he was dividing his attention amongst all three children.

She had been loath to reveal the subjects they had covered thus far, certain that he'd scorn her limited knowledge, but he didn't seem to care at all. He took them on imaginary journeys to uncharted places filled with curious facts, weaving a treasure trove of information into a spellbinding tapestry. They rode a train pulled by a locomotive steam engine from Richmond to Washington, where they climbed into a hot air balloon and floated all the way to New York. There they watched a baseball game and ate ice cream in the middle of August, rode an omnibus to the circus and saw a mermaid and a man with two heads. Next he launched into silly stories that he told in clever verse, and when he couldn't think of a word that rhymed, he made one up. The children's giggles bounced off the walls, their faces radiant with wonder.

As the second hour neared its end, Charmaine began to fathom John's subtle, yet artful tactics. She had never known a man to seek out children as he did. If it were possible, he had won them over again, and she realized that this would be the first of many such lessons. They would benefit from his knowledge, and he, in turn, could escape to this oasis of acceptance in a home where he was mostly spurned.

She marveled at how effortlessly he captivated them. She'd never seen them so happy, not even when Colette was alive. Grudgingly, she acknowledged that he was a better tutor than she could ever hope to be. How could she compete? Did she want to? Age, experience, travel, and the privilege of wealth gave him the undisputed advantage. This was a fortuitous opportunity for the girls, even Pierre.

When the twins pleaded him to visit the next day, John awaited her consent. *Her consent!* She almost laughed aloud at the idea. He didn't need her permission to return, and she wondered why he had even bothered to look her way. Why was he suddenly showing her respect? What had happened to bring about his drastic change in attitude?

The more she pondered the question, the more perplexing it became. Was it the spanking incident with Pierre? That seemed to be the turning point, but she quickly dismissed the notion. Since the night he arrived home, he hadn't disguised his belief that she was promiscuous – his brother's paramour. So how could Pierre's spanking have changed *that* opinion? Yet now, he was treating her like a lady!

Whatever the reason, she wouldn't lament her good fortune, and she certainly wouldn't jeopardize it by barring him from his sisters' studies. As long as he treated her amicably, she'd reciprocate. Today's turn of events heralded good times at last, good times indeed!

Friday, September 1, 1837

It was close to midnight when the French doors began opening again. Jeannette was frightened and stood quaking at the foot of her governess' bed.

"Yvette probably opened them," Charmaine reasoned. "It was hot today."

"I did not!"

Yvette's denial from the room beyond seemed a bit too vehement. They'd been through this same scenario two weeks ago. Clearly, a hoax was being perpetrated. The girl's fascination with the morbid had continued to grow: monsters, vampires, and now ghosts.

Charmaine sighed and ushered Jeannette back to her own room, fixing a pointed stare at Yvette once Jeannette was settled back in bed.

"You think *I* opened them?" Yvette demanded.

"I thought you wanted to prove *Joseph* the ninny, not your sister."

Yvette folded her arms in a huff, denying any hand in the opening doors.

Charmaine did not believe her; unfortunately Jeannette did and could not be reassured. When footfalls resounded in the hallway, Charmaine was ready to seek assistance. "If your brother tells you that there's no such thing as ghosts, will you believe him?"

Jeannette nodded halfheartedly.

Charmaine looked down at Pierre, clutching his stuffed lamb. He slept soundly, oblivious to it all. She slipped on her robe and departed.

Paul's dressing room door stood slightly ajar, soft light spilling through the crack. Charmaine raised her hand to knock, but hesitated.

"Second thoughts?"

She jumped, heaving a sigh of relief when she pivoted around to find John ascending the last steps of the staircase. "You startled me."

"I'm sure I did," he commented wryly. "Next time, use the French doors. They're less conspicuous."

"The French doors?" Charmaine queried innocently. The light dawned. "Oh, you don't understand! I was only going to ask your brother for a favor."

"A favor?" he snickered, his lips curling into a lopsided smile. "Shouldn't he be asking you?"

"Sir, you misunderstand."

John shook his head, chuckling this time, and stepped toward his bedchamber door mumbling, "I don't think so."

"Sir?"

"Mademoiselle?"

There was no turning back. He was the preferable choice for comforting his distraught sister. "Do you have a moment?"

"I have a whole night."

Her cheeks grew warm. "That is not what I meant! Oh, never mind! I can handle this myself."

"Wait a minute," he insisted, meeting her at the nursery door and grasping her arm. "What is it that you actually wanted, Miss Ryan?"

He listened patiently as she explained, then entered the children's bedroom, crossed to Jeannette's bed, and set his efforts to comforting her.

"Miss Ryan tells me that you're frightened."

"The French doors keep opening all by themselves," she moaned, glancing toward Yvette, who remained awake, but silent.

John's gaze followed. "And you don't know who opened them?"

"No, but when it happened the last time, I saw somebody. This time, I only heard a noise."

"It was just your imagination – the result of all the ghost stories you've been reading."

"No, it can't be," she countered. "The first time it happened was before I started any of those books. Besides, doors don't open by themselves."

"Sometimes they do," John replied.

"They do?" both girls asked in unison.

"They do," he affirmed, demonstrating how a draft could cause a door to swing open. Finally Jeannette smiled, admitting that she was no longer afraid.

"But how did the latch come undone?" Yvette asked.

"These doors don't lock, Yvette. Sometimes a latch doesn't catch properly. That's probably what happened tonight. Wouldn't you agree, Miss Ryan?"

"Absolutely."

Yvette only grunted and stretched out once again on her bed.

He walked over to the French doors to reopen them. "It's going to be hot again tomorrow. Best to enjoy the breeze while it lasts."

"No!" Jeannette cried. Then seeing that she'd disturbed Pierre, she continued more softly, "Please close them – the right way, Johnny. I'm still frightened."

"But you told me you weren't."

"Not of the doors, just of someone creeping in here, like the last time."

"The only person creeping around the house at this late hour," John remarked lightheartedly, "is George, pillaging treats from Cookie's kitchen."

The girls giggled, as he knew they would, but their laughter finally succeeded in waking Pierre.

Charmaine sighed. The disruption had turned into a midnight party.

John read her displeasure and stepped over to the boy. "Back to sleep," he gently admonished, ruffling the lad's hair. "There is nothing to be afraid of in here. You have Miss Ryan in the very next room, and if you need me, I'm close, too. All you have to do is call."

"Thank you," Charmaine whispered as he reached the door, disconcerted by his nearness.

"Any time at all," he replied.

"Johnny?" Jeannette called. "Do *you* believe in monsters?"

He faced her again. "Definitely."

"Have you ever seen one?"

"Saw one this morning at breakfast."

"*You did?*"

"Didn't you?"

"No."

"I don't know how you could have missed her," he continued with a straight face, giving them a moment to absorb his irreverent humor. "She was sitting right at the foot at the table with her great big nose in the air."

They burst into laughter, and Charmaine stifled a giggle of her own.

"You know," he offered, stepping toward their beds again, "Paul was frightened of Cookie when she first came to work here."

"*Why?*"

"Well, we were very young when she became our cook – only about five or six years old. But Paul thought she was the boo-bock."

"The boo-bock?"

"Yes, the boo-bock – a monster," John explained, delving into an extended story of how he had tricked Paul into believing that the jovial and kindhearted cook was attempting to poison him. The children hung on his every word, chortling more than once, and especially when their disgruntled father threatened Paul with the switch if he persisted in his disrespect. Although Charmaine knew the tale was meant to be a diversion, she was certain every word was true and found the deception cruel.

John read her disdainful expression. "Surely you can find humor in a childhood prank, Miss Ryan. I assure you Paul played his fair share on me."

"Well taught at your hands, no doubt."

"No doubt," he agreed. "I apologize if my inadequate stories offend you."

Charmaine regretted the remark. "I'm sorry. I never had brothers, so I suppose I'm not a fair judge of how boys behave. I do appreciate your help."

"Very well," he replied, winking at the children, "we'll leave it at that."

"You know, Johnny," Jeannette mused, "I'm not afraid when you're here. Do you think you could sleep with us tonight?"

"And where would I sleep, Jeannie?"

"With Pierre. He wouldn't mind. Would you, Pierre?"

The boy immediately lit up. "No, I wouldn' mind!"

"*See?* Please stay!"

John canted his head as if considering the request, and Charmaine cringed at the begging chorus that followed, mindful of the adjoining door and its easy access to her room.

"You're not being fair to Pierre," he said. "You've talked him into this."

"No they hav'n," the child replied, his chubby cheeks rosy in the lamplight. "I want you to stay wight here, too!"

Charmaine waited for John's response, struck by the tenderness – vulnerability perhaps – that fleetingly crossed his face. "It seems I'm outnumbered. If Miss Ryan has no objections," and he looked directly at her, "then I suppose I must stay."

"I've no objections," she murmured, hugging herself against his perusal.

He nodded and turned away, the resemblance he bore to his father at that moment, striking – mostly in the magnetism he radiated. It was uncanny. *John and Frederic are alike in so many ways... and both of them would vehemently deny it if they heard me say so.* No wonder they clashed; two such intense personalities in one family couldn't possibly coexist without someone getting hurt.

This revelation impelled her to study him more closely. He sat next to Pierre now, pulling off his boots. Even the physical traits were strong: the thick head of hair, squared jaw, curved nose, and thin lips. Although Paul was unmistakably a Duvoisin, with John, the similarity to Frederic went beyond appearance. John was so self-assured, directed himself with such purpose, that Paul couldn't hope to compete. Suddenly, she was ill at ease with her mutinous musings.

"Will you monitor my bedtime preparations like you do Pierre, my Charm?" he quipped as he worked at his belt buckle. "Or must I beg for some privacy?"

The twins giggled, and Charmaine's cheeks flamed red, realizing that she'd been absentmindedly scrutinizing him. "I – I'm terribly sorry!" she sputtered. "I didn't mean to – I mean I was–"

"I'm sure you didn't," he interrupted with a chuckle as he cast the belt aside.

Realizing the shirt was coming off next, Charmaine hurried to the door. But when she looked over her shoulder to bid them one last goodnight, she saw that he'd merely unbuttoned it and was already stretched out alongside Pierre.

"I'm bunking with you tonight, Pierre," he said, unaware of her nettled regard.

She'd show him that she wasn't embarrassed by his goading capers! She marched straight to Jeannette's bed. "Let me tuck you in, Sweetheart," she said, pulling the coverlet up and giving her a kiss. She did the same to Yvette. "No talking," she ordered mildly, walking over to Pierre next. She picked his lamb off the floor and placed it in his arms, giving him a kiss on the forehead.

"Don't I get one?" John asked in feigned disappointment.

The twins giggled.

"I only kiss *good* boys."

The twins giggled again.

"Bad boys are more fun to kiss."

The giggles grew louder.

"Goodnight, *Master* John."

The children's glee followed her into her bedchamber.

"You two had better quit laughing," he warned, "or else Mademoiselle Ryan will tan my hide. Kissing I can take. A spanking? Never!"

Paul was exhausted, but couldn't sleep. The day had been blisteringly hot and his chambers were uncomfortably warm. Presently, he stood on the balcony taking in the cool night air. It was impossible to keep up the exacting pace of running Charmantes and developing Espoir at the same time. Thankfully, George was back, but even so, critical problems ultimately fell into his lap, the biggest of all, the infant tobacco fields. Not so terrible if he wasn't needed on Espoir, but he was. Supplies had arrived, new construction had commenced, and fresh cane tracts planted. It demanded a week of his time. His brother had experience with tobacco. Paul wondered if John would agree to help out while he was away.

Voices seeped into Charmaine's dreams, melded, then abruptly broke away, snapping her awake. It was dark, but the voices came again – from the children's room – one of them deep and irate. She jumped up and opened the door.

John stood in the center of the room, holding a distraught Joseph Thornfield by the scruff of the neck and pointing to a crumpled sheet that lay at his feet.

"I told you, sir," the boy stuttered fearfully, "I didn't mean any harm!"

"*Didn't mean any harm?*" John expostulated. "You come creeping through the French doors in the middle of the night, draped in a white sheet, and you're telling me you didn't mean any harm?"

"No sir."

"John – I mean, sir," Charmaine corrected, "please – let him go."

"*Let him go?* Can't you see what he's been up to tonight?"

"I can see, but it's not all his doing. Is it, Yvette?"

John's brow knitted, befuddled, but when Yvette threw Joseph a murderous scowl, he understood.

"It was only a wager," she replied defensively. "And I tell you now, Joseph Thornfield, you did not frighten me, so you have not won the bet."

"*A wager?*" John railed, shaking the lad hard. "You're telling me that you've crept into this room – God knows how many times – just to win a wager?"

"It was only tonight, sir!"

"That's a lie!" Yvette blazed. "You know you frightened Jeannette before!"

"I did not! I swear I didn't! This was the very first time!"

"You're just saying that so you won't lose your dollar!"

"No, I'm not! Here, take the money and see if I care." Joseph fished a crumpled dollar from his pocket and shoved it toward Yvette.

John quickly snatched it away, knowing that it was a great deal of money for the boy. "Is this your half of the wager?"

"Yes, sir, but –"

"And you think you've lost your stake because you failed to frighten her?"

"No, sir, but –"

"*Then why the hell are you handing over your money?* Never mind. I'll just hold onto this for safe keeping." He waved the note under the boy's nose, before shoving it into his trouser pocket. "When you've shown me that you won't throw away a month's wages on a ridiculous gamble, you can have it back. Now pick up that sheet and get out of here before I change my mind!"

"Yes, sir!"

The boy grabbed the linen and dashed through the French doors.

John raked his fingers through his tousled hair, stopping at the base of his neck. His eyes had lifted to Charmaine and his momentary massage stopped. Her hair was plaited in a thick queue that hung over one shoulder and past her breast. She'd forgotten her robe in her haste to reach the nursery, and the thin nightgown highlighted her unbridled curves and heaving bosom. Apprehension played in her large brown eyes, lending her an innocent quality that he found disarming. No wonder Paul was attracted to her. He couldn't have conquered her yet. She seemed too wide-eyed and naïve to have been with an experienced man.

"He's just a boy," she was saying, unaware of his sensate thoughts.

"Yes, he's just a boy," John agreed, "but he startled the life out of me creeping over to Jeannette like that. *I* should be paying him!"

Charmaine smiled, and Yvette snickered.

"Too bad he didn't find the right bed."

"He wouldn't have frightened me even if he had," Yvette objected haughtily.

"I'm sure," John laughed, finally seeing the humor in the whole affair. "Let's get back to bed. Move over, Pierre, and make some room for me."

"Johnny?"

John regarded Jeannette, who'd remained ever so quiet.

"Joseph said he didn't come into our room until tonight. So who was it that other time?"

"It was Joseph. He was just too afraid to admit it."

"I don't think so," Jeannette reasoned. "Because the first time it happened was *before* Yvette and Joseph made the wager."

John frowned skeptically. "You've mixed up the dates, Jeannette."

"I'm sure I haven't. The first time was the night you came home – the night of that terrible thunderstorm. Remember, Mademoiselle?" Jeannette looked to Charmaine for confirmation. "The storm was so bad, it even frightened you. That's when you went to fetch us some cookies and milk to help us go back to sleep. You remember, don't you, Mademoiselle Charmaine?"

"I remember," Charmaine whispered, conscious of John's eyes upon her, worried that her heady memories were publicized on her burning cheeks.

"That explains a few things I was wondering about," he murmured thoughtfully. "But it doesn't tell us when the wager began."

"It sort of does," Yvette interjected. "You gave me *Frankenstein* the first morning you were home, and Joseph challenged me *after* he saw me reading it."

"*Frankenstein*," John grunted. "So, it's my own fault that I'm not getting any sleep tonight."

Charmaine was tickled with his assessment.

"All right. Back to my original theory," he concluded, "the breeze and a faulty latch, which I'll fix in the morning."

"But Johnny, I really did see someone else in here!" Jeannette pressed.

"No, Jeannette, you didn't. You were dreaming. I promise, nobody has been creeping into this room at night."

"Somebody has," Pierre piped in.

"Really?" John smiled. "And who would that be?"

"I'm not 'aposed to tell," he averred.

"Please?"

"Well… sometimes… Mama comes to see me."

Everyone inhaled in unison, a huge sibilant sound that held.

John grasped the boy's shoulders, stern in disbelief. "What did you say?"

Pierre remained unaffected, a winsome smile on his face.

"Pierre," John persisted, "who did you say visits you at night?"

"Mama," he reiterated happily. "She plays with me and tells me things."

"He's lying!" Yvette protested, but when Charmaine told her to hush, she grumbled under her breath: "Well, he is."

"What does she tell you, Pierre?" Charmaine asked, stepping closer.

"Can't tell. I'm not 'apposed to."

"Why aren't you supposed to?" John asked.

"Mama… she says never to tell."

"Pierre," Charmaine offered, "maybe you've been dreaming."

"Oh no," he replied resolutely. "She wakes me up and sometimes she visits me when I take my nap. She took me to her big room that day when that auntie spanked me…"

Jeannette began to weep, all the old turmoil resurrected, the wounds laid open.

With an instinct born of love, Pierre crawled from his bed and cuddled next to her. "Don' cry, Jeannie. I sorry I made you cry."

Charmaine was at a loss and turned to John, but one look at his face – the pallor that rivaled the goose flesh that crawled up her neck – and she knew he'd be of little help. What was wrong with him? Men were supposed to be strong.

"He's obviously been dreaming," she reasoned with weak conviction.

Sometime later, she climbed back into bed, but Pierre's bizarre story kept her awake, amplified by John's grave eyes staring at the French doors, as if he fully expected the ghost of Colette Duvoisin to float through them.

Saturday, September 2, 1837

Surprisingly, Charmaine awakened very early the next morning, so early in fact, that she heard Paul descend the stairs at the crack of dawn. Coming to an abrupt decision, she threw back the covers. She'd breakfast with him. Perhaps he could make some sense of last night and the fantastic chain of events that had shaken all of them. Unlike John, Paul would prove sensible: laugh at her and then supply some logical explanation.

As she dressed, she wondered if John had remained in the children's room the entire night. She crept to the connecting door and gingerly opened it. All four occupants were sleeping soundly. Pierre was cuddled in the crook of John's body, his back pressed against John's chest. He clutched his elder brother's hand, a substitute for the stuffed lamb, which had fallen to the floor again.

Charmaine was captivated, the similarities between man and boy remarkable. Though Pierre's hair was a shade closer to his mother's, the cut of his face, the almond shaped eyes – Frederic's eyes – were the same. Even in sleep, they worked beneath closed lids. So, too, did John's, though the movement ended there. He was totally relaxed, his face youthful. He was rather handsome now, his even breathing stirring the fine locks atop Pierre's head. Her gaze roamed further, to the two arms, juxtaposed, Pierre's creamy white against its swarthy counterpart. Paradoxically, the limbs drew strength and comfort from each other.

She closed the door, freezing when it creaked on swollen hinges. It roused Pierre. He turned over, found John in his bed, and sat up. Yawning, he leaned forward until his face was only an inch from his brother's and tried to pry open an eyelid. John turned onto his stomach and buried his face in the pillow. The three-year-old immediately straddled his back.

"Have mercy on me, Pierre," the man groaned as the boy began bouncing. "If I were a horse, I would have slept in the stable last night."

Charmaine stifled a giggle, watching as Pierre slipped to John's side and squeezed into the space between man and wall. To her surprise, he stuck a thumb in his mouth and closed his eyes. She shut the door and finished her toilette.

Paul sat alone at the table, sipping his coffee and reading a newspaper. When Charmaine stepped closer, his eyes slowly lifted, and a smile broke across his face. "This is an unexpected surprise. Why are you up so early?"

"I don't know," she fibbed, dissembling under his charismatic charm. "I guess I just couldn't sleep." *Stupid answer! Tell him the truth... that is why you came down here!*

"Well then," he said, "your insomnia has become my good fortune."

He stood and helped her with her chair. She breathed deeply, intoxicated by his presence, the light scent of shaving lotion and cologne that lingered in the air. Impressions of last night's haunting receded.

Fatima broke the spell, bustling into the room to lay a plate before him, taking Charmaine's breakfast order as she poured two cups of coffee.

"I'm glad we have this quiet moment," he said. "I have a few things I need to discuss with you."

"Yes, so do I..."

Again he smiled, and she hesitated, waiting for him to speak first.

"I'll be leaving for Espoir on Monday," he continued.

"Leaving?"

The word erupted with childish fervor, yet he seemed pleased.

"Only for a week or two. I've neglected her for a while. But there are important matters that can't be postponed any longer."

"Two weeks?" she asked sullenly. The day had quickly turned dismal.

"The time will pass rapidly, and I'll be home before you know it. Why the glum face? This isn't about John, is it? He hasn't been troubling you, has he?"

"No, he's been unusually courteous this past week."

Paul scowled. "So I've noticed. What is the matter, then?"

She was about to tell him, but faltered. "It was nothing."

"Are you certain?"

"Yes, quite certain. I'll be fine while you're away. We'll all be fine."

He cocked his head to one side, his expression thoughtful while Fatima served Charmaine's food. "How are the children?" he finally asked.

"Lately, they've been very happy, especially with John entertaining them."

"John?" he queried, rankled by her use of his brother's Christian name, which fed his growing unease. *In that case, she is fair game. We shall see who is the better player.* "I don't like it," he objected. "He shouldn't be 'entertaining them'. He's a bad influence."

Not one week ago, Charmaine would have readily agreed, but John's conduct had been exemplary over the past few days.

"I will put a stop to it. I don't want him taking advantage of my absence."

"Put a stop to it?" she exclaimed. *Easier said than done!* John had gone from minding Pierre, to helping with the girls' lessons, to sleeping in the nursery with them. One look at Paul's face, and she prayed that he'd not find out. "I don't see how you can possibly order your brother around," she reasoned. "He comes and goes as he pleases."

"I will speak to him. He shouldn't be interfering."

"But you can't do that!"

"Why not?" he asked, puzzled by her vehemence.

"What I mean is – that won't be necessary. There is no sense in stirring up a hornet's nest. He's been cordial to me lately, and the children enjoy his visits. Besides, if you tell him not to pester us, he is sure to do just that. I'm certain that if we do nothing, make him think we don't care, he will tire of visiting the nursery all on his own."

Paul considered her comment. "You are probably right," he finally relented, allowing her to breath easier. "At any rate, there are duties on Charmantes that he'll have to take care of while I'm away. That should keep him occupied during the day. Even so, you should remain wary of him, Charmaine. I know him well, know how he operates, the little games he loves to play. He will use the children to toy with your affections. I'll not allow him to hurt you."

Charmaine was certain that his gallantry was sincere, but she smiled halfheartedly, ate quickly, and left his company.

She had just reached her room when John stepped out of his own chambers, bleary-eyed. Clearly, he'd be glad to be back in his own bed tonight.

"Good morning… I think," he said, securing the last button at his collar. "Did you get any sleep last night?"

"I finally drifted off, but it was close to dawn. Are the children still asleep?"

"Surprisingly, no, but they appear well rested and are already begging to visit the stables to curry the foal. They are working on a surprise for you. We thought you were still asleep, and I suggested they not disturb you. So they're attempting to get themselves dressed, Pierre included, though I think his knickers might wind up on backwards. When I left, he had a leg in the arm of his shirt, but refused to let me help."

"I see," she replied with a chuckle.

"I'll take them down to breakfast if you'd like to rest for a while."

He shouldn't be interfering. Charmaine cringed. Paul might still be eating. "That won't be necessary," she replied a bit too adamantly, then quickly added, "But, thank you all the same."

"Is there a reason why I shouldn't take them down to breakfast?"

"No," she lied, not wishing to kindle *his* suspicions. Would she now be forced to effect a balancing act between Paul and John? She groaned inwardly. "I couldn't possibly impose on you again this early in the day. Of course you're welcome to join us. It is just that the children are my responsibility."

"Yes," he pondered aloud, but his knitted brow indicated doubt.

"He's so beautiful!" Jeannette exclaimed, petting the colt's sable coat.

"Not beautiful," Yvette countered, "handsome. Johnny, do you remember Rusty?"

"Yes," the man answered, throwing a saddle over Phantom's back. "Why?"

"Remember how you taught Jeannette and me how to ride him?"

"Uh-huh."

"It's a shame he died, because we never go riding anymore. All the other horses are too big for us, and Mademoiselle Charmaine doesn't know how."

"So they are," John agreed, securing the saddle straps.

"If only there was another pony…"

"What are you getting at, Yvette?" he asked, turning to study her. "Are you hinting around so that I'll purchase one for you?"

"*Oh, could you, Johnny?*" she cried, her face transfused with excitement. "Two would be nice! One for me and one for Jeannette. *Please?*"

Jeannette's face mirrored her sister's, and John couldn't help but smile. "We'll see," he said, taking hold of Phantom's reins. "Now, step aside. I'm off to town. I have some business to take care of at the bank."

"Do you really have to go on Saturday and so early in the morning?"

"I'm hoping to inconvenience the clean Mr. Westphal into opening his bank before nine. If I time it just right, I may catch him in his nightgown and cap."

Jeannette and Yvette sniggered.

John had just reached the stable doors when Charmaine and Pierre appeared. She carried a letter she'd written to Gwendolyn Browning the day before and, realizing that John was leaving for town, bravely asked him to post it.

"What is this?" he chuckled. "You'd entrust me with so *personal* an item?"

Instantly, she regretted her impulsive request. "I'm sorry I asked!"

"Just a minute," he laughed again. "There's no sense in storming over nothing. Let me have the letter. I'll see that it gets to the mercantile intact."

Her eyes shot daggers at him, for he never missed an opportunity to bait her, but he was further entertained as he took the correspondence from her hand.

The morning wore on, and the children grew cranky. After lunch, Charmaine suggested a nap. Though Yvette objected, in five minutes, even she was sound asleep. Charmaine picked up the discarded vampire book and tiptoed from the room. She'd return it to the library and choose another for herself.

The study was occupied. John sat at the desk with his head buried in his hands, so deep in thought that he was unaware of her presence.

"Sir?" she queried.

He came up immediately from his contemplation, but quickly averted his gaze, wiping a forearm across his eyes. They appeared glassy, red even, undoubtedly the result of his restless night. She wondered whether the strange events were still on his mind.

"Sir, are you all right?"

"Sir?" he mimicked, finally looking at her. "I thought we'd dispensed with that formality last night. I prefer John."

"Very well," she replied guardedly, recalling Paul's warning.

"I returned from town two hours ago," he said, "but I've yet to see our resident ghost, Joseph Thornfield. Does he only come out at night?"

"Why do you want to see him?"

"Because I visited the bank on his behalf this morning, and I want to give him this account voucher before he complains that I confiscated his money."

"A bank voucher?" Charmaine asked in astonishment. "Have you placed his dollar in the bank for him?"

His expression turned cross. "As I said last night – for safe keeping."

"Of course," she nodded, smiling buoyantly now.

"You think I'm being too lenient with the lad, don't you?"

"Oh no, sir. I mean, John."

She was laughing at him, and he didn't like it. "Are you here for a reason, Miss Ryan?"

She considered the book she held and sobered. "I'm glad you were lenient with Joseph. Yvette is a different matter."

His frown deepened. "Yvette? Why?"

"You may think she's clever, but her escapades are getting out of hand. After her mother's death, I indulged her. Her precocity was preferable to lethargy, and her antics had a positive effect on Jeannette. They were smiling again. But lately, she's lost all sense of decorum."

John snorted. "I'd be more concerned about Jeannette."

"Jeannette?"

"Yes, Jeannette. She's far too good, far too kind. Unlike Yvette, who's learned to stand up for herself, who will never be manipulated, Jeannette is a sweet innocent who might easily be destroyed one day."

Charmaine's bewildered expression gave him pause; he hadn't meant to say so much. "Yvette was born into money," he quickly added. "She is playing the part of a little rich girl."

The final remark chafed Charmaine. "A *spoiled* little rich girl," she corrected defensively. "Her mother would not approve. Colette demanded good manners of all three children, grace and charity taking precedence over wealth. Yvette respected that, responded to her mildest of reprimands."

John's eyes turned dark. "Each to his own opinion, Miss Ryan. But I hold it is better to be bold than meek."

Monday, September 4, 1837

John sat slumped in one of the study's large leather chairs and fiddled with one of Pierre's blocks, lacing it through his lean fingers, waiting for Paul, who held his position behind the huge secretary, to finish speaking. His brother had requested this meeting last night, but John had brushed it off until the morning, saying that he was too tired and would be up before seven. Thus he sat, the early riser, if not the serious businessman Paul expected him to be.

"That is where we're at, financially. Any comments?" Paul looked up from his ledger, instantly losing his patience. "What are you snickering at now?"

"You, Paulie. You take this all so seriously."

"You're damned right I do–"

"I don't know where Father and I would be without you," John interrupted blithely. "In the militia, perhaps."

"You sit there and laugh, but this is not some trivial game to be scoffed at. You're in for a rude awakening someday. By then, it may be too late. Don't come crying to me when you find a fortune has slipped through your fingers."

"Whose fortune, Paul? Father's or mine?"

"You know when Father dies it's all yours."

"The only fortune I'm worried about is mine, the one I acquired on my own."

"On your own?" Paul scoffed. "Beyond your salary, I think you're overlooking all the other conveniences that Father's shipping, plantation, and good name have afforded you in making your *own* fortune."

"I'd have been a fool not to take advantage of them," John replied in kind, "but Father's enterprises benefit from my charity as well."

"Charity?"

"Let's start with the staples that I ship to the island on a regular basis at no charge: feed, flour, corn, tobacco–"

"Grown on Duvoisin land, John, land that has belonged to the family for three generations–"

"And farmed by workers whom I pay out of my own pocket. I haven't been reimbursed for that."

"That is your own folly!" Paul bit back. "You weren't forced to free your slaves. The land could be farmed for a pittance of what you pay your tenants!"

"Yes, Paul, my folly and my conscience."

"Conscience?" Paul snorted in derision. "Since when has conscience concerned you? They're only slaves."

"Yes, Paul, they're only slaves. And Cookie is only our cook, and Buck only your foreman. You've never been to a slave auction. If you had, you'd be revolted, and you certainly wouldn't abide such degradation, free labor or no."

Paul exhaled. The argument was moot. He'd learned long ago, starting with Colette, that the abolitionist could never be persuaded to think logically.

"Never mind, John. I've not called this meeting to debate with you. Obviously, we view things differently. You, of course, know that and have led me far from the point."

"I didn't know there was a point. I thought we were sitting here rambling on and on to kill time until you leave."

Paul ignored the remark. "The island is short of supplies. For all your so-called *charity*, we haven't received a shipment of staples for months now."

"You must be mistaken. Before I left for New York, I left instructions at the Richmond warehouse that your last order be shipped no later than mid-April. I couldn't have spelled it more clearly–"

"Well, no such packet arrived."

"–if I had drawn a picture for them."

Paul's eyes narrowed. "Don't tell me that was the vessel with the missing invoices!"

"Missing invoices? I don't handle the paperwork."

"No – you only draw on it!"

John chuckled. "Now Paul, don't lose your temper over a harmless joke–"

"*A harmless joke?* Is that what you call it?"

"When did you lose your sense of humor, Paul? You're no fun anymore. Anyway, you received the supplies, so why the scolding?"

"Because, dear brother," Paul snarled between clenched teeth, "I sent the vessel back to you!"

"*Back to me?* In God's name, why?"

"Because it was your confounded mess. I don't pay my crews to dig through holds, break open casks, and take inventories!"

"What are you talking about?"

"The ship arrived here, all right, via Liverpool, with a cargo for Richmond. Your incompetent captain insisted that – under your orders – he stacked our supplies at the very back of the hold, instead of off to one side. Once he took on the European wares, our casks were buried!"

"I don't give loading instructions," John replied. "Stuart does, and he knows what he's doing, so the mix-up must have occurred in Britain."

The response was sincere, and Paul surmised that the new captain had been pressed to weigh anchor and leave port, so to save time he'd cut corners and ordered the European goods loaded haphazardly.

"The British invoices were legitimate," John continued, scratching the back of his head, "and the casks for the island were marked with the Duvoisin crest. So between the European invoices, your original order, and the crest on the barrels, how difficult could it have been to locate your cargo?" John's deep chuckle erupted into a hearty guffaw. *"And you sent it all back!"*

"It isn't funny, John!"

"Yes it is!" he averred, wiping a tear from his eye. "Tell me, Paul, were you wearing trousers or a skirt the day you made that decision?"

Paul's face blackened. "Laugh all you like, John, but you couldn't have been very happy when the ship returned to Richmond. In the end, it was your loss."

"What loss? I wasn't in Virginia to receive the ship. I was in New York."

"Jesus Christ!" Paul exploded. "Do you realize what that means?"

"Yes," John snickered, "either the cargo is sitting in my warehouse losing market value – which doesn't affect me, since I wasn't selling it anyway – or, Stuart figured you didn't need it, and put it up for auction. That brings in money I hadn't counted on. If I were you, Paul, I'd pray that it's stored in the warehouse, but I wouldn't bank on it."

"Damn it, John, your bright idea for these new shipping routes is just not working! Now, you're going to set this matter right before the day is out!"

"And how do you suggest I do that?"

"You are going to write to Edward Richecourt and have him arrange another shipment of the staples we need, straightaway. No stops in New York or Baltimore, no stops in Europe. It's leaving Richmond and coming directly here, within the month, with accurate invoices. And from now on, I want a dedicated packet running a Charmantes to US circuit at least once a month."

"*Edward Richecourt?* That stiff ass wouldn't know the first thing about handling this," John replied. "I'll take care of it my own way. But since I'll have to pull a ship off its normal route, I'm going to charge all the associated expenses to the island's account, not mine. And if you want a dedicated bark running half-empty between here and the States, weighted down with blocks my crew will have to load and unload for ballast, why not use one of *your* new ships? That way the family business can benefit from your charity, too."

"Just be about it, John. I'll see to it that you're paid."

John stood to leave, but Paul stopped him. "I'm not finished yet."

"No?" What more could you possibly have to say?"

Paul ignored the gibe. "I'd appreciate your help while I'm on Espoir, looking in on operations, especially the tobacco. We're new at it."

"Why in the hell did you plant that?" his brother continued in the same vein.

"I don't know. Now that I've seen all the additional work it has caused me, I wish I'd gone with cocoa instead. But that's neither here nor there. Harold, Wade, and George handle day-to-day production well enough, but Charmantes requires necessitous hands. Things always run smoother when I'm around."

"Then can you really afford to place her in my *incapable* hands?"

"I never said you were incapable, John, just bent on irritating me. You have more authority than George if a crisis erupts, which always seems to happen when I'm away."

"Don't worry, Charmantes will be shipshape when you return."

"Good," Paul nodded, feeling at ease for the first time that morning.

Then he remembered something else. Despite Charmaine's request that he leave well enough alone, he forged forward. "There's one more thing, John. I'd like to talk to you about the children."

John's expression turned stern. "What of them?"

"I don't want you annoying them."

"Annoying them?"

"You know what I mean, distracting them from their lessons, seeking them out in the afternoon, playing nursemaid."

"I didn't realize you had such a sharp eye," John replied curtly, "especially when you're away from the house all day. So how *would* you know what's going on? Unless, of course, you have an informant."

"I have no informant. I see for myself what's happening. You know Father wouldn't approve. He doesn't want you around them."

"Approve?" John queried derisively. "I don't give a damn what he wants, and I certainly don't care if he approves. I will seek out the children whenever and wherever I like, and you can tell him that for me."

"Damn it, John! When will you desist from this need to hurt him?"

"*Hurt him?* What about me? There was a time when you were sympathetic to me." Disgusted, he added, "Just remember, Paul, he started it all."

"And he's paid."

"Has he? Well then, so have I."

Sunday,
September 10, 1837

Chapter 3

An hour before Sunday Mass, Yvette announced that she was not going. "The benches are too hard, and Father Benito talks gibberish. If Johnny doesn't go, why should I?" Charmaine had reasoned, cajoled, and finally threatened to take the matter to Frederic – all to no avail.

John! She simmered. *This is all his doing!* He hadn't set foot in the mansion's chapel since he'd arrived. Plainly, Yvette was utilizing Paul's absence to pit her governess' authority against John's. *Well,* Charmaine fumed as she headed toward Frederic's chambers, *we'll just see about that!*

She didn't get very far. Agatha emerged from the south wing corridor, blocking her path. Few words had passed between them since Pierre's spanking, and Charmaine wasn't about to strike up a conversation now. With a cursory nod, she changed direction and scooted down the stairs.

As her initial fury ebbed, common sense took hold. To whom could she turn to convince the headstrong eight-year-old that attending Mass was essential for her moral welfare? Rose? Possibly. John? She almost laughed aloud at the thought; he was the root of the problem. Still, he didn't know a thing about it. Perhaps if he did, he'd accompany them to the chapel, and Yvette would abandon her protests. Hadn't he lent a hand before?

She found him in the dining room, alone, eating a large breakfast, even though the rest of the household observed the Church's decree of a strict fast before Communion. She had seen less of him this week. With Paul gone, he'd assumed the reins of responsibility. Nevertheless, he had managed to spend time with the children before he left the house or directly after dinner. It was becoming less difficult for her to speak to him. Even so, she stepped forward gingerly.

"Excuse me, sir."

John's eyes left his newspaper. "Miss Ryan," he returned, irritated by her persistent formality. "Is there something I can do for you?"

"Yes, there is," she jumped in, mustering a radiant smile.

She was rewarded for her efforts, for he smiled in return, apparently disarmed by her ebullience, and she braced herself for a suggestive remark.

"And what would that be?" he asked instead.

"I'd like to invite you to attend Mass with us this morning," she said, carefully choosing her words. "I know the children would love your company."

His smile vanished. Still, he hadn't refused.

She took courage and pressed on, hoping to fan his enthusiasm again. "And then there's Pierre. He can be quite fidgety in church, but I thought that if you were there – well, you're so good with him and–"

"*Really?*" he interrupted, fixing steely eyes upon her. "You know, Miss Ryan, your tactics are quite duplicitous, yet rather transparent. You play the helpless heroine to a fault, seeking out my aid when it suits you, then complaining to my brother afterward."

"I'm afraid I don't understand."

"Don't you? Well, no matter."

The seconds gathered into an uncomfortable silence.

"Was there something else, Miss Ryan?"

"Something else?"

"Yes. I'd like to return to my meal."

Dumbfounded, she dropped her hands to her sides and blurted out, "Won't you even consider accompanying us to the family service?"

"Miss Ryan," he replied slowly, "as a boy, I heard enough of Father Benito's fire and brimstone sermons to last me well into eternity. I had no choice then. I do now and have no intention of suffering through even one more. I need no pretentious priest to measure my pain. I do that well enough on my own. Does that answer your question?"

"Surely you can't mean that!"

"Haven't you learned by now that I always mean what I say? Apparently not. So, let me spell it out for you: I will not accompany you or the children to Mass. Not today, nor next week – not ever."

"But you must!" she objected, anger eclipsing her dismay. This man was wreaking havoc in the household with his heathen ways, and it was time someone told him so. "You may not care a farthing about your own soul, but it is unforgivable that you've neglected the children's!"

Bemused now, his brow arched. "What have they to do with it?"

"Everything and more! You ought to consider the effect your bad example has on them. What do you think crosses their impressionable minds when week after week, they see you reject God by refusing to partake of His son's holy celebration? How do you propose that I explain it to them?"

"So," he scoffed, "this has nothing to do with an invitation to join you after all. And here I thought that you worried over my sooted soul."

"Have no fear about that!" she rejoined pointedly. "I'd be a fool to think that I could ever sway the likes of you!"

"A very Christian attitude," he replied mordantly.

"How dare you mock my values?"

"Your values, my dear, are not, by my estimation, worth holding."

"Oh, you – you–"

"Scoundrel? Infidel?" he offered. "No, I think *demon* would be more to your liking."

"Yes, demon is perfect!" she exclaimed furiously, but instantly repented the words. "I'm sorry. I didn't come here to call names."

"No? A lecture in morality then?" he pressed, irritated that she felt at liberty to confront him this way. Wasn't *she* the hired help and *he* the family? When she refused to answer, he continued. "Miss Ryan, let me clear something up right now. I don't take kindly to people – especially righteous women – who nurture a bit of good will with me and then assume that I can be manipulated into doing their bidding. For the moment, I'd like to think that you and I have come to a truce of sorts; however, I guarantee that I will put an end to that truce within the hour if you persist in attempting to bend me to your will."

His deadly tone left no doubt that she had pushed him too far. Even so, she felt unjustly accused. She had approached the situation from the wrong angle and had to find a way to salvage her self-respect and regain the ground of civility they had cultivated over the past fortnight. "Sir, that was not my intention."

"Then what is this all about?"

"I've told you – the children, specifically Yvette. She refuses to attend Mass because, as she puts it, 'If Johnny doesn't go, why should I?' I thought if you accompanied us, she would give up this stubborn nonsense."

He did not immediately respond, though Charmaine could tell that a barrage of retorts raced through his quick mind. When he did speak, she was aghast.

"Leave her behind with me, then. The Mass is, after all, a ritual for which the soul is supposed to yearn, is it not?" Sarcasm laced his query. "If Father Benito's preaching leaves her empty, what is the point in forcing her?"

"*The point?* The point is that we are speaking of a child's soul, a soul that will not reach its Maker if it does not partake of the sacred ceremony that you ridicule! I cannot believe that you're suggesting she is old enough to decide this for herself!"

He remained calm in the face of her resurrected rage. "And what need does an innocent eight-year-old have of that damned doctrine? Perhaps your comprehension would not be so limited, so obtuse, if you answered that question without prejudice, Miss Ryan. What terrible sin has she committed, is capable of committing, that would damn her to your God-forsaken hell for all eternity? What morality need she learn that her own family cannot teach her?"

"What morality indeed!" she rejoined contemptuously. "If her mother were still alive, I might agree with you. But even the mistress Colette did not limit her Christian example to good deeds alone. She marched the children to the chapel each and every Sunday. Can't you see? It is what *she* wanted."

"*By God, woman!*" he exploded, slamming a fist into the table. "What makes you think I give a *damn* about what the mistress Colette wanted?"

"Because–" Charmaine stammered, wide-eyed and trembling "–because she was a kind and decent woman who lived her faith, a faith she wanted her children to embrace." Foolishly, inexplicably, she babbled on, even though her mind screamed: *flee*. "Besides, she was your father's wife and mother to your siblings. Surely as such, you should respect her wishes!"

"Miss Ryan," he snarled, "the mistress Colette was a very different woman than the one you have made her out to be, and my feelings toward her were far from noble. She should *never* have become 'Mrs. Frederic Duvoisin'. In fact, I approved of her less in that role than I do the third Mrs. Duvoisin. So why don't you keep your angelic apparitions to yourself? I cannot stomach such a large dose of piety and virtue this early in the day!"

With his last words, Charmaine did indeed flee, her dignity in tatters.

Colette, dear sweet Colette! How could the man degrade her so? Charmaine couldn't understand it! Paul's assertions echoed in her ears: *Even Colette, as good and kind as she tried to be to him, suffered at his hands.* It was true! True! How could she have allowed her guard to slip these past weeks? How could she have thought that there was anything more to the man than her initial impression of turpitude? What a fool she had been! Paul had warned her, and still, she had discounted his wise judgment and allowed John to ingratiate himself to the children. No wonder Paul was wary! John *was* depraved! Thank God she had seen him for what he was before it was too late!

Yvette faltered when she entered the nursery. "Did you speak with Father?"

"No, I did not. I spoke to your brother instead."

"Johnny?"

"I'd hoped he'd reason with you, but he refused. In fact, he scorned your mother's beliefs. What a shame you've chosen his bitterness over her goodness."

Jeannette stood from her bed. "Yvette is hurting Mama by not going to Mass, isn't she, Mademoiselle?"

"Yes, I'm afraid she is," Charmaine whispered.

"See, Yvette, I told you so. You mustn't hurt Mama anymore. She won't rest in peace unless she's pleased with everything we do."

Rose walked in. "What is this?" she asked, taking in their somber faces. "I've seen happier people at a funeral."

It was too much; Jeannette erupted into tears, and Yvette's frown deepened.

"Whatever is the matter?" Rose clucked. "There now, child, don't cry."

"Yvette won't go to Mass!" she sobbed. "She doesn't care that Mama–"

"I didn't say that!" Yvette countered. "And I've changed my mind. I'll go, Jeannette – only *please stop crying!*"

The night was black. An open carriage swayed as it gained momentum. The dark, dusty road was barely negotiable, treacherous to the inexperienced hand, and fear suddenly gripped the driver. She pulled back on the reins and the horse shied and whinnied, then slowed to a steady prance. Although the buggy's lamp would help illuminate the way, it was wiser to leave it unlit. The deserted road finally leveled off, and a dim light appeared through the trees off to the right. The driver yanked on the reins, and the horse all but stopped. Locating the turn, the animal proceeded gingerly, and the conveyance moved toward the beacon, squeaking to a halt before a solitary structure nestled in the dark forest. Still, the real journey had yet to begin, and she steeled herself against the impending trial, descending the coupe, her black skirts cascading to her ankles as she reached the ground. Although she stepped stealthily, gravel crunched underfoot, signaling her trek. As she mounted the steps, the door cracked open.

"You are late," a deep voice accused from within. "Six hours late."

She crossed the threshold, and the portal closed behind her. With an air of indifference, she ripped off her gloves, pushed back the hood of her cloak, and faced the enemy. "I told you I would come, and I have."

She was angry. He could see it in her set jaw and flashing eyes, but she was worried too, her discomfiture poorly concealed beneath a mask of cool contempt.

"You seem to believe that you can keep me waiting," he stated coldly, "and I have never tolerated waiting for anyone, least of all the likes of you."

"How dare you–"

"Mrs. Duvoisin," he admonished, irritated by her outrage. "Don't play games with me. You are here for a very unseemly reason, one that you hope will go away if you just ignore it, a supposition that you thought to test by arriving late today. So let me spell it out for you. I never forget, and I am not a tolerant man. Next time, don't be tardy, or my patience will reach its limit before the very first hour has passed."

"Next time? I assure you, there will be no next time," she hissed. "You are mad if you think that you can blackmail me!"

"On the contrary. Not only will you continue to pay me, but as of today, my silence costs twice as much."

"You have been paid enough already!"

"If that were the case, you would not be here tonight, would you?" He paused, letting his remark sink in. "Let me decide when I have been paid enough. Even at double the price, my fee is not at all unreasonable for the wife of Frederic Duvoisin. After all, look at the heights you have scaled thus far. And isn't that what this is all about – how you've benefited from plotting and planning? So why not share the wealth with someone who understands you?"

"I've no idea what you are talking about!"

"No? Your husband might be interested in learning of the duplicitous life you've been leading. And then there's a theory I've been toying with. Frederic might find a visit from me most… 'revealing', shall I say?"

"There are ways to deal with you!"

His eyes turned evil. "*Do you take me for a fool, Madame?* I hope not. Because if you try to get rid of me, the truth *will* come out."

He watched her fear deepen and nodded. "Yes, I have taken precautionary measures. Now, let me relieve you of this."

He stepped forward and slipped the reticule from her fingers. Loosening the cinches, he fingered the cold cash within. Satisfied, he pulled the strings closed. "Very good. Very good indeed. From today forward, we will meet every other Saturday at three o'clock sharp. I do so enjoy your visits. Goodnight, Mrs. Duvoisin."

"Saturday? Why Saturday?"

"Surely you can see the wisdom of a Saturday rendezvous. If you fail to keep that appointment, I can kill two birds with one stone come Sunday morning." He chuckled wickedly, pleased with his pun. "At any rate, I doubt your husband will be pleased to see me. Our last private meeting was disastrous enough. Another could prove fatal." His keen eyes rested pointedly on her, and for the moment, she ceded defeat.

Monday, September 18, 1837

The children were asleep, and Charmaine climbed into bed, exhausted. Last week had been difficult, and this one was off to a bad start. It had rained every day, and they had been housebound. To make matters worse, John hadn't come near them, his absence feeding the children's boredom and restlessness. Of course, they begged for his company, but he used Paul's trip to Espoir as an excuse: he was busy with work, a justification that acquitted him while branding Paul the despot. Nevertheless, Charmaine hid behind the same white lie when they complained to her, and wondered what fib she would use when Paul returned. She didn't have to worry about that just yet. Paul had sent word that he would be detained on Espoir a week longer. If the rain persisted, it meant another seven days cooped up in the house, another week that would consume John's time. She suspected that he was avoiding them out of spite to prove some enigmatic point. For all his preoccupation with 'work', she was certain those responsibilities wouldn't have prevented him from setting time aside for the children if he had been so inclined.

Once John passes judgment on somebody, it sticks. He rarely changes it. Obviously, his unfavorable opinion of her hadn't changed, despite his conciliatory comportment in the days leading up to last Sunday. What had he called it? A truce? A truce was a suspension of fighting between enemies. So, John still viewed her as an enemy. But why should that matter to her, anyway?

She'd considered forgiving his unholy remarks – words spawned in the heat of the argument – but abandoned that idea yesterday when they ran into him on their way to the chapel. "So, Miss Ryan," he'd observed wryly, his eyes on Yvette, "I see you have risen from the battle victorious." It was too much! She seethed throughout Mass. The man was incorrigible, no worse, barbaric, without principle, unable to communicate on a level shared by the whole of civil society. He didn't deserve her clemency.

Still, he dominated her thoughts, and her mind lingered on something Millie Thornfield had said earlier when she had drawn her bath. "My Mum likes him. She claims that any man who loves children the way Master John loves his sisters and brother has to have a kind heart." Charmaine wondered. Was his affection for the children genuine, or were his motives perfidious? Did he cultivate the work of the angels or that of the devil? She fluffed her pillow, resolved to travel the path of caution.

Thursday, September 21, 1837

Pierre trained his weary legs on the portico steps, teetering when he reached the summit. He hardly appeared the youngest lord of the island, rather a guttersnipe without family or home: his face smudged black, his fine clothes soiled, and his shoes muddied beyond repair. Yet, he drew a triumphant breath and trudged along the wide colonnade, dragging a fishing pole twice his height behind him.

The day turned black. Suddenly, the sky ripped apart, sending torrents of rain soaring toward the anxious earth. Certain that her worst possible fears had come to fruition, Charmaine recommenced her pacing. A commotion in the foyer drew her out of the drawing room.

"Oh, Miss Ryan," Travis Thornfield lamented as he ushered the little ragamuffin toward her, "look what the wind has blown in! I'm afraid he is in dire need of your tender care."

"I'll see to him immediately," she replied, her eyes never leaving Pierre. She was shaking all over, a palpitating surge of relief that surpassed her receding distress. "And just where have you been, young man? Do you know how upset I've been?" The boy's eyes welled with tears. "Oh, Pierre!" she sobbed, instantly regretting the trenchant reprimand and hugging him close, unmindful of his soggy state or that his clothes reeked of dead fish. "I should spank you for frightening me so." She did not notice the man who towered above her.

"If you must scold somebody, Miss Ryan, it ought to be me."

She straightened up. "How dare you take him away without my knowledge?"

"Miss Ryan," he attempted to placate, appreciating her concern, if not the tone of voice, "didn't Rose tell you he was in safe hands?"

"Yes, she told me!" Charmaine snapped. "But you had no right to take him anywhere without my permission!"

"*Permission?*"

"Yes, permission! The boy is my responsibility, not yours! He was out of my care the entire day. God only knows what harm could have befallen him!"

"Miss Ryan," John snarled with set jaw. "I am not a pestiferous beast. I have feelings just like you, am capable of–" He shook his head and forced himself calm. "I apologize for your distress, but I didn't think you would worry over Pierre's welfare."

"Then why did you go behind my back to abduct him?"

"I didn't *abduct* him," John answered in exasperation. "I went to Rose in the hopes of avoiding the nasty dispute we're having now."

"And how would I have explained Pierre's whereabouts if your father had visited the nursery today?" Charmaine retaliated. "I'm certain he would be very displeased with my lax guardianship – that someone was able to take his son from the house without my knowledge."

John clenched his fists, and it was a moment before he trusted his response. "He didn't 'visit the nursery', did he?" When Charmaine held silent, he relaxed. "I hope you've learned a lesson today. Maybe now you will admit that I can be trusted with the children. For all of your worry – fed no doubt by my brother – I have returned Pierre safely. Yes, he's filthy, but happy. At least he was until you dampened his gaiety." John looked down at the boy, who stood mute at Charmaine's side, eyes wide as saucers.

"Don' be angwee, Mainie," Pierre sniffled. "Johnny took me fishin'. We had fun. We didn't do nothin' bad."

His beseeching voice mollified her. "I'm not angry with you, Pierre," she whispered, clasping his hand and throwing John one last meaningful glare as she turned toward the stairs.

Pierre pulled away. "I don' wanna go to the nurswee. I wanna see my fishes."

"Your fish?" Charmaine asked, noticing for the first time the discarded fishing pole and the repugnant odor.

"Yes, my fishes that I caught in my fishin' boat," he explained.

"Your fishing boat?" Charmaine looked to John, who was smiling now.

"Johnny bought it for my birfday, and we went fishin' today."

"How very generous," she replied tightly. "Only it's not your birthday."

"I know that," Pierre agreed. "but the boat didn't, so we be-tended it was."

Charmaine read the approving twinkle in John's eyes, then Pierre's pure joy. His innocent charm vanquished her ire. "And where are these fish you caught?"

"Right here," John said, dangling a variety of dead specimens from a hook.

"I wanna put 'em in some water and see 'em swim," Pierre insisted.

"Oh no," John chuckled, holding them out of the boy's reach. "We're giving these to Cookie so she can fix them for dinner."

"You mean eat 'em?" Pierre asked apprehensively. "I don' wanna eat 'em. I wanna see 'em swim."

"But they can't–" John began, and then "–come with me."

Minutes later, they were in the kitchen, staring into a large tub of water that John had placed on the wooden table. Pierre poked a finger at one of the floating fish, perturbed when it did not dart away like the others in the lake.

"Why ain't he swimmin'?" Pierre finally asked.

"Why *isn't* he swimming," John corrected.

"Why isn't he swimmin'?" Pierre repeated, his eyes fixed on John.

"Because he's dead," John replied levelly.

"Did it hurt?"

"I don't think so. Anyway, he's mighty happy to know that he's going to be a delicacy dinner tonight, cooked by the world's greatest chef here–"

"Oh go on with ya, Mastah John," Fatima exclaimed bashfully.

"–and devoured by the likes of George, a man renowned for his discriminating taste in fine cuisine – and anything else that's edible."

As if on cue, George stepped into the kitchen, eliciting Pierre's giggle. "What is he laughing at?" George asked, looking from a smiling Charmaine, to an embarrassed Fatima, and finally, a mischievous John.

"Dead fish, George," his friend answered. "Only some dead fish."

Sunday, September 24, 1837

When Frederic showed up at the nursery door directly after breakfast, Charmaine wondered if the afternoon outing she had planned would be spoiled. But he only nodded when the girls told him that they were going into town for the remainder of the day.

"I'll only visit with you for a short while then," he said.

Charmaine retreated to her room, allowing them some private time together.

John had slept late and it was nearly eleven-thirty when he left his chambers. Assuming that the children would be back from Sunday Mass, he headed for the nursery, but as he lifted his fist to knock, his father's voice stopped him. He quickly lost his desire to see them and changed course. Breakfast...

He was halfway down the stairs when he noticed the tall stranger standing in the foyer. Though dressed in Sunday attire, his clothes were threadbare. Yet, his stance was confident, arrogant even, as he studied the portrait of Colette. John bristled at his perusal, the seeming right he had of being there.

"Excuse me," John called gruffly, continuing his descent. "Can I help you?"

The stranger tore his gaze from the painting and focused on him. "Yes."

The dark eyes grew intense, so much so that John was confounded.

"Are you John?"

"I am. And who might you be?"

"Wade Remmen," he replied casually, extending a hand in greeting.

John stepped forward to take it. "Ah yes, the illustrious Mr. Remmen," he derided. "I've heard a great deal about you."

"And I you," Wade returned, "more than you could ever imagine."

John's brow raised, intrigued. *Very self-assured,* he thought. No wonder Paul has placed him in charge. "What can I do for you, Mr. Remmen?"

Wade looked down at the papers he held in his other hand. He passed them to John. "Your brother told me that you'd be taking over while he's on Espoir. I expected him back by now, but, as you know, he's been detained. Anyway, these are for him. It's a tally of the wood delivered into town over the past two weeks as well as the shipments sent to Espoir."

John scarcely glanced at the invoices. "I'll see that he gets them."

"Actually, I'm to deliver them back to the warehouse with a signature. If you could look them over now, I'd appreciate it."

"Mr. Remmen, today is the Sabbath. I always honor the Sabbath."

Wade frowned momentarily. "Very well. If you could possibly get them to me at the mill tomorrow, I'll take them into town after I've finished work."

"I'll do better than that," John said. "I'll deliver them to the warehouse tomorrow morning. How would that be?"

"That would be fine."

John saw Wade to the door, then stared down at the documents. Inspired, he took the steps two at a time and, without knocking, entered the nursery. He found Jeannette on his father's lap, Pierre playing at his feet, and Yvette reading a story to them. Charmaine was nowhere to be seen.

Frederic looked up in surprise as Yvette greeted him with, "What are you doing here? Joseph said you were still sleeping."

"I have something for Father," he answered curtly, stepping into the room and depositing the invoices on the desk nearest the man. "Wade Remmen delivered these. They need to be signed by tomorrow morning."

"Wade?" Jeannette queried excitedly. "Is he still here?"

"He just left."

She jumped from her father's lap and scurried across the room.

"What is this?" her father called after her, but she paid him no mind as she raced out onto the balcony in the hopes of catching a glimpse of the man who had caught her fancy.

Yvette rolled her eyes. "She's in love."

Frederic chuckled. "Is she now? With Mr. Remmen?"

"All because Mama told her how very handsome he was."

Frederic's eyes turned black.

"What is the matter, Papa?" Yvette asked.

"Nothing," he bit out.

John was just at puzzled, but he quickly discounted his father's strange reaction when it looked as if the man were about to speak to him. A second later, he was out the door, ignoring his sister's calls for him to stay.

"Will there be something else, Miss Ryan?"

"No..." Charmaine hesitated, stroking the more expensive bolts of yard goods. As Maddy Thompson returned them to the shelves, Charmaine bit her bottom lip. "On second thought, I *will* take the paisley taffeta and blue muslin."

"It will raise the amount of your purchase considerably."

"Yes, I know," Charmaine murmured.

A short while later, she stepped out of the mercantile, package in hand. Though she was light of coin, she did not regret her extravagance. The twins' birthday was only four days away, the first without their mother. Charmaine intended to make it the happiest of occasions, much as they had hers only nine months ago. The unexpected memory evoked an acute sense of loss and loneliness. She missed Colette and sighed deeply, hoping to shake off the melancholy. She thought of the girls again. She'd spend the next few evenings sewing, a labor of love made possible by the wages she had saved.

She squinted against the bright sun and headed toward the livery. George was where she'd left him, on the boardwalk, amusing Pierre, who sat on his lap, and the girls who were climbing on the casks beside him. Clutching her parcel, she picked her way past buckboards and carriages and the strolling townspeople.

"Get everything you needed?" he asked when she reached them.

"Yes, and thank you for minding the children."

"I was happy to do it," he replied, standing to lift Pierre into his arms. "And a good thing, too, that the mercantile is open on Sundays," he finished.

Charmaine reserved comment, having refused to shop on the Sabbath on more than one occasion, doing so only today because he had offered his nursemaid services. It had been an ongoing dispute – *Keep Holy the Lord's Day.* Charmaine embraced the Third Commandment and stood as the exception among the churchgoing islanders who, every Sunday, directly after noon Mass, discounted Father Benito's vehement threat of eternal damnation and patronized the many businesses that opened their doors.

"Would you like me to drive you back to the house?" George proceeded. "Or would you prefer to visit Stephen Westphal?"

His teasing induced a frown and then a giggle. "We had better head home, or we will be late for dinner."

"Not yet," Yvette protested. "We've been waiting to see Bummy."

"Who?"

"Bummy Hoffstreicher," the girl reiterated. "You remember – the boy who stole sandwiches from Johnny and George. He comes past here every day."

"Yvette, he's just a man," Charmaine reasoned, "there will be other chances to meet him, and when you do, I hope that you remember that he is a human being, and should be treated as such, no matter what stories you've heard."

Yvette rolled her eyes, prompting George to intercede. "Charmaine, I'm sorry. We were just jesting a bit."

"I know, George, and I don't hold *you* responsible–"

She was interrupted by shouts from the dock and the push of bodies gravitating to the wharf. "What is it?"

"A ship must be arriving," he replied, shielding his eyes to look.

Charmaine did the same, concentrating on a smudge of white passing into the cove. They, too, pressed nearer the quay.

"Can you see it?" Yvette asked excitedly, tugging on George's shirt. "Where's it coming from? Can you tell by the mast? Is it flying our flag?"

"Yes," George replied. "It must be the Gemini. The Raven isn't due in port until next week. Paul will most likely be aboard."

"Wonderful," Yvette mumbled in sudden disgust.

The girl's reaction did not dampen Charmaine's soaring spirits as she peered longingly at the white masts that were steadily growing larger. Finally, everything would be right again.

Not ten minutes later, the creaking vessel thumped against the dock. With admiration, Charmaine watched Paul command her crew, throwing himself into the mooring, much like the day she'd arrived on the Raven, one year ago. He was even more handsome now, the finest figure of a man she had ever beheld, and her quickening pulse forced her to look away.

Paul donned his discarded shirt and left the sailors and longshoreman to finish up. As he descended the planking, he noticed the welcoming party, Charmaine in particular, a bit of loveliness he hadn't expected to see until he got home and a painful reminder of his lack of female companionship for the past three weeks. When he reached them, their eyes locked. *Was that lust in her gaze?* Instantly, his ignited passion raged out of control. As if perceiving his need, she averted her face. He focused on George, determined to quell his rutting instincts.

"Good afternoon, weary traveler," that one greeted jovially, "and how is the work coming along on Espoir?"

"Quite well, and what a nice greeting this is," Paul returned, putting an arm around Jeannette, his eyes traveling to Charmaine again. "Charmaine, you are looking lovely."

"So are you," she blundered. "I mean – you are looking well."

The girls laughed, bolstering the deep blush that rose to her cheeks.

"I *am* well," he replied, "though I'm looking forward to Fatima's cooking. I won't even tell you what the men prepared at the camps. Some of it wasn't fit for consumption. I'm glad to be back. Espoir doesn't have the feel of home."

"One day it will," George replied, "just give it a little time."

"I suppose so," Paul concurred. "Have you missed me, Pierre?" he asked, gesturing for George to hand the boy over.

"Uh- huh. But I wanna go home. I'm hungwee."

"So am I!" Paul agreed, holding Pierre high in his arms. "Home it shall be."

George ran ahead to the livery, leaving Paul, Charmaine, and the children to walk slowly down the boardwalk. "Well then," Paul mused, "you'll have to tell me everything that's happened while I was away." His words were directed at the children, though his eyes remained trained on their pretty governess.

Frederic paced his chambers for the remainder of the afternoon and well into the evening, his quandary mounting in the dark. So, Wade Remmen was Colette's lover. Or was he? Should he bring the man in and question him? He snorted at the thought. The young man would admit nothing. Nevertheless, Frederic knew he would be able to read the truth in Wade Remmen's eyes. And then what? What could he do? What should he do? And what of his children? Did he want his children to know? They would certainly find out if he pursued it. They loved their mother, thought of her as an angel. Sadly, he realized that he still loved her; even in her infidelity, *he still loved her.* Paul was right: Colette *was* good and kind. If she had taken another lover, it was because of him and his deplorable disposition. He was through blaming her for every miserable thing that had befallen him, and he refused to torture his children with facts about her unfaithfulness. Let them hold onto their precious memories. Colette was dead and buried, and this nasty affair would be as well. Reaching that resolution, he stretched out on his empty bed and finally slept.

Charmaine had intended to sew tonight, but after three aborted attempts, she set the fabric aside. Her mind was not on task. It ran rampant with images of Paul and the overwhelming feelings that his arrival home had incited, foreign desires that tingled her fingertips one moment and drained her limbs the next, leaving her strangely agitated. She recalled the indescribable look he had leveled upon her at the harbor, the rush of blood that had left her lightheaded. Even now, she shuddered in wanton yearning. Dear God, what was wrong with her?

It had been difficult to converse with him for the remainder of the day. She was grateful when he, John, and George retired to the library after dinner, and she and the children were able to slip upstairs unnoticed. Thankfully, they crawled into their beds without so much as an argument and fell asleep earlier than usual.

Right now, she longed for a walk in the gardens, but quickly dismissed that idea. Though it might help clear her mind, she couldn't chance meeting up with him. She no longer trusted herself. No, until these inexplicable sensations dissipated, she would avoid Paul at all costs. Thus, she said her prayers and climbed into bed.

Paul stepped out onto the balcony. It had been a productive evening. Come morning, he would see if his brother had accomplished all that he purported. According to George he had, lending an invaluable hand – with the tobacco in particular. If that were true, Paul wouldn't be swamped tomorrow.

Thoughts of Charmaine took hold again. He longed to corner her alone and finish what he'd postponed for far too long. She wanted him, perhaps as much as he wanted her. But she had escaped to her room, leaving him to chomp at the bit. *Was she sleeping?* On impulse he decided to find out...

The nightstand lamp burned low, but his eyes quickly adjusted to the dim light. She was asleep. He stepped up to the bed and stared longingly down at her. Lovely... she was so lovely, with dark lashes fanned against creamy white cheeks, kissable lips slightly parted, a stray hand raised beside her pillow, and her luscious breasts rising beneath the thin fabric of her nightgown. How he yearned to make love to her. What would she do if he awoke her with a kiss? His pulse accelerated as he imagined any number of reactions. She might struggle, and he found that possibility highly sensual. But no, it would be her first time, and he wanted the experience to be exquisite, an awakening that she would agree, perhaps even beg, to engage in again. With that thought, he backed out of her room. He would never sleep tonight – *Never!*

Charmaine's eyes flew open, and she grabbed hold of her coverlet for support. How long had she held her breath? *You weren't holding it, silly! You feigned absolute serenity. And all the while, your heart was thundering in your ears.* Surely he had heard it! How could he not? She had waited for the kiss that never came. Prayed that he wouldn't – longed that he would. Then he was gone... *Gone!* With a moan, she turned over and attempted to breathe, to sleep.

Thursday, September 28, 1837

Chapter 4

"Will you marry me, Charmaine?"

The words were soft in her ear, caressing her neck, and at first she was certain she was dreaming. Yet Paul pulled her closer, his plundering mouth returning to her lips, his desperate plea speaking to her body as well as her heart...

Charmaine woke with a start, and it was a full minute before her erratic breathing lulled. Then, as the euphoria of impassioned sleep waned, piercing reality took hold, and she groaned. Paul had disturbed her slumber for four consecutive nights, ever since he'd crept into her chamber and stood over her bed. The recurrent dream was so vivid that it plagued her waking hours as well.

A dream, only a dream! Dare she hope for more – for the ardent proposal whispered only in sleep? Or was she doomed to stand on a summit of uncertainty, expectant one day, disappointed the next? There were no answers, only a wistful wish spun upon one word: perhaps. She rose and began her daily routine.

The clip-clop of horse's hooves drew her to the veranda. She watched Paul lead his white stallion from the stable, mount, and gallop away. Since his return, he'd been so busy, it was no different than when he was on Espoir, almost as if he were avoiding her. But that was silly. She knew what he demanded of himself. It was only six in the morning, and already he was gone, probably for the day. Once again, she'd have to wait. *But, for what?* Another indecent breach of her bedchamber? It was just as well that he kept away.

Forget him, she told herself as she turned to dress. *It's the twins' birthday. Use the occasion as a distraction.* She had promised that they could spend the day in any manner they wished, and that would certainly keep her mind occupied.

She had been quite sly in her preparations. They knew nothing of her late night efforts with needle and thread, nor the presents she had wrapped and neatly stacked on the dining room table only a few short hours ago. Jeannette would be delighted with the dresses for her china doll. Yvette was a different matter. Charmaine hoped that the girl would be pleased with the feminine breeches she'd concocted. Certainly, Agatha would disapprove. However, the damage was done; best not to fret over the consequences now.

A rap fell on the connecting door, and Charmaine opened it to a sleepy-eyed Pierre. "Good morning, my little man," she greeted, scooping him into her arms. "What do you think of your lazy sisters? Should we let them snooze their birthday away, or should we wake them up?"

"Wake 'em up," he directed, squirming from Charmaine's embrace and bouncing on Yvette's bed.

The girl groaned. Then, realizing that her birthday had indeed arrived, she was across the room, coaxing her sister to rise. When Charmaine mentioned presents in the dining room, they dressed hastily and were gone.

Ten minutes later, she and Pierre found them seated empty-handed at the table, their presents nowhere in sight, their eyes flashing at their elder brother.

"That's not fair!"

"Ah, but it is more fun," John replied, sipping his coffee.

Charmaine stepped up to the table, annoyed. "What is this?"

"Good morning, Miss Ryan," he responded, ignoring her displeasure.

"Good morning," she returned stiffly, helping Pierre into his chair.

John's eyes traveled to the three-year-old. "How are you, Pierre?"

"Good," the boy answered. "Can we go fishin' again?"

"Not today. Today I have other plans."

Charmaine interrupted. "Where are the presents I wrapped?"

"They're hidden," John replied.

"Hidden? And who hid them?" she demanded, as if she really had to ask.

"Now, my Charm, please allow me to explain. First, seeking them out can be as much fun as opening them. And second, your gifts aren't the only ones hidden. Rose supplied me with a few, and there were the two large ones that I–"

"*Really?*" the girls exclaimed in tandem. Sanguine anticipation replaced anemic disappointment, and Charmaine was forgotten as Jeannette and Yvette bombarded their elder brother with questions.

"I'm not about to tell you where they are," he chuckled. "It took me the whole night to hide them. It is up to you to conduct a treasure hunt."

"Treasure hunt?" they queried, the words echoed by Charmaine.

John noted her smile. "I take it you approve of this innovation in gift giving?"

"I suppose so," she answered honestly, unable to remain hostile, her attention snared by Yvette, who had pushed away from the table. "Oh no you don't, young lady. Breakfast first."

"But–"

"No buts," John admonished, enforcing Charmaine's edict. "Besides, I have a few clues that you might be interested in hearing while you eat."

Yvette eagerly complied, and they ate quickly. The girls' alacrity was contagious, and even Charmaine was caught up in it, fed by John, who committed to nothing, but seemed to promise everything. She began to worry that they would be disappointed. Her presents were sadly lacking next to the picture he was painting, and though his gifts also awaited discovery, she doubted that even they could measure up to the twins' expectations.

"Now remember," he warned when they finally rose from the table, "with every treasure hunt, there is always an adversary – a rival – who is searching for the treasure as well. So, you must be careful not to be caught."

"Caught? By whom?"

"Who else?" he snickered. "Auntie Agatha – the deadliest enemy of all!"

The ease with which he garnered their mirth still astounded Charmaine.

"Don't laugh," he chided seriously. "If she catches you, the fun is over."

"Yes, yes," Yvette said, and tugging her sister's arm, they bounded off.

"Me too!" Pierre declared, pushing away his bowl of half-eaten porridge.

"You too what?" Charmaine asked, tucking in the napkin that had come loose from his collar.

"I wanna look for them presents, too."

"When you've finished," Charmaine answered, lifting a spoon to help him.

He grabbed at it, insisting, "I do it myself!"

Charmaine relinquished the utensil with a squeeze of his shoulder and a kiss on his head. But as she turned back to her own food, she caught John's warm gaze upon her, a self-conscious moment when their eyes locked. To her surprise, John broke away first, returning to his newspaper.

"Good morning, everyone!" George hailed from the hallway. He spied the serving bowl of porridge, sat down, and pulled it in front of him. "Is anybody eating this?"

John snickered. "Have all you like, though the hogs will be disappointed."

George ignored John's japing and poured liberal amounts of cream and sugar atop the oatmeal, and then, to Pierre's delight, ate from the large dish using the serving spoon.

"I suppose, George, that you have come to the table for another reason?" John interrupted. "Aside from a second breakfast, that is."

"Reason? Oh yes. I'd almost forgotten. The children's birthday..."

He caught John's swift shake of the head and fell silent. *Too late!* Charmaine's attention had been snared, her inquisitive eyes on him. "It is the twins' birthday," he repeated, attempting to mask his blunder, "isn't it?"

"Yes," she agreed suspiciously, "but you knew that."

"And I was just wondering how you were celebrating it. Do you have something special planned for the day?"

"Only their presents and now this treasure hunt. But I did promise them no lessons. They can decide what they'd like to do, within reason, of course."

"Of course," George nodded, his brow arched in John's direction.

Though Charmaine's curiosity was piqued, John smiled passively in return; the strange exchange yielded no clues.

"So George, did all go well?" John finally asked.

"I moved the shipment early this morning, if that's what you want to know."

"Then everything is settled?"

"Everything is in order, just the way you wanted it, except–" George held up one finger "–there is the matter of finances."

"Finances?" John queried. "I gave you the money weeks ago, or have you forgotten?"

"No, John, I haven't forgotten. But neither am I a fool. That money was for the payment of the p– eh... the merchandise. It did not cover *my* fees. Now, I do admit that I am your friend, but after I spent a good portion of yesterday avoiding Paul to work on this *project* for you, I do believe you owe me something in return, and I don't mean gratitude." With that, he held out his hand, palm up.

Charmaine giggled, for he looked like a beggar. Intrigued, she watched John pull out a wallet and hand him a sheaf of bank notes, a sum that rivaled her week's wages. *What favor could have merited such a hefty allowance?* George straightened the bills, counted them meticulously, and smiled at her as he tucked them into his pocket. She was oddly disconcerted by that smile, as if she had somehow become an involuntary participant in the transaction. Her eyes traveled to John for an answer, but he was reading his newspaper again. She did not trust him. George, however, was her friend, and as such, wouldn't lead her to harm. Neither would he lie to her. She'd question him about it when they were alone.

Pierre scattered her thoughts when he began banging his spoon on his empty dish. She quickly confiscated it, sending him into a fit of tears.

"I'm sorry, Pierre," she said, "but it's impolite to make such a racket."

He continued to wail, refusing the milk she offered him and turning his face aside when she tried to wipe it.

John abruptly stood and stepped behind the boy's chair. Certain that he intended to usurp her authority and seize the utensil, her grip tightened on it. But he ignored her completely and lifted Pierre from his seat, holding him high in his arms. "What is all this fuss about?" he asked. "Surely you're not crying over a lost spoon? Or maybe you are not the Pierre I know. Could that be it? Maybe you're some other lad come to take his place, because the Pierre I know never cries. He is always smiling, especially at Mainie. Isn't that so?"

The tears stopped. "I'm Pierre," the boy declared. "But I have to go potty."

"No," John corrected wryly, "you *had* to go potty."

"Oh my!" Charmaine groaned, immediately comprehending the boy's crankiness. "Come, Pierre, let's go to the nursery and change you."

But John drew back as she reached for the child. "Let me carry him. There's no point in soiling your dress as well."

Before she could object, he headed into the hallway. There they found Jeannette, sitting on the landing, knees drawn up to her chin, shoulders sagging.

"What is this?" John asked. "Have you uncovered all your gifts already?"

"No," she pouted, her eyes fixed on the floor. "I've only found one... a rock! Yvette found three of hers, and they were all real presents: candy, a book, and some funny looking knickers. But all I got was a wrapped up rock!"

"Well, maybe that's all there is for you," he jested.

"Don't say that!" Charmaine hissed. "You'll have her crying as well!"

He took her point to heart. "Don't give up so easily, Jeannette. There are just as many presents for you."

"But where can they be? I've searched everywhere!"

"Everywhere?" he probed.

"Everywhere but out–" Her words gave way to comprehension, and her face brightened. "They're not in the house, are they?"

"One clue is all you get."

It was enough. Jeannette stormed the front portico, leaving John to chuckle all the way to the nursery.

He's having as much fun as the girls, Charmaine thought.

"Put him on his bed," she directed over her shoulder, retrieving a set of undergarments, knickers, and a towel from the armoire.

John deposited his wet charge, then stood with arms spread wide, surveying his saturated shirt and damp jacket. Charmaine stopped in her tracks, dropping everything but the towel on a nearby chair. "Oh, no! Your jacket is ruined! And your shirt! Oh, I'm sorry!" Without thought, she began to wipe vigorously across his shirtfront and down to his belt buckle, blotting the fabric dry. Suddenly, she realized her impropriety, and her hands dropped to her sides. Cringing, she looked up at him, then slowly stepped away. "I – I'm sorry."

He didn't move, his raised arms mourning the space she had vacated, his crooked smile nourishing the blush that was deepening upon her cheeks.

"I – I'd better see to Pierre."

"Yes," he agreed, his smile broad now, "and I had better leave before I develop a further complication that won't be remedied with a dry cloth."

Once Pierre's clothes had been changed, Charmaine led him out onto the balcony to look for Jeannette. The main doors opened below and George and John came into view. John had changed into a white shirt, fawn colored pants, and high boots. Completing the ensemble was the leather cap he wore, the garb lending itself to a day in the saddle. Evidently, he and George planned on riding out together.

They were absorbed in conversation, and although Charmaine couldn't catch the phrases, their easy banter bespoke a deep-rooted friendship. Even after six weeks, she puzzled over their camaraderie: a chuckle here, the shake of a head there, a raised hand to emphasize a point, or an arm clasped around the other's shoulder. Most brothers would envy such a bond.

A squeal of delight punctuated the air, and the twins bounded from the stable, racing to their brother. Yvette reached him first, hugging him fiercely. "Oh, they're beautiful, Johnny! Wherever did you get them?"

His response was too soft to hear. Then both girls were dancing around him, grabbing his arms, and attempting to pull him toward the paddock. "We can go right now!" They stopped when he spoke again. "Yes!" Jeannette laughed.

"Let's get her!" Yvette added, turning toward the house, espying Charmaine in the process. "There she is!"

The troop took a few steps in her direction. "Mademoiselle Charmaine!" Jeannette shouted. "Wait until you see what Johnny gave us!"

"Stay right there," Yvette interjected, "and we'll bring them out!"

Charmaine surmised what the presents were, and she watched as the girl disappeared into the stable with George. Jeannette continued across the lawn with John, her face radiant. "Just wait until you see!" she reiterated. "They are the most wonderful presents in the whole world! Better than anything I expected this morning! Better than any treasure!"

George led two ponies through the stable door. They were gorgeous creatures, meticulously groomed for the occasion and perfectly matched to the twins' dispositions. One was coal black, a proud animal, prancing wickedly against the bit in its mouth, its head held high. The other was powder white, docile, but no less handsome.

"They're beautiful, girls," Charmaine said, anticipating their next request.

"Johnny said that he would take us riding if you gave your permission."

"There's no point in owning a pony if you cannot ride him, is there?"

"No!" Jeannette agreed. "And will you come along, too?"

"Me?" Charmaine asked in flustered surprise. "No, I'm afraid you'll have to enjoy your ride without my company. I'll just remain behind with Pierre and worry over your safety."

"Oh, please come, Mademoiselle!" the girl implored. "It won't be fun without you, and you promised to spend the day any way we wished."

"And I will," Charmaine reaffirmed, "as soon as you return. Now don't look so glum. It is you who have received such fine animals, not I, therefore, you should enjoy them."

"But Johnny purchased a horse for you, too!"

Charmaine paled. "I'm afraid I don't understand..." But she understood all too well, and already her mind was racing for a suitable excuse to extricate herself from the promises she had made over the past two days.

John read the turmoil on her face. "Miss Ryan," he called up to her, "I took into consideration your diligent supervision of the children and knew that you would insist on joining us today."

When George stepped out of the stable this time, he led a speckled horse over to the corral. The dappling gray was just as majestic as the ponies, its silver coat shimmering in the morning sun, its dark mane and tail rippling in the breeze.

Charmaine was dumbfounded. All that had passed between the two men at breakfast was suddenly clear: the raised brows, the riddle conversation, and the monetary transaction. "I cannot accept such a gift from you! It is quite inappropriate."

"Do not think of it as a gift," he replied. "Think of it as a tool, one required for your job. Then it becomes entirely appropriate."

"*What?*" she fumed.

"The twins will want to ride frequently, and I won't always be around to accompany them. As you've often reminded me, the children are your responsibility, so you will need a horse if you are to go with them."

"You must hurry, Mademoiselle Charmaine!" Yvette beckoned from below. "You can't stand there all day. The horses will grow impatient!"

"And so will we!" Jeannette added.

"That's right," John concurred. "Change into something more comfortable, a dress you can afford to soil, and come down quickly."

"I can't!" Charmaine protested, angry at his matter-of-fact attitude, his confidence that she would do his bidding. "I have to stay with Pierre." She looked to her young charge, who had grown bored and was now running up and down the length of the balcony.

"Pierre is coming with us," John asserted.

"Really? And where do you propose we put him?"

"He can ride with me. Now, we are wasting precious time. Find a suitable garment and get down here before dusk is upon us and the day is gone."

"I'm sorry to disappoint you, but I am not going anywhere on that animal. I won't be held responsible for him."

"Her," John corrected, "and I told you, the horse is yours."

"I don't believe you. No one in their right mind would purchase an expensive animal like that for a governess."

"Whether you believe me or not, Miss Ryan, *I have* and you *are* going to accompany us on our outing," he persisted, matching stubbornness for stubbornness. "As the children's governess, you are obliged to supervise them throughout the day. Isn't that right?"

"Yes, but–"

"But what?"

"I don't know how to ride!" she finally blurted out, stung by the twins' laughter and Yvette's exclamation of: "I told you!"

John's frown struck them mute. "We shall teach you," he said, his manner thoughtful and persuasive. "The mare is gentle. So, no more excuses. We will wait at the stable. If you haven't joined us in ten minutes, I shall come for you." He grasped the girls' shoulders and walked them back to the paddock.

Charmaine sighed. "Now what are we to do?" she asked Pierre as he scurried past her.

He stopped and looked up at her. "Go."

She chuckled ruefully. "Then go, we shall."

Millie Thornfield hesitated before knocking on Frederic's antechamber door, drawing a deep breath when he bade her enter and tightening her grip on the basket she carried. He looked up from the periodical he was reading and beckoned her to come closer. "Well?"

"I have them, sir," she whispered. "The prettiest two of the litter."

"May I see?"

She set the basket down and uncovered it, revealing two kittens, one gray, the other orange. They immediately awoke, and as the marmalade feline yawned and stretched, the gray tabby pounced on her, igniting a fierce tussle. Millie giggled despite her surroundings. Then, remembering where she was, she reined in her sudden joy and looked back at the master of the house, surprised to find him smiling as well.

"Thank you, Millie. You had an excellent idea. My daughters should be very pleased. Even Pierre will enjoy watching them play."

Charmaine arrived at the stable with Pierre, clothed in a timeworn dress. Jeannette was ecstatic, exclaiming that it was going to be a marvelous day. Charmaine shuddered, knowing that John would return and the real disaster would begin. If only Paul were around; he would put a stop to such folly. But no, her fate rested in his brother's hands.

The twins had named their ponies Spook and Angel, and were asking George about their gender when John appeared with Phantom. "Angel is female, and Spook is male," George said. "I believe they will be serving more than one purpose."

"And what is that?" Jeannette innocently asked.

Yvette clicked her tongue. "Now what do you think? Making foals like Phantom and Chastity did. Isn't that so, Johnny?"

"Exactly."

"And can we watch this time?" she inquired, eliciting an embarrassed frown from Charmaine. "I don't understand what happens, and I'd like to find out."

"You would, would you?" he queried, unfazed.

George, however, pulled at his collar, which bolstered Charmaine's fear that an explanation of conception and birth was at hand.

"It will have to wait, Yvette," John said instead. "The day is wasting away. Fetch the picnic basket while I help Jeannie and Miss Ryan into their saddles."

"*Picnic basket?*" Charmaine exclaimed.

"Now, my Charm, what would a picnic be without a picnic basket?"

"It wouldn't be a picnic," she supplied. "I don't want to go on a picnic with you. One was quite enough, thank you."

"You'll disappoint the children… on their special day."

Trapped! John and George's clever interrogation at breakfast had uncovered her plans for the day. She had played right into John's cunning hands. "I'm not wearing my bonnet," she rallied. "I refuse to ride far from the house!"

"Not far at all," he reassured, though she was certain he lied. "What are you waiting for, Yvette?" he pressed. "Go and fetch the basket!"

She immediately jumped to do his bidding.

The nursery was unusually quiet, both bedchamber and playroom empty. "Set the basket on the floor, Millie," Frederic directed. "I thought they'd be here for lessons."

"Would you like me to go and find them, sir?" she offered.

Laughter wafting off the front lawns drew him to the French doors. "That won't be necessary," he muttered, hobbling out onto the balcony. There he stood, inconspicuous in the shadow of the large oak, watching the drama unfold.

John finished adjusting the girth strap on Jeannette's pony. Once secured, he motioned to her. In the next instant, she was seated squarely on Angel's back, laughing gaily. He raised her stirrups a hair higher, then stepped back. She knew what she was doing, for she nudged the animal, and it loped away.

John turned to Charmaine next, and a violent panic rose up inside her. There would be no escape now, and wide-eyed, she looked to George for reassurance. He smiled in return, stroking the mare's speckled neck. "Don't be alarmed, Charmaine. She's quite complacent and easy to ride." He led the horse to her side and relinquished the reins to John, taking charge of Pierre while the man worked the mare's saddle straps.

"Are you ready?" John asked when he was finished.

Her mouth was so dry that she was unable to reply. Though the animal was not as large as Phantom, it was imposing. "It's so high," she finally whispered, her eyes fixed on the saddle that was level with her anxious gaze.

"Yes it is," he conceded, his regard assuasive when she faced him, "but it's quite easy to mount."

"I've never ridden before," she pointed out again, trembling. "I have no idea how to get up there."

"There's a first time for everything," he reasoned devilishly.

She glared at him, finding no humor in her present predicament.

He ignored her disdainful air. "Don't worry, my Charm, I'll not allow your first ride to end in failure."

She caught sight of George's snigger. "I don't intend to be patronized! If that is your game, then you may prey on some other woman!"

"But Miss Ryan, you do me a great injustice," he protested mildly. "I am merely attempting to assist you in a new undertaking. Allow me to demonstrate."

He did so, offering step by step instructions as he swung up and into the saddle. "Easy enough," he concluded. "Do you understand?"

She nodded, even though she knew her struggles were just beginning.

Then he was off the horse and standing beside her again. "Well?" he queried brightly, entertained by her apprehension, his audacity maddening.

"All right!" she snapped, tearing her eyes from his mocking face. Without hesitation, she took hold of the dark mane and the rim of the saddle. To her amazement, the horse did not move.

"Very good," he observed, "but you need to place your foot in the stirrup."

"I know that!" she shot back. But as she lifted her leg, her undergarments were exposed, and in her haste to veil them, she missed the iron. She tried again, releasing the mane to steady it, and still her contorted efforts proved futile. She burned in shame, aware that the men were exchanging smirks behind her back.

"Miss Ryan," John reproved, arresting yet another pathetic attempt. "I am past the age of lusting after your petticoats. If you worried less about your underskirts and more about getting into that saddle, you'd have already mounted!"

"Stop taunting me! If it weren't for your rude jests, I'd be able to do this."

"Really?"

"*Yes, really!* Besides, it is not proper for me to ride a horse this way. No wonder I'm finding it difficult. A lady should ride side-saddle!"

"There you are mistaken, Mademoiselle," he contradicted with a laugh, amused by her numerous excuses to avoid the inevitable. "In Paris or London ladies ride side-saddle, but here on Charmantes, women straddle their mounts..." His words trailed off as his thoughts turned ribald, his eyes going to George. "You're less likely to fall off that way. Besides, this *position* is quite *natural*, and worlds more *comfortable*, especially to the inexperienced horsewoman."

George chuckled softly.

"I'll take no assurances from you," Charmaine rejoined.

"Do you doubt my riding experience?" he queried in pretended offense. "I've been proficient in the art for quite some time now, and some – those who've had the *pleasure* that is – have congratulated me on my skill."

She eyed him speculatively, unable to fathom George's mirth. Obviously, the man was speaking in riddles, and only George understood what he really meant. Wishing only to place the entire ordeal behind her, she gestured to the stirrup. "It is far too high. Could you at least lower it for me?"

"Why, my Charm, I'm afraid that wouldn't do at all."

George roared with laughter and John joined in, all at her expense.

Miserable, she stepped away from the horse, reliving the incident with 'Fang', a thick lump lodged in her throat. She was about to flee when Yvette returned lugging a picnic basket, protesting that her governess had yet to mount up.

"I'm sorry, Charmaine," John apologized, taking in her forlorn face. It was clear how very innocent she was, and he suffered a pang of contrition. "We're not laughing at you. The stirrups have to be high so that you can pull yourself up and into the saddle."

His vulgar mien was gone, leaving Charmaine confused.

"I offer my shoulder. Lean on me while you put your foot into the stirrup, and you'll be atop the mare in no time."

She couldn't object; he was already crouching next to her. She rested her right arm tentatively across his back. Oddly secure, her foot found the iron.

"Grab the saddle and mane," he directed. "That's it. Now, pull up."

She barely left the ground, her attention riveted on the warm hands that encompassed her waist.

"Try again," he coaxed before she lost courage.

This time, she pushed off, and somewhere between earth and saddle, John's strong arms propelled her upward. When she exhaled, she was astride the mare, looking down at him. Though she focused on his smiling face, her mind lingered on her waist where his hands had branded her.

In the next moment, a wave of paranoia seized her – her familiar surroundings turned perilous from the lofty perch, and she clutched the horse's mane desperately, letting go only when John pulled the reins over the mare's head and handed them to her. She hardly noticed his familiarity when he shortened the stirrups and took hold of each ankle to test the length. To her horror, he turned away, tending to his own mount.

Instantly, the horse shifted. "*Where are you going?*" she cried.

"One moment," he assured her.

"You can't leave me here! I've no idea how to control this animal!"

As if on cue, the mare ambled toward the grassy knoll where the ponies grazed. "She's moving!"

"Let her go," John replied, as he hitched the surcingle about the small picnic basket and fastened it to Phantom's saddle, "she just wants to graze."

As predicted, the mare stopped when she reached the ponies, and her head plummeted to the lawn. Petrified, Charmaine held onto the reins for dear life, certain that she was going to slide down the horse's neck, breathing easier only after some minutes had elapsed and she remained in place.

John untied Phantom and swung up into the saddle. The horse snorted loudly and shook his head, fighting the bit and the iron hand that held him in check.

"Are you more at ease now?" John asked as he drew even with her, eyeing the leather straps entwined in her white-knuckled fingers.

"Yes," she replied, pushing the inconsequential inquiry aside. "Do you still plan on having Pierre ride with you?"

"Of course. Why do you ask?"

"I think we should leave him with Rose."

John's brow furrowed and his eyes grew stormy.

"I'm concerned for his safety," she added. "That beast is so fierce."

His visage softened, then the anger was gone altogether. "Mademoiselle, for all those you would love to see me land on my backside, he has yet to throw me. Pierre will be fine. Besides, you wouldn't want to disappoint him, would you?" His eyes traveled to the patiently waiting boy, whose face was alight with anticipation.

Charmaine knew she had been manipulated, emotion pitted against common sense. She could also tell that John's mind was made up.

"This day belongs as much to him as it does to his sisters. Do you think we could leave him behind in tears and then hope to enjoy the afternoon ourselves?"

"I suppose not," she conceded. "But sometimes things are beyond our control and–"

"Charmaine, must I give my solemn word? Pierre is the *last* child who will come to harm because of me." Dismissing further protest, he nudged the stallion toward George and the boy was placed in front of him.

As John prodded Phantom into motion, Pierre squealed with glee. Now, she was glad they had not left him behind. He would have been miserable cloistered in the house all day.

Yvette balked at her elder brother's riding instructions. "I mounted all by myself didn't I?"

So, once again, John drew up alongside Charmaine, and gave her a brief demonstration on how to prod the horse and use the reins. It seemed too simple to work. He cautioned her to loosen up on the straps, warning that clutching them too tightly wouldn't prevent her from falling off, but could provoke the animal into throwing her. "The mare doesn't need to be broken. That has already been done for you," he finished, chuckling at her renewed anxiety.

Yvette tugged on her reins and Spook abandoned his grazing for the cobblestone drive. Jeannette quickly followed suit. Their unquestionable ability left Charmaine shaken, and she breathed deeply when John nodded to her.

"Your turn," he said.

In imitation of the twins, she steered her horse in the same direction, awed when the beast complied. They were on their way, bidding George goodbye and clopping through the iron fencing to the dirt road. Charmaine's tension faded with the rhythm of the animal beneath her. As long as the route remained straight, the mare walked steadily along, obediently following the ponies.

Frederic remained on the veranda, haunted by fragmented memories. *You're never home to spend time with them... I'd much prefer to have a horse... It wouldn't have to be in a box, Papa... You could have him hidden in the stables with a big blue ribbon around his neck... John loves them... He'll see to it that they are well cared for... The colt thinks we're his masters, maybe he could be mine... Colette wrote to me... to supply the children with the love and affection that they'd never get from you... He's the very last child who will come to harm because of me...*

The riders were long out of sight when Frederic turned back into the nursery. He was alone and only had himself to blame. With a plaintive sigh, he looked down at the basket. The kittens were once again sleeping.

Kittens... Yvette had begged him for a horse on her last birthday, and he had decided to give her a stray kitten instead. Why did he think such a gift would please her? He knew what she longed for. But had he listened? John, on the other hand, had been home less than six weeks and already knew her deepest desires. His son was fulfilling Colette's dying request.

Then there was Pierre. He was too young to lament what he could never receive from his sire – what his childhood and the circumstances surrounding his birth would deny him. But it wouldn't be long before he, too, was turning nine and, like his sister, would grow disenchanted and unhappy.

Nine... was it possible that Yvette and Jeannette were already nine? Frederic stared across the room and time. Nine years ago today, his prayers had been mercifully answered; his young wife had survived the difficult labor and birth of twins.

Twenty-nine years ago tomorrow, he had not been so blessed, and he trembled with the memory. Images of that bleak night, just past midnight, assaulted him as if it were yesterday, and his chest tightened with the overwhelming loss of that first delivery.

"John," Elizabeth had moaned, suffering another violent contraction. "If it's a boy, Frederic, name him John." They were her dying words.

Colette's labor had mirrored Elizabeth's, and though he'd always been stalwart, Frederic had been terrified the night the twins were born, certain that he was going to lose his second wife as surely as he had lost his first twenty years earlier.

But God had been merciful, and Colette was spared. *Why?* Had the Good Lord heard his petition in those last few hours before midnight? Was Colette's recovery a result of the vow he had made to the Almighty and to himself? He realized now that, if nothing else, it had propelled him to this point, scripting the present and marking the lives of his children in the most disastrous way. He sat down hard on Yvette's bed and rubbed his throbbing brow. Would he allow the past to dictate the future? *Dear God,* he murmured, *what am I to do?*

"Do you like the ride, Pierre?"

John's voice interrupted the thud of hooves in the dust.

"Yes!" the boy giggled. "I like this big horse!" He craned his neck back to regard his saddle-mate and exclaimed, "You're upside down!"

"No, I'm not, you are."

Pierre looked down at himself thoughtfully. "No, I'm not!" he disagreed, eventually noticing Charmaine. "I like this ride, Mainie!"

"I can tell," she replied with a smile.

John smiled as well. "Have you put aside your misgivings?" he asked.

"Most, but not all. I'm becoming used to her movements. However, I'm not looking forward to getting down."

"Don't worry. It is much easier than mounting."

Their short conversation lapsed into silence, and Charmaine began to enjoy the scenery around her. She directed her gaze away from John, taking in the foliage and wild birds, turning back to him only when her neck began to ache. She found him studying her thoughtfully and braved his unnerving regard. "Is something wrong?" she asked.

"Wrong?" he queried with arched brow. "Why should anything be wrong?"

"The manner in which you are staring at me leads me to assume the worst. Perhaps I've grown a wart on the end of my nose?"

"A wart? No, my Charm, your nose is just fine… perfectly shaped." His gaze came to rest there.

"What then?" she pressed.

"Am I not permitted to admire your accomplishment? I do not mean to ogle you, Miss Ryan. It's just that I never thought to see you sit a horse so well. Quite an accomplishment for a beginner."

"Compliments are of no use," she remarked, certain he mocked her.

But his next words were quick and sure, leaving her befuddled. "No compliment intended, merely an observation that answers a score of questions."

"Such as?"

"Why you were employed as the children's governess."

"Surely you are not suggesting that riding a horse has led to my present occupation? But then, the workings of your mind never cease to amaze me."

His lips broke into a rakish grin. "I'm glad to hear that no matter what else I might be, I haven't been a bore."

"You haven't answered my question," she rejoined.

"I wasn't aware that you had asked one."

"What exactly is the connection you've made between my employment as the children's governess and my achievement upon this animal?"

"Oh, that question. Well now, I was contemplating your ability to conquer a new endeavor, in this case, riding the mare. That particular facet of your character led me to understand how you gained the position you now hold. Even in fear, you pressed on. I commend you on your determination."

"You mock me, sir," Charmaine replied sheepishly.

"No, Miss Ryan, I do not mock you. That *was* a compliment. You play a very important role in the children's lives."

"You've just now realized that?"

"No. In fact, it was the reason I doubted your capabilities at first."

"At first?" she asked in great surprise. "And you don't now?"

"No, not anymore, not since I gave you a chance – watched you with them."

She was too astounded to speak.

"You enjoy your job, don't you?"

"Yes, I do. I love the children."

"Do you?"

Though his words were not unkind, they rattled Charmaine. "Yes!" she averred. "Don't you believe me?"

"I believe you," he answered resolutely. "I just wanted to hear you say it again, to reassure me perhaps."

"Reassure you? Certainly that's a curious remark?"

"Why should it be curious, considering the state of their lives? My father is a recluse, their mother is dead, and their stepmother hates them. They need somebody to love them."

He grew pensive, his gaze traveling to the edge of the forest. She preferred the silence to his disturbing statements. Their odd discourse had taken its toll. She was certain of only one thing: she'd never in a million years understand him.

John Duvoisin. The man *was* an enigma, and more often than not, a thorn in her side. Life on the island, in the house, hadn't gotten back to normal since his arrival. Granted, the great storms that had shaken the manor that first week were all but gone, and yet, his presence affected everyone.

Thoughts of his departure, one that had grown less likely with each passing day, came unwittingly to her lips. "When are you planning to leave?"

John's attention was snared, his expression sharp, then devilish. "I'll bet you can't wait until that day arrives, can you?"

"I – I didn't mean for it to sound that way," she gushed.

"Really? Forgive me if I fail to believe you this time. No," he laughed, "I'll wager you meant every word and are just now regretting having said them."

"I just wanted to know–"

"Know what? When you can expect things to get back to normal on Charmantes? When you and my brother can recommence your love affair?"

"It's not a love affair!" she objected fiercely.

"No? I suppose I just imagined the passionate scene I walked in on that night. The question is, how much further has it all gone?"

Charmaine turned away in heightening embarrassment.

"Your red face would lead me to believe the worst. However, my growing faith in you would not." He paused a moment as if in deep thought. "I'm feeling generous today, so I'll offer you a word of warning concerning my brother."

"Don't bother!"

"Oh, but I feel it is my obligation."

"Your obligation?" she queried incredulously. "Since when have you become so noble? Or do you think that by maligning your brother, you'll promote yourself?"

"I'm the first to admit that I'm far beyond redemption, Miss Ryan." He chortled anew. "Now, don't lead me off track. We were speaking about Paul and all the trouble he could get you into."

"And I told you that I've no interest in what you have to say."

"Interest," he repeated. "A perfect word, for it's at the heart of my very next point. You should be *interested* to know that Paul has but one *interest* in you."

Charmaine gaped at him.

"Don't be offended. I'm only stating the facts as they are."

"*Facts?* What would you know of facts?"

"Plenty. If you would like to–"

"I would like nothing, and I'll not believe a word of it, anyway."

"I assure you my facts are not fabricated," he pressed on. "But perhaps you'd prefer a more reliable source, someone who could provide concrete evidence. I'm certain that the maids of the manor could tell tales that would shock even me. You see, Paul has quite an affinity for the young ladies in my father's employ. He must have been quite disheartened when your more distinguished position of governess placed an unusual obstacle in his one-track path."

"What is that supposed to mean?"

"Must I be more explicit, my Charm? My brother is a Don Juan with an insatiable appetite for women. Not that I'm condemning him morally. What is a man to do when the mansion is so well *stocked*? Before I left a few years ago, there was many a night when some young maid, who should have been sleeping virtuously in her own bed on the third floor, found *comfort* in my brother's bed one floor below. I doubt those fair times have changed, especially if you are holding him at bay."

"*If?*" she choked out, even as a distant memory surfaced. *I'm speaking of comfort – yours and mine.* "Well, if you're hoping to trap me into affirming your crude speculation, allow me to dash those hopes right here and now! I have no intention of carrying this conversation any further."

"I'm not speculating. I grew up with him. My brother is many things, but celibate is not one of them. He's sampled the fruit many times, in assorted varieties. I know."

"Really? And how do you know? Did you place a glass against the wall?"

"I didn't have to," John chuckled softly, amused by her feisty reply. "Paul never guarded his liaisons. In fact, he often boasted about them."

"Many people boast," she reasoned, "I'd hardly call that concrete evidence."

"My, you are determined to defend him, aren't you?"

"I'm not defending him!"

"No?"

"No!"

"Then why turn a deaf ear to information that is in your best interest to know?"

"Whatever went on between Paul and someone else is none of my business."

"Why do you use the past tense?"

She was appalled by his tenacious debasement of his own brother. "I refuse to believe your lies."

"Believe what you will," he snorted, certain she could not be *that* naïve, "but don't cry into your pillow later on, for I did warn you."

"I don't need your warning!" she retorted, ripping her gaze from him.

"That maid," he pursued, forefinger to lips, "Travis' daughter, Millie…"

Charmaine's eyes shot back to his taunting face.

"The voluptuous Felicia was his favorite, but I believe he's allowing that field to lay fallow for a while, a good guess considering how she's been acting toward me lately. If Paul gets nowhere with you, I'd place money on Millie."

"But she's only sixteen!"

"The perfect age – no diseases."

"Enough!" Charmaine cried out. "I've heard enough!"

The twins turned round in their saddles. But John only smiled and waved to them. A moment later, he and Charmaine were forgotten.

"Of course," he pressed on, "Paul may have a bit of trouble seducing Millie with her father about. Therefore, Miss Ryan, you'd best be on guard, unless of course, you are willing..."

"You are very crude," she hissed. "As for your *chivalrous* warning, it was unnecessary. I'm not some trollop who'd give herself to a man without sacred vows exchanged before a priest and God, so take your lecherous insinuations elsewhere!"

"*Marriage?*" he laughed. "You think he would marry you?"

His boisterous reaction gained the twins' sidelong glances a second time.

Crushed, Charmaine bowed her head to the decimation of her most cherished dream. How foolish those girlish fancies suddenly seemed! Marriage. Of course Paul wouldn't marry her, a lowly servant girl. Oh, yes, she was the governess, but as Felicia had said only a week ago, an employee just the same.

"I'm sorry if you were misled," John proceeded, "but my brother could never marry you, even if that were his most ardent desire. You see, money marries money, especially when the money is limited. Paul isn't heir to my father's estate. Not yet, anyway. So, *if* he marries, he'll invest any money he has in a rich wife."

Her pain diminished. This man, in his great analysis, had never touched upon love and all its glorious possibilities. Unable to love, having never loved, he thought of marriage only in terms of capital and investments, of buying a wife like one would a mare or a new ship. He could never hope to appreciate an emotion so strong that it could impel a decent man to snub convention and break society's code by choosing a partner lowly born and financially poor, yet rich in love.

"Yes, Paul will be forced to seek a wealthy wife," John continued, "I, on the other hand, can marry whomever I choose." He chuckled wryly, a laugh born of pain, not pleasure.

Charmaine regarded him again, perceiving the irony in his voice. Was he afraid that his father would disown him? But as she searched his face for an answer, he turned away, leaving her to puzzle over the cryptic remark.

Yvette's shout drew their eyes to the road ahead. "Look Johnny – a rider!"

"Speak of the devil," John muttered.

Though not the devil, it might well have been. Atop his white stallion, Paul was quickly approaching, and Charmaine worried over his reaction. Surely if he didn't like John pestering the children during lessons, he'd find their late morning excursion intolerable. She was grateful when Jeannette greeted him enthusiastically.

"Good day, Paul! How do you like our presents?"

"Very nice," he said, reining in Alabaster shoulder to shoulder with Phantom.

"Johnny purchased them for us," she added, unmindful of his twitching jaw.

"So I imagined," he replied tenderly, his cold eyes reserved for John.

Charmaine waited with bated breath. It would be wise to proceed with caution, but she knew that John would never do that.

"What brings Paulie home so early today?" he asked merrily.

"Yeah," Yvette echoed, "what brings Paulie home so early today?"

Ignore them, Paul thought as he tore his gaze from his heckling brother. "Good morning, Miss Ryan," he greeted debonairly.

"Good morning," she returned, relief rushing in.

John couldn't restrain himself, the endearing exchange fanning his knavery. Leaning forward, he addressed Yvette. "Good morning, Miss Duvoisin."

"Good morning," his young sister mimicked, catching on quickly.

Satisfied that he once again commanded Paul's attention, John continued. "You didn't answer my question, Paul. Aren't you feeling well?"

"I'm fine, John."

"Then why have you rushed home so early in the day? There must be a score of projects just waiting for your – how did you put it – 'necessitous' hands?"

"They're finished, John. I was out of the house early–"

"Mr. Proficiency."

"–with the intention of celebrating the twins' birthday this afternoon." His eyes rested on Charmaine, a hint of a promise reflected there.

"What a shame," John sighed with the snap of his fingers.

"And why is that?"

"Isn't it obvious? You are hours too late! We're on our way to a picnic! You're welcome to join us, of course. Not even I would be so cruel as to exclude you from the outing. You look like you need a break." *Besides,* John thought, *it would be entertaining to watch Paul in action with the governess.*

Paul's demeanor hardened. "I'll see you later," he told Charmaine, "at the house." He yanked on the reins, drawing his stallion away.

As he galloped off, Charmaine experienced a pang of regret; Paul's companionship had slipped through her fingers. But there was no point in crying over spilled milk.

"I think someone's in trouble," John teased in a singsong children's chant.

She ignored him.

They nudged their mounts into motion again, leaving the dusty road and trekking south across a wide meadow, tall of grass and abundantly speckled with wild flowers. As they meandered along, Yvette asked to race her pony, but John set aside the petition; Spook could step into a hole and break a leg.

"Like Charity?" the girl asked.

"Possibly."

"Not like Charity," Jeannette corrected, "because Charity didn't really break a leg. I remember Mama crying and saying that Dr. Blackford destroyed her horse for no good reason."

"You never told me that, Jeannette! Is that true, Johnny?"

"Yes," he pronounced flatly, "it's true."

"But why? Why would Dr. Blackford do that?"

"Because the man is a pompous imbecile. He calls himself a doctor and can't diagnose a fracture correctly..." Then he mumbled under his breath, "I could be dying, and I wouldn't let him near me."

Charmaine shifted uneasily in her saddle, relieved when she realized the girls hadn't heard the last comment. The man was criticizing the physician who had ministered to their mother. Even so, she was curious about the story. At first, she had assumed they were talking about Chastity, the mare that had foaled only weeks ago. Now she realized they were talking about an entirely different animal.

John explained that Paul had purchased Chastity for Colette some weeks after Charity was destroyed in the hopes of brightening her spirits. "But Colette loved Charity," he concluded, "and Chastity never quite took her place."

They came to a wooded area, and John prodded Phantom to the front of the entourage, leaving Charmaine to take up the rear. He uncovered an obscure trail hidden in a dense copse. The horses entered single file, and the leafy lane closed in around them. Though it was cool here, Charmaine would have preferred the heat of the meadow. Now she had to work at guiding her mount, lest she stumble over a dead branch. The heavy vegetation offered its share of obstacles as well. Low hanging twigs accosted her, scratching her face, catching at her dress, and loosing strands of her hair. Dodging them, she soon forgot about the horse beneath her, and the mare abruptly stopped. Charmaine nudged her sides, but the animal was already chewing on a patch of tall weeds and refused to budge. Frustrated, she looked to John, but he was nowhere in sight. Yvette and Jeannette disappeared next, directing their ponies around a bend up ahead.

"Come on, you silly horse!" she scolded. "You can't eat now! Move! Please move." The mare, however, chewed away, its reins pulled taut against its craning neck. Gritting her teeth, Charmaine yanked on the leather straps. The horse only whinnied, then returned to the vegetation. "Oh no you don't!" she hissed, jerking the reins again and nudging the beast's flanks. The animal shook its head and stepped backwards. Paralyzed with fear, Charmaine pulled harder. The mare trumpeted loudly and began prancing in place, then turned, wedging herself on the narrow path, her wide neck bowed sideways, head pointed in the direction from which they had come.

"John! Dear Lord, John!" Charmaine screamed.

John looked back. "Good God! Where is she?"

The twins only shrugged.

"Stay put. I'll be back."

He angled Phantom around them and set the steed on a fast trot, rounding the bend just as Charmaine cried out again. The mare was on her hind legs, front hooves pawing the air. "Stop pulling on the reins!" he shouted.

Charmaine was too petrified to hear him.

Pierre burst into belly-shaking laughter. John jumped off Phantom, lifted the boy from the saddle, and set him down a safe distance away. "Stay here."

He approached the mare, dodging the thrashing hooves. "Grab her mane! For God's sake, Charmaine, let go of the reins and grab her mane!"

Their eyes connected, and Charmaine finally heard the command, but at the moment she released the leather strap, the crazed horse reared again. John winced as her hands came up short of the mane, clutching air instead. She sailed over the horse's rump, and her backside met the ground with a painful thump. There she sat, too stunned to move, her hair combs askew, the copious tendrils tousled and sagging in defeated glory. Unburdened, the mare loped over to the weeds that had instigated the unfortunate episode.

John swiftly knelt beside her. "Are you all right?"

The twinkle in his eyes and the smile on his lips belied the concern in his voice, and Charmaine's eyes narrowed on him as she brushed the tangled locks from her face. "It's not funny! I could have been hurt!"

"Then you are all right?"

"I think so," she answered, finally accepting the hand he extended to help her up. The loosened combs fell to the ground, and the abundant tresses tumbled over her shoulders in a riotous waterfall of curls. In growing displeasure, Charmaine stomped her foot. "This is entirely your doing, I'll have you know!"

"My doing?" John asked, placing a hand to his chest.

"Yes, your doing!" she accused. "Just look at my hair!"

"I'm looking," he replied wickedly, "and I like what I see."

"Oh, you would!"

"What is that supposed to mean?"

"Never mind. I'll not waste my breath explaining it to you. Why couldn't leave me behind today? Why did you have to press me into this – this–"

"Adventure?" he offered.

"Stop ridiculing everything I say!"

"Stop blaming me for your mistakes," he retaliated. "It was your fault that the mare threw you. I warned you this morning not to pull so fiercely on the reins, but did you listen? No. She might have upset you, but you panicked and yanked too hard on the bit. Now admit it, Charmaine, you confused the poor beast into throwing you. It was entirely your doing."

"*My doing?*" she raged. "I told you that I didn't know how to ride, and still you insisted that I join you, promising that no harm would befall me! *And the poor beast?* What about me?"

He was chuckling before she had finished, and quite unexpectedly, her anger ebbed. Then she was laughing with him, her anxiety yielding to relief, returning Pierre's hug when he ran over to them and wrapped his arms around her legs.

"What am I to do with my hair?" she complained.

"Here," John replied, retrieving her combs. "These should keep it out of your face. A prim bun never belonged to the day in the first place."

"But it's too hot to leave down! I should have worn my bonnet, but I didn't think our *little* ride was going to turn into a full day's outing."

"You can borrow my cap," he offered, scratching vigorously behind his ear with a laugh. "The last time I looked it was nit free."

She clenched her jaw and refused to comment.

"Not to worry. It's cool where we are going, and I prefer you this way."

She reached for the combs, but he stepped forward with arms extended. "I'll do it, thank you," she said, snatching them away.

Once the locks were coifed, she brushed the clinging twigs and moist leaves from her dress, relieved to find that the garment was not soiled beyond repair. When she looked up, John was walking the gray mare toward her and Pierre. "Ready to try again?" he asked.

"You cannot be serious!"

"Quite."

"No, sir. I'm not getting back in that saddle, not for a million dollars!"

"Why not?"

"*Why not?* You saw what just happened! I value my life!"

"You have one of two choices, Miss Ryan. You can either get back on your own mount, or we can place Pierre in that seat and you can ride with me."

"Oh, goodie!" Pierre laughed. "I want my own horse!"

"And I have a third choice, sir. I'll walk."

"Walk?" John expostulated. "At that rate, we won't picnic until sunset!"

"I doubt that," she said, brushing past him and trekking up the trail.

John ran his hand through his hair, then scooped up Pierre and placed him in the mare's saddle. "Hold on tightly," he admonished as he grabbed Phantom's reins as well and lengthened his strides to catch up with the willful woman.

"How did you find this path, anyway?" she asked, clearly recovered.

"George and I uncovered it when we were boys," he replied. "We used to track through this area whenever we went hunting, and came upon it accidentally one day. Occasionally it's used by the bondsmen."

"Occasionally? Why only occasionally?"

John was about to explain that the trail was too narrow to accommodate buckboards, but was suddenly inspired. "The men use it when they're in a hurry, and only when on horseback."

"But why?"

"Because of the wildlife," he replied.

"What kind of 'wildlife'? Certainly not *dangerous* wildlife?"

John didn't answer.

"It wouldn't be what you and George used to hunt as boys, would it?"

"Actually, yes," he conceded.

"Yes what? They are dangerous creatures, or they're what you hunted?"

"Both. We trapped and killed a few rattlesnakes here."

"Rattlesnakes?" Her eyes shot to the ground and darted about. "Why come this way then?"

"There's nothing to worry about," he mollified. "We cleaned this area out long ago… haven't seen one in years, not since George shot his trophy."

"But if it's been cleaned out, why don't the bondsmen–"

"They're just a pack of ninnies," he cut in, "afraid of their own shadows and spreading tales about old man Lavar, who insisted that he'd been bitten by one before he died. Robert Blackford claimed it wasn't a snake bite at all."

"But you said that Dr. Blackford couldn't be trusted in his judgments."

"True. Still, if you are atop a horse you're safe, and if not, you're clad in boots. What are the chances of a snake biting through thick leather?"

"Probably none," she mumbled, noting John's boots next to her shoes and stockings. Suddenly, she wanted the protection of the lofty saddle. "I suppose I could give riding another try. It wouldn't be fair to impede our progress."

"Good," he said, smiling down at her.

They rounded the bend and reached the twins. "Did she fall?" Yvette asked.

"Yes, she fell. Just like you did the first time."

Yvette was miffed into silence.

With a soft chuckle, John helped Charmaine mount up. Amazingly, she replaced Pierre in the saddle with only a flash of white petticoats. He returned the lad to Phantom's back and led the stallion to the front of the procession.

"Is Mademoiselle Charmaine all right?" Jeannette asked him.

"She's fine. Her horse was just hungry."

They were on their way again, and this time, Charmaine kept her mind on task. After a while, she relaxed, taking in her surroundings: the cabbage and royal palm trees towering eighty feet above them, the sapodilla and calabash blooming in white and pale yellow flowers, the bearded figs with their thick trunks, sporting heavy growths of hanging roots, like ropes gone awry off the rigging of a ship, their interlaced branches harboring the tropical birds that hopped from limb to limb. The soft breezes intensified as they advanced, and soon the foliage began to thin. When the trail widened, John drew back to ride alongside her. Salt was heavy in the air, and they could hear waves thundering on the beach to their right.

Charmaine turned to ask him how long they would ride parallel with the shoreline when she caught sight of Pierre, who reclined against his chest, eyelids sagging. John's gaze followed hers. "He's quite a boy," he murmured, stroking Pierre's hair.

"Yes, he is," she whispered, touched by his gesture of affection.

The trees opened to sprawling sea grape shrubs, white sand, and aquamarine water as far as the eye could see. "Oh, my!" she breathed, reveling in the buffeting gales that unfurled her long, wild hair.

"The perfect place for a picnic," John added, regarding her when she didn't immediately respond. "You're not displeased with the location, I hope."

"Displeased? Not at all! I love the ocean. Don't you?"

"That depends on where you are when you're looking at it," he replied thoughtfully, casting his gaze out to the water.

Charmaine studied him, but he said no more.

"Where to now?" Yvette called.

"Why don't you find a spot where we can have our picnic?" John suggested.

"All right," Yvette agreed enthusiastically, "follow us."

They continued down the parched beach, the horses' hooves throwing sand high in the air. Not far ahead was a small cape, the curved projection forming a charming, secluded inlet, a natural barrier against the open ocean. Jeannette pointed to an enormous silk cotton tree, its towering branches spread far over the sandy shore, an inviting haven from the blistering sun.

Once there, the girls jumped from their ponies and led them into the woods where they could graze in the protection of the shade. Charmaine sat indecisively in her seat, apprehensive of dismounting.

"The sooner you take courage, my Charm," John remarked, "the sooner I can hand Pierre over to you. I don't want to awaken him."

Realizing that the ordeal would be over quickly if she just got on with it, Charmaine swung her leg over the saddle rim and descended to the ground, quite gracefully for an amateur. She took charge of Pierre, cradling his limp body to her breast while John led the horses into the woods.

When he returned, the twins helped him spread the blanket, and they settled in, delving into the basket that had been packed with a feast fit for a king. Pierre slept while they ate, Charmaine and the twins on the blanket, John reclining a few feet away against the tree trunk. Few words were spoken until the twins had swallowed the last of their dessert. "Johnny," Jeannette queried, "why didn't you ever bring us here before? I know Mama would have loved this spot."

He didn't answer, and Charmaine looked up. *Would he tell the girl the truth, that he loathed her mother? Or was he remorseful for having scorned her?*

"Yes," Yvette piped in, "why *didn't* you bring us here when you and Mama planned all those picnics together?"

The statement shook Charmaine, thundered in her ears.

"It was too far to walk," he finally replied, grabbing his cap and walking to the water's edge. There he stood, gazing out at the horizon.

"But we used to walk much farther plenty of other times!" Yvette called after him. He didn't respond, and she shrugged. "Oh well, come, Jeannette, let's go collect seashells." They raced down the beach, paying little mind to Charmaine's admonition that they not stray too far, leaving her to study the man.

What was he thinking? Surely those thoughts could answer a score of questions. She attempted to dismiss the possibilities and began collecting the lunch plates. But her mind betrayed her: *Why didn't you bring us here when you and Mama used to plan all those picnics together? We used to walk much farther plenty of other times! My dearest John... John has hurt many people; even Colette suffered at his hands... He's a menace to certain members of this family... you'll not speak of him again! Nobody likes John, they either hate him or love him, and it's usually in that order...*

Dear God, where did it all lead? Hate or love? Or something else? She regarded him again. He hadn't moved. The man was many things, but a seducer of his father's wife? No, she couldn't believe that.

Colette would have loved this spot. As in a daydream, Charmaine's vision blurred, and the blue-green waters melded into the eyes of her dear, kind friend. Just one year ago today, Colette was defending John to her husband. What secrets had she taken to the grave? It was better – safer – not to know.

And the letter. Did Frederic know that his wife had written to John a month before her demise? What telling words were contained within its pages? *It is not my intention to cause you greater pain...*

Yes, John had known pain. That was obvious. He had remained closeted in his chambers for days after he had learned of Colette's death, brooding in the oblivion of alcohol.

My God! Charmaine thought with quickened pulse. Colette and John. John and Colette. Intimate lovers? Never. Chaste lovers? Possibly. But how? Why? It made no sense and made perfect sense. She refused to believe it, certain that her mind was playing tricks on her, yet the more she tried to suppress the unholy thoughts, the stronger they became. She closed her eyes in wild confusion, hoping to calm her raging mind. It did not. They opened to a sound at her feet. John had returned to the blanket.

"Tired?" he asked.

"A bit," she murmured as he settled next to her.

"Riding can be tiring," he said as he pulled his knees up and encircled them with his arms, his eyes trained on the water.

Because he did not perceive her profane thoughts, she felt at ease to study him in a new light. The breeze caressed them, mussing his wavy hair. The sun's rays glinted reddish-blonde off the lighter strands, which curled about his ears, over his sideburns and white collar. The locks framed his profile: the wide brow, intense eyes, and clean-shaven cheeks. As he raised a hand to rake back the tousled strands, her gaze traveled to his flexed arm and the play of muscle against his shirtsleeve. Disconcerted, she breathed deeply against her thudding heart and the strange feeling building inside her. She looked at him as a woman looks at a man, perhaps in the manner in which Colette had.

He leaned back on his elbows, stretching out his long legs and crossing them. Self-consciously, belatedly, she looked away, carrying with her that last glimpse of him – his hair windswept. She wanted to touch those locks, savor their texture between thumb and forefinger, to go further and run her hands through them. Oddly, she felt cheated at residing so close to the object of such wanton desire and unable to act on it. He was affecting her in a most perplexing way, and she was not pleased. *Imagine, wanting to stroke his hair! What was wrong with her?*

Pierre stirred beside her, opening sleepy eyes. Dazed, he looked around, then settled his head in her lap, muttering, "Mama".

"He really loves you, doesn't he?" John mused.

"I suppose so," she said, stroking the child's hair, "but he misses his mother."

"Does he?"

"Very much. Colette cherished the children. They were her life. Although her health restrained her in that last year, she spent as much time with them as she possibly could, even if it was only to be in the same room as they, or hold Pierre on her lap. I know he misses that."

"And the twins?"

"The wound is healing, but the scars remain," she answered. "I'm sure you can appreciate the pain they've suffered. I know the feeling all too well myself."

"I never had a mother to lose," he replied dispassionately, "so I suppose I don't know what they're experiencing."

"Experience isn't the only teacher. Sympathy is easy, defeating their misery, another matter. Time and routine have seen them through the worst. They've finally accepted the fact that their mother is gone."

"And what of you, Miss Ryan? Surely you've given them the love they've needed. Isn't that the most important component in their recovery?"

"Yes, it's important, but I can never replace Colette."

"Perhaps you can," he contradicted. "Perhaps you already have. They're quite fond of you, and fondness can grow into love. You, too, could become as irreplaceable as their mother."

"I seriously doubt it. They turn to me because they have no other choice. But if Colette were here, I know to whom they'd run." She met his quizzical gaze, then boldly said, "Colette was a fine lady, good and kind."

He didn't disagree, though a wry grin broke across his face. "And you are not?"

"I didn't say that." When his smile broadened, she backtracked, "I mean, I try to be a good Christian, but Colette... she was perfect."

"Nobody is perfect, Charmaine."

"Not even you?" she challenged, unable to quell the urge to best him.

His eyes only sparkled. "There's an exception to every rule."

She clicked her tongue and rolled her eyes. Pierre turned his face into the folds of her skirts, calling for his mother again.

"Does he do that often?"

She massaged the boy's back. "Only when he's sleeping. Sometimes I think he feels the loss more than either of his sisters."

"Surely memories of his mother have faded. He's so much younger."

"True, but Colette spent the most time with him."

"Why was that, do you think?"

"Pierre was content to play near her, whereas the twins were always running off, and she couldn't keep up with them."

He seemed displeased with the answer, compelling her to explain. "It's not that she didn't want to chase after the girls. In fact, she often complained of how her malady restricted her. That is why she insisted on a governess. She didn't want her infirmity to stifle them. She sought to make them happy, to see them run and play, to…"

"Go ahead," John pressed, "I'm listening."

"I'm afraid I'm talking too much."

"No, you're not talking too much," he said. "In fact, this is the first time you've really talked *to me*. I must admit, I'm enjoying the conversation."

"Circumstances never permitted me to speak otherwise, sir," she tersely replied, aware that they now tread upon dangerous territory.

"Ah, but I kept the faith," he proceeded lightheartedly. "I knew that given enough time, I would break through all your raging righteousness and reach the real Charmaine Ryan."

"Really?" she snapped, annoyed that he presumed to know her so well, that he blamed her for their strained conversations.

"Yes, really," he smiled placidly. "Now, let us not destroy such a hard-won accomplishment. Finish what you were saying, Mademoiselle."

"And what was that?" she asked coolly.

"About the Mistress Colette, and why she favored Pierre over her daughters."

"Favored? That wasn't the word I used." *Why the misinterpretation?* "She loved the twins just as dearly."

"But, according to you, she spent more time with Pierre. Isn't that favoritism?"

"Not necessarily. I told you, the girls were more active than he. Beyond that, I think Colette knew she was dying and wanted to leave him with as many good memories as possible. I suppose she thought the girls would remember her because they were older. With Pierre, she wanted to be especially sure. Even to the end, when most days she was bedridden, she'd find the strength to come to the nursery before he fell asleep at night."

"Does he ask about her when he's awake?"

"I don't think he has to. I think she is with him always, and he happily accepts her presence."

He didn't respond, his eyes shadowed as he looked down at the sleeping boy, and Charmaine knew he'd fallen into his contemplative mood again.

They turned to the sound of laughter and the girls racing toward the blanket. Yvette reached them first. Out of breath, she greeted John by dropping a finely shaped seashell in his lap with the word, "Look!"

"A very nice discovery," he said, holding it up for inspection. "How far did you travel to find it?"

"Oh, not too far. A few miles or so."

"A few miles?" he queried, receiving a shrug.

"You know, Yvette," Charmaine interjected, "if you place the opening to your ear, you'll be able to hear the sound of waves crashing upon the shore."

"Now why would I do that when I'm standing right here and can hear them without some stupid old shell?"

John chuckled. "You were gone all that time and only collected one shell?"

Yvette turned a triumphant smile upon Jeannette. "See? I told you he'd ask that question!" She produced a badly battered chalice that she had concealed in the folds of her frock. "This is the real treasure we found!" she bragged, handing him the tarnished item. "Isn't it magnificent?"

"Yes," he agreed as he studied it, the encrusted jewels sparkling in the sun. "Where did you find it?"

"Over by the reef. It was buried in the sand, but I saw something shining, so I decided to investigate. Do you think it's valuable?"

"Valuable? Why, this may be the Holy Grail itself!"

"John," Charmaine admonished, "don't blaspheme!"

"Blaspheme?" he objected. "Mentioning the grail isn't blasphemy."

"What is the grail?" Jeannette asked.

Charmaine explained that it was the cup that Christ had used at the Last Supper, expressing her doubts that Yvette had found the genuine article.

"But is it valuable?" the girl pressed again.

"Let George have a look at it," John suggested with a chuckle. "He knows almost as much about religious artifacts as he does money. The two together should really interest him."

"Where do you suppose it came from, Johnny?" Yvette asked.

"Well now, I'm not certain, but I have a good idea."

"Really? Where?"

"It is probably a relic from the shipwreck that brought that other 'relic', Father Benito, to our shores some fifteen years ago."

"*Really?* You never told us about a shipwreck before!"

"That is because it wasn't something to brag about. If Paul and I had known whom we were dragging from the surf, we would have left him to drown. But we didn't find out that he was a priest until it was too late."

Jeannette spoke before Charmaine could protest. "You saved his life?"

"Unfortunately, yes."

Again Charmaine was on the verge of a reprimand, but what good would it do? "What about the others?" she asked instead.

"There weren't any survivors, other than Benito."

His eyes grew distant as if he could see it all before him. "It was a terrible night, fog covered the entire island, and a fierce storm was rolling in. The water was rough, the coastline invisible, the lighthouses useless. The ship crashed into the reef, probably near where Yvette found this. The town's men signaled the alert and came to the house, demanding the aid of the bondsmen. Then Father was off, forbidding us to leave the grounds. But Paul, George, and I weren't about to miss all the excitement. What did we know of devastation and loss of life? So, we sneaked out of the compound and reached the shore before most of the men. George saw him first, floating in the surf. Paul dove in before we could stop him. I knew I'd have my head handed to me if he drowned, so I plunged in after him. We dragged the body out together, fearing that we'd rescued nothing more than a corpse. We realized he was alive when he moaned. The tide washed many others to shore the next day, all dead. Very little of the wreck was recovered, until this."

He studied the chalice again and shook his head. "Benito remained on the island. Father offered him the post of chaplain, and when he recovered, he decided to stay. He wrote to his bishop in Rome and gained permission to minister to our sooty island souls."

"Humph!" Yvette snorted. "You should have let him drown."

"Yvette!" Charmaine scolded, appalled by the recalcitrant remark. She turned on John. "Do you see where your twisted gibes lead?"

"I see," he muttered, massaging his brow, "so let us drop the nasty subject."

Yvette snatched the chalice from him and put it in the picnic basket for safe keeping, declaring that she would not return it to Father Benito. If he hadn't missed it in fifteen years, then it belonged to her.

"We saw a boy swimming!" Jeannette volunteered.

"Yes," Yvette nodded, "and I wanted to join him, but Jeannette said she would tattle on me if I went in the water."

"It's a good thing, too," Charmaine said. "Proper young ladies don't swim."

"That means it's fun," Yvette rejoined scornfully. "It's unfair that *proper* young ladies are never allowed to do anything that's fun."

"Would you really like to learn to swim, Yvette?" John asked.

"Yes! Oh yes!"

"Very well then, take off your shoes and stockings and get out of your dress, but leave on your petticoats, and I'll see what I can do."

"Do you really mean to teach me?" Yvette didn't wait for her brother's affirmation. In a matter of minutes, she was standing on the blanket, barefoot and clad only in her undergarments. "Well? Let's go!" she cried. With a jump, she was off and running.

"Yvette!" Charmaine gasped. The ruse had gone too far. "Yvette, come back here! You'll ruin your petticoats and–"

"Who cares?" she called back. "We're rich! Besides, I have a hundred other ones just like it in my armoire!" She was already knee-deep in the bubbling surf of the cove, squealing as the waves slapped against her legs. She took a step further out, and Charmaine shifted uneasily and began to rise.

John stopped her. "Leave her be," he chided gently.

She looked up at him, and her eyes grew wide, for he had doffed his shirt and was now bending over to pull off his boots. "Are you serious about this?"

"Of course. Yvette will be fine. She has the good sense to wait for me."

The boots were tossed to the far side of the blanket. His socks followed, leaving him barefoot as well. Next came his belt, and to Charmaine's utter humiliation, he began working at his trouser buttons, as if he fully intended to peel them off right there, in broad daylight. "Sir!" she gasped, quickly averting her gaze, mortified by what seemed a diabolical chuckle.

"Come, Charmaine, take a look. I know you're dying to."

"I'm not!" she objected, looking to Jeannette, whose eyes were trained on him, a bewildered expression giving way to a wide smile. She pulled the girl down beside her, certain she'd die of shame. "I'll never forgive you for this!"

"For what?" he asked and, stepping before her, laughed the louder when she clamped her eyes closed. "Such modesty, even for a woman! What will you do, my Charm, when you have a husband?"

"Put your trousers back on!" she demanded. "Please!"

Crouching before her, he pried free the hands that cupped her eyes. Though they remained closed, he coaxed them open with the words, "I *have* them on."

She took in the cut-off breeches that the field workers wore, and her temper flared. "I'm sure you're quite proud of yourself, tricking me like that!"

"Perhaps, but then, I hadn't planned to. Once again, you've brought it all down upon yourself, my Charm. You concluded the worst without allowing me the chance to explain. Do you really consider me so low as to disrobe in front of my own sisters?"

"Oh yes, you had it planned," she returned, "or you wouldn't have been wearing those – those things beneath your trousers in the first place!"

"I was wearing them, yes, but not to embarrass you. I had hoped to enjoy a swim today. That's why I chose this particular spot for our picnic."

Defeated, she refused to say more.

"And you, Jeannie?" he asked. "Would you like to learn to swim, too?"

"I don't know if I should," she faltered, not wanting to cause her governess further distress. But she grew exuberant when Charmaine encouraged her to go.

"It is so warm!" Yvette shouted as they approached, standing waist deep in the surf. "And there are so many fish! Hundreds of them!"

Jeannette dashed ahead, but as the first wave lapped at her feet, she squealed and scurried toward the sand. Then, with arms raised, she danced toward her sister. John followed, and together they made their way further out, until the girls were shoulder-deep. There they commenced a splashing fight, dousing each other gleefully. When Yvette noticed that her brother's hair was still dry, she shouted: "Let's get Johnny!" and turned on him. But he dove into the next wave, resurfacing some feet away, drenched. "I'll show you!" she protested. With that, another battle ensued, the girls showering him with a salty deluge that pelted his face and stung his eyes.

"Careful, Yvette," he warned, "you're setting yourself up to get dunked!"

"Don't threaten me!" she jeered, splashing him harder, screeching when he dove for her, laughing triumphantly when she dodged him. But he continued to stalk her, and with his second lunge, she scrambled to shore, laboring against the strong undertow. "You can't catch me!" she teased, miffed when he ignored her and waded over to Jeannette instead. It wasn't long before she rejoined them.

John took them beyond the breaking waves where they could ride the undulating swells. Clinging to him, they squealed each time they were lifted and dropped, not truly swimming, but swimming all the same.

Pierre awoke to a hearty appetite and ate greedily. He gazed out at the water, and his face lit up. Standing, he pointed to his siblings. "Look!"

"Your sisters are learning to swim."

"Me too!" he declared, pulling off his shoes and socks. He ran toward the water as fast as his little legs would carry him. No sooner had he reached the shoreline and he was fleeing the bubbling surf that chased him up the beach. When the water receded, he planted himself where dry sand met wet. There he stood, mesmerized by his sisters' antics.

Yvette continued to throw water into John's face, knowing he wouldn't dunk her out there. Charmaine laughed aloud as the man sputtered and objected. She waved merrily back at Jeannette, who had spotted them at the water's edge.

When they tired of their play, John began to teach them to swim. Yvette mastered the strokes with ease, but Jeannette remained timid, clutching John repeatedly. Later, the threesome headed toward the beach, emerging from the breakers. They were soaked from head to toe, a sight to behold with tangled hair and clinging garments.

"Mademoiselle Charmaine," Jeannette heaved, "you should have come swimming, too! It was wonderful!"

"And easy!" Yvette added.

"So I see," Charmaine said, looking from the excited twins to John. He was pushing back a mop of hair from his saturated face.

"Yvette," he called, pointing to the horizon, "I think you forgot something."

With a frown, she squinted out to the water. He snatched her and dragged her back into the churning waves, swiftly dunking her under. She came up sputtering, her eyes shooting daggers that stifled Jeannette's hearty guffaw. John laughed harder. "And what was that for?" she demanded.

"Just evening up the score. Next time, you won't splash me every second."

"You make it sound like a terrible sin!"

"Do I? Well now you've been absolved." He reached heavenward. "Repent and sin no more!"

"Who do you think you are anyway – *John the Baptist?*" With that, she sloshed to shore.

Charmaine looked at John, who seemed to have met his match; he had no retort for his precocious sister. He shook his head and laughed anew. Then Yvette was forgotten as he noticed her at the water's edge, his gaze as purposeful as his approach, his bare chest glistening in the blazing sun. She looked down at Pierre, who was squatting at her feet and scribbling with his finger in the wet sand. She picked him up and faced John again, quelling the urge to step back, somewhat fortified with the boy between them.

He smiled down at the lad. "What is that in your hand, Pierre? Some hidden treasure?" The boy giggled and shook his head. "Can we see it?" John probed, poking at the pudgy knuckles.

Pierre pulled his fist away, grazing Charmaine's cheek and spilling its contents into her windblown hair. To her horror, the 'treasure' moved, scrambling to safety in her dark tresses.

"Get it out!" she shrieked, sending Pierre into a fit of laughter. She deposited him on the ground, her hands flying to her head, blindly searching for the tiny intruder, recoiling when she touched it. "Get it out!" she cried with each tug of her locks, imagining the cocoon it wove. "Please get it out!"

Now she had an audience. "What's wrong?" Yvette asked.

"Miss Ryan has just made a new friend, and he's building a nest in her hair."

"You're absolutely no help!"

"I didn't think I was permitted to touch your hair, or perhaps you've changed your mind."

"Just get it out!"

"Very well," he chuckled, "now that I have permission, let's see where our little friend has disappeared to..."

Her eyes riveted to the flex of muscle in his arm, and her stomach fluttered as he placed a palm against her temple and raked his fingers through her long hair. Those butterflies soared when his thumb caressed her cheek. "It's somewhere in the back!" she hissed, pulling away from his tormenting hand, unable to meet his eyes. He stepped behind her, working at the tangled strands on her neck, lifting and separating the thick curls, unafraid of what lie beneath.

"There it is!" Yvette directed. "See – the hair is moving!"

Charmaine groaned in misery, but in the next moment, the nasty incident was over. The twins screamed and jumped back as her unwanted 'guest' toppled out of its knotted lair, hit the sand, and scrambled to the safety of the breaking waves. It too, had had enough.

"Just a tiny sand crab," John shrugged, looking from Charmaine to Yvette. "Nothing to be frightened of."

"I wasn't frightened!" Yvette objected vehemently.

"No? Then why did you jump so high?"

"I was playing it safe."

"And now, Miss Ryan is safe as well. Delivered from one black monster..." He let his words trail off, leaving her to draw her own conclusions. "I believe I should thank you, my Charm."

"Thank me? For what?"

She received a rakish leer for an answer as he lifted Pierre into his arms. "That was not a very nice thing to do to your governess," he chided lightly.

"Yes it was!" Pierre giggled.

"Aren't you going to say you're sorry?" John probed.

"No. It was funny."

"Well then, if you're not going to apologize, you will have to be punished."

Shocked, Charmaine was momentarily anchored to the spot. John was already walking back to the blanket, where he set Pierre down. He couldn't be serious. He didn't seem angry. She rushed up the beach after them.

Yvette shook a finger at the boy. "You should have apologized while you had the chance, Pierre. Now you'll catch it!" She grinned crookedly at John, as if savoring thoughts of the boy's chastisement. "What will the treatment be?"

"The usual, of course."

Charmaine began to tremble as he bent toward the boy, intent upon carrying out his ambiguous threat. To her horror, Pierre only chortled and slapped his hand away.

"So… it's a battle you're after!" John declared, his voice bordering on the wicked. He caught Pierre in his grasp – easy prey.

"No!"

Charmaine's cry was muffled by John's proclamation: "Now I've got you!"

He sat squarely on the blanket, tucked the boy between tented legs, and began tickling him. Pierre's laughter intensified to a fevered pitch as he squirmed and writhed. But no sooner had he blocked one part of his body and another was exposed. "Stop it! Do it again!" the three-year-old cried over and over again, heaving and out of breath. He finally managed to roll beneath John's knees and crawl to safety. Exhausted, John did not pursue him.

"Now I get the punishment!" Jeannette exclaimed, stepping forward.

"Only those who've offended Miss Ryan get the punishment."

"Let's all tickle Johnny then!" Yvette suggested. "He's offended Mademoiselle Charmaine lots of times!"

The girls fell on him, pressing the battle. He met their onslaught with one of his own, pinning and tickling each in turn. Recovered, Pierre attempted to join in, but was unable to penetrate the melee. He devised his own plan of attack, scooping up sand and dumping it on John's head. When he delivered a second load, John tore away and stood up. "Good God!" he complained, raking his fingers through his matted hair. "My head feels like an ant hill."

Charmaine's happy laughter drew him around. "You find this amusing?" he asked, sand still clinging to the wet strands.

"You laughed when he put a sand crab in my hair!"

"True, but I also attempted to coax an apology out of him. What's your excuse for not intervening?"

"I have no excuse. I believe you've gotten exactly what you deserve." She threw him a mischievous look.

"That is a most offending statement if ever I've heard one," he mused. "Don't you agree, girls? I think Miss Ryan deserves the punishment."

"Oh, no!" Yvette reproved. "That's only fun for you!"

John missed Charmaine's blush as he regarded his sister in astonishment. "Fun for me?" he inquired tactlessly. "And how would you know that?"

"Because I've had experience."

"Experience?" John reiterated facetiously. "With whom? Joseph?"

"No, not with Joseph. Not with anybody. But I have eyes and ears. I know when things are happening."

"Oh really? And you've seen and heard these 'things' first hand?"

"That's right," she nodded haughtily.

"When?"

"When we were alone in our rooms about a year ago – the week before Mademoiselle Charmaine came to live with us."

"Really? And what exactly happened?"

"Mama had just left us. She had one of those long appointments with Dr. Blackford. He kept coming to the house... at least once a week. And each time he left, Mama seemed worse. She kept saying he was helping her with his elixirs, but I didn't believe that. I knew she wasn't telling us the truth, and I was worried, so I decided to find out for myself. I told Jeannette to tell anybody who came to our room that I had gone to the privy. That way I'd have time for my spy mission. First, I ran to the kitchen, and I got a glass from the cupboard – the one that picks up the sound best. Then I–"

"Yvette," John interrupted, "what are you talking about?"

"Let me finish!" she huffed. "Since it was too risky to listen from the hallway, especially with Auntie Agatha patrolling the house, I decided to use Paul's room. That spot would be perfect, because the wall of his bedchamber meets Mama's dressing room wall, and I figured Paul wouldn't be home since it was the middle of the afternoon. Well, was *I* wrong! Not only was he home, but he was *in* his room, and he wasn't alone, either. That rude maid Felicia was with him, and she was only wearing her chemise. At first I was surprised, so I just stood at the bedroom door and watched. She was laughing because he was tickling her. Then, he pulled her real close and bit her neck like a vampire."

Mortified, Charmaine suffered through the narrative, certain that her burning cheeks branded her the fool, and that John basked in the heat of her misery.

"Oh, it was disgusting!" Yvette continued. "And I told them so. I suppose I should have tiptoed out of the room, or better still, hid and watched, but I didn't think of that until much later."

John burst into uproarious laughter, imagining his brother's stunned surprise when he was caught red-handed in Felicia's buxom embrace, his rapacious appetite whetted, but not satiated.

"What's the matter?" Yvette demanded, sure that he was laughing at her.

"Nothing, Yvette," he breathed, "just continue the story; I'd very much like to hear how Paul extricated himself from this one." He continued to snicker and shake his head, vivid images of the man's volatile temper coming to the fore.

"Well, I don't have to tell you how angry he was!" she elaborated, confirming John's thoughts. "In fact, I've never seen him so angry! First, he chased me around the room a couple of times–"

"Don't flower it up, Yvette. Just tell me what happened. That's all I want."

"All right. He did cuss something fierce... words I've never heard before, not even on the docks. I tried to remember them all, and even Joseph didn't know what some of them meant. Anyway, I knew that I was in *real* trouble, and if I wanted to stay alive, I had better get out of that room. So, as he grabbed his shirt, I ran out as fast as I could and raced down the stairs. But he was behind me before I could hide. Was I glad when Auntie Agatha walked into the foyer with a tray of food! I ducked behind her, and Paul stopped in his tracks when he realized that I'd been rescued."

"Rescued?"

"Well, I'm not stupid," Yvette declared. "I knew that Paul didn't want *her* to know what he was doing. He didn't want anybody to know, so before he could say a word, I just mentioned Felicia's name. Then he told Auntie that I'd gotten into some 'mischief' in his room and that he was taking me back to the nursery. Once we were alone, he gave me a hard shake and warned me never to tell anyone what I had seen. He even threatened me with a spanking. But I only glared at him and promised nothing. After all, what could he really do? I suppose I'm still safe, even though I've told you."

"Unbelievable," John muttered, laughing all over again. "You seem to have a knack for uncovering the inconceivable, Yvette, and your story couldn't have come at a better time."

"Why is that?"

"Miss Ryan and I were discussing a similar matter on our ride here this morning. Isn't that right, my Charm?" he insisted, humiliating her all the more. "That is about as concrete as evidence gets."

"What do you mean?"

"Never mind. Oh, what I would have paid to have seen his face."

"I could do it again," Yvette offered, "and you could wait outside his room. How much are you willing to pay?"

"No, dear sister, I'm afraid I'll have to decline."

"I'll give you a discount if you listen carefully for all the swear words and tell me what they mean."

"I think not," he said, as he walked around the blanket and retrieved his clothing. "Your vocabulary is diverse enough."

"Huh! You're just afraid that he'll say words you don't know!"

"You are probably right, Yvette," he answered. "But I hope that was the last time you went into Paul's room to eavesdrop."

"Don't worry, the next time I used the back staircase that opens right into Mama's old bedroom. But Doctor Blackford didn't say anything interesting, so I never tried again."

Charmaine's utter shock gave way to acute disapproval. "Well, young lady, I will be keeping a better eye on you from now on."

Yvette looked at her askance, smiling when she received another soft chuckle from her older brother.

Ignoring him, Charmaine directed the twins to slip out of their wet undergarments. Yvette protested, begging to go back into the surf, but John responded with a firm 'no', saying that the sea was unusually rough, the cove unnaturally turbulent, and that a storm was likely brewing. A second swimming lesson would have to wait for another day.

Charmaine turned from them and bent low to Pierre, who had been tugging incessantly at her skirts to gain her attention. "What is it, my little man?"

"I need to go potty!" he insisted.

She hadn't thought to ask him about such necessities and realized that she, too, was in need of such an accommodation. But before she could usher him to the seclusion of the brush, John intervened. "Let me take him."

"No, it's all right. He needs to... relieve himself."

"And I have similar business to attend to. Please, let me take him."

Realizing that John's absence would allow her to see to her own needs, she agreed, and he and Pierre disappeared into the woods.

The bedraggled girls wiggled out of their wet petticoats, giggling when they realized that they'd be wearing very little beneath their dresses for the remainder of the afternoon. Charmaine slipped away, glad to find them working out the knots in their tangled hair when she returned.

John reappeared, fully dressed, with Pierre riding upon his shoulders. The three-year-old laughed hysterically when the man broke into a trot, bouncing him higher. "Guess what, Mainie?" he said when John set him at her feet. "Johnny has a really big–"

John's hand clamped over Pierre's mouth, muffling the remark. Frowning, Charmaine looked up at the man, his reaction as baffling as his crimson face. Then she understood, and a mixture of discomfiture and amusement washed over her. She'd never seen John embarrassed before, and a part of her longed to laugh out loud, but when he hoisted Pierre high in his arms again and whispered in his ear, "I told you not to say that," she turned away.

For the next half-hour, Pierre squealed as the foamy waves trickled over his feet. Charmaine had taken off her shoes and stockings as well and stood in the shallow surf, enjoying the cool water lapping around her ankles. It was as if it were washing away the pain of the past, replacing it with warm memories. Her mother's presence was very strong, not in sorrow, but in contentment. Once, when she was a child, they had visited an aging friend who resided near the ocean. During that month, she and her mother had spent hours on the beach, enjoying a tranquil respite from their harsh life.

Presently, she looked up to the azure sky. Thick clouds were moving in from the southeast. A gull circled high above the water, its wings outstretched, gliding effortlessly. A battering gale sent it careening toward the water in a screaming dive. The bird was inches from the surface when another gust catapulted it upward. It flapped its wings vigorously and finally reclaimed its lofty flight, soaring out to sea. So near disaster, a brush with death.

Death. Charmaine thought of her mother again, but now she dwelled on the memory of her demise, those miserable days when her mother lie unconscious before finally passing away. Death. She remembered Colette and those anxious days when everyone was praying and hoping for a miracle. Death. With growing unease, Charmaine feared it stalked her still, the gull a tenebrous warning that it wasn't yet satisfied and would take charge of her life again.

"Charmaine?" John's gentle voice brought her around. "You were awfully far away. Richmond, perhaps?"

"Yes, Richmond," she nodded.

"It is difficult to forget the past," he said, as if he understood her deepest insecurities. Odd how he had read her mind. He was holding Pierre against his chest, and she found she liked the combination. Her mother's presence grew strong again, washing away her anxiety.

As they turned back to the blanket, she noticed the twins were missing. "Where are the girls?"

"They ran off into the woods. They promised to return shortly."

"The woods? *My God!* What about the rattlesnakes?"

"Snakes?" John asked, and then, "Good God! How could I have forgotten!" His hand went to his chest and his brow creased in a show of concern, yet he made no move to find them.

Dismayed, Charmaine dashed up the beach. John raced after her, wearing a wide grin now, finally catching up and grabbing her arm.

"How can you laugh? I've just this minute had a premonition!"

"Charmaine," he said when she tried to wrench free, "there are no snakes."

The struggle ceased. Still, he held her. "What?"

"There are no snakes, rattlers or otherwise. I fabricated the story to get you back on the mare."

She twisted free with an irascible snarl. "*You lied?* I can't believe it! I can't believe you would go to such lengths to get me to ride!"

He chuckled deeply. "Ah, Charmaine, you can't begin to imagine the lengths I've gone to. And if they could get you to ride, it would be worth the retribution of a thousand lies."

"Oh, you crude, dirty-minded–"

Unexpected thunder muted her barrage of insults, and the amusement faded from John's face. He had dismissed the episode, his eyes on the inky sky, leaving Charmaine to fume all the more. But the next rumbling report caught her attention, too. The gathering clouds had darkened considerably.

"Pack up the food while I fetch the horses," he directed as he turned toward the woods. "This storm is moving in rapidly. The sky was clear a half-hour ago."

"What about the girls?"

"They hear it, too," he called over his shoulder, "they'll be back shortly."

"But Yvette's not frightened by thunder!"

"I'll lay money down that she's running faster than Jeannette when they come out of the woods."

Charmaine hurried back to Pierre, who continued to play contentedly in the sand. She dusted him off, carried him over to the blanket, and quickly slipped on his stockings and shoes. She did the same for herself, then gathered up the remnants of their picnic.

Just as predicted, the girls appeared, racing up the beach. Another shudder shook the heavy air. Yvette turned a worried eye to the sky. "I think it's going to be a bad one," she whispered.

John returned with all four animals, and they quickly mounted and headed back the way they had come. Although they took the same route, everything was silent and menacingly still. Not a leaf rustled, nor a branch bowed.

On the main road, the skies to the southeast were black, dense and churning. The winds picked up, buffeting them with gusts that caught at their hair and unfurled the horses' manes. Day was ahead of them, behind them, a vision of night. Thunder shook the air again, and the twins squealed in delight. The horses were agitated, flicking back their ears and whinnying loudly. Pierre squinted closed his eyes. In growing trepidation, Charmaine's regard shifted to John, whose attention was on the sky, often looking over his shoulder. Her apprehension heightened when he shook his head.

Two riders approached at full gallop, and in a matter of seconds, Paul and George were reining in their steeds. Paul leaned forward to speak to John, his eyes cutting away from Charmaine and her disheveled appearance, her windswept hair. "I'm glad you're on your way back. It's a hurricane, and by the look of it, a bad one."

"I just got in from town," George said, "the Raven laid anchor not two hours ago. Jonah Wilkinson outraced the storm by forty leagues or so. We had trouble mooring her. The ocean is very rough."

"George is going to the mill," Paul continued, "and I'm headed into town to batten down the smaller ships and secure the quay. Can you come along?"

Charmaine braced herself for John's response. "What of the house?"

"Travis and Gerald are seeing to it. I need your help more than they do."

"Very well," John replied.

Another shaft of lightning and the horses whinnied again, pawing at the dirt, a crack of thunder and they shook their heads, prancing in place.

"But what about the children and me?" Charmaine protested.

"You're to go back to the house," Paul directed.

"Just follow the road," John added gently.

"*But what if the horses panic?*"

John read the fear in her eyes and turned to George. "Can you go with them before you head to the mill? That way I can help Paul."

George nodded and took Pierre from John's lap. Then they were off: John and Paul at a breakneck gallop for town, Charmaine, George, and the children at a quickened pace for home.

They reached the safety of the portico none too soon, pelted by pebbles and twigs hurled on high winds. Even the branches of the great oaks bent to nature's will, their boughs dipping close to the ground. At the far end of the colonnade, two stable-hands labored to nail the shutters closed.

Travis Thornfield greeted them in the foyer. He stood erect like some sentry guarding his post. His normally stoic face was set in lines of concern. "We have six men securing the windows," he said. "Once they're finished, the very heavens may break open, and we will be prepared for it."

"Good," George nodded.

"Is it truly a hurricane?" Yvette asked, eyes dilated with fearless excitement.

"By all outward signs, yes, it is a hurricane," George confirmed soberly.

"Oh, good!" she piped with pleasure. "The house is sure to rumble tonight, and Cookie will be telling her stories!" She recounted the superstitious tales and severe damage sustained during the last hurricane, which had hit Charmantes a year prior to Charmaine's arrival.

"Are such storms really that destructive?" Charmaine asked, disquieted by Yvette's disturbing description. "Surely this one won't cause injury?"

"Charmaine," George soothed, "they can be very bad, but not always. All we can do is wait and pray that it doesn't hit us directly."

"But Paul – and John – they're still out there!"

"They have plenty of time to secure the island before the worst of it arrives. Remember, they were born and raised here. They know how to deal with a hurricane. Now, I have to get to the mill. I'll be back as soon as I can."

Despite George's reassurance, Charmaine remained worried. It was best to focus on other things, so she ushered the children upstairs for baths and fresh attire. The bedchamber was so dark that she had to light the lamps.

She bathed Pierre first. He was very nervous and reached for her each time the wind howled or the thunder rumbled. "Let us talk about our day," she cajoled, certain that if she could take his mind off the storm, he'd relax. "What was the best part of our picnic?"

"Ridin' on Johnny's horse," he said with a timid smile, allowing her to strip off his clothing. His gaze traveled up from the floor, his cheeks puffed up in the widest of grins. She smiled in return. Her ploy was working. "Now I know what that's called, Mainie," he declared, pointing to his crotch. "Johnny told me. It's a penis." Charmaine's smile vanished.

"What did he say?" Yvette asked.

"Nothing," Charmaine scolded. "He said nothing."

She quickly turned back to the boy. "That word is very private, Pierre. You mustn't say it again."

"Why?"

"Because it is impolite to talk about. Do you understand?"

"What did he say?" Yvette persisted.

"He is not repeating it. Are you Pierre?"

He obediently shook his head 'no', and the matter was put to rest.

The girls had just finished their baths and were brushing out their wet hair when Travis Thornfield appeared at their door. "Your father would like to see you in his chambers," he told them.

Charmaine's face paled, but Jeannette hugged her with a happy smile. "Papa probably has a present for us." Charmaine wasn't so sure. She hadn't even thought of Frederic this morning and felt ashamed that, without a word, she had whisked his children away for the day. Last year, he had specifically set aside time for them. Memories of that first encounter still disturbed her, but that was no excuse for not bringing them to his chambers for a visit. Would he be angry that they had spent the entire day with their older brother – that their governess had agreed to the excursion without his permission?

A short while later, they were sitting in the man's antechamber, and to Charmaine's chagrin, the girls immediately dove into a recounting of their most adventurous of birthdays. "We even learned to swim!" Yvette finished.

Frederic nodded, his eyes intense. "I gather you had a nice time then?"

"It was fun!" Pierre replied blithely. "I got to ride on a great big horse!"

Frederic smiled down at the boy who sat in his lap, and Charmaine breathed easier. It was the first sign that he wasn't upset. "And you weren't frightened?"

"Oh no, Johnny was holdin' me tight."

"Johnny?"

"Uh-huh," Pierre nodded. "I love him, Papa," he went on in earnest, hugging the man to emphasize his simple declaration. "I'm glad he came home."

Frederic's eyes turned sad and distant.

Yvette spoke across his thoughts. "Those ponies are the best presents we've ever gotten!"

"Yes, I suppose they are," he replied. He smiled again, a mechanical smile by Charmaine's estimation, and she wondered over his sudden melancholy. "I've something for you as well, but I'm afraid it is nothing as grand as your ponies."

"What is it?" Jeannette asked.

"If you look over there in that basket," he answered, nodding toward a corner of the room, "you'll see."

The two girls quickly crossed the chamber, and finding the furry bundles snuggled together, they began to 'ooh' and 'ah' over them. Pierre quickly jumped from his father's lap and scampered over to his sisters. In the next moment, the kittens were lifted from the basket and tucked under each girl's arm. "Look, Pierre," Jeannette said as she sat on the floor, "a kitten."

"He's so soft!" Pierre observed once he'd stroked the marmalade fur.

The small animal began to purr, and Pierre's eyes grew wide in wonderment. "What's that noise?"

"He's purring," his sister explained. "It means he likes you."

"It means *she* likes you," her father corrected. "Millie tells me that both cats are female."

Jeannette smiled brightly. "Sit down, Pierre, and I'll let you hold her."

He complied, and she placed the kitten in his lap. He giggled uncontrollably as the orange tabby circled once and twice, then jumped from his embrace. It was time to play, and Yvette's kitten also struggled to be free. In the next moment, the two balls of fur were scooting across the room, wiggling their bottoms and hunching their backs before pouncing upon one another. Then they were wrestling and tumbling, swiftly springing apart to begin the fray all over again, eliciting everyone's laughter. The children drew their happiness from the kittens, Charmaine and Frederic, from their carefree glee, the storm forgotten.

Yvette crossed to her father and threw an arm around his shoulders. "You're right, Papa, they're not as good as the ponies, but they are a lot better than the dolls you gave us last year."

Frederic gave her a fierce hug. "You are a wonder, Yvette."

She moved away, and Jeannette took her place. "I love them just as much as the ponies," she offered sincerely, bestowing a kiss. "Thank you, Papa."

Pierre said nothing. He was mesmerized by the feline's antics and giggled each time they darted from behind a chair and scurried across the floor.

They returned to the nursery, the kittens sound asleep in their basket. Pierre took heed; no sooner had he settled on his bed and his heavy eyes closed, oblivious to the howling hurricane.

With nothing to do, the girls insisted on resuming their treasure hunt. Charmaine agreed – Pierre slept blissfully – and so, they headed downstairs, the girls in search of their remaining gifts, Charmaine, a cup of tea.

As they reached the foyer, George dashed inside, drenched. "The mill's secured," he said with a shiver. "How are you faring?"

"Glad that I'm not out there," Charmaine replied. "Is the storm very bad?"

"It's bad, but the worst is yet to come."

"Surely it can't be any worse than what we've already heard?"

"This is only the edge of it. It *will* get worse and last the whole night. I'm soaked and need a good hot cup of tea."

"I was just going to get a cup myself."

"Let me join you then, as soon as I change into dry clothing."

George returned just as she was pouring hot water from the teakettle Fatima had set on the dining room table.

"Still nervous?" he asked, taking the chair across from her.

"Yes. I hate these storms. They were never like this in Virginia. When I see how unaffected the twins are, I feel like a ninny. Will I ever get used to them?"

"No one gets used to them, Charmaine. I've lived here all my life, and even I get the jitters."

She smiled gratefully. "How long does it take to secure the harbor?"

"That depends. But if you're still worried about Paul, you needn't be. With such a lovely lady here to fret over him, he'll be eager to return safe and sound."

She bowed her head with his compliment.

"Besides," he went on, "John is there to lend a hand."

"Will he – lend a hand?" Charmaine asked dubiously.

"Of course he will," George said, brow knitted. "Don't you believe me?"

She only shrugged, belatedly realizing that she had offended him.

"That's hardly an answer, Charmaine."

"I'm sorry, but I've seen them together. You can't deny that there's little love lost there. Surely you can understand my reservations."

George put his teacup down. "There has always been a rivalry between them. It goes back a long way, even to when we were boys."

"Yes, and John never misses an opportunity to make Paul angry."

"It works both ways," he replied gruffly.

"What do you mean?"

"Paul does his share of provoking, only it's harder to see."

"Don't tell me that John has won you over to his side?" she rejoined.

"There are no sides, Charmaine. I've known them for as long as I can remember. They are brothers to me. I also know what motivates them." He read the confusion on her face, and expounded. "When we were growing up, they vied for their father's approval, but that approval *always* weighed in on Paul's side."

Charmaine was not swayed. "And I can understand why a father would favor a son who is well behaved over one who is bad mannered."

George shook his head. "Frederic was downright mean to John. So, imagine how John felt when he watched his father's *adopted* son claim that man's love, while day after day, week after week, year after year, he, the legitimate son, came up empty-handed. Perhaps then you can understand his cynicism."

Perturbed by the revelation, Charmaine had no rebuttal.

"Even so, I know that John does not hate Paul for it, and I *know* that he would come to Paul's aid if he were in jeopardy. And Paul would do the same for John. You might not believe this, but there was a time when they were close, all three of us, we were *very* close."

"So why the fighting now?"

"Most of it is not as serious as you think. You've seen enough of John to know that he's a mischief-maker, and Paul is his favorite target because he takes everything so seriously, always rising to the bait. Most of their quibbling doesn't go any deeper than that."

The late afternoon wore on, and the family gathered in the dimly lit drawing room. Suddenly, there was a commotion in the foyer, a whistling whoosh and the heavy thud of the main door slamming shut against the elements. Charmaine and the twins raced to the archway, followed closely by George. There stood a badly beaten, but laughing, John, who was saturated from head to toe in exact replica of the night he arrived home. The only thing missing was his cap.

"What happened?" Yvette demanded.

"Where is Paul?" Charmaine added.

The door banged open again, and Paul stumbled in, fighting to secure it behind him. He was equally battered, but was laughing as well.

"What happened?" Yvette echoed.

"Johnny tried to moor a dinghy on his own and took a little dive in the harbor instead!" Paul chortled. "Why you didn't wait for me, I'll never know."

"I did," John replied, his guffaws louder than his brother's, "in the water. It was worth staying under just to get you to jump in after me."

Paul grunted jovially. "I should have left you there, but I care too much."

"If you had really cared, you would have retrieved my cap," John objected facetiously. "I've lost it because of my tomfoolery."

"Well worth the swim, dear brother," Paul snickered, slapping John across the back, "well worth the swim."

"The second one I've had today, only this time I had all my clothes on. I should have brought some soap along."

Paul stopped laughing, and the smile froze on his lips. "Funny, but I didn't know you were so fastidious about washing, John. I always thought your tastes ran toward the tainted and soiled."

"Tastes can change," John quipped.

Paul didn't respond, his clenched jaw twitching, his hardened eyes on Charmaine. He stalked off, taking the stairs two at a time. The assembly stood in awkward silence, flinching with the slamming of his chamber door.

John shrugged. "I suppose all good things must come to an end."

"Especially when you ruin them!" Charmaine blurted out. "You said that on purpose!"

"Actually, it was quite spontaneous, my Charm."

Furious now, she took a threatening step forward. "Oh! If you call me that – that – *stupid* name one more time, I'll – I'll–"

"You will what, *my Charm*?" John pressed, stressing the endearment as he, too, advanced.

"Oh, just leave me alone!" she cried, whirling on her heel and sidestepping George, who eagerly retreated, and the twins who stood their ground, snickering.

John pursued her up the stairs, entertained by her fiery temper. "You should be glad I call you 'my Charm'," he proceeded to explain. "It's very individual, you see. Not at all like the standard 'y' or 'ie' endings that I usually employ. Nothing so common as Paulie, or Auntie, or even Cookie."

Charmaine bit her tongue, determined to say nothing as she reached the crest of the staircase. Raising a hand, she purposefully pushed him aside. With her path cleared, she strode briskly toward her bedchamber door.

Still, he trekked after her. "I had considered an 'ie' ending," he mused, "but, I didn't think 'Charmainie' had quite the right ring to it. For Pierre, 'Charmainie' might be fine, but for *me*, well, it just wouldn't do. What do you think?"

She turned on him to deliver one last retort when their eyes locked. He stood there, soaked to the skin, yet he was smiling, his hands folded behind his back, as if he were the most respectable gentleman come to call on his lady. Unmindful of where her anger had fled, she only knew the absurdity of the situation and the ridiculous dilemma he wished to resolve.

"Well?" he asked. "Will it be 'my Charm' or 'Charmainie'?"

She answered with a genuine giggle that ended in a soft smile.

"There now," he nodded, "you're not so very angry after all."

He stepped closer, the flickering lamplight of the wall sconces dancing in his amber-brown eyes. His fingers raised to her cheek and brushed aside a stray lock of hair. Her stomach lurched at the contact and she broke away. His hand remained suspended momentarily, as if to lure her back.

"I – have to check Pierre," she said and headed toward the nursery.

Again John followed her. "He's all right, isn't he?"

"Yes," she whispered as she opened the door and tiptoed in. "He has been napping for nearly two hours now."

At the sound of her voice, Pierre sat up in bed and rubbed his bleary eyes.

"So, you're not asleep," she greeted affectionately, sitting beside him and giving him a hug. He yawned and shook his head. Charmaine looked up at John and found his admiring regard fixed on the boy.

The moment was broken by Yvette's loud entrance. "Cookie told me to inform you that dinner will be served at the usual hour of seven."

Pots and dishes clattered in the kitchen, but for all the ruckus, dinner had yet to be served. Agatha pursed her lips and reserved comment, raising a winged brow in a show of impatience. Two chairs remained unoccupied. John was always late, but Charmaine fretted over Paul's unprecedented tardiness. Would he hold his brother's knavish remark about swimming against her?

"So, Miss Ryan," Agatha commented. "I've been told that you took the children on a picnic today."

Charmaine regarded her warily. Though the query seemed innocent enough, the woman never addressed her without a hidden agenda.

"Did you have a pleasant day?" she pursued.

"Yes, we did," Charmaine answered simply, hoping to end the discourse.

"And my nephew, John – he accompanied you?"

"He purchased ponies for the girls' birthday. The picnic was his idea."

"I see," Agatha replied. "So, how did you spend all those hours *alone*?"

"We weren't alone," Charmaine responded sharply, the insinuation clear. "We were minding three children."

"I'd hardly term them qualified chaperones, Miss Ryan. For all we know, you could have deposited them anywhere on the island and then…" She artfully let her words drop off.

Seething, Charmaine retaliated impetuously. "Oh dear, you've found us out. We dumped the children in the woods and passed the afternoon in one another's embrace. Does that clarify the day's events to your liking, Mrs. Duvoisin?"

The mistress gasped, her slackened jaw falling further open in unadulterated revulsion. But the rest of the diners chortled, their glee led foremost by George.

Charmaine instantly regretted the sullied remark. *What was she thinking? Dear God, the ramifications!* She blushed profusely and quickly bowed her head. When the merriment subsided, she took courage to look at George, whose eyes applauded her. Just as she smiled in return, John entered the room, humming.

Though informally dressed, his attire was respectable once again, with finely tailored shirt and trousers that highlighted each masculine angle. His hair was wet, but neatly combed, curling deviously over his sideburns and collar. He threw Jeannette a wink as he took his seat.

Footsteps resounded in the hallway and Paul walked into the room. Her heart skipped a beat with the handsome figure he cut. Like John, his hair was still wet and combed in place, save one glossy black lock that fell on his forehead. His jaw remained set, his brow creased. As he stepped up to the table, Charmaine admired the crisp dinner jacket, white shirt and black trousers he wore, the fabric catching against the well-toned muscles in his legs. She averted her gaze to John, certain that he watched her, but he was staring up at Paul.

"Take your feet off my chair," Paul growled.

John abruptly sat up, snickering.

When Paul was seated, Agatha addressed her nephew. "I have been informed that you spent the day with Miss Ryan."

"Informed?" John asked lightly. "To be informed, one must have an informant. Who would that be, Auntie dear?"

"Rose."

"Ah..." John nodded. "And I'm sure Rose also told you that I was spending the day with the children and that their governess accompanied us to assist in their care. So, why are you insinuating that I spent the day *only* with Miss Ryan?"

George's chuckle snagged his attention. "Did I say something funny?" he asked, receiving from his friend a shake of the head.

"I know why he's laughing," Yvette spoke up, her smug smile fading when she caught Charmaine's harsh glare.

George opened his mouth, but a bellowed: *"Ouch!"* was all that came out. He reached under the table and rubbed the shin that Charmaine had kicked.

John regarded her next. But she wore the same innocent expression that he so often employed when making mischief. Something was definitely brewing here.

Pierre's small voice came from out of nowhere. "We went on a picnic, and Mainie said you dumped us in the woods–"

"–and then you spent the afternoon in each other's embrace," Yvette piped in, eager to be the one to divulge the juicy information.

John's eyes shot to his sister. "*Mademoiselle Ryan said that?*"

When he looked to Charmaine for confirmation, he caught Paul's steely eyes on him. The topic was too hot to drop, and he couldn't restrain himself. He leaned across the table and, to Charmaine's utter shame, clasped her hand much as a lover might. "I always fancied our little tryst a secret, my Charm," he murmured, "something just between the two of us, a–"

"Steady, John," George interceded, ending the amorous pledge; Paul could be pushed just so far. "Charmaine was only engaging in a bit of humor. Surely, she's allowed an innocent gibe now and then?"

"I'll gibe with her whenever she likes," John responded with a wicked chuckle, his eyes never leaving Charmaine's bowed head.

"And guess what Jawj?"

Pierre, having enjoyed his moment's attention, spoke enthusiastically. Grateful for the distraction, George regarded the boy. "What is it, Pierre?"

"Johnny has a *big* penis! And mine's gonna be that big someday, too!"

"Good Lord!" Agatha squawked. "Of all the scurrilous comments!"

Charmaine hid her face behind a trembling hand, wishing that there were a hole nearby. Crawling into it would have been preferable to enduring Agatha's gasps of outrage, Paul's fists striking the table beside her, George's uproarious laughter, or Yvette's declaration: "So that's what Mademoiselle Charmaine told you not to talk about!" John's merry: "There's no substitute for a positive outlook," didn't help matters. There was nothing to do but remain mute and allow the humiliating hullabaloo to die down.

Dinner was served, but it was consumed in relative silence. Paul did not speak at all, and Charmaine dared not look his way. She prayed that when he calmed down, he'd accept her remark as nothing more than a joke. As for Pierre, surely he could comprehend what had happened there. Still, his rigid form bespoke a man who was beyond angry. So, tonight, he, and not John, perpetrated a quiet misery.

As dessert was served, he pushed away from the table, declining the cup of coffee that Felicia offered him. Charmaine's stomach twisted as she looked up at him, chilled by his curt manner. "I would have a word with you privately, Miss Ryan." When she moved to stand, he halted her. "Later."

She felt like a scolded child and lowered her gaze, avoiding eye contact with everyone, especially John.

Paul had been gone all of a minute when Fatima presented a huge cake to the twins. "Happy birthday Miss Yvette and Miss Jeannette. I made your favorite just for you." She placed it in front of the girls and began slicing it. "Oh, no you don't, Miss Yvette," she scolded, "Mastah John gets the first piece."

"John gets the first piece?" Charmaine reiterated in annoyance.

John leaned forward. "I have to taste everything that leaves Cookie's kitchen. Poison, you see."

The twins giggled, but Charmaine was not amused. "A very clever excuse, but the girls should be served before you. It is *their* birthday." The twins giggled again, and she grew befuddled.

"Tomorrow is Johnny's birthday," Jeannette explained. "Whenever he comes home, we celebrate the two days together. Didn't you know that?"

"No, I didn't know," she replied, looking back to John. "Is tomorrow really your birthday?"

"Yes, tomorrow is really my birthday."

"Why didn't you tell me? We spent this whole day together, and you never said a thing."

"Why should I have?'

"Because, I would have wanted to know."

"Why? Were you planning on giving me a gift?" he quipped. "I know how eager you would have been to choose something special."

"I would have at least liked to wish you well," she answered feebly.

He didn't believe her, his visible skepticism aggravating the awkward moment. Self-conscious now, she babbled on. "I can't believe that no one mentioned it in preparation for tomorrow."

"Preparation?" John asked. "What preparation?"

"To celebrate – as we do with everyone else in this household."

"Jeannette has already told you that we combine the two days. I'm a big boy now, Miss Ryan, further celebration is not necessary."

For the first time that evening, he seemed disturbed, heightening her confusion. Unwisely, she did not let the matter rest. Had she looked to Rose or George, she would have bitten her tongue. "But a piece of cake is hardly a celebration."

"My birth is not a celebrated event in this house," he said in a low voice. "More important than marking the day I entered this world, it marks the date my mother passed from it. Therefore, my father has never permitted any type of festivity, birthday or no."

"But that's – that's ridiculous," Charmaine sputtered, stunned by his stolid declaration. "Your birthday was *never* celebrated?"

"No," he replied coldly. "To commemorate such a day would have been nothing less than blasphemy. You see, my father holds her memory *sacred*."

She was incredulous, her heart tied in a painful knot. She took in Rose's bowed head and George's grim face. Only Agatha remained indifferent, her shoulders thrown back, chin jutting in the air.

As everyone began to eat, Charmaine studied John again. He seemed to have dismissed the conversation. Or was he concealing his anguish behind a mask of apathy?

Charmaine preceded Paul into the study. He closed the door, crossed his arms and legs, and leaned one shoulder into the panel as if guarding against possible escape. She had dreaded this confrontation as she waited in the children's nursery after dinner. Now she silently cursed John. He could have denied the fabricated encounter, doused the fire, but no, everything was a joke to him, and pushing the sticky situation to the limit had been so wickedly pleasant, he'd banked it instead.

Paul's face remained stern, like a father about to discipline a disobedient child. Apprehension was now a tangible thing, a demon that somersaulted inside her belly and made her ill. The lengthening silence told her that she was already condemned. Then he spoke. "I never thought I'd be forced to this, but your conduct, the example that you've set for the children, leaves me no other choice."

She was cut to the quick and could not summon the anger needed to refute his claim. Would he dismiss her? At this moment, she didn't care, for nothing, not even the loss of her position, could cause her greater pain than the censor in his eyes and the rebuke in his voice.

"Have you nothing to say?" he demanded as he pushed away from the door. "Have you no defense?"

"You leave me none!" she choked out.

"*I leave you none?* You blame me? I wasn't the one who acted improperly today, traipsing about the island with a man renowned for his debauchery. Your behavior was at best depraved!"

"*Depraved?* It was an innocent birthday picnic!"

"Come, Mademoiselle," he snorted in vexation, "don't pretend that you don't understand. You continue to ignore my warnings and allow John to use you, in front of the children – *and* – by every indication, have very much enjoyed it."

"How can you say that?" she objected. "You know I've tried to avoid him!"

"Forgive me if I no longer believe it. I'm not a fool. I've seen many a woman play your little game. But your slip of the tongue? *That* was a major blunder."

"A slip, yes!" she pleaded through tightened throat. "But you can't possibly believe that what I said actually occurred today! I swear–"

"Miss Ryan," he interrupted, "you spent the entire day in John's company."

"With the children ever present!"

"And–" he held up a hand to silence her "–did not seem to be avoiding him."

"I had no choice! He insisted that the children were my responsibility – that I must accompany them."

"Exactly. He used you – *with your consent.* You even let your hair down for him!" he declared childishly, his lips twisted in rueful triumph. "Don't think I didn't notice that bit of incriminating evidence when I met you on the road this afternoon. You needn't deny it, Charmaine, for I know that you would never have said what you said this evening if you didn't feel comfortable with my brother, *very* comfortable."

"That is not true!"

A shriek penetrated the closed doors of the nursery. When no one answered his knock, John went in. Pierre was playing the kittens in the middle of the floor, but Jeannette was in the far corner of the room, cowering, while Yvette dangled something above her head.

"Keep it away!"

"Yvette!"

The twins turned toward John's voice, and Yvette rapidly tucked her hand behind her back. "What have you got there, Yvette?" he demanded as he advanced on the girl, his eyes trained on her reddened face.

"It's only a spider," she answered, presenting the creature that wriggled lamely against a trapped leg.

"Throw it down!"

With a click of the tongue, Yvette complied.

John looked about the room. "Where is Mademoiselle Ryan?"

"Paul called her away a little while ago," Jeannette responded.

"To take her to his dungeon, no doubt," John contemplated aloud.

"Dungeon?" Jeannette queried. "Does he truly have a dungeon?"

"No, not literally, Jeannie. But when Paul gets his dander up, being cornered by him is tantamount to torture. Tonight we must act as Miss Ryan's champion."

"Champion?" Yvette asked suspiciously.

"We must rescue her from his clutches," he explained. "The question is, who would like to help me with this chivalrous endeavor?"

"I would!" Yvette volunteered excitedly. "How much do I get paid?"

"Paid? Since when do I have to pay you to help me?"

"Oh, all right, I'll help you for free."

Charmaine was near tears, certain that the worst was yet to come – that at any moment Paul would mention Pierre. "I cannot believe you are saying this to me!"

"Do you deny that he went swimming?"

"He took the twins into the water, and they were all wearing their clothes!"

Paul snorted. "I used to believe that you were the epitome of decency."

"And now you don't?" Charmaine queried in a tiny voice.

"Now I think you were playing me for an idiot! All these months I've respected your wishes, treated you as a gentleman should, have waited patiently in deference to your *innocence.* I was taken in by your professed virtue, until today. Should I have acted differently? Would you have preferred a direct attack? Is that how my brother has succeeded where I have failed?"

"What – what are you saying?"

"Don't you know? Damn it, Charmaine, I want you – have wanted you from the start. And damn you if you'd prefer to spend the day in John's embrace!"

"But I told you that didn't happen! I was angry with Agatha. She had passed innuendoes at the table, and I lashed out at her sarcastically without thinking. I swear, there is nothing between John and me! Please believe me!"

It was too much! She burst into tears.

"Damn it," he swore under his breath, his anger flagging, "don't cry. God, how I hate it when you cry." He pulled a freshly laundered handkerchief from his dinner jacket and pressed it into her hand, contrite.

Even with his change of mood, Charmaine could not stop crying.

His remorse increased. "He's done it again, hasn't he?"

"What has he done?" she heaved.

"Connived and twisted an innocent situation to his advantage. He knew his remarks would lead me to believe the worst – send me on this rampage. He counted on it. I suppose I'm no better than he." He drove his fingers through his hair. "I've asked for your forgiveness before. I do so again, though I would understand why you might not find it in your heart to pardon me."

His voice was sincere, his eyes just as earnest, and, as he grasped her shoulders, the electrified atmosphere swiftly changed.

Without warning, the door swung open, and Yvette crossed the threshold. "Mademoiselle Charmaine?" she queried in an unusually meek voice.

"Damn!" Paul swore again, oblivious to his sister's apparent distress.

Charmaine ignored the man's rekindled temper. "What is wrong, Yvette?"

"Well…" she began reluctantly as she fiddled with her fingers.

"*Well and what is it?*" Paul barked. "Let's have it out and over with!"

"Pierre had an accident!"

"An accident!" Charmaine gasped, racing halfway across the room before the girl spoke again.

"In his knickers."

"*Jesus Christ!*" Paul sneered. "And did you think that this 'accident' warranted an interruption, young lady?"

"If you were in our room you'd think so," she rejoined. "It smells something terrible up there!"

"Then you'll just have to endure the stench until your governess and I are finished. Now, return to your chambers and do not leave them again."

"But it's awfully messy up there," Yvette complained. "Jeannette tried to change Pierre's pants, but he only giggled and pulled away from her and… and…

he ran into your dressing room. He even locked the door and refuses to come out!" she added, as if on an afterthought.

"My room! What in the name of God is he doing in there?"

"Hiding I suppose."

"You suppose? *You suppose?* You have two minutes – two minutes to get him the hell out of there. Do you hear me, young lady?"

"But–"

"No buts!" he shouted. "Just do it!"

"Paul–" Charmaine interposed "–I've left them unattended for far too long. I really should return to the nursery."

"No! John is problem enough. I'll not have the pestering of a passel of brats continually trespass against my time with you."

He faced Yvette. "Go back up those stairs and get your brother out of my chambers immediately – soiled knickers and all!"

Confident that she had presented a convincing act worthy of John's praise, Yvette strutted from the volatile room. Beyond the doorway, she met him. He was fighting the urge to laugh aloud, biting down hard on a white-knuckled fist.

"You had better make it good," she warned in a whisper. "He's fit to be tied."

John subdued a last chuckle, wiped the moisture from his eyes, and rapped on the doorframe. "May I come in?" he asked with dramatic courteousness.

"What do you want?" Paul growled.

Charmaine stepped forward "I shall leave the two of you to speak privately. I must see to Pierre."

John agreed, clearly entertained. "Having just now spoken to Yvette in the hallway, I would say he is in dire need of Miss Ryan. Yvette is in quite a dither."

Paul's scowl blackened, his rancor proportionate to his brother's delight, and he fired a barrage of French expletives.

"Watch your tongue, dear boy," John warned as if shocked. "What will Miss Ryan think, since she doesn't know the language? Why, it's like talking behind her back."

"That's right, John, you just keep it up!" Paul sneered, teeth bared.

"I fully intend to."

"You lewd, despicable–"

"How despicable must I be before you storm from the room again?"

"So – you want me to leave? Is that it?"

"I want you to *leave* Miss Ryan alone," John responded. "We all know why you've cornered her this evening, demanding that you speak with her *privately.* I'd call it a brow-beating, and I decided to put an end to it."

"Since when have you become her paladin?"

"Let us just say that I've grown *fond* of her," John answered.

"Let's not. Let us get to the real point, John."

"The point, Paul, is that *you* are jealous," John replied, his voice high with merriment. "So there is no point in trying to uncover your point. Get the point?"

"Fine, John, just fine!" Paul threw up his hands and strode to the door.

"Where are you going?" Charmaine called after him, her turmoil resurrected. Everything she had believed to be reconciled was once again in the balance.

"Out!" he blazed. "To get some air!"

"But Paulie, there's a hurricane about!"

"Aye, and its company is preferable to yours!" With that, he was gone.

Charmaine turned to John. "He wouldn't really go out there, would he?"

"I wish he would," he replied flatly.

Her perturbation spiraled into fury, his cruelty solidifying every misery he'd caused her that day. *"Oh! How I despise you!"*

"Someday that will be different."

The statement seemed a promise, and she balled her fists in outrage.

He stepped in close. "Do you realize how dark your eyes become when you are angry? How the tip of your nose wiggles when you rant and rave?" He placed a forefinger on it.

She tried to swat it away, but his fingers deftly encircled her wrist, lowering and then pinning it to the small of her back. He drew her against him until their bodies met in the most agonizing of places. She pushed futilely against his chest with her free hand, turned her face aside, but he grasped her hair at the base of her neck, entwining it round his menacing fingers. Ever so slowly, he pulled her head back, dashing any hope of escape. Insidiously, he lowered his lips to hers until they touched – a gentle, teasing caress – his embrace like iron, demanding, his kiss tender, pleading. His mouth moved on to the hollow of her neck, and she could feel an intake of breath as if he were savoring her scent. She renewed her efforts to break free, stumbling back a step when he decided to release her.

"As delectable as I had imagined," he murmured.

The sentiment was not reciprocated. Charmaine's hand lashed out, but for all her swiftness, John caught her wrist again. "You weren't going to slap me, were you, my Charm? Not a very kind gift to bestow on the eve of my birthday."

Twisting away, she glared at him defiantly. "Don't ever try that again!"

"Saving yourself only for Paul, are you?"

"That's right!" she retaliated, and she rubbed her forearm viciously across her mouth, proof of her revulsion. Unmoved, his smile broadened. She gritted her teeth and marched to the doorway.

"Where are you off to, my Charm?"

"To see to the children. You've detained me from my duties long enough!"

"Duty?" he called after her. "There is none."

She came to an abrupt halt and eyed him suspiciously over her shoulder. "What do you mean, 'there is none'?"

"Duty," he reiterated. "There is no *duty* – or should I say, doo-doo? The story about Pierre was a little ruse."

"A ruse?" she asked in stupefaction.

"Yes, a ruse. Concocted to rescue you from my furious brother."

"Saved from his grasp only to fall into yours," she threw back at him.

"A brilliant observation, my Charm," he commented rakishly. "But wasn't it worth it? After all, now you have a basis for comparison."

After a brief lull, the tempest raged again. Charmaine remained in the nursery long after she tucked the children in for the night, but when they refused to settle down, she withdrew to her own room, taking Pierre with her. At the girls' insistence, she left the door open, and slowly, their chattering subsided.

Pierre was asleep in no time. Unfortunately, the arms of Morpheus evaded her. The house moaned and creaked with each ferocious gale, a mimicking reminder of all that had happened that day. Try as she might, she could not get John out of her mind: his taunting, the awkward attraction, his kiss! Her pulse quickened as she recalled his hard body pressed against hers, his lips – not displeasing – a tender caress. She had made certain that he didn't know how he had affected her. At least he could not say that she'd enjoyed it.

She chided herself for her desire to uncover the soul of the man, to figure out what made him tick. She thought about his quarrel with Paul and wondered if the whole of his waking hours were spent trapping and tormenting his opponents. But he had other sides, too. She had never known a person to display such an array of dispositions. Hate – love, and everything in between.

My birth is not a celebrated event in this house... Had Frederic truly spurned him? What happened to this family so long ago? To the adult brothers? *They were close once... very close...* And where did Colette fit in? *The mistress Colette was a very different woman than the one you have made her out to be... She should never have become Mrs. Frederic Duvoisin...*

Yes, the hatred was there, manifested in moments of apathy, bitterness, and anger. But John loved as well. This morning, Charmaine had denied his capacity for love, but she was losing stock in that axiom. He loved his younger siblings. At first she thought he sought them out to infuriate her, but she didn't believe that anymore. *They need somebody to love them.* He'd spoken those words earnestly.

She wrapped an arm around Pierre.

For all the love he'd been denied, he hadn't begrudged his sisters any. He had spent the entire day making their birthday special: from the treasure hunt, to the ponies, to his undivided attention. No wonder they loved him so much.

It seemed unfair that a piece of cake presented by the cook would be the only acknowledgment of his birthday. *They ought to reciprocate – show that they love him, too.* She quickly formulated a plan, and thus reconciled, cuddled closer to Pierre and finally slept.

The clock tolled eleven, and John rose from the desk in the study where he'd been reading through documents that Stuart Simons, his production manager in Virginia, had forwarded to him. In the hallway, he met Paul, who glared at him. Neither spoke as they strode toward the staircase, reaching it at the same time.

"After you, by all means," John invited, stepping back.

As Paul ascended the three steps to the landing, John's voice halted him. "Oh, Paul, I think you dropped this in the study earlier," and he extended a crumpled handkerchief embroidered with the initials PJD to his brother, dangling it between forefinger and thumb. Paul ripped the linen from John and shoved it into his pocket. His eyes were smoldering, but he refused to speak.

"Don't make her cry too often, Paulie. You wouldn't want to lose a gem like Charmaine."

"I don't intend to."

John's smirk infuriated Paul more than his words. "And not even your manipulation of Pierre will serve your purpose to the contrary," he added.

John's face turned turbulent for only a moment, then he was chuckling. "What's the matter, Paul? Afraid you don't *measure* up?"

"Just stay away from her," Paul sneered, "or I'll be forced to–"

"To what, Paul, inform Father that his bad boy son has turned an eye upon the governess? That can hardly hold a candle to my other, more serious, offenses."

"There are other ways to deal with you, brother," Paul enjoined, "and let that be my warning to you."

John only yawned and walked past him, mounting the north staircase. Paul ascended the opposite flight, and had just placed his hand to doorknob when John's voice cut across the stillness. "Step carefully in there. There was a terrible stench coming from beneath that door an hour ago." John chuckled again and entered his bedchamber.

It reeked of cheap perfume. Felicia reclined in his bed, an inviting smile on her lips, a blanket clasped to her bosom. She sat up, lifting her hands to the back of her neck, removing hairpins, the coverlet dropping to her waist, revealing generous breasts that were quickly veiled beneath the black mane she had loosed.

Without a word, John stepped closer, his eyes never leaving her. She shook her head, and the straight tresses scattered wildly, offering another tantalizing glimpse of her wares. When she spoke, her voice was husky. "Good evening, Master John."

He inhaled and watched as she artfully raised her hands to the base of her neck and pulled her hair up and over the pillow, exposing everything to his view. He moved closer still. "Aren't you in the wrong room, Felicia?" he demanded as he tried to ignore her seductive display. He concentrated instead on holding his anger in check, anger at himself that he was tempted to take advantage of the maid's invitation. In his younger days, he wouldn't have thought twice about it. But then, life had taught him some hard lessons, so perhaps he was learning from his mistakes.

"I was frightened by the storm," she pouted with a giggle. "I thought you would protect me."

Her reply did not soften his stern visage. Instead, his scowl deepened. He scanned the room for her clothing, finally spotting it strewn over the far chair. In three strides, he was across the chamber to retrieve it. She jumped when he flung the articles at her. "I am sorry to disappoint you, my dear," he said in a low, threatening voice, "but I'm in no mood to entertain a frightened housemaid."

"Then allow me to entertain you," she purred.

"No, Felicia. I don't settle for cheap entertainment. But Paul's room is just a short walk away. Perhaps he'd be interested. A word of warning, though: Once he's tired of a woman, he rarely invites her back to his bed."

She was stung by the truth of his words and fell mute.

"Now, I'm leaving this room for five minutes. When I return, you'd better be gone. Otherwise, I'll be forced to evict you, which might rouse the entire house. I doubt that even you could bear such humiliation."

The nursery was peaceful, punctuated only by the sound of wind, rain, and deep breathing. John stepped closer to the beds and looked down at his sisters. Next, he turned an eye toward Pierre's bed, but the soft lamplight did not penetrate that quarter of the room. He approached it carefully, and with his palm flat, he brushed over the thin coverlet, searching for a limb, a shoulder, or a tousled head. His hand came away clean. He scanned the mattress again, spanning its full length. It was empty. Alarmed, he turned back to the twins. Perhaps Pierre had settled in with one of them. But his initial impression of the sleeping arrangement was correct; his sisters slept alone.

It occurred to him that Pierre was with Charmaine. He stepped through the open doorway, relieved to discern two forms in the four-poster bed, the flickering lamplight dancing over them.

Pierre was sleeping in the bend of Charmaine's body, his back pressed against her bosom and belly. Like his sisters, his breathing verged on a snore, his mouth agape in total relaxation. Charmaine held him fast, her right arm encircling his waist possessively. Her face was expressionless, her locks, usually plaited into obedience were loose and curling over her pillow and shoulders.

She was pretty, more so than the first night he had laid eyes on her, certainly more desirable. John shook his head, now filled with the lovely vision. *Ah my Charm*, he thought, *if only you had surprised me in my bedchamber tonight. I would not have evicted you.* He studied her face: so innocent. The temptation to exchange places with the boy, to lose himself in the young woman's inviting embrace, was strong. But he wouldn't make that mistake either. Charmaine Ryan was the kind of girl a man married if he took her to his bed. But it was pleasant to dream, and fantasies didn't hurt anyone, so long as they remained fantasies.

As if she heard his thoughts, she sighed in her sleep.

Realizing just how closely he stood over them, John quietly withdrew. When he returned to his chamber, the only vestige of Felicia's presence was perfume in the air and the rumpled sheets she'd thrown on the floor.

From the moment Paul settled his weary body on the bed, he knew slumber would evade him. Tomorrow would demand more of his time in the wake of the storm, and he'd be a fool not to get some sleep tonight. But, he was haunted by a young woman's face: large dark eyes imploring his trust, trembling lips begging to be kissed, long wild tresses swirling about him. Yes, Charmaine Ryan was a temptress, an innocent, unknowing temptress. He'd been an oaf thinking she was anything else, yet she made him so damned angry when she permitted John that sweet glimpse of her vulnerability. John would only use her, hurt her.

He punched his pillow and turned onto his side. Why did it all matter so very much? Why did he lose sleep over it? He'd never lost sleep over any woman before, but then, the others had spent their nights beside him, and he had known exactly where he stood. Charmaine was different, so very different.

Odd, but in her innocence, she was more woman than those with years of experience, a woman he desperately wanted. Their aborted encounters had become increasingly painful, and though he admitted to lusting for her, he also knew that she meant more to him than the shallow housemaids whom he had previously used at leisure. Charmaine was far from shallow. She was intelligent, vivacious, and capable of reciprocating any man's passion as long as he loved her.

He tossed in the bed, uncomfortable with the word. *Love*... It had always been absent from his romantic vocabulary, a word he avoided to keep his life on an even keel, less complex. He'd seen the games a woman could play with a man's head, the lasting scars she could leave on a heart laid bare, and he wasn't eager to step into that role. Better to keep the upper hand, sample the fruit and move on.

But would a taste of Charmaine be enough? Did he want it to be enough? Where once he believed a simple conquest would vanquish his need for her, now he was uncertain, acknowledging that he would not tire of her quickly. In fact, he knew she would please him more than any of the others that had gone before. Was this then love? Somewhere deep inside, he acknowledged that possibility. But he had never been in love before; so how could he know for certain?

Then there was his brother to consider. Charmaine had become exceedingly enticing now that he had to compete for her attention. He would have seduced her the night John returned if they hadn't been interrupted. And so the game had begun. He'd lost his temper thrice this night on John's account. He would not allow it to happen again.

He was confident that Charmaine could not be attracted to the likes of John, no matter how well his brother played his hand. Sooner or later, John's pranks would push her away, and John would be forced to throw in his hand. Yes, John would definitely lose; he always did. But if he hadn't learned who would take all, Paul would oblige him with one last turn of the card. It was a game they had indulged in many times, ever since childhood, and John had never claimed the winning hand. All Paul needed to do was sit back, enjoy the spectacle his brother would make of himself, and wait for Charmaine to come running back to him. And when she did, the companionship he would offer would not require a commitment. Yes, John would unwittingly resolve all, including this gnawing fear of love and entrapment.

Friday,
September 29, 1837

Chapter 5

Charmaine's eyes fluttered open. The bedside lamp cast a glow around the nursery, but it took a full minute to realize where she was and why she had spent a part of the night in Pierre's bed. Close to three in the morning, a branch from the oak tree had crashed through the shuttered French doors of her bedchamber, rousing the entire house. Within minutes, a crowd had congregated in her room: the children, Paul, John, and George were all there, discussing what to do. Even the servants loitered in the hallway. Agatha appeared and took charge.

John grimaced. "Auntie, why don't you leave?"

"Leave?"

"Yes, leave. This bedchamber – now. The house – tomorrow. Charmantes – forever."

"*That's it!*" she shrieked. Pursing her lips, she flounced from the room.

Charmaine stifled a giggle and withdrew to the nursery, settling into bed with Pierre. She drifted off to sleep to the sounds of Paul and John removing the large branch, their discourse congenial, brotherly even.

Now, the storm was gone, and all was peaceful, slivers of morning light springing through the seams of the shuttered French doors. She snuggled deeper under the covers and closed her eyes, content. It was too early to rise. The girls were still asleep and Pierre…

She bolted upright in the bed. Pierre was not there, and the hallway door stood ajar. She flew into the corridor, pulling on her robe as she went. Everything was shrouded in darkness, save the same broken rays that sprung through the boarded up staircase windows overlooking the gardens. Another shaft of light poured from the slight crack at John's dressing room door. Charmaine moved toward it. A soft giggle confirmed her suspicions.

"Pierre, are you in there?" she whispered.

A moment's pause, and the door opened, revealing a magical elf. Pierre beamed up at her, sporting a white beard concocted of shaving lather.

"Oh Pierre! What have you gotten into?"

When she bent over to pick him up, he kissed her, and half of his moustache came away on her cheek, branding her a conspirator. The door opened entirely, and Charmaine's eyes swept upward – from stocking feet to trousers, bare chest to manly face. John was laughing down at her, his own face blanketed in white.

"Is there something you desire, my Charm?" he asked.

She straightened up quickly. "I was looking for Pierre."

"He found his way into my room, so we were using the time wisely. I'm teaching him how to shave."

"Isn't he a bit young for that?"

"You can never learn too soon." He stepped in front of the washstand, took up the straight razor, and caught her eye in the mirror. "It's a very tedious chore."

Pierre scurried after him, perching on a chair set to one side of the basin, completely absorbed with the first stroke of the razor.

"Would you return him to the nursery when you've finished?"

"Certainly," John replied, throwing a wink to the boy.

Five minutes later, Charmaine returned to the doorway. Now John was entertaining his twin sisters as well; they weren't about to miss all the fun.

"But I want to learn, too!" Yvette insisted.

"Girls don't shave," came the answer, and then: "Welcome back, Miss Ryan. I suppose you'll be demanding a lesson as well?"

"Not in shaving, thank you."

He chuckled, mumbling that there was hope for him yet.

She comprehended his meaning when his eyes traveled to the bed, and her cheeks grew warm.

"Why do you shave anyway, Johnny?" Jeannette inquired.

"Because he doesn't wanna grow a beard," Pierre answered.

"Exactly," John nodded as he cocked his head to one side and drew the razor across the remaining strip of foam, his voice distorted when he spoke. "I like my face nice and smooth for the ladies I kiss."

"You kiss ladies?" Jeannette asked, astounded.

"Once in a while – if I'm lucky."

"You like kissing them?" Yvette questioned, equally incredulous. "Do you kiss them on the lips like Paulie does?"

"On occasion," he replied, setting the razor aside and wiping his face clean.

"When was the last time?" she interrogated.

Charmaine's eyes met John's in the looking glass and her blush deepened.

"Yvette," he admonished mildly, "that is not a proper inquiry to place to any man, even your brother."

"Just answer the question. When was the last time?"

"Hmm… let me think…"

"It's disgusting!" Yvette gagged. "I'll never allow a boy to do that to me! All that spit! Yuk!"

John finished drying his hands, then faced them. "Thank you, Yvette."

"For what?"

"For clearing something up for me. You see, one lady I kissed quite recently did not seem to enjoy it at all and responded to my gesture of affection by wiping away my 'spit' with the back of her hand. I suppose she must feel the same way you do. It's certainly an explanation to keep in mind. Then again," he pondered offhandedly, "it could be that she prefers a bristly face to a clean-shaven one."

Agatha did not pass a pleasant night. John's newest affront rifled through her mind relentlessly, inducing a maddening headache. Why was life so complicated, hazardous? Why did it constantly throw stumbling blocks in her path? Well, she'd not stumble, had no intention of stumbling. By the crack of dawn, she was composed. She knew exactly how to proceed.

She entered her husband's dressing room just as Paul arrived. Camouflaging her delight, she quickly augmented her strategy and spoke decisively. "I don't want to add fuel to an already blazing fire, Frederic, but this condition extends far beyond John's insults. You've asked me to swallow my pride, even in front of the servants, and, for you, I have, enduring the ridicule he constantly dishes out. However, I guarantee his abominable behavior is only a prelude of what is yet to come." She paused, her voice waxing with concern. "Last night, I finally figured out his motives, why he has returned to Charmantes after all these years."

Frederic's pulse quickened. "And what are they, Agatha?"

"Isn't it obvious? He's uncovered the plans for Paul's Christmastide gala and is determined to undermine the event. Stephen Westphal has mentioned a number of things he's already done to hinder the endeavor. He wants to see Paul fail."

Frederic said nothing, in fact, he seemed relieved, and Agatha bristled, frustration riding high in her voice. "I warn you now, Frederic. I refuse to be humiliated in front of your prestigious Richmond associates and their wives. If John is allowed to remain on Charmantes – if you permit him to play his little games at Paul's expense – then I will remove myself from the planning of those festivities."

She sent beseeching eyes to Paul. "I'm sorry, but I won't participate in the spectacle that I am certain your brother intends to manufacture. We will become the laughing stock of influential southern society."

"Agatha," Frederic attempted to appease, "I hardly think John has any intention of manufacturing–"

"On the contrary," Paul cut in, his eyes stormy. "Agatha is right, Father. We all know what John is like. If he remains on Charmantes, he *will* wreak havoc on this event. He already has."

"How?"

"When the Raven laid anchor yesterday, she carried disturbing documents from Edward Richecourt. I was out to the harbor at dawn and received these." He flashed the folder he'd been holding. "They're the reason why I'm here this morning. John definitely knows of our plans, learned all about them as early as last February. He's questioned the directives I left with Richecourt in January. Thanks to him, important papers have been delayed and will not reach New York until Richecourt receives word from you overriding John's power of attorney."

"The Raven?" Frederic asked. "How long will she remain in port?"

Paul was confounded. He'd noted the man's intense eyes and thought they reflected anger over John's interference. Why then this inquiry about the Raven? "A few days," he answered with a frown. "Why?"

Frederic shook his head, his gaze fixed on the far wall. "No reason… I'd like to speak with Jonah Wilkinson before he sets sail."

Again, Paul puzzled over his father's reaction, the peculiar request, and was quickly becoming annoyed with his parent's disinterest in the more important issue at hand. "Can we get back to the subject of John?"

"Yes," the elder murmured, his mind feverishly working. Last night, he had debated his choices and struggled with a decision, frustrated to conclude that it lacked direction. The Raven pointed the way, provided the rudder. Frederic rubbed his brow, detesting this course of action, his thoughts sinking like deadweight on his chest. If only John and he could speak civilly. But that option was closed to them; John would only accuse him of scheming – exactly what he was forced to do.

"Father?" Paul pressed, shattering Frederic's perplexing thoughts.

"Yes… John," his sire acknowledged, regarding Paul once again. "I have good reason to believe that he will be leaving before week's end."

Though stunned by the prediction, Agatha and Paul remained doubtful.

"If it pleases you," Frederic continued, his eyes traveling to Agatha, "I will speak to John tonight at dinner."

"At dinner?" she asked. "You'll be taking dinner with the family?"

"Am I not allowed to dine at my own table?"

"Of course you are. It's just–"

Perturbed, Paul didn't allow her to finish. "You realize what day it is?"

"Yes," Frederic said, his voice dispassionate, chilling in its emptiness.

Charmaine and the children sat down to a late breakfast. The house had been an exciting place all morning as the barricades from yesterday's storm were pulled down, restoring the manor to its palatial glory. John was at the table, sipping the last of his coffee, and leaned back in his chair as the foursome took their seats. Paul was right behind them.

"Have you been abroad to survey the damage?" John asked amiably.

"Hours ago," his brother replied just as congenially. "We were fortunate. I don't think the storm struck us directly. Some of the fishing boats are in need of repair, but we didn't lose the Raven."

"Good. And the mill?"

"Minimal damage, the only casualty the sugarcane, which will require a few days' salvage work, but if we get on it quickly, it shouldn't be a total loss."

Astounded, Charmaine listened as Paul and John exchanged ideas. They conversed like brothers. *There was a time when they were close – very close.*

The conversation turned to the news of the day. The Raven carried various periodicals from England. King William was dead, and the new monarch, his young niece, had ascended the throne. What effect would Queen Victoria's reign have on Duvoisin commerce?

George emerged from the kitchen. Charmaine had hoped to catch him this morning, but when she realized he was only passing through the room, she slipped from her chair and called after him. "George, may I speak with you?"

"Certainly," he smiled, surprised when she boldly took his arm and led him toward the hallway where they could converse privately.

Paul's regard followed the departing couple. He looked at John, but received only a shrug. By the time Charmaine returned, John and he were talking with Pierre.

"And how did you like sharing your bed last night?" Paul asked.

"I wuved it!" the three-year-old replied emphatically. "It was nice and warm when Mainie cuddled me."

"And did you cuddle Mademoiselle Ryan, too?"

"Uh-huh."

"Now there's a boy who knows how to treat a lady," John interjected for his brother's benefit.

Paul ignored the remark. "Wasn't it a bit crowded, Pierre?"

"Nope," the lad replied, shaking his head twice and crossing his hands over his protruding abdomen. "And the next time there's a huwacane, I'm gonna stay with Mainie in *her* bed. And I'm gonna puh-tect her, too, 'cause I'm not a'scared of no stupid branch."

"But what if we don't have any more hurricanes?" John asked, treating the boy's proclamation quite seriously.

"I can *still* sleep with her – *if* I'm very good. Wight Mainie?"

Charmaine nodded quickly, aware of John's laughing eyes on her, certain of what he was going to say next.

"And if *I'm* very good?"

Pierre supplied the answer. "You can sleep with us, too!"

Charmaine was shocked when Paul chortled, his hearty guffaws eliciting contagious giggles from Pierre, who was quite proud of himself.

John, on the other hand, held silent, his chin perched on a fist, a faint smile tweaking his lips, and tender eyes caressing the boy, as if the sight of the child's uninhibited joy was enough to sustain him for the day.

Pierre and Yvette watched the reparations underway. The huge branch had been pushed out of Charmaine's room and onto the veranda last night, the glass removed this morning. Soon, Charmaine joined them, and the three stepped back as John and Joseph detached the splintered shutters and doorframes. Panels from one of the guestrooms awaited installation.

Wiping his brow with his forearm, John turned to the thick tree limb, lifting it as high as the balustrade. Joseph struggled to do the same with his end, but failed. On the third attempt, the branch splintered, falling on John's foot. "Damn!" came the muttered oath, born of frustration rather than pain. Again he blotted his brow dry and turned to Joseph.

"I'm sorry, sir!" the lad blurted out. "I didn't mean to–"

"It wasn't your fault," John ceded, though his voice was rough and his scowl black. "I need a more able-bodied assistant. Where is your father?"

"He's busy with the stable-hands pulling the shutters off the windows. But I'm willing to try again, sir."

"*Try again?*" John echoed incredulously. "Try again to break my foot?"

"No sir. I'll be extremely careful, sir."

"I'll help, Johnny!" Yvette volunteered. "And I won't break your foot!"

John sent his eyes heavenward. "You think you can lift something that Joseph can't hoist above his knees?"

He missed Yvette's determined nod as he faced the servant boy. "Go downstairs and find my brother. I believe he's in the study with Auntie having his ear gnawed off. I'm sure he'll appreciate an excuse to leave her."

"But–"

John took a step toward the argumentative youth.

"Yes, sir!" the boy agreed. "Right away, sir!"

He dashed from the room, nearly colliding with Jeannette, who was rushing through the doorway.

"George is back!" she cried, disappearing into the nursery with her sister.

John's curiosity was piqued when Charmaine and Pierre quickly followed. "I've never received that much attention," he grumbled, wondering where they were headed. He was befuddled when they exited the French doors adjacent to him and leaned over the balustrade excitedly.

George was still at the stable, retrieving a wrapped package from his saddlebag. He threw it under one arm before heading to the house.

"George!" Yvette called as he approached. "We're up here!"

John frowned. The girl had never behaved like this toward George before, waving vigorously to be sure that he saw her. And Charmaine. She had pulled George aside just this morning. Something was definitely brewing here.

He smiled down at his friend. "Good afternoon, Georgie."

"John," he nodded before turning to Charmaine, the package he carried now raised. "I was able to locate the item you requested."

"Thank you, George," she replied sweetly, "I owe you a favor."

"It was my pleasure. Do you think you can catch it?"

With her nod, he tossed it up, and Yvette quickly snatched it.

"Don't rip it open here," Charmaine ordered, her eyes meeting John's.

"What was that all about?" he inquired when George disappeared below.

Charmaine basked in the moment. "Aren't the employees allowed a bit of privacy, sir?" she asked coquettishly.

Without waiting for a reply, she grasped Jeannette and Pierre's hands and stepped back into the house. Yvette smiled up at him smugly, then waved the mysterious parcel in front of him, spun on her heel, and joined her siblings.

Paul arrived, and the branch was hoisted over the banister. Joseph appeared below and was told to remove it from the drive.

"That should take him the better part of a week," John sniggered.

"Do you need me for anything else?" Paul asked as Charmaine and the children entered the partially restored room.

"No, that should do it."

"What about those?" Paul gestured toward the doors that needed to be installed.

"I can manage. Why don't you hurry off before Auntie corners you again?"

Paul's countenance sobered. "John," he started cautiously, "I meant to speak to you after breakfast, but we were interrupted. Agatha is extremely annoyed with what you said to her last night. She's finally made good her threat. She went to Father this morning and complained about it."

"I could care less," John snorted and, as if to emphasize his indifference, turned his attention to the new glass panels.

"You should care," Paul contended.

"And why is that? What is her charge – defamation of character? Auntie doesn't need me to do that. She does it well enough on her own."

"John..."

Paul's faltering appeal seemed to reach the man, for he stopped working and regarded his brother.

"I think you should know that Father plans to dine with us tonight and has promised Agatha that he would speak to you."

"Isn't *that* nice," John sneered, cocking his head to one side and folding his arms over his chest. "Thank you for warning me. I'm just *quaking* in my boots."

"It's not a warning, John, it's just..."

"Just what, Paul? Just what?"

"Nothing," Paul replied with a shake of his head, "it's nothing."

"*Just what, Paul?*" John shouted as his brother left the room, waiting a moment longer as if Paul might return. Then he set the French doors in place, muttering "Just what?" one last time.

Charmaine reflected upon Paul's entreaty. Had it been meant as a warning? But to what end? A curbing of John's tongue? Or his abstention from the table? This seemed more logical, and her musings found voice.

"Will you be joining us for supper tonight?"

"Why wouldn't I?" John asked gruffly.

"I thought–"

"It doesn't matter what you thought, Miss Ryan," he cut in. Then his voice grew heavy with sarcasm. "This is my home, too, and much as some people wish it weren't so, I'm a member of this *great* family. I have every right to take a seat at the dinner table tonight, one that I fully intend to exercise."

Charmaine toyed with the ribbon that decorated the present in her lap. The children had been so excited when she told them about her idea this morning, accepting her recommendation that they wait until dinner to offer their gift to John. They'd watched the clock all day long, their ebullience near bursting. She couldn't disappoint them now. Nevertheless, she feared the possible outcome of celebrating John's birthday; she was flouting Frederic Duvoisin's prohibition of the event. Was she mad? She'd never even seen the two men in the same room together, save that chilling encounter after Pierre's spanking. And now, here she was stirring up a hornet's nest.

They entered the dining room to find Frederic already there, seated at the foot at the table, and not the head. That chair remained vacant, and with growing anxiety, Charmaine questioned the master's intent. If John did dine with them as he vowed he would, then he and his father would be facing each other across the great expanse, setting the stage for what could very well become an out-and-out confrontation.

Agatha sat regally to Frederic's left, her hands folded demurely in her lap, a soft smile plastered across her lips. She'd mastered the deceptive portrayal of beneficent mistress – statuesque, beautiful in fact.

"Good evening, Papa," Jeannette greeted blithely, pausing to kiss his cheek as she circled round his end of the table.

"Good evening, Princess. And how are you tonight?"

"Very well, thank you," she responded as she settled into the chair next to her sister. "How are you?"

"I'm feeling quite fit," he said, his eyes traveling to his other daughter and the parcel that she clutched. "What have you there, Yvette?"

"A present," she remarked flippantly, "for Johnny. It's his birthday, you know."

Charmaine inhaled, but was confounded by his benign reply. "Yes, I know."

Then his eyes were on her, and he nodded. "Miss Ryan."

"Good evening, sir," she breathed, quickly turning her attention to Pierre.

The greetings were exhausted and the room fell silent, an uneasy calm in which the seconds gathered into minutes. Charmaine was relieved when Paul's voice resounded in the hallway and he entered the dining room with Rose. He helped her with her chair, then took his own seat next to Charmaine. "Good evening everyone," he said, and in particular, "Father."

Felicia and Anna entered the room and glided around the table, pouring beverages from wine carafes and water pitchers. They exited and then reappeared, bearing abundant trays of savory meats, fresh green vegetables, fluffy white potatoes and bread. This spread rivaled any meal that Charmaine had partaken in the manor, and she realized that Fatima had spared nothing when she learned that the master of the house would be dining at the table this evening.

When everyone had been served, Frederic struck up a conversation with Paul. "Did you uncover any other storm damage this afternoon?"

"Not really, sir," Paul replied, his respectful response affecting Charmaine in an odd way, having never heard him address his father before. "Our efforts to secure the important areas paid off."

"Good," Frederic nodded. "I can always depend on you."

"Sir?"

Frederic didn't elaborate. "Espoir," he said instead, "any word from there?"

"No. But we secured the harbor in anticipation of hurricane season. The house is well built, and I imagine the burgeoning sugarcane is fine. Most of the plants are small, so I'm not overly concerned. I'll find out on Monday."

"Would you like some company?"

"Father?"

"I'd like to see the progress you've made first hand."

Paul sat in awe of the statement, as did everyone else at the table. Even Agatha's expression betrayed astonishment. "You want to come with me?"

"Of course I do. Is that unfathomable?"

"No, sir. It's just that – I didn't think you were up to such an excursion."

"A few miles at sea aboard a sound ship is hardly an excursion. I'll be fine."

Frederic spoke to his wife. "What about you, Agatha? Would you like to join us on Monday?"

"Yes," the woman greedily agreed.

"Then it's settled," Frederic concluded, raising his wineglass in a toast. "To Monday and Espoir."

"To Espoir," Paul concurred, warming to the inconceivable idea as he, too, raised a glass.

The cheers died down and varied conversations sprung up among those sitting near one another. More than once, Charmaine's eyes traveled to the vacant chair at the head of the table. Obviously, John had decided to stay away, and though she was certain that his decision was for the best, inexplicably, her heart was heavy. She turned back to her plate when voices carried from the main foyer. The table fell silent as all eyes turned to the delinquent intruders. John and George didn't seem to notice as they casually took their seats, talking still.

Frederic laid down his fork and considered John across the table. He'd best initiate the second stage of his plan. There was no point in dallying. His family could not go on this way. It was time his son made a choice. "You're late," he reproved flatly and, after a moment's pause, added, "dinner is served at seven."

John leaned back in his chair, and Charmaine was certain she read sadness in his eyes. But they quickly turned turbulent, a shield erected for battle.

"Sir," George began, "it's my fault that we're late. I asked John to help me in the tobacco fields–"

"Don't make excuses for me, George. No matter what you have to say, my father will choose to believe the worst. Isn't that correct, *sir*?"

The sneered title stood in stark contrast to Paul's respectful address.

"My judgment could never rival the Almighty's," Frederic rejoined.

Unnerved, Charmaine's pulse accelerated. Yet, John was smiling. She scanned the table. Everyone stared at their plates, save Agatha, whose satisfied eyes sparkled. Charmaine looked askance at Paul. His brow tipped upward, confirming her silent appeal. So this was how father and son behaved toward one another, the hostility that hardened their hearts.

John's regard remained fixed on Frederic. Finally he stood, grabbed George's plate, and piled it high with all the food within his reach. He placed the heaping dish before his friend, receiving a nod of appreciation. Then he served himself, sat down, and began to eat. After a few hearty mouthfuls, clearly a deliberate tactic to prove that his appetite had not been affected, he spoke.

"How are those kittens of yours, Jeannie?"

"They're fine," the surprised girl replied, not daring to expound.

Yvette was not intimidated. "Smudge slept in Jeannette's bed last night."

"Is that the orange one?" he asked, seemingly oblivious to his sire's glare.

"No, that's Orange." When John snickered, she added, "Pierre named her."

"Well, Orange woke me up this morning by walking all over my face."

The children giggled, but Agatha clicked her tongue in disapproval. "The kittens are very sweet, Jeannette," she said, "but they should be sleeping in their own bed, not yours."

The twins' faces dropped, but not John's.

"So, Father," he goaded scathingly, "how is married life after being a bachelor for so very long? Is my *dear* aunt the perfect wife or does my *good* mother still hold that title and fill that special place in your heart?"

Frederic responded swiftly and without thought. "Elizabeth's goodness has never been reflected in you."

"Ah, Father, if not my mother, then who *do* I take after?"

"Good question," Frederic volleyed. "Since the day you were born, you've brought nothing but pain and sorrow to this household."

"Since the day I was born?" John retaliated softly, pensively, the query's message brutally clear.

Frederic winced. *Damn! Why had he said that? Damn!* The wounds would never heal. Their only hope: stay out of each other's way. Tonight's stratagem would see it to that end. It was for the best, he resolved.

Charmaine toyed with her food, wishing only to leave the table. This dinner was all too reminiscent of those she'd partaken of as a girl. Why would a father say such a thing to his son? And why did John deliberately provoke the man?

The minutes ticked by, and the meal labored on. Out of the corner of her eye, she saw John return his knife and fork to his plate. He sat for a moment with head bowed, and then, in a rush, pushed back from the table. He would not be staying for dessert, and in premature relief, Charmaine sighed. They would give him his gift later, at a safer time.

Yvette was not of the same mind and called out as he stood. "Johnny, wait!" She jumped from her own chair, hastened around the table, and extended the wrapped package to him. "Happy Birthday."

Dumbfounded, John made no move to take the gift, so she placed it before him, waiting patiently as he fingered the ribbon that held the wrapping in place. "You're the best brother in the whole world," she declared adamantly, "and we love you!"

He swallowed hard and released the ties. The paper fell away to reveal a leather cap. He sat back down, placed an arm on the table, and leaned his forehead heavily into his hand.

"Thank you," he choked out.

"Don't you like it?" Pierre's voice carried across the table.

Fighting for control, John lifted his head and opened his mouth to speak, but Frederic's command halted him. "Pierre, come to me."

The boy looked back and forth between the two men before choosing. His gaze rose above his father's right shoulder. Smiling, he scrambled from his chair and climbed into Frederic's lap, wrapping his arms around the man's neck.

"I love you, son," Frederic murmured, his voice heavy. The words were sincere, and though they were spoken to Pierre, Frederic's eyes were on John, leaving Charmaine to wonder for whom they were meant.

"I love you, Papa," the lad responded brightly.

Wood scraped against wood, and John's chair crashed to the floor. He loomed over the table, palms planted on either side of his plate, face contorted and flushed, eyes glassy with tears. *"I hate you!"* he cried out, the air rushing from his lungs as if he had sustained a violent blow. He grabbed the cap and fled the room.

Charmaine slowly faced Frederic. She found him stroking Pierre's hair, a twisted smile marking his drawn face, though his eyes were dark with sorrow.

The nursery offered little respite from the pathetic episode. Charmaine remained numb and, much like the children who sat lethargically in the playroom beyond, was unable to concentrate on any task. Her mind raced on, one thought dominating all the others: hatred, definitely hatred. It was an emotion she knew well, for hatred had been her close companion those tender years when she was growing up. But she'd always kept it inside, her bitter devotion ever silent to the world. Not so with John.

And what of Frederic? His disdain was just as apparent, just as nauseating. Charmaine was revolted by the polar extremes she'd witnessed: the healthy accolades he'd bestowed upon Paul and the dark slanders he'd hurled at John, all in front of his impressionable young daughters. It didn't make sense. Why didn't he just banish John from Charmantes? And why did John, for all his proclaimed hatred, remain? Didn't she know? No, her mind revolted, she didn't know.

She jumped with a knock on the door, surprised to find John standing there. "I'd like to speak with you," he said softly. "May I come in?"

She hesitated. He was the last person she had expected to see. "Of course."

He stepped into the room. "I apologize for my behavior this evening. I didn't intend–"

"You needn't apologize to me," she interrupted, uncomfortable with his strained words, relieved when Yvette appeared in the playroom doorway, smiling for the first time since dinner.

"Did you try on your cap?" she asked, walking over to him. "Does it fit?"

"It's perfect. In fact, that is the reason I'm here. I came to say thank you. Though it may have seemed I didn't appreciate it, I do, and I shall wear it as proudly as I did the last one."

"Really?

"Truly," he replied, nodding to Jeannette and Pierre as they, too, entered the bedroom. "Actually, I like it better than the one I lost."

"Why did you tell Father you hate him?" she abruptly asked.

John's eyes dropped to the floor. "It's a long story. It took twenty-nine years to live, and it would take almost as much time to explain."

"Well, if you hate him, then so do I!"

"No, Yvette!" he objected, falling on one knee before her. He took hold of her shoulders and looked her straight in the eye. "You mustn't hate somebody just because someone else does. Hatred is a terrible thing. It destroys lives."

"Then why do *you* hate him?"

"I shouldn't have said what I said tonight. I said it because I was angry, but I shouldn't have said it."

"Why were you angry?"

"You are too young to understand," he tried to reason. "But Father loves you, and it would hurt him to hear you say that you hate him."

"Didn't you hurt him?"

"I don't know. But *you* wouldn't want to hurt him, would you?"

He patted her head when she said 'no', then stood and whispered a few last words to Charmaine. "I thank you also, Miss Ryan."

"For what?"

"For attempting to make my birthday a special occasion."

Saturday, September 30, 1837

The house was painfully quiet for a Saturday afternoon. It seemed that everyone had taken heed of the past night's persecution and had either fled the house or tucked themselves in some remote quarter. Paul was gone at the crack of dawn. The mistress, usually a late riser, followed shortly afterward, leaving by carriage at the unheard hour of seven. And finally, Rose and George departed for town, taking the twins with them. Charmaine had decided to remain behind with Pierre. Now, hours later, she wondered why she hadn't joined them, for the desolate manor feasted upon her melancholy heart. Even Pierre's innocent smile could not lift her downtrodden spirit.

He must have comprehended her somber state, for he gave her a hug and jumped from her lap, dismissing the alphabet book they had been reciting. Presently, he was playing with his blocks, constructing a simple structure.

Charmaine's eyes left him and traveled across the room, settling on the large painting that hung above the fireplace. Funny, of all the times she'd sat in this elegant parlor, she never once studied the portrait. Now she did, with startling clarity: a man and two boys, that's all it had been before. Today it was Frederic, embracing his adopted son, Paul, while his legitimate son, John, stood off to one side, dejected and alone. Her mind wandered far afield, and George's words rang in her ears: *They vied for their father's approval, but that approval always weighed in on Paul's side... Frederic was downright mean to John. So, imagine how John felt when he watched his father's adopted son claim that man's love, while day after day, week after week, year after year, he, the legitimate son, came up empty-handed...* Her dismal mood plummeted further. Was the portrait displayed just to smite John?

Pierre's tower clattered to the floor. Charmaine watched as he clambered under chairs to retrieve the scattered blocks, building it once again. As it grew taller, it inevitably swayed and crumbled. But the three-year-old was not defeated, and she watched with wonder as the edifice was erected a third and fourth time.

Could John's life be so easily reassembled? Charmaine frowned, greatly disturbed with the comparison. *Why had she thought of him in those terms? Why had she thought of him at all?* More importantly, when had she *not* been thinking of him? She was uncomfortable with the realization that he had been foremost in her mind for two full days.

Of all the people who had run away this morning, only he and Frederic remained behind. How were they faring? She shuddered again with the memory of the fierce hatred she had witnessed and the conclusions she'd drawn. What if the children became pawns in their despicable game of animosity? Dear God, she'd be in the middle of it. How was she to handle it? There were no answers, but if she were to know any peace today, she had to cleanse her mind of such questions and move forward. With that resolution, she stood.

"Pierre?" she called, setting the primer aside on the table. He looked up. "I have to go upstairs for just a minute."

"Why?"

"I want to write a letter to my friends in Virginia, but I need some paper to do that and it's up in my room. Can I leave you here all by yourself?"

"Uh-huh," he nodded.

"And you'll play nicely with your blocks? You won't go wandering off?"

"No, Mainie. I'll stay wight here and wait for you."

She winked at him, her heart brimming with love. "I'll be right back."

He attempted to return the gesture, but both eyes blinked at the same time. He tried again, succeeding only when he held one eyelid open with his fingers.

Charmaine laughed heartily.

John leaned his shoulder into the doorframe that connected the study to the drawing room. He had been drawn away from the desk where he'd been reading by the sound of happy laughter, and now he considered the small boy who was singing softly to himself while crawling about on hands and knees, gathering his blocks. A quick scan of the room confirmed that they were alone, and he savored the moment that permitted him to watch Pierre inconspicuously. This time belonged to him. Finally, he stepped forward. "Good morning!"

Pierre immediately turned around. "Whatcha doin' here?"

"I was about to ask you the same thing."

Pierre pointed to his blocks. "I'm buildin' a house."

"A house, is it? And when you're finished, who's going to live in it?"

"Me and Mainie and Jeannie and Yvie and... you!"

"I'd like that," John said, and looking about the room again, he asked, "Where is Mainie, anyway? I thought I heard her laughing."

"She was. But now she went upstairs. She tol' me to wait wight here and she'll be wight back. Then she's gonna make me do the albabet again."

"The albabet, eh?"

"Al-*fa*-bet!" Pierre corrected, annoyed with John's mispronunciation.

John's eyes twinkled. "So you *can* say it properly."

"Yep! Do ya wanna hear it? I can say it real good now and I don' even make no more mistakes."

John listened, nodding his approval when the boy had finally finished.

Pierre pushed up from the floor and walked over to him. "Do ya know what letter I like the bestest?" he asked.

"No, what letter is that?"

"M."

"M?" John queried. "Why M?"

"'Cause the two peoples that I love the bestest in the whole wide world start with that letter. Jeannie tol' me so."

John was bewildered. "Really? And who would they be?"

"Mainie and Mama, silly."

"Of course."

Pierre grew serious. "Do you know my Mama? She's very boo-ti-ful."

"So I've heard," the man mumbled.

Pierre tugged on his hand. "I'll show you her."

John's face went white; he followed the boy nonetheless.

Their pilgrimage ended at the landing of the north and south wing staircase, there where the portrait of Colette Duvoisin hung – reserved beauty, breathtaking in her unadorned loveliness. Cast in shades of blue, she could have been the Blessed Mother had she worn a veil; her eyes radiated a compassion born from the scars of her own burden of pain.

"Lif' me up!" Pierre demanded, yanking the harder on John's shirt when he didn't respond. "Lif' me up higher!"

John complied and stepped closer to the huge painting. They were directly beneath it now and had to crane their necks to look at the lifelike image.

"That's my Mama," Pierre whispered as if he might awaken her. "Isn't she boo-ti-ful?"

"Yes," John whispered in kind. "She's very beautiful."

Following the man's example, Pierre stretched out a tentative finger and caressed the ivory hands folded on the woman's lap. At the contact, his brow creased in displeasure. The texture of the canvas destroyed the artist's illusion, for it mocked the splashes of color that had so vividly captured the essence of his mother. "She's not alive no more," he said, his candid regard on John now.

"No," John muttered, the words catching in his throat, "she's no longer alive."

Pierre tilted his head to one side, studying John's glassy eyes. "Why are you cryin'?"

"I suppose I... miss her," John answered softly.

"Do you love her?"

"Yes."

"How much?"

"As much as you." John gulped down his pain, grasped the boy tightly to him, and buried his lips in his soft hair, taking succor from the embrace.

By the time Charmaine reached the landing, his emotions were in check.

"Good morning, Miss Ryan," he greeted. "Pierre and I were just keeping one another company."

She was pleased to find a smile on his lips, if not in his eyes. "I'm sorry I left him unattended. I only ran upstairs to–"

"No need to apologize. We were enjoying our chat, weren't we, Pierre?"

The boy nodded, but was ready to return to his blocks. John set him on his feet and watched him race back to the parlor. He faced Charmaine, waiting for her to reach the landing. Together, they rejoined Pierre, who had resumed his construction of houses and towers. John took a chair closest to him.

Charmaine set the stationery aside and sat opposite the man. He seemed intensely interested in the newest structure being erected until he looked up and their eyes locked. She spoke rashly. "Are you… well?"

He puzzled a moment. "If you are asking if I've recovered from last night's ordeal," he commented blandly, "I'll survive. There are no visible scars."

"Only well-concealed ones?"

Again a befuddled frown, and then, a twisted smile. "Why Miss Ryan, could it be that you are coming to understand me?"

"No," she replied, shaking her head. "I'll never pride myself of that."

"Ah," he breathed, "but you are trying."

"I didn't mean to pry," she apologized, uncomfortable with the sardonic smile that now danced in his eyes.

"I don't believe you did. In any case, I don't fault you your curiosity." He leaned back in his chair, lending his full attention. "We've spent the better part of two months together, and in that time you've been exposed to quite a few facets of my personality, many of them ugly. I think it is only natural to contemplate my motives."

He paused for a moment, and Charmaine wondered if he were waiting for her to comment. When she didn't, he pressed on, arms folded across his chest. "I'd very much like to hear your assessment – your *honest* assessment of me."

She was flabbergasted. *Was he serious?* "I'm afraid I couldn't!"

"And why not?"

"Because – because – I just couldn't."

"I guarantee that you've seen the worst of my temper, if that is your concern. And remember, you did survive." He chuckled. "Come now, I *know* you've waited for this moment – the moment of truth, so to speak – when you could tell me exactly what you thought of me, and force me to listen."

"You are wrong!"

"Am I?" he asked dubiously, her flushed face at odds with her assertion. "Well, no matter. I'd still like to hear your evaluation. What if I promised to remain passive and keep a level head? Better yet," he added on an afterthought, "if you pledge honesty, we'll shake on it, and I shall be honest with you. I'm certain there is some family secret you would like to inquire about, something concerning Paul, perhaps? If I can, I will answer any question you place to me."

Charmaine's eyes widened. He had whetted her appetite and knew it.

"Is it a bargain?"

Suddenly, he was towering over her, and she quickly came to her own feet, unsettled by the overpowering variance of height. She was uncertain of his intentions until he extended his hand half the distance between them. Slowly, she placed her cool palm in his warm one, her eyes fixed upon the union. She met his gaze, losing herself in the caramel-colored eyes, warm and understanding.

"It's a pact then," he finally murmured, holding the appendage a moment longer than necessary. "To truthfulness and honesty."

"And you'll answer my questions?"

"As soon as you reveal the real me," he replied with a crooked smile.

She didn't know where to begin... Then she did. Hadn't conjecture mercilessly plagued her these past two days? "I think you are a man with a past," she began cautiously, watching for the first sign of discontentment. "Something has either hurt you or left you disenchanted. Hence, you hide behind a shield of sharp gibes and joviality. Life has dealt you a heavy blow, and you intend to repay it in kind. It is easier to be cruel than to forgive, to laugh than to cry."

"On the contrary, my Charm. Most times it is easier to cry than to laugh. Laughter is a hard-won, diligent effort. It must be refined day in and day out to bar despair and ruin. Only then can one subsist–"

"Did you love her?" she whispered, realizing too late her blunder. Already his eyes had hardened. "I'm sorry. I shouldn't have asked–"

"Don't apologize," he snapped. "I shook on our pact." He chuckled hollowly. "It's just that that particular question is becoming quite tiresome. Pierre asked the very same thing not ten minutes ago."

"And your answer?"

"What do you think I said to a boy inquiring about his deceased mother?" he replied caustically. "Of course I loved her. She was, after all, my *stepmother*."

He closed the conversation as swiftly as he turned his back on her. *So much for honesty.* But even in the lie, she glimpsed the truth.

Paul bathed quickly; Stephen Westphal was due within the hour. Much as he'd have liked to postpone the meeting, the banker had flagged him down in town, insisting that his proposal could wait no longer. It was time to bring Espoir's construction phase to a close and her commercial phase to a beginning. With the first ship arriving any day now, Paul needed to cement ocean routes, buyers, and sellers. To that end, Westphal had worked tirelessly for him, his stateside business connections invaluable, thus the reason for this evening's meeting.

Paul entered the drawing room. It might as well have been deserted, for John stood solemnly at the far end, studying something through the French doors, while the banker fiddled with the starched collar that pinched his reddened neck. "Good evening, Stephen," he greeted.

The man's regard bespoke undying gratitude, as if he'd just been raised from the depths of hell. "Paul," he returned, jumping to his feet, arm extended for a hearty handshake, "I didn't realize how early I was."

Paul moved to the liquor cabinet. "I apologize for keeping you waiting. I was delayed at the cane fields. We're still cleaning up after Thursday's storm."

"Of course, of course," Stephen nodded.

"May I pour you a brandy?" Paul inquired over his shoulder, his eyes going fleetingly to his brother, who already held a glass.

"That would be wonderful," Stephen answered, "if it isn't any trouble."

Paul considered John again. "Couldn't you offer our guest a drink, John?" he inquired sharply.

John turned. "It's not mine to offer. Not yet, anyway."

Paul's eyes narrowed. Obviously, the two men had exchanged words; the question was, what had John said? Agatha's assertions played heavily in Paul's mind. John's behavior toward Westphal could be a preview of what was yet to come, disaster right around the corner if potential investors and business partners were led to believe that his brother was undermining him.

Agatha entered the room and showered the banker with exaggerated salutations. "Stephen, it's been too long! How nice to have you as our guest!"

"Agatha, I assure you, the pleasure is all mine."

John winced, muttering, "He's easy to please."

Paul fought the mounting tension. Much as he'd like to tell John to run off and play with the children, a vulgar retort came to mind, and he knew that his brother was not above voicing it.

"Will Frederic be joining us?" Stephen asked.

"I'm afraid not," Agatha stated. "He asked me to extend his apologies."

"I'm sorry that he cannot be with us." The banker's eyes shifted to John. "Your nephew mentioned a family gathering the other night. Might I presume that there has been an overall turn for the better?"

"In fact, there has," Paul interjected charily. "This Christmastide conference was his idea. He's assisted in every aspect of its preparation, his advice and know-how as invaluable as the funds he's supplied. None of us would be where we are today if it weren't for him, now would we?"

"I'll drink to that," John mordantly agreed, raising his brandy glass.

Paul cast him a murderous glare before suggesting that they sit down. "Dinner will not be ready until seven, so we have a bit of time to get started."

Agatha settled into an armchair, but Stephen moved to the desk, unfastened the straps of a leather portfolio, and withdrew some papers. "First, the invitation list," he said, handing it over to Paul. "Those are the men you should invite: farmers, investors, and brokers. The farmers will provide the cargo, and of course, the investors will be critical as the business expands, but it will be the brokers who bid on your cargo space. If you're to commission additional ships as you've indicated, these men, especially the wealthier farmers, could certainly provide the finances. That would, of course, be contingent upon your success. Most would be interested in a long-term return, say, over a five year period."

Paul looked over the names, his eyes gleaming with pleasure. If only half these men came in December and a mere quarter invested, the cornerstones of financial success would be laid and he, Paul Duvoisin, the illegitimate son of the renowned tycoon, Frederic Duvoisin, would be on his way.

"I recommend Williamson, Brockton, Carroll, and Farley," Westphal was saying. "They own some of the largest and most lucrative plantations in the South, and are always seeking alternate carriers. Every year their harvests increase, so I suggest that you approach them directly. They usually deal with Hiram Gimble. His brokerage is well known, his success due to his bidding clout. If these farmers gain a vested interest in your shipping line, then I'm certain it would affect how they negotiate with Mr. Gimble, bringing their influence to bear, so to speak."

Paul embraced the clever proposal, reveling in the excitement of making his first business deal, the delectable fruits of years of labor.

"These men will indeed be invited, including Mr. Gimble!" Agatha chimed in, her face alight in voracious anticipation, as if the strategies being discussed couldn't be executed quickly enough.

Paul concurred. "But once I've finalized this list, we'll need to meet again and discuss these men in greater detail. Some of the names I know well, but the ones you've just mentioned I've only heard in passing."

"They're all cotton farmers."

Paul faced his brother, who had spoken from the settee where he now reclined. "You say that as if it's a problem, John."

"In the short run, no. Potentially, yes."

Paul weighed the remark. "Do you care to expound, or must I pay you, like you do Yvette, for more information?"

"You're paying Stephen," John returned glibly. "Maybe he can tell you."

Stephen bristled in unmasked aggravation, his hand going to his waist. "If you're trying to trivialize my knowledge, John, I am the first to admit that I am not an expert in farming. I *am* a banker, however, and common sense dictates that the men with the largest bank accounts know the most about commerce."

John considered Westphal's monologue for a moment, head cocked, legs extended and crossed, one hand clasped over the other in his lap. "No wonder you doubt my observation. I don't bank with your establishment."

"This conversation is ridiculous!" Agatha expostulated. "Why do you listen to him, Paul? He's trying to distract you. No worse – undermine you! I don't trust him! You should make him leave!"

Paul ignored the woman. Much as he hated it to admit it, he was curious. "What is your point, John?"

Agatha jumped up. "Paul!"

"Auntie," John cut in coolly, "sit!"

Paul did not intercede. Furious, Agatha bit her tongue and sank back into her chair. Then, realizing she was obeying the command much as a dog would its master, she straightened, pretending at grooming her skirts.

"I concede that all the men you mentioned are well-established cotton farmers," John proceeded. "But is cotton the only product you want to ship? Cotton isn't in demand this year. In fact, prices are quite low. Next year, that might change. But the risk always remains high when you place all your coins on one bet."

Westphal took further offense. "Cotton is more than fifty percent of the market. In addition, Williamson, Brockton, Carroll, and Farley afford cargo contacts from regions other than Virginia. Should blight damage the tobacco harvest – or a hurricane, even – Paul would have a second crop to fall back on. Even so, he wouldn't be dealing in cotton alone. The other farmers on that list harvest tobacco, and his Caribbean contacts would be supplying sugar."

The man smiled smugly, and John knew he had devised his reasoning as he spoke. "Ingenious."

Paul frowned. "What else, John? There's something else."

"There are rumblings of a war. It may not happen next year, it may not happen in ten years. But do you really want to take that chance? Throw all your money and hard work into southern commodities alone?"

"Don't tell me that you're preoccupied with this war talk, too? I can't believe this explosion is just around the corner as so many claim."

John shrugged derisively. "I'm surprised you're so indifferent about it. Now, I know all of this speculation is coming from nasty-no-good John, but isn't it just *common sense* to have all the facts before making a decision? This slave business will not go on forever. The Negroes have had enough of it. Nat Turner proved that in '31. Maybe invention will beat confrontation to the finish line, but a war almost happened last year. What are you going to do if all of your ports of call are blockaded? Remember, you'll be labeled the southern sympathizer, so your flags won't be welcome in New York or Boston. Then what are you going to ship, and to where are you going to ship it?" He sighed and shrugged again. "Just a little insight from someone who's been on the mainland for ten years now and knows what the talk is from day to day, in the north as well as the south."

Paul settled into the desk chair, eyes trained on his brother. John's rationale made a great deal of sense, but could he trust the source? John would enjoy seeing him fail at this costly undertaking. "If what you say is true, surely it doesn't bode well for you either. After all, you're a tobacco farmer and a southern shipper. So, what are you doing about it, John?"

"Come now, Paul, you've bucked and complained over the changes that I've instituted over the last few years. Anything else shall remain unspoken, all in the spirit of fair play."

"What are you driving at, John?"

"I was not privy to any of the plans you were making here and on Espoir before I came home in August. In fact, there was a concerted effort to keep it all a secret from me."

John looked pointedly at Stephen Westphal, who squirmed in his seat for the second time that evening. "What I did find out, I had to coerce out of father's solicitous solicitor, Mr. Richecourt. What I don't understand is: *why?* But, since you felt it necessary to leave me out of the equation, two can play at that game. I've been quite generous in giving you this bit of advice."

Paul rolled his eyes, unmoved. "You know very well why I prefer to leave you out. You've alienated all of influential Richmond with your sharp tongue, and when it's not that, it's your rebellious behavior. You released all of your slaves, without Father's permission, when the rest of the South has been struggling to preserve its right to keep them. And you're telling me about good business decisions? Does it make sense to throw away free labor? And don't sermonize about slave degradation. They can be treated civilly and still be slaves. And what about the people you associate with? They're barely fit to walk the face of the earth, let alone move in the circles of proper society. Edgar Allen Poe. Really! Then you wonder why I don't want you involved in this?"

John leaned forward, placed his empty glass on the table, and smiled. "Nevermore." He stood and strode to the open doorway, turning back as he reached it. "Go ahead and listen to Mr. Westphal, Paul. I'm sure he knows much more about all this than I do. I think I'll see if dinner is ready."

Paul stared at the vacant archway, then faced the banker. "I'm sorry for that disruption. If you don't mind my asking, Stephen, what did my brother say to you before I arrived? I hope he wasn't insulting."

"It was nothing," Stephen countered with a gracious wave of his hand.

"Nothing?" Paul probed, unconvinced. "Was there some sort of dispute?"

"It was my own fault. Let us not speak of it."

"No, Stephen. You should tell me," Paul insisted, determined to get the details of a discussion that could have serious repercussions on his interests. "I'll take the matter up with my father, if need be. John has no right to insult a guest."

"No need to upset your father, Paul. For some reason John assumed that Frederic had invited me to the house. He sarcastically lamented that my daughter wouldn't be interested in him once his name was removed from the will."

Agatha jumped in. "You must take these remarks from whence they come, Stephen. I've learned to ignore anything my nephew has to say. But speaking of Anne, you must give us with her address. She must attend our affair this winter. After all, what will the event be without a sophisticated, cultured young woman to grace its festivities?"

Stephen lit up with the suggestion.

Paul, in turn, considered the invitation, appreciating the prospect of Anne London's presence on Charmantes. For all of his brother's assertions to the contrary, John must have encouraged the Richmond widow at some point, thus fanning her forwardness. He pondered the panorama ahead. If John had succumbed to Anne's charms once, he could be vulnerable again, and how would the naïve Miss Ryan feel about him then? It was just the insurance Paul needed, should John remain on Charmantes.

"What about John?" Stephen questioned worriedly, as if reading Paul's thoughts. "I don't think he'll be very pleased–"

"It is not *his* invitation," Paul cut in smugly, "it's mine."

Stephen brightened again. No doubt his daughter would be pleased to meet Frederic's other handsome, soon-to-be-wealthy, bachelor son.

Sunday, October 1, 1837

Charmaine finished changing out of her Sunday dress and into her everyday apparel. The girls shouted to her from the other side of the closed door. "We're done! Now may we go down to the stable to see our ponies and the kittens?"

"Yes, but be careful!" Charmaine called to them. "And don't go near any other horses except Angel and Spook!"

"We won't," came the reply.

"And be back in a half hour for breakfast!"

No answer... they were already gone. Charmaine shook her head, grateful that they remained happy amid the undercurrents of pain that plagued the house.

Just this morning John had convinced them to move the kittens to a more sensible home: the barn. "You can make a nice bed for them there, and they will keep your ponies calm and happy." When Yvette appeared unconvinced, John insisted that she ask Paul and George if she didn't believe him. "Cats are good animals to have around horses. And I'll get a better night's sleep," he added. Apparently, three nights of kitten paws across his face was enough. Now the girls had three reasons to visit the stable: the foal, their ponies, and the felines.

Charmaine entered the nursery moments later and found John reclining on the floor alongside Pierre. They were sailing the boy's model ships across the floor. She paused in the doorway, enjoying the endearing scene. "Are you hungry, Pierre?" she finally asked. "Time for breakfast."

John looked up. "Hungry?" he queried, noting the late hour. "I'd be famished. I hope Holy Mass was worth the fast."

"It was," Charmaine declared, offended by the irreverent tone of his voice.

John chuckled. "Have Benito's homilies become inspirational?"

She refused to answer, to lie. The priest's fire and brimstone sermons had grown worse, making Sunday Mass nothing more than an obligation.

John's chuckle intensified sagaciously. "I guess some things never change. How can you abide his sanctimonious airs?"

"He is a priest!" Charmaine objected.

"Not by my estimation. Do the words compassion and kindness ever enter into his vocabulary? Better yet, has he ever exemplified them?"

Charmaine bit her tongue. Though John's words rang true, she felt he mocked more than the island priest, using Father Benito's poor example to ridicule her religious beliefs.

"I can see you are angry with me," he said. "I'm not faulting all priests. A good friend of mine is a priest, a kind and compassionate man, who could teach our Father Benito a thing or two. Though, I daresay, he is beyond redemption."

"Who?" she retaliated, "Father Benito or your friend?"

Before he could respond, Paul entered the nursery. He took in John's prone form and the deep frown that creased Charmaine's brow.

"Is he annoying you, Charmaine?"

"No," she answered, throwing John one last disdainful look, "not really."

"We were just discussing Father Benito," John supplied mildly. "What would you call him, Paul: good priest or bad?"

Paul grunted, refusing to side with his brother. "I don't have time for this, John. I need to discuss something with you."

"And what would that be?"

"Privately," Paul replied. "I'd like to speak with you privately."

John mumbled something under his breath, but stood and followed his brother into the hallway.

When they were closeted in the study, John flopped into the sofa.

"We will be leaving first thing in the morning," Paul began.

"We?" John puzzled aloud.

"Father, Agatha, and myself, as well as a number of the servants."

"What are you talking about?" John asked, completely baffled now.

"We discussed it at the table the other night. Father wants to see my progress on Espoir. We shall be gone for the week."

John's brow gathered, his mind working. "I don't remember that."

Paul rubbed the back of his neck. "Maybe we talked about it before you came in. At any rate, we'll be traveling there first thing tomorrow, and I'd like to know that Charmantes is running smoothly while I'm gone. My biggest concern is the sugarcane. Two fields were salvaged from the storm, but the pressing will take all the manpower we've got if we're to minimize the loss. George said he'd oversee all that, but he could use a hand loading the Raven once the casks are filled."

"The Raven?" John queried, his interest further piqued. "She should have been on her way to Richmond by now."

"She would have been, if not for the storm. Now I need her to transport the sugar extract." Paul paused a moment, but when John did not respond, he asked, "Can I count on your help?"

An eerie silence pervaded the room. John's gaze was fixed on the book-lined wall far across the study, and Paul knew that his brother had dismissed the query. He wondered if John had heard him at all.

Paul changed the subject. "There is another thing. I'd like your word, as a gentleman, that you'll not bother Charmaine while I'm away." Again, his brother didn't answer. "John," Paul snapped impatiently, "are you listening to me?"

John's eyes focused on him. "Don't worry, Paul, don't worry about a thing."

Monday,
October 2, 1837

Chapter 6

Chaotic commotion gripped the front lawns. A throng of servants, house staff and grooms alike, ran helter-skelter between manor and paddock. Frederic Duvoisin intended to travel abroad this day, and his employees zealously embraced this extraordinary event. Two horses were led from the stable and harnessed to the spanking new brougham, manufactured in Britain, ordered by Paul during his visit there last winter, and shipped to Charmantes only a month ago. The meticulously groomed animals pranced nervously against the bit as the final straps were secured. It took not one, but two footmen to hold them steady when they pulled up to the portico. Still, their skittishness did not deter Travis Thornfield as he hoisted another trunk into the carriage.

Standing out of harm's way, Charmaine and the children watched in wonder. Then the moment was upon them, and the front doors opened for the last time.

Frederic limped out of the house, his ebony cane striking sharply against the stone terrace. He stumbled only once, misjudging the first step, but he quickly righted himself, shooing away his fawning wife when she rushed forward to assist him. "Leave me some pride!" he snarled, the scolding nearly inaudible.

As Agatha backed away, Frederic's stormy gaze followed. Realizing that his attention had been arrested, she turned to find the children and their governess loitering at the drawing room casement. "Have you nothing better to do, Miss Ryan, than to gawk at my husband? Surely, the girls have lessons? Or is this frivolous wasting of time a prelude of the week to come when I shan't be here to monitor your shabby supervision of them?"

"That is enough, Agatha," Frederic reprimanded, his words tight. "Miss Ryan is diligent in her care of the children."

"I fear you have been misinformed," Agatha protested, attempting to save face among the many servants who stared at her.

Frederic's ire was rising, but he concealed it beneath honey-coated words. "Have I? By whom? At least Miss Ryan loves my children."

Insulted, Agatha lifted her chin, descended the three steps of the porch, and ensconced herself in the carriage.

Charmaine cheered inwardly, grateful that her utter shock forestalled a chuckle. The man was moving toward her, and she quickly composed herself. "Miss Ryan, I would like to say goodbye to my children. Do you have a kiss for me, Pierre?"

"What for?" the boy asked.

"To remember you by."

Frederic stooped over and the lad kissed his cheek, but before Pierre could pull away, the man's unencumbered arm wrapped around his shoulders and squeezed him fiercely. After a prolonged moment, Frederic straightened up, aware of Charmaine's eyes on him. "One never knows when the last day might be," he offered.

"The last day? But you mustn't say–"

"Yes, I must," he corrected. "I've been very pleased with your service to this family, Miss Ryan. My wife, Colette, was correct about you. You have been a wonderful mother to our children. Therefore, remember, I'll not hold you responsible for any circumstances beyond your control."

"Sir?"

"Just remember, Charmaine Ryan. When you become upset, remember." He nodded rigidly, stifling a reply, then turned away, never once requesting a kiss from either of his daughters.

As the brougham passed through the front gates, Charmaine noticed John standing in the shadows of the maimed oak. She couldn't read his expression, but his hand raked agitatedly through his tousled hair. Then he abruptly marched off.

Exhaling, she ushered the children into the house and, allowing for the favorable occasion, permitted them to run off and explore the unguarded homestead. Few had remained behind. The Thornfields boarded a smaller carriage and followed the family coupe to town. Felicia and Anna were already there. Charmaine could only wonder over Paul's whereabouts. He'd left very early, and she doubted she would see him before the ship departed.

So consuming were her thoughts that she walked headlong into George, who was charging across the foyer. Excusing herself, she looked down at the baggage he carried and was horrified to learn that he was deserting her as well.

"It was all discussed last night at dinner," he said. "We have to press every stalk of cane that we can. Time is of the essence, and I can get a lot more accomplished if I just camp out with the men. Frederic has promised me a bonus if the entire crop is processed before he returns."

Charmaine's trepidation spiraled, and George regarded her bemusedly. "Why should my absence from the house upset you, anyway?"

"I'll be here all alone tonight."

"Alone? You won't be alone. John is still here."

"Exactly. John and *only* John."

With the dawn of comprehension, George burst out laughing.

"It isn't funny!"

"Oh, but it is!" he wheezed.

"*How can you say that?* Don't you see, I won't feel safe knowing John is prowling about, worrying that at any moment he could–"

"Could what?" he prompted, noting Charmaine's flushed cheeks, a condition that fed his merriment.

"I thought you were my friend!" she threw back.

"I am," he avowed, his laughter finally sobering to a chuckle. "Don't be angry, and don't fret over John. He's the last person you need fear."

"That is easy for you to say."

"Easy because it's true." He was laughing again, a hearty laugh that followed him out of the house, across the lawns, and into the stable.

Agatha studied her husband as intently as he studied the foliage that sped past them. He had scarcely glanced her way since falling into the cushioned seat opposite her. But that mattered very little, as little as his caustic remarks in front of the servants. He didn't mean what he said, hadn't realized how cruel he sounded. His comportment was always sharp, spawned by his handicap and, therefore, easily forgiven. If he were harsh, she would remember that they were finally married – that she was his wife, a title that soothed any injury. If the present with its many obstacles was at times difficult to swallow, the promise of tomorrow lighted such days with a shimmering ray of hope. The future was hers, secured by the title of Mrs. Frederic Duvoisin, a title that guaranteed her time to win back his love. Hadn't she waited her entire life, spent every waking hour planning to attain what was finally hers? She was his wife. Though Robert had scoffed at her purpose, attempted to expunge it, she refused to admit defeat, never permitted the word to whisper through her mind. How could she, when her sole desire was Frederic and only Frederic?

From his first kiss, she knew she could never be satisfied with another, never be whole without him. Dear God, how she loved him. After all these years, she was still in awe of her intense yearning, drawn to him like a moth to a flame. He might very well be her undoing, but she'd gladly lay down her life if just once he'd whisper the three words she longed to hear. Then she'd know that no matter what she had done in the name of love, it could not be considered wrong.

Frederic... he was handsome still. For all his three score and two years, he could still set her heart to hammering, her limbs quivering, her mind reveling in the memory of wanton passion. Since their marriage, they had shared a few moments of intimacy. For the past two months, however, he had brushed her aside. She pined for his touch of years gone by, before his seizure had sapped his virility. Could it ever be the same again? Dare she hope? With a half-smile, she promised herself that she'd do more than that. Thirty years ago, she had been but a novice at the game of love. If only she could have had the experience then that she had now. Frederic would never have dismissed her so easily, would never have been distracted by the wiles of a sister five years her junior.

Elizabeth... the fountainhead of her pain, the ruination of her life. Elizabeth... eager to snatch away what didn't belong to her. Elizabeth... married to Frederic with the change of a season. Elizabeth... snickering at her conniving conquest, leaving Britain without a backward glance, without a care for her desperate sister. But, the Almighty had rendered a severe punishment. For all the newlyweds' so-called love, Elizabeth had not survived, a sign that their love was not love at all.

Frederic... Once again she studied him across the carriage, longed to squeeze alongside him. She'd brush back the lock of hair that had fallen onto his stern brow and caress away his dark scowl. He'd seen so much sorrow, endured so much pain. First Elizabeth, and now John. Like mother, like son. How she longed to set it right for him. But in his bitterness, he overlooked the one person who loved him more fiercely than the sum of all those he claimed to cherish: not his adoring Elizabeth, nor his youthful Colette, not his simpering Pierre, nor his pampered daughters, not even Paul loved him as surely as she did. Someday very soon, he'd see that. He'd realize how blind he'd been, how very wrong to allow John to ridicule her, how convoluted to place obligation and the mores of society first when distributing his wealth. Someday, he'd turn to her as a husband turns to a wife and she would be there for him.

Frederic leaned back into the soft cushions and feigned sleep, contemplating his wife beneath hooded eyes. In a rush, the past spilled into the brougham. It was the year 1807. He was thirty-two, a wealthy bachelor in the prime of his life. She was twenty-two, young and beautiful, very beautiful. But his eyes weren't on her as the carriage sped to Charmantes' harbor. His eyes had found Elizabeth, head slightly bowed, hands folded demurely in her lap, cheeks slightly flushed from their brief exchange in the stable.

Audaciously she had asked, "Are you in love with my sister, Mr. Duvoisin?"

He responded to her intrepid, yet curious, query with one of his own. "What has love to do with a sound business decision?"

She should have been offended; yet, he read something very different in her brown eyes. It intrigued him.

"But my sister loves you, doesn't she?"

Irritated now, he frowned. "How old are you, Elizabeth?"

"I've just turned seventeen."

"All but grown up," he remarked derisively.

Moments later, she dared not meet his gaze, her manner suddenly diffident. But that did not deter him from feasting his eyes upon her as he had done for the better part of two weeks: not half so beautiful as her older sister, but lovely, animated, and captivating. He had misread her inquiries, thinking it a puerile interrogation borne of concern for her sister. He'd grossly underestimated the power she would wield over him and, even today, thanked the Good Lord he had. That had been the spring of his love. God, how she had haunted him since. The attraction to Colette had been the same, but then, they were alike in so many ways. He recalled the stable; even their private encounters had been similar, uncanny.

Sadly, only Agatha occupied the bench across from him today. At times such as these, he was guilt-ridden. He had probably ruined her life as surely as he had his own. Paul was right: He should never have married her. He prayed that his present purpose ended more favorably than their courtship had. He would offer the two in atonement for his many sins.

"But *you'll* be there!" John appealed earnestly. "I want you to come. I'm begging you to come!"

"I'm sorry, John, I can't. That's *not* what Colette wanted. Beyond that, you haven't even considered Yvette and Jeannette. They'd be crushed."

"Nan–"

"John – I can't. I just can't."

Rose turned away slowly, her heart fraught with despair.

Charmaine froze in the archway. "I'm sorry. I didn't mean to–"

John pivoted round, his face contorted, anguished, like the morning he'd learned of Colette's death. He swiftly masked the emotion and forced a sheepish smile. "Come in, Miss Ryan. Rose and I are finished."

The remainder of the day passed on the same eerie note, escalating Charmaine's initial anxieties. Not even Yvette's exclamations of: "We have the run of the house!" and "No Auntie Agatha to scold us!" or "Just Johnny and us for a whole week!" could quell her misgivings.

Just Johnny and us… therein lie the rub. Charmaine didn't need a week of 'just Johnny and us'; didn't want one night of it. Johnny was acting too peculiar, as were the others. At dinner, Fatima Henderson insisted that he take extra helpings, as if his meals to come would be sparse. And Rose had taken supper in her room, leaving Charmaine and the children alone with him at the table. He had studied her keenly, a scrutiny that bordered on an assessment, as if he were weighing her worth. Extremely uncomfortable, she had eaten quickly and retreated with the children to the nursery.

Now it was ten o'clock, and they were long asleep. Determined to remain wide-awake until John retired as well, Charmaine needed a book. When she reached the foyer, she hesitated. Did she really want to intrude on the man?

John had closeted himself in the study after dinner, relentlessly pacing. Evidently, it hadn't lessened his turmoil; he was marching still. She'd be a fool to walk into the lion's den. She returned to her room.

The night was a precipice of indecision punctuated by malicious moments of desperation. Seconds turned into weary minutes, minutes accumulated into unending hours, and the hours begged for dawn. The great clock struck twice in the foyer. As the tolls diminished, the walls grappled for the reverberating sound and, in the end, surrendered to the void.

John lay abed, listening to his amplified breathing. For the first time in many minutes, his mind was blank. Too long had he deliberated his present crucible, weighing each option, rejecting those that suited him best, realizing – even from the onset of this miserable day – that he could not wrest what he had never claimed, for in so doing, he would forfeit the precious, meager contentment he had been rewarded these past weeks.

His happiness depended on that of another. And since no one would conspire with him, he would be wise to surrender to the hopelessness of it all, his inability to proceed in any direction save the one thus far charted. Float with the tide… the course destined to govern his life.

God, how he hated this prison that had shackled him for so many years now! He could not advance, he could not retreat, he could only remember and curse heaven for the hard hand dealt him, the hand he had chosen to pick up and play. And yet, something had to be done. If nothing else, he'd be damned if he'd pass another three hours in his rumpled bed, tossing and turning in exhausted turmoil.

He threw aside the linens and jumped from the bed. But as he started pacing again, piercing memories took hold, crucifying his soul. He had devoutly embraced those recollections, hoping that the future would set them free. The future had never come; the past had never died. It was time the two met and were buried, peacefully. Perhaps there was a chance for that, if only he could evoke his passion and release his despair. Suddenly, he knew where to turn. He pulled on his robe and, unmindful of those he might disturb, stormed the hall, slamming the door behind him.

Charmaine bolted from a fitful slumber, feverishly tracking the tread of heavy footsteps diminishing in the corridor beyond. She knew who was stalking the house at this late hour. She strained to detect the returning steps of her predator, certain they would be menacingly soft, perhaps imperceptible. Even though she'd locked her door, she feared access from the veranda or the unused dressing room, or even the nursery. Seconds gave way to minutes and, as her racing heart lulled, so too did her breathing. Nothing – no sinister sound of danger. Had the man left the house or merely his chambers? Was he once again pacing in the study, perhaps plotting his assault of the vulnerable governess? John wasn't like that, she reasoned. He'd never given her reason to believe him capable of rape. After all, she'd been just as defenseless the night of his arrival. Still, that first night had not offered the same unencumbered opportunity. Tonight, there was no Paul, no servants, no one to come to her aid should she scream. Rape... She shuddered. But wouldn't he have accosted her sooner? The night was half spent and, save the fact that he could not sleep, would be no different than any other.

Then it came: an abandoned melody. *Was she dreaming?* She canted her head, but could only capture wisps of the blossoming sonata. Instantly, she was out of bed. She wasn't dreaming! Someone was mastering the incredible score, calling her to come and listen. She rushed out of the barricaded room, pulling on her robe as she went, following the music that floated up to her on silken wings. If only Colette were here...

She found herself standing barefoot in the drawing room doorway without memory of her descent. John was seated at the piano, his back to her, head slightly bowed. At first, his hands caressed the keys, coaxing from the instrument a heart-wrenching loneliness, a fervent yearning. Abruptly, his irate fingers struck out, evoking a tidal wave of passion. Her eyes were drawn to the candelabrum, mesmerized by the flickering flames that danced wildly to the amplifying rhapsody, the man's movements displacing the air nearest them. She felt akin to the wick, scorched and devoured, spent in the wake of such power and majesty, yet transformed and at peace, like the hot wax that wept onto the piano's ebony surface.

As the climax broke, John faltered. A jarring dissonance echoed off the walls, and he pulled away as if cauterized. Then, his hands came crashing down again, as if he could pound his mistake from existence. The keys locked, and a deliberate, brutal cacophony seized the air.

Charmaine grimaced, aching for the loveliness that had been annihilated.

Slowly, the punishment ebbed. Laying both arms across the keyboard, John buried his face there, weathering the constricting thud of his battered heart. He'd hoped to exorcise his demonic desolation, not conjure it. He inhaled deeply, then shuddered as he released the pent-up breath, unaware of the young woman who stood in the shadows, observing him in this new light.

Much later, Charmaine would wonder why she didn't escape back to her room. "Don't stop," she implored, stepping into the parlor.

John turned and scowled. Tonight he needed to be alone.

"What I mean is – you play very well."

John grunted. "The one thing I'm able to do right."

"Except for the last few measures."

"Except that," he agreed, his voice hard.

She took no offense. He seemed to be chastising himself. "Even so, one mistake shouldn't cause you to dismiss the piece entirely. After all, look how well you've played most of it. Mrs. Harrington used to always say–"

"Isn't it a bit late for you to be up, Mademoiselle?" he cut in brusquely.

Charmaine faltered. "I was awakened by the music."

"My apologies."

"No need to apologize. I happen to love that particular piece."

"Do you?" he mocked. "I've never heard you play it."

"I don't do it justice. Colette used to encourage me, but after she died, I was forbidden to–"

"*Forbidden?*" he demanded, his vexation giving way to full-fired wrath. "Who forbade it?"

The truth had stood just behind a doorway, awaiting the portal to be thrown open, and comprehension, with all its answers, came crashing down upon Charmaine. *Forbidden…* the word that unlocked so many doors and shed light on so many questions. Playing the music – forbidden. Mentioning John's name – forbidden. Writing to him – forbidden. John seeking out the children – forbidden. Bearing more children – forbidden. John and Colette – *forbidden!* Everything Charmaine had surmised was true! *Had to be true!* Pray God it wasn't true!

"I – shouldn't have come down here," she stumbled aloud. "I'm sorry."

But before she could reach the archway, John caught her arm from behind. "Not so quickly!" he ordered, pulling her around with one cruel twist. "You haven't answered my question."

She didn't flinch, neither did she pull away, and John drowned in the melancholy eyes that lifted to his. He was shaken by her silent submission, his fiery reaction abruptly doused. "Please… don't go," he whispered, releasing her arm. "It was my father, wasn't it? He was the one who wouldn't allow you to play the piece, wasn't he?"

"Yes," she conceded. "I'm sorry."

"Why? Why should you be sorry?"

"Because I don't want to make matters worse between you and your father."

He snorted in disgust. "Colette used to say the very same thing, but you have less control over this miserable situation than she did, and she had precious little then. As I've said before, it took twenty-nine years to live. Nothing can worsen what is already the most deplorable of relationships between a father and son."

"Even so," she argued, "it must pain you, though you try to deny it."

"I deny nothing, save the fact that neither you nor Colette are to blame."

"But I am responsible for mentioning it. It doesn't please me to know that I've hurt you."

The statement seemed to confound him. "Why would you harbor any compassion for me?"

"I don't know," she answered truthfully. "Perhaps it's because I'm beginning to comprehend your past. I'm not certain what happened here so very long ago, but I think it transcends your childhood and..." She hesitated, reticent.

"And?" he probed.

"I think I've grown to like you, in some ways, even respect you. In either case, I don't think you deserve to be hurt."

"No one deserves to be hurt, Charmaine, least of all an innocent child."

At first she thought he spoke of himself and his father, but his eyes betrayed no sign of self-pity or resentment. He appeared instead to be at peace, as if he finally understood something that had eluded him for hours. When he spoke again, she was completely baffled. "Would you like to hear the entire piece?"

With her affirmation, he returned to the piano, and she followed. He sat, rested his fingers on the keys, and contemplated the first flourishing stroke.

The initial measures were soft, poignant. Then the room exploded with sound. Not once did his fingers falter, rather they bent to his will, summoning from the instrument a fine-tuned cadence, an unfathomable longing that swelled and ebbed like the tides of a tempestuous sea. Without warning, the last strains cried out, heralding the final chord.

Doleful, yet satiated, Charmaine could not speak, sighing deeply instead.

"You seem displeased, my Charm."

It was a moment before she realized John had spoken.

"Displeased?" she queried. "No, I'm not displeased, just sad that it is over."

"I shall play it again whenever you wish," he promised with a lopsided smile, "that is, if you can abide this particular rendition."

"Oh, yes – I can!" she answered fiercely. "Those last few measures are extremely difficult. I'm certain that the composer would be quite satisfied with your conclusion."

"It was the only one open to me."

Before she could reflect upon the bizarre remark, he approached her.

"I'd like to apologize for my behavior today," he said, standing only a breath away. "I know it must have been unnerving."

Charmaine inhaled slowly. "I feel quite safe at present."

He chuckled softly, just now savoring the femininity before him, a vision imbued with the tantalizing fragrance of purity, an invasion of the senses. At this moment, she was more desirable than ever before. "Perhaps you shouldn't."

Suddenly, she was in his arms, and his mouth captured hers. He kissed her completely, stealing her breath away, his lips playing a seductive, coveting game, soft one moment, intense the next. She did not resist, nor did she respond, rather she caught hold of him and drew strength from his solid form. Her heart soared and every nerve in her body, down to the tips of her fingers, tingled. Her legs turned liquid, and she clung more tightly to him, submitting completely to his will. She was certain that the moment lasted an eternity, yet it was only a moment, she told herself, one unexpected moment. Later, she would argue that if she had been forewarned, she would have fought off his advance – successfully. For now, she permitted John his embrace, her eyes closed to reason and reality, her senses open to the sweet sensations this man stirred inside her: his warm palm on her cheek, his sinewy arm cradling her head, his hard chest pressed to her breasts. He traced kisses along her jaw until his face burrowed deep in the hollow between her neck and hair, where his lips nuzzled the ivory column and his tongue caressed an aching earlobe. She was paralyzed by his magnetism, her agony most manifest when his head lifted and his arms fell away. She swayed on unsteady legs and could hear her heart pounding in her ears.

"We had best leave it there," he whispered raggedly.

He, too, was bereft and studied her for one hopeful moment. When she said nothing, he smiled. She was an innocent, completely unaware of the effect she had on him, the blood that thundered in his veins and quickened in his loins. She certainly didn't deserve to get mixed up with someone like him.

"Dawn is only a few hours away," he continued determinedly, "and we both need some sleep. It shouldn't be too difficult to find that golden slumber now."

She disagreed, but wisely held her tongue as he lit a candle and snuffed the candelabrum. When he grasped her elbow, she began to speak, but he put a finger to her lips. "No need for words, my Charm. They'd only mar the moment and spoil the calm." She took heed.

They walked through the foyer and ascended the staircase, a climb that seemed endless in the shadowy darkness. As they neared the crest, her apprehension mounted, and she drew her robe more tightly around her.

"Cold?" he asked, misreading the action. "Not to worry. You'll soon be warm beneath the covers."

She was reassured that he hadn't mentioned joining her there. Still, she mistrusted herself and looked up at him slowly when they reached her door. His regard was intense, an unusual warmth in the amber-brown orbs. He bent forward and placed a fatherly kiss on her forehead. When he stepped back, his eyes caressed her face. "Thank you," he said, looping a stray lock behind her ear.

"For what?"

"For the past few moments, for tonight. It wasn't the resolution I'd expected to reach at the onset of this day, but it's not one I scorn. You've given me something very precious just now, something I couldn't have given myself."

"What's that?" she asked, greatly intrigued.

"Hope – in the future. I'll float with the tide, not against it, and maybe someday, it *will* right itself. Goodnight, my Charm."

He walked away, but Charmaine stared after him until the light from his candle died with the closing of his chamber door. Sure that she would not sleep even if he did, she heaved a perplexed sigh and went into her own room. But as she nestled into bed, the rhapsody resounded in her head, and she felt John's strong arms enfolding her in a cocoon of contentment.

Tuesday, October 3, 1837

Much as Charmaine longed to shirk her duties, she could only groan at the light, yet insistent, knock on her bedchamber door. "Come in," she beckoned as she stood and retrieved her discarded robe.

Mrs. Faraday pushed into the room carrying fresh bed linens. Bleary-eyed, Charmaine watched as, without a word, the woman bustled about the chamber, drawing a drape here, extinguishing a lamp there. She turned to the bed.

"That won't be necessary, Mrs. Faraday. As I've told you before, I'm capable of making my own bed."

"Be that as it may," the older woman commented sharply, "today is Tuesday, wash day. The mattress must be stripped and fresh linens spread."

"And I'm capable of doing that as well."

"If you were capable, Miss Ryan, it would have been done already. I cannot afford to have my schedule upset by someone who sleeps the day away. As it is, I'm short staffed."

Charmaine frowned. "What time is it?"

"Nearly eleven."

"But it can't be! The children would have awakened me!"

"It is, and they would have had Master John not interceded on your behalf." She clicked her tongue in evident disgust, tearing the sheets from the bed without a glance in Charmaine's direction. "Why the master of the house would take it upon himself to mind three children when his father is paying a governess to do so is beyond my comprehension. I'd say it's a trifle queer that she's in bed, regaining her – how did he put it? – needed sleep, when he's up and about, full of vim and vigor. Very queer indeed, if you ask me."

Charmaine groaned inwardly, certain that her crimson cheeks condemned her. "I *didn't* ask you, and I'm sorry that you've misconstrued a kindness for something lewd."

Mrs. Faraday scoffed. "Miss Ryan, I'm no simpleton. That remark you made at the dinner table has the whole house talking. I thought you were attempting to make Master Paul jealous at the time, but now – well, now I don't know."

Humiliation yielded to outrage. "Mrs. Faraday! You may pick up your linens and kindly leave my room!"

The woman was silenced. She pursed her lips and bundled the sheets.

"And the next time I'm sleeping," Charmaine added, "do not disturb me! I'm not being paid to endure your verbal abuse."

The door thundered shut, but Charmaine remained planted in the center of the room, fists balled at her sides, teeth clenched in unspent fury. She was proud of her mettle, yet, still so very angry. The audacity of the woman! At this moment, Charmaine was certain that she was worse than Agatha.

Slowly her ire ebbed. As she turned to make her bed and get dressed, John seeped into her thoughts, reviving those exquisite feelings of the night before.

She had slept peacefully; nevertheless, she knew, without specific recollection, that John had occupied all of her dreams. How would he greet her this morning? How would she greet him? Unlike the first time he had kissed her, she could not hide behind a façade of injured pride or pretended disgust. She had enjoyed his embrace – completely – and her pulse raced with the memory of it. She prayed that he'd heed his own declaration and keep silent about the intimate encounter. But knowing John as she did, she feared he would not.

"Anything?"

"Anything within reason," John answered, his gaze fixed on Yvette across the dining room table. They were eating lunch!

Pierre spotted Charmaine first and scrambled from John's lap. "Mainie's here!" he announced, grasping her hand and drawing her into the room. "Come… you hafta help us plan the week!"

"What week?" she asked, avoiding eye contact with John.

"This week, silly," he giggled. As she sat down, he climbed into his own chair and gave John his full attention. "All wight," he said most maturely, elbows propped and chin cradled in his hands, "we're weady now."

"As I was saying to the children, Miss Ryan, the week belongs to them."

She looked directly at him in spite of herself, surprised to find his smile assuasive rather than sardonic, and her heart skipped a beat.

He turned back to the twins. "Your wish is my command," he continued. "We'll spend the next four days in any manner you'd like. And, to be fair, I'll give each of you a day of your own. We'll begin with Pierre. Today will be his day. Tomorrow, Jeannette may decide what we'll do. Thursday will belong to Yvette, and Friday will be Mademoiselle Charmaine's. How does that sound?"

"Why do I have to wait until Thursday?" Yvette objected.

"I thought you would like time to plan the best possible excursion."

"Oh," his sister pondered aloud, quickly warming to the idea. "Yes, I suppose I would, and I promise it will be something extra special, something that no one else will ever dream of."

"I'm certain," he said. "So, Pierre, what should we do today?"

"I want Fwiday," the boy insisted. "I need more time, too!"

John chuckled. "I suppose that can be arranged, if Mainie doesn't mind exchanging days with you."

He looked at Charmaine, and she quickly consented, realizing too late that she would now have to contrive some fabulous plan for the afternoon. *But what?*

John folded his arms across his chest and, with an exaggerated yawn, propped his boots atop the tablecloth. He pushed back, and balanced the chair on two legs.

"Johnny!" Jeannette scolded, "Cookie is going to tan your backside if she comes in here!" Yvette and Pierre giggled.

"I said anything," he replied, ignoring his sister's reprimand as he rocked the chair to-and-fro. "Miss Ryan, we are awaiting your pleasure."

"It would please me to see you sitting properly in that chair. You are teaching the children terrible things, and if you're not careful, you'll topple over and injure your back."

As if on cue, the chair wobbled precariously, then fell away from the table entirely, spilling John on the floor. The children screeched, but Charmaine flew to his side, worry creasing her brow. "Are you all right?"

"I think I've fractured my spine!" he groaned, his face a mask of pain.

"I knew it!" she gasped, crouching closer and looping an arm around his shoulders. "Do you think you can get up?"

"I – I don't know."

"Please try," she coaxed, so focused on assisting him that she was unprepared for his swift movement that stole a kiss. *Tricked!* John was laughing up at her, and her cheeks burned red from the momentary contact.

"Johnny kissed Mademoiselle Charmaine!" Jeannette squealed in delight.

"On the lips!" Yvette gagged.

Charmaine shot to her feet. *"Ssh! Do you want the entire house to hear?"*

"What's goin' on in here?" Fatima Henderson demanded as she barreled into the dining room, her thick girth heaving. "What are you up to Mastah John?"

"Nothing, Cookie," he reassured as he slowly stood and righted the chair. "I took a little spill, but I'm fine."

Unconvinced, she cocked her head. "Mastah John, I don't know what mischief you' calculatin' in that handsome head of yours, but I say it's about time you went about yo' business for the day. Didn't Mastah Paul ask you to do some work for him?"

"He asked, but I didn't answer."

The children laughed, but Fatima sucked in her cheeks.

"Later," he promised, "I'll do some work later. Right now I'm waiting for Miss Ryan–"

"Miss Charmaine ain't your concern. She hasn't even eaten yet, and already you're in here harrassin' her."

"Harassing? Me? I assure you that was not my intent. As soon as she tells us how we are to spend the day, she may eat in peace."

"A swing," Charmaine replied, drawing all eyes to her.

"What?" John queried, confounded.

"A swing," she repeated, wondering how such a novel idea had popped into her head. "I would like you to construct a swing for the day's enjoyment."

"A swing?"

"Yes, a swing. S-W-I-N-G," she repeated for a third time, smiling triumphantly as she imagined John high in the branches of one of the great oak trees and far from her. Unable to instigate trouble from there, she'd be quite safe from his schemes.

"You spell quite well," he complimented with a twisted grin. "Still, I don't see much fun–"

"Are you saying you won't do it?"

"No, I didn't say that. It's just that I don't think–"

"That you can't do it?" she pressed.

"I didn't say that either," he argued, his amusement fading. Damn, she was playing the game too well.

"What then?" she asked with arms folded across her bosom, eliciting a chuckle from Fatima Henderson as she returned to her kitchen.

"If you'd let me finish, I was going to ask: where would we hang it?"

"From one of the oak trees nearest the front portico. Yes, that should do very nicely... A capital way to spend the day."

John only snorted. "Actually I think it's rather–"

"It doesn't matter what you think, does it? You said the day was mine and that I could spend it in any manner I wished. That was what you said, wasn't it?"

"Yes, that was what I said."

"In that case, why don't you locate the materials you will need: a nice smooth board and a good length of rope. When I've finished eating, the children and I will join you."

Yvette clicked her tongue. "But I've already eaten. I want to go with Johnny!"

"Me, too!" Pierre chimed in. "I wanna build me a swing!"

"See," Charmaine pointed out, "they like the idea."

"So they do," John replied debonairly, "so a swing we shall build."

He winked at Pierre as if the idea had been his all along, then took the children with him.

An hour later, the swing was suspended, a feat less difficult than Charmaine had at first imagined, especially with the aid of the stable-hands. Presently, she sat on the terrace and watched the children as they took turns on it. Yvette quickly mastered the rudiments of pumping the board to dizzying heights, squealing each time she dropped toward the earth. Next, it was Jeannette's turn and finally Pierre's. The latter had to be pushed gently, a chore eagerly assumed by Jeannette once Yvette plopped in the grass some feet away.

"Well, my Charm, you have your swing," John said as he climbed the steps of the colonnade and came to sit next to her. "Aren't you going to at least try it?"

"Later," she answered, "when the children have tired of their play."

He considered her, his eyes finally resting on her lips, a point of interest that caused her to shiver. "I thank you for this favor," she said, hoping to distract him, relieved when his regard lifted to her eyes. "I would ask another."

"And what would that be?"

"That you refrain from displays of affection toward me," she replied.

"Displays of affection? If you're speaking about my *passionate* kiss this morning–"

"Exactly," she interjected, not allowing him to finish.

"I'd hardly call such an overture passion, my Charm. I assure you, it was completely innocent."

"Innocent to you, perhaps," she argued, fighting hard to retain her poise, "but what do children know of innocence and passion? To them, the two are one and the same."

"And to you, Charmaine?"

She'd lost the battle, and she felt her face grow warm. She couldn't answer; neither could she look his way.

"Very well, my Charm. I do not want to spoil our week together, so you need not fear any further overtures from me, passionate or otherwise."

"Thank you," she whispered, studying the hands in her lap.

"And I'll speak to Mrs. Faraday as well, if you'd like."

Stunned, her eyes flew to his face. "How did you know–"

"I didn't. Not for certain anyway. But the look she gave me this morning when I insisted that you not be disturbed... let us say, I realized my mistake. Don't worry, Charmaine, she won't be telling Paul. And even if she does, it could work in your favor."

Charmaine's shame turned to anger, but she bit her tongue when she noted the deviltry in his eyes, that familiar expression that meant he was teasing her.

"You know," he goaded when she refused to retaliate, "a bit of jealousy could work wonders at bringing my brother around."

"Bringing him around?"

"To the altar, Charmaine. That *is* your deepest desire, is it not?"

Holding silent, she stared out across the lawns. John allowed the minutes to accumulate, and Charmaine knew he studied her. Then, he dropped the subject altogether. "So, what are we going to do for the remainder of the day?" he asked. "It's still early. Perhaps a visit into town?"

"You could play the piano for me – and the children."

His smile broadened as if he'd extracted a confession from her. He waved off the idea. "You play for them every day, surely there's something else–"

"Not nearly as well as you do. After last night, I understand why you..."

"Why I what? Why I inferred that your musical ability was lacking?"

She didn't answer.

"You play very well, Charmaine, and I enjoy hearing the children sing along when you sit at the piano. I was an ogre those first few days home, especially to you. I misjudged you. George tried to tell me I was wrong, so did Paul, but I guess because I was hearing it from my brother, I refused to believe it."

"Why?" she asked. "Why do you mistrust one another? Why are you constantly at odds?"

"There are a number of reasons. Most of them revolve around my father."

"Are you angry with your father for giving Paul the other island?"

"No, I'm not angry. At least, I don't think I am."

She frowned at his curious reply. "Is it the enthusiasm he's given Paul's endeavor? I imagine you must have your own accomplishments in Virginia that deserve recognition."

"If my father knew of my accomplishments in Virginia, he'd probably put Paul in charge there, too."

She digested the derisive statement, the twisted smile. "Still, it means a lot for a parent to show an interest in an offspring's undertakings. I know how it feels to be unappreciated, to be scorned."

"You were scorned?"

"Yes, by my father I was."

"Well then, my Charm, it seems we *do* have something in common." He was quiet for a while and then asked, "What happened to your mother?"

Charmaine inhaled. Even after two years, the memory was painful. Strangely, she didn't feel she had to hide the truth from him any longer. She could tell him about it, and he would understand.

"My father, he was drunk and angry. He brutally beat my mother, and she died of the injuries he inflicted. He disappeared, and nobody has seen him since." Tears sprang to her eyes without warning. "It was my fault," she choked out, turning her face aside.

"Your fault?"

"I was hiding my wages from him. He was a lazy bum, who rarely worked. When he did, the money was spent on spirits. Most times he relied on my mother to tarry. When I found employment with the Harringtons, he felt he was entitled to what I earned as well. Then one night, when he was good and drunk, he came to their house looking to collect my wages. When he didn't find me there, he went after my mother instead, assuming that we were conspiring together to hide my salary. He would never have touched her if I had handed the money over to him."

"No, Charmaine, it wasn't your fault," he refuted in acute disgust. "There is no excuse for a man to beat a woman. I've known men like him. If it weren't about money, it would have been about something else. Don't blame yourself. You shouldn't blame yourself."

She was comforted by his sincerity. She'd never told anyone that she held herself responsible for her father's dastardly deed. She wondered why it had been so easy to tell John, why his reaction relieved her burden of guilt.

"What is your father's name?"

"His name? Why do you ask?"

John shrugged. "Just curious, I guess."

"His name is… John Ryan."

A sudden, perspicacious grin broke across his lips. "John, eh?"

Uncomfortable that he'd be examining her soul next, Charmaine redirected the conversation. "Your father has scorned you as well, hasn't he?"

The smile vanished. "You were there the other night, Charmaine. You tell me? It is just another reason why Paul and I don't get along."

Understanding dawned. "So that is why you're not interested in Duvoisin business. Without your father's love and acceptance, you have little desire to promote his enterprises." When he didn't respond, she continued. "Paul has your father's love, but longs for legitimacy, while you long for your father's love, caring little about your legitimacy."

"No," John bit out, amazed, yet annoyed with her astute assessment. "Paul longs for it all, but he won't get it! You see, my father enjoys having him dangle as well."

"Dangle?"

"You wouldn't understand, Charmaine. Frederic Duvoisin is the master of manipulation, the consummate puppeteer."

She was saddened by his summation. "I've found your father to be forthright," she insisted.

"*Really?*" he scoffed sourly. "That just proves how very naive you are." She bristled at the insult, but John was just as vexed. "I don't want to ruin my day with talk of my father. If we're going to continue our little heart-to-heart, let's restrict it to Paul. Anything you'd like to know about him?"

He was right; Paul was a far more interesting topic. But she was also wary of the insights John might offer. There was one question that seemed benign. "Who is older, you or Paul?"

John's brow lifted, and his eyes darted around, mischievous again. He leaned in close and whispered as if the mansion had ears. "Well now, my Charm, that's the *big* family secret. No one knows for sure. Some say that the baby – that would be Paul – was brought to my father before I was born, from origins unknown and in the middle of the night." He straightened up and answered directly. "I don't put credence in that, though. I've often wondered how my mother accepted Paul's arrival, if she had to accept it at all. It seems more logical that Paul was born after she died. My father's philandering wouldn't have mattered. Either way, he was a very busy man, sowing his wild oats, so to speak."

"And Paul's mother?"

John shrugged. "Dead, according to my father. But my father never doubted that Paul is his son, bastard though he be."

Charmaine winced, stung by the harsh words.

"Come now, my Charm," he cajoled, "Paul has accepted what he is. There's no need to pity him. There are a great many men who would gladly trade places and take the title of bastard if it would insure them a share of the Duvoisin fortune. I know George would." He chuckled softly, ignoring her frown.

Pierre bounded over to them. "This time I go very high!" he declared, tugging on John's hand and coaxing him up and out of the chair.

Charmaine stood as well and meandered across the lawns to the girls. They were at the paddock now, petting the two-month-old colt, Sultan.

"May we bring the ponies out?" they called.

Thursday, October 5, 1837

"I still don't like it," Charmaine feebly protested from where she sat in the swaying brougham. The twins had petitioned to ride atop the conveyance on either side of the driver, and their governess found herself closeted in the plush carriage with John and Pierre.

"I assure you there's nothing to be alarmed about, my Charm," John replied.

"Why couldn't she have been satisfied with a day similar to the one we passed yesterday? The ride was lovely, the picnic pleasant, even the rain didn't spoil our time, and–"

"–Yvette will never be content in the shadow of repetition," he finished for her. "She's not Jeannette, and the only similarity that will ever exist between them is their looks. You should know that by now, Charmaine. Besides, I find her choice a singular idea."

"Singular indeed," she mumbled. "And what will your father say when he finds that you've escorted your sisters to Dulcie's? I know–" she held up a hand to ward off his answer "–you don't care!"

"I wasn't going to say it quite like that, but in a manner of speaking, yes."

"You can afford to be incorrigible, but what about me? I'm responsible for their welfare. I'll rue the day I compromised my morals for this little escapade."

"And what morals could possibly be in the balance if we visit a saloon? I guarantee that only Dulcie will accost us."

"A saloon?" Charmaine scoffed. "Aren't you being a bit generous? It's a gambling establishment, not to mention–"

"Yes?" he probed with brow raised.

She could not speak what thundered in her mind. She recalled Felicia's tales of the barmaids who cavorted with the seamen in the bedrooms above the common room.

"Don't fret, Charmaine," John proceeded knavishly, "Dulcie's can't be completely condemned if my brother patronizes it."

"Paul is a grown man! Not a child!"

"Exactly! And as such, is more susceptible to the evils of a brothel than any child could ever fear to be."

Charmaine's cheeks flamed red with the declaration. "You think you have all the answers, don't you?" she squeaked out.

"Usually," he replied proudly, "and if you pay close attention, you may recall them should anyone confront you on the matter."

Her eyes narrowed, bolstering his lighthearted mood. "Don't be angry with me. We've enjoyed two splendid days with the children. Today can be just as wonderful if only you'd make it so. And, if anything should go wrong at Dulcie's, I promise to intervene and assume full blame. Isn't that right, Pierre?"

"Wight," the lad chirped.

"I still don't like it," Charmaine reiterated. *Remember, I'll not hold you responsible for any circumstances beyond your control. When you become upset, just remember.* Charmaine sighed. She certainly couldn't order Frederic's son around, Yvette's excursion was definitely out of her control, and she was quite upset. Did this then annul her responsibility? She hoped so. With that thought, she leaned back into the cushions and attempted to enjoy the scenery.

John was correct; there was nothing to fear. When they left the bright boardwalk and slipped into the saloon, Dulcie was expecting them. She ushered them to a prepared table where she sat lemonade before them, followed by a delicious meal. They were treated regally and, to Yvette's chagrin, did not behold the true workings of the quiet tavern. Few were about, and not a single gaming table was being used.

John explained the rules of one card game he called 'poker', informing them that George had concocted it from a few European games they had played at university. The twins remained skeptical, certain that their brother was telling another tall tale. But he insisted that every Friday night was 'poker' night at Dulcie's, and for their benefit, suggested they play a hand. Demonstrating the stakes usually bid, he threw an imaginary coin into the center of the table and dealt them each five cards. Surprisingly, Jeannette caught on more quickly than Yvette and pretended to rake in the kitty four out of five times, but since the pot was imaginary, even she grew bored.

"I wonder what is upstairs," the kind-hearted twin sweetly mused. "I would really like to see."

John's eyes narrowed suspiciously. "What game is this – *Yvette*?" he inquired pointedly of Jeannette.

She shrugged.

"Have you done this before?" he demanded, no longer duped.

"Done what before?" came the innocent question.

Charmaine was baffled, her eyes drawn to Yvette who now stepped forward, an unusual expression on her face.

"I'm Jeannette, Johnny," she said, leaving her accomplice, who'd given one of her braids a fierce yank, scowling. "And only a couple of times."

Charmaine stood amazed and vexed by the clever deception.

The real Yvette stomped her foot, annoyed that nothing was going as planned, unmoved by her governess' look of disapproval. "I still want to see upstairs," she insisted. Her petition ended there, however. John's scowl had deepened, his refusal firm and nonnegotiable. She'd have to devise another scheme to satisfy her curiosity.

They departed the saloon to amble along the boardwalk, which took them directly to the harbor and the Raven. Pierre and the girls begged to go aboard, and Charmaine was happy to comply. She wondered if she'd see Captain Wilkinson. What would he think when he found her walking the ship's deck on John's arm? Maybe he wouldn't remember her at all.

It was an odd sensation ascending the gangway. Not since the day the Harringtons had embarked for Virginia had she done so – a full year ago! She marveled over all that had happened in that time, how she herself had changed.

The vessel sat dormant. According to John, she awaited the salvaged sugarcane harvest before setting sail for New York. With little to do, Jonah Wilkinson had abandoned her, leaving an abbreviated crew to holystone and caulk the decks, tar the masts, and mend the frayed canvases.

Yvette and Jeannette sidestepped them, scurrying across the ship's waist, leaning over the starboard wall, attempting to swat the shrouds or catch a swooping seagull. They climbed atop the forecastle deck, surveying their surroundings from that lofty summit.

John and Charmaine meandered leisurely, starting at the prow, stopping when they spotted something of interest to point out to Pierre, John a wealth of information, the sailors nodding respectfully to him, he reciprocating. When they reached the quarterdeck, he dragged an empty crate over to the helm and stood the lad behind the huge wooden wheel. Charmaine leaned back against the rail and watched as he demonstrated how to grip the wooden spikes and steer the vessel, his eyes alive, indicating that, for all his repudiation of his heritage, he was proud to be a Duvoisin.

"My turn!" the boy demanded, instantly immersed in the imaginary task, supplying the sounds of lapping water against the hull as he guided the bark out of the harbor.

John patted his back, then stepped away and joined Charmaine. She smiled up at him, charmed by his attachment to the lad. "What are you laughing at?"

"You," she answered. "I think you'll make a very good husband someday."

"Really?" Now it was his turn to smile. "And why do you say that?"

Embarrassed, she quickly backtracked. "What I meant to say was 'father'. You'll make a very good father."

His expression sobered. "I fear that avenue is closed to me."

"But you're so good with children," she countered mindlessly, unnerved by his abrupt change of mood. "You should have many of your own."

"Have you forgotten I'm a bad influence?"

"I was wrong about that. You've showered Pierre and the girls with more love and affection than I thought possible of any man."

He forced a smile, but didn't answer.

"I'm sorry..." she murmured. "I've offended you."

"No, my Charm. I appreciate your accolades, but you are mistaken. I'd be a poor substitute for a father." When she opened her mouth to object, he rushed on. "Fortunately, I do have Pierre and my sisters to be content with."

"They will miss you when you leave," she said, startled by her sudden heaviness of heart.

"They won't have to," he replied, turning away from her and gazing out across the peninsula. "I plan on staying around for a while. I didn't realize how lonely my homes in Virginia and New York were until I ventured back here."

"Really?"

"Unless my father permits me to take the children to Richmond for a visit."

"Are you planning on asking him?"

He faced her, his eyes intense. "Would you come with us if I did? If my father gave his consent? They would need to have you there, especially Pierre. And you'd be able to visit your friends."

His voice held a note of expectancy – excitement – as if his happiness depended on the case he now put to her. Then, like quicksilver, he chuckled disparagingly, brushing the fanciful thought aside. "Not to worry, Charmaine. We won't be traveling anywhere together. I know what my father's answer would be, so why bother to ask?"

Charmaine held silent. Sadly, she knew he was right.

They left the Raven shortly afterward and strolled along the town's main thoroughfare. Charmaine felt many eyes upon them and was proud to have John as her escort. Not so long ago, she would have recoiled from such attention, scorned any conclusions drawn by the islanders. But today was different. John was not the man she had so sharply misjudged him to be, and for the first time, she acknowledged her gladness for having come to know him.

Friday, October 6, 1837

Children's laughter wafted off the lake, much like the afternoon breeze that caught at Charmaine's hair and loosed strands from the bun tucked beneath her bonnet. They settled as stray ringlets, framing her pretty face. Still, she was unaware of the picture she painted, sitting on the blanket that John had chivalrously spread for her. Her eyes were on the man who, with his back to her, sat some hundred feet away in the small dinghy he had purchased for Pierre a few weeks ago. With the lad in his lap and his sisters seated across from him, he continued to paddle out to the lake's center, pretending all the while that Pierre was propelling the vessel. Charmaine's smile widened as they finally glided to a stop and John bent over, retrieving the fishing rods he had carelessly thrown in the bottom of the small craft. Few complete sentences reached her ears, but the manner in which he worked at the rods led her to believe the worst: the lines were dreadfully tangled. Well, she had warned him, but the children had been so excited that he hadn't listened. Now he was paying the piper, for already Yvette was tugging at her pole and Pierre, his. A lighthearted laugh escaped her lips. It was swallowed when the fishing boat swayed precariously. John stilled the motion with outstretched arms and shook a finger at Yvette. Charmaine smiled again, glad that she had had the good sense not to further encumber the crowded boat. She was safe where she sat. Finally, the lines were cast. As their activity lulled, she studied her surroundings once again.

They were nestled within a forest, an idyllic clearing that ran along the perimeter of a central reservoir, which, according to John, was dug from a small pond by his grandfather and fifty laborers over seventy years ago. She had been astonished when they had walked not fifty yards, entered the line of thick pine trees from the grounds at the rear of the manor and, in less than ten minutes, practically stumbled upon the pristine fresh-water lake. Only a small bungalow and dock marred nature's untamed beauty. All else remained unspoiled.

Charmaine breathed deeply in great contentment. Presently, a pair of flamingos meandered to the water's edge and waded along the bank. This beautiful glade, just beyond the mansion... She thought of the twins' birthday picnic on the beach and that first picnic on the bluffs. Because of John, she'd experienced first-hand the majesty of Charmantes. John. Again, her eyes were drawn to the man. How many times during their week together had this happened? It was an unsettling question, and she marveled at the great distance they had traveled in two short months. She could not know that the journey had just begun.

It was late, yet a brilliant half-moon illuminated Charmantes' cove. The Falcon reduced sail and drifted into the harbor. As she was moored, Frederic stood stoically at the rail. The Raven was gone, and a foreign ship was berthed in her place, a fact that should have pleased him. His torment would haunt him for the rest of his days. However, what was done was done, and what he had set out to accomplish this week had been accomplished. Downtrodden, he wondered if he'd ever see his son again. He swallowed against the thick lump lodged in his throat, impeding speech.

"Father, we'll be going ashore now."

Frederic averted his gaze. "By all means," he coughed, "lead the way."

A half-hour passed before a conveyance was obtained from the livery and the luggage hoisted into it. In that time, Frederic surveyed the new merchantman.

"The Wanderlust," Paul breathed with pride, slapping her hull. "The first of the new fleet. One hundred fifty feet of the finest white oak the States have to offer. I shall meet with her captain in the morning. Would you like to accompany me – look her over?"

Frederic said nothing, and Paul stood bewildered when his father turned and limped down the pier. The man had shown great interest over the past five days, his enthusiasm ever expanding, and now this. Clearly, he was exhausted.

After Agatha and the servants were settled inside the landau, Frederic declined the seat saved him. "You go ahead. The carriage is far too crowded. I'll await its return at Dulcie's."

"Dulcie's?" Agatha objected. "That place is nothing more than a–"

"Agatha, I'm acquainted with the establishments that operate on Charmantes. Paul and I will wait at Dulcie's."

The vehicle pulled away, and Frederic faced his blatantly confused son. "Don't tell me you're concerned about the trouble I could get into there?"

Paul laughed. "No, sir. It's just that it has been a long five days. I know you must be tired and–"

"Before all that, I'm the master of this island," his sire interrupted. "I'd like to find out what has happened while we were gone. What better way than to visit the tavern where the gossip is high and everything known?"

Bawdy music spilled into the street just outside Dulcie's, a syncopated rhythm livened by the boisterous laughter of men and women alike: the shout of a longshoreman, the squeal of a doxy, the snap of the spinning wheels, which drew huddles at the gaming tables.

George Richards strode into the raucous common room looking forward to a stiff drink. The week's work had been grueling: first the sugarcane harvest, then the loading of the Raven. The vessel hadn't embarked until late that afternoon, and then he'd helped secure the new ship that pulled into port just behind her. After that, he'd traveled to the mill, relieved to find it running smoothly. Still, George would be glad when Paul returned. Managing Charmantes was too much for one man, and though John was there, he had been no help whatsoever, informing George at the onset of the week that his father's work was Paul's work, not his. Therefore, everything had fallen into George's lap, and tonight, he was bone-weary and spent.

He sat at the bar and swiveled around on his stool. He watched as one surly sailor coaxed a barmaid into his embrace, only to find her less than willing when he didn't hand over the coin that he jangled. Though the man's grip tightened, the buxom wench pushed hard on his chest, sending his chair tumbling to the floor. She rubbed her hands together and turned a proud nose upon his compatriots. "You don't pay, you don't get no service." She sauntered toward another, more promising table, a mound of cold cash just now doubled at its center. George smiled as the strumpet leaned heavily into the shoulder of the man dealing the next hand. He shooed her aside with a slash of his arm, a sure sign that he was losing. Indifferent, she moved around the table. George's eyes followed as he raised a frothing tankard of ale to his lips. He took a long draw off the top, but spewed it down his shirtfront, choking.

There, sitting in the circle of the gaming table, her back to the door and five cards clasped firmly to her chest, was Yvette Duvoisin, disguised as a guttersnipe, her meek sister, similarly garbed, standing directly behind her and sorely out of place.

He jumped to his feet and was at the table in the bat of an eye. "What in blazes are you doing here, Yvette?" he roared.

Alarmed for only a moment, she quickly recovered and raised her chin in defiance. "Playing poker. Five-card draw, to be precise. Isn't that what you called it?" and she turned back to the men for affirmation.

They nodded with a grumble, awaiting her bid.

"I'll raise it ten," she announced, fingering a stack of gold coins before pushing it into the pot.

George grabbed her by the arm and yanked to her feet. "The game is over! Throw in your hand, we're going home!"

"No, I won't!" she protested, wrenching free. "I'm not leaving until the pot is broken. I have over ten dollars in there!"

But for all her recalcitrant bravado, she stumbled backward, cards still clasped to her chest, her resistance wavering under George's uncommon fury.

"Wait a minute, bud," one of the gamblers objected, anticipating the outcome of the showdown, "no need to rush the little lady. She ain't your kin is she?"

"He's only a friend," Yvette swiftly answered. "He can't order me around."

"Well then," another bolstered. "Why don't you leave our little missy alone? She's doin' a fine job takin' care of her herself. Won a hefty sum of our money, she has, and we'd appreciate the chance to win it back."

George turned on the men in disbelief. Evidently, they were new to Charmantes, off the maiden ship that had docked that afternoon and ignorant to Yvette's identity. Her ragamuffin apparel didn't help. Still, she was a mere child. "*Have the lot of you gone mad?*" he exclaimed. "She's a nine-year-old girl–"

"Hold it right there, fella!" the dealer warned. "She came in here with a hefty purse and insisted that we allow her to play. Anyone can game if he has the money to lose, them's the rules of any reputable gamblin' house. At first, we thought we'd humor her. But she's won a few hands, and now it's become serious. So why don't you leave us be?"

"You can go to–"

"George!" Yvette cut in. "One more hand – just let me play one more hand, and Jeannette and I will go home. I promise."

George eyed her suspiciously, still simmering. But reason cautioned him a level head. Her consorts were less than friendly, especially in the face of their losses, and the last thing he needed was an out-and-out brawl. He was, however, going to wring John's neck. When the man had ridden over to the bondsmen's keep and bragged about his weeklong escapades, George had been dismayed and warned him that his visit to Dulcie's would come back to haunt him. John had only mocked him for sounding like Charmaine. But of course, the instigator of this unfolding calamity was at home, while he, George, his so-called friend, was dealing with the consequences. And where in God's name was Dulcie? Did no one know who the twins were?

"One hand – that's all you're getting – one hand!" he relented. Whirling on his heel, he strode back to the bar and the drink that he desperately needed. It would be a miracle if he escorted her home without a scandal. "Whisky – straight," he ordered after downing the ale in one gulp, "and make it a double."

Again he pivoted on the stool and observed the ludicrous scene. Jeannette was bending to her sister's ear, probably whispering some urgent plea that they leave the saloon. Yvette, in turn, shook her head once and proceeded to fold two cards from her initial hand of five. Three of a kind, George surmised as he watched her draw two more from the dealer.

A gush of cool night air, refreshing in the malodorous, smoke-filled tavern, heralded the arrival of newcomers. Snared by the hush that fell over the large room, George turned an eye to the entryway. There, on the threshold of Dulcie's saloon, stood her benefactor, Frederic Duvoisin.

Panic-stricken, George reached the door in three enormous strides. Frederic and Paul lingered there, surveying the establishment and its occupants, who slowly turned back to their vices. "Frederic – ah hum – Paul," he coughed, thanking heaven itself when they gave him their undivided attention. "I didn't expect you back so soon."

"Didn't you?" Paul queried with a frown. "I said the end of the week."

"So you did, so you did," George laughed falsely, taking hold of Paul's elbow and firmly pulling him round. "I suppose I've just been so busy that I didn't realize what day of the week it was. Friday night already, my, my!"

"George, is something wrong?" Paul interrupted, looking down at his arm.

"Wrong? No, nothing's wrong," he replied with another hollow chuckle. "Why would you think that?"

"You seem harried, and you're pulling on my arm."

"So I am," he responded, releasing the limb as if burned. He mustn't be conspicuous. "Actually," he said, inspired, "there was a bit of a problem while you and your father were away. But I need a breath of fresh air. It's so hot in here. Why don't we go outside?"

Frederic observed George with a mixture of satisfaction and regret. "If you have something to tell us, George, I prefer to hear it now, where I stand."

"Sir?" George gulped, by all signs a man with something to hide.

Suddenly, a piercing screech rent the air. George cringed and cursed under his breath. "You've cheated!" Yvette cried, jumping to her feet and throwing a branding finger at the dealer. "You drew the third ace from your sleeve!"

"Prove it!" the man retorted with a wicked chuckle.

"There!" she spat, tossing the same card on the table. "I was holding the ace of spades in the hopes of drawing a higher pair!"

In unison, all five sailors shot to their feet, chairs clattering to the floor. Yvette was certain they were going to devour her, but one look at their faces and the cards they'd cast aside, and she realized she held the winning hand. She'd uncovered the dealer's underhandedness, and now, with George beside her, she could claim her winnings and go home, just as soon as the snake who had raked in the pot pushed it back in her direction. "All of those coins are mine!" she proclaimed flippantly. "And those, too! Tell them, George!"

From nowhere, a black cane struck the table, jolting it like the crack of a whip against the flank of a horse, leveling stacks of gold and silver coins and sending them tinkling to the floor. Others rolled in indecisive circles before toppling to rest. Her mind a blur for only an instant, Yvette recognized the familiar staff, stole a sidelong glance at the broad hand that clutched it, thick veins protruding against taut skin. Murmurs went up around her: "Frederic Duvoisin".

Ever so slowly, she faced her father and fought the urge to cower, looking up into his livid features, braving the clenched jaw – there, where a muscle twitched fiercely – the turbulent eyes, and the sharply creased brow. Worse still was his rabid silence, and she dreaded his leashed wrath. Never before had she seen this side of his ferocious temper. Now, here she was, the object of it.

"Sir?" she gulped with colossal courage.

"What are you doing here, daughter – and in those clothes?"

The query was menacingly soft, yet devastating. Out of the corner of her eye, she took in the ashen complexions of her fellow gamblers.

"Mr. Duvoisin," one man dared to interrupt, "we thought she was a street waif. We had no idea she was your–"

"*Silence!*" Frederic thundered, striking the table again. "You indulge in gaming with a child – *a girl no less* – and then you attempt to extricate yourself by pleading ignorance? By God man, you tread upon perilous ground! And you, young lady!" he growled, sweeping the table clear of its booty and leveling his gaze once again on his wayward daughter. "You will wait for me outside!"

Yvette bobbed her head, then dashed around him and through the doors.

As if seeing Jeannette for the first time, Frederic's visage softened. "Go," he indicated with a jerk of his head. She nodded woefully, then departed the tavern exceedingly slower than her sister, her head bowed in contrition rather than fear.

Yvette was halfway down the street when her sister called after her, but she didn't stop running until she reached the livery. "Yvette!" Jeannette scolded once she'd caught up. "Father said to wait for him outside Dulcie's!"

"I know what he said," Yvette heaved, rubbing the pain in her side, turning to the bleary-eyed man who stepped out of the building. "Martin, I want my pony now," she ordered, "and my sister's as well."

Grumbling, the farrier disappeared into the livery.

"If you know," Jeannette rejoined, "then why didn't you do as he said? You're only going to make matters worse this way!"

"*Worse?* Jeannette, how could it *be* any worse? I probably won't be alive tomorrow morning. But I'm not going to die without a fight!"

"How, by running away?"

"Yes! Don't you see? Down there–" and she pointed to the vacant street just outside the saloon "–I'd be murdered on the spot! But at home, I can hide behind Johnny or Charmaine!"

"Yvette, you can't! You know how terrible things are between Father and Johnny, and if you get Mademoiselle Charmaine involved, Father might dismiss her! Please–"

"*And what about me?*" Yvette demanded. "I'm your sister! Don't *I* count? *Do you want to see me killed?* How would you feel then?"

"Yvette, I don't think Father is going to–"

"Oh dear, oh dear!" Yvette fretted, ignoring her sister altogether as she began to wring her hands. "Where is that man? If he doesn't come back soon, I'll be done for before I even have a chance to run away!"

Endeared to be home, Agatha issued a spate of orders from the foyer, then watched as each servant hastened to follow her directives. Her satisfaction was short lived, however. John, paper in hand, stood in the study archway.

"Well," he said with a tight smile, his shoulder propped against the doorframe, "you're back."

"Yes," she said proudly, "in *my* home."

"Tell me Auntie, has my father accompanied you tonight, or did he have his fill of you this week and decide to remain on Espoir instead?"

"It's not like that between your father and me," she refuted with dignity. "He loves me. And yes, he has returned, by my side."

"Really? Oh well, I knew heaven couldn't last forever, but I *was* hoping to avoid hell. Where is he, anyway?"

"I have no intention of playing your little game," she replied haughtily. "The week we spent on *Paul's* island was too marvelous, and not even you can spoil its lasting pleasure. Goodnight."

She'd just reached the landing when shrieks echoed from the front lawns, followed by thundering footsteps on the portico. The oak door was attacked, and Yvette stormed into the house as if demons chased her, Jeannette right on her heels. "*Johnny! Charmaine!*" she cried. "*Help! Please help me!*" She spotted

John and threw herself into his outstretched arms, sobbing mercilessly, "Oh no! He's right behind me!"

"What the devil's going on?" John demanded, attempting to peel her free.

But she offered no explanation, clinging to him fiercely, her face buried in his shirtfront, moaning the incantation: "Oh Johnny!" over and over again.

This is not a farce, he finally realized. Dismayed now, he looked to Jeannette for an answer. "What's happened? Why are you up and out of the house at this late hour? And why are you dressed like this? Where is Charmaine?"

"Here!" she called from above, belting her robe as she hurried down the stairs. "The cries awoke me." She took one look at the tattered twins and her worry increased. "What is going on?"

"That's what I'm trying to sort out," he said in growing vexation. "*Yvette?*"

Still the girl whined. "You must save me! He's going to kill me, I know he is! At the very least, he'll beat me, whip me!"

"Who – who's going to–?"

Frederic stepped across the threshold, and all went silent. Yvette choked back her tears, sniffling pitifully. She sidled behind her protector, her beseeching eyes lifting to Paul and George, who had drawn up alongside her father.

"I told you to wait for me outside Dulcie's," Frederic growled.

"Dulcie's?" John queried in compounded shock. "She was at Dulcie's?"

Frederic's regard, which had been riveted on his delinquent daughter, shot to John, and his rage flared, spawning the words: "*Why are you still here?*"

The inquiry took everyone by surprise, save John, who smiled belligerently. "I apologize for foiling your devious plot, Father," he sneered, "but I decided not to follow in your footsteps."

Checked, Frederic hurled his fury at an easier target: his trembling daughter. "You have much to answer for this night, young lady. Come here!"

"No!" she retaliated. But when he took one scraping step toward her, she fled the safety of her brother, skirted past Jeannette and Agatha, and raced up the staircase, hiding behind Charmaine. "Don't let him touch me!"

"Miss Ryan, bring her down here!" Frederic demanded.

John had had enough. "Take her back to her room, Charmaine."

"Miss Ryan, stay!" came the master's command, his eyes trained on her and not the son who was attempting to usurp his authority. "I hold you responsible. Bring Yvette to me – *now!*"

"Charmaine–" this time Paul stepped forward "–do as John says and take Yvette to the nursery."

"Damn it!" Frederic bellowed. "This is *my* house! She will do as I say! Get out – all of you! This is between my daughter, her governess, and me!"

"That's right, Father! You wield your whip!" John fired back virulently. "But don't expect me to cower before you!"

The man swung round, his cane slicing up and over his shoulder. John didn't move, his sardonic semblance piercing Frederic's heart and staving his intent. Nauseated, he lowered the crutch slowly. "Get out of my sight," he croaked. "You pretend at being a man, but don't have the backbone to claim what is yours."

The declaration wiped clean John's inveigling smile, and his face paled as if he had suffered a mortal injury. He bowed his head and exited the house, deserting them all. To Charmaine's horror, Frederic turned on her.

Mercifully, George stepped forward. "Sir, as I said in the carriage, this little calamity cannot be blamed on Miss Ryan. Certainly, she was asleep when–"

"Mr. Richards," Frederic cut in, "I have no intention of discussing this matter any further with you. I've yet to discern how you are involved; however, I do know that you were at Dulcie's while my daughter tried her hand at a game of cards, and, by every outward sign, meant to divert my attention from her. Now, don't press your luck. Excuse yourself from this inquisition."

"Father–"

"And the same goes for you!"

"No!" Paul rejoined heatedly. "The same does not go for me! Now, I realize that Yvette's behavior was depraved, and she should be punished. But your anger exceeds the bounds of rational thinking when you turn on Miss Ryan and hold her responsible. She couldn't have known about this. Or George and accuse him of conspiring with Yvette. Surely he was only trying to protect her!"

Paul's reasoning took hold, and Frederic's ire flagged.

The terrible ordeal ended when Jeannette valiantly stepped forward. "Paul is right, Father," she whispered. "Yvette and I waited until Mademoiselle Charmaine was asleep. Then we dressed in the clothes Yvette *borrowed* from the stable and slipped from the house. We knew we were doing wrong, but we didn't think we'd be caught, especially in our disguises. We just wanted to see what Dulcie's was really like, at night. When George saw us there, he was very angry, but Yvette had a good hand. She promised to leave after she'd played it out."

Charmaine held her breath, relieved when Frederic's response held a note of empathy. "And your sister couldn't tell me this? It was her idea, wasn't it?"

"Yes, sir."

"Then why you? Is she such a coward that she cannot assume responsibility for her own actions, speak for herself?"

"She was afraid you would kill her," Jeannette answered simply. "But I didn't think you would. I suppose that's why I wasn't afraid to tell you the truth."

Frederic absorbed the statement with a mixture of surprise and regret. He looked up at Yvette, just now realizing the effect his naked wrath had on the nine-year-old. It was not the first time he had humbled someone to such quaking depths, and he was unhappy to admit that he had not changed.

"I will speak with you tomorrow – the two of you," he finally said. "You needn't fear death, but you will be punished for your bad behavior."

He spoke to Charmaine. "Take them back to their rooms and make certain that they remain there until I call for them."

"Yes, sir," she said. Beckoning to Jeannette, she turned Yvette around, and they proceeded up the staircase.

"I'm sorry, Father," Jeannette offered. "Truly I am."

But he did not seem to hear as he labored toward the study, his hesitant gait mocking the swiftness with which he had stormed the house minutes earlier.

"Oh Mademoiselle Charmaine, what have I done?" Yvette moaned from Charmaine's bed, her head buried in the safety of her governess' lap. "I've been so very naughty, and now everyone I love has been hurt!"

"There, now," Charmaine soothed, stroking the girl's blonde head. She'd never seen Yvette so repentant and was deeply moved. "It's not quite so terrible as you imagine it to be."

"Yes, yes it is! First Johnny. I didn't mean to get him into trouble, but I did. Jeannette warned me it would be so, but I refused to listen. And then you. She warned me about that, too. But I didn't think Father would rant and rave at you like that! Even Paul and George. Oh, George will never forgive me! He didn't deserve any of Father's anger. He was only trying to protect me, and now he might lose his job. And Jeannette. She should hate me for all the trouble I've gotten her into."

"I don't hate you, Yvette," her sister reassured. "Really I don't."

"You should," Yvette argued, slowly lifting her head. "Tomorrow you will be punished, too, and it's all my fault! Everything!"

Again she was sobbing. "I don't know why I do the horrid things I do! I don't even know why I think of them! Oh, why did I have to go to Dulcie's tonight? Why couldn't it have been last night when Father was still on Espoir?"

"Because you said there would be more action on a Friday night," Jeannette reminded her. "You wanted to play poker, remember?"

Charmaine was shocked. Yvette wasn't contrite over her bad behavior, just sorry that she'd been caught.

"And I was winning!" she wailed. "I'd more than tripled my money!"

"But that's good," Jeannette encouraged.

"*Good?*" Yvette exclaimed. "How can you say that? I ran out and left it all behind! Almost eighty dollars! One hundred, if you count the last pot! And those greedy, stinkin', cheatin', no-good lot of dirty swindlin' seamen probably shoved it all into their filthy pockets when Father left! We're out twenty dollars!"

George found John in the stable brushing Phantom's flank to a brilliant luster, as if the chore could draw out all of the poison that festered in the wound his father had so deftly reopened.

"Isn't it a bit late to be currying your horse?" George queried lightly.

"It's a bit late for a lot of things, George," the man bitterly replied. "I'm a fool, one damned fool."

"No, John, you're not. You did what was best. Don't allow your father to lead you to believe otherwise. You did what was best."

"Did I?"

"You know you did," George finished. "Now, come on, this is Yvette's night for mischief, not yours. No sense in acting the spoiled boy just because she's stolen center stage from you."

The remark brought a smile to John's eyes, and he laughed with his friend in spite of himself.

"Look!" George weighed a hefty purse in his hand before tossing it over.

"What is this?"

"Count it," George directed, watching John rake his fingers through the contents. "There's over a hundred dollars there. More than eighty-five in winnings by my estimation."

"Winnings?" John questioned bemusedly.

"Yvette's winnings. According to the men she was playing poker with, she took a seat at the table with a purse of twenty dollars. She won the rest."

"Won?" John asked incredulously. "Are you saying she won this off a surly lot of seamen?"

"Fair and square," George replied, "though I'm certain her manner of play was at best baffling. On more than one turn of the card, she held a high ace, hoping to draw a second pair. But the men misread the three cards she kept as beginner's luck, assuming she'd been dealt three of a kind. If your father hadn't stormed the table, it would have been downright entertaining."

"And how did you come to be there, Georgie?"

"Just stopped in for a drink," his friend answered. "But I don't mind telling you, I nearly died on the spot when Paul and your father walked in."

"I'm sure you did," John agreed, a deep laugh erupting. "So, tell me more. From the beginning, if you don't mind."

"Not at all," George chuckled, and he launched into the entire story.

Saturday
October 7, 1837

Chapter 7

Spent of curses, Frederic found the morning less to his liking than the night before. Cloistered in his private chambers, he could spare others his miserable disposition. But for himself, his refuge was nothing more than a prison, an incarceration of the mind, plagued by the memory of the life he had lived, the many opportunities he had wasted, the schemes he had forged in their stead. Another plan had failed. When would he learn that he could not bend destiny? The Almighty was determined to prolong the agony of his failure: failure as a father, failure as a husband.

Voices floated up from the gardens, drawing him to the French doors. John was there, squatting and settling Pierre on one knee, his arm encircling the child's small shoulders. "Now let me see," he said, taking hold of the boy's hand and turning it over for inspection. "Where is this terrible splinter Mainie can't see?"

"There!" Pierre pointed out. Charmaine moved behind John, watching from over his shoulder.

"Not a very big one," John commented softly, pulling the palm nearer his face, "but there all the same. They say the smaller ones hurt the most."

Pierre looked up at his governess, and John's gaze followed, the sun catching in his hair. He was talking to the lad again, the love in his voice disarming. "You won't cry when I take this out, will you?"

Pierre shook his head, and John stood, hoisting him into his arms. The sun glinted again, playing a color game with the reddish tints in the brown-blonde hair, Elizabeth's hair. The shade and texture were identical.

The boy was a man already. Only yesterday, Frederic thought he had so much time. Suddenly, he was in a tunnel of events that transported him back to a time when John was a similar age to Pierre suffering his splinter. The ship pitched and plunged through the roiling waves. Bursts of thunder exploded, an untamed beast. The cabin door flew open, and the frustrated nanny rushed in, fretting over his wailing son. John could not be calmed, the darkness too great and the storm too fierce to dike his turgid tears. He was placed in Frederic's care, a father vaguely known to him, a father who had all but disowned him, but could not bring himself to completely renounce the only remaining part of the woman he still loved. Frederic held the lad for the first time that night, knowing that, if nothing else, his strength and size could shield the three-year-old from the tempest and perhaps soothe him. As they settled in the cot, John buried his head in Frederic's shoulder and his breathing grew steady. Frederic began to fancy the feel of Elizabeth's son cuddled in his embrace. Then he remembered Elizabeth in that spot and began to cry, hot tears trickling into his hair as he mourned the woman he had lost...

"*Damn,*" he cursed aloud, ignoring the blur of his vision. Why hadn't John just taken Pierre and fled? *Why?*

Yvette stood meekly before her father ready to accept her comeuppance, comforted only by the fact that her sister stood next to her. It had been little over a week since she had last visited the master's chambers; now she'd be pleased never to step into these rooms again.

"Two things I would have from you," Frederic began roughly, his shrewd eyes scrutinizing the child from where he sat.

He did not delight in her submissiveness. Remembering Jeannette's declaration of the preceding night, he berated himself for snuffing out the rebelliousness that he very much admired. Still, she had recklessly hatched more trouble than even John and Paul at that age and comprehended little of the danger she could have faced had he not intervened. Therefore, it was best to deal with her sternly.

"First," he said, "I would have your promise, your word of honor, that what happened last night will *never* happen again. Beyond that, I want it understood that you will never, under any circumstance, leave this house or its grounds without permission from either myself or your governess."

"Yes, sir," she replied softly, meeting his eyes. It appeared that the man's apoplectic anger had indeed dissipated, and she regained her aplomb with the pledge, "I promise."

Frederic cocked his head. "I don't want the words given casually. I expect you to hold by them, and not just when you think you may be caught. When you leave here, I want to know that I can trust you, that your vow won't be broken."

"On my life, sir," she pronounced, "I give my word. I won't *ever* do anything so very naughty again."

He smiled for the first time, and Yvette wondered what he found so amusing. "I believe you," he said.

"And the second?" she probed; he had mentioned two things.

"I want you to apologize to Miss Ryan. You could have caused her great alarm if she had gone to your room and found your beds empty. As it was, she was unjustly blamed for your misconduct, something she didn't deserve."

"Is that all?" Yvette asked, convinced that the worst had yet to come.

"Isn't that enough?"

"Yes, but aren't you – I mean, I thought you–"

"No, I'm not," the man interrupted, his brow raised. "As angry as I was when I found you gambling at Dulcie's, I had no intention of beating you, Yvette. However, if something like this should happen again, I'll not be so lenient."

"Then – there's to be no punishment?" the girl asked hopefully.

"I didn't say that. After some consideration, I've decided that my untimely arrival at the tavern last evening will stand as punishment enough."

Yvette frowned. "I don't understand."

"Then let me explain." Frederic rifled through his desk drawer, producing the reticule the girl had laden with an assortment of gold coins and one-dollar notes only twelve hours earlier.

Relief washed over her when the pouch jangled, and in unmasked delight, she quickly calculated the value of the purse.

"There's more than the twenty American dollars you started with," he said, as if reading her mind, "close to five times that amount by George's count."

"George?"

"He confiscated all of your winnings. If your little adventure weren't so naughty, I'd have to congratulate you. However," he continued, his voice growing hard and uncompromising, "no daughter of mine is going to gamble – let alone with dirty, low-class seamen. Is that understood?"

"Yes, sir," Yvette muttered, her moment's elation squashed with the realization of what was coming next.

"Unfortunately, lessons are often learned the hard way. And the best lesson for you, my dear, is to lose this."

"But–"

"I'm donating it to the poor."

"Just the winnings, Papa, please, I promise that I won't–"

"No, Yvette, not just the winnings. You see, it was only luck that prevented you from losing last night. Do you realize what those men would have done had you continued to win? You feared a beating from me, but I guarantee they would have inflicted far worse. They would have followed you and cornered you alone."

She shuddered and meekly mumbled, "Yes, sir."

Frederic eyed his other daughter. "What of you, Jeannette? Was any of this money yours?"

"Yes, Papa. Half of it was mine. Yvette said we'd split whatever she won."

"Well then, you've shared equally in the punishment. It had better not happen again."

"No, sir, it won't."

They watched as Frederic slid open the deepest drawer in the desk, fumbled curiously with what looked to be a false back, deposited the purse there, and replaced the wooden panel.

"It would be safer in the safe," Yvette offered.

"No, my dear, it won't remain in the house for very long. I'm certain there are a few families in town who could benefit from your generosity. I shall speak to Paul about it."

He smiled at them, a self-satisfied smile that riled Yvette. She resisted uttering the recriminations that were rifling through her head, certain they would induce his wrath if they found their way to tongue.

"That will be all," he finished.

Once they were in the south-wing corridor, Yvette took to grumbling. "Just wait until I see George. He snatched all of my winnings and told Father about it instead of me! Why would he do that? "

"I don't know, Yvette," her sister attempted to console. "But if Father didn't use the money as our punishment, we could have gotten worse."

"*Worse?* I don't see how! All that loot and we didn't even get to count it! It's unfair, I tell you."

"Tired?"

Startled, Charmaine looked up from the lawn and squinted against the sun that silhouetted the man looming over her. He stepped forward, blocking the rays altogether. Disappointed, Charmaine smiled halfheartedly up at Paul.

"Not tired," she answered as he sat beside her, drawing his knees up and locking his arms about them. "Just discontent, I suppose."

"Discontent? You're not blaming yourself for what happened last night?"

"Partially. I'm waiting for the girls now."

She focused on Pierre, who was pushing the swing back and forth.

"Everything will turn out for the best," he soothed, studying her with a sympathetic eye and an indefinable ache in his breast. "Charmaine, look at me."

She faced him, surprised by the raw emotion in his eyes.

"I missed you," he stated simply, his hand catching hers, squeezing it in understanding and support, instilling her with renewed strength. "How was your week?"

John stepped back into the house. The terrace offered little respite. Charmaine was already occupied. He no longer commanded her attention. His week had come to a close. Hadn't he realized that last night? He'd be wise to shut the door. He rubbed his forehead and swallowed hard.

Why was he always denied? Why did he allow himself to be denied? He grunted across the words that chastised him, the gentle petition that continued to haunt him: *Take care of them... live and love again, John...*

Coming to an abrupt decision, he crossed the foyer hurriedly and took the stairs two at a time. He knew it was a last resort, but because he had nothing more to lose, he set his pride aside and entered his father's sanctum.

Frederic looked up from his desk.

John read the surprise in his eyes and got right to the point. "I will be returning to Virginia tomorrow. I request your permission to take Pierre and the twins with me."

Frederic was stunned by the direct petition, awed by his son's valor to take this step, especially in light of the ugly episode of the evening before. Wasn't this what he wanted, an honest give and take?

"For how long?" he asked.

"Forever."

"And who will see to their care when you are occupied with business?"

Was his father actually considering this request? John had expected a swift and unequivocal 'no'. "Miss Ryan, if she is willing. She has friends there. A move back will allow her to be closer to them."

Frederic breathed deeply and stood up. He walked to the French doors, weighing the advantages and disadvantages of such an arrangement. Here was an opening to begin setting things aright with his son, but in so doing, would he estrange his remaining offspring?

"And what of Yvette and Jeannette?" he finally asked.

"What of them?" John rejoined, exasperated. "What will they miss here, except a shadow of a father closeted in a room who pays them no mind, or when he does, rants and raves like a lunatic, and a stepmother who despises them? Where do *you* think they will be better off?"

Frederic smarted with the truth of the declaration, remembering his cowering daughters. Another grave mistake he needed to correct – for Colette, for himself. He turned back to John. "Why don't you stay here?" he offered. "Wouldn't it be easier if you just stayed on Charmantes?"

"Easier for you," John replied. "I refuse to participate in this – this *evil charade* any longer. You keep your children close not by giving them what they need, but by withholding it." He snorted in disgust when his father didn't respond. "Obviously, your answer is 'no'. I knew it would be. I come to claim what is mine – the courage you didn't believe I had – and *still* I am denied!" Not waiting for a reply, he retreated.

But Frederic called after him, "Not all of it is yours to claim," and then to the empty doorway, "I cannot release my daughters... certainly not forever."

"I'm listening, John," Paul said, annoyed when his brother quietly took a seat. "Surely you didn't summon me here to watch you recline–"

"Sit down, Paul," John interrupted mildly. "I have a number of things to discuss with you. And no, I'm not kindling a row. I would like to speak civilly."

Paul indulged him. "What is it?"

"I'd like to talk to you about Charmaine."

"What about her?" Paul queried cautiously, warily.

"Charmaine is a decent woman, good and kind."

"You don't have to tell me that, John. Remember, it was I who knew her first, I who informed you of her integrity. It took you long enough to recognize it, the noble attributes that you sought to scorn and scandalize."

John concurred. "But I did recognize them. I admit that I misjudged her at first. Likewise, you must agree that few women can match Charmaine in worth."

"I don't discredit that observation," Paul replied, his brow a study of a mind working. "But where is all of this leading?"

"Have you considered marriage?"

"Marriage?" Paul sputtered. "Are you suggesting that I marry her?"

"In a word, yes. Is it so revolting an idea?"

Severely suspicious now, Paul pressed his chin into the palm of his hand and considered the man. "What is this about, John? What is this *really* about?"

"I'm fond of Charmaine. I wouldn't want to see her hurt."

"And you think marriage to me will prevent that?"

"Yes, I do. She loves you, you know, more deeply than I think even you realize. The night I came home, she kissed you with all the passion and love a woman can give a man. I didn't comprehend how neatly her heart was sewn into the bargain until I came to know her better, heard her speak about you. She doesn't deserve to be hurt – not by me, and not by you."

"Then why don't *you* marry her?" Paul baited, suddenly angry that the man was placing them on the same plane.

"Like I said, Paul, she doesn't deserve to be hurt," John returned, his voice dead serious. "I confess to my little games, but they're over now. George tells me the Raven pulled back into port at dawn, something about a ripped spanker and a splintered mast. When she sets sail again, probably tomorrow afternoon, I'll be going with her."

"*What?* Just like that?"

"Yes, Paul, just like that. I plan on telling Charmaine and the children later, but I wanted to speak with you first."

"I can't believe it," Paul muttered.

"But you must, for it's true. And it is for the best."

"*Really?* You come back here, upset the children's lives, make certain that they're attached to you all over again, and then you just pull up and leave. Why? To punish Father for what happened last night? To make him look like the fiend you believe him to be?"

John's eyes narrowed, but he marshaled his anger and forced himself to answer calmly. "No Paul, believe it or not, this has nothing to do with Father.

But it has everything to do with the children. I, too, have become 'attached' as you put it, and such a relationship cannot be, can it? So, what I can't take with me, I relinquish altogether." He bowed his head momentarily, then met Paul's intense regard with one of his own. "For that reason alone, I will be aboard the Raven tomorrow afternoon, and I won't be back."

Disconcerted, Paul turned to safer ground, more comfortable with anger than misery. "And what does all this have to do with Charmaine and me?"

John didn't answer, but Paul puzzled over the question until all the pieces fell in place. "You're worried that Father will dismiss her, aren't you? *Aren't you?*"

"No, Paulie."

"Yes, Johnny!" the man mocked in kind. "And what better way to prevent that from happening than to see her married to me, wife to the children's brother? That would certainly insure her position in the household, wouldn't it? *Wouldn't it, goddamn you?*" When John refused to respond, Paul pressed on. "You amaze me, you really do! Banking on me to fix the atrocious mess you've made of things!"

John's eyes hardened. "You're a fine one to sit in judgment, Paul – you, who've conquered woman after woman without a care in the world."

"Really? Well, *unlike you,* John, I haven't maliciously seduced a woman who didn't belong to me just to get revenge!"

"Is that how you see it?" John muttered, the blood running cold in his veins. "All these years – and that's what you think happened? No wonder you sided with Father."

Momentarily deflated, Paul drew himself up. "Don't play me for the village idiot, John. We both know how you hate him. You've made that *abundantly* clear. And don't point a finger at me because I refuse to be pulled into it. You know what? You're pathetic!"

"Pathetic?" John rejoined ferociously. "You call *me* pathetic? Look at yourself, Paul. There isn't anyone in this house more pathetic than you! That's right, brother. Take a good look at yourself – sitting next to Father at the table like a loyal dog, anxiously awaiting the scraps of gristle he might throw your way. And like a *loyal dog,* you're blind to how he abuses you! Instead, you defend him to the end, hoping that if you just show him how capable you are, how very diligently you can work, maybe one day he will acknowledge you and your exceptional efforts. Work! Work! Work! Oh yes, Paul, you're good enough to get the job done. You go above and beyond! But where has it gotten you? John can shirk his responsibilities. John can shame his father with the ultimate affront, but John is still first on the will! And what about you? After all your toil, dedication, and loyalty, you're not even legitimate yet, are you? If you were *my son,* you would be! But be my guest, Paul – keep blaming me for all the evil in this house. It's all very tidy that way, isn't it? By placing everything on my shoulders, you don't need to examine the truth." John pointed at him emphatically. "*You're* the pathetic one, Paul, and *damn you* for not claiming Charmaine while you have the chance. You would rather chase after Father's unrequited love than return her love, freely given. Mark my words: you will rue the day you were ever so blind as to throw away happiness with both hands!"

Charmaine studied the pacing man apprehensively. John had said he had something important to speak to them about, and now she and the children waited for him to find the words to begin. He finally came to a standstill, as if immobility would help him overcome his impasse. He faced the twins who sat on their beds, his back to her and Pierre.

"I'll be leaving tomorrow," he said, his trembling voice belying the ease with which he delivered the simple statement.

"*Leaving?*" The single gasp fell from everyone's lips.

"*Charmantes?*" Yvette added, horrified. "You're leaving Charmantes?"

"That's right. I'll be aboard the Raven when she sets sail for the States. It's about time I returned home and got some work done there."

"But *this* is your home!" the girl objected. "Here, with us!"

"No, Yvette, not anymore. I have another home, you know that, one that I've neglected for too long now."

"So you'll neglect us instead? Virginia is more important than us?"

"Yvette, you know that is not true," he answered softly. "But I do have other responsibilities that–"

"Responsibilities?" his sister countered. "What responsibilities? What could be more important than your family – taking care of us?"

"Yvette, you were fine before I arrived home two months ago, and you will be fine after I've departed."

"No, I won't! And you're wrong about two months ago, very wrong! I wasn't just fine, none of us were, not until you came back and made everything right! We were so unhappy, but you made us laugh again! You can't leave now! You just can't! I won't let you!"

"You are making this very difficult for me, Yvette, but I must leave, and no matter how much you beg, I won't change my mind."

"But why? *Why?*"

"I've told you, I have business to attend to in Virginia *and* New York. I cannot postpone it any longer." He inhaled and drew strength from a new thought, infusing his voice with a note of excitement. "What if I promised to invite you, Jeannette, and Pierre for a visit? Perhaps next spring, when the weather warms. By then, the work I've ignored will be behind me, and I'll have plenty of time to spend with the three of you. How does that sound?"

"It sounds like a lie!" she spat back, "a lousy lie!"

"Yvette!" Charmaine scolded, her heart pounding with the climaxing scene.

"It's true!" the girl retaliated, her blue-gray eyes widened more in pain than anger, riveted first on her brother and then her governess. "He's lying, just like before. Right after we turned five, he left, promising that we could visit, promising to write, promising to send passage in the springtime. But that passage never came and neither did the letters, and no one would even let me speak about it! And then, when I was finally allowed to write, I begged him to send for me, but do you think he answered? No! He just ignored that part of my letters, as if he didn't care! His letters talked about everything *but* a visit to Virginia."

She faced him again, her anguish masked by her rage. "I won't listen to your lies anymore! Father's right. All you bring to this family is pain and sorrow! You don't care about anybody but yourself! Go back to Richmond. See if I care. I swear I won't!"

"Yvette! That's enough!" Charmaine reprimanded.

John swallowed hard, the agony he experienced more for the child's woe than his own. "It's all right, Charmaine, she doesn't know what she's saying. I know she doesn't really mean it."

"I do mean it!" she protested, twisting away from him when he tried to embrace her. "Don't touch me! Just leave me alone!"

Having exhausted all avenues of reasoning, John dropped his arms to his sides, bowed his head, and left the misery-ridden room.

The evening meal, long in arriving, commenced in silence, an indication that the wretched tableau had yet to come to an end. Whether gladdened or disheartened, one sweep of the room revealed that each member of the family, from adult to child, contemplated John's sudden decision to depart the island, speechless, heads bent to plates.

Best to hold quiet as well, Charmaine thought. No need to make pleasant conversation and pretend at happiness, to deal with the situation the way Yvette was. The nine-year-old was demonstrating a hearty appetite, a punishment intended for John, though he did not seem to notice. She didn't comprehend her brother's pain, the vile situation that forced his hand. But Charmaine understood, understood enough to know that the big family secret was bigger and more terrible than she had been prepared to believe.

A familiar click, followed by a retarded thud, punctured the dismal silence, awakening everyone to the realization that the master of the house intended to preside over the unhappy table. Charmaine held her breath. No one said a word as Frederic approached his family. Mercifully, he didn't stop near John, but made his way toward the foot of the table and the wife who threw him a curious look before surrendering her chair and slipping into the one to his left. Anna moved Agatha's plate and quickly laid a new place setting. As the minutes gathered, so too did the tension.

Pierre's candid voice shattered the uneasy calm. "Johnny?"

John looked up for the first time, his gaze locking on Frederic before traveling to the boy. "Yes, Pierre," he asked, clearing his throat, "what is it?"

"I've decided somethin'."

"Have you now?"

"Uh-huh," he stated with a resolute nod. "I've decided I'm gonna go with you tomorrow to that place... Vir – gin – ni – a."

John paled, but his response was chillingly unemotional. "I'm afraid you can't. You'd have to leave too many of the things you treasure behind."

"No, I don't," the lad refuted ingenuously. "I got me a trunk. I can put all my stuff in there."

John didn't know whether to laugh or cry. "The type of trunk you'd need would be entirely too big. It wouldn't fit in our cabin."

"That's silly," Pierre giggled. His older brother was just teasing him, as he'd so often done in the past. "I've seen that ship, 'member? It's tremenjus!"

"And what about the people you'd have to leave behind? Your sisters, Mainie? You love them very much, don't you? Wouldn't you miss them?"

"They can come, too! Jeannie wants to come. She tol' me so." Pierre looked toward his sister, who nodded with a weak, yet hopeful smile. "See?"

"What about Yvette? She's extremely angry with me."

"She'd come. Wouldn't you, Yvie?" he asked, his eyes imploring the girl for a similar response. But she was guarding a severe silence and refused to look his way. "Well, she would anyway... if you asked her."

"Even so, I still can't take you with me."

"Why not? You asked me before."

Involuntarily, John's eyes traveled to his father again, and Charmaine's regard followed. Was it sadness or turmoil she read on the elder's face? Perhaps both.

"That was before," John choked out, "not now."

"Why? Don't you love me anymore?"

"Yes, I love you!" John barked, belatedly leashing his strife. "It has nothing to do with that. I'd be far too busy in Virginia to take care of you properly."

"I can take care of myself. I won't get in no trouble. I promise."

"No."

"But I wanna go!"

"*I said 'no'!*"

With bottom lip quivering, Pierre blinked twice and held in check the burgeoning tears that threatened to erupt. "If you don't take me, I'll go anyway. I'll get in my boat and I'll row there all by myself!"

"You'd never last the trip," John muttered.

"I will! You'll see. And once I'm there, you can't send me back!" He turned his attention back to his plate and said one last time, "You'll see."

John propped an elbow on the arm of his chair and pressed his forehead into the palm of his hand. Frederic did the same, looking up only when his son pushed away from the table. He started to speak, but John was gone before the words were out. The moment was lost.

Charmaine quietly closed the door to the children's bedroom. They were finally settled for the night, a difficult chore in the face of all that had happened in the past twenty-four hours. Rose said 'goodnight' and hobbled toward her rooms in the north wing. But Charmaine had no intention of retiring. She'd never fall asleep now; her mind was too full, the hour too early.

She descended the staircase, coming up short as John appeared on the landing. His gaze swept upward until his clouded eyes locked on her, turning keen and holding her captive. Thus they stood, neither one speaking.

"Will I see you before you leave?" she finally asked.

"The Raven doesn't set sail until late afternoon. So, yes, you'll see me."

"The Raven... It was the ship that brought me to Charmantes. Now it takes you away."

"You sound displeased, my Charm," he attempted to quip. "Could it be that you, too, will miss me?"

"Yes, I shall miss you," she whispered, struggling to contain her burning emotions, disturbed by his soft chuckle. "Is that so inconceivable?"

"Somewhat, considering you've awaited this date for two months now."

She ignored the comment that held some truth not two weeks ago. "You'll write?" she asked instead.

"Yes, I'll write."

With his portion of the dialog exhausted, John turned toward the opposite staircase to place some distance between them. Despite his valiant effort, she refused to release him. "Why *are* you leaving?"

He faced her slowly. "Don't you know?"

"No," she lied, wanting only to hold him to the spot.

"Sweet, innocent Charmaine," he murmured reverently. "Better that you don't know or you would despise me as well."

"I no longer despise you... I could never despise you."

His eyes caressed every feature of her face. "I will carry you with me, my Charm. You've provided me with a perfect two months, a time that will have to suffice, memories to hold dear."

The scraping of wood on wood interrupted them. Pierre appeared at the crest of the stairs, struggling to push Charmaine's trunk across the floorboards.

"Pierre, whatever are you doing?"

The boy swiftly straightened, his face a mask of guilt. "I'm goin'," he admitted, expelling one exhausted breath, his determined eyes traveling from Charmaine to John.

"Going where?"

"To Johnny's other house just like I said I was."

"Oh no, you're not!" she argued, marching up the stairs with John close behind her. "Come," she said, grabbing his hand, "back to bed with you."

"No!" he objected, pulling away. "I don't wanna go to sleep! I wanna go with Johnny!"

Before the boy could sidestep her, Charmaine lifted him up, allowing John to take charge of the trunk. "Johnny is not leaving until tomorrow afternoon."

"I don't believe him," Pierre protested, struggling to get down.

"You must, because it's true," Charmaine said, holding him tightly and returning him to the nursery, where she found Yvette and Jeannette wide awake. "You are to stay in bed and go to sleep, and if you're a good boy you will see John first thing in the morning before we go to Mass."

Pierre pursed his lips. "I bet I won't! I bet he's gonna leave without sayin' goodbye, just like Yvie said."

John looked at Yvette. "No, Pierre, she's wrong," he countered angrily. "I'd never leave without saying goodbye, and you *will* see me in the morning just like Mademoiselle Charmaine promised, but only if you go to sleep."

The boy brightened. "And you'll take me with you?"

"Not this time, and no more begging."

He burst into tears. "But I wanna go with you! Please let me go. I'll be very, very, *very* good! I promise. Please, Johnny, please take me!"

"No!" John shouted. "Now, stop crying or I won't visit at all!"

The severe threat had a devastating effect. Pierre fought to stem the deluge that glistened upon his flustered face, but only succeeded in gasping for breath. Charmaine gathered him in her arms, yet could not console him. With rigid jaw, she glared at John.

It was the final blow. Disgusted, John confronted his sisters. Yvette refused to look at him, but Jeannette presented a vulnerable target, her frown of disapproval feeding his rising ire. *"Why didn't you stop him?* Why didn't you call Charmaine when you saw what he was doing?"

Jeannette's eyes flashed fire for fire. "Pierre can do just as he likes," she answered callously, her voice unnaturally sharp, an indication that although she had remained silent, her pain was no less malignant.

"Do as he likes?" John asked incredulously.

"That's what you always do, don't you? Go ahead and run away – run away because it's easier than trying to be nice to Father. And when you're back in Virginia, you can forget about us, just like you did the last time. Yvette is right. You don't care about anybody in this family."

"Jeannette, that's not true!" he choked out. "I hate seeing you like this."

"Then why are you going?" she moaned, leaping from the bed and hugging him fiercely until he was forced to hug her back. "Please don't go! Say you'll stay! Or take us with you! We'll do anything – anything if you'd only–"

"I can't," he muttered, ripping away from her and rushing out of the room.

Charmaine lie on her back staring at the ceiling, seeing nothing of the room save her memories of John in it. It had begun that first night he'd come home.

John – when had he come to mean so much to her? When had the thought of him changed from frown to smile? Displeasure to pleasure? *He's an enigma – a one of a kind… You either hate him or love him, and it's usually in that order…* When had the Good Lord revealed the real man?

John – heir to his father's immense fortune. The thought of such wealth commanded by one individual would send some women swooning, others salivating at his feet. How sad for them; they'd be blind to the bounty beneath. John could be a beggar, and still she would count herself the richer for having known him.

John – sleeping just down the hall, or perhaps he wasn't sleeping at all.

Dismally, she wondered if she'd ever see him again. How barren the future appeared. No more picnics, excursions into town, endeavors that courted trouble and made life worth living. No more exchanging of words, matching of wits, conversations that scoffed at boredom or plans that dismantled the most carefully laid routine. Each day, each encounter had been different, unexpected, rich and rewarding. Would the dawn steal it all from her? How was she to endure without him?

She ached for his melancholy, the decision he was forced to make, one that cut more deeply than his innocent sisters fathomed. But Charmaine understood. The pieces of the elusive puzzle pointed to one horrible, yet logical conclusion: Colette and John had been lovers; had, in fact, conceived a child together. Pierre was Frederic's grandson! It couldn't be true! But it must be true!

How could it have happened?

Colette – married to a man old enough to be her father. Was this the reason she had turned to John? It couldn't be! Surely her sacred vows had meant something. And she had admitted to loving Frederic, had told Charmaine that she had been attracted to him from the moment they'd met. Why, then, would she take her husband's son as a lover?

Frederic – he must have been devastated when he learned that his wife had been unfaithful – that his son had betrayed him. Charmaine could just imagine John and Frederic fighting over the woman they both loved, the truth of Pierre's conception spilling out and inducing the seizure that left Frederic crippled.

John – why would he enter into an adulterous affair with his father's wife? Was this his revenge for the scorn he'd endured as a child? It had to be more than that. John loved Colette. Charmaine could feel it, knew it to be true. And he desperately loved Pierre, the precious remnant of that love.

How could Colette have allowed this to happen? She had wreaked havoc in this house, her love for father and son tearing the entire family apart. And yet, Charmaine couldn't condemn her. What a terrible tragedy! Everyone had been affected, would suffer the repercussions for generations to come. This was the reason Colette's ghost roamed the house: her soul was not at peace!

And what of little Pierre? Would he grow up believing that Frederic was his father and think of John only as an elder brother? *John had wanted to take him away,* Charmaine suddenly realized. That was the cataclysmic impasse he had reached that night she'd found him at the piano. *No one deserves to be hurt, least of all an innocent child.* So, John would sacrifice his own happiness for Pierre's welfare. But would the boy be happy without him?

Charmaine shook with the ferocity of her thoughts. Would she ever know the whole incredible story? Could this family ever bury the past? No, a situation this heinous could never be forgotten, let alone reconciled, for it lived on.

Tears sprang to her eyes, but she didn't fight them back. Grasping her pillow, she turned her face into its downy softness and cried, cried in the hopes that her tears would wash away her depraved conclusions.

Sunday, October 8, 1837

Pierre was ill. Though he wasn't running a fever, his face was flushed and he complained of a headache and stomachache. Obviously, he was suffering from a battered heart and a poor night's sleep.

"If Pierre is not going to Mass," Yvette announced, "then neither am I!"

"Yes you are, young lady," Charmaine remonstrated lightly. "Your little brother isn't feeling well, but you are just fine."

"Who will mind him while we are gone?" she asked peevishly.

"I'm sure John will look after him for an hour."

The declaration sent Yvette into a huff, and like the preceding night, she turned her sullen face to the wall.

Charmaine smiled to herself. Yes, John would lend a hand. *This might be his last chance to spend time alone with Pierre.*

John sat on the bed beside the boy, gently stroking the tousled hair, placing each strand back in place. The house was so very quiet, the lad's heavy breathing the only sign of life in the great manor. The silence mocked the wailing of John's heart, the piercing pain so intense that he could no longer fight it, and the first tears spilled on his extended hand.

Two months, he'd been granted two months. It would have to be enough, last the rest of his days. Eight weeks of laughter. Funny, he couldn't recall the heartache and frustration of having reached Charmantes too late. Only this day's anguish persecuted him now. Two months... If there was a God, he thanked Him.

A bloodcurdling howl rent the air, and John shot to his feet, racing out to the balcony. Across the lawns, pandemonium ruled. A stableman was doubled over in pain, the arm he cradled bent at an odd angle. Another man skirted across the paddock, shouting over his shoulder, "He's over there!" Two other men ran toward the house.

Highly agitated, Phantom snorted loudly and pranced in a circle, tossing his massive head from side to side. Abruptly, he stopped and rubbed his muzzle against a leg, then reared and pawed the air, trumpeting his unfathomable anger to the heavens. He repeated the fierce dance again and again, his hooves clattering on the cobblestone.

Three grooms approached gingerly, bridle and rope in hand. But the stallion charged them, a surprise attack that caught one man off guard and clipped his shoulder, catapulting him backward. Before he could jump to his feet, the beast reared again and the lethal hooves came pounding down, missing him by inches.

Cursing, John dashed through the nursery. Pierre slept on. Without a thought, he reached the hallway and took the stairs three at a time.

John was leaving. Frederic paced his chamber, allowing the words to reverberate in his mind. His son was leaving – for good, this time. Damn him for going now. Damn him for going alone!

Frederic hadn't slept last night; nevertheless, he savored the burning sensation behind his eyes, the fatigue that was creeping in. He relived the scene at the dinner table over and over again. Would his family never know happiness? Would this be his legacy to his children?

Poor little Pierre – so young, so beautiful, so innocent. Frederic loved the boy in a way he'd never loved John, or even Paul at that age. He'd been given a second chance with Pierre. And what had he done with it? He'd spurned it. With bitter remorse, he remembered the months following his seizure, those wretched days when he'd languished as a mute cripple. He recalled the first time Rose had placed the tiny babe in his arms. The woman had been wise, for ironically, it had been that innocent infant who had coaxed him out of miserable non-existence. Now, when the child had come to mean the most, when holding the three-year-old on his lap was the closest thing to happiness, he realized it was time to let go. John deserved Pierre's love far more than he did. But John wasn't about to hurt the boy by tearing him away from all the things he treasured, namely his sisters and his governess. That was why John had asked for the girls, why he'd set all pride aside and practically begged to have them. Where Frederic had schemed, John had been honest, braving his contempt and asking for the children even though he could have stolen them the week before. And what had he, his father, done? He had denied him, again. *You keep your children close not by giving them what they need, but by withholding it.* Dear God, John was right.

Frederic raked his hand through his hair. He knew what he should do, what Colette, even Elizabeth, would want him to do. Reaching a resolution, he opened his safe and pulled three documents from his will. He sat and scrawled a last declaration on each one.

A movement at the French doors caught his eye. He blinked twice. Colette stood in the casement, an apparition so real that he questioned his sanity. Perhaps he'd fallen asleep. In a rush, he stood, but for every step he took in her direction, she remained out of reach, a sad imitation of their marriage. He exited the room and pursued her along the veranda. But the wraith floated westward, slowly dissolving into the morning air. He shook his head once, twice, unsure if he tried to rid his mind of her image or recapture it.

His eyes were drawn to the edge of the pine forest. He thought he'd seen some movement at the base of the trees. Something was definitely there; something had grabbed his attention. He didn't know what precisely, and he cocked his head to better see. It did not help. Still, his eyes remained riveted to the spot – the opening that marked the path that led to the lake.

His heart quickened, and blood surged through his veins. He tried to discount the anxiety that gripped him, but could not. Unmindful of the cane that clattered to the balcony floor, he hastened back into his room, reaching the bell-pull in five large, unencumbered strides. Someone would come. Not everyone was at Mass. Again, he yanked on the rope, praying that someone would respond, cursing when another minute passed and still, nothing. Enough! He was down the hallway before Felicia had reached the top of the stairs.

"Sir? You wanted something?" she asked, curious as to why his face was ashen, why he was even in the corridor.

"Get Travis."

"But he's at Mass, sir, as is the rest–"

"*Get him, damn it, and get him now!* Tell him to go into the forest – behind the house! Something's wrong at the lake!"

"Sir?"

"Just do it, girl!" he shouted, his fervor sending her racing down the stairs. "If Paul is there, tell him the same! Remember – they're to check at the lake!"

The churchgoers congregated in the small vestibule and spoke in hushed tones, attempting to make sense of the interruption that had halted Sunday Mass and sent Paul and Travis on a crazed mission to the lake.

"I want some answers," Agatha demanded, dismissing Benito's outrage.

"I don't have any, Ma'am," Felicia replied. "Like I told you, the master, he rung while everyone was at Mass. But before I could reach his apartments, he was rantin' and ravin' in the corridor, demandin' that Travis and Master Paul be sent to the lake to check on something."

"To check on what?" the mistress pressed. "What was to be checked?"

"A problem of some kind. He didn't say what."

As the hour lengthened, and it became apparent that the Mass would not resume, the assembly slowly dispersed.

"Come, girls," Charmaine urged, "let us check on Pierre."

The nursery was unusually quiet. Then Charmaine knew why: John and Pierre weren't there. For all the times she'd found the boy's bed empty, experienced that heart-stopping panic that left her limbs painfully weak, this time it did not, this time she smiled. Pierre was with John. John had him. One last hour together, they needed that.

A chilling scream annihilated the happy thought, then thundering footsteps.

Paul's desperate voice reached them – rapid-fire orders shot from the foyer. "Get Blackford! Now, damn it! And blankets, I'll need blankets – all you can gather! Then Rose – find her and find her fast!"

Silence – a second's silence and then: "John – my God, *where were you?*"

Another voice – John's. "What the hell–"

Then Paul again: "We've got to get him upstairs! *Damn it, John!* He's swallowed a great deal of water! We've got to–"

"What water? *Where in God's name did you find him?*"

"The lake! Jesus Christ, John, there's no time to explain! We've got to get Robert!"

"Give him to me, Paul. *Goddamn it, give him to me!*"

Wednesday, October 11, 1837

For the third consecutive morning, the sun broke free of the horizon and captured the navy-blue heaven, blessing the world below with its promise of a new day. And for the third morning in succession, this was not so within the great manor, where family and servants alike awaited word from the governess' bedchamber.

Pierre lie in a state of delirium. A raging fever swept him along a maelstrom of hallucinations in which his amber eyes grew wide, perceiving monstrous images crawling on the ceiling. Charmaine called to him, but he did not respond.

Again, Rose changed the saturated bed clothing, but no sooner were the fresh linens tucked in place and the boy was drenched in sweat. With a click of her tongue, she returned to the task of bathing his fiery brow, laying a chilled cloth upon his forehead. He vaulted against the polar contact, but she held it in place. The compress was instantly branded. Undeterred, she removed it and tried again. Thus far, her remedies had been ineffectual, but she refused to cave in to despair. Instead, she relinquished the cloth to Charmaine, picked up her worn rosary beads, and knelt beside the bed, petitioning the Lord's Blessed Mother to intercede. Her lips mouthed the prayers while her crooked fingers counted off the smooth beads one by one, decade by decade.

As the day wore on, Pierre's condition changed. His limbs flailed against the blankets that suffocated him one moment and failed to warm him the next, his small teeth chattering in his scarlet mouth. He began to moan and call out names, incoherent phrases that slurred into 'Mama' or 'Mainie'. Charmaine consoled him with gentle caresses and endearing whispers, cursing her inability to do more.

The shadows lengthened, and at the toll of seven, an uneasy calm descended on the infirm chamber. The tossing and turning stopped, but Pierre's lungs labored to capture what little air the selfish room offered, his wheezing amplified, though the rise and fall of the coverlet was imperceptible. Rose tiptoed from his side, and Charmaine quickly took over her post, refusing to succumb to fatigue. She would not leave the boy until she was certain of his recovery.

Her resolve was not singular. Of all who had come to check on the boy's condition, those who remained an hour or two, or those who had milled in the hallway beyond, one person had not abandoned Pierre for more than a minute at a time, departing only to see to necessaries, eating nothing. Charmaine's regard traveled across the bed to John. He had finally fallen asleep, his neck arched and head pressed into the back of the armchair. She sighed, grateful that her eyes had not met his. She despised the desperation and guilt she read there. His momentary surrender to exhaustion was just as disconcerting. Yet, at least he was not pacing, a march that tore at the carpet as surely as it tore at her sanity.

For three days, he had measured the room by the length of his stride, an eternity of steps interrupted only when a knock fell on the outer portal. The chamber had become a fortress that he fiercely guarded, barring most, allowing entry to those few he himself selected: Paul and George, Fatima, bearing trays of food. The rest did not question his restrictions; perhaps they thought him mad. By all outward signs, the apathy apparent in his unkempt state, he was. His face had become drawn and ashen, the cheeks hollow, the chin prominent. Both carried the stubble of a beard. His sunken eyes were listless. The usually tousled, glossy hair was matted and coarse, clinging to his dampened brow. He looked like a man possessed.

Time drew on. Rose returned, though not alone. Paul was beside her. Neither of them spoke as they stepped deeper into the room and stopped at the foot of the bed. Paul clasped a bedpost, his visage grim. Finally, he regarded Rose, nodding slightly to her. Taking the cue, she moved to John's chair.

Sensing her presence, he opened his eyes. She considered him, noting the lassitude that had taken hold, his faltering lucidity. Inhaling, she spoke. "John, I've asked Paul to call on Robert. If you'd give your consent, he'll leave immediately."

The bleary mind was instantly sharp and attentive. "No," he growled.

"But John–"

"*No!*" he bellowed. "I don't want him near the boy!"

"John, I'm not a physician. I'm not schooled in the remedies employed–"

"You are," he stated vehemently, his rough voice growing earnest. "When we were young, never once did you fail us. No matter the illness, you always found the cure. Though you doubt your ability, I know you can help Pierre."

"You expect too much of me. I've done everything within my ability."

"If you can't help him, then no one can."

"You don't know that, John. We have a physician on the island who–"

"*I said no, damn it!* I won't allow that incompetent ass to touch Pierre. My God, the man killed the boy's mother. He killed *my* mother!"

"John, you're wrong," she whispered woefully.

"Think what you like," he snarled, "but I swear, if Robert Blackford takes one step across that threshold, I'll wring his neck with my bare hands. I swear I will."

"Very well," Rose soothed in resignation. "I'll not press you on the matter. However, you will go downstairs and have something to eat. Fatima has prepared some broth, and after you've finished that, you must get some sleep."

"No."

"Charmaine and I will remain right here," she persisted. "If there is any change in his condition, we will come and get you immediately."

"No."

"John, I won't take no for an answer. You need nourishment and sleep."

"No! I said *no*!" he barked, "I won't allow you to sneak Blackford into this room by shooing me away!"

Rose gritted her teeth, unintimidated. "I wouldn't do that, not to you or to anyone else to whom I'd given my word."

The planes of the man's face remained set, far from contrite.

Rose proceeded with care. "You're working yourself into a state of collapse, and then I'll have not one, but two patients to attend to."

"I'll be fine. Just minister to the boy and forget about me."

"Rose is right," Paul interjected, stepping forward. Though his words bordered on a command, they also rang with compassion. "John, please listen to her. You know that she has Pierre's best interest at heart. I'll take up your vigil for a while."

"*You?*"

"Yes, me," Paul answered softly, impervious to the snide query. "It would benefit me to stay. If I hadn't wasted precious time arguing with Travis outside the chapel, if I had rushed to the lake right away, I might have gotten there before the boat capsized. I'd like to do something, know that I've helped in some way."

"You're not at fault," John refuted, his tone tight. "I know who's to blame."

"John, please. I'll not fail you this time. I swear I won't."

Paul awaited his brother's response, unsure if his pledge had met its mark.

Finally, John pushed out of the chair, swayed, then cast imploring eyes to Charmaine. "Promise me that you will not leave Pierre – that you won't permit Blackford access to this room."

"I – I promise," she stammered.

"Swear it."

"I swear it."

Satisfied, John stared down at Pierre, combed his fingers through the boy's hair, and staggered from the chamber. Charmaine watched him go, disturbed by a sudden sense of desolation. Even in his incapacitated state, John had radiated an intensity of purpose that had guarded against the enemy. She feared his abandonment and turned worried eyes to Paul.

"No need to fret, Charmaine," he said, "John will not hold you responsible."

"Responsible? What do you mean?"

But he hadn't heard her, for he'd already turned to Rose, who was speaking urgently to him. "You'd best leave immediately if you are to get Robert here before it's too late."

Charmaine reeled with the plot being hatched. "*What are you talking about?* You mean to bring Dr. Blackford to this room when you know how John feels about him?"

No answer, their muteness branding them guilty.

"I can't believe it! You gave your word!"

"Charmaine–"

"Child," Rose soothed. "There's no time for explanation. Pierre is dying."

"No!" Charmaine refuted fiercely. "You're wrong, terribly wrong!"

"I wish I were. Like John, you deny in your heart what you know to be true. The boy *is* dying and if we don't call on Doctor Blackford now, tomorrow John will blame himself for more than just this terrible accident."

"No, he can't be," she whispered, her eyes sweeping to Paul, desperately seeking some ray of hope from him, finding only defeat. "You're betraying John. You deliberately deluded him – tricked him into leaving this room. And I won't believe that Pierre is dying. God wouldn't claim the life of an innocent boy, not when there are so many who love him, not when we're all praying for his recovery."

Her words echoed off the walls, then died. No one spoke, though their minds raced, searching for solutions, finding none, aware only that there was no hope to be found in hopelessness, no miracle to be wrested from the firm hand of the Almighty. Charmaine studied Paul. He quickly diverted his distraught gaze. When Rose cast her eyes to the floor, taking on the yoke of the accused, Charmaine turned away, a tear trickling down her cheek.

Silence reigned. She slumped into John's chair and took succor from the silence, reveling in its blanketing void. It was an unsullied silence, offering a peace that she had not enjoyed for three long days. But suddenly, it seemed as if the room had become overwhelmingly silent, as a deeper, more intense silence enveloped her, severing itself from time and becoming an entity in and of itself. She concentrated on the silence, wondering what made it different. It was a silence that negated the gravity of the situation, a silence that lulled one into a false sense of security, a silence undisturbed. The wheezing had stopped.

Charmaine bolted to her feet and threw herself at the bed, grasping Pierre. "Rose! He can't breath! I don't hear him breathing!" She tore away the suffocating blankets and shook him. "Pierre – breathe! *Dear God – breathe!"*

Her petition went unanswered, and slowly, painfully, the terrible truth took hold. Charmaine looked down at the feeble head that lolled against her arm, the long eyelashes fanning flushed cheeks. With an agonizing groan, she cradled the limp body to her chest, buried her lips in his matted hair, and sobbed.

"Charmaine..."

From far away, she discerned Paul's voice, felt him loosen her hold on the boy, watched Rose restore the lifeless body back to the center of the bed, was cognizant of being drawn further from it, her vision blurred, then further still...

"Let me go!" she protested savagely, reclaiming her sanity, attempting to reach Pierre again.

"Charmaine! Don't do this!" Paul commanded. "The boy is gone. You've held on long enough."

With the strength of one possessed, she wrenched free, but came up short as she stormed the bed. Pierre lie so very still.

"He's at peace now," Rose murmured.

The statement was like a knife in her heart and, refusing to accept it, she thought to outrun it.

"Charmaine – wait!"

"Let her go," Rose advised, grabbing hold of Paul's arm. "She needs to be alone, and I need you here."

Charmaine reached the stairs and stumbled down them, for blinding tears distorted the shadows around her. More than once, she clutched the banister, catching herself before she fell to the landing below, still, she did not falter in her demonic pace, not even when she reached the foyer. Her legs carried her through the disused ballroom and toward the chapel doors. With muffled sobs, she closed her burning eyes, a fervent prayer racing through her mind, already on her lips: *Dear Lord, help me to accept Your will and bereave the loss of my loved one. Please... give me the strength to go on...*

She passed through the vestibule's archway before she saw him. Head bowed, John was half-sitting, half-kneeling in the pew nearest her. His elbows were propped on the bench in front of him, his forehead pressed into the white knuckles of his entwined fingers.

She rushed forward, and his head lifted. He crossed the aisle and grabbed hold of her. "*What is it?*" he demanded. "*Pierre – is he all right?*"

She hesitated, until he shoved her aside and raced for the doorway.

"John – don't go up there! You shouldn't go back up there." She bowed her head, unable to face him. "Pierre is dead. Oh God, John, he's dead."

He stared, unseeing, as her words amplified – laid siege to his heart and ravaged his soul. Then silence reigned, carrying with it a cross and nails. He threw back his head and laughed pitifully. "And I came here to beg mercy from a God who has none!"

Charmaine's head jerked up, horrified. "You mustn't say that!"

"*Why?*" he growled. "*Because I'll provoke His wrath?*"

He stepped back and shouted at the crucifix suspended above the altar. "*Must you punish me forever? Will I never see an end to it?*"

"John! Stop it! Please stop!"

"He's taken everything from me – everyone I've ever loved."

"No, John, it wasn't the Lord's doing. He has no reason to persecute you, and you need Him now – the solace that only He can offer."

"I don't want His damned solace!" he exploded. "I want my son! Can't you understand that? *I want my son!*"

"Merciful God," she murmured. *She had been right!*

Unconsciously, she stepped back, her reaction catching his eye. "Poor Charmaine Ryan," he snarled diabolically, "subjected to evil and decadence. See, you were right about me all along! I fathered that child you loved. He was nothing more than a bastard." His voice cracked, the anger failing him, though he strove to hold it, command it. "I require no audience, my dear, so why don't you run along, back to your pristine world of morality and self-righteousness? I'm capable of dealing with this on my own, have been for quite some time now."

His cruel remarks did not affect her; no words remained to chase her away.

John damned her for holding fast to the macabre sanctuary, for gawking at him. He'd make a fool of himself soon; invading visions of Pierre assaulted him with such clarity that he could feel the boy's hand in his, the brush of his pursed lips on his cheek – a swift, piercing embrace.

"Dear God," he groaned, "I loved him. Why did you take him away? *Why?*"

He drove a trembling hand through his matted locks and swallowed hard, as ineffectual at dislodging the lump in his throat as he was at barricading his grief. The tears gathered, so he tilted his head back to catch them, but they spilled over, trickling into his hairline. He was losing the battle and, with a moan, the fortress caved in.

"Oh God, Colette!" he implored, his head still thrown back as if he could see through the stone ceiling to the heavens, as if she could hear him. "Why did you abandon me? *For what?* What did you gain – but misery and death? I loved you and I needed you, but you sent me away. Why didn't you turn your back on this evil place when I begged you to? You would still be alive – *our son* would still be alive! Why did you think that this – *this* was for the best?"

"John, don't do this! Please, don't do this to yourself!"

Someone was beseeching him, tugging on his arm. Suddenly, that someone was in his arms, and he was clinging to her for dear life, unable to let go, certain that he'd be submerged in a cauldron of fire if he let go. His world was crumbling; the lofty summit upon which he was perched was quaking precariously, and the jaws of madness waited hungrily below.

Charmaine returned his fierce embrace and caressed his broad back, her yearning to be held just as desperate. His head was buried between her shoulder and cheek, and she could feel his tears on her neck, the desolate phrases he uttered, incoherent at times, painfully clear at others.

"Colette… Hold me! Please, hold me!"

Her arms tightened around him, pulling him closer. Then she turned her face into his chest and wept bitterly. She didn't know for whom she cried: Pierre, the tender lad, Colette, the melancholy woman, or John, the brooding man, full of life, laughter, tears, hatred, and love. A man she had yet to understand. Her heart ached for them all. And she cried for herself, the immeasurable loss she was just now beginning to experience; would have to live with for the rest of her days.

"I killed him! Dear God – I killed him!"

"No!" Charmaine countered, pulling away. "No, you mustn't blame yourself! It was an accident, a terrible accident."

"Accident? No, Charmaine, it wasn't an accident. Accidents happen when people have no control over a situation. When I learned of Pierre's conception, he became my responsibility. I should never have abandoned him, but I did. I set everything on course to this end. The sins of the father were laid upon the son. He's dead because of me."

"No, John," she disputed fervently. "You are wrong. God wouldn't hurt Pierre to punish you. He was a dear little boy, whom God loved as much as you did. As for your past transgressions, they are in the past. Pierre had nothing to do with them."

"He was at the center of them!"

His voice was heavy with guilt. What was she to say to a man who had taken his father's wife and witnessed that woman bear his child?

"I should *never* have come back," he bit out. "He would have been spared if I had never entered his life. I should have remained a distant brother, a name occasionally mentioned, a name without a face. But Colette insisted that I come, and once I'd seen him – he was such a fine boy – I couldn't turn away, I just couldn't. I knew I was making it harder on myself – on him – but I thought that if I gathered enough memories, I would be able to make the final break. I never meant to hurt him."

He turned aimlessly to the pews again, slumped onto the bench, and buried his head in his hands.

"I know you didn't, John," Charmaine soothed, joining him there.

"I didn't deserve him," he ground out. "He was too fine a boy to have a father the likes of me."

"That's not true!"

"It *is* true! If I were any kind of a father, would I have left him alone?"

"John, you had no way of knowing that Pierre would leave the room!"

"Didn't I? He was determined to go to his boat only the eve before! I knew he didn't want me to leave, knew he wanted to come with me. And what did I do? I refused him, and I hurt him. I broke his heart. I saw the pain on his face – saw him choke on his tears, and then, because I couldn't stand to see him cry, I turned my own misery on him and threatened to desert him without a final farewell. God forgive me," he sobbed, "that was the gravest sin of all! Is it any wonder that when he awoke he'd assumed I'd left and ran to the lake to follow me?"

"You didn't know. How could you know?"

"No, I didn't know, but I could have prevented it! I could have told him what he wanted to hear. I could have taken him with me. Or I could have stayed. But my father was right," he sneered. "I wasn't man enough to claim what was mine. I abandoned him – not once, but twice. All these years I've hated my father for the very same thing. What a hypocrite I am, and my, how he must be laughing!"

"He's not laughing, John," she averred. "I know he's not laughing."

"Oh God, Charmaine, I did love him," he cried. "I swear I did. The only reason I didn't take him from this God-forsaken place was because I didn't want to hurt him, or his sisters. How could I tear them apart? Let the girls believe I had chosen him over them? How could I even dream of taking him away from you? I knew that eventually he'd despise me if I did. But I was growing too attached to stay any longer. That's why I thought it best to leave, before it became impossible to live the lie."

Charmaine dabbed at her own tears and put a hand on his shoulder. "John, it serves no purpose to torment yourself."

He was quiet for a time, head buried on his arms. "Why couldn't God have taken me instead? He could have prevented me from hurting anyone else."

"Don't say that, John!"

"But I have. First Colette – I loved her more than I'll ever love anyone. She was never really mine, and still I took her, and I hurt her…"

"John, please – you're turning in circles. The past cannot be changed, but you have your entire future to look to."

"Future?" he snorted dismally. "My future will always be shadowed by the sins of the past."

"Those sins were pardoned long ago," she replied with fierce determination. "They no longer exist. If you continue to dwell on them, they will destroy you. It is far better to remember your love for Pierre and pray for him." She cleared her throat. "Pray that he has joined his mother in heaven."

"Heaven," he murmured, comforted by her forgiving heart. "If only I could believe that such a realm exists, that they share it. Perhaps I could find some peace then."

"It does exist, John," she promised, "and I know they are there, together, praying for you."

He was quiet again, as if weighing her sincere words. "Sweet Charmaine," he whispered, "I know you grieve, too. I shouldn't have burdened you with this, forced you to become my confessor. You should be appalled, and yet, you are compassionate. You haven't condemned me. Why?"

"Because I know you loved Pierre. I do not think you are wicked."

"Then what?"

"Lonely."

"Aye," he nodded, "lonely and alone."

"Again, you are wrong," she argued softly. "You have your sisters. You have Rose and George, even Paul. And you have me. If you ever need a friend, I will always be here for you."

"Aren't you afraid that I might tarnish that friendship?"

She chuckled plaintively. "If you didn't succeed in tarnishing it in the beginning, then it certainly won't happen now."

Her response brought a doleful smile to his face, but it swiftly took wing.

"If you'd prefer to be alone, I'll retire."

"No, stay with me," he said, taking her hand in his and clasping it lightly.

They remained that way for a long time, contemplating the consuming sorrow, drawing solace from the peaceful sanctuary and one another.

Charmaine sighed deeply. *The greater the wealth, the deeper the pain...* Sadly, her mother had been right. For all their fortune, the Duvoisin family had suffered greatly, would continue to suffer. Marie's presence was strong now, and Charmaine took succor from the aura of commiserate love.

When they finally left the chapel, they found Fatima waiting for them outside the doors, dabbing at her eyes with her apron. She insisted that they come to the kitchen for something to eat. They followed her lead, though neither of them ate much of the soup she set before them.

Charmaine faltered first, bowing her head as she succumbed to weariness. Visions of a dimpled-faced Pierre besieged her. She closed her eyes, and they grew stronger, distorted by her exhaustion. "Dear God," she whispered.

"Charmaine," John called, his hand tightening over hers.

Her head came up at the sound of his voice.

"Come, we must get you to bed."

She felt his arms enfold her, leading her through the dining room to the staircase. She was at the top step without remembering how she got there, and suddenly, she was facing that room again – her room, John's room – knowing what lay inside. Her mind snapped into focus.

The chamber door flung open, and Father Benito stepped out. He assessed them, his dark eyes condemning John. "I've blessed the body," he said curtly. Charmaine was certain he wanted to say more, but he turned away.

"I'd like to look at him one last time," John whispered once the priest had left them. "Then I will take you to a guest chamber. Will you come with me?"

She nodded, allowing him to lead her into the chamber that had been their prison for so many days. Rose was still there, preparing the small body for burial. She looked up from her labor, her worried eyes waxing thankful when John moved forward. Paul pushed away from the wall where he had been leaning, exhaling once he noted his brother's lucidity. George was there, too. He'd spent the past few days with the twins, and suddenly Charmaine fretted over them, wondering if they knew, and if not, how she would tell them.

John stepped up to the bed. Charmaine stayed close behind, fearful of leaving his side, knowing that the last time she had allowed him to depart, the gravest disaster had befallen her.

He looked down at Pierre for untold minutes. The boy was no longer drenched in perspiration, his face no longer twisted in pain. The desperate struggle had ceased, the battle relinquished, and now a desolate solitude settled upon the room. Pierre was at peace. John studied him still. Had he come to grips with his death? In that moment, it became Charmaine's sincerest prayer.

Then he was speaking, not to his son, or to those gathered in the stark room, nor to God, but to Colette. "I entrust him to you, my love. Take him and keep him safe until the day when we are all together."

The supplication sent shivers down Charmaine's spine. A stillness greater than death came to life in the room, and she was infused with the power of its resurrection. Her eyes swept across the chamber, yet no one seemed affected by the tangible presence vibrating through every fiber of her being. Just as quickly as it coursed through her veins, the invader retreated, draining her of every sensation save the thud of her hammering heart. When she looked down at Pierre, a smile kissed his lips, one that had not been present before. Colette had claimed her son.

Chapter 8

Thursday, October 12, 1837
Midnight

Paul raked his hand through his tousled hair, breathed deeply, and entered his father's chambers. The man was as he had left him hours ago, despondent and disheveled. He hadn't moved from the chair near the French doors. He wore the same clothes as the day of the accident, his eyes were red and distant, and three days growth of beard marked his drawn face. His visage mirrored John's.

Paul walked over to him, and slowly, his gaze lifted. "He's gone," Paul rasped, swallowing hard against the blistering pain in his throat.

Frederic's head bobbed forward.

Realizing his sire was crying, Paul turned to leave.

"And John?" came the deep voice, cracking.

"He's dealing with it."

Again Paul attempted to leave. After the last three days, he didn't want to take on the burden of his father's agony as well. But this time, a piece of paper lying on the floor halted his step. He picked it up, his eyes skimming over the document as he walked to the desk to return it. His face paled as he found two replicas atop the secretary. "What is this?" he asked incredulously.

His father looked up, then averted his face. "My legacy to John – too little too late."

"You were signing custody of the girls and Pierre over to him?"

"It doesn't matter now, does it?" Frederic whispered.

"But Yvette and Jeannette as well as Pierre?"

"John asked me for custody of all three children on Saturday. But because I refused to take a good look at myself, I denied him again. By the time I thought better of it, it was too late."

Frederic breathed deeply, his face masked in sorrow. "My grandson is dead because of me. Colette forgive me… he's dead because of me."

Moonlight spilled into the chamber, cascading across the carpet, illuminating the foot of the bed and the man who could not sleep. In a daze of fragmented slumber, John contemplated the room, his wretched life, the dust motes suspended on moonbeams above him, moving neither this way nor that, silently mocking him.

This time he had floated with the tide. The outcome was worse than when he attempted to twist circumstance in his favor. Stupid fool! When would he learn that his actions always led to disaster? Never! He had continued to challenge God, his father. And because of that, Pierre was dead, Pierre and…

The night air blew into the room carrying with it the scent of lily. She had come, a presence as alive as the past. It was not the first time she had haunted him in the hours before dawn, so he knew he was dreaming.

Colette… on the threshold of his chamber, her limitless charms unbridled for the hour's love, her flaxen hair unbound, suspended on the buffeting breeze, her eyes, pools of blue, her full lips slightly parted, inviting his impassioned kiss. The moonlight silhouetted her naked body beneath a sheer gown of cerulean silk.

With a groan, he closed his eyes. Undaunted, she floated to the bed, certain that he could not resist. "John," she whispered, "my dearest John."

Never before had she spoken, and thunderstruck, he jumped to his feet. With hand outstretched, he tentatively touched her arm, expecting the apparition to evaporate. It did not, and he was overcome by rage, his fingers closing over her shoulder and digging into her delicate flesh. "Leave me alone! You've tormented me enough!"

She placed her cheek against his chest and encircled his waist with her arms. "Don't send me away," she implored. "Not yet."

"Send *you* away? It's you who've abandoned *me* time and again!" He shook her until her head jerked back and tears spilled from her eyes. Still, he persisted. "Go away! You're dead, goddamn it, you're dead!"

"Not while you suffer. I longed for you to come back to Charmantes, John, but not for this. You know what you have to do, what I've begged you to do."

Death... So simple a solution.

He pulled her to him, and his lips snuffed out her petition. He lifted her into his arms and laid her on the bed, tearing away the transparent veil. He pressed himself upon her, making love to her more fiercely than ever before, entwining her dark hair through his fingers, kissing the hollow of her neck, that delectable spot he'd tasted only once before. Her soft panting and timid endearments heightened his desire. She was so unlike the woman he remembered, and he reveled in this unfamiliar innocence, her virginal touch.

The clean redolence of morning dew invaded his senses, an airy breeze liberated of the heavy essence of lily. His mouth traced her jaw, coming to rest on her parted lips. Her inexperience re-ignited his ardor, and he took her again, his breathing ragged when finally he lifted his head to behold her.

"Charmaine..." he whispered hoarsely in confusion. Her arms were slipping from him, and though his embrace tightened, she melted into the bedclothes, and he awoke.

"Damn!" He sat up and buried his throbbing head in his hands, his eyes burning like white-hot coals. "Damn," he murmured again.

Paul loitered indecisively in the empty hallway. More than once, his fist lifted to the guest chamber door before dropping again to his side. Ten steps forward and another ten back brought him before the same plaguing portal. She was probably asleep; he shouldn't disturb her. Yet, perhaps she wasn't. Perhaps she needed a shoulder to cry on. He wanted to be there for her, had wanted to comfort her and hold her last night. But Rose had detained him.

Now, hours later, with the body prepared, he remembered Charmaine, how she had returned to Pierre's deathbed, dry-eyed and standing stalwart beside his brother. Her pretense at inner strength was as heart wrenching as her initial bout of hysteria. He knew her fortitude was a drama enacted for John's benefit. She'd been there for John, enabling him to return to the death chamber and behold his son's corpse. But who had been there for her? With new resolve, Paul quietly stepped into the room.

Agatha sat before the looking glass and studied her reflection. For all her years, she was still quite fair. She smiled prettily at her flawless ivory neck framed by the stark black collar of her unadorned gown. A touch too drab, she decided. She flipped open the jewelry case and selected one of the few pieces that remained. She'd been using Elizabeth and Colette's jewels to pay the blackmailer, occasionally dipping into her monthly allowance, but never touching the estate she'd inherited from her deceased husband. What a sage decision, that! Her crafty eyes narrowed. She'd have to accept the loss of some of her hard-earned wealth. It was an investment, and today that investment would pay off. *All of this will soon be behind you, my dear.* She pinned a diamond-encrusted brooch to her widow's weeds, and patted back the wisps of hair at her temples. Peering into the mirror again, she subdued her enthusiasm and twisted her face into a mask of remorse. Satisfied, she stepped gracefully into her next, most promising, role.

Charmaine stirred, rolling from her cramped side onto her stiff back. It hurt to breathe deeply, a pain that comes from crying for too long, and she had a terrible headache. Still, she smiled as she awoke. She'd been dreaming! Thank God it had only been a terrible nightmare.

She stared at the white ceiling, finally turning her head. *This was not her room.* She shifted uneasily and clutched the coverlet. Not a dream. *Dear God – not a dream!* She closed her eyes to the searing pain, but they flew open, taking in the man slumped in the armchair across the room. *Paul.*

She turned her face aside and whimpered into her pillow. Horrific, indelible images assaulted her: the death room, Pierre, the chapel, John – each one impossible to suppress. And yet, to get through this day, she must.

Slowly, she mastered her anguish and forced herself to sit up, then stand. She crossed the short distance to the sleeping man. Kneeling beside the chair, she laid a gentle hand on his brow, furrowed in exhausted slumber, and chased the lines away, placing that one stray lock back into place. He did not stir, his breathing even and deep. She studied his handsome face in the first rays of dawn, so youthful in sleep, dark lashes fanning his cheeks. Her hand dropped to his arm and patted it once. "Thank you," she whispered, heartened by his protective presence. Then she withdrew to dress.

"Did you hear me?"

"Yes, Agatha, I heard," Frederic grumbled from the French doors, gracing his wife with a slight turn of the head, his grim profile silhouetted in the early light of dawn. He'd just finished bathing, making himself presentable for the agonizing day ahead, and already his wife was pestering him. "Charmantes is lacking in social graces," he reiterated as if by rote, "and I should consider sending the girls to a female academy in London."

His thoughts were far away, his senses reeling from lack of sleep. *He'd have to visit his daughters first. This time he wouldn't allow them to suffer their loss with only a governess to comfort them...*

"...and you, my dearest, will rest easier knowing they are in safe hands."

"Agatha, please, I don't want to discuss this–"

"I know," she interrupted compassionately. "You are troubled by more pressing concerns. But this will be the last time John hurts you."

Frederic faced her with a scowl. "What are you talking about?"

"John is unfit to be called your son," she pronounced rigidly. "Surely you can see that now."

"I see no such thing," he countered, his voice deadly.

"Then you are blind!" she rejoined, steeling herself to meet his ire. "The boy was placed in his care, and John abandoned him for that beast of his. He knew the child was desperate, but did he care? No. In fact, he reveled in Pierre's heartache."

Frederic stood stunned at his wife's incredible assertion. "Are you mad, woman? John loved the boy – is grieving this terrible tragedy."

"A tragedy that could have been averted. Perhaps John didn't foresee Pierre reaching the lake, but you can be sure that he hung his hat on the hopes that the child would wake up, become hysterical, and throw this family into turmoil again. He's deviously exploited all three of your children, Pierre in particular."

"That's preposterous. I'm to blame for what happened, no one else."

"Really?" she asked wryly. "Then you've been duped, duped into believing that everything is your fault. Granted, you may have been roused to anger, Frederic, but that does not make you culpable – naïve, perhaps, but not culpable. I, on the other hand, have sat back and watched, and what I've witnessed over the years has been difficult to stomach. The first night you joined us for dinner is a perfect example. John spoiled our meal that evening. He was hostile from the start, cleverly bringing his mother into the conversation, ridiculing your love for her, ridiculing me." She paused momentarily in disgust. "How dare he behave like that in front of family and servants?"

"He has every right to hate me," Frederic replied sadly.

"No, he does not," Agatha refuted. "You've been far too clement with him. How long will you allow your love for Elizabeth to be the reason for excusing him? She's been dead for thirty years, and she doesn't live on – not in her son!"

His eyes turned black, but she was not shaken. "You yourself admitted that Elizabeth was never reflected in him. What is left then – the seed of a brigand?"

"My seed," came the deadly response, "*mine.* Anything that he is comes directly from me. I am his father."

"But–"

"Don't," he snarled contemptuously, "don't resort to your ugly premise concerning John's paternity. I ceased to believe it long ago. He is *my* flesh and blood."

"That is impossible!"

"I thought so once, but not anymore."

"But you cannot be certain!" she objected vehemently.

"I am certain. One has only to look at him to know he is mine. You said I was blind. Well, in fact, I was, and it has cost me dearly. I believed your brother when he delivered John, worrying over his small size, determined to convince me that John was born a month early. I believed him when he blamed the babe for his mother's death. And, God forgive me, I believed him when he calculated the date of conception and – even though he knew Elizabeth and I had been lovers before her abduction – concluded that he was no son of mine, rather the spawn of some heinous crime against her. But I believe him no more, Agatha. I'm through listening to this nonsense."

"But Frederic," she implored, "Robert would never mislead you. You do him a great injustice."

"There is only one person in this house who has suffered an injustice, and that is my son. For the first ten years of his life, I scorned him. By the time I realized what I was doing, it was too late. I know that now, know it will always be too late for John and me. I wasn't fit to be called a father, and he has every reason to hate me. But I won't ever do anything to hurt him again."

"But you'll allow *him* to hurt *you*," she bit out, marshaling her rage in order to make the most of this opportunity. "Is that how Colette conceived his child? You were so determined not to hurt him that you overlooked the most reprehensible of behaviors – the seduction of your wife! What's next?"

Frederic's eyes turned blacker. "How do you know that?" he growled.

Agatha grimaced in disgust. "Then Robert *was* right."

"Robert – always Robert!"

"What else would he think? Yes, he told me all about the twins' birth, how Colette cried out for John during their delivery. Tell me, are they his, too?"

"No, Agatha," he ground out, "they are mine."

"Then how can you be certain of Pierre?"

"Let us just say, I'm certain." He smiled bleakly at her. "So you see, John wasn't exploiting anybody. He loved Pierre and only wanted to be a father to him."

"I'll never believe that. He puts on an admirable performance, but the truth is he despises you and you'll *never* gain his love. He's determined to destroy this family."

"And how is he going to do that?"

"By alienating you from your other children," she declared. "You've allowed him to feast on his jealousy – jealousy over his own siblings, jealousy over Colette. He won't be satisfied until you're in the grave. Just look at the way he treats Paul! He envies the bond you share. And now that Paul has the other island, his envy has soared. But has he ever tried to be the son that Paul is? *Never!"* she exclaimed with an emphatic slash of her hand. "He has, however, fostered discord and acrimony whenever possible. You want to believe that he came back here to be a father to Pierre. But I say he came back only to make you suffer. Why can't you see this? You're too good, Frederic! He's had two months to ingratiate himself back into the twins' lives – Pierre's life. And for the whole of those two months he's been able to endure your presence in the house. Then, quite suddenly, he can't tolerate you anymore? How gullible can you be?

"He plotted the events that have branded you the villain, starting with his little excursion to Dulcie's. Why, in heaven's name, would he take the children *there*? I'll tell you why, he set Yvette up. He set *you* up! And you took the bait! All he needed was the remark you made in the foyer that night to hang his head and flee. My, what an actor he is! And it all worked out just as he planned. By the next day, everyone was pining over his banishment from Charmantes, believing that his tyrannical father had made his life so miserable, so unbearable, that he was forced to desert his sisters, forced to desert his own son! I can just imagine what he said to them: 'I wish I could stay, but I'm no longer welcome here. Father hates me. No, you can't come with me, Pierre. He won't let you.'

But you *were* willing to give the boy up, weren't you? That was the reason for our visit to Espoir, wasn't it? You gave John five days – five days to claim

Pierre as his son. There was a ship available. If he wanted to be a father to the boy, why didn't he just take him? Answer me that! And don't tell me it was because he couldn't bring himself to break Pierre's little heart. He certainly didn't have trouble breaking it four nights ago at the dinner table, did he?"

She shook her head in revulsion when Frederic didn't answer. "Pierre might have been too young to understand what was going on, but John saw to it that your daughters understood only too well. It's sad that they've been manipulated into blaming you. What did you say months ago? You were tired of being viewed as the sinister patriarch? Well, my dear husband, you'd better get used to it. You'll end up being blamed for Pierre's death, too. And why not? You've welcomed everything else that John has dished out." She feigned a vile taste in her mouth. "Not me, I've had enough of it! You think I hate him? Well I do. I hate him for all the misery he's put you through. But that's fine; he despises me as well. Why? Because I see him for what he is.

"Believe what you will, Frederic. Believe he's your son. But the next time he stabs you in the back, don't get angry with me. Just remember Colette and how he wormed his way into her bed. He will stop at nothing, *nothing* I tell you. Continue to protect him if you must, coddle him, use his inheritance to keep him close, but don't lament when he succeeds in destroying your family. You'll be left with naught. And John? He will have it all – that smug smile painted across his face, your fortune – everything. Just remember, Frederic, I warned you."

Frederic cleared his throat, attempting to dislodge the lump that had tightened there, and faced the French windows once again. "Send Miss Ryan in to see me when she awakens," he said as Agatha turned to leave.

He knew she was astonished, intrigued. Maybe he could do something right today, something that would please everyone in his family, even his wife. First he'd find out if the young governess would consider visiting Richmond with his daughters.

Agatha leaned against the portal and breathed a sigh of relief. It hadn't gone quite the way she had planned, but a window of opportunity definitely remained open. Her husband wanted to speak to the governess. Yes, opportunity knocked.

Think, don't rush into this! Think!

She crossed the narrow corridor and entered her own apartments. It was still early and she had plenty of time, time to plot and plan. *And while you work out all the important details, your husband will be dwelling on what you told him.*

She smiled wickedly. Though Frederic longed to make peace with his estranged son, the bad blood remained, and if John provoked him, Frederic's volatile temper would rule.

Robert's suspicions had turned out to be true: Colette was a tramp. Agatha's delight increased. She had attempted to verify her brother's hunch the morning John arrived home, surreptitiously slipping into her nephew's room, snooping through his desk drawers, and finally locating the letter everyone had been whispering about. Unfortunately, the meddlesome governess had charged into the room, forcing her out onto the balcony, a narrow escape. When she returned to the bedchamber a few days later, the letter was gone. Nevertheless, she had pieced the story together over the weeks that followed. Today, everything made sense, all her speculation confirmed.

Yes, John had good reason to loathe Frederic. She would stir that cauldron of hostility until it boiled over into the final showdown. *Oh yes, dear nephew, this morning, I will provide the rope and you will hang yourself!* Moments ago, she'd set the stage. Now, she had to arrange the players. She would even help them with their lines. Then, she'd sit back and enjoy the theatrical.

Frederic slumped into his chair. *Oh God, Elizabeth, what have I done?*

The years fell away and she was trembling before him, fearful that he'd send her packing. That had been his intent. He'd spent days convincing himself that England was the proper place for her. But here she stood, offering herself to him as long as he'd let her stay. His pitiful assumption that she was too young for him was laid to waste that night. She gave him everything, even her heart, asking nothing in return, save the safety of his arms and a home on Charmantes. Even the next day, she remained innocent to how she had affected him, her eyes welling with tears when he insisted she forget the sensual experience they had shared. He should have been grateful that she believed the worst, that she meant nothing to him. After all, he was taking her back to her family. He had other plans that did not include her, a promise to keep.

But fate intervened. His infatuation only intensified during their crossing, and instead of avoiding her, he found himself seeking her out. By the time they reached Britain, she held his heart in the palm of her hands. He loved her.

Had he known what awaited them in Europe, he would have turned back to Charmantes, coveting their sanctuary there. But hiding from Elizabeth's family was not a solution. Beyond that, he wanted to wed her and needed a priest. And so, they forged ahead for the sake of respectability. But before the final banns were posted, their future was irrevocably tainted.

In late January, she was abducted and savagely raped by a band of highwaymen. For the better part of a week, he had nearly gone insane combing the countryside, finally praying when there was nothing else to do, thanking the very angels when, by the mercy of God, she was miraculously returned to him. Her fate at the hands of the ruffians did not matter to him, as long as she was alive.

For weeks she was despondent, and the wedding postponed, but he refused to leave her side. Slowly, he coaxed her recovery. It was then that her disapproving parents had a change of heart. If Frederic married their daughter and whisked her away, the shame of her abduction would be forgotten. So, they wed in late March and returned to Charmantes, putting aside thoughts of her brutal violation.

In early April, Elizabeth announced the wondrous news. She was with child. Frederic should have been elated, but the worry in her eyes confirmed his fears: the child might not be his. Thus, an innocent babe was on his way into the world, a world that would not receive him well.

Just after midnight on September 29, 1808, eight months after her abduction, John was born. His parents had been married for all of six months, and yet, he was, according to the mores of society, their legitimate son.

The delivery had been long and hard, the bleeding effusive, and though the infant was very small, his position had been breech, stealing his mother's life-blood. Frederic cried into her dampened bedclothes, felt her feeble hand caress his tousled hair, heard her rasp some final endearment with a plea that he name their son after her deceased brother, John. Then she departed him forever, leaving him desolate in the wake of so miraculous an event as the birth of a son.

He turned his blind rage on Robert, blaming him for Elizabeth's death. The man quaked in fear, but Rose interceded, stepping between them, the newborn in her arms, petitioning Robert to assess the baby's health. In a matter of minutes, Robert was clicking his tongue and muttering, "Certainly not a full nine months in the womb. To think that they killed her in the end."

"Who? Who killed her?"

"The brigands. I'm sorry Frederic, he's far too small to be yours..."

More than a week passed before Frederic even looked at the baby, quickly turning away in disgust. *If you were not half Elizabeth, I'd cast you to the dogs and be damned.* Revolted by his insane hatred, yet unable to shake it off, he held fast to his disdain and spurned John.

Paul's presence only made matters worse. Frederic knew that he was this baby's father. In fact, he often thought of *Paul* as Elizabeth's son, cherishing the fond memory of her mothering him in those weeks before her death. Here was a happy child, who grew into a genial lad. John, on the other hand, was an obstinate fellow, who took pleasure in vexing everyone. True, there had been moments when Frederic felt a certain closeness to him, an ember of contrition, but bitter memories always intruded, snuffing out the fragile flame. If not for John, Elizabeth would still be alive.

The years fell in upon themselves, and suddenly, John was a young man. "He's such a handsome boy," Frederic's eldest sister, Eleanor, had admired. She resided in the States, but, on one rare occasion, had ventured home. "The picture of you at that age, Frederic... the very picture..."

Yes, he had been blind, but the damage had already been done: John bitterly resented him.

Joseph faced John and prayed that Yvette's remarks concerning her elder brother were true: "It's just a charade to make everyone tremble. He's really a coward. He told me so."

Charade or no, the man was giving one fine performance, for John scowled down at him, seemingly oblivious of the water he had drawn for his bath.

"That will be all, Joseph," he finally muttered as he settled into the brimming tub. "Oh and Joseph, Miss Ryan is sleeping in the guest chamber next to mine. She shouldn't be disturbed until she rings for someone."

"But she's already up and about, sir."

John turned a bleary eye upon the lad. "Yes, I suppose she would be."

"Sir?" Joseph queried.

"Nothing, it was nothing."

"Sir?" the lad began, courageous in the face of John's debilitated state. "I just wanted to say that I'm sorry about your younger brother, sir. I know–"

John closed his eyes.

"–that you loved him, sir. We all knew that. And well, I just wanted to tell you how sorry we are about what happened."

John could not answer. He wondered how he would survive the day's condolences, the unbidden reminders that would trespass upon his guarded heart and prey on his vulnerability.

"Joseph?" he rasped as the boy reached the door.

"Yes sir?"

"Thank you."

"Yes, sir," the boy nodded. He exited the somber room, allowing John to take up soap and brush and scrub his body clean.

"That's right, Jeannette, cry," came the soothing voice, "cry until you can't cry anymore, and then, you'll feel better."

"I'll never, *never* feel better," the child sputtered.

"You don't think so now," Charmaine comforted, "but you will. Someday, when you remember Pierre, it will be of the happy times we spent together..."

John leaned his forehead against the closed portal and shut his eyes to the piercing pain. He should go in, attempt to console the girls as Charmaine was doing, but he couldn't. He had neither the strength, nor the desire to embrace his sisters' loss. His own was too great, too fresh.

"But why did he die?" Jeannette sobbed.

"God was probably punishing him for pretending to be ill on Sunday."

"Yvette!" Charmaine remonstrated sharply. "You know that's not true!"

The girl burst into tears. There was a moment's pause, and then Charmaine's voice penetrated the portal again, her words indiscernible, though John strained to hear them.

"Why did God do this to us?" Jeannette implored. "Wasn't Mama enough?"

"Oh, Jeannette, I don't have those answers. But you still have each other, and you have me. You know that I love you very much, don't you?"

"Yes," came the two trembling voices.

"And you have John. He needs your love more than ever."

"Why?"

"Because he loved Pierre, and he is very sad, too. If we comfort each other, one day the wound *will* heal and this terrible time will fade. Then you'll smile when you think of Pierre, and you'll laugh when you say: 'Remember when we went picnicking at the beach and Pierre dumped sand on Johnny's head?' or..." Charmaine's voice broke off.

"It's all right, Mademoiselle," John heard Jeannette say. "You loved Pierre as much as we did, so you don't have to be strong for us."

"She's right," Yvette added, "you should cry, too."

"No, Yvette, I've cried too much already."

With head bowed, John walked away.

"You are dismissed, Miss Ryan. Your services are no longer required."

Jaw slackened, speech stymied, Charmaine stared aghast at Agatha Duvoisin.

"My dear," the mistress reprimanded with head canted, "don't look so surprised. And please, close your mouth. It is quite unbecoming."

"But – why?"

"Surely you're not serious. The reason is quite obvious. Pierre is dead."

Charmaine flinched. It was one thing to speak of the boy's accident herself, quite another to hear his death uttered heartlessly. "And I'm just to leave?"

"You have until week's end."

"But that's–"

"Tomorrow," Agatha supplied, her lips curled in a ruthless smile.

"And if I refuse to go?" Charmaine demanded, no longer impeded by confusion and pain, but quite fired up by the mistress' edict.

"Refuse? My dear, you have no say in the matter."

"And who does have a say, Mrs. Duvoisin? You? Does anyone else know of this decision? Your husband? Paul? Should I take this matter up with them?"

"Miss Ryan, do you really think Paul would question his father's authority for a little trollop who has caught his fancy? Surely he's tired of you by now."

"You are a vile woman!" Charmaine accused.

"And you are an impudent little fool," Agatha hissed. "But this shall be the last time you address me in such a manner! You are responsible for the death of an innocent three-year-old. My husband, blind to your neglect up until now, has finally seen the light. The twins are to be sent to a boarding school, a fine English academy, and a governess is no longer required."

"You cannot be serious!" Charmaine objected.

"Oh, but I am, Miss Ryan. The past three days have forced my husband to take stock of his posterity. He's contemplated all his options concerning the welfare of his remaining offspring, and when I spoke with him earlier this morning, he asked to see you."

Charmaine's eyes widened.

"Yes, Miss Ryan," she acknowledged, eyebrow arched, "this is his decision, not mine, and I warn you now, he is not happy with you, not happy at all!"

Charmaine paled, fear clashing with her anger.

The chamber door slammed shut, and Agatha was once again alone. She smiled in self-satisfaction. She'd played it just right, had struck the most promising chords, and now, Charmaine Ryan, incensed by the injustice of it all, would stand before Frederic, her temper ablaze. With any luck, she'd overstep her bounds and seal her own fate. More importantly, she'd initiate the final confrontation between father and son.

Agatha hesitated as a wave of apprehension swept over her. *What if Frederic suffered another seizure? Worse still – what if this battle proved fatal?* She brushed aside such a possibility. It was a risk she was forced to take.

Her eyes hardened. She mustn't waste time. The governess' audience with her husband would be brief; therefore, every second counted. It was time to speak to the twins, Yvette in particular. She'd be quite upset to learn that her father had summoned her precious 'Mademoiselle' to his apartments and was, at this very moment, dismissing her. She'd run to John, inform and infuriate him, spur him into mindless action. Agatha had made certain he was in the house before setting her stratagem in motion. When John stormed into Frederic's chambers, there would be no rational truth seeking, only that vicious hatred they doggedly shared. And her husband would, for all his righteous resolve, deliver the final blow.

Charmaine's palms were sweating, and her stomach churned violently. Where was her valor now? Even her zealous rage had simmered down. As she stepped into the master's quarters it evaporated completely, like a drop of dew before the gates of hell. Damn her impulsive temper! Agatha had baited her.

The man she faced was no demon; he sported no fangs, sprouted no horns. His staff was a crutch that supported his crooked frame, a body that appeared to have further withered. This could not be the man who had bred contempt in his own home, abandoned one son and embraced another. Reason insisted that both sides were guilty, that John had wronged as well. But John had also loved. Where was Frederic's love?

Instantly, Charmaine repented her rush to judgment. Frederic *had* loved Pierre! She had only to look at him to know that. He couldn't run and play with the boy, but he had loved him and had feared that John might whisk him away. Suddenly, it all made sense. Frederic hadn't flaunted that love to enrage his estranged son; he was merely gathering his own memories. Charmaine wondered if John could ever understand this. Sadly, Frederic seemed prone to injuring those who should have been closest to him. But she realized now, the older man had been backed into a corner with no escape.

Frederic assessed her much as she did him, his eyes sweeping upward, searching her face and measuring her pain. It was a moment before Charmaine realized he had addressed her. "How are you faring?"

The concerned query took her by surprise. Unexpectedly, she experienced great compassion for him. He blamed himself; it was etched across his face.

"As well as can be expected, sir," she murmured, fighting back tears, grateful that he didn't know she had been privy to the truth about Pierre's conception and birth. "I'm sorry about Pierre."

"Charmaine, you don't have to apologize to me. It was an ugly accident and no one, least of all you, is to blame. But I do accept your condolences."

She nodded, cleared her throat, and then changed the subject. "Is there a reason you wanted to see me this morning, sir?"

"Yes, but why don't we sit down?" He motioned to a chair opposite his desk, and as he moved behind the secretary, she cautiously crossed the room.

Fatima told George that she had sent breakfast into the study for John. George found him there, gathering up the papers on the desk. George didn't say anything, but put a comforting hand to his friend's shoulder, then poured him a cup of tea from the untouched tray.

"I haven't seen Paul this morning," John said. "Has he left?"

"He's upstairs."

"I've lost track of the days, George – don't even know when the next ship is due in port."

"Why?"

"I'm going back to Richmond, after the funeral."

George bowed his head to his tightening chest and stinging eyes. The study fell silent, but for the rustling of papers that John mindlessly shoved into a valise.

The door burst open, and Yvette charged in, followed closely by a sobbing Jeannette and a concerned Paul.

"Johnny," she blurted out, "Father is sending us to a boarding school, and he's called Mademoiselle Charmaine to his chambers. He's going to dismiss her!"

"*What?*" John's face twisted in feral disgust. He abandoned the papers and headed toward the door.

"John!" Paul called after him, but George grabbed Paul's arm.

"Let him go."

"But they'll kill each other–"

"Leave them be," George advised sharply, holding fast Paul's arm. "They need to have it out, once and for all. You can't keep protecting them from each other. You'll only end up being blamed for interfering."

Frederic waited for Charmaine to be seated. "How are my daughters?" he asked. "I assume they know about Pierre?"

"Yes sir, they know." She looked down at her hands, reliving the girls' grief, witnessing the horrific disbelief that contorted their faces when they learned that their younger brother would no longer be a part of their lives. "They were asleep last night," she whispered hoarsely, "but I was there when they awoke. They're extremely upset and have been in tears all morning. I should be getting back to them soon."

Frederic nodded. Charmaine Ryan was the only ray of hope on this dismal day. God had sent his family a blessing when she had come to live in his house. "They are not going to face their loss alone," he vowed. "This time I will console them. I wanted you to know that."

Charmaine silently thanked God. "They would welcome seeing you, sir."

"Would you like to bring them here or would you prefer I visit the nursery?"

Charmaine relaxed with the query, choosing to answer it with one of her own. "Sir, you're not going to dismiss me, are you?"

His brow lifted. "Why would you ask that?"

"Mrs. Duvoisin said you were sending the girls to a school in Europe."

Frederic mastered his instant ire. "Her idea, not mine," he ground out. "That's the last place my daughters need to be right now. They need their family, and you, Charmaine. They've suffered two terrible tragedies this year. I want to see them emerge from the second as successfully as they did from the first. I want to see them whole and happy again."

"So do I, sir."

"That brings me back to the reason I wanted to speak to you this morning. John came to my quarters on Saturday morning and asked if–"

The unfinished statement hung in the air. Charmaine grimaced, and Frederic read the torment in her eyes. "What is it, Miss Ryan?"

"Nothing, sir," she lied, suppressing another urge to weep, the sudden chill that left her trembling.

Her shallow denial left Frederic unconvinced. "Have you seen John this morning?" he asked, dreading some unfathomable answer.

"No sir, not this morning."

Apprehension gripped her. She did not want to discuss John with his father.

"Last night?"

"Yes, sir." She was back in the chapel, back in John's arms, reliving his piercing pain, powerless to her tears.

Frederic was moved by her compassion. "Would you like to talk about it?"

"He blames himself!" she blurted out. "He lays all blame on himself."

Frederic's eyes grew turbulent, but before he could comfort her, there was a wild commotion from beyond. The outer door banged open, and John charged in, slamming the portal shut behind him.

"You lousy bastard!" he shouted, taking in Charmaine's tear-stained face. "You've reduced her to tears already? How despicable can you be?"

Frederic's eyes narrowed. "What's going on, John?"

"You tell me, Father! Why don't you tell me?"

Charmaine jumped up. "John! Listen to me!"

Her petition fell on deaf ears. For all his apparent outrage, he wasn't seeing her at all. "You enjoy watching the women in this house cry, don't you?" he sneered, stepping deeper into the room. "It makes you feel powerful, doesn't it?"

Frederic shot to his feet, fists clenched, Agatha's allegations ringing in his ears. "I don't know what you think is happening here, John, but–"

"*But what, Father?* What don't I understand? I'll tell you what I don't understand – how you can rob your children of love and affection! Are you out to hurt the girls now, or just me? Maybe that's it: hurt Yvette and Jeannette, hurt John. After all, it worked with Pierre, didn't it? *Didn't it, goddamn you?*"

Frederic paled, the calumnious words a minor attack when set against the torment in his son's face. "John, I'm sorry about Pierre. I never –"

"Don't! Don't even say it, because I'll never believe it. Pierre was only a pawn in your cunning game of subterfuge and power."

"Please, John, you misunderstand," Charmaine interrupted, stepping directly between the two men.

He looked at her for the first time. "No, Charmaine, you're the one who doesn't understand. I told you once: my father is the master of manipulation. Pierre was a valuable piece in his scheme, valuable because he was my–"

"Watch what you say in front of the governess!" Frederic warned.

"Why, Father? Are you afraid she'll find out that she works for a fiend?"

"John!" Charmaine gasped. "Please, don't–"

"She knows everything, anyway," John announced, ignoring her protests.

"So," his father snarled in derision, "you've shared your intimate relationships with the hired help?"

John chuckled ruefully. "When the 'hired help' offers more compassion than my own family – yes. Charmaine knows that Colette had a husband and a lover. What she doesn't know is that the lover should have been the husband!"

"That's enough! I want you out of here – *now!*"

"No," John growled with a fierce shake of the head, "I'm not going anywhere. I want to know why Charmaine is being dismissed? *Why, damn it?"*

"But John, I'm not!" Charmaine countered in surprise.

He wasn't listening. "You wouldn't give the girls to me when I asked for them, but a boarding school will suit them just fine! Is that how you shower them with love and affection? Or is this just another way to hurt Colette? Even though she's in the grave, you still want to hurt her! Damn you! Damn you to hell!"

"John, stop it! Please stop it!"

"No! I want some answers! You manacled Colette to you by withholding her daughters. You attempted to do the same to me. And now they're to be sent away? Cast aside? Why, because they're no longer of use to you?"

"John, I had no intention of sending them away. I was–"

"*Liar!* Always deceit and lies with you! God, how I loathe them! How I loathe you! How can you stand there and lie again and again to me – *to Colette?"*

"I don't know what you're talking about!"

"Don't you? She loved me! *Me!* We were to be married! But somehow you manipulated her into breaking the banns!"

Charmaine gasped.

"That's right, Charmaine, I knew Colette first, but my father convinced her that I'd never amount to anything – that I didn't have a penny to my name, save what I would inherit from him one day. The *great Frederic Duvoisin,* on the other hand, could take care of her family here and now, rescue them from poverty. So, Colette sacrificed herself for her poor crippled brother. And what did it gain her but a miserable cripple of a husband instead?"

"It wasn't all about money, John," his father murmured dolefully.

"What then? *Love?* Don't tell me she loved you! She was so sad when I came back into her life that she had forgotten how to smile. It didn't look like love to me!"

"What would you know of love?" Frederic lashed out.

"Nothing that came from you!" John fired back, a volley that met its mark. "You say that you loved my mother, but I don't believe that either. If you did, you would never have done what you did to me. But unlike you, I loved my son. And now he's dead – dead because of your hatred for me!"

Frederic inhaled, wounded. *Agatha was right: John loathed him and he'd never change that. But what gave him the right to hope that he could?*

Still John persisted. "You've taken everything from me, haven't you? Anything – anyone I've ever loved, you've managed to wrench them free."

"John," his father attempted again, "I'm sorry."

"Don't! Don't you dare grovel with an apology now, for I will *never* forgive you! And I'm glad Colette came back to me, that she finally followed her heart. When she looked upon you, it was with pity – pathetic pity, nothing more. If only you had died first, that fair lady would now be *my* wife!"

Charmaine recoiled, the agony on Frederic's face piercing. "John!"

But Frederic was armed for his own battle. "That *lady*, as you call her, was far below such a title. You blame *me* for her death, but you don't even know how she died. She miscarried a child that was not mine. Yes, John," he sneered smugly, savoring the befuddled expression on his son's face, "she loved you *so much* that she took *another* lover."

John laughed scathingly, the consternation gone. "Who fed you that shit?"

"Blackford–" Frederic faltered "–ask Blackford."

"No, I won't ask Blackford. He's a filthy liar who'd say anything to cover up his incompetence – *if he told you that at all!*"

The logic of John's assertion took hold, making it difficult to breathe.

When Frederic didn't respond, John continued, his words low and tight. "I loved her, Father. I loved her because I knew her, knew her to be decent and good. Maybe you can't comprehend that, and I pity you for it, but I loved her. And unlike you, I doubted her only once. So your newest lie falls upon deaf ears."

He shook his head. "You always believed the worst about her, didn't you? Even when I first brought her here, you were disdainful of her. She could feel it, she fretted about it. But I told her not to worry, that you'd come around. Little did I know. I suppose that after she accepted your proposal, it confirmed your opinion of her – that she was out for the Duvoisin money. But she cared about her family – her brother – and that is why she married you. What a fool I was to desert her, not once, but twice, to honor her perverted sense of duty! I should have known you'd destroy her! I should have protected her from that."

"John, I never meant–"

"If only I could do it over again," John ranted on, "I would never be so stupid as to leave her here with you. I wouldn't care if you disowned me. I never gave a damn about your fortune. I'd forfeit every penny of it for just one more second of her time!"

Frederic bowed his head to remorse, the poignant sincerity of his son's declaration. He was swept back to those last two nights, holding Colette in his arms again, and tears sprang to his eyes. "I know you'll never believe this John, but I, too, would forfeit it all."

"You're right, I don't believe you. It sounds good, but it's just another lie."

Suddenly, everything made sense to Frederic: that one deception, conceived nearly ten years ago, had led to this. "You've only been lied to once, John," he whispered. "I thought you knew the truth. These last few years, I thought Colette must have told you the truth."

"Told me what?" John prompted, confused.

Frederic glanced uncomfortably at Charmaine, then pressed on. "I was attracted to Colette when she first came to Charmantes." John snorted, but Frederic ignored him. "I mistook her coquetry for something else, and late one night, I seduced her."

"I don't believe it!" John railed, bombarded by a fleeting glimpse of Colette flirting with his father. The nocuous image sent his innards plummeting. "Seduced or raped?" he demanded venomously.

The chamber fell deadly silent, and in those mounting seconds when no denial came, John's face drained of color. The memory was gone, replaced by an uglier scenario: the painful truth. "*You forced her!* Goddamn you to hell, she was pure and innocent, and you forced her!"

He dove at his father maniacally, but Charmaine was there, throwing herself in his path, grappling for his arms. "No, John! Stop it! You're not going to change anything this way! Please stop!"

The sanity of her petition penetrated, and John faltered. He glanced down at the hands that held him, took in Charmaine's desperate face. Finally, he looked back at his father, but Frederic had collapsed into his armchair, head bowed, by all outward signs a man condemned.

John stepped back, but when Charmaine's hands dropped away, he clasped one of them, turned, and pulled her from the iniquitous room. Together they snaked through the crowd loitering in the corridor. There was Agatha, aquiver with anticipation, the worried twins, a concerned Paul, George, even the servants.

The next thing she knew, they were in her room. Pierre's body had been removed, the bed made, the furniture dusted, and the French doors thrown wide to catch the soft morning breezes. The tenebrous reminders of those four terrible days were gone. Everything was immaculate, mocking the turmoil that tainted their hearts.

John leaned heavily on the doorframe, his head resting against a raised forearm, eyes staring down at the emerald lawns. When it seemed he'd never speak, Charmaine said, "Your father has no intention of sending the girls away. I wasn't called to his quarters to be dismissed."

He glanced over his shoulder. "You shouldn't have been exposed to that."

"I should have left," she concurred.

But he wasn't listening. "Rape," he muttered in revulsion. "But why? Did he hate me that much? Or is he really that evil? Never once, in all those years, did it occur to me that that was the reason she deserted me. My God! I wronged her so many times in my mind, chastised her, and still she loved me. She knew I was consumed with jealousy, yet she never told me the truth. Why did she allow me to believe the worst – that she had chosen my father's fortune over me – that *she* was to blame?"

When the quiet room yielded no answers, he looked back at Charmaine.

"I didn't realize you knew Colette first," she said. "Were you truly betrothed?"

He stared outdoors once again, transfixed. Charmaine held silent. When he spoke again, the story unfolded.

The year had been 1827 and George, Paul, and he were attending university in France. "We were hell-raisers then, at least I was," he said, with a sad chuckle, "spending less time at the books and more time carousing. The spring semester was half-spent before I first glimpsed the young lady whom Paul had been escorting from one Paris soirée to another. She was beautiful," he whispered reverently, "and the moment she wrinkled her fine aristocratic nose at me, I was determined to have her. Such an objective proved more difficult than I had initially imagined, and once I had lured her away from my brother, I found that, although she pretended at being a woman of the world, she was quite proper and innocent. But it was too late for me. I had fallen in love with her, and she, with me, or so I thought. Torture became my reward, and since I'd been unable to seduce her, I realized that the only alternative open to me was marriage. True, I was young, but if seventeen was not too young for a woman to marry, then nineteen was not unreasonable for a young man.

"Her mother objected fiercely. The woman did not fancy the likes of me for a son-in-law. But thanks to the gossip of a family friend, she was finally assured of my family's wealth and the inheritance that would eventually fall to me, and not Paul, as she had originally believed.

"That same friend suggested the wedding take place on Charmantes so that Colette's mother could meet my father and ascertain my standing as heir to the family's holdings. I was reluctant to involve him, but Colette persuaded me to return home for the wedding. Her childhood friend would accompany us, along with Paul and George. It would be romantic, she reasoned, and although I didn't want to wait, I loved her and wanted to please her.

"So, we laughed over the workings of the adult mind and surmised that Colette's mother hoped to snare my widower father. Her husband had lost most of his fortune to the revolution, and after his death, she had to rely on any device, including Colette, to see that she and her son, Pierre, were cared for.

"Such assumptions were close to the truth. As soon as we arrived on Charmantes, Adèle Delacroix set her sights on my father. He was not interested… not in Colette's mother, at least." John snorted in contempt as he contemplated his sire's true motives.

"Over the years that followed, I wondered if Adèle had taken my father's snub in stride, then manipulated Colette into his arms in her stead. Had she used her son's infirmity to convince Colette to forfeit me for the immediate security of his fortune? I had walked in on several conversations that supported that possibility. The woman was intuitive, alert to every word my father and I exchanged. It didn't take her long to size up our strained relationship. When we argued, it only served to heighten her anxiety. He didn't think I was prepared to step into marriage and work for a living, an assertion I was determined to prove wrong. I started by lending a hand in the fields..." John's words dropped off, and Charmaine watched him work through the details, his scowl darkening. "Suffice it to say, Adèle fretted over the inheritance that might be withdrawn if I didn't behave myself. If nothing else, she burdened Colette with talk of responsibility and family loyalty, exploiting Colette's love and concern for her younger brother.

"All I knew was that one day we were planning our wedding, and the next, Colette was breaking the banns. She wanted nothing more to do with me. At first, she was diplomatic, telling me that she had grown *fond* of me, that she didn't want to hurt me, that the charade had gone on for too long. She had been out to catch a rich husband, and when Paul didn't fit the bill, she had turned to me. She had to think of her family, her crippled brother, in particular. His medical bills were mounting, and she had planned to send her mother home with an allowance to pay them. But when it became clear that my father controlled the purse strings, she had turned her sights on him. I begged her not to sacrifice our love. I told her that I would work harder, that I could provide for all of them. She shook her head and told me it wasn't enough. She needed the money now. When I asked her how she could throw our love away, she broke down and cried. When I tried to embrace her, to reason with her, she turned away. She swore that she'd never loved me. I became furious, though I knew her words were ludicrous. I threatened to tell my father that she was a tramp – a sly, conniving whore. But she only laughed, saying, 'He knows what I am, and he doesn't care. He wants me anyway!'

"I ran from the house, and I didn't stop. I stumbled over my own two feet with that last vision of Colette, her eyes swollen from crying, swearing that she didn't love me, had never loved me. I boarded the ship that was in port and awaited its departure. Even then, a part of me wanted to go back, to hold her and shake the lies from her, certain that she wouldn't have cried if the lies were true! But another part of me was crushed, so I didn't go back, and I swore that I'd never return to Charmantes, that I'd forget her as easily as she could me.

"I went to Virginia and took to running my father's business there, determined to gain independence from the damned fortune that had always kept me under his thumb and had now ruined my life. But in the months I was there, I was consumed with anger and hatred. I hated her mother, even her brother. I hated my father for interfering, even though I concluded that he'd married her to save me from the mistake he had insisted I was making – saddling myself with a money-grubbing wife. But mostly, I hated myself for still wanting her, loving her, my self-loathing paramount only to my hatred for her. I was not very different from my father at that time. Many nights, I raped her in my dreams, driven by one single desire: to inflict pain on those who had hurt me, pain upon Colette, and pain upon my father. So, I broke my vow and returned home.

"He and Colette had been married less than a year, and she was heavy with child, close to delivering. She greeted me cordially, as if I were a long-lost brother, as if nothing had ever happened, as if we were one big, happy family – my father included. It made me want to vomit. But they dropped that charade once they realized I wasn't about to accept the cozy life they were now living. For a week, not one word passed between us, but my hatred continued to fester. Then, one night, I cornered her in the drawing room, and we had it out. I enjoyed making her cry, was even more satisfied when my father barged in. We would have come to blows, but Colette collapsed onto the sofa, and he ran to her. She was in labor.

"I left for Virginia right away, unaware that she had delivered twins, and didn't go back for four years. When I did, it was obvious that something had changed between them. My father's foul moods were worse, and Colette rarely smiled. At first I gloated over her sadness; she was finally getting what she deserved. I decided to spend time with the twins. They were sweet and innocent, and winning them over was easy. More importantly, here was an opportunity to be cruel to their mother. I'd ignore her completely, exclude her from excursions I planned with the girls, and when my father put a stop to that, I convinced Yvette and Jeannette that their mother was responsible. Colette knew what I was doing, but she never turned them against me. It made me angrier. I wanted her to regret that she had chosen my father's fortune. I invited women to the house for dinner and openly flirted with them. She disapproved, but never said a word. After a while, I grew disgusted with the game. Then, one morning–" he inhaled deeply, held the breath, seemed to savor it, but when he expelled it, he said "–I left. A little distance and time, and I'd get on with my life. I was wrong. When I got back to the States, I couldn't stop thinking about her. I realized that she was more miserable than I was. I remembered our happy times in France, her radiant smile that could light up a room. My father had robbed her of that, and it wasn't fair. And so, I went back again.

"My father had begun developing Espoir. He was seldom on Charmantes that summer. The girls' enthusiasm threw us together, and it was easy to pretend he didn't exist. I fell in love again, this time with a very different woman. As the weeks went by, instinct told me that she loved me still. Her misplaced sense of responsibility had gotten us into this mess, and although she tried time and again to shift any blame away from my father, how I hated him for it. I knew he could have helped her family *without* demanding payment in return. If he loved me, that's what he would have done. But no, he didn't want *me* to benefit from his charity. Instead, *he* greedily enjoyed the pleasures his money could buy, making Colette his whore as easily as he set me aside. Their marriage was a sham.

"When Colette told me she was carrying my child, I pleaded with her to leave him. I'd acquired my own fortune. We could go to New York, where nobody would know about the past. But my father denied her custody of the girls, and she refused to desert them. That led to a vicious row. My father and I said things to each other that can never be forgiven. I vaguely remember him collapsing, and still, I shouted at him. Then Colette was screaming at me, demanding that I leave, and Paul was there, pulling me out of the room…

"I loved her, Charmaine, will always love her. Now, after all these years, I know the truth: Colette wasn't a mercenary, and she wasn't a saint. She married my father because she was humiliated, and she stayed with him because of the girls and her guilt. He exploited those emotions, but she never loved him."

John faced her, his eyes fierce. "You know the rest," he murmured, his voice suddenly raspy. "She refused to leave him – to *ever* leave him. When I realized he wasn't going to die, I went back to Virginia, alone." He turned back to the French doors. "No longer will I be haunted by the image of her kneeling before him begging his forgiveness. I finally know the truth. She loved me."

Frederic gave Jeannette one last squeeze, and the girls left him. His gaze lifted to Paul. "See that they get back to the nursery," he directed. "Perhaps Rose could look in on them if Miss Ryan is not there."

Paul nodded. "I'm sorry about this, Father. I tried to calm Yvette before she went running in search of John. You're certain you're all right?"

"Yes, I'm fine. You can send Agatha in now."

Agatha drew a chair even with her husband. "I'm sorry," she whispered. "I know I caused all of that."

Surprised, Frederic scrutinized her expression, looking for a flaw in the genuine contrition he heard in her voice. "Why did you tell Miss Ryan that I was sending the girls to a boarding school?"

"We did discuss it," she replied evenly. She studied the hands in her lap, her long fingers rotating her wedding band thoughtfully. "I know. Nothing was decided, and I should have held my tongue. But Miss Ryan can be quite insolent, and I lashed out imprudently. I'm sorry."

"And John – you made certain he heard the same tale."

Agatha squared her shoulders. "When has he believed anything I've said?"

Frederic was given pause. Agatha was right. Sadly, he realized that his son had been looking for an excuse to lambaste him; doing so in front of the children's governess was vindictive, at best.

Before he could think about it, Agatha was speaking again. "I've been fretting over what I said to you this morning, Frederic. I was wrong, terribly wrong, to say what I did. You've been hurt by so many of your loved ones, and I ache with the knowledge that I have gathered with them."

"Agatha – please," he beseeched, warding off the sympathy she seemed wont to bestow. "The funeral will be in less than an hour's time, and I need a moment's peace before that ordeal begins."

"As you wish, my dearest, as you wish." She departed his company, uncertain as to the outcome of the morning's row.

Friday
October 13, 1837

Chapter 9

Charmaine woke with a start and sat upright in Pierre's bed. Someone was crying. She stood and crossed the room, settling next to Jeannette who was moaning in her sleep. "Wake up, Sweetheart. You're having a bad dream."

Slowly, the girl surfaced from the dregs of a disturbing slumber. "Oh, Mademoiselle Charmaine," she whimpered. "We were in the fishing boat with Johnny. It started to rock and – and Pierre fell out! But then he started to swim. I think he was all right." She groaned woefully. "Oh, why couldn't that have really happened? I miss him so much!"

"I know, Sweetheart, I know," Charmaine consoled. "But he's with your Mama now. She's watching over him, and she's no longer alone."

Charmaine cuddled the distraught child for a very long time, stroking back her hair until her breathing grew regular. When she was certain that Jeannette slept, she eased her head back onto the pillow, drew the thin coverlet over her, and kissed her cheek.

Standing, she stepped out onto the balcony, happy to find that it had stopped raining. She breathed deeply, drinking in the night air that carried the wisps of hair off her neck and eased the pain in her breast. Her moment's reprieve was swiftly stolen; she hung her head and choked on the tears she fought to subdue.

Just one week ago, they were living in paradise. One week ago today, she and John, the twins and Pierre had traveled to the lake nestled in a hidden forest and passed a wondrous day together. One week ago tonight, that flawless week came to a jarring end when cries from the front lawn ruptured her sleep, and Yvette tore into the house. Now, one week later, Charmaine could almost laugh with the insanity of it. This tragedy over a silly game of cards!

At least it was behind her. Pierre had been buried yesterday, a brilliant day that mocked all that had transpired earlier that morning: the confrontations and revelations, the lies and the truths. The breeze had been mild, the sun's rays strong, the day clear and bright, full of mendacious promise. John's eyes had been as dry as the day had been splendid, and that had been a lie as well.

So many lies…

Frederic had also made the journey from chapel to burial ground, one arm around Jeannette's delicate shoulders, the other hand clasping his cane as the entourage escorted the small coffin to its final resting-place next to Colette's grave.

Yvette had attempted to console John, but he remained aloof, and after a while, she moved to Charmaine instead, head bowed, sniffing back her tears.

Everyone from the manor had been there, even Rose and George this time. The latter clasped John's shoulder supportively, remaining with him to the end, watching as the overturned earth was shoveled onto the small pine box, his arm quickening when Jeannette stepped forward and placed Pierre's stuffed lamb on top of the mound.

Not once did father or son look one another's way, and no sooner had the company arrived home, the clouds rolled in and the skies opened up, shedding the tears the two men refused to weep. The remainder of the day had passed in solemn misery. Today had been no better.

Charmaine wiped her tears away. She should retire to her own room, but she had no desire to sleep in the bed in which Pierre had died. Sooner or later she must, but not tonight.

A sound from the end of the balcony drew her round. She was surprised to find Paul there. He strolled closer, standing before her now. She had not had a moment alone with him since finding him asleep in the armchair just yesterday morning. But that was an eternity ago.

She read the sorrow in his eyes, realizing how much he, too, grieved.

"It is very late," he whispered. "Are you having trouble sleeping?"

"Any sleep I've had has been fragmented and disturbing," she replied. "I keep hoping that I'll become too tired to think and..."

Her words dropped off as Paul gathered her in his arms. She grabbed hold of him, buried her face in his chest and willed herself not to cry. He stroked her hair and caressed her back. When the tears did not come, he squeezed her tightly. "Go ahead and cry, Charmaine," he encouraged. "You've been strong for so many others. Let me be strong for you." They came in a deluge.

Paul battled his own anguish, taking solace from the feel of her in his arms. "I wanted to be there for you yesterday," he rasped.

"I know you did," she whimpered weakly, her tears still effusive, face pressed firmly to his shirtfront, unwilling to pull away.

"We're going to get through this. There will be happy days again."

"I pray God you're right, Paul, because I don't know how I'm going to go on without him. I miss him so much already."

"You will, Charmaine, I promise you will."

They remained entwined for a very long time. When her pain subsided, she stepped slightly away, but Paul leaned back into the balustrade and drew her next to him, his arm resting possessively around her shoulders.

"Maybe we can do something with the girls tomorrow," he offered. "Perhaps a ride into town together."

Charmaine hugged him closer, her cheek resting upon his chest, conveying how much she appreciated his concern.

Much later, he retreated to his rooms. It had begun to rain again. Brushing his lips across hers, he bade her goodnight. Charmaine watched him go.

Entering her own chamber, she strode to the bed, tore back the blanket, and climbed in. It was a very long time before she slept, but as she hugged her pillow, she relived the security of Paul's embrace, and her eyes grew heavy.

Saturday, October 14, 1837

If you want to believe the worst about me, you continue to do so, Frederic... Frederic awoke with a start. He'd been arguing with Colette, her eyes flashing fire at him, so much like those first few weeks of their marriage. And yet, her words were not of long ago. They had been spoken to him recently, only a month before her death.

He closed his eyes again, hoping to recapture his dream. But as the minutes ticked by and sleep eluded him, he rose from the bed.

Dawn was upon the island, and although the French doors faced north, the early morning sun shone through the rain-spattered panes, spraying a spectrum of colorful dots across the morbid room. Frederic slumped into the armchair and stared at the pinpoints, their intense brightness blinding. Still he contemplated them; if he stared long enough, everything became black and white.

He was bored of this room, weary of his prolonged internment. He thought of John, his son, and a feeling welled up inside him, a feeling that he had only begun to acknowledge. His eyes blurred with the realization that he loved his estranged son, loved him intensely. More than that, Frederic admired him. For Frederic, it had been so much easier to be angry than sad, cruel than kind. And so, he had allowed jealousy and pain to keep him away from the one precious thing that could heal him: his own flesh and blood. But unlike him, John had borne life's wounds, accepted the suffering. He hadn't passed his cross onto an easy victim. And, for all his anger and hurt, even his mistakes, John could live with his decisions, live with himself.

Frederic bowed his head. When had he become such a pathetic fool? There would be no forgiveness, hadn't John said so? But then, why should there be?

Pierre was dead, and the cold truth pierced like a knife. *Pierre is dead because of your hatred for me.* Frederic had never considered the far-reaching consequences of his obstinate bitterness, never thought that it could bring such ruin down about him. Had he become so depraved that he would allow the destruction of his own family, or worse yet, the death of an innocent three-year-old? Now he had to face it. He'd betrayed Elizabeth, John, and Colette.

Colette... He had misjudged her from the outset. When she arrived on the island at the age of seventeen, her delicate beauty took his breath away. More disturbing was her demeanor – something in her manner of speech and behavior that constantly reminded him of Elizabeth, an attraction that grew stronger and more difficult to suppress each day.

Colette's motives were equally disconcerting. Although John was obviously smitten, Frederic grew wary. First, there was her mother. He read the woman quickly, the worry of looming poverty in her eyes. Then there was Paul, who'd been dropped as a suitor when Colette learned that John was the legitimate heir to the Duvoisin fortune. And finally, there was Colette herself, born and bred in decadent France. Frederic had experienced its depravity first hand, was certain that this young lady could teach his son a thing or two, a supposition reinforced by a few saucy conversations he'd overhead. She'd even gone so far as to flirt with *him*. So, he had serious doubts about her innocence, concluding that her purported virtue was merely a hook to reel John into marriage. She wasn't about to give up her body without a ring on her finger and money in the bank. Clearly, this was a near-destitute family capitalizing on an unprecedented opportunity to mitigate their woe.

As for John, he didn't object to his son sewing his wild oats with her, but Frederic felt he was far too young and undisciplined for marriage. Unlike his industrious brother, John was hardly the model student at university. With the exception of his music studies, John just did not have the patience to sit through long lectures, nor the interest in doing the work to make his grades. Frederic had received numerous letters from the university complaining of John's lackadaisical attitude and disruptive presence in class. Few instructors were willing to have him in their lectures, as John was always bent on challenging their assertions or, once he had homed in on their flaws, humiliating them in front of the other students, who would laugh uproariously at his jokes. When it became clear to the professors that the Sorbonne was not about to spurn the Duvoisin money, they resorted to giving John passing marks just to avoid another semester of his grating presence. Since university had not settled him down, Frederic felt that John needed hard work and worldly experience before he married.

When Frederic overheard Colette telling her friend that the game she played with John was far more complicated than kissing stable-hands in the hayloft, he had had enough. He wasn't about to allow her to perform favors for some commoner and then play the virgin for his naïve son. No, Frederic concluded, the time had come for Colette to be confronted by a man who had the experience to see through her façade and handle her appropriately. If money was what she was after, he would spare his son the mistake of marrying a mercenary, young and beautiful though she was. Oh yes, John would be furious with him, but he was used to that. There would be plenty of other young ladies to conquer. In time, the dispute would be smoothed over, and Frederic's intervention applauded.

Unbidden, came vivid images of the sultry night that sealed Colette's fate...

He had arrived home very late, tired and aching from a grueling day in the sugarcane fields. The house was dark, save for the lamps flickering in the corridor. He'd assumed that everyone was abed and headed toward the kitchen to get a drink. He had reached the dining room when he heard the giggling and whispers of young women carrying from the garden beyond. He moved into the archway, which afforded him a view of the courtyard. Colette and her friend emerged, bubbling over in animated conversation, and although they conversed in French, he remembered enough of the language to understand their banter.

"I still say Paul is far more handsome," her friend said, "but alas, he won't be the rich one."

Frederic strained to hear Colette's response, but her voice was hushed.

"Their father is just as handsome," her friend continued. "Such a waste to leave him to your mother! Maybe I can have him!"

"Ssh!" Colette admonished, moving closer. "Someone might hear you!"

"You know, *you* could have him!" the friend pressed on. "I think he's attracted to you!"

"Stop it, Pascale!" Colette warned, but with a wicked chuckle added, "Then again, I could practice kissing with him!"

"Yes," the shameless girl giggled, "I'm certain he knows just how it's done, and if he tutored you, then you would have nothing to worry about on your wedding night." Their laughter increased.

"Pascale, you are terrible!" Colette reprimanded with a click of her tongue.

They laughed again. Finally, Pascale said, "We should be seeking our beds. Are you coming?"

"I need something to drink first. It is so hot here, I'll never get used to it. You go ahead, Pascale, I'll see you in the morning. Goodnight."

Colette passed through the swinging kitchen door, but drew herself up when she found him standing at the table, pouring himself a glass of water.

"So, Mademoiselle Delacroix, I understand you are thirsty?"

She nodded, but blushed under his piercing gaze, her poise shaken. He poured a glass, his hand brushing hers as he handed it to her. She finished it quickly. "More?" he asked.

"No, thank you," she murmured.

"Then if you are retiring, let me escort you to your room."

They walked down the hallway, Colette leading the way. Frederic considered her feminine figure, the delicate arch of her neck, the graceful undulating of her hips as she climbed the stairs.

When they arrived at her chamber door, she swung around, and he stepped in close. He turned the doorknob behind her, swinging the door inward. She stepped into the room, and he followed her. She was surprised by his impropriety, but did not appear alarmed.

"I also understand you wish to practice the art of kissing to prepare for your wedding night," he stated, closing the door behind him. He stepped very close to her again.

She giggled nervously. "You overheard my conversation with Pascale," she replied with a tremulous smile.

"Yes." He cupped her chin, gently nudging her face upward toward his.

"We were only being silly!" she laughed, surprising him when she didn't immediately pull away. "We are both giddy from this adventure and the excitement of being here."

"Are you?"

"Yes," she laughed again tensely, though her blue eyes sparkled, as if titillated by the encounter unfolding between them.

She can't wait to tell Pascale about this.

He abruptly released her chin, grabbed the hair at her nape, and pressed his lips to hers. Whether dumbfounded or excited, she did not step back, and he swiftly took hold of her shoulders, pulling her hard against him. Then his mouth was cutting across hers, his fingers entwined in her flaxen locks, urging her head back, his tongue parting her lips, probing and caressing.

"Monsieur!" she exclaimed breathlessly when he finally drew away.

"What else would you like to practice, Mademoiselle?" he asked, similarly shaken, his voice husky in his ears. He boldly caressed the length of her back, his hand coming to rest on her buttocks. "That is, if you need any practice."

"Monsieur, really, I think you misunderstood."

"Oh, I understand very well," he replied, as he began to work at the buttons of her bodice. The fresh smell of her was as intoxicating as her lips, fanning the passion he thought he was capable of controlling. "Come now, we both know that French girls can be coy – skilled at the art of acting virginal when, in fact, they are not. Especially society girls such as yourself."

"Really, you do misunderstand!" she insisted shakily.

She backed away, but came up against the bed, stumbling backwards onto it. There she lie, the bodice of her gown open, revealing the lovely swell of her breasts above her corset.

He followed her, stooping to pull off his boots, ripping open his shirt and undoing the buttons of his trousers. When she finally attempted to scramble away, he chuckled and lunged across the bed, pulling her back into the center of it. She struggled for only the moment it took to pin her beneath him, her protests snuffed out as his mouth captured hers. He worked at her corset until the stays were released and the beauty of her firm, round breasts revealed. He squeezed the pliable orbs, taking delight in how they molded to the shape of his hands, his senses inflamed by the guttural groan that rumbled in her throat.

"Mon Dieu," she whimpered when his mouth left her lips to sample first one and then the other delectable nipple, trembling fiercely, though the room was quite warm.

Even when he knelt above her to pull off the last of her clothing, and stood to quickly remove his own, she did not move, did not scream, apparently realizing the futility of resisting and the embarrassment it would cause her. Her only protest was a modest, "Non, s'il vous plait!"

But his ardor was piqued. "Too late, demoiselle," he said, lust heavy in his voice. "Of all the instruction your mother gave you about cornering a rich husband, did she not teach you that if you play with fire, you will get burned?"

She frowned up at him, and he read defeat in her eyes, submitting as he parted her legs. He covered her with his body and, after kissing her passionately, penetrated her with one hungry thrust, surprised when she vaulted against the rending intrusion, a muffled cry of pain erupting from her throat. It was then that he realized her innocence, but his own need was great and would not be quelled.

She struggled anew, attempting to push him away, but he grabbed her buttocks and pressed deep inside, all the more eager to have her. When she had accepted the full length of him, he lay very still, enjoying the feel of her breasts against his chest. He devoured her lips, drinking in her agony, cupped her face between his hands and rained kisses along her jaw to her cheek, wet with tears. She refused to look at him, so he tenderly tasted each moist eyelid, waiting for her to relax beneath him. When she sighed, he began to move against her, gently at first, and then, when he could no longer contain himself, harder. She grasped him tightly, her nails digging into his shoulders, her eyes still closed to what was happening. Her arms fell away once his passion was spent and, as he released her, a sob escaped her bruised lips.

When he rose from the bed, he took in the bloodstained linen and the second onslaught of tears. They confirmed what he already knew: she had been a virgin, exactly what everyone else had believed her to be, and he experienced a sharp stab of shame. He had made a grave error, his assumptions concerning her virtue had been unfounded, and he was overcome with regret, comprehending the implications of his vile behavior. He had soiled this young woman, spoiling her prospects as a future bride to his son, or anyone else for that matter.

He stared down at her for a moment longer, but when he tried to speak to her, to sit on the edge of the bed and wipe the tears from her eyes, to apologize, she only moaned, pulled the covers up, and turned away, refusing to even look at him. At a loss, he quickly dressed and abandoned the room.

The next day she remained closeted in her chambers, claiming illness, refusing to see John, her mother, even her friend. Late that evening, when all were abed, Frederic breached her chamber again, this time to propose marriage. She had no choice but to accept.

Over the next few days, Colette's heartache became his pain. She insisted on speaking to John alone, and although Frederic was of a mind to tell his son the truth, she vehemently objected. He never knew precisely what she said to John, but surmised that she accepted the unjust title of 'mercenary' and 'harlot' in order to prevent greater repercussions. John was devastated, nonetheless.

Today, Frederic grieved with the weight of it. Because he'd been uncomfortable with his son's bitterness, he chose to brush it off. John would recover from his broken heart. He was young, he'd find another, he'd forget Colette. As for himself, Frederic worked at making Colette forget as well. She was in his blood and he couldn't concentrate for thinking about her. For all her feeble protests, she hadn't truly fought him, hadn't attempted to push him away until it was too late. *Why?* Was she frightened of him, or did she only fear her own intense attraction? He grew to believe that their encounter hadn't been rape, but seduction.

The first few weeks of their marriage had been tumultuous, and his pulse quickened with the memory. He recalled her fiery mettle, the times she fought his conjugal forays, the many nights she succumbed to passion and moaned in his arms. She never cowered before him, though he felt she worked hard at the poise she displayed.

Thrown into the mix was her vehement opposition to human bondage. Here was a mere slip of a girl who avoided speaking to him, yet had the effrontery to question his morality over holding slaves. He remembered their many altercations and thought specifically of the slave, Nicholas. She had been unconventionally vocal arguing the Negro's plight. Determined to rule his domain with an iron hand, Frederic turned tyrannical. It became a contest of wills. And only when he took her to his bed did she momentarily retreat. A familiar warmth spread through his loins as he thought about it. No other woman had satisfied him like Colette, save Elizabeth. But then, he often thought of them as one and the same.

Weeks turned into months, and their stormy relationship turned tender. The consuming fire remained, but Colette no longer sidestepped his passion behind a pretense of injured pride. She welcomed his lovemaking and slept contentedly in his arms night after night. Then she was with child, and his heart nearly burst with joy. During that year, he felt blessed; he'd been given a second chance.

He often thought about John, wrestled with the letters he could write, what he might say to make amends. But somehow, he knew he'd only make matters worse. In the end, he could only hope that time would heal all.

And then that time came: John returned. Colette was heavy with child, and though she greeted him congenially, John could scarcely look her way, his eyes simmering in unmasked repugnance when she and Frederic occupied the same room. As the days wore on, Frederic bristled with the intended slights and silent insults. Why had his son come back? He obviously still loathed them both. John's motives became painfully apparent toward the close of the week – that wretched night when his voice rang out from the drawing room, his wrath so intense that Frederic could hear him from the second floor. Frederic flew down the stairs, horrified when he came upon the scene. The only thing that prevented them from coming to blows was Colette, prone on the sofa in the early throes of labor.

The twins' delivery was difficult, lasting over twenty-four hours, but Frederic remained by her bedside, refusing to leave even when Blackford demanded he do so. He was paralyzed by fear, reliving Elizabeth's labor some twenty years earlier. It was then that he prayed, bargaining with the Almighty to spare Colette. "Give her something for the pain, damn you!" he blazed as she writhed in agony.

Blackford complied, and he calmed down when the laudanum took effect. Even so, her breathing remained ragged, and from time to time, her head twitched on the pillow. He soothed her, smoothing the hair from her sweaty brow and murmuring words of encouragement close to her ear. She became delirious and called for John over and over again. When she couldn't be comforted, he turned away in misery.

Hours later, it was over, and two healthy girls were presented to him. But the love he was wont to bestow upon them only the day before was gone.

He never touched Colette again. Sadly, he accepted the fact that her heart would always belong to his son. He had robbed them both. That she eventually took John as a lover shouldn't have come as a surprise, or hurt as it did. He'd acknowledged the inevitable years earlier when she had openly flirted with his business associates at dinner one night. Her desires were quite clear, and they did not include him. When she admitted to her affair with John, begging him to understand, denouncing their marriage as a mistake, he assumed that she had finally told John the truth. But she hadn't.

Looking back on those years, he realized that Colette had continued to protect him. Even in her suffering, she had placed the precious tie between father and son above her own yearnings, in the beginning as an unwilling bride, and later as his wife. She'd only stopped trying when he had succeeded in breaking her spirit, not by taking her to his bed, but by setting her from it, by denying her that fragile bond of love that had just begun to blossom between them. He gulped back a wave of blistering emotion. To prevent an irreversible rupture, Colette had concealed the truth from John to the end. She had cared about them both so very much that she had protected them from each other.

Frederic bowed his head to the saddest fact of all: after everything he had done to her, the havoc he'd wrought, his continual condemnation, Colette had never once condemned him. Instead, she had believed the best about him, cherished him more than he ever knew. She must have known his innermost insecurities, understood the ferocious front that was his shield, and comprehended what would be most important to him in the end. Now she was dead, and he had allowed that to happen as well. Even in the grave, he had not relieved her of her terrible crucible, though he owed her a great debt. *If you want to believe the worst about me, you continue to do so, Frederic... You don't trust me... even now, you don't trust me...*

No, ma Fuyarde, he vowed, *I do trust you. I will never believe the worst again.* Blackford had lied. *Why?*

Frederic rose from his well-worn seat. This would be the last time he languished here all day.

Robert received Frederic's one-line message before he opened his small clinic for the day. As he closed the office door behind Joseph Thornfield, he wondered about the urgency of the dispatch. Was the man ill? He dismissed the thought quickly, certain that his sister would have informed him first. Perhaps *she* was ill. This, too, he ruled out. Surely the note would have contained words to that effect. Why, then, was he needed immediately at the manor? Maybe the truth was out.

He counseled himself calm as he donned a waistcoat and jacket. Now was not the time to lose his composure. This probably had very little to do with him and quite a lot to do with his errant nephew, who refused to seek a physician's care for Pierre. Now that the initial shock had passed and the funeral was over, these unresolved issues could be properly addressed. Certainly Agatha would be pleased with the outcome. Hadn't this been what she was pressing for all along? John had definitely dug a hole for himself this time.

Robert grabbed his hat and physician's bag and stepped out of his small abode. Best to be punctual.

Charmaine hugged herself against the chill in the house and shivered. The foul weather of yesterday had not broken. The rainy season of late August and September had come at last, a constant drizzle, tenacious in the wake of the brilliant sunshine that had mocked Pierre's funeral barely two days ago.

Lies. That one word continued to plague her, scream at her.

"You should have accompanied Paul and the girls into town."

Rose shook off the brooding silence, and slowly, Charmaine turned away from the tear-splattered panes. "Not in this weather," she said.

"It will be clear by afternoon," Rose predicted as she looked up from her knitting, her dexterous fingers blindly feeding the wool to the clicking needles.

Charmaine agreed absentmindedly. "No doubt Paul is annoyed with me. He didn't have just his sisters in mind when he offered the outing at breakfast."

"I'm surprised that Yvette decided to go," Rose conferred.

"I'm not," Charmaine replied, finally leaving the drawing room casement and sitting beside the woman. "John left the house early, and since she hasn't been able to engage his attention here, she's hoping to catch him in town."

Rose shook her head. "She's a wonder. So much like her mother."

Charmaine heard the woman's tears and fought to control her own misery. "Dear God, Nana," she breathed. "What a mess!"

Rose set her knitting aside. "Would you like to talk about it?"

Charmaine hesitated, uncertain of what Rose knew. But the elder's melancholy eyes told Charmaine that she knew everything. "Oh Nana, that day in the master's chambers... it was terrible. And John, he said things I should never have heard."

"There, now," Rose soothed with a pat of the hand, "I thought as much. But you must use this revelation to cultivate understanding for all those involved."

"Understanding?" Charmaine queried incredulously. "How can I possibly understand a hatred that has existed for twenty-nine years – a hatred that has bred so much evil here?"

"Evil? Charmaine, you're speaking about people, people whom you've grown to love, who are fallible and have made mistakes, grave mistakes, but mistakes, nonetheless." Rose paused a moment, and then with a half-smile said, "All is not so lost. You're reaction is only natural. But time will be the greatest healer, time and companionship. The girls need you more than ever now."

Charmaine contemplated the wise statements. "But what if I'm dismissed? Mr. Duvoisin did not want me to hear the ugly things John accused him of. Now I'll stand as a constant reminder of his humiliation."

"Frederic will not send you away," Rose declared resolutely.

Charmaine was not so certain. She thought of Agatha and the confrontation she had generated. "Why did Mrs. Duvoisin lie to me? To what end?"

"To set John and his father at one another's throats again, to have John expelled from Charmantes once and for all."

"But why? Why does she hate him so? He's her nephew."

"Come, Charmaine," Rose reasoned, "you remember what it felt like to be the target of John's sharp tongue. Agatha has never bowed meekly to his ridicule, though she's endured it for years. Now that she is Frederic's wife, she's set her teeth in. John has dug his own grave where his aunt is concerned."

Charmaine snorted. "I should have seen through her little game."

"Not a little game," Rose whispered ominously. "Suffice it to say, Agatha bears her own scars, and though they should have healed long ago, she nurses them often, lamenting the cross she was given to carry. In the future, take heed."

"I intend to," Charmaine bit out, "with both the master and the mistress."

Rose's brow gathered. "Charmaine, don't be so quick to judge Frederic. Remember, he has been wronged as well."

"That is a result of his own doing."

"Perhaps, but perhaps not. He is, for all his faults, a good man. I came to Charmantes when I was your age, Charmaine. Frederic was *my* little Pierre. I helped to raise him, and it does not please me to witness his pain. I know he feels a grave responsibility for all that has happened between John and himself. I believe he would like to make amends. This is, however, a difficult thing for a man who lost the woman he loved and allowed his grief to turn into a knot of resentment. John's mother had a dauntless, spirited character. It's a trait that she passed on to her son, a trait that served John well in withstanding Frederic's bitterness in those early years, but ironically, one that constantly reminded Frederic of his dead wife." She sighed, her eyes deepening in sadness. "The rumors are true. Frederic *did* blame John for Elizabeth's death. But Frederic's animosity was not without foundation; it was erected on the belief that John was not his son."

Charmaine's eyes widened in shock, and she listened intently as Rose retold the story of Elizabeth's abduction and rape. "Frederic and Elizabeth had been married only six months when John was born," she finished.

"But surely John is Frederic's son! One has only to look at them."

"Yes, Charmaine," Rose said, "they are most definitely father and son. But when John was only a boy, there was no way to tell. That doubt added to Frederic's torment and nurtured a subtle hostility. By the time Frederic accepted John as his own flesh and blood, it was too late. John had grown to despise his father as much as he believed his father despised him. It seemed that no matter what Frederic said or did, he could not rectify the situation. In fact, when he attempted to, he made matters worse. John delighted in testing Frederic's patience, his antics and caustic barbs limitless, always determined to have the last laugh. In time, the need to inflict injury became an ugly habit that we grew accustomed to living with."

"Does John know what happened to his mother?" Charmaine asked.

"No," Rose whispered. "It's something that Frederic never talked about, and it wasn't my place to speak to John on his behalf. Either way, it wouldn't have made one whit of difference."

Charmaine pondered this newest revelation. It did not exonerate Frederic, far from it. How could he have blamed an innocent babe for something over which he had no control? How could he have been so malicious, so cruel? Charmaine bit her tongue against the accusations and said instead, "That explains John's childhood, but what of Colette?"

"Frederic thought of her as his salvation, his second chance. You met Colette when her health and spirit were already failing her, but she was quite mettlesome when she first arrived on Charmantes, much more like Yvette than Jeannette. For all her fairness of feature, her personality mirrored Elizabeth's. She held her own with John much the same way Elizabeth did with Frederic. I noticed it, and so did Frederic. She turned that spunkiness on him, and though he tried to ignore the disturbing similarities, they also charmed him. He resorted to avoiding her, dismissing her with barely any decorum. Colette, in turn, wondered how she had offended him. In an attempt to win him over, she unwisely initiated conversations that bordered on flirting." Rose breathed deeply and let out a soft sigh. "Then there were those times when..."

"When what?" Charmaine probed.

Rose rubbed her brow, seemingly disturbed with the memory. "Colette knew things – it was strange really, as if..."

"As if what?"

"As if she'd been here before." Rose chuckled, a false, uncomfortable chuckle. "But listen to me, an old woman rambling on, losing her sanity. It was just fate, sad, twisted fate that pushed Frederic and Colette together until..."

Her words trailed off, and Charmaine wondered if Rose had any idea of what had really happened. *Rape...* She grimaced with the word. Then, swift and sure came Colette's declaration of long ago: *"I love him still... so very much,"* leaving Charmaine very confused.

"Just give me the truth. All I want is the truth."

Robert Blackford was dumbstruck in the face of Frederic's wrath, having all but written the man off. But here he stood – imposing – the clothing freshly laundered and pressed, the cane more a scepter than a crutch. His cheeks and chin were clean-shaven, the hair well groomed, and the eyes flashed the workings of a keen mind.

"The truth?" Blackford hesitated. "What are you talking about?"

"My wife – my deceased wife, Colette. I have, on good authority, reason to believe that the condition that led to her death was not the one you purported it to be. Now, as I've said, man, I want the truth."

"Frederic," Agatha gasped in dismay, "are you suggesting that Robert has lied to you?" She, too, had been summoned to her husband's quarters and was visibly surprised to find her brother there.

"Isn't that obvious, woman?" Frederic sneered, his steely gaze settling on her for the moment.

Blackford applauded the interruption, her stupid comment clearly designed to give him time to think his way out of this unexpected attack.

"And you," the man was saying to her, "will do well to hold your tongue. You had very much to gain from the unhappy outcome of Colette's infirmity."

Agatha's eyes welled with tears, severely wounded.

"Who maligned my diagnosis, Frederic?" Blackford interjected. "I was the only physician who treated your wife. Who told you–"

"*Never mind who told me! I found out!*"

Robert faltered. *Who was the informant?*

"I'm waiting, man. Your muteness is branding you guilty."

His mind spinning unprepared, Blackford acknowledged only two avenues open to him: the lie or the truth. There was no choice but to gamble and stay the original course. "If you have reason to doubt me, then I have every right to know what information has contradicted my diagnosis."

"You have no rights!" Frederic seethed. "Your practice on this island is a product of my good will. I am your benefactor, but that can change in the blink of an eye. Now, I know that my wife was not unfaithful to me; therefore, she could not have miscarried a child. Why did you lie to me?"

The tableau held until Agatha stepped forward. "Robert is not to blame, Frederic," she said softly. "This was all my doing. I'm at fault."

She bowed her head to Frederic's piercing gaze, his eyes narrowed in disbelief over her sudden confession. She breathed deeply before braving his regard once again, tears trickling down her cheeks. "Robert never wanted to mislead you, but I implored him to intercede. He did it for me."

She seemed at a loss for words and groped fruitlessly for a handkerchief. Coming up empty, she used the palms of her hands to wipe away the deluge.

"What are you saying?" Frederic pressed.

"I love you, Frederic!" she choked out. "You know I've always loved you! After Colette's death, your mourning turned to madness, and my heart ached for you. When I realized you were hell-bent upon destroying yourself, I couldn't stand by and watch you slip away from me. I convinced Robert to cast Colette in a bad light so that she wouldn't be worth the grief you were expending on her. I thought it would bring you to your senses, back into the world of the living. Then there were your children to consider. They were struggling to overcome the loss of their mother, and you weren't there for them. Instead, they heard the rumors about you and began starving themselves, too."

When Frederic's brow arched in dismay, Agatha paused, allowing that bit of information to seep in, certain he would question Rose or the governess about it. She pressed on, the contrition in her voice heavy and convincing. "I was wrong to do what I did, I know, but I was beside myself with worry, frightened that if drastic measures weren't taken, your children would lose you. You had so much to live for: your sons and your daughters, and yes – *me.* I prayed to God that you'd live for me!"

Frederic took the story in, his gaze shifting from the silently sobbing Agatha to the solemnly resigned Blackford. *So... John had been right.* Disgust welled up in the pit of his stomach, disgust for himself and his pathetic conduct after Colette's death, which had led to this vicious lie about her. He couldn't blame these two, not when he'd set the stage for their tactics. Nevertheless, he couldn't bear to look at them. "Get out of my sight!"

They departed quickly, leaving Frederic to his disgust and a surge of pity that congealed in his breast, pity for Agatha and her continued degradation.

By early afternoon, the relentless drizzle had ceased, and the sky cleared, the only evidence of the two-day downpour teardrops that sparkled on the tip of each blade of grass. Charmaine marveled at the wonder, her pain ebbing in light of the beauty around her. Paul had not yet returned with the girls, and now that the day had turned fair, she didn't expect them for another hour. She cherished her time alone, meandering down the long, cobblestone drive, remembering Pierre.

With no destination in mind, she walked into the stable, located the stall of the dapple-gray mare she'd ridden just two weeks ago, and stroked the horse's soft muzzle. "She's a beauty," came a voice from the shadows.

"Yes, she is," Charmaine agreed, allowing the speckled head to nuzzle her as she faced the groom who approached. She had seen the man often enough, though surprisingly, she didn't know his name.

"One of the few in this paddock that can be called gentle," he continued, massaging the arm that was cradled in a sling. "Handpicked her myself when Master John was determined to find you a suitable mount. He sent me all the way to Virginia, he did."

"Really?" Charmaine asked in astonishment.

The middle-aged man nodded. "Mr. Richards made all of the arrangements and covered the cost of the livery fees once the horses arrived on Charmantes, but I do take credit for the choice of mare and ponies."

She sighed, her heart momentarily light. "And I thank you, Mister...?"

"Bud," he supplied, "just call me Bud."

"Bud," she smiled. "Have you seen Master John?"

"No ma'am, not since early this morning when he rode off."

"Into town?"

"No ma'am, into the west fields. I think he needed to be alone. He's nursin' a bit of guilt, what with Phantom distracting him the way he did. Here he comes to my aid and leaves the child alone. But he didn't know what was gonna happen."

Astounded, Charmaine listened to the scenario. Up until now, she'd only heard bits and pieces of the events that had drawn John away from Pierre's bedside. "Phantom? He'd gotten loose?"

"Yes, ma'am, as was a regular occurrence. Sometimes he can act downright demonic. On Sunday morning, the look in those black eyes was near lunacy, and when he cornered me, well, I confess, I thought I'd seen my last day on God's green earth! Thank the Lord above that Gerald diverted his attention and saved me from those hooves, else I'm sure I'd have been trampled to death."

"And John?" she asked.

"He must have heard the commotion from the house, 'cause the next thing I know, he was circlin' the horse and tamin' him a bit. But Phantom didn't calm as quickly as he normally does when he catches sight of his master, and it took some time to get him corralled. Then Master John tended to me. Now I wish he hadn't. I hold myself responsible and wish it were me instead of that little boy..."

"Don't," Charmaine countered, "there's no point in blaming yourself. We all feel responsible for what happened. But then, nothing we did or didn't do would change what God intended all along, would it?"

"Thank you, ma'am," Bud muttered emotionally, "thank you."

Charmaine smiled up at him, experiencing for the first time in many days a sense of reward. She eyed the mare. "Would you saddle her for me?" she asked.

"What – to ride?"

"Yes," she answered quickly, lest she lose her daring.

He obliged, and not ten minutes later, she rode off, slowly at first, taking the trail that led to the back of the house and the west fields. Her initial nervousness yielded to determination, and she repeatedly told herself: *If I encounter any trouble, John will soon be along to help me.*

It would be good if she met up with him. She needed to see him, talk to him, reassure herself that all would be well with him. At the house, he had all but ignored her these past days, and she worried over his continued isolation. True, he eschewed everyone's company, but she was different. She knew his pain better than anyone else. He had confided in her, a baring of his soul that must have meant something. And yet, perhaps he regretted his confession and avoided her now because of his shame.

Robert Blackford stared at his sister in disbelief as they made their way down the hall. She held silent, her expression warning that he should do the same. It wasn't until they had climbed into his buggy and it rolled through the front gates that she let out a cheer of unmitigated delight.

"Oh, what a stroke of wonderful, extraordinary, marvelous luck!"

He was horrified. "Woman, are you mad?" he enjoined, his eyes flashing anger as he searched her face for some sign that her senses had returned. "I nearly lost my head to the executioner in there!"

"Robert, Robert, Robert," she cajoled, taking his hand into her lap and patting it reassuringly. "Do you really think I would have allowed that to happen? No, quite the contrary. Things could not be better. You fail to see the benefits we now stand to reap. You must learn how to find the good fortune in a setback! Fortune, Robert," she chortled once again, "fortune! The truth is out now, my dear brother. I'm sure that our extortionist will be quite disappointed. Poor man, he thought he had everything arranged so comfortably." She pouted prettily for emphasis. When his laugh blended with relief, she went on. "What did you think of my acting? Was I convincing?"

"You practically had me crying, dear sister!" he laughed again, suddenly in awe of her ability to think under pressure, her stately beauty. "You should consider the theatre. It's not too late, you know. Think of it – New York!"

"No, no, Robert. This production is far more profitable."

"But what about Frederic? How do you suppose he knew about Colette?"

"It doesn't matter. If he had any more information, he would have challenged my story. Personally, I think he was bluffing."

"Yes, but that means he's suspicious of us."

"And we admitted that he had reason to be suspicious," Agatha replied. "But now he views any unscrupulous tactics on our part as concern for his welfare. How can he fault us for that? No, Robert, we needn't worry about Colette anymore. We have other matters to set our minds to."

"John?"

"Yes, John."

"Agatha, he is leaving Charmantes. Paul said as much when I ran into him after the funeral."

Agatha eyed Robert speculatively. She did not doubt his assertion, but leaving was quite different from expulsion, her good humor suddenly shattered.

"You are Frederic's wife now," he continued, "mistress of the manor, of Charmantes. What more do you want?"

"I want it all, Robert. I want the rightful heir named sole beneficiary to the Duvoisin holdings. Don't tell me you won't sleep more soundly knowing that Frederic's fortune will pass to Paul and Paul alone. As it stands now, John will cast us to the dogs the moment Frederic dies."

Robert cringed, silently acknowledging the accuracy of his sister's prediction, and whipped the mare into a brisk trot.

Charmaine didn't cross paths with John, and found upon her return that she hadn't left the paddock but five minutes when he arrived home by way of the main road. She handed the reins to Gerald and headed toward the house.

John was not in the study, nor in the drawing room, but just as she returned to the foyer, she noticed the correspondence sitting on the table there. The letter crowning the odd assortment was addressed to her. It was from Loretta Harrington, and she quickly broke the seal and devoured its contents.

> *Dear Charmaine,*
> *Your last letter upset me. You know I am not one to judge others before I have actually met and come to know them, but I cannot help but be deeply troubled over your description of John Duvoisin. I pray the man is not quite so intolerable as he seems, but still, you have me worried. Perhaps there are other reasons behind his dark moods...*

Dear Lord, Charmaine groaned. She would have to answer Loretta tonight, scripting a letter that would erase the scurrilous image she had painted of John. She did not know how she would bring herself to write about Pierre's death.

The hour was late. Charmaine had just finished her prayers and was getting into bed when a knock fell on her door. She pulled on her robe and opened the portal. John was standing there. "Were you asleep?" he asked.

"No, not yet," she replied.

"I must speak with you for a moment, Charmaine," he said, gesturing for her to come into the hallway.

She felt uneasy, knowing she wasn't going to be happy with what he had to tell her. She followed him to his dressing room and stepped inside. He closed the door and leaned back against it. She turned to him, waiting for him to speak.

"I am leaving for Virginia before daybreak tomorrow."

She drew a deep breath and closed her eyes. Didn't she already know that this was coming? *The girls will be devastated.*

"I have imposed upon your kindness already, Charmaine," he continued, "but I hope you will do me another favor, and give Yvette and Jeannette my goodbye. I didn't tell them myself because I cannot endure their pleading for me to stay. I do not want to refuse them."

"Do you really have to leave?" she whispered.

"Aside from my sisters, there is nothing left for me here. If I could, I would take all three of you with me, far away from this hell. But my father rejected that request a week ago, and he will be less inclined to allow it now."

She was stunned and could see the bitterness smoldering in his eyes, aware of his thoughts. If he had been allowed to take them, Pierre would still be alive.

"Don't tell them that," he enjoined, reading her expression, his voice dead serious. "They will hate him for it. I do not hold my father responsible for what happened, only myself. None of us would be suffering this misery if it weren't for my terrible judgment four years ago." The room fell silent until he spoke again. "So, will you tell the twins goodbye for me?"

"Yes, of course I will," she ceded. "Will you come back?"

"I don't know," he replied. Then, seeing the despair in her eyes, he added, "In the spring, perhaps my father will change his mind and allow the girls to visit Virginia, once the turmoil has settled here."

"They are going to be very upset with this," she said, in spite of herself. "They will miss you. And what of you? You will be all alone. You should not be alone right now."

"I cannot stay. In Virginia and New York, I have work to occupy me, and I have friends there. I neglected much while I was here." He sighed. "So, I will take a page from my brother's book and keep busy."

She nodded in resignation. Though she wanted to press him to change his mind, she knew he wanted to avoid an emotional scene. It would be cruel to attempt to sway him. She said instead, "I will miss you."

He smiled for the first time, a hint of warmth reaching his eyes. "Well then, at least one good thing came from my visit." He took hold of the doorknob and opened the portal. "I will miss you, too, my Charm."

As she reached the doorway, she hesitated and looked up at him.

"Thank you," he murmured.

She knew what he was doing could not be easy. She was compelled to comfort him, to convey some small measure of mercy and kindness before he set out to bear his crucible alone. She breached the short distance between them and encircled his waist with her arms. Closing her eyes, she pressed her cheek against his chest and listened to the steady beat of his heart. She took comfort from his arms closing around her shoulders, his chin atop her head. "Goodbye, John," she whispered, pulling him tighter to her, emotion now rising painfully high in her throat, "goodbye." Then she pulled away and fled the room.

Sunday, October 15, 1837

The next morning, George greeted her and the twins at the chapel doorway. They were early for Mass and stood in the empty ballroom, smiling sadly as he walked toward them. He'd come to convey the news that Charmaine already knew and had told the girls when they awoke: the Falcon had set sail at dawn, and John was aboard, heading back to Virginia.

"He left notes for you," George said. "They're on the table in the foyer."

As the girls ran to retrieve them, Charmaine looked back at George. "I'm worried about him, George. He'll be all by himself."

"He wants to be alone, Charmaine," George replied softly. He never thought he'd hear such concern for John from her. "He will be all right."

The girls returned with their letters; one was for her. She ushered them through the vestibule and sank into the nearest pew as she opened and read the brief words penned in masculine scrawl.

> *Charmaine,*
> *I am grateful for your kindness these past days. Mostly, I thank you for the love you gave Pierre. You are a fine person, and the twins are fortunate to have you. I know you will give them the comfort they will need in the days to come, and I hope they will do the same for you. If you are ever in need of anything, do not hesitate to call on me. George knows where I can be reached.*
>
> *John*

Charmaine folded the letter and slipped it into her pocket. She looked up at the crucifix some distance away. The words in the note left her empty: very kind, friendly, detached. *And who will comfort you, John?* her mind screamed.

But she understood John's departure in the same way she now understood why he had come home. The things that had drawn him to Charmantes no longer existed. Colette and Pierre were gone, and he was estranged from his father. And though she knew he cared deeply for the twins, they belonged to Frederic, not him. He no longer had a reason to stay.

She looked to the girls and read the disappointment in their blue eyes. They turned away in misery and slowly walked to their usual seats at the front of the chapel. Charmaine marveled over their fortitude; neither of them pressed the matter with the lamentations they had used before. Perhaps they knew they could never recapture those happy, carefree days before Pierre's tragedy.

Charmaine resigned herself to that reality as well and began to pray that she'd be able to accept it. There was nothing she could do. John's decision had been made, and there was no turning the Falcon back now. It was time to move forward, to find comfort in the mundane and routine. They had done so before, they would have to do so again, difficult though it might be. But as she willed herself to look to the future, a terrible loneliness washed over her. It was as if she were losing Colette all over again, and for the first time, she realized that John had swept that feeling of loneliness away the moment he had stepped into her life.

She was just about to rise when Frederic entered the chapel. She didn't breathe as he limped past her and joined his daughters. She watched in wonder as Jeannette swiftly stood, hugged him, and coaxed him to sit first.

Agatha was equally surprised when she entered the sanctuary moments later. Charmaine heard the woman whisper, "Why didn't you tell me you were attending Mass? I would have come down with you," but she couldn't discern Frederic's response. To Yvette's displeasure, her stepmother sat next to her.

Charmaine remained exactly where she was, leaving without a word as soon as the Mass was over. She had no desire to converse with the master of the manor and knew the twins could find her in the nursery. She even avoided breakfast. But at lunch, Travis informed her that Frederic wanted to see her privately in the study at one o'clock sharp.

She was stunned by the message. Why the study? Why the meeting in the first place? He'd had days to mull over what she knew. Had she become a liability, a shameful reminder of his terrible secret, just as she'd suggested to Rose? Would he dismiss her after all? Rose had assured her that this would not happen. Still, she was very upset.

At five minutes to one she left the girls in their room and made her way to the library. She was trembling as she knocked on the door.

"Come in."

The room was unusually bright with both sets of French doors thrown open, sunbeams splashing onto the large desk and across the carpet. Frederic was seated at the secretary, papers strewn over it, stacks of ledgers piled on the floor nearby.

"How are you, Miss Ryan?" he asked, motioning for her to sit down.

"I am well, sir," she lied, unable to read his intent from the polite opening. "You wished to speak to me?"

"Yes. I won't detain you for long. I wanted to let you know that I am making some changes in my daughters' schedule."

Charmaine gulped back her dread. *Here it comes.*

"From now on, they will spend their Saturdays with me. They are to be dressed and in the dining room at nine o'clock this coming Saturday morning. They will be in my company for the whole of the day, so from nine in the morning until seven in the evening, you are released of your duties."

"Released of my duties?" she repeated, confused, noting only the word 'released'. *Was he dismissing her?*

"You are free to spend your Saturdays as you wish. I will only infringe upon that freedom on those days I am indisposed or otherwise occupied. Is this satisfactory to you?"

Charmaine paused, unsteady. "It is not a matter of what is satisfactory to me, sir, but to respect your wishes regarding your daughters."

"Miss Ryan," Frederic smiled, "I am giving you a day off each week. Your wages will not be affected, as I will expect you to be able to change your Saturday plans if you are needed. Is this not satisfactory?"

"It is quite satisfactory, sir."

"Good. Then you will have my daughters ready at nine o'clock six days hence. That is all, Miss Ryan. You may return to the twins."

Charmaine let out a great sigh of relief as she closed the study door behind her. Not dismissed! More importantly, Frederic had acted as if nothing had happened between them. She was immensely grateful.

Yvette was not happy with the news, decrying this latest turn of events. "He's just trying to copy Johnny! He'll never be like Johnny! Now our Saturdays are ruined!"

Charmaine looked at Jeannette, who remained ever so quiet, then back to Yvette. "Perhaps your father wants to make time for you both while he's still able. Even if he is imitating John, is that such a bad thing?"

Yvette pondered Charmaine's reasoning, then flung herself into a chair. "But what are we going to *do* with him all day long?"

"Why don't you start thinking of some ideas? I'm certain your father will appreciate the help."

The girls took up her suggestion, leaving Charmaine to wonder just how Frederic would execute the grand plans they had already conjured: picnics, excursions into town, ship rides, and lawn games. He had barely left his chambers in four years. Would he really be out and about with two nine-year-olds? Charmaine shook her head and laughed in spite of herself. What other changes would they face in the coming days?

There was a knock on the door. Yvette jumped up, but her hopeful face dropped when Paul stepped into the room. "Good afternoon," he smiled.

She grumbled a greeting and trudged back to her desk.

"Good day, Paul," Jeannette greeted cheerfully.

"I've brought you a surprise," he offered pleasantly.

Yvette looked up in renewed interest.

"A cargo came in from England yesterday with a whole cask of sweets made from the sugar grown on Charmantes. I thought you'd like some." He produced a paper bag from behind his back and offered it to Jeannette.

She snatched it from him quickly, exclaiming an enthusiastic 'thank-you'. Yvette joined her sister to inspect the booty and pick out the choice pieces.

Paul looked to Charmaine. "There were fresh kegs of tea as well. Fatima is brewing some now. Would you like to join me for some on the porch?"

"I would love to," she answered, leaving the girls to their plans.

"You were working today?" Charmaine asked once they were sitting outdoors.

"It couldn't wait. But the cargo was inventoried by early afternoon."

"The cargo was from the Falcon?"

"Yes," he replied, his eyes never leaving hers.

"Did you see John this morning?" Charmaine asked softly.

"We rode into town together."

"Did he say anything to you?"

"Not much." He sighed. "John wanted to go back to Virginia, Charmaine. I don't blame him. It's been unbearable here the past few days. He's neglected a lot the last two months, and at least in Virginia he'll have the distraction of work." His voice was sympathetic. "I knew the girls needed some cheering up. They couldn't have been happy with the news."

"They did, and the candy helped. It was kind of you to think of them."

Fatima arrived with the tea and poured two cups.

"How are you faring?" Paul asked. "Any better since Friday night?"

"I'm doing what I need to do to get through the days," she replied honestly. "I try not to think about it. And still, I curse myself for leaving Pierre that morning." Tears sprang to her eyes.

"It wasn't your fault, Charmaine," he comforted, taking her hand. "It wasn't John's fault either. How many times had you left him to nap or come downstairs at night when you were certain he was asleep in his bed? You only did so knowing that he was safe and sound. It wasn't a lapse of responsibility to do that, Charmaine. Every parent does the same."

"I know you are right," she replied, dabbing her eyes. "Still it's difficult not to think 'if only I'd done this, or if only I'd done that.' And it doesn't help because I miss him terribly."

"I know you do," he replied, his warm hand stroking hers. "I do, too."

They fell silent, sipping the piping hot tea, until Charmaine broached the subject of John again. "John told me everything that morning," she mused tentatively, a little nervous that Paul might grow weary or angry with the topic.

He looked at her, but did not seem annoyed. "But you're still curious."

"I'm curious to know how you feel about it. I didn't realize that you had met Colette first."

He leaned back in his chair and drew another long sip from his tea. "I was not in love with Colette, if that's what you would like to know. I cared for her as a friend, a friendship that grew deeper with time. When we first met, I was attracted to her. She was beautiful. She knew her way around Paris society and introduced me to her circle of friends. So when John caught her fancy, I wasn't jealous, not after a while anyway. There were plenty of women to pick and choose from, most of them willing…"

She could feel a blush rising to her cheeks. "But you were so angry at John those first few days after he came back."

He shook his head. "He was bent upon provoking me. So, in my anger, perhaps I overreacted. Still, I never understood why John took the relationship as far as he did, and I blame him for that. Granted, he was engaged to Colette, and yes, my father should never have interfered. But once Father did, and Colette made her choice, John should have left it alone. Instead, he chose to torment her. He hated our father so much that he drew her into a terrible situation from which she could never extricate herself."

"And Colette had no free will in the matter? John controlled everything?"

Paul massaged his forehead. "Charmaine, neither Colette nor John ever provided me with the details on how their affair started, or how long it lasted. What I do know is that John was not lacking for other prospects. There were many women who, at the drop of a coin, would have fallen at his feet, ready and willing if he'd only given them the time of day. So why a love affair with a married woman – no, worse – *his father's wife*, when the alternative is so easy and clear? I do know that John hurt my father deeply, and not just physically. Imagine how it felt to be cuckolded in his own home, by his own son, and afterwards, wonder how many others in the house knew about the scandal. It wasn't an easy thing for him to deal with."

Live by the sword; die by the sword, Charmaine thought, though she didn't say so. "But John loved her," she insisted instead. Fleetingly, she read surprise in Paul's eyes, as if that possibility hadn't occurred to him before.

"Then maybe I don't understand love," he replied, exasperated now. "Perhaps I haven't experienced it yet to judge whether one loses his rational mind over it."

Enormously disheartened, she couldn't respond, and again they fell silent. But as her distress dissipated, she measured his remark and, for the first time, understood his disdain for John's actions. Even so, his view of the matter was highly impersonal – that one woman could so easily be replaced by another.

She poured him a second cup of tea, not wanting the conversation to end on this contentious note. "Your father called me to the study earlier this afternoon."

"The study?" Paul asked quizzically.

"Yes. It looked like he was working there. He'll be taking charge of the girls on Saturdays from now on. I'll have that day off," she finished on a laugh.

Paul was astonished and finally smiled. "I'll have to work harder during the week so that my Saturdays are free."

Frederic was present at the dinner table that night, and although he worked at being cordial, his efforts fell short. The girls spoke to him, but only to answer his questions, their responses stilted. With a resigned smile, he finally dropped the artificial repartee, allowing his daughters their melancholy.

Before the meal was over, Yvette asked to be excused, complaining of fatigue and a stomachache. She promised to go straight to her room. But when Charmaine reached the nursery, the girl was nowhere to be found. The week, culminating with John's unannounced departure that morning, had taken its toll on the headstrong nine-year-old.

After a quick search of the house, Charmaine found her in the stables, sitting on a pile of hay in the corner of Phantom's stall, clutching her kitten and crying. Her stoic façade had finally crumbled.

"Johnny took Phantom with him this time, Mademoiselle Charmaine," she sobbed, rocking back and forth. "That means he's *never* coming back! Oh God! I want my brother. I just want my brother!"

Charmaine did not offer encouraging words to the contrary. The last time she'd insisted on miracles, disaster had stepped in to laugh at her. She'd stopped believing in miracles, anyway. Thus, she knelt down beside Yvette and hugged her close, allowing the child to embrace her misery and shed her bitter tears.

Book Three

****

The Choice

Friday, October 20, 1837
Freedom... 56 miles west of Richmond

Chapter 1

Brian Duvoisin was black. Born on the Duvoisin plantation thirty-five years ago, he had been a slave for most of his life, that is, until the day John Duvoisin signed the document that freed him. Having no surname to place on the legal paper, John suggested he use Duvoisin. Brian agreed. Grinning, John shook his hand and called him 'brother'.

At first, Brian was wary of John's motives, but he remained on the plantation. He really had no choice. Where else in the South could a penniless, unskilled colored man go?

John emancipated many other men, women, and children that week, and his indignant neighbors swiftly dubbed the Duvoisin estate 'Freedom'. Within the month, John erected an elaborately carved sign above the plantation's main gates. Freedom it was.

John grew to respect Brian and, with each passing season, placed greater responsibility upon his shoulders. The field workers respected him as well. If John wanted the plantation to remain productive, especially when he was away, Brian was the man to have there.

Brian's wife was also free, for John had purchased Wisteria Hill, the adjacent estate where she lived, releasing those slaves as well. At first, Brian puzzled over his wife's emancipation; leaving Virginia was possible now. He'd gained some skills beyond the backbreaking field labor. He could travel north, take Nettie with him, earn a living, and keep a roof over their heads. Why he didn't go, he couldn't say, other than John relied on him.

Today, he was the only black overseer in the entire county. It did not sit well with John's neighbors, who opposed paid Negro help. But John never caved in to the pressure; rather, he seemed to revel in the controversy, holding firm to his decision. His staunch resolve garnered Brian's steadfast loyalty and trust. Now, four years later, the two men were close friends.

Stuart Simons was white. Though born and raised in the south, he was a northern sympathizer, a posture embraced by his Quaker parents, who had instilled in him a deep sense of right and wrong. Because he rebuked a number of southern viewpoints, finding employment had been difficult until he met John. Eventually, he became Freedom's production manager.

John knew that Brian needed the protection of a white man, especially when he was abroad in Richmond or New York. Therefore, John situated Stuart on the plantation to discourage his neighbors from harassing the black overseer when he was away. It proved a wise move. The first time John had left Freedom on an extended trip, there had been an incident, one easily quelled when Stuart appeared to greet the men who just happened to stop by for a 'visit'.

Because Stuart had an easy manner, and because he also respected Brian, they became friends. Stuart quickly learned the workings of a tobacco plantation. He already knew the ins and outs of the shipping business, overseeing the loading and unloading of Duvoisin vessels in Richmond after the fall harvest. This year, John had relied heavily on both men, for he had been away the entire summer and fall. But the plantations rested in capable hands, so Freedom and Wisteria Hill's harvests were the least of John's worries.

Tonight, the two men sat at the kitchen table, discussing the year's production. Cotton prices were down fifty percent, and although cotton was not grown at Freedom, John wasn't going to like it. The brokers in New York were not buying. If the newspaper reports were correct, Congress had just authorized the issue of ten million dollars in short-term government notes to stem the panic that was sweeping across the country.

It was thus that John found them – deep in worried conversation.

Though John's comings and goings were always unpredictable, they looked up in surprise. He'd notified them some months ago that he had traveled to Charmantes. They knew him well, having spent many a night with him after an onerous day in the fields, drinking and talking into the wee hours of morning. For John to go home, something had to be wrong. One look at his face and they knew they were right.

"Good God, man," Stuart breathed, "you look awful."

John grunted and slumped into a chair.

"What's the matter?" Brian asked.

"Everything," John chuckled wryly, "as always."

Stuart leaned forward. "Did you see them?"

"Just my son," John said softly, tenderly. "Colette was dead before I reached Charmantes." Propping his elbows on the table, he drove his fingers through his tousled hair before whispering, "Pierre died just over a week ago."

"John," Stuart murmured, "I'm sorry."

"Me too, John, me too," Brian consoled. When the silence became uncomfortable, he asked, "What are you going to do now?"

"Try to forget… try to forget."

"Maybe this will help," Stuart offered, extending the paper with the rankling financial figures.

For the next few hours, they examined plantation documents, discussed the tobacco yield and production costs, shipping, the New York brokers, and the economy. John seemed unconcerned with the rumors of the dissolution of the conservative Bank of the United States and the failure of three banks in England. Stuart just shook his head; the man obviously knew what he was doing.

When all topics had been exhausted, John stood up and stretched. "I've had enough for one night."

As Brian and Stuart rose, he broached another subject. "You'll be going into Richmond tomorrow?"

Stuart nodded. "I'll be leaving at the crack of dawn."

"Do me a favor then, would you?"

"What's that, John?"

"Visit Sheriff Briggs and find out if a John Ryan was ever apprehended."

"John Ryan?" Stuart puzzled. "He used to work for you."

John's brow lifted in interest. "Really?"

"I believe he was being sought in connection with his wife's death."

"That's the one."

"I remember Briggs coming to the wharf and questioning the men. I don't think he was found. Why in heaven's name are you interested in him?"

"Locating him is important to a friend of mine and its important to me."

"I'll see what I can find out. If the authorities aren't a help, I'll make a few inquiries of my own around town."

John nodded a thank you and turned to leave.

"How long are you planning to stay in Virginia?" Stuart asked.

"Aside from a trip north, you'll be seeing more of me from now on."

Both Brian and Stuart smiled, happy to be in the man's company again, but reading John's face, they knew the sentiment was not reciprocated.

The next afternoon, Stuart went directly to the sheriff's office. Briggs seemed annoyed, grumbling something about 'white trash' and that wife beating wasn't a crime. Disgusted, Stuart realized he was getting nowhere fast. He might turn up something at the wharf. With the Duvoisin clout, the authorities might be persuaded to reopen the case. He was not disappointed. A few longshoremen had seen Ryan scrounging around for odd jobs, but his appearances were sporadic, and no one remembered exactly when they'd seen him last.

John was displeased. "Could you ask the men to keep an eye out for him?"

"Sure, John," Stuart agreed, "next time I'm in Richmond."

Saturday, October 21, 1837 Charmantes

Charmaine and the girls arrived in the dining room well before nine o'clock. Today was the first Saturday they would spend with their father. True to his word, Frederic was waiting for them. After breakfast, the threesome departed the manor, leaving Charmaine alone.

Yvette dragged her feet, her father's steps quick and sure by comparison.

"What is the matter, Yvette?" he asked as they arrived at the paddock.

"Nothing," she grumbled sullenly.

Frederic only smiled.

Gerald appeared with Spook and Angel, and Yvette perked up. "We're going to go riding today?"

"That and other things."

Paul emerged from the barn with a meticulously groomed stallion.

"Papa," Jeannette breathed in alarm, "you're riding Champion today?"

"I'm going to try, Jeannette."

Paul had his doubts, but he'd been unable to talk Frederic out of this folly and knew it would be futile to try again now. "I ran him hard yesterday," Paul said, "so he shouldn't be straining at the bit today."

"That's fine, Paul. I might need some help getting in the saddle, though."

Frederic swallowed his pride and endured the humiliation of mounting the horse he'd ridden countless times. He stumbled only once, his lame arm buckling under him as he pulled up and into the saddle, his chin hitting Champion's neck hard. His eyes shot to Paul, who'd swiftly averted his gaze, pretending he hadn't seen. The awkward moment passed as Frederic situated himself atop the steed. Paul secured the cane to the saddle, finally nodding in approbation. They were all set. Frederic breathed deeply. "Come girls," he encouraged, "we've Duvoisin business to attend to."

His smiling daughters were already on their ponies. Together, they trotted down the cobblestone drive and out the gates.

"Where are we headed, Papa?" Jeannette asked enthusiastically.

"The mill."

"The lumber mill?"

"I have a great deal of catching up to do," he answered, "and I'd like to start by meeting the newest men working for me. Wade Remmen is first on the list."

Jeannette was beaming. This was going to be a wonderful Saturday! As for Yvette, it was going to take more than a visit to the mill to please her; however, the ride was pleasant.

Paul watched them go, then headed toward the house. Charmaine was all his today. He found her in the gardens reading a book. A melancholy smile greeted him, causing his heart to hammer in his chest. He remembered the feel of her in his arms just one week ago, and he longed to hold her again, to comfort her. He sat next to her on the bench that they had shared an eternity ago.

"So, Miss Ryan, what are we going to do today?"

She regarded him quizzically. "You're not working?"

"I said we'd spend time together."

Her smile turned sweet.

"A visit into town?" he suggested. "Or perhaps a walk along the beach?"

The mill was abuzz. Yvette and Jeannette's eyes widened as they approached, for they had never imagined the sweaty toil here. A score of men labored with teams of draft horses, pulling long, thick logs to a central building where they would be milled. A huge waterwheel rotated briskly at the far end of the structure, plunging into a deep ravine. Planks were emerging on the other side, where they were swiftly hoisted onto a buckboard for transport to town. The screech of saws, the shouts of men, and the whinny of horses punctuated the air.

"Yvette, Jeannette?"

They tore their eyes from the engrossing commotion and looked down to find that their father had already dismounted.

"Are you coming?"

As Frederic and his daughters approached, one man looked up, then another, until all work was suspended. Jeannette searched for Wade, finally spotting him near the tree line, speaking to a young woman. Her smile vanished. "Now where is this Mr. Remmen?" her father asked, puzzled by her glum face.

"Over there," she pointed.

Frederic eyed the couple. The young woman was quite lovely, with straight black hair. She didn't belong at the mill, and apparently Wade Remmen was telling her so, his voice raised in agitation.

"I don't care if it *is* Saturday, nor that you're bored, I've work to do!"

Dismissing her, he turned back to the mill, immediately spotting Frederic and the girls. His momentary shock gave way to a frown. He strode toward them with a determined gait. "Mr. Duvoisin," he pronounced, extending a hand. "Yvette," he continued with a nod, "Jeannette. What can I do for you, sir?"

"My daughters and I are abroad for the day, and having heard a great deal about you, Mr. Remmen, I thought it was time that we met." Frederic glanced over Wade's shoulder to the edge of the forest, but the woman was gone. "We didn't mean to interrupt–"

"No," Wade replied, "that was just my sister. She wanted to spend the day with me, but Paul asked me to work. She's young, and I don't like her going into town on her own. So what does she do?" He threw up his hands in exasperation. "She walks here instead." He exhaled loudly, then shook it off. "Would you like to see the mill in operation?"

An hour later, they set off again, this time toward town and the warehouse, where they would reconcile invoices against lumber deliveries and finish up the day's business at the bank. Frederic had something he wanted to show Yvette.

Stephen Westphal was astounded when Frederic stepped up to his desk. He scrambled to his feet, sputtering, "Well – isn't this a surprise?"

"Yes, Stephen, the first of many."

"What I can do for you today, Frederic?"

"The mill account – I'm going to put Yvette in charge of it."

"*What?*" the banker exclaimed loudly, his astonished query overpowering Yvette's identical response. "But she is a mere child – a female!"

"She is also a Duvoisin and my daughter," Frederic replied. "Like her mother, she has a keen head for figures. Now that Paul is preoccupied with Espoir, I'm going to make use of other resources." He draped his arm affectionately across her shoulders and drew her close. "I'm willing to *gamble* on Yvette's ciphering abilities and see if she is up to handling the books. If her sister shows some interest, I'll find something for her to accomplish as well. Now, if you'd be so good as to provide a ledger of this month's transactions, I'll go over everything with her this evening."

They lunched at Dulcie's, a place Yvette thought never to see again, let alone in her father's company. The townsfolk stared openly at them, which made her feel very important. *So this is what it means to be a Duvoisin.*

"Did you ever give that money to the poor?" she courageously asked.

"What money, Yvette?"

"You know what money."

"Actually, no."

When her father didn't elaborate, she dropped the subject. Still, their banter was easy, and she truly enjoyed being with him.

"Papa?" Yvette asked as they rode home. "Will I really be in charge?"

"Of the lumber mill books? Yes." She smiled exultantly. "But I warn you now, Yvette, it is not going to be easy."

"Don't worry, Papa," she assured, "I'm up to it. I won't disappoint you."

Frederic chuckled, unable to remain serious. For the first time in years, his heart swelled with pride.

"What about you, Jeannette? Would you like take charge of something?"

"Well, I'm not as good with figures as Yvette is, Papa, but I'll help if I can."

"Only if you want to, Princess, only if you want to."

They arrived home just after three o'clock. At the girls' insistence, Frederic allowed them to groom their ponies in the paddock. He retreated to the house.

They had just finished currying Spook and Angel when their stepmother swept past them without so much as a word of greeting. Yvette eyed her suspiciously as Gerald rushed over. They exchanged a few words and the stable-master nodded toward the carriage house, where a chaise stood ready. Agatha climbed in, flicked the reins, and steered the buggy through the manor gates.

"That's strange," Yvette murmured.

"What is?" her sister asked.

"Auntie going out for a buggy ride."

"Why is that strange?"

"When have you ever seen her riding out alone – without a driver?"

"Never?" Jeannette supplied thoughtfully.

"That's what I thought."

Agatha was in no rush to be on time for her customary three o'clock appointment. She was close to an hour late when the carriage rolled up in front of the tiny abode. She alighted from it and stepped up to the door, not bothering to knock. Her adversary sat at a small table near the hearth, pen in hand. He looked up, seemingly unaffected by her unannounced entrance. When he did not speak, she took charge. "This will be my last visit," she announced.

"Your last visit? Why? You haven't run out of resources, have you?"

Agatha looked around the room, noticing the bottle of expensive wine on the table, the well-stocked pantry, and the silk curtains adorning the windows. The man was living well at her expense. "My *resources* are of no concern to you. I'm through providing your finances."

He was surprised. "What are you saying, Mrs. Duvoisin?"

"I've informed my husband of the small matter over which you've been extorting money," she replied triumphantly. "He knows all the details and has been most forgiving. Your threats are inconsequential now."

A low, deliberate laugh erupted from his unctuous smile. "Mrs. Duvoisin," he started magnanimously, "I've grown quite accustomed to my stipend. It has helped offset my humble circumstance. Do you really think I would place it in jeopardy without insurance?"

Her eyes narrowed. She was not following him, so he hurried to explain. "I reflected for hours on your little lie, pondered your motives, puzzled over the role your brother played in it all. Robert's situation has dramatically improved as well: his new house, lavishly furnished. Has his medical practice really grown that much? Or was he rewarded for assisting you?"

Agatha's pulse throbbed, apprehensive yet irate over what was coming.

The man chuckled at her tightlipped reply. "Yes, I've done some investigating, gleaned a bit of *evidence* that would be of great interest to your husband."

"I don't believe you!" she expostulated furiously. "You are bluffing."

"Ah, but do you really want to take that chance, Mrs. Duvoisin?"

She stood before him in stony silence.

"I thought not. So, since you arrived empty-handed today, shall I see you next week at the appointed time? Oh, and by the way, my silence has become more expensive. Let us make your visits weekly ones from now on. So, do come prepared. Good day, Mrs. Duvoisin."

After dinner, Yvette and Frederic disappeared into the study. Charmaine had been told all about their wondrous day. 'Wondrous' was how they'd described it. Thanks to their father, their healing had commenced, and Charmaine was grateful. Her own heart was another matter.

An hour later, Yvette looked up at her father, who was reading over her shoulder. "This is not so difficult, Papa. I can cipher the rest tomorrow afternoon when lessons are over, and you can check my work in the evening."

"I have a better idea," Frederic said. "I think I can persuade Miss Ryan to substitute your arithmetic problems with this bookkeeping. After all, what is the purpose of education if not to benefit from its application?"

"You're absolutely right, Papa."

"I thought you'd agree," he chuckled. "Shall we finish tomorrow then?"

"Yes, Papa, I'm quite tired." She rose, stretched, and placed a mild kiss on his cheek, but as she reached the hallway door, he called her name. "Yes, Papa?"

"You are quite a young lady – so very much like your mother."

"Mama?" she asked in astonishment. "But Jeannette is much more–"

He didn't allow her to finish. "No, Yvette, *you* are like your mother."

She rushed across the study and gave him a fierce hug. Then, embarrassed, she raced from the room. With a heavy heart, Frederic watched her go. Not so long ago, Colette had sat at this desk doing the very same job.

The warm days of October turned unusually cool and blustery, heralding the onset of the Caribbean winter. Charmaine marveled at Frederic's transformation. Most days, he ventured out with George to monitor work on the docks, at the mill, or in the sugarcane fields, master of his empire once again. When he was at the house, he was usually working in the study. He was hardier, his weak side growing stronger. Though he still favored a cane, his limp had also improved.

True to his word, he spent every Saturday with his daughters, and though it was a challenge at first, he managed quite well. In fact, Charmaine was impressed with the things he taught them, the engaging outings he embarked upon, all of which revolved around Duvoisin business. Although he and Jeannette had always been close, Yvette flourished under his guidance. Both girls looked forward to Saturday now, often speculating as to what the next excursion might be.

Charmaine remained uncomfortable in his presence, preferring to keep her distance. Though she tried to suppress them, she could not forget the revelations of that bleak October morning. Sadly, she could not regard Frederic with the same respect, despite his titanic effort to begin anew. She often contemplated the ugly word uttered only by John, though not denied by his father: *rape.* Had Frederic raped Colette or was it as *he* claimed – a seduction? Instinctively, Charmaine knew the latter had to be closer to the truth. She recalled Colette's remarks: *I was attracted to him from the moment we met... He's handsome still... I love him still...* No woman would use such words to describe a man who had raped her; there had to be more to the story. Nevertheless, pardoning Frederic of rape did not acquit him of stealing Colette from John.

The frenzied pace Paul had previously kept abated when Frederic reassumed control of Charmantes. Espoir's development was suddenly unimpeded, and he spent most weekdays there. But every Friday night, he ventured home. *She* commanded his Saturdays now. A stroll on the lawns, afternoon tea, even lunch at Dulcie's became a ritual. She was amazed that he chose her companionship over his fledgling enterprise. Their discourse was direct, free of the previous games and guile, and they chatted and laughed together as never before. His attentiveness was comforting, a welcome distraction from the grief over Pierre, a piercing emptiness that often gripped her unexpectedly.

Agatha was not pleased. Charmaine often caught her disapproving glare. The woman continued to ingratiate herself to Paul, mindful of her future and the comfortable lifestyle she'd grown accustomed to as Mrs. Duvoisin. Clearly, she hadn't forgotten her disdainful nephew's threats to cast her out, so she curried Paul's respect in an effort to secure her future in the manor. She certainly didn't want Charmaine around to interfere.

To Agatha's chagrin, Frederic postponed the christening of Espoir. She objected, but he could not be swayed, insisting that such a celebration was inappropriate so soon after Pierre's death. Paul agreed, and so the affair was set for early April, just before Easter, when the weather warmed. Better accommodations could be arranged, and travel to the islands would be easier.

There had been no word from John. The twins missed him fiercely and were downtrodden when ships arrived from Richmond carrying no letters. But Charmaine understood; the wounds were still fresh, the happy memories too painful. She often reminisced about that winsome time, especially the two weeks before Pierre's death. They had been a family then, a loving family. She had lost more than Pierre in October; she had lost John as well. But even if he returned today, those carefree days could never be recaptured. Pierre was gone forever. Far better to cherish her recollections than dwell upon what wasn't meant to be.

In mid-November, a young physician arrived in town. Recently graduated from medical school, he'd jumped at the prospect of opening up a practice where there would be little competition. Charmaine had unexpectedly encountered Caroline Browning one day, who lost no time in asking whether John had made the arrangements. It was rumored that he distrusted his uncle's competency and was subsidizing the new doctor until a clientele of patients could be established. Charmaine didn't doubt the assertions, the traumatic hours before Pierre's death foremost in her mind, but she cut the conversation short when Caroline inquired about the accident, asking why Pierre had been left in John's care.

Saturday, November 25, 1837

Paul turned an admiring eye on Charmaine. She was seated confidently on the dappling mare, handling the steed competently, unaware of his regard from astride his own mount.

The Saturdays they spent together were the one silver lining in the cloud of disasters that had befallen his family over the past months. He wanted Charmaine more than ever. Those bleak days in October had served to make her more alluring: the quiet dignity with which she bore her grief, her warmth in comforting his sisters, her forbearance to move on. He longed to take her in his arms and teach her about the pleasures of the flesh, yet he did not press her. Although there was a candor between them now, her passion lay dormant. She was still grieving Pierre, he reasoned, desire would return in time.

"How is Espoir coming along?" she asked, glancing his way.

"It's nearly finished," he replied, pleased with her interest. "The light will be installed in the lighthouse next week. I intend to launch some limited shipping. It's impractical to delay until April. Some early runs will also allow the crews to become acquainted with navigating the port." Impulsively, he asked, "Would you like to see it?"

Her eyes left the road altogether, taking in his broadening smile, white teeth flashing against bronzed skin. He was serious! "Yes, I would!" she exclaimed.

"Why not next week? We can take the girls and spend a few days there."

He noted her fading enthusiasm, signaling her concern over an unchaperoned voyage. "I'll ask Rose to join us and give you all an extended tour."

Mentioning Rose did the trick; her face brightened again. "I think it's a wonderful idea!" she said.

For the first time in weeks, she was looking forward to something.

Monday, December 4, 1837

The twins welcomed their first excursion on a Duvoisin vessel, their alacrity unrestrained. With Paul in close attendance, they took turns at the helm, though he did the work. Most of the time they were at the bow, arms extended, flaxen hair and skirts dancing in the headwind. Occasionally, the ship cut into deep waves, hurling sea-spray over her sides, startling them into squeals of delight.

They arrived by late afternoon and headed straight to the new house. Aside from Frederic and Agatha, they were the first to take up temporary residence there. The house was magnificent, constructed with the highest quality materials. Paul noted that though the main floor was sparsely furnished, many of the bedchambers were fully appointed in anticipation of the guests who would be visiting in the spring. He showed them to their rooms; the twins would share one, but Charmaine and Rose had their own. He also brought them to the master chamber suite, which was larger than Charmaine's childhood home. She imagined the life of the mistress of this manor, and fleetingly, fancied herself in that role. But she quickly brushed those thoughts aside. Even as the governess to the Duvoisin children, she enjoyed comforts and privileges she could never have fathomed. Could she ever go back to her humble beginnings? Someday she might have to, so it was wise to stay anchored in reality.

Millie set up the kitchen, serving them a simple meal by late evening. Afterward, they retired to the drawing room, where Rose took up her knitting and Charmaine, Paul, and the twins played a game of cards, which, along with chess and checkers, they had brought for evening entertainment. Jeannette tired of the game and went to Rose, asking for a knitting lesson. With an extra pair of needles and spare yarn, Rose set up a basic stitch. Jeannette caught on quickly. After completing a few rows, she brought her handiwork to Charmaine.

"Very good!" she praised. "I think you have a knack for knitting."

Yvette boasted that she could knit just as well, and when Paul insisted that she didn't seem the domestic type, she pressed Jeannette to show her the stitches.

He regarded Rose. "Every night you take up that knitting, Nan. What do you do with your finished work? Nobody can use it here."

"I send it to family in the States, and they usually donate it to the poor."

Yvette tired of the tedious task much as Paul had predicted.

"What are you knitting, Jeannette?" he asked.

"I don't know. What *am* I knitting, Nana Rose?"

"Why, a scarf, of course."

"But you don't need a scarf, Jeannette!" Yvette exclaimed.

"No, I don't," she replied, "but I can send it to Johnny for Christmas!"

"That's a wonderful idea," Rose said with a smile, "and I'll show you how to knit his initials into it when you near the end."

Jeannette happily agreed.

"Just make sure he knows that I helped make it, too!" Yvette insisted.

"I'm sure he'll know exactly which two rows you did," Charmaine chuckled, eyeing Yvette's loose, uneven stitches.

Friday, December 8, 1837

The weather was fair, and the week on Espoir sped by quickly. In the mornings, Charmaine and the twins worked on lessons. After lunch, Paul joined them, and they ventured out on horseback to the sugarcane fields, some under preparation for planting, others growing tall. One afternoon they passed endless stretches being cleared of vegetation. The twins enjoyed riding along the trails that bordered the fields, traveling the entire circuit connecting one to the next.

On the last day of their excursion, the weather turned brisk. It had drizzled overnight, and cold air followed the rain. After dinner, they settled into the drawing room. Paul struck a fire in the hearth to chase away the chill, and the girls sat in front of it, Jeannette with her knitting and Yvette with a book. Before long, both had fallen asleep. Paul carried them to their room, where Charmaine tucked them in for the night. When she returned to the parlor, Rose stood and announced that she, too, was retiring.

For the first time that week, Charmaine was alone with Paul, and she could feel herself growing tense – a strange mixture of excitement, anxiety, and reluctance. She remained on the sofa, watching him. He was banking the fire with fresh kindling, his masculinity silhouetted by the glowing embers. She admired the play of muscle in his thigh as he crouched low to press the logs deeper into the blaze. His handsome face was striking in the orange light. He rose and moved to the sideboard where he poured two glasses of wine.

Paul inhaled as he handed a glass to her. She was lovely tonight. He hadn't kissed her in months, and the urge to do so now was overpowering.

Charmaine blushed as he settled on the sofa next to her, his arm cast across the back of it. He was so close that she could feel the heat of his body. "I don't drink," she said, gesturing with the glass.

"Try it, Charmaine. It's a vintage wine. It will help you relax."

"Very well," she said, taking a sip. It was smooth and warm going down.

"So, did you enjoy the trip here?" he asked.

"Very much. I'm impressed. I see what kept you busy all those months."

"There is still much to do before Espoir will stand on its own merit."

"With all the care you've taken, it will be very successful."

"I hope so. Still, it has distracted me from other important things."

She looked at him quizzically. He was studying her intently. "You'll find time for those things," she said quickly, wishing to redirect the conversation.

"I'm trying to." His hand, warm and persuasive, caressed her cheek, found her chin, and coaxed her head back. With her face upturned, he leaned forward, his lips meeting hers. "You are lovely, Charmaine Ryan," he murmured against her mouth. "It has been so long since I've kissed you, I was afraid this week would pass without the opportunity."

His kiss deepened, and his arm slid off the sofa, closing around her shoulder. The minutes gathered, and his ardor grew, his hand stroking her hair, her shoulder, and coming to rest on her thigh. She felt feminine and desirable, yet as the sensual moment heightened, a visceral tide of resistance took hold. She pressed her hands against his chest and slowly drew back.

He looked down at her searchingly. "Are you all right?"

"Yes, yes," she replied, standing up and moving to the fireplace. This situation was very dangerous.

"Charmaine," he started, coming to stand behind her. "I know you have been very sad these past two months. I had hoped to comfort you."

She faced him. "And you have. You have been a great comfort, a good friend, and I appreciate your concern."

"Are you in better spirits now?" he asked, not relishing the title 'good friend'.

She smiled. "Some days I am. This week I have been."

The silence between them seemed endless.

"What do you want, Charmaine Ryan?"

"What do I want?" she queried, awed by the unexpected question.

"Yes, what do you want – for your future, for your life?"

Was this trite banter, or was he asking how she felt about him? Somewhere inside, she knew the answer to his question, but it was too sublime, too frightening – *too impossible* – to even ponder.

"Six months ago, I could have answered," she replied. "Now... I don't know." She paused, then turned the question over to him. "What do *you* want? And don't say me."

"And if I did say I want you?" he asked sincerely.

"I would say that I'm flattered."

"But?"

"But what do you *mean* when you say you want me?"

"It means I want you at my side. It means I want to make love to you."

"Does it mean you want to marry me?" she inquired brashly.

His smile faded, and she was strangely relieved. "What does it matter, anyway?" she chuckled lightheartedly, waving away the frivolous query, intent upon soothing him. "It's not even in the realm of consideration, is it? After all, I'm just a governess, hardly a suitable spouse."

Marriage... Not exactly the subject he wanted to broach right now. *Marriage...* Why was it so frightening? Why did he hesitate? *You will rue the day you threw away happiness with both hands.* If it weren't Charmaine, who then? *Marriage...* What was he waiting for?

"I don't think of you as just the governess, Charmaine," he replied. "You are a fine woman: compassionate, intelligent, attractive. Social mores have never been important to me, and they certainly won't dictate whom I marry. Look at my parentage. In society's eyes, I am less worthy than you."

She was surprised and heartened by his words. "And?"

He didn't have to make a commitment this moment, and he wouldn't be lying if he told her that he had considered marrying her. "And, to answer your question, I've never felt for any woman what I feel for you. So yes, I would consider marrying you, have, in fact, contemplated it more times than you would imagine. But I'm a rogue, Charmaine. I don't want to hurt you, have you grow to hate me." He paused, still thoughtful. "Marriage, the vows, they are simple. But how can either of us be certain of our feelings years from now? Yes, I want you tonight, desire you greatly, and yes, I love you. But I'm a man. I can't promise that another woman will never turn my eye. That is what I fear most. A pledge to love, honor, and cherish for all eternity? I won't make such a vow lightly."

He pulled her into his arms and his lips snatched away her reply. Slowly, her hands encompassed his back, relishing the feel of his sturdy body, the warmth of his flesh under her palms. He coaxed her back to the settee, his caresses extending to her breasts and hips, awakening sensations that teased her insides. She relaxed into the cushions, he half-kneeling, half-prone above her, his kisses growing furious, his breathing heavy and unsteady. Then he was shifting his position, pressing her further back. As he lowered himself, she could feel the weight of his body, something hard against her thigh, and an inkling of reluctance washed over her again. She pushed onto her elbows, coming up for air.

"Charmaine..." he murmured, his voice husky, "if you're worried about conceiving a child, you needn't be–"

She frowned, disconcerted. Curiously, that thought hadn't crossed her mind, but she quickly capitalized on it. "That is easy for you to say."

He leaned in close again. "There are ways–"

She turned her face aside, hands braced against his chest. "I can't," she whimpered, "I'm sorry, I just can't."

Disappointed, he moved the end of the sofa. She stood to bid him goodnight. "Don't leave," he said. "It's our last night here. I won't press you if you're not ready. Please, come and sit with me."

Again, she was gladdened by his words and returned to him. His arm closed around her, his hand stroking her hair, finally nudging her head onto his shoulder. They stayed there late into the night, talking and staring into the fire...

Christmas Eve, 1837

Charmaine and the girls spent the day decorating the house: weaving pine and holly sprigs, fastening fruit to them with string, and garnishing the balustrade, mantle, and French doors with the festive boughs.

After dinner, the family gathered in the drawing room. It was quite chilly, lending the day a true holiday air. Paul lit a fire in the hearth. Frederic invited the staff to join them, and so, the Thornfields, Jane Faraday, and Fatima settled in for eggnog and Christmas cookies. Felicia and Anna were spending the night in town with Felicia's parents. The girls sang to the Christmas carols that Charmaine played on the piano. When she tired, Paul took over at the keyboard and entertained his sisters, who were as surprised as Charmaine to hear him play.

The twins begged to open the packages that had arrived yesterday. They were from John; the first they had heard from him since October. Charmaine acquiesced; there would be more gifts tomorrow. They dove into the wrapping, revealing two finely tailored riding jackets in royal blue, complete with tan jodhpurs, velvet riding hats, boots and crops.

Agatha began to object to Frederic's daughters wearing boys' clothing, but her protests over the breeches Charmaine had sewn for Yvette last September had gotten her nowhere, so she took a sip of her brandy instead.

The package also contained a book for Yvette and Jeannette: *The New-York Book of Poetry*. A note from John was inserted like a bookmark at the page where the poem *A Visit from St. Nicholas* appeared. They greedily read the brief letter aloud, then the poem, and the letter again...

Dear Yvette & Jeannette,

Perhaps St. Nick will fill your stockings this Christmas Eve – that is, if his eight tiny reindeer don't need snow, Auntie allows them to land on the roof, and Yvette is well behaved. The odds are not very good. If St. Nick does not visit, then I hope my gifts will do. Happy Christmas.

Love, John

Agatha gripped tight the arms of her wing chair, offended. John continued to ridicule her, even across the Atlantic. The girls, however, were thrilled, and the poem sent them scrambling to find stockings to fasten to the mantle.

Charmaine was heartened by their enthusiasm, amazed once again at how John could cast a whimsical spell on them, even from so far away. She looked to Frederic, who observed the tableau with intense interest. When he realized she studied him, he turned away, his gaze lifting to the painting that hung above the fireplace. *What was he thinking?* Her heart answered: *He never imagined it would be like this. He doesn't want it to be like this.*

There was also a small package for her.

"Open it, Mademoiselle," Jeannette said. "What do you think it can be?"

Charmaine glanced at Paul, who had moved to the fireplace, staring into the flickering flames. She untied the ribbon and pulled the wrapping aside. Inside was a simple ivory hairbrush. She smiled, running a finger lightly over the smooth handle. It was much finer than the one John had broken that first night last August.

"A most pleasant evening," Agatha declared. "It truly feels like Christmas: a warm room, a crackling fire, and the family together. So much like England this time of year. Everything Christmas should be."

Charmaine bristled at the callous remark. She glanced around the room: at Paul, with head bowed, George hiding behind a magazine, Frederic with his turbulent eyes, and Rose with her mournful face, even Fatima Henderson, lips pursed indignantly. She wondered where John was this evening. Instinctively, she knew he was alone.

Later, as she turned down the lamps in the nursery, Charmaine nearly cried when Jeannette innocently asked, "Do you think Saint Nick can bring Pierre and Mama back to us for Christmas?"

She looked with a heavy heart at Pierre's empty bed and remembered sleeping there with him, remembered John sleeping there. She would be glad when this Christmas was over. As she completed her nightly toilette, she thought of her mother… of Colette and Pierre… She lay down and wept. But tears were futile, so she prayed, prayed for her deceased loved ones and comfort for her grieving. But mostly, she prayed for the Duvoisins.

Christmas Day, 1837 Richmond

The cold, crisp air frosted John's breath as he descended the steps of the St. Jude Refuge. He tightened Yvette and Jeannette's scarf around his neck, unhitched Phantom, and pulled up into the saddle. It was early, and although the Richmond streets were deserted, the refuge was busy. He had stopped in to see Father Michael Andrews before morning Mass and the ensuing bustle of the refuge's customary turkey dinner for the poor.

"Why don't you join us, John?" the priest had asked. "We can have dinner together after the soup kitchen has closed."

"No, no. You would have to hear my confession, and that could take all day," John had quipped hollowly. "You'd best direct your efforts where you'll have some success. There's no redemption for me."

In truth, John wanted to be alone this day. He couldn't think of anybody he cared to be with, save perhaps Charmaine. Pulling his woolen overcoat closed against the cold, he prodded Phantom into a brisk trot, setting him west on Wilderness Road toward Appomattox. He would ride to Freedom, a trip that would take most of the day. The road would be empty and the plantation house deserted, precisely what he wanted.

Michael had hoped that John would spend Christmas day with him and had purposely set time aside yesterday to stop by his Richmond townhouse and extend the invitation. When the butler let him in, he found John at the piano. Michael knew from the steward that John had gone home to the family's islands late last summer. He surmised that something grave had happened there. Michael had seen this distant mood before – the day they had met at the refuge four years earlier. Then, John had drowned himself in alcohol, seeking succor in drunken oblivion. This time, he was sober, and Michael thought it best not to probe. Yesterday, they had conversed briefly. As Michael pulled on his coat, he was encouraged when John agreed to stop by the refuge. But today, it was painfully apparent that John was spurning his company, for he'd stayed all of ten minutes.

A disturbing disquietude welled up in Michael. *I was naïve to think that I could make a difference in this pitiable world. Another year of useless ministering to those I serve – of meaningless existence for myself...*

He turned away and opened the leather purse that John had handed him at the door. Twenty banknotes were inside; the sum easily exceeded the soup kitchen's expenses for the day, not to mention the Christmas donations he expected to collect at Mass. "You *are* redeemed, John," he intoned with a shake of his head, his moment's antipathy assuaged. He entered the church to lay out his vestments for the Christmas Day celebration.

Saturday, January 6, 1838

Yvette insisted that she and her sister wear their new riding habits. When they arrived at the breakfast table, she was beaming. Frederic's brow raised in amusement as she sashayed before him like never before in any feminine apparel. "What do you think, Papa?" she queried. "Do you like it?"

"No," he answered, "but I can see you do, and that is all that matters."

She pretended to pout, but her happiness quickly bubbled over.

Rose chuckled. "I'd say she looks like a Duvoisin ready to do business."

Frederic nodded as he considered his other daughter. "What of you, Jeannette? Do you like wearing boy's clothing?"

"It feels strange, Papa. I think I prefer a dress."

When they left for the day, Charmaine sighed. Paul was preoccupied as well, and she would be alone. She and Rose talked for a while, but when the older woman went upstairs complaining of her rheumatism, Charmaine stepped outdoors for a peaceful stroll.

She meandered about the grounds, finding herself at the family cemetery. It was no longer gnarled and ill kept. She surmised that Frederic had ordered it manicured and maintained. A bench had been placed near the two newest graves, and she sank down on it, as she had often done over the past few months, lifting and hugging Pierre's soiled lamb. She closed her eyes to her gathering tears and jumped when Paul placed a comforting hand on her shoulder.

"I'm sorry," he said, "I didn't mean to startle you."

Unable to speak, she just shook her head.

"Gerald said you were headed this way," he commented, allowing her a moment to compose herself, offering her his handkerchief.

She read compassion in his eyes as he sat down beside her. "I thought you were working today," she finally said.

"I was. But Father and the girls caught up with me and sent me home." He chuckled softly. "Yvette is a wonder. She's starting to impress even me."

Charmaine smiled. Yvette had indeed taken over the mill's books, and Charmaine had yet to find a mistake in her ciphering. Even Frederic was pleased; he checked her figures only once a month now.

"Do you come here often?" Paul asked.

"Occasionally," she whispered, her grief regrouping. "Oh Paul," she murmured, surrendering to it, "when my mother died, I didn't think the pain could be any worse. But I was wrong! I miss him every day. I think of him every morning. Sometimes I even forget and go into the nursery..."

"There now," he soothed, gathering her in his arms, cradling her head against his shoulder. "This is only natural. You loved Pierre like a son."

She sobbed until her body shuddered, and still Paul held her.

"I scolded the girls after Colette died!" she declared angrily. "Their mother had been dead for only a month, and I scolded them. And now, look at me! It has been three months and... How could I have done that to them?"

"Charmaine, you did what was best. You brought them out of despair and made them whole again. With time, the same will be true for you."

Charmaine nodded, deeply consoled.

Paul closed his eyes to agony. *Why had this happened to his family?*

He was nine years old again. The sun was setting, the harbor cast in long shadows. He watched anxiously with John and George on the quay as the last casks were rolled off the ship. The crew was loitering nearby, waiting for their mates to finish up. Then, they all fell in together, a boisterous, smelly, backslapping procession making its way to Dulcie's. Frederic had taken the captain into the warehouse office to reconcile invoices. The brigantine was theirs!

Paul scrambled up the gangplank with his brothers. Tonight John, George, and he were pirates. They battled the crew with pistols and swords, vanquished them and commandeered the vessel. They made the captain walk the plank and crept into the bowels of the ship, plundering the coffers of gold and jewels nestled in the hold. Down below, they could barely see, but they could hear their father calling for them. The fantasy was over.

Paul swallowed hard and pulled Charmaine closer. Little boys didn't die on Charmantes. This was, after all, paradise. But then he remembered: three little boys had lost their lives on this paradise island, over fifty years ago, during a pirate raid. His father had been little more than two, with an elder brother and sister, ages fourteen and twelve, and three brothers in between, ranging in ages from five to nine. The boys slumbered peacefully in their beds as a fire was ignited over their heads, destroying in one short, horrific hour, the first house ever constructed on Charmantes.

Charmantes had enjoyed twenty years of peace, guaranteed by the deal Jean Duvoisin had struck with the pirates who roamed the waters of the West Indies. He allowed them safe haven in the hidden coves of his three islands as long as they did not set foot on the beaches. The quietude nurtured a false security; Charmantes should have been wary of the carnage wreaked upon neighboring islands, should have been careful about boasting of its own prosperity.

According to Frederic, the renegades waited until his father traveled abroad, landing on the western shore in the middle of the night and penetrating the island's limited fortifications in less than an hour. They spent the remainder of that bleak night pillaging and destroying. Frederic's mother was only able to carry her youngest son to safety, perishing when she attempted to rescue her remaining children from the inferno. By the following afternoon, only ashes remained.

When Jean returned, he proclaimed the ground hallowed. Embittered, he turned from his life on the seas and became a farmer. He built the mansion in which they now lived, complete with back staircases: escape routes should they ever be threatened again. He settled in with his three remaining children, hired Rose to help raise Frederic, and nursed a broken heart for the rest of his days.

Today, there was little threat of a pirate attack. With Great Britain's sovereign claim to the Bahamas, the British navy patrolling her waters, and Frederic's allegiance to the crown, complete with tithing and the upholding of British law, Charmantes enjoyed military protection that had not existed fifty years earlier, when Caribbean raids were commonplace. And yet today, the sorrowful past lived on. *Little boys did die on Charmantes.*

With a deep sigh, Paul leaned his cheek atop Charmaine's head. Her arms encircled his waist, and he drew strength from her vulnerability. Taking solace from each other, they finally rose and walked back to the house.

New York

John looked out the bedroom window of his row house and stared, unseeing, at the street below. It was busy, even for late Saturday night. The noise of the city had awoken him. But then, he hadn't been sleeping very well these days. He breathed deeply and sighed. The woman in his bed stirred. He regarded her for a moment, but when she didn't awaken, he turned back to the window.

He thought of Colette. He thought of Charmaine. Strange, last night, Charmaine had been the centerpiece of his fantasies. *Charmaine...* How he'd love to hold her, cry with her, laugh with her again.

Saturday, January 13, 1838 Charmantes

Charmaine had plans to meet Paul in town. The sun was quite bright for January and because she would be riding Dapple, the name that Jeannette had dubbed her gray mare, she turned back to the house to fetch her bonnet.

From her room, she could hear the twins conversing with their father in the nursery. Apparently, they were remaining at the house today. The door stood slightly ajar, and Charmaine listened, appreciating the easy banter between them.

"Papa, do you think Pierre is really in heaven with Mama, now?"

A moment's silence, then, "Yes, Yvette, I'm certain he's with your Mama."

Charmaine could hear tears in Frederic's voice. He changed the subject. "I was late today because I was involved with some of the planning for Paul's celebration. We're to meet with Mr. Westphal tonight."

"I don't think this celebration is *ever* going to arrive," Jeannette lamented.

"April isn't far off. It will be a splendid affair – the first one on Charmantes in many, many years." Frederic sounded enthusiastic, and Charmaine realized that he, too, was looking forward to the event. "There will be a great ball, elegant ladies and gentlemen, and musicians."

"Will we go to the ball?"

"Of course, and you shall wear beautiful dresses, which have already been ordered."

"Where will all the fine ladies and gentlemen come from?"

"Georgia, the Carolinas, Virginia, Maryland, and even New York. Some Caribbean farmers have also been invited."

"Will Johnny come?" The inevitable question came from Yvette, and the room fell into another awkward silence.

"No, Yvette, I'm afraid not," Frederic murmured.

"You won't allow him to come, will you?"

"He can come if he likes," her father answered in earnest.

Unconvinced, she added, "It wasn't his fault, Papa. He loved Pierre."

"I know he did, Yvette, but there is more to it than just Pierre."

"But you're better now!" she insisted. "Why do you still hate him?"

"I don't hate him. He is my son."

"So why won't he come?"

"Because he is very angry with me."

"But why?" Jeannette asked searchingly.

"I made many mistakes with John and did things that hurt him terribly."

"What things?"

"Things that you are too young to understand," he replied, "things that are difficult for me to explain to you."

"Then why don't you tell him that you are sorry?" Yvette offered. "That's what Mademoiselle Charmaine tells us to do when we've made a mistake."

"I'm afraid it is not that easy," Frederic faltered.

"Yes it is!" Jeannette chimed in. "I have an idea, Papa. You can write him a letter and tell him you're sorry. We can help you write it, can't we, Yvette?"

"Yes! We'll make it the best apology ever! And you can invite him to come to Paul's celebration, too!"

"Come, Papa, let's find some paper! *Please?*"

"Perhaps you are right, my dear daughters," Frederic mused. "Very well, let us see what kind of a letter we can write."

With tears in her eyes, Charmaine left her room, thanking the heavens above and praying that John would receive the invitation with an open heart.

Later that afternoon, Frederic's letter sat atop others on the table in the foyer. Agatha noticed her husband's scrawl as she swept by, and she scrutinized the address. She was not pleased that he was writing to his errant son.

Bending closer to the mirror, Paul fumbled with his cravat. The sun was fast setting, the peer glass cast in shadow. Travis should have arrived long ago to light the lamps. He'd do it himself, but the tinderbox was nowhere to be found, so he swore at his reflection and ripped the atrocious knot apart again. A man shouldn't have to suffer the nonsense of proper attire after a full day's labor. He had spent most of the afternoon in the cane fields, his intervention urgently needed when the press broke down and half a tract of produce was in jeopardy of being lost. That catastrophe had forced him to abandon his outing with Charmaine, but both problems had been easier to deal with than his tie. Irritated, he leaned into the mirror again.

Travis finally arrived.

"Where have you been?" Paul gruffly inquired.

"With Mr. Westphal."

"Damn! Is the man never late?"

"No, I'm afraid not, sir."

The butler was about to say more, but thought better of it, stepping up to the ill-humored Paul with arms extended. "Allow me, sir," he offered, smiling when Paul's arms dropped to his sides. "What you need, Master Paul," he mused as he worked at the cravat, "is a wife to see to tasks such as this."

Paul snorted. "Travis, if I take a wife, it will not be to dress me."

The man blushed. He would never get used to the ribald remarks of Frederic's sons. To Travis, they would always be the lads he chased after to keep out of such trouble. "There," the steward sighed, "that should do it, sir."

"Thank you," Paul praised, patting the knot, satisfied with his reflection.

"I think you should know, sir, that the mistress is with Mr. Westphal."

Paul shrugged. "Better if she talks with him first. Then he'll be free to speak with my father and me without interruption."

"Yes, sir."

"Where is my father, anyway?"

"He arrived back quite late with the girls, sir. I'm to see to him next."

Paul grunted. He suddenly thought of Colette, and how little his father had relied on Travis that first year they were married. *A wife...*

He left his dressing room and, with head down, walked straight into Charmaine. Catching her in his arms, he set her from him with a stern frown. He apologized curtly and descended the stairs quickly, leaving her puzzled.

Much to his relief, dinner was relaxed. All his hard work was finally coming together. Following the meal, he spent over two hours in the study with his father, Agatha, and Stephen discussing the arrangements for the monumental spring event. The invitation list had been finalized, guest transportation and accommodations planned, and the week's expenses estimated.

The clock struck eleven, and Agatha noted that Stephen and Frederic shared her exhaustion. The financier's tie had long been loosed, dinner jacket doffed, waistcoat unbuttoned, and now, in the dim library light, he stole a yawn as Paul leaned forward to scribble some last particulars. Her husband had closed his eyes more than once in the armchair where he now reclined.

"Paul," Agatha interjected, gaining the man's regard, "maybe you should continue this tomorrow–" she looked to the banker "–as I fear our guest is growing weary."

"Tomorrow would be fine," Stephen concurred wholeheartedly.

Paul had lost track of the time. It *was* late. "Forgive me Stephen," he apologized, laying down his quill. "I've forgotten that this is not quite as exhilarating for you." He stood and went to the door. "I'll see to it that your carriage is brought to the portico. Would you like an escort home?"

"That's unnecessary. I doubt I shall encounter any highwaymen."

Everyone but Frederic laughed. "I'll say goodnight then," Frederic said.

Agatha was pleased when Paul and her husband departed. She grabbed the banker's jacket and helped him slip it on. Gathering his belongings, she walked him into the foyer. "Stephen, you mentioned contacting Mr. Richecourt."

He nodded.

"When you do, could I trouble you with a favor? You've done one of this kind for me before."

"Miss Ryan again?" Stephen queried with cautious interest.

"No, she is insignificant. This concerns John. He's been spending a great deal of time in New York. He said as much months ago, before Pierre's tragic accident. Perhaps you could bring your influence to bear on Mr. Richecourt to find out exactly what his transactions are in the North. I'm concerned over these bank accounts he's been closing out, and I'm afraid my husband has been more trusting than wise."

Westphal nodded in disdain. "I've thought the same thing myself, but wouldn't presume to say so to Frederic. John is–"

"You needn't expound," Agatha interrupted, patting his hand in understanding. "Rest assured that you will be compensated for your efforts."

"I'll see what I can find out, Agatha. Goodnight."

Agatha's smile turned radiant. "Goodnight, Stephen."

He stepped out onto the portico to await his carriage.

Saturday, January 20, 1838

Yvette had a plan. She was going to find out where her stepmother went every Saturday afternoon and why she went alone. Naturally, there were obstacles to surmount: she'd have to get around her father, and she'd have to pick a day when Charmaine was off with Paul. Today was that day. Frederic was planning to take them to the harbor. So, when Charmaine set off for town after breakfast, Yvette complained of a stomachache and asked to stay home in bed. Frederic acquiesced, leaving her in Rose's care. She went straight to her room, pulled on her nightdress and lie on her bed with her knees pulled up to her chest. She heard Frederic and Jeannette leave in the carriage. When Nana Rose came in to check on her, she pretended she was asleep. She was starving by lunchtime, but she dared not show up in the dining room. Nana checked in on her again around two o'clock, bringing some toast, tea, and a fresh pitcher of water, soothing her when she pushed the tray away, moaning that her stomach still hurt. She closed her eyes and pretended to doze again. She heard Rose step softly from the room, pleased with herself. She still had the knack, completely fooling the woman. Rose would not return for another two hours. Perfect! She could be out and back without anyone ever knowing she was gone.

She jumped up, pulled on her breeches, and shoved her hair into Joseph's cap, which she'd lifted just yesterday. She could pass for a boy from a distance. She tiptoed from her room, dashed down the staircase behind her father's suite of rooms, and darted furtively out of the house toward the stables. It was a blustery afternoon. Thankfully, all the stable hands were off to town, except Gerald, who was napping in the tack room. She saddled up Spook and led him out of the stable, noting the chaise awaiting her stepmother, the horse already harnessed and tied to the fence. Pulling up and into her saddle, she set her pony into a trot, passing quickly through the main gates. When she found a spot alongside the road with heavy underbrush, she dismounted, led Spook into the concealing thicket, and waited.

About fifteen minutes later, she heard the rhythmic beat of hooves and the squeak of a buggy coming up the road. It passed her hiding spot, and she saw Agatha plying the whip to the horse's back. When it rounded a bend just up the road, she scrambled from the thicket and jumped back onto Spook, in pursuit until she caught sight of the chaise again. She followed at a safe distance. About a mile further, it turned onto the thickly wooded road that led to Father Benito's cabin. Yvette was surprised. *Why would Auntie be visiting Father Benito?*

Yvette held Spook back as Agatha alighted and entered the priest's abode, carrying a leather pouch. Yvette tied Spook to a tree behind a copse a good distance away and approached the cabin surreptitiously. There was a window on one side, a pile of wooden crates and refuse scattered below it. Yvette climbed the crates and peered in. The window was closed, the voices inside muffled. The curtains were also drawn, but she could see the priest's kitchen and living area through the slit. Agatha and Benito were engaged in a heated dispute, Agatha's rigid posture betraying her anger. Yvette held her breath, straining to hear. Benito took the pouch from Agatha and opened it. Jewels sparkled.

Suddenly, the pile of crates teetered, caving under and spilling Yvette onto the ground. She clambered to her feet and ran to the outhouse, taking cover behind it. She prayed that Benito wouldn't think to look there. She stole a peek around the corner and saw the priest walking around the cabin, stopping at the toppled crates. Agatha was behind him. He looked around, casting his gaze up to the road. He eyed the woman suspiciously.

"It must have been the wind," Agatha theorized. He considered her again, then retreated, slamming the cabin door behind him. Agatha left.

Certain that the priest was peering out his window, Yvette crept deeper into the woods, picking her way through brambles and underbrush and arcing around to Spook. Once she'd led him safely to the road, she kicked him into a gallop, frowning when she realized she didn't have her riding crop. It couldn't be helped; she'd dropped it along the way and would have to complain about misplacing it the next time she went out to ride. All told, she'd been gone just over an hour and was back in bed when Rose came in to check on her again, exclaiming that the nap had helped. She felt much better now and was hungry for dinner.

Sunday, January, 28, 1838

Paul snapped the portfolio shut. He and his father had spent two hours going over Charmantes paperwork, and he was of a mind to take the rest of the day off. He'd arrived home very late last night and, because he'd been on Espoir for the better part of the week, had promised Charmaine and his sisters at Mass this morning that he'd spend the afternoon with them. Time was getting on.

"There is one more thing," Frederic said as his son stood to leave.

Paul eyed him thoughtfully. His father seemed anxious. "Yes?"

Frederic hesitated. "I've invited John home for your celebration."

"*What?* In God's name, why?"

"Jeannette and Yvette requested it."

Paul ran a hand through his hair. "He won't come," he finally said.

Frederic was disheartened. "You are likely right, though I hope he does."

"For the girls' sake," Paul supplied.

"And mine. I'd like to make amends, even at this late date."

"It wasn't your fault. None of this was your fault."

"It *was* my fault," Frederic refuted. "He loved her, Paul, more deeply than I wanted to believe."

Paul scoffed at the idea, but Frederic's earnestness gave him pause.

"Pierre's death put everything into perspective," Frederic continued, "everything. It was easier, *safer*, to discount John's feelings. But in so doing, I made this place a living hell for everyone – including you. You were forced to choose sides, which undermined the camaraderie you once shared with John. I should *never* have stolen Colette from him."

"And Colette had no say in the matter?" Paul threw back at him.

Frederic's eyes hardened, but he didn't respond.

Exasperated, Paul exhaled loudly. "I don't understand. He's had months to stew over this tragedy. That's all it was – a terrible tragedy. And now you unleash Pandora's box? If he decides to come home, it won't be to make amends."

"We shall see. All I ask is that we try to move forward – as a family."

With his initial anger spent, Paul accepted his father's plaintive plea and was moved to remorse. "Very well, Father. I'll welcome him home. I just hope John accepts the invitation for what it is."

Wednesday, February 9, 1838

Agatha had been holding interviews in the study for two days now. Since early Monday morning, a steady stream of villagers had made their pilgrimage to the manor in the hopes of securing one of the fifteen positions that would be available here and on Espoir during the weeklong festivities in April. An inside glimpse of the Duvoisin mansion was as much a motivation to make the nine-mile trek as the employment opportunity, for even those whose names did not make it into the mistress' little book smiled as they left.

Yvette and Jeannette stole away from the nursery many times during those two days, observing the strangers in the foyer or those walking up the drive. They conjured games, wagering over which ones would be selected.

Travis escorted one after the other from entrance hall, to drawing room, to library. The few that gained Agatha's approval were ushered into the ballroom, where they met with Jane Faraday or Fatima Henderson. The rest were released and walked to the portico, where they lingered before heading back to town.

At the close of the day, Agatha shut her ledger and leaned back in her chair.

"Finished?"

Frederic drew her away from her preoccupation. She nodded contentedly.

"I have three cooks and six maids assigned to Espoir. Fatima has chosen an additional two for our kitchen. On the morning of the ball, those from Espoir shall be transported here to assist. Jane will spend the next month training the housekeepers, including the four I've hired for us. All ten should perform splendidly; they know that five permanent positions are available on Espoir. In addition, Anne London has graciously arranged a retinue of waiters and table staff to depart her country estate and arrive here a week before the banquet."

"Agatha, you've assumed the role of mistress with the authority it demands," Frederic praised. "Paul's debut will be remembered for years to come."

Her heart soared with his admiration. "Thank you, Frederic," she murmured tearfully. "With all the money you've spent, how could I not lend it my best effort? I've done this as much for you as I have for Paul. I'm so pleased to see you up and about again, as strong as ever."

She stood and went to him, running her hands down his arms, brushing a stray lock of hair back into place. "I love you, Frederic."

He caught hold of her wrist and brought her fingers to his lips. "I thank you for all you've done."

Sunday, February 25, 1838

George Richards was smitten.

He'd accompanied Paul to the harbor because the Destiny was due in port. Stephen Westphal's daughter, Anne London, was expected to be aboard. Since Paul planned to escort her back to the house, George would take charge of unloading the vessel. The ship arrived, and the mooring went very smoothly.

Anne was above deck, anxiously waiting for the gangplank to be lowered. Paul, George, and Stephen climbed the ramp to greet her. George took an immediate disliking to her. She was pretentious and cloying, and she wore too much rouge. In a matter of seconds, she gave her father a dismissive kiss on the cheek and turned her smothering attention upon Paul. Irked, George jumped at the opportunity to get her luggage from her cabin.

It took a moment for his eyes to adjust to the light as he stepped inside. Then he saw her: a young woman gathering up parcels. She had long auburn hair, hazel eyes, olive skin, and high cheekbones. She was exotic and took his breath away.

"Good day," he greeted, "I'm here to collect Mrs. London's things."

She nodded and blushed, lowering her eyes to the floor before scurrying through the doorway.

He hastily grabbed a few bags and rushed out in pursuit. It was bright and warm above deck. The young woman was not far ahead of him. As she reached the gangplank, she stumbled and grasped for the railing, the parcels spilling out of her arms. George dropped his baggage and hurried to help her.

"Are you all right?" he asked, taking her elbow until she regained her balance. He picked up the packages, their eyes locking as he straightened up.

"Thank you," she replied with another blush.

"You're welcome," he smiled. "Here, take my arm."

She slid a delicate hand into the crook of his elbow, and he walked her down the ramp to Paul and Anne.

"You're going to need another carriage," he commented.

"I'll hire one from the livery," Paul replied, "if you'd get the other trunks."

George agreed, but by the time he'd returned, the first carriage was rolling away, Anne, Paul, and the lovely young lady inside. *Who was she?*

A ruckus resounded in the hallway. Charmaine stepped out of the nursery with the twins close behind. Travis and Joseph had just deposited a mountain of leather traveling cases outside John's bedchamber door, then disappeared down the steps. Charmaine looked at the twins, who returned her regard with quizzical shrugs. Yvette dashed back into the nursery and out onto the balcony.

"Come and see, Mademoiselle!"

Jeannette and Charmaine followed. Two carriages had pulled up in front of the portico, and two women were on the lawn, one of them conversing with Paul and Stephen Westphal. She was elegantly garbed in a pale yellow dress, cut low to reveal the swell of her ample bosom. A wide-brimmed hat was cocked to the side of her head, and she held a parasol. She had strawberry-blonde hair that was swept up and pinned neatly under her hat. Her face was heart-shaped, with expressive brown eyes and a finely arched brow. Her cheeks were rosy, and she had a curvaceous body. She was quite attractive, though she did not come close to the delicate, graceful beauty of Colette Duvoisin. Anne London, Charmaine surmised. The woman's eyes were locked on Paul, her head tilted back and a smile tugging at her lips.

Her companion was younger, perhaps Charmaine's age, and dressed in plain clothes. She was tall and slender, her long hair tied back with a ribbon and falling to her hips. She was busy unloading hatboxes from the second carriage, which was piled high with luggage. The top box wobbled, then fell altogether, spilling a frilled bonnet onto the lawn.

"Really, Mercedes," Anne London exclaimed with a click of the tongue, "do be more careful! I haven't even worn that hat yet, and already you've managed to soil it!" Mercedes scrambled to pick up the expensive item, blushing in embarrassment as both Stephen and Paul turned to see. "Why don't you follow the butler and bring the boxes up to my room?"

"Who is it, Mademoiselle?"

"Mrs. London," Charmaine replied, gaining Yvette's grimace.

"Good thing Johnny isn't here!"

Charmaine chuckled.

Again, they heard the commotion in the hallway. Travis had opened John's dressing room door and was carrying two trunks into the chamber. Charmaine was instantly annoyed. "Mr. Thornfield," she called when he reappeared empty handed, "what are you doing?"

"Delivering Mrs. London's things to her room, Miss. Why do you ask?"

"You have the wrong room," she replied.

"Master Paul told me to bring them here, Miss Ryan."

"Take them to another room," she insisted. "Two doors down will be fine."

"I beg your pardon?"

Paul and Anne arrived. "Is something the matter?" Paul interrupted.

"Miss Ryan seems to think that I'm placing the baggage in the wrong room."

Paul turned quizzical eyes on Charmaine, and Anne's gaze followed.

Charmaine watched her nose wrinkle disdainfully and knew what she was thinking: *So this is the governess, Miss Ryan, the daughter of a murderer – worse than common.* Charmaine tore her eyes away and looked pointedly at Paul.

"May I speak with you privately, Paul?" she pressed, pleased when Anne appeared aghast that she had used his given name. "It will only take a moment."

Paul seemed oblivious to the silent exchange. With a courteous smile, he excused himself and led Charmaine into the nursery.

"Those are John's quarters," she said when he had closed the door behind him. "Mrs. London can stay in another room."

"What difference does it make?" Paul asked, entirely befuddled.

"Those chambers belong to John and shouldn't be disturbed. He was pushed out when I took his room. Now it's happening again. It's not right."

"But he's not here, Charmaine. I don't think he would care…"

"*I* care," she replied, unmindful of his annoyance. "And what if he should come home for your celebration?"

"That is not likely," Paul replied, taken aback by her disappointed expression. "Very well," he replied, rubbing the back of his neck.

He returned to Anne and directed Travis to move her bags to the next suite. "The children are early risers, Anne," he explained urbanely. "You'll have peace and quiet if we place a little distance between your quarters and theirs."

"How kind of you," she smiled artificially, glancing Charmaine's way.

"Would you like to join us for lunch?" Charmaine asked from the door.

The young woman turned from her task of hanging dresses in the armoire. "I have to unpack all these gowns first," she told Charmaine and the twins.

"It's getting late," Charmaine remarked. "You must be hungry. Can't you finish this after lunch?"

"I had better do it now. Mrs. London will be furi– upset if they're wrinkled."

"Well then, let us help, so you can have lunch, too. Come, girls."

Charmaine stepped into the chamber, followed closely by the twins, and proceeded to take one beautiful garment after another out of the traveling cases.

"I'm Charmaine Ryan, Yvette and Jeannette's governess," she offered, extending a hand to the lady's maid. "Welcome to the Duvoisin manor."

"I'm Mercedes Wells. It is nice to meet you." For the first time, the young woman smiled. Charmaine knew she had just made a friend.

Thursday, March 1, 1838

George admired Mercedes from the armchair where he sat, as he'd done for the past three nights after dinner. Paul had invited Anne London's personal maid to join them. Though George was pleased to enjoy her company, if only from afar, the words he'd exchanged with Paul earlier at the mill still rankled him.

"Not this one, Paul – you're not going to have this one."

Paul threw him a puzzled look. "What are you talking about?"

"You know goddamn well what I'm talking about – encouraging Miss Wells to join the family after dinner."

Paul remained bewildered. "She and Charmaine have struck up a friendship. Don't tell me you're annoyed that I've invited her to…" Suddenly, Paul was laughing. "Oh, now I understand. You're jealous."

George's face reddened. "Just leave her alone."

"She's not beautiful, George," Paul teased, "comely, but not beautiful."

"The hell she's not!"

Paul chuckled again. "If she were beautiful, my friend, do you think she'd be Anne London's attendant? I assure you, Anne would never place a delectable dish so near her own plate. She's far too vain."

George remained tightlipped, simmering.

"I'm not interested in Miss Wells, George. I leave her to you."

Mercedes Wells *was* beautiful – in George's eyes, the most beautiful woman in the room. Abruptly, he stood and walked over to her chair.

She looked up in surprise.

"Miss Wells," he heard himself say, "will you take a stroll with me in the gardens?" He was elated when she murmured, 'Yes'.

In the days that followed, Charmaine saw very little of Paul. He was busy with preparations for the celebration, and when he was free, Anne London rarely left his side. She now commanded his Saturdays.

Charmaine and Mercedes' friendship continued to grow. Mercedes was a sensible, down-to-earth woman, with a keen perception of people and their motives. Because she was Anne London's lady's assistant, she was at the widow's beck and call for anything and everything. Up and out of bed well before dawn, she laid out Anne's clothes and placed her breakfast order before she awoke. When Anne did rise, Mercedes didn't know a moment's peace until long after lunch, shuttling food trays to and from the widow's chambers and helping with her morning toilette and coiffure, a laborious process that took hours. Afterward, she ran errands: posting Anne's letters, acquiring incidentals from the mercantile, bringing her drinks, or fetching her books from the library. Anne was condescending and abusive, constantly threatening to dismiss her for the most minor infraction or mishap.

Anne and Agatha got along famously. When Paul wasn't around, they spent much of their time together. Agatha was engrossed in planning every detail of the affair, from receiving invitation responses to selecting flower arrangements, preparing menus, organizing table settings, hiring musicians, establishing lodgings and other accommodations. Anne advised Agatha on all these matters, and they spent many an hour locked away in Agatha's boudoir.

Mercedes despised Anne London, but she was paid well, and she needed her job. Like Charmaine, her mother had died a few years earlier, after a prolonged illness. Mercedes' father was a stable-master on a Virginia estate, and she had an elder brother, also a stable-master, who had a wife and children. Her father was rarely around, and Mercedes felt it was time that she set out on her own in the world. Because she'd grown up around horses, she was an experienced rider.

When Yvette told Frederic this, he gave the young woman free rein to ride Colette's mare, Chastity, since the horse was in dire need of regular workouts. So in the afternoons when Anne went off with Agatha, Charmaine, Mercedes and the twins went riding to all corners of the island, having a fabulous time.

Whenever he could, George returned to the manor for lunch, and after work, he avoided Dulcie's, preferring to go straight home. Occasionally, he'd get lucky and Mercedes would go for a walk with him after dinner. He despised the way Anne London treated her. Much as he wanted to defend her, he didn't dare, certain that Anne would dismiss her on the spot.

Some weeks before Paul's gala, George asked Mercedes to be his partner at the banquet and ball. She accepted eagerly, but the very next day, she told him that Anne had forbidden her to attend.

"This isn't a servant's affair," Anne had remonstrated sarcastically. "It's a business engagement and a society soirée, reserved for gentry with social status. It will be very embarrassing for Mr. Duvoisin and for me if you show your face there. I will not allow it."

Friday, March 9, 1838

Anne had been on the island less than two weeks, and already Paul had had enough of her. Out of deference to her father, and because she knew a good many influential men from Virginia, he escorted her around Charmantes, as every polite host should. He was glad when she went off with Agatha to gossip and plan. Guests would begin arriving in just over a fortnight.

Today, he was with his father, handling routine business that had been neglected with the imminent unveiling of the new island and fleet of ships.

Frederic rubbed his brow. "I hope there's enough cash to cover this," he mused. "We may have to liquidate other assets."

"I thought the same thing," Paul agreed. "I'll talk to Stephen about it later."

"You'll be seeing him again?" Frederic asked with surprise.

Paul sighed. "With Anne here, Agatha has invited him to sup with us."

Frederic leaned back in his chair and considered his son for a moment. "And this 'relationship' with Anne London," he proceeded cautiously. "Are you interested in this woman?"

Paul shook his head. "There is no relationship, Father, but it is in my interest to be hospitable while she's here. Anne knows many people, has many connections through her deceased husband."

"I see," Frederic breathed. "And what of Charmaine Ryan?"

Paul was confounded. "What about Charmaine?"

"You've spent a good deal of time with her over the past five months. I have eyes you know. I can see how you look at her."

Paul was embarrassed. He'd never had a heart-to-heart talk with his father about a woman before. When he didn't speak, Frederic continued. "You could do worse than Charmaine, you know."

"What are you saying, Father?" Paul asked, stupefied.

"You could do worse than Charmaine," he reiterated. "You don't need to marry for money. Why not choose a woman who will make you happy? I could be mistaken, but I think you'd be far happier with Charmaine than with Mrs. London."

Paul smiled broadly. "There is no comparison."

"I thought not," Frederic nodded, turning back to the documents before him, happy that he'd finally found the right moment to speak his mind.

Paul was heartened that Frederic cared – was concerned that money might influence his choice in a spouse.

He suddenly thought of the banquet and ball. As yet, he had no partner. Inspired, he coveted Charmaine in that role. *She should be very pleased if I ask her. How many other governesses have received such an invitation?*

His mind raced ahead to that night. Charmaine was in his arms, and they were dancing the first waltz. She was smiling sweetly up at him, blushing, like she had that first year, before John had come home and interfered. The evening would be magical, and anything could happen.

Charmaine Duvoisin – yes – he liked the sound of it.

Sunday, March 11, 1838

Like every evening since Anne London arrived, Charmaine ushered the girls from the dinner table straight to their rooms. "I don't want to go up there yet," Yvette complained, but Charmaine had given her a reprimanding scowl.

An hour later, Paul said goodnight and went to the nursery. He found Charmaine reading to his sisters, who groaned when he asked to speak to her privately. "Why don't you go down to the drawing room for a few minutes?" he queried. "Fatima has set out some delicious pastries."

Charmaine gave her consent, sighing as they left. "You'll send them back up to me?" she asked, certain that she'd struggle to extricate them from the parlor later on.

"There is something important I want to ask you," he said instead.

Disconcerted by his stern face, she was sure she'd done something wrong.

"Has anyone asked to accompany you to the dinner and ball?"

Charmaine looked down at her folded hands. "No," she whispered. She thought of Mercedes, and her throat constricted. He was about to forbid her to attend the spectacular affair, too.

"Well then," he inhaled. "*I* would like to be your escort."

Astonished, her head snapped up before she could conceal her tears, but they told Paul that he had made her very happy. He smiled devilishly, and she felt like throwing herself into his arms.

"I gather that is a 'yes'?" he asked.

"Yes!" she cried with disarming exuberance.

He pulled her to him and savored the kiss she was willing to give. His embrace tightened, and his kiss grew passionate. Abruptly, he tore away, unsettled by the spell she had cast upon him, his breathing ragged, his eyes smoldering with desire. "I had better say goodnight, Mademoiselle," he said lustily, "lest I take you to my room."

Her blush thrilled him, his desires fanned by the realization that his words still affected her. "I will send the girls up to you," he murmured.

Charmaine waltzed around the nursery when he was gone. *The ball! Paul's partner! It didn't seem possible!* She needed a gown! Tomorrow, she would have to ride into town. She would invite Mercedes to come along. Yes, Mercedes could help her pick out the very best one!

On his way back to the drawing room, Paul wondered why he had been content to wait so long to make love to Charmaine Ryan. She was the only woman he had ever waited for, and yet, if he desired her, if he loved her as he was beginning to believe he did, why was he content to wait? Sometimes, he was able to put her from his mind completely, but other times, her stubbornness not to submit vexed him to distraction. Didn't she realize that if she pleased him in bed, he'd do the gentlemanly thing and marry her? Perhaps he'd just grown comfortable knowing that she would always be here waiting for him. Sooner or later, desire would prevail, and they would consummate their love. Sooner or later, she would scorn her empty bed and fall into his. Sooner or later she would want to become a woman, his woman. Perhaps she'd succumb sooner than later – on the night of the ball.

Chapter 2

Sunday, March 18, 1838
Richmond, Virginia

Michael Andrews had heard talk of Paul Duvoisin's gala celebration every Sunday now for the past month. Greeting his congregation after Mass, it was a favorite topic of conversation among the clutches of chatting parishioners gathered outside St. Jude's. Anticipation was building for the weeklong event.

Michael last saw John two months ago. He was headed for New York and hadn't mentioned anything about his brother's debut. Michael wondered if he planned to attend. Though he knew John wouldn't have dreamed of going home to Charmantes last year this time, John's unexpected trip last summer made *this* visit a possibility. Something urged Michael to find out, so after dinner, he went to John's townhouse. The butler answered and told him that John had returned from New York, but had gone directly to the family plantation for the planting season. He wasn't due back in Richmond until mid-April. Perplexed, Michael climbed back into his buggy and flicked the reins. He was only a short distance down the street when intuition compelled him to turn back. The steward opened the door again and gave Michael directions to the plantation. He would set out first thing in the morning. Mondays were quiet at the refuge, so he could afford to be away.

Monday, March 19, 1838

Michael arrived at Freedom around four o'clock in the afternoon. Only the house staff was at the quaint plantation house. John had left with his overseer at dawn and might not return from the tobacco fields until dusk. A manservant let Michael in, and he settled into the parlor with tea, biscuits, and a book. Michael tried to read, but his thoughts meandered.

He'd been worried about John for months now, seeing through his jovial front, disturbed by the despair in his eyes, like the John he'd met four and a half years before. Michael wondered again about the man's trip home – the single place on earth where John had vowed never to return. *Give him time. You gave him time before and he talked...*

Michael shuddered with the memory of that 'talk'. They had known each other for only six months. John had just received news from Charmantes, upsetting news. With Marie's insistence, Michael finally drove to John's Richmond townhouse and heard the man's confession that fine spring day.

He was angry that Michael was there. "Did Marie send you?" he bit out, half-drunk. "That's the last time I tell a woman anything."

"She didn't *tell* me anything, John," Michael refuted, "she's just worried."

John scoffed at the answer, but Michael was not easily dismissed. "John... when are you going to tell *me* what happened? Perhaps I can help."

Gulping down a mouthful of whisky, John eyed the priest derisively. "I don't need you to hear my confession, *Father*."

"Not a confession, John. Just a heart-to-heart, between friends."

Taking another long draw off the glass, John gazed out the window.

"You're not the only one who has done things he's not proud of, John," Michael offered when the accumulating minutes became uncomfortable.

"Oh, really?" John sneered dubiously. "And what could you have possibly done, Michael? A little nip and tuck in the sacristy with the consecrated wine?"

Michael welcomed the sarcasm. "I'll confess if you confess."

John's brow raised in interest. "You've got a deal, Father."

Michael froze. He hadn't thought John would take the bait.

"Well?" John nudged, eyes intent, relishing his distress. "I'm waiting..."

Michael cleared his throat. "When I was much younger..."

"Yes?" John prodded again, leaning back against the liquor cabinet, crossing his legs and folding his arms over his chest.

"I broke my sacred vows of celibacy – with a woman, whom I loved..."

Silence. "That's it?" John asked disappointedly. "That's all?"

"*That's all?*"

John chuckled and shook his head. "At least it was with a woman. That will be nine *Hail Marys*, three *Our Fathers,* and one *Act of Contrition*."

With downcast eyes, Michael smiled, but he wasn't going to release John from his end of the bargain. "Your turn, John."

John leveled a piercing gaze on him, his reticence gone. "I took my father's wife to my bed and fathered a baby with her. When I bragged to him about our affair, we nearly came to blows, causing a seizure that's left him an invalid. I fled Charmantes, leaving her to contend with his wrath alone. I hated him so much that I prayed, in *your holy sanctuary,* for him to die so that I could be with her and my child..." Swallowing his pain, John laughed wickedly. "Tell me, Father, does it get any worse than that?"

Michael saw through the evil. "You love this woman, don't you?"

"More than my own life," John freely admitted, turning away as if to barricade his grief. "My son was born three weeks ago... Pierre," he whispered hoarsely, "his name is Pierre." After an interminable silence, he looked over his shoulder. "Tell me, Michael, if I suffer a lifetime never knowing the boy, will I be forgiven?"

"You've been forgiven already, John."

"No, Michael," John denied fervently, irately. "To be forgiven, one must feel remorse. I'm not sorry; Colette belonged to me!"

Michael learned the whole story that night, leaving John close to dawn. John had vowed never to return to Charmantes, allowing Colette, the love of his life, to live the life *she* had chosen. He would punish himself by never beholding his little boy. And the world would know Pierre Duvoisin as his younger brother. It was Colette's choice, and now it would be his.

But, John *had* returned to Charmantes. *Why?*

Around dinnertime, Michael finally heard voices and looked out the window. John was walking up to the house with another man, presumably his overseer. They were dirty and sweaty.

"What the hell are you doing here?" John asked when they walked through the door, his crooked smile broadening, hand extended. "No, let me guess... Pope Gregory found out the truth about you, and you need a job."

"The truth about me?" the priest asked warily, taking his hand.

"Admit it, Father, you've been using your priestly powers to turn bread and wine into steak and ale. So where's dinner?"

Michael laughed along with John's overseer, sending his eyes heavenward. They went into the kitchen for drinks, and John introduced Michael to Brian. John grew serious and asked, "What brings you all the way out here?"

Michael looked at Brian, who took the cue that he wanted to speak to John privately, stepping out the back door and heading toward a row of cabins in the distance. The cook, who'd been running furiously between cookhouse and kitchen, disappeared as well. Michael and John sat down at the table, cold glasses of water in hand.

"Parishioners have been mentioning your brother, Paul, lately," the priest began. "There's talk of a big celebration for the launch of his shipping concern."

John shrugged. "He's been developing another of the family's islands for over a year now. My father gave it to him. He'll run his own shipping line from it. So?"

"I don't mean to meddle, but a few of my congregants say that they'll be leaving shortly for the affair. Aren't you going?"

John leaned back in the chair. "I wasn't planning on it."

"Why not? Wouldn't your brother appreciate your support?"

John scratched his head. "Have you forgotten my vow, Michael?"

"John," the priest breathed, "I know you traveled there this past fall."

John was surprised, but Michael continued. "Your butler told me."

John bowed his head to the unwelcome memories and his heart began to race.

"Are you going to tell me what happened? Why did you go back? You said you'd never go back."

John massaged his brow, and the room fell disturbingly quiet as he searched for words. "Colette wrote to me. My friend, George... he delivered the letter.

He had trouble finding me. I was in New York, and it took him weeks to track me down. By the time I got home, Colette was dead." John's throat tightened, and he could say no more.

He still loves her, Michael realized sadly. *After all these years, he still loves her.* "And the boy?" Michael braved to ask.

"I killed him, too," John pronounced somberly, his voice cracking. "I killed him, too." When he regained his composure, he told Michael the whole story.

"It's over now," Michael comforted. "It's time to move on."

"I know that," John agreed, "and I am."

"Then why not go back?" Michael prodded. "You are invited, yes?"

"In effect."

"In effect? What does that mean?"

"My father invited me, which is as good as Paul inviting me."

"Your father?" Michael asked in surprise. "So why aren't you going?"

John's grim silence was his reply.

"Are you angry at your brother?"

"No. I hope his business succeeds beyond his wildest dreams."

"It's your father. That's the issue," Michael pressed. "You still hate him."

John clenched his jaw. "I'm not going back because every time I do, there's a disaster. It's best for everyone concerned if I just stay away."

"But your father has invited you. That means he's forgiven you."

"That means," John sneered, "that he wants all his guests to believe that we are one big, *happy*, wealthy family – for my brother's sake."

"No, John. It means he's forgiven you. I know it. I think you know it, too. He's never invited you home before, has he?"

"No, he hasn't."

"John," Michael implored, "if you ever want to get on with your life, you have to face this. Do it now, while your father wants it, while he's willing to forgive you. You may never have this chance again."

"I don't want his forgiveness," John confessed acidly. "And he certainly won't get mine."

Astounded by the ferocious declaration, the depth of John's prolonged bitterness, Michael shook his head sadly. "Perhaps there is more to it than you understand, John. Is it possible that your father loved this woman, too?"

John snorted, repulsed by the idea. "He married my aunt not three months after Colette died, Michael. So you tell me – is that love?"

Michael inhaled sharply. The sordid story only grew worse. Even so, he rejected the obvious answer. "Perhaps you can't forgive your father now, but you should accept *his* forgiveness," he reasoned. "Go back for your brother's sake – and your sisters'. I'll wager they'll be thrilled to see you."

John pondered Michael's words. He thought about his last visit to the island and how dramatically his life had improved. Though Colette's death had cut deeply when he'd first arrived, it changed nothing really. He had long resigned himself to life without her. And lately, even the pain of Pierre's death was subsiding. Because he didn't discount the existence of God, entertaining the belief that Pierre was with his mother in the afterlife consoled him. He was beginning to step away from the past. Charmaine had been right; now he *could* think of Pierre dumping sand on his head and chuckle about it, rather than fight back tears. He knew Yvette and Jeannette would be overjoyed to see him, and then there was Charmaine. In fact, seeing her motivated him to go back more than anything else. He might even be lucky and find that she wasn't married to Paul yet.

"Where has this anger gotten you and your family anyway, John?" Michael asked. "Isn't it time to let it go? It appears your father wants to bury it, so why not you? The future might be brighter than you believe possible."

Suddenly, John was disgusted with the whole matter. Michael made it sound so simple. Why go through that again? "I'll think about it," he lied.

The priest decided it was best not to pressure him and walked to the vestibule.

John followed, dismayed and disgruntled, certain that he had prodded Michael into a hasty departure. "You're not setting out now," he objected. "The sun will soon be setting."

"I have a lamp in the carriage," Michael replied, pulling on his coat, "I also passed an inn along the way. If need be, I can stop there. In either case, I have to get back."

"Would a bit more money help?" John asked, certain that his friend was working himself into the grave.

"You've been far too generous already, and it's better if I keep busy."

"Busy with work or with killing yourself?"

Michael's brow lifted. "Is it that obvious?"

"I'm surprised that Marie hasn't put her foot down and made you take some time off," John said with a twinkle in his eye, perplexed when the priest's face went white. "What's the matter?"

"Marie is dead," Michael pronounced. "I thought you knew, John. I thought everyone knew. It's been over two years now."

"*Dead?*" John was shocked. During his few brief visits to the refuge, he hadn't thought to ask for her, taking it for granted that she was alive and well. Two years and he hadn't seen her! He was immediately angry with himself. Was he so caught up in his own misery that he overlooked his friends? Marie had been a savior, a sympathetic confidant who had helped him through the worst times of his life – the months following Pierre's conception and birth. "Dead," he reiterated as the truth set in. "But how?"

"It was terrible–" Michael struggled to explain.

John just shook his head, for he knew that the priest, this good man, this equally good friend, had loved Marie. "Michael, I'm sorry, so sorry."

"She was a very special woman, John."

"Yes, Michael, she was."

Words exhausted, they pondered the finality of death. The bleak mood was broken when John strode into the small library and rummaged through his desk drawers. He finally found what he was looking for and walked back to the hallway, studying the envelope in his hands.

"Funny," he said, "Marie gave this to me years ago, and–" he looked up at Michael "–she asked me to give it to you should anything happen to her." He gingerly extended the missive to the priest.

Michael accepted the letter, cradling it as if it were a precious gift.

"Aren't you going to open it?"

Michael broke the seal, removed the single paper, and began to read. His hands were trembling by the time he'd finished. He looked up at John, tears in his eyes. "I have a daughter," he whispered. "Dear God… a daughter."

Burying his face in his hands, he slumped into the nearby armchair. Now he knew why Marie had deserted him twenty years ago. He believed it was because of that one intimate encounter. For nearly six years, he'd worried over what had become of her and chastised himself for having shamed her. When she did return one bitterly cold day, she had a young girl with her – her daughter. She was married, she was happy, she told him. She and her husband had started a family. Marie kept him at arm's length, so Michael believed her story. They never talked about what had happened between them, but he wondered if she thought about it as often as he did.

Suddenly, he was furious: furious with himself – the priesthood – God. He should have turned his back on the ministry when he knew he loved Marie. She would still be alive if he had just walked away!

"Are you all right?" John asked, shaken by the man's expression.

"I'm not even certain where she is," Michael said, his anger gone, enervation seeping in.

"Perhaps Marie placed her with a good family. She's likely surrounded by brothers and sisters."

Michael looked up at him quizzically. "No, John. She'd be a young woman by now – nineteen or twenty."

John was surprised once again.

"I knew Marie for many years," Michael explained. "She was orphaned and raised at St. Jude's. I was young when I was assigned there, and she was beautiful, inside and out. It's no excuse for what I did, but I did love her. I still love her."

"I know that. So why berate yourself? You loved her, and she you."

"That *love* forced her into a loveless marriage."

"Marriage?" John puzzled. "She never mentioned a husband to me."

"She rarely spoke of her life outside the refuge," Michael whispered. "Apparently, she chose it to spare me the shame of fornication. According to this, she didn't want me to leave the priesthood, something she feared I'd contemplate if I had known about the baby. So she sacrificed herself instead."

Laying the letter in his lap, Michael pressed his hands together in prayer and brought his fingers to his lips, tapping them in deep thought. "Now, what am I to do, John? Do I track down my daughter? Do I tell her that I'm her father? I know she despised the man she thought was her father."

"How would you know that?"

"She grew up at the refuge, attended Sister Elizabeth's school. I heard many of her confessions."

"Find her first," John suggested, "and make certain that she's all right. You can decide about telling her the truth later."

"You're right," the priest nodded, reconciled. "Marie would want that."

A rap on the door drew them away from Michael's problem. Annoyed by the interruption, John opened it to five men staring up at him from the lawn below, their horses tethered to the hitching post at the edge of the drive.

"Good evening, Mr. Duvoisin," said a sixth man who'd parted from the pack and stood on the porch. "We'd like a moment of your time."

"Concerning?" John queried.

"Two runaway slaves. We have reason to believe they are in the area and traveling at night."

John listened, expressionless. When he didn't respond, another man stepped forward with a newspaper clipping, which he shoved into John's hand. John glanced down at it. "A strong buck and his woman – spotted about thirty miles south of here the night before last. Take a good look at that paper, Mr. Duvoisin, and tell me if you've seen any nigger fittin' that description."

A reward of one hundred fifty dollars was offered for the fugitive. The article gave the date of his escape, the state he'd fled from, his owner's name, and a description. The bounty increased the further from home the slave was captured.

John shrugged, passing the paper to Michael. "They all look alike to me."

The men grunted in agreement, the remark putting them at ease. The ringleader remained staunch. "We understand that you've freed all your slaves, Mr. Duvoisin, that they work for you here. There'd be a high price to pay if your niggers were harboring someone else's property. Best we speak with them."

"The men and women on this plantation know better, Mr....?" and John waited patiently for the name.

"Reynolds," the man supplied.

"Mr. Reynolds," John acknowledged. "They'd lose their position here. Unlike the Yankees, I don't fault the South for using slave labor. After all, my family's wealth has been built on it. Freeing my slaves was a business decision, nothing more. I find they work harder because they're paid; I don't need a whip, and I don't have to hire expensive bounty hunters like you to track them down. They don't run."

The men eyed him suspiciously, but could not refute what he said.

"All the same, we'd like to see their quarters," the first man replied.

"As you wish," John relented.

He descended the porch and led them to the humble Negro quarters behind the plantation house, passing Stuart's abode first. He stepped out and nodded to them. "My production manager," John explained.

As they approached, the children swiftly abandoned their games. John singled out one cabin and rapped on the door. Brian opened almost immediately, evidence that he'd been watching anxiously from the window.

"Brian," John began, "these gentlemen are looking for two runaway slaves from North Carolina. They were spotted south of here two nights ago. Is that right, gentlemen?" They nodded. "Have you or anyone else seen them?"

"No, sir."

"Unfortunately, I cannot take your word for it," John said. "I'm sure these gentlemen will not rest until they have searched your home."

The men mumbled in agreement.

"Yes, sir," Brian answered. Stepping aside, he allowed two of them in.

The others paired off and searched each cabin. They came up empty handed, and Reynolds turned to John. "We're sorry to have troubled you, Mr. Duvoisin."

John smiled. "No trouble at all. I'll keep an eye out for your runaways."

They trudged back to the main house and mounted up. John climbed the front steps, rubbing the back of his neck. When they were out of sight, Michael came out onto the porch. "They're gone?" he queried anxiously.

"They're gone," John affirmed.

Michael still clutched the news clipping in his fist.

"May I have that?" John asked. "I keep them," he explained, "every one of them, as a reminder of what I'm doing and why."

Michael handed the paper over. John slipped it into his pocket and said, "Let us see if they made it to *Freedom* last night."

Michael chuckled, and together, they retraced John's steps to the cabins.

Stuart came out onto the porch again, smiling in relief.

"So they *are* here?" John asked.

"Yes, John, since dawn, but I didn't know you were up at the house."

"No harm done," John replied. "Today continues to be their lucky day. Since there are only two of them, and Father Michael will be setting out for Richmond in the morning, he can transport them to the refuge in his buggy."

Michael nodded; it looked as if he'd be spending the night.

They slid a heavy, crude hutch off two moveable floorboards, and the couple emerged from the crawlspace beneath Stuart's cabin. Nettie gave them dinner, then prepared a bed for them, and at the crack of dawn the next morning, they were on their way. The pregnant woman sat beside Michael and did not look out of place; the advertisement had not described her and she could pass for his housekeeper. Her husband, however, was tucked uncomfortably behind the carriage seat, concealed under a blanket. Still, it was better than walking.

John wished them well and pressed some money into the woman's hands.

"Thank you, sir," she whispered, grabbing hold of his arm and cradling it to her heart. "God bless you and your family."

"And you, Ma'am," he rejoined. He shook Michael's hand and said, "I'll stop by when I'm back in Richmond."

The priest flicked the reins, setting the buggy in motion.

Saturday, March 24, 1837   Charmantes

Charmaine and Mercedes stepped out of Maddy Thompson's cottage, in no hurry to return to the manor. Charmaine sighed contentedly. Two weeks ago, she had worried about what she would wear. She was determined to turn every eye at the banquet and ball, but the dresses on display in the mercantile were far from elegant. Certainly, the other maids and matrons would be wearing gowns purchased abroad, in Paris and in London. Paul had said as much when he insisted that he purchase her entire ensemble. Thankfully, he and Maddy had come up with a solution. Fashionable gowns were advertised in the magazines on the mercantile counter. Charmaine would choose amongst the finest fabrics in stock, and Maddy, who had been a seamstress for a couturier in Charleston, would do the rest. So, for the past two Saturdays, Charmaine had stood like a statue on a pedestal in Maddy's parlor as the gown took shape. One final fitting and it would be ready, and Mercedes would take care of any minor adjustments at the house.

They crossed the busy street and headed toward the livery. A large sign hung in Dulcie's window: *Attention Sailors: No Vacancies*, and in small letters: *lodging available at the warehouse.* The most influential guests would be staying in the mansions on Charmantes and Espoir, and Frederic was paying Dulcie well to accommodate the others. Earlier in the week, the saloon had been whitewashed, and the shutters repainted. Today, the second story windows were thrown wide, and six women were in the side yard bleaching the bed linens. The whole town was busy preparing for this unprecedented event.

When Charmaine and Mercedes turned their mounts onto the main road toward the manor, Charmaine couldn't contain her excitement. "Thank you, Mercedes, thank you so very much. I just wish you could be there, too."

Mercedes discounted the sympathetic remark. "Don't worry about me. You'll enjoy it for the two of us. And on Paul's arm, no less! I just can't believe it. I really thought he'd ask Anne. She had her eyes fastened on his brother last year. She'd kill for that spot, you know."

Charmaine smiled, the pleasantness of the day expanding.

"Why *did* he ask you?" Mercedes queried, making the most of Charmaine's elation, yet hoping she wouldn't think her impertinent.

"Paul and I have grown very close, especially over the past five months."

"Close?"

"He's a friend, Mercedes, a very *good* friend."

"A friend?" Mercedes mused doubtfully. "Charmaine, do you realize how many girls would give an arm and a leg to be in your shoes? How jealous they will be? And you're telling me that you're just 'good friends'? Aren't you attracted to him? Why, if he looked my way, I'd blush scarlet!"

Charmaine laughed in spite of herself, recalling those early heart-thundering days when all she did was blush. Nowadays, she kept her composure around Paul without a worry, and she wondered what had changed.

"Well?" Mercedes asked, leaning forward.

"Well what?"

"Well – are you in love with him? Is he *interested* in you?"

"Interested," Charmaine mumbled. *You should be interested to know that Paul has but one interest in you...* Why had she thought of that? "Yes," Charmaine smiled, "he is interested in me."

"Then what are you waiting for?"

"What do you mean, what am I waiting for?"

"Go after him! Don't let him get away! Don't allow Anne to sink her claws in! You'll never have an opportunity like this knocking at your door again."

Saturday, March 31, 1838

The ball was fast approaching, just a week away. Travis had been stationed in town days ago, receiving ships as they made port and establishing the prestigious visitors at their assigned lodgings. Many had already arrived. Tomorrow afternoon there would be a reception at Dulcie's to commence the weeklong conference.

This morning, the breakfast table buzzed with happy conversation, filled to capacity with guests. Everybody was talking except Frederic, who remained distant, his eyes solemn. Charmaine wondered if he was as downtrodden as she. *Was he thinking of John? Did he remember that today was Pierre and Colette's birthday? That his grandson would have turned four or that the anniversary of Colette's death was just a week away?* Charmaine sighed with a heavy heart.

As if reading her thoughts, Frederic spoke directly to her. "Miss Ryan, you seem unusually pensive today. Is something wrong?"

"You have been uncommonly quiet this morning, too," she courageously replied, "for the very same reasons, I believe."

All eyes were instantly on them, the noisy table falling silent.

"What reasons?" Agatha queried, eyeing Charmaine suspiciously.

Frederic smiled sadly and answered laconically. "Miss Ryan is very astute. I'm afraid I shall be busy all day, Miss Ryan, and need you to mind the twins. Perhaps a ride with my daughters will lift your spirits."

"Yes sir," she whispered dismally, certain that *nothing* could do that.

Yvette and Jeannette lit up with Frederic's suggestion and quickly ran off to the kitchen to invite Mercedes. As Anne opened her mouth to object, Frederic intervened. "Mrs. London, I assume you will be assisting my wife today?" With her slight nod, he said, "Then why not allow Miss Wells to accompany my daughters? Agatha's itinerary should only require the services of the house staff."

Not wishing to appear cruel, Anne smiled unhappily. She would have a private word with Mercedes later.

Heading toward the paddock, Jeannette noticed a cloud of dust kicked up on the dirt road beyond the entry gates. "A rider!" she exclaimed.

Yvette stopped dead in her tracks, eyes riveted to the road.

"What is it, Yvette?" Jeannette queried, turning to her sister.

"It's Phantom!" she screamed, dashing across the lawns, "and Johnny!"

Jeannette broke into a run behind her, arriving at the gates just as Phantom cantered through them. "Johnny!" they squealed, grabbing at him before he could dismount. He jumped off the stallion and hugged them with a jubilant laugh. "This is wonderful! You must see Mademoiselle Charmaine! And Papa, too!"

A stable-hand hurried over and took charge of Phantom. John slung his knapsack over his shoulder and walked up the lawns, the girls on either side of him. Jeannette's arm was clasped tightly around his waist, and Yvette beamed up at him as if he were a mirage that might disappear if she dared to look away.

"So, what have I missed while I was gone?" he asked, squeezing Jeannette's shoulder.

"Papa spends Saturdays with us," she gushed, "and we have ball dresses!"

"I'm the bookkeeper for the mill!" Yvette interjected.

"We went to Espoir, and Mademoiselle Charmaine can ride Dapple now!"

John was gladdened by their enthusiasm. Their joyous reception always made him feel welcome here, that this *was* his home. He pulled them closer, wondering where Charmaine was.

Charmaine stepped out of the house, adjusting her bonnet as she went. Her heart caught in her throat. There was John, walking toward her! Her eyes feasted on him: the cap cocked to the back of his head, his wavy brown hair falling on his brow, his self-assured gait. In that rush of joy, the urge to fly down the steps and throw her arms around him was overwhelming, and she had all she could do to hold to her spot. He looked up as he arrived with the twins at the foot of the portico, and their eyes finally met.

He drank in the sight of her: the plain, well-worn riding dress, her shaking fingers belatedly tying the strings to her bonnet under her chin, and her large brown eyes betraying her excitement to see him. Instantly, he was indescribably pleased that he had come back, and he inhaled slowly, relishing the ineffable elation expanding in his breast. He *had* missed her, more than he'd realized. Jeannette scurried into the house, eager to tell her father the good news. He hardly noticed.

"You look well, Mademoiselle," he said in that crisp voice, long denied.

Blood thundered in her ears, and her heart pounded in her chest. His regard was warm as he and Yvette climbed the steps. A crooked smile broke across his lips, bathing her in another wave of happiness. "I am," she breathed, tilting her head back to study his face. "How are you?"

"I'm fine – just fine."

"You've come home for the celebration?" she commented more than asked.

"Yes," he replied, "my father invited me. Apparently, he'd like to mend some fences." She nodded, and his eyes went to Mercedes, who had stepped out of the house with her. "Good morning, Miss Mercedes."

Mercedes murmured a quick greeting and looked at the ground.

Charmaine suffered a pang of jealousy before remembering that Mercedes had made John's acquaintance through Anne London. She was delighted when he chuckled and turned back to her.

"Will you be staying long?" she asked, hopeful that the answer was yes.

"That depends," he replied, sizing up her attire. "I see you are on your way out."

Charmaine was about to respond when the front door opened and Frederic joined them. His eyes glinted, and his smile widened.

"John," he started, "welcome home."

John fought a sure and congealing repugnance, the impulse to retreat.

"Come inside," Frederic motioned. "There is cool lemonade in the study."

John hesitated, then forced himself forward. The twins tagged along, but Frederic stopped them. "Girls, go for your ride with Miss Ryan and Miss Wells. You will have time with your brother when you return."

"Come, girls," Charmaine commanded, "the ponies are waiting, and if we dally any longer, it will be too hot to go."

They reluctantly capitulated, turning away from their beloved brother. But Charmaine's eyes followed the men into the house. There was Agatha, standing in the foyer, her hate-filled regard reserved for John. Then, the door closed.

Mercedes stepped nearer Charmaine. "You're in love with him," she murmured close to her ear.

Charmaine spun round, shocked. "Don't be silly!"

Mercedes chuckled knowingly. "No wonder Paul is just a 'good friend'."

Paul greeted John with a handshake, amazed that he had returned. John clasped an arm around his shoulder. "So, Paul, this is your big week. Are you ready?"

"Never more in my life," he replied, surprised by John's affable manner.

Anne descended the staircase and turned her head aside in blatant disdain when she saw John. That suited him just fine.

Everyone stepped into the study, rejoining Stephen Westphal, whose anxious eyes darted from John to Frederic, a folder clasped tightly to his chest. Frederic resumed his seat behind the desk, while Paul and John took the chairs across from it. Agatha walked over to the French doors, and Anne perched on the settee. Felicia scurried in with lemonade and poured everyone a glass.

"I gather you came on Paul's ship," Frederic said. "How was the crossing?"

"The sea was calm, the wind strong. We made the voyage in no time. A fine packet, Paul. Those makeshift apartments were very cozy. When your guests got a glimpse of Dulcie's, they ran back to the captain to make reservations for the week!" Agatha frowned, but John's deviltry only intensified. "Yes, a fine vessel, perfect once the leaks are repaired, but there are always flaws on a virgin voyage."

Paul's eyes darkened apprehensively. "Leaks? There shouldn't be any–"

"Not to worry, Paulie," John chuckled. "Everything was just fine."

The jest registered, and Paul laughed, too. "What is the latest news from the States, John?"

"That depends where you are in the States."

"Why not start in New York?" Agatha interjected, her gaze steely upon him.

He eyed her suspiciously. "What would you like to know, Auntie?"

"It's not what I'd like to know," she returned smugly, her voice sweet, "it is more a matter of what your father would like to know."

Befuddled, Frederic's attention shifted from his son to Agatha.

"Stephen," she continued, "why don't you tell John what you've learned about his dealings in New York?"

Westphal squirmed. Agatha was supposed to divulge the information he'd garnered. But Frederic's eyes were leveled on him, a hardened regard that Stephen knew all too well. There'd be no release until Frederic's curiosity had been satisfied. Stephen glanced at John, who wore the same expression, and he shifted uncomfortably, not wanting to get on either man's bad side. "Perhaps we can discuss this at some other time..." he sputtered.

"No, we'll discuss it right now," Frederic pronounced, his confusion growing. He thought to shoo Anne out of the room, but what was the point? She could extract the story from her father or even Agatha, if she didn't know it already.

Westphal cleared his throat. "My banking contacts have mentioned things..."

"Go on," Frederic pressed in irritation.

"They've written that John has been investing heavily in canals and railroads in the North, using the Duvoisin bank holdings withdrawn from the Bank of Virginia."

Paul glared at John in astonishment. Westphal hesitated to say more.

"And?" Frederic urged.

The man cleared his throat again. "I also have it on good authority that John is an abolitionist. He has ties to the Underground Railroad – provides them with financial support."

"Underground Railroad?" Frederic queried, the term unfamiliar.

"The name hasn't made its way into print yet, but it's an association that many southerners whisper about."

"What exactly is it?"

"A group of southern and northern abolitionists who aid and abet runaway slaves. It is rumored that John is one of them – that he uses Duvoisin vessels to transport slaves from Richmond to New York."

"Is this true?" Frederic asked, his eyes shooting to John. Memories of his early days with Colette took hold. She was in this room, with them right now. He could feel her at his side.

"Have you taken to spying on me now, Father?" John asked, his voice mildly amused, though his face was stern. "Is this why you invited me back? I'm not here five minutes and already I'm under interrogation. Why the inquisition?"

"Is it true about the Virginia bank accounts?"

"Yes, it's true. Did your brilliant Mr. Westphal tell you there was a bank panic last year? That hundreds of farmers lost everything when the US bank was dissolved? But not you, Father. Why? Because of the northern securities

I purchased in your name *before* the panic. Your banker, Mr. Westphal, hasn't noticed that you're already the richer for it. No, he's been too busy discrediting me to see past the nose on his face!"

"Since when are we in the canal and railroad business?" Frederic demanded.

"I thought I was in charge on the mainland, Father," John jeered. "Shipping is shipping. What does it matter if it's ships or canals or trains? Whenever I've found a sound investment, I've purchased it – with my own money as well."

"Why not make these investments in the South, where we have our roots?"

"The South as it stands will not last," John replied. "I'll be long gone from Virginia when it comes tumbling down. If it were up to me, I'd transfer *all* your assets north."

"And what of this 'Underground Railroad'?"

"I support it," John replied simply, "with my money."

Frederic sighed in exasperation. Ten years ago he'd waged this battle with Colette. John had embraced her views, while he had suavely sidestepped them.

"And you've used Duvoisin vessels to smuggle runaways?" he pursued.

"Occasionally."

Frederic's anger began to percolate. "If this gets out, it will be devastating to my holdings and trade in Virginia. Harboring runaways is against the law! Imagine what the authorities will do if they find you've been pirating them!"

Agatha gloated. Finally, they were getting somewhere.

"You are right," John declared, satisfied when Frederic's expression turned to one of bewilderment. "So, I have a solution. I'm resigning as manager of your Virginia estates, and I demand that you remove *my* name from *your* will."

"John–" Paul sputtered "–you can't do that!"

"Oh yes, I can."

Anguished, Frederic murmured, "Now you use my wealth to thwart me?"

"I've learned well from you, Father," John answered flatly.

"I won't do this," he rejoined.

Agatha stepped forward. "Why not, Frederic?" she demanded, afraid that John might rescind his request. She indicated Paul. "Surely you can place it in more worthy – competent – hands?"

"Silence, woman!" Frederic thundered, before turning back to John. "Why –why are you doing this?" he beseeched, nonplussed.

"Because the price of your great fortune has been evil, misery, and tears," John replied in disgust. "I've had my fair share of it, and *I don't want it anymore*."

Frederic gaped at him, reluctance and dismay branded on his face. Agatha beamed ecstatically. Anne leaned forward, savoring the unfolding story.

"I can accept your resignation," Frederic finally said, "but I will not remove you from my will."

"If you leave my name on it," John sneered, "I swear, on the day you die, I will turn every parcel, every ship, every penny over to the Underground Railroad. Why not give it all to Paul? He deserves it far more than I do."

Paul shifted uncomfortably, looking from Frederic to John. "John –" he started again, but his brother waved him off, his eyes fixed on Frederic.

"John is right, Frederic," Agatha desperately chimed in. "You'd be wise to agree to this proposal immediately. It is the right thing to do. You have overlooked your worthy son for far too long."

"Agatha! I said–"

"For once we agree, Auntie," John concurred, cutting his father off. "What I don't understand is why you're such an advocate for my brother. He hates you as much as I do. One might think you were his mother."

Paul's eyes shot from Agatha's injured face to his astonished father, a spark struck, a thought ignited.

"Frederic, you have no choice!" Agatha pursued irately. "Would you really see the family fortune tossed to the dogs? *Why do you hesitate?"*

"Silence, woman!" Frederic bellowed a third time. He studied John sadly. The chasm between them was growing wider.

John watched Frederic, confused by the genuine regret on his face. Why had the man spent the better part of a lifetime setting him aside, pushing him away, scorning him, even undermining him, if he really cared?

"You leave me no choice, " Frederic muttered, echoing a triumphant Agatha.

"Don't worry, Father," John offered sarcastically, "I do have one redeeming request of you."

"What is it?"

"Guardianship of my sisters when you die. They are all that matter to me."

Frederic's eyes welled with tears, but he quickly hid them behind the hand he brought to his brow. Once composed, he nodded his assent.

"I'm sure Edward Richecourt will be here this week," John continued. "Shall I make the arrangements for a meeting with him, or will you?"

"I will make the arrangements," Frederic rasped, his plaintive eyes going to a stunned Paul. With a nod, John pushed out of his seat and left.

Frederic turned on Westphal. "Why wasn't I given this information sooner?"

"I – I–" Westphal sputtered, red-faced. He didn't want to betray Agatha because she had paid him well for the information.

"Stephen," Paul jumped in, "we can finish up later – at your house."

"Very good," Westphal replied gratefully, hastily grabbing his portfolio and shoving the folder into it as he scurried from the room, Anne on his heels.

Frederic waited out their departure, his fury rising. "I warned you, Agatha," he snarled, "yet you deliberately interfere with John and me time and again!"

Her chin jabbed up, but she did not speak.

Paul stepped between them. "Is what John said true, Father?" he asked, eyeing them both, reading their expressions as they glared at one another.

"Is what true?" Frederic asked, bewildered again.

"About Agatha."

Frederic bowed his head, but Agatha smiled victoriously.

"You *are* my mother, aren't you?" Paul demanded, incredulous, yet enlightened.

"Tell him, Frederic," Agatha pressed. "Isn't it time that your grown son know the truth about us?"

Frederic looked at Paul's harrowed face, a testimony to the total betrayal that he now felt. "Paul, I need to explain. It's a complicated story."

"I'm sure it is," Paul snorted, holding up a hand to hold him silent, "especially with all the lies you built around it. But I don't want to hear it now! I have guests to greet and the reception tomorrow. I don't want my plans for the week spoiled by this odious admission. I've worked too hard!"

John entered his room and threw his knapsack on the bed. He'd just walked into an ambush! With his head pounding, he considered returning to town and boarding the first ship to Richmond, but he couldn't disappoint his sisters, or Charmaine. He sat down and massaged his brow, breathing deeply to calm himself. The entire conversation came back to him now, and he wondered whether Westphal had taken his father by surprise. After all, Agatha had prompted Westphal's diatribe. Yes, she hated him, but John hadn't realized just how much until now. Though his taunting infuriated her, he doubted that alone motivated today's tactics. There had to be another reason. *But what?*

When Anne London dined with her father later that evening, he forbade her to repeat a word of what she'd learned that afternoon, threatening to reveal her best-kept secrets if she dared to jeopardize his position on Charmantes.

Sunday, April 1, 1838 4 am

Paul could not sleep, yesterday's incredible revelation magnifying in the darkness. He'd avoided his father for the remainder of the day and brushed aside two Caribbean farmers he should have made time to speak with. His mind was not on ships, steam propulsion or export commodities. The looming week was suddenly a heavy yoke, a burden to bear. He paced his bedchamber, grinding his left fist into the palm of his right hand, grappling with the truth that he'd have to come to grips with and shake off, lest all his hard work go to waste. Agatha was his mother – the mother that was supposed to be dead. According to his father, she was dead! It wasn't possible! But it was logical.

How had it happened? What had brought them together? Had Agatha offered Frederic succor after the death of his beloved Elizabeth? Was that it? But it couldn't be. He was told that he was older than John. Or was that just another lie, too? Why did he even want to know? *You don't want to know*, he tried to convince himself, *not yet anyway. Set it aside. Don't let it distract you.*

He needed air. With that thought, he left his rooms for the stable. He saddled up Alabaster and rode the stallion hard into town. Once there, he boarded the Bastion, the ship that had brought John to Charmantes. Standing on her empty decks, he cast his eyes beyond the thin peninsula, out to sea. A light rain was falling, and he breathed deeply of the salty air, letting the gentle drops wash away his turbulent thoughts. *You will forget. Until the week's end, you must forget!*

Frederic lay abed, listlessly contemplating the ceiling. *Paul knew... he finally knew.* Frederic had dreaded this day, dreaded it with a passion. He had lied to Paul all those years ago. When the bright five-year-old found out that he and John did not share the same mother, telling Paul that his mother had died as well seemed the simplest, least painful, solution. It also protected Agatha. She was married and living a respectable life; it became important to keep the secret for her sake. Though Paul had never asked about her again, Frederic wondered if he longed to know more. Evidently, he did. Frederic recalled the torment in his son's eyes, and he worried where his dishonesty would lead.

Then there was John. This afternoon's fiasco had been another setback, not the step forward Frederic had hoped for. Though he'd always allowed John free rein on all mainland business matters, he'd been embarrassed to learn about the family's financial business through Westphal, so he'd lost his temper. Still, he'd endured far worse where John was concerned. The investments, though not traditional, were sound enough, reassuring Frederic that the Duvoisin fortune was in capable hands. As for the abetting of runaway slaves, he had grave misgivings. Yet now, hours later, he knew that John's crusade had nothing to do with retaliation or revenge. It was a cause that John believed in.

Frederic sighed deeply. Thanks to Agatha, both sons were angry with him. Somehow, he had to repair the damage. He would begin by speaking with John, alone. After that, he'd direct his attentions to Paul. For the first time, the son who had always honored him was more difficult to approach. He'd respect Paul's wishes and wait until the week was over.

When John had first returned to Virginia last October, fitful sleep and fragmented dreams tormented him, despite long days of strenuous work. Nearly every night, he had nightmares that transported him to remote places where he roamed aimlessly along unfamiliar streets and spiritless strangers passed him. They were all ugly. He would turn a corner onto a crowded thoroughfare littered with refuse, carts, and animals. In the midst of the throng, he could see Pierre, lost. The boy's face was streaked with dirt and tears, his clothes tattered and filthy, his eyes searching the faces around him. As John hastened to rescue him, the boy would move just beyond his reach until the pushing and shoving bodies swallowed him up. Ultimately, his powerlessness would startle him awake.

By Christmas, the dreams were all but gone. Then, on the night of Michael's visit to Freedom, the harrowing dream recurred, and it plagued him relentlessly over the days that followed. But unlike before, when he dismally attributed the nightmare to his guilty conscience, this time he felt it meant something more. Inexplicably, it pointed to Charmantes, telling him that he had rushed back to Virginia too quickly – that he would never put the past behind him until, for some unfathomable reason, he returned home. Stranger still, he slept peacefully every night once he decided to return. That is, until tonight...

Succumbing to fatigue, bizarre images beset him. Colette was coming to him again, the first time since last October. She sent the breeze as her scout, clearing the way into this room of clandestine encounters. The drapes billowed with a gust of wind, coaxing the French doors open. John turned on his side, determined to ignore her, but the air was already imbued with her scent, and her shadow fell upon the threshold. He didn't want her there, but she seemed to need him tonight. As she glided closer, he rose, transfixed by the blue eyes desperately beckoning him. As he lifted his hand to touch her, she grabbed it, pulling him across the room toward the French doors. But he planted his feet firmly and wrenched free. When she grabbed at his hand again, he cried out as if burned, and awoke.

He stared, unseeing, at the shadowed ceiling. Had he screamed? He threw a forearm over his eyes, feeling the sweat on his brow. The bedclothes were damp from perspiration. He sat up, his head spinning and stomach nauseous. Inhaling deeply, he rose and went to the bowl and pitcher on the nightstand. He splashed water in his face and on his chest and braced his hands on the edges of the table to steady the lurching room.

Charmaine could not sleep, and in the early hours of dawn, she finally abandoned her futile sheep counting and Hail Marys. Pulling on her robe, she left her bedchamber and went downstairs. Perhaps a book from the study and a warm glass of milk would do the trick.

The house was deathly quiet, but to her surprise, she found John seated at the desk in the study, his eyes closed and head tilted back against the leather cushions. The lamp was burning low.

"John?" she whispered. "John?" she called again, touching his arm lightly when he did not respond.

Startled, his eyes flew open. "Thank you, Miss Ryan," he muttered, "the first bit of sleep I've had all night, and you've come to spoil it."

"I'm sorry," she sputtered, stung.

He leaned forward and propped a throbbing head in his hand, closing his eyes once again. In the awkward silence, she turned to leave, but his voice stopped her. "Why are you up and about at this hour?"

"I couldn't sleep either," she replied, facing him. "My mind kept turning, and I couldn't stop it. Hasn't that ever happened to you?"

He was smiling now. "Far too often I'm afraid, my Charm."

She relaxed with his use of her pet name.

"Why couldn't you sleep?" he asked.

"I'm nervous about the coming week and the social graces needed to see it through."

"You'll do fine," he reassured. "Are you attending the ball on Saturday?"

"Oh yes!" she exclaimed eagerly, her eyes lighting up. "Maddy Thompson has sewn the most exquisite gown! The fittings have taken hours and I've had to stand stock-still the entire time."

His smile grew in proportion to her enthusiasm, his chin propped on a fist, his eyes sparkling. "Will you accompany the twins, or do you have an escort?"

She hesitated. *Is he offering to take me? Why am I reluctant to tell him?* "Paul has asked me," she finally said, battling a pang of disappointment.

His eyes betrayed no reaction. "I must admit I'm surprised. I thought the fair Lady London would be his consort. She was glued to his side yesterday."

"But he has invited me as his partner," Charmaine replied defensively.

"You must be very pleased about that."

"I am. We've gotten to know each other better over the past months."

John frowned slightly.

"Is there something wrong with that?" she probed.

"Nothing at all. Has he made any plans with you beyond this week?"

She knew what he was getting at and did not answer.

"You realize, of course," he expounded, "that after this celebration is over, Paul will be living on Espoir. You will see much less of him."

The observation hit her head-on. She hadn't thought of it before, but it was true. "The future will take care of itself," she said. "I will have to wait and see."

"You've done a lot of 'waiting and seeing' with my brother." When she appeared indignant, he harassed her further. "Do you still harbor hopes for him?"

"Should I not?" she asked directly. "What is your advice?"

John grew quiet, and she could tell that he debated what to say. "I don't think my brother is ready to make a commitment to any woman," he replied. "He has yet to understand himself, and he won't be ready to marry until he does."

"What do you mean by that?" she asked, baffled by his last remark.

"It doesn't matter," he said. "To state it more simply, he has had plenty of time with you and hasn't proposed marriage yet. His romantic overtures could turn out to be a seduction and nothing more. That is my honest assessment of the matter, but you have heard it before."

"Your opinion could be wrong."

"It could be," he conceded, thinking that his advice had once again fallen on deaf ears. The room fell silent. "So how long are you willing to 'wait and see', Charmaine, before you grow tired of it?" he asked pointedly.

"He is not my only prospect," she objected, realizing how foolish she appeared.

"He's not?" John teased. "Who else has arrived on the scene? Have you been kissing someone behind my brother's back?"

"He's not the only man I've ever kissed!" she insisted heatedly, blushing when his brow rose in merriment, the discourse reminiscent of their early days.

"*Now* we have the confessions," he pursued devilishly. "Who else have you kissed, my charm? You can tell me. Wade Remmen, perhaps?"

"I've kissed you!" she gushed, annoyed that he'd forgotten the two occasions he'd taken her in his arms. Belatedly, she realized that she'd put her foot squarely into her mouth.

He leaned back and chuckled. "Ah, but that doesn't count… Or does it?"

"Of course it does!" she expostulated. "I mean no – it doesn't!"

His sagacious grin widened. "Then why did you mention it?" he asked.

But as her mouth flew open again, he waved off her retort and rushed on. "I think we had better drop this conversation, because you are growing annoyed with me, and I'd hate for the week to be spoiled so early on."

"What about you?" she rejoined, her chin lifted in miffed vexation.

"What about me?"

"Will you be escorting a lady to the ball?"

"I have no plans yet. Who knows? Perhaps they'll change."

She wondered what he meant, but didn't ask. She grew serious. "Will you be staying on after the ball?"

"I'll be returning to Virginia."

"Right away?"

"I might stay a few days longer – for the twins, but not many." He rose from the desk. "I'm going to retire. I'd like to get some sleep before everyone begins to stir. Goodnight, Charmaine."

After he'd left, she stood in the center of the study for a long time. She abandoned the idea of a book and sought her own room, determined to get dressed. She wouldn't be able to sleep now.

Three days sailing and the unpleasant confrontation with his father caught up with John, and he finally fell into a deep sleep. He rose after lunch and found that nearly everyone had left the house to attend the kick-off festivities in town. He was pleased; he needed the afternoon to himself. Memories of Pierre were strong, so after he ate, he saddled up Phantom and rode to the family cemetery to contemplate, pay his respects, and come to terms with the past. He meandered around the island for the rest of the day, visiting old haunts and letting go.

Right now, the night air was balmy, and the leaves rustled, riding the easterly breeze. Crickets chattered in the grass, and the moonlight cast long shadows on the lawns. Voices from the drawing room carried on the gentle wind. Since George and Mercedes had gone off for a walk, and Charmaine had disappeared with the twins, John shunned Agatha and Anne, his father and Paul, for the peaceful haven of the portico.

Charmaine was headed for the drawing room when she heard Anne London's pretentious laugh. She walked straight to the main doors instead; she'd enjoy the refreshing breeze before she retired.

She was surprised to find John sitting on the top step of the portico, his elbows propped on his knees, his fingers entwined between them. He turned to see who was coming out of the house.

"I'm sorry," she apologized, turning back toward the doors, even though she wanted to sit down next to him, "I didn't know you were out here."

"You don't have to leave, Charmaine," he called after her, halting her step. "I was just enjoying the peace and quiet. Come, sit with me."

She gladly joined him.

"We didn't see you all day," she commented, arranging her skirts.

"The journey caught up with me, and I slept late," he replied. "Why aren't you abed? You didn't sleep well last night either."

"I'm not tired. I suppose I won't feel tired until the week is over."

John smiled at her ingenuous remark, his eyes coming to rest on her face.

"How did you fare with your father yesterday?" she asked, daring to broach the subject that had slipped her mind last night.

"It didn't go well," he replied. "Westphal had a long list of my latest transgressions. My father and I were at it again in all of five minutes. I don't understand why he invited me back."

"Your father didn't ask Westphal for that list," Charmaine replied, her anger swift and sure, "Agatha did."

"Really?" John asked, surprised she'd come to the same conclusion he had.

"She had Westphal get information on me, too," Charmaine explained. "He's the one who found out about my father, and Agatha tried to use it to have me dismissed. Fortunately for me, it didn't make any difference to Colette or Paul."

She studied John for his reaction to Colette's name, but he remained impassive. "It was fortunate for the children, too," he said.

"Not if it had been up to Agatha. She'll stop at nothing to get rid of anybody she doesn't like. I'd lay money down that she instigated yesterday's confrontation sure as she plotted the one last October. Your father wasn't sending the twins to a boarding school, but she made the girls believe he was, knowing that Yvette would run to tell you. I can't stand her. I don't know what your father sees in her or why he ever married her."

"He married her to punish Colette."

Charmaine grew quiet, the silence catching his attention. "I don't think so," she replied softly, debating her next thoughts. She was treading on dangerous territory. "He loved her, John."

John scoffed at the assertion, impelling her to speak her mind. "I don't know if I'll ever understand the relationship that your father and Colette shared, but I'm certain that he loved her." She hesitated before adding, "And Colette told me that she loved him."

"Of course she'd tell you that," John said derisively, "to keep up appearances."

"Perhaps," Charmaine replied, realizing that John wasn't willing to entertain such an idea. There was no point in pressing it. "Still, your father *didn't* have a confrontation in mind when he invited you home. I know that he is very sorry about what happened. He has changed since you left: coming out of his isolation, taking charge of business again, and spending time with the girls."

"It didn't appear as if he'd changed yesterday," John mused.

"Perhaps he was taken off guard." She sighed deeply. "He invited you back to make amends. I'm *certain* of it."

John mulled over her words; they echoed Michael's sentiments. "I trust what you say, my Charm," he finally ceded. "Still, he's off to a pretty bad start."

"I'm sure he is, but old habits die hard, so give him a chance."

She thought to lighten the mood and changed the subject. "What are your latest transgressions?"

"The list is long, my Charm," he chuckled. "I wouldn't want to bore you."

"Then tell me about Virginia. You never talk about it."

"I go back and forth between Richmond and the plantation."

"Do you like it there?"

"I hate it: the slave business, the classes, the games that one must play to survive. But, a few people there depend on me, so I'm bound to it."

"What would you rather be doing?"

"Live in New York, play the piano, be a composer. But there isn't any money in it, and I like having money too much to do without it."

Charmaine laughed. "You don't realize how true your words are. You've never been poor, but I have. There's no going back!"

John laughed, too. When their mirth died down, she asked, "Why do you like New York so much?"

"It will be the center of the world before long – bigger than London, bigger than Paris. In New York, if you've got ambition, you've got a chance. The only thing to hold you back is yourself. In New York, you can start over."

"Is that why you go there – to start over?"

"Perhaps, but right now, I travel between two worlds."

"I'd love to see it," she stated with conviction, turning her regard to him.

"And I'd love to show it to you," he replied, his eyes captivating her.

She could not look away, thrilled by the plummeting lurch in her stomach, her quickening pulse, and her heart thudding in her breast. Slowly, almost imperceptibly, John leaned in to her.

The door opened behind them, and Paul stepped out of the house. "Here you are!" he exclaimed. "Jeannette had a bad dream and is calling for you."

Blushing, Charmaine quickly stood and, without a backward glance, rushed past him. Paul watched her go, then considered his brother. But John had turned back to the lawns, apparently disinterested in Charmaine's departure.

Monday April 2, 1838

"No, John," Paul said, "they are not paddlewheels. The European engineers are manufacturing what they've termed a corkscrew propeller, which they claim will cut Atlantic crossing time by half."

"Well, if locomotives are possible, I suppose anything is," John rejoined.

"Do you realize what this could mean for Duvoisin shipping?"

Charmaine listened to their civil banter, amazed by it. The girls were playing outside, and she could keep an eye on them from the open French doors, so she meandered to the drawing room casement and paused in the archway.

Presently, Paul was asking John's opinion on the New York guests and how to persuade them to use his fleet for their exports. The Duvoisin barristers were due to arrive shortly, and he was waiting for them. When a carriage rolled up and two distinguished gentlemen stepped out, she assumed it was them.

One man was middle aged, of medium height, with liberal touches of gray in his hair and beard. The younger was short, but good-looking in a pretty sort of way: with blue eyes, long aristocratic nose, protruding chin, and oiled-down blonde hair.

"Mr. Pitchfork," John exclaimed, extending a hand to the elder solicitor when George showed them into the drawing room, "you've arrived!"

The man's face twisted into a grimace, but his associate snickered. George laughed outright. "I'd appreciate it if you would use my proper name," the lawyer replied curtly, "Richecourt – Edward Richecourt. When are you going to realize that you've worn out that witless name?"

"When you've worn out getting angry at it," John quipped.

George chuckled again, and Richecourt's assistant joined in. Though the latter had never met John before, he'd heard talk of the man's acerbic wit. He was quite funny.

Scratching the back of his head, John turned mischievous eyes to the young lawyer. "Who's your friend here, Pitchie?"

"This is our most promising junior associate," Richecourt offered, ignoring John's gibe, "Geoffrey Elliot the Third."

"There are three of you?" John exclaimed, eyeing the younger man.

Geoffrey extended a hand to John, still chuckling in camaraderie. "My father was Geoffrey Elliot the Second."

"Ah, that explains it: if at first you don't succeed..." John shrugged. "Are you the one who consigned two shiploads of sugar here when my export broker took ill last January?" he continued, leveling his gaze on Elliot while ignoring Paul's deepening frown.

"Why, yes, I am!" Elliot replied proudly.

"And where do you suppose those boatloads of sugar came from, Geoff?"

Momentary confusion washed over Elliot's face as John finally shook his hand. "I'm pleased to make your acquaintance, Mr. Idiot," he declared merrily. "What else are you promising at, Junior?"

Elliot's face dropped in injured astonishment. "Why – I'm a lawyer. I'm a graduate of William and Mary – I've – I've – I've–"

"Yes – yes – yes?" John asked unimpressed, the devil in his eyes.

"Mr. Duvoisin!" Elliot rejoined angrily, his back stiffening. "I warn you now, I am not Mr. Richecourt! I'll not tolerate name-calling. Do so again, and I'll not hesitate to remonstrate you!"

"Mr. Idiot," John cut in, "I have no doubt about your ability to remonstrate or reprobate. I'm concerned with your ability to contemplate and concentrate. And while you ruminate on that, this will make you fulminate: tell me, do you ejaculate when you mastur–"

"We get the idea, John," Paul cut in sharply, averting his face from Elliot as he crossed the room, the scowl replaced by a snicker that threatened to erupt into something more. He didn't dare look at George, who was howling hysterically.

Instead, he turned to Richecourt. "Welcome to Charmantes," he greeted, once he could speak without laughing. "Sit down and make yourselves comfortable. I'll ring for refreshments. No doubt you're weary from the journey."

As they found seats, Paul turned to the bell-pull, casting murderous eyes upon John, who smiled sheepishly back at him. Elliot glared at John in utter disbelief, his face beet red, but he didn't dare open his mouth, lest he be cut down quickly.

John is in rare form today, Charmaine thought. She wondered why he called Mr. Richecourt 'Mr. Pitchfork'. There had to be a reason.

Richecourt summarized the business matters he would address in detail later on in the week, then eyed John, who lounged in an armchair, thumbing through a magazine, his booted legs propped on the low table. "John," he called, "Geoffrey has prepared some important documents at your broker's request."

"Really?"

"Yes," Geoffrey jumped in, composed and ready to begin anew, "and I will personally bring them back to Richmond. Mr. Bradley needs them posthaste if he is to finalize agreements before others step in to undercut your price." He placed his valise on the table and fished out a thick stack of papers, a quill and a bottle of ink. "Here, I can show you where to sign."

"Just leave them with me, Geffey," John replied, "I want to read them first."

"I assure you that everything is in shipshape order, just as your broker specified." He dipped the pen and extended it to John. "Now allow me–"

"No, Geffey, I'll read them first," John insisted, "lest I end up shipping ladies' undergarments to West Point instead of tobacco to Europe."

Elliot's face reddened again.

The twins came skipping across the porch, petitioning Charmaine to take them into town to fetch their dresses. When she agreed, she caught Geoffrey Elliot's interested gaze on her. "We'll have to take the carriage," she said.

Yvette nodded, then turned to her brother. "Johnny? Will you come, too?"

"Yes, I'll come," he agreed, happy to disengage himself from the pompous Geoffrey Elliot the Third. "Will you show me your dresses?" he asked. "Or will you hide them away until Saturday?"

"We'll show you!" Jeannette exclaimed. "They came all the way from Paris! Stepmother ordered them for us last fall, but we've grown since then, and Mrs. Thompson had to make quite a few adjustments. I can't wait to try mine on!"

"And what of Mademoiselle Charmaine? Will she model hers as well?"

Paul's eyes shot to Charmaine. He had yet to see the expensive finery.

"Why?" Yvette questioned.

"I want to see if it meets with my approval," John replied.

Paul's scowl darkened, and Charmaine's cheeks burned, knowing the twins waited for her to respond. When she didn't, John only chuckled. "I'll ask Gerald to ready the carriage," he offered, tossing the magazine onto the table.

"But Mr. Duvoisin," Geoffrey objected, "what about your contracts?"

"Don't get your knickers twisted, Geffey," he called over his shoulder, already out the door, "or there won't be a Geoffrey Elliot the Fourth."

Paul watched as Charmaine and the twins followed, disconcerted by the expression on Charmaine's face. She looked pleased. He'd seen that expression a few times already this week, and he didn't like it – he didn't like it at all.

John heard the twins' voices as he climbed the stairs, and he strode to the open bedroom doorway to say goodnight. He was surprised to find his father there, sitting on Jeannette's bed, telling them a story about a gentleman pirate, Frederic's father, Jean Duvoisin II. Apparently, he was tucking them into bed. Perhaps this transformation that Charmaine had talked about yesterday *was* real.

"Did he really steal ships and plunder treasures?" Jeannette asked.

"He always claimed he did," Frederic chuckled. "But I think he exaggerated a bit for my sake. What he actually did was look the other way when pirate ships entered Charmantes' coves. They found safe haven here, and in return, they didn't attack my father's merchant ships."

Frederic looked up to find John standing in the doorway. They hadn't spoken since Saturday afternoon, and he didn't want the week to go on like this, cringing again with the memory of Saturday's dispute. If the mood remained strained, John would leave for Virginia as soon as Paul's gala ended.

"Come in, John," he encouraged with a smile. "I was just telling Yvette and Jeannette about your grandfather."

"He was a pirate!" Yvette exclaimed as John hesitated and then stepped across the threshold, settling on the end of Yvette's bed.

"So I've been told," John replied mildly.

Frederic's eyes danced. "And your brother is following in his footsteps," he declared, looking pointedly at John and gaining all of their quizzical regards.

"He is?" Yvette queried.

"First of all, he's named after his grandfather. Jean means John."

"But Johnny is not a pirate, Papa," Jeannette reasoned.

"He *is* – of sorts."

Again, Frederic's gleaming gaze met John's raised brow.

"But Johnny wouldn't smuggle diamonds and gold," Yvette countered, certain that her father was telling a tall tale. "He's already rich!"

"There are other things to smuggle besides treasure, Yvette," Frederic replied. "But let us save that story for another night. It is time to turn down the lamps."

Despite their protests, he leaned heavily on his cane and rose from the bed. He doused the light and kissed them goodnight. He and John stepped into the hallway together.

As John turned toward his own chambers, Frederic called to him. "John, we have guests arriving during the week, brokers from Boston and New York. I've been told that you suggested they contact Paul."

"I did," John nodded.

"Since you know these gentlemen, would you be willing to entertain them at the celebration Saturday night? I understand that tensions run high between southerners and northerners these days, and I want everyone to keep a level head. I thought I'd have them at their own table with you seated there."

"That's fine, Father," John said.

Frederic hadn't moved, and John could tell that he wanted to say more. Finally he spoke, his voice earnest. "I'm glad that you came home, John. I wasn't spying on you, and I didn't ask Westphal to get that information. I was as astonished to hear about it as you were."

"My aunt has been very busy then. I'm not surprised. She has always hated me. I deserve it now, but I didn't when I was a child."

Frederic nodded. He thought about asking John to reconsider his request to be taken off the will, but stopped short of broaching the topic. He knew John had made up his mind, so he turned toward the stairs instead. "Goodnight, John."

"Goodnight, Father."

Tuesday, April 3, 1838

John rose early, but not early enough. His sisters were not in the nursery. He turned from the doorway, but had a change of heart and stepped into the room.

Unlike last night, all was peaceful. He was alone, alone with his memories. He crossed to Pierre's empty bed and sat gingerly. He caressed the pillow, remembering the last time he sat here.

Charmaine was three steps into the children's bedroom before she realized John was there. Embarrassed, he stood and turned away, wiping at his face with his forearm. She wanted to cross the chamber and comfort him, but knew that he wanted to bury his sorrow, not reopen the healing wound. *Most times it's easier to cry than to laugh.* Now she understood, truly understood.

"We are going for a stroll. Would you like to come along?" she offered.

"No," he rasped. "I'd rather be alone today."

Charmaine hesitated, then turned away, leaving him to his mourning.

Wednesday, April 4, 1838

Charmaine grabbed the doorknob and pushed into the study, coming up sharply as she found herself in the midst of a meeting between John, Edward Richecourt, Geoffrey Elliot, and another man she did not recognize. All three men shifted in their seats as she entered, conversation suspended, their eyes fixed on her. She, in turn, regarded John, who lounged in the large desk chair, his elbows propped casually on the armrests, one booted leg crossed over his knee, and Jeannette's cat in his lap. Fleetingly, she thought he was angry, perhaps for barging in so unceremoniously.

"I – excuse me," she stammered and began to back out of the room, groping behind her for the doorknob.

John's voice cut across her apology. "Miss Ryan, where are my sisters?"

She was stunned by his formality, the annoyance on his face.

"They are with your father. I had some time to myself."

"You mean leisure time," he corrected tersely.

"Yes," she capitulated, still taken aback. *Was the meeting confidential?*

"Miss Ryan, you are not paid for leisure time. So, since you have nothing to do right now, I will have to find something."

Charmaine stood dumbfounded. Was he Agatha in disguise or was he showing off in front of the lawyers? Maybe he was just out of his mind.

"Come, sit beside me." As he leaned over to drag a chair nearer the desk, the cat leapt out of his lap. "Here is a pen and paper. Take notes on our discussion."

He couldn't be serious! She didn't know whether to frown or laugh.

"Come now, Miss Ryan," he pressed, "time is marching on."

He *was* serious, but she was too stupefied to reply. As she settled into the chair and took up the pen, she began to simmer. He *was* showing off!

John introduced her to the stranger, one Carlton Blake. He was good-looking and tipped his head, smiling suavely at her. He was about the same age as John, and she surmised that he already knew John from the States.

Edward Richecourt resumed the conversation, and Charmaine was transfixed with this talk of prices and exports, supply and demand, contracts and deals, and she found herself enjoying this eye into the Duvoisin's world. She tried her best to take notes, but her pen struggled to keep pace with the issues that bounced back and forth, and changed on a dime. She wondered why John needed her there, noticing he'd taken up a quill as well.

As Carlton Blake turned the conversation to Midwest shipping via the Erie Canal, Charmaine became aware of John's eyes upon her. She was wary of meeting his gaze, but the caramel orbs were warm now as he reached over nonchalantly, took her sheet of paper and looked over her notes, his chin poised upon thumb and forefinger. He tucked her paper under the one he'd been writing on and passed both sheets back to her. She looked down at his sloppy scrawl. *How long do you think it will take Geffey to ask me if I've signed his papers yet?* Her eyes flew from the paper to Geoffrey Elliot to John, whose face was poker-straight as he listened to Mr. Blake. Charmaine read the next line. *I think Mr. Blake is enamored of you, my Charm. Perhaps I won't invest with him after all.* She smiled and looked at John. His eyes were trained on her, as if daring her to laugh first. Feeling a tickle bubbling forth, she looked down at the paper again. *Mr. Pitchfork has to relieve himself, but he'd rather sit there and hold it than ask to be excused.* Charmaine stole a sidelong glance at the man, who was squirming in his chair. She giggled, gaining the stoic stares of all three men, the room suddenly silent, save her laughter echoing off the walls. Highly embarrassed, she dropped her gaze to the paper, dramatizing great interest in it.

"Miss Ryan," John commented coolly, "is something amusing? Perhaps you'd like to share it with us?" He leaned cockily back in his chair.

"Only your handwriting," she responded smugly, lifting the paper as if she fully intended to hand it to Carlton Blake. "Perhaps your guests would like to see it. I think they'd agree."

"No," John countered curtly, snatching it away. His eyes sparkled with admiration. "That won't be necessary. They've seen it before. May we proceed?"

"Certainly. Do excuse me."

She retrieved her paper and pretended at note taking, realizing now that she'd been duped, John's stern demeanor bolstering the success of his prank. She looked at him again, but he'd turned his attention back to his associates. She eyed the paper in front of him, and noticed that he'd written yet another line meant for her eyes only, the sheet tilted in her direction so that she could read it. His last message held the promise of long-denied distraction: *If I can finish my business with these gentlemen today, I will take you and the girls out on a riding excursion tomorrow.*

Thursday, April 5, 1838

When Jeannette spilled the beans at breakfast that they were going on a picnic, Geoffrey Elliot invited himself on the outing. Edward Richecourt followed suit with his wife Helen. Anne insisted that Paul had run himself ragged for the first half of the week and deserved a leisurely afternoon, then told Mercedes she'd require her services. And so it went, until the small party became a crowd.

They met at the paddock at eleven o'clock, where the grooms were readying the horses. When Gerald emerged from the stable with Champion, Geoffrey stepped up to take the stallion's reins.

"I'm sorry," George intervened, "but that is Mercedes' mount today."

"Mr. Richards," Geoffrey objected, "do you think it advisable that the young lady sit such a spirited animal? I am an experienced equestrian. Please, allow me to take charge of this one."

"She's an experienced rider, too," George replied, as Mercedes swung up into the saddle, "she'll be just fine."

Geoffrey suspended his protestations when Gerald tied Phantom to the fence. John noticed his avid interest. "You'd best forget that idea, too, Geffey. Fang bites."

"Fang?" the lawyer queried. "Certainly, that's a queer appellation."

John snickered and glanced toward Yvette who was giggling softly. "Not so queer. I'll explain – later. That is, if you're fearless enough to look into Fang's mouth. Right now, Bud has found you a suitable mount: a nice docile gelding."

Geoffrey simmered, but didn't say a word as Bud led the horse, one usually reserved for the carriages, over to him. Though insulted, he took the reins.

Charmaine had just mounted Dapple when a fierce whinny drew her around. There was the old gelding, frantically circling in place, saddle askew, and a terrified Geoffrey hanging off his side. The lawyer gripped the horse's flank like a vise, one leg looped over the beast's back, the other tangled in the stirrup that had slipped under its belly. The horse continued to trumpet furiously, finally bucking to shake loose its clumsy burden, hind legs shooting out like pistons and jolting Geoffrey about like a kernel of popcorn in a hot kettle.

Paul guffawed at the pathetic spectacle, wiping away tears of mirth with his forearm. The twins and George were laughing, too, but not John. He stared in disbelief, uncharacteristically silent.

The beast pivoted once more, and George had seen enough. Lunging forward, he grabbed the gelding's bridle, and the animal quickly settled, its anger evident only by its flattened ears.

Geoffrey hung on still, looking up at George helplessly.

"Let go," the latter ordered, but the red-faced solicitor just stared up at him from the horse's side. "Let go of the saddle and reins!"

Reluctantly, Geoffrey obeyed, dropping to the ground like a sack of potatoes. He kicked his foot free of the stirrup and stood, patting the dust from his trousers.

"I thought you were an experienced equestrian," George remarked dryly, pulling the saddle up and onto the gelding's back. "Or was that just one of your maneuvers?"

John laughed loudly. "Good one, George!" he commended.

"That's not humorous!" Geoffrey protested testily, his humiliation gone. "Anyone can suffer a mishap. I assure you, I know what I am doing!"

"Then why didn't you tighten the girth strap?" George rejoined.

"That service should have been performed by the grooms."

"And it was. But any *experienced* equestrian knows to check it again."

"Ah, leave him be, George," John interrupted, his merriment settling into a crooked grin. "He'll never admit that he wanted to ride side-saddle."

An hour later, they were enjoying a scrumptious lunch on Charmantes' western beaches. Paul began complaining that he was wasting the day away. "I should have used the time to take another group of guests on tour of the island."

"How many times do they have to see Espoir to know that you're well on your way to financial success?" John chided facetiously.

"Not Espoir. *Charmantes.* I should have shown them Charmantes."

"You're showing me," Anne London piped up. "Don't I count?"

Paul smiled blandly. "I was talking about the plantation," he responded, realizing that he hadn't exploited his ten years' experience here.

John chuckled knowingly. "Don't show them the tobacco fields, or they will jump in the harbor and *swim* straight home! A tobacco farmer you're not. Those fields should have lain fallow for a while."

Paul only grunted.

When they finished eating, Yvette and Jeannette asked to go exploring. Only John and Charmaine seemed eager to join them, so they parted company, heading north to some caves that John had discovered as a boy.

"This is more like it," he commented as they strolled down the beach. "That 'picnic' was just about as bad as it could get. Then again, Auntie could have decided to come along."

Yvette's brow gathered, as if she had just remembered something. "You know Johnny, Auntie Agatha is up to something," she said.

John's curiosity was immediately piqued. "What do you mean, Yvette?"

"I've been keeping an eye on her."

"Keeping an eye on her?" Charmaine asked suspiciously. Since Pierre's death, the girl had abandoned her mischievous jaunts.

"Well..." Yvette faltered, reticent with Charmaine present. "It's just a suspicion. Sometimes Auntie acts very strange. That's all I meant."

They arrived at the caves, where the beaches turned craggy and cliffs jutted toward the sky. The tide was low, and John suggested they go inside. Charmaine decided to wait for them on the dry beach.

"So, Yvette," John pursued once they'd left her behind, "tell me about Auntie's strange behavior."

"You have to promise not to tell Mademoiselle Charmaine."

When he'd given his vow, she said, "Every Saturday at three o'clock, Auntie goes for a carriage ride. I thought it was strange because she always goes alone, without a driver. So one day, I pretended I was sick when Father took Jeannette into town. Then I followed her on Spook. She went to Father Benito's cabin. I peeked in the window. She gave him a pouch. I think there was jewelry inside."

John canted his head, eyeing her doubtfully. "What did she say to him?"

"The window was closed," she replied with the click of her tongue, annoyed that she didn't have more information for him. "You believe me, don't you?"

John didn't know what to make of it. "Yvette, you're not to follow Agatha anywhere, understand? If she catches you, you'll be in trouble with Father."

"Yes," she brooded, disappointed with his reaction.

"Why do you call Mr. Richecourt, 'Mr. Pitchfork'?" Charmaine asked John as they walked back to the blanket.

John grinned. "My Charm, you're the first person who has asked me that."

"Well?" she pursued.

His smiled grew wicked. "Late one evening, I stopped by Mr. Richecourt's office and caught him in an unsavory act with a woman who was not his wife."

"And?" Charmaine pressed, though her cheeks were stained a deep crimson.

"And... when his face turned redder than yours, I pictured little horns growing out of his head, so I said to him, 'Mr. Richecourt, you little devil, you – from this day forward, I dub thee Pitchfork.' So there you have it. Lucky for him, you're the first person who's been intuitive enough to realize that there's more to that name than meets the eye."

Charmaine giggled in spite of herself.

When they returned to the picnicking area, they found Paul and George arguing over who would tell John the news. "What news?" he asked, his eyes narrowing.

"Geoffrey rode off – on Phantom. After the gag you and the twins pulled on him with 'Fang', I suppose he wanted to prove himself. He kept insisting that your stallion was not too much horse for him to handle."

Cursing, John threw up his hands. "He's going to break his neck."

"Then you won't have to sign his papers," George offered.

"We had better find him before he breaks Phantom's neck," John added.

Edward Richecourt stepped forward. "May I make a suggestion?"

Paul, George, and John regarded him derisively. "Suggest away, Pitchie."

"Perhaps you're overreacting," he ventured with courteous concern, "Geoffrey will bring the beast back in good condition. He is an extremely gifted horseman."

"Geffey is an extremely gifted horse's ass," John rejoined.

"May I make another suggestion?" Richecourt offered with an infinite amount of patience. "We should establish a search party."

"That's a brilliant idea, Mr. Richecourt," John agreed.

"Thank you, John," Richecourt responded modestly, "I always knew that a worthy compliment was not above your character."

"Neither is lying," John commented dryly. "Now, since a search party was your idea, I'm going to put you in charge of returning to the mansion and rustling up some stable-hands to go out on a search. Can you handle this?"

With his assent, John explained that there was a shortcut back to the house. Richecourt was to proceed directly into the woods for about one hundred yards and made a left at the great cabbage palm tree. If he continued straight, he would arrive at the compound in about fifteen minutes time. Richecourt repeated the directions to the word and set off on his horse.

George and Paul looked at one another bemusedly.

"I never knew about that shortcut," George said, scratching the back of his head. "A great cabbage palm? Come to think of it, I don't see how those directions could possibly take him to the estate."

"They won't," John replied, low enough that Richecourt's wife couldn't hear, "but you know that old gelding – when he gets hungry, he'll wander back on his own, and we'll be spared Pitchie's brilliant suggestions for the remainder of the afternoon."

They found Geoffrey Elliot on the logging road about a half-hour later. Phantom had jumped over a fallen tree at full gallop and had thrown Geoffrey some ten feet away. The horse lie whinnying in pain, abrasions on his chest, though by Mercedes' estimation, his legs were not broken. Geoffrey Elliot the Third's incessant groans echoed through the forest.

George stared down at him reproachfully. "How could you be so stupid? Don't you realize the value of that animal?"

It took them some time to coax Phantom to his feet. George did the same with Geoffrey, and they staggered back to the mansion. George suggested that they send for Martin, the farrier, but Mercedes convinced John that she could nurse the stallion back to health, as she had seen her father do over the years.

Charmaine and the twins were on their way to dinner when they found Dr. Blackford treating a badly battered Geoffrey Elliot in the drawing room. Seated in the large armchair near the hearth, his hair was a tousled mess, flecked with leaves and twigs, one sprig hanging off the side of his head. His face was bruised and dirty. His bleached, starched shirt of that morning was speckled with blood and soiled beyond repair. His right pant leg was split down the seam.

"What happened?" Charmaine asked as the physician pulled the shirtsleeve off Geoffrey's right arm, ignoring his yelp of pain.

"He has fractured his arm," Blackford replied.

"But what happened?" Charmaine asked again.

"That blasted animal threw me!" Geoffrey cursed.

"At least you're not seriously injured," Charmaine comforted, turning reproving eyes on Yvette and Jeannette, who were snickering.

"Not seriously injured?" he protested. "I've never experienced such pain in my life! And the rest of them – why, they're all outside with that vicious beast. One would think it was he and not I who nearly sustained a broken neck!"

John, George, and Mercedes came in from the stables very late and finally sat down to eat. Fatima had just served up a light meal when the foyer door banged open. A few moments later, Edward Richecourt appeared in the archway.

"Where have you been?" John asked, "I thought you were organizing a search party. We were about to send one out for you!"

"I'm afraid I got lost. Am I too late for dinner?"

Friday, April 6, 1838

"That should do it, Charmaine," Mercedes smiled, securing the last pin on the bodice of her new gown. "We can finish up after lunch."

Charmaine stepped down from the stool, glad to have an hour's respite, equally glad that John had taken the girls swimming today. They would have found the morning, as well as the afternoon to come, tedious.

"I'd like you to look over the seating arrangements, before I hand them off to the staff," Agatha was saying to Paul as Charmaine and Mercedes passed through the dining room on their way to the kitchen.

"Where will I be seated?" Anne queried coquettishly, smiling for Paul.

"At the head table, next to Paul, of course," Agatha replied. "You are, after all, our special guest, your invitation written at his request. He will be honored to be your escort for the evening."

As Anne said, "That's wonderful!" Paul glared at Agatha in astonishment.

"Agatha–" he began. Instantly, he thought better of it, his eyes traveling helplessly to his father instead. But the exchange was lost on Frederic, who was absorbed in the newspaper at the side of his plate and hadn't heard a thing.

Charmaine sped up her steps, disappointment rushing in. She could feel Mercedes' regard on her, as well as Paul's, but she didn't dare look around. She declined lunch and fled back to her chambers via the servant's staircase. The new gown was spread out on the bed, but she had no desire to pick up needle and thread. She wanted to cry, but forced herself to the task, lest she give in to the building tears. Now, all her dreams had been laid to waste, again by the inveigling Agatha Duvoisin.

She grimaced when a knock resounded on her door. She could not ignore the second rap and opened the portal to a grim-faced Paul.

"Charmaine, may I speak with you?" He gestured to the hallway, but as she stepped out of her room, he scanned the corridor, frowning. Voices indicated the approach of guests. "Come," he said, "the gardens will offer some privacy."

He didn't speak again until they were near the center of the courtyard. "I'm sorry about what happened at lunch," he began, his hands clasped behind his back. "I had no idea what Agatha was planning."

She looked up at him, trying hard to conceal her dejection. "Perhaps you could tell Anne that there has been a misunderstanding," she offered.

His brow darkened. "I'm afraid that would be in poor taste. Anne would be highly insulted. It could spill over to my guests and spoil the entire affair."

"I understand," she forced herself to say, head bowed.

"Charmaine," he tried to soothe, taking her hands in his, "I'm sorry about this. I really am." When she remained quiet, he felt helpless. He wanted to appease her. "I was looking forward to escorting you. I will make this up to you."

She looked up at him, befuddled, yet hurt, nonetheless.

"Charmaine..." he murmured, struggling to find the right words. He started again, fearful of what he was about to say, yet realizing that the time was right. "Anne will be at my side tomorrow night, but I want you at my side always. Will you marry me?"

She was flabbergasted. Even though they had spent so much time together over the past months, she never expected this. She couldn't react; so incredible was his proposal. The heart-thumping excitement she should have experienced wasn't there, leaving her acutely confused.

Paul was disturbed by her muteness. He'd anticipated an immediate and unequivocal 'yes'. *Why was she so quiet?* "Well, Charmaine, you have me in suspense. What is your answer?"

"I – need to think about it," she replied, her face flushed.

"Very well," he muttered curtly, thinking all the while: *She is angry with me.* "I will give you some time."

When she didn't respond, he left the gardens hurriedly, stung that this monumental step had elicited such a tepid response.

Saturday,
April 7, 1838

Chapter 3

"Will you marry me, Charmaine?"

Charmaine woke with a start and stared unseeing at the ceiling above. On a moan, she turned onto her stomach and cried into her pillow. *Not a dream!* The impossible fantasy was no longer a dream. Then why was she weeping?

Stupid, stupid question! You know why! John. The answer was as simple as whispering his name. Mercedes was right. She was in love with him.

Dear God! What was she to do? What answer was she to give Paul? Little more than six months ago, that answer would have been a resounding 'Yes!' Last year, she had loved him. Why then had she suddenly turned fickle? Was she no better than he? *The marriage vows are simple, Charmaine, but how can either of us know how we will feel towards one another years from now...*

Years from now? Again she moaned. In mere months, her love for Paul had vanished. And if her feelings could change that quickly, could she rely on them? Yes, she yearned for John now, but how could she be certain that it was love when so many other emotions were involved: loneliness, sorrow, and empathy. What if it wasn't love at all? What if it was only a tidal wave of commiseration? Perhaps it had engulfed her desire for Paul, and in time, that desire would reemerge. Yes, that made sense, she decided.

Her relief was short-lived. She was fooling no one, least of all herself. The elation she had experienced when John returned – the memories of his lips upon hers – mocked all logic. She'd been attracted to him long before Pierre had died. *She loved him!* Much as it would be simpler to deny it, she loved him.

But what of John? Did he feel the same about her? He hadn't given her any reason to think so. Yes, he'd returned, but he'd told her that if he extended his visit, it would be for his sisters' benefit. So, where did she fit in? Did she fit in at all? He had walked away from her six months ago. If she had meant anything to him, why had he abandoned her when she had needed him most?

She gulped back her burning misery. Paul had comforted her during those months of agony, had cared and cried with her, held and sheltered her. Could she set aside his compassion so easily – hurt him?

And even if John told her today that he loved her, was she willing to gamble on such a declaration? Now that she was forced to think about it, she realized that she was afraid of loving John. *I'd forfeit every penny for just one more second of her time! I loved her, Charmaine, will always love her...*

Fool! Fool! Fool! She could never compete with Colette.

Charmaine wept again.

When she finally rose, she was grateful that she wouldn't be attending the ball, wouldn't have to face Paul. She had a full day to deliberate her dilemma, a full day before Paul would expect an answer; she still had time to decide.

Richmond

Michael Andrews stood in the Harrington's front parlor, wringing his hands nervously. He'd rehearsed what he would say many times over the past week, and still his pulse raced. Finally, Loretta appeared, as surprised as her housekeeper with this visit. "What brings you here, Father Michael?"

"Actually, I had hoped to catch you after Mass the last two Sundays."

"Joshua has not been feeling well for the past fortnight," she offered by way of a hasty excuse. "He's much improved this week, however."

Michael chuckled. "Good Lord, that's not why I'm here," he reassured and, suddenly inspired, plunged ahead. "Actually, it's Charmaine Ryan that I've been concerned about. I haven't seen her at Holy Mass for some time now. I had promised Marie, her mother, to watch over her."

"Charmaine?" Loretta queried, bewilderment supplanting her initial surprise. "Why Father, she left Richmond well over a year ago. She's living in the West Indies now."

"The West Indies?" he asked, astonished.

"She's working for the Duvoisin family," she continued. "They're prominent shippers here in Richmond and own an island in the Caribbean. Frederic Duvoisin and his wife were looking for a governess for their three young children. Charmaine was able to obtain that position."

"Governess, you say?"

The timbre of his voice and his furrowed brow were disconcerting. Loretta attempted to alleviate his anxiety. "She's quite well. My sister and brother-in-law live there. That is how we learned of the job. I'm sorry, Father, but I was unaware of your concern for Charmaine. If I had known–"

"No – no," the priest interjected, belatedly camouflaging his emotions. "Any miscommunication is owing to long hours at the refuge and my thoughtlessness. Over a year, you say?"

"Yes. She was extremely distressed after her mother's passing, especially when her father was never apprehended. I thought distance and new faces would provide a solution, the start of a new life, so to speak."

"You are probably right. Is she happy there?"

Loretta sighed. "The Duvoisins have endured two tragedies over the past year. Naturally, they were upsetting, but overall, yes, I think she is happy."

"The next time you write to her, please let her know I was asking for her."

"I'll do that, Father."

On his way back to the refuge, Michael's mind was reeling. Charmaine was living with the Duvoisins! She'd been there for the two deaths: the boy, just six months ago, and the child's mother. She must have suffered heartache all over again. And John… she must know him, and he, her! Michael couldn't focus on anything else for the remainder of the day.

Likewise, the priest's visit perplexed Loretta. If Michael Andrews had promised Marie Ryan to look in on her daughter, why had it taken him so very long to do so? And why had he seemed so emotionally involved? *Yes,* Loretta thought, *very intriguing indeed!*

Charmantes

The fine ore captured the lamplight, a quicksilver glint that traced the delicate engraving within: *My Love, My Life.* The locket snapped shut in Agatha's trembling hand. Gingerly, she placed it on the dressing table and stared at it. The charm had been Elizabeth's wedding present from Frederic.

Bitter memories faded when Agatha beheld herself in the mirror. Elizabeth had not won. The tables had turned in Agatha's favor. Through years of careful planning and maneuvering, she had orchestrated the ultimate victory. Tonight was the culmination of her triumph. Tonight, her genius prevailed. Agatha laughed lightly with the irony of it all. She had won. Elizabeth lie, long disintegrated in the cold earth, a brief six months of marriage the only thing she'd given Frederic.

Tonight, the true joy of Frederic's life was the loyal and long lasting treasure that Agatha had given him: Paul. He was Frederic's pride this night, carrying on the lofty Duvoisin legacy.

Agatha studied the locket again. She would have been the happy recipient of this fine piece if Elizabeth had not interfered. Now, that didn't matter. Yes, time had been on her side. Tonight, she would enter the ballroom on Frederic's arm. Tonight, she reigned victorious.

Dinner was to be served at six o'clock. The twins wore their new chiffon dresses, pale blue with white lace, accentuating their eyes – Colette's eyes. Soon they would look just like her. They milled about the nursery, anxious to go down to the festivities. As voices floated up from below, Charmaine decided to humor them. She looked longingly at the lovely gown she would not be wearing tonight. Thanks to Agatha, she would be attending as the girls' governess, nothing more, so she wore her best Sunday dress, as was appropriate. Frederic expected his daughters to attend the dinner and had given permission for them to participate in the first hour of the ball, which was scheduled to begin at eight-thirty. After that, Charmaine would retire with a good book and try not to think about what she was missing.

The twins' new shoes tapped loudly on the marble floor as they crossed the foyer to the ballroom. The doors were open wide, the room as Charmaine had never seen it: splendid beyond description, the crowd clustered and abuzz with anticipation. It was intimidating. She took Yvette and Jeannette by the hand and they passed under the archway together.

Flickering candles in the huge chandeliers cast sparkling light on the place settings of fine china and crystal. The lamps on the wall glowed warmly on the Italian murals. Bouquets of freshly cut flowers crowned four round tables at the far end of the banquet hall. Guests strolled in, with glasses in their hands, gentlemen with ladies on their arms, all elegantly dressed. While they waited to be seated, they ambled about the dazzling room, conversing and enjoying hors d'oeuvres.

As the twins sped over to a waiter with a serving tray, Charmaine eyed the place cards on the tables. She and the twins would be seated with Frederic, Agatha, Edward Richecourt and his wife, Geoffrey Elliot, Robert Blackford and a couple from North Carolina.

Paul and Anne London walked into the room. His impeccable formal attire of gray waistcoat and jacket, black trousers and white shirtwaist accentuated his sleek, muscular form. Many women were looking his way. Anne wore an off-the-shoulder gown, skin-tight at the bust with ruffled sleeves, full and flowing from the waist – the newest Paris fashion. The ivory satin was cut scandalously low at the bodice, revealing the generous swell of her creamy white bosom. Delicate lace-trimmed gloves covered her arms, and her ears glittered with diamonds. Her blonde hair was meticulously coiffed into tight braids looped high on her head, where a shimmering tiara held them in place. Charmaine knew it had taken her the entire day to dress, for she had not seen Mercedes since breakfast.

John and George appeared next, conversing with the guests from New York and Boston, a corpulent businessman chewing their ear. Charmaine's breath caught in her throat at the sight of John in formal attire. He was dressed entirely in black, save a white shirt and an ivory carnation pinned neatly to the velvet lapel of his jacket. The finely tailored suit accentuated his lean body, catching his broad shoulders and tapering to his slender waist. His hair was combed back, his short sideburns neatly trimmed, his face clean-shaven. He talked easily with the northern gentlemen, his eyes lively, a window to his keen mind. He was so handsome and projected such confidence that Charmaine could not tear her eyes from him.

John, too, had caught the attention of quite a few young ladies. One of them broke away from her mother, who nodded approvingly, and boldly crossed the room, producing a dance card before she reached him. Clearly, these farmers' and brokers' wives had their own agenda. While their husbands sought business partners for their clients, they sought marriage partners for their daughters. In a wave of despair, Charmaine turned away.

The waiters began to usher the guests to their tables, and Charmaine quickly located Yvette and Jeannette. As an attendant helped Agatha with her chair, Charmaine sat down with the girls on either side of her, but Frederic remained standing, waiting for everyone to find their seats before he himself reclined. As she gestured to his daughters to place their napkins in their laps, she looked up to find his intense eyes on her. She resisted the urge to look away, only doing so when his attention was drawn to Edward Richecourt. In the corner of the room, a string quartet tuned up and began playing a divertimento. As the first course was served, Charmaine felt her tension ease.

She glanced around the room, noting that a Duvoisin family member hosted each table. Paul and Anne were at the table directly opposite hers, where the company was engaged in quiet conversation. Her eyes caught Paul's momentarily, and he smiled at her. Charmaine could tell that Anne was trying hard to be charming, her hand resting possessively atop his. Rose and George were at the table behind her. Though George chatted amicably, his face was forlorn. John was at the next table, which was animated in a lively discourse. As usual, he commanded the banter; all the guests at his table were laughing.

Geoffrey Elliot watched her throughout the endless meal, engaging her in conversation whenever their eyes met. Helen Richecourt chatted with Jeannette and Yvette. They responded confidently, golden curls bouncing on their shoulders as they nodded, their manners exemplary. Colette would have been proud.

As the dishes were cleared away for dessert, Charmaine looked to John again, leaning forward in his chair, arms folded casually before him, a hand clasped to his chin, engrossed in the recounting of some story. He hadn't looked her way all evening. Had he even noticed that she was there?

After dessert, the waiters ushered everyone out of the banquet hall so that it could be rearranged for the ball. Some of the guests wandered into the drawing room and study for after-dinner drinks, while others left the house to stroll on the lawns or in the courtyard.

Charmaine accompanied the girls to the parlor, where their father introduced them to several of his guests. All were very gracious. Helen Richecourt had learned that both girls knew how to play the piano, and she asked Jeannette to play. Before long, a small audience had gathered around to listen as the twins took turns with their favorite pieces. Frederic looked on with pride, and Charmaine was satisfied that she could take some credit for these two cultivated young ladies.

"Charmaine? Charmaine Ryan?"

She turned toward a couple she recognized. "Mr. and Mrs. Stanton! It is so good to see you!"

Raymond Stanton was a Richmond merchant and business associate of Joshua Harrington. He and his wife, Mary, had not attended dinner, so Charmaine assumed they had just arrived for the ball.

"It is good to see you, too, dear," Mary rejoined. "Loretta and Joshua asked us to look for you. They send their love." She smiled, assessing Charmaine from head to toe. This polished young woman could not be the same insecure girl she'd met at the Harringtons a few years ago.

"I'm always pleased with news of the Harringtons. How are they?" Charmaine inquired, ignoring her discomfiture over the woman's blatant perusal.

"Quite well and getting ready for a visit with Jeremy in Alexandria."

"That's wonderful. Travel will be much easier now that it is spring."

"Yes, yes," Mary agreed, dismissing the topic, her eyes surveying the room. "My, this house is truly magnificent! What is it like to live in such opulence?"

Charmaine glanced over her shoulder. Frederic was only a few feet away and within earshot. "I enjoy my life on Charmantes, Mrs. Stanton. It is certainly very different than Richmond."

"I'm sure you do. That Paul Duvoisin is quite a handsome fellow. I daresay, he must turn many a maid's eye. Do you see him often?"

"Almost every day, Mrs. Stanton. He lives here, too."

"And I see Mrs. London is with him tonight. That is quite surprising. The talk last year was that she was as good as engaged to his brother, John."

Charmaine was about to speak, but Mary babbled on. "Is *he* here?"

"Yes..." Charmaine sighed, as the woman's eyes lit up.

"You'll have to point him out to me. I've heard so much talk about him, but have yet to meet him. Raymond's partners complain that he can be very difficult."

Before Charmaine could respond, the twins came dancing over. She introduced them to the Stantons quickly, as Yvette was tugging on her arm. "C'mon Mademoiselle Charmaine, let's go and find Johnny!"

Mary's eyebrow arched, but Charmaine quickly murmured an apologetic 'good evening' and allowed Yvette to draw her into the foyer, relieved to be rescued from the gossipmonger. When John was nowhere to be found, she suggested that they return to the nursery to rest and freshen up.

George was miserable. He could not stop thinking about Mercedes and how he wished she were at his side this evening. John had tried in earnest to convince him to propose to her. The widow London's threat of dismissal would be moot, and Mercedes would be free to attend the ball. But last night when George had walked Mercedes to her door, he'd grown cold feet, his tongue thick in his mouth. He knew he'd come off the utter oaf if he managed to stammer out those four fateful words.

As Frederic stepped onto the portico to share a cigar and talk politics and commerce with two gentlemen, he noticed Paul on the lawn with a small group of guests. Anne was still at his side. Frederic had been surprised when his son escorted the widow and not Charmaine Ryan to the dinner table. After his conversation with Paul some weeks ago, he was convinced that Charmaine meant more to him than just a casual affair – that Paul intended to escort her tonight. And Jeannette had mentioned something about a new gown. So why had she appeared for dinner plainly dressed and with the twins by her side? Frederic thought back on his affairs with Agatha and Elizabeth and shuddered, uncomfortable that his son was so much like him. He could only hope that Paul wouldn't make the same mistake.

John knocked on Mercedes' door on the third floor. It opened partway, only her face visible, her eyes red and swollen. "You've been crying," he said.

She looked away.

"I've come to take you to the ball."

"But – I can't," she stammered. "Mrs. London will dismiss me if I dare."

"She won't make a scene. She's trying too hard to impress my brother."

"Really, I mustn't. She will be furious and dismiss me in the morning."

"I have a hunch that it won't matter tomorrow, Mercedes," John replied with a crooked grin, "but if it puts you at ease, I will see to it that you're taken care of, one way or another. I'm in desperate need of a farrier at my plantation."

She smiled, and the door opened completely. "Really?"

"I owe you this for ministering to Phantom."

"But I haven't anything appropriate to wear!"

"Sure you do," John countered. "The armoire in Mrs. London's dressing chamber must be packed with expensive gowns. Pick one she has never worn."

Jeannette and Yvette began to fidget. The hum of voices and instruments tuning up drifted upstairs, and Charmaine could tell that the crowd had grown larger. She and the twins watched from the balcony as carriage after carriage rolled up and men in top hats alighted, lending assistance to elegantly dressed women. The last one pulled away, and it was time to go down. As they stepped out the door, Charmaine took one last look at her lovely gown.

The twins charged jubilantly into the glittering ballroom. Couples were already on the dance floor, and the first number was coming to a close. George was partnered with a very pretty young lady. Her jet-black hair was tied back with a simple ribbon, her dress plain. She had to be an islander. Anne was dancing with Paul, her eyes fixed on his face, her arms ensnaring him whenever the cotillion brought them together. Though the woman irked her, Charmaine was indifferent to the sight of them in one another's embrace. Perhaps she'd just grown accustomed to seeing them together.

Robert Blackford stood in the shadows close to the orchestra and watched his sister. As the musicians tuned up for the first waltz, Agatha led Frederic to the dance floor, where she placed one possessive hand on his shoulder and the other on his waist. Her exquisite blood-red gown accentuated a curvaceous figure that every woman her age would envy. Her fine jewelry glittered in the light of the chandelier. Robert admired her anew. She was still beautiful, the most beautiful woman in the room. As Frederic stepped into the waltz, Robert fantasized... He walked across the room with an authoritative step, tapped Frederic's shoulder, and took the man's place. But now, as the couple drifted past him, his sister's radiant face shattered his idyllic musings. Though Frederic worked hard at the cumbersome steps, Agatha's eyes were suffused with pride, satisfaction, and love as she looked up at him. Yes, love was the word. After all these years, the truth struck Robert like a full broadside. His sister was, and always had been, in love with Frederic Duvoisin.

As the second waltz began, Yvette and Jeannette took to dancing together, until Yvette caught sight of Joseph Thornfield leaning against the wall holding a tray. She broke away, grabbed the tray, and deposited it on a table. She paired him off with her sister, prodding them to waltz together. They danced off awkwardly, much to the guests' amusement.

A hush and then murmurs near the main archway caught Charmaine's attention. She froze as John walked in with Mercedes on his arm. She wore a gorgeous tawny gown, her long auburn hair falling with scandalous abandon to her waist. She was stunning. *But why was she with John?* Charmaine felt betrayed, paralyzed by a consuming wave of jealousy. Her eyes searched the dance floor to see George's reaction, but he was still partnered with the black-haired girl.

Yvette ran over to her brother and pointed out Jeannette and Joseph. A smile broke across John's face, but Mercedes' gaze was riveted on George.

Finally, the music stopped. John grasped Mercedes' elbow and led her to George, who was now quite alone. They exchanged a few words, and George's smile widened when Mercedes fell in at his side. He placed a possessive hand on the small of her back, and Charmaine's envy ebbed. Mercedes was beaming.

The three stood chatting until Rose grabbed John's arm and pulled him into a Scottish reel. She broke into a spry step that belied her advanced years, and John had to work to keep up with her. They danced two more numbers before John wiped the sweat from his brow, and handed her off to George.

Charmaine felt miserable – isolated – anxious for her hour with the twins to be over so that she could barricade herself in her room and cry herself to sleep.

Frederic was glad when the waltz ended. It had been a test of stamina, not only of body, but mind, as well. And now, as he walked off the dance floor and left Agatha with a clutch of prattling matrons and their vacuous conversation, he dropped his constrained smile.

A group of men were arguing heatedly in a corner of the room. He headed their way. "... no Percival, I'll leave the first runs to you. You test the waters with *your* goods and *your* money."

"Once Paul has an established market, there may not be space next year."

"I'll take my chances. There are always shippers out there."

"Yes, but at what price? The Duvoisin fees are too good to pass up."

There were murmurs of agreement, quickly quelled when the first man pressed his point. "Yes, with a five-year commitment. I've heard too much talk of discord. Some say that Frederic and John aren't even on speaking terms.

"Advantageous to Paul – and anyone using his shipping line. He might very well take charge of his father's fleet one day."

The man grunted. "But in the interim, pandemonium may reign."

Another man butted in. "I've watched the three of them together throughout the week. I'm not fond of John, but I haven't heard one word that alarms me."

"A word? No. But what about the hostile undercurrents? Even Paul has turned curt. I met him last year at Edward Richecourt's office. He was quite affable then. I get the distinct impression that he's annoyed that his brother is involved. I also think that all three of them are putting on a grand façade for us."

"When has John ever 'put on a façade', Matthew? He doesn't care–"

"When it involves money, and his fortune to boot, he cares. He loves to flaunt his wealth. Take that sign above his plantation gate. It must have cost–"

"Excuse me, gentlemen," Frederic interrupted, the small group falling silent. "Allow me to respond to some of your concerns." He looked at the man who was arguing most vehemently and smiled. "You make a good point, Matthew. I would ask the same questions if I were in the market for an intercontinental carrier. John and I have often disagreed – it stems from a desire to be in charge – but those disagreements have never adversely affected Duvoisin business. You see, I respect John's judgment as surely as I do Paul's. During the ten years he has been in charge in America, my assets have more than tripled there." Frederic paused, allowing his words to sink in. "Nevertheless, John is not the issue here, Paul is. *His* fleet of ships, *his* shipping concern, the routes *he* has set up, are just that – *his*. Everything you have seen this week, he has planned and built on his own. The only help I've provided is financial backing. Neither John nor I will have any dealings with his enterprise, other than to give advice when and if he asks for it. In fact, that should be your primary concern, Matthew – that Paul does, in fact, ask. This area of Duvoisin business is fairly new to him. John has dealt with most of the shipping thus far, and knows, even better than I, the ins and outs that make it lucrative, not only for the Duvoisin family, but for the brokers who utilize his transport. It is the main reason he is here this week – to share his knowledge."

"Frederic, I meant no offense."

"No offense taken," Frederic replied expansively. "Your objectivity in reviewing all aspects of these contracts indicates a sound business mind." He extended a hand to the gentleman and shook each in turn. "Now, if you have any other concerns, please come to me. That is why you've been invited here."

Anne was incensed. Her personal lady's maid had just waltzed by in the arms of her smitten suitor, George Richards, wearing *her* finest gown, a gown she had yet to wear, a gown that had cost a small fortune. Her couturier had designed it expressly for her, and she had been saving it for Mass tomorrow, determined to surpass tonight's stunning effect. That plan was foiled now, and Anne's blood boiled. How dare she? How dare that snip of a girl deliberately flout her mistress' authority? Anne inhaled deeply, holding the violent breath for untold seconds. *Well, Mercedes Wells... you will regret coming down here! On Monday, after all the guests have departed, I will dismiss you. Then you shall see just how much your beau cares about you!*

John was simmering by the time Charmaine and his sisters left the ballroom. Anne had been his brother's dinner partner and had returned on his arm, obviously his companion for the entire evening. Charmaine was dressed in her drab governess garb, seeing to his sisters. Apparently, Paul's invitation had been rescinded.

The twins were already asleep. Charmaine had changed into her nightgown and had just settled into the armchair with a book in hand when there was a rap on her door. She was astounded to find John waiting in the corridor.

"I thought Paul was to be your escort for the evening," he stated directly.

"I didn't lie to you, John."

"I know you didn't lie," he replied. "So what happened?"

"Agatha invited Anne London to the ball on Paul's behalf yesterday at lunch. She spoke for him, and he couldn't refuse."

"So *he* lied to *you*."

"It wasn't a lie. He wanted to escort me."

"Right," John remarked doubtfully.

"Agatha threw them together. Paul didn't want to embarrass them."

"I wouldn't have cared about embarrassing them."

"You enjoy embarrassing people, John," she retorted. "Paul doesn't."

"No. Paul enjoys having a woman on his arm while another waits for him in the wings."

Charmaine smarted with his words. "You're wrong. He wanted to take me. He regretted what happened and apologized."

"So you humored him and are cheated out of this evening, while *she* enjoys his company."

Charmaine didn't care to be reminded of her disappointment. Still, she knew that the slight had not been intentional and felt compelled to defend Paul. "You don't understand, John, and you are being unfair. He has promised to make it up to me. What does one silly night matter anyway, when the future–"

She caught herself, certain that she'd revealed too much, John's brow already furrowed in swift comprehension. Embarrassed, she turned back into the room, but he followed her.

"Paul proposed to you?" he asked. "Is that what you're trying to hide?"

"Is that so inconceivable?" she rejoined, pivoting round to face him, nettled that he didn't think her worthy.

"What? That he proposed to you, or that you're trying to hide it?"

"I'm not trying to hide it!" she exclaimed. "And yes, he proposed to me."

"So *he's* trying to hide it."

"No, he's not!" she objected.

John's frown deepened. "So when does Paul plan on announcing this engagement, Charmaine? At the ball tonight, with you in your room and Anne at his side?"

His words stung like salt in a fresh wound. Again, she was baited into saying more than she wished to. "We're not betrothed yet. I told him I would think about it."

John's eyes betrayed surprise, but his words were cutting. "How generous of you and convenient for him. One last stand before he's a happily married man!"

"I haven't made it convenient for him!" Charmaine countered defensively, her anger and shame melding into one sickening lump of foolishness. "I've told you, he was embarrassed by Agatha and forced into a situation out of his control."

John snorted in disgust. "So tell me, Charmaine – if Agatha tells Anne tonight, '*Anne, Paul has asked for your hand in marriage*', my brother will be too embarrassed to tell Anne, '*I've already proposed to Charmaine*'. Do I have it right now?"

She glared at him furiously. There was no point in responding.

"Now that we've figured that out, get dressed. *I* will take you to the ball."

She hesitated, stunned and thrilled by his offer. She opened her mouth to accept, but the implications of doing so stopped her. "It wouldn't be appropriate for me to accompany another man until I give Paul an answer."

John stood incredulous. "But it's acceptable for him to escort another woman to the ball with a standing marriage proposal to you?"

Charmaine sighed in frustration. "Why does it matter to you, anyway?"

John fell mute, debating his answer. He must drop talk of his brother if he were to convince her to accompany him. "It matters to me because I know you've been looking forward to this night," he finally replied. "You've talked about little else the entire week. I could see how disappointed you were at dinner."

She was surprised. He *had* noticed her. Suddenly, her mood lifted.

"Now, Charmaine," he coaxed, "there isn't a woman alive who wouldn't give her right arm to be downstairs tonight. This opportunity may never come your way again. You can tell anyone who asks that we are merely friends."

Her resolve was weakening, even though she knew no one would believe that they were just friends.

"Please come, my Charm," he pressed on. "I've attended many such parties, and it won't matter to me if I miss this one. But I *will* take great pleasure in seeing you enjoy it. If you don't accompany me, we shall both be disappointed."

Charmaine mulled over his petition. Why *should* she miss such a splendid affair, perhaps the opportunity of a lifetime? She desperately wanted to go. Then there was her daring side, chuckling inwardly, wondering how the likes of Mary Stanton and Anne London would react when she arrived on John's arm.

"Very well," she capitulated. "I'll go. But I'm warning you now, if you embarrass me even once, I will leave."

"I won't, I won't," he replied, waving off her threat as he headed toward the door. "You have ten minutes," he directed, as he stepped out of the room.

"*Ten minutes?*"

"Ten minutes." His face was bright with satisfaction. "I'll be waiting."

The portal closed behind him, leaving her to her hasty toilette. In a flurry, she was ripping off her nightgown and pulling the evening gown from her armoire. It hugged her bust and waist, flaring out at her hips and tumbling to the floor. The champagne silk complimented her skin and dark hair, pronouncing her natural innocence, while the sash at her waist accentuated her slim, yet curvaceous figure, and the sheer frill that trimmed her décolletage drew attention to the swell of her breasts. She'd have to get used to the low-cut neckline as well as the feel of the delicate satin slippers on her feet. Quickly, she brushed out her hair and swept the curls off her face with ivory combs. She deftly twisted the thick mane into a queue that fell over her left shoulder, cinching it with a fancy hair clip. With a pinch, she coaxed her cheeks to a rosy hue. Before long, she was standing at the looking glass, wondering if she were the same girl of only twenty minutes ago. She turned from side to side and was pleased with what she saw. She considered her glowing face one last time, then stepped confidently to the door.

John leaned over the balustrade, his impatient eyes on the landing below. At the sound of the portal opening behind him, he straightened and turned. The vision of loveliness standing in the doorway surpassed any that he'd conjured up. If he didn't look away, he'd lead her right back into the bedroom and forget about the ball. He trained his eyes on her pretty face. She was oblivious to the effect she had on him, for although her cheeks were flushed, her eyes sparkled girlishly.

Charmaine was unnerved by his perusal, which compelled her to speak. "Could it be that *you* of all people are speechless?"

He laughed, glad that she had broken the spell. "You are a sight to behold, my Charm," he replied. "A vision of perfection."

His compliment made her feel attractive and feminine. "And you are very handsome this evening," she returned. "Black becomes you."

"Not the first time you've voiced words to that effect."

She giggled, her giddiness rising.

"Be careful, my Charm," he warned, "you are so beautiful tonight, I may have to live up to my black reputation, and we may never make it to the ball this evening."

She smiled with his brash flattery, happy to know that he found her desirable. He took her arm and led her to the staircase.

A heady blend of apprehension, joy, and excitement reached its pinnacle as they began their descent. She broke away, and he chuckled when she raced ahead, throwing him a backward glance from the landing. Leaning over the banister, she could see into the ballroom, where the mélange of color, fragrance, and music was irresistible. Hems of gowns flashed past the arched doorway, a kaleidoscope of sight and sound. The waltz was fast and catchy – the newest craze – the Bohemian Polka – the instruments perfectly tuned. Only John held her back.

"Am I not the escort, my Charm?" he smiled wryly as he caught up with her. He extended his arm, and she slipped her hand through the bend of his elbow, reveling in the feel of muscle beneath the fabric.

"I feel like Cinderella," she whispered, "and you're my fairy godmother."

"How can that be, my Charm?" he queried devilishly, "I haven't taken out my magic wand yet." He laughed at her confusion, then guided her down the remaining steps and through the foyer. They crossed the threshold of the great hall together.

The music had just stopped and Charmaine looked around the room. Her eyes met those of quite a few guests, who considered her with intense interest. She was dressed like an elegant society lady, yet she knew that had little to do with it. The world had suddenly noticed her because she was with John. Two words – 'the governess' – passed in murmurs behind her. Undaunted, John led her further into the room, tall at her side, his gait unrushed and confident. She felt protected next to him, his firm hand at the small of her back.

"Charmaine, you look lovely!" George exclaimed when they reached him. "I'm glad that you've returned. Everyone is having a fabulous time!"

With eyebrow arched, Mercedes passed Charmaine a knowing nod.

A bellowing voice called for silence, and the noise of the crowd died down. Charmaine glanced around, and once again, caught many eyes upon her, Mary Stanton gaping from the sidelines. At the center of the room, Edward Richecourt climbed atop a chair, a makeshift platform for his announcement.

John elbowed George. "You slip on the noose, and I'll kick out the chair!"

George's raucous guffaws echoed to the rafters, and people turned to see who was laughing.

"Ladies and gentlemen!" Richecourt shouted magnanimously. "I'd like to propose a toast." He lifted a glass of champagne to Paul. "To our fine host," he continued loudly, "he has treated us like royalty this week, culminating in this exquisite celebration. May this intrepid endeavor become his triumph! Cheers!"

A round of applause gripped the hall. A call went up for Paul to take the platform. As he did, Charmaine felt John's hand slip around her waist, pulling her close, the feel of his sturdy frame quite pleasing.

"Thank you for your kind wishes," Paul stated cordially.

Charmaine stiffened as his eyes roamed over the spectators, arcing in her direction. She tried to step away from John, but his arm was like a vise, holding her in place.

"And I thank you all for journeying here," Paul continued. "I hope that this evening will be your best yet on Charmantes–" His gaze alighted on John "–I look forward to a prosperous relationship with each and every one of you–" then settled in blatant astonishment on her. He took them in as a couple, and Charmaine read fury in his eyes, his speech ending between clenched teeth. "My father and I hope you enjoy the remainder of the evening." Though the audience cheered enthusiastically, he didn't seem to notice, for his reproachful gaze never left her.

As the clapping died down, John snatched a glass of champagne off the tray of a passing server. He raised it to propose his own toast, his crisp, resonant voice halting Paul before he stepped down. "To you, Paul," he declared full-voiced. "I admire your persistence. In less than two years, you've kindled a budding empire from a deserted island. When you really know what you want, *nothing* holds you back. Here's to making dreams come true."

Paul's mouth flew open to retaliate, but a third round of applause drowned him out. The crowd closed ranks, shouting good wishes and drinking to his success.

"I'm leaving!" Charmaine huffed, her eyes flashing.

"Not yet," John argued, his voice sympathetic, though he held fast.

"And how am I to face Paul after this? We both know what he thinks."

"What does he think, Charmaine?" John demanded evenly.

"That we're together."

"And we are," he replied simply. "That's his fault. So why worry about facing him? If you'd left it up to him, you'd be up there–" and he nodded toward the ceiling "–reading some goddamn book, wishing you were down here!"

"Why did you have to embarrass me like that?"

"I didn't embarrass you. He was going to find out sooner or later, wasn't he? He doesn't deserve you, Charmaine."

He released her, acknowledging that ultimately, it was her choice to stay or to go. The band tuned up, and the crowd dispersed to clear the floor.

"May I have this dance, my Charm?" he petitioned softly, innocently, prompting her to decide. She wanted to stay, and as her eyes met his, the plea in their soft brown depths gave way to the rogue, chasing the little boy away.

"I'm not sure I remember how," she hesitated.

"I'm not very good at it either," he smiled, pleased with his second victory of the evening. He held up a finger. "But if we stumble, we can always consult an expert." He nodded in Geoffrey Elliot's direction, where the solicitor looped around a cluster of dancers, writhing and twisting grotesquely before a comely partner, drawing disdainful glares.

Charmaine giggled when the couple whirled past them.

"With Geffey on the floor," John expounded, "nobody will even notice us!"

With that, he opened his arms, inviting her into his embrace. She placed one hand in his and the other on his shoulder. His warm hand clasped her waist as they stepped into the beat of the music. She followed his lead, quickly realizing that he knew every step. Her lessons with Loretta came back slowly, and her eyes finally left her sluggish feet for John's face.

He smiled down at her, and she was bound to his regard until the room and crowd fell away, and there was nothing but the music, the mild air imbibed with the fragrance of tropical flowers, and this man. For months now, not a moment had gone by when some corner of her mind had not coveted precious thoughts of him. Her throat constricted, and a deep flush suffused her cheeks.

She stepped back as the waltz ended, thankful that he misinterpreted her crimson face. "It's warm in here, isn't it?" he remarked, leading her to the French doors. "I'll get us something to drink."

She welcomed his departure, for she needed time to compose herself.

Frederic stood on the sidelines of the huge hall watching Charmaine Ryan dance with John. He was intrigued when she'd returned to the ballroom on his son's arm. They were drawing a lot of attention, the room abuzz with speculation. He studied Charmaine's expression, one he'd never seen when she was around Paul, and he understood why that relationship hadn't progressed these many months. *She was in love with John.*

Pondering it now, Frederic realized that he'd often thought of the governess and John as a couple. It had started the first time he'd seen them together, the day that Agatha had ruthlessly spanked Pierre, that day when he'd been acutely aware of Colette's presence in the house. Then there was the twins' birthday, when he observed John helping Charmaine onto the dappling mare. And the night when Yvette had been gambling at Dulcie's; Charmaine's eyes had flown to John for protection, not Paul. He'd never forget those terrible days when Pierre lay dying, the untold hours they'd spent at his bedside, or Charmaine's compassion for John afterward, her heartfelt tears over his suffering. And just a week ago, her face had brightened with unabashed joy when John returned.

A glimmer of hope heartened Frederic as he watched them now. For the first time in ten long, dismal years, John looked happy. The cynicism that John had worn like a badge was gone. Frederic closed his eyes and uttered a silent prayer that his son had finally found someone to call his own.

"So, Mademoiselle, you've rejoined the festivities," Paul commented politely as he came to stand before her. The strains of the next waltz had just begun. "May I have this dance?"

Charmaine nodded charily. John was still off getting drinks, and she knew she could not turn Paul down without embarrassing him. He took her hand, and they walked to the center of the dance floor. There, she stepped into his embrace, not daring to look up. Instead, she cast her eyes aside, noticing that some of the guests, especially the women, were scrutinizing them avidly.

Anne London could hardly conceal her ire when she caught sight of the couple. First Mercedes, now this! *Charmaine Ryan... I have underestimated you. You have beguiled not only John, but Paul as well. What is this game you are playing?*

Throughout the evening, Anne had itched to reveal all concerning the rewriting of Frederic Duvoisin's will and John's abolitionist activities. But her father's warning forced her to glumly hold her tongue. Charmaine Ryan had been the least of her concerns. She was a servant girl, riffraff. But here she was, escorted by John to this high-society affair, and dancing with Paul – blushing in his arms! *What was going on?* It was time to intervene! Her father hadn't forbidden gossip about the governess; so that was where she'd start. Then, she'd throw caution to the wind and use her experience with men to make Paul forget the woman.

For a few minutes, Charmaine and Paul danced in painful silence. She did not feel the thrill of being in his arms as she had so many times before.

"It didn't take you long to make other plans for the evening, Charmaine."

His words stung. "I didn't make other plans," she countered. "John invited me to join him, and it only happened a short while ago."

She caught sight of Mary Stanton watching amidst a bevy of matrons.

"Why didn't you tell me that you were angry, Charmaine?" he asked, drawing her eyes back to him.

"Angry? About what?"

"Obviously you are getting even with me by returning on John's arm."

"Getting even?" she asked, his reasoning beginning to register.

"Because of what happened with Agatha and Anne – to give me a taste of rejection. Isn't that it?"

"No, that is not it!" she refuted, offended that he would think her so petty.

Paul chuckled derisively, inciting her more.

"I was not angry, but I was disappointed. John saw that, and invited me when he realized I would miss the ball."

"John is very good at stealing other men's women," he replied, his voice low so that only Charmaine could hear. "Do you want to be his next victim?"

Her temper flared, but she resisted the urge to tear away. Instead, she looked him straight in the eye, mustered a pleasant voice and said, "He wouldn't have been able to steal me tonight if you had brought me here yourself."

"Then you *are* angry," he rejoined, his minor victory dissatisfying.

"I'm angry now."

They danced the rest of the waltz in icy silence. Paul watched her return to his brother, who was waiting with two drinks.

"You look annoyed, my Charm," John commented as he handed her a glass.

"I don't want to talk about it," she replied.

"Why? Because he scolded you?" John quipped.

"I told you, I don't want to discuss it."

"You should have given him a piece of your mind, Charmaine."

"No! I refuse to make a scene here. This event means too much to him."

"He didn't seem too concerned about that," John scoffed derisively. "He's very fortunate that you care."

"Paul has been very good to me," she retaliated. "Although you might not understand it, John, I care for him very deeply."

He relented. Best to drop the subject, though her words 'care very deeply' were perplexing. She hadn't accepted Paul's proposal, so what did she mean?

They had danced nearly every dance, and now they were in the lush gardens, where they'd stolen away from prying eyes. George couldn't stop kissing her. How John had managed to coax Mercedes down to the ball, George could only wonder, but whatever he did, George thanked him now. This was the most exciting night of his life. He bent low to kiss her again. On Monday, she'd return to Richmond. He didn't want her to leave, for he loved her so. "Mercedes," he murmured in her ear.

"Yes…?" she whispered, hugging him close.

"Will you marry me?"

Her embrace quickened. "Yes! Oh, yes!"

"May I have this dance with the lady?"

John turned to Geoffrey Elliot, who had tapped him on the shoulder, his avid eyes on Charmaine. "Is your name written on her dance program?" John rejoined.

"Well – actually – no."

"There is your answer." John prodded Charmaine into the steps of the next reel, leaving an insulted Geoffrey alone in the center of the floor.

The next dance was a quadrille. Charmaine squared off with George, and Mercedes with John. Charmaine had thought that no one could be as happy as she, but George's eyes twinkled brighter than ever before. As the music died down, Rose once again stepped in and stole her grandson away. Charmaine laughed as George tried to keep pace with his wiry grandmother.

Throughout the evening, John had been the perfect gentleman. Like a debutante, Charmaine stole admiring glances at him: his height, the fine tailoring of his jacket, the lamplight playing its color-game with his hair. She was oddly exhilarated when his warm hand lightly brushed hers or their shoulders touched when they sat side by side.

The ballroom was dreadfully hot, and many guests lingered close to the French doors where the air was cooler. Exhausted, Charmaine took a seat close to them. John stood nearby, four gentlemen chewing his ear. They were embroiled in a debate that by Charmaine's estimation had been ongoing over the past week. They could not bend the radical's mind, their discussion spiraling, touching upon an array of current events: the new president (Martin Van Buren), the dissolution of the Bank of the United States, and inevitably, the slave question. Though the men talked about these subjects with absolute gravity, John remained jocular, his bemusement growing proportionately with their anger. One stalwart Virginian nearly screamed the word 'traitor' in his face when he insisted that he welcomed protectionist tariffs on foreign imports. Though detrimental to shipping, they would fuel manufacturing in the North and benefit his investments there.

"Well, why should tonight be any different?"

A sandpaper voice caught Charmaine's ear. She turned slightly to find two plump, middle-aged women six feet away, heads tilted together, eyes on John.

"You know, the Palmers were in New York on business last February and he actually had the nerve to bring that quadroon woman along with him to the dinner party thrown by the Severs. Sarah Palmer told me that the woman was a slave on his plantation, but that he freed her a few years ago and brought her to New York." The woman smiled smugly. "We all know what *she* did to earn *her* freedom!"

The other woman manufactured a scandalized expression. "I've heard that whenever he's in New York, she stays with him at his house. It is common knowledge that she is his – his–"

"–mistress," the second supplied.

Charmaine was stunned, and her eyes went to John. His futile conversation had taken its toll; he was shaking his head.

"I wonder if his mistress in New York knows that he has one here!"

"And the governess of all people!" the first woman exclaimed. "I can just imagine the lessons she's taught his sisters!"

Both women shared a hearty laugh at Charmaine's expense, indifferent that she was now looking at them, their heads bent close together, though she caught snippets of their continued abuse. "White trash… what can you expect? Imagine, someone like that being hired to such a position?" Their eyes condemned her, while their remarks cut deeply into her dignity.

John's tender voice drew her away from their flagrant condescension. "Don't pay them any mind, Charmaine." Then he spoke loud enough for the women to hear. "They're two fat, ugly cows who haven't been touched by a man in decades, and they're jealous because you are young and beautiful."

Their mouths dropped open in apoplectic indignation, but they didn't dare utter another insulting word.

Paul found a moment's peace in the cool kitchen, a breeze coming through the open back door. Fatima wasn't there. She was working from the cookhouse behind the ballroom tonight. For as long as he could remember, this was his favorite place to go when he was frustrated. Although it was Fatima's territory, she never shooed him away. She'd been feeding him since he was old enough to beg for her cookies, and understood his moods. So, when he came in search of solace, she'd pile a plate high, pour a glass of milk, and set them on the table before him. Then, she'd turn back to her chores: the potatoes that needed peeling or the dough that needed kneading. In her deep, melodious voice, she'd hum a pitch-perfect tune while she worked, a yearning, soulful strain.

The soothing elixir of childhood memories did not have an enduring effect. Aggravated, he flung himself into one of the chairs, cradling his aching head in his hands. He'd been stupid yesterday, and he'd played the lout tonight. Damn!

Suddenly, he sensed somebody watching him, and he lifted his gaze to the door. He was thunderstruck by the girl standing there. Straight black hair framed the loveliest face he'd ever laid eyes on. Thick, dark lashes hooded her extraordinary green eyes. She stepped into the room, revealing a body that rivaled her face. She was young, more than ten years his junior, he surmised. He wondered why she hadn't caught his eye before. It was impossible not to notice such a comely lass. He stood, uncomfortable with the way she silently assessed him.

Rebecca hadn't expected to find him here, in fact, she was certain that she wouldn't find him at all. Now, as she had so often dreamed, they were in a room together, alone, and she was tongue-tied.

"Are you lost?" he asked, the question reverberating foolishly off the walls.

"No," came a husky alto voice.

"Then what can I do for you? Perhaps you are hungry," he suggested, his hand sweeping about in indication of the room.

"No."

The short response left him wondering if she had spoken at all. For all her beauty, she was odd, standing there staring at him. If she were the daughter of one of his guests, why hadn't he seen her before?

"I can't say I remember meeting you, Miss…?"

No answer.

"To which family do you belong?"

"None," she finally replied, her voice mellow and sensual. It did not match her youth. "I mean, I'm not one of your formal guests. My brother brought me. He is in your employ."

"Your brother?"

"Wade Remmen."

"Ah, yes," Paul murmured, the light beginning to dawn. "Our impressive Mr. Remmen. I had forgotten he had a sister."

His mind continued to work. What was it now – two years or three – since the indigent siblings had stowed away on a Duvoisin vessel? Amazing, the generosity of time. Or was his memory of a wide-eyed, half-starved, filthy girl deceiving him? "And what might your name be, Miss Remmen?"

"Rebecca."

"A lovely name," he commented gregariously, comfortable now that the conversation had begun to flow. "And what brings you to my kitchen, Miss Remmen? Have you a complaint that you would like to bring to the cook?"

"I came to see you," she answered simply, much to his astonishment.

"To see me?" he reiterated. "I don't even know you, Rebecca. What could you possibly have to say to me?"

"That I love you."

He laughed outright at the ingenuous declaration, the naked honesty that nevertheless gave him pause. *What the hell was this? An adoring adolescent pouring out her heart and soul?* He groaned with the thought of her tagging after him now, appearing at inopportune times, as if her ardent proclamation gave her that right. Well, there was an easy way to deal with this. "You love me."

"Yes."

The green eyes shone brilliantly in the lamp-lit room. If she weren't so young, he'd taste the fruit right here in the kitchen, but he was certain that she'd never been with a man. If she had, she wouldn't be standing here laying bare her feelings. He preferred an experienced wench, anyway.

"And what do you intend to do about this?" he asked, commencing a stroll along the perimeter of the room.

"I wanted to tell you," she answered evenly, her eyes following him.

"To what end?"

"To the end of becoming your wife," she declared, eliciting another hearty laugh. Undaunted, she held her head high. He'd never be hers without a fight. The battle would require time, but time was on her side. Tonight was a victory.

"As I pointed out before, Miss Remmen," Paul rejoined, "I don't even know you, and I needn't indicate the difference in our ages. What could you possibly offer me that would make me consider marrying you?" He assessed her rakishly, his eyes boldly running over her body, certain that this approach would quell her amorous overtures. However, if she remained open to his advance, he'd be a fool to deny his manhood, especially with such an exceptional prize.

"I don't understand..." she faltered in that all too familiar innocence that fanned his ire.

Damn, it was his own fault that his pursuit of Charmaine had become so complicated. He'd lost control of the game when he'd begun playing it her way. Had he but stayed the normal course...

He abruptly closed in, towering over the girl. He'd always been victorious in his romantic conquests; she proved it. He could have her now if he wished.

The green eyes were watching him, her head craned back to meet his regard, her composure shaken. But she was too proud, or perhaps wanted him too much to back away. For the moment, he savored this delectable bit of femininity, fought to ignore the young girl he knew lay beneath this deceptive display of blooming womanhood. He leaned forward to kiss her ruby lips, to possess her body, ripe and ready for the plucking.

The door slapped open and the quiet kitchen was violated with a barrage of noise, stale air, and Anne London. With artful timing, he stepped back and was straightening his jacket before she spotted him.

"Here you are!" she bubbled, seizing his arm and prodding him toward the door. "Everyone is looking for you. You've abandoned your own celebration!" She glanced in Rebecca's direction, but turned back to him so swiftly, he wondered if she'd noticed Rebecca at all. He had no chance to protest, and thoughts of Rebecca Remmen were left behind with Anne's fulsome laughter.

Charmaine relished the momentary peace of the terrace. John was perched on the marble balustrade, his arms folded across his chest. He was so close – so alive. A soft breeze tousled his healthy crop of hair so that it fell enticingly low upon his brow, just a stroke away from her aching hand, if only she braved the wifely caress. Instead, she stepped into the breeze, moving toward the end of the colonnade where it would be more plentiful.

John grasped her hand to hold her back. "You are lovely tonight, my Charm."

"Thank you," she murmured.

"Why haven't you accepted my brother's marriage proposal?" he abruptly asked, his eyes unusually stormy.

The answer thundered in her head: *Because I'm in love with you!*

Suddenly, someone was calling from the French doors. "Charmaine? Charmaine is that you?"

Charmaine turned. A young woman stood in the archway, silhouetted by the bright light of the ballroom. "There you are!" she exclaimed. "I've been searching for you since I got here, but nobody knew where you were!"

Gwendolyn Browning stepped into the circle of torchlight.

"Gwendolyn!" Charmaine laughed, rushing forward and hugging her affectionately. "What are you doing here? When did you get back?"

"Mother wrote to me, bragging over Father's unexpected invitation, and of course, I wouldn't miss this for the world! We should have been here hours ago, but there was a mix-up at the livery. All the carriages had been dispatched with you-know-who's guests, and we were forced to wait until one returned. Mother worked herself into a dither, telling Father that he should have secured a coupe for us. Father insisted that he was the hired help and the guests came first. Before I knew it, they were arguing. I thought we'd never get here!"

John chuckled and walked to the end of the terrace, allowing Charmaine some time with her garrulous friend, who gesticulated emphatically with her hands.

"Oh, this is just so wonderful, Charmaine, isn't it? This house is beautiful. And look at you! You're gorgeous! Oh, Charmaine, you are *so* lucky!"

"Yes, Gwendolyn you've said that before. I am very fortunate."

"Charmaine, some of my friends from Richmond are here. They've heard about you-know-who and are jealous."

Charmaine wasn't surprised that Gwendolyn's talk turned to Paul. It never took her more than a few minutes to get around to her favorite topic.

"They didn't believe me when I told them the real man is ten times as handsome as the rumor. Anyway, tonight they know that I wasn't lying."

"Gwendolyn…" Charmaine chided, casting a sidelong glance at John. He was leaning against the railing some distance away, but still within earshot. For the moment, he seemed inclined to allow her this reunion with her friend.

"When word about the banquet started to circulate, I told them that I've known about it for months. When they expressed doubt, I told them I could prove my story – that my best friend actually works in the mansion where you-know-who lives – and the next letter I received from you, I read to them. You should have seen them turn green with envy!"

"Gwendolyn!" Charmaine expostulated in embarrassment, "you didn't!"

"I did!" she averred unabashedly. "Have you seen you-know-who tonight?"

"Of course I have," Charmaine answered, "but I–"

"Lord, I nearly swooned when I saw him," she bubbled, "I thought perhaps my memory had exaggerated how fine he is, but I swear, Charmaine, he is the most beautiful man my eyes have ever been blessed to see! His broad shoulders and muscular chest, his narrow waist and finely tailored trousers... Mother had to scold me three times when my eyes lingered on his manly bulge–"

"Gwendolyn!" Charmaine admonished sharply. "With whom have you been associating? Mrs. Harrington would be appalled–"

"Oh, don't be a prude, Charmaine!" she laughed in naked happiness, ignoring Charmaine's shocked erubescence. "All my friends whisper about such things, and of course I've told them that you-know-who is the most perfect specimen to behold! Why, he's the best part of being home. If only I could dance with him tonight. Oh, those girls would just shrivel up and die! It would be a dream come true for a fat, ugly girl like me!"

"Really Gwendolyn!"

"*Ssh...!*" the girl warned, her eyes cast down the veranda. Charmaine turned round and nearly jumped out of her skin to find John standing right behind her.

"Are you ready, my Charm?" he asked with a grin, his eyes twinkling.

Gwendolyn became tight-lipped, cowering slightly in John's presence, and Charmaine realized that her friend did not know who he was. Likewise, Gwendolyn surmised that Charmaine knew this man quite well.

"Miss Browning," John greeted, his voice sharp and masculine in the stilted silence. "I'm pleased to make your acquaintance."

"How – how do you know my name?" Gwendolyn stammered.

"Oh, I remember you. You're Harold's daughter," he replied. "You used to tag along after your father in the cane fields when you were just a little girl."

Confused, Gwendolyn blushed. "Who are you?" she demanded, now feeling quite foolish.

"You don't remember me? Well, now that you've shared your most coveted secrets, introductions are in order."

Gwendolyn's eyes flew helpless to Charmaine.

"This is John Duvoisin, Gwendolyn."

John's brow lifted devilishly. "You-know-who's brother."

Gwendolyn's eyes grew wide as saucers. Never before had Charmaine seen a face so red, not even in a mirror.

Wiping his hands clean, John returned to Charmaine's side. He considered the couple dancing a few feet away and could scarcely suppress his mirth.

"I can't believe you managed to do that," Charmaine declared with the shake of her head, watching her radiant friend in her glorious moment, dancing in Paul's arms. "How did you get him to agree?"

"He wasn't about to say 'no' in front of two important business prospects and their wives."

Charmaine giggled gaily as Gwendolyn and Paul glided by, Gwendolyn actually tearing her eyes away from the man to smile happily at her. "It was kind of you to do this," she said. "You've made her dream come true."

"I did it for selfish reasons," he confessed.

"Selfish reasons?"

"I'm dying to see her swoon in my brother's arms!"

The statement had barely left John's lips when the room resounded with a loud gasp of: "Dear Lord!" and fell into a hush. The crowd edged away from the dance floor, and the band tuned down, disparate violins carrying fading strains of the melody. The circle of bodies burst open, and Paul labored toward them, a lifeless Gwendolyn in his arms and accusatory eyes leveled on John. Out of breath, he deposited her in a chair. Caroline appeared from nowhere to angrily shoo him away. She produced a fan from her purse and flapped it vigorously in her daughter's face. Charmaine's eyes shifted to Paul, who was shaking his head.

"What happened?" someone finally had the courage to ask him.

"How in hell am I to know?" Paul expostulated gruffly, "obviously she's of a rather weak constitution."

In the time it took John to snicker, Caroline turned on Paul. "Her constitution was just fine until you accosted her! She is of fine stock, sir, descended from an established bloodline!"

"Do you have her papers?" John demanded loudly. "Fine breeding requires official certificates. My brother always demands certificates. He loves the little seals, you see."

If there were a hole nearby, Charmaine would gladly have crawled into it, for each and every eye had turned upon them. Even Caroline Browning was speechless. Mercifully, Gwendolyn sighed.

"What happened, Gwendolyn?" Charmaine probed.

The bewildered girl sighed. "I swooned!"

John's hearty laughter brought the unfortunate episode to an end. Taking Charmaine's arm, he led her back to the dance floor, muttering, "I told him those trousers were too tight."

"I just wanted to prompt your recollection, John. You will permit me to call you John, won't you?" Geoffrey Elliot asked rhetorically. "I'll be making my departure tomorrow and do require your autograph on the legal instruments I proffered to you on Monday."

"Did you write those contracts?" John asked.

"Why yes, I did."

"I gave them back to Richecourt," John lied.

"To Richecourt?" Geoffrey asked. "Why?"

"They need to be translated."

Geoffrey's face twisted into a confused frown. "Translated?"

"To English."

"But – they *were* in English," he stammered. "I don't understand...?"

"Neither did I, Geffey. But, that's neither here, there or anywhere. There's a lovely young lady I'd like you to meet. Her bloodlines rival your own..."

They'd danced their last dance of the evening, and John escorted Charmaine to her bedchamber door. The clock tolled one, but music and voices still resounded in the corridors. She stood against the portal with arms clasped behind her. "Well, my Charm," John said, "I suppose this is goodnight."

"Yes, I suppose it is," she replied with a smile. "I have to check on the girls," she added, suddenly very nervous. "I hope they've stayed in their room..." The words caught in her throat as John closed the short distance between them, looking down at her, so very silent. "Thank you," she murmured, her head tilted back.

"Thank you?"

"For a wonderful evening – for escorting me."

"You're welcome."

His voice was low, his eyes inviting as his head dipped forward, his lips stopping just shy of hers, his breath buffeting her face. She closed her eyes to the moment, awaiting his touch. His hands closed over her shoulders and she fell willingly against him, her heart throbbing when his mouth finally initiated a long sultry kiss that tied a knot of pleasurable pain deep inside of her. With limbs trembling, she savored the pleasing warmth of his body, the strong arms that held her, his wet lips moving over hers, and without thought or hesitation, she grasped him tightly. Regret marred the sweet sensations when his arms dropped away. "Goodnight," she whispered hoarsely.

In a rush, she pushed into her room, closed the door between them, and collapsed against it. By dint of will, she held rigidly to that spot, for the urge was strong to turn around and fall back into his embrace.

With the sweet memory of Charmaine in his arms, John escaped to the stable and settled on a bale of hay in the corner of Phantom's stall, a bottle of wine in hand. The injured stallion watched him impassively as he took a swig. But the spirits had little effect.

After a time, he stepped out of the barn and looked up at the house. Lights still burned bright in the ballroom and on the terrace. His eyes found Charmaine's room. A lamp glowed there, softly penetrating the leaves and branches of the oak tree. *Is she awake? Best not to think about her or you'll never sleep tonight.*

He slumped back against the doorframe. Seconds accumulated into minutes, and he willed his mind blank, breathing deeply of the cool night air.

Paul and Anne stepped out of the house and ambled along the portico, finally descending to the lawns. When they were a discreet distance from any onlookers,

Anne wrapped an arm around Paul's waist, and pressed her hips and breasts into his lean body. She raised a champagne glass and toasted his success. He bent down and kissed her long and passionately. Her hands moved over him brazenly, intent upon bringing the evening to the close she desired. Paul pulled her to him again. Abruptly, they stopped. "Not here," he muttered. "There's a boathouse not far away." He grabbed her hand, and they rounded the deserted north terrace, disappearing into the night.

"Damn you!" John cursed, walking back to the house unnoticed.

Charmaine had no desire to retire once she had slipped into her nightgown. She turned the lamp down low, and sat in the wing chair, wide awake as seconds grew into minutes and minutes approached a full hour. Why hadn't she just let him in?

Ashamed, astonished, and ultimately dismayed, she set her mind on the ball, reliving every splendid moment of it, could feel John's warm hand on her back, see his crooked smile, hear his resonant voice, smell the pleasing scent of light cologne and flesh, taste his kiss. Each sensual recollection evoked such sweet yearning that she jumped from the chair and stepped through the French doors.

Two figures emerged from the veranda below. In the torchlight, she recognized Paul and Anne, arms entwined. Anne raised a glass of champagne and lavished him with blandishments. "You are the toast of the evening, the envy of the shipping world." She tossed her glass aside and boldly looped her hands around his neck. On the tips of her toes, she drew his head forward, kissing him squarely on the mouth. He responded by pulling her hard against him. The sound of heated kisses and murmured endearments soon punctuated the rhythmic chirping of crickets. Charmaine's cheeks burned as Anne touched him in places a wife might hesitate to venture. "Not here," he murmured, "there's a boathouse not far away."

Charmaine stepped back. No need to watch. She knew where they were headed. At first, she wanted to cry, not out of disappointment, but innocence lost. And then, even that impulse vanished. She was a woman now and ready to leave the naïve girl behind.

She turned her face into the breeze and luxuriated in the cool night air. She had already recovered from the lascivious scene, for she knew the truth about Paul. Hadn't he told her so himself? *I'm a rogue, Charmaine...* But it didn't matter! She didn't care! Minutes passed, perhaps more. She didn't know how long she stayed there, reveling in the lightness of her mind.

Finally, she returned to her room. She paced the floor, once, twice, and once again. She was still wide-awake; the fresh evening air had dusted all the cobwebs of sleep from her head. She settled into the chair, but she couldn't close her eyes. Not now... not tonight... She sprang up and circled the stifling, oppressive room again, this room where she didn't feel whole.

John couldn't sleep, so he started reviewing Geoffrey Elliot's contracts. They took his mind off Charmaine. The thought of her accepting his brother's marriage proposal would drive him mad if he dwelled on it any longer.

He came up from his contemplation with the rap on his door. The rap came again. Who could be knocking at this hour? The ball had broken up long ago. He left the bed and the many papers strewn over it and opened the door, indifferent to the fact that he was clad only in his swimming breeches. It was probably only Paul, back from his romp.

He was astounded to find Charmaine there. "What is it?" he queried softly, worried by the look on her face.

She stood mute, then breached the distance between them, encircling his waist in a tentative embrace. Her cheek caressed his naked chest, instantly triggering a quickening in his loins.

They stood that way for a time; she, apprehensive, yet savoring the sensation of his sturdy body against her own; he, dumbfounded, wondering what had prompted this uncharacteristic display of sensual affection. Was this what he thought it was? He stroked her hair and asked again, "What is it?"

"Nothing," she said, oblivious to anything save his embrace.

She didn't know what force had drawn her to his chamber; she didn't have a purpose in mind, other than her need to see him. And, unlike his cavalier brother, John was in his room, alone. When she beheld him half-naked in the doorway, all rationality fled and animal instinct took over. Now, here she was, in his arms.

John was aroused, her soft breasts pressing into his chest, sweet agony. Did she know the trouble she was courting with her hands stroking his back? When she turned her head the other way, laying a cool cheek against his skin, he silently groaned, his resistance rapidly dwindling. Throwing caution to the wind, he clasped her shoulders, stepped back into the room, and pulled the portal shut, turning the key in the lock. He no longer hesitated, his hands coursing the length of her, firmly grasping her buttocks and pulling her hard against his manhood.

She was surprised, but not displeased. Looking into his eyes for the first time, she wrapped her arms around his neck and met his mouth halfway. Like before, his lips brushed over hers ever so lightly, barely touching, playing. His kiss deepened, and he pulled her closer yet, his tongue finding hers in an erotic, catapulting caress.

He pulled away and stepped over to the bed. Hastily, he began to gather his papers, depositing them unceremoniously into the armchair. She looked on in expectation, so when he gestured toward the bed, she walked to it straightaway and climbed in, ignoring the rational voice that screamed: *Return to your room!* It was of no use to her now. The sensible Charmaine had been left there to contemplate right and wrong. This Charmaine wanted to know, touch, become part of the flesh and blood John. She lay back against the pillow, trembling, yet alert to his every movement.

Aware of her inexperience, John used the task of clearing the bed to cool his ardor. Yes, she was here with him, but was she ready for intimacy? Unless he had sorely misjudged her, this was her first time. Better to approach the encounter delicately, slowly. He wouldn't undress just yet.

Her rapt eyes followed him as he moved about the room, lowering the lamp, drawing the curtains, and securing the dressing room door. A strange exhilaration was building inside as she freely perused the inviting expanse of his back, the muscles in his shoulders where they met sinewy arms.

He settled into the bed next to her, and their eyes finally met. Surprisingly, she found voice to speak, something to break the awkward silence of anticipation. "Do you always wear your swimming breeches to bed?" she asked.

"When it's hot," he smiled, noting that she had pulled the coverlet up to her neck, clutching it with white-knuckled fists. Not that she needed such fortifications; she was wearing a robe over her nightgown. "Do you mind?" he queried softly with a gesture that he'd prefer to leave the blanket down.

"No," she replied unsteadily, releasing it.

She caught his grin as he pulled the coverlet aside and sized up her amply clad body. "Aren't you hot?" he asked. In fact, the chamber was suffocating. Realizing how silly she appeared, she doffed her robe.

He remained half-prone, his back resting against the pillows and headboard. They lie there, not touching. His eyes took on a pensive gleam, and he regarded her quizzically. "Why did you come here, Charmaine?"

"I don't know," she answered honestly.

"Are you sure you want this? You won't be crying in the morning?"

"Should I be? Crying, I mean?"

"No, my Charm. I'd never intentionally make you cry. I can make you very happy. I want to make you happy."

"I couldn't stand being apart from you for another second," she murmured, lost to her love for him. "When you were away, I missed you terribly."

He pondered her response and smiled. "I've fantasized about this moment many times. Now that it's arrived, I feel like a little boy let loose in Cookie's kitchen after she's spent the entire day baking nothing but treats."

He raised his arm and invited her closer.

She snuggled in, laying her head against his hard shoulder, slipping her arm over his bare chest. The feel of his flesh, his solid body next to hers, sent a pleasing thrill into her soul. Ever so lightly, he pulled her hair to the side, his fingers brushing her neck and playing with the thick, unbound locks.

They remained that way for minutes on end, quiet, yet communicating all the same. She closed her eyes to the ecstasy of his hand sliding over her back and shoulders, caressing her arm. She knew he was enjoying it, too, for she could feel his heart racing under her palm. Suddenly, he seemed agitated, as if this closeness were not enough. He tugged at her nightdress. She looked up at him.

"Charmaine," he murmured, "why don't you take this off?"

Had she been anywhere else at this moment, she would have shrunk back at the bold request or scurried away like a frightened rabbit. But here she was, pulling the garment away, watching bashfully as he did the same.

It was close to dawn when they consummated their love. Charmaine was anxious, but John calmed her with tender words. He kissed her again, his rough cheek brushing hers as his lips moved to her ear and the hollow of her neck. His hands moved freely over her now, stroking her breasts, her bottom and thighs. His touch evoked erotic sensations she had never experienced before. A sweet ache throbbed in her belly, leaving her quivering with lust and wondering why she had avoided this for so long. He explored the most intimate of places, places she should have been embarrassed to permit, and yet, she was certain if he stopped, she would beg him for more.

He held his passion at bay as he covered her body with his and penetrated her slowly. She whimpered, and he perceived her pain across his own elated revelation that she really was innocent to a man – that she had chosen him to be her lover. She was his alone; he wouldn't have to share her with anyone. As he pressed deeper, she went rigid beneath him, and he reined in his heightening urge to climax, holding still for her, allowing her time to adjust to these new sensations, time for the pain to ebb. "It's all right, Charmaine," he whispered, his hands cradling her face, his thumbs caressing her tears away. "I love you. Let me show you how much I love you…" He kissed her tenderly again, his tongue tasting its fill when she responded with parted lips. He could feel her relax as her tension yielded to passion.

Charmaine was hostage to pleasure – the indescribable oneness she felt with him. The chaffing discomfort was gone, and she pulled him closer with unbridled abandon, as even in their intimacy, she couldn't have him close enough. For the first time, she understood her desperate yearnings and felt complete. As she breathed deeply, tiny tentacles tantalized her insides, intensifying her desire.

Unable to hold himself in check any longer, John began to move above her, the rhythm soothing, yet carnal, the persistence of each stroke so sensate that it evoked a deeper need within her: a mystical unity, a divine splendor, an unfathomable crescendo that crested without warning. Her body responded with one tremendous jolt, a series of quick convulsive tremors following in its aftermath. John groaned and fell upon her, breathless and satiated.

They lay entwined, quiet for many minutes, basking in ebbing ecstasy. Charmaine's sigh drew John's attention, and he propped up on an elbow, his eyes sparkling. She was ready for any number of comments, but to her amazement, he held silent. He relieved her of his weight, then lifted a strand of her hair and played with it between thumb and index finger, before letting it fall on her breast. She resisted the urge to pull up the coverlet and allowed him to behold her naked body, glowing in the soft lamplight. His hand caressed her shoulder, moving over the curve of her hip and coming to rest on her thigh. She shivered in anticipation, incredulous that she wanted him all over again.

He plumped the pillows and drew her to him, so that her head rested upon his chest and his arms encircled her. As they lay with eyes closed, a potent contentment settled over her. He stroked her hair and her shoulder again. "I finally have my life back…" she heard him murmur as he drifted off to sleep.

Tears of joy trickled down her cheeks. "I love you, too, John," she whispered into his chest. She reached up and, at long last, ran her fingers through his tousled locks. Almost immediately, she succumbed to a peaceful slumber.

Closing her sitting room door, Agatha sighed in deep satisfaction. The evening had been magnificent. She couldn't be happier. Paul had been brilliant, a star that outshined her sister's son in every respect. And Frederic – he had been the perfect host, as handsome as the day they had first met. Tonight, she had finally claimed the coveted place by his side.

There was only one flaw in the entire week. She'd been unable to tell everyone that Paul was her son, too. But at least he finally knew the truth, and was not, as Frederic had predicted, offended by it. They should have ended the deception years ago. She longed to speak to him, to proclaim her love for his father and explain the unfair twists of fate that had deprived him, until now, of his birthright and everything he deserved. She shook her head of the troublesome thoughts. She'd give it a bit more time. Tonight was too glorious to waste on sad memories, not when it was *she* who had danced in Frederic's arms. Tonight, she would seek his bed.

She undressed slowly, donned a sheer nightgown, brushed out her hair, and sprinkled perfume behind her ears. Frederic hadn't made love to her since the day she had spanked Pierre, and though she'd attempted to seduce him since then, he'd set her aside. But not tonight. Tonight, she'd break down the fortress he'd once again erected around his heart. She had done so before and could do it again.

She was surprised to find him standing beside the French doors, staring down into the gardens. He turned as she closed the door behind her.

"It was a wonderful week, an exquisite evening," she praised. "You've made our son very happy. You've made him proud to be called a Duvoisin."

"Yes," Frederic murmured, turning back to the glass portals.

"I'm proud to be your wife," she whispered in a husky voice. Coming up behind him, she looped her arms around his waist and leaned her cheek against his back. "I love you."

Frederic pulled away, placing distance between them before facing her again. The ball was over, the week behind him. He could stop pretending.

"Agatha," he began, "I don't love you. I thought perhaps something akin to love could grow between us – companionship, perhaps – but we've grown apart these past nine months."

"I don't understand."

"Don't you? You despise my children even though they are a part of me."

She bristled at the statement. "I love Paul."

Frederic was saddened by her lame defense. "Exactly. You love your son. As for John – your own nephew – time and again you've set out to alienate him from me. This last time, the worst of all."

When she started to speak, he held up a hand, and she wisely let him finish.

"I know you have always wished to legitimize Paul's birth. God knows I've wished for the same thing. But to usurp John's rights because of what happened between us – that, I cannot understand, refuse to accept. I thought our marriage would heal your pain, but sadly, it hasn't. You're still filled with bitterness and hate."

"I can change, Frederic, I promise I can!" she pleaded.

"Then there are my daughters," he pressed on. "We both know how you feel about them. And when Pierre was alive–"

"Is this still about that spanking?"

"No, Agatha. The spanking was just a manifestation of your true feelings for my children. It is something I should have taken the time to notice, to realize would never change."

"I'm sorry if I've hurt you," she whimpered softly. "I never meant to hurt your children, especially Pierre. As for the girls, I thought a school for young women would be best for them."

She hung her head, and he realized she was crying. He hadn't intended to inflict pain, not tonight when she'd been so happy. But he *was* through pretending. "Agatha, I'm tired," he said softly, compassionately. "Why don't we wait until things get back to normal here? Then we can talk again – with Paul."

She looked at him lovingly. "Yes, Frederic," she eagerly agreed. "We *should* speak with Paul and explain everything to him." She crossed to him, stood on her toes, and kissed his cheek. "I do love you," she whispered, "more than you will ever know." She quietly left his room.

He closed his eyes to his agony, the agony he read on her face. He turned back to the French doors. Perhaps Colette would come to haunt him tonight.

Agatha leaned against the portal, breathing deeply, allowing the stabbing sorrow to subside. She'd pushed Frederic too far, too fast. But she loved him and, in the end, that love would vanquish his disillusioned heart. She'd gained too much to think otherwise. Wasn't the prosperous week and triumphant evening testimony to that fact? Frederic might be upset, but she'd weathered setbacks before. Now that John was removed from the will, she would back off. In time, he would be banned from Charmantes. She must concentrate on getting back into Frederic's bed. He would come around.

Frederic lay abed, listening to the silence. One year… it had been one year since he had held Colette in his arms, one year ago tonight that he had prayed for a miracle that never came. She had breathed her last while he slept, his arms wrapped protectively around her. Now, a year later, he closed his eyes to the piercing pain he'd experienced when he'd awoken to find her cold in his embrace, when he had cuddled her for hours and wept for the love he had chastised, the happiness he had thrown away. *Colette, I'm sorry, and I promise, if it's the last thing I do, I will make amends. I love you, ma fuyarde… I will always love you.*

He did not remember sleeping.

Sunday
April 8, 1838

Chapter 4

Paul awoke at the crack of dawn with a splitting headache. He lay in bed considering the week's accomplishments, yet he felt disenchanted and depressed. His tryst with Anne London had satiated his manly need, but in every other way, it had left him empty. She'd wanted to accompany him back to his bedchamber, but he turned her down flat, relieved when she rushed to her rooms in an insulted huff. If he had made love to Charmaine in the early hours before dawn, he would now be sound asleep, content with her in his arms.

Charmaine – therein lie the rub, the root of his depression and the headache that awoke him. He should never have allowed himself to be manipulated into escorting Anne to the grand gala, not when he had already invited Charmaine. What had he been thinking? He had proposed marriage to her! He should have used the event to present her as his future wife, but that opportunity had slipped through his fingers. Now, when he announced his betrothal, he would really appear the fool. He could hear the gossip already: *You know, the governess. No, Paul didn't escort her to his ball; he was with Anne London all evening. Remember? Yes, the young woman who tended to his two sisters. The woman who returned on John's arm! Isn't that the most curious thing you've ever seen?*

Damn! Last night had been a debacle. And John had certainly made the most of it. Paul couldn't understand why Charmaine was so smitten with him, but he should have read the signs. They'd been obvious all week long. Still, nothing rankled him more than seeing her rejoin the festivities with John. It was his own fault. If he had proposed sooner, Agatha would not have dared meddle.

Paul left the rumpled bed, dressed quickly, and headed to the dining room, grateful that no one was there. He needed peace and quiet.

Unfortunately, his sisters came out of the kitchen, bright and bubbly.

"Good morning, Paul," Jeannette greeted. "Wasn't the ball magnificent?"

"Magnificent," he answered gruffly.

"Have you seen Mademoiselle Charmaine?" Yvette asked.

"No," he said. "Isn't she with you?"

"We haven't seen her since last night," Yvette replied in exasperation.

"She's not in her room," Jeannette added, "and her bed is made, so we thought she'd already come downstairs, but Cookie hasn't seen her either."

Paul was intrigued. It had been well past midnight when Charmaine left the banquet hall with John. Why would she have risen, made her bed, and left her chambers so early? And if she had, why hadn't she let the twins know of her whereabouts? Suddenly, he was uneasy and suspicious.

"I have an idea," he said. "Let's find John and see if he knows where she is. Yvette, I'll pay you five dollars if you can get him to open his bedchamber door and come out."

Yvette eyed him dubiously, but she wasn't about to turn down a sum like that, no matter how odd the request. She'd worked harder for a lot less.

Once they were at John's door, Paul nodded for her to go ahead and knock.

Charmaine awoke slowly, the room bathed in the early light of dawn. She was lying on her side, with her knees curled up, and John cuddled behind her, his chest pressed against her back, his warm legs tucked under hers, an arm draped possessively across her shoulder. She could feel his even breathing close to her nape and sighed contentedly. She had slept for only a short time, but it had been a deep and satisfying slumber. She belonged to John now. *Please, Dear Lord, let him belong to me as well.*

As if she'd spoken, he stirred, and his arm tightened around her. He kissed her neck, and she could tell that he was smiling. They reveled in the warm cocoon until he broke away and rolled onto his back. When Charmaine turned to face him, he plumped up her pillow, tucked it under his arm, and beckoned to her. She had just snuggled in when someone knocked on the door.

Startled, she bolted up in the bed, clasping the sheet to her breasts. The knock came again, but John put a finger to his lips. "Who is it?" he called.

"It's me, Johnny," Yvette answered in a loud whisper. "Can I come in?"

"What do you want?" he asked, rising from the bed and pulling on his swimming breeches, suppressing a chuckle when Charmaine turned away in embarrassment.

"Jeannette and I are looking for Mademoiselle Charmaine," she answered.

John helped Charmaine slip into her robe, then led her into the dressing room. "Stay here," he whispered, brushing his lips across hers, "and don't leave this room without me."

He pulled clothes from his armoire, grabbed his boots, and stepped back into the bedchamber, closing the connecting door behind him.

"...she's not there either," Yvette was saying as he yanked on his trousers. "Have you seen her?" The silence behind the door annoyed her. "Open up!"

"I'm getting dressed," he called. "Did you look downstairs?"

"I just told you – we can't find her. Open up!"

"I'm coming," he said, pulling on his shirt.

Yvette snatched the five-dollar note out of Paul's hand and pocketed it before John opened the door. He was astounded to find Paul there, too.

"Good morning, Paul. Are you looking for Charmaine as well?" he inquired nonchalantly, fastening the buttons at his neck.

"In fact I am," Paul replied, peering over John's shoulder and into the empty room. "We're concerned. Apparently, she didn't sleep in her bed last night."

"And you suspect that she slept somewhere else," John remarked sarcastically, glaring at his brother in disgust. "Is that it?"

Paul thought better of responding.

John returned to the bed. "Did you check in the chapel?" he asked as he sat and pulled on his boots.

Yvette wrinkled her nose. "It's too early to be there."

"Well, that's where I'll look," he stated, his eyes on Paul as he stepped out of the room and closed the door. "Perhaps she was upset about something and went there to be alone." He turned to his sisters. "Why don't the two of you check upstairs? Maybe it was too noisy last night, and she decided to sleep there. And Paul, why don't you check the boathouse?"

Paul's eyes narrowed. John must have seen him with Anne last night.

"The boathouse?" Jeannette asked. "What would she be doing there?"

"Just a thought," he said with a shrug. Then, with a wicked smile and lighthearted gait, he left them.

The twins headed toward the servants' quarters, but Paul hesitated at John's door, his eyes riveted on the knob. Charmaine might have taken cover in the dressing room. Indecisive, he contemplated going in, but decided against it. If Charmaine had slept with his brother last night, John would have flaunted the conquest. Besides, she wouldn't do something that dim-witted.

Suddenly, he was very hungry. Dismissing the thought of Sunday Mass, he went back to the dining room for breakfast.

Not a half-hour later, John returned to the dressing chamber with fresh bed linens and clothing for Charmaine. He found her working out the tangles in her hair with his comb. He hadn't thought to retrieve her brush.

She turned quickly when he entered the room and blushed, memories of their night together rushing in.

She was radiant, and John's heart missed a beat as her shy manner swiftly aroused him. There would be time for that later. He smiled joyously, knowing he would have limitless nights with this woman.

"The coast is clear, my Charm," he said, taking her in his arms. "The girls are searching for you upstairs, and I'm to find you in the chapel, awaiting Mass."

He wondered if she had heard his brother's voice in the hallway, but didn't ask. Instead, he cupped her chin and kissed her tenderly.

It served as a stirring reminder of their lovemaking and left her so incredibly giddy that she grabbed hold of him for support.

"It was worth the wait, my Charm."

He stepped out of the dressing room so that she could dress. When she returned to his bedchamber, she found him spreading a clean sheet over the soiled one and looked at him quizzically. "You'll understand tomorrow," he explained. Without a word, she helped him make the bed.

"Now, come with me," he commanded, scanning the hallway before he led her from the bedroom.

They descended to the foyer and walked through the messy ballroom. The staff had retired late, and the tedious task of cleaning up hadn't begun. The lavish hall was empty and quiet.

"It's early for Mass," Charmaine finally said as John led her to the chapel doors. Like a bolt of lightning, a new thought struck her, and she froze.

"What is the matter?" he queried.

"I'm in a state of mortal sin," she moaned, bringing her hands to her mouth. "Everyone will know when I refuse communion."

"Don't fret, Charmaine." Though his voice was kind, she was certain that he would mock her religious conviction. Instead, he said, "We haven't come for Mass. We've come to exchange marriage vows. That is – if you'll have me?"

Charmaine was dumbfounded. When John had left her this morning, cold reality set in, and she'd chastised herself for succumbing to her physical yearnings. She was a good girl, had always been a good girl! Not even the memory of their intimacy – that crowning moment when she had been one with him – could assuage her belated misgivings. Yes, she had given herself to this man, but until this very moment, she had been afraid to hope that he wanted her as completely as she wanted him.

"*Have you?*" she asked incredulously. "Surely you jest?" But one look at his earnest face, quietly waiting, and she knew that he was dead serious. Her joy burst forth, and she threw herself into his arms. "Of course I'll have you!" He lifted her clear off the floor and whirled her around. By the time he set her back down, she was shaking all over, tears streaming down her cheeks.

They stepped into the chapel and found Father Benito preparing for a large congregation of worshipers. John grasped her hand and pulled her to the altar with him. When he explained his reason for being there, the priest immediately objected, contending that he could not officiate over the holy sacrament of matrimony during the solemn Lenten season. "Today is Passion Sunday. It is entirely inappropriate. And there is the matter of confession," he continued. But before he could finish protesting, John fanned a wad of ten-dollar notes under his nose. Charmaine gaped in disbelief as Benito snatched them and, without so much as one repentant word from either of them, made the sign of the cross and intoned a general prayer of absolution.

The chapel door opened, and George and Mercedes stepped in.

"Our witnesses, my Charm," John explained.

In less than five minutes, they had spoken their vows and were husband and wife. Charmaine thought she was dreaming.

"Where to now, my Charm?" John asked. "Mass doesn't begin for another hour, and we can't hide here forever."

"No," she agreed, "and the girls are probably still looking for me."

"Why don't we go back to the nursery?" he suggested. He wanted to take her back to his room, but that would have to wait until tonight.

They passed a few guests as they made their way upstairs, all too exhausted to pay them much notice. Still, Charmaine breathed a sigh of relief when they reached the nursery. She didn't fancy coming face-to-face with Paul just yet. It was short-lived, however; Paul's chamber door swung open, and he stepped into the hallway.

"So, you've found her," he said.

Charmaine wondered what he meant. Paul's assessing eyes raked her from head to toe as if plumbing for secrets, making her terribly uncomfortable.

"She was precisely where I said she would be," John replied, "in the chapel, praying."

Yvette's voice rang out from the north wing. "There you are! Jeannette and I have been looking for you everywhere."

"Where have you been, Mademoiselle?" her sister asked, rushing forward. "We were worried when we didn't find you in your room."

Charmaine looked at each of them, quickly formulating an answer under Paul's scrutiny. "I couldn't sleep after all the excitement."

"You didn't go to bed at all?" Paul interrogated.

To John's amazement, she looked him in the eye and replied, "I was upset by something I saw from the balcony last night."

Paul appeared shaken.

"What was it?" asked Yvette.

"Nothing important," Charmaine answered laconically, turning to the girls and reminding them that they had best get ready for Mass.

A short while later, she entered the chapel again, this time with Jeannette and Yvette on either side of her. It was empty.

They had just finished their prayers when John appeared in the doorway. Yvette saw him first. "What are you doing here?" she whispered incredulously as he lifted Jeannette over his lap and placed her to his right so that he could sit next to Charmaine.

"Attending Mass," he stated simply, a twinkle in his eyes.

Charmaine was astounded as he took her hand and cradled it affectionately on his warm thigh. He had left them to bathe and shave, and she'd assumed that she wouldn't see him again until breakfast. But now, here he was beside her, feeding her pride. Blissful beyond compare, she looked up at him with a brilliant smile. In reply, he raised her fingers to his lips and kissed them tenderly. The twins exchanged glances and giggles.

Charmaine could only wonder what the other family members thought when they saw John there. She kept her head bowed, more in thanksgiving than to avoid suspicious eyes. John, however, gave a friendly nod to anyone who looked his way. Frederic's brow rose, Agatha's eyes narrowed, Anne stuck her nose high in the air, Rose's lips curled with a knowing smile, and Paul simmered.

The entire congregation stood as Father Benito entered the sanctuary. Charmaine hardly heard the opening prayer, but her pulse quickened with the pronouncement: "This Mass is being offered for the repose of the soul of Colette Duvoisin at the request of her husband and her children."

Charmaine's eyes closed in silent agony. *One year ago today! How could she have forgotten?* John grasped her hand and squeezed her fingers. She stole a glance at him; he was smiling. The sorrowful moment passed, and her heart grew light.

She couldn't concentrate on the Mass, her mind possessed of her incredible experience the night before. She blushed, and noticing that John studied her, the color in her cheeks deepened.

During the Consecration, she began to fret over taking Communion. But when the time came, John nudged her up and out of the pew, his hand under her arm. He remained close and prodded her toward the altar. Unable to protest without making a scene, she found a spot to kneel with John beside her. Father Benito reached him first, and with great reverence, the host was placed on his tongue. John bowed his head and waited for Charmaine. They rose together and rejoined the twins in the pew. As she knelt down once again, she offered up her petition and asked the Lord to bless her new family this day, most especially her husband. *Forgive me for receiving your precious gift when in a state of sin,* she silently whispered, *but I do love him so.* John's head remained bowed long after she had finished.

Later, she asked him why he had prompted her to receive the Holy Eucharist when they were both in a state of mortal sin. He looked at her with a mischievous smile. "Of all the grave sins in this world, my Charm," he replied, "making love to you will *never* be one of them." His wise words were a tender absolution.

The ceremony ended, but Father Benito detained the assembly a moment longer. "Godspeed to our guests who will be journeying home. Before you leave, John would like to say a few words."

To everyone's surprise, John stood and walked to the front of the chapel. "Good morning," he greeted, glancing over the congregation. "Because you are all here, family and friends alike, this is the perfect time to introduce you to my wife – the woman I love – Charmaine Duvoisin."

Charmaine heard her married name pronounced for the first time, and her heart leapt.

His eyes rested momentarily on the twins. "We were married earlier this morning, and we want to share our happiness with all of you."

He gestured for Charmaine to stand, and though disconcerted by the large, attentive crowd, she proudly rose to her feet. He went to her side and took hold of her arm. Someone started clapping and the twins immediately joined in gleefully.

"Oh, Johnny, oh, Mademoiselle Charmaine, is it true? Is it really true?"

"Yes, Jeannie, it's really true."

They were stopped numerous times as they wended their way to the chapel doors, guest after guest stepping forward to offer congratulations. The family held back until the end. Rose shook a crooked finger at John, but hugged him close, a long, heartfelt embrace. George nudged his grandmother along, giving John another hearty clap on the back. Mercedes hugged Charmaine again. Paul was next. His eyes were dark, and Charmaine shivered. He had to be told sooner or later, and this was the best way for him to find out. He said nothing, but glared at John, who, undaunted, stared him down. Agatha extended them cordial good wishes.

Frederic was the last to leave the sanctuary, offering his hand to John. To Charmaine's surprise, John took it. "Congratulations, son," he said, his voice husky, "may you be truly happy."

"I intend to be," John responded without acrimony.

"And you, Mrs. Duvoisin," Frederic added, "welcome to my family. I hope you know what you're getting yourself into," he quipped.

"I think so, sir," she said timidly as he bent forward and embraced her, his lips lightly brushing her cheek.

"Shall we break the fast?" He gestured toward the dining room, allowing Charmaine and John to lead the way.

The twins remained by his side, bantering happily as they skipped along. "Isn't it wonderful, Papa? Charmaine is part of the family now! We told you that it would be a good thing to invite Johnny home. We were right, weren't we?"

"Yes," the man breathed expansively, "you were both very right. Come now, I'm starving. Let us go and see what Fatima has prepared for us."

Charmaine enjoyed Cookie's reaction most of all. Choking back tears, she exclaimed, "Only one thing coulda made me happier today, Mastah John, and that woulda been if you'da married me."

John gave her a huge hug, and Fatima had all she could do to contain herself.

"Mastah John, you know better than to kiss me like that. Now look what you did, you gone and made me cry! Now you get outta here and save your hugs for Miss Charmaine."

If there was any gossip about the early morning wedding, Charmaine was unaware of it. Throughout the day, she received many warm wishes, and John happily introduced her over and over again to anyone who approached them.

She saw little of Paul. After breakfast, he left with two of his guests. She was thankful he kept his distance, but she dreaded the inevitable confrontation.

For the first time in years, John and Frederic carried on a cordial conversation at the table. Charmaine looked away when she caught their eyes on her. If she could have read Frederic's thoughts, she would have been abashed.

He wondered about the hasty marriage. Had John seduced his daughter-in-law last night? Her crimson face led him to think so. But no matter; John had chosen well, and Frederic felt a fondness for his son as never before. John had finally buried Colette and was willing to accept Charmaine's wholehearted love. Frederic knew that Paul was angry. Nevertheless, Paul wouldn't have allowed Charmaine to slip away if his feelings ran as deeply as John's. Frederic hoped that Paul would accept the marriage without interfering – that history wouldn't repeat itself.

As the day drew on, the guests departed, sent off with endearing farewells. They would get settled for the night on the Falcon, the Raven, and two of Paul's new merchantmen, setting sail for home at the break of dawn.

Agatha breathed a sigh of contentment when the last carriage pulled away. The week had been well worth her grueling efforts. This was her destiny. For the first time, she was truly recognized as the mistress of the Duvoisin manor. John's marriage to the governess was the icing on the cake, a balm for her little setback with Frederic last night. When John finally left Charmantes, perhaps in the next few days, Charmaine Ryan would go with him. Perhaps they'd even take the twins. Then she'd send Paul to Espoir and have her husband all to herself. They could finally relive that blissful rapture before cruel, twisted fate had wrenched him from her all those years ago. It was time to pay her brother a visit and relate the good news…

Robert expected to a find a desperate patient on his doorstep, but was surprised to see his sister instead.

"Oh, Robert," she declared as she stepped over the threshold, "the gods have smiled down upon us this day!"

She spun around to greet him, a brilliant smile lighting the whole of her face. But he had already returned to his bedchamber where he had been busy before she came calling. Agatha followed him. Something was amiss. A trunk was open at the foot of his bed, packed with clothing.

"Are you going somewhere?" she queried in consternation.

"Yes. I'm leaving."

"*Leaving?* You can't be serious. Things are finally looking up. Our plans–"

"Your plans, dear sister, not mine," he said softly.

"What do you mean, *my* plans? You've shared in all my dreams and desires."

"Yes, *your* dreams and *your* desires."

"Now, Robert," she soothed, "what is that supposed to mean?"

"I have *desires*, too," he sneered, his eyes finally meeting hers. "I thought you understood that. You led me to believe that I mattered. But last night, watching you *admire* your husband, I realized that I've been a dolt these many years, a simpering, adolescent dolt, happy with the scraps you've tossed my way."

She bristled, but he continued. "*Frederic offers us security*," he mimicked in an effeminate pitch. "*I must right the wrongs perpetrated against me – and then, Robert – then we will be together.*" Suddenly, his voice was no longer mewling, but hard and clipped. "You've no intention of leaving Frederic, even now when you have everything you want, even after all he has done to you. *You love him!* Have always loved him, even when you've hated him!"

"Yes I love him!" she screamed.

"Then why pretend with me? You used me. I know that now. That was why you kept me around. You used me for your own conniving ends."

"Now, Robert," she purred, coming close to him, "that's not entirely true. And you yourself conspired in the beginning."

"Because I loved you – and cursed the man who nearly destroyed you!"

"And I shall always love you," she whispered, brushing her lips across his sallow cheek. "You are my brother, after all."

"Enough! No more games!" He shoved her aside and grabbed more clothing from his armoire. "You don't need me anymore. And I think I've finally had enough of you. Like your guests, I, too, will be aboard the ship that departs for Richmond tomorrow. And I shan't be back."

"But how will I explain your departure?"

He eyed her with a crooked smile and snapped shut the trunk. "You don't need me to come up with ideas, dear sister. After all, duplicity suits you."

She did not press him and left without a backward glance.

Through the slit between curtain and window, Robert watched her go, combating tears as she climbed into the carriage. All hope that she would beg him to stay faded as it lurched forward and rolled away.

Agatha Blackford, the other half of his soul, was gone – forever. But he had never really possessed her. He'd spent the whole of his life convincing himself that she loved him, that someday, when she was completely healed, when she was vindicated, she would belong to him. But in his heart of hearts, he knew the truth. He sat hard on his bed and, with head in hands, looked back on the thirty years that had brought him to this despicable moment.

As children, he and Agatha had been close, even into adolescence – too close, as their father would say. But their mother indulged that 'love'; they were twins after all. Lucy Blackford idolized her eldest children and spurned her daughter, Elizabeth, five years their junior and the apple of their father's eye. Lucy turned a blind eye to the ridicule Elizabeth endured at Robert and Agatha's hands.

Robert Blackford senior had been a merchant on the Mersey River in the heart of Liverpool, a modestly wealthy man. And so, he could afford to send Robert to university to study medicine. But only men went to Oxford, and Robert missed Agatha terribly while he was away. He did not know that one of their father's wealthiest suppliers, Frederic Duvoisin, had caught her eye, or he would have hastened home earlier and put a stop to the blossoming love affair. Even now, he was consumed with jealousy as he remembered those first few months when Agatha's eyes lit up at the mere mention of Frederic's name.

"Don't be silly, Robert," she'd soothed. "I'm a spinster, for God's sake, and people are talking about us! I don't love him, and I will always have you close. Marrying him will give us *both* security. Besides, I *do* want to be a mother."

Soon they were planning a wedding. Frederic Duvoisin loved her, Agatha averred. In truth, Frederic was sealing a business deal with Robert senior, forging a robust family enterprise. The two men had included Robert in a late night conversation, tallying the benefits both sides would reap from the union. Frederic would supply the imports; Robert senior would secure buyers and distributors.

"So much the better if Agatha fancies herself in love with Frederic," his father confided that night as they left the inn where Frederic was lodged.

"She is not in love with him, Father," Robert bit out.

"How would you know that, son?"

"She told me."

"She is a woman, Robert, and a beautiful one at that. She's held many a swain at bay, but now it is time. Frederic and she make a handsome couple. It is wise for the family business. With Agatha as his wife, Frederic will not think of negotiating with other merchants in England. Medical practice is a shaky undertaking. The family business, on the other hand, is established. You'll have something to fall back on after I'm gone. And there is Elizabeth to consider."

"I don't need something to fall back on, Father. I can take care of Agatha and myself. And if you're so worried about Elizabeth, why don't you offer *her* to Mr. Duvoisin? It's obvious he's charmed by her, and she, him."

When his father did not comment, Robert knew he had noticed the attraction, too. At that precise moment, the idea of sabotage took root, and Robert silently vowed that Frederic and Agatha would never be married.

But the wedding date was set, and Frederic invited the Blackfords to his Caribbean home for a glimpse of the paradise island where he and Agatha would live as man and wife. They spent five months abroad and a fortnight on Charmantes. Agatha had fawned over Frederic, while he played the role of an eager groom-to-be, his hand always possessively under her arm, pretending interest in her every word.

But Robert saw how he watched Elizabeth, and how his younger sister reacted. He had had enough. The night before their departure for England and the impending nuptials, Robert cornered Elizabeth alone in the mansion's gardens. For nearly a week, he had carefully planned exactly what he would say. But then, the plot had been simple really, thanks to Frederic and his announcement that he would not be returning to England with them – that he had business to attend both in Virginia and New York, and would follow on a separate ship.

"Oh, Robert," Elizabeth sighed when she saw him. "I'm going to miss Charmantes. It's so unlike our rainy England."

"Are you sad that we're leaving, or that Frederic is remaining behind?"

"Robert, why ever would you say that?"

"Isn't it obvious? You're smitten with him."

She squirmed on the bench, and he continued. "I daresay, Frederic has eyes for you, too. *And*, I think you know it."

She objected. "He's in love with Agatha – is going to marry Agatha!"

"A shame really," he pondered aloud.

"What do you mean?"

"She doesn't love him," he stated sourly. "She's just going through with this marriage for Father's sake and the business connections it will secure for him."

"You're wrong, Robert," she countered. "Agatha loves him dearly. I've seen them together. She dotes on his every word."

"As a good wife should," he bit out, smarting with the remark.

Elizabeth studied him curiously, and his anger settled into one enormous knot of jealous resentment. It fueled his zealotry, the focus he needed to execute his plan. "She's told me that she does not love him," he declared. "In truth, she does not wish to marry at all."

Elizabeth shook her head. "I can't believe that."

The resentment grew. *Let her see how it feels – let the axe fall!* "Here you are, attracted to him," he continued, "wishing you didn't have to leave, yet you are to be taken home and wed off to that pompous fop, Henry Davenport."

"*What?*" Elizabeth went white, and Robert delighted in her anguish. Evidently, thoughts of the odious man could make her physically ill, for her hands reflexively clasped the edge of the bench as if to steady a teetering world.

Fat, bald, and thrice her age, Henry Davenport had asked for Elizabeth's hand in marriage on a number of occasions. Even Robert senior had been repulsed.

"That's right," Robert proceeded, prepared to drive the last nail in the coffin. He knew her well: She would claw her way out, then act impulsively. "The night before we left Liverpool, he chewed Father's ear at the tavern, and Father finally relented."

Her hand flew to her mouth. "Father would never do that! He knows I despise that man!"

"Yes, but Mr. Davenport has made an impression on Mother, and she refuses to let the matter rest. Father has grown weary of her nagging. It's a shame that you and she don't get along. She *is* bent upon getting you out from under her roof, especially now that Agatha will no longer be there."

"Well," Elizabeth said, her chin slightly raised in a burst of defiance, "I'll just have to speak with Father and let him know –"

"And what if your pleas fall on deaf ears, Elizabeth? Father has to live with the woman, after all. In the end, Mother *always* gets her way."

Grim reality seeped in, and she buried her face in her hands and wept. "What am I to do? Dear God, Robert, what am I to do?"

"There, there," he soothed compassionately, as if he'd gladly shift the burden of her anguish to his shoulders, his hand placed gently on her arm. "You know... there might be a way."

Her head lifted slowly. "What do you mean?"

"You could remain behind!" he declared, as if thunderstruck.

"Remain behind? But–"

"Just think," he hurried on, "you'd be alone with Frederic, have him all to yourself."

"Remain behind?" she muttered again.

"Yes – when we leave. Without Agatha here, you could confirm his feelings for you, perhaps save Agatha and yourself from a dismal and unjust future."

Robert studied her vacuous expression, certain that the amber-brown eyes were deceiving; her quick mind was turning furiously. And then she spoke. "But if he has no feelings for me, my reputation will be ruined."

"Exactly. And if nothing comes of this 'experiment' with Frederic, Mr. Davenport will surely withdraw his proposal. That sort of man would never consider marrying a maid who'd been compromised, soiled or not."

A sudden smile broke across Elizabeth's face. "You are right," she said, clearly relieved. Just as abruptly, her manner changed, and Robert knew her conscience had intervened. "But Robert, what about Agatha?"

He answered dispassionately. "I would say you are doing her a service."

"Even so–" she wavered "–this is so very devious. What if–"

He didn't allow her to finish. "Better to make your own decision than have it made for you."

"But how – how do I remain behind? I can't announce that I'm not going. I will have to board the ship along with everyone else."

Finally! "You have a point…" he said, pretending at deep concentration, settling his chin atop his fist, even though he'd formulated an elaborate solution days ago. "Vessels are always bustling before departure, and I can distract Father and Frederic. It shouldn't be terribly difficult to slip off unnoticed. As for Mother and Agatha, they will be preoccupied in their cabins and assume you've remained in yours."

"But what if a sailor waylays me?" she asked, dismay heavy in her voice.

"Simply tell them you left something behind in the carriage."

"And what happens when Mother and Father discover I am missing? Surely they'll demand the Captain turn back."

"All the more reason not to dally. Make the most of this opportunity – *quickly*."

"I should tell Agatha," she suddenly decided.

"Do that, and I guarantee she will speak to Mother," he replied coldly, having expected such a thought. "You know she resents you and would cut off her nose to spite her face if it meant making you miserable as well." He smiled to himself when she grimaced; she knew he was right. Agatha despised her.

How she carried out the plan, he never really knew. He distracted Frederic and his father as promised, and later, when the ship was underway, he went to Elizabeth's cabin. It was empty. He'd been correct in counting on his family's disinterest in his younger sister. Meals had been served up in the cabins, and nobody even noticed her absence.

To ensure that the vessel would not turn back, he executed the next phase of his scheme. Just before daybreak, he hoisted a ballast stone over the ship's railing and into the ocean. Immediately, a cry went up from the rigging, "Man overboard!" Within an hour everyone, except Elizabeth, was accounted for. Dinghies were dispatched, but the search was futile. They concluded that she'd gone above deck to see the sunrise and had somehow fallen to her death. A funeral service was held, and they spent the remainder of the journey in mourning. Even Agatha did not suspect the truth, not until three months later, when Frederic stepped off the ship with Elizabeth on his arm.

Never had Robert seen Agatha turn so ugly, lashing out like a cornered cat. But Frederic was unmoved and broke the banns, vowing to marry Elizabeth instead. When Robert senior objected, Frederic told him that he'd compromised Elizabeth's reputation. Agatha wailed that her good name had been compromised first, but Frederic pointed out that Agatha's visit to Charmantes had been chaperoned; no one need ever know of their tryst as long as she kept her mouth shut. She was outraged and insisted that she was carrying Frederic's child. Frederic hesitated, then called her a liar, scrutinizing her slim form. She prostrated herself at her father's feet, demanding that he hold Frederic accountable. But Robert senior was in a difficult quandary. Agatha was capable of lying, his dear Elizabeth could be pregnant as well, and he didn't fancy alienating his most lucrative trade partner. Frederic's marriage to either of his daughters achieved the same economic ends he'd been cultivating all along.

The next day, Agatha enlisted Robert's aid and showed up at Frederic's lodging, confident that if she were alone with him, she could win him back. But Frederic, though contrite, remained resolute. He loved Elizabeth. And so, he gave Agatha a sizable sum of money, promising that he would provide for any child she produced within the next five months. When she cried at his feet, he offered to raise the baby himself, but she refused, vowing to revile him for all time.

For two weeks, she wallowed in anger and despair, refusing to eat. Elizabeth, in turn, lamented the part she had played. Robert turned mediator, interceding whenever Elizabeth seemed on the verge of forfeiting Frederic for Agatha's happiness.

Then, quite suddenly, a glimmer of hope punctured Agatha's black despair. Elizabeth had vanished. She'd gone off riding, and hours later, only her horse trotted home. Anticipation flickered in Agatha's eyes as day after day, no one, not even Frederic, could uncover a trace of her. A week passed, and she was found – left for dead at the side of a road. Still, Agatha waited with bated breath, smiling when she learned that Elizabeth had been raped repeatedly at the hands of a band of highwaymen. She was soiled – had gotten precisely what she deserved.

It didn't matter to Frederic. He remained by her side and nursed her back to health. Seeing her great shame, he broached the subject of his own disgrace – his lust for Agatha and the babe she might carry to term outside of wedlock. Later, Elizabeth told Robert that this single admission, accompanied by his vow to take care of the child, alleviated her humiliation. Weeks later, they wed and returned to the Caribbean, leaving behind a hollow, disillusioned Agatha.

Agatha was indeed carrying Frederic's child, and so, the Blackfords closeted her away, determined to keep her dishonor a secret. She seemed impervious to rebuke, speaking to no one, not even Robert, who finally delivered the baby.

After months of apathy, a ray of happiness lit her eyes. The babe was handsome, a miracle amidst such anguish, and she cradled him so tightly that it was often difficult to pry him from her arms. It soon became apparent that she was not in her right mind, and their parents only made matters worse. Appalled, they refused to even look at the infant. *A bastard! A scandal!* they swore. He would not remain under their roof! Despite Agatha's wailing, Robert whisked him away. It was for the best, he decided, as he set off with a wet nurse and the tiny bundle, boarding a ship bound for the Caribbean and the boy's father. *We will be together when I return, Agatha. I will make you forget Frederic.*

Such was not to be the case. Robert arrived on Charmantes to find Elizabeth heavy with child. The couple took in Paul with open arms and asked Robert to stay and deliver Elizabeth's baby. He longed to return to Agatha, but could not refuse Elizabeth's pleading, and so, he was there on that bleak night that brought one life into the world and snuffed out another.

He did everything in his power to save Elizabeth. God knew he didn't want Frederic left a widower. The man might repent and marry Agatha after all. The delivery was torturous, the babe breech, and Robert could not stem the hemorrhaging. Elizabeth succumbed hours later with Frederic at her side.

Robert thought that his own life would end in those hours before dawn, as Frederic's grief congealed into a feral rage. "Man, you are a butcher – a murderer! You delivered Agatha safely, but not my wife!"

Though Robert quailed, a new, more potent loathing took hold, its ferocity paramount to any terror he suffered. How could Frederic so hardheartedly wish Agatha dead? It had been satisfying to point the finger of blame on the men who had raped Elizabeth. In so doing, Robert cemented Frederic's latent fear that the baby was not his. "I did everything I could!" he protested. "She was not fit to deliver a child after her ordeal!" With Frederic's darkening scowl, he added, "The baby is most surely born of their seed."

Frederic blanched and turned away, but as the days passed, his anger gave way to grief again. Remorseful over his irrational accusations, he finally apologized to Robert, asking him to stay on Charmantes; the island needed a physician. Robert declined the offer; his beloved Agatha awaited him in England. When Frederic entrusted him with a letter for her, Robert's worst fear was realized. Frederic intended to set things right: he would marry Agatha and legitimize Paul's birth.

On the journey home, Robert worried over what to do, indecisive to the end. It didn't matter. Robert senior had married Agatha off to Thomas Ward, a former suitor who did not know about her confinement and thought she loved him. Despondent, Agatha had accepted the man's proposal, obedient to her parents' demands for the first time in her life. Robert couldn't say why he gave her the letter, but it evoked a poignant response: she cried on his shoulder, then allowed him to make love to her completely that night.

Later, when they lay entwined, she had whispered, "We are not defeated, Robert. We will build on this – *you* must build on this. I cannot be with my son right now, but you can. Elizabeth must pay for her deeds. What better way than to make *her* son suffer? Go back to Charmantes and set up your practice. Watch over Paul and never fail to remind Frederic that *he* is the firstborn, the rightful heir. He must shine while Elizabeth's babe..."

Robert gazed incredulously into her tormented face. Noting her faltering sanity, and guilty over the part he had played, he told her what she wanted to hear. "For you, my love, I will do anything."

"I love you, Robert," she had sighed, "will always love you. You are the only one who has ever cared about me. Someday, I will come to you, and we shall be together... someday..."

Her earnest pledge seized hold of his heart, and his shallow promise became a quest. He returned to the West Indies, where he carried on her mission until yesterday. But last night, he embraced the truth that he had doggedly brushed aside for all those years: she was obsessed with Frederic. With a final sigh, he dragged his trunk to the door.

John shut the door and faced his father. He didn't relish meeting in this room. Some of their most damaging confrontations had taken place here.

"Be civil, John," Charmaine had cautioned. "Your father is trying very hard." Though he placated her, he was not pleased. *Why did all the women in his life champion his father?*

"Come in, John," Frederic beckoned from the desk.

They were alone. "Richecourt is late?" John asked.

"Not late," Frederic explained. "I wanted to speak with you first."

John braced himself for the worst. Frederic lifted a sheaf of papers and handed them to him. "I believe they're all in order," he stated, "however, before you read them, I'd like to explain my decisions to you."

"Your decisions? I thought everything had been decided."

"By you, perhaps, but not by me."

John began to object, but Frederic waved him off. "John, I'm not about to get into a row with you; I only ask that you listen to what I have to say. Then, if you object, we can discuss it."

Shaking his head, John slumped into a chair. "First, custody of Yvette and Jeannette will be turned over to you upon my death. Doing so makes a great deal of sense, especially now that you are married to Charmaine."

That's the good news. Now for the bad, John thought.

"As for the plantation and Richmond holdings, they will be left to Yvette and Jeannette. I know your misgivings concerning an impending civil war; however, the land is there, and at present should be accounted for. The girls will soon be women, and when they are introduced into society, it will likely be with you, in Richmond. When they come of age, the properties can be divided equally. However–" he drew a long breath "–the property needs to be managed until then. I ask you to remain on as guardian to their interests."

"No."

"John, hear me out. I believe this Underground Railroad business is dangerous for any plantation owner, but I cannot fault you for upholding your ideals. It is a trait that I honestly respect in you."

John was taken aback. Certain that he was being set up, he said nothing.

"Obviously, this escape system involves more than smuggling runaways aboard a Duvoisin ship. I gather that Freedom is a stop on this 'railroad'. Can it afford to do without you?"

John hadn't thought of this. He was, after all, Freedom's mainstay. Brian and Stuart might elect to remain at the plantation, but a new manager would not give them the protection he did. He'd discounted switching the station to Wisteria Hill long ago. Freedom was ideally situated on the Appomattox River, making hound tracking nearly impossible. "What exactly are you saying, Father?" he asked. "You *want* me to run your plantation as a stop on the Underground Railroad?"

"Run it however you wish – until your sisters come of age," he said simply. "And lastly," he went on, as if the previous matter were settled, "Charmantes–"

What was the score now? John wondered.

"–I didn't know what to do about that until this morning. Paul has Espoir, and I will give George Esprit. He deserves it for his many years of dedicated service to this family. However, Charmantes will be left to your children, my grandchildren. If you refuse guardianship, I will place it in Paul's hands until your sons come of age."

John swore fiercely. "You're still vying for the upper hand, aren't you?"

"I'm not surprised you see it that way, John. I've never given you a reason to think otherwise. However, there is only one reason why I've made these adjustments. Leaving you and your children a piece of my estate is the only thing, other than life, that I have been able to give to you." Frederic struggled for words. "I wish that were not so, but for you and me, it is too late for many things."

John didn't know what to say. He was uncomfortable with his father's naked emotion, and his anger ebbed. All these years, he had craved approval – affection – from this man. Now that it was offered to him, the feeling was alien and disquieting. He changed the subject. "And what of the ships?"

"Upon my death, they will be left to Paul, with the stipulation that any transport you require is free."

John snorted. One more point for him. He'd sooner find another carrier than rely on Paul's generosity. "What of all your investments?" he pursued.

"They will be divided equally between you and Paul."

"I told you I'd–"

"Do whatever you wish, but they will be equally distributed by the week's end. I have more than enough money to see me content until the end of my days. I don't want the Duvoisin fortune to dominate and undermine our relationship any longer." He paused for the moment it took to swallow against the lump in his throat. "I invited you home to start anew, John. I'm sorry about Agatha and Stephen. She got exactly what she wanted, and now Paul is angry with me, too."

"Angry?" John asked bemusedly. "With you?"

"He learned that Agatha is his mother."

"You can't be serious," John chuckled, his incredulity fanned by his father's grim expression. But he didn't need Frederic's affirmation. In its insanity, it made sense – perfect sense. Agatha championed Paul because he was her son.

"I knew Agatha before I met your mother. After I pledged my troth to her, we became lovers. For her, it was love, for me, just another business proposition. Then I grew to know your mother and experienced love for the first time. In the beginning, I held fast to my promise – attempting to ignore my feelings for her. But eventually, the idea of sacrificing that love became incomprehensible, so I broke the banns with Agatha, and married Elizabeth instead, even though I knew Agatha was carrying my child."

John was shocked. "No wonder she hated my mother…"

"And by extension – you," Frederic finished.

"So Paul *is* older than I am."

"By three months," Frederic answered.

The rest of the story unraveled slowly, Frederic speaking plaintively. When he finished, John inhaled. "Why didn't you tell Paul the truth?"

"Because I was ashamed," Frederic answered.

John was astonished. To him, Frederic was only a bitter, vindictive man with a hardened heart. "But why was I promoted as your heir?"

"Because you were the son born into wedlock, because you belonged to Elizabeth, and because, as you got older, I thought it was the only way to make amends for your childhood – my scorn."

Strange words, John thought. "So now, Paul knows, and he's upset."

"Yes, though he put on quite a front for his guests this week. But what is done is done, and it had to be told sooner or later. I just thought that you should know as well."

John nodded. After a moment, Frederic gestured to the documents he still held. "Are you agreeable to them?"

"Not really, Father," John smirked, "but what does it matter?"

Yvette tried to ignore the giggling in the hallway. She had promised she would be good and stay in the nursery with Jeannette until Charmaine or John came for them. After all, the morning had been so wonderful, the news that John had married Charmaine so gratifying that she truly intended to keep her word. John had gone off to speak with Father, and Charmaine was napping. Yvette turned her back to the door, which was slightly ajar, and stared hard at the book in her lap. Not a moment later, a man's devilish chuckle echoed just outside the room. She glanced at Jeannette, who was deep in concentration at her desk, practicing her script. Yvette crept to the portal and peered through the crack.

John gathered up the last of Geoffrey Elliot's papers. Except for one, he hadn't signed any of them. The contracts, which should have been simple renewals, had been completely rewritten, and now each one had a mistake.

John met Travis in the foyer. "Is Richecourt still with my father?"

"No, John," the manservant replied "He was quite alone when I left him."

"Wonderful," John muttered, "now I'll have to ride into town to catch him."

"No you won't, Johnny," Yvette called from the stairs.

John walked over to the landing. "You've seen Richecourt, then?"

"Maybe…"

He let out an exasperated sigh. "How much do you want, Yvette?"

"Ten dollars."

"You're mad."

"One dollar."

"Not worth it."

"Yes it is," Yvette countered in a singsong voice. "You'll see."

John canted his head as if to read her mind. "Very well – one dollar."

"Oh goody!" she exclaimed. "With the five dollars Paul gave me this morning, that's the most money I've ever earned in one day!"

John eyed her in astonishment, the implications of her declaration and Paul's curious behavior that morning sinking in. "So, where is Richecourt?" he asked, mindful of the more pressing matter at hand.

Yvette's lips curled into a smile. "In Felicia's room. When do I get paid?"

John threw open the door to Felicia's room. There was Edward Richecourt suspended on all fours above the maid, his bare buttocks soaring high in a sea of blankets and discarded clothing, his manhood dangling in all its decrepit glory. In a panic, he dove under the covers, pulling them up to his neck.

"Holy coconuts, Pitchfork!" John exclaimed.

"This is not what you think!" the solicitor sputtered, his face flaming red.

"So, you've given her legal counsel," John expounded, stepping into the room, his shock giving way to a crooked grin. "and instead of getting paid, you're getting laid. Ah... I always knew I'd get to see your horn one day, Pitchie, but the rest I could have lived without."

"I have no horns!"

"Then you're bound to disappoint Felicia over there."

"I hardly think it proper to barge in on us like this!" Richecourt growled. "Was there something you wanted?"

"I've finished with Junior's papers," John replied, displaying the contracts. "I thought you'd like to look them over before you throw them out. They need a little work."

"Give them here," Richecourt ordered, arm outstretched.

"Come and get them."

The lawyer glared at him, then shifted uneasily. "Leave them on the bureau. I'll read them later."

"No, I've made some notes that I want to show you now." John smiled devilishly, waving the documents in indication that Richecourt come and get them.

Felicia, nestled quite comfortably next to the flustered barrister, giggled.

Richecourt glanced around the room in search of his clothes, but they were piled on the floor next to John's feet. He hesitated a moment and swung his hairy legs over the bed, clutching the linens about him. Reluctantly, he stepped across the room until he ran out of covers just shy of John's extended hand. He reached out to grasp the papers, but John pulled them back. Humiliated, Richecourt took the last three steps and the coverlet fell away, revealing sagging shoulders, flabby arms, and a paunchy middle.

With an exaggerated grimace, John considered the specimen, then regarded Felicia in disbelief. "*You went from my brother to this?* You've lowered your standards, Felicia – or dropped them altogether."

"Give me those!" Edward barked and, snatching the papers out of John's hand, quickly lowered them to his groin to cover himself.

"Junior would be shocked to learn that his papers have been reduced to fig leaves hiding the dried – I mean – forbidden, fruit."

"*Get out! Just get out!*"

Despite her short nap, the heady day caught up with Charmaine, and her eyes grew heavy after dinner, burning when she blinked. The twins were exhausted, too. She coaxed them upstairs, leaving John with George and Mercedes, who were celebrating their engagement in the drawing room. She was startled when the nursery door opened behind her and Paul stepped in.

"Yvette, Jeannette, I want to speak to Charmaine *alone*," he stated sharply. "And if you know what is good for you, you won't go running to John."

They sent anxious eyes to Charmaine, intimidated by his dark demeanor.

"It's all right, girls," she said. "Please wait for me in my room."

When they were gone, Paul studied her for a moment. She braced herself for the worst, but it was best to get this over with.

"What happened last night?" he finally asked.

She was surprised and heartened by his even tone. Perhaps this discussion wouldn't be as unpleasant as she anticipated.

"I don't know what you mean," she answered softly. She was not about to tell him that she had spent the hours after the ball in his brother's arms.

"You know damn well what I mean," he snarled. "I thought we had an understanding. I proposed marriage to you. I thought that was what you wanted, have always wanted!"

Charmaine bowed her head. "I thought I wanted it, too."

"*Thought?* Didn't you *know*?" He was seething. "Let me understand this, Charmaine. You spend week after week in my company. You allow me to kiss you, to caress you, to make plans with you. You lead me to believe that you desire me, too, but because of your morality, you require a commitment before you'll come to my bed. And then, when I give you that commitment, you marry my brother instead? *Have I been taken for an idiot here?* What is going on?"

"I couldn't sleep last night," she began, hoping to provide answers that would not widen the rift between him and John. "When I walked out onto the balcony, I saw you with Anne London."

He inhaled. "So, you ran to my brother's arms. Is that what happened?"

"No!" she railed, insulted that he was making light of his tryst, while scorning hers.

Paul was satisfied with the response. He'd been right in assuming that if John had bedded her, he would have bragged about it. No, his brother had simply capitalized on her vulnerability when she grew disillusioned with her fiancé's dalliance. "Don't be a fool, Charmaine," he proceeded. "John is never going to make you happy."

"*And you will?*"

"I've been honest with you," he reasoned. "I'm a flesh and blood man. You refused me time and again. Last night meant *nothing* to me."

"How can you say that? How can you stand there and say that to me?"

"Really Charmaine, you are very naïve about men. Do you think that John hasn't taken a woman to his bed since he left here last fall?"

"But he wasn't the one who proposed marriage to me. You were! If you cannot be faithful when you are engaged, how will you be faithful when you are married?" *And John was alone in his chambers last night*, she thought, *not cavorting with the easiest woman at hand.*

"Be a fool then. But you are the first and only woman I've ever loved. John, on the other hand, will *never* forget Colette. You know that, and I know it."

"You're wrong!" she objected vehemently.

"Am I?" he shot back, further annoyed when she turned her back on him. But when he realized she was crying, his anger abated. "Charmaine," he cajoled, "let us set this situation straight, right now. Let us go together and find Father Benito. The vows have not been consummated. The marriage can be annulled."

"No!" she sobbed, wrenching free of the hands that closed over her shoulders, free of the lies he was spinning to confuse her. She whirled around to face him. "I love John! I don't love you!"

She saw the pain in his eyes and softened her words. "I thought I loved you, Paul. But when John was gone, I missed him so. If he hadn't come back, I would have believed that I meant nothing to him. But he did come back, and he loves me, too. He *does* love me! Last night when I saw you with Anne, I should have been hurt, but I wasn't. If it had been John in her embrace, I would have cried myself to sleep."

Her remarks cut deeply. "You're lying," he snarled, his anger barely in check.

"No, Paul. Truly, I don't want to hurt you, but I *do* love John."

He didn't hear her, for his mind was racing. "You saw me with Anne last night, but you say that didn't upset you. Yet, John finds you praying in the chapel this morning and claims that you were *very upset…*" His thoughts trailed off as he pieced the puzzle together. Then he glared at her through smoldering eyes. "You spent the night with him, *didn't you?*"

Her silence was affirmation enough.

"You little fool! You've thrown away the happiness we could have shared just to get even with me! John knew how vulnerable you were. *Can't you see he's using you to get to me?*"

When she shook her head in denial he pressed on, determined to hurt her as she had hurt him. "Do you know that he came to me and suggested that I marry you before he left here six months ago?" He smiled in satisfaction at her stunned face. "It's true. Ask him. He doesn't love you, Charmaine. He's just using you. And when he's had enough–"

"Stop it!" she screamed. "I hate you! Get out!"

When he didn't budge, she flew at him, pummeling his chest with both fists. "Get out, I tell you! *Get out!*"

Frederic heard the cries coming from the nursery and pushed into the room to find Charmaine in hysterical tears. "*What is going on?*"

Paul spun around. "I was just leaving," he bit out.

"It's best that you do," Frederic warned, catching hold of Paul's arm as his son attempted to brush past him.

Paul stopped, looked down at his sire's hand, then met the man's eyes. "Charmaine is John's wife now," Frederic said. "Remember that."

Paul had no intention of heeding his father like a scolded child, and he tore away. Frederic watched him leave, then turned to Charmaine.

She fought to master her emotions, wiping away her tears. "I knew I was going to have to face him. But it was terrible. I've hurt him deeply."

"Perhaps," Frederic offered, walking over to her. When she wouldn't meet his gaze, he placed a finger under her chin and forced her to look at him. "I would say it's more a matter of wounded pride."

"I wish it were so simple," she murmured.

"Do you love my son, Charmaine?" he asked.

She knew that he meant John. "I love John deeply."

"Good, because he needs that love, and I believe he loves you just as much. He has had many hard knocks in his life, but because of you, his future looks very bright. This marriage has made me very happy today."

John was highly agitated to find them together. It was apparent that Charmaine had been crying. "What is this all about?"

She went to him in relief. "Paul and I had words. Your father intervened."

John's eyes darkened, but he said nothing. After Frederic bade them goodnight, he put an arm around her and led her back to his room. Once there, she reveled in a soothing bath, leaning her head back against the rim of the tub and closing her burning eyes. Perhaps the water would wash away Paul's bitter remarks.

John left her to put the twins to bed, but returned long before she was finished. He sat on the rim of the tub. Embarrassed, she sank modestly into the water to conceal her breasts. But he wasn't looking at her, his thoughtful gaze cast beyond the room. "Are you going to tell me what Paul said to you?" he finally asked. "I know you were crying."

She closed her eyes and whispered, "It was terrible. I knew it would be."

"I'm sorry, my Charm," he said. "I had hoped to spare you his wrath. When he disappeared today, I thought you were safe."

"If it hadn't been today, it would have been tomorrow," she said, though she knew Paul had cornered her in the hope of sabotaging her wedding night.

"Did he hurt you?"

"Only with his words, but I hurt him, too. John – what he said doesn't matter. I don't want it to come between the two of you."

"It matters to me," John replied heatedly. "We need to understand each other if this marriage is to be a success. What did he say?"

She studied him, then plunged ahead. "He called me a fool – that you could never love me as he could – that your heart would always belong to…"

"Colette," he supplied.

"Yes," she whispered.

"Damn him," John swore, but to Charmaine's chagrin, he did not deny the assertion. She looked at him with tear-filled eyes, and John read her pain. "You don't believe that, do you? Charmaine, you can't possibly believe that."

"I don't think I do," she choked out. "I don't want to."

"Charmaine, I love you, and only you. Colette is dead. Yes, I loved her, but I had resigned myself to a life without her before I came back last August. Still, the love I shared with her has made me a better man, one who understands what is valuable in life. I'm not about to lose you now that I know you love me in return."

"Is it true that you told Paul to marry me before you left for Virginia?" she asked, dreading the answer.

John regarded her pensively. "I suggested that he marry you *before* Pierre died, when I knew I had to leave. I had feelings for you, but I was afraid – afraid that I'd only hurt the children if I stayed – afraid that I'd hurt you. When Pierre died, all those fears were confirmed. I left because I had interfered in everyone's lives: my father's life, Paul's life, the twins', yours, and most importantly, Pierre's, and the consequences were devastating. I didn't want to live that way any longer, to do the very things my father did to me, be the hypocrite."

"Then why did you come back?"

"I came back because a friend convinced me to. I came back because I missed my sisters, because I missed you."

"Would you have returned without an invitation?" she asked apprehensively.

"I would have stayed away," he confessed. "As I said, I didn't want to interfere. I missed you Charmaine, but I didn't realize I loved you until I walked up to the house a week ago and saw you standing there. I was amazed that Paul hadn't married you yet. I was *happy* that he hadn't married you."

"And you didn't interfere last night?"

"When I took you to the ball, yes, I interfered." he replied. "I was angry at Paul – the way he was treating you. He had six months, Charmaine, *six months* with you all to himself, and still, he threw away his opportunity to have you!"

"And after the ball?"

"You came to *me*, Charmaine. I asked you if you were sure before we even started. So, you tell me – did I interfere?"

"No," she murmured, the color rising to her cheeks again.

His eyes searched hers, then he asked, "And you, Charmaine, did you come to my room last night because you saw Paul with Anne?"

She was astonished, uncertain if he were serious. "Self-assured John Duvoisin needs to ask me that?" she teased, but when his eyes remained earnest, she realized that he was just as vulnerable as she. "No," she answered honestly, "I wasn't upset. I came to you because I love you, John. I suppose I realized it when Paul proposed, but I didn't know how to tell him, or how to tell you. I was *frightened* to tell you. When I watched Paul and Anne go off to the boathouse, everything became clear. Paul's walking away didn't matter. But I would have been heartbroken if I had to watch you walk away. I don't want you to ever leave me again. I love you, John."

His heart expanded jubilantly, and he leaned forward to kiss her.

"One more thing," she interrupted, forefinger to his lips.

"Yes?"

"Do you really have a mistress in New York?"

His brow lifted innocently, but his smile turned rakish. "Not anymore."

The water was growing cold, and she shivered. "Come," he coaxed, "it is time you were about your bath."

He rolled up his sleeves and lathered the sponge. When she leaned forward to take it from him, he held it out of her reach, chuckling when she blushed. He lifted a shapely leg out of the water and washed her ankle, her calf, then her thigh. He started on the other leg, and she could feel her tension falling away. He moved behind her and pressed the sponge to her back, massaging it over her shoulders, down one arm and up the other. She closed her eyes to the soothing caress. He nudged her forward and washed her back. She felt his lips on her neck, then on her shoulder, sending a shiver of pleasure down her spine. He discarded the sponge, and his hands traveled down her arms, moving to her breasts, cupping them, brushing his thumbs over her nipples and coaxing them erect with desire. Charmaine groaned and closed her eyes to overwhelming, burning passion. His hands traced over her belly and stroked the inside of her thighs.

When she could stand it no longer, she pushed up from the tub and stepped out of the water. John grabbed the towel off the armchair and, coming from behind, draped it over her shoulders. She was shaking uncontrollably, but not from the cold. He dried every inch of her slowly, then turned her around so that she faced him. Using the towel, he pulled her naked body to him, dropping it as he encircled her in his arms and kissed her. His hands roamed freely, finding her womanhood, where ever so lightly, his fingers stroked and teased until she was moist with anticipation. Her loins pulsed with desire, and when he drew away, she looked up at him and pleaded, "Don't stop."

He quickly stripped off his own clothing and led her to the bed, pressing her gently into the soft mattress as he rolled on top of her.

"I do love you, Charmaine," he affirmed in a husky voice.

"I know you do." She smiled as she closed her eyes to the ecstasy of being in his arms. She didn't believe that their lovemaking could be any better than it had been the night before. She was thrilled to learn that she was wrong.

Monday, April 9, 1838

When they awoke the next morning, they were still in one another's embrace. Much later, they rose and John stripped the clean linen off the bed, revealing the stained sheet beneath.

"Let them think what they will," he stated with a wry smile.

"I'd prefer no one see that," Charmaine stated anxiously.

"Then the gossips in this house will have reason to whisper, my Charm. You are my wife, and I want them to treat you with respect." With that, he opened the door and glanced up and down the hall. No one was about. He took the clean sheet with him, depositing it in the laundry service room.

When he returned, she smiled warmly at him. "John?"

"Yes?"

"I didn't thank you for all you did yesterday: the way you treated me, your concern, our wedding, attending Mass and your beautiful announcement afterward." Her eyes welled, and her voice grew raspy. "You never cease to amaze me. The day was perfect in every way, and I shall *always* cherish it."

He inhaled contentedly, his happiness compelling her to say more. "Only your lovemaking surpassed it."

His expression turned wicked, lips curling deviously. "I told you long ago that I'd not let your first ride end in failure – that I'd go to great lengths to insure its success. We've given new meaning to Passion Sunday!"

They arrived at the dining room in time to watch a gratified George chastise an indignant Anne London. "I'm afraid you'll have to pack your own trunks. I won't permit my future wife to do so for the likes of you. It would be far below her rank in society." Anne marched away in a fulminating huff.

John chuckled. "Well, George, she hates all three of us now." He pointed to himself, George, then Paul's empty seat. "Shooed, booed, and screwed."

When they had finished eating, John gave Charmaine a quick peck on the cheek and headed toward the study, where he knew he'd find his brother. As he closed the door behind him, Paul lifted his eyes from the paperwork on the desk.

"We need to talk, Paul."

Paul pushed back in his chair and folded his arms across his chest. "I'm listening."

"I want you to leave Charmaine alone," John stated directly.

"Do you now?"

John didn't respond.

Annoyed, Paul added, "In other words, the game is over, and you've won. Is that it, John?"

"It hasn't been a game for a very long time. Maybe if you had realized that, Charmaine would be your wife right now instead of mine. However, she is my wife, and you will respect her as such. So, no more cornering her when she's alone, no more making her feel that she wronged you when, in fact, it was the other way around."

Paul snorted. "What I said to Charmaine was between the two of us."

"No, Paul, you hurt her with your accusations, accusations that included me, and I won't allow it to happen again. I realize you were upset, but you've had your say, and there won't be a repeat performance."

"*Aren't you a fine one to talk?*" Paul roared. "When Father married Colette, you couldn't keep from tormenting her – even on the night the twins were born!"

"Colette has nothing to do with this," John stated softly, controlling the anger his brother was desperately trying to incite. "And if you think you can shake Charmaine's feelings for me by throwing Colette in her face, you're wrong. She knows Colette is a part of the past – that my love belongs to her alone."

"You're awfully sure of that, John. But I'll be right here when your 'love' fails her."

Agatha studied the portrait of Colette Duvoisin. Over the past week, many who entered the manor marveled over its opulence. Amongst its palatial splendors, this one item, this exquisite painting, rendered each and every guest momentarily speechless. She recalled their open admiration – the comments, the questions. *Oh my, isn't she breathtaking! Who is she?* Once again, the bile rose in Agatha's throat. She had forced a stiff smile, then uttered Colette's name nonchalantly, unprepared for the final insult: the astonished eyes, the almost imperceptible nod that measured the third wife against the second in the space of one awkward moment. She would never suffer such humiliation again!

Agatha confronted her adversary – the woman who taunted her, even in death. *You frivolous little whore... the father and the son! Why do men always fall for trollops like you?* The blue eyes stared back, so lifelike, they condemned her from the lofty perch upon the wall. *Condemn all you like, but this is the last time you will harass me.* Like the wife, it was time for the painting to go.

She rang for Travis Thornfield. "I want that canvas removed," she stated blandly, her arm sweeping upward in a dismissive gesture, "immediately."

The butler hesitated. The portrait had hung in the foyer for nearly a decade, serenely greeting those who entered the mansion, and he knew how ferocious Frederic could be in all matters concerning the Mistress Colette.

"Immediately!" Agatha shrieked. "I said immediately!"

Frederic had come abreast of the upper staircase and heard the strident command. "*What is this?*" he seethed as he labored downward.

"Why Frederic," Agatha soothed, "this painting should have been removed a long time ago. After all–"

"Leave it alone!" he barked over his shoulder to Travis as he grabbed hold of Agatha's arm and marched her into the study.

Paul and John were there, but before Frederic could ask them to leave, Agatha pulled free of his grasp and allied herself with her son. "Tell your father that I am the mistress of this manor."

Paul scowled and looked away.

"Agatha," Frederic began, "I have made a grave mistake."

Oddly, she seemed placated, but when he continued, she grew horrified.

"A year ago, I thought to right the wrong I perpetrated against you long ago, but I have only made a sad situation worse. Had I married you when Paul was a baby, things might have been different. However, we are two very different people now. I cannot continue with this ruse."

"Ruse? *You call our marriage a ruse?*"

"Agatha, I told you Saturday night – I don't love you. I have directed Edward Richecourt to draw up the documents required to–"

But she didn't allow him to finish, her long-contained agony erupting. "Now let me tell you something! You ruined my life! I loved you! I gave you everything! You proposed to me! *We* were betrothed! And then, oh God, you took Elizabeth instead – first to your bed and then to the altar! How could you do that to me? How could you turn your back on me when you *knew* I was carrying your child? *How?*"

Paul paled, and John surmised that Frederic hadn't told him the entire story.

"Do you know how it felt to have my baby ripped from my arms because he was a bastard – because I had shamed my parents?" she accused, genuine tears streaming down her face.

John pitied her.

"–how it felt to have them call me a whore because I had loved you? And Elizabeth, your *precious* Elizabeth, she knew my heart was breaking, but she stole you anyway. I hope she's rotting in hell!"

"Enough!" Frederic roared, his eyes glassy. "Any pain you endured was my doing, not Elizabeth's."

She abruptly composed herself, wiping away the moisture with the back of her hand. "That's right, Frederic, you excuse her, but I know what she did. *She* was the whore, for she did not have your vow when she went to your bed."

"*Damn it woman!*"

"I'm already damned," she pronounced proudly, chin raised. "You remember the money you threw at me?" When his brow gathered in confusion, she continued. "You said it would provide financial security for my child. You do remember, don't you? Tell Paul you remember!" She looked directly at her son. "Your father didn't intend to raise you as his own. He thought to buy me off – abandon us in England so that he would never have to look at us – at you." She turned back to her husband. "I took that money, Frederic, and I *invested* it."

"Invested it?"

"I used it to bribe some men. They did not refuse my hefty purse."

Frederic felt the blood drain from his limbs. "What are you saying?"

"Just that I can inflict pain, too." Her eyes turned maniacal. "I took great pleasure in knowing that Elizabeth was raped over and over and over again. Those ruffians were only too glad to take *your* money! If only it could have purchased her murder as well!"

Frederic descended on her in a deranged fury, his hands around her neck before anyone could react. Paul grabbed hold of his arms, John Agatha.

"Father! Stop! *Stop!*"

It was all they could do to tear them apart, Frederic's burst of strength dissipating the moment he was disengaged. He slumped into a chair and buried his head in his hands. Agatha collapsed into the sofa, sobbing pitifully.

"I'm sorry, Frederic, but I love you!"

"Get out! Get out, damn you, and never come back!"

"But, Frederic, I'm your wife!"

"Not anymore!" he snarled, his face set in stone, her future inexorable.

"But, Frederic! I love you!" she implored. "Truly I do!" When she got nowhere, she turned pleading eyes on Paul. "I only did it for you…"

With great pity, Paul went to her. He knew his father would not change his mind and resentment consumed him. Placing an arm around his mother, he coaxed her up. "Come with me. You'll be comfortable on Espoir."

"But I'm the mistress of *this* manor," she objected, her expression strangely blank. "Frederic needs me here. He doesn't know what he's saying. He'll realize his mistake and..." Her words trailed off as Paul ushered her from the room.

John shook his head and sat opposite his father. "Are you all right?" he asked, amazed that he felt sympathy for the man.

"Dear God," Frederic groaned. "I've made such a mess of things."

"From the deepest desires often come the deadliest hate," John murmured.

"She has every right to hate me."

"And my mother as well," John said, suddenly understanding why Agatha had despised him all these years.

"No, Elizabeth didn't do any of those things," Frederic insisted. "I was enamored of your mother just as my affair with Agatha began. Elizabeth had no idea that we had been intimate until after she and I were lovers." Frederic bowed his head again. "But for Agatha to have wanted her dead – to have hired those men to..." His words fell away under the weight of the incomprehensible, the realization that he'd seriously underestimated Agatha, her pernicious animosity. "She fostered more evil than you can imagine, John. For the first ten years of your life, I thought you were born of that vile crime against your mother, and I believed the rapes caused her death. Blackford convinced me of it. I suppose he was avenging Agatha."

John was astonished.

"It's no excuse," Frederic said, his hand massaging his forehead. "You were only a baby; it shouldn't have mattered. But I missed Elizabeth desperately, and you were an easy scapegoat." He breathed deeply, and the minutes gathered before he spoke again. "What is wrong with me? Will my decisions ever prove sound? When will my family know peace?"

John had no answers. Hadn't he often asked the same questions of himself, cursed his propensity for hurting those closest to him? Unexpectedly, he was beginning to understand his father and was uncomfortable with the realization that they were alike in many ways.

Yvette protested when she learned that she and her sister were not invited to the newlyweds' picnic. "But we want to go, too!"

"Charmaine and I are on our honeymoon," John attempted to explain.

"I know what that means: you want to be alone so you can hug and kiss."

"Exactly," John affirmed, sending her into a pout.

Charmaine's face was beet-red. "They know we've been kissing, my Charm," he chuckled.

"In your bedroom," Yvette interjected. "Does it have to go on all day, too?" She spoke to her sister. "I liked it better *before* they were married, Jeannette."

"I think it's wonderful they're married," Jeannette countered.

"I have an idea," John offered. "Father has had a bad morning and could use a bit of company right now. If the two of you can cheer him up, we'll take you on a picnic tomorrow. How would that be?"

"I guess it's better than nothing," Yvette relented.

With John's smile of encouragement, they went off in search of Frederic.

Charmaine enjoyed having John all to herself. He told her about his father's will and all that had happened with Agatha. "Paul's mother for Christ's sake," he muttered, still incredulous. "All these years, all the times we pondered it, and I never thought of Agatha."

Although astounded, Charmaine was happy to learn that the woman would no longer reside at the house.

"That makes you mistress of the manor," John quipped. "You're Mrs. Faraday's boss now!"

Charmaine smiled wickedly. She'd never been anybody's boss!

"And you must look the part," he continued. "It's time for the governess garb to go. Tomorrow morning, I'm taking you to the mercantile to select a more appropriate wardrobe."

"I don't think we will find anything grander than what I've been wearing."

"We shall order them out of Maddy's catalogs. My wedding present to you." He kissed her then, a long, delicious kiss.

The twins awaited their return, having prepared them a wedding gift. "You are going to be so happy!" Jeannette bubbled from the steps of the portico.

"Oh, yes!" Yvette agreed. "It's the *best* present you'll ever receive!"

"Really?" Charmaine asked as they stepped inside the house and Jeannette nudged them up the stairs.

"Truly!" the girl gushed. "And best of all, *we* can enjoy it, too!"

The declaration drew a swift glare from Yvette, but it did not succeed in stifling Jeannette's jubilance. "They're going to see it anyway," she reasoned.

Yvette rushed ahead and stopped at Charmaine's dressing room door.

"Is this where your gift is hidden?" John asked, eliciting wide-eyed nods. "Well, what are we waiting for? The suspense is killing me."

Jeannette giggled, but Yvette scowled. "Go ahead and make fun of our present," she dared, "but you'll see how unique it is!"

"Unique? Why don't you let me be the judge of that? Open the door."

Jeannette led them into the immaculate room. Not one piece of furniture was out of place, not one speck of dust marred the polished wood floor. Nothing was out of the ordinary. The twins snickered at John and Charmaine's confusion.

"Well?" he demanded.

"Well what?" Yvette inquired innocently.

"Where or what is our wedding gift?"

"Can't you see it, Johnny? It's right before your eyes." Yvette turned to Charmaine. "Maybe Mademoiselle Charmaine knows what it is."

"Yvette, this isn't fair," Jeannette interjected, "we haven't shown them everything." She opened the door to Charmaine's bedchamber and gestured for them to step in.

John's large armoire sat opposite them, against the wall that abutted the nursery. "How did you get that in here?" John asked Yvette.

"Joseph helped us push it along the balcony so that nobody would see."

"And what is it doing here?" he probed curtly, his eyes narrowing. "And I hope it's not the reason I think it is."

"It's part of your present, silly!" Yvette giggled, unaffected by his stern regard. "Both rooms are your present."

"Isn't it wonderful, Mademoiselle Charmaine?" Jeannette asked. "Just think, you'll be right next to us again, and so will Johnny!"

"That's right," Yvette piped in, "now we can bring you breakfast every morning and keep you company during thunderstorms and–"

"*Damn it, girl!* Don't you know when you've gone too far?" John's heated query sent Jeannette scurrying to Charmaine's skirts, tears welling in her eyes. Yvette stood her ground, pretending confusion, though her eyes blazed brightly. "Whose idea was this–" he growled "*–as if I really have to ask?"*

"A fine brother you are!" Yvette spat back. "This gift took us all afternoon to organize! You'll never get another one from me! That's a promise!"

They matched scowl for scowl. Finally, John strode to the bell-pull, and yanked it violently. When Travis appeared, he instructed him to install a lock on the adjoining nursery door, then he asked for George.

"He's in the drawing room with Miss Wells," the manservant informed him.

"Can you send him up here?"

As Travis left, Jeannette looked at John woefully. "I thought you'd be happy with our present, Johnny," she lamented. "We could have so much fun."

John was at a loss for words in the face of the girl's innocence. Yvette, on the other hand, had ulterior motives.

George appeared in the doorway. "You wanted something?"

"I need help moving this bed into the dressing room. Yvette has decided that the wedding present we need most is a new bedroom – this one in particular."

"How cozy," George chuckled under his breath.

"Aren't you taking this a bit far?" Charmaine finally interjected.

John looked at her in disbelief. "My Charm, on some future morning when we are 'occupied', you will be thankful that the door is bolted."

Charmaine blushed. "I wasn't talking about the lock. I don't understand why you want to move the bed into the other room."

"Why don't you ask Yvette how many glasses she has hidden in the nursery?"

When the bed had been moved and all was in order, Charmaine sighed in relief. She didn't relish the idea of sleeping with John in the room he had more than likely shared with Colette, the room with so many sad memories, Pierre's death the most potent. In this room, they would make their own memories.

John came up behind her. He must have sensed what she was thinking, for he said, "That should do it, my Charm. I didn't fancy sleeping in the other chamber, anyway."

Edward Richecourt turned his face into the wind, heaved a deep sigh, and looked at Helen. She stood at the railing with friends. They certainly had plenty of gossip to bring back to Richmond. The ship lurched in the turbulent sea, and the ladies grasped the railing or clutched an arm to steady themselves. Helen... In her younger days, she was the belle of Richmond. But they had drifted into middle age together, Helen more so than he.

It had been convenient, practical to marry Helen Larabbie. She was the eldest of three daughters, and her father, Neil, ran a respectable law firm in Richmond. Edward was young and ambitious, so when he began to pay court to the eldest Larabbie daughter, Neil couldn't have been more pleased. The family firm could be passed along to a son-in-law. Edward had an amiable relationship with the man, both professionally and personally. And Neil Larabbie was content with the two grandchildren Edward and Helen had given him, especially his grandson, who was studying law. Neil trusted Edward, expecting only that he uphold the firm's good name and keep his daughter happy.

Edward was always discreet about his infidelities. And what harm? Helen had little interest in the marital bed, and he'd found relief with youthful beauties who viewed him as distinguished and worldly.

Paul Duvoisin's triumph... It could well be Edward's waterloo! Old man Larabbie had at best ten years left. *Ten years!* God, what if he found out? Or Helen? He didn't want to think about it, hated the fact that it all depended on the whim of one man: John Duvoisin. Would he tell Larabbie? Edward hadn't even consummated the adulterous encounter, and yet, he'd literally been caught with his pants down. The last time this had happened, John extorted information about Paul's shipping venture. But John didn't seem to care about Paul's business plans anymore. Now Edward could only pray that he'd come up with something to offer John in exchange for his silence. His future depended on it.

Tuesday
April 10, 1837

Chapter 5

Jane Faraday appeared in the bedroom doorway. "May I have a word with you, Ma'am?" she asked.

Charmaine nodded, disconcerted by the woman's formality.

"As you know, Mrs. Duvoisin – Agatha, that is – hired a temporary staff for last week's festivities. She indicated that the five most competent employees would earn permanent positions on Espoir. I'm assuming that she has chosen from the servants that are already there."

Charmaine listened patiently, wondering, *Why is she telling me this?*

"There is one girl working here who is most deserving, and I recommend that she be added to *our* staff."

The monologue ended, and Jane seemed to be waiting for a response. Puzzled, Charmaine said, "I suggest you bring the matter to Master Frederic."

"No, Ma'am. He told me to bring it to you – that you are the mistress now."

Charmaine was flabbergasted. *You're mistress of the manor now!* Evidently, Eric thought so, too. It was incomprehensible! She rubbed her brow. "If you feel she is qualified, Mrs. Faraday, I trust your judgment."

The woman smiled and turned to leave, stopping just shy of the doorway. She pivoted around, hesitant. "Ma'am, I apologize for what I said to you last fall."

"Apologize? I don't under–"

"I was in the laundry service yesterday morning when Felicia and Anna brought in the linen–" Charmaine felt her cheeks grow warm, but Jane talked on "–and I just wanted you to know that I realize I was wrong, terribly wrong. I hope you won't hold it against me."

"No, Mrs. Faraday," Charmaine whispered. "I won't hold it against you."

A few minutes later, John found Charmaine humming happily to herself.

"Something I did?" he roguishly laughed.

"If only you knew!" she giggled.

Sunday, April 22, 1838

Benito Giovanni stood before Frederic Duvoisin with brow creased. The priest had demanded this meeting directly after Mass, but now found it difficult to begin. Agatha had not kept her weekly appointment last Sunday; the reason confirmed first thing this morning. Her husband had literally banished her to Espoir. But why? Benito didn't fear exposure. If Frederic had knowledge of his unscrupulous dealings with the woman, *he* would have called this meeting. Even so, Agatha's exile could potentially prove disastrous.

"You wanted to speak with me?" Frederic prodded.

"Yes." Benito cleared his throat. "There have been rumors circulating, rumors concerning your wife. As your spiritual advisor, I think you should apprise me of your intentions."

"Do you?" Frederic queried laconically.

Benito cleared his throat again. "I do."

Frederic leaned back in his chair, a faint smile tweaking the corners of his mouth. "Very well. Perhaps you can be of service to me, Father. I have renounced Agatha as my spouse and have had legal documents drawn to that effect. Of course, we are still united in the eyes of God. I would like you to write to Rome and obtain a dispensation that will dissolve the marriage entirely."

"I can't do that!" Benito objected. "She is your wife. You spoke the words 'for better or for worse, until death do us part'. Rome will refuse. You will face excommunication if you proceed further."

Frederic merely chuckled. "Then the legal document will stand as my repudiation of the marriage. In either case, she'll no longer be called my wife."

Benito's eyes narrowed. This was not going well at all. He'd hoped to sway Frederic, reinstate Agatha to her post of mistress, and continue with his extortion. One more year, and he'd have accumulated enough wealth to retire comfortably. Suddenly, his source of income had been cut off, and the fervor of Frederic's declaration left no doubt that it would remain that way. The only option open to him now was to leave Charmantes. He had no reason to stay. Nevertheless, he must carefully disengage himself, lest his departure raise suspicion. Best to set that in the works now.

"I am extremely displeased," he remarked condescendingly. "The lack of morality... I tell you now Frederic, I intend to retire by year's end. I've received word from family in Italy, a nephew who is ill. If you wish, I can write to my superiors in Rome and request a replacement."

Frederic grunted. "Do what you like Benito." He refrained from adding that he doubted the priest would be missed.

Tuesday, May 1, 1838

The days fell in on themselves, a heady blend of lovemaking, picnics, and laughter, all of which left Charmaine glowing. Paul had moved to Espoir, venturing home only twice, and then for only a night. He had three reasons to keep his distance: Agatha, his father, and her. He barely acknowledged her during those visits, so she was glad he stayed away.

This morning they were breakfasting together – a true family – for Frederic was at the table, along with the girls, Rose, Mercedes and George. Charmaine marveled over the change between John and his father, their discourse no longer baiting and angry. Yvette had just told a joke that left everyone chuckling. The girls were benefiting most from this newly won harmony.

Fatima bustled in with coffee and biscuits, frowning when she reached Charmaine. "Miss Charmaine, you ain't touched a bit of your food."

"I'm sorry, Cookie, but I'm not feeling very well this morning."

John leaned forward. "Are you all right, my Charm?"

"Yes, I'm fine. I just feel a bit queasy." She pushed her plate away.

John's eyes lifted to his father, who was smiling at them, a knowing look that bewildered Charmaine. "Sir?" she queried, as if he had spoken to her.

"Charmaine," Frederic said, "you are part of this family, and I'd be pleased to have you call me Frederic."

"I don't know if I could feel comfortable–" she began. Then she was muttering an apology, overcome by a wave of nausea. She pushed away from the table and ran for the kitchen, reaching the sink just in time.

"Miss Charmaine," Fatima soothed, "are you all right?"

In the next moment, John was there, placing a hand to her back. Another knowing look passed between the cook and her husband. "Come, Charmaine," he coaxed, "why don't you sit down?"

"I'm fine now, really I am."

"Yes, I'm certain you're fine," John chuckled.

"Stop laughing!" she snapped.

"I'm not laughing. After all, I feel responsible."

"Responsible?" Charmaine asked, completely baffled. "For what?"

"Your condition." Then, he bent close to her ear and whispered, "Do you think it will be a Michael or a Michelle?"

She blushed a deep crimson, her innocence warming his heart. "I love you, Charmaine Duvoisin!" he shouted, sending Fatima into peals of robust laughter. "Come! Everyone will want to hear the good news."

"John – wait!" she protested. "Are you sure? How can you be sure?"

"I suppose nine months or your tummy will tell."

Monday, May 7, 1838

When Frederic arrived at the tobacco fields, John was already there. John wiped his soiled hands on a rag and walked over to him. "What are you doing here?" they asked simultaneously.

Frederic chuckled, but John answered first. "Charmaine doesn't fancy leaving for Richmond just yet, so I thought I might help out. And you?"

Frederic tethered his stallion to a tree. "I ride out every day now. It does me good to work."

John nodded in understanding.

His father turned and gazed critically across the terrain. "I'm thinking of turning the ground over. The first crop wasn't what it should have been. Paul's initial assessment was correct; the fields need to breathe for a while. Then we can go back to sugar."

John frowned. "I thought Espoir's bumper crop flooded your market."

"Paul has done very well," Frederic agreed.

"It would be a shame to abandon this investment," John continued, gesturing toward the tobacco fields. "Perhaps the first yield was poor, but Harold says the tracts due for planting have lain fallow for four years. The crop should flourish in that soil, and I know a few tricks that will bring top-dollar at auction."

Frederic was inspired. "What do you suggest?"

"Fire-curing for one," John responded. "Add a little charcoal, and your tobacco will have a distinct smoky aroma and flavor. We'll have to build a couple of barns, but that shouldn't be too difficult."

"Let's do it. Where should we erect them?"

John was astounded that Frederic hadn't challenged his expertise. As they walked off to find a spot for the barns, he realized that it was the first time they had worked side-by-side in over ten years – not since the day Colette had made her choice.

Saturday, May 12, 1838

Paul sat alone in the study of his grand new mansion. It had been a month since the life he had known had crumbled. His triumphant ascent into the world of commerce had been tainted from the outset. He reflected on John's return, the confrontation that had removed his brother from Frederic's will and revealed the truth about his own parentage. Agatha was his mother. Even after a month, it was hard to believe. For years, he had longed to know the details of how he had been placed in his father's custody. Today, he wished he didn't.

He had achieved more than he'd ever dreamed possible, stood to inherit much of his father's fortune. Yet, it left him empty. John was legitimate, John had Charmaine, and John was man enough to stand on his own. What had John called him months ago? A pathetic fool? Yes, he was pathetic. He had revered his father, but had it earned him the man's admiration or respect? No – just his money, and *that* only when John had turned it down.

Then there was Charmaine. She had been lovely the night of the ball. He'd allowed himself to be manipulated and distracted, taking it for granted that she'd always be there. But John had been man enough to pass up frivolous temptation and claim what he truly desired. Paul was certain that this had played a part in Charmaine's decision to marry him, John's apparent propriety set in counterpoint to his salacious behavior with Anne London, confirming that he would always be a rogue. He rubbed his brow, remembering how she'd pummeled his chest and screamed her hatred of him. He could have loved her, but now she, too, was lost to him.

John, who had nothing, now had everything, even his father's love. Frederic might storm and rage, but in the end, he really loved his legitimate son. As for his bastard son? Frederic was willing to pay Agatha to raise him in some far off place, choosing never to know him. After all these years, Paul finally knew why he had never measured up.

A great shame laced with pity seized him. How often had he scorned Agatha, and still, she had championed him? Yes, she had done some terrible things, but he could empathize, and therefore, forgive. She had been egregiously wronged, had suffered at his father's hands. He would never allow her to suffer again.

Voices from the hallway brought him up from his contemplation. Agatha was talking to someone. "Go away! Frederic loves me! He'll be coming soon, and I don't want him to find you here!"

Piqued, Paul strode to the doorway, only to find her staring off into the distance. "Agatha?" he queried, uncomfortable with calling her 'Mother'. "Who are you talking to?"

She spun around and smiled at him. "Paul, you're here," she breathed. "When will your father return?"

"Father?" he asked in growing alarm. "My father won't be coming here, Agatha. He's in his home on Charmantes. Are you feeling ill?"

"I'm fine, Paul. But he'll be here shortly, and I have to explain things to him. Once I do, I know he'll understand."

"Agatha," Paul cajoled, "why don't you retire? I'll call for a maid to assist you."

"No, no, I'd rather be up when your father arrives," she stated resolutely, sweeping into the study.

It was the last straw. This deplorable situation was his father's fault. He'd gotten off too easy. It was time they talked.

"Are you feeling better now, Charmaine?" John asked. She had reached the water closet just in time. The last week and a half had been very unpleasant.

"This is going to be a terrible nine months if I feel this way the entire time."

"Rose insists that it will only last a month or two," he reassured.

"That's easy for her to say!" she moaned, sitting hard on their bed. When he snickered, she fumed. "Go ahead and laugh! You had all the pleasure–"

"*All* the pleasure, my Charm?" and he raised a brow that set her cheeks crimson. "You're still blushing."

"Out!" she ordered, pointing to the door.

"Before I leave, I have something to discuss with you."

She eyed him apprehensively, his change of demeanor disconcerting.

"I've been here for six weeks now," he began, "but I have other matters to attend, both in Virginia and New York. I'd like to take you and the girls with me when I go. I spoke to my father yesterday, and he'll allow them to accompany us. I also want to show you our home."

She had stiffened even before he'd finished. Richmond... home... it did not beckon to her at all. Yes, she would be able to see the Harringtons, proudly introduce her husband to them. But thoughts of John Ryan raised the hair on the back of her neck. He was still out there. Charmantes was her haven; she did not have to worry about him here. "I don't think I could go right now," she replied, shaking her head. "I'm afraid I'd be ill the entire journey."

"Very well. We shall wait a bit longer and see if Rose is right. My father should be pleased. He's beginning to realize how much Paul did for him."

"You won't be *over*working, I hope?' she asked, mindful of the grueling schedule Paul had always kept.

"Me? Never. But we won't be picnicking every day, either." He studied her for a moment longer, then encouraged her to venture outdoors for some fresh air.

They had just reached the foyer when the door swung open and Paul strode in. His punishing gaze settled on her. "John," he acknowledged caustically.

"Paul," John rejoined, stepping behind her and placing a reassuring hand on either shoulder. "We have a bit of good news. Charmaine is expecting."

"Congratulations," Paul bit out, his day turning darker. "Where is Father?"

"In town with Yvette and Jeannette. Isn't that right, Charmaine?"

"Yes," she murmured, her eyes fixed on the floor.

Paul swore under his breath. He had hoped to corner Frederic at home; now he had to ride back the way he had come. Without another word, he was gone.

"Charmaine," John chided softly, squeezing her shoulders, "you have to stop giving him the satisfaction of upsetting you."

Goosebumps rose on her arms, and her blood ran cold. "John," she murmured, dismissing his comment entirely, "would you take me into town?"

"Why?"

"I have a very bad feeling about Paul going there."

He stepped in front of her and canted his head. "Very well," he finally said.

She chose to take the horses; they were faster to ready. In less than ten minutes, they were on their way. She quickly set aside any concern that the mare's jostling might endanger the baby; she felt no differently than any other time she had ridden and began to enjoy being out in the fresh air.

In town, they found Yvette and Jeannette shopping at the mercantile. The girls hadn't seen Paul, but Frederic had ventured to the dock; they were to meet him at Dulcie's in a half-hour. Leaving Charmaine with them, John promised to do the same. He headed toward the harbor.

"Haul them off with the nets, then," Frederic commanded, "I'll stay down here and direct you when they're ready to lower the boom." The worker went off quickly, leaving him alone on the pier.

Frederic was enjoying himself today. He was thankful for his improving health, that he had not died as he had once prayed. John and he had finally come to a truce, and though they would never be completely reconciled, he was glad that the interminable acrimony had subsided. His son had a wife, a baby on the way, and a future. This grandchild would be welcomed into the family with joy, rather than sorrow.

His two beautiful daughters were growing lovelier each day. In a few years, they would be turning many a young man's eye. For this reason, he had agreed to let John take them abroad. It was time they got a taste of the world beyond Charmantes' shores. He would miss them, but John would bring them back, granting him more time to mend their healing relationship.

Despite his clash with Agatha and Paul's anger over it, it had been years since he'd felt this optimistic. Regrettably, he couldn't change the circumstances surrounding Paul's birth. Still, if he and John could take a positive step forward, Paul would certainly come around.

Frederic had wasted so much time, but here on the wharf, watching the men unlading the Black Star, he had a purpose once again. If only Colette were alive, waiting for him at home, life would truly be complete.

A large net was hoisted off the deck of the merchantman, cinching around nearly a ton of grain sacks. The vessel had weathered rough seas. Casks in the hold had collided and split open. The crew had bagged the grain that could be salvaged, but unlike the barrels, this cargo couldn't be rolled off the ship and had to be discharged with a boom and net.

Frederic cringed as the frayed ropes pulled taut, wondering why the crew hadn't divided the haul. Suddenly, the boom let go of its tether and swiveled wildly over the wharf in a one-hundred-twenty-degree arc, slamming into the foremast rigging. Puffs of dust exploded from the sacks as the spinning net bobbed back and forth, the mast's tapered yards puncturing the burlap with each collision. Amid the shouts of deckhands, the tether was slowly reined in, grain trickling onto the decks below. Frederic eyed the tattered, yet bulging net, certain the load was too heavy. "Buck!" he shouted, "You need to–"

"Father!" Paul approached, scowling darkly, his teeth clenched.

"Paul, I didn't know you'd–"

"We need to talk," Paul cut in, dispensing with false greetings.

"Come back to the house and have dinner with us. We can talk there."

"I don't have time, but I would like to clear up a few things."

His father took courage to say, "Paul, I know you are angry with me–"

"You can't begin to imagine how I feel about you!"

"I'd like the chance to explain," Frederic insisted, "but not here." Mindful of the dangerous work overhead, he took hold of his son's arm to lead him away.

"*A chance to explain?*" Paul laughed insanely, yanking free, appalled that his father was still determined to keep the secret. "I'd say you've had over twenty years to explain! Now, when you're cornered, you want more time?"

"Paul, I never meant to hurt you. You are my son and I will always–"

"Don't – don't you dare say it! When I wanted your love – your acceptance – your approval, what did I get? Name calling, nothing more!"

Seeing the rampant confusion on his father's face, Paul stormed on, all the angrier with the realization that the man was unaware of the ridicule he had endured as a young boy, even into adulthood. "It was easier for you to turn a blind eye to the taunting than to be honest with me. *Oh, Paul Duvoisin*," he mimicked, "*the bastard Duvoisin? No, he doesn't know where he came from – but his father must have had one hell of a good lay with his whore of a mother if he took her bastard under his wing! All that money, but he's a bastard still!* That's what I heard day after day, and why? Because my father wouldn't do the gentlemanly thing and marry her... No, he sent her away with a hefty purse and wed her sister instead! How did you live with yourself all those years, Father – looking at me, knowing what you had done to my mother – *to me?* Answer me that? Did you think that taking me into your home absolved you? That telling me she was dead legitimized my birth? That I–"

Suddenly, there was a shout from above. Frederic and Paul looked up just as the boom swung over them, one rope rapidly unraveling down to a single ply of hemp. The strand snapped and the netting broke open, touching off an avalanche of fifty-pound sacks. Some of the punctured bags exploded with the forceful shift, showering their meal below. The rest fell in rapid succession, hitting the quay with thundering thuds, most splaying open and spilling forth a mountain of grain.

Charmaine and the girls stepped out of the mercantile and into the bright sunshine carrying two bundles of goods. "The two of you go on to Dulcie's," Charmaine directed, passing her purchases to Jeannette. "I am going to find your father and John. We shall meet you there."

Frederic fell on the settling heap of grain. Not a hand, not a boot, not a trace of Paul. He cast his cane aside, digging barehanded into the pile. He cried out for help, yanking at the heavy sacks, clawing at the fluid mass that caved in upon itself as quickly as it was cleared. Surely Paul was unconscious – would suffocate. *Pray God, he wasn't dead already!* He cursed his feeble arm, less hale than he'd thought, and cried out for help again. *Did no one hear him? Would no one come?* The longshoremen were suddenly there beside him, tackling the pile in the same frantic frenzy.

John felt a series of shudders rumble the wharf. Charmaine's earlier premonition took hold, and he broke into a run along the boardwalk, swiftly coming upon the disaster. Pandemonium ruled, then he heard George's voice: "*What is it?*" followed by his father's: *"Paul – he's buried under all of this!"*

"Good God!" George exploded, and seeing John running toward them, he let out a blood-curdling yell that incited anyone within earshot to come post-haste. "It's Paul! He's buried alive!" He, too, jumped into the fray.

Men were grabbing sacks and tossing them aside, some landing with huge splashes in the water, others splitting open on the quay. Still, there was a mountain of grain to clear away.

John spun around. Spotting Charmaine, he shouted to her. "Ring the bell at the meetinghouse and raise the alarm!"

Propelled by fear, she pressed herself to run. She looked back only once, remembering a similar accident long ago. Everyone had escaped injury then. Today, she prayed for the poor soul trapped beneath.

Paul was breathing. Through God's mercy, they uncovered his head first. Slowly, they cleared the remaining meal away.

"Paul, can you hear me?" Frederic beseeched, but his son lay unconscious. "Damn it, where's Blackford?" he snarled.

There was a murmur before Buck stepped forward. "He's gone, sir."

"Gone?"

"Yes, sir, left a month ago. But we sent for Doc Hastin's."

Charmaine's fist flew to her mouth when she reached the scene. "Is he–?"

"Alive," John answered, breathing easier. "We're waiting for the doctor."

"Oh John, I knew something was going to happen. I just knew it!"

Frederic hobbled a few feet away and slumped torpidly on a cutoff pile at the pier's edge. John wondered how much more the man could endure in his life. He had to give him credit; somehow, he always managed to pull through.

Doctor Hastings arrived, and Paul was placed on a makeshift stretcher. Broken ribs, he concluded, which could be wrapped once Paul was home.

As the litter was raised, Charmaine picked the grain from Paul's hair, a gesture that disturbed John even in its seeming innocence. Paul groaned, and John noted the relief that swept over his wife's face. Before they began their trek down the boardwalk, Paul's eyes opened, and he slowly scanned the crowd that had gathered around, reading the concern on their faces. He attempted to sit up.

"Lie still," Charmaine admonished, chasing more granules from his shirtfront.

He grabbed her hand and pressed it to his lips, then lost consciousness again, his arm falling away.

"Don't be cross, John!" Charmaine beseeched as they rode home together. "He was hurt, and I was frightened for him."

"So was I, but I didn't brush his hair clean for him."

"You're jealous!" she accused and then laughed.

John squeezed Phantom's flank, nudging the stallion into a gallop. Charmaine was left behind to ponder his ill humor.

When the doctor deemed Paul fit for visitors, Frederic seized the moment. He had almost lost his eldest son, the son he had taken for granted. He was not about to squander this second chance. "I'm sorry, Paul," he whispered, standing over the bed.

Paul closed his eyes to the pain on his father's face. He knew what had happened on the pier, the effort everyone had exerted to pull him out alive.

"You gave us a fright," Frederic continued, searching for words. "Son – I don't know what I would have done if…" He faltered. "You have every right to hate me, but I *do* love you, and I'm proud – have always been proud – to call you my son. If you ever doubted that, then I'm sorry. I only kept the truth from you because I was ashamed of myself. I hope someday you can forgive me."

Paul could not open his eyes for the tears that burned there. Though he fought to suppress them, small rivulets chased down his cheeks and into his hairline. His throat was dry, and it was painful to swallow, to breathe. He finally opened his eyes, only to find that his father's countenance mirrored his own. As Frederic turned to leave, he rasped, "Father – I'm not angry any longer."

Charmaine eyed John surreptitiously from her mirror on her dressing table. He hadn't spoken two words to her since they had arrived home. His morose mood was quite amusing, and she thought to have a bit of fun with it.

"How is Paul?" she asked sweetly.

He only grunted, provoking a smile that danced in her eyes. But he wasn't looking her way. He sat hard on the bed, pulling off a boot.

She put on a serious face and stepped in front of him. "You wouldn't mind if I nursed Paul back to health, would you?" she asked nonchalantly, stooping to help him with the second boot and tossing it aside.

"The hell you will!" he exploded, nearly coming to his feet.

She ignored the outburst and pushed him back onto the bed. Propping herself atop him, she giggled. "John Duvoisin – the man who's so good at getting everyone else's goat – can't take a bit of teasing himself."

As his eyes narrowed, her fingers traced his hairline, and she studied every feature of his handsome face. "If you don't know by now that my heart belongs only to you, then you *are* a fool, Mr. Duvoisin!" Before he could reply, she kissed him passionately, entwining her hands behind his head.

His arms encircled her and he rolled over with her in his embrace. When he lifted his head, his eyes sparkled with mischief. "You saucy, brazen wench." He kissed her again and all other thoughts fled him.

Saturday, May 19, 1838

Paul spent the next two days trying to cleanse his body of the grainy odor that permeated his hands, his hair, and his nose. His throat was parched and he couldn't drink enough to quench his persistent thirst. His body ached from head to foot, his chest raw and throbbing. Doctor Hastings had bound the ribs tightly, and the wrap offered support, but he grimaced every time he moved. Still, he counted himself lucky to be alive. Everyone in the household bent over backwards to see to his comfort, and he soon grew weary of their hovering.

Charmaine used the time he spent recuperating to carve out a new friendship with him. Though John might not understand, she liked Paul and regretted their estrangement. He had been her protector – a fortress, and she was ashamed that she'd told him she hated him.

Near the end of the week, she caught him alone in the study, sitting in an armchair with a newspaper. When she stepped in, he rose as quickly as his mending ribs would allow.

"How are you feeling?" she asked.

"Much better. And you?" he inquired, aware that she suffered with morning sickness. Even so, she looked radiant; pending motherhood brought a new beauty to her face.

"I'm fine, just fine."

The room fell into an awkward silence. He moved closer, putting her ill at ease. When he was but a breath away, he spoke again. "You're happy now, aren't you?" he asked, as if it were very important for him to know that her marriage to John was what she really wanted.

"Yes," she sighed, "I'm very happy."

"I could have made you happy, too."

"Yes, you could have, if I had never met your brother."

Paul's eyes were sad, realizing again what he had lost. Charmaine belonged to John, and he *would* do well to remember that. He raised a hand and gently tucked a stray lock behind her ear.

She did not cringe. Inexplicably, she wanted to cry. "I would like for us to be friends, Paul," she whispered.

"I'll always be here for you, Charmaine," he said, "all you have to do is call." With that, his hand dropped away.

Friday, May 25, 1838

John was livid. He had stewed for the better part of the afternoon, and now it was time to have it out.

Charmaine jumped when he slammed the bedroom door shut behind him. "What is the matter?" she queried with concern.

He paced back and forth, then abruptly stopped. "I'm very angry."

Instantly, she realized his ire was directed at her, but she was at a loss as to what she had done to upset him so. "What is the matter?" she asked again.

Her seeming innocence riled him more, and he raked a hand through his hair twice. "Don't pretend not to know what I'm talking about!" he stormed.

"I *don't* know what you are talking about!" she responded in kind, annoyed with his childlike behavior. "*Why don't you tell me why you're upset?*"

"I was coming out of the stable this afternoon," he bit out. "I saw Paul's arms around you – the two of you were laughing together!"

Charmaine let out a relieved giggle, but John did not find her sudden gaiety humorous. *"This is funny?"* he choked out.

"No," she soothed, "but you mistook what you saw. I tripped on the top step of the portico. I was running to help Jeannette with the heavy lemonade tray, and I tripped. Paul was right there, and he caught me. I knew I looked foolish, so I started to laugh. He laughed, too."

The explanation did not put him at ease, and she was at a loss as to what to say. "Surely you're not upset over an innocent stumble? The girls were right there, John. I slipped!"

"Yes," he muttered, his eyes still simmering, "that's how it starts – with a slip, an innocent slip."

Charmaine considered the strange remark. "What are you saying?" she asked, her eyes narrowing. "Is that how your affair with Colette began? She stumbled into your arms?"

He was uncomfortable with her swift comprehension, and he turned away, but before he could leave, Charmaine charged after him. "Well let me tell you something, John Duvoisin!" she shouted, standing in front of him now. "I am not Colette! And I will not meekly stand by while you compare us!"

"Charmaine–" he started, his voice soft and repentant.

"No! I don't want to hear it!" She charged from the room, slamming the door behind her.

John sighed, feeling quite the buffoon. Clearly, his wife would not be bullied into feeling guilty over something quite innocent. *I must learn to trust her; otherwise, our marriage is a farce.*

Quite abruptly, he realized that his worry had little to do with his faith in her and quite a great deal to do with his mistrust of Paul, who seemed bent upon pursuing her, even though she was married now. Suddenly, he was ashamed of his own behavior, not with Charmaine, but with Colette.

Grace Smith, Paul's head housekeeper, was glad when he returned to Espoir. Though the manor was back in order, and things were finally running on an even keel, Agatha Duvoisin had been rattling her nerves, roaming the mansion and talking to herself. Even more disturbing was the voice that Grace heard answering. The moment Paul stepped through the door, she confronted him with the news of his mother's condition.

Tonight, he sat alone in his library, sipping a brandy. He felt like a different man; he should have been dead. Charmaine was lost to him forever. Earlier today, he'd almost come to blows with his brother. John had cornered him in the stable, incensed that he'd dared touch his wife. The stumbling incident had been spontaneous and innocent, but Paul could still hear the blood thundering in his ears as he hugged her, holding her a moment longer than necessary. She had laughed with embarrassment, he with happiness. John had had a right to be angry with him. To avoid another such encounter, he would stay far away from

Charmaine – best to remain on Espoir. With a sad sigh, he drank the last of his brandy and rose for bed.

Voices in the hallway drew him quickly to the door. Agatha stood in the foyer: her hair knotty, robe askew, eyes vacant. Grace's disquietude appeared warranted. Two weeks ago he'd attributed his mother's condition to duress, but now he was really concerned. She wasn't talking to herself, but to people she believed stood before her: her brother, Elizabeth, and, he suspected, Colette.

"Agatha, what is wrong?"

"Frederic," she sighed, "there you are. I heard the baby crying, but I can't find the cradle where Robert has laid him. Help me find him."

"Agatha," Paul implored. "It's me – your son – Paul. Agatha?"

Her head was cocked to one side, straining to listen. "Do you hear that?" she queried, oblivious to what he had said. "I think… I think I hear *two* babies crying. *You haven't allowed Elizabeth in here, have you?"*

"Agatha–"

"I'll not allow her bastard son in this house, *do you understand me?*"

Paul was beside himself. He grabbed her shoulders and shook her hard, forcing her to look at him. "Agatha! Mother!"

Recognition dawned. "Paul?"

"Yes, it's me," he said, relieved. "I think you've been sleepwalking. Why don't we get you to bed?"

"Yes," she murmured, "I'm quite tired. Tell your father I'm in my chambers when he's ready to retire."

"I'll do that, Mother."

John found Charmaine in Pierre's bed, cuddled under the light coverlet. He had searched most of the house, overlooking the most obvious place. Now, he felt the dunce. "Charmaine?" he whispered.

When she didn't stir, he scooped her up and headed to the door. She murmured something in her sleep and, with a sigh, shuddered deeply, the kind born of many tears. He was ashamed that he had made her weep. He cradled her close, kissing her head. Before he got to their room, he realized she was awake. He laid her gently on the bed, and she looked up at him through heavy eyes.

"I'm sorry," he said, his voice thick, "I won't–"

She put her fingers to his lips, not wanting to hear Colette's name again. He grabbed her hand and kissed it. Settling next to her, he drew her close. They lay quietly, Charmaine sad, yet content with the feel of his chest rising and falling beneath her cheek, he relishing her arm wrapped around his waist, a sense of forgiveness. He stroked her hair and kissed her head again and again. Finally, he pressed back into the pillows and closed his eyes.

She awoke at dawn, not knowing when she had fallen back to sleep. John's arms were still around her, his breathing deep.

When he rose, he found that she remained annoyed with him, and even though he apologized again, she had to speak her mind to put the event behind her. "I chose you, John," she said, "not Paul. I waited for *you,* even though Paul was here while you were away. Why would I turn to him now? I love you."

He believed her and vowed never again to brood over Paul. Still, he was happy that his brother had returned to the other island.

Paul threw himself into work on Espoir. There was plenty to keep him busy from dawn to dusk, and he'd ride home exhausted, unable to think about anything but sleep. If he wasn't overseeing the planting or nurturing of a field of sugarcane, he was directing the clearing of the first harvest. It had taken nearly twelve months for the stalks to grow a full twenty-four feet high. He had staggered plantings to pace the yield. Though the harvest should have heralded the end of the grueling labor, it was, in fact, the beginning of another brutal phase. After the cane was cut, it was hauled and shredded. Finally, the stalks were immersed in water and passed through large rollers to express the sugary extract, which ran into casks that were sealed and carted to the warehouse for transport.

He had many valuable workers. His father had suggested he take three of the best men from Charmantes, indentured servants who had paid their time of service. He put them in charge of planting and weeding, cutting and shredding, pressing and transport. Others had ventured from Charmantes on their own, those without families, eager to work harder in the hopes of carving out a more elevated position on the fledgling island.

Although the plantation could run itself, toil helped Paul forget. His drive and ambition inspired the laborers, and he got more out of them than before. After three months, he was able to stand back and smile. Three shipments had already left port – not bad, considering his crew had tarried through the rainy season of May and June, and this was still a virgin undertaking.

He threw a party to celebrate at the end of July, giving all the freed men a bonus. Presently, most of them were living in tents, so he encouraged them to build cabins near the harbor, supplying the lumber at a nominal fee.

As busy as he was, he checked in on his mother almost every day. She seemed to improve for a while, but if he missed a visit, Grace Smith would give him a disturbing report. It was almost always the same: she heard voices. Agatha usually carried the conversation, but Grace often heard a whisper from the other side of the room. Paul laughed off her superstitious speculation, until one day, she claimed she'd had enough of the frightening episodes and quit.

Saturday, June 10, 1838

Mercedes was radiant when she stepped into the chapel.

George had the jitters waiting for her at the altar. Paul and John were with him, doing little to calm his nerves. Paul kept teasing him that it wasn't too late to back out: plenty of good years of bachelorhood left, no more late nights at Dulcie's, no more flirting with the barmaids, no more courting the maidens in town who pined for him. "No more hoarding all your money," John added.

When Mercedes followed Jeannette and Yvette up the aisle, George was beaming, and Charmaine was certain that the smile would be permanently etched across his face.

A small group of friends had been invited: Wade Remmen and the Brownings among them. John and Charmaine stood as witnesses for the bride and groom. After the ceremony, they were the last to congratulate the newlyweds. Charmaine kissed Mercedes on the cheek and gave George the fiercest hug she could muster.

At the luncheon reception on the portico, Caroline Browning approached Charmaine. "My dear Charmaine, you are looking well!" Her eyes darted to Charmaine's stomach.

"I *am* well, Mrs. Browning," Charmaine replied cautiously.

"Harold and I are so happy for you, dear. I just *knew* I was right in convincing my sister to bring you here. And look how well you have done for yourself, marrying such a fine gentleman!"

Charmaine was astounded, recalling the woman's scathing remarks about the Duvoisin brothers. "I'm very fortunate, Mrs. Browning, and very blessed."

"I can see that marriage agrees with you." The fulsome compliments continued to pour forth as Caroline assessed Charmaine from head to toe.

"Good day, Charmaine," Harold Browning greeted as he walked over to them. "Congratulations to you, too! John is a smart man choosing you for his wife."

"Of course he is!" Caroline exclaimed, clapping her hands together. "You must bring him over here, Charmaine, so we can congratulate you properly."

Charmaine reluctantly called to him.

He broke away from George and Mercedes and joined them.

"Welcome to our family, John," Caroline purred sweetly.

"*Your* family?"

"Why yes! Charmaine is practically a daughter to my sister and a niece to Harold and me. She is family, John. I may call you John, yes?"

"That was my name this morning."

Charmaine could see the devil in his eyes, but Caroline was oblivious.

"I was just telling your wife that if it weren't for me, she wouldn't have learned about the position of governess here. It took some coaxing, but I finally convinced my sister that Charmantes was the right move for her."

"Then we have you to thank for bringing us together, Mrs. Browning."

"Please don't be so formal. We're family now. Do call me Caroline."

Harold fidgeted uncomfortably with his collar as Caroline blabbered on. "I owe you a thank-you, too, John. Gwendolyn has written us that the distinguished Mr. Elliot has come calling on her. If it weren't for you–"

"Oh, don't thank me," John replied with a magnanimous wave of the hand, "that was an accident – I mean – match just waiting to happen."

"Oh, but I must!" Caroline gushed effusively. "It was just what my dear Gwendolyn needed – a handsome young man to pay her court..."

And so it went. Mercifully, Rose glided by, announcing that it was time to cut the cake. Charmaine and John fell in behind the Brownings as they headed toward the small crowd that had gathered around Fatima's splendid concoction.

"What do you think she wants, Charmaine," John muttered when Caroline was out of earshot, "a ship, a plantation, or a loan?"

Charmaine giggled and hugged him close.

For the few months, John kept busy helping his father. In the evenings, the family dined together, then retired to the drawing room to relax. Frederic, John, and George taught the twins a wicked game of checkers, and when Yvette begged enough, poker. "I promise never to play outside of the family," she had implored one night, her liquid-blue eyes beseeching her father. He finally relented. To their amazement, neither girl needed much instruction.

Charmaine continued to complain of morning sickness, though she wasn't as ill as she had been at the onset of her confinement. Still, John did not press her concerning his need to travel abroad. She seemed so content, and surprisingly, so was he. He was enjoying his days on Charmantes as he never dreamed possible. Before he knew it, July melted into August. He could hardly believe that just a short year ago, his entire life had been about to change.

Friday, August 24, 1838

Agatha stared across her lovely room. Thanks to Paul, she wanted for nothing, and yet, she wanted nothing but Frederic. *Frederic, how can I convince you that I did what I did because I love you?* She cursed her many misfortunes: Elizabeth, her parents, her marriage to Thomas Ward, Colette, and now, this! But it all stemmed from Elizabeth, revolved around Elizabeth, and ended with Elizabeth. Elizabeth, Elizabeth, Elizabeth! *How I hate you, Elizabeth!*

Life with Thomas Ward had been the same as her life now. He had been a British naval officer, the only son of a modestly wealthy family, destined to one day inherit his father's small fortune, for Commodore Thomas Wakefield Ward Senior had no intention of leaving any money to his five daughters. Thomas Junior had adored Agatha for many years, and when his frigate made port, courted her in a bashful sort of way, long before she met Frederic. Because he was at sea during her time of confinement, he knew nothing of the dashing rogue who had captured her heart. When they wed, his good name cleansed the stain of her humiliation. He worshipped the ground upon which she walked, and with him, she enjoyed a comfortable life. But her heart was scarred, and she passively submitted to his lovemaking, leaving him to wonder over her melancholy moods.

Her parents were another matter. Even after Robert had departed with her illegitimate son, their contempt persisted, and they refused to look at her. Agatha's despair turned to resentment. Only her maternal grandmother, Sarah Coleburn, defended her, later convincing her to accept Thomas Ward's marriage proposal.

"You have been through a great deal, Agatha. Learn from it. Thomas is a fine young man. As his wife, you shall want for nothing, and someday, God willing, you will be a widow with resources. You are at the mercy of your parents now. Is that what you want?"

So Agatha stepped into the role of wife, departing her parents' home without a backward glance. It didn't matter. They were relieved to be rid of her and showed no remorse the day Robert returned to Liverpool with Frederic's letter. When she learned that he had been willing to marry her after Elizabeth's death, her resentment festered into unmitigated hatred. If they hadn't driven her from their home, she could have wed the man she loved.

She began to believe she was cursed. By the time she had received Frederic's letter, she had been Mrs. Thomas Ward for nearly six months, and though no one knew it, she was pregnant again. The fate of her unborn child was sealed with Frederic's second proposal. She cried on her brother's shoulder, insisting that he return to Charmantes and become Paul's guardian. She kissed him, finally took him to her bed, and pledged undying love for him, all in the name of revenge.

The day he departed, Agatha aborted Thomas' baby, refusing to be bound to her husband by his brats. If Thomas were to die, she would be free to pursue her heart's desire: Frederic. She nearly bled to death from the resulting miscarriage. Thomas was granted a leave of duty to minister to her. He remained by her bedside for nearly a month, and, quite unexpectedly, she grew fond of this tender, compassionate man. He never learned that she had destroyed his baby.

When she recovered, she resigned herself to a life without Frederic. Like her unborn baby and Paul, he was lost to her forever.

"There will be other children," Thomas had promised, finding succor in her genuine embrace. But the months turned into years, and she never became pregnant again. Agatha knew she had done irreparable damage when she'd jabbed the sharpened twig between her legs and terminated the life of his unborn child.

"I worry for you, my dearest," he fretted over the years that followed. "My father wants a grandson to carry on his name and has threatened to leave his fortune to my sister's son should I die without an heir. We must get you in the family way again. Let us seek the advice of a physician."

Fearing that her husband might discover the cause of her infertility, Agatha pacified him by insisting that she take the matter up with Robert. "During your next voyage abroad, I shall travel to Charmantes," she suggested. "Robert will know if something can be done."

That was the summer of 1813, and Paul had just turned five. He was growing into a fine lad. If she was apprehensive over her reception on Charmantes, she needn't have been. Frederic welcomed her into his home and insisted that she stay as long as she like.

As handsome as ever, he remained aloof. She valiantly kept him at arm's length, resisting his magnetism. She should hate him, she reasoned. He had stolen Paul away, and now, she would never know the joys of motherhood. She was irrevocably barren; there would be no other offspring. When she passed from this life, only Paul and the children he would someday sire would mark her existence. Paul became her obsession.

Then there was Robert, always sniveling at her feet. She knew he still adored her in his own possessive, repugnant way, so occasionally, she allowed him to make love to her. He repaid the favor by denouncing John and promoting Paul as Frederic's flesh and blood. Because of Robert, Frederic believed the lie, doting on Paul and scorning John. Though she basked in that knowledge, she could not rest until Paul was the sole heir to the Duvoisin fortune – his birthright.

When she left Charmantes, she resigned herself to three things. First, her struggle to forget the past was futile. She was hopelessly in love with Frederic. When she returned to Charmantes she would seduce him. Second, she would not leave Thomas. Sarah Coleburn was right; he would be a well-off man someday, so long as he outlived his father, and if she remained by his side, she would benefit from his wealth. She would always desire Frederic, but she'd learned not to rely on his love. He had used her and discarded her when she'd been most vulnerable: in love, pregnant, and alone. If she were widowed tomorrow, she could not bank on a proposal from him. His guilty conscience had prompted the last one. Never again would she be without resources. Third, time was on her side. With Elizabeth dead and John spurned, she could bide her time.

By the following summer, she was living two very different lives: a respectable British officer's wife when in England and a sultry seductress when her husband's naval obligations took him far from British soil. She ventured to Charmantes as often as possible, and she and Frederic became intimate again, resurrecting all those glorious feelings. Leaving him grew more and more difficult, but Thomas' father was growing feeble, and it was only a matter of time before Thomas inherited his estate. When Thomas died, she could count herself an independent woman, something she deserved after all she had suffered and sacrificed. No matter what the future held, she'd be secure.

Thus, the years slipped by, and she and Frederic remained lovers. But this satisfactory arrangement was most unexpectedly eradicated.

In the spring of 1829, Agatha met Colette Duvoisin. Paul had been off to university in Paris, and she hadn't traveled to Charmantes in nearly four years. She was horrified to find that Frederic had married this young woman, thirty-four years his junior. A whirlwind wedding they called it. Robert surmised it was something else, for Colette had come to the West Indies on John's arm. But Agatha's raging intuition dismissed his assertion. She shuddered with the memory of that introduction, Frederic's desperate, consuming love for his child-bride branded on his face. He had barely looked Agatha's way, and she was on fire with covetous hatred. Elizabeth had returned, the battle for him resumed.

She turned to Robert. But he made light of her predicament with a shrug. "Frederic is married to her now. There is nothing you can do."

"Nothing? She is Elizabeth reborn, can't you see that?"

Robert laughed incredulously. "Don't be ridiculous!"

"I tell you, she *is* Elizabeth. Frederic knows it, too. I can see it in his eyes! She's come back I tell you, she's come back to – to–"

"To what, Agatha?"

"To curse me – and Paul – to patch things up between Frederic and John!"

"You are wrong, my dear, very wrong."

"Can't you see? John stole her away, and John has brought her back!"

Robert laughed at the preposterous premise. "John and Frederic's questionable kinship has finally ruptured. John loathes his father now, his departure permanent. I should think this would please you, my dearest. So, if you hate Frederic as much as you say you do, let *this* be your revenge. Frederic may very well disinherit John if you use Colette as the wedge between them, and then Paul *will* have it all. It has a better chance at succeeding than any of our lies."

Agatha was desperately forlorn when she returned to England, and Thomas was at a loss. His father's death and mother's widowhood distracted him, however, affording Agatha time and space to ponder this newest adversity.

Her sour disposition abated when news arrived that all was not well between Frederic and Colette. *She cried out for John over and over again during her labor*, Robert had written, *though Frederic was there.*

Agatha finally recognized the potential in exploiting the discord between Frederic and John, but first, she had to get back into Frederic's bed. It was simpler than she had imagined. Robert helped set the stage with three simple words that he repeated like a mantra to both Colette and Frederic: *No more children.*

Another visit and it became obvious that husband and wife were no longer intimate. Agatha couldn't quite piece the puzzle together. Frederic obviously lusted for his young wife, and intuition told her that Colette desired him as well, yet they remained estranged. Why? Was John truly to blame?

Agatha capitalized on Frederic's frustrated desire and seduced him before he returned to Colette's bed. Then Colette had her affair with John. Betrayed, Frederic never made love to his wife again.

So where had she failed? Somehow, Elizabeth had won; even in death, then in life and in death again, she had won.

Agatha rubbed her brow with both hands, her torment manifest in an excruciating headache that threatened her sanity. She closed her eyes, and her sister's caramel-colored eyes swam before her, taunting her as they turned smoky blue.

Elizabeth, the war is not over. I am not defeated! Frederic belonged to me first. I've shared his bed more times than you and Colette combined. Very soon, he will realize that I did what I did for him, our son, and our undeniable love.

Saturday, August 25, 1838

Paul scoffed down a light dinner and had just retired to his study when the door banged open. His mother stood silhouetted in the low lamplight.

"Frederic?" she asked timidly. "Is that you?"

She stepped deeper into the room, and the light illuminated her face. Her cheeks were pale, her eyes vacant, yet searching, as if he weren't there.

Paul stood. She attempted to compose herself, sweeping the disheveled hair from her brow, smoothing the wrinkles from her robe.

"Frederic," she sighed, "it *is* you."

"No, Agatha, it's not Father, it's me – Paul."

"Frederic – I need to tell you, I need to explain. You'll understand–"

"Agatha, you're still asleep. Let me–"

"–I'm going to explain everything. Then you will love me again…"

Sunday
August 26, 1838

Chapter 6

The house was quiet. Everyone was at Mass, and John was catching up on paperwork. He couldn't put off a trip to Richmond much longer, but he didn't have the heart to tell Charmaine. She still suffered from morning sickness, but intuition told him that she was avoiding Richmond because of her fugitive father. Still, he'd have to leave soon if he hoped to be back before she delivered.

The study door opened, and John looked up, astonished to see Paul walk in. He'd only visited Charmantes once since their confrontation in the stable: for George's wedding. *He's grown tired of Agatha and is returning her to Father,* John snickered to himself.

Paul took the chair across from the desk, his face somber.

"What brings you back here on a Sunday morning, Paul?" John asked, refraining from a barb about not being able to make a go of it without Father.

"John…"

Something was wrong. The man was perturbed: his face ashen, his keen eyes turbulent, his demeanor shaky.

"What is it?" John demanded. "You look as though you've seen a ghost."

"Agatha," he began. "It's Agatha. She's deranged – gone mad."

"You're realizing this just now?" John quipped.

"I'm not joking, John. She's been grief-stricken since Father cast her out, and last night, she just snapped. She's in a state of delirium – she thinks *I'm* father. She makes little sense, but she's saying things…"

John's eyes narrowed. "What has she been saying?"

"She goes on and on about meeting Father before your mother did. She rants about Elizabeth stealing him away."

John sighed. "We know all this. Why is she still crying about it, Paul? She managed to bring Father around to her way of thinking. You have your fair share now, so what else does she want?"

"She wants *Father!* She's insane, I tell you! She's confusing your mother with Colette, and she's been saying things. I don't know if they're true, but…"

"What has she been saying, Paul?" John reiterated.

"Things about Colette," Paul replied, his eyes searching John's.

"What about Colette?"

"She claims that she and Robert saw to it that Colette was – removed."

Dumbfounded, John leaned back in his chair. *"Removed?"*

"John," Paul murmured, dreading what he was about to say. "That last year when Colette was so ill… Agatha set herself up as Colette's personal companion, insisting that she was not well. She had Robert here treating Colette every week, then twice a week, and finally, every day. In the beginning, Colette tried to avoid him, complaining about feeling worse after he left. He changed his compounds, or so he said, and she seemed improved. After Christmas, I was away, and I assumed that I'd find her completely recovered when I returned. But Charmaine insisted that she only grew worse. Blackford blamed it on a lung infirmity, but now, now I don't know... Colette's death enabled Agatha to become Father's third wife. John–" Paul's face went white, and he hesitated to state his next horrific speculation. "Pierre was on Father's will. He was named as successor to the estate after you. Agatha found out and was very upset, probably furious."

Like the light rushing into a darkened room, comprehension dawned, and Paul's words melded with a kaleidoscope of incidents that were suddenly most logically connected: Agatha's persistent efforts to alienate him from Frederic, her triumphant face when he'd finally removed himself from his father's will, Blackford's abrupt departure, a demonic Phantom escaping his stall, Pierre getting past all eyes to make it to the lake – even his nightmares! *I followed Auntie... She gave him a pouch. I think there was jewelry inside...*

John jumped to his feet and headed for the door, but Paul caught his arm before he reached it. "Where are you going, John?"

"To church!"

The Latin phrases of the consecration echoed in monotone off the walls of the chapel. The coolness was rapidly dissipating as the heat of summer penetrated the sanctuary on beams of sunlight plunging down to the nave and altar. With the small congregation behind him, Father Benito sped up his lengthy recitation. Grasping the host, he held it up to the crucifix before him, uttering the Latin intonation: "Hoc est enim corpus meum..."

The chapel doors banged open, and though he held a reverent silence as he cast the bread heavenward, he cursed the inopportune interruption at the pinnacle of the holy celebration. Footsteps echoed hollow on the floor, but Benito resisted the urge to look back, lowering the bread to the plate. He raised the chalice when a shadow loomed behind and his arm was violently wrenched away from the altar, knocking the cup from his hands. It spiraled off the table and clattered to the floor, splattering wine across the white linens. He was brutally twisted around and came face-to-face with a livid John. *"What do you know, old man?"*

Charmaine cried out as Benito's vestments were abruptly gathered in two balled fists, his face pulled up close to John's. From the corner of his eye, the priest saw Paul draw up behind his brother. *"What do you know?"* John demanded full-voiced.

"I don't know what you're talking about!" Benito sputtered.

"You know goddamn well what I'm talking about, and let's have it out before I choke the life from you right here and now!"

Charmaine jumped to her feet, but Frederic grabbed her arm, holding her to the spot, his eyes riveted on the scene unfolding in front of the altar. "What are you doing, John?" she cried. "What is going on?"

But John's eyes were locked on the petrified priest, his grip tightening around his neck. "You were taking payments from my aunt! Why?"

"They were contributions for my mission for the needy," Benito croaked.

"Do you want to *die*, old man?" John shouted, his hold so violent that Benito's eyes were beginning to bulge from their sockets.

"John, stop it! Stop it!" Charmaine screamed, her horror increasing. She looked to Paul. *Why was he here? Why wasn't he intervening?*

"You have one choice right now," John snarled. "Tell me what happened, and I won't kill you. *Understand?"*

Benito's face took on a bluish hue. The tableau held for what seemed endless minutes, the clergyman's cyanotic complexion now ghastly. Charmaine's desperate gaze traveled helplessly from Frederic to Paul; both were equally bent on facilitating this inquisition, refusing to intervene. The gaping congregation was standing, frozen, the chapel deadly silent. Just when Charmaine thought the priest would pass out, he rasped. "Your aunt and uncle poisoned Colette..."

Benito's eyes rolled back in his head and his eyelids fluttered shut.

"What else, *Father*?" John seethed, adjusting his grip enough to revive him. "Speak up, you bastard!"

"Blackford... abducted the boy... and drowned him... in the lake."

The terror on the priest's face climaxed as John, insane with fury, twisted the garments ferociously, lifting Benito Giovanni up and off the floor.

Charmaine screamed again, but Paul had already grabbed hold of his brother, and George was charging the altar. John shoved Benito away, the man tumbling backward to the floor. "I should kill you, you greedy charlatan!"

Paul was between them now, allowing the gasping Benito to rise to his feet. "George," he directed, "take a stable hand with you and lock him in the bondsmen's keep."

"No!" Frederic countermanded. "Take him into the barn, tie him up, and wait for me there."

George shoved Benito toward the back of the church. The grooms who had attended the service fell in alongside him, then they were gone.

Jeannette had begun sobbing uncontrollably, her arms flung around Charmaine's waist, her head buried in her bosom. Yvette remained silent, standing ramrod straight, her eyes clouded in disbelief.

"John!" Charmaine implored desolately, rushing to his side when Frederic released her. "Oh, John!"

But he wasn't hearing, his mind racing. He headed toward the chapel doors.

"Where are you going?" she called after him.

He didn't answer, and she looked helplessly to Paul again.

Paul chased after him. "Where are you going, John?"

"To see Westphal," he replied. "Come with me."

When Paul did not return, the austere company migrated to the drawing room. Frederic settled into an armchair and cradled Jeannette in his lap. She buried her face in his shirt and whimpered pitifully, hugging him fiercely. He stared beyond the walls, stroking her hair and patting her back until the tears finally subsided.

Charmaine closed her eyes to the piercing pain in her heart. It was as if Colette and Pierre had died all over again. *Poisoned!* How had she not seen it? No wonder Colette had been so ill! All the signs were there. And Pierre! His death had not been a horrible accident! Charmaine groaned. *I didn't protect him! Dear God, I didn't protect him!* But why murder an innocent, beautiful boy? Agatha had much to gain from Colette's death, but Pierre – *why?*

"Why, Papa?" Yvette asked, her voice quivering. "Why did they kill Mama and Pierre?"

"Because they are evil," he said quietly, his voice hard and heavy. He nudged Jeannette's chin off his chest so that she would look at him and gently wiped away the tears that smudged her cheeks. "Better now?" he tenderly asked.

"I think so," she heaved.

"Good. I have to speak with Father Benito. Will you be all right if I leave you with Charmaine and Nana Rose?" When she nodded, he kissed her forehead and rose, setting her back into the chair. He patted Yvette's head. "They will be punished, Yvette. I promise you that."

She smiled up at him mournfully. "Be careful, Papa," she warned.

"I shall."

He looked across the room at Rose and Mercedes. The old woman shook her head sadly. He walked to the doorway where Charmaine stood. "I won't be long," he told her. He squeezed her shoulder and was gone.

The greater the wealth, the deeper the pain...

John and Paul rode into town together. Westphal's house was directly across the street from the bank. They dismounted, and John rapped on his door. Finally, it opened.

"What is it?" Stephen asked, astonished to find both Paul and John there.

"Get your keys and open the bank," John stated flatly.

"Open the bank? It's Sunday!" Stephen objected. "I'm eating right now!"

"Open the bank."

The banker looked at Paul.

"Stephen, just do as he asks," Paul said.

They waited at the doorstep as the man went inside to retrieve his keys. They crossed the street to the bank.

"What is it that you want?" Stephen queried, clearly annoyed as he fumbled with the lock.

"I want to see Blackford's account," John answered.

"I can't do that!" Westphal roared. "That would be a breach of privacy!"

"Blackford is a murderer," John replied. "He left the island in April, and he's not coming back. He had to have taken all his money with him. I want to know how much and what bank you endorsed his money to."

"You can't be serious!" Westphal objected.

John considered him for a moment. "Westphal, what I've told you is true. Benito Giovanni corroborated it. Now, I'm losing my patience. Will you give me Blackford's file, or do I have to get it myself?"

Westphal's eyes went helplessly to Paul. "It *is* true, Stephen. We need to find out where he headed after he left in April."

Shaking his head, Westphal entered his office. He retrieved the file and handed it to John, who flipped it open and settled into the desk chair to study it.

After a few minutes, John looked up at Paul. "Agatha paid her brother well for his work. There are quite a few hefty deposits here starting in April of '36. I would imagine that's when the poisoning began. But the big payoff didn't come until the week after Pierre's death. That's when she signed Thomas Ward's entire estate over to this account."

John paused a moment, rubbed his forehead, and turned to the banker. "This shows that Blackford drew all his funds in a voucher, signed by you, Westphal, to the Bank of Richmond. I doubt he remained in Virginia. Did he tell you where he was headed?"

"No," Westphal replied. "He only said that he planned on retiring comfortably. But maybe this will help."

John was surprised when the banker handed him a letter from Benito Giovanni. "Benito entrusted it to me for safekeeping," Stephen explained. "I was told to pass it on to your father should anything happen to him."

John didn't need to read the letter to know that it was the clergyman's insurance against an untimely death.

George and Gerald stood guard over Benito, who sat on a crate with his hands bound behind his back. Both men were scowling at him when Frederic entered the stall. "Leave us alone," he ordered.

"We'll be right outside," George said.

Frederic waited until the large barn door closed, then he lifted a horsewhip off the peg from which it hung and stepped closer to the priest. Benito's head lifted for the first time, and he cringed.

"Now, my *good* man," Frederic growled, slapping the butt of the whip across the palm of his hand, "I am going to ask you a few questions, and unlike the last time, you are going to answer each and every one of them, or you will hang for your corrupt deeds before sunset. Do you understand?"

The priest remained mute, but nodded slightly.

"Good. Now, how did you come by the information you just revealed?"

Benito inhaled and swallowed. "When you called me to your chambers that night after your wife's death, I realized that lies were being spread about her."

"Lies?"

"Although years ago she had confessed her affair with John, on her deathbed, she did not confess any other adulterous liaisons. Therefore, I concluded that she had not been unfaithful to you." He hung his head and waited.

"And yet, you led me to believe otherwise!"

"I never claimed she had committed adultery," Benito objected obliquely. "If you think back on that night, I merely refused to reveal her private confession."

The whip whistled through the air, missing its mark by inches. "Liar!" Frederic shouted, outraged. "You led me to believe that there was a secret to keep, and when you escaped my chambers unscathed, you used that information to extort payments from Agatha and Blackford! Now – be truthful."

"On the contrary," Benito whispered to the floor, "I didn't request money from Agatha until she had married you." When the whip did not crack again, he bravely looked up. "It was only after she succeeded in bringing you to the altar that I surmised her motives. Until then, I thought she and her brother had lied to you to save your life!"

"Really? And I suppose you, too, meant to save me by guarding that lie?"

Benito brightened. "Actually – yes. If it could bring you to your senses–"

"Don't!" Frederic snarled. "If you want to live, you'd be wise to drop the act, *Father*. Your pretense at piety is revolting. Now – when did you find out that Colette had been poisoned? The truth man, I want the truth!"

"I only guessed that," he admitted. "It was strange that Agatha paid as willingly as she did, despite her protests. It became clear that she had something more important to hide. So, I was prepared for the day she told me it was her last visit, claiming that you knew the truth – that Colette had not been unfaithful. I gambled on my speculation and told her that I knew Colette had been poisoned. Agatha accused me of not having proof, but she didn't deny it. When I said that Pierre's death was a strange coincidence, her face went white. Only then did I realize how unscrupulous and heartless they were."

"You are an evil beast," Frederic sneered, appalled by the man's candor. "If you had come to me with this information, Pierre would still be alive."

"No, I wasn't certain! Not until it happened – *after* the boy's death."

"But you had your suspicions. You enjoyed the luxuries my money could buy at the expense of two innocent lives!"

The priest eyed him meekly, his brow raised in contrition, fanning Frederic's ire. *"How dare you attempt to excuse yourself now?"*

Frederic jerked the crop back and delivered a blistering *thwack* across Benito Giovanni's face, slicing open his cheek and the bridge of his nose.

The priest yelped in agony. "I'm sorry!"

"How much did she pay for your silence?" Frederic demanded.

When Benito didn't answer, Frederic launched the whip again, the bloodied thong lashing across his shoulder and neck this time. *"Was it worth this?"*

Again, the priest screamed. "Mercy! Please, have mercy!"

"My sons saved your life, you ungrateful, despicable bastard! What kind of priest are you? Or have you been pretending all these years?"

"No, I am a priest. I swear, I am!"

"Worse for you, you demon!"

Frederic raised the whip again and Benito winced, curling into a ball. "Please, no more!" he implored.

"Where's Blackford now?"

"I don't know – he just left!"

"Why? Why did he just leave? Was he afraid of you? Was he unable to pay? Did you push him too far?"

"No – I mean, I don't know! Agatha was paying for both of them," he attempted to mollify. "I don't know why he left Charmantes! He just did!"

"You know more than that!" Frederic countered. "You'd better tell me something, man! Why was Blackford involved? His sister had plenty to gain, but what was in it for him?"

"Agatha said he despised you for blaming him all these years."

"Blaming him?"

"For your first wife's death."

"Retribution? He was driven by retribution? No, that's not it," Frederic refuted. "Why harm the boy? *Why?*"

Benito was shaking with terror. "I – I don't know. He didn't say anything else. I only know that he was receiving money from Agatha as well."

"Yes, Agatha was behind it all, but what hold did she have over her brother that he was willing to murder for her? He was well established on Charmantes. Why did he risk everything for her?"

"I don't know, I tell you!"

"And you weren't interested in finding out? I find that hard to believe!"

"Believe what you will, but I don't know!"

Frederic coiled the thong again and Benito quickly added, "It must have been for the money!"

Frederic's eyes narrowed with his lame reasoning. "Then why flee?"

"I swear, I don't know! Maybe he was frightened it would come to this."

"Come to what, Benito, the moment of truth?" He studied the crop, then disgusted, flung it into a stall.

Benito looked up, an ugly welt running down his forehead and joining the blood that oozed from the bridge of his nose and his right cheek. "What are you going to do with me?" he beseeched.

"John saved your life. I think he should decide how it will end."

Frederic called for George and Gerald. "Take him to the bondsmen keep and make certain he's well guarded. John can *visit* him later."

John was a maelstrom of emotions: despair, helplessness, guilt, anger, and loathing. *Colette and Pierre had been murdered. He hadn't protected them.* Blackford's tidy escape fed his torment. How had his father allowed this to happen? Paul had an excuse. He had been toiling and then was abroad, but his father had been there – right next door – as the sinister plot was being executed. His hatred for his uncle did not rival his searing contempt for Frederic.

They rode home in silence. Paul knew what John was thinking and fearlessly said, "John, I know you blame Father, but he was just as ignorant to what was happening as we all were. He had no idea that Colette was being–"

"Really?" John bit out, not allowing him to finish, looking him in the eye. "Do you think it would have happened if either you or I were married to her?"

Paul inhaled. *John loved her – had loved her deeply.*

"*Would it have?*"

"I don't know, John."

"*Don't you?* Well, you keep making excuses for him – protecting him. I, on the other hand, will remember *everything* I've suffered at his hands, to this very day. I've been a fool these last four months," he chuckled derisively, "pretending that the past was behind us. But here it is – right in my face again."

"John, he's tried to right those wrongs."

"*Has he?*" John growled. "How – by throwing me a bone now? What about last summer, when it would have made a difference? No, Paul. He was jealous of my love for Pierre, and he was out to destroy it. He set me up to abduct Pierre – to tear him away from his sisters and Charmaine, just so the boy would grow to hate me. By proving I was as terrible a father as he, he could feel vindicated. That was his objective, nothing more and nothing less."

"You're wrong, John. I know there are some things Father can never change, but he didn't want to hurt you anymore. When he realized you were leaving, he wanted to make amends. He signed custody of the girls and Pierre over to you the morning you were to leave. I saw the papers – signed *before* Blackford ever laid a hand on Pierre."

John's eyes betrayed great surprise, but before he could retaliate, Paul pressed on. "During the ordeal with Pierre, Father stayed away out of respect for you and your grief, not because he didn't care. I went to see him each time I left Pierre's bedside. He didn't eat or sleep. He was suffering just as much as you were – was beside himself with guilt. He loved Pierre and still blames himself for what happened." Paul turned away, his anguish poorly concealed.

The minutes gathered, the only sound the clip-clop of horses' hooves. Paul wrestled with his thoughts, wondered whether it was wise to voice them. "Father loved Colette, too, John. You may not believe that, but it's true, and though you may not want to hear it, she loved him as well. She told me so. The last thing Father wanted was to see her suffer. He was devastated when she died."

John clenched his jaw in renewed rage. *Is this what he allows to happen to those he loves?* But his rebuttal withered away when he read the desolation in his brother's eyes and realized that Paul was only stating the facts as he saw them.

"I don't know what tore them apart, John, but I realize now, it transcended you and Colette. I fear my mother was involved in that, too." Bearing his own burden, Paul could say no more, and they rode the rest of the way home in silence.

"You cannot be serious!" Charmaine exclaimed. "You cannot mean to leave me alone here when our baby is on the way!"

Her eyes followed John around the dressing chamber, as he pulled clothing out of drawers and threw them into a knapsack on the floor. He did not respond and doggedly continued packing. She couldn't stand his silence and stepped in front of him to block the path he was beating.

"This is pure folly!" she protested. "It is far too dangerous!"

"The man murdered my son, Charmaine," he finally replied, stopping to regard her. "He is not going to get away with it."

"You will never find him! He is long gone!"

"I *will* find him. If it's the last thing I do, I will find him."

"John, it could take years to hunt him down. Why won't you let the authorities apprehend him? They are better equipped to do this than you are!"

"Like they apprehended your father, Charmaine?" John asked derisively. "If you could find your father and make him pay for what he did to your mother, what would you do?"

His question left her momentarily mute. "And what of the life we've made together?" she murmured. "You can walk away from it that easily?"

He strapped the knapsack shut. "There is no life if I do nothing."

She turned away, head bowed, tears stinging her eyes. "I will be alone here, worrying for your safety."

"You won't be alone. You have the twins, you have Rose, George, Mercedes. You will be fine. *I* will be fine. I will send word." He came up behind her, placing his hands on her shoulders, but she pulled away.

"You love her more than me," she choked out, "still – you love her more."

"Don't do this, Charmaine..."

"If you loved me more, you wouldn't leave!" she cried.

"Don't make this a choice between you and a dead woman, Charmaine."

"Then don't leave," she whispered.

John reached out and turned her in his arms to embrace her, but she pulled away again, setting her face in stone as he bent down to kiss her cheek. He stepped back and considered her for a moment longer. He grabbed his cap off the dressing table, placed it squarely on his head, and left the room.

Charmaine ran into the bedchamber and threw herself on the bed, burying her face in her pillow, fighting her tears, swearing that she would not allow herself to cry over him. She lay there for minutes on end; the reality that he had left consumed her. *He would be in great danger. Would he be safe? She might never see him again!*

She sprang from the bed, flew out of the room and down the stairs, through the foyer and across the lawns to the stable. She entered the dim enclosure and ran headlong into Gerald.

"What is it, Ma'am?"

"John – is he still here?"

"He's already left, Ma'am – gone a good five minutes now."

Travis had just finished packing Frederic's trunk, saying, "That should do it, sir," when Frederic's outer chamber door banged open. Charmaine stood in the archway, out of breath, tears streaming down her cheeks.

"He's leaving!" she sobbed, casting beseeching eyes to Frederic, then Paul. "Please stop him!"

"This ship is setting sail for Richmond in thirty minutes," John pronounced, as he boarded the Raven.

One look at John's face and Captain Wilkinson knew there was no point in objecting. "May I ask why?" he queried, wondering when his cargo would ever reach England.

"I'll explain later," was all John would say.

Taking heed, Jonah began barking orders to the crewmen who were milling about. Grumbles went up, unhappy that they were turning back to the States without so much as a layover on Charmantes. But Jonah brooked no resistance, and they dutifully fell in with John, preparing the ship for departure.

When the last of the staples had been hastily loaded, Jonah gave the order. The mooring was released, and the vessel pushed off.

A shout from the quay brought all eyes around. Jonah frowned in consternation when he saw Paul, running down the pier, frantically waving both arms at the ship. The men standing on the boardwalk began to shout after the Raven as well. John came to the railing next to Jonah.

"We'd best throw out the ropes," Jonah said.

But John only called to his brother, *"What is it?"* thinking Paul had uncovered something pertinent relating to the monstrous revelations of a few short hours ago.

"Bring the ship back in!" he called. "Bring her back in!"

As Jonah looked from John to Paul, he caught sight of Frederic, laboring down the wharf. "Bring her back in!" Frederic demanded.

John had seen him, too. Swearing under his breath, he turned on the Captain. "Keep going! *Do not* turn back!"

"But John–" Jonah faltered.

"*Go! Just go!*"

Jonah Wilkinson looked across the water to Frederic, who was ordering him to return, then back to John. "Throw out the lines!" he finally commanded.

The crew scrambled to do his bidding.

"Damn him!" John swore, punching the railing. His rage smoldered when the ropes were cast to the dock and secured round the pilings on the quay. The ship clapped against the pier, and the gangway was lowered. Frederic finally boarded the vessel.

"What are you doing here?" John snarled in his face.

"Charmaine sent me," he replied. "She doesn't want you to leave, John. She's frightened for you."

"This is something I must do. I've explained that to her."

"She's your wife. You shouldn't be leaving her, not now."

"Don't you *dare* tell me what I should or shouldn't do!" John shouted. "Now, if you'll get off this ship, I'll be about my business."

"Don't do this, John. No good will come of it!" Frederic implored.

"Do you really think I could live knowing that the man who killed my son and *your wife* is out there – living, breathing? *What kind of man are you, Father?* How can you let him get away? Did Colette mean nothing to you at all? And what of Pierre? He was an innocent child who had the lousy luck of being born into this rotten family."

"You are right," Frederic breathed dolefully, startling John and momentarily quelling the fire in his eyes. "I want you to stay here and allow me to do this – on my own."

"What?"

"You heard me. You have a new life, John. Charmaine doesn't deserve this. She's carrying a child – your child. She needs you by her side right now. I have nothing to tie me to Charmantes. I will see to it that Robert Blackford is apprehended. I promise you that."

"No!" John stated vehemently. "This is something *I* have to do. Someday Charmaine will realize that it's the only way to put the past behind us."

Frederic sized his son up and nodded in understanding. "All right, we'll do it your way."

"We'll?"

"I'm coming with you."

"No you're not," John refuted.

"Then we are at an impasse. This ship is not sailing without me."

Frederic ordered his trunks carried below deck.

John turned away in chafing frustration; as usual his father held the upper hand. But this time, it didn't matter. He would dump the man when they reached Richmond and pursue Blackford on his own.

"Set sail, Jonah," Frederic commanded. Then he shouted to Paul who waited on the pier. "Tell Charmaine that I will bring him home safe and sound."

With his son's dismal nod, the Raven cast off a second time.

Yvette and Jeannette watched Charmaine pace the portico, arms crossed, brow knitted, and tears still smudging her cheeks. Yvette looked to her sister in silent communication. Jeannette shook her head when it seemed she would speak.

"Johnny will be all right, Mademoiselle," Jeannette comforted, "you'll see."

"Only if he drops this foolhardy idea and comes home!" she agreed hotly.

"He's *got* to find Doctor Blackford," Yvette declared. "I hope he kills him for what he did to Mama and Pierre!"

Charmaine was aghast. *"And what if Doctor Blackford kills him first?"*

Neither girl had considered this. Earlier, when they were alone, Yvette had accused Charmaine of not loving Pierre or her mother. "Why else would she be angry with Johnny for what he wants to do?" Now she felt ashamed of that question and grew concerned.

Jeannette was more optimistic. "Don't worry, Mademoiselle Charmaine, Papa will protect him. Please don't be upset."

A rider approached, and they soon recognized Alabaster. Paul rode directly to the house, dismounted, and climbed the portico steps. He shook his head to Charmaine's unasked question. "They're gone – both of them."

She turned her back on him, her rage caving in to anguish, her anguish rekindling her rage.

"Charmaine," Paul placated. "He'll be fine. Father is with him. He promised to bring John home to you." When she didn't answer, he continued. "It's something John felt he had to do. Surely–"

"No, Paul," she bit out over her shoulder, "you were right. He will never love me as he loved her. That's why he's gone, and I hate him for it!"

Yvette and Jeannette stole quizzical glances at one another. One look at their faces, and Paul spoke sharply. "This is neither the time nor the place to discuss it, Charmaine. You'll feel differently when John gets back."

She began to cry. "He's never coming back! I feel it – I just feel it!"

Paul came up behind her and turned her in his arms. He held her until she calmed down, his head resting atop hers. "You know," he finally said, "dwelling on this cannot be good for the baby. Come, let us find a distraction." He led them into the house.

Monday, August 27, 1838

The ocean was so blue Frederic could not see where it met the sky. It was the color of Colette's eyes. How had he allowed this to happen to his beautiful wife? To sweet, innocent Pierre? With an aching heart and paralyzing remorse, he looked at John. Like yesterday, his son had not moved from the bow, his eyes fixed on the sea ahead, as if he could spur the vessel on simply by staring into the distance. Frederic knew they must talk, and breathing deeply, he joined John at the railing. They stood silently for many minutes.

"What are you thinking about?" Frederic finally asked.

John gritted his teeth. He had no intention of talking with the man. Their camaraderie of the past four months had been a farce. They'd only turned a blind eye to their hatred for one another, but it was there, would always be there. Today, John loathed him more than ever.

"John?" his father pursued.

John dragged his eyes from the cerulean sea and, wearing a twisted, satanic smile, turned on Frederic. "Thinking about? You want to know what I'm thinking about? I'm thinking about my aunt and uncle, and how it took them nearly a year to poison and kill Colette. And I'm thinking about her *dear* husband, who stole her from his son, loved her *so much* that he set her up for a love affair and then punished her for being unfaithful, yet didn't suspect a thing." John shook his head in revulsion. "Your own daughter sensed what was going on."

Seeing Frederic's surprise, John pressed on, all the more disgusted. "That's right. Yvette told me that her mother always seemed worse after her visits with the *good* doctor. She was so suspicious that she even took to spying on him and Agatha. But her father – my father – no, *he* didn't suspect a thing – had no idea that anything was amiss. *Or did you?* Was that how you punished her, Father? *By offering her up to the executioner?*"

The heated remarks, raised to near shouting, had caught the ears of the crew, and they began milling nearby, pretending not to listen.

"Is that what you think happened?" Frederic queried plaintively.

"Not what I think – what I know!"

"John, I had no idea–"

"Shut up! *Why don't you shut your goddamn mouth?* There will never be an end to your evil! I blame Agatha and Blackford, yes. But I blame *you* more!"

His agony increasing, unbearable now, Frederic exploded. As John turned away, he grabbed his shirt and threw him back into the railing. John gaped at him, unable to react. "Let's get one thing straight," Frederic growled, "Colette was *my* wife and *I love her*! Go ahead and accuse me of turning a blind eye to what was happening, but you were just as blind! Where were *your* eyes when Pierre was snatched from the house? I'll tell you where: on that damned horse of yours!"

"I should kill you for that!" John snarled, fists at the ready.

Frederic stepped forward, his face inches from his son's. "I'm sick and tired of your self-pity – your vicious ridicule – your tantrums!"

John laughed diabolically. "Tantrums? Ridicule? Self-pity? *You wrote the book, Father!* They're the only reason Colette didn't leave you!"

"You'd like to believe that!" Frederic fired back. "But if she really loved you, she wouldn't have given me a backward glance when you begged her to leave!"

"Damn you! *Damn you to hell!*"

John lunged at him, but Frederic caught him by the wrists, warding off the assault. John shoved harder, and they staggered across the deck, crashing into the capstan with such force that the gears shuddered.

"Enough!" Jonah Wilkinson shouted, jumping into the escalating brawl. The sailors took his lead and pulled them apart. *"Are the two of you mad?* Save your fight for the murderer!" he admonished, planting himself squarely between the two men, knowing they'd go at each other again if he stepped aside. "What's gotten into you?" he demanded of Frederic. "He's your son, man. And you–" he said, turning his eyes on John in a deep scowl "–this is your father. You'd best respect him."

"He'll *never* have my respect," John vowed tightly, "not while there's a breath left in my body!"

They stared each other down, and not another word was spoken that day.

John fumed over his father's declarations, and they turned his mind inside out. *If she really loved you, she wouldn't have given me a backward glance...* He picked up the chair in his cabin and slammed it into the wall, wood splintering in all directions. His anger spent, he studied the rungs he clutched. *Your vicious ridicule, your tantrums...* He sat hard on the cot and put his head in his hands. *Damn the man, damn him to hell! He wouldn't have the final say!*

The sky was dark when he left his cabin, but the deck was bathed in moonlight. He couldn't sleep, and the sea breeze might clear his churning mind. At the stern, a skeleton crew cast lots while they kept vigil under the star-studded sky. Their banter and the serenity of the ocean provided a peace he'd not enjoyed for two long days. Leaning on the rail, he contemplated the choppy water, the small waves catching the moonlight and sparkling brilliantly as they clapped together.

He was surprised when Jonah Wilkinson drew up alongside him. He respected the man and made an effort to smile.

The minutes gathered before Jonah spoke. "Why do you hate him, John?"

"You know why, Jonah." John swung round and leaned back. "Some things will never change."

"But you have a wife now and a baby on the way, maybe a son. Isn't it time to bury the past?"

"If only it were that simple," John murmured, his chin tucked to his chest, arms folded. "You know what's gone before and what's happened over the past two days. The wound has been opened again. It was left untended, and now it festers with poison, just waiting for the kill."

"The two of you have made it so," Jonah said. "Why can't you accept the fact that your father loved this woman – *deeply* – and that she loved him as well?"

John's head came up. "Why is everyone trying to convince me of this? She didn't love him – *not ever*."

"That's not how I saw it," Jonah countered "When I returned to Charmantes after they were married, I watched them together, in town and at the estate. Frederic invited me to dinner, as he always did back then. Colette was radiant; there was no doubt that she was in love with him. And your father, he doted on her as if she were a princess – acted like a young man again."

John's turbulent eyes did not faze Jonah. He had known John since he was old enough to climb the Raven's gangplank and had weathered this expression before. Suddenly, it became imperative to make the younger man see reason. The resentment that ate away at his heart would destroy him if he didn't let it go. "I know you loved her, John," he continued, "and perhaps she loved you. But she loved your father as well."

"If she loved him," John ground out, "why did she turn to me?"

"I don't know," Jonah replied. "Why don't you ask your father? But when you do, why don't you *listen* to his answer? Your father is a good man, John. It would be a shame if you left this world not knowing that."

Tuesday, August 28, 1838

Paul swore under his breath as he dumped out the last drawer and tossed it to the cabin floor. George kicked a stool aside and, wiping his hands together, said, "That's it. He must have spent it all, just like he said."

Paul shook his head and rubbed the back of his neck. "I doubt it. Yvette insists that Agatha handed him jewelry. He wouldn't have been able to pawn that so easily – not here on the island."

George sighed. "Well, there's nothing here."

"I don't trust him, George. I'm going to move him out of the bondsmen's keep to a place where he'll be all alone, where it will be difficult to escape."

"What do you think your father will do with him?"

"I don't know. But I want him alive and well when he and John return."

Paul strode to the window and stared at the wooded grounds beyond. "I can't go back to Espoir," he murmured. "If I do, I might strangle her."

George walked over to his friend and placed a reassuring hand upon his shoulder. "It's not your fault, Paul. None of this is your fault."

Paul nodded, tears stinging in his eyes. "I know it's not. But I'm so goddamn angry George, I feel like–"

"We're all angry, and we all feel helpless," George reasoned. "Give it some time. We'll get over it. You'll get over it. As for Agatha, Jane Faraday will keep an eye on things there. And, if you'd like, I'll venture over every so often."

Paul faced him. "You're a good friend, George. I'm lucky to have you here."

John found his father at the rail, leaning forward, contemplating the vast Atlantic. He steeled himself for another confrontation. He doubted Jonah's words. His father had raped Colette. How could she have loved such a man?

"So, Father," he said as he came abreast of him, "she didn't love me?"

Frederic turned around and folded his arms across his chest. "I shouldn't have said that to you."

John was not happy with his answer. "So, you're saying you were wrong."

"No. I'm saying I shouldn't have said that to you."

"If she didn't love me, Father, why did she come from your bed to mine?"

Frederic didn't answer, and John pressed on. "And unlike you, I didn't have to force her. She came to me of her own volition."

Frederic bowed his head, and John reveled in the delicious pain he was inflicting. "So what was it, Father?" he smiled crookedly, virulently, "you tired of forcing her or–"

"You're not ready for the truth," Frederic cut in.

"Try me."

Frederic eyed him speculatively. "Colette only chose you because I hadn't made love to her for five long years. She was lonely, nothing more."

John laughed outright, the comment insane, but his father's sober eyes gave him pause. Shaken, he blurted out, "I loved Colette!"

"That is where you and I are different, John. For I love her still."

"How *touching*!"

"But true," Frederic responded, turning back to the ocean. "I was also hurt."

"*You* brought it down upon all of us – not I!" John accused.

"Yes, I did," his father ceded, "but not for the reasons you think."

"Then why?"

Frederic inhaled deeply, held the breath, then released it, all the while staring across the water as if he could see beyond the barriers of time. "The moment I saw Colette, I was struck by her resemblance to your mother – not in her looks, but in her mannerisms: the way she walked into a room, her self-confidence, her smile, the mischievous fire that lit up her eyes. Even the small things: the sweep of her hand and the lilt of her voice. They disturbed me, and though I struggled to ignore the similarities, the attraction only grew."

"So, because she reminded you of my mother, that gave you the right to rape her?"

"No," Frederic replied softly.

"Then why did you force her? Why did you steal her away? Do you really hate me that much?"

"I don't hate you, John!"

"*No?*" John cried, spurred on by the cruelty he'd endured and suppressed the whole of his life. "Were you so angry that I took Elizabeth from you that you took Colette from me? I loved her, couldn't you see that?"

Frederic stood stunned, moved by his son's unmasked torment. *Dear God, is that what he thinks?*

"*How could you do that to me?*" John demanded.

"I didn't do it *to you*, John," Frederic refuted. "And though you may never believe it, I *am* sorry." He paused, at a loss, fearful of saying more. John continued to stare at him, his disbelief and misery increasing, an awesome front. For Frederic, it was now or never. "I misjudged Colette," he began hesitantly, his chest constricting. "I was certain she was playing you for the fool – *me for the fool.* I'd overheard a few conversations between her and her friend and could see her mother's fear of poverty. So I assumed Colette didn't love you at all, that she was simply out for a rich husband. That night, I only thought to shake her up, to make her realize she was playing with fire. But that fire got out of hand. Once I'd kissed her, the years fell away, and it was as if I had your mother back in my arms again. I know it's not an excuse, but I was lost to desire."

Frederic breathed deeply, the ache in his breast acute now. "She didn't fight me. I realized later that she was too frightened to fight. But when it was happening, I believed I was right about her: she had had other lovers. I couldn't stop. I didn't want to stop. I didn't hurt her, John, not physically, anyway."

He gulped back his pain. "When it was over, I realized my mistake. She *was* pure and innocent, and I was ashamed over what I had done. At the same time, I was elated that my speculations had proven wrong. The next day, I couldn't concentrate for thinking about her. That night, I went to her and offered marriage. I promised to help her family. Yes, I wanted to set things right, but more than anything, I wanted her to be *my* wife. I convinced myself that what happened between us was destiny: she belonged with me and not you. You were young, I reasoned, too young to be married. You weren't in love, merely infatuated. Eventually, you'd find another. So, I brushed your feelings aside." Frederic closed his eyes, struggling valiantly to rein in his rampant emotions. "I convinced Colette this was true and warned her that she might already be with child, my child. She realized she couldn't go to you a soiled bride and agreed to marry me."

He regarded his son, wondering how his words had been received. The perfidious story had to be as difficult to hear as it was to tell. "It wasn't planned, John. It just happened."

"I don't want to hear any more," John sneered.

"Very well," Frederic rasped, grabbing hold of John's arm before he could walk away. "Just answer me this: why is it that I am willing to accept your love for Colette – forgive your affair – but you refuse to consider that I loved her, too?"

John yanked free, unmoved by his sire's beseeching voice. "I'm not asking for your forgiveness, Father! I didn't do anything wrong. I just took what belonged to me in the first place."

Frederic shook his head, knowing that John couldn't possibly believe that. "I should have released her," he murmured. "I tried to deny loving her for those five years. It would have been easier just to let her go."

"Then why didn't you?"

"*Because* I loved her," he said simply. "I loved her, and I couldn't bear to see her walk out of my life. Having her there, even without her love, was preferable to never seeing her again."

"So, you admit that she didn't love you," John rejoined.

"I *thought* she didn't love me," he corrected softly. "The first year we were married, we were happy – I was happy, happier than I'd been in a very long time. I had a reason for living again. I thought Colette was happy, too. Though she never said it, I felt in my heart that she'd grown to love me.

"Then she was expecting and we were overjoyed, until the night the twins came into the world. It was a terrible ordeal, the labor long and hard. Blackford finally gave her something for the pain. I stayed with her, frightened that I was going to lose her all over again, just like on the night you were born. Then the laudanum took effect and she became delirious. She called for you over and over again, leaving me no doubt who she really loved."

Frederic bowed his head with the painful memory, and John recalled the fierce argument he'd had with Colette that night, one that had induced her labor, perhaps ravaged her mind.

"I begged God to spare her, John – vowed that I'd never touch her again if He'd just let her live. And so, when she recovered, I stayed away. At first, I was able to accept my promise, but as time passed, I began to pray that she would come to me. When she didn't, I ached with the belief that she had never loved me.

"I threw myself into work – first on Charmantes, then on Espoir. Then you came home, and things went from bad to worse. I don't blame you, John, and I don't blame Colette, I blame myself. At that time, however, I wanted to blame everyone *but* myself.

"After the stroke, I prayed to God to take me, so that you and Colette could be together. But death didn't come.

"The years passed and suddenly, she was gravely ill. I was going to lose her all over again, and I damned myself for the pain I had caused her, the time I had wasted. I finally bared my heart to her – told her I had always loved her and asked her to forgive me. She said she'd forgiven me years ago – that she loved me, but thought I hated her for what she had done – that I no longer wanted her. Dear God, how could she think I wouldn't want her?"

His eyes grew glassy, his hoarse voice nearly inaudible. "She died in my arms that night, John. When I awoke the next morning, she was gone. She died in my arms..."

Frederic's tears fell freely now, and John, with eyes stinging, walked away.

Wednesday, August 29, 1838

In less than four days, the Raven reached Richmond. John threw his knapsack over his shoulder and rushed down the gangplank, bent on abandoning his sire. He glanced back to see Frederic laboring far behind him, trying his level best to keep up. *It wasn't planned... It just happened... That's how it starts – with a slip, an innocent slip...*

"Shit!"

John hailed a carriage, then turned back to his father, grabbed his bag, and helped him into the conveyance.

"Good luck!" Jonah Wilkinson shouted after them.

"Don't leave port until I speak with you tomorrow!" John called back. "We may need the packet."

The bank was busy for a Wednesday, but John and Frederic went straight to the platform and inquired for the bank manager, Thomas Ashmore, an acquaintance of John's. "I need some information on a Robert Blackford," John stated, once his father had been introduced and handshakes exchanged.

"Well, John," the bank manager proceeded cautiously, "what kind of information are we talking about?"

"Robert Blackford left Charmantes four months ago," he offered. "At that time he had closed out a sizeable account with the island's bank and had a promissory note drawn up payable to this bank. We are trying to track him down. Therefore, I need to find out when he deposited that note, if, in fact, he still holds an account here, or whether the money was endorsed to another bank."

"Well, John," Thomas Ashmore replied, "you're asking for personal information. Can you give me a good reason why I should release it to you?"

"The man is a murderer."

"Well, John, why don't you go to the authorities?"

"Because I want to track him down myself, Ash-hole," John replied through clenched teeth, missing Frederic's snigger.

"Well, John–"

"Is 'well John' the only thing you know how to say?" Frederic interrupted.

Thomas gave Frederic a sidelong glance. "Well, sir–"

"Obviously, it is," Frederic bit out. "Mr. Ashmore, this institution was one of the few unscathed by last year's bank panic, was it not?"

Thomas nodded, but his eyes grew wide as saucers.

"I daresay, I had a lot to do with that, considering my substantial backing here. Now, if this bank wishes to avoid another such panic today, you had better go and find the information my son has requested. If you are not back here in ten minutes' time, information in hand, I will close out every account that I have in this establishment, and demand each balance in cash. Do you understand?"

"Yes, sir," Ashmore gulped out before fleeing his desk.

Very good! John thought.

Joshua Harrington overheard the dispute at Thomas Ashmore's desk and was taken aback when John Duvoisin turned around and flopped down in the nearest chair as the banker scurried away.

"Mr. Duvoisin?" Joshua inquired, determined to speak to him.

John looked up and, canting his head, tried to place name to the man's face.

"Mr. *John* Duvoisin?" Joshua asked again.

"What can I do for you?" John responded. Frederic looked on in interest.

"I'm Joshua Harrington. We met quite a few years ago... I was wondering if your wife was with you – here in Richmond?"

"Charmaine?" John asked in bewilderment. *Who was this man?* His name sounded familiar.

"Yes, Charmaine lived with my wife and me before becoming governess on Les Charmantes."

John rubbed his forehead. *Of course!*

"We are a bit concerned about her," Joshua rushed on. "Her last letter – well, we'd love to see her and make certain that she is – in good health."

"Yes," John breathed, irritated by the tacit message that Charmaine was in some sort of peril married to him. "Unfortunately, she did not accompany me. I had urgent business to attend, and she wasn't up to making the voyage in her condition."

Joshua's brows raised in what appeared to be ghastly comprehension.

"She is fine," John quickly added, "but preferred to stay behind."

Thomas Ashmore returned, and with a nod, Joshua retreated.

Frederic and John left the bank with the information they needed. Blackford had deposited the monies on the fifteenth of April and drawn on the new account immediately. The family's finances had facilitated his escape: The Charmantes' seal guaranteed the note and the Duvoisin funds were held against it. He had taken a quarter of the money in cash and the remainder in another note payable to a New York bank.

They headed back to the harbor to check the ships' manifests for the month of May and ascertain exactly when Blackford had headed to New York City.

The carriage was quiet. John stared out the window. Frederic watched him. "Do you love Charmaine?" he abruptly asked.

John faced him, brow creased. "What do you mean, do I love her?"

"It's a simple question, John."

"Yes, I love her."

Frederic turned and looked out his window.

"That's it, Father?" John queried. "That's all you wanted to know? I know you better than that. What was your real reason for asking that question?"

"You certainly didn't give Mr. Harrington the impression that you love her," Frederic replied, ignoring John's dismissive grunt. "The man was obviously concerned. You did nothing to alleviate his disquiet. In fact, he appeared more worried when he walked away."

"He'll get over it," John replied dryly.

"Yes, but what of Charmaine? Do you think she'll get over it?" He gave John a moment. "You may have told her that you needed to do this for Pierre, and I understand that. But on the ship, your anger was about Colette."

"My *anger*, Father," John ground out, "was directed at you, no one else. Do you want to hear how I hate you for robbing me of the three short years I could have spent with my son? If you had seen Agatha for what she was, Pierre would still be alive, wouldn't he?"

"Yes, he would," Frederic capitulated softly. "But Charmaine sees only one face when she thinks of you running off and leaving her, and that face is not Pierre's. You should go back home and allow me to find Blackford."

"No," John snarled. "You're not going to deprive me of the satisfaction of seeing *his* face when I confront him. He will wish he had died and gone to hell."

"We're of a similar mind, but are you willing to forfeit Charmaine for that?"

"Charmaine has waited for me before, Father. She will wait for me again."

"Are you certain?" Frederic probed. "Your brother loves her, too, you know. I've seen it in his eyes."

John grunted again, and again Frederic paid him no mind. "*Your eyes,* when you looked at Colette after I married her."

"My eyes were filled with loathing."

"And deep pain and longing," Frederic finished. "Strange how one can desire something the most when it is no longer theirs to claim."

"Charmaine doesn't love Paul," John reasoned, "or she would have gone to him long before I returned."

"I pray you are right. But she has a woman's heart now, one that you've broken. In her pain, she may turn to the nearest arms that offer her solace."

John was ill at ease with Frederic's words, but as the carriage drew near the docks, he refused to be deterred. He resolved to write Charmaine that night and let her know that he loved her despite their strained goodbye.

Charmaine sat at the piano, absentmindedly picking out a disjointed melody. Mercedes and George had taken the girls into town, for she had been dismal company the past five days. Even the news of Mercedes' pregnancy had not lifted her spirits. In the quiet solitude, her mind wandered to the sea and Richmond. Any hope that John would change his mind and turn back dwindled by the day. She had been a fool to ever love him – a stupid fool! She did not hear Paul step into the room.

He considered her momentarily, her sorry state. Nobody could make her see reason. His assertion on her wedding night had met its mark. How easy it would be exploit it now, to side with her and bolster her doubts.

He walked over to the piano and put his hands on her shoulders. "It is quiet now," he said when she turned to face him. "We need to talk." He drew up a chair and took both of her hands into his. "Charmaine, I know you're angry with John, but you can't go on like this. He and my father may be gone for weeks. Do you really want to be miserable the entire time they're away?"

"You are right," she said. "Why should I sit here pining for John, when I know he hasn't given me a second thought?"

Inspired, Paul agreed. "Exactly! I told you that I'd always be here for you, Charmaine. When you've had enough of this, my arms are wide open."

She was aghast and jumped to her feet. "If you think that I could forget John that easily, you insult me! I may be angry with him, but–"

Her anger instantly ebbed, for Paul's eyes were laughing up at her. "I thought you hated him," he said.

"I do," she sputtered, sinking back down to the bench. "I *do* hate him and when he gets back, he's going to hear it! But–"

"–you love him, too," he finished for her, "so much so that you hate him for leaving you in pursuit of Blackford. And there's nothing wrong with that."

"But what if he doesn't come back, Paul?" she implored, voicing her darkest fear. "I'm so *worried* for him."

"Charmaine, *nobody* is as slick as John. He knows what he's doing. If he can't find Blackford, nobody can. And Father is there to watch out for him. I doubt anything will happen to either of them." He paused for a moment and added thoughtfully, "Don't you find it strange that they've been thrown together to set this terrible thing right, as if it is meant to be? Providence perhaps. Maybe they will come home reconciled, not only with the past, but with one another."

Charmaine listened quietly, wishing his wisdom true. Clearly, he had been pondering the nefarious events almost as much as she and cared enough about her to offer comfort. She lifted her hand to his rough cheek. "I pray you are right," she said softly. "And I promise not to be so very miserable from now on."

He took her hand and pressed her palm to his lips. "I just want you to be happy, Charmaine."

The Duvoisin ship manifests revealed that Blackford had left Richmond on the Seasprit on the sixteenth of May, which would put him in New York by the eighteenth. He'd had over three months to dissolve into the hubbub of the burgeoning city.

With Frederic waiting on the wharf, John boarded the Raven and spoke to Jonah. They would set sail on the morrow, and the cargo of tobacco and sugar intended for England would be sold at auction in New York instead.

They settled back in the cab, and John turned to Frederic. "If you don't mind, I would like to make one last stop before calling it a day. It won't take long."

Frederic nodded, wondering what John had in mind.

Joshua Harrington arrived home, heavy of heart. He entered the front parlor with head down, wondering how he would tell his wife what he had learned.

Loretta immediately knew something was wrong. "What is it?"

"I ran into John Duvoisin at the bank today."

Her face lit up. "Was Charmaine with him?"

"I'm afraid not, my dear, and I fear things are not good between Charmaine and her husband. She was left behind because she *is* expecting. I knew no good would come of this."

Loretta wondered if he meant Charmaine's marriage to John or her idea to send Charmaine to Charmantes. Over the last two years, the letters they'd received from Charmaine often conveyed a disconcerting gloom. She wrote of Colette's death, Frederic's marriage to Agatha, the prodigal son's return, and little Pierre's terrible drowning accident. Both Loretta and Joshua surmised that something more dreadful than Pierre's death had happened to this family, and they had second thoughts about Charmaine living there. Yet, she gave no indication that she wanted to return to Richmond. Instead, she wrote of her resolve to stay by the twins' side, John's departure, Frederic's slow recovery, and Paul's preparations for the unveiling of his fleet of ships and island. Obviously, she was spending a great deal of time with Paul, though she never mentioned her feelings, nor speculated where that relationship might lead. Loretta worried often, but Charmaine was a woman now, twenty years old, certainly old enough to make sound decisions.

Michael Andrews' peculiar visit nearly five months ago rekindled their concern. Not two weeks later, Joshua and Loretta entertained Raymond and Mary Stanton, just returned from Charmantes and Paul Duvoisin's commercial debut. Mary was burning to recount the most unexpected and quiet wedding that had capped the week's events.

"You knew nothing about this, Loretta?" Mary had exclaimed, reading Loretta's surprise, raven for more gossip. "Surely Charmaine wrote that she had feelings for this man – that he was courting her? No?"

When Loretta remained speechless, the woman rushed on, tickled to tell what she knew. "It was so strange – the whole thing." Then she paused, reliving the grandiose event. "Oh, it was a most impressive affair. Charmaine, however, was there in the capacity of governess, nothing more. I caught up with her before the ball. She was plainly dressed, with the children at her side. She said nothing about having an escort for the evening and disappeared not two hours later, settling the girls for the night, no doubt. I can assure you that no one expected her to return – certainly not on John Duvoisin's arm, anyway, and so elegantly garbed! She remained at his side for the rest of the evening, danced nearly every dance with him. And Paul – well he might have escorted the widow London to the festivities, but everyone could see that he was preoccupied with Charmaine. He appeared highly agitated. Either he did not want her there or he greatly disapproved of her partner." Mary shook her head as if she could not fathom it.

"My, you should have heard the talk when *he* danced with her! Something was amiss to be sure!"

Loretta shuddered, displeased that Charmaine was the subject of much Richmond gossip. Though she dreaded the rest of the scandalmonger's narrative, her desire to know was greater than the woman's humiliating glee, and so, Loretta allowed her to prattle on.

"I heard that at Mass the following morning, John was seated beside her again, a most unexpected sight, as everyone who is anyone knows that he *never* attends church services. They say Charmaine's head remained bowed for the entire time, feeding speculation as to what was going on between her and the heir to the Duvoisin fortune. But *nobody* was prepared for the announcement that John made at the conclusion of the service. They were wed not two hours earlier! And I have it on good authority that Paul was furious."

"What of Charmaine?" Loretta probed worriedly. "What was her reaction?"

"Anne London insists that she couldn't stop blushing, as if–" Mary lowered her voice to a whisper "–as if she had something to be embarrassed about."

"Mary," Loretta chided sharply, horrified, "you don't know that. After all, Mr. Duvoisin must feel strongly for Charmaine if he proposed marriage to her."

"Really?" Mary rejoined. "Well, if he feels *strongly* for her, why didn't he arrange a proper ceremony and celebration? He can well afford it, can he not?"

Why indeed?

For weeks, Loretta and Joshua fretted over Mary Stanton's news.

Finally, they received word from Charmaine, the correspondence lively and gay. She *had* married John. *I know this will come as quite a shock to you and Mr. Harrington,* she wrote, *but almost two weeks ago, I married John Duvoisin. Tell Mr. Harrington not to worry. I am very happy. As I insisted some months ago, John is not the man I thought him to be when first we met.*

Though Loretta remained confused, she was at ease with Charmaine's decision to wed. She had no reason to feel otherwise. The young woman had, in fact, done very well for herself, even if the man she had chosen was notorious.

But today, all of Loretta's concerns were revived. She was dismayed that Charmaine was already pregnant and left behind while her spouse traveled abroad. She considered her husband woefully. "What has happened, Joshua?" she whispered. "What do you suppose has happened to our dear Charmaine?"

"I'm afraid to guess," Joshua bit out, "but I'm going to find out."

"How?"

"I will book passage to Charmantes," he said determinedly. "And if you think you're up to the voyage, my dear, you are welcome to join me."

"Do you think I'd allow you to travel there without me?"

The carriage pulled to a stop in front of the St. Jude Refuge, and Frederic allowed John to help him down to the cobblestone. "What are we doing here?" he queried in surprise.

"A bit of investigating," John explained, as they entered the sanctuary, "I have a friend here who I'm hoping will be able to find out more about our good Father Benito. We mustn't forget the part he played in this atrocity."

A nun opened the door. John pulled off his cap, and she led them into a tiny interior room, a makeshift office with sparse, worn furniture. They were seated for only a few minutes when a tall priest entered. His face brightened when John stood to greet him with a handshake. "John," he breathed, belatedly noticing Frederic. "This must be your father."

Frederic read the priest's stunned expression and surmised that he knew all about their stormy relationship. As John introduced them, Michael stepped forward to shake hands. Something in his manner, his directness perhaps, put Frederic at ease.

"Please, have a seat," Michael offered, pulling up a chair close to them. "I'm glad you decided to stop by. I've tried to get in touch with you for months now."

"We've just arrived in Richmond," John said.

The priest's eyes returned to Frederic. "I gather your visit went well?"

"At the onset," John answered grimly, "but this is not a social call, Michael. We found out that the deaths of my son and Colette were not accidents. They were murdered."

He recounted the evil plot that had taken the lives of Colette and Pierre. Michael listened without a word, reading the pain on each man's face. "May God rest their souls," he murmured compassionately when John had finished. "I'm very sorry. What can I do?"

John marshaled his emotions. "We need some information about a Father Benito St. Giovanni. He shipwrecked on Charmantes almost twenty years ago and, when he recovered from nearly drowning, was asked to stay on as the island priest."

"He claimed to be a missionary," Frederic explained, "his destination another Caribbean island. During his recovery, he grew adamant about 'converting' Charmantes, assuring me that the Vatican would approve such a mission, eventually boasting that he'd received papal blessing from Rome. Of course, his work on my island could hardly be called missionary, but suggesting it was afforded us a priest."

John snorted. "If you could call him a priest."

"Why do you say that, John?" Michael queried.

"He knew of the murders and was blackmailing my aunt."

"Are you certain?"

"Oh, I'm certain," John affirmed. "He confirmed all of Agatha's mad ranting and raving. We even have a letter, penned in his own hand, as proof."

"Dear God," the priest sighed. "I'll do what I can. It may take some time to receive word, but I'll write to the Vatican and find out whatever I can about Father Benito St. Giovanni of Italy. When do you think you will return to Richmond?"

"That depends on how long it takes me to find Blackford in New York and–" John stopped short, but his manner and the fire in his eyes shook the priest.

"And?" Michael pressed, but John would say no more. "You don't intend to take the law into your own hands, do you?" The silence collected and Michael looked to Frederic. "You're not going to allow him to murder this man, are you?" With Frederic's muteness, Michael grew alarmed. "John, you must not do this! You may think that retribution will satisfy you, but I promise, it will not. Please tell me that you will not seek revenge on this man."

"I can't promise you that, Michael."

Michael shook his head fiercely. "John – track him down, call the authorities, but leave it in *their* hands and in the hands of the Good Lord."

"The *Good* Lord," John bit out venomously, "allowed that man to take my innocent son, hold his head under the cold water and callously watch his arms and legs flail in unfathomable distress until the life was snuffed out him." Suddenly, he was crying. "Don't tell me that seeking revenge won't satisfy me – bring me peace – because, *goddamn it,* I won't *know* peace until the very last breath is snuffed out of him!"

Again Michael looked to Frederic. "You have to talk him out of this. He'll be a wanted man – a murderer!"

"I can't," Frederic stated solemnly. "I want to see Blackford suffer just as much as he does."

"You are not in your right minds! Can't you see that this man is not worth your own souls? He's already damned. Do not damn yourselves!"

Silence.

When the answer congealed into a knot of cold dread, Michael finally implored, "Is there nothing I can say to change your minds?"

"Pray for us, Father," Frederic replied.

Michael shook his head, and John hurriedly stood, wanting only to end the meeting. "Depending on how long we're in New York, we may head directly back to Charmantes. When you receive word from the Vatican, I'd appreciate it if you would send it to Stuart. He'll make certain that it gets to me."

"I may deliver the correspondence myself," Michael said softly, still shaken.

The statement piqued John's curiosity. "Why?"

"I need to check on someone there," Michael replied. "Actually, someone in your employ, Frederic."

"Who?" Frederic asked, equally befuddled.

"The governess to your daughters – Charmaine Ryan."

Though Frederic was surprised, John's confusion ran rampant. "Charmaine?" he queried. *How did Michael know her?*

The priest was smiling again. "I took your advice, John, and contacted Loretta and Joshua Harrington shortly after you left for Charmantes. Charmaine was working for them when Marie passed away."

Michael had never seen John speechless, let alone dumbstruck. "John, are you all right?"

"He's in a bit of shock," Frederic interjected. "You are the second person today who has inquired about his wife."

"His wife?" Michael uttered. *Impossible!* The incredible coincidence had instantly grown fantastic. "But you never told me you knew her!"

"You never mentioned her name!" John rejoined.

"But surely you knew she was Marie's daughter?" the priest pressed.

"I never knew," John murmured, his memory jarred. That first morning he had come home, Charmaine had looked familiar. Marie – Charmaine was Marie's daughter! His mind raced – John Ryan had killed Marie! His eyes darkened once more.

"My God," he breathed as all the pieces fit together. *John Ryan wasn't Charmaine's father!* The insanity of it all hit him full force, and quite abruptly, he threw back his head and laughed. "Wait until Charmaine hears this!"

"No, John," the priest warned, eyeing Frederic, intent upon keeping the story confidential. "You mustn't tell anyone! I want to see her first."

"Not tell her?" John queried in waxing glee. "Of course you've got to tell her! She hates the man she thinks is her father."

"John, please," Michael cut in, searching Frederic's face.

John's eyes traveled to his father as well. "Your little secret won't shock him, Michael. He's done plenty of things he's not proud of. Believe me, he keeps secrets better than you keep confessions."

Later, as John and his father traveled to his townhouse, Frederic asked him about Charmaine's mother.

"I met her a few years ago. She was working at St. Jude's and came to my aid when I no longer wanted to live. Like Charmaine, she was my savior of sorts, and through her, I befriended Michael. Together, they turned my life in a new and, I think, better direction. If I had known about Marie's hardship, I would have helped her. But I'm ashamed to say that we only talked about me."

He looked out the window, introspective with the wrenching revelation. He thought of Charmaine and realized just how much he missed her.

They spent a quiet evening together. After dinner, John withdrew to his desk and wrote to her, carefully choosing the words he put to paper, telling her that he loved her and longed to put this ordeal behind him. He then penned a quick letter to Paul. When he was finished, he said goodnight to his father.

Frederic stayed awake long into the night, contemplating all that had gone before, all that had been revealed today, and all they had yet to face. He walked to the hearth and studied a small sketch tacked there. It was a picture of a black horse rearing high in the air with the words: *Fantom misses you, Johnny! So do we! Love, Yvette.* With a sad sigh, he traced a finger over the drawing. It was faded and curled at the edges. *What was I thinking when I tore this family apart?* He retired, praying to God that, for once in his life, he was doing the right thing.

Michael prayed fervently that night as well, kneeling before the crucifix that hung above his bed. By dawn, he had come to a decision, inspired by his prayers. He found Sister Elizabeth, told her about his plans and, throwing some clothing into a threadbare satchel, left St. Jude's.

Silence stalked the halls, cloaked the rooms, and seeped into the cracks and crevices, joining the darkness in an eerie, unholy communion. It was near midnight. Agatha crept up the staircase, her head cocked to one side, listening, groping, grasping the balustrade. "Frederic?" she whispered. "Is that you? Robert! Where are you? Is it accomplished?"

She found a lamp on a table and blindly lit it, chasing the dark away to lurk with the shadows. *"Who is it?"* she cried. Sensing a movement far off to her left, she whirled around. "Elizabeth – is that you?" Undaunted, she stepped closer. "I told you never to come back here! Frederic is mine now!"

A cold gust of air swirled about her lithe form, carrying upon it a whisper. "He's gone now… never to return…" Her eyes darted about the corridor, tracking the breeze back down the cavernous flight. It was true; Frederic had left days ago, hadn't returned since she'd explained everything to him. She thought he would understand, but now, she was apprehensive.

Paul hadn't awakened. He should be hungry by now, should have wanted to nurse. Panic seized her. Had Frederic taken her babe away? Or had Robert taken him again? She'd told him to take Pierre! The air whispered from below, as if reading her thoughts. "Pierre, mon caillou…"

Agatha flew down the stairs, tripping on her robe and nearly dropping the lamp. She followed the wraith into the drawing room, her eyes distended in recognition. There stood Colette, grasping the hand of her small son.

"You!" Agatha hissed. "Where's Robert?" she demanded, searching the room. "He was supposed to take your boy away – forever!" She laughed cruelly. "Finally, Frederic will know how it feels to have a child ripped from *his* arms!"

"My boy is safe," Colette whispered, "with me."

Again Agatha's eyes darted about. "Where's Robert? *Where is he?*"

Colette smiled. "He's gone… with the other babe…"

"Elizabeth's bastard?"

"No, John is with Frederic… is safe with his father."

Fear seized Agatha. *"Paul?"* she cried, flying to all corners of the room and out to the foyer. "*No!* Robert promised me! He promised to make me happy – that he'd never take Paul from me again!"

"But you didn't make *him* happy," Colette breathed. "He's angry with you."

It was true; Robert hated her now. Agatha had used him, and he knew it.

The front door flew open and the night air beckoned to her. "Where did he go?" she pleaded. "Where did he take my baby?"

Colette led the way. "You told him to drown the boy…"

Instantly, Agatha knew. Desperate, she ran after the apparition that remained just out of reach. "*Oh God!*" she sobbed.

"Agatha… you deserted Him long ago…"

It was true. "Please!" she shrieked. "Not my son! Please, not *my* son*!*"

The dock was just ahead, and Agatha flew across it, possessed. She could see a dinghy bobbing in the waves. "Robert! *No!* Please! *You have the wrong boy!*"

There were cabins near the wharf. The men inside thought they heard a cry, but they stepped out too late, rubbing sleepy eyes. They heard a splash. Or was it just the clapping waves? They shrugged and returned to their quarters.

Thursday, August 30, 1838

The Richmond harbor was already buzzing when John and Frederic arrived at the Raven. Jonah was on the quay with Stuart Simons, and John was pleased. He thought it would be months before he saw Stuart again.

"John," he greeted, "I was expecting the Destiny to land today, but certainly not the Raven and you." He noticed Frederic and politely extended a hand. "You must be Frederic," he said jovially. "I'm Stuart Simons."

John let Frederic reply, then took Stuart aside, walking the length of the boardwalk with him.

"Jonah told me what happened," Stuart said. "I'm sorry, John."

"I'm dealing with it," John replied, abruptly brushing the matter aside. "Remember when you made inquiries about John Ryan?"

"Yes. What about it?"

"Have any of the longshoremen seen him?"

"I don't know." When John frowned, Stuart added, "I never really pursued it, so he may have been around."

"Do me a favor. Spread the word that I'm offering a reward to anyone who can identify him. When you know who he is, pay him so well that he can't *wait* to come to work each day."

"Why?" Stuart asked in bewilderment.

"Once he's consistent about showing up, promote him to a better paying job onboard a Charmantes-bound packet. When he's on that ship, notify me."

"But how am I to know where you are?"

"Send the information with the cargo invoices. If I'm not on the island, Paul will be there and know what to do. I've written to him." John pulled two letters from his shirtfront. "Make sure these are on the Destiny."

"But she's headed for Liverpool. We're packing her hold with tobacco."

"Load only half," John directed. "The Raven will return to Richmond by next week, ready to take on a full cargo. As for the Destiny, Paul can fill her hold with sugar." He handed Stuart the letters. "It's important that these get to Charmantes."

John didn't know that Michael Andrews had boarded the Raven. Frederic told him to stay below deck until they were far from port. When he did emerge, John was annoyed. "What's this?" and he looked from his father to Michael. *"Now I have two fathers to contend with?"*

"You're stuck with me," Michael said, casting his eyes heavenward. "Rant and rave all you like, but I've been sent by a higher authority."

"I hope you can walk on water, Michael. Any preaching, and I'm throwing you overboard."

The news of Agatha's death reached Paul when he arrived in town early that morning. In less than an hour, he stepped onto Espoir. The corpse was left as it had been found on the beach, with a blanket draped over it. With a mixture of disgust and guilt, hatred and sadness, he looked down at Agatha's bloated body. His heart heavy, he ordered two men to construct a pine box for the burial.

That night, he sat in his grand mansion, alone and lonely. So this was what commercial success meant. In the past four months, three vessels had departed his island; their cargo would fetch tidy purses. Yet today, he didn't feel the deep satisfaction he'd always experienced when he'd worked hard for his father. He retired, the empty hallways echoing his desolation. He could not sleep.

Michael knocked on John's cabin door, then entered the cubicle on an indrawn breath and a prayer. John was seated at a small desk, his brow furrowed. "I'm not here to preach," Michael promised. "I'd like to talk about Charmaine."

John leaned back and propped his feet atop the desk, inviting him to sit on the small cot. He was smiling now. "I love her," he said decisively.

Michael returned the smile and asked, "How did this happen?"

"God, Michael, I don't know. When I returned home to find Colette had died, Charmaine was already there caring for the children. I didn't like her at first. Actually, I misjudged her." *I misjudged Colette...* John frowned with the unbidden thought, rubbed his brow, and addressed Michael again. "We were thrown together day after day. I wanted to spend as much time as possible with Pierre, and of course, she was always there. She was a mother to him. When he died, she was as devastated as I was, and yet, she comforted me. Looking back on it now, I know I was in love with her when I left last fall, but with everything that happened, I wasn't ready to admit it until I went back home last April and saw her again." He grinned with the heady memory. "It was a taste of heaven to find that she felt the same way about me."

John grew thoughtful. "If your God *is* out there, Michael, he sure planned this one pretty well, didn't he? And I promise you this: we couldn't protect Marie, but you needn't ever worry about Charmaine."

"What of Colette?" Michael mused. "You said you couldn't love another."

"I didn't believe I could," John murmured. "But I do."

"Enough to forgive your father and yourself?"

John's face hardened. "I don't know."

"He's forgiven you, hasn't he?" Michael probed.

John was uncomfortable and rose swiftly from the desk. Michael wisely changed the subject. "When were the vows spoken?"

"On the island, after Paul's party. It was very private with Father Benito–" John's words broke off, and Michael followed his thoughts: *What if the priest wasn't a priest at all?* "When we are finished in New York," John decided, "we will have a ceremony on Charmantes with you presiding this time, Michael."

"I would be honored."

"There is something else you should know. You are going to be a grandfather."

Michael wondered if the surprises would ever end, but this was just the sort of announcement he could capitalize on. "A baby on the way," he pondered softly. "When is he or she due?"

"Around Christmastide."

"And you think it wise to be away from Charmaine at such a time?"

"You sound like my father," John pronounced as he began to pace.

"We're concerned for you, as well as for your new son or daughter."

"Yes, I'm sure you are," John muttered, then he stopped in his tracks. "So – is the sermon coming now or are you still leading up to it?"

"John–"

"You're wasting your time, Michael."

"John, you are one of the most honorable men I know. For that reason alone, my time is not being wasted. But you are also married to my daughter now. I can't keep silent. We each have our missions here."

John's tumultuous eyes mocked his crooked grin, but he did not argue.

Friday, August 31, 1838

Agatha Blackford Ward Duvoisin was not buried beside Frederic's other two wives. Paul had her grave dug on the far side of the cemetery. Charmaine, George and Mercedes were the only ones attending the small funeral, for the girls had refused to go, and even for Paul's sake, Charmaine could not force them to pray for the woman who had murdered their mother and brother.

Without a priest, it fell to Paul to offer a eulogy, one sad sentence that chilled Charmaine's soul: "May God forgive you and bring you the peace you never found in this life." With bowed head, she allowed her tears to fall, not for Agatha, but for her son.

Late that night, Charmaine found Paul in the dark library; he'd allowed the lamp to burn out. She stepped into the room, the hallway sconces sending a shaft of light across the chair in which he lounged. As she moved closer, she found he slept. Her eyes filled with tears again. It would have been easier to love this man, she realized. Today, he had desperately needed someone to love him. Her mind wandered back to that time of innocence, when a bare chest and a lazy smile made her legs go weak. She'd always treasure those profound feelings of first love.

"Paul," she whispered. "Paul?"

He stirred, his eyes fluttering open, and then, almost in a daze, he realized where he was. He rubbed his brow and then his eyes. "I must have fallen asleep."

"Why don't you go to bed? You've had a draining day."

"No, no," he dissented. "I wouldn't be able to sleep if I retired."

He stood, stretched, and went to the decanter to pour himself a drink. "Would you like some?" he offered, but she only shook her head.

"I felt the baby move today," she said, attempting to break the melancholy.

His half-smile told her that she hadn't succeeded. "And how have *you* been feeling?" he asked.

"Much better. Rose was right. The first few months were the worst."

"You look beautiful, Charmaine," he told her, his smile finally reaching his eyes as if he'd read her thoughts, "even if you are in the family way."

Why this silly small talk? She inhaled, then plunged headlong into the source of their misery. "Paul, we haven't spoken about this, and perhaps now is not the time, but John told me everything about your father and Agatha, and–" she paused, searching for the right words "–you should know that you're one of the finest men I've ever known. I hope you don't hold yourself responsible for what's happened to this family. I don't, and I'm certain John doesn't either."

He was listening intently, but she was uncertain of his reaction.

"I've lived with that terrible feeling of helplessness," she continued, "and I've finally realized that *I* could never have changed my father or prevented what he did. Agatha is only a bad memory now, but she did bless this world with something very good – *you.*"

Sunday, September 2, 1838
New York City

Chapter 7

When Frederic and Michael stepped off the ship with John, they were awed by the bustle on the docks and the throngs in the street. They hailed a carriage and headed for John's row house near Washington Square. Manhattan made Richmond look like a country village.

"This is where the future of shipping is, Father," John said as the conveyance rolled through the streets.

They settled into the vacant row house on Sixth Avenue, opening windows and lighting the lamps. The next day, they set up house with supplies and foodstuffs, and began planning how they would track down Robert Blackford.

The bank where he'd deposited his small fortune proved to be a dead end. The account had been closed as soon as the Richmond banknote had cleared. The financier yielded little information. Robert was shrewd. The money had not been transferred; he'd taken his funds in cash. There was nothing to do but start scouring the city, hoping for a clue or a lead. They agreed that Michael would accompany Frederic, and John would go out on his own because he knew New York better.

"I'm sure he's taken an assumed name," John said.

Frederic concurred. "But how do we begin to guess what that might be?"

"Start with the obvious ones," Michael suggested, "Smith, Jones, Brown…"

"He won't go from Blackford to Brown," John quipped derisively. "Is there anything darker than black? That's what he is."

"No, John," Michael replied grimly. "Black is as dark as it gets. Try then the names Black and Ford."

They grew quiet, discouraged by the daunting mission ahead of them.

"I just want to know why he did it," John finally muttered. "It wasn't for the money, I just know it wasn't. There was something else."

Frederic looked up, not surprised that his son had come to the same conclusion. Their eyes locked, and John addressed the other problem they would have to face. "What are you going to do about Agatha when we get back?"

"I don't know, John. From what Paul told me, she is in her own private hell already."

That night, John had his recurrent dream of Pierre, lost in the streets of New York. But this time, after Pierre disappeared in the crowd, John found himself in a dark factory, where veiled black figures shoveled coal into large ovens. The flames flared up and burned brightly, greedily devouring the coal.

Friday, September 7, 1838 Charmantes

They had fallen into a routine. Paul and George made a point of being home before dinner, and the table was laid for seven each night: Paul and Charmaine, the twins and Rose, Mercedes and George. Charmaine marveled at how the girls were maturing. They showed an interest in nearly any topic and participated in each conversation; Yvette in particular often questioned Paul about his workday. She continued to be an asset to the mill operation, the only bookkeeping he didn't have to worry about. Her knowledge of the family business astounded him, and as his respect grew, so, too, did the camaraderie that had sprung up between them.

Tonight was the same, and when the dishes were cleared away, everyone stood to retire to the front parlor. Yvette and Paul were involved in a heated discussion concerning the benefits of building a sugar refinery on Charmantes. "It can't be done!" Paul argued. "Purification must be accomplished abroad."

"But the ships could carry far more condensed extract than raw, and you could charge a higher price for a nearly finished product."

"Fresh water is limited here, Yvette, and there's the wood supply to consider. We'd be burning a great deal each day just to fire the plant."

"Then what about cocoa?" And so it went.

Charmaine exchanged a chuckle with Rose and, seeing one last plate on the table, turned to the kitchen to deliver it to Fatima. Pots and pans were piled high in the middle of the wooden table, and the cook was shuttling dishes and cutlery to the new girl, Rachel, who was scrubbing them in the adjacent scullery.

"Oh, Miss Charmaine," Fatima scolded lightly, "let me have that plate."

"Cookie, where are Felicia and Anna?"

The woman grunted. "Seeing to Mastah Paul, I suspect."

Charmaine felt her ire rising. Evidently, this was not the first time that the duty of washing the dishes had fallen to Fatima. "But this is *their* job, isn't it?"

"With Missus Faraday mindin' Mastah Paul's house and Mistress Agatha gone, they been gettin' outta a lot of work they know they should be doin'."

"Have they?" Charmaine mused before marching from the room.

She'd suspected that the two lazy maids had been slacking off, but that wasn't the only reason she was furious when she entered the front parlor. Two days earlier, she had overheard their whispers behind the doors of John's old room.

"...and now that he's away, you see how she fawns over Paul?"

"Even with John's baby growin' inside of her."

"Well maybe it's not John's at all!"

The room echoed with vicious giggles.

Charmaine had turned away, not allowing them the victory they would certainly savor if they knew they had hurt her. But not tonight! Tonight she was armed for battle.

Sure enough, she found the two at the liquor cabinet, Anna pretending to wipe up, while Felicia strolled across the room with hips swaying, presenting a glass of port to Paul, who looked up and smiled.

"Felicia, Anna," Charmaine called from the doorway, her arms crossed.

The two women turned to face her.

"Have you finished with the dinner dishes already?"

"Fatima said she'd see to it," Felicia lied.

Charmaine responded sternly. "I told *Mrs. Henderson* that she is not to do any dishes, pots, pans, knives, forks, spoons or utensils of any sort. She is our cook, not the cleanup help. However, if I do find her cleaning up after a meal, I will give her a day off, and the chore of cooking will fall to you. Understood?"

Both maids appeared shocked, but when Anna opened her mouth to speak, Charmaine rushed on. "Now, if I were you, I'd run to that kitchen and make myself busy. You're not being paid to pour drinks."

Felicia's eyes flew to Paul, as if to say she'd only take orders from him, perhaps hoping he'd come to her rescue, and Charmaine held her breath. But one look at his face told her that he was of no mind to interfere. Felicia must have recognized it, too, for she stomped from the room in an insulted huff. As she passed through the door, Charmaine added, "In future, we won't be requiring your services after dinner. This is *family* time."

When they were alone, Yvette and Jeannette began to laugh, and George quickly joined in. "What was that all about?" Paul asked.

"If I *am* mistress of this manor, it is time I start acting the part."

Paul raised his glass in a toast and winked. For the first time in two long weeks, Charmaine felt happy.

Three days later, Felicia was sent packing. Charmaine hadn't a clue why.

Paul fired the trollop on the spot and didn't give her a backward glance as she scurried from the house. Returning to the study where he'd been working, he thought back on the morning. Anna and Felicia had been making his bed, thinking him gone for the day. They were also talking about Charmaine.

"My blood boils every time I think how that hussy sauntered into this house," Felicia was saying, "wormin' her way into the family by playin' the virgin."

"You'd best get over it," Anna advised in a whisper.

But Felicia could not curb her temper. "I'd rather have Agatha back."

"Charmaine's not that bad. You're just jealous, is all."

"Jealous of what? Her big belly? I think that baby was growin' inside of her long before she snared John."

"Felicia, you saw the bed linen, same as I did!" Anna stated.

"She probably cut herself and bled on them sheets just to trick everyone, John included. You see the way she's sprouting? It won't be long before Paul is disgusted by the sight of her, and then he'll be looking my way again."

Paul had heard enough and barged in, slamming the door behind him.

"Master Paul!" Anna shrieked.

His scowl was directed at Felicia, and she recoiled. "Pack your things," he growled. "You'll not spend another night in this house."

"But where will I go?"

"Your parents live in town, don't they? Maybe they'll take you in. If not, there's always Dulcie's. You're more suited for that type of work, anyway."

Felicia blushed and fled the room.

Paul turned on Anna, and she unconsciously took two steps backwards. "Sir," she implored. "I didn't like listening to her."

"You had best make me believe that," he warned, his jaw still clenched. "I don't want to hear that Charmaine has had to speak to you again. *And* she had better not be the subject of any of your conversations. Do I make myself clear?"

"Yes, sir," she murmured meekly and, with a swift curtsy, flew out the door.

Tuesday, September 11, 1838

Paul was in town when the shout went up that a ship was docking. He stood on the wharf as Matt Williams navigated the Destiny to the pier. Once the ship was moored, he jumped aboard. "What brings you to us, Matt?" he queried. "I thought you'd be running shipments for John out of Virginia."

"That was the original plan, but according to Stuart Simons, John and your father changed all that. They've taken the Raven on to New York and sent me to deliver these." He handed Paul two letters, the envelopes addressed in John's scrawl. "I'm carrying only a half-cargo of tobacco. John thought the trip wouldn't be a total loss if I filled the remainder of the hold with sugar."

"Take a break for now," Paul said. "We should be able to get her loaded tomorrow, and you can set sail in two days' time."

Matt nodded, then informed his crew. With a whoop of appreciation, they quickly finished securing the vessel, motivated by thoughts of Dulcie's and an afternoon of leisure.

Paul went down into the captain's cabin and tore open his letter. When he'd finished reading it, he looked at the envelope addressed to Charmaine and abruptly decided to postpone the work he had planned for the afternoon.

Charmaine was sitting on the swing listening to the girls as they took turns reading to her. The weather was mild and the day too beautiful, so she had suggested that they finish the novel in the shade of the oak tree. She was surprised to see Paul ride through the gates and rein Alabaster in their direction.

He dismounted quickly, tucked both hands behind his back, and suggested she pick one. Bewildered, she chose the right, but when it came up empty, he quickly presented his left. "A little present," he said with a debonair smile.

Charmaine recognized John's handwriting and gasped in relief. She turned the envelope over, carefully broke the seal, and sat absentmindedly on the swing.

"Is it from Johnny?" Jeannette asked.

"What does it say?" Yvette demanded.

Paul put a finger to his lips and motioned the girls to follow him to the stable. Without an argument, they fell in step beside him, Alabaster in tow. When they were a distance away, he said, "Give Charmaine some time alone. She needs a few moments of happiness."

They smiled up at him.

"Besides," he continued, "John wrote to you in my letter."

"*Really?*" they queried in tandem. "What did he say?"

"He wrote that he misses you and will be home as soon as possible."

"That's all?" Yvette asked. "Did he say if he killed Doctor Blackford yet?"

"No, Yvette," Paul frowned, "he didn't write about that. According to his letter, he's still searching for him."

"Well he's sure taking his time, isn't he?"

"What about Papa?" Jeannette asked. "Did Johnny write if he's all right?"

"I don't know," Paul admitted, "but I'm certain Father is fine."

"I just hope they're not fighting," Yvette proclaimed. "That will surely slow things down."

Paul shook his head with his sister's words of wisdom. "Let it be, Yvette."

Charmaine feasted on John's letter from the tender opening: *My dearest Charm,* to the poignant closing: *Tell our beautiful baby that I love him as much as I love his mother.* She learned that his pursuit of Blackford was taking him and his father to New York and that he'd unexpectedly run into Joshua Harrington. Then came his love words, words that melted Charmaine's heart.

> *I'm sorry about the way I left you that day. Please understand that I am compelled to see justice done. I could never live with myself knowing that the murderer of my son was still at large, and that I did nothing about it. And yes, I am also doing this for Colette. I would be a liar if I didn't admit that to you or myself. But it is not because I harbor a fierce love for her. She was a good and kind person who didn't deserve to die so young – to be murdered. If she were alive today, I would still choose you. You are more woman than I could ever hope to love me. I learned something incredible today – something that made me smile amidst all this gloom, but that news will have to wait. This revelation made me realize how much you mean to me, my Charm, and how very much I love you. It's so lonely here*

tonight, and I long to hold you in my arms and make sweet love to you. I promise that when I return, we will make up for all the time these weeks have stolen from us.

Blinded by tears, Charmaine pressed the signature to her lips and savored the contact, as if she could drink in John's presence through the kiss. She closed her eyes to bittersweet happiness and breathed deeply. When she had finally composed herself, she looked up and realized she was quite alone.

Later that evening when Yvette and Jeannette were asleep, Charmaine wrote her first love letter. She poured out all her emotions and found herself crying before she had finished. Like John, she, too, apologized for the things she'd said before he left and told him how much she longed for the day he'd return home to her. When she was finished, she kissed the missive. Paul promised to put the post on the first vessel bound for New York. Thanks to George, they knew John's address there.

Thursday, September 13, 1838

Robert Blackford stood behind a middle-aged woman who spoke softly to the clerk at the apothecary counter. He smiled to himself when she asked for a small vial of arsenic, and he wondered whose demise she was planning, most likely her husband's or perhaps a lover's. The clerk produced a ledger that he asked her to sign. She paid him, and he handed over the poison.

Simple, Robert thought, *so very simple.* If Colette had lived on the mainland, Agatha wouldn't have needed his services. But the mercantile on Charmantes stocked few medicinal items, and she had had to rely on him to procure the arsenic from Europe, which he did after she'd given Colette that first, nearly fatal dose in the early spring of 1836.

Robert stepped out into the bright sunshine moments later. He breathed deeply of the unusually brisk autumn air – crisp, but not clean. The booming factories soiled the afternoon breezes with thick smoke. Ah well, he couldn't have everything.

As he walked along the bustling streets, his mind returned to Charmantes, that faraway place where he'd passed the better part of his life. Agatha had neatly sewn up the future for him, situating him here. He remembered his joy when she had arrived on Charmantes to stay. He thought it was the beginning for them; in reality, it was the beginning of the end.

Her husband had died, and even now, Robert wondered if Thomas Ward was the first of her victims. She had left Britain with enough arsenic to kill Colette overnight. But her rush for revenge was thwarted. Perhaps Colette was stronger than she realized, perhaps the entire draught was not consumed. Whatever the reason, Colette recovered, and Agatha had little poison left. When she confided in Robert, he upbraided her.

"You fool! What if Frederic were to find out? He'd have your head!"

She threw herself into his arms and cried on his shoulder. He basked in her embrace. When her tears subsided, she cajoled him, and promised that she loved him as well. "I must rid Charmantes of any memory of Elizabeth. Please help me, Robert!" she implored.

She was determined to do away with Colette, marry Frederic, and effect John's disinheritance, ensuring Paul the security that had been robbed from him on the day of his birth. Only then could they be together and enjoy the wonderful life that Frederic's money could buy.

He believed her. And because he loved her fiercely, he took command of the murder plot. He procured the arsenic and administered it in minute doses. "So that it will be a slow, unexplainable death," he reasoned. In truth, he dragged his feet for a full year before he finally killed Colette, hoping that Agatha would change her mind and return to him.

"Yes," her eyes glittered. "Let it be painful."

When Colette began to complain about her 'illness', her mistrust of Robert apparent, it was easy to allow Agatha to take over. A strict schedule was developed, doses carefully calculated. A dash of poison was sprinkled on Colette's food three days prior to Robert's appointment, a tad more the following day, and a full measure the day after that. Colette was so ill by the time Robert arrived that she welcomed his visits. Agatha withheld the poison on the days he came, and Colette would feel better after he left, as the severe side effects of the arsenic were wearing off. After three days, Agatha began the dosing all over again.

For months, she took enormous pleasure in watching Colette suffer, gleefully describing the grisly details: the headaches and dizziness, the vomiting and soiled undergarments, the ghastly face and hair loss. But in time, Agatha grew anxious to be done with the act, accelerating their routine to two appointments per week.

Colette should have died sooner, but pneumonia made poisoning difficult. Though arsenic was undetectable in food and liquids, Colette consumed very little of either, and when she did, there was always someone hovering over her: Gladys, Millie, Rose, and on occasion, Frederic. Toward the very end, Robert grew apprehensive; both Paul and Frederic were asking too many questions, and he prayed that the pneumonia would kill her. When Colette pulled through, he seized the moment and liberally laced her broth and coffee with a lethal dose. But he wasn't allowed in her room, and the tray he carried from the kitchen was left with Frederic. He feared the worst: what if Frederic sampled the poisonous fare?

Robert was lucky. Colette swallowed every drop and, within the hour, was violently ill. He was surprised that she lasted the day, more amazed that no one ever contemplated her many symptoms. But then, they had been gradual and endured over a long period of time.

His cunning had worked in their favor; their treachery met with only one hitch: Benito Giovanni. The island priest had been just as clever and ruthless. It could not be helped, but Robert let Agatha handle that. Benito's extortion did not deter her. She was certain that she'd find a way to shake him off. Besides, there was more to do: Pierre was next.

"He is on the will," she complained. "Pierre may inherit it all, and Paul won't get a red penny of his birthright. We must set this injustice right, Robert! Help me, my dearest, please! I promise we shall be together as soon as we've taken care of this one last detail."

"John is first in line," he'd reasoned. "I thought you were out to get him, that *he* was the problem."

"Of course he is! But I want him to suffer as I did. It's just a matter of time with John, anyway. I guarantee this event will be his undoing. I'll make it so."

Her hollow pledge haunted him still. Unconsciously, he'd embraced the truth: she was only using him. He didn't want to believe it, and so he finally agreed to the diabolical deed, praying that she'd finally see how much *he* loved her. But just in case she didn't, just in case he needed to flee Charmantes, he set a high price for the part he would play.

The fateful night arrived. Agatha swept into his abode, a hungry gleam in her eyes. The perfect opportunity had unexpectedly presented itself. Pierre had set the stage at dinner. "We must strike while the iron is hot," she eagerly declared, her mind racing, "now, while Frederic is furious with John – before John returns to Richmond. We must stoke the rage into an inferno!"

Robert shuddered at her maniacal euphoria. "How much are you willing to pay?" he inquired coolly.

She was momentarily deflated, but quickly recovered, signing a promissory note that turned Thomas Ward's entire estate over to him.

The next morning, she slipped a minute dose of arsenic into the boy's milk. He became ill within the hour, complaining of stomach cramps and a headache, and as Agatha had predicted, John was asked to mind him while the family attended Mass.

In the meantime, Robert visited the stables. Few were about; most of the hands were also at Sunday service. His greatest fear that morning had been the great black stallion, but even that was easy. Phantom greedily devoured the mango that he had pitted and filled with lye. Within seconds, the horse was writhing in agony. Robert unlatched the stall door, and the stallion bolted, knocking him over as he galloped out of the stable. He jumped to his feet and fled through the rear door, charting the shouts and high-pitched neighing that rose from the front lawns.

Within minutes, he reached the second floor of the manor, taking the back stairway that originated behind the ballroom and opened onto Agatha and Frederic's chambers above. He watched John run from the nursery, and before the front door slammed shut, he was at Pierre's bedside, scooping him up. The boy's eyes were closed, and Robert looked away, racing back the way he had come, out across the rear lawns, and into the safety of the tree line. Capsizing the boat and the actual drowning took longer than anticipated. He was distracted by shouts in the distance. "The lake – my father said the lake!"

He fled and watched from the boathouse, petrified when he realized the boy was not dead. *What if he awoke? What if he talked?* For three agonizing days, Robert could only pace. There were no ships in port – no means of escape. He waited to be called upon; he'd waste no time finishing what he'd begun. But Pierre died all on his own.

Even today, the memories remained vivid. Robert breathed a sigh of relief. Fate had smiled down on him eleven months ago. It was just as well that he had left Charmantes. Here, he was far from Benito, even Agatha, and he was safe. No one, neither Frederic nor John, could ever track him down. Smiling smugly, he ambled down the busy road with a lighthearted gait.

Saturday, September 15, 1838

Maddy Thompson shook out the last lovely dress. The wardrobe that John had ordered for Charmaine had finally arrived from Europe. But the new garments held no joy for Charmaine. The dresses didn't fit, and even if they did, John wasn't there to see her in them.

"What's the matter?" Jeannette asked. "Don't you like them?"

Even Yvette was disturbed by Charmaine's apparent dissatisfaction. "They're all beautiful," she said.

"Beautiful, yes," Charmaine murmured, "but I'll not be wearing them for quite some time."

Maddy returned the garment to its box. "Your condition won't last forever," she said. "By springtime you'll have your figure back. For the moment, however, I think I could sew you something a bit more comfortable than that." The widow's eyes rested on Charmaine's protruding belly and tight bodice. Every dress Charmaine owned had been altered, each pleat, each seam, let out, and soon, not a one would fit. "If you want to stop by my house in an hour's time, I could take some measurements and have a few dresses ready for you by next week. How would that be?"

"It would be wonderful," Charmaine replied gratefully.

The bell sounded above the mercantile doorway and Wade Remmen stepped in with a beautiful young woman at his side – the girl George had been dancing with the night of the ball. "Good afternoon, Yvette," he greeted. "I left this week's invoices at the warehouse just a few minutes ago."

She nodded, but like her sister, her eyes were reserved for the woman.

"This is my sister, Rebecca," he offered, seeing their interest. "Rebecca, this is Yvette and Jeannette Duvoisin, and this is Charmaine Duvoisin, John's wife."

Charmaine extended her hand, but received only a hostile glare.

Later, outside the general store, Wade berated his sister. "What was that all about?"

"What?"

"You know what, Rebecca! Charmaine was being friendly, and you were downright rude to her."

Rebecca raised her nose. "I don't like her, that's all."

Friday, September 21, 1838

Paul was determined to get some work done. Riding out at dawn, he headed to Charmantes' tobacco fields.

He'd just spent a week on Espoir. One man in particular had proven an asset. With Peter Wuerst in charge, Paul was confident that he could reside on Charmantes and venture to Espoir once a week. Her sugar crop was hardy, and his laborers had been through the production routine a number of times.

Tobacco, on the other hand, was a time-consuming and tricky business: transplanting early in the season, pests and mold to manage, and painstaking fire curing over a three to twelve week period. The curing barns had been constructed. But now, with another harvest upon them, each field required a half dozen pickings, starting from the bottom of the stalk up. After curing, the tobacco needed to age for a year before being sent to market. The leaves were bundled into 'hands' and warehoused in town near the wharf, where they were regularly inspected for insect infestation. Charmantes' tobacco hadn't turned a profit yet, making Paul wonder why he'd ever gotten involved with it. At the time, he'd reasoned that if John had been successful, it had to be easy. *Easy?*

He arrived at the southern fields not a half-hour later and cursed as he looked out over the sloping terrain. The paid help and indentured servants were milling around. Paul urged his horse forward. "What's going on here?" he demanded.

"We're waitin' for Mr. Richards," one man answered. "He said he'd come out first thing this mornin' to show us what needed doin'."

"What about Mr. Browning?"

"He took some men with him into town. They're stackin' the kegs from yesterday's cane pressin' in the warehouse."

"So because he's not here, and Mr. Richards hasn't arrived yet, the lot of you don't know what to do?" Paul growled, jumping down from the saddle.

He strode through the nearest row of tobacco plants, plucking off several dark green leaves, bending each one over, noting they were brittle. Returning to Alabaster, he pulled up and into the saddle and shouted out to all the men. "I want the remaining leaves of this entire tract gathered and bundled. Tomorrow, I want them hung in the curing barns."

The workers began to grumble, "We just went through this field a day ago."

Though irritated, Paul knew that losing his temper wouldn't get the work done, especially if George remained absent. "I know John has shown you what to do. These leaves are ready. If they are reaped by sunset, I will grant a day off for every man here – *after* the harvest. For those of you who've paid your time, an extra day's wages!"

A whoop of approval went up, and the men threw themselves into the toil.

Paul turned Alabaster around, intent upon locating George. He checked the mill next and found the same situation there. Unsupervised, the men were taking advantage. "Have any of you seen George Richards?" he queried in rising agitation.

"No, sir, he don't usually drop round 'til noon."

"Where the hell is Wade Remmen?"

"He's normally here by now, sir, but he was feelin' poorly yesterday."

Paul swore under his breath. "Very well, Tom, how would you like to be in charge for the day?" When the man frowned, he added, "Double wages if you mill as much lumber as Wade usually does."

"Yes, sir!"

Paul spoke to the other men who had gathered around. "Tom's in charge. Follow his orders, get the work done, and there will be a bonus at sunset."

Before Paul had mounted up, Tom was barking orders.

What to do? He had been lax lately, and the word had gotten out: Frederic and John were gone, and he was rarely around. *Had everyone gone on holiday because he wasn't breaking his back?* He had no idea where to look for George, but Wade Remmen was going to find out that he couldn't take a day off on a whim. The man was paid well to be reliable.

Twenty minutes later, he was riding along the waterfront road on the outskirts of town, where the cottages were humble. Near the end, he reined in Alabaster, dismounted, and tied the horse to the whitewashed fence that enclosed the bungalow's small front yard. Of all the abodes along the lane, this one was the most charming, with flower boxes under the windows and a fresh coat of paint on the front door. Paul smiled despite his foul mood.

He knocked and waited. The door finally opened. There stood the young woman who had approached him in Fatima's kitchen on the night of the ball. *Of course! She was Wade's sister.* Even in her plain dress, she was stunning. "Is your brother here?" Paul inquired curtly, attempting to camouflage his surprise.

"Yes," she said softly.

"May I speak to him?"

"He's not well."

"I would still like to speak with him," Paul persisted. *It would be nice if she invited me in.*

"He's sick with fever," she argued. "I don't want him disturbed."

Paul snorted in derision. Obviously, she was lying. Her manner alone branded her guilty, for she refused to budge.

"May I come in?" he bit out, quickly losing patience.

When she protested again, he placed palm to portal and pushed it aside. As he strode into the plain but tidy room – a kitchen and parlor of sorts – the young girl tracked him, spitting fire over his audacity.

"How dare you? This is our home and if you think that you can barge in here because you're the high and mighty Paul Duvoisin, you've got–"

Paul headed toward one of the bedroom doors.

Just as swiftly, Rebecca scooted past him and flattened herself against it. "I told you – Wade is ill! You can't disturb him!"

"Miss Remmen – step aside, or I will move you."

"You just try it!" she sneered through bared teeth and narrowed eyes.

She was a little vixen, but he wasn't about to be deterred, or worse, ordered around by a sassy snip of a girl, lovely or not. In one fluid motion, he swept her up in his arms and deposited her unceremoniously in the nearest chair.

Astounded, she scrambled to her feet, but he'd already entered the bedroom.

The curtains were drawn and someone was abed. Wade's breathing bordered on a snore. As Paul's eyes grew accustomed to the dim light, he could see beads of perspiration on the young man's brow. He placed a palm to his forehead. Wade's eyes fluttered open, and he murmured something in delirium. "He's burning up," Paul stated irately. "Why didn't you summon the doctor?"

"Doctors cost money," she defiantly whispered. "Now please, he's resting. You're going to wake him up, and then I'll have him arguing with me as well."

"Arguing with you?" Paul declared incredulously. "He's delirious! I pay your brother decent wages. He can afford a doctor when he's this ill."

"Wade insists on saving his money."

Paul glowered at her, and she added, "So we don't ever go hungry again."

The last remark brought her shame, and she turned away, glad when another knock fell on the outer door.

Paul followed her out of the bedroom, somewhat contrite. He, too, was grateful for the distraction. George was standing on the threshold.

"Where have you been?" Paul demanded.

"Looking for you," George replied. "When Wade sent word that he wouldn't be going to the mill, I figured one of us would have to oversee his work. You left the house before me. I missed you at the tobacco fields, then I went to the mill–"

"All right, George, I understand," Paul ceded. He rubbed the back of his neck, the day's work far less pressing than Wade.

George volunteered to fetch Doctor Hastings, and before Paul knew it, he was once again alone with Rebecca. Her face remained stern.

"You were much lovelier at the ball," he commented with a lazy smile. "Remember – in the kitchen – when you were in love with me?"

"Mr. Duvoisin," she responded flatly, feigning disinterest in his flirtatious compliment, "I told you my brother won't waste his money on a doctor. Thanks to you, he has a fever. With a bit of rest, he will heal all on his own."

"Thanks to me?"

"Yes. You see, Wade kept on working in the pouring rain last week – to make things easier for you. He caught a chill, and now he's paying for it."

Paul ignored her statement. "Why didn't you tell me you had sent word?"

"I thought that was the reason you were here." When he seemed confused, she continued, "I thought you were going to force him to work, anyway." She bowed her head. "I love my brother. He's all I have."

"And that is why George is fetching Doctor Hastings," Paul interjected. "You needn't worry about his fee. I'll take care of it."

"Wade wouldn't like that," she argued, her head jerking up, eyes flashing again. "It would be like taking charity."

"Miss Remmen," Paul countered, "if your brother remains ill for days on end, I will lose a great deal more money than the cost of a doctor. Right now, I'm shorthanded. I need Wade up and about. He's invaluable."

She looked at him quizzically, and it occurred to him that she didn't understand. "I can't do without him," he explained, distracted by the sparkling green eyes that changed on a dime, speaking volumes.

Apparently, his reasoning met with her approval, for she was smiling now, the orbs even more captivating with this new expression. She was lovely.

"Would you like a cup of coffee or perhaps tea?" she offered, grabbing the kettle and swinging it over the embers in the hearth.

"That would be nice. I'd like to hear what the doctor has to say."

Rebecca grew dismayed. "You don't think it *is* serious, do you?"

"No, you are probably right. Wade will mend all on his own."

She sighed, her smile returning. Then, as if suddenly shy, she began to stoke the fire. Paul sat back and watched her.

Doctor Hastings' diagnosis was similar to Rebecca's: overwork and a chilling rain had brought on the fever, bed-rest and nourishment, the cure. Paul told her to keep Wade home until Monday and that he wanted to know if there wasn't an improvement. Then he and George were saying their farewells.

As they turned their horses onto the main road, George spoke. "Rebecca is smitten with you."

Paul snorted.

"It's true! You should have seen her at the ball. I danced with her once, but she couldn't keep her eyes off you the entire evening. If you hadn't been so damn busy, I would have introduced you."

Again Paul snorted. He didn't tell George that Rebecca had introduced herself.

George pressed on. "Whenever I go to the cottage, she always brings the conversation around to you."

Paul's brow arched, and though he tried not to, he smiled. "She wasn't too happy with me this morning."

"She can be a regular spitfire," George confirmed. "She bullies Wade like no man's business. But she is quite lovely."

"And young – she can't be more than sixteen."

"Just seventeen, I believe." He paused for a moment. "You know, Paul, a bit of a diversion is what you need – take your mind off things."

Paul scoffed at the idea. "The last time I had a 'bit of a diversion' I *lost* the one thing that meant the most to me."

"Maybe Charmaine wasn't yours to find," George replied evenly. He let the remark sink in before saying, "John is going to be home before you know it, Paul. And when that happens, you'll be nursing a broken heart – again."

Paul looked away. "Is it that obvious?"

"Yes, it is."

Paul shook his head. "When did things become so complicated, George? I remember when we were young. Everything was so very simple. We enjoyed life, and the women were free for the picking."

"I guess we grew up," George supplied.

"I guess we have."

Another knock resounded on the Remmen door. Rebecca collected herself and walked slowly to the portal. Perhaps it was Paul again. She lamented his departure, treasuring the private moments she'd had with him. But when she opened the portal, she frowned in disappointment. Felicia Flemmings stood in the doorway. "What was Paul Duvoisin doing here?"

"My brother is not well," Rebecca answered, "Paul was checking on him."

"Paul is it?" Felicia asked as she pushed into the cottage.

Rebecca eyed her speculatively. She didn't think she liked the older girl, though Felicia had tried to ingratiate herself to Rebecca from the moment she'd moved back into her parent's home next door. Rebecca suspected that it was because Wade was so good-looking. But she had allowed Felicia her visits over the past few days because the older girl was willing to divulge a plethora of information concerning the goings-on in the Duvoisin mansion, details about Paul the most interesting of all. Felicia had told her that she'd quit her domestic job at the manor because she couldn't stand John's new wife, Charmaine, an opportunistic trollop, who means to Paul in her husband's absence. "I couldn't watch it any longer," she had complained. "Poor John!"

Poor Paul, Rebecca had thought.

Presently, Felicia was sizing her up, chuckling perspicaciously. "You have your sights set for Paul, don't you?"

"I'm going to marry him."

Felicia guffawed until she realized that Rebecca was serious, the girl's tight expression giving her pause. When Wade didn't appear, she wished her luck with another flippant chuckle and promptly left.

Rebecca tucked the woman's ridicule to the back of her mind and indulged in memories of Paul: his rough hands on her, strong arms lifting her up, carrying her... She was alone; her brother slept soundly. Intoxicated, she entered her bedroom and, with heart accelerating, closed the door.

Friday, September 28, 1838

Yvette and Jeannette's tenth birthday dawned bright and warm. But the brilliant day did not lift Charmaine's spirits. She left her bedchamber with a heavy heart, dwelling on cherished memories of last year. She wondered where John was and what he was doing. Did he remember what day it was? Was he thinking about their wonderful picnic just one short year ago?

The girls were downtrodden, too, making no inquiries about gifts when they reached the dining room.

Mercedes and George were there. "Why the glum faces?" George asked. "I thought everyone was happy on their birthday."

"We don't feel like celebrating," Yvette grumbled. "Not without Johnny."

"Is that so?" he queried. "Mercedes and I thought the two of you would like to try out the new saddles and tack that Paul purchased for your ponies." He was smiling now, noting their faltering sadness. "That's right. Mercedes placed the order. And I've taken the day off just so we can go riding."

Sparks of happiness lit the girls' eyes. Soon they were departing. Charmaine couldn't join them in her condition. Instead, she sat with Rose on the portico and thought about John. Tomorrow, he'd be spending his birthday with his father...

Monday, October 1, 1838

The days melted into weeks, and Frederic and Michael spent them visiting the city post office and the shipping offices, combing address listings and immigrant registers for Blackfords. Though common sense suggested the man *had* changed his name, they couldn't be certain, and with nothing to go on, they were compelled to track down every Blackford, Black, Ford, and finally Smith, Jones, and Brown they came across. Frederic was able to exert his influence on the owners of other shipping lines to gain access to their passenger manifests. Not a one listed a Blackford leaving New York recently, but they found a number of Blacks and Fords in the post office registry. Though it did not provide a street address, the public roll did help narrow down the neighborhoods where these men lived. Frederic and Michael passed hours scouring the streets and visiting places of business in the hopes of turning up the fugitive doctor. Even with the remotest of leads, they often waited an entire day for the resident to return, only to head home disappointed.

John wore street clothes like the immigrant factory workers, making the trip every day to the shipping wharfs downtown, the mercantile exchanges on South Street, or the textile factories on the lower East side, talking to dockworkers, visiting taverns, and casing houses of ill-repute. He asked passersby if they'd seen anyone meeting Blackford's description, or if they knew anyone who went by that name. He'd inquire of local doctors and mention the names Black and Ford, Smith and Brown. He'd walk the residential avenues of red brick row houses and meander through the slums south of Wall Street, hoping to get lucky and spot his uncle.

He liked this face of the city: the immigrants pouring off the merchant ships, longshoremen heading home for dinner after twelve hours of grueling labor. He watched children playing in the streets and mothers doing laundry in wooden tubs and hanging the clothes out to dry. New York was where they all wanted to be, and he enjoyed being in their midst, even though his own privileged life was so different than theirs. As hard as the labor was, they all tarried with such purpose, leaving hopeless existences in Europe for the chance at something better. John was sure that the city would one day be the jewel in the crown of the nation, for the Erie Canal had made the city the gateway to the west, a merchant's magnet.

Tonight, he sat at the desk writing a letter to Charmaine. In his rush to press on to New York, he hadn't given her the address where he could be reached. George knew it, but John wanted to send it along, just to be sure. How ironic that tonight his father was in this house with him. He'd scrupulously kept the residence a secret in the hopes that one day he, Colette, and the children could start a new life here. If they fled to New York, nobody, especially Frederic, would ever find them. Last year, it had taken George weeks to track him down, resorting to staking out the Duvoisin shipping offices until, one day, John stopped by.

A month had already passed since he'd last written to Charmaine. Tomorrow, he'd put this letter in the mail to Richmond, and Stuart would place it on the next Duvoisin vessel bound for Charmantes. He had held off writing, hoping that he'd have encouraging news. But at least he could write that they were ruling out each Blackford one by one. He was anxious for news from Charmantes.

The parlor was chilly. He left the desk to stoke the fire with fresh logs, pushing them back with the iron poker. The logs hissed, throwing out angry embers that lit the hearth like tiny fireworks. Frederic and Michael reclined in the armchairs on either side of it.

Frederic considered John in the tranquil room. He had been pensive, distant all day. A year ago this week, Pierre had died. Obviously, the bleak anniversary was on his son's mind.

He looked above the mantle. John had tacked a small drawing there. *I gave Mama and Pierre the hug and kiss you sent* Jeannette had written below a picture of five figures standing on a beach. Frederic remembered Yvette's sketch in John's Richmond townhouse, and he bowed his head regretfully.

"All these empty houses, John... in Richmond – here. All these empty, lonely houses."

Michael looked up from his bible, as did John from the fireplace. "I'm in Richmond and New York frequently, Father. Houses are more comfortable than hotels," he replied placidly, wondering over Frederic's thoughts.

"You wanted to bring them here – always hoped that someday you'd bring them here, didn't you?" Frederic mused more than asked.

Michael stood up to leave.

"You can stay, Michael," John said, his eyes fixed on his father, astonished by his parent's sagacity. He looked away and stared into the hearth, propping an arm against the mantle. Perhaps for the first time, he really understood Frederic, the deep regrets the man harbored. If his father could turn back time to that fateful day five years ago – the day of their vicious row and Frederic's debilitating seizure – he would let Colette go, just so she could be alive today. Suddenly, everything was very clear. Frederic hadn't coveted Colette to smite him, or to exact revenge. His father had done so because he loved her and couldn't bear to let her go. Now remorse plagued him, and he desperately needed to be forgiven. But there was no one to offer comfort, no one who comprehended his pain. The room had fallen silent, and the minutes gathered.

"When I came back here after Pierre died," John finally murmured, "I asked myself a million times, *why didn't I protect him?* How could I have left him alone that morning? I should have realized that he'd wake up, find me gone and go looking for me. He'd told me at dinner what he was going to do. I should have seen it coming."

John sighed against the crushing pain in his chest. "I wasn't in the room the night he died, either. Charmaine found me and told me. She was as devastated as

I was. She could have blamed me, but she didn't. Instead, she was compassionate. I held onto her words for months afterward, remembered them when I didn't want to go on anymore..."

John stopped to collect his rampant emotions. "No, Pierre didn't go looking for me," he rasped, "but if I'd taken him seriously, I would never have left that room, and Blackford wouldn't have been able to snatch him away. Sometimes it can be right under your nose – *so damn obvious* – and still, you just don't see it." John looked back at Frederic, struggling for words. "Colette's death wasn't your fault, Father. I was furious when I found out what happened, but I shouldn't have blamed you. Agatha and Blackford are to blame – not you."

John went back to the desk, sat down, and picked up the pen.

Michael was astounded. He looked at Frederic. The man's face was awash with relief and hopefulness, and Michael's heart swelled with pride for Charmaine. Her influence was at work here with these wounded, but healing souls. His own soul rejoiced with a gladness he hadn't experienced in three long years. Marie was gone, but her kindness and empathy lived on. *This* was why he'd become a priest, remained a priest even through his apathy and self-doubt. Michael closed his eyes and offered up thanks.

Tuesday, October 2, 1838

When Jeannette heard a carriage approaching, she scampered to the balcony, and her sister quickly followed. Charmaine's heart caught in her throat and the baby gave a violent kick. She, too, rushed out the French doors. *John! He's injured and they're bringing him home in the carriage because he can't...* She refused to entertain the horrific conclusion.

An unfamiliar coach had passed through the front gates. She watched a moment longer, then composed herself and followed the girls downstairs. They stepped onto the front portico just as the carriage door swung open and Joshua Harrington stepped down, turning to assist his wife.

"Mrs. Harrington!" Charmaine gasped, consumed with relief, disappointment, surprise, and joy. "Mr. Harrington! *What are you doing here?*" She rushed down the portico steps and fell into Loretta's embrace.

"My dear!" Loretta exclaimed, tears brimming in her eyes as she held Charmaine at arm's length and assessed her from head to toe. "So it *is* true?" she said, her gaze rested momentarily on Charmaine's middle.

Charmaine blushed. "Yes, it's true. Didn't you receive my letter?"

Loretta shook her head, but seeing the happiness in Charmaine's eyes, felt reassured that things were not as bad as she and her husband had feared.

Yvette and Jeannette stepped forward and were reintroduced.

Charmaine clicked her tongue. "What's the matter with me, having you stand out here in the blazing sun? Let's go inside where it's cool."

Joshua turned to retrieve their luggage, but Charmaine scolded him. "Leave that, Mr. Harrington. I'll have Travis get your bags." She led the company back up the porch steps, instructing the butler to see to the Harrington's belongings. "Take them up to John's old room. Our company should be comfortable there."

"Very good, Miss Charmaine," the manservant nodded with a smile.

Loretta and Joshua exchanged astonished glances. Charmaine had regally assumed the title of Mrs. John Duvoisin. But was Frederic's wife, Agatha, happy with the young woman's air of authority?

They settled in the drawing room, and Charmaine rang for lemonade. She joined Loretta on the settee, her eyes sparkling, still astounded that she was truly there. "What has brought you to Charmantes?"

"We were concerned for you," Loretta began, glancing at the twins.

Charmaine understood and addressed the girls. "Since we have visitors, why don't we postpone your lessons for the day?"

They eagerly agreed. "May we visit the stables and curry our ponies?" Jeannette asked. With Charmaine's assent, they said goodbye and hastened happily from the room.

"They love you very much," Loretta commented when they were gone.

"And I love them," Charmaine whispered, and then, "Oh my, I still can't believe this! I'm so glad you're here!"

"Are you well?" Loretta pressed, leaning forward to clasp her hand.

Charmaine noted the worry in Loretta's voice and replied, "When I first found out that I was expecting, I was ill most mornings. But that passed, and I've been feeling much better."

Loretta and Joshua exchanged looks of relief.

"Joshua met John in Richmond," Loretta offered.

"Yes, I know. John wrote to me saying that you'd run into one another at the Richmond bank." She looked up at the older man with a smile, then back to his wife, reading her misgivings. "Mrs. Harrington, I'm fine. I don't know what you've heard, but truly, I'm fine."

"But are you happy?" Joshua asked.

Charmaine tilted her head, trying to read him. "Yes, I'm happy…"

"But?" Loretta probed.

"But," Charmaine breathed, "I miss my husband."

"And the only reason you're not with him in Richmond is because of your morning sickness?"

"That is not the reason," Charmaine admitted. "And John is no longer in Richmond. He's traveled to New York."

"Charmaine," Loretta began slowly, not wishing to alarm the young woman, but determined to make sense out of all that she had heard. "There is much gossip going around Richmond, and it concerns your hasty and most surprising marriage to Mr. Duvoisin."

Charmaine grew dismayed. "What are they saying?"

"It is not what they are saying, it is what they are insinuating. And as much as I hate to admit it, some lies often stem from truths." When Charmaine didn't respond, Loretta pressed on. "Were you forced to marry this man?"

"No!" Charmaine denied, aghast with the canards that had obviously prompted the Harrington's trip. "John was my choice and I love him."

Loretta was happy with the vehement answer, but Joshua wasn't convinced. "Then why has he left you alone at a time like this?"

Charmaine studied the hands in her lap. "Something terrible happened here a month ago." Slowly, painfully, she told them about the murders.

"But why is your husband tracking down this doctor?" Joshua asked. "I thought he and his father didn't get along."

Charmaine grappled with an excuse, for the truth could never be revealed, and Loretta realized that there was a great deal more to the story.

"There, there, Charmaine," she soothed, "we don't mean to upset you." She eyed her husband and added, "After all, it's not good for the baby. I would like to freshen up and rest a bit. The voyage was extremely unsettling. Could you show us to our room?"

"Certainly," Charmaine said, grateful that Loretta understood. "How long will you be staying?"

"For as long as you would like," Loretta offered with abundant love.

"At least until the baby is born," Charmaine hoped aloud.

"I'm certain we could manage that, now couldn't we, Joshua?"

Monday, October 15, 1838

John's second letter to Charmaine was delivered to the Duvoisin warehouse in Richmond. One of the employees paid the mail dispatcher the postage fee. Seeing that the post was sent 'Care of Stuart Simons', he tossed the envelope atop a pile of mail for the man. Stuart wasn't due in Richmond for another fortnight.

Friday, October 26, 1838

The jeweler handed John the ring for his inspection. He'd fashioned it precisely to his customer's specifications. It had taken weeks to locate the diamond; a difficult task, since Mr. Duvoisin wanted a flawless stone weighing at least three carats. The jeweler watched John as he examined it. Even in this dim room, the stone flashed with fire and light. It was set on a thick, unadorned band, engraved inside with the simple sentiment, 'For my Charm, with my love, J.D.'

The jeweler could see that his client was satisfied, so he placed the ring back in its box. John paid for it in cash, tucked the box into the pocket of his overcoat, and stepped out of the shop into the overcast day.

Nearly two months had passed since they'd arrived in New York and their efforts had proven fruitless, all their leads dead ends. His father had begun suggesting that they take their search to London or Liverpool. After all, Blackford's roots were in England. But John was adamant that they stay in New York, certain that Blackford had not gone any further than the anonymity and the work that the large city had to offer, especially with the burgeoning immigrant population. He had only his intuition to support this hunch, but he could not shake the certainty of it, nor ignore the recurrent dreams of Colette and Pierre that reinforced those assumptions every night.

He walked to the post office. He'd finally received a letter from Charmaine earlier that week and had been relieved to hear news from home, the most important, that Agatha was dead. It was one less thing to plague him, to have to face. He was happy to know that the twins were well, Mercedes expecting, and Charmaine had forgiven him his hasty departure. She'd written that she could feel the baby moving. He longed to put this crusade behind him so that he could return home; he was missing so much. The letter he'd send off today admitted they hadn't uncovered anything new concerning his uncle's whereabouts, but reassured her that it was just a matter of time until he was holding her again.

Like his last letter, he'd placed it within another envelope addressed to Stuart in Richmond with instruction for its immediate delivery to Charmantes. With Paul's packets running supplies to Charmantes at least once a month, John was certain that Charmaine would receive the correspondence by early December.

That night, John showed Michael the ring. "Beautiful," the priest admired.

"I know what you're thinking," John said. "I should have given the money to the poor."

"No, John. Charmaine deserves to be happy." Michael looked at the ring again, turning it over in his hand. "*This* should make her very happy."

John smiled, watching as his friend read the inscription.

"My Charm?" he asked.

John's grin widened, his eyes lighting up as well. "My pet name for her," he explained. "She used to hate it when I called her that, but I'd say it again and again just to see her eyes flash."

Michael could tell that John relished the memory.

"Like Marie's eyes…" John mused.

Michael nodded. "Yes," he breathed. "I remember that look…"

He handed the diamond back to John, who replaced it in its box, then locked it away in his desk. "If anything should happen, Michael, please make certain that Charmaine gets it."

Michael's heart lurched with the tenebrous request.

November, 1838

Charmantes didn't have a jail, so Benito Giovanni had spent the last two months incarcerated in the storeroom beneath the town's meetinghouse. The cellar had been used for petty infractions in the past, and so, Paul had transferred the priest from the bondsmen's keep three days after his arrest to keep a better eye on him.

The edifice was built into the side of a hillock, and those attending Sunday Mass climbed eight steps up to a small wooden platform that opened into one large room. Inside, a staircase led down to a dark, cool basement, where perishable items were stored. The chamber was six feet deep with an earthen floor, its front wall constructed of rock and clay mortar, the rear wall, little more than heavy stones embedded in the hillside. Three rows of shelves lined the back of the cellar. They were stacked with preserves, wine, vegetables, and exotic fruits. The priest was pleased to discover that the furthest shelf was set about two feet away from the stone and dirt wall. It was tight, but there was room to move behind it.

Giovanni had spent the first two weeks of his imprisonment cursing his rotten luck, his scheme to leave Charmantes at the end of the year, foiled. He'd prepared for the possibility of betrayal from the start, but when Blackford departed and Agatha was banished, that ceased to be a concern. Certainly, he never expected this! Before he could escape from the island, he had to escape his cell. As long as he had time, there was a chance. Within two weeks, he had formulated a plan.

Twice a week, either Paul or George would check in on him. Sometimes the door would open, other times he'd hear their voices on the other side and knew that a sentry stood guard. He wondered why John or Frederic had not come to confront him again, concluding that they had left Charmantes in search of Blackford. He wondered what had happened to Agatha and puzzled as to how the truth had been unraveled and their treachery revealed.

Twice a day, he was brought food: breakfast early in the morning, and around five, supper. At that time, his chamber pot was removed and returned clean. Buck Mathers had been taken from the docks and charged with delivering these meals and any other needs. The priest knew better than to attempt an escape when Buck came through the door. Giovanni used the time to strike up several conversations with the man, however, gradually putting him at ease. Buck religiously attended the Sunday noon Mass with his wife and five children. Like everyone else on the island, he was astonished that a man of the cloth could be guilty of blackmail, blackmail over two murders.

"I don't know how this happened," Benito murmured humbly one evening.

Buck looked up from the chair he had posted near the door.

"Surely Frederic realizes that I'm bound by the Holy Father's precepts to hold confessions secret." Giovanni stole a glance at Buck and was pleased with the Negro's look of consternation. He softly added, "It pained me to hear Agatha Duvoisin's confession, but I was not allowed to divulge her terrible sin."

"The way I hear it," Buck bristled, "there wasn't a confession. You were blackmailin' her."

"I am sad to say she was very sly," the priest admitted, head bobbing forward. "She attempted to bestow gifts upon me, perhaps to ease her guilt. If only I had known that she was tricking me into sharing the blame..."

He said no more for a week, allowing Buck to mull over his remarks.

One day, he managed to lift a spoon off his food tray and was pleased it went undetected. That evening he calculated where he would dig and how he would conceal the hole. Using the utensil, he pried the first stone of the crude foundation free, and like unraveling a knitting stitch, the rocks next to it dislodged easily. When the hole was big enough, he lifted the rocks back into place. He wasn't quite ready to begin digging. The shelves would help to conceal the breach, but a rearrangement of goods was necessary first. He moved a sack of fruit one day, a few jars the next, a bucket or a crate after that, until slowly and imperceptibly, the excavation site was concealed. Then he began to dig, spending hours in the dim room, timing his work on the light that came through the narrow, barred window, stopping a half-hour before meals were delivered. He'd fill an empty bucket to the top and sprinkle the loose dirt evenly on the ground, trampling it under foot until it compacted with the earthen floor. He prayed that he'd break through to the other side before time ran out.

His contrition had garnered Buck's sympathy, and Giovanni read pity in the black man's eyes every time he delivered meals. The Negro was speaking freely to him now, and the priest learned that John and Frederic had indeed left the island in pursuit of the evil Robert Blackford. Paul was in charge while they were away, and Agatha had committed suicide, or so everyone assumed.

It could take months, possibly years, to track down Blackford. Benito had plenty of time to tunnel his way out of his prison, recover his stash of jewels, and flee Charmantes on the fishing boat he'd hidden near his cabin. Of course, Paul might discover he was gone before he was off the island, but the man would search the ships in the harbor first. Giovanni had practiced an escape. His maps were stowed with the rowboat. The nearest uninhabited landmass was tiny Esprit, half a day's trek in the dinghy. No one would think to look for him there, but with the jars of fresh water and foodstuffs that he'd stored on the isle, he could survive for two weeks, if necessary. From Esprit, six hours rowing would take him to any of three inhabited Bahaman islands. He would melt into the populace and leave for civilization when it suited him. All he needed was calm seas, grit, and some luck. Thanks to Agatha, he could kiss the priesthood goodbye.

Thursday, November 15, 1838

John was dreaming. He was at home – on Charmantes – in his room. Colette was beckoning to him from the French doors. This time he followed her: out onto the balcony, across the side lawns, behind the manor and to the edge of the woods and the small, unbeaten footpath to the lake.

He was on the shore when he noticed Colette was gone, her only trace the faint scent of lily. A dark, faceless figure loomed just beyond his reach at the water's edge. Even though the sun shone high in the sky, everything was shrouded in darkness. Shards of light flashed on the rippling water.

Then he saw the boat and the boy in it, bobbing perilously on the churning lake. Predictably, it capsized, toppling its passenger out. He started forward to save Pierre, but he could not lift his feet. It was as if they had sprouted hearty roots, holding him fast. There was no time to lose, yet he watched, horrified and helpless. His eyes went desperately to the morbid specter, standing an easy distance from the tumult, but it only backed away, dissolving into the tree line.

John awoke with a start, a cry shattering his nightmare. He jumped up, rushed into the dimly lit hallway, and crossed to his father's room. As he reached for the knob, the door opened.

Frederic was standing there, bleary-eyed. "What is it?" he asked.

"I heard you cry out."

"I heard *you* cry out," Frederic rejoined, baffled.

"It wasn't me," John replied. "Maybe it was Michael." He walked down the corridor and opened the door to a third bedroom, but the priest was snoring loudly. "Maybe that's what we heard," he quipped lightly, quietly closing the portal. "The windows are rattling." He walked back to his room.

Frederic followed. "I had a dream about Pierre," he offered in a low voice. John stopped dead in his tracks. "First he was at the lake," Frederic continued, "in the boat. It was very dark. The dinghy capsized–" Frederic's voice cracked.

"And?" John pressed, his eyes keen.

"I was powerless to get to him, just like the morning Blackford–"

"*You've had this dream before?*"

"No," Frederic muttered. "I was awake the morning Blackford abducted Pierre, wide-awake when Colette came to me. She led me out onto the balcony, then evaporated. I thought I was going mad, until I saw a movement in the tree line. I was gripped with dread. That's why I sent Paul to the lake."

John stared at him in mute consternation. He'd never learned why his brother had gone to the lake, assuming that Charmaine had returned to the nursery, found Pierre missing, and had sent Paul in search of him. Vexed, John exhaled. He turned toward his room, but Frederic halted his step. "There's more."

John frowned, facing his father slowly.

"The dream changed. Suddenly, I was here, in New York. I saw Pierre. He was lost in a busy street, but when I tried to reach him, he was swallowed up by the crowd."

John gaped at him in utter disbelief. "What happened next?"

"There were furnaces and flames – burning coal. I thought I was going to fall into them. Maybe that's when I cried out in my sleep."

"Does burning coal mean anything to you?" John asked, gooseflesh raised on his arms and up the back of his neck.

"Why?"

"Because I've had the same dream."

Frederic's eyes widened. "I don't know," he said. But as he lay in bed, an oblique memory hit him: Elizabeth's mother's maiden name had been Coleburn.

Friday, November 16, 1838

Stuart Simons swore under his breath when he found not one, but two letters from John addressed to him at the warehouse. Sickness at Freedom and Wisteria Hill had kept him away from the Richmond harbor for over a month now, but he had left explicit instructions that any correspondence from John should be opened and forwarded to Charmantes as appropriate. Someone had screwed up. He was relieved when he read John's notes to him and realized that there was really no news to tell. John just wanted to make certain that the accompanying letters reached his wife. She wouldn't have to wait much longer. The ship dedicated to Charmantes was due in port any day now.

Stuart smiled. Although John's search had proved futile thus far, Stuart's had not. John Ryan had turned up nearly two months ago.

Saturday, December 1, 1838

Charmaine's birthday was a short two weeks away and the twins wanted to get her a present, something special, they told Paul. He agreed to take them into town. Charmaine declined to accompany them, reluctant to appear in public in her condition. "I'll rest," she said. "I didn't sleep very well last night."

When Loretta showed concern, Charmaine reassured her, saying, "I had dream after dream. My mother was there–" she laughed hollowly "–talking about John, of all people!"

After Paul and the girls left, Charmaine remained contemplative, wondering whether her dreams meant more. She had not received word from John since his letter ten weeks ago and, as the days accumulated, she grew more and more worried, a gnawing dread plaguing her late into the night. Loretta sent Joshua off with George, and stayed with Charmaine all afternoon. It was then that Loretta finally learned all about John and most of what had happened on Charmantes.

Leaving the livery, Paul draped his arms over Jeannette and Yvette's shoulders and they strolled down the thoroughfare, drinking in the sunshine despite the brisk breeze.

"Aren't Sundays pleasant now that we don't have to attend Mass anymore?" Yvette mused.

Paul raised a dubious brow. "Charmaine had better not hear you say that or she'll be sending for a new priest." His mild warning ended in laughter. "I have to admit, I don't miss Father Benito's sermons either."

"But what will happen if someone wants to get married?" Jeannette asked.

"I suppose the couple will have to travel to America or Europe," Paul speculated, "or do as father's sister did and exchange vows before a ship's captain."

They had just reached the mercantile when Wade and Rebecca stepped out. Paul and Wade immediately fell into easy banter, but Rebecca pretended disinterest, turning her head aside.

Paul noticed her coy reaction and found it appealing. He spoke to her directly. "You see, Miss Remmen, your brother is no worse for the fever he suffered a few months ago."

"It's as I told you, Mr. Duvoisin," she replied levelly, though her legs were like liquid and butterflies fluttered in her belly, "all he needed was bed rest."

"And a tender touch," Paul added with a dashing smile, his eyes holding her captive. "Now, if you'll excuse us, we have some shopping to do."

"Paul is going to help us pick out a gift for Mademoiselle Charmaine," Jeannette explained. "It will be her birthday soon."

Wade nodded, not interested in the least, but Rebecca was miffed.

Less than a half-hour later, Paul and his sisters left the mercantile carrying a box of sweets and a new book of poetry. He had ordered a rocking horse months ago, and although it had arrived, it would be delivered to the house later that day.

The girls teased him. "The baby won't be able to ride it until next year!"

"Nevertheless, it will be in the nursery when he's ready," Paul rejoined, "and I'm sure the two of you will be eager to teach him how to rock on it."

"You're as bad as Johnny!" Yvette chided.

"I'm going to take that as a compliment."

"It was."

Paul laughed as they crossed the busy street, turning around when shouts resounded from the wharf, heralding the arrival of a ship.

As always, the pedestrians pressed toward the harbor, and soon, the pier was a sea of people. Paul hastened to the boardwalk, guiding his sisters through the throng that obligingly parted for them. They passed unimpeded until they were standing abreast of the huge ship. Paul cautioned the girls to wait for him on the wharf. He saw no sign of John or his father, but was anxious for news. The ship had most likely come from Richmond. Before the last mooring lines were secured, he was boarding the vessel.

The captain rushed over, clearly relieved to see him.

"What is the matter, Gregory?" Paul queried anxiously. "You haven't brought us bad news from my father or John?"

"No, sir, no," he reassured. "But I do have some important documents that Stuart Simons instructed me to hand over to you as soon as we made port." He produced the shipping invoices. They confirmed what Paul had already guessed: John Ryan was on board.

"Excuse me, gentlemen!" Paul shouted, waiting for the crew to quiet down. "I'm looking for a Mr. Ryan."

John Ryan was not surprised to hear his name called. According to Stuart Simons, Paul Duvoisin was looking for efficient, reliable laborers. Having learned of John Ryan's exemplary work in Richmond, Paul wanted to meet him as soon as he reached Charmantes. Ryan snickered to himself. *How dim-witted could the man be?* Snickering again, he confidently stepped forward.

"Mr. Ryan?" Paul queried through narrowed eyes. "Mr. John Ryan?"

"That's me," Ryan nodded, his chest puffed out like a bantam cock.

"You're just the man I've been looking for," Paul said, hiding his revulsion behind a smile. "These documents tell me that you've been an invaluable help to my brother. I believe I can use you up at our meetinghouse."

"Oh, I'm valuable all right," Ryan boasted. "I just hope this job pays what I'm worth."

"It does better than that," Paul confided, placing an arm around the man's shoulder in fraudulent camaraderie. "It includes free meals, room and board."

Astounded, John Ryan happily allowed Paul to lead him down the gangplank, eager to learn about this unprecedented windfall. His ship had finally come in!

Yvette and Jeannette suspiciously eyed their brother's motley companion as the two men approached. "Girls," Paul called, "let us lunch at Dulcie's. I'll be there in ten minutes time."

"Who is he?" Yvette asked, when Paul offered no introduction.

"The name's Ryan," the man blurted out. "John Ryan."

Paul swore under his breath. Recognition had dawned on his sisters' faces.

Yvette overcame her surprise and studied her brother. A fleeting scowl had crossed his face, accompanied by a nearly imperceptible shake of his head. Reading his signal, she grasped Jeannette's arm and began to nudge her down the pier. "Very well, Paul, we'll meet you at Dulcie's."

Paul thanked God that she was growing up and turned back to John Ryan. "My sisters," he explained nonchalantly, noting the man's interest. He indicated the boardwalk. "Shall we?"

Ryan nodded, and Paul struck up some small talk as he escorted the older man to the meetinghouse. They climbed the steps, and Paul allowed John Ryan to step in first, closing the door behind him and leaning back against it.

"Well," Ryan began when it seemed as if Paul would not speak, his eyes darting around the empty room. "What work do you want me to do here?"

"Prayer work," Paul said softly.

"Prayer work?" the elder asked, laughing outright at the inane suggestion.

"Yes, Mr. Ryan," Paul pronounced rigidly, his brow suddenly furrowed. "You'd best start praying, because I believe you're a wanted man." Seeing John Ryan's stupefaction, Paul continued, arms folded across his chest. "I have it on the most reliable authority that you murdered your wife."

The older man did not like this conversation and grew belligerent. "I mighta hit her on occasion, but she had it comin'."

"Had it coming?" Paul asked incredulously, his jaw clenched.

"She was a mouthin' off hen-pecker who needed to be put in her place. And that's what I did – put her in her place."

Paul's hand shot out so fast, Ryan didn't know what grabbed him. With a fist-full of shirtfront, Paul lifted him clear off the ground and sent him sailing. He hit the floor with a loud oomph, his legs and arms splayed in four directions. "Why'd you do that?" he demanded from where he lay. "*Why'd you bring me here?*"

"So you can pay for your crime."

John Ryan jumped to his feet, but Paul rushed him, grabbing his forearm and yanking him around. He squealed in pain as Paul guided him down the stairwell, wrenching his arm ever higher behind his back. The guard unlocked the door and swung it open, and Paul shoved him inside. Again, he stumbled to the floor.

Paul eyed Benito, who had scrambled to the center of the room. "The two of you should be great company for one another," he commented wryly, wiping his hands on his trousers. "Why don't you tell your new inmate who my brother's wife is, Benito? Mr. Ryan should be very interested to know."

When the door was bolted, Paul cautioned the burly guard to remain alert.

By the time he reached Dulcie's, his sisters were already eating. After he'd ordered his own meal, Yvette bluntly asked, "Was that Charmaine's father?"

"Unfortunately, yes," Paul admitted. "But you mustn't tell her he's here."

"Why *is* he here?" Jeannette asked, her eyes clouded with worry.

"John wants to deal with him. He's responsible for his wife's murder."

"What will Johnny do to him?" Yvette asked.

"I don't know, Yvette."

"What would you do?" Jeannette queried.

Paul raked his fingers through his hair. "I don't know that either. I'd have to think long and hard on it. Are the two of you going to keep quiet about this?"

"If that is what you want Paul, that's what we'll do," Yvette promised.

"Thank you," Paul said with a warm smile. "And thank you for heeding my warning on the quay. I wanted to make certain that John Ryan was locked up with our good Father Benito before he learned why he was here."

Yvette smiled wickedly. "I'll wager he had the surprise of his life."

"That he did," Paul affirmed. "That he did."

New York

After a long day walking the streets of lower Manhattan, Frederic had grown weary and Michael, hungry. They hailed a ride near the harbor and headed back to Washington Square. Frederic had had enough of New York City. After weeks of scouring her streets, their paltry leads had turned up nothing. Even their breakthrough with the name Coleburn had led nowhere. He stared out the window of the quiet cab, contemplating their futile search, frustrated, angry, and homesick. It was growing dark, and people were spilling onto the streets, stopping along the way to buy bread or a slab of meat for dinner.

He closed his eyes and dozed to the lull of the rocking carriage. It rolled over a hole as it negotiated a turn, jolting him awake. He shifted and looked out the window, the silhouette of a man about a block ahead snaring his attention. Tall, dark, and slender, he was just now reaching the street corner. His black overcoat billowed against a stiff breeze. One hand was planted on his top hat; the other toted a black bag.

Frederic's heart leapt into his throat. Their carriage was turning away! He pushed the door open with his cane, shouting up to the driver to stop. He scrambled out of the conveyance, nearly falling as the cabman yelled at him to wait. "Get back here, man! You ain't paid the fare!"

Bumping shoulders with pedestrians, Frederic ignored the indignant voice that followed him and leaned hard on his cane, dodging the hogs and goats that wandered the road, scavenging street refuse for food scraps. When he reached the next corner, heaving and breathless, the man was nowhere in sight. Had he continued straight ahead, turned left or right? Frederic pivoted in all directions, straining to see beyond the press of people, hoping to catch a glimpse of the dark figure again. It was useless; he was gone. Downtrodden, Frederic turned back to the cab in mute resignation.

Even though Michael was convinced that he'd imagined it, Frederic thought about the incident for days. Every evening afterward, he left Michael at the townhouse and headed downtown, strolling the streets in the same neighborhood. When night fell, he would step into a local tavern for dinner, sitting near a window with a tankard of ale as he watched people walk by.

Tonight, the waiter had just set a plate of hot food before him when a commotion erupted two tables away. A barmaid was screaming at two men, who had shot to their feet. "You told me you loved me, you lyin' bastard!" she spat at him, her face red, tears streaming down her cheeks. "I ain't doin' this, I seen other girls bleed to death!"

When one of them shrugged sheepishly, she hurled a crumpled piece of paper into his face and flew at him. The patrons nearby scrambled from their tables, and two waiters rushed over to break up the fracas. Frederic came to his feet as well. The barmaid was hissing and spitting fire at the longshoreman, even as the waiters pulled her away. The dockworkers threw a few coins on the table and fled the tavern. The proprietress put an arm around the sobbing girl and, with comforting words, led her into the kitchen.

Frederic sank back into his seat and lifted his fork, noticing that his napkin had fallen to the floor. As he reached down for it, he saw the crumpled paper under his chair. He picked it up and smoothed it open, his heart nearly stopping when he read: Coleburn Clinic. 27 Water Street.

According to John, the address was in a seedy section a few blocks from the wharfs. He would check it out the next day. Frederic insisted on going with him, but John objected. "We'll be too conspicuous together."

Frederic capitulated reluctantly. "If it is Blackford, promise me that you won't take action on your own. We must decide together how to proceed."

John nodded placidly, but Frederic was unnerved.

The next day, John went to the address. It was a row house with a continuous stream of people going in and out. He approached a woman with two young girls as they left. "Is this the doctor's office?" he asked.

The woman looked at him quizzically. At first, he didn't think she spoke English. "Yes," she finally replied in a thick Irish brogue, "it's Doctor Coleburn. Why do you ask?"

"I wasn't sure if I had the right address. Thank you."

She nodded and nudged her children along.

John waited in the street until long after dark. As dusk fell, the clientele changed. Mostly young women and tarts entered the building, hesitating before their hands alighted upon the knob, their eyes darting surreptitiously to and fro to be certain nobody saw them enter. Finally, the last patient left, and the lights in the first floor windows went dark. A few minutes later, a tall dark figure appeared in the doorway and descended the steps, setting a brisk pace up the street. John followed, keeping a safe distance behind, walking gingerly so that his footfalls would not call attention to his presence. The man turned a corner and walked a few blocks further, turned again and ascended the steps of another row house. John marked the address.

Before dawn the next day, he was seated on the steps of the row house across from 13 Stone Street, his collar drawn high around his neck, his cap cocked low over his forehead. At exactly eight o'clock in the morning, Robert Blackford stepped out of the door and headed toward his clinic.

"We can have a ship ready. Now that we know his address, all we have to do is corner him. He'll be no match for the three of us, and we can take him to the ship straightaway."

"I agree with your father, John," Michael offered, stirring his tea. "This is the least dangerous way to handle it." Though John did not argue, his dissatisfied frown bolstered Michael's dismay. Clearly, the man was keeping his own counsel. "Once he's on Charmantes," Michael continued, "your father will have free rein to punish him however he sees fit."

With hands clasped behind his head, John leaned back in his chair and looked from his father to Michael, deliberating. Michael could read a hundred thoughts flashing in his eyes. "All right," he finally replied, his face suddenly stolid. "When do we start?"

"We'll make arrangements for the ship tomorrow," Frederic replied. "The next Duvoisin vessel in port will be rerouted to take us back to Charmantes."

"I plan on keeping an eye on Blackford while we wait," John interjected. "He's not going to get away again."

"Fair enough," Frederic agreed.

John pushed from the table and turned to retire. Michael stared after him, very uneasy. He couldn't shake the feeling that John had plans of his own. "John, while your father arranges for the ship tomorrow, I want you to show me where Blackford lives."

John faced him. "It's too risky. He might spot us."

"We can go after he opens his clinic. It's just a precau–"

"Fine," John interrupted sharply. "I'm going to bed."

Wednesday, December 5, 1838

The evening air was raw, and it was going to rain. Lily Clayton made her way up Washington Square past the elegant row houses of Greenwich Village and turned onto Sixth Avenue. Even though it was Wednesday, her employer had allowed her to go home early, an extremely rare act of generosity, and for that, Lily was grateful. Now she had two hours to spare before her sister, Rose, who was minding her children, expected her home. That free time brought her here.

She stopped on the walk outside of row house number nine and noticed that the lamps were burning inside. She smiled. The lights meant that John Duvoisin was back in New York. She missed him, for she hadn't seen him since February. Over the past months, she had worried about him, because he never stayed away from New York this long. Now she wondered when he'd gotten back and why she hadn't heard from him. He always came by to check on her as soon as he arrived in town.

Lily and her sister, Rose, had been house servants at the Duvoisin plantation in Virginia. They were quadroons and became the property of John Duvoisin when he purchased Wisteria Hill, the plantation adjacent to his father's, in late

1834. They were thrilled when they heard that John was interested in buying the property, because they knew all the slaves at Freedom had been freed. On his first visit to Wisteria Hill, she'd been attracted to him. He was young and handsome and, unlike other plantation owners, he had spoken to her, even though she was a slave. Within months of purchasing Wisteria Hill, John freed her and Rose. She moved to the plantation house at Freedom and became the resident housekeeper there, while Rose remained at Wisteria Hill for the same purpose. Rose was a mere two miles away.

Lily was beautiful, her skin a light, creamy tan. She was tall and lithe with straight dark hair, black eyes, sensual lips and an aristocratic nose. Lily had twin sons and a daughter by her husband, Henry, who had been sold south to a North Carolina cotton planter before John had purchased Wisteria Hill.

Henry was a mulatto, so their children were also light-skinned; the casual observer would never suspect their black ancestry. John had tried to purchase Henry to work at Freedom, but his owner, a viciously stalwart southerner, was unwilling to sell him for any price, for Henry was big and strong and worked hard. Furthermore, his new master held great disdain for border-state plantation owners who freed their slaves, and bristled at the thought of even one more black, especially a mulatto, being freed.

Lily knew that she would never see Henry again. Over three years ago, she had received word that he'd been 'crippled' during an unsuccessful escape attempt. Three runaways had made it as far as Freedom, delivering into Lily's hand a short letter from Henry. According to the runaways, Henry had been brutally mutilated, the toes on his right foot hacked off so that he would never run again. Lily became resigned to life without him.

When John began making frequent trips to New York, she begged him to take her, Rose, and her children there. She wanted to start over, to be independent. She wanted her children to be more than just free; she wanted them to be educated. In New York, they could go to school. John was reluctant to bring her north. Lily and Rose kept the plantation houses running smoothly when he wasn't there, which was more often than not. But with her incessant begging, he finally gave in, and nearly three years ago, she arrived with him in New York.

John helped both women find jobs as housekeepers for affluent New York merchants; for the first few months, Lily worked for his aging aunt. He located a tiny house for them in lower Manhattan, gave her money for a full year's rent, and accompanied her when she enrolled her children in a New York public school. The schoolmaster assumed that John was her husband and the children, white. When he asked John where he was employed, he simply said the Duvoisin shipping line, which satisfied the schoolmaster and wasn't a lie. So, even without Henry, Lily's life had never been better.

Lily loved Henry and longed to be with him again, but Lily also loved John. She loved him because he treated her with a respect that other white men reserved for white society ladies. She loved him because she could tell him anything and he always listened without passing judgment. She could cry about missing Henry, and he understood, because instinctively, she knew that he also had been separated from somebody he loved. She loved him because he was kind to her children and he made her laugh. She loved him because he had never forced himself on her, as every one of her other white owners had. Even so, she had shared his bed many times. John had joked that if Henry ever found out, he'd overcome his infirmity and escape bondage solely to find and kill him.

Tonight, she would seek out John. He'd relieve her gnawing need, one that hadn't been satiated since February. After her children were fed and put down to sleep, she would leave them with Rose and return to Sixth Avenue.

John pulled his collar up high around his neck and his cap down low on his forehead, his back to the hallway as he rapped on the landlady's door. The building had been sectioned so that each floor was a two-room apartment. The ground floor corridor was shrouded in darkness, as evening was falling and rain pounded on the muddy street outside. Most of the longshoremen had already arrived home, the connecting houses resonating the sounds of clattering dishes, muffled voices, and children's play.

The landlady opened the door. She was a stout, middle-aged woman, her greasy, gray-streaked hair tied back into a ponytail that reached her hips. She looked up at him, chewing on a mouthful of her dinner.

"Whaddaya want?" she asked before swallowing, one front tooth missing.

"I am looking for Dr. Coleburn."

"Did ya knock on his door?"

"There was no answer. When does he usually arrive home?"

"Who wants tuh know?" she boldly asked, sizing him up. He'd probably knocked up his girlfriend and needed the doctor's services.

"A patient."

She eyed him skeptically.

He flashed her a one-dollar note.

"He gets back late. After nine o'clock, gen'rally. You'd best come back then." She snatched the bill from his hand.

"It's raining. I've come a long way, and I'd rather wait for him here, in his apartment."

Though suspicious, she didn't object. "What's it worth tuh ya?" she asked, fingering the keys that hung on a chain at her waist.

John extended his hand again; a crisp five-dollar note sat neatly in his palm. Her greedy eyes grew wide. "How's about two of those?" she replied.

Frederic pushed through the front door and found Michael in the parlor reading a newspaper next to the burning hearth. Dusk had fallen and all the lamps were lit. It had been a long, yet gratifying day.

Late last night, the Heir had reached New York. Frederic had spent the hours just after dawn closeted in the captain's cabin while John showed Michael where Blackford lived and worked. In the two hours they were gone, Frederic explained to Will Jones, the Heir's captain, what had happened and what he planned to do. By the time John and Michael arrived at the wharf, Will knew that if, for any reason, Frederic, John, or Michael had not contacted him in three days' time, he was to sail back to Charmantes without them. There he would tell Paul that Blackford had indeed been found under the assumed name Coleburn and that Frederic and John had attempted to apprehend him on the sixth of December. Frederic was confident that nothing would go wrong, but it was best to be prepared for the worst.

The Heir carried a letter from Charmaine, and Frederic had watched as John eagerly ripped into it, the third he'd received. He'd been happy with all her news, especially pleased to learn that the Harringtons had decided to remain on Charmantes until the baby was born. He was befuddled as he read on; Charmaine had not received any of his letters, save the first one. Frederic had assured him that that mattered very little now. By tomorrow, everything would be resolved and they'd be on their way home, arriving a month before the birth of his child.

The remainder of the morning had been grueling. Frederic and John unloaded the ship's cargo onto a partially laden vessel that had berthed in New York en route to Liverpool. They had hastily commissioned the other carrier while the cargo space was still available, and threw themselves into the laborious task of shifting goods, since hired help was short that morning. In this way, the Heir could return directly to Charmantes, and the sugar and tobacco promised for Europe would arrive on time. Frederic had felt extremely lucky that morning. He'd been certain they'd have to wait at least a fortnight before a Duvoisin vessel reached New York.

A crew had been hired by lunchtime, and Michael realized he was of little use standing around. He was only getting in their way. So, he left them and spent the afternoon and early evening walking the streets, visiting a myriad of churches and buildings, many of them magnificent. In the weeks they had been there, he'd rarely gone exploring, and by tomorrow, they'd be traveling to Charmantes, so this was his last chance. When it began to rain, he headed home.

He'd been at the house for nearly two hours and looked up when Frederic entered, pulling off his wet overcoat, shaking it out, and hanging it in the foyer. "Where is John?" he asked when the door did not reopen.

"What do you mean?" Frederic queried. "I thought he was with you. He said he was going to meet you when he left the merchant's office a few hours ago."

Their eyes locked, and Frederic's face grew stormy. "What is Blackford's address, Michael?"

"13 Stone Street," he answered, praying that John had taken him to the right building, that he hadn't purposefully misled him. "It's just south of Wall Street."

"Thank God."

"I should go with you."

"No. Wait for me here – just in case we're wrong."

Michael looked at him skeptically. "I should check the clinic in case something happened there. We will meet back here."

Frederic agreed, then rushed upstairs, taking the stairs as swiftly as his lame side would allow. Rifling through his trunk, he found the revolver and bullets he'd purchased their first week in New York. He hastened back down to the foyer, where he pulled on his coat, loaded the firearm, and shoved it deep into a pocket. Grabbing his cane, he threw one last look at Michael, who was also ready to leave. Together, they set off, hailing two cabs.

Robert Blackford climbed three flights of stairs to his cramped rooms. The cry of a baby and the couple fighting on the floor below echoed upward, the odor of food fried in rancid suet melded with the must of the damp hallway. Although the row house afforded him anonymity, he eschewed such squalor whenever possible. Practically every evening, he visited the affluent neighborhoods north of this hovel, where he could enjoy the finer things in life that the city had to offer. Tonight, he was returning from dinner at the Astor House Hotel. Tomorrow, he would go to a playhouse. He liked it here in New York. Indeed, life was better than he imagined it could be, even without his beloved Agatha.

He walked to his door, put the key in the lock, and turned it. He tried to push the portal open and realized he had locked rather than unlocked it. Funny, he always locked up when he left.

He stepped into the dark flat and groped his way to the lamp on the table. Finding the tinderbox, he struck the flint and lit the wick, the flame flaring up in the lamp and illuminating the cold room. He rubbed his hands briskly together to warm them against the chill and decided to leave his cloak on. After thirty years in the Caribbean, he'd never grow accustomed to the penetrating cold.

It wasn't until he turned to light a fire in the stove that he saw the shadow of a man sitting in the chair next to it. Recognition spurred him into motion, and he swung around swiftly, flying to the door.

John was out of the chair in an instant, reaching out and clutching his billowing cloak. Robert managed to pull the door open before he was forcefully jerked backward. John immediately threw an arm around his neck and grabbed his wrist, yanking it high behind his back. Robert howled in pain.

"It's reckoning time, Blackford," John growled against his ear, pushing him toward a large wooden dish tub set on the floor next to the stove.

As they got closer, Robert could see that it was still filled with the morning's dishwater. John wrenched his arm even higher, then violently kicked the back of his legs so that they buckled under him, and he fell to his knees before the tub.

John followed him down. "Tell me why you did it, Blackford."

"I don't know what you're talking about, John," he croaked, as he felt his nephew's hand move to the back of his head. "There must be some kind of mistake. What is this about? Can't we just talk about it?"

"Tell me why you did it, and I'll let you live."

"I don't know what you're talking about!"

"Then why are you hiding here under an alias?"

"Please, John..."

John ignored his pitiful appeal and began to push his head slowly, purposefully down toward the water. "How do you think it felt, Blackford?" John cried. "How can you live with yourself knowing what you did to Pierre?"

Robert resisted, struggling to turn his head aside as his face met the cold water. Then he was totally submerged, held fast, immobile. He concentrated on mustering all his strength to throw his body backward, but that effort proved futile. John finally released his head, and he came up sputtering and gasping for air.

John took tighter hold of him, pressing a knee deep into his back. "Are you ready to tell me why you did it now?"

"It wasn't my idea – it was my sister's! Paul is her son, *he* should have been the heir."

"That's not good enough, Blackford!"

John propelled his head toward the water again. "Do you think this is how it felt, you evil fiend? he sobbed. "Did you take great pleasure in drowning an innocent child? I want *you* to know how it felt, *you Satan!*"

He plunged Blackford's head deep into the tub again, pressing down upon him for endless seconds. Great air bubbles churned violently to the surface, and water sloshed over the sides of the bucket. Blackford's legs thrashed and kicked across the slippery floor, catching the chair and toppling it over. His free arm flailed in every direction, blindly grappling for anything within reach. John released his head, and Robert emerged, heaving and gulping in air.

"Are you ready to tell me now?" John sneered, his fingers entwined in the man's hair. "It wasn't just for the money. So tell me, *why did you do it?*"

"I loved my sister. Your father ruined her life," Robert wheezed, gasping to catch his breath, the water dripping off of his face and hair.

"Not good enough, Blackford!"

Robert's head dipped toward the water a third time, the room deathly silent, save his desperate struggle to wrench free of the strong hands guiding him forward. "All right, John, all right!" he begged. Then came the murmured admission. "I was *in love* with my sister... I would have done anything for her."

John felt the blood drain from his limbs and, with a tormented curse, relaxed his grip. Robert instantly threw himself backward, and John staggered, slipping on the wet floor. Robert rolled over to face his attacker. But John was up and on him again, straddling and pinning him down, hands around his neck. Robert's head was cocked at an awkward angle, shoved against the side of the tub. He sputtered for air, and his fingers furiously clawing at John's hands. But the vise continued to constrict. John was going to strangle him.

He had one last hope. Straining to the right, he groped inside his boot for the knife he carried for protection against the street thugs who loitered around his clinic. The tips of his fingers brushed against the smooth handle. Stretching further, he finally loosed the dagger from its sheath, pulling it free. He drew it back and plunged it viciously into John's flank.

John cried out and, clutching his side, collapsed next to him.

Choking, Robert's hands shot to his throat, the knife clattering to the floor. He threw his head back and closed his eyes, inhaling rapidly, his pulse thundering in his ears. When he could breathe again, he fumbled for the knife at his side. He knew he had to finish John off – slit his throat quickly and flee.

As he opened his eyes, a tall shadow loomed above him, and he found himself looking up the barrel of Frederic Duvoisin's revolver.

Frederic looked away and pulled the trigger. There was a flash and a loud report. He glanced down at the grisly sight, threw his cane aside, and dropped to his knees beside John.

"John! Get up!" he insisted nudging John fiercely. "We have to get out of here – *now!"*

"Father..." John groaned, pushing himself onto his knees.

Already the room reeked of fresh blood. Frederic hurriedly looped his arm around John's waist and shouldered a portion of his weight. Then he struggled to his feet, dragging John with him.

Somebody screamed, and Frederic looked up, the pistol concealed in the folds of his coat. A young woman stood in the doorway, gaping at them. "*Murderers!*" she shrieked, raising the alarm. "*Murderers! Police!"*

He advanced, his arm tight around his son. The girl blocked their path. "Move aside," he demanded. When she didn't, he pointed the firearm at her. She stepped back quickly, but screamed again after they passed. More voices sounded from the dark hallway below.

Frederic forced himself calm. "John, you have to walk down the stairs. You have to help me." Trembling, Frederic released him, his hand covered in thick, syrupy blood.

John grabbed hold of the railing and started down, enduring the searing pain that radiated into his chest and down his leg.

Frederic followed, gun drawn.

John managed the first two flights, fighting to breathe, each aspiration shallow and excruciating. Three steps further, and his knees buckled beneath him. He tumbled down the last flight, landing in a crumpled heap at the foot of the stairwell.

Frederic raced after him. The landlady's door cracked open as he reached the bottom, and she peered out. Frederic dropped to one knee, but swiftly straightened as two men confronted him. He flashed the pistol again, and the two backed off. "Get up, John!" he shouted, holding the firearm level against them. "You have to get up!"

His father's command echoed as if at the end of a tunnel. Though everything was fading, John grabbed the railing and pulled himself to his feet.

Frederic put an arm around him again, and John leaned heavily into his body, forcing Frederic to carry most of his weight. Staggering across the foyer, they pushed through the doors and out into the rainy night.

Thankfully, the hired carriage was still there. Frederic had promised the driver a double fare for the return trip if he waited. He shoved John in and climbed onto the seat across from him, directing the cabby to make haste uptown. The old man set the horses into a brisk trot, and finally, they were rolling away.

As they turned the corner a few blocks up, they passed two mounted policemen heading toward the row house.

John moaned and his head fell back against the seat cushions. Frederic crossed to his side and pulled him into his arms. John jerked forward, then slumped across his lap, shivering uncontrollably, his clothing soaked through.

"Hold on, John," Frederic pleaded in a whisper, enfolding him in his cloak, his anxiety rising in proportion to his hammering heart.

"How could he, Papa?" John beseeched, his voice a strained sob, his face contorted in pain. "How could he murder my little boy?"

"I don't know, John," Frederic soothed, pulling John closer, gathering the dry cloak tighter around him. "I don't know."

"Is he dead?"

"Yes, he's dead."

John looked up at his father. He hadn't heard the answer, for the world was slipping away. "Is he dead?"

"Yes, John, he's dead."

John closed his eyes. "Charmaine..."

"Hold on, John. Just hold on. You're going to be all right. We'll get you a doctor." Frederic looked at the blood on his hands again, his own coat stained red, and was petrified that his son was going to die in his arms.

The carriage rolled up to John's row house, the driver glancing furtively back into the enclosure of his cab.

Michael heard them and ran outside. He'd been back all of ten minutes, having found the clinic closed. Frederic had already alighted, his expression imploring Michael to keep silent.

Frederic addressed the coachman, pulling the double fare from his wallet. "You'll get twice this tomorrow night if you keep your mouth shut," he enjoined, pressing the coins into the man's hand. The cabman nodded, and waited as Frederic and Michael pulled an unconscious John from the vehicle. They struggled a moment, throwing his arms over their shoulders. Finally, they dragged him inside and up the stairs to his bedchamber.

"What happened?" Michael asked, alarmed by John's blood-splattered coat, horrified when Frederic removed it to reveal his blood-soaked shirt beneath.

"They were in a scuffle," Frederic replied brusquely, ripping open the shirt and pressing a handkerchief to the wound. "Blackford knifed him."

"Is he alive?" Michael asked fearfully, placing a hand on John's chest in search of a heartbeat.

"Yes, but there is no time to lose. He needs a doctor before he bleeds to death. I'll find one as fast as I can. Lock the door behind me and douse the lights."

"Why?"

"Blackford's dead. There were witnesses. The police will be looking for us."

Michael regarded Frederic in dismay. "Did John–?"

"No. I did."

A knock on the front door silenced them.

"Damn!" Frederic cursed, moving to the window. To his relief, a woman was on the stoop. "Probably a meddling neighbor. Can you get rid of her, Michael?"

Michael hurried to the first floor. *Sweet Jesus, how did he wind up here, aiding and abetting a murderer? What lies would he have to make up now?* Closing his eyes, he drew a deep breath and intoned a "Hail Mary". He opened the door, stunned to see a woman he recognized. They had met in Richmond nearly three years ago when John was bringing her to New York. *"Lily?"*

"Father Andrews? What are you doing here?" Lily queried.

"Come in, come in," he insisted, gesturing emphatically for her to step inside quickly and out of the rain.

"Where is John?" she asked, looking across to the parlor, disconcerted by the priest's white face and disquietude.

"He's been hurt."

"Hurt?" Her eyes shot back to Michael. "How? Where is he?"

"Upstairs."

Lily flew up the stairs and charged into John's bedroom, running headlong into Frederic. He grabbed her arms, keeping her from the bed. "Who are you?" he demanded as she struggled to pull free, her eyes riveted on John.

Michael stepped through the door.

"My God!" she cried.

"Who are you?" Frederic demanded again.

"I'm his friend!" she replied, trying to wrench free, looking for the first time at Frederic. "John brought me here from Virginia. Who are you?"

"John's father."

Frederic read her astonishment. He released her, and she ran to John, clutching his cold hand. "John! John! Can you hear me?" She brought his hand to her lips and kissed it. "Sweet Lord!" she cried, caressing his face and stroking back his hair. "There's so much blood! Wake up, John! Please wake up!"

She looked over her shoulder at Frederic and Michael. "He's soaking wet. We have to get him out of these clothes and warm him up! And the blood – this cloth isn't working. We have to stem the blood!" She started to pull the shirt from John's arms. "Get some clean towels!"

"I will do this, Miss," Frederic declared, uneasy with her familiarity. John and she were obviously more than just friends. "Do you know a doctor who can help us? We need one right away. Neither of us know the city well enough–"

"Yes, I do."

"Can you get him to come here tonight?"

"I think so."

"Then please take Michael, go find him, and bring him back here," Frederic implored. He handed Michael his wallet. "Spend whatever it takes, Michael, but bring him back as quickly as possible."

Frederic followed them downstairs. Without another word, Lily and Michael slipped out into the dark city.

After they left, Frederic locked the door and doused the lamps in the parlor. He returned to John's bedchamber, pulling the curtains shut, leaving only a single candle burning on the floor as he tended to his son.

Within the hour, the clopping of horses' hooves resounded from the street and men's voices carried up to the quiet bedroom. There was a rap on the door. Frederic snuffed the candle. The rap came again, louder this time, and he peered through a crack in the curtains down to the street. Two men with uniforms and nightsticks stood at the door. The cabdriver must have ratted on them. Frederic prayed that they would not try to enter. The police rapped again and waited, and he worried that Lily and Michael would return while they were there. A carriage rattled up the street, slowing as it passed the row house, but then it lurched forward, turning a corner just a few blocks up. The officers paced around the yard a few times, glancing up the façade of the building, until finally, with shrugs, they mounted their horses, and trotted away. Not long afterward, the same cab of only minutes before pulled up to the house, and Lily, Michael, and another man alighted.

Lily returned to John's side as Doctor Hastings came away from the bed and washed his hands for the last time in a bowl of water on the dresser. Grabbing a towel and his medical bag, he motioned for Frederic to step out of the room.

They descended to the first floor, where Michael stood sentry in the darkened foyer, waiting for the police to return.

"It's just as well he's unconscious," the doctor stated, their only light the small candle that Frederic carried. "Stitching a deep wound can be very painful."

"Will he be all right?" Frederic asked.

"He has lost a lot of blood, but the bleeding has stopped, and I don't think any important organs were damaged, else he'd be dead already."

Frederic sighed in thanksgiving.

The doctor noted his relief and was compelled to speak again. "I am worried about his left lung. It may have been punctured. And there's the greater danger of infection. I saw this in the wounded in 1812. The infection will eat beyond the wound. It can kill him. He's likely to become very ill in the next few days."

Frederic's alarm was rekindled. "Then what are we to do?"

"Keep the fever down. Keep a tub of water and some ice on hand. If he gets very hot, submerge him in an ice bath. It's my own remedy. I've found it works. Other than that, there's nothing to do but wait. It all depends on how strong he is. It doesn't help that he's lost so much blood."

Frederic closed his eyes in dread. He'd hoped to leave on the Heir first thing in the morning, but now that was too dangerous. "What will it take to keep this just between us, doctor?" he pursued in another vein.

"Nothing," Dr. Hastings replied. "Your son is a good man, Mr. Duvoisin. He helped my nephew set up a practice – on your island. I hope he recovers." He removed his cloak from the coat rack and pulled it on. "Send for me if you need anything else."

Frederic returned to the bedroom once the physician had left. "We have to move him," he declared. "The police will be back."

"You can stay at my house," Lily offered. "It's small, but we'll make room."

Frederic nodded, and once again, Lily and Michael went out into the gloomy night, this time in search of Lily's friend, who owned a livery service. She would borrow a carriage that they could use to transport John downtown.

By dawn, they had settled John into her humble, two-bedroom home. Lily's children and Rose were moved to the tiny parlor, leaving the second bedroom to Frederic and Michael.

Michael caught a few hours sleep before setting out in search of ice. He got lucky when he went to a neighborhood tavern. The proprietor gave him the name of an ice supplier, and by the afternoon, a buckboard had pulled up in front of the house. Curious neighbors paused to watch as the massive block was unloaded. It had been cut out of a lake well north of the city in Rockland County and floated down the Hudson River. Now it sat on a wooden pallet in the backyard of the small house, covered in burlap. The December weather had turned mercifully cold, snow blowing in, and the ice would stay frozen.

Friday, December 7, 1838

Frederic came away from John's bedside early, nodding to Michael who now took up the vigil. As he stepped into the front parlor, he found Lily hastily tying her daughter's shoelaces, her twin brothers impatiently waiting.

"I can do it, Ma!" she complained. "We're gonna be late!"

Lily stood, gave both sons' coats a final tug, nodded her approval, and shooed all three out the door with the words, "No stopping along the way and come directly home after school!"

"We will, Ma!"

She sighed, then turned around, surprised to find Frederic studying her.

"You love them very much," he said.

"Yes," she admitted with a smile, "my pride and joy. How is John?"

"The same: still sleeping, no fever."

"Good." She moved toward the hearth. "Rose has already left for work. Can I make you something to eat?"

Frederic waved away the offer. "Not just yet. I'd like to talk, if you can spare the time."

"My time is my own. Rose will make my excuses at work."

She settled into an armchair and motioned for Frederic to do the same. When he had, he rubbed his brow, wondering how to broach the subject that had plagued him since Lily had rushed into John's bedroom not two days ago.

"You're quite a woman, Miss Clayton," he began. "Again, I thank you for your hospitality – what you've done for my son."

Lily smiled knowingly. "I'm also a woman of color, Mr. Duvoisin – a quadroon." She chuckled deeply at his astonishment. "You're surprised."

"Yes."

"Don't worry, sir, John is not the father of my children. I was a slave at Wisteria Hill, the plantation near Freedom. When John purchased it, we – that is my children, Rose, and myself – became his property as well, though not for long. We were emancipated within the year. Your son is a good man, sir, an *honorable* man. If not for him, I would never have made it north, my children would have remained uneducated, not much better off than those in bondage, and life would hold little hope for them."

"And what of their father?"

Lily bowed her head, the lump in her throat making it difficult to speak. "Henry, *my husband*, remains a slave. He was sold south nearly five years ago. I will never see him again."

Frederic heard the despair in her voice and knew a greater dread. "You love your husband."

Lily's head lifted. "With all my heart."

"All your heart?"

"Yes," she averred.

A lengthy silence descended on the room. Frederic wondered where John fit into the picture. It was obvious that this woman had feelings for his son. But were they deep? Or did John merely fill a void left in the wake of a family torn apart – the dismal abyss of loneliness? The possibility stirred a memory and thoughts of Hannah Fields clouded his musings. Hannah had not only filled a void; she had seen first-hand the atrocities of slavery, escaping to this very same city. *Did she and Nicholas still live here?*

"I know what troubles you, sir," Lily was saying.

Frederic was drawn back to the present. "Do you?"

"John was there when I needed him most," she answered slowly. "But I love John as surely as I love Henry. I will always love John."

Frederic scoffed at the assertion, and Lily raised an irate brow in return.

"I see you don't believe me."

"Pardon me, Mrs. Clayton, but you avow your love for your husband and, in the very next breath, proclaim your love for another."

"Is it so hard to believe that a woman could love two men?" Lily's voice cracked, her tears accumulating. "I assure you, sir, it isn't. I know I have two hearts. One was broken five years ago. The other is breaking now."

Frederic was dumbfounded and profoundly moved. Without warning, he thought of Colette, and everything was clear, crystal clear. "John is married now," he pronounced solemnly, "with a son or daughter on the way."

Lily digested the information, and her sadness intensified. She collected her emotions and whispered, "Then I pray he will be happy. He deserves to be happy. But first, I pray that he will recover."

Frederic nodded. Declining breakfast, he stood and retired.

The second day was as tranquil as the first. John remained unconscious, though he groaned now and then. His eyes would sometimes flutter open, and he'd mutter incoherently before they'd close again.

That evening, he showed signs of fever, shivering under the blankets as a sweat broke on his brow. Lily continuously applied a cool cloth to his forehead, but by morning, the fever was raging. He shuddered uncontrollably, and his teeth chattered violently. He bucked against the compresses and pulled at the bedcovers to get warm, even though Lily kept pulling them away. Frederic and Michael prepared an ice bath. They stripped off his nightclothes and submerged him in the frigid water. He cried out in agony, struggling against the arms that held him down, but the bath worked, and as they settled him back into the bed, he finally fell into a peaceful sleep. Within hours, the fever rose again, and he began to hallucinate, uttering fragmented phrases, reliving the confrontation with Blackford and calling out for Charmaine. Michael and Frederic submerged him in the water again, and again they succeeded in bringing the fever down.

Saturday, December 8, 1838

Frederic stirred in the cramped chair next to John's bed, the glaring sunlight streaming through the window slats, shocking him awake. He looked at John, who lay deathly still. Jumping up, he grabbed his son's hand and gasped in relief. It was cool, but not cold. Still, John was unresponsive to anyone's voice or touch, his breathing shallow, his face colorless.

Lily ran for Dr. Hastings again. An hour later, he examined John, then stepped out of the room with a grim shake of the head. "I'm sorry… I wish I could do more."

Michael studied Frederic, whose eyes were dark with grief, and pitied him. So valiant an effort, and now this. Michael looked down at John, his good and generous friend. The face was ghostly white, a face the priest had seen too many times while presiding over a bedside, administering the Last Rites. It was the face of death. He thought of his daughter. She would not be here to say farewell to the husband she loved.

Michael's eyes filled with tears. Silently, he recited the prayers for the dying, finishing with: *Sacred Heart of Jesus, pray for us... St. Jude, helper of the hopeless, pray for us... Father in Heaven, restore him to us…*

Late Evening

Frederic sat beside his son's lifeless body. With head bent, he clutched one of John's hands between his own, and brought it to his mouth in a fervent prayer. "Dear Lord," he murmured, "don't take him from me – not now!" He squeezed the hand harder as if he could infuse it with his own vitality. "I promised Charmaine that I would bring you home, but not this way, Dear God, not this way!" He buried his head in the bed clothing and wept.

John looked down upon the curious scene unfolding below. His father was praying over his body, but he didn't feel the man's pain, only serenity. *Was he dreaming?* Someone was calling his name – not from the room, but from above and behind him. He turned slowly, and the corner of the ceiling opened wide, bathing everything in splendor. Far off, a woman was walking toward him, silhouetted against the bright light, and he shielded his eyes to better see her. She called his name again, her voice unfamiliar. Her hair was golden brown, her eyes like honey. She was plain, yet beautiful in her placid mien, and something in the way she moved reminded him of Colette. He knew she was his mother.

"John," she breathed again. "I've longed to see you."

There was a great distance between them, but his heart swelled with her greeting as if she were only a breath away. He took one last look at his father and turned back to her.

Charmantes

Chapter 8

Beneath a blackened sky and cold, steady rain, the sorrowful procession picked its way along the craggy path to the cemetery. They finally stood before the open grave, where Michael Andrews intoned the dirge: *Eternal rest give unto him, O Lord, and let perpetual light shine upon him.* The men lowered John's casket into the deep hole, and the first shovelfuls of dirt were thrown on it. Charmaine closed her eyes and wept pitifully into Frederic's shirtfront, his strong arms encircling her. The twins were wailing. Paul was at their side, his eyes stormy. Flanked by Rose and Mercedes, George's head bowed further to hide his tears, though his shoulders shook with grief. Charmaine couldn't bear it. She was going to die, too... *Oh God, let me die, too!*

She awoke, her heart pounding and her body saturated in a cold sweat. She was staring at the ceiling. It had been a dream – just a dream, yet she knew John was dead. She struggled out of bed, rolling with her cumbersome belly, but as her feet touched the floor, she doubled over in pain. She was in labor.

Elizabeth smiled at John as he approached, but oddly, the distance between them remained constant. His eyes left her face for the small child she held by the hand. It was Pierre, smiling up at him. John broke into a run and, after an eternity, reached them. He lifted Pierre up, and the boy flung his arms around his neck. "Papa," he said. "Where were you?"

"Right here, Pierre," John whispered. "I was right here."

"We missed you! Mama and I missed you!"

John turned to his mother, but Colette smiled up at him now. He reached for her, and she stepped into his embrace. "You did well, John," she murmured. "You righted the wrong, and now it is over."

"Colette," he breathed, "Colette." He hugged mother and son tightly to him and savored her sweet fragrance. He was finally at peace.

Charmaine groped through the darkness to Paul's room, hunched over with another contraction. She rapped on his door, pounding harder when he didn't answer.

"Charmaine?" he queried when he opened to find her there. "What is it?"

Then he knew. The baby was on the way, one month early. He lifted her into his arms and quickly carried her back to her room. "Stay here, I'll get Rose and Loretta and set out for Doctor Hastings."

"Paul!" she called as he reached the door. He turned to face her. "John is dead. Dear God – I know he's dead!"

He returned to the bed, grasping her hand and holding it tightly as another contraction seized her, waiting for the pain to subside. "You don't know that, Charmaine."

"I had a dream," she moaned, her breathing rapid, "but I know it was real! I've lost him!"

"You're in labor, Charmaine, and your mind is playing tricks on you. Now try to relax, and I'll be back soon."

He left her again, beset with worry.

Marie Elizabeth Duvoisin was born not two hours later, a loud wail greeting the doctor, who arrived too late. It had been a surprisingly easy labor, especially for a first child, and Rose beamed at her prowess as midwife.

Doctor Hastings stayed until he was sure that mother and child were fine. The babe was small, but quite healthy, he reassured. Her early delivery was induced by anxiety, he diagnosed, which he admonished Charmaine to subdue, lest she bring on complications. He spoke to Paul on his way out. "I hope your brother won't be disappointed with a daughter."

"No, Adam," Paul murmured, "John won't be disappointed."

Charmaine gazed down at her infant daughter, who was already searching for a nipple. She wept, her tears falling onto her daughter's head, a baptism of abounding love.

"Marie, my sweet little Marie, if only your father were here..."

Leaning over, Charmaine kissed her head, the fuzz of red-blonde hair, soft as down. The baby looked like John, already she looked like John, save the blue eyes, the beautiful blue eyes that opened now and then. Her tiny fist clutched Charmaine's finger, and Charmaine brought it to her lips for another tender kiss.

Rose and Loretta bustled about the room, removing the soiled linens, shooing people away from the door. "Give Charmaine a moment's peace. She wants to have the babe all to herself for a spell." The twins had been awoken with all the commotion, and they were the most anxious to see the newest Duvoisin.

Marie began to fuss, letting out a fierce cry that turned rhythmic, the volume increasing. Rose quickly dropped what she was doing and came around the bed. "She wants to nurse," she stated mildly and proceeded to show Charmaine the proper way to offer the infant her breast. The tiny lips rooted around and latched firmly onto the proffered nipple. The suckling sensation was both uncomfortable and exquisite. Together they fed a burgeoning contentment, and Charmaine was blanketed in an unfathomable peace.

When Marie fell asleep, she made herself presentable, allowing her pillows to be fluffed before sitting back into them. Twice Loretta attempted to put Marie in the cradle, but Charmaine cuddled her daughter all the closer. "No, let me hold her. I need to hold her." Loretta nodded in understanding. Rose invited the family in for their first visit.

Yvette and Jeannette danced with delight as they beheld their niece.

"Wait until Johnny comes home," Yvette said.

"He's going to be so proud," Jeannette added.

Paul stood at the foot of the bed, admiring the tender vision. Charmaine looked radiant, bearing the twins' comments with quiet dignity, a faint smile on her lips. He wished she were cradling his child. He loved her, he suddenly realized. If John didn't return, he vowed to take care of her and perhaps, if she'd have him, marry her.

Sunday, December 16, 1838

Charmaine had enjoyed a wonderful birthday, as wonderful as it could be without John. Next year would be different, everyone reassured her. This year, the entire household had taken great pains to make it a happy occasion. She even felt better, nearly restored to the woman she'd been before her confinement.

Now, with Marie sound asleep in her cradle, she stroked the mane on the rocking horse. She turned to the other birthday gifts, most of them for her daughter. Charmaine didn't mind; she enjoyed looking at the pretty little dresses and stockings. She spent the next hour or so rearranging drawers to make room for Marie's layette. She decided to combine John's clothing into five drawers, as there was more room in his chiffonier than hers.

She was working on the second drawer when she found it – tucked between two shirts, neatly folded and worn. As if scorched, she dropped Colette's love letter, her shaking hands flying to her mouth, the sheets fluttering to the floor.

Charmaine composed herself. She didn't know it was a love letter. She had only read a small portion of it that day almost a year and a half ago.

The days, the weeks, the months fell away, and she was back in John's room, searching for the twins, rankled by the draft that had strewn so many papers on the floor. She was picking them up again, rearranging and reading them. It didn't seem possible that it was John, *her John,* who had stormed into the room that morning – that such terrible rage and hatred had ever existed between them. And yet, she'd gladly go back, if only he could be with her now.

The letter remained on the floor, yet, like a magnet, tugged at her heart. Indecisive, she stepped back. She shouldn't read it. *But John may never come home, and he is your husband. You have a right to know! You have that right.* But did she want to know? *It's no longer private,* her mind screamed. *John has told you everything... But has he really? Isn't it better to know for sure?*

Swiftly, she snatched it up. The last page was on top, and she read the closing: *Until we meet again, Your loving Colette.* She closed her eyes and swallowed hard. Why was she putting herself through this? She folded the pages, angry that she'd started at all. John had been furious when she had read his private correspondence before. She would not be guilty of doing so now. Besides, she didn't want to know Colette's innermost feelings for John, refused to give them power over her.

Drawing a ragged breath, Charmaine quickly replaced the letter in the drawer. Her terrible nightmare took hold, and a chill chased up her spine. If the dream were real, if John *had* died, he was finally with Colette. He had her all to himself now, for his father had remained behind with the living. This letter that John cherished and cradled amidst his personal belongings was testimony to his desperate love for her, even unto death. No wonder he wasn't afraid of dying in pursuit of Robert Blackford. He knew Colette was waiting for him in the afterlife.

Charmaine thought of the single letter that she had received from him over three months ago. *If Colette were alive today, I would still choose you.* But Colette wasn't alive. She was in paradise with Pierre at her side. John was with his family now. She knew it. Charmaine just knew it. She closed her eyes to the vivid vision of them embracing him, and she fought back tears. "Oh God!" she moaned, and threw herself on the bed, sobbing bitterly.

Thursday, December 20, 1838

Paul was alarmed to find the Heir docked in the harbor. She had left Charmantes late November and should have been well on her way to Europe by now. "Will!" Paul called as he climbed aboard, "what has happened?"

The captain frowned. "I'm afraid I have some disturbing news, Paul."

He recounted the Heir's arrival in New York, and the disturbing events that followed. Paul rubbed the back of his neck, not knowing what to make of it, Charmaine's premonition taking root.

"Your father told me to weigh anchor on the ninth if they didn't show up, but I waited an extra day to be certain. I even sent a man in search of your brother. Apparently, the police were all over his place. They came snooping around the harbor, too – on the docks and at the warehouse – but were tightlipped, so I don't know what happened. I would have been here sooner, but the weather down the coast was rotten, blizzard conditions nearly half the way."

Will read the dread on Paul's face and added, "Perhaps your father and John knew about the police and laid low. I know your father was concerned about police involvement."

"Or," Paul countered aloud, "Blackford injured them, and the authorities were looking for someone to contact the family."

Will shrugged. "At this point, we don't know enough to assume the worst."

"True, but how are we going to find out?"

Paul spent the rest of the day working alongside the dockworkers and sailors. The grueling labor of reloading the ship helped clear his mind so that he could think rationally. He toyed with the idea of setting sail for New York immediately, but ruled that out when he thought of Charmaine. He couldn't tell her what he'd learned. She'd be terribly upset, and if he left before Christmas, she'd *know* something was wrong. That would add up to two more weeks of worry. No, the answers would have to wait just a bit longer – until Christmas was over.

With dusk on the harbor and the lading finished, Paul came to a decision. The Tempest, his newest ship, was due in port any day now. After the holiday, he'd take her on to New York himself.

Christmas Eve, 1838

Charmaine sat on the sofa in the drawing room, little Marie comfortably nestled in her arms, sound asleep. This dismal Christmas Eve mocked last year's sad holiday, for although the manor was serene, it was a shaky peace. They hadn't heard from either John or Frederic for three months now. Though Paul assured her that no news was good news, Charmaine knew that her premonition had signaled some dire event. As she adored her babe, she offered up another petition to the litany of those that had gone before.

Rose and the twins fastened the last of the festive decorations to the mantel, their stockings hanging from the fireplace in anticipation of St. Nicholas. The girls had even fashioned a stocking for Marie. When Charmaine warned them about expecting too much, Yvette had countered that St. Nicholas was bound to come this year, since there was no Agatha to frighten the merry old elf away. Charmaine looked at Paul, but he seemed unaffected, his eyes twinkling in knowing merriment.

Joshua and George were playing a game of chess (they got along famously) while Loretta and Mercedes leafed through a catalog of baby items. Mercedes was large with child, her own days of confinement nearing their end. Soon little Marie would have a playmate.

Paul stood at the fireplace, deep in contemplation, his eyes going frequently to Charmaine. His attentiveness was not lost on Loretta or Rose. Espoir had been all but forgotten, and though he was needed more desperately here, they knew that Charmaine was the reason he stayed on Charmantes.

George was worried, too, but his concern centered on John and Frederic. Paul had told him about the Heir's aborted mission, and although he'd advised Paul not to jump to conclusions, he'd conjured a few terrible scenarios himself. When Paul decided to head for New York, he was relieved. If Mercedes weren't so near her time, he would have volunteered to go. But he wouldn't put his wife through what Charmaine was enduring.

Presently, he stood and conceded the game to Joshua. Helping Mercedes out of her seat, they bade everyone goodnight.

Charmaine looked to the yawning twins. "It's time you found your beds as well. You don't want St. Nicholas to pass you by. I hear that he only visits the homes of sleeping children." They went off with Rose.

With an expansive stretch, Joshua said goodnight, and with some reservations, Loretta said the same. Paul walked over to Charmaine and sat beside her. He didn't say a word, but he studied her with a faint smile.

Despite her sadness, Charmaine treasured the happiness that Marie stirred in her heart. She looked at him and saw the laughter in his eyes. "What are you smiling at?" she asked.

He shook his head and gave a slight shrug as if to say 'nothing'. When he was certain that no one would return, he reached behind the sofa and retrieved four packages. Though each one was small, they were wrapped, complete with ribbons.

"What is this?" she asked in surprise.

"St. Nicholas has arrived," he said, before walking to the hearth and depositing two gifts in each stocking.

"What are they?"

"A set of playing cards for Yvette and dice."

"You're joking!" Charmaine laughed.

"On the contrary," Paul replied.

"But your father will be furious!"

"If he comes home, I'll be happy to face his punishment."

The spontaneous comment annihilated the cheerful moment, and Charmaine bowed her head to a sudden surge of tears. "I'm a coward, Paul," she whispered, looking down at her daughter. "If I faced reality, maybe this emptiness in my heart would begin to heal."

Her declaration reverberated about the room. Hadn't he come to believe the worst himself – John and his father had attempted to apprehend Blackford on the sixth of December and something had gone terribly wrong? *Were they dead?* Paul clenched his fists angrily, a violent reaction that he had been unable to quell since the day the Heir had docked on the island.

Charmaine distracted him from his murderous thoughts. "What is in the packages for Jeannette?" she asked, changing the subject.

"A locket and a miniature horse," Paul replied, forcing a smile.

"Would you hold Marie for me?" she asked, wondering whether he would be comfortable with the request. *Had he ever held a newborn?*

But the invitation pleased him, and he plucked the baby out of her arms, cradling her as if he had done so many times before. Charmaine realized that he'd probably held Pierre and the twins when they were infants.

"Where are you going?" he asked.

"You'll see," she answered, sweeping from the room.

She came back with her own gifts and stuffed them into the girl's stockings, which were now bulging with booty. Satisfied, she faced him. "Marie won't sleep much longer, so I had best get some rest."

He nodded, for he had often heard the baby's cries during the night, but when she reached for Marie, he shook his head. "I'll take her," he offered.

Nestling the infant in the crook of his arm, he stood, put his other arm around Charmaine's shoulders, and accompanied her upstairs. The lamps burned low in the sconces, the house ever so quiet. When they arrived at her door, Paul strode into the room and gently laid Marie in her cradle.

He turned back to Charmaine, considering her in the lamplight. Finally he spoke. "What would you like for Christmas, Charmaine?"

"John," she gushed without thought, her throat constricted, "only John."

Just the answer he wanted! "Well, Charmaine," he proceeded, "I've been giving that a great deal of thought – ever since the night Marie was born. The day after Christmas, I'm going out in search of your errant husband and my father. It's about time we found out what has happened." Seeing her surprise, he continued. "One of my ships is in port and is scheduled to travel to New York and Boston. I'll be on board when she sets sail."

"Paul? You'd do that?" she asked, her heart leaping with hope.

"My Christmas present to you. However–" he hesitated, hoping to provide a beacon in the storm he feared she had yet to weather "–I want a promise from you."

"What is it?"

"If I come back with bad news – and I'm not saying I will – I want your promise that, after a reasonable time has passed, you will consider marrying me."

Charmaine lowered her gaze to the floor, bombarded by many emotions.

"Is marriage to me so revolting an idea?" he queried, misreading her.

"No, Paul – of course it's not," she choked out, her eyes meeting his.

Realizing that she was about to cry, he enclosed her in his arms. She grabbed hold of him and wept softly. He stroked her hair and kissed the top her head, his heart aching with the feel of her in his embrace. When she lifted her head, he could hold back no longer. He lowered his lips to hers and tenderly kissed her. She accepted his gentle overture, then stepped back. "I love you, Charmaine," he whispered hoarsely. "I want to take care of you and Marie."

She was astounded, and new tears filled her eyes; now she ached for him.

"I – I know you do, Paul," she murmured, wiping her cheeks dry. "And I thank you for being here for me. But I can't–"

"Very well, Charmaine, I won't press you. I just want you to know that you need never be alone."

She inhaled raggedly, aware that she would have to face reality sooner or later. "I will consider your offer," she said. "But only after I know what has happened, when all hope is lost."

Paul retreated to the door. "Goodnight," he murmured, then slowly retired to his lonely chambers.

For a moment, Charmaine considered running after him. She longed to sleep in someone's arms, not to make love with him, but to be held, to feel protected once again, to shake off this overwhelming despair.

Marie began to stir, and she knew she wasn't alone at all. She lifted her daughter and climbed into bed. Marie nuzzled close, eagerly accepting her breast. Soon they fell into a peaceful, symbiotic slumber.

Christmas Day, 1838

Rebecca Remmen placed the boiled potatoes on the table and settled into her chair, watching Wade carve thin slices of the ham he'd brought home for their Christmas dinner. With fresh bread and sweet green beans, it was their finest meal of the year. They'd have the ham for a few days, and Rebecca would coax a soup from the bone, stretching this rare indulgence into a week's worth of meals.

It was pleasant having Wade home for the day. Usually, she was alone, and more often than not, lonely. She'd just turned seventeen, and Wade would not allow her to work anywhere in town, fearful that a young woman as lovely as she would get herself into more trouble than she could handle, especially with surly longshoremen coming and going daily. She could take care of herself, but she hadn't convinced Wade of that, so other than the weekends when they'd stroll into town together to shop for necessities and socialize, Rebecca scarcely went further than their tiny yard. Paul Duvoisin's grand ball had been the single most enchanting event in her short, disenchanting life, an occasion that she treasured.

Three years ago, she and her brother had reached Charmantes, and life had drastically improved. They had food on their table, clothes on their backs, and a roof over their heads. Rebecca wanted more: to write a letter, to read a good book, to cipher so that *she* could pay Maddy Thompson for their purchases. She was tired of cleaning the spotless cottage, sick of weeding the flowerbeds, hated tending the vegetable garden. She'd darned enough socks and mended enough shirts to clothe an army. But if she must do it, she'd rather do it for a husband. When her chores for the day were done, she would step out of the cottage and sit under a palm tree in the backyard, waiting for Wade to come home. Each night as dusk fell, she fantasized about a life of adventure, but most of all, she dreamed about Paul.

Her life had changed forever on the day the Captain of the Black Star had marched them in front of the man and declared them stowaways. Paul did not scoff at her brother's daring scheme to start over. He listened when Wade described the squalid slums of Richmond. He understood their unorthodox pilgrimage to the 'promised land' – Les Charmantes – the fabled paradise island of the Duvoisin dynasty. He nodded when Wade insisted that he was strong and willing to work, that given a chance, he would make the Duvoisin family proud.

Those first few days, Paul saw to it that they were fed and clothed. He set them up in the neglected cottage where they now lived and put Wade to work. Part of her brother's wages would go toward the purchase of that property. Over time, Wade did prove himself, assuming greater responsibility, ignoring the grumbles of some of the older men. Now three years later, he was in charge of the mill and had the respect of many, all because of Paul. For this, Rebecca's innocent heart placed Paul on a pedestal. He was her hero.

Though he hardly knew she existed, she was thrilled when she and Wade were invited to his spectacular ball. But Wade didn't want to go, insisting that they'd be out of place. She disagreed, and for weeks she'd pestered, wheedled, and begged, until finally, he gave in. Unfortunately, he was right. She was unprepared for the cruel disillusionment of stepping into that grand banquet hall and beholding the most elegant of women in their finest garb. Paul would never notice her in her plain dress, certainly wouldn't dream of asking her to dance.

On a whim, she sought him out alone. All she needed was a few moments of his time; he'd have to notice her then. She knew she was attractive. She'd heard the whistles and catcalls from the sailors when she and Wade passed by Dulcie's. But she had botched her opportunity in the Duvoisin kitchen, had acted like a ninny. She'd vowed to be truthful with him. Yet, where had it gotten her? In his eyes, she was little more than a silly, tongue-tied girl, blurting out her childish adulation. For months, she had fretted over her behavior that night.

Her brother's illness last September changed all that. Although Paul might not like her, at least now he knew she wasn't some simpering simpleton. She could stick up for herself *and* her brother. Like Wade, she had strength of character.

"Rebecca?" Wade interrupted her deep contemplation. "What's the matter with you?" he demanded. "Why are you always daydreaming?"

She smiled brightly at him. "I'm sorry. What were you saying?"

"Just that I'm going to be extremely busy for the next few weeks."

"Why? Is Paul going to Espoir again?"

"Weren't you listening to anything I said?" he chided with a scowl. "He's leaving for New York tomorrow to track down his father and his brother. He'll be on the Tempest when she casts off at dawn."

"But why is he going to do that?" she queried in alarm, remembering Felicia's words just yesterday. *Charmaine has him wrapped around her little finger. Why, he's so blind he'll do anything for her.*

"He's worried," Wade explained. "He hasn't had word from them in over three months. He'll be gone for at least two weeks and he's putting me in *total* control of the sawmill. That means no George checking in."

Rebecca cared little about her brother's gratification. She was very upset and ate most of her meal in silence, her brother's comments doing cartwheels in her head. When he left the table to leaf through a newspaper, she slipped next door to wish the Flemmings a happy Christmas and speak privately to Felicia.

"Did you know that Paul intended to follow his father and brother to New York?" she asked when she and Felicia stepped out the back door.

"I'm not surprised," the woman said flippantly. "Charmaine's probably cried on his shoulder, and now he wants to make her happy by bringin' John home."

"But if she's after Paul as you say, why would she do that?"

Felicia laughed. "She doesn't *really* want her husband back. She just wants Paul to think that she does."

"But why would she want him to think that?" Rebecca pressed.

Irritated by the obtuse question, Felicia's face twisted in haughty contempt. "Agatha got rid of Pierre for the money, and Frederic and John are probably dead at her brother's hands. Charmaine will have it all if Doctor Blackford kills Paul, too – her baby the sole heir to the Duvoisin fortune."

"Do you really think that Doctor Blackford has killed Frederic and John?"

"You figure it out! Why else haven't they sent word?"

Rebecca was truly worried. If Paul's brother and father *were* dead, then he was headed for the same trap.

Felicia babbled on. "I wouldn't be surprised if she's working *with* Blackford."

"Oh, Felicia, I can't believe that!" Rebecca objected.

"No? Well, you don't know the woman like I do. Everyone knows that her father's a murderer. She's been sly from the start. I'd even lay money down that her daughter isn't a Duvoisin. She married John in April, one week after he came home. Babies take nine months to arrive. Hers came in eight."

Rebecca could not sleep that night. She didn't believe everything Felicia had told her, but still, she was concerned. Lying there in the dark, in the dismal quiet that mimicked her life, she decided that she was sick and tired of sitting back and doing nothing.

Rising, she tiptoed into her brother's room and groped furtively through his drawers, pulling out trousers and a shirt. She couldn't write, so she couldn't leave him a note, and she wasn't fool enough to wake him up. If she told him where she was going, she wouldn't get out the door. No, let him think she'd gone off somewhere on the island to be alone. She dressed quickly, pulling a length of rope through the belt loops of the baggy trousers and knotting it at her waist. She grabbed his cap off the peg by the door and tucked her hair into it, then took a chunk of leftover bread from the cupboard and crept out of the slumbering cottage.

In no time, she was on the wharf, standing before a tall ship, majestic and still on the rippling water. Stealing a glance in both directions, she quickly scurried up the gangplank. A couple of sailors were asleep on the open deck, but she hastened past them with her head bowed. Nobody could see her face in the darkness.

Where to hide? When she and her brother had stowed away over three years ago, they had squeezed between the large casks in the hold, squatting there for nearly a day. She did not fancy doing that now, but it was the best way to lay low until the vessel was well into the Atlantic. Then the activity on the deck would die down, and she could meander up above. If she kept her head down, no one would take much notice. She'd wait for the right moment to slip into Paul's cabin and hide there. She hoped that he would stay above deck until nightfall. By the time he found her, they'd have voyaged a fair distance, and she'd have time to reason with him.

Wednesday, December 26, 1838

Paul left the house while the stars still studded the sky, a gibbous moon bathing the front lawns in heavenly light. He had said his goodbyes the night before, savoring his last few minutes with Charmaine.

"Take good care of Marie while I'm gone."

"You don't know how much this means to me, Paul," she had whispered.

"I think I do."

By the time he boarded the Tempest, the first rays of sunlight streaked the eastern sky. The sailors were preparing for departure in the predawn light. Philip Conklin, the Tempest's captain, greeted him. Philip knew this was not a typical voyage, although the tobacco in the hold would be sold at auction in New York. Paul assisted with the preparations, and in less than a half-hour, the Tempest was pushed from the pier. The tide was going out and the wind took hold of the sails. The ship sped out of the harbor, through the cove, and onto the open sea.

Six days, Paul surmised, six days and he'd finally have some answers. What would they be? Was he prepared for them? Never had he known turmoil of this magnitude, and he prayed that God would be merciful. Did he want his brother dead? Certainly not. He was glad that John had found happiness, even at his own expense. John and Charmaine loved one another. For that reason alone, he wanted to bring him home alive. But if John didn't return, Paul was prepared to step in and attempt to cherish her as his brother had. Don't think about it, his reasonable mind cautioned, for he knew her pain would be devastating. *What is done is done. Very soon, you will know the truth.*

Rebecca paced the cramped cabin. Her plan had gone off without a hitch. Since early afternoon, she had sat quietly in the stuffy cubicle awaiting Paul. She was tired and ached all over from hours squashed between hogsheads in the hold. The small bed looked inviting, but they hadn't traveled far enough yet, and she had to be awake in case somebody ventured into the cabin before dark. If that happened, she would bow her head, mumble an excuse, and scurry away. Once darkness fell, she began to breathe easier. The first day was over.

The hour grew late. Six bells rang out, signaling the sixth half-hour of the night watch – eleven o'clock – and still Paul did not come. She began to think she was in the wrong cabin, though this one was next to the captain's quarters and spacious in comparison to the first mate's cell. So much the better if he didn't bed down here. She'd wait an extra day before confronting him. There would be time enough to convince him not to do anything dangerous, especially for his scheming sister-in-law. She, Rebecca Remmen, loved him – was *free* to love him! Perhaps she wasn't as old and as sophisticated as Charmaine Duvoisin, but she had never belonged to another man either. Closeted together for days on end, he would recognize her love and hopefully return it.

She espied a knapsack tossed beneath a small table and opened it. It was filled with essential, finely tailored clothing. This was definitely Paul's cabin. She concluded that he had chosen to sleep above deck, under the starry sky. Rubbing her eyes, she realized her fatigue was rivaled only by her hunger. She ate the last of her dry bread and washed it down with fresh water from the bucket that sat in the corner, then stretched out on the small cot and turned toward the wall. The rocking ship lulled her to sleep.

Paul entered the cabin near midnight and groped his way to the desk where an anchored lamp sat. Blindly, he struck the flint and ignited the wick with a tiny spark, illuminating the room with a low, glowing light. He rubbed the back of his neck, sitting down on a stool to pull off his boots and shirt. He stood to unfasten his trousers when he noticed the bundle in the middle of his bunk. Frowning, he stepped closer, staring down in irritation at the young man with long hair sound asleep in his bed.

"What in hell?" He gave the lad a sharp nudge.

The boy groaned and turned over. His eyes fluttered open in confusion, and he scrambled from the bed, brushing the hair from his face.

"*Jesus!*" Paul swore angrily. This was no lad at all, but one Rebecca Remmen. "What the hell are *you* doing here?" he roared.

"I – I stowed away," Rebecca muttered.

"How? When?"

"Last night," she said anxiously. "It was easy. Everyone was asleep."

Paul rolled his eyes in utter amazement. "Why?"

Rebecca took a deep breath and bit her bottom lip. "Because I was afraid for you. I don't want you to – to get hurt – to be murdered."

Paul drove both hands through his hair. *"Don't you think I can take care of myself?"*

"No – I mean – I don't know," she stammered. "I was just–" She threw her hands up in the air. "It's just that I love you – and I don't want to lose you."

Terrific! Paul thought, his jaw clenched. *Just what I need! An imbecile chasing me up the North Atlantic Coast!* "Are you mad or just stupid?" he expostulated.

Rebecca's eyes flashed fire. She had bared her heart, and all he could do was call her names. "Go ahead and make fun of me!" she blazed. "But I'm the only one who cares what happens to you!"

"I don't need you to care. I don't want you to care! Now get out, I'm tired!" He thrust a finger toward the cabin door.

"What?" she asked, aghast.

"Get out," he reiterated indifferently. "Find somewhere else to sleep."

"But – I can't go above deck. When the men realize I'm a woman they'll–"

His derisive laugh struck her dumb. "*Woman?* You have nothing to fear, my dear," he countered, his eyes raking her from head to toe. "They'll see that you're just a little girl. Or is it a boy?" He thought of Charmaine, and added, "After all, no *woman* would ever do what you've just done."

Her throat stung, yet she gritted her teeth. "I'm more woman than your precious Charmaine!" she hissed, as if reading his mind.

His eyes narrowed. "What would you know of Charmaine?"

"More than you can guess," she answered, raising her chin a notch.

"Try me," he growled. This girl was more trouble than she was worth.

"I know she's using you to get what she wants!" Rebecca exclaimed callously. "She doesn't love you, but she knows *you* love *her!* She's certain that you'll do anything for her if she just acts shy and occasionally looks your way. She throws crumbs at your feet, and you grovel for the few you can catch!" In her insane jealousy, Rebecca blathered on. "It's disgusting really, and everyone on Charmantes is laughing at you!"

"Out – *get out!"* he bellowed. In two strides, he grabbed her by the arm and pushed her toward the door.

"No! You can't send me out there!" she shrieked, slapping him across the cheek with all her might. "Let go of me!"

He was astonished, and his eyes turned steely, infuriated by her smug face, her hand poised to strike again. "Oh no you don't!" he snarled, catching her wrist and giving her one hard shake.

"Let – me – go!"

"I've had enough of you, Rebecca Remmen. It's high time somebody put you in your place."

He dragged her across the cabin and sat hard on the cot, pulling her across his lap. She didn't scream, but she fought like a wild animal, and he had all he could do to pin her flailing limbs with one hand while he wrenched the rope belt free with the other. He yanked the pants down, baring her firm, creamy bottom. His palm smarted with the first crack of his hand, but he was gratified when she cried out. She thrashed violently, nearly squirming free. He readjusted his grip until she lay taut across his thighs. This time, he spanked her harder. She yelped, then sunk her teeth into his forearm. He released her with a loud oath, the bite deep, blood trickling from his wrist. *"You damn little wench!"*

She clambered from his lap and tripped over the trousers bunched around her ankles, lying sprawled at his feet. He threw back his head and laughed, lunging forward and grabbing hold of the pants, pulling them free. She was up in a flash, streaking bare-bum to the portal. But before she could throw the door open, he was upon her again, yanking her around. His anger had evaporated, vanquished beneath a rush of passion, the animal instinct to dominate and conquer, and he relished the arousal her struggles had ignited.

"Now where will you go without any pantaloons? Or aren't you afraid of those men anymore?" She pushed hard against him, but he didn't budge. "I know," he chuckled. "You aren't frightened. You're a strapping lad! Let me see your muscles."

Before she could react, he ripped the shirt open, revealing perfect little breasts, round and inviting. Aghast, she pummeled his hairy chest with both fists, but he ignored the admirable attack as he swept the tattered garment from her shoulders, leaving her naked before him. He pinned her to the door, grabbing her bottom with one hand and the hair at her nape with the other. He pulled her head back and kissed her passionately, forcing her lips apart and thrusting his tongue into her mouth. His hand traveled from her buttocks along the curve of her hip and up to her breast, which he cupped and kneaded.

The sensual assault left Rebecca reeling. She relinquished the battle with a feeble punch, prisoner to Paul's blistering kiss and her own smoldering passion. If he didn't release her mouth she would faint, and yet she hungrily kissed him back, quickly noting how it was done. Her mutinous hands grabbed hold of his corded arms and swept over his broad shoulders. She savored the feel of his skin under her palms, her breasts crushed against his rock-hard chest, and luxuriated in the arousing heat of his body.

He abruptly tore away, and she teetered on weak legs until he scooped her up and turned toward the bed. She didn't fight him when he laid her there, observing him through hooded eyes as he ripped off his trousers and joined her.

"So you want to be a woman?" he queried, his voice husky.

"Your woman," she murmured, titillated by the unbridled lust in his eyes.

Her words were as intoxicating as her unadorned beauty, and his loins ached for her, the fire that burned there volcanic. His mouth possessed hers again, a consuming, breathless kiss. When he released her, she sighed, but his lips pursued their sensual assault, tracing a searing path along her jaw and down her throat. His coarse moustache raked her soft flesh, meeting the callused hand that fondled a firm, yet pliable breast, sampling the delectable orb, teasing the nipple with his tongue until it stood erect.

The familiar wanton desire that was triggered whenever she looked upon him was stoked to an unbearable degree, and she dug her fingers into his shoulders, joyous tears trickling into her hairline. His roving hands continued to explore the curve of her hips, her belly, the inside of her thighs. Upward he stroked, until his fingers found and probed that most delicate of spots, already moist in anticipation of his lovemaking, the center of all pleasure, craving him now in unchaste abandon. She groaned with expectancy and agony when he finally mounted her.

She was a virgin. In all his thirty years, he had had many women, but never a virgin. The thought that this young woman had never lain with another fanned his ardor. He would make certain that she yearned for him when this was over, so he fought to subdue his soaring need and lay still until her pain ebbed, basking in the sweet sensations of rapacious lust, until he could stand it no longer, her supple body responding beneath him. Shifting on his elbows, he began to slowly move inside of her, each throbbing stroke exquisite.

Rebecca pressed her head back into the pillow and closed her eyes to ecstasy. He kissed her all over, his lips constantly coming back to hers, then roaming afield again. His rhythmic invasion evoked familiar, ravenous sensations in her loins. As he grabbed her buttocks, she wrapped her legs around his hips to receive more of him. He rode her harder, faster, plunging ever deeper, and her body answered with a will of its own, hips writhing, the sublime sensations indescribable – building – the summit nearly reached. Suddenly, he groaned and, with one final thrust, collapsed upon her, clutching her closely in resplendent gratification. Surprisingly, it was his stillness, the press of his body, that catapulted her into the realm of rapture, an upheaval of such enormous proportion that she shuddered violently, the spasm sucking him into the very depths of her womanhood, leaving her tummy and pelvis quivering, surpassing any act she'd initiated in her lonely bedroom. She lay with her eyes closed, astounded, her heart pounding, her breathing as ragged as his. When he moved, she hugged him closer, reveling in the feel of his blanketing body.

Finally he rolled on his side, still very close in the cramped cot.

"That shouldn't have happened," he muttered, more to himself than her.

She frowned up at him. "I thought it was wonderful."

He smiled in spite of himself, a plaintive smile. She was lovely, and she was a woman. He'd just made her *his* woman. But he was already thinking about Charmaine and was ashamed. This was the second time he had proposed to her and the second time he had dishonored that proposal. *What was the matter with him*? He rose and began to dress.

"I love you," Rebecca whispered, desperate tears welling in her eyes. "You'll marry me now, won't you?"

Paul looked back at her and saw her anguish. "No, Rebecca, I won't marry you. Like I said, what just happened between us – it shouldn't have happened."

"It's your precious Charmaine!" she lashed out. "*Fool!* You *think* you love her!"

"Don't!" he warned, angry with himself when she faced the wall. She was crying, but he feared that if he consoled her, he'd take her all over again. Unsettled by that thought, he grabbed the blanket that had fallen to the floor. As he shook it out to spread over her, he noticed a strange scar on her derrière, just below the curve of her hip.

"What's this?" he growled, touching the mark, irritated by the imperfection.

She vaulted as if branded, then recoiled. "It's from my father," she ground out. "He was cruel, too!"

The declaration hit its mark, and Paul stepped back, duly chastised. He tossed the coverlet on the bed and deserted the cabin. He needed time to think.

The night sky was black. Dense clouds roiled above, blocking even the brightest stars, the deck illuminated only by a series of dimly lit lanterns. Paul picked his way around the sleeping sailors, who preferred the open air to the stuffy forecastle quarters below. He went to the railing and stared out into the dark void, breathing deeply of the salty air.

What had he done? Not so long ago, he would have already dismissed this romp. But then, this experience had been different from any other.

He remembered his first sexual encounter. He had just turned fifteen, and John and George thought it was high time they pay his way at Dulcie's. John wagered George ten dollars that he wouldn't get through it successfully, but John lost that bet. Of course, Paul never let John know that he had left the brothel concerned. Even though the strumpet had had more men than she could count, he worried that he'd impregnated her; no child should ever endure what he had.

There was no turning back, however. He'd tasted the pleasures of the flesh, and it eclipsed his fear of fathering a child. And there was no more paying. Paul knew he had charisma, and many of the women he met at home and abroad were ready and willing. They were always older or experienced, and he let them know from the start that they would not leave his bed carrying his babe in their bellies. There were ways around it. He learned how to elicit great pleasure and to withdraw before he ejaculated. If the woman was responsive, especially if she had shared his bed before, she might satisfy him in her own way. His love life was robust, yet he was confident that he had never spawned a bastard.

Tonight with Rebecca, that nagging fear hadn't even crossed his mind. He had taken her fiercely, spilling every bit of his seed deep inside of her. *What were the odds that she'd conceive from this one time? Slim, very slim.* His heart mocked his rational mind. *Not slim enough...* Their lovemaking had been dynamic – intoxicating. Who had dominated whom?

He had heard tell that a virgin did not experience the full depth of her womanhood, but Paul knew Rebecca had been deeply satisfied; even now, he could feel her hips undulating, hear her moaning in ecstasy. Was it because she loved him? He inhaled deeply, reliving those intense moments of consuming pleasure. Was this love? It couldn't be. He hardly knew her.

He raked his hands through his hair and thought once again of Charmaine. He had wronged her. But he had wronged Rebecca as well... just like his father and his mother and Elizabeth. *Don't think about it! Don't be a fool. Watch and wait. That's all you need do.*

When he grew tired, he went back into the cabin. Rebecca hadn't moved, and he assumed she had cried herself to sleep. Fully clothed, he lay down next to her and quickly dozed off. Almost as quickly, he began to dream.

He rode up to the manor on Alabaster. Charmaine was sitting on the swing, and little Marie was crawling on a blanket next to her. She saw him and waved. As he dismounted, she picked up Marie and walked over to him. Together, they strolled into the house and climbed the staircase. She put Marie to sleep and opened his bedchamber door, sauntering in. He followed her, closing and locking it behind them. She undressed and stepped into his embrace. He kissed her and lifted her into his arms, carrying her to the bed. He made love to her, but when he was finished, she rolled away from him, tears in her eyes, leaving him empty.

Next, he was headed for a day's work, checking on the mill and nodding to Wade. He turned his horse toward town. Then, he was walking up to the Remmen house. No one answered when he knocked, so he pushed his way in. Rebecca was standing there, her eyes flashing. She knew he'd been with Charmaine, and she spurned him. But he was certain that if he kissed her, she'd be a slave to her passion. She attempted to flee, but he crossed the room in two strides and pulled her into his arms. She ceased to struggle when his lips conquered hers. He kicked the bedroom door open and took her to the bed. He rode her hard until all his passion was spent, then cradled her in his arms, satiated, savoring his ebbing pleasure.

"Paul – what are you doing?"

John was standing in the doorway.

Paul's eyes flew open. His breathing was ragged, his pulse quick, and beads of perspiration dotted his brow. He stared up at the ceiling, slowly realizing where he was and that it had only been a nightmare.

Rebecca had turned in her sleep and was now cuddled close to him, her head resting on his shoulder, an arm thrown across his chest. Despite his resolve, he pulled her closer. "...but I do love you," she murmured. Paul swallowed hard, befuddled, for he wanted to cry. He closed his eyes to the urge and, after a long while, succumbed to exhaustion.

Light pouring through the porthole awakened Rebecca. Her head hurt, her eyes burned, and her body ached all over, especially between her legs. She shifted and realized that her cheek rested on Paul's chest. She rolled away, rousing him. As his eyes opened, she was filled with shame and tried to cover herself.

"Here," he gently offered, stripping off his shirt and draping it over her bare shoulders. She pulled it tightly around her, dropping her gaze to the bed. "I'm sorry about last night," he remarked.

"You said that already," she replied hotly.

"We need to talk," he pursued, aware of her anguish despite her ire. "You're very beautiful, Rebecca, and someday you will find someone who will make you happy. But that someone is not me."

Her eyes glistened with tears, and once again, she averted her face. But he cupped her chin and forced her to look at him. "Last night, you said that I loved Charmaine. You are right, I do. I set out on this voyage to find my brother, but if I don't bring him home alive, I'm going to marry her. I promised her that before I left, before all of this happened. Do you understand?"

She refused to answer him and pulled away.

"Do you understand?"

"Oh, I understand, all right! She's sending you to your death, just like she did her husband and your father!"

Unlike the night before, Paul didn't get angry, though his brow furrowed. "What are you talking about?"

"If your father and John are dead, and Doctor Blackford kills you, Charmaine's baby will inherit the entire Duvoisin fortune. Isn't that true?"

Paul put his head in his hands and let out an incredulous laugh.

"Isn't it true?" she pressed, offended by his sardonic bemusement.

"Yes, I suppose it's true," he finally conceded. "But Robert Blackford is not going to kill me."

"He might – if you chase after him!"

"I'm not chasing after him, Rebecca, and Charmaine didn't want *John* chasing after him either. I'm just going to New York to find out what happened to my brother and father – to bring them home, one way or another. Where did you get these ideas, anyway? Not from Wade, I hope."

"He doesn't know anything about this," she hastily replied. "It was Felicia, Felicia Flemmings."

Paul scowled. "Did Felicia tell you that I fired her for spreading lies?"

"No," she whispered. "She said she quit because she couldn't stand…"

"Charmaine," he supplied.

"But not everything she said was a lie!" Rebecca rallied, unhappy that he still revered his sister-in-law.

"Perhaps she told you that *she* has lain with me – many times," he continued sharply. "That she hoped our romps would turn into something more. That she's jealous because Charmaine married into my family and she did not."

Rebecca's face bore her injured pride. "And now you think that I'm trying to do the same thing," she murmured, casting her eyes to the floor.

"No, Rebecca," he replied softly. "I don't think that of you."

She heard none of it, rising from the bunk and retrieving her pants from the floor. She pulled them on through her tears. "Don't worry," she whimpered. "Once we get back to Charmantes, you'll never have to see me again."

"When we get to New York," he said, ignoring her desperate promise, "I'll buy you something more appropriate to wear. Then, if I do find my father and John, I'll tell them that you stowed away, hoping to see the city sights. Is that acceptable?"

She didn't answer, and he was uncertain if anger or pain left her mute.

Thursday, December 27, 1838

Benito Giovanni took the intrusion of John Ryan in stride. Things could be worse: the tunnel that he'd nearly completed could have been discovered, or his time could have run out. When Ryan came careening into his prison almost four weeks ago, Benito had cautiously observed him for a week.

"What's this about John Duvoisin's wife?" Ryan had demanded.

Benito did not immediately answer, his thoughts lingering on the new Mrs. Duvoisin. *So, this was her family background. How revolting!*

When Ryan pressed the issue of John's wife, Benito finally said, "Does the name Charmaine Ryan ring a bell?"

John Ryan eyed him speculatively. *How did this man know his daughter's name?* Enlightenment came slowly.

The priest smiled. "That's right old man. Charmaine is John Duvoisin's wife. I'd say your daughter did quite well for herself. You, on the other hand, have not." Giovanni allowed the words to sink in. "It's common knowledge that Charmaine's father – that would be you – beat her mother to death. John's not going to be happy when he returns to find you here. He's got quite a temper, if you didn't already know."

"Whaddaya mean, when he returns?" John Ryan sneered.

"He's abroad right now," the priest supplied, "chasing down another murderer. Then he'll be back for us – you and me."

John Ryan pulled two rumpled letters from his pocket. "So these must be from him," he mumbled.

"Where did you get those?" the priest asked, his interest instantly piqued. Charmaine's name was written across both envelopes.

"Aboard ship. I heard Simons talkin' to the captain, heard my daughter's name mentioned, and I saw him hand these here letters over with a whole pile of others. Later, I just moseyed on over to where they was settin' and helped myself. I can't read none too good, but I know how my daughter's name is spelled."

Giovanni smirked. "Would you like to know what they say?" Clearly, Ryan wanted outside information, but when Giovanni motioned for the letters, the man refused to hand them over.

"What did *you* do?" Ryan asked.

"I'm not prepared to talk about that."

"Well, maybe you ain't interested in readin' these," Ryan responded in kind.

So... Benito thought, *you and I speak the same language.* "Blackmail," he finally answered, "only blackmail."

Satisfied, Ryan shoved the letters toward the priest. Giovanni quickly ripped into them, then smiled broadly. They had plenty of time. John and Frederic were still searching for Blackford in New York, working on the assumption that he had changed his name. It could be months before they returned.

By the next day, Giovanni decided that he had no choice but to include John Ryan in his escape. In fact, Ryan might prove useful for some things along the way, and in the end, he'd rid himself of the degenerate. Benito smiled with the thought. Once they were on the open sea, that wouldn't be difficult at all.

During the second week of John Ryan's incarceration, he learned how to dig a tunnel with a spoon. By the end of his third week, they had broken through. In four months, Benito's only apprehensive moment was Buck Mathers' simple declaration, "Either I'm getting taller or this ceilin's getting' lower."

As December came to a close, their plan came together. Buck informed them that Paul had left in search of Frederic and John. The time was ripe. An hour after sunset on the twenty-seventh of December, Giovanni and Ryan crawled out of the meetinghouse cellar and escaped into the night.

Luck was with them. The brilliance of the nearly full moon muted the star-spangled sky and cast eerie gray shadows on either side of them. They trudged the seven miles to Benito's cabin, reaching it just before midnight. They had planned carefully in jail, so there was no need to talk now, Giovanni insisting on silence, alert to any unnatural sound.

Taking a lantern from the cabin, John Ryan went into the pine forest behind the outhouse and searched until he found the fishing boat tucked in a dugout and covered with brush. Turning it over, he placed the oars inside and dragged it along a path that Giovanni had told him would take him to the shoreline. Dusting off his hands, he headed back toward the small abode.

Giovanni prayed that the four items he'd secreted away months ago were where he'd left them. He wasn't surprised to find his home ransacked. He shook his head. Did they really think that he was stupid enough to hide his booty here? Or were they the stupid ones? They hadn't even uncovered the pistol hidden beneath a loose floorboard under his bed. He dropped a bullet into the chamber and pocketed the extra ammunition. He retrieved his compass hidden in a cup in the cupboard, and took a length of rope from the laundry spilled all over the floor. Finally, he lifted a silver key off a hook concealed behind a painting of the Savior. It unlocked the gates to the Duvoisin compound. He also possessed another key, one that had been hidden on his person since the morning of his arrest. It unlocked his future.

Ryan returned just as the priest stepped outside. They nodded to one another and Ryan fell in step behind Giovanni. Their next stop: the Duvoisin mansion.

Wade Remmen sat at the kitchen table, running his hands through his hair. Rebecca had been missing for two days now. He knew his sister had been unhappy. She'd complained often enough of her boredom in the tiny bungalow, but he had ignored her, and now, he was beside himself with worry. When he awoke the day after Christmas and found the house empty, he hadn't been too concerned. He didn't like her going off on her own, but lately, she'd grown exceedingly headstrong. Real anxiety took hold yesterday when he'd returned home from work and she was still missing. Where had she gone?

Felicia Flemmings hadn't helped. She seemed to think Rebecca's disappearance revolved around her 'love' of Paul Duvoisin. Wade was cognizant of his sister's infatuation, but Paul was a mature gentleman and Rebecca an uneducated girl with silly romantic ideas. When Wade finally extracted himself from Felicia, he was no closer to knowing where his sister might be. Paul had departed the island on the Tempest; Rebecca knew that. Had she gone off to moon over Paul until he returned? *No,* he reasoned, *she's probably just angry with me.*

Tonight, he knew he was deceiving himself. Something terrible could have happened to her. He hadn't been able to go out looking for her during the day; however, he wasn't needed at the mill until morning. That gave him hours to search Charmantes. He stepped out into the night, a bright gibbous moon lighting his way. Why he headed toward the Duvoisin estate, he didn't know, other than it was Paul's home. Perhaps Rebecca was drawn there, even if he was away.

Jeannette couldn't sleep. It had been a long time since her French doors opened all by themselves. Ever since Pierre's death, the 'ghost' had become a distant memory. Not so tonight. Tonight she heard the door unlatch and blow open, even though there wasn't a breeze in the air. Unlike before, she wasn't afraid, though she would have felt a lot safer if her father, Johnny, or Paul were home. She woke her sister.

"What's the matter?" Yvette asked, rubbing sleepy eyes.

"The doors," Jeannette whispered, "they opened by themselves again."

Unperturbed, Yvette jumped up and pulled them closed, slipping the latch in place. "Let's see what happens now," she said.

"Can I sleep with you?" Jeannette queried, not at all pleased that her bed was closest to the glass panels.

Her sister smiled. "Sure."

They snuggled under the covers, staving off the chilly December air. Minutes later, the doors blew open again. The girls looked at one another. Yvette rose and approached them guardedly this time. Then, on impulse, she stepped outside, determined to confront the elusive specter. There was nothing there.

She turned back into her room when a noise from below drew her around. She peered over the balcony just in time to see the outer door to the chapel close, a reverberating 'thump' assuring her that she wasn't imagining things and that the manor had indeed been breached. She frowned. Who would be going into the chapel at this time of night?

Giovanni and Ryan walked purposefully up the short aisle of the sanctuary. Their escape had gone without incident. Before long, they'd be far out to sea, watching the sunrise. While Ryan held the lantern, Giovanni stepped up to the altar. The chalice and ciborium had been restored to the sacrificial table, but not returned to the tabernacle. A good sign – only he possessed the key. *Idiots, the lot of them, not to question me about it!* He inserted the key and opened the small ark. The coins and precious jewels he'd extorted from Agatha Duvoisin were still cached there. Weighing the heavy treasure in his hand, he tied the bag around his middle with the rope, then carefully concealed it under his shirt.

"Is that all?" John Ryan whispered, his eyes narrowed in displeasure.

"It's enough," the priest assured.

"Enough for you," Ryan muttered, scanning the stone enclosure until his gaze returned to the vestibule by which they had entered. He began to formulate his own, very different plan. "This is some grand house. There's got to be a lot more in there," he said, throwing a thumb toward the side portal that opened into the manor. "We got plenty of time before the sun comes up. Let's see what else we can find."

"No!" Giovanni ordered. "We've been over this before. It's too dangerous!"

"*You've* been over it before," Ryan growled. "Now it's my turn to make some of them decisions."

"Go in there, and I leave you to your own devices," the priest threatened. "There will be no boat when you reach the shore!"

"And what if I jus' rouse the family," John Ryan rejoined. "You wouldn't want me to do that, now would ya?"

Giovanni hesitated. Ryan was shrewd. He should have shot the slovenly albatross back at his cabin where the report of the pistol would have been swallowed up by the forest. Now, he had no choice but to give in.

Gloating, John Ryan attempted to placate the priest. "With all the men gone, it should be easy to get some more loot. You know this place like the back of your hand. Where should we look first?"

Yes, Giovanni mused, *why not pillage the house? Ryan is anxious to carry any additional treasure to the boat, and I'll be that much richer when I shoot him later on.* "The master and mistress' chambers," he finally breathed, allowing the old man his momentary victory.

"Lead the way."

Yvette shrunk into the shadows of the ballroom just in time. She hadn't expected the chapel door to suddenly swing open, and she gulped back a startled scream. Her eyes widened further as Father Benito stepped through the doorway. She didn't have to be a genius to figure out who was with him. Charmaine would be very upset to know that her father roamed the manor.

Wade stood just outside the Duvoisin compound. The imposing mansion was bathed in moonlight, but every window in the house was dark. He leaned into the gates, surprised when they gave way. The stable hands usually secured them by ten o'clock each night, unlocking them at dawn. Strange – they weren't locked tonight. He pushed them open and walked up the drive.

Jeannette began to fret when her sister did not return. She went out on the balcony again and peered over the balustrade to the chapel doors below. They were still shut, and all was quiet, but as she straightened up, she nearly jumped out of her skin when she saw the figure of a man approaching the house. She quickly ducked back into her room. It was time to go and wake up Charmaine.

Yvette followed the two intruders, keeping a safe distance behind them. They slunk across the banquet hall and passed through the ballroom kitchens before entering the rear service stairwell. They were headed for her parents' chambers. For a moment, Yvette debated taking the main staircase back up, but she discounted that idea, deciding it was safer to keep the two men directly in front of her. She waited until she heard the upstairs door close before racing up the steps herself, clutching the railing in the blackness. Reaching the second floor, she put an ear to each portal and listened. All was quiet. Not knowing which door they used, she chose her mother's, slowly pulling it open and peeking around it. Moonlight spilled into the room through the French doors. No one was there. She tiptoed forward, past her mother's bed to the sitting room door. She listened at the door again. Nothing. She waited unending minutes, her breathing thundering in her ears, fearful of where the two men might be – perhaps in her father's chambers. Biting her bottom lip, she turned the doorknob gingerly, cracking the portal, her eye pressed to the small opening. No one was there either, and she sighed in relief. She would head for her father's quarters next.

She pushed through the door and stepped into the room. Without warning, a filthy hand clamped over her mouth from behind, and a man growled near her ear. "You better stop your goddamn thrashin' if you know what's good for ya, girl!"

She continued to punch and kick until Father Benito stepped out of the shadows, brandishing a pistol.

"You've spied once too often, Yvette," he whispered.

When she struggled anew, he cocked the trigger, and she immediately stopped. "I believe you lost a riding crop behind my outhouse a year ago." He shook his head and clicked his tongue. "To think your dear stepmother thought it was the wind that spilled those crates to the ground."

Her brow tipped upward, and the priest chuckled in glee. "Yes, I thought so. And now you'll learn what happens to meddlesome children." He looked at his compatriot. "I do believe we have a hostage, Mr. Ryan."

Ryan's lips curled into a greedy grin, his covetous eyes upon the girl he held. Giovanni smiled as well. "Tell us, Yvette," he said, stepping over to the table and relighting his lantern, "where did your mother keep her most valuable jewels? In a whisper, please. I'd hate for something to happen to your sister or your governess' new baby."

Charmaine was sitting in the armchair nursing Marie when Jeannette came in. "What's the matter?" she asked, reading the fear in the girl's eyes.

Jeannette quickly explained, but Charmaine was not alarmed. After all, the mysterious ghost had never materialized. This was just another of Yvette's escapades. As for the apparition on the front lawns, it was probably a stable-hand stepping out of the carriage house apartments to relieve himself. Still, she couldn't permit Yvette to wander about the mansion at two in the morning.

Handing the squirming Marie to Jeannette, Charmaine stood and tightened her robe about her waist. "Come," she said, taking the baby back from the girl. "We'd best go find your sister."

Wade circled the entire house, but finding nothing out of the ordinary, he decided to head home. Why had he come here in the first place? Now he feared he would not find his sister until she decided to return home, if she were able.

Rounding the corner nearest the stables, he heard voices. It was one of the twins and John's wife. "I don't know where she could be," the girl was saying as the two peered out the chapel door. "She said she was coming down here."

She sounded worried, as worried as he, and Wade was compelled to step forward, his presence eliciting a shriek from the pair of them. "Sorry – I'm sorry!" he apologized. "I didn't mean to startle you. It's me – Wade Remmen."

Jeannette was happy, but Charmaine frowned deeply, annoyed that her horrified reaction had frightened Marie, who let out one fitful cry that instantly turned into a rhythmic wail. "What are you doing here," she demanded, "creeping up on us like that?"

"I didn't mean to frighten you," Wade averred, "and I wasn't creeping. I was looking for my sister, Rebecca. She's been missing since yesterday morning."

"What would your sister be doing here, Mr. Remmen?" Charmaine probed suspiciously, not at all pacified by his excuse, shifting Marie to her shoulder and patting her back until she quieted.

"Don't be angry with him, Mademoiselle," Jeannette implored. "At least now we know who was walking up to the house." Her adoring eyes rested on Wade. "You haven't seen *my* sister, have you?"

"No, Jeannette, I haven't."

Yvette knew she'd get herself out of this scrape somehow, but she was terribly frightened for her sister and little Marie. Therefore, she did exactly as she was told. She showed the priest her mother's hand-carved jewelry chest, vexed to find it nearly empty. "All of Mama's best pieces are missing!" she objected loudly, her eyes leveled on Benito.

"Quiet!" he ordered, wagging the pistol at her. Evidently, Agatha had purloined Colette's valuables first. "There must be money – a safe in these chambers," he growled. "Where is it?"

Yvette took them into her father's rooms. She went to his desk and pointed out the dummy drawer that not only concealed important documents, but also a moneybag filled with gold coins and, surprisingly enough, her own gambling purse. She didn't mention the safe in the wall. Apparently, it was enough; there was an avaricious gleam in Benito's eyes as he set the lantern down and emptied one into the other, then weighed the bulging sack in his hand. "Any more than this and we wouldn't be able to carry it," he commented wryly. "You and I should be set for life, Mr. Ryan."

John Ryan was pleased as well, snatching the satchel from the priest and strapping it around his waist with his belt.

"Now are you going to let me go?" Yvette asked defiantly.

"All in good time, my dear, all in good time."

"But my sister is going to be worried if I don't return soon."

The priest chuckled. "If she's as stupid as you to come looking for trouble, we'll just have to give her some, now won't we?"

Yvette smarted with the insult, then realized it bolstered her intrepid spirit. She wasn't defeated yet, and if she kept a level head, she'd get through this calamity with no greater harm done than the loss of her father's money, money that could easily be replaced.

They marched her back down the stairwell, Benito lighting the way, John Ryan wrenching her arm behind her so she couldn't escape him. They scurried across the ballroom, coming up sharply when the chapel door swung open.

Charmaine jumped and stifled a scream when Father Benito pointed the pistol at her, but her horror climaxed as her eyes flew to Yvette and the man who restrained her. Then, she did scream, for here she was, face to face with her nightmare: John Ryan!

"What are *you* doing here?" she cried, recovering enough to speak, oblivious to her daughter's renewed wailing that echoed loudly off the walls of the empty banquet hall.

"Well, Haley," her father snarled, "word got out that you came into a bit of money, and jes' like before, you been leavin' your Pappy out. I reckon it's high time you shared the wealth."

"But how – how did you get here?"

"I ask the questions," Benito declared, turning to his young hostage. "Your sister did come looking for you, Yvette. Too bad she didn't have the good sense to stay in her room." He waved the gun at Charmaine, demanding that she calm Marie down.

"She's upset!" Charmaine objected. "There's nothing I can do!"

"She's gonna wake up the whole goddamn house!" John Ryan barked.

Giovanni grew more agitated and quickly discarded the lantern. "Come here!" he ordered, leveling the weapon on Jeannette. *"Now!"* he shouted, grabbing hold of her arm and viciously yanking her to his side.

Charmaine gasped as he pressed the muzzle to the girl's temple. "No – please!" she begged. "Please let her go!"

"Now," Benito instructed coolly, "you go quietly up to your bedroom and you nurse that baby back to sleep. Then get down on your knees and pray that I am merciful enough to release the girls when I've finished with them. However, if you alert even one person in this house as to what is happening, I guarantee that you will never – *never* – see Yvette or Jeannette alive again."

Jeannette whimpered.

"Please!" Charmaine implored. "Please release them now, and I promise we won't say a word to anyone!"

The priest coughed sardonically. "I think not."

Charmaine turned beseeching eyes on her father. "You're my father! Don't do this! Just let the girls go!"

"*Your* father?" the man sneered. "You ain't my goddamn flesh and blood! Your mother was a whore from the day I met her 'til the day she died!"

Charmaine choked back a sob, her grip on Marie tightening with the perverted assertion.

Benito cocked the firearm. "We are wasting precious time here. On the count of ten, Madame. *Must I count?*"

"*Dear God!*" Charmaine moaned and, by dint of will alone, fled the ballroom as the countdown began.

Wade had reached the gates when he heard a scream inside the chapel, but he concluded that Charmaine and Jeannette had come upon a surprised Yvette. He started home, heading south toward the beach. He'd walk back to his cottage along the coastline, hoping to turn up something along the way.

Giovanni and Ryan prodded the twins forward, Benito with a shove to Jeannette's back, and Ryan with a boot in Yvette's backside. The girl turned on him. "No wonder Mademoiselle Charmaine hates you so much!" she grumbled.

"Shut up!" the priest snarled. "No more talking – just walk!"

"Where are we going?" she demanded, unintimidated.

"Shut up or I'll blow a hole through your sister's head!" Benito threatened.

Yvette did not speak again, her mind feverishly working.

Charmaine was at George's bedchamber door in all of two minutes, banging frantically on the portal until it opened.

"What is it?" he asked, panic-stricken.

"Father Benito – my father," she gasped, shaking violently. "They were here! They've taken Yvette and Jeannette!"

"Where? When?"

"Just now! But I don't know where! They warned me not to tell anyone. Benito has a pistol! Oh God, George – *what if he kills them?*"

George dashed back into the room and swiftly pulled on his boots. "Show me where they were headed," he urged, grabbing his shirt.

Marie was still crying and Mercedes coaxed her from Charmaine's arms.

George took Charmaine by the arm and they ran down the hallway. "Mercedes," he called over his shoulder, "wake up Travis and Joshua!"

The front lawns were deserted. George swore under his breath. "Damn it! I'll kill John for this!"

Charmaine looked up at him in surprise. "John? What do you mean?"

"It was his idea to send your father here."

Belatedly, he realized he should have kept his mouth shut. He lengthened his stride toward the paddock.

"What do you mean *his* idea?" she pressed, rushing after him.

"I'll explain later!"

Though she badgered him, he refused to say more. "Right now, we have to find the girls."

The horses were swiftly saddled and rifles pulled from the stable. They would search the harbor and Benito's cabin first.

"You must be careful," Charmaine enjoined. "If they see you coming, they may very well shoot the girls. They warned me not to tell anyone!"

"We can't just sit here and wait, Charmaine," he stated.

He swung into the saddle and spurred his horse forward, taking the main road toward town. Gerald and three stable hands whipped their own mounts into motion and fell in after him. Minutes later, Joshua, Travis and Joseph Thornfield reached the lawns and headed north on foot.

Charmaine paced, unable to quell the urge to do something herself. She ordered Bud, the only man who had remained behind, to saddle up Dapple.

"But Madame," he implored, "you can't go out on your own." Then, realizing that he could not dissuade her, Bud did as he was told.

She was soon guiding her horse toward the southern shoreline, the only direction not taken by the search party. Moments later, she heard the clopping of hooves behind her and Bud reached her astride Champion. "I couldn't live with myself if something happened to you, Ma'am," he said when their eyes locked.

The unlikely foursome trudged through the underbrush toward the white beaches about three miles away. The strenuous walk became more exerting once their feet hit the sand, and Giovanni and Ryan were panting, laboring under the burden of their plunder. More than once John Ryan wanted to stop, but the priest, tired though he was, pressed on. Jeannette was glad they'd slowed down, hoping that someone from the manor was in hot pursuit, but Yvette kept her strides brisk, determined to wear the men out. When Jeannette regarded her, Yvette said not a word, but yanked on one braid. Jeannette nodded slightly, acknowledging the signal, then thought of Wade. He was out here somewhere. Perhaps he would come to their rescue before her sister did something rash.

Wade frowned down at the fishing boat, thinking it curious that any boat was sitting on this particular part of the beach miles from town. No one came this far north to fish, especially with the bondsmen's quarters so close. He walked around the dinghy, noting the footprints and a furrow in the sand that suggested it had recently been dragged from the edge of the forest. Scratching his head, he followed the tracks and discovered a path at the edge of the woods. He continued along, coming upon Father Benito's dormant cabin. Again he scratched his head, wondering if his sister had come here.

By the time Benito and Ryan reached the rowboat, they were perspiring profusely. John Ryan plopped down in the sand, winded. Benito remained vigilant, his pistol drawn, but he released Jeannette to check for his maps.

Coming away from the dinghy satisfied, he faced the twins, who stood side-by-side, complacent and maddeningly identical in the moonlight. "Jeannette, come here," he commanded.

Both girls stepped forward, though one eyed the other with a tilt of the head, her baffled expression visible even in the dim light.

Benito chuckled sagaciously. "Do you take me for a fool?" he asked pointedly of the girl staring straight ahead. "Now, I'll ask one more time. Jeannette, come here."

There was a moment of indecisiveness, and finally his suspicions were confirmed. The 'confused' twin took another step forward. "I'm Jeannette," she whimpered. "Sorry, Yvette," she added, looking back at her frowning sister.

The priest's smile turned wicked. "Get in," he growled, motioning toward the craft with the gun.

"But I'm afraid of the ocean!" she objected fiercely. "Especially at night!

"Get in or I'll shoot your sister!"

She hurriedly complied. John Ryan jumped in, too.

"Not you!" Giovanni barked. "Help me get her into the water!"

Grumbling, Ryan climbed out, and together, they pushed the dinghy into the foaming surf.

"What about me?" Yvette queried anxiously from the shore.

"You'll behave better on the sand!" Benito shot over his shoulder, struggling for a firmer grip on the rowboat as they confronted the first white-capped wave. "Stay put if you want your sister to live!"

Yvette nodded, her worried eyes riveted on Jeannette.

"Sit down!" he ordered Jeannette. "Not there – in the center!"

Jeannette obeyed, eyeing the pistol, watching the priest fumble with the rim of the boat, the gun becoming a hindrance. As the water got deeper and the breakers exceedingly rougher, Benito deposited the firearm onto the first bench, shoving the vessel forward unimpeded now. "Push harder!" he snarled at John Ryan. "One more–" he heaved "–and we're home free!"

As the next wave broke, Jeannette shot to her feet. "Run, Jeannette! Run!" she screamed.

Predictably, Benito and Ryan looked back at the beach, confounded. The girl in the boat instantly snatched the pistol and leveled it on Benito. Though startled, the priest laughed. "So – we didn't take Jeannette after all. You think you're very clever, don't you, *Yvette?* But now what are you going to do? Shoot me?"

Yvette's frown was met by the next wave, and the two men had all they could do to hold onto the boat. "There's only one bullet in the chamber," Benito growled. "Shoot me and Mr. Ryan will strangle you! Shoot him and I'll strangle you! Now put the pistol down, like a good little girl."

The firearm was heavy. Yvette used both hands to raise it over her head and pull the trigger. The recoil sent her tumbling backward. Swearing viciously, Giovanni pulled himself up and into the vessel. Too late! Yvette flung the gun with all her might out to sea. Seething, he grabbed her by her hair and slapped her hard across the face. Unshaken, she kicked out, catching him in the crotch. He doubled over in agony, a high-pitched yelp rending the air. She smiled triumphantly, grateful for all the refined things she had learned from Joseph.

"Forget about the girl!" Ryan shouted. "Let's get this goddamn boat beyond the breakers! Everyone on the island musta heard that shot!"

Catching his breath, Benito took heed and jumped from the dinghy. With a final heave, they thrust past the surf and finally climbed in. Giovanni tossed an oar to Ryan, then grabbed one for himself. "Sit!" he commanded Yvette when she made a move to stand, threatening her with his raised paddle.

Pretending contrition and fear, she hunched over and cast hooded eyes to the shore. Jeannette was standing there with her hands to her face, oblivious to the fact that someone was running full speed toward her from the woods, or that two figures on horseback were bearing down on her from the west. As Benito Giovanni and John Ryan sunk their oars into the ocean, they saw them, too.

Wade had torn off his boots and stockings. He charged the water at breakneck speed, ripping off his shirt and diving headlong into the breakers.

The priest swore, pumping the oar harder. "Pull, damn it, pull!" he yelled to John Ryan, letting out a pent-up sigh when they finally reached deeper water.

Suddenly, Yvette stood up and began stripping down to her undergarments.

"Damn it girl!" Giovanni scolded. *"Are you daft? Sit!"*

"Why don't we throw her overboard?" Ryan demanded, aware that the swimmer was closing in on them. "We're havin' to pull her weight, too."

"No – don't!" she cried, trembling. "I don't know how to swim!"

The two men exchanged smiles. Needing no further encouragement, John Ryan jumped up and reached for her. But the dinghy dipped sharply to the left, and he quickly forgot her, his attention drawn to his feet, planting them far apart, alarmed when the craft continued to rock.

"Sit down man!" Giovanni shouted, dropping his oar and splaying his arms wide, then clutching the sides of the careening boat. "Do you want *us* to end up in the water?"

"He's too stupid to figure that out!" Yvette baited, eyes flashing.

Furious, Ryan advanced again. "No little girl's gonna sass me like that!"

This time, the boat lurched steeply to the right, its rim plunging under the water's surface for one paralyzing moment, taking on water as it righted itself.

Petrified, the priest screamed. "You're going to kill us both! Sit down before we capsize!"

Seizing the moment, Yvette began to bounce from foot to foot, giggling hysterically. The boat oscillated back and forth, the water within sloshing from side-to-side, the waxing momentum growing more and more precarious.

Benito held on for dear life. "Throw her overboard!" he finally bellowed.

She was ready for John Ryan. When he dove at her, Yvette threw all her weight in the same direction, and the small vessel rolled with them, spilling them all into the sea.

Cold water engulfed her, and she held her breath for untold seconds. Finally, she surfaced, gulping in precious air, treading water to stay afloat. Then, she was yanked back under, her foot ensnared. She thrashed violently, but could not loosen the human manacle that dragged her deeper. She bent over, using her hands to pry back the fingers that dug into her flesh, certain her lungs were going to burst.

Suddenly, she was free! Cupping great handfuls of water, she kicked up and out of the tenebrous depths, sputtering and coughing as she surfaced again, her chest on fire. Another second longer, and she'd not have survived.

Wade was there, encouraging her to swim back to shore. She marshaled every aching muscle and swam as hard as John had taught her. But when she reached the breakers, she was too tired to propel herself any further. The waves curled over her and carried her the rest of the way in, depositing her in ankle-deep water, battered and shivering. Bud and Charmaine rushed forward and helped her to dry ground, where they wrapped her tightly in Charmaine's robe. Wade was not far behind, crawling out on hands and knees.

Within minutes, George and the stable-hands reached the shore, searching the sea for the fugitives. The capsized boat bobbed just beyond the breakers, but there was no sign of Benito Giovanni or John Ryan.

"They stole gold and jewelry from the house," Yvette said through chattering teeth. "John Ryan tied a sack of coins around his waist. It must have weighed him down. And I don't think Father Benito knew how to swim. He was terrified out there!"

"I don't think my father did either," Charmaine added, turning away from the horrific scene. "Let's get you home," she whispered, trembling from head to toe.

Jeannette was kneeling beside Wade, who had donned his dry shirt and now sat, heaving on the sand. "Thank you for saving my sister's life!"

The man smiled at her. "Any time."

"I thank you, too," Charmaine added. "If you hadn't been here tonight, I don't know what would have happened to Yvette."

"You should be thanking Johnny!" Yvette exclaimed. "He's the one who taught me how to swim."

"You weren't swimming anywhere with Benito's hands around your ankle," Wade responded.

Yvette cocked her head to one side, suddenly realizing that it was Wade who had freed her from the ocean depths. "I'm sorry," she whispered. "Thank you for saving me."

By dawn, they were all sitting around the dining room table rehashing the incredible events of that night. George explained John Ryan's arrival on Charmantes and his incarceration with Benito Giovanni. When all was told, Charmaine could not remain angry with her husband, remembering his words the day he had left in search of Blackford: *If you could find your father and make him pay for what he did to your mother, what would you do?* John had known her innermost fears, had understood her desperate desire for justice, and had cared enough to do something about it. Unlike the authorities, he had pursued John Ryan, had sent him to Charmantes to face retribution for his crime, jailing him in secret to spare her any alarm. Neither he nor Paul could have guessed what would happen in their absence.

The sun was just rising when the company disbanded. Charmaine invited Wade to stay and wash up at the house, but he refused. He needed to go home in case his sister returned. George offered to help search the island for her, telling Wade to take the day off work. "I'll see to it," George reiterated as Wade departed atop Champion. "By tomorrow, I promise no stone will be left unturned."

According to Mercedes and Loretta, Marie had screamed herself to sleep. Charmaine took the slumbering infant from Loretta's comforting arms and retired. In her peaceful chambers, she knelt down and thanked God that nobody in her family had been harmed.

Sunday, December 30, 1838

Rebecca refused to speak to Paul. When he ventured into the cabin, she would turn away. She didn't eat the food he brought her either, and at night, he lay on the bunk alone, wondering in the morning where she had slept, or if she had slept at all. He decided that if she wanted to sulk, that was fine by him. After all, he hadn't pursued her – she had pursued him. And he had given her ample opportunity to leave his cabin that night. Even so, he was angry that he dwelled on her predicament – that she was ever in his thoughts.

On the last night of their voyage, he found her asleep when he entered the cubicle, concluding that she slept during the day when he wasn't there. He put the tray of food he carried down on the table. Tonight, he would force-feed her if necessary. She hadn't touched a morsel in four days. If this continued, she would make herself ill.

"Rebecca," he called, nudging her awake.

She rubbed her eyes, befuddled at first as to where she was.

"I've brought you dinner," he said gently. "You need to eat."

She sat up, watching him warily. She swung her legs over the edge of the bunk, his shirt and her men's trousers still in place.

Paul made light conversation, hoping that the sleep had put her in a better mood. "It's quite good actually. About the best meal I've tasted aboard this ship." He'd been stirring some soup, which he now carried over to the bed.

When she realized he meant to feed her, she turned her head aside.

"Rebecca," he said sharply, "you have to eat something! You can't go on like this." Her clenched jaw began to quiver. "Please try it," he insisted, no longer cross.

She jumped from the cot and retreated to a corner of the room, taking her misery with her. When he approached, her back stiffened. "Leave me alone!" she moaned. "Why won't you just leave me alone?"

At his wit's end, he brusquely deposited the bowl on the table, the soup sloshing over the edges. "Suit yourself," he stated irascibly. "Starve and see if I care."

"I know you won't," she said, but he had already stormed from the cabin.

Hours later, the food remained just as he'd left it. He shook his head. She was stubborn, he had to give her that, and determined to make him feel guilty.

Monday, December 31, 1838

New York City came into view with the dawning of the sixth day. The Tempest made port in four hours' time, the delay caused by an icy Hudson River and the tremendous snowstorm suffered by a vast stretch of the Atlantic seaboard three weeks earlier.

As she docked, Paul returned to the cabin one last time. He threw on his cape, for the air was frigid, much colder than it had been two years ago. He caught Rebecca's intense eyes upon him, but she swiftly looked away. He hesitated. Her manner hadn't changed, yet something about her disturbed him this morning, something he couldn't quite put a finger on.

"I'll be back by dark," he said. "I don't want you leaving the cabin. Do you hear me?" Unlike the past five days, she acknowledged him with a slight nod. Suddenly, he knew.

He left the cubicle and closed the door behind him, retrieving the key hanging above the doorframe. He locked the portal, the 'click' sounding within the cell. Rebecca flew to the door, yanking on the knob. She banged on it with both fists, her escape plan neatly foiled. "Let me out!" she screamed.

For the first time in nearly a week, Paul felt satisfied. "You stay put!" he shouted back. With a smug smile, he disembarked, his destination John's row house on Sixth Avenue, the address George had given him.

As he left the wharf, he marveled once again at the throngs of people, the endless buildings, the noise, the very magnitude of this booming city. In the two years since he'd commissioned the building of his ships, the city had grown. Tonight, it was blanketed in white, a light snow falling atop the mountainous heaps already obstructing the roadway.

He hailed a cab, calling the address up to the driver who sat shivering beneath a thin overcoat and frayed lap-blanket, collar drawn up and cap pulled down low, breathing heavily into the hands he occasionally rubbed together to keep warm.

Paul, a mite more protected from the elements, settled back in the seat of the enclosed carriage, taking in the sights, the smells, and the sounds. Still, his mind was far away, wondering what he would find.

John's house was locked tight. It was New Year's Eve, and Paul found some Greenwich Village residents at home. However, all of John's immediate neighbors had little information to offer. They hardly knew John except to say a passing 'good day' when he was in town. One woman told him about the unprecedented event in early December when the New York City police had breached and then searched John's residence, questioning neighbors for the next two days, tightlipped the entire time, offering not one reason why they were there.

Although relieved, Paul was confused; most of their inquiries had involved John's possible whereabouts and any family he had residing in the city. He began to wonder if his brother and father were on the run.

When he left Sixth Avenue, he headed for the shipping offices at the busy seaport. He was back at the New York harbor by mid-afternoon. The warehouse ledgers carried the names of other prominent New York shippers, and he combed over them, hoping to find the name of someone who might have offered John a place to stay. The clerks were brusque and lent little aid. By late afternoon, he decided to call it a day. Perhaps he'd have better luck tomorrow and run into somebody who could help him.

He hailed another cab and asked to be taken to a fashionable shopping block in the city. For Rebecca, he picked out a lovely dress in pale green – it would match her captivating eyes – as well as undergarments, a nightgown, and plush robe. For himself, he bought a heavy redingote, a hat, and gloves. He'd been freezing all day in the bone-chilling cold. At least he'd be warm when he began his hunt tomorrow.

Darkness had already fallen by the time he boarded the Tempest. Though his day had proven unsuccessful, his evening did not. He found Captain Conklin talking to one Roger Dewint, John's New York shipping agent. Roger hadn't recognized the Tempest, but he had noticed the Duvoisin flag flying high on her mast and stopped by to introduce himself. Dewint had no news about John or Frederic; he did have a list of men who worked for John when his ships laid anchor in New York. Most were freed slaves. He agreed to meet Paul on the merchantman early the next morning, and together, they would make the rounds, locating as many of these men as possible. Finally, Paul was getting somewhere.

It was quiet when he unlocked the cabin door. For a moment, he held his breath, wondering if Rebecca had figured another way to escape. But she was there, sitting in the dark on the bunk, wrapped in a blanket. He closed the door, pocketing the key. He deposited his bundle on the stool and lit the lantern.

There was a knock on the door, and he stepped in front of Rebecca as the porter dragged in a large tub. "I'll be back with the water, sir," he said.

After he'd left, Paul turned the lamp down low, obscuring Rebecca in the shadows. She eyed him suspiciously, but held silent.

The porter returned numerous times, and slowly, the tub was filled with steaming water. He left soap, a cloth, and a towel before retreating altogether.

Paul faced her with arms crossed over his chest. "You're taking a bath. Now, you can either bathe yourself, or I will do it for you. You have a half-hour to decide." She didn't move. "Very well," he said as he grabbed hold of the door, "but remember, when I return, the water will be cold. The clothes I promised you are in that package–" he indicated the bundle "–if you change your mind."

Certain that he'd carry out his threat, Rebecca undressed and settled into the tub as soon as he left. The cubicle had been mercilessly cold all day, and she relished the piping-hot water, closing her eyes and resting her neck against the tub's rim. After a while, she washed clean all the reminders of the days gone by. When tears welled in her eyes, she dunked her head under and washed her hair.

In less than a half-hour, she left the tub, shivering, wrapping the towel quickly around her. She fingered the package on the stool, and against her own will, opened it. Inside, she found a gorgeous dress, accompanied by various undergarments and stockings. There was also a nightgown and robe, which she chose to wear now.

When Paul returned, he found her garbed in the thick robe. She looked lovely, her damp hair framing her beautiful, yet drawn, face.

He carried a tray of food. "Will you eat something now?" he asked, surprised when she meekly nodded.

There was a knock on the door, and she melted into the shadows. Paul told the porter that he wasn't finished with the tub yet and would keep it until the morning. "I'd like to bathe, too," he explained when the portal closed.

They sat at the table and ate quietly. Although she consumed only a small portion of the fare, at least it was something. Setting his knife and fork down, Paul studied her. "Why were you going to run away today?"

She stopped chewing and stared down at her plate.

"Don't you realize how cruel a big city such as New York can be? Am I so horrible that you won't let me take you back to Charmantes?"

She could scarcely swallow for the burning lump in her throat. When she looked at him, her green eyes sparkled. "I don't want to shame my brother," she whispered. "He will know what has happened when I return. Better he doesn't know. Better if I just disappear."

She blinked back tears, and Paul experienced her pain. Embarrassed, she left the table and turned her back to him. "I've grown up a lot these past few days," she rasped, "and I don't think I like being a woman."

Paul fought the consuming desire to take her in his arms and kiss her, to carry her to the bunk and make tender love to her, to prove her wrong. But his mind screamed: *Charmaine – remember your pledge to Charmaine.*

He drew a deep breath to calm himself. "Rebecca, no one needs to know what happened between us," he said evenly. "If all goes well tomorrow, I may have my father and brother with me when I return. If so, this cabin will be yours alone. I will tell everyone that I found you in the hold, that you wanted to see the New York City sights, and that now I'm bringing you home to your brother. I'll spend the remainder of the trip in the common quarters with the crew, and no one will question me."

It was not what she longed to hear. He seemed certain that he was going to find his brother alive. Charmaine would have her husband back, and he would no longer be bound by his promise. Still, he made no pledge to her, not a single word of encouragement. She meant nothing more to him than a tawdry encounter that had claimed her virginity. She was like Felicia: out of sight, out of mind. In fact, she meant less to him than Felicia, for Felicia had shared his bed many times, and she, only once. He showed no desire to make love to her again. He *did* think she was just a little girl. She'd best accept that, or her heart would break, and she would not allow him that final triumph.

He waited for her to face him again, surprised and relieved to see that she was smiling. She appeared pleased with his plan, and he breathed a bit easier. Perhaps everything would work out for the best.

Later, while he bathed, Rebecca studied him surreptitiously from the shadows. Even though he'd rejected her, she yearned for him still and battled the urge to offer herself to him. She remembered his rough hands, his impassioned kisses, and her eyes stung with tears. She had all she could do to hold tight to her spot on the bunk. When he rose from the tub, she turned away. He was lost to her. She *was* a little girl – a foolish little girl, with big, foolish dreams.

New Year's Day, 1839

Early the next morning, Paul left the ship, telling Philip Conklin that he'd been down in the hold and discovered a stowaway, a young girl charmed by the notion of living in the big city. "Her brother will be distressed," he explained, "so I've locked her in my cabin until we leave port."

The captain raised a dubious brow, but said not a word. The hold had been unloaded the day before, and none of his crew had spotted her.

Paul found Roger Dewint waiting for him on the quay. Together, they walked along the many piers in the harbor, stopping from time to time to engage somebody in conversation.

By noon, Paul got lucky. Samuel Waters worked for John, had in fact, arrived in New York aboard a Duvoisin vessel. He was a runaway slave. It took quite a bit of coaxing, but Samuel finally capitulated, telling Paul that he knew a Rose Forrester, whose sister was a good friend of John's. He gave Paul their address.

Chapter 9

Sunday, January 13, 1839
Charmantes

Charmaine woke with a start. Had Marie cried out? The infant's tiniest squeak could bring her out of the deepest slumber. She rolled over and peered into the cradle. Marie was still sleeping.

Paul had been gone for nearly three weeks, and Charmaine had counted the days, his journey ever on her mind. She had traveled to town every morning for the past week. Today would be no different. As before, the girls and the Harringtons insisted on accompanying her.

She visited the chapel before departing. Without a priest, she hadn't attended Holy Mass for over four months, but she found solace in the serene sanctuary and petitioned the Almighty to bring her husband home to her. She had not missed a day in her novena, nor would she until her prayers were answered.

Just before ten, they were on their way. Because it was Sunday, nearly everyone was strolling along the main thoroughfare, greeting neighbors and enjoying the cool breezes that would not last much longer. They did a bit of shopping and went to Dulcie's for lunch, but Charmaine ate very little.

Loretta looked at the food on her plate. "Charmaine," she chided lightly, "you haven't touched your meal."

"I've no appetite," Charmaine replied.

"But you must eat," Loretta proceeded, "for your daughter's sake. Starving yourself with worry will never do."

Charmaine had heard the lecture before and was grateful when Yvette interrupted. "Can we go down to the wharf after this?"

Charmaine nodded. "I'd like that."

Marie, who'd been content for hours, began to fuss. "Please, finish eating," she insisted as she stood with her baby. "I'll be back once I've fed Marie."

Loretta nodded, and Charmaine left them in pursuit of the carriage that was parked in the livery. Once there, she rearranged the cushions within the brougham, drew the curtains, and began nursing her daughter.

Marie's mouth opened wide, and Charmaine smiled down at the infant, watching her pursed lips worked the nipple, stopping only to swallow. The tiny eyes rolled heavenward, satiated, her delicate eyelids, already fringed with dark lashes, closing slowly. Charmaine basked in the moment, just as she did each time the child suckled at her breast. "My little Marie Elizabeth," she breathed. "What will this month bring for us?"

Was John still alive? Or would she be forced to face Paul's marriage proposal? Charmaine struggled to suppress the thought. But today, it was so vivid she could not ignore it. Would she wed Paul? Probably. Not so much for herself, but for her daughter and for him. She knew he was suffering, realized now how poignantly he loved her. Yes, if she were forced to recover from another loss, she would consider marrying him.

She was still staring into the distance when the carriage door was yanked open. "What goes on in here?" A toothless man peered in, tobacco-tainted saliva drooling from the side of his mouth. He wiped it away with the back of his grimy hand.

Horrified, Charmaine quickly drew her bodice together. "Sir! This is my carriage!"

He squinted at her. "Are you the new Mrs. Duvoisin?"

"Yes, I am. Who are you?"

"Martin St. George," he replied, dark spittle spraying in all directions.

The name triggered an ancient memory. "Martin, the farrier?"

"That's me. And what'er you doin' in this coach all the way back here?" Oblivious to the baby she held, his eyes darted about, as if he'd find her lover hidden in the corner.

Suddenly she was laughing, laughing as she hadn't laughed in a very long time, laughing so hard that she shook. *I mistook John for this man the night we met. Impossible!*

Marie squeaked in her sleep, and Charmaine subdued her mirth.

"What's so funny?" the noisome stableman demanded.

Charmaine sighed, wiping away happy tears. "Nothing, nothing at all!"

He shook his head, spat into the hay, and walked away.

She giggled again and then, making herself presentable, climbed out of the carriage, the slumbering Marie clasped firmly to her breast.

Loretta and Joshua had just stepped out of Dulcie's with the girls when she returned. Together, they strolled toward the harbor.

A shout went up, and Charmaine's heart leapt into her throat, missing a beat when just beyond the peninsula, out on the open sea, she caught sight of a ship's sails, bellied out. Pray God it was a Duvoisin vessel! Pray God it was from New York! Pray God it was Paul bringing John!

Pedestrians migrated to the wharf, and soon there was a throng of onlookers. They stepped aside when they saw Charmaine and the twins, sensing the importance of the merchantman that was wearing into the mouth of the cove. Joshua led them to an unobstructed spot, where they waited for what seemed an eternity. Finally, the vessel entered the inlet, and someone shouted, "It's the Tempest!" as it closed the distance to the quay. Charmaine's trembling hand flew to her mouth. She'd have her answer today.

"Look, Mademoiselle," Jeannette exclaimed, "it's Wade!" The man had drawn up alongside them, but Charmaine's eyes never wavered from the ship.

"May I hold Marie?" Jeannette asked, wanting to show off the babe.

Charmaine surrendered her daughter without a thought, and Jeannette giggled when Marie objected with a squeak and a squirm.

The Tempest grew in size and majesty, sailors now visible fore and aft, making ready to moor the one-hundred-fifty-foot vessel, some high on the forecastle deck, others on the quarterdeck, many climbing the ratlines to reef the sails, all immensely busy. When Yvette made a move to run ahead, Joshua grasped her shoulder, urging her to stay put. Charmaine didn't recognize anyone on board, and she brought folded hands to her lips, uttering a swift Hail Mary.

Loretta patted her arm. "God's will be done, Charmaine."

Charmaine inhaled, praying that she could accept her cross and go on.

A scrape of wood on wood, a great groan, and the ship finally settled into place. Ropes were thrown overboard, and the longshoremen scrambled to loop and tie them to the pilings. Finally, the gangplank was lowered, and in consternation, Charmaine recognized Father Michael Andrews, lending an arm to Frederic as they stepped forward to disembark.

"Papa!" Jeannette cried exuberantly and hurried to him with Marie in her arms, welcoming his embrace as he stepped onto the stable quay.

Charmaine's eyes flew back to the deck above, but there was no sign of John or Paul. She looked at Frederic again and read sorrow in his eyes, even though he smiled her way. Her heart froze. *He hasn't come back with John! He's come back with a priest – my family's priest!* She had her answer. *He's brought Father Michael here to comfort me.*

Gulping back a violent sob, she turned away and buried her face in Joshua's shirtfront. As his arm encircled her, she caved in to her grief.

Yvette's squeal sliced through the hum of the crowd. "Johnny! It's Johnny!"

Charmaine pivoted around, the name reverberating, sundering her every emotion. Miraculously, she beheld her husband hobbling down the gangplank, supported by Paul, who clutched his arm. He was there – thin, his face pale and drawn – but really there! Although his expression was pained, his eyes lit up when he saw her. Incredulous, she stood rooted to the spot, the entire boardwalk strangely hushed. Behind her she heard Loretta ask, "Is that John?" When he reached the pier, he smiled his familiar, crooked smile. "Will you have this prodigal husband back, my Charm?"

All of her anxiety evaporated, and she ran to him. He pulled free of Paul and stepped forward. She fell into his open arms, his name on her lips. Tears of joy replaced those that were still moist on her cheeks, and she felt his arms quicken, his face buried in her hair, his embrace so fierce she could scarcely breathe. Then his head lifted, and his hand spanned her face, thumbs stroking her cheeks to wipe her tears away, his fingers cupping her head. He leaned forward to kiss her, and she wrapped her arms around his neck, meeting his lips in impassioned fervor. There they stood in broad daylight, unconcerned about friends and family, the ship's crew, or the multitude watching them.

Frederic's heart swelled as Charmaine uttered his John's name over and over again. Loretta and Joshua hugged one another, overjoyed for the reunited couple. Michael combated a tide of emotional exultation, lest he weep, watching as Charmaine caressed John's face and ran her hands through his hair, categorizing his every feature, as if to confirm that she was not dreaming.

Finally, John held her at arm's length, perusing her from head to toe. "Well?" he queried. "Where is she?"

Although Charmaine frowned, Jeannette stepped forward, offering up the small bundle she lovingly held. "Here she is, Johnny. Here's little Marie."

John tenderly took his daughter into his arms, looking down at her in awe, chuckling softly when she wiggled, yawned, and cooed in contentment. "She's beautiful," he whispered hoarsely, his gaze meeting Charmaine's. "You did an exceptional job, my Charm."

"We both did," she replied.

She was suddenly aware of the many onlookers around her. John's regard shifted to Michael, and Charmaine wondered why he was there. She noted the knowing look that passed between them, and her eyes narrowed.

John smiled innocently. "What?" he asked.

"I know you're up to something," Charmaine supplied. When John shrugged sheepishly, she said, "Are you going to tell me what is going on?"

His crooked smile deepened, dimples visible now. "What do you mean?"

"Never mind," she said, dismissing him with a wave of the hand. She'd find out sooner or later. She found Michael Andrews studying her intently. She couldn't begin to guess what he was thinking.

Mostly, he was pleased to know that his daughter could read her husband so well. The couple obviously liked one another as much as they loved each other. God had smiled down upon their union.

"So, Father Michael," she said, stepping over to him and clasping his hand, "what has brought you all the way to Charmantes?"

"John, actually," he answered simply. "I've known him for five years. He's a close friend."

Charmaine's astonishment made John laugh. "You see, Charmaine," he said, "I'm not in league with the devil as you once believed."

She rolled her eyes and turned back to the priest.

"John has been a generous benefactor to the St. Jude Refuge," Michael expounded.

Charmaine's expression grew incredulous. "My husband? The man who doesn't believe in God?"

"But I do believe in good people and good causes, my Charm."

Frederic interrupted the exchange. "Come, John," he prodded with concern, "you've been on your feet long enough. It is time we get you home."

Charmaine was amazed by the man's display of affection.

"He was gravely ill, Charmaine," he explained, "and is still recovering from a serious injury. He's been advised not to exert himself."

"I'm fine, Charmaine," John reassured, seeing the worry on her face. "The worst is over, but Father is right. I would like to sit down."

She nodded and took Marie from his arms. The babe slept on.

"Did you get him, Johnny?" Yvette finally asked. "Did you kill Doctor Blackford?"

The wharf fell silent until Frederic spoke. "He's dead, Yvette." Deciding it was best to get the story out and over with, he added, "When he attacked your brother with a knife, I shot and killed him. He's no longer a threat to our family."

"Good!" Yvette exclaimed.

Paul offered to arrange transportation from the livery, but as he turned to leave, Charmaine grabbed his arm, holding him there a moment longer. A hint of a smile reached his eyes, and she could see that he was happy for her.

"Thank you," she whispered hoarsely, "for everything."

His smile grew dynamic. "You're welcome. Now – no more tears!"

Rebecca tore her burning eyes from Paul and Charmaine, hurried down the gangplank, and headed home. Since the afternoon that John and Frederic had boarded the ship, Paul hadn't said two words to her. Now she knew why. It didn't matter if John was dead or alive. He would always love Charmaine. She must forget him.

The Duvoisins ambled down the pier toward the road. Charmaine had completely forgotten about Loretta and Joshua, but found them smiling at her. She went to them with John's arm looped through hers and Michael Andrews flanking him on the right.

"John, this is Loretta and Joshua Harrington," she stated proudly, "Mr. and Mrs. Harrington, this is my husband."

"Ah, yes," John grinned devilishly, "the Prophet. I'm sorry I didn't remember you in Richmond, but you weren't wearing your robes–"

"John!" Charmaine admonished, her eyes shooting from Joshua to Father Michael, who was snickering behind a raised hand. "I've told the Harringtons that you're not as incorrigible as they've heard. Are you out to prove me wrong?"

"Actually, I'm worse," John replied. Catching her frown, he turned serious. "No, my Charm, I'd never do that." He took Joshua's hand. "Thank you for bringing your wife to Charmantes and looking after Charmaine in my absence." He turned to Loretta and gave her his most charming smile. "Mrs. Harrington."

"Pleased to meet you," Loretta nodded dubiously before speaking to Charmaine. "Let me take Marie so you can help your husband to the carriage."

The twins accompanied their father, bantering effervescently. "Papa," Jeannette exclaimed, "you don't have your cane!"

"I lost it somewhere along the way," he commented, his arms encircling their shoulders. "But I don't think I need it any longer. Not with the two of you to lean on and all the excitement behind us."

"You and Johnny are not the only ones with exciting news!" Yvette cut in. "Wait until you hear what happened to us!"

"Let me help John into the carriage. After that, you'll have my ear all the way home."

The brougham came to a standstill at the end of the wharf. John waved off the hands that offered help and, with some difficulty, pulled himself up and in. He exhaled with a grimace, which he tried to conceal by asking to hold Marie. Charmaine obliged.

As the coach pulled away, she grabbed hold of John's arm and hugged it, her eyes devouring every line of his face. He was studying his sleeping daughter again, marveling over every delicate feature.

Michael's heart once again expanded with gladness as he watched them, the interior of the vehicle bathed in a very tangible love.

"I'm dreaming," she finally whispered, drawing John's eyes from Marie. "I know I'm dreaming."

"No, my Charm," he smiled, "I'm really here."

"But I had a premonition – the night Marie was born – that you had died!"

He put his arm around her and pulled her close. "I did die," he whispered. "But your mother sent me back to you."

She gaped at him. "*My mother?*"

"Yes," John nodded, regarding his slumbering daughter again, "your mother, Marie... She was my savior long before I met you, my Charm. Only I didn't learn that she was your mother until last August. *She* was the one who helped me through that terrible time before and after Pierre's birth, and *she* introduced me to Michael."

"Dear God!" Charmaine gasped, goose bumps rising on her flesh.

"What is it?"

"It was *you*," she whispered. "My mother once told me, 'the greater the wealth, the deeper the pain'. I didn't understand what she meant, had no idea who she was talking about. But after Pierre's death, her presence was so strong. I felt her there beside me in the chapel. And then the next day, during the funeral, those words kept coming back to me. For days they went through my mind. Now I'm certain she was talking about you, John – you and your pain!"

John remembered telling Marie that his father's fortune had ruined his life, firmly believing that Colette had forfeited their love for it. He looked from his wife to Michael. "It appears she brought us together, Charmaine." He shook his head with the weight of it.

"If I had known anything about your mother's life with John Ryan, I swear I would have put a stop to it. But she never burdened me with her troubles. She was only concerned for mine. I didn't even know her last name or that she had died. I was in New York when it happened. And I certainly didn't make the connection between you, your father, or her." When he spoke again, there was anger in his voice. "I promise you now, Charmaine, John Ryan will be punished."

She took a deep breath. "You don't have to worry about that."

The remark shook him. He knew from Paul that Ryan had been incarcerated on Charmantes in early December. "What has happened?" he asked in dismay.

She related the story of Benito Giovanni and John Ryan's escape. More than once, John swore under his breath, his scowl deepening as he contemplated the danger in which Charmaine, his daughter, and the twins had been. But the finale brought a twinkle to his eye, and he couldn't resist saying, "Good thing I taught Yvette how to swim."

"That's exactly what Yvette said," Charmaine replied, "but my father could have killed her." She bowed her head. "The Good Lord's mercy spared her."

"He wasn't your father, Charmaine," he said. "You mustn't blame yourself."

She looked up in surprise. "How do you know that?"

John was equally astonished. Obviously, she knew at least a portion of the truth. *But how?*

"Charmaine," Michael whispered softly, cautiously. "I'm your father."

Charmaine gaped the priest, her expression bordering on the mortified, but John squeezed her hand, encouraging her to listen compassionately.

"I loved your mother deeply," Michael affirmed, clearing his throat. "I didn't know she was carrying my child, Charmaine. I didn't know the truth about you until nine months ago."

His confession came hard.

"She just left one day. When she returned to St. Jude, you were already a little girl. I thought you were John Ryan's little girl." He pulled a letter from his pocket and offered it to her. "It's from your mother."

Charmaine took it, studied the neat, familiar handwriting on the envelope.

"Marie gave it to John years before she died," Michael continued.

"She asked me to pass it on to Michael if anything happened to her," John interjected. "But I didn't learn about her death until this past spring."

"Even then," the priest continued, "John didn't make the connection between you and Marie because I never mentioned your name. I went to the Harringtons the week of Paul's celebration. That is when I found out where you were – when I realized that John must know you. But it wasn't until he came to me for information on your island priest that all the pieces of the puzzle fell into place."

There was a long silence, Charmaine speechless, John and Michael giving her time to absorb the incredible story.

"I loved her, Charmaine," he reverently proclaimed, "and I would have left the priesthood if I had known she was with child. But she didn't want me to do that, and she guarded her secret until she wrote that." He nodded toward the letter Charmaine still held in her hands. "She sacrificed her own happiness for me..."

Michael lowered his head, and Charmaine knew he was fighting back tears. She reached across the carriage and took his hand. "All these years, I believed my mother never knew a moment of happiness. I'm glad to discover I was wrong – that you loved her dearly. I know she loved you."

He looked up, his eyes sparkling, and no further words were necessary. Hands clasped, they basked in the miraculous revelation that they were family.

The baby stirred and John gazed down at the wriggling infant. "Would you like to hold your granddaughter?" he asked.

When Michael nodded, Charmaine scooped Marie from John's lap and passed the little bundle to him. He snuggled her in the crook of his arm and his tears fell freely. Charmaine grasped John's arm with both hands and laid her head against his shoulder. She closed her eyes in a prayer of thanksgiving, certain she would be weeping tears of joy for many days to come.

They were nearly home when Marie began to cry, refusing even the comfort of her mother's arms. "She's hungry," Charmaine explained, and then more softly for John's ears, "She fell asleep before she had her fill and needs to be nursed."

He tilted his head and whispered, "Can I watch?"

She blushed scarlet, her eyes flying to her father, hoping that he had not heard. He was only smiling tenderly at her, and she turned to John, pleased to find that wonderful, familiar deviltry dancing in his eyes.

"If you'd like," she answered sweetly, that lopsided smile now dominating his handsome face, his brow raised in astonishment over her bold response.

As the carriage rolled through the front gates, Michael sat in awe of the majestic mansion and its grounds. The coach drew up to the portico steps.

Charmaine placed the fidgeting Marie in John's arms and alighted, holding up a hand to wave off any assistance. Marie started wailing immediately, but she was right there to take her back.

George emerged from the house, laughing heartily when he caught sight of John climbing from the carriage. "How are you, weary traveler?" he called, rushing forward and eyeing Michael who had also alighted.

"A bit frayed around the edges," John chuckled, "but no worse for the wear." He introduced George to Michael.

"Did you get the bastard?"

"My father did," John answered somberly.

The other coaches had also arrived, and their passengers spilled out, flooding the cobblestone drive, a clamoring crowd of family and friends.

Charmaine's voice rose above the others as she issued a spate of orders to the servants who appeared at the doorway. "Travis, please take Father Michael's luggage up to one of the guest rooms. Joseph, could you summon Doctor Hastings? Tell him I'd like him to check on John. Millie, would you take Marie and change her, then bring her to my bedroom. Cookie, could you put up a pot of coffee and prepare us a nice spread of food? Mrs. Faraday..."

A great hush blanketed the terrace, save Charmaine's authoritative voice.

"I told you," Paul said to Frederic and John, "she's in charge now."

Charmaine swung round to face them. "And you–" she pointed to John "–up to bed!"

"I'm ready whenever you are, my Charm."

George chortled, but Charmaine shook her head, choosing to ignore the ribald comment. "George, Father Michael, would you help him manage the stairs?"

In no time, John was in his room. She pulled down the coverlet of their bed. John winced as he sat and slowly drew his legs up and onto it. Suddenly, she was aware of the great effort he had exerted at the quay, remembering the pained expression he'd attempted to camouflage when he'd climbed into the carriage. "Now are you going to tell me what happened?"

"Blackford stabbed me in the side," he grunted, releasing the breath of air he'd held. "My father got there just in time to keep him from doing worse."

"I knew it!" she said, concern giving way to anger. "You *were* in danger!"

"It's over now, Charmaine. Don't be angry with me."

"Why didn't you write?"

"I *did* write – at least three or four letters."

"I only received one – from Richmond!"

"I wrote twice from New York."

His face contorted as he readjusted himself on the pillows, and her ire flagged. "Lie still," she admonished, brushing the hair from his forehead and dabbing away beads of perspiration.

When she'd finished, he grasped her hand and drew it to his mouth, kissing it tenderly. "I missed you, Charmaine. I promise I'll never leave you again."

"You'd best remember that," she warned, "because I intend to hold you to it."

With a soft rap on the open door, Millie brought in the wailing Marie. "Thank you, Millie," Charmaine said. "Please, close the door on your way out."

John looked on in amusement as his wife reclined alongside him and unbuttoned her blouse, offering the greedy infant a large pink nipple. He drew an uneven breath, the quickening in his loins oblivious to his injury. His hungry eyes consumed every inch of her. "It might be a while before I can make love to you, my Charm," he whispered, "but I long to do so right now."

"I yearn for you, too," she murmured, leaning over her daughter to steal a kiss from him. His hand cupped the back of her head, and he held her lips to his for a few moments longer.

When Marie was asleep and swaddled comfortably in her cradle, Charmaine turned back to the bed. John had fallen asleep as well, and she shook her head, alarmed by his weakened constitution. Rest was what he needed.

She closed the door quietly behind her, wondering if Joseph had returned with the doctor yet. Voices drew her to the dining room. She found all of her loved ones at the table: Joshua and Loretta, George and Mercedes, Rose, Yvette and Jeannette, Michael, Paul, and Frederic. Her eyes met Frederic's. He rose, and she went to him, wrapping her arms around him, laying her cheek against his chest.

"Thank you for bringing him home to me – alive."

Frederic closed his eyes. "We have God to thank," he murmured, "and the people who love my son. I didn't realize how many they were."

Marie was wailing, waking John with a start. He sat up in bed and looked into the bassinet. The babe was squirming, her face beet-red. He lifted her to his shoulder and rocked her gently, to no avail. His eyes traveled to the door, wondering why Charmaine hadn't yet appeared.

Loretta heard Marie crying from the staircase. She'd left the large company in the drawing room, where Charmaine was entertaining the family. When the pulsating protests did not abate, she quickly went to the bedchamber and knocked. There was no answer, so she opened the door and stepped in to pacify the babe before she woke her convalescing father.

She found John sitting at the edge of the bed with Marie in his arms. He turned at the sound of her entrance, and his face dropped. "Not the milkman yet, Marie," he soothed.

Loretta smiled and went to him. Marie was wriggling fiercely, working her way down his chest in search of a nipple.

"She was on my shoulder just a moment ago," he commented helplessly.

"She's looking for her mama's bosom," Loretta supplied delicately.

"Well, she's at the wrong address."

Loretta chuckled. "Here, let me take her. She could be wet or soiled." She lifted Marie from his arms, put a nose to her bottom, and sniffed.

John frowned. "Any other way to check?"

Loretta smiled again as she hastened toward the changing table in the adjoining chamber. "She needs her nappy changed."

John followed her. Loretta laid the babe on the soft table. Marie immediately stopped crying. "She knows where she is," John mused.

"They learn quickly," Loretta replied, as she worked at the diaper pins.

Loretta changed Marie adeptly. Lifting her off the table, she offered her, clean and happy, to John. He took her into his arms. "You're quite good at that," he said.

"I've had a lot of experience – five boys."

"How long do babies stay in those?" he asked, nodding toward the diapers.

"About two years, or a bit longer. It depends on the child."

"You know, we don't have any plans for that room you're staying in. Are you sure you want to leave? Free room and board for two years, or a bit longer, depending..."

"I would love to stay, but Joshua is anxious to get back to Virginia, and I miss my sons and grandchildren." She eyed John pensively. "I trust that you are back for good, Mr. Duvoisin?"

"Yes I am, Mrs. Harrington. I had a score that needed to be settled. It has been, and I'm not going anywhere now."

Somewhat satisfied, Loretta pressed on. "Charmaine is the daughter I never had, Mr. Duvoisin. I want her to be happy. I love her, you know."

"Not as much as I do, Mrs. Harrington."

Loretta nodded, reassured by the declaration and his apparent sincerity.

"If Charmaine is your daughter, that makes me your son-in-law," John continued. "So why don't you call me John? That is, if your husband will have it. I believe he has some other names for me."

Loretta laughed heartily; this man was quick and quite irreverent. No wonder her mild-mannered husband didn't like him. "Very well. As long as you call me Loretta."

Rebecca closed the door to the cottage and leaned back into it. She was home, but it offered no security. She closed her eyes for a moment, hoping that the spinning room would settle, certain that the floorboards below her feet rocked like the ship. When the wave of nausea ebbed, she headed listlessly toward her bedroom. She would remove her beautiful dress and never wear it again.

The door banged open behind her, causing her to jump, and Wade strode into the room, eyes furious, jaw set. He slammed the door behind him, and Rebecca shivered. *"Where the hell have you been?"* he growled.

There was no point in lying. "On board the Tempest," she whispered.

He swore under his breath, eyes raking her from head to toe. "You little slut!" he blazed, satisfied by the pain he read on her face. But she raised her chin a notch, and he struck out again. "Are you his mistress now?" When she frowned in confusion, he pressed on in disgust. "Those fine clothes must have bought a great deal."

She looked down at the lovely gown, blinking back tears. Without a word, she walked toward her bedroom.

Wade charged across the kitchen and blocked her path, swatting away her hand as she reached for the doorknob. "Damn it, Rebecca! *Answer me!* How could you have done this to me – to yourself? That's what we ran from – why we stowed away! We've built a new life here. How will we face our friends now? Doesn't that matter to you?" When still she refused to respond, he ran his hands through his hair. "It matters to me!"

"I'm glad they're more important to you than I am!" she sobbed. Unable to bear his abuse any longer, she shoved him out of her way and pushed into her room. Slamming the door shut, she fell facedown on her bed and wept.

Paul entered his bedchamber and breathed a sigh of relief. It had been an exhausting three weeks, and he was glad to be back home, in his own room and in his own bed. But as he sat down to pull off his boots and unbutton his shirt, he felt forlorn, the empty room, desolate. Tired as he was, he pushed off the bed and walked out onto the balcony.

Rebecca Remmen, what are you doing tonight?

He hadn't seen her slip off the Tempest. Then again, he'd been preoccupied with helping his brother and making the arrangements to get everyone home. During the nine-day voyage from New York to Charmantes he had guarded his silence, speaking very little to her to bolster his stowaway story and protect her honor, even though he had tarnished it. Everyone on the ship had accepted his explanation, seemed to believe him, though John had raised a dubious brow.

Paul wondered over his own deception. When he feared his brother was dead, he'd had a reason to pretend disinterest in Rebecca, but now he was free to court her. So why hadn't he done so? There was nothing stopping him from bringing her home to his bed tonight. His heart thundered in his ears as he relived the heady memory of her naked in his arms, inexperienced, yet meeting his inflamed ardor with uninhibited carnal zeal.

But Rebecca wanted more than his bed. She wanted to be his wife, wanted his love. Was marriage to her so repulsive? No, he realized without trepidation. He would savor making love to her each night, would be content to claim that right. He had thought of little else the last eighteen days – since the night of their unbridled union. Never had a woman obsessed him so, not even Charmaine. Even if Rebecca ignored him, he would enjoy having her here just to look at her. He admired her stubbornness, and he burned to tame her. But mostly, he longed to hold her, to comfort her, to make her happy.

Tomorrow, he would visit her, just to see her again, to be intoxicated. Finally, he was able to settle into bed, and after a while, sleep.

Diabolical dreams beset him, fragmented visions of Rebecca running frantically through a sinister forest with hooded fiends close on her heels, dogs barking and tracking her down. She was crying, calling for him, and his heart raced. He awoke in a cold sweat and jumped up.

The consuming need to know that she was all right spurred him to action. In less than ten minutes, he was dressed and in the stable saddling a confused Alabaster. He thanked the gods that the night sky was clear and the moon bright. It was nearly one o'clock in the morning when he rode down the deserted dirt road and stopped in front of the Remmen cottage. A soft glow spilled out of the kitchen window. Someone was still awake. He tied Alabaster to the picket fence, strode up to the small porch, and rapped on the door.

Wade was drunk and scowled darkly at him. "What the hell do you want?"

"May I come in?"

"No," he growled, his words slurred, "you may not come in!"

"I would like to see Rebecca," Paul pressed.

Wade's wicked laugh ended in a hiccup. "Of course you would," he sneered sarcastically, astounded by the man's imperious gall. "She's only seventeen years old! If you think I'm going to stand back while you satisfy your lust on her, you'd better think twice! You just try to step into this house – you just try to touch her – and I swear I'll break your goddamn neck!"

"You're drunk," Paul said softly, disheartened that Rebecca had told her brother about them.

"You're damned right I'm drunk!" he cried. "How do you think I felt this afternoon when my sister stepped off that ship, dressed in the most elegant gown a rich man's money could buy? What do you think everyone else was thinking? She disappeared for three weeks, and suddenly, she's back? They all know she's a whore now – *your whore!"*

Paul's blood boiled, but he knew that Wade was right. Many were at the harbor today; surely they had come to the same conclusion. And the dress! Paul had only longed to make her happy. Now he realized that he'd unconsciously wanted everyone to know that she belonged to him, the gown an emblem of his desire. But in so doing, he had exposed her to public censure, Wade a harbinger of the castigation that was yet to come. Fleetingly, he thought of Yvette and Jeannette, and what his reaction would be under similar circumstances. *I'd throttle the bastard!*

"I want to speak with Rebecca," he insisted.

"And I told you to go to hell!" Wade snarled.

Paul's mind was made up, and he easily pushed his way into the cottage.

Wade went after him with a vengeance, and before Paul knew what had hit him, they lay sprawled on the floor. Then the shock was gone, and Paul grabbed Wade's shirtfront, rolling over and pinning him down. "Now listen to me," he growled. "I *will* speak with your sister. Whatever you think about her, you're wrong, and I'll hear no more of it, do you understand? I love her, and I'm going to marry her. *That's* why I'm here."

Paul pushed up and off the floor, then extended a hand to Wade, whose anger had turned to confusion. "Marriage…?" he murmured, making no move to rise. "But you can't – I mean, you don't–"

The strange response ended there, as apparently he fought off the effects of his inebriation. Finally, he grabbed hold of Paul's proffered hand and stood. "I'll get Rebecca," he said soberly.

Paul's relief was momentary, for the bedroom was empty, the green dress spread reverently across her bed. He drove a hand through his hair, gripped with worry. Where had she flown to now? Her grief had been great, and certainly, Wade had made it worse. *I don't want to shame my brother. Better I just disappear.* Well, Paul wouldn't let her just disappear. He'd find her – *tonight!*

"Do you have any idea where she might have gone?" he asked.

"No," Wade whispered, suddenly ashamed, cringing with the memory of how he had treated her. "I said some rotten things this afternoon."

"We have to find her."

"Felicia!" Wade suggested. "Next door. She might know."

Paul hastened to the house, rousing all within with a heavy fist on the door. Felicia's gruff father opened it, capitulating grudgingly when it was clear Paul would not leave without speaking to his daughter. Felicia was standing before them moments later.

"Where is Rebecca?" Paul demanded.

Her sleepy eyes turned shrewd, and suddenly, she was smiling. "I saw that beautiful gown," she replied sweetly. "But Rebecca said she wasn't going to be bought and paid for – even by you."

"What else did she say?" he pressed through clenched teeth.

"Just that she's moving on – to a new life," Felicia answered smugly. "I tried to warn her about you, but she wouldn't listen. She kept insisting that she was going to marry you. Some girls have to learn the hard way. Anyway, now she knows better."

"Really?" Paul scoffed. "Well, Felicia, if you happen to see Rebecca, tell her that I *do* intend to marry her."

He didn't wait for a reaction, but clamped an arm around Wade's shoulders and led him back to his cottage. "I know where to look. Stay here and sleep it off. Meet me at the mansion first thing in the morning. I'll be there – with Rebecca."

Wade began to object, but Paul insisted again that he knew where Rebecca was and needed to speak with her – alone. "Go to bed," he reiterated. "And don't worry about your sister." He headed toward the Tempest and the cabin they had shared.

Moonlight spilled through the porthole, illuminating the cubicle. Rebecca was sound asleep in the bunk, her raven-black hair fanned across the pillow. An ineffable happiness seized him. If he hadn't come tonight, she would have been gone in the morning, lost to him, perhaps forever. Why had he been so foolish? Why hadn't he just married her on the ship? There was a priest right there to see the vows exchanged and the union blessed. He had vacillated again, but no more. This might be the worst mistake of his life – or the very best beginning. For Rebecca, he was willing to take that chance.

Sitting gently on the edge of the bed, he took her hand in his, and brushed the hair from her face. She stirred, and her eyes fluttered open. She stared up at him for a moment, dazed. He smiled down at her and could tell that she thought she was dreaming.

"I've come to take you home," he said softly. "To *my* home."

She pulled her hand away and rubbed her eyes. Her brow gathered and she pushed herself onto her elbows. "What are you doing here?"

"I couldn't sleep, Rebecca. I was worried about you, so I went to your house. Your brother did not put me at ease."

"He hates me now," she murmured, her head bobbing forward. "I knew he would."

"He doesn't hate you."

"He's ashamed of me. He has a right to be ashamed of me."

"No, Rebecca," Paul refuted, gently gripping her chin and persuading her to look at him, "he doesn't have that right. And after tomorrow, no one will dare insult you. If they do, they will have me to deal with."

She was bewildered, but he stood and extended a hand to her, inviting her up and out of the cot. "Come," he said. "Let's get you home."

"No!" she said. "I want to go far away from this place."

"Come," he insisted. "This is your home – here, on Charmantes, with me."

"I won't be your mistress!"

"I'm not asking you to be my mistress, Rebecca," he declared. "I'm asking you to be my wife."

Her green eyes swiftly filled with tears, but then she was shaking her head 'no'. "I don't want to marry you now."

Nonplussed, he felt as if the air had been knocked out of him. "Why?" he managed to utter. "Why not?"

She gulped back her agony. "I want you to love *me.* I couldn't live knowing that you wished I were Charmaine. You've only come because she's lost to you."

"No Rebecca, that's not true. I swear it is not true."

"*Isn't it?*"

"Rebecca, since I made love to you, I haven't been able to think straight. At first, I was confused. I was worried over my brother and Charmaine. What happened between us was so exquisite that it frightened me. Even after I knew John was alive, it frightened me. But tonight, when I was alone in my bed, I realized how unhappy I was. Not because I had lost Charmaine, but because I had lost you – *you,* Rebecca. You're the one I want."

He bent forward and kissed her, a slow, tender kiss that deepened in intensity. Her hands found their way to his shoulders, and she pulled herself up and into his embrace. Abruptly, he drew back. "Now, will you marry me?"

"Yes, oh yes!" she sobbed, pulling him close and kissing him ardently.

His resolve to wait until they were back at the mansion crumbled, and in seconds, they were stripping off their clothes and making fierce love. When they had finished, he enfolded her in his arms. She nuzzled against him and sighed in quintessential happiness. He could feel the moisture of her tears on his chest, and he relished an unprecedented sense of contentment.

Monday, January 14, 1839

They woke to the caterwaul of seagulls and the sun's light.

"We'd better get up," he urged, "or Captain Conklin will be setting sail again with us aboard."

Rebecca smiled up at him. "What made you change your mind about me?"

"I never changed my mind, Rebecca," he said honestly. "I think I loved you from that very first night."

"But you called me a little girl then."

"You're not a little girl, Rebecca. You're all woman – my woman." He kissed her passionately, then sighed. "I've had many women, but not one has ever made me feel the way you have, Rebecca, and no woman has ever loved me the way you do. I'd be a fool to throw that away, wouldn't I?"

Her arms encircled his waist, and she rested her check against his chest. "I've loved you – for such a very long time."

He kissed the top of her head, squeezed her tightly, and then stood to dress. She followed suit, pulling on her breeches and shirt. Paul chuckled.

"I told your brother to meet me at the manor this morning," he said. "We'd best hurry if we're going to get there ahead of him."

Rebecca puzzled over the remark, but didn't question him about it.

They left the ship to find an agitated Alabaster waiting for them, hooves pawing the dirt at the end of the pier, ears flicked back. Paul quickly untied the stallion and patted his neck in apology. He mounted, reaching down for her. Rebecca hesitated, but he grabbed her arm.

"Everyone will be looking at us!" she objected, holding back.

"Let them look!" he laughed.

His words touched her heart. She pulled up behind him, wrapped her arms around his waist, and pressed her cheek against his back, certain she would awaken at any moment.

John and George had just stepped off the last stair of the landing when they walked through the doors. One look at their disheveled appearance, Rebecca's outlandish garb, and John chuckled knowingly. "What have the two of you been up to – a nature walk?"

"Cut it, John," Paul said. Rebecca was blushing, but he put his arm around her and pulled her close. "Where is Michael?"

John's grin grew wider. "Has my brother finally come to his senses?"

"Steady, John!" George warned, despite Paul's confident smile.

"That's right, John, I have. Rebecca and I are going to be married – this morning, if possible."

"Well then, Paulie, congratulations are in order." John extended his hand in a gesture of genuine goodwill, even as he was thinking: *You should have married her on the ship last week, you horny bastard!*

The morning was spent making all the arrangements. Rebecca was closeted in one of the guestrooms, where Millie helped her bathe and dress in the wedding gown that Mercedes had kindly offered. Though the fit wasn't perfect, a few hasty alterations made the garment more than acceptable. Paul also bathed, donning the suit he had worn for the ball. Father Michael prepared the chapel for its first Mass in nearly five months.

At precisely noon, Rebecca Remmen grasped her brother's arm and walked down the short aisle of the chapel. Jeannette blushed as they passed by her pew and Wade smiled down at her. She looked up at her father, hugged his arm, and giggled softly when he winked at her. Paul stood tall at the altar, ready to receive his bride. Wade handed her over, and the couple stepped before Michael.

Frederic looked on with pride, thankful that Rebecca had become Paul's obsession. During the voyage home, it had been obvious that Paul was smitten with the girl, going out of his way to keep her at arm's length, as if she'd swallow him whole if he came too close. Though everyone wondered what had happened between them, Frederic didn't have to guess. He read the hunger in his son's eyes, knew the feeling all too well, even the circumstances. Paul's desire for Rebecca mirrored his fierce love for Elizabeth. God had been very good to his family.

After the ceremony, Paul led his beautiful wife to the archway, where they received heartfelt congratulations. Wade was the last to embrace his sister. Paul noted the guilt in his eyes. Or was it something more? Apprehension? But Rebecca hugged him close, too happy to hold a grudge. When he smiled shamefaced at Paul, Paul clapped him on the back, letting bygones be bygones.

Michael rearranged the altar, placing the chalice and ciborium off to one side in preparation for the other two marriage ceremonies he would perform later that day. It could be months before they ascertained the legitimacy of Benito St. Giovanni's priesthood, and Michael planned on returning to Richmond very soon. He'd been away from the refuge and church far too long already. John and Charmaine, as well as George and Mercedes wanted to be certain that God sanctified their unions, so Michael gladly accepted their invitation to preside over the reaffirming nuptials.

Fatima Henderson whipped up an afternoon fete, and family and friends gathered on the porch and lawn to celebrate Paul and Rebecca's wedding in the mild, winter breezes. Overseeing all the details, Charmaine finally headed to her chambers to nurse Marie and check on John. As she reached the portico, she espied Paul and Rebecca alone for the first time that day and changed direction.

"Congratulations," she said when she reached them. Looking pointedly at Rebecca, she added, "welcome to our family. You've made Paul and the entire family very happy today."

Rebecca was amazed by Charmaine's genuine warmth, and she nodded slightly.

"I'm glad you made the voyage in search of John," Charmaine said to Paul, "We both benefited from it."

Paul responded with a dashing smile, pleased that she had gone out of her way to put Rebecca at ease. "Thank you, Charmaine," he said simply, though Charmaine read much more in the depths of his green eyes. They had journeyed a long way together, and she treasured the unique bond they would always share.

Wade joined them, followed immediately by Frederic. "Mr. Remmen," Frederic declared, "my daughter insists that I thank you for saving her sister's life."

Wade coughed uncomfortably. "It was nothing, sir."

Frederic refuted the modest denial. "Charmaine has confirmed the entire story. I am forever in your debt."

Wade rubbed the back of his neck self-consciously, and Rebecca smiled, intensely proud of her brother. "Wade is bashful about compliments, sir."

"Be that as it may," Frederic continued. "I am grateful and will, from this day forward, consider Wade a member of this family."

"Thank you, sir," Wade replied, taking Frederic's hand and shaking it heartily, a smile breaking across his face.

Charmaine shooed John into the dressing room so that she could complete her toilette alone. "It's my wedding day, and you mustn't see the bride until she enters the church."

"All right, all right," he laughed as she gave him a final shove through the doorway. "I know when I'm not wanted."

An hour later, she descended the great staircase, wearing the gown that she'd donned the evening of Paul's ball, her hair cascading down her back. Today, as she walked down the aisle on Joshua's arm, she looked more spectacular than on that wondrous night nine months ago. Motherhood agreed with her, her figure curvaceous to a fault, her ample bosom straining against the décolletage of her bodice. She was radiant and took John's breath away. When she reached him, she gave him a brilliant smile before turning her eyes to her father, whose happiness mirrored her own.

Family and friends looked on, overjoyed to share in their second, more profound wedding ceremony. The chapel echoed with sniffles and sighs, and to the congregation's amusement, Marie shrieked now and then, adding her own two cents to the proceedings.

As the Mass neared a close, Michael asked for the rings. Charmaine watched quizzically as John searched his pockets for the simple wedding band that he'd shown her earlier in the day. It had belonged to his mother. When her smile turned to frown, he whispered, "Not to worry, my Charm, I know it's here somewhere." He finally dug it out of his waistcoat pocket and presented it to her – the largest, most brilliant diamond ring she had ever beheld. Her eyes grew nearly as wide as the stone itself, and out of the corner of her eye, she could see her father smiling broadly at her. A murmur shook the chapel as John lifted her left hand and slipped the beautiful stone on her finger.

"With this ring, I thee wed," he pronounced solemnly.

She stared at the fiery diamond a moment longer, felt the weight of it. She looked up into John's happy eyes, the delight born of her astonishment sparkling there.

It was her turn. She slipped off the plain, loose band she'd worn around her index finger and reached for his hand. "With this ring, I thee wed," she choked out, as she pushed the ring over his finger, tears evident in her voice.

When she was composed, Michael proclaimed, "You may kiss the bride!"

John pulled her into his arms and brushed his lips across hers. Then he buried his face in her wild locks and savored the fresh scent of her.

She hugged him close. "I can't wear this ring, John Duvoisin!" she murmured heatedly near his ear. "It is huge and very heavy!"

"Then I will just have to find another young lady who will," he whispered back, squeezing her the harder. "I love you, Mrs. Duvoisin. That ring is only a small token of my love and affection."

"I love you, too!" she averred.

Someone coughed, and Charmaine realized they had prolonged their embrace beyond the realm of decorum. She broke away, but John kept a possessive arm around her shoulder, and together they received the congratulations of all those in the chapel.

She was conscious of the ring all day, its size alone making it impossible to ignore, and her fingers rotated it continuously. At dinner, John caught her studying it, her fingers splayed upon the linen tablecloth. "Do you like it?" he asked.

"No," she breathed, looking at him beseechingly, "I love it. But it wasn't necessary, John. All I'll ever want is you. You know that, don't you?"

"Yes, I know that, my Charm." He nodded toward it. "Read the inscription."

She hadn't thought to look inside the band. She removed it and read the writing there. Once again, her eyes filled with tears. "I'll always be your charm, as long as you'll have me."

"Forever," he whispered. "I'll have you forever."

He grasped her hand and brought it to his mouth, his titillating kiss sending wisps of pleasure up her arm. He read the look of longing in her eyes. "Later, my Charm," he promised, setting her heart to a rapid beat. "Later..."

Having cleared the altar of the final wedding feast, Michael headed to the dining room for dinner, crossing through the ballroom and into the foyer. For the first time since his arrival yesterday, all was quiet there, and he stopped for a moment to study the portrait of Colette Duvoisin, the painting that had given him pause the moment he had first stepped into the mansion yesterday.

So this was the woman who had started it all, her pulchritude unrivaled, just as John had once told him. He was so deep in thought that he didn't hear Frederic's approach until the older man was standing beside him.

"She was very beautiful," Michael said.

"Yes," Frederic replied. "In a few more years, my daughters will look exactly like her, especially Yvette."

This surprised Michael. Frederic smiled now. "Personality plays a great part in one's looks. Yvette is more like her mother than her sister will ever be. Colette was full of fire and very vocal about her beliefs and crusades. She would have approved of your work, Michael."

Before Michael could ask him what he meant, footfalls echoed from the hallway. Frederic turned slightly to regard John.

Michael considered both men. The mending kinship was fragile and, he feared, easily broken.

Frederic's eyes returned to the magnificent portrait. "I think I shall have the canvas taken down," he commented.

"No, Father," John breathed, "don't remove it. I feel secure knowing that Colette is watching over us."

The remarkable declaration intensified in the sudden silence. Frederic broke the aura. "I'm afraid I've forgotten something in the chapel," he murmured and walked away.

John watched his father disappear through the archway, staring after him pensively.

Michael permitted John his far-away thoughts. "Shall we go in to dinner?" he finally asked.

"You go ahead," John replied, never looking at him. "I'll be there in a minute."

The light of the joyous day was waning, and in the chapel, the shadows lengthened. The stone enclosure was cool, and Frederic lit the candles on the altar. He edged into the front pew and knelt. Burying his face in his hands, he offered a prayer of thanksgiving. His prayers had been answered. When his Maker called him home now, he could go to Him in peace – clear of conscience. He had done everything within his mortal power to atone for his many mistakes and sins.

He lost himself in the quiet sanctuary, the consuming peace here, and opened his heart and soul, inviting Elizabeth and Colette's guiding presence.

A hand came down on his shoulder, and his eyes lifted to John, standing just behind him. He watched in surprise as his son settled next to him. They sat for many minutes without speaking.

"Thank you," John finally murmured, fighting the moment's reticence.

Frederic turned to find his son's earnest eyes locked on him.

"I would be dead if you hadn't been there for me." John sighed deeply. "When you had the seizure, I left you for dead. I didn't care if you lived or died. I *wanted* you to die. After everything I did to you, you could have – *should have* – left me for dead, too. I didn't deserve to have you stay by my side."

Frederic looked back at the altar, struggling for words. "Thirty years ago, I abandoned you, John. Even though you were innocent and vulnerable, I abandoned you." He swallowed hard. "No matter what you had done to me, I wasn't going to abandon you again."

Another lengthy silence took hold.

"I saw Pierre that night, Father," John whispered. "I saw my mother, and I saw Colette. I was with them." He looked at Frederic again. "They are in a peaceful place. Mother wants you to know that she loves you still. And Colette... she loves you, too."

Frederic turned tear-filled eyes to the altar. "I loved her, John," he rasped.

"I know you did, Father. I know you did."

Frederic could say no more.

John rose and placed a comforting hand on his shoulder, held it there for a moment, then turned and left.

The dinner table was lively and animated, filled to capacity. Only the head and foot of the table remained vacant. John finally joined them, followed a few minutes later by Frederic. Each in his turn smiled at Charmaine, and she wondered where they had been. Now all twelve chairs were occupied. John and Frederic were quickly drawn into various conversations, often talking across the great expanse to one another. Charmaine sat back, overwhelmed by the wholesome banter of a loving family.

How many dinners she had passed in her parents' home on tenterhooks, fearful of incensing her father? Even when she lived with the Harringtons, she had always yearned for a family of her own. Here it was before her now: a feast of boundless abundance. Her mother's presence was strong, and she bowed her head in renewed thanksgiving. Finally, peace and love reigned under this roof.

When the table was cleared, everyone migrated to the drawing room. Even John, who had rested again after their wedding ceremony, insisted on joining them. As additional chairs were pulled from the study, Michael sat on the piano bench near John.

"This pianoforte is similar to the one you have in New York," the priest commented.

"Piano, Michael," John corrected, "and it's identical. I purchased them from the Bridgeland and Jardine Company when they were first introduced five years ago. Perhaps you've heard of them?"

When Michael shook his head 'no', John continued. "The sound of this particular piano is powerful and brilliant. The manner in which it is strung heightens that quality, making it a far superior instrument to the pianoforte or harpsichord. I was quite taken by the demonstration they gave and, once I'd played it myself, immediately ordered four."

"*Four?*" Michael queried. "You purchased *four*?"

John chuckled. "One for New York, one for Richmond, the other for the plantation, and the fourth for here. It was quite a feat to secure it on the ship. But it did make for an interesting welcome when I arrived here. I thought my sisters would enjoy learning to play, and thanks to Charmaine, they have."

Frederic joined the conversation. "John is quite an accomplished pianist himself. It was the one thing at which he excelled when I sent him to university."

"I've heard him play," Michael remarked, unmindful of John's snicker. "Unfortunately, I've always interrupted him."

"Well then," Frederic said, "maybe he'll perform something for all of us now. That is, if you feel up to it?" He regarded his son, his eyes filled with pride.

Yvette and Jeannette moved closer and took up the petition, "Yes, Johnny, please! You used to play for us all the time. We'd love to hear something now."

"What would you have me play?"

"Anything!"

"Something special!"

"Why don't you play the piece you composed?" Frederic suggested.

John's eyes turned turbulent, and he looked to Charmaine. She was chatting with the Harringtons.

"I... I don't think I could," he hesitated.

Frederic read his misgivings. "It would please me to hear it, John."

John scratched the back of his neck, then acquiesced. Frederic and Michael found vacant chairs. Yvette sat in her father's lap. Jeannette grabbed Paul and Rebecca's hands and pulled them into the gathering, then settled next to Frederic, who patted her head as John began to play.

The opening chord echoed and all banter ceased, eyes turning to the man at the piano. His fingers traveled the familiar path across the keys, resurrecting the melancholy rhapsody. Pouring out his life and soul, John played, arpeggios rising in a frenzied fugue, turbulent and discontent, effete and hopeless, surrendering at last to a tender, tumbling cadence of bittersweet yearning. Then a sweet, new melody rose from the despair, a delicate strain that wed the somber with the bright, the harmonious threads amplifying in a reverberating crescendo. Then it ended: a triumphant, solitary chord.

Someone started clapping. John raised his head and turned slowly around. His eyes traveled to Charmaine, who sat spellbound. He winked at her. It had been accomplished; he'd found the resolution to his composition.

"Johnny," Yvette broke in, "I didn't know you wrote that!"

Charmaine was astounded. *John... of course John had composed the piece!* Why hadn't she guessed it? But more importantly, when was she going to realize that he would never cease to amaze her?

"You didn't know your brother was so talented, did you?" Frederic asked his daughter.

"Yes, I did!" Yvette countered, eliciting everyone's laughter.

The merriment died down, but Frederic remained pensive. He hugged Yvette and Jeannette close, giving each a tender kiss atop their heads. He could feel Colette's presence close by and savored the poignant moment.

John stood and crossed the room, drawing Charmaine out of her chair. She, too, was thinking about Colette. *I hope you were listening, my dear friend.* A distant memory answered: *Perhaps your touch is exactly what the piece needs...*

bend the masterpiece... possess it, as it has possessed you... then, when your love is the music, the harmony will be perfect. Colette had been speaking of John. Colette knew; somehow, she knew!

Looping her arm through John's, Charmaine allowed him to lead her from the room. They strolled along the front terrace, where it was cool and quiet. When they were just outside the ballroom, they stopped, and John leaned back against the balustrade. Charmaine stepped into his embrace.

"That was beautiful," she finally murmured.

"You've made it so, my Charm," he answered, studying every inch of her face, stroking her cheek with his hand. He pulled her against him and kissed her tenderly. "I love you, Charmaine, more than you'll ever know."

Rebecca trembled as Paul led her into his suite of rooms, closing the door quietly behind them. The day had been overwhelming. Now here she was with him, on her wedding night. She felt giddy and intoxicated, but mostly frightened. The grandeur and sophistication she'd experienced today were a world apart from her servile background, all of it quite intimidating. As the day had progressed, she began to question her foolhardy belief that she could ever live up to the role that she had coveted for the past three years. She turned to face her husband, anxiety written on her face.

"What is this?" Paul queried with a chuckle. "You're not suddenly afraid of me? This isn't the wench who scarred me for life, is it?" He rolled up his shirtsleeve, extending his wrist toward her so that she might see the bite mark she'd left there three weeks ago.

"I could never be afraid of you. But this house–" she indicated the lavish room "–and your family – who they are – all the things they know and own and can do! I was stupid to think I could fit in – that I was old enough to fit in. I don't even know how to read and write!"

She began to cry and Paul felt a painful twinge in his breast, his love for her fierce and daunting. He went to her and pulled her into his embrace. "Rebecca... Rebecca..." he murmured into her hair. "You have made me so happy! You're honest and strong and proud. You're not afraid to stand up for yourself."

Her cheek was pressed to his chest, and as he chuckled again, she found comfort in the deep rumble beneath her ear.

"You've plagued me, Mrs. Duvoisin: my thoughts by day and my dreams at night! Now don't tell me you don't belong here with me. You're as much a Duvoisin as anyone else in this family."

"But we hardly know one another. There are things–"

"No buts."

He held her at arm's length, studying her intently. "You want to learn to read and write? Then you'll learn. Anything you want to do – just tell me, and it will be done. Do you understand?"

"Yes. I think so."

"Good," he said, and his smile turned wicked. "Now, I don't want to hear any more of this nonsense or I'll be forced to put you across my knee and give you something to cry about!"

"You wouldn't dare!" she taunted, her heart suddenly pounding, her cheeks flushed in anticipation of his lovemaking.

Paul savored undressing her, and she, him. He carried her into his bedchamber and laid her on the mattress, making love to her through the night. By dawn, they were spent.

"You will soon be carrying my child, Rebecca, if every night is like this," he said huskily.

She smiled down at her flat belly and stroked it. "I think I already am," she murmured shyly, grateful that he had pursued her last night, his resolution that they wed putting to rest her brother's volcanic protestations.

Paul's hand quickly covered hers, his dark fingers spreading across her creamy flesh. "I thought as much," he replied, his ardor inflamed with the knowledge that their first passionate encounter had made them a part of one another. His hand moved down from her tummy and stroked between her legs. When a guttural groan escaped her lips, he rolled on top of her and took her again.

John lay with Charmaine asleep in his arms, pondering the miracle that had brought him home. He remembered and relived that surreal place – that place in the light where his mother, Pierre, and Colette had embraced him. In his mind's eye, he was there once again in paradise, holding his lost family in his arms – his son and the woman who should have been his wife.

"John," Colette breathed when he relaxed his embrace. "How is your father?"

The peace that enveloped him was shaken. "My father?"

"He is crying. He is praying for you. He doesn't want you to die."

"Why do we have to talk about him, when *I'm* here with you? Now I can take care of you."

"You did take care of me," she whispered. "Agatha and Robert – they have chosen to go to that other place..."

"And we can finally be together," John stated vehemently, "with our son."

"We are not meant to be together," she dolefully replied. "That is not our destiny. Frederic is part of me, John. I belong to him, and he belongs to me." She brought his hand to her lips and kissed it tenderly, tempering the blow. "You must go back and reconcile with him."

"I don't understand...?"

"He never meant to hurt you, John. He loves you. Don't you hear how he weeps for you?"

Her melancholy eyes bore into him, and he could hear his father crying.

"Charmaine has abundant love to give – to my children – to you. She needs you as much as your father needs me. You've known that for a long time, haven't you?"

The blues and blondes melted into mellow browns, and his mother was smiling up at him once again. Pierre was no longer in his arms, but nestled at her side. Behind him, John heard a baby cry. "You don't belong here, John," she affirmed. "Go back. Go back to your father and tell him I love him. Tell him *you* love him. Go back to your beautiful new daughter, and go back to Charmaine. She loves you so..."

The baby cried again. His father was talking to him, begging God's mercy, and John could feel the man's deep sorrow, his Gethsemane. He yearned to comfort him, take away the agony. His breast ached, and he drew a deep breath to ease the pain. He longed to hold Charmaine. If he could just get back to his father, he knew he would hold her again.

John turned away from the light. Then he was back on the ceiling of the room. His father was still there, bent over the bed. A priest was mumbling prayers; it was Michael. He looked back at the light, but it was quickly fading away. His gaze shifted, and he saw a woman at the foot of his bed. She looked so much like Charmaine. It was Marie, and she was smiling and beckoning to him. John reached for her. He had too much to live for. He'd fight to live.

He was no longer on the ceiling. He was sleeping, and for a few moments longer, he reveled in oblivion, at peace knowing that his son was safe and happy in his mother's care. When his eyes fluttered open, he saw relief and joy wash over his father's face. Frederic grasped his hand even tighter, and John was comforted by the contact. "Father," he groaned before closing his eyes again, content that he'd chosen life over death...

Thinking back on that incredible experience now, with his beautiful wife asleep in his embrace and his newborn daughter slumbering in the cradle beside their bed, John realized that a miracle *had* brought him home. Elizabeth, Colette, and even Marie had sent him back to Charmaine. But he couldn't tell her that. Not that she wouldn't believe him, but she didn't want to hear about Colette. He would never allow Colette to come between them again. Colette had told him that she belonged to his father, and he was willing to accept that. It didn't matter anymore; it was over; it was finally over. With a deep sigh, John hugged Charmaine tightly and closed his eyes. A resplendent serenity settled over him, bathing him in hopefulness.

Epilogue

Friday, March 8, 1839
Accomplished

The day dawned bright and glorious, but today they would be leaving, leaving Charmantes to travel to Richmond and on to New York City. Charmaine attempted to combat another onslaught of sentimentality. John came up behind her, reading her thoughts as she took the last of the clothing from her dresser drawers. "Don't be sad, my Charm. We won't stay away forever." She turned in his arms and kissed him. When he had gone, she finished packing.

Colette's letter was not where she had left it, though John's shirts were still there, and she wondered if he now carried it with him. Did he realize that it had been moved, possibly read? She was going to ask him about it, tell him that she had found it, had almost read it. Someday, she decided, but not today. Today was sad enough.

He had been home almost two months now and, by all signs, fully recovered. The mild weather of March was upon them and, over the last few weeks, they had spent many happy moments together. Her father and the Harringtons had returned to Virginia in late January, and she was looking forward to seeing them soon. Why then was she downtrodden? Charmantes. *This* was her home, would always be her home.

She no longer wore the fiery diamond on her finger, choosing Elizabeth's wedding band instead. The spectacular ring was suspended on a long gold chain that Frederic had presented to her as a wedding gift and rested under her clothing, near her heart. "I'll wear it on my finger for special occasions," she had promised John. "But for now, I feel it's safer here," and her hand had gone to her breast.

"I'm certain it is," he had responded devilishly. "However, that diamond will be on your finger when we arrive in Richmond. I want those gossipmongers to *really* have something to wag their tongues about!"

"John!"

"You can't tell me that you're not looking forward to seeing them turn green with envy when you flash that ring their way… Admit it, Charmaine!"

Unable to deny it, she had blushed, making John chuckle.

At breakfast, Frederic's countenance was melancholy. Mercedes was also pensive, cradling her newborn son in her lap. George ate heartily, but said little. Sniffles carried from behind the kitchen door. Only the girls were bubbly, excited to be traveling abroad with their brother out into that other world they'd heard so much about. Charmaine was certain that if they were not coming along, the room would erupt into tears.

Marie began to fidget, but before Charmaine could get up, Frederic went to the bassinet. With her nod, he returned to the table with his granddaughter, holding her on his lap. "You're to bring her back," he enjoined.

"I will," Charmaine vowed, but Frederic's eyes were fixed on John.

"Don't worry, Father," John appeased. "Charmaine won't allow us to stay away for very long. We'll be back by the fall."

"The fall?" Yvette protested. "We want to go to New York and see snow! Why would we want to come back here in the fall when it's usually rainy anyway?"

John gave her a lopsided smile. "It doesn't normally snow until January or February in New York, Yvette. We can always venture there in winter. And perhaps Father will come with us then."

"No," the man stated. "I've had enough of New York to last me a lifetime."

"And we can't be away when Rebecca's baby arrives," Jeannette interjected.

"Rebecca's baby, huh!" Yvette reproved. "Wade is the only reason you want to come back. You are hoping to see more of him once the baby is born." Jeannette smiled with the thought of it, but Yvette bristled in disgust. "I think New York and snow are far more interesting than him!"

Rose shook her wizened head. "We won't be seeing much of anybody if Rebecca and Paul decide to make a home of Espoir, and I am getting too old to travel all the way there and wait on that little bundle's arrival."

John laughed. "To think that in a few more years, there will be a new generation running around Charmantes, instigating madness and mayhem."

"I don't know, John," George countered. "You have a daughter, not a son. It won't be the way it used to be with the three of us."

"Thank heavens!" Rose replied, making Frederic chuckle.

"You never know," John said devilishly. "Marie could wind up as bad as Yvette. Everyone knows she's worse than all three of us put together!"

"Hey!" his sister objected, though her eyes twinkled loftily. The entire room roared with laughter, the solemn mood lifting.

Shortly afterward, they departed in three carriages filled to capacity, waving goodbye to Mercedes and Rose, who stayed behind.

The town was busy, with two ships moored in the harbor. Paul descended the gangplank of the smaller vessel. "I arrived in time," he said, taking in the entire company as they alighted from the carriages. "I wanted to say goodbye."

With immense pride, Frederic watched his two sons exchange handshakes. "Take care of yourself, John. And don't stay away too long."

"I won't be allowed to," John replied. "And don't you work too hard either, Paulie. Save some energy for that lovely wife of yours."

"I get more rest when I go to work," Paul rejoined rakishly.

He turned to Charmaine just in time to note the blush that spread across her cheeks. His eyes fell to her slumbering baby, cradled in her arms. "By the time you get back, we might have one of own to show off," he said affectionately.

"We hope to return before your baby arrives," she replied, smiling up at him.

He stepped closer and embraced her, placing a gentle kiss on her cheek. "Take care, Charmaine. We're going to miss you."

"Come on, come on!" Yvette insisted. "You act as if you're never going to see each other again. I want to get going!"

"Just a moment longer, Yvette," John cajoled. "Why don't you and your sister scoot up the gangplank and find your cabin?"

Yvette scrambled away, but Jeannette turned to her father with tears in her eyes. She hugged him tightly and whispered, "I'm going to miss you, Papa."

"And I, you, Princess," he answered hoarsely. "But you're going to have a wonderful time and will come back to Charmantes with many stories to tell me."

Before her tears spilled over, she turned to Paul and gave him a quick kiss, too. Then she hurriedly boarded the ship in pursuit of her sister.

John watched his father, realizing just how empty the manor would be with almost everyone away. "So, Paul," he said, hoping to dispel what could quickly turn into a maudlin farewell, "you just came to see us off, did you?"

"Actually, no," Paul chuckled. "Rebecca is still in the cabin. We've decided to move back here, at least until the baby is born. None of the servants want to stay in the house, anyway. They insist it is haunted."

"And what do you say?" John asked, piqued by his brother's uncomfortable laugh.

"I'm more comfortable at home. No one cooks like Fatima, not even Rebecca. And she is lonely there. Her friends are on Charmantes, and Mercedes is up at the house."

George agreed, knowing that his wife missed Rebecca and would grow lonely with Charmaine away. Rebecca and Mercedes had struck up a friendship, and Mercedes had begun to teach Rebecca how to read and write.

"Well then," John breathed, "I guess it's time we were on our way." He looked to his father and extended his hand.

Frederic seized it and pulled John into his embrace. "I'll miss you, son. Don't stay away for too long."

"I won't, Father," John answered, grabbing hold of his father before stepping back. "Don't let the tobacco wilt while I'm gone."

Inhaling deeply, Frederic chuckled and nodded.

With a happy heart, Charmaine embraced the man next. "Thank you – for everything," she whispered, but Frederic held her at arms' length and looked at her quizzically as if to say he should be thanking her.

"Take care of my granddaughter."

"I secured the cradle to the cabin floor," George told John, "so Marie should be comfortable during the voyage."

John clapped his friend on the back, put his arm around his wife, and together, they embarked. When the last of the luggage had been loaded, the girls joined them at the rail, waving goodbye. The gangplank was raised, and the ship pushed from the pier. The first sails were released and instantly snapped in the wind, the lofty gales taking hold and pulling each canvas taut. The girls scampered off again, but Charmaine and John remained starboard side, watching as Frederic, Paul, and George finally turned away, heading for a typical day of grueling labor.

Additional sails were unfurled, and the packet began to pick up speed, easily propelled through the inlet.

Charmaine looked up at John, who'd turned Marie in his arms so that she could see everything around her, her back propped against his chest. She could hold her head up now and was alert, her large brown eyes riveted first on the gulls that squawked and darted in and out of the rigging, then on the aquamarine water.

Charmaine hugged John's arm and sighed. He had convalesced quickly, strong once again, thanks to rejuvenating rest and Fatima's good cooking.

"Don't be unhappy," he coaxed.

"I'm not," she said. "Now that the departure is behind me, I'm looking forward to seeing your homes in Virginia and New York.

"*Our* homes," he corrected.

As they forged into the open sea, the winds increased, the sails billowing like giant pillows on towering spars high above them. Those on the deck were buffeted by gales that caught in their hair and whipped at their clothing. Jeannette and Yvette squealed in delight, sidestepping sailors who tried to concentrate on their work. Soon, there was nothing to see but ocean, and Marie began to fuss.

"She needs to nurse," Charmaine remarked. John smiled down at the protesting babe, then escorted his wife and daughter to their cabin one deck below.

When Paul returned to the other ship, Frederic spoke to George. "I've a favor to ask of you. I'd like you to make a trip to North Carolina and a plantation known as Silver Maple, west of Durham and just south of Burlington."

George's interest was piqued as Frederic produced a paper from his pocket and handed it him. "Maximilian Krait owns the Silver Maple plantation and a slave named Henry Clayton. I want to purchase that slave. Actually, I want you to purchase him under your name. I don't want the Duvoisin name mentioned in any of the negotiations."

"Why?" George asked, further intrigued.

"Mr. Clayton has a beautiful wife, who is free and lives in New York City with their three children," Frederic explained. "Lily Clayton helped save John's life, and I would like to repay her." The memory of Nicholas Fairfield and Hannah Fields was potent, a driving force. They were of another time, and yet so much a part of everything that had happened. That realization allowed him a glimpse of Colette's smiling face, and he knew that, wherever she was, she greatly approved. He relished the vision a moment longer, then turned back to George, who remained attentive. "It is the least I can do for her and her children."

George nodded, having met Lily two years ago when he had gone in search of John, bearing Colette's letter. "But why me?" he queried.

"Because, according to Michael Andrews, Maximilian Krait would not sell Henry to a northern sympathizer like John. His southern loyalty runs as deep as John's abolitionist views, and Mr. Krait was not about to sell a slave who would ultimately be freed. Therefore, he must never know your intentions concerning

Henry Clayton. He must believe you are purchasing him to work – that he'll be set up on another plantation. To that end, you are to tell Mr. Krait that you've purchased a plantation and are interested in buying three strong men. Henry mustn't be singled out, or Krait will grow suspicious."

"And what if Henry is no longer at Silver Maple?" George queried.

"According to what I've heard, he was too powerful a man to lose, lighter skinned and very big. However, if he has been sold south, do whatever it takes to find him and spend whatever amount to purchase him."

"And after I've done that?"

"That second address is Lily's home in New York," Frederic said, nodding at the paper George now held in his hands. "Once you've secured the purchase, sign the documents entitling him to his freedom and transport him there."

"And the other two men?"

"I'm certain John can set them up with work in New York."

George nodded, but Frederic could read hesitation in his eyes. "If you're concerned about leaving your wife behind, why not take her along on an extended holiday?" The younger man's reservation disappeared, and Frederic produced a sizeable purse. "If you need more than this, there are signed notes within. They can be redeemed in the States through the Bank of Richmond."

"Well then," George said. "I guess it's just a matter of asking Mercedes."

They turned together to begin the day's labor. When Frederic reached the end of the boardwalk, he looked up at the meetinghouse, remembering his precious Colette. *For you, ma fuyarde, for you...*

It was dark when John left the cabin. The twins were finally asleep, giggling for the longest time before succumbing to the lull of the rocking the ship. Marie had been fussing since they left port, but Charmaine had finally gotten her to accept the nipple she had refused all afternoon. She'd sleep soundly once she had nursed her fill.

John strode to the railing and contemplated the endless ocean, the choppy water that no longer mirrored his life. With great contentment, he breathed deeply of the salty night air. After a while, he reached into his shirt pocket and withdrew Colette's letter. He unfolded it, and his eyes roamed over the delicate script. It was impossible to read her words in the poor light, for there was only a crescent moon, and the lamps on deck burned low. It didn't matter. He had memorized every line. He brought the stationery to his lips and savored the delicate scent of lily that still clung to the pages. Slowly, he allowed the sheets to slip from his fingers. The ocean breeze caught them, catapulting them high into the air, tossing them about like the seabirds that had careened around the ship that afternoon. The leaflets were carried far off, three white specters flying effortlessly in the freedom of vast openness, luminescent against the inky night. They relinquished the buffeting updrafts and fluttered to the water, settling on the swells and floating serenely away.

Charmaine grasped his hand.

Startled, he turned a guilty face to her. But she said nothing; rather she squeezed his fingers and looked out at the vast emptiness.

"Charmaine–" he began.

"I found the letter," she whispered before he could say more. "I didn't read it. I was *afraid* to read it."

"It's over, Charmaine," he promised. "It doesn't matter now."

"But you kept her letter – *all this time*."

He heard the despair in her voice, wanted to put it to rest forever. "And you should know why. You should know what it said," he murmured, beckoning her to step into his embrace as he leaned back against the railing. With his arms around her waist and chin atop her head, he recited:

My dearest John,

I cannot know your present state of mind. It is not my intention to cause you greater pain. I pray that you receive this letter. I have every faith in George to deliver it into you hands.

I know that I have few days left in this life. If I am to go to the afterlife clear of conscience, I must do what I can now to end the terrible hatred between you and your father. I desire eternal serenity, but without your help, this is impossible. Your father is in a miserable state, consumed with jealousy, anger, and sadness. If he leaves this life this way, then I will be responsible, because I am the one who came between you. I do not want to die knowing that he will shortly follow me in such a state of mind. The ferocity of his rage belies the depth of his love, but he needs somebody to show him the way. I was unable to do so, but I know that you are. If you have ever truly loved me, please take my dying prayer to heart, return home, and make amends with your father.

I also beg your forgiveness. I am sorry for turning to you in my loneliness and selfishly taking your love, only to abandon you to suffer all on your own. I think of you every day, wonder how you are, and pray that you will be happy again. I long to see you just one more time before I leave this earth. If I could only behold your smiling face before I finally close my eyes, I wouldn't be so frightened of going into that dark, endless night.

Our son is a beautiful child, John. I beg you to come home to see him. I want Pierre to experience the excitement for life that only you can show him, and I want you to know his innocent love. He has so much of it to give, and you need that love desperately.

I beg you to look after Yvette and Jeannette's happiness, too. If your father cannot put his bitterness behind him, the only love my children will have when I am gone is that of their young governess and Nana Rose. It is important that they know the love of family, so please, please take care of them for me. Show them how to run and play, how to laugh and sing.

I love you, John. I love you for the comfort and happiness you brought to me, not once, but twice. I love you for showing my daughters how to seize the day during that miraculous time when we were all together. I love you for your courage in letting go, for sacrificing your own desires in the noble interest of doing what was best for everyone. Live and love again, John. There is somebody in this world who deserves the privilege of sharing your unique zest for life and your beautiful, intense love.

Even though I know I am dying, I have hope for the future and for my children – hope that their lives will be happy and that some day, a true family will surround and embrace them. I have hope that you will find contentment in this life and a loving wife and children you can call your own. And finally, I have hope that you will find empathy in your heart for your father. Forgive him, John, so that we can be forgiven. If God is so good as to take me into his perpetual light, I will watch over and pray for you and all of my loved ones here on earth.

Until we meet again,
Your loving Colette

Charmaine was weeping by the time he had finished, her arms wrapped tightly around him. On a ragged breath, he finally spoke. "Yes, I came home, but selfishly, it wasn't to answer Colette's prayer."

"And yet," Charmaine said in amazement, "her prayer *was* answered all the same." Suddenly, the tears she shed were bittersweet and joyous. "You saw her, didn't you?"

"Yes, Charmaine, I saw her."

"But you came back to me," she choked out, lifting her eyes to his. "Why?"

"I had a choice," he rasped. "And I chose you."

He pulled her further into his embrace, buried his head in her hair, and held her more fiercely than ever before. He was weeping, and she could feel his tears trickling down her neck, uniting with her own. "She never belonged to me, Charmaine," he breathed. "But you do. You're all mine."

"Always," she promised, "and forever."

Sneak-preview: two scenes from the sequel to *Colette's Prayer*

Les Fuyards

November, 1827 Charmantes

Frederic arrived home shortly before seven, having passed two carriages along the way – part of his guests' entourage he suspected. They were pulled to the side of the road, fixing a disabled wheel, and Frederic stopped to see if he could be of assistance. Evening was settling upon the island and in the shade of the avenue, it was becoming difficult to see. But the coachmen had already replaced the broken spoke and were just about ready to set out again. They thanked him for his concern and congratulated him on his sons' return, dwelling on the news John had shared with them. Frederic nodded stiffly and, bidding them a good evening, rode on.

Briefly, he wondered how long this entire ordeal was going to take. It sounded as if John and this Colette of his were contemplating a large wedding, complete with festivities. At least that's what the men from the livery had led him to believe. Frederic snorted – just what he needed. That should cut very nicely into his workload. Then something different occurred to him, and he smiled wickedly. He had three young men home – three *strong* young men. Perhaps it was time that they learned what a day's work meant – how to toil for the clothes on their backs and the food on their table. *Yes,* Frederic mused as Champion cantered through the manor's gates and reached the paddock, *let the women plan the wedding while his two sons and George lent him a hand.* Once the vows were spoken, all three would eagerly board the next available ship back to France and scurry back to their studies, taking their guests with them. Frederic savored the thought as he dismounted and, with a nod, handed the stallion off to Gerald. His mood was still improving as he strode across the front lawn and entered the house.

Voices from the drawing room drew his immediate attention. Though he was in sore need of a bath and a change of clothes, curiosity got the better of him. Without ceremony and quite unannounced, he strode into the animated room, swiftly arresting the varied conversations in mid-sentence and gaining every eye.

Paul spoke first. "Father, you're home."

"Yes," came the clipped response, his keen eyes swiftly assessing everyone there. The company numbered seven, but that mattered little as his gaze came to rest on the young woman on the settee, John sitting opposite her in one of the armchairs. *Nothing special.*

"I suppose I should ask what the three of you are doing here," Frederic continued, "but I've heard the tale from nearly all of Charmantes already. It's always nice to be the last to know. So John, why don't you make your introductions?"

Bemused, John stood. "Good to see you too, Father," he returned.

The sarcasm met its mark, and Frederic hesitated. "Look," he stated, a bit more cordially this time, "I'm tired. I've worked a long day. So, why don't we get the formalities behind us? Are you going to introduce me to your fiancée – Colette, I believe?"

Frederic crossed to the sofa, closer to the young woman with whom John had been conversing. He looked at her, surprised when John said, "This is not Colette, Father. This is her friend, Pascale Drouet. And this is Pascale's mother, Madame Renée Drouet and Colette's mother, Madame Adèle Delacroix."

"Monsieur Duvoisin," Adèle purred, her eyes nearly popping out of their sockets as she extended a hand to the handsome, yet irascible gentleman. "It's a pleasure to finally meet you."

Not yet recovered from his blunder, Frederic accepted the proffered hand with a cursory nod, letting it drop as he turned a questioning frown upon his son. "And your fiancée?"

John's gaze traveled over his father's shoulder and his smile broadened. "She's just returned," he answered.

Frederic pivoted round just as Colette swept into the room, a soft smile lighting her translucent eyes.

She'd begun to speak when she caught sight of the two men staring at her, and the words died on her lips. For the briefest moment – an eternity – she couldn't breathe and was certain the blood drained from her face. But John rushed forward, oblivious to her inexplicable discomfiture. With a hand under her elbow, he propelled her forward. She followed as if in a trance, offering a hand to the man who loomed before her.

"Colette, this is my father," John was saying, "Father, Miss Colette Delacroix."

He was strikingly handsome, with chiseled face, square jaw, intense brown eyes, plunging nose and thin lips. He wiped at a sweaty brow with his forearm, and Colette took in his dark, mussed hair, broad shoulders and muscular chest – thoroughly masculine in contrast to the house-kept physiques of his two youthful sons. He was very tall – taller than John and Paul.

From somewhere far away, she heard herself saying, "Enchantée, Monsieur."

Frederic brought her hand slowly to his lips and, with eyes never wavering from hers, brushed an electrifying kiss across her fingers.

"Mademoiselle," he murmured, his voice deep, resonant, and inviting. When he released her hand, she bowed her head and unconsciously rubbed the spot his lips had scorched. He looked down at her a moment longer and then disengaged himself from the group. "I really must change before dinner. Please, feel free to begin without me," he invited.

It was only after he'd gone that Colette was able to draw an even breath.

John was chuckling. "Don't let him fluster you, Colette," he whispered close to her ear. "He'd just love that." When she looked at him askance, John continued. "He's never so happy as when he's intimated someone. Trust me, I know."

"Stop it, John," she scolded, "you'll only make it worse for me."

"On the contrary, Colette, the worst is behind you. Now that you've met the notorious Frederic Duvoisin, what else is there to fear?"

October 1847 Espoir

Elise Duvoisin tiptoed through the master's chambers and into the mistress' boudoir, pulling her five-year-old sister, Michelle, behind her. Like the other rooms, cobwebs hung from the ceilings and a thick coating of dust blanketed the chamber's lavish appointments. With heart pounding in her small chest and goosebumps crawling up the back of her neck, she vowed out loud, "Brett Richards – Marie Duvoisin – I'm going to kill the two of you!"

She left Michelle standing in the center of the room, and began searching behind doors, inside armoires, and under the four-poster bed, clicking her tongue in dismay when she turned up nothing.

"I'm scared, Ellie," the younger child moaned.

Elise sighed deeply in feigned bravado. "Come along," she insisted.

Entering the corridor, she cracked the door of her late grandmother's quarters, the only rooms not yet searched. A stiff draft sucked through the open portal, catching their dresses and whipping them around their legs.

"I'm scared!" Michelle cried again, more forcefully this time.

"There's nothing to be scared of," Elise reasoned. "Now come, or next time I'm going to tell Pa to leave you at home."

Michelle's eyes were wide as saucers, but following her older sister into the dreadful chamber was preferable to remaining out in the hallway alone. Their footsteps echoed hollow in the vacant sitting room, and Elise briefly wondered if the stories Brett had told her only yesterday were true – the servants who used to work in the abandoned manor had burned Agatha Duvoisin's belongings one by one. The words *ghost, haunted, and possessed* raced through her mind, and though she put on a courageous mien for her sister, in truth, she was frightened out of her wits.

Gritting her teeth, she shook her head of the cowardly thoughts. After all, she was Paul Duvoisin's daughter. Brett Richards purposely had fed her those tales during the short crossing from Charmantes so she'd be scared silly now! He was probably lying in wait, stifling his glee until he pounced on her, hoping to make her scream in terror. If he succeeded, she'd never hear the end of it. Well, she'd not allow that to happen!

By dint of will, she crept across the room, wondering where the breeze had come from; not a window was open. Only two pieces of furniture remained: a desk and a tall, ornate armoire. Elise reached a trembling hand toward the knob of the latter, fighting her apprehension.

"Don't!" Michelle whispered.

Elise glared at her sister over her shoulder, then trained her eyes on the knob. Another gust of air lapped up her arms, carrying upon it a faint whisper. *Elizabeth... is that you?*

Elise's hand froze in mid-air. "What was that?" she asked, fear rising in her voice. "Did you hear that?"

"What?"

"Someone whispering! You didn't hear it?"

"No – I – I don't think so," Michelle whimpered. "You're scaring me, Ellie. I wanna go home!"

"You're such a baby!" Elise scolded, drawing courage from her anger. She grabbed hold of the armoire door and yanked it open.

A hooded specter dove out at her, spilling her backwards into her dainty sister and toppling them both to the floor. The petrified squeal that burst from Michelle muted the long, shrill shriek emitted from the depths of the apparition's billowing cloak. Suddenly, the cape was thrown off, and the wraith took on a human form.

Before her stood Brett Richards, laughing gleefully.

"She was right!" he chortled. "Yvette was right! She said it would work."

"*What would work?*" Elise spat out as she rolled off her sister and came to her feet. Her green eyes flashed angrily, but Brett paid her no mind. He was savoring his triumphant moment, declaring victory to Marie, who appeared in the doorway.

"Ellie..." he finally called ever so softly "...is that you?"

She threw him another disdainful glare. "You didn't frighten me," she refuted flippantly, dusting off her hands and backside.

"No?" he chuckled again. "I'd say you nearly pooped your pants!"

"I'm not wearing pants!" she rejoined in kind.

She turned to Michelle, who was still sniffling. "That was a cruel thing to do to Michelle, Brett Richards. I think I shall tell your mother about it."

Brett only shrugged. "It's your own fault. I told you I could frighten you, but you didn't believe me."

"And I told you – you didn't!"

Their argument ended when a door banged open on the first floor and booted feet echoed in the marble foyer. "Elise? Michelle? Marie?"

Relief flooded across the younger girl's face. "Papa!" she cried in sheer joy.

She raced from her squabbling companions, through the second floor corridor, down the huge staircase and straight into her father's arms. He chuckled as he lifted her high in the air and settled her against his chest.

"And what's this?" Paul queried. "You look as if you've seen a ghost."

"I did!"

Paul raised a dubious brow. "You did?"

The query was directed at Michelle, though his eyes lifted to Elise and Brett and his niece, Marie, as they descended the stairs. "What have the three of you been up to?" he asked when they reached him. "You haven't been teasing Michelle, have you?"

"No, sir," George's eldest son responded. "Well... not much anyway."

"I see," Paul said with a scornful scowl.

The silent accusation ruffled Elise. "It was all Brett's doing, Pa. But he was trying to frighten *me*, not Michelle. He didn't though!"

"Come," Paul prodded with a smile, "it's time we traveled home. Your Ma will be worried about us."

They made their way down to the harbor. Michelle skipped ahead, squealing each time the buffeting winds whipped her skirts high about her waist. Her hair danced on the gusty gales, and Paul admired the color game the early evening light played with the dark, curly tresses. As they neared the waiting ship, he rushed forward, scooped her up and ran across the gangplank, relishing her giggles of sheer delight. Marie, Elise, and Brett followed in hot pursuit, heaving in exhaustion when they were safely aboard the vessel. In short order, the gangplank was raised, and the ropes released. With a mighty groan, the Tempest was pushed from the pier, her sails unfurled to harness the wind that would propel them back to Charmantes.

Elise stole one last glimpse at the sandy beaches that were swiftly receding behind them, her eyes traveling to the dormant manor overlooking the harbor. Even now, it beckoned to her, raising the hackles on the back of her neck. Brett likened the mansion to a fishing pole, reeling them in each time they visited Espoir. But she didn't believe that, just like she didn't believe in ghosts. A movement in the upper windows caught her eye. She shook her head. Impossible! The stately house had been vacant nearly five years now. She turned her face back into the wind and squinted against the fierce rays of the setting sun, forcing herself to ignore the uneasiness creeping up her spine and down her arms...

About The Author

DeVa Gantt is a pseudonym for co-author sisters, Debra and Valerie Gantt. Inspired by romantic and historical fiction, they set out to write their own love story on a whim. *Colette's Prayer* was conceived twenty-five years ago and completed after a long hiatus, which bridged the gap between the age of the typewriter and the personal computer. Debra is a clinical writer for a major pharmaceutical company and Valerie, an elementary school teacher. Both women are married with children. Charmantes is their escape from the mundane, and they often refer to the Duvoisins as their 'other' family. *Colette's Prayer* is just the beginning. Look for the sequel, *Les Fuyardes.*

Printed in the United States
39389LVS00004B/11

9 781420 821512